WORKS OF
H. G. WELLS

WORKS OF
H. G. WELLS

THE WONDERFUL VISIT

KIPPS

THE WIFE OF SIR ISAAC HARMAN

LOVE AND MR. LEWISHAM

Plus 14 Short Stories including
The Crystal Egg, The Star, In the Abyss,
and A Dream of Armageddon

Edited by George Gesner

AVENEL BOOKS · NEW YORK

This 1982 edition is published by Avenel Books,
distributed by Crown Publishers, Inc.

Library of Congress Cataloging in Publication Data

Wells, H. G. (Herbert George), 1866–1946.
  Works of H. G. Wells.

  I. Gesner, George, 1954–   II. Title.
PR5772.G47   1982   823′.912   82-11401

ISBN: 0-517-371537

Manufactured in the United States of America.

h g f e d c b a

CONTENTS

INTRODUCTION

There comes a time in the continuing saga of English literature that a man rises from the ranks of the common man to achieve a position of world renown. Herbert George Wells was such a man—a man whose supernormal energy and prophetic vision led him to new worlds of imagination and propelled him to be a major social and political reformer.

Wells was born in Bromley, Kent, in 1866 to a father who was an unsuccessful shopkeeper and semiprofessional cricketer and to a mother who was a domestic servant. Society was rapidly changing as he was cast into a lower middle-class existence with a modern world-state coming of age. As Wells observed, "The germinating forces of that Modern World State were already thrusting destructively amidst the comparative stabilities of the old eighteenth-century order before I was born." Railway stations, suburbs, and slums had made their way into his world. Having to battle with poverty and the prospects of being doomed to a life of normality, Wells saw too clearly the desperation and futility of his situation.

Wells, as in the case with most boys his age, saw his education terminated in his early teenage years, only to be "put to a trade" and bound to employment before there was any choice in the matter. Following in the footsteps of his two older brothers, he was "bound" to be a draper's apprentice. Wells said that his two years in that trade were the most unhappy and hopeless period of his life. He was able to break free from that life of industrial boredom by seizing every free opportunity in his hectic life to educate himself. With such a voracious appetite for learning he set a rule for himself to never read a work of fiction or play a game. Wells knew the seduction of a good story and disturbance of a game of skill and said his abstinence was not evidence of an intense and concentrated mind but evidence of an acute sense of the need for concentration. He said, "I was not attacking the world by all this effort and self-control; I was making my desperate get-away from the shop and the street. I was bracing myself up tremendously."

A big opportunity came for Wells when he was awarded a scholarship to study at the College of Science in South Kensington. It was here that he came under the tutelage of his boyhood hero, T. H. Huxley, the world-famous biologist whose son Aldous would go on to write the science-fiction classic *Brave New World*. Huxley was a major influence for Wells, a young man whose horizons were expanding dynamically. Wells was undergoing a "sudden irruption of new ideas of scientific precision and confirmation." It was this specialized learning experience that gave Wells such a fresh perspective on the world of science and the stories it could yield. Wells said, "If I had been the son of an instructive-minded astronomer and had been bothered with early lessons about the stars, I might not have made my first contact with the starry heavens in a state of exaltation, nor pursued Jupiter with the help of *Whitaker's Almanack* until with my own eyes, I saw him and his moons quivering in the field of my telescope, as though I were Galileo come back to earth." But as Wells said, "Before one breaks or climbs fences one must look over them or through them for a time." It was a difficult time for Wells following his brief term as a science student at South Kensington. He was struggling at his first attempt to write professionally and continued to develop his ideas on socialism.

Wells probably had his first introduction to socialism when he read Plato's *Republic* as a young boy. It was here that he was presented with, in his words, "the conception of society in which economic individualism was overruled entirely in the common interest." Wells saw himself in a social order where all the good things went to people who "constitutionally and necessarily watch, grab and clutch all the time." He said, "In a world of competitive acquisitiveness the natural lot of my sort of people is to be hustled out of existence by the smarties and pushers. A very strong factor in my developing socialism is and always has been the more or less conscious impulses to anticipate and disarm the smarty and the pusher and make the world safe for the responsive and candid mind and the authentic, artistic, and creative worker."

Two major forces were now shaping up in the life and thoughts of H. G. Wells. His fascination and knowledge of biology and evolution were merged with his conviction to political and social reform. These forces influence most of his writings. It was during his days at University Correspondence College, as a teacher, that Wells turned from an amateur to professional writer. He regularly wrote articles of scientific journalism for the *Pall Mall Gazette* and was hired in 1894 as a regular contributor to the *Saturday Review*. His big break came when he sold *The Time Machine* to the *Pall Mall Gazette* for one hundred pounds. This was the first major work by Wells, and it established him as an imaginative writer. It was works such as *The Time Machine*, *The Invisible Man*, *The War of the Worlds*, *The Island of Dr. Moreau*, and others that would establish Wells as one of the founding fathers of science fiction. But Wells wanted to be remembered as a serious novelist—a man who in his day achieved a proportionate amount of popularity for his non-science-fiction works.

The Works of H. G. Wells is presented to the reader to introduce the various writings of H. G. Wells that have been overshadowed by his science-fiction classics. In this collection one will find a combination of his "serious novels" that lean more toward his socio-political and realistic self, and the short stories that are trademarked with the Wellsian tales of fantasy and the macabre.

Included here is *The Wonderful Visit*, his first novel dealing with social criticism, which followed right on the heels of the success of *The Time Machine*. It is the story of an angel who falls to earth and the hopeless situations he is confronted with in late Victorian society.

The short stories included here were written in the mid-1890s as well. Some of the most vivid and imaginative ideas ever presented by Wells appear in these short stories. One will find tales of the macabre in "Pollock and the Porroh Man," "The Cone," and "The Moth." "The Star," written in 1897, is a cosmic disaster story that may have been the forerunner of Edwin Balmer and Philip Wylie's science-fiction classic *When Worlds Collide*, published in 1933. Also included is the magical fantasy "The Man Who Could Work Miracles," which was extended and adapted in the 1930s and made into a film of the same name. Other fantasy-science-fiction tales include "The Plattner Story," "The Crystal Egg," "In the Abyss," "A Dream of Armageddon," and more.

In the novels *Love and Mr. Lewisham*, published in 1900, and *Kipps*, in 1905,

Wells drew heavily on his own life and situations he encountered in the lower mid-dle-class. Wells said, "I set out to write novels, as distinguished from those pseudoscientific stories in which imaginative experience rather than personal conduct was the matter in hand, on the assumption that problems of adjustment were the essential matter for novel-writing. *Love and Mr. Lewisham* was entirely a story about dislocation and an adjustment." In this novel, Wells drew on his experiences as a science teacher and used scenes from his early days in the biological laboratory at South Kensington. It is the story of one man's "schema" of a career and how it was disrupted by love. In order to raise a family, the young science teacher-student must tear up his "schema" and settle down. Wells shows his subconscious fear of being caught in a similar type of household using a term he calls "domestic claustrophobia."

In a letter to his father at the close of 1898, Wells wrote, "Just now I am writing rather hard—though this is between ourselves—at a comic novel rather on the old-fashioned Dickens line, a lot of entertaining characters doing ordinary things." He was, of course, referring to *Kipps*. In his tenure as a draper's apprentice and assistant, Wells met a new apprentice who had an "amusing simplicity of mind and a carelessness of manner," and he made him the model for Mr. Kipps. Probably one of Wells's most popular novels, *Kipps* is the story of a young draper's apprentice who inherits a fortune and is forced to rise above his station in life. Wells makes his social comment by poking fun at the upper crust of society with Kipps as his traditionally meek hero.

In *The Wife of Sir Isaac Harman*, Wells expands his social and political comment. At the same time he presents a sterling romance. His insights on the suffragette movement and urban living are candid and sensitive. About the novel Wells said, "The interest centers not upon individual character but upon the struggles of common and rational motives and frank enquiry against social conditions and stereotyped ideas." Wells's motive in writing this novel was done with conviction and good intention. He said, "The old feminist movement of the early nineteenth century had undergone a sort of rejuvenation in the 1880s and '90s. It had given up its bloomers and become smart, energetic, and ambitious. I tried to explain to myself and my readers the suppressions and resentments that might lead a gentle woman to smash a plate-glass window."

One can see when reading through his works that Wells is still very timely today. He was so acutely aware of his own time and society that many thought he was ahead of his time. *The Works of H. G. Wells* includes only a small portion of the more than one hundred books that H. G. Wells wrote. There are many other works that have escaped the public eye, and it is collections such as this that reintroduce these works to the serious devotees of good literature and all H. G. Wells enthusiasts.

GEORGE GESNER
New York
1982

THE
WONDERFUL
VISIT

TO THE
MEMORY OF MY DEAR FRIEND,
WALTER LOW.

The Night of the Strange Bird

I

ON THE NIGHT of the Strange Bird, many people at Sidderton (and some nearer) saw a Glare on the Sidderford moor. But no one in Sidderford saw it, for most of Sidderford was abed.

All day the wind had been rising, so that the larks on the moor chirruped fitfully near the ground, or rose only to be driven like leaves before the wind. The sun set in a bloody welter of clouds, and the moon was hidden. The glare, they say, was golden like a beam shining out of the sky, not a uniform blaze, but broken all over by curving flashes like the waving of swords. It lasted but a moment and left the night dark and obscure. There were letters about it in *Nature,* and a rough drawing that no one thought very like. (You may see it for yourself—the drawing that was unlike the glare—on page 42 of Vol. cclx. of that publication.)

None in Sidderford saw the light, but Annie, Hooker Durgan's wife, was lying awake, and she saw the reflection of it—a flickering tongue of gold—dancing on the wall.

She, too, was one of those who heard the sound. The others who heard the sound were Lumpy Durgan, the half-wit, and Amory's mother. They said it was a sound like children singing and a throbbing of harp strings, carried on a rush of notes like that which sometimes comes from an organ. It began and ended like the opening and shutting of a door, and before and after they heard nothing but the night wind howling over the moor and the noise of the caves under Sidderford cliff. Amory's mother said she wanted to cry when she heard it, but Lumpy was only sorry he could hear no more.

That is as much as anyone can tell you of the glare upon Sidderford Moor and the alleged music therewith. And whether these had any real connection with the Strange Bird whose history follows, is more than I can say. But I set it down here for reasons that will be more apparent as the story proceeds.

The Coming of the Strange Bird

II

SANDY BRIGHT WAS coming down the road from Spinner's carrying a side of bacon he had taken in exchange for a clock. He saw nothing of the light but he heard and saw the Strange Bird. He suddenly heard a flapping and a voice like a woman wailing, and being a nervous man and all alone, he was alarmed forthwith, and turning (all a-tremble) saw something large and black against the dim darkness of the cedars up the hill. It seemed to be coming right down upon him, and incontinently he dropped his bacon and set off running, only to fall headlong.

He tried in vain—such was his state of mind—to remember the beginning of the Lord's Prayer. The strange bird flapped over him, something larger than himself, with a vast spread of wings, and, as he thought, black. He screamed and gave himself up for lost. Then it went past him, sailing down the hill, and, soaring over the vicarage, vanished into the hazy valley towards Sidderford.

And Sandy Bright lay upon his stomach there, for ever so long, staring into the darkness after the strange bird. At last he got upon his knees and began to thank Heaven for his merciful deliverance, with his eyes downhill. He went on down into the village, talking aloud and confessing his sins as he went, lest the strange bird should come back. All who heard him thought him drunk. But from that night he was a changed man, and had done with drunkenness and defrauding the revenue by selling silver ornaments without a license. And the side of bacon lay upon the hillside until the tallyman from Portburdock found it in the morning.

The next who saw the Strange Bird was a solicitor's clerk at Iping Hanger, who was climbing the hill before breakfast, to see the sunrise. Save for a few dissolving wisps of cloud the sky had been blown clear in the night. At first he thought it was an eagle he saw. It was near the zenith, and incredibly remote, a mere bright speck above the pink cirri, and it seemed as if it fluttered and beat itself against the sky, as an imprisoned swallow might do against a window pane. Then down it came into the shadow of the earth, sweeping in a great curve towards Portburdock and round over the Hanger, and so vanishing behind the woods of Siddermorton Park. It seemed larger than a man. Just before it was hidden, the light of the rising sun smote over the edge of the downs and touched its wings, and they flashed with the brightness of flames and the color of precious stones, and so passed, leaving the witness agape.

A ploughman going to his work, along under the stone wall of Siddermorton Park, saw the Strange Bird flash over him for a moment and vanish among the hazy interstices of the beech trees. But he saw little of the color of the wings, witnessing only that its legs, which were long, seemed pink and bare like naked flesh, and its body mottled white. It smote like an arrow through the air and was gone.

These were the first three eye-witnesses of the Strange Bird.

Now in these days one does not cower before the devil and one's own sinfulness, or see strange iridescent wings in the light of dawn, and say nothing of it afterwards. The young solicitor's clerk told his mother and sisters at breakfast, and, afterwards, on his way to the office at Portburdock, spoke of it to the blacksmith of Hammerpond, and spent the morning with his fellow clerks marvelling instead of copying deeds. And Sandy Bright went to talk the matter over with Mr. Jekyll, the "Primitive" minister, and the ploughman told old Hugh and afterwards the vicar of Siddermorton.

"They are not an imaginative race about here," said the Vicar of Siddermorton, "I wonder how much of that was true. Barring that he thinks the wings were brown it sounds uncommonly like a Flamingo."

The Hunting of the Strange Bird

III

THE VICAR OF Siddermorton (which is nine miles inland from Siddermouth as the crow flies) was an ornithologist. Some such pursuit, botany, antiquity, folk-lore, is almost inevitable for a single man in his position. He was given to geometry also, propounding occasionally impossible problems in the *Educational Times,* but ornithology was his *forte.* He had already added two visitors to the list of occasional British birds. His name was well-known in the columns of the *Zoologist* (I am afraid it may be forgotten by now, for the world moves apace). And on the day after the coming of the Strange Bird, came first one and then another to confirm the ploughman's story and tell him, not that it had any connection, of the Glare upon Sidderford moor.

Now, the Vicar of Siddermorton had two rivals in his scientific pursuits; Gully of Sidderton, who had actually seen the glare, and who it was sent the drawing to *Nature,* and Borland the natural history dealer, who kept the marine laboratory at Portburdock. Borland, the Vicar thought, should have stuck to his copepods, but instead he kept a taxidermist, and took advantage of his littoral position to pick up rare sea birds. It was evident to anyone who knew anything of collecting that both these men would be scouring the country after the strange visitant, before twenty-four hours were out.

The Vicar's eye rested on the back of Saunders' British Birds, for he was in his study at the time. Already in two places there was entered: "the only known British specimen was secured by the Rev. K. Hilyer, Vicar of Siddermorton." A third such entry. He doubted if any other collector had that.

He looked at his watch—*two.* He had just lunched, and usually he "rested" in the afternoon. He knew it would make him feel very disagreeable if he went out into the hot sunshine—both on the top of his head and generally. Yet Gully perhaps was out, prowling observant. Suppose it was something very good and Gully got it!

His gun stood in the corner. (The thing had iridescent wings and pink legs! The chromatic conflict was certainly exceedingly stimulating.) He took his gun.

He would have gone out by the glass doors and veranda, and down the garden into the hill road, in order to avoid his housekeeper's eye. He knew his gun expeditions were not approved of. But advancing towards him up the garden, he saw the curate's wife and her two daughters, carrying tennis rackets. His curate's wife was a young woman of immense will, who used to play tennis on his lawn, and cut his roses, differ from him on doctrinal points, and criticize his personal behavior all over the parish. He went in abject fear of her, was always trying to propitiate her. But so far he had clung to his ornithology. . . .

However, he went out by the front door.

IV

IF IT WERE not for collectors England would be full, so to speak, of rare birds and wonderful butterflies, strange flowers and a thousand interesting things. But happily the collector prevents all that, either killing with his own hands or, by buying extravagantly, procuring people of the lower classes to kill such eccentricities as appear. It makes work for people, even though Acts of Parliament interfere. In this way, for instance, he is killing off the chough in Cornwall, the Bath white butterfly, the Queen of Spain Fritillary; and can plume himself upon the extermination of the Great Auk, and a hundred other rare birds and plants and insects. All that is the work of the collector and his glory alone. In the name of Science. And this is right and as it should be; eccentricity, in fact, is immorality—think over it again if you do not think so now—just as eccentricity in one's way of thinking is madness (I defy you to find another definition that will fit all the cases of either); and if a species is rare it follows that it is not Fitted to Survive. The collector is after all merely like the foot soldier in the days of heavy armor—he leaves the combatants alone and cuts the throats of those who are overthrown. So one may go through England from end to end in the summer time and see only eight or ten commonplace wild flowers, and the commoner butterflies, and a dozen or so common birds, and never be offended by any breach of the monotony, any splash of strange blossom or flutter of unknown wing. All the rest have been "collected" years ago. For which cause we should all love Collectors, and bear in mind what we owe them when their little collections are displayed. These camphorated little drawers of theirs, their glass cases and blotting-paper books, are the graves of the Rare and the Beautiful, the symbols of the Triumph of Leisure (morally spent) over the Delights of Life. (All of which, as you very properly remark, has nothing whatever to do with the Strange Bird.)

V

THERE IS A place on the moor where the black water shines among the succulent moss, and the hairy sundew, eater of careless insects, spreads its red-stained hungry hands to the God who gives his creatures—one to feed another. On a ridge thereby grow birches with a silvery bark, and the soft green of the larch mingles with the dark green fir. Thither through the honey humming heather came the Vicar, in the heat of the day, carrying a gun under his arm, a gun loaded with swanshot for the Strange Bird. And over his disengaged hand he carried a pocket handkerchief wherewith, ever and again, he wiped his beady face.

He went by and on past the big pond and the pool full of brown leaves where the Sidder arises, and so by the road (which is at first sandy and then chalky) to the little gate that goes into the park. There are seven steps up to the gate and on the further side six down again—lest the deer escape—so that when the Vicar stood in the gateway his head was ten feet or more above the ground. And looking where a tumult of bracken fronds filled the hollow between two groups of beech, his eye caught something parti-colored that wavered and went. Suddenly his face gleamed and his muscles grew tense; he ducked his head, clutched his gun with both hands, and stood still. Then watching keenly, he came on down the steps into the park, and still holding his gun in both hands, crept rather than walked towards the jungle of bracken.

Nothing stirred, and he almost feared that his eyes had played him false, until he reached the ferns and had gone rustling breast high into them. Then suddenly rose something full of wavering colors, twenty yards or less in front of his face, and beating the air. In another moment it had fluttered above the bracken and spread its pinions wide. He saw what it was, his heart was in his mouth, and he fired out of pure surprise and habit.

There was a scream of superhuman agony, the wings beat the air twice, and the victim came slanting swiftly downward and struck the ground—a struggling heap of writhing body, broken wing and flying bloodstained plumes—upon the turfy slope behind.

The Vicar stood aghast, with his smoking gun in his hand. It was no bird at all, but a youth with an extremely beautiful face, clad in a robe of saffron and with iridescent wings, across whose pinions great waves of color, flushes of purple and crimson, golden green and intense blue, pursued one another as he writhed in his agony. Never had the Vicar seen such gorgeous floods of color, not stained glass windows, not the wings of butterflies, not even the glories of crystals seen between prisms, no colors on earth could compare with them. Twice the Angel raised himself, only to fall over sideways again. Then the beating of the wings diminished, the terrified face grew pale, the floods of color abated, and suddenly with a sob he lay prone, and the changing hues of the broken wings faded swiftly into one uniform dull grey hue.

"Oh ! *what* has happened to me?" cried the Angel (for such it was), shuddering violently, hands outstretched and clutching the ground, and then lying still.

"Dear me!" said the Vicar. "I had no idea." He came forward cautiously. "Excuse me," he said, "I am afraid I have shot you."

It was the obvious remark.

The Angel seemed to become aware of his presence for the first time. He raised himself by one hand, his brown eyes stared into the Vicar's. Then, with a gasp, and biting his nether lip, he struggled into a sitting position and surveyed the Vicar from top to toe.

"A man!" said the Angel, clasping his forehead; "a man in the maddest black clothes and without a feather upon him. Then I was not deceived. I am indeed in the Land of Dreams!"

The Vicar and the Angel

VI

NOW THERE ARE some things frankly impossible. The weakest intellect will admit this situation is impossible. The *Athenæum* will probably say as much should it venture to review this. Sunbespattered ferns, spreading beech trees, the Vicar and the gun are acceptable enough. But this Angel is a different matter. Plain sensible people will scarcely go on with such an extravagant book. And the Vicar fully appreciated this impossibility. But he lacked decision. Consequently he went on with it, as you shall immediately hear. He was hot, it was after dinner, he was in no mood for mental subtleties. The Angel had him at a disadvantage, and further distracted him from the main issue by irrelevant iridescence and a violent fluttering. For the moment it never occurred to the Vicar to ask whether the Angel was possible or not. He accepted him in the confusion of the moment, and the mischief was done. Put yourself in his place, my dear *Athenæum*. You go out shooting. You hit something. That alone would disconcert you. You find you have hit an Angel, and he writhes about for a minute and then sits up and addresses you. He makes no apology for his own impossibility. Indeed, he carries the charge clean into your camp. "A man!" he says, pointing. "A man in the maddest black clothes and without a feather upon him. Then I was not deceived. I am indeed in the Land of Dreams!" You *must* answer him. Unless you take to your heels. Or blow his brains out with your second barrel as an escape from the controversy.

"The Land of Dreams! Pardon me if I suggest you have just come out of it," was the Vicar's remark.

"How can that be?" said the Angel.

"Your wing," said the Vicar, "is bleeding. Before we talk, may I have the pleasure—the melancholy pleasure—of tying it up? I am really most sincerely sorry . . ." The Angel put his hand behind his back and winced.

The Vicar assisted his victim to stand up. The Angel turned gravely and the Vicar, with numberless insignificant panting parentheses, carefully examined the injured wings. (They articulated, he observed with interest, to a kind of second glenoid on the outer and upper edge of the shoulder blade. The left wing had suffered little except the loss of some of the primary wing-quills, and a shot or so in the *ala spuria,* but the humerus bone of the right was evidently smashed.) The Vicar stanched the bleeding as well as he could and tied up the bone with his pocket handkerchief and the neck wrap his housekeeper made him carry in all weathers.

"I'm afraid you will not be able to fly for some time," said he, feeling the bone.

"I don't like this new sensation," said the Angel.

"The Pain when I feel your bone?"

"The *what?*" said the Angel.

"The Pain."

" 'Pain'—you call it. No, I certainly don't like the Pain. Do you have much of this Pain in the Land of Dreams?"

"A very fair share," said the Vicar. "Is it new to you?"

"Quite," said the Angel. "I don't like it."

"How curious!" said the Vicar, and bit at the end of a strip of linen to tie a knot. "I think this bandaging must serve for the present," he said. "I've studied ambulance work before, but never the bandaging up of wing wounds. Is your Pain any better?"

"It glows now instead of flashing," said the Angel.

"I am afraid you will find it glow for some time," said the Vicar, still intent on the wound.

The Angel gave a shrug of the wing and turned round to look at the Vicar again. He had been trying to keep an eye on the Vicar over his shoulder during all their interview. He looked at him from top to toe with raised eyebrows and a growing smile on his beautiful soft-featured face. "It seems so odd," he said with a sweet little laugh, "to be talking to a Man!"

"Do you know," said the Vicar, "now that I come to think of it, it is equally odd to me that I should be talking to an Angel. I am a somewhat matter-of-fact person. A Vicar has to be. Angels I have always regarded as—artistic conceptions—"

"Exactly what we think of men."

"But surely you have seen so many men—"

"Never before today. In pictures and books, times enough of course. But I have seen several since the sunrise, solid real men, besides a horse or so—those Unicorn things you know, without horns—and quite a number of those grotesque knobby things called 'cows.' I was naturally a little frightened at so many mythical monsters, and came to hide here until it was dark. I suppose it will be dark again presently like it was at first. *Phew!* This Pain of yours is poor fun. I hope I shall wake up directly."

"I don't understand quite," said the Vicar, knitting his brows and tapping his forehead with his flat hand. "Mythical monster!" The worst thing he had been called for years hitherto was a 'mediaeval anachronism' (by an advocate of Disestablishment). "Do I understand that you consider me as—as something in a dream?"

"Of course," said the Angel smiling.

"And this world about me, these rugged trees and spreading fronds—"

"Is all so *very* dream-like," said the Angel. "Just exactly what one dreams of—or artists imagine."

"You have artists then among the Angels?"

"All kinds of artists, Angels with wonderful imaginations, who invent men and cows and eagles and a thousand impossible creatures."

"Impossible creatures!" said the Vicar.

"Impossible creatures," said the Angel. "Myths."

"But I'm real!" said the Vicar. "I assure you I'm real."

The Angel shrugged his wings and winced and smiled. "I can always tell when I am dreaming," he said.

"*You*—dreaming," said the Vicar. He looked round him.

"*You* dreaming!" he repeated. His mind worked diffusely.

He held out his hand with all his fingers moving. "I have it!" he said. "I begin to see." A really brilliant idea was dawning upon his mind. He had not studied mathematics at Cambridge for nothing, after all. "Tell me please. Some animals of *your* world. . . . of the Real World, real animals you know."

"Real animals!" said the Angel smiling. "Why—there's Griffins and Dragons—and Jabberwocks—and Cherubim—and Sphinxes—and the Hippogriff—and Mermaids—and Satyrs—and. . . ."

"Thank you," said the Vicar as the Angel appeared to be warming to his work; "thank you. That is *quite* enough. I begin to understand."

He paused for a moment, his face pursed up. "Yes. . . . I begin to see it."

"See what?" asked the Angel.

"The Griffins and Satyrs and so forth. It's as clear. . . ."

"I don't see them," said the Angel.

"No, the whole point is they are not to be seen in this world. But our men with imaginations have told us all about them, you know. And even I at times. . . . there are places in this village where you must simply take what they set before you, or give offense—I, I say, have seen in my dreams Jabberwocks, Bogle brutes, Mandrakes. . . . From our point of view, you know, they are Dream Creatures. . . ."

"Dream Creatures!" said the Angel. "How singular! This is a very curious dream. A kind of topsy-turvey one. You call men real and angels a myth. It almost makes one think that in some odd way there must be two worlds as it were. . . ."

"At least Two," said the Vicar.

"Lying somewhere close together, and yet scarcely suspecting. . . ."

"As near as page to page of a book."

"Penetrating each other, living each its own life. This is really a delicious dream!"

"And never dreaming of each other."

"Except when people go a dreaming!"

"Yes," said the Angel thoughtfully. "It must be something of the sort. And that reminds me. Sometimes when I have been dropping asleep, or drowsing under the noon-tide sun, I have seen strange corrugated faces just like yours, going by me, and trees with green leaves upon them, and such queer uneven ground as this. . . . It must be so. I have fallen into another world."

"Sometimes," began the Vicar, "at bedtime, when I have been just on the edge of consciousness, I have seen faces as beautiful as yours, and the strange dazzling vistas of a wonderful scene, that flowed past me, winged shapes soaring over it, and wonderful—sometimes terrible—forms going to and fro. I have even heard sweet music too in my ears. . . . It may be that as we withdraw our attention from the world of sense, the pressing world about us, as we pass into the twilight of repose, other worlds. . . . Just as we see the stars, those other worlds in space, when the glare of day recedes. . . . And the artistic dreamers who see such things most clearly. . . ."

They looked at one another.

"And in some incomprehensible manner I have fallen into this world of yours out of my own!" said the Angel, "into the world of my dreams grown real."

He looked about him. "Into the world of my dreams."

"It is confusing," said the Vicar. "It almost makes one think there may be (ahem) Four Dimensions after all. In which case, of course," he went on hurriedly—for he loved geometrical speculations and took a certain pride in his knowledge of them—"there may be any number of three-dimensional universes packed side by side, and all dimly dreaming of one another. There may be world upon world, universe upon universe. It's perfectly possible. There's nothing so incredible as the absolutely possible. But I wonder how you came to fall out of your world into mine. . . ."

"Dear me!" said the Angel; "There's deer and a stag! Just as they draw them on the coats of arms. How grotesque it all seems! Can I really be awake?"

He rubbed his knuckles into his eyes.

The half-dozen of dappled deer came in Indian file obliquely through the trees and halted, watching. "It's no dream—I am really a solid concrete Angel, in Dream Land," said the Angel. He laughed. The Vicar stood surveying him. The Reverend gentleman was pulling his mouth askew after a habit he had, and slowly stroking his chin. He was asking himself whether he too was not in the Land of Dreams.

VII

NOW IN THE land of the Angels, so the Vicar learnt in the course of many conversations, there is neither pain nor trouble nor death, marrying nor giving in marriage, birth nor forgetting. Only at times new things begin. It is a land without hill or dale, a wonderfully level land, glittering with strange buildings, with incessant sunlight or full moon, and with incessant breezes blowing through the Æolian traceries of the trees. It is Wonderland, with glittering seas hanging in the sky, across which strange fleets go sailing, none know whither. There the flowers glow in Heaven and the stars shine about one's feet and the breath of life is a delight. The land goes on forever—there is no solar system nor interstellar space such as there is in our universe—and the air goes upward past the sun into the uttermost abyss of their sky. And there is nothing but Beauty there—all the beauty in our art is but feeble rendering of faint glimpses of that wonderful world, and our composers, our original composers, are those who hear, however faintly, the dust of melody that drives before its winds. And the Angels, and wonderful monsters of bronze and marble and living fire, go to and fro therein.

It is a land of Law—for whatever is, is under the law—but its laws all, in some strange way, differ from ours. Their geometry is different because their space has a curve in it so that all their planes are cylinders; and their law of Gravitation is not according to the law of inverse squares, and there are four-and-twenty primary colors instead of only three. Most of the fantastic things of our science are commonplaces there, and all our earthly science would seem to them the maddest dreaming. There are no flowers upon their plants, for instance, but jets of colored fire. That, of course, will seem mere nonsense to you because you do not understand. Most of what the Angel told the Vicar, indeed the Vicar could not realize, because his own experiences, being only of this world of matter, warred against his understanding. It was too strange to imagine.

What had jolted these twin universes together so that the Angel had fallen suddenly into Sidderford, neither the Angel nor the Vicar could tell. Nor for the matter of that could the author of this story. The author is concerned with the facts of the case, and has neither the desire nor the confidence to explain them. Explanations are the fallacy of a scientific age. And the cardinal fact of the case is this, that out in Siddermorton Park, with the glory of some wonderful world where there is neither sorrow nor sighing, still clinging to him, on the 4th of August 1895, stood an Angel, bright and beautiful, talking to the Vicar of Siddermorton about the plurality of worlds. The author will swear to the Angel, if need be; and there he draws the line.

VIII

"I HAVE," SAID the Angel, "a most unusual feeling—*here*. Have had since sunrise. I don't remember ever having any feeling—*here* before."

"Not pain, I hope," said the Vicar.

"Oh no! It is quite different from that—a kind of vacuous feeling."

"The atmospheric pressure, perhaps, is a little different," the Vicar began, feeling his chin.

"And do you know, I have also the most curious sensations in my mouth— almost as if—it's so absurd!—as if I wanted to stuff things into it."

"Bless me!" said the Vicar. "Of course! You're hungry!"

"Hungry!" said the Angel. "What's that?"

"Don't you eat?"

"Eat! The word's quite new to me."

"Put food into your mouth, you know. One has to here. You will soon learn. If you don't, you get thin and miserable, and suffer a great deal—*pain,* you know—and finally you die."

"Die!" said the Angel. "That's another strange word!"

"It's not strange here. It means leaving off, you know," said the Vicar.

"We never leave off," said the Angel.

"You don't know what may happen to you in this world," said the Vicar, thinking him over. "Possibly if you are feeling hungry, and can feel pain and have your wings broken, you may even have to die before you get out of it again. At any rate you had better try eating. For my own part—mahem!—there are many more disagreeable things."

"I suppose I *had* better Eat," said the Angel. "If it's not too difficult. I don't like this 'Pain' of yours, and I don't like this 'Hungry.' If your 'Die' is anything like it, I would prefer to Eat. What a very odd world this is!"

"To Die," said the Vicar, "is generally considered worse than either pain or hunger . . . It depends."

"You must explain all that to me later," said the Angel. "Unless I wake up. At present, please show me how to eat. If you will. I feel a kind of urgency. . . ."

"Pardon me," said the Vicar, and offered an elbow. "If I may have the pleasure of entertaining you. My house lies yonder—not a couple of miles from here."

"*Your* House!" said the Angel a little puzzled; but he took the Vicar's arm affectionately, and the two, conversing as they went, waded slowly through the luxuriant bracken, sun mottled under the trees, and on over the stile in the park palings, and so across the bee-swarming heather for a mile or more, down the hillside, home.

You would have been charmed at the couple could you have seen them. The Angel, slight of figure, scarcely five feet high, and with a beautiful, almost effeminate face, such as an Italian old Master might have painted. (Indeed, there is one in the National Gallery [*Tobias and the Angel,* by some artist unknown] not at all unlike him so far as face and spirit go.) He was robed simply in a purple-wrought saffron blouse, bare kneed and bare-footed, with his wings (broken now, and a leaden grey) folded behind him. The Vicar was a short, rather stout figure, rubicund, red-haired, clean-shaven, and with bright ruddy brown eyes. He wore a piebald straw hat with a black ribbon, a very neat white tie, and a fine gold watch-chain. He was so greatly interested in his companion that it only occurred to him when he was in sight of the Vicarage that he had left his gun lying just where he had dropped it amongst the bracken.

He was rejoiced to hear that the pain of the bandaged wing fell rapidly in intensity.

Parenthesis on Angels

IX

LET US BE plain. The Angel of this story is the Angel of Art, not the Angel that one must be irreverent to touch—neither the Angel of religious feeling nor the Angel of popular belief. The last we all know. She is alone among the angelic hosts in being distinctly feminine: she wears a robe of immaculate, unmitigated white with sleeves, is fair, with long golden tresses, and has eyes of the blue of Heaven. Just a pure woman she is, pure maiden or pure matron, in her *robe de nuit,* and with wings attached to her shoulder blades. Her callings are domestic and sympathetic, she watches over a cradle or assists a sister soul heavenward. Often she bears a palm leaf, but one would not be surprised if one met her carrying a warming-pan softly to some poor chilly sinner. She it was who came down in a bevy to Marguerite in prison, in the amended last scene in *Faust* at the Lyceum, and the interesting and improving little children that are to die young, have visions of such angels in the novels of Mrs. Henry Wood. This white womanliness with her indescribable charm of lavender-like holiness, her aroma of clean, methodical lives, is, it would seem after all, a purely Teutonic invention. Latin thought knows her not; the old masters have none of her. She is of a piece with that gentle innocent ladylike school of art whereof the greatest triumph is "a lump in one's throat," and where wit and passion, scorn and pomp, have no place. The white angel was made in Germany, in the land of blonde women and the domestic sentiments. She comes to us cool and worshipful, pure and tranquil, as silently soothing as the breadth and calmness of the starlit sky, which also is so unspeakably dear to the Teutonic soul. . . . We do her reverence. And to the angels of the Hebrews, those spirits of power and mystery, to Raphael, Zadkiel, and Michael, of whom only Watts has caught the shadow, of whom only Blake has seen the splendor, to them too, do we do reverence.

But this Angel the Vicar shot is, we say, no such angel at all, but the Angel of Italian art, polychromatic and gay. He comes from the land of beautiful dreams and not from any holier place. At best he is a popish creature. Bear patiently, therefore, with his scattered remiges, and be not hasty with your charge of irreverence before the story is read.

At the Vicarage
X

THE CURATE'S WIFE and her two daughters and Mrs. Jehoram were still playing at tennis on the lawn behind the Vicar's study, playing keenly and talking in gasps about paper patterns for blouses. But the Vicar forgot and came in that way.

They saw the Vicar's hat above the rhododendrons, and a bare curly head beside him. "I must ask him about Susan Wiggin," said the Curate's wife. She was about to serve, and stood with a racket in one hand and a ball between the fingers of the other. *"He* really ought to have gone to see her—being the Vicar. Not George. I—*Ah!"*

For the two figures suddenly turned the corner and were visible. The Vicar, arm in arm with—

You see, it came on the Curate's wife suddenly. The Angel's face being towards her she saw nothing of the wings. Only a face of unearthly beauty in a halo of chestnut hair, and a graceful figure clothed in a saffron garment that barely reached the knees. The thought of those knees flashed upon the Vicar at once. He too was horrorstruck. So were the two girls and Mrs. Jehoram. All horrorstruck. The Angel stared in astonishment at the horrorstruck group. You see, he had never seen anyone horrorstruck before.

"MIS—ter Hillyer!" said the Curate's wife, "This is *too* much!" She stood speechless for a moment. *"Oh!"*

She swept round upon the rigid girls. "Come!" The Vicar opened and shut his voiceless mouth. The world hummed and spun about him. There was a whirling of zephyr skirts, four impassioned faces sweeping towards the open door of the passage that ran through the vicarage. He felt his position went with them.

"Mrs. Mendham," said the Vicar, stepping forward. "Mrs. Mendham. You don't understand—"

"Oh!" they all said again.

One, two, three, four skirts vanished in the doorway. The Vicar staggered half way across the lawn and stopped, aghast. "This comes," he heard the Curate's wife say, out of the depth of the passage, "of having an unmarried vicar—." The umbrella stand wobbled. The front door of the vicarage slammed like a minute gun. There was silence for a space.

"I might have thought," he said. "She is always so hasty."

He put his hand to his chin—a habit with him. Then turned his face to his companion. The Angel was evidently well bred. He was holding up Mrs. Jehoram's sunshade—she had left it on one of the cane chairs—and examining it with extraordinary interest. He opened it. "What a curious little mechanism!" he said. "What can it be for?"

The Vicar did not answer. The angelic costume certainly was—the Vicar knew it was a case for a French phrase—but he could scarcely remember it. He so rarely used French. It was not *de trop,* he knew. Anything but *de trop.* The Angel was *de trop,* but certainly not his costume. Ah! *Sans culotte!*

The Vicar examined his visitor critically—for the first time. "He *will* be difficult to explain," he said to himself softly.

The Angel stuck the sunshade into the turf and went to smell the sweet briar. The sunshine fell upon his brown hair and gave it almost the appearance of a halo. He pricked his finger. "Odd!" he said. "Pain again."

"Yes," said the Vicar, thinking aloud. "He's very beautiful and curious as he is. I should like him best so. But I am afraid I must."

He approached the Angel with a nervous cough.

XI

"THOSE" SAID THE Vicar, "were ladies."

"How grotesque," said the Angel, smiling and smelling the sweet briar. "And such quaint shapes!"

"Possibly," said the Vicar. "Did you, *ahem,* notice how they behaved?"

"They went away. Seemed, indeed, to run away. Frightened? I, of course, was frightened at things without wings. I hope—they were not frightened at my wings?"

"At your appearance generally," said the Vicar, glancing involuntarily at the pink feet.

"Dear me! It never occurred to me. I suppose I seemed as odd to them as you did to me." He glanced down. "And my feet. *You* have hoofs like a hippogriff."

"Boots," corrected the Vicar.

"Boots, you call them! But anyhow, I am sorry I·alarmed—"

"You see," said the Vicar, stroking his chin, "our ladies, *ahem,* have peculiar views—rather inartistic views—about, *ahem,* clothing. Dressed as you are, I am afraid, I am really afraid that—beautiful as your costume certainly is—you will find yourself somewhat, *ahem,* somewhat isolated in society. We have a little proverb, 'When in Rome, *ahem,* one must do as the Romans do.' I can assure you that, assuming you are desirous to, *ahem,* associate with us—during your involuntary stay—"

The Angel retreated a step or so as the Vicar came nearer and nearer in his attempt to be diplomatic and confidential. The beautiful face grew perplexed. "I don't quite understand. Why do you keep making these noises in your throat? Is it Die or Eat, or any of those. . . ."

"As your host," interrupted the Vicar, and stopped.

"As my host," said the Angel.

"*Would* you object, pending more permanent arrangements, to invest yourself, *ahem,* in a suit, an entirely new suit I may say, like this I have on?"

"Oh!" said the Angel. He retreated so as to take in the Vicar from top to toe. "Wear clothes like yours!" he said. He was puzzled but amused. His eyes grew round and bright, his mouth puckered at the corners.

"Delightful!" he said, clapping his hands together. "What a mad, quaint dream this is! Where are they?" He caught at the neck of the saffron robe.

"Indoors!" said the Vicar. "This way. We will change—indoors!"

XII

SO THE ANGEL was invested in a pair of nether garments of the Vicar's, a shirt, ripped down the back (to accommodate the wings), socks, shoes—the Vicar's dress shoes—collar, tie, and light overcoat. But putting on the latter was painful, and reminded the Vicar that the bandaging was temporary. "I will ring for tea at once, and send Grummet down for Crump,'' said the Vicar. ''And dinner shall be earlier.'' While the Vicar shouted his orders on the landing rails, the Angel surveyed himself in the cheval glass with immense delight. If he was a stranger to pain, he was evidently no stranger—thanks perhaps to dreaming— to the pleasure of incongruity.

They had tea in the drawing-room. The Angel sat on the music stool (music stool because of his wings). At first he wanted to lie on the hearthrug. He looked much less radiant in the Vicar's clothes, than he had done upon the moor when dressed in saffron. His face shone still, the color of his hair and cheeks was strangely bright, and there was a superhuman light in his eyes, but his wings under the overcoat gave him the appearance of a hunchback. The garments, indeed, made quite a terrestrial thing of him, the trousers were puckered transversely, and the shoes a size or so too large.

He was charmingly affable and quite ignorant of the most elementary facts of civilization. Eating came without much difficulty, and the Vicar had an entertaining time teaching him how to take tea. ''What a mess it is! What a dear grotesque ugly world you live in!'' said the Angel. ''Fancy stuffing things into your mouth! We use our mouths just to talk and sing with. Our world, you know, is almost incurably beautiful. We get so very little ugliness, that I find all this . . . delightful.''

Mrs. Hinijer, the Vicar's housekeeper, looked at the Angel suspiciously when she brought in the tea. She thought him rather a ''queer customer.'' What she would have thought had she seen him in saffron no one can tell.

The Angel shuffled about the room with his cup of tea in one hand, and the bread and butter in the other, and examined the Vicar's furniture. Outside the French windows, the lawn with its array of dahlias and sunflowers glowed in the warm sunlight, and Mrs. Jehoram's sunshade stood thereon like a triangle of fire. He thought the Vicar's portrait over the mantel very curious indeed, could not understand what it was there for. ''You have yourself round,'' he said, *apropos* of the portrait, ''Why want yourself flat?'' and he was vastly amused at the glass fire screen. He found the oak chairs odd—''You're not square, are you?'' he said, when the Vicar explained their use. ''*We* never double ourselves up. We lie about on the asphodel when we want to rest.''

''The chair,'' said the Vicar, ''to tell you the truth, has always puzzled *me*. It dates, I think, from the days when the floors were cold and very dirty. I suppose we have kept up the habit. It's become a kind of instinct with us to sit on chairs. Anyhow, if I went to see one of my parishioners, and suddenly spread myself out on the floor—the natural way of it—I don't know what she would do. It would be all over the parish in no time. Yet it seems the natural method of reposing, to recline. The Greeks and Romans—''

''What is this?'' said the Angel abruptly.

''That's a stuffed kingfisher. I killed it.''

''Killed it!''

''Shot it,'' said the Vicar, ''with a gun.''

''Shot! As you did me?''

''I didn't kill you, you see. Fortunately.''

''Is killing making like that?''

''In a way.''

''Dear me! And you wanted to make me like that—wanted to put glass eyes in me and string me up in a glass case full of ugly green and brown stuff?''

''You see,'' began the Vicar, ''I scarcely understood—''

''Is that 'die'?'' asked the Angel suddenly.

"That is dead; it died."

"Poor little thing. I must eat a lot. But you say you killed it. *Why?*"

"You see," said the Vicar, "I take an interest in birds, and I *(ahem)* collect them. I wanted the specimen—"

The Angel stared at him for a moment with puzzled eyes. "A beautiful bird like that!" he said with a shiver. "Because the fancy took you. You wanted the specimen!"

He thought for a minute. "Do you often kill?" he asked the Vicar.

The Man of Science
XIII

THEN DOCTOR CRUMP arrived. Grummet had met him not a hundred yards from the vicarage gate. He was a large, rather heavy-looking man, with a clean-shaven face and a double chin. He was dressed in a grey morning coat (he always affected grey), with a checkered black and white tie. "What's the trouble?" he said, entering and staring without a shadow of surprise at the Angel's radiant face.

"This—*ahem*— gentleman," said the Vicar, "or—*ah*—Angel"—the Angel bowed—"is suffering from a gunshot wound."

"Gunshot wound!" said Doctor Crump. "In July! May I look at it, Mr.— Angel, I think you said?"

"He will probably be able to assuage your pain," said the Vicar. "Let me assist you to remove your coat?"

The Angel turned obediently.

"Spinal curvature?" muttered Doctor Crump quite audibly, walking round behind the Angel. "No! abnormal growth. Hullo! This is odd!" He clutched the left wing. "Curious," he said. "Reduplication of the anterior limb—bifid coracoid. Possible, of course, but I've never seen it before." The angel winced under his hands. "Humerus. Radius and Ulna. All there. Congenital, of course. Humerus broken. Curious integumentary simulation of feathers. Dear me. Almost avian. Probably of considerable interest in comparative anatomy. I never did!— How did this gunshot happen, Mr. Angel?"

The Vicar was amazed at the Doctor's matter-of-fact manner.

"Our friend," said the Angel, moving his head at the Vicar.

"Unhappily it is my doing," said the Vicar, stepping forward, explanatory. "I mistook the gentleman—the Angel *(ahem)*— for a large bird—"

"Mistook him for a large bird ! What next? Your eyes want seeing to," said Doctor Crump. "I've told you so before." He went on patting and feeling, keeping time with a series of grunts and inarticulate mutterings. . . . "But this is really a very good bit of amateur bandaging," said he. "I think I shall leave it. Curious malformation this is! Don't you find it inconvenient, Mr. Angel?"

He suddenly walked round so as to look in the Angel's face.

The Angel thought he referred to the wound. "It is rather," he said.

"If it wasn't for the bones I should say paint with iodine night and morning. Nothing like iodine. You could paint your face flat with it. But the osseous outgrowth, the bones, you know, complicate things. I could saw them off, of course. It's not a thing one should have done in a hurry—"

"Do you mean my wings?" said the Angel in alarm.

"Wings!" said the Doctor. "Eigh? Call'em wings! Yes—what else should I mean?"

"Saw them off!" said the Angel.

"Don't you think so? It's of course your affair. I am only advising—"

"Saw them off! What a funny creature you are!" said the Angel, beginning to laugh.

"As you will," said the Doctor. He detested people who laughed. "The things are curious," he said, turning to the Vicar. "If inconvenient"—to the Angel. "I never heard of such complete reduplication before—at least among animals. In plants it's common enough. Were you the only one in your family?" He did not wait for a reply. "Partial cases of the fission of limbs are not at all uncommon, of course, Vicar—six-fingered children, calves with six feet, and cats with double toes, you know. May I assist you?" he said, turning to the Angel who was struggling with the coat. "But such a complete reduplication, and so avian, too! It would be much less remarkable if it was simply another pair of arms."

The coat was got on and he and the Angel stared at one another.

"Really," said the Doctor, "one begins to understand how that beautiful myth of the angels arose. You look a little hectic, Mr. Angel—feverish. Excessive brilliance is almost worse as a symptom than excessive pallor. Curious your name should be Angel. I must send you a cooling draught, if you should feel thirsty in the night. . . ."

He made a memorandum on his shirt cuff. The Angel watched him thoughtfully, with the dawn of a smile in his eyes.

"One minute, Crump," said the Vicar, taking the Doctor's arm and leading him towards the door.

The Angel's smile grew brighter. He looked down at his black-clad legs. "He positively thinks I am a man!" said the Angel. "What he makes of the wings beats me altogether. What a queer creature he must be! This is really a most extraordinary Dream!"

XIV

"THAT IS AN Angel," whispered the Vicar. "You don't understand."

"*What?*" said the Doctor in a quick, sharp voice. His eyebrows went up and he smiled.

"But the wings?"

"Quite natural, quite . . . if a little abnormal."

"Are you sure they are natural?"

"My dear fellow, everything that is, is natural. There is nothing unnatural in the world. If I thought there was I should give up practice and go into *Le Grand Chartreuse*. There are abnormal phenomena, of course. And—"

"But the way I came upon him," said the Vicar.

"Yes, tell me where you picked him up," said the Doctor. He sat down on the hall table.

The Vicar began rather hesitatingly—he was not very good at story telling—with the rumors of a strange great bird. He told the story in clumsy sentences—for, knowing the Bishop as he did, with that awful example always before him he dreaded getting his pulpit style into his daily conversation—and at every third sentence or so, the Doctor made a downward movement of his head—the corners of his mouth tucked away, so to speak—as though he ticked off the phases of the story and so far found it just as it ought to be. "Self-hypnotism," he murmured once.

"I beg your pardon?" said the Vicar.

"Nothing," said the Doctor. "Nothing, I assure you. Go on. This is extremely interesting."

The Vicar told him he went out with his gun.

"*After* lunch, I think you said?" interrupted the Doctor.

"Immediately after," said the Vicar.

"You should not do such things, you know. But go on, please."

He came to the glimpse of the Angel from the gate.

"In the full glare," said the Doctor, in parenthesis. "It was seventy-nine in the shade."

When the Vicar had finished, the Doctor pressed his lips together tighter than ever, smiled faintly, and looked significantly into the Vicar's eyes.

"You don't . . ." began the Vicar, falteringly.

The Doctor shook his head. "Forgive me," he said, putting his hand on the Vicar's arm.

"You go out," he said, "on a hot lunch and on a hot afternoon. Probably over eighty. Your mind, what there is of it, is whirling with avian expectations. I say, 'what there is of it,' because most of your nervous energy is down there, digesting your dinner. A man who has been lying in the bracken stands up before you and you blaze away. Over he goes—and as it happens—as it happens—he has reduplicate forelimbs, one pair being not unlike wings. It's a coincidence certainly. And as for his iridescent colors and so forth—. Have you never had patches of color swim before your eyes before, on a brilliant sunlit day? . . . Are you sure they were confined to the wings? Think."

"But he says he *is* an Angel!" said the Vicar, staring out of his little round eyes, his plump hands in his pockets.

"*Ah!*" said the Doctor with his eye on the Vicar. "I expected as much." He paused.

"But don't you think . . ." began the Vicar.

"That man," said the Doctor in a low, earnest voice, "is a mattoid."

"A what?" said the Vicar.

"A mattoid. An abnormal man. Did you notice the effeminate delicacy of his face? His tendency to quite unmeaning laughter? His neglected hair? Then consider his singular dress . . ."

The Vicar's hand went up to his chin.

"Marks of mental weakness," said the Doctor. "Many of this type of degenerate show this same disposition to assume some vast mysterious credentials. One will call himself the Prince of Wales, another the Archangel Gabriel, another the Deity even. Ibsen thinks he is a Great Teacher, and Maeterlink a new Shakespeare. I've just been reading all about it—in Nordau. No doubt his odd deformity gave him an idea. . . ."

"But really," began the Vicar. "No doubt he's slipped away from confinement."

"I do not altogether accept . . ."

"You will. If not, there's the police, and failing that, advertisement; but, of course, his people may want to hush it up. It's a sad thing in a family. . . ."

"He seems so altogether . . ."

"Probably you'll hear from his friends in a day or so," said the Doctor, feeling for his watch. "He can't live far from here, I should think. He seems harmless enough. I must come along and see that wing again tomorrow." He slid off the hall table and stood up.

"Those old wives' tales still have their hold on you," he said, patting the Vicar on the shoulder. "But an angel, you know—Ha, ha!"

"I certainly *did* think . . ." said the Vicar dubiously.

"Weigh the evidence," said the Doctor, still fumbling at his watch. "Weigh the evidence with our instruments of precision. What does it leave you? Splashes of color, spots of fancy—*muscae volantes.*"

"And yet," said the Vicar, "I could almost swear to the glory on his wings. . . ."

"Think it over," said the Doctor (watch out); "hot afternoon—brilliant sunshine—boiling down on your head. . . . But really I *must* be going. It is a quarter to five. I'll see your—angel (ha, ha!) tomorrow again, if no one has been to fetch him in the meanwhile. Your bandaging was really very good. I flatter *myself* on that score. Our ambulance classes *were* a success you see . . . Good afternoon."

The Curate
XV

THE VICAR OPENED the door half mechanically to let out Crump, and saw Mendham, his curate, coming up the pathway by the hedge of purple vetch and meadowsweet. At that his hand went up to his chin and his eyes grew perplexed. Suppose he *was* deceived. The Doctor passed the Curate with a sweep of his hand from his hat brim. Crump was an extraordinarily clever fellow, the Vicar thought, and knew far more of anyone's brain than one did oneself. The Vicar felt that so acutely. It made the coming explanation difficult. Suppose he were to go back into the drawing-room, and find just a tramp asleep on the hearthrug.

Mendham was a cadaverous man with a magnificent beard. He looked, indeed, as though he had run to beard as a mustard plant does to seed. But when he spoke you found he had a voice as well.

"My wife came home in a dreadful state," he brayed out at long range.

"Come in," said the Vicar; "come in. Most remarkable occurrence. Please come in. Come into the study. I'm really dreadfully sorry. But when I explain . . ."

"And apologize, I hope," brayed the Curate.

"And apologize. No, not that way. This way. The study."

"Now what *was* that woman?" said the Curate, turning on the Vicar as the latter closed the study door.

"What woman?"

"Pah!"

"But really!"

"The painted creature in light attire—disgustingly light attire, to speak freely—with whom you were promenading the garden."

"My dear Mendham—that was an Angel!"

"A very pretty Angel?"

"The world is getting so matter-of-fact," said the Vicar.

"The world," roared the Curate, "grows blacker every day. But to find a man in your position, shamelessly, openly . . ."

"*Bother!*" said the Vicar aside. He rarely swore. "Look here, Mendham, you really misunderstand. I can assure you . . ."

"Very well," said the Curate. "Explain!" He stood with his lank legs apart, his arms folded, scowling at his Vicar over his big beard.

(Explanations, I repeat, I have always considered the peculiar fallacy of this scientific age.)

The Vicar looked about him helplessly. The world had all gone dull and dead. Had he been dreaming all the afternoon? Was there really an angel in the drawing-room? Or was he the sport of a complicated hallucination?

"Well?" said Mendham, at the end of a minute.

The Vicar's hand fluttered about his chin. "It's such a round-about story," he said.

"No doubt it will be," said Mendham harshly.

The Vicar restrained a movement of impatience.

"I went out to look for a strange bird this afternoon. . . . Do you believe in angels, Mendham, real angels?"

"I'm not here to discuss theology. I am the husband of an insulted woman."

"But I tell you it's not a figure of speech; this *is* an angel, a real angel with wings. He's in the next room now. You do misunderstand me, so . . ."

" Really, Hilyer—"

"It is true I tell you, Mendham. I swear it is true." The Vicar's voice grew impassioned. "What sin I have done that I should entertain and clothe angelic visitants, I don't know. I only know that—inconvenient as it undoubtedly will be—I have an angel now in the drawing-room, wearing my new suit and finishing his tea. And he's stopping with me, indefinitely, at my invitation. No doubt it was rash of me. But I can't turn him out, you know, because Mrs. Mendham— I may be a weakling, but I am still a gentleman."

"Really, Hilyer—"

"I can assure you it is true." There was a note of hysterical desperation in the Vicar's voice.

"I fired at him taking him for a flamingo, and hit him in the wing."

"I thought this was a case for the Bishop. I find it is a case for the Lunacy Commissioners."

"Come and see him, Mendham!"

"But there *are* no angels."

"We teach the people differently," said the Vicar.

"Not as material bodies," said the Curate.

"Anyhow, come and see him."

"I don't want to see your hallucinations," began the Curate.

"I can't explain anything unless you come and see him," said the Vicar. "A man who's more like an angel than anything else in heaven or earth. You simply must see if you wish to understand."

"I don't wish to understand," said the Curate. "I don't wish to lend myself to any imposture. Surely, Hilyer, if this is not an imposition, you can tell me yourself. . . . Flamingo, indeed!"

XVI

THE ANGEL HAD finished his tea and was standing looking pensively out of the window. He thought the old church down the valley lit by the light of the setting sun was very beautiful, but he could not understand the serried ranks of tombstones that lay up the hillside beyond. He turned as Mendham and the Vicar came in.

Now Mendham could bully his Vicar cheerfully enough, just as he could bully his congregation; but he was not the sort of man to bully a stranger. He looked at the Angel, and the "strange woman" theory was disposed of. The Angel's beauty was too clearly the beauty of the youth.

"Mr. Hilyer tells me," Mendham began, in an almost apologetic tone, "that you—ah—it's so curious—claim to be an Angel."

"*Are* an Angel," said the Vicar.

The Angel bowed.

"Naturally," said Mendham, "we are curious."

"Very," said the Angel. "The blackness and the shape."

"I beg your pardon?" said Mendham.

"The blackness and the flaps," repeated the Angel; "and no wings."

"Precisely," said Mendham, who was altogether at a loss. "We are, of course, curious to know something of how you came into the village in such a peculiar costume."

The Angel looked at the Vicar. The Vicar touched his chin.

"You see," began the Vicar.

"Let *him* explain," said Mendham; "I beg."

"I wanted to suggest," began the Vicar.

"And I don't want you to suggest."

"Bother!" said the Vicar.

The Angel looked from one to the other. "Such rugose expressions flit across your faces!" he said.

"You see, Mr.—Mr.—I don't know your name," said Mendham, with a certain diminution of suavity. "The case stands thus: My wife—four ladies, I might say—are playing lawn tennis, when you suddenly rush out on them, sir; you rush out on them from among the rhododendra in a very defective costume. You and Mr. Hilyer."

"But I—" said the Vicar.

"I know. It was this gentleman's costume was defective. Naturally—it is my place in fact—to demand an explanation." His voice was growing in volume. "And I *must* demand an explanation."

The Angel smiled faintly at his note of anger and his sudden attitude of determination—arms tightly folded.

"I am rather new to the world," the Angel began.

"Nineteen at least," said Mendham. "Old enough to know better. That's a poor excuse."

"May I ask one question first?" said the Angel.

"Well?"

"Do you think I am a Man—like yourself? As the checkered man did."

"If you are not a man—"

"One other question. Have you *never* heard of an Angel?"

"I warn you not to try that story upon me," said Mendham now back at his familiar crescendo.

The Vicar interrupted: "But Mendham—he has wings!"

"Please let me talk to him," said Mendham.

"You are so quaint," said the Angel; "you interrupt everything I have to say."

"But what *have* you to say?" said Mendham.

"That I really *am* an Angel . . . ."

"Pshaw!"

"There you go!"

"But tell me, honestly, how you came to be in the shrubbery of Siddermorton Vicarage—in the state in which you were. And in the Vicar's company. Cannot you abandon this ridiculous story of yours? . . . ."

The Angel shrugged his wings. "What *is* the matter with this man?" he said to the Vicar.

"My dear Mendham," said the Vicar, "a few words from me. . . . ."

"Surely my question is straightforward enough!"

"But you won't tell me the answer you want, and it's no good my telling you any other."

"Pshaw!" said the Curate again. And then turning suddenly on the Vicar, "Where does he come from?"

The Vicar was in a dreadful state of doubt by this time.

"He *says* he is an Angel!" said the Vicar. "Why don't you listen to him?"

"No angel would alarm four ladies. . . ."

"Is *that* what it is all about?" said the Angel.

"Enough cause too, I should think!" said the Curate.

"But I really did not know," said the Angel.

"This is altogether too much!"

"I am sincerely sorry I alarmed these ladies."

"You ought to be. But I see I shall get nothing out of you two." Mendham went towards the door. "I am convinced there is something discreditable at the bottom of this business. Or why not tell a simple straightforward story? I will confess you puzzle me. Why, in this enlightened age, you should tell this fantastic, this far-fetched story of an Angel, altogether beats me. What good *can* it do? . . ."

"But stop and look at his wings!" said the Vicar. "I can assure you he has wings!"

Mendham had his fingers on the door-handle. "I have seen quite enough," he said. "It may be this is simply a foolish attempt at a hoax, Hilyer."

"But Mendham!" said the Vicar.

The Curate halted in the doorway and looked at the Vicar over his shoulder. The accumulating judgment of months found vent. "I cannot understand, Hilyer, why you are in the Church. For the life of me I cannot. The air is full of Social Movements, of Economic change, the Woman Movement, Rational Dress, The Reunion of Christendom, Socialism, Individualism—all the great and moving Questions of the Hour! Surely, we who follow the Great Reformer. . . . And here you are stuffing birds, and startling ladies with your callous disregard. . . ."

"But Mendham," began the Vicar.

The Curate would not hear him. "You shame the Apostles with your levity. . . . But this is only a preliminary enquiry," he said, with a threatening note in his sonorous voice, and so vanished abruptly (with a violent slam) from the room.

XVII

"ARE ALL MEN so odd as this?" said the Angel.

"I'm in such a difficult position," said the Vicar. "You see," he said, and stopped, searching his chin for an idea.

"I'm beginning to see," said the Angel.

"They won't believe it."

"I see that."

"They will think I tell lies."

"And?"

"That will be extremely painful to me."

"Painful! . . . Pain," said the Angel. "I hope not."

The Vicar shook his head. The good report of the village had been the breath of his life, so far. "You see," he said, "it would look so much more plausible if you said you were just a man."

"But I'm not," said the Angel.

"No, you're not," said the Vicar. "So that's no good."

"Nobody here, you know, has ever seen an Angel, or heard of one—except in church. If you had made your *debut* in the chancel—on Sunday—it might have been different. But that's too late now. . . . *(Bother!)* Nobody, absolutely nobody, will believe in you."

"I hope I am not inconveniencing you?"

"Not at all," said the Vicar; "not at all. Only—. Naturally it may be inconvenient if you tell a too incredible story. If I might suggest *(ahem)—.*"

"Well?"

"You see, people in the world, being men themselves, will almost certainly regard you as a man. If you say you are not, they will simply say you do not tell the truth. Only exceptional people appreciate the exceptional. When in Rome one must—well, respect Roman prejudices a little—talk Latin. You will find it better—"

"You propose I should feign to become a man?"

"You have my meaning at once."

The Angel stared at the Vicar's hollyhocks and thought.

"Possibly, after all," he said slowly, "I *shall* become a man. I may have been too hasty in saying I was not. You say there are no angels in this world. Who am I to set myself up against your experience? A mere thing of a day— so far as this world goes. If you say there are no angels—clearly I must be something else. I eat—angels do not eat. I *may* be a man already."

"A convenient view, at any rate," said the Vicar.

"If it is convenient to you—"

"It is. And then to account for your presence here."

"*If,*" said the Vicar, after a hesitating moment of reflection, "if, for instance, you had been an ordinary man with a weakness for wading, and you had gone wading in the Sidder, and your clothes had been stolen, for instance, and I had come upon you in that position of inconvenience; the explanation I shall have to make to Mrs. Mendham—would be shorn at least of the supernatural element. There is such a feeling against the supernatural element nowadays—even in the pulpit. You would hardly believe—"

"It's a pity that was not the case," said the Angel.

"Of course," said the Vicar. "It is a great pity that was not the case. But at any rate you will oblige me if you do not obtrude your angelic nature. You will oblige everyone, in fact. There is a settled opinion that angels do not do this kind of thing. And nothing is more painful—as I can testify—than a decaying settled opinion. . . . Settled opinions are mental teeth in more ways than one. For my own part,"—the Vicar's hand passed over his eyes for a moment—"I cannot but believe you are an angel . . . Surely I can believe my own eyes."

"We always do ours," said the Angel.

"And so do we, within limits."

Then the clock upon the mantel chimed seven, and almost simultaneously Mrs. Hinijer announced dinner.

After Dinner

XVIII

THE ANGEL AND the Vicar sat at dinner. The Vicar, with his napkin tucked in at his neck, watched the Angel struggling with his soup. "You will soon get into the way of it," said the Vicar. The knife and fork business was done awkwardly but with effect. The Angel looked furtively at Delia, the little waiting maid. When presently they sat cracking nuts—which the Angel found congenial enough—and the girl had gone, the Angel asked: "Was that a lady, too?"

"Well," said the Vicar *(crack)*. "No—she is not a lady. She is a servant."

"Yes," said the Angel; "she *had* rather a nicer shape."

"You mustn't tell Mrs. Mendham that," said the Vicar, covertly satisfied.

"She didn't stick out so much at the shoulders and hips, and there was more of her in between. And the color of her robes was not discordant—simply neutral. And her face—"

"Mrs. Mendham and her daughters had been playing tennis," said the Vicar, feeling he ought not to listen to detraction even of his mortal enemy. "Do you like these things—these nuts?"

"Very much," said the Angel. *Crack.*

"You see," said the Vicar *(Chum, chum, chum)*. "For my own part I entirely believe you are an angel."

"Yes!" said the Angel.

"I shot you—I saw you flutter. It's beyond dispute. In my own mind. I admit it's curious and against my preconceptions, but—practically—I'm assured, perfectly assured in fact, that I saw what I certainly did see. But after the behavior of these people. *(Crack)*. I really don't see how we are to persuade people. Nowadays people are so very particular about evidence. So that I think there is a great deal to be said for the attitude you assume. Temporarily at least I think it would be best of you to do as you propose to do, and behave as a man as far as possible. Of course there is no knowing how or when you may go back. After what has happened *(Gluck, gluck, gluck*—as the Vicar refills his glass)—after what has happened I should not be surprised to see the side of the room fall away, and the hosts of heaven appear to take you away again—take us both away even. You have so far enlarged my imagination. All these years I have been forgetting Wonderland. But still—. It will certainly be wiser to break the thing gently to them."

"This life of yours," said the Angel. "I'm still in the dark about it. How do you begin?"

"Dear me!" said the Vicar. "Fancy having to explain that! We begin existence here, you know, as babies, silly pink helpless things wrapped in white, with goggling eyes, that yelp dismally at the Font. Then these babies grow larger and become even beautiful—when their faces are washed. And they continue to grow to a certain size. They become children, boys and girls, youths and maidens *(Crack)*, young men and young women. That is the finest time in life, according to many—certainly the most beautiful. Full of great hopes and dreams, vague emotions and unexpected dangers."

"*That* was a maiden?" said the Angel, indicating the door through which Delia had disappeared.

"Yes," said the Vicar, "that was a maiden." And paused thoughtfully.

"And then?"

"Then," said the Vicar, "the glamor fades and life begins in earnest. The young men and young women pair off—most of them. They come to me shy and bashful, in smart ugly dresses, and I marry them. And then little pink babies come to them, and some of the youths and maidens that were, grow fat and vulgar, and some grow thin and shrewish, and their pretty complexions go, and they get a queer delusion of superiority over the younger people, and all the delight and glory goes out of their lives. So they call the delight and glory of the younger ones, Illusion. And then they begin to drop to pieces."

"Drop to pieces!" said the Angel. "How grotesque!"

"Their hair comes off and gets dull colored or ashen grey" said the Vicar. "*I*, for instance." He bowed his head forward to show a circular shining patch the size of a florin. "And their teeth come out. Their faces collapse and become as wrinkled and dry as a shrivelled apple. 'Corrugated' you called mine. They care more and more for what they have to eat and to drink, and less and less for any of the other delights of life. Their limbs get loose in the joints, and their hearts slack, or little pieces from their lungs come coughing up. Pain. . . ."

"Ah!" said the Angel.

"Pain comes into their lives more and more. And then they go. They do not like to go, but they have to—out of this world, very reluctantly, clutching its pain at last in their eagerness to stop. . . ."

"Where do they go?"

"Once I thought I knew. But now I am older I know I do not know. We have a Legend—perhaps it is not a legend. One may be a churchman and disbelieve. Stokes says there is nothing in it. . . ." The Vicar shook his head at the bananas.

"And you?" said the Angel. "Were you a little pink baby?"

"A little while ago I was a little pink baby."

"Were you robed then as you are now?"

"Oh no! Dear me! What a queer idea! Had long white clothes, I suppose, like the rest of them."

"And then you were a little boy?"

"A little boy."

"And then a glorious youth?"

"I was not a very glorious youth, I am afraid. I was sickly, and too poor to be radiant, and with a timid heart. I studied hard and pored over the dying thoughts of men long dead. So I lost the glory, and no maiden came to me, and the dulness of life began too soon."

"And you have your little pink babies?"

"None," said the Vicar with a scarce perceptible pause. "Yet all the same, as you see, I am beginning to drop to pieces. Presently my back will droop like a wilting flowerstalk. And then, in a few thousand days more I shall be done with, and I shall go out of this world of mine. . . . Whither I do not know."

"And you have to eat like this every day?"

"Eat, and get clothes and keep this roof above me. There are some very disagreeable things in this world called Cold and Rain. And the other people here—how and why is too long a story—have made me a kind of chorus to their lives. They bring their little pink babies to me and I have to say a name and some other things over each new pink baby. And when the children have grown to be youths and maidens, they come again and are confirmed. You will understand that better later. Then before they may join in couples and have pink babies of their own, they must come again and hear me read out of a book. They would be outcast, and no other maiden would speak to the maiden who had a little pink baby without I had read over her for twenty minutes out of my book. It's a necessary thing, as you will see. Odd as it may seem to you. And afterwards when they are falling to pieces, I try and persuade them of a strange world in which I scarcely believe myself, where life is altogether different from what they have had—or desire. And in the end, I bury them, and read out of my book to those who will presently follow into the unknown land. I stand at the beginning, and at the zenith, and at the setting of their lives. And on every seventh day, I who am a man myself, I who see no further than they do, talk to them of the Life to Come—the life of which we know nothing. If such a life there be. And slowly I drop to pieces amidst my prophesying."

"What a strange life!" said the Angel.

"Yes," said the Vicar. "What a strange life! But the thing that makes it strange to me is new. I had taken it as a matter of course until you came into my life.''

"This life of ours is so insistent," said the Vicar. "It, and its petty needs, its temporary pleasures (*Crack*) swathe our souls about. While I am preaching to these people of mine of another life, some are ministering to one appetite and eating sweets, others—the old men—are slumbering, the youths glance at the maidens, the grown men protrude white waistcoats and gold chains, pomp and vanity on a substratum of carnal substance, their wives flaunt garish bonnets at one another. And I go on droning away of the things unseen and unrealized— 'Eye hath not seen,' I read, 'nor ear heard, nor hath it entered into the imagination of man to conceive,' and I look up to catch an adult male immortal admiring the fit of a pair of three and sixpenny gloves. It is damping year after year. When I was ailing in my youth I felt almost the assurance of vision that beneath this temporary phantasm world was the real world—the enduring world of the Life Everlasting. But now—''

He glanced at his chubby white hand, fingering the stem of his glass. "I have put on flesh since then," he said. [*Pause*].

"I have changed and developed very much. The battle of the Flesh and Spirit does not trouble me as it did. Every day I feel less confidence in my beliefs, and more in God. I live, I am afraid, a quiescent life, duties fairly done, a little ornithology and a little chess, a trifle of mathematical trifling. My times are in His hands—''

The Vicar sighed and became pensive. The Angel watched him, and the Angel's eyes were troubled with the puzzle of him. "Gluck, gluck, gluck," went the decanter as the Vicar refilled his glass.

XIX

SO THE ANGEL dined and talked to the Vicar, and presently the night came and he was overtaken by yawning.

"Yah—oh!" said the Angel suddenly. "Dear me! A higher power seemed suddenly to stretch my mouth open and a great breath of air went rushing down my throat.''

"You yawned," said the Vicar. "Do you never yawn in the angelic country?''

"Never," said the Angel.

"And yet you are immortal!—I suppose you want to go to bed.''

"Bed!" said the Angel. "Where's that?''

So the Vicar explained darkness to him and the art of going to bed. (The Angels, it seems sleep only in order to dream, and dream, like primitive man, with their foreheads on their knees. And they sleep among the white poppy meadows in the heat of the day.) The Angel found the bedroom arrangements quaint enough.

"Why is everything raised up on big wooden legs?" he said. "You have the floor, and then you put everything you have upon a wooden quadruped. Why do you do it?" The Vicar explained with philosophical vagueness. The Angel burnt his finger in the candle-flame—and displayed an absolute ignorance of the elementary principles of combustion. He was merely charmed when a line of fire ran up the curtains. The Vicar had to deliver a lecture on fire so soon as the flame was extinguished. He had all kinds of explanations to make—even the soap needed explaining. It was an hour or more before the Angel was safely tucked in for the night.

"He's very beautiful," said the Vicar, descending the staircase, quite tired out; "and he's a real angel no doubt. But I am afraid he will be a dreadful anxiety, all the same, before he gets into our earthly way with things."

He seemed quite worried. He helped himself to an extra glass of sherry before he put away the wine in the cellaret.

XX

THE CURATE STOOD in front of the looking-glass and solemnly divested himself of his collar.

"I never heard a more fantastic story," said Mrs. Mendham from the basket chair. "The man must be mad. Are you sure—."

"Perfectly, my dear. I've told you every word, every incident—."

"*Well!*" said Mrs. Mendham, and spread her hands. "There's no sense in it."

"Precisely, my dear."

"The Vicar," said Mrs. Mendham, "must be mad."

"This hunchback is certainly one of the strangest creatures I've seen for a long time. Foreign looking, with a big bright-colored face and long brown hair. . . . It can't have been cut for months!" The Curate put his studs carefully upon the shelf of the dressing-table. "And a kind of staring look about his eyes, and a simpering smile. Quite a silly looking person. Effeminate."

"But who *can* he be?" said Mrs. Mendham.

"I can't imagine, my dear. Nor where he came from. He might be a chorister or something of that sort."

"But *why* should he be about the shrubbery . . . in that dreadful costume?"

"I don't know. The Vicar gave me no explanation. He simply said, 'Mendham, this is an Angel.' "

"I wonder if he drinks. . . . They may have been bathing near the spring, of course," reflected Mrs. Mendham. "But I noticed no other clothes on his arm."

The Curate sat down on his bed and unlaced his boots.

"It's a perfect mystery to me, my dear." (Flick, flick of laces.) "Hallucination is the only charitable—"

"You are sure, George, that it was *not* a woman."

"Perfectly," said the Curate.

"I know what men are, of course."

"It was a young man of nineteen or twenty," said the Curate.

"I can't understand it," said Mrs. Mendham. "You say the creature is staying at the Vicarage?"

"Hilyer is simply mad," said the Curate. He got up and went padding round the room to the door to put out his boots. "To judge by his manner you would really think he believed this cripple was an Angel." ("Are your shoes out, dear?")

("They're just by the wardrobe"), said Mrs. Mendham. "He always was a little queer, you know. There was always something childish about him. . . . An Angel!"

The Curate came and stood by the fire, fumbling with his braces. Mrs. Mendham liked a fire even in the summer. "He shirks all the serious problems in life and is always trifling with some new foolishness," said the Curate. "Angel indeed!" He laughed suddenly. "Hilyer *must* be mad," he said.

Mrs. Mendham laughed too. "Even that doesn't explain the hunchback," she said.

"The hunchback must be mad too," said the Curate.

"It's the only way of explaining it in a sensible way," said Mrs. Mendham. [*Pause.*]

"Angel or no angel," said Mrs. Mendham, "I know what is due to me. Even supposing the man thought he *was* in the company of an angel, that is no reason why he should not behave like a gentleman."

"That is perfectly true."

"You will write to the Bishop, of course?"

Mendham coughed. "No, I shan't write to the Bishop," said Mendham. "I think it seems a little disloyal. . . . And he took no notice of the last, you know."

"But surely—"

"I shall write to Austin. In confidence. He will be sure to tell the Bishop, you know. And you must remember, my dear—"

"That Hilyer can dismiss you, you were going to say. My dear, the man's much too weak! *I* should have a word to say about that. And besides, you do all his work for him. Practically, we manage the parish from end to end. I do not know what would become of the poor if it was not for me. They'd have free quarters in the Vicarage tomorrow. There is that Goody Ansell—"

"I know, my dear," said the Curate, turning away and proceeding with his undressing. "You were telling me about her only this afternoon."

XXI

AND THUS IN the little bedroom over the gable we reach a first resting place in this story. And as we have been hard at it, getting our story spread out before you, it may be perhaps well to recapitulate a little.

Looking back you will see that much has been done; we began with a blaze of light "not uniform but broken all over by curving flashes like the waving of swords," and the sound of a mighty harping, and the advent of an Angel with polychromatic wings.

Swiftly, dexterously, as the reader must admit, wings have been clipped, halo handled off, the glory clapped into coat and trousers, and the Angel made for all practical purposes a man, under a suspicion of being either a lunatic or an impostor. You have heard too, or at least been able to judge, what the Vicar and the Doctor and the Curate's wife thought of the strange arrival. And further remarkable opinions are to follow.

The afterglow of the summer sunset in the northwest darkens into night and the Angel sleeps, dreaming himself back in the wonderful world where it is always light, and everyone is happy, where fire does not burn and ice does not chill; where rivulets of starlight go streaming through the amaranthine meadows, out to the seas of Peace. He dreams, and it seems to him that once more his wings glow with a thousand colors and flash through the crystal air of the world from which he has come.

So he dreams. But the Vicar lies awake, too perplexed for dreaming. Chiefly he is troubled by the possibilities of Mrs. Mendham; but the evening's talk has opened strange vistas in his mind, and he is stimulated by a sense as of something seen darkly by the indistinct vision of a hitherto unsuspected wonderland lying about his world. For twenty years now he has held his village living and lived his daily life, protected by his familiar creed, by the clamor of the details of life, from any mystical dreaming. But now interweaving with the familiar bother of his persecuting neighbor, is an altogether unfamiliar sense of strange new things.

There was something ominous in the feeling. Once, indeed, it rose above all other considerations, and in a kind of terror he blundered out of bed, bruised his shins very convincingly, found the matches at last, and lit a candle to assure himself of the reality of his own customary world again. But on the whole the more tangible trouble was the Mendham avalanche. Her tongue seemed to be hanging above him like the sword of Damocles. What might she not say of this business, before her indignant imagination came to rest?

And while the successful captor of the Strange Bird was sleeping thus uneasily, Gully of Sidderton was carefully unloading his gun after a wearisome blank day, and Sandy Bright was on his knees in prayer, with the window carefully fastened. Annie Durgan was sleeping hard with her mouth open, and Amory's mother was dreaming of washing, and both of them had long since exhausted the topics of the Sound and the Glare. Lumpy Durgan was sitting up in his bed, now crooning the fragment of a tune and now listening intently for a sound he had heard once and longed to hear again. As for the solicitor's clerk at Iping Hanger, he was trying to write poetry about a confectioner's girl at Portburdock, and the Strange Bird was quite out of his head. But the ploughman who had seen it on the confines of Siddermorton Park had a black eye. That had been one of the more tangible consequences of a little argument about birds' legs in the "Ship." It is worthy of this passing mention, since it is probably the only known instance of an Angel causing anything of the kind.

Morning

XXII

THE VICAR GOING to call the Angel, found him dressed and leaning out of his window. It was a glorious morning, still dewy, and the rising sunlight slanting round the corner of the house, struck warm and yellow upon the hillside. The birds were astir in the hedges and shrubbery. Up the hillside—for it was late in August—a plough drove slowly. The Angel's chin rested upon his hands and he did not turn as the Vicar came up to him.

"How's the wing?" said the Vicar.

"I'd forgotten it," said the Angel. "Is that yonder a man?"

The Vicar looked. "That's a ploughman."

"Why does he go to and fro like that? Does it amuse him?"

"He's ploughing. That's his work."

"Work! Why does he do it? It seems a monotonous thing to do."

"It is," admitted the Vicar. "But he has to do it to get a living, you know. To get food to eat and all that kind of thing."

"How curious!" said the Angel. "Do all men have to do that? Do you?"

"Oh, no. He does it for me; does my share."

"Why?" asked the Angel.

"Oh! in return for things I do for him, you know. We go in for division of labor in this world. Exchange is no robbery."

"I see," said the Angel, with his eyes still on the ploughman's heavy movements.

"What do you do for him?"

"That seems an easy question to you," said the Vicar, "but really!—it's difficult. Our social arrangements are rather complicated. It's impossible to explain these things all at once, before breakfast. Don't you feel hungry?"

"I think I do," said the Angel slowly, still at the window; and then abruptly, "Somehow I can't help thinking that ploughing must be far from enjoyable."

"Possibly," said the Vicar, "very possibly. But breakfast is ready. Won't you come down?"

The Angel left the window reluctantly.

"Our society," explained the Vicar on the staircase, "is a complicated organization."

"Yes?"

"And it is so arranged that some do one thing and some another."

"And that lean, bent old man trudges after that heavy blade of iron pulled by a couple of horses while we go down to eat?"

"Yes. You will find it is perfectly just. Ah! mushrooms and poached eggs! It's the Social System. Pray be seated. Possibly it strikes you as unfair?"

"I'm puzzled," said the Angel.

"The drink I'm sending you is called coffee," said the Vicar. "I daresay you are. When I was a young man I was puzzled in the same way. But afterwards comes a Broader View of Things. (These black things are called mushrooms; they look beautiful.) Other Considerations. All men are brothers, of course, but some are younger brothers, so to speak. There is work that requires culture and refinement, and work in which culture and refinement would be an impediment. And the rights of property must not be forgotten. One must render unto Cæsar. . . . Do you know, instead of explaining this matter now (this is yours), I think I will lend you a little book to read (*chum, chum, chum*—these mushrooms are well up to their appearance), which sets the whole thing out very clearly."

The Violin
XXIII

AFTER BREAKFAST THE Vicar went into the little room next his study to find a book on Political Economy for the Angel to read. For the Angel's social ignorances were clearly beyond any verbal explanations. The door stood ajar.

"What is that?" said the Angel, following him. "A violin!" He took it down. "You play?" said the Vicar.

The Angel had the bow in his hand, and by way of answer drove it across the strings. The quality of the note made the Vicar turn suddenly.

The Angel's hand tightened on the instrument. The bow flew back and flickered, and an air the Vicar had never heard before danced in his ears. The Angel shifted the fiddle under his dainty chin and went on playing, and as he played his eyes grew bright and his lips smiled. At first he looked at the Vicar, then his expression became abstracted. He seemed no longer to look at the Vicar, but through him, at something beyond, something in his memory or his imagination, something infinitely remote, undreamt of hitherto . . .

The Vicar tried to follow the music. The air reminded him of a flame, it rushed up, shone, flickered and danced, passed and reappeared. No!—it did not reappear! Another air—like it and unlike it, shot up after it, wavered, vanished. Then another, the same and not the same. It reminded him of the flaring tongues that palpitate and change above a newly lit fire. There are two airs—or *motifs*, which is it?—thought the Vicar. He knew remarkably little of musical technique. They go dancing up, one pursuing the other, out of the fire of the incantation, pursuing, fluctuating, turning, up into the sky. There below was the fire burning, a flame without fuel upon a level space, and there two flirting butterflies of sound, dancing away from it, up, one over another, swift, abrupt, uncertain.

"Flirting butterflies were they!" What was the Vicar thinking of? Where was he? In the little room next to his study, of course! And the Angel standing in front of him smiling into his face, playing the violin, and looking through him as though he was only a window—. That *motif* again, a yellow flare, spread fanlike by a gust, and now one, then with a swift eddying upward flight the other, the two things of fire and light pursuing one another again up into that clear immensity.

The study and the realities of life suddenly faded out of the Vicar's eyes, grew thinner and thinner like a mist that dissolves into air, and he and the Angel stood together on a pinnacle of wrought music, about which glittering melodies circled, and vanished, and reappeared. He was in the land of Beauty, and once more the glory of heaven was upon the Angel's face, and the glowing delights of color pulsated in his wings. Himself the Vicar could not see. But I cannot tell you of the vision of that great and spacious land, of its incredible openness, and height, and nobility. For there is no space there like ours, no time as we know it; one must needs speak by bungling metaphors and own in bitterness after all that one has failed. And it was only a vision. The wonderful creatures flying through the æther saw them not as they stood there, flew through them as one might pass through a wisp of mist. The Vicar lost all sense of duration, all sense of necessity—

"Ah!" said the Angel, suddenly putting down the fiddle.

The Vicar had forgotten the book on Political Economy, had forgotten everything until the Angel had done. For a minute he sat quite still. Then he woke up with a start. He was sitting on the old iron-bound chest

"Really," he said slowly, "you are very clever."

He looked about him in a puzzled way. "I had a kind of vision while you were playing. I seemed to see—. What did I see? It has gone."

He stood up with a dazzled expression upon his face. "I shall never play the violin again," he said, "I wish you would take it to your room—and keep it—. And play to me again. I did not know anything of music until I heard you play. I do not feel as though I had ever heard any music before."

He stared at the Angel, then about him at the room. "I have never felt anything of this kind with music before," he said. He shook his head. "I shall never play again."

The Angel Explores the Village

XXIV

VERY UNWISELY, AS I think, the Vicar allowed the Angel to go down into the village by himself, to enlarge his ideas of humanity. Unwisely, because how was he to imagine the reception the Angel would receive? Not thoughtlessly, I am afraid. He had always carried himself with decorum in the village, and the idea of a slow procession through the little street with all the inevitable curious remarks, explanations, pointings, was too much for him. The Angel might do the strangest things, the village was certain to think them. Peering faces. "Who's *he* got now?" Besides, was it not his duty to prepare his sermon in good time? The Angel, duly directed, went down cheerfully by himself—still innocent of most of the peculiarities of the human as distinguished from the angelic turn of mind.

The Angel walked slowly, his white hands folded behind his hunched back, his sweet face looking this way and that. He peered curiously into the eyes of the people he met. A little child picking a bunch of vetch and honeysuckle looked in his face, and forthwith came and put them in his hand. It was about the only kindness he had from a human being (saving only the Vicar and one other). He heard Mother Gustick scolding that granddaughter of hers as he passed the door. "You *Brazen* Faggit—you!" said Mother Gustick. "You Trumpery Baggage!"

The Angel stopped, startled at the strange sounds of Mother Gustick's voice. "Put yer best clo'es on, and yer feather in yer 'at, and off you goes to meet en, fal lal, and me at 'ome slaving for ye. 'Tis a Fancy Lady you'll be wantin' to be, my gal, a walkin' Touch and Go, with yer idleness and finery—"

The voice ceased abruptly, and a great peace came upon the battered air. "Most grotesque and strange!" said the Angel, still surveying this wonderful box of discords. "Walking Touch and Go!" He did not know that Mrs. Gustick had suddenly become aware of his existence, and was scrutinizing his appearance through the window-blind. Abruptly the door flew open, and she stared out into the Angel's face. A strange apparition, grey and dusty hair, and the dirty pink dress unhooked to show the stringy throat, a discolored gargoyle, presently to begin spouting incomprehensible abuse.

"Now, then, Mister," began Mrs. Gustick. "Have ye nothin' better to do than listen at people's doors for what you can pick up?"

The Angel stared at her in astonishment.

"D'year!" said Mrs. Gustick, evidently very angry indeed. "Listenin'."

"Have you any objection to my hearing . . ."

"Object to my hearing! Course I have! Whad yer think? You aint such a Ninny . . ."

"But if ye didn't want me to hear, why did you cry out so loud? I thought . . ."

"*You thought!* Softie—that's what *you* are! You silly girt staring Gaby, what don't know any better than to come holding yer girt mouth wide open for all that you can catch holt on? And then off up there to tell! You great Fat-Faced, Tale-Bearin' Silly-Billy! I'd be ashamed to come poking and peering round quiet people's houses . . ."

The Angel was surprised to find that some inexplicable quality in her voice excited the most disagreeable sensations in him and a strong desire to withdraw. But, resisting this, he stood listening politely (as the custom is in the Angelic Land, so long as anyone is speaking). The entire eruption was beyond his comprehension. He could not perceive any reason for the sudden projection of this vituperative head, out of infinity, so to speak. And questions without a break for an answer were outside his experience altogether.

Mrs. Gustick proceeded with her characteristic fluency, assured him he was no gentleman, enquired if he called himself one, remarked that every tramp did as much nowadays, compared him to a Stuck Pig, marvelled at his impudence, asked him if he wasn't ashamed of himself standing there, enquired if he was rooted to the ground, was curious to be told what he meant by it, wanted to know whether he robbed a scarecrow for his clothes, suggested that an abnormal vanity prompted his behavior, enquired if his mother knew he was out, and finally remarking, "I got somethin'll move you, my gentleman," disappeared with a ferocious slamming of the door.

The interval struck the Angel as singularly peaceful. His whirling mind had time to analyze his sensations. He ceased bowing and smiling, and stood merely astonished.

"This is a curious painful feeling," said the Angel. "Almost worse than Hungry, and quite different. When one is hungry one wants to eat. I suppose she was a woman. Here one wants to get away. I suppose I might just as well go.''

He turned slowly and went down the road meditating. He heard the cottage door re-open, and turning his head, saw through intervening scarlet runners Mrs. Gustick with a steaming saucepan full of boiling cabbage water in her hand.

'' 'Tis well you went, Mister Stolen Breeches,'' came the voice of Mrs. Gustick floating down through the vermilion blossoms. "Don't you come peeping and prying round this yer cottage again or I'll learn ye manners, I will!''

The Angel stood in a state of considerable perplexity. He had no desire to come within earshot of the cottage again—ever. He did not understand the precise import of the black pot, but his general impression was entirely disagreeable. There was no explaining it.

"I *mean* it!" said Mrs. Gustick, crescendo. "Drat it!—I *mean* it.''

The Angel turned and went on, a dazzled look in his eyes.

"She was very grotesque!" said the Angel. "*Very*. Much more than the little man in black. And she means it.— But what she means I don't know! . . .'' He became silent. "I suppose they all mean something,'' he said, presently, still perplexed.

XXV

THEN THE ANGEL came in sight of the forge, where Sandy Bright's brother was shoeing a horse for the carter from Upmorton. Two hobbledehoys were standing by the forge staring in a bovine way at the proceedings. As the Angel approached these two and then the carter turned slowly through an angle of thirty degrees and watched his approach, staring quietly and steadily at him. The expression on their faces was one of abstract interest.

The Angel became self-conscious for the first time in his life. He drew nearer, trying to maintain an amiable expression on his face, an expression that beat in vain against their granitic stare. His hands were behind him. He smiled pleasantly, looking curiously at the (to him) incomprehensible employment of the smith. But the battery of eyes seemed to angle for his regard. Trying to meet the three pairs at once, the Angel lost his alertness and stumbled over a stone. One of the yokels gave a sarcastic cough, and was immediately covered with confusion at the Angel's enquiring gaze, nudging his companion with his elbow to cover his disorder. None spoke, and the Angel did not speak.

So soon as the Angel had passed, one of the three hummed this tune in an aggressive tone.

Then all three of them laughed. One tried to sing something and found his throat contained phlegm. The Angel proceeded on his way.

"Who's *e* then?" said the second hobbledehoy.

"Ping, ping, ping,'' went the blacksmith's hammer.

"Spose he's one of these here foweners,'' said the carter from Upmorton. "Däamned silly fool he do look to be sure.''

"Tas the way with them foweners,'' said the first hobbledehoy sagely.

"Got something very like the 'ump,'' said the carter from Upmorton. "Dää-ä-ämned if'E ent.''

Then the silence healed again, and they resumed their quiet expressionless consideration of the Angel's retreating figure.

"Very like the 'ump et is," said the carter after an enormous pause.

XXVI

THE ANGEL WENT on through the village, finding it all wonderful enough. "They begin, and just a little while and then they end," he said to himself in a puzzled voice. "But what are they doing meanwhile?" Once he heard some invisible mouth chant inaudible words to the tune the man at the forge had hummed.

"That's the poor creature the Vicar shot with that great gun of his," said Sarah Glue (of I, Church Cottages) peering over the blind.

"He looks Frenchified," said Susan Hopper, peering through the interstices of that convenient veil on curiosity.

"He has sweet eyes," said Sarah Glue, who had met them for a moment.

The Angel sauntered on. The postman passed him and touched his hat to him; further down was a dog asleep in the sun. He went on and saw Mendham, who nodded distantly and hurried past. (The Curate did not care to be seen talking to an angel in the village, until more was known about him). There came from one of the houses the sound of a child screaming in a passion, that brought a puzzled look to the angelic face. Then the Angel reached the bridge below the last of the houses, and stood leaning over the parapet watching the glittering little cascade from the mill.

"They begin, and just a little while, and then they end," said the weir from the mill. The water raced under the bridge, green and dark, and streaked with foam.

Beyond the mill rose the square tower of the church, with the churchyard behind it, a spray of tombstones and wooden headboards splashed up the hillside. A half dozen of beech trees framed the picture.

Then the Angel heard a shuffling of feet and the gride off wheels behind him, and turning his head saw a man dressed in dirty brown rags and a felt hat grey with dust, who was standing with a slight swaying motion and fixedly regarding the Angelic back.

Beyond him was another almost equally dirty, pushing a knife grinder's barrow over the bridge.

"Mornin'," said the first person smiling weakly. "Goomorn'." He arrested an escaping hiccough.

The Angel stared at him. He had never seen a really fatuous smile before. "Who are you?" said the Angel.

The fatuous smile faded. "No your business whoaaam. Wishergoomorn."

"Carm on:" said the man with the grindstone, passing on his way.

"Wishergoomorn," said the dirty man, in a tone of extreme aggravation. "Carncher Answerme?"

"Carm *on* you fool!" said the man with the grindstone—receding.

"I don't understand," said the Angel.

"Donunderstan'. Sim'l enough. Wishergoomorn'. Willyanswerme? Wontchr? gemwishergem goomorn. Cusom answer goomorn. No gem. Haverteachyer."

The Angel was puzzled. The drunken man stood swaying for a moment, then he made an unsteady snatch at his hat and threw it down at the Angel's feet. "Ver well," he said, as one who decides great issues.

"*Carm* on!" said the voice of the man with the grindstone—stopping perhaps twenty yards off.

"You *wan* fight, you—" the Angel failed to catch the word. "I'll show yer, not answer gem's goomorn."

He began to struggle with his jacket. "Think I'm drun," he said, "I show yer." The man with the grindstone sat down on the shaft to watch. "Carm on," he said. The jacket was intricate, and the drunken man began to struggle about the road, in his attempts to extricate himself, breathing threatenings and slaughter. Slowly the Angel began to suspect, remotely enough, that these demonstrations were hostile. "Mur wun know yer when I done wi' yer," said the drunken man, coat almost over his head.

At last the garment lay on the ground, and through the frequent interstices of his reminiscences of a waistcoat, the drunken tinker displayed a fine hairy and muscular body to the Angel's observant eyes. He squared up in masterly fashion.

"Take the paint off yer," he remarked, advancing and receding, fists up and elbows out

"Carm on," floated down the road.

The Angel's attention was concentrated on two huge hairy black fists, that swayed and advanced and retreated. "Come on d'yer say? I'll show yer," said the gentleman in rags, and then with extraordinary ferocity; "My crikey! I'll show yer."

Suddenly he lurched forward, and with a newborn instinct and raising a defensive arm as he did so, the Angel stepped aside to avoid him. The fist missed the Angelic shoulder by a hairsbreadth, and the tinker collapsed in a heap with his face against the parapet of the bridge. The Angel hesitated over the writhing dusty heap of blasphemy for a moment, and then turned towards the man's companion up the road. "Lemmeget up," said the man on the bridge. "Lemmeget up, you swine. I'll show yer."

A strange disgust, a quivering repulsion came upon the Angel. He walked slowly away from the drunkard towards the man with the grindstone.

"What does it all mean?" said the Angel. "I don't understand it."

"Dam fool! . . . say's it's 'is silver weddin'," answered the man with the grindstone, evidently much annoyed; and then, in a tone of growing impatience, he called down the road once more; "Carm on!"

"Silver wedding!" said the Angel. "What is a silver wedding?"

"Jest is rot," said the man on the barrow. "But 'E's always avin' some 'scuse like that. Fair sickenin it is. Lars week it wus 'is bloomin' birthday, and *then*'e ad'nt ardly got sober orf a comlimentary drunk to my noo barrer. *(Carm* on, you fool.)"

"But I don't understand," said the Angel. "Why does he sway about so? Why does he keep on trying to pick up his hat like that—and missing it?"

"*Why!*" said the tinker. "Well this *is* a blasted innocent country! *Why!* Because 'E's blind! Wot else? (Carm on—*Dam* yer). Because 'E's just as full as 'E can 'old. That's *why!*"

The Angel noticing the tone of the second tinker's voice, judged it wiser not to question him further. But he stood by the grindstone and continued to watch the mysterious evolutions on the bridge.

"Carm on! I shall 'ave to go and pick up that 'at I suppose . . . 'E's always at it. I ne'er 'ad such a blooming pard before. *Always* at it, 'e is."

The man with the barrow meditated. "Taint as if 'e was a gentleman and 'adnt no livin' to get. An' 'e's such a reckless fool when 'e gets a bit on. Goes offerin out everyone 'e meets. *(There* you go!) I'm blessed if 'e didn't offer out a 'ole bloomin' Salvation Army. No judgment in it. (Oh!*Carm* on!*Carm* on!). 'Ave to go and pick this bloomin' 'at up now I s'pose. 'E don't care, *wot* trouble 'e gives."

The Angel watched the second tinker walk back, and, with affectionate blasphemy, assist the first to his hat and his coat. Then he turned, absolutely mystified, towards the village again.

XXVII

AFTER THAT INCIDENT the Angel walked along past the mill and round behind the church, to examine the tombstones.

"This seems to be the place where they put the broken pieces," said the Angel—reading the inscriptions. "Curious word—relict! Resurgam! Then they are not done with quite. What a huge pile it requires to keep her down. . . . It is spirited of her."

"Hawkins?" said the Angel softly, . . . *"Hawkins?* The name is strange to me. . . . He did not die then. . . . It is plain enough,—Joined the Angelic Hosts, May 17, 1863. He must have felt as much out of place as I do down here. But I wonder why they put that little pot thing on the top of this monument. Curious! There are several others about—little stone pots with a rag of stiff stone drapery over them.

Just then the boys came pouring out of the National School, and first one and then several stopped agape at the Angel's crooked black figure among the white tombs. "Ent 'e gart a bääk on en!" remarked one critic.

" 'E's got 'air like a girl!" said another.

The Angel turned towards them. He was struck by the queer little heads sticking up over the lichenous wall. He smiled faintly at their staring faces, and then turned to marvel at the iron railings that enclosed the Fitz-Jarvis tomb. "A queer air of uncertainty," he said. "Slabs, piles of stone, these railings. . . . Are they afraid? . . . Do these Dead ever try and get up again? There's an air of repression—fortification—"

"Gét yer *'air* cut, Gét yer *'air* cut," sang three little boys together.

"Curious these Human Beings are!" said the Angel. "That man yesterday wanted to cut off my wings, now these little creatures want me to cut off my hair! And the man on the bridge offered to take the 'paint' off me. They will leave nothing of me soon."

"Where did you get that *'at?"* sang another little boy. "Where did you get them clo'es?"

"They ask questions that they evidently do not want answered," said the Angel. "I can tell from the tone." He looked thoughtfully at the little boys. "I don't understand the methods of Human intercourse. These are probably friendly advances, a kind of ritual. But I don't know the responses. I think I will go back to the little fat man in black, with the gold chain across his stomach, and ask him to explain. It is difficult."

He turned towards the lych gate. *"Oh!"* said one of the little boys, in a shrill falsetto, and threw a beech-nut husk. It came bounding across the churchyard path. The Angel stopped in surprise.

This made all the little boys laugh. A second imitating the first, said *"Oh!"* and hit the Angel. His astonishment was really delicious. They all began crying *"Oh!"* and throwing beechnut husks. One hit the Angel's hand, another stung him smartly by the ear. The Angel made ungainly movements towards them. He spluttered some expostulation and made for the roadway. The little boys were amazed and shocked at his discomfiture and cowardice. Such sawney behavior could not be encouraged. The pelting grew vigorously. You may perhaps be able to imagine those vivid moments, daring small boys running in close and delivering shots, milder small boys rushing round behind with flying discharges.

Milton Screever's mongrel dog was roused to yelping ecstacy at the sight, and danced (full of wild imaginings) nearer and nearer to the angelic legs.

"Hi, hi!" said a vigorous voice. "I never did! Where's Mr. Jarvis? Manners, manners! you young rascals."

The youngsters scattered right and left, some over the wall into the playground, some down the street.

"Frightful pest these boys are getting!" said Crump, coming up. "I'm sorry they have been annoying you."

The Angel seemed quite upset. "I don't understand," he said. "These Human ways. . . ."

"Yes, of course. Unusual to you. How's your excrescence?"

"My what?" said the Angel.

"Bifid limb, you know. How is it? Now you're down this way, come in. Come in and let me have a look at it again. You young roughs! And meanwhile these little louts of ours will be getting off home. They're all alike in these villages. *Can't* understand anything abnormal. See an odd-looking stranger. Chuck a stone. No imagination beyond the parish. . . . (I'll give you physic if I catch you annoying strangers again.) . . . I suppose it's what one might expect. . . . Come along this way."

So the Angel, horribly perplexed still, was hurried into the surgery to have his wound redressed.

Lady Hammergallow's View
XXVIII

IN SIDDERMORTON PARK is Siddermorton House, where old Lady Hammergallow lives, chiefly upon Burgundy and the little scandals of the village, a dear old lady with a ropy neck, a ruddled countenance and spasmodic gusts of odd temper, whose three remedies for all human trouble among her dependents are, a bottle of gin, a pair of charity blankets, or a new crown piece. The House is a mile-and-a-half out of Siddermorton. Almost all the village is hers, saving a fringe to the south which belongs to Sir John Gotch, and she rules it with an autocratic rule, refreshing in these days of divided government. She orders and forbids marriages, drives objectionable people out of the village by the simple expedient of raising their rent, dismisses laborers, obliges heretics to go to church, and made Susan Dangett, who wanted to call her little girl 'Euphemia,' have the infant christened 'Mary-Anne.' She is a sturdy Broad Protestant and disapproves of the Vicar's going bald like a tonsure. She is on the Village Council, which obsequiously trudges up the hill and over the moor to her, and (as she is a trifle deaf) speaks all its speeches into her speaking trumpet instead of a rostrum. She takes no interest now in politics, but until last year she was an active enemy of "that Gladstone." She has parlor maids instead of footmen to do her waiting, because of Hockley, the American stockbroker, and his four Titans in plush.

She exercises what is almost a fascination upon the village. If in the bar-parlor of the Cat and Cornucopia you swear by God no one would be shocked, but if you swore by Lady Hammergallow they would probably be shocked enough to turn you out of the room. When she drives through Siddermorton she always calls upon Bessy Flump, the post-mistress, to hear all that has happened, and then upon Miss Finch, the dressmaker, to check back Bessy Flump. Sometimes she calls upon the Vicar sometimes upon Mrs. Mendham whom she snubs, and even sometimes on Crump. Her sparkling pair of greys almost ran over the Angel as he was walking down to the village.

"So *that's* the genius!" said Lady Hammergallow, and turned and looked at him through the gilt glasses on a stick that she always carried in her shrivelled and shaky hand. "Lunatic indeed! The poor creature has rather a pretty face. I'm sorry I've missed him."

But she went on to the vicarage nevertheless, and demanded news of it all. The conflicting accounts of Miss Flump, Miss Finch, Mrs. Mendham, Crump, and Mrs. Jehoram had puzzled her immensely. The Vicar, hard pressed, did all he could to say into her speaking trumpet what had really happened. He toned down the wings and the saffron robe. But he felt the case was hopeless. He spoke of his protégé as "Mr." Angel. He addressed pathetic asides to the kingfisher. The old lady noticed his confusion. Her queer old head went jerking backwards and forwards, now the speaking trumpet in his face when he had nothing to say, then the shrunken eyes peering at him oblivious of the explanation that was coming from his lips. A great many Ohs! and Ahs! She caught some fragments certainly.

"You have asked him to stop with you—indefinitely?" said Lady Hammergallow with a Great Idea taking shape rapidly in her mind.

"I did—perhaps inadvertently—make such—"

"And you don't know where he comes from?"

"Not at all."

"Nor who his father is, I suppose?" said Lady Hammergallow mysteriously.

"No," said the Vicar.

"*Now!*" said Lady Hammergallow archly, and keeping her glasses to her eye, she suddenly dug at his ribs with her trumpet.

"My *dear* Lady Hammergallow!"

"I thought so. Don't think *I* would blame you, Mr. Hilyer." She gave a corrupt laugh that she delighted in. "The world is the world, and men are men. And the poor boy's a cripple, eh? A kind of judgment. In mourning, I noticed. It reminds me of the *Scarlet Letter*. The mother's dead, I suppose. It's just as well Really—I'm not a *narrow* woman—I *respect* you for having him. Really I do."

"But, *Lady* Hammergallow!"

"Don't spoil everything by denying it. It is so very, very plain, to a woman of the world. That Mrs. Mendham! She amuses me with her suspicions. Such odd ideas! In a Curate's wife. But I hope it didn't happen when you were in orders."

"Lady Hammergallow, I protest. Upon my word."

"Mr. Hilyer, I protest. I *know*. Not anything you can say will alter my opinion one jot. Don't try. I never suspected you were nearly such an interesting man."

"But this suspicion is unendurable!"

"We will help him together, Mr. Hilyer. You may rely upon me. It is most romantic." She beamed benevolence.

"But, Lady Hammergallow, I *must* speak!"

She gripped her ear-trumpet resolutely, and held it before her and shook her head.

"He has quite a genius for music, Vicar, so I hear?"

"I can assure you most solemnly—"

"I thought so. And being a cripple—"

"You are under a most cruel—"

"I thought that if his gift is really what that Jehoram woman says."

"An unjustifiable suspicion that ever a man—"

("I don't think much of her judgment, of course.")

"Consider my position. Have I gained *no* character?"

"It might be possible to do something for him as a performer."

"Have I—*(Bother! It's no good!)*"

"And so, dear Vicar, I propose to give him an opportunity of showing us what he can do. I have been thinking it all over as I drove here. On Tuesday next, I will invite just a few people of taste, and he shall bring his violin. Eigh? And if that goes well, I will see if I can get some introductions and really *push* him."

"But *Lady,* Lady Hammergallow."

"Not another word!" said Lady Hammergallow, still resolutely holding her speaking-trumpet before her and clutching her eyeglasses, "I really must not leave those horses. Cutler is so annoyed if I keep them too long. He finds waiting tedious, poor man, unless there is a public-house near." She made for the door.

"Damn!" said the Vicar, under his breath. He had never used the word since he had taken orders. It shows you how an Angel's visit may disorganize a man.

He stood under the veranda watching the carriage drive away. The world seemed coming to pieces about him. Had he lived a virtuous celibate life for thirty-odd years in vain? The things of which these people thought him capable! He stood and stared at the green cornfield opposite, and down at the straggling village. It seemed real enough. And yet for the first time in his life there was a queer doubt of its reality. He rubbed his chin, then turned and went slowly upstairs to his dressing-room, and sat for a long time staring at a garment of some yellow texture. "Know his father!" he said. "And he is immortal, and was fluttering about his heaven when my ancestors were marsupials. . . . I wish he was there now."

He got up and began to feel the robe.

"I wonder how they get such things," said the Vicar. Then he went and stared out of the window. "I suppose everything is wonderful, even the rising and setting of the sun. I suppose there is no adamantine ground for any belief. But one gets into a regular way of taking things. This disturbs it. I seem to be waking up to the Invisible. It is the strangest of uncertainties. I have not felt so stirred and unsettled since my adolescence."

Further Adventures of the Angel
in the Village
XXIX

"THAT'S ALL RIGHT," said Crump when the bandaging was replaced. "It's a trick of memory, no doubt, but these excrescences of yours don't seem nearly so large as they did yesterday. I suppose they struck me rather forcibly. Stop and have lunch with me now you're down here. Midday meal, you know. The youngsters will be swallowed up by school again in the afternoon."

"I never saw anything heal so well in my life," he said, as they walked into the dining-room. "Your blood and flesh must be as clean and free from bacteria as they make'em. Whatever stuff there is in your head," he added *sotto voce*.

At lunch he watched the Angel narrowly, and talked to draw him out.

"Journey tire you yesterday?" he said suddenly.

"Journey!" said the Angel. "Oh! my wings felt a little stiff."

("Not to be had,") said Crump to himself. ("Suppose I must enter into it.")

"So you flew all the way, eigh? No conveyance?"

"There wasn't any way," explained the Angel, taking mustard. "I was flying up a symphony with some Griffins and Fiery Cherubim, and suddenly everything went dark and I was in this world of yours."

"Dear me!" said Crump. "And that's why you haven't any luggage." He drew his serviette across his mouth, and a smile flickered in his eyes.

"I suppose you know this world of ours pretty well? Watching us over the adamantine walls and all that kind of thing. Eigh?"

"Not very well. We dream of it sometimes. In the moonlight, when the Nightmares have fanned us to sleep with their wings."

"Ah, yes—of course," said Crump. "Very poetical way of putting it. Won't you take some Burgundy? It's just beside you."

"There's a persuasion in this world, you know, that Angels' Visits are by no means infrequent. Perhaps some of your—friends have travelled? They are supposed to come down to deserving persons in prisons, and do refined Nautches and that kind of thing. Faust business, you know."

"I've never heard of anything of the kind," said the Angel.

"Only the other day a lady whose baby was my patient for the time being—indigestion—assured me that certain facial contortions the little creature made indicated that it was Dreaming of Angels. In the novels of Mrs. Henry Wood that is spoken of as an infallible symptom of an early departure. I suppose you can't throw any light on that obscure pathological manifestation?"

"I don't understand it at all," said the Angel, puzzled, and not clearly apprehending the Doctor's drift.

("Getting huffy,") said Crump to himself. ("Sees I'm poking fun at him.") "There's one thing I'm curious about. Do the new arrivals complain much about their medical attendants? I've always fancied there must be a good deal of hydropathic talk just at first. I was looking at that picture in the Academy only this June. . . ."

"New Arrivals!" said the Angel. "I really don't follow you."

The Doctor stared. "Don't they come?"

"Come!" said the Angel. "Who?"

"The people who die here."

"After they've gone to pieces here?"

"That's the general belief, you know."

"People, like the woman who screamed out of the door, and the blackfaced man and his volutations and the horrible little things that threw husks!—certainly not. *I* never saw such creatures before I fell into this world."

"Oh! but come!" said the Doctor. "You'll tell me next your official robes are not white and that you can't play the harp."

"There's no such thing as white in the Angelic Land," said the Angel. "It's that queer blank color you get by mixing up all the others."

"Why, my dear Sir!" said the doctor, suddenly altering his tone, "you positively know nothing about the Land you come from. White's the very essence of it."

The Angel stared at him. Was the man jesting? He looked perfectly serious.

"Look here," said Crump, and getting up, he went to the sideboard on which a copy of the Parish Magazine was lying. He brought it round to the Angel and opened it at the colored supplement. "Here's some *real* angels," he said. "You see it's not simply the wings make the Angel. White you see, with a curly wisp of robe, sailing up into the sky with their wings furled. Those are angels on the best authority. Hydroxyl kind of hair. One has a bit of a harp, you see, and the other is helping this wingless lady—kind of larval Angel, you know—upward.''

"Oh! but really!" said the Angel, "those are not angels at all."

"But they *are*," said Crump, putting the magazine back on the sideboard and resuming his seat with an air of intense satisfaction. "I can assure you I have the *best* authority. . . ."

"I can assure you. . . ."

Crump tucked in the corners of his mouth and shook his head from side to side even as he had done to the Vicar. "No good," he said, "can't alter our ideas just because an irresponsible visitor. . . ."

"If these are angels," said the Angel, "then I have never been in the Angelic Land."

"Precisely," said Crump, ineffably self-satisfied; "that was just what I was getting at."

The Angel stared at him for a minute roundeyed, and then was seized for the second time by the human disorder of laughter.

"Ha, ha, ha!" said Crump, joining in. "I *thought* you were not quite so mad as you seemed. Ha, ha, ha!"

And for the rest of the lunch they were both very merry, for entirely different reasons, and Crump insisted upon treating the Angel as a "dorg" of the highest degree.

XXX

AFTER THE ANGEL had left Crump's house he went up the hill again towards the Vicarage. But—possibly moved by the desire to avoid Mrs. Gustick—he turned aside at the stile and made a detour by the Lark's Field and Bradley's Farm.

He came upon the Respectable Tramp slumbering peacefully among the wildflowers. He stopped to look, struck by the celestial tranquillity of that individual's face. And even as he did so the Respectable Tramp awoke with a start and sat up. He was a pallid creature, dressed in rusty black, with a broken-spirited crush hat cocked over one eye. "Good afternoon," he said affably. "How are you?"

"Very well, thank you," said the Angel, who had mastered the phrase.

The Respectable Tramp eyed the Angel critically. "Padding the Hoof, matey?" he said. "Like me."

The Angel was puzzled by him. "Why," asked the Angel, "do you sleep like this instead of sleeping up in the air on a Bed?"

"Well I'm blowed!" said the Respectable Tramp. "Why don't I sleep in a bed? Well, it's like this. Sandringham's got the painters in, there's the drains up in Windsor Castle, and I 'aven't no other 'ouse to go to. You 'aven't the price of a arf pint in your pocket, 'ave yer?"

"I have nothing in my pocket," said the Angel.

"Is this here village called Siddermorton?" said the Tramp, rising creakily to his feet and pointing to the clustering roofs down the hill.

"Yes," said the Angel, "they call it Siddermorton."

"I know it, I know it," said the Tramp. "And a very pretty little village it is too." He stretched and yawned, and stood regarding the place. " 'Ouses," he said reflectively; "Projuce"—waving his hand at the cornfields and orchards. "Looks cozy, don't it?"

"It has a quaint beauty of its own," said the Angel.

"It *'as* a quaint beauty of its own—yes . . . Lord! I'd like to sack the blooming place. . . . I was born there."

"Dear me," said the Angel.

"Yes, I was born there. Ever heard of a pithed frog?"

"Pithed frog," said the Angel. "No!"

"It's a thing these here vivisectionists do. They takes a frog and they cuts out his brains and they shoves a bit of pith in the place of 'em. That's a pithed frog. Well—that there village is full of pithed human beings."

The Angel took it quite seriously. "Is that so?" he said.

"That's so—you take my word for it. Everyone of them 'as 'ad their brains cut out and chunks of rotten touchwood put in the place of it. And you see that little red place there?"

"That's called the national school," said the Angel.

"Yes—that's where they piths 'em," said the Tramp, quite in love with his conceit.

"Really! That's very interesting."

"It stands to reason," said the Tramp. "If they 'ad brains they'd 'ave ideas, and if they 'ad ideas they'd think for themselves. And you can go through that village from end to end and never meet anybody doing as much. Pithed human beings they are. I know that village. I was born there, and I might be there now, a toilin' for my betters, if I 'adnt struck against the pithin'."

"Is it a painful operation?" asked the Angel.

"In parts. Though it aint the heads gets hurt. And it lasts a long time. They take 'em young into that school, and they says to them, 'come in 'ere and we'll improve your minds,' they says, and in the little kiddies go as good as gold. And they begins shovin' it into them. Bit by bit and 'ard and dry, shovin' out the nice juicy brains. Dates and lists and things. Out they comes, no brains in their 'eads, and wound up nice and tight, ready to touch their 'ats to anyone who looks at them. Why! One touched 'is 'at to me yesterday. And they runs about spry and does all the dirty work, and feels thankful they're allowed to live. They take a positive pride in 'ard work for its own sake. Arter they bin pithed. See that chap ploughin'?"

"Yes," said the Angel; "is *he* pithed?"

"Rather. Else he'd be paddin' the hoof this pleasant weather—like me and the blessed Apostles."

"I begin to understand," said the Angel, rather dubiously.

"I knew you would," said the Philosophical Tramp. "I thought you was the right sort. But speaking serious, aint it ridiculous?—centuries and centuries of civilization, and look at that poor swine there, sweatin' 'isself empty and trudging up that 'ill-side. 'E's English, 'e is. 'E belongs to the top race in creation, 'e does. 'E's one of the rulers of Indjer. It's enough to make a nigger laugh. The flag that's braved a thousand years the battle an' the breeze—that's *'is* flag. There never was a country was as great and glorious as this. Never. And that's wot it makes of us. I'll tell you a little story about them parts as you seems to be a bit of a stranger. There's a chap called Gotch, Sir John Gotch they calls 'im, and when *'e* was a young gent from Oxford, I was a little chap of eight and my sister was a girl of seventeen. Their servant she was. But Lord! everybody's 'eard that story—it's common enough, of 'im or the likes of 'im."

"I haven't," said the Angel.

"All that's pretty and lively of the gals they chucks into the gutters, and all the men with a pennorth of spunk or adventure, all who won't drink what the

Curate's wife sends 'em instead of beer, and touch their hats promiscous, and leave the rabbits and birds alone for their betters, gets drove out of the villages as rough characters. Patriotism! Talk about improvin' the race! Wot's left aint fit to look a nigger in the face, a Chinaman 'ud be ashamed of 'em. . . .''

"But I don't understand," said the Angel. "I don't follow you."

At that the Philosophic Tramp became more explicit, and told the Angel the simple story of Sir John Gotch and the kitchen-maid. It's scarcely necessary to repeat it. You may understand that it left the Angel puzzled. It was full of words he did not understand, for the only vehicle of emotion the Tramp possessed was blasphemy. Yet, though their tongues differed so, he could still convey to the Angel some of his own (probably unfounded) persuasion of the injustice and cruelty of life, and of the utter detestableness of Sir John Gotch.

The last the Angel saw of him was his dusty black back receding down the lane towards Iping Hanger. A pheasant appeared by the roadside, and the Philosophical Tramp immediately caught up a stone and sent the bird clucking with a viciously accurate shot. Then he disappeared round the corner.

Mrs. Jehoram's Breadth of View

XXXI

"I HEARD SOMEONE playing the fiddle in the Vicarage, as I came by," said Mrs. Jehoram, taking her cup of tea from Mrs. Mendham.

"The Vicar plays," said Mrs. Mendham. "I have spoken to George about it, but it's no good. I do not think a Vicar should be allowed to do such things. It's so foreign. But there, he . . ."

"I know, dear," said Mrs. Jehoram. "But I heard the Vicar once at the schoolroom. I don't think this *was* the Vicar. It was quite clever, some of it, quite smart, you know. And new. I was telling dear Lady Hamergallow this morning. I fancy—"

"The lunatic! Very likely. These half-witted people. . . . My dear, I don't think I shall ever forget that dreadful encounter. Yesterday."

"Nor I."

"My poor girls! They are too shocked to say a word about it. I was telling dear Lady Ham —"

"Quite proper of them. It was *dreadful*, dear. For them."

"And now, dear, I want you to tell me frankly—Do you really believe that creature was a man?"

"You should have heard the violin."

"I still more than half suspect, Jessie—" Mrs. Mendham leaned forward as if to whisper.

Mrs. Jehoram helped herself to cake. "I'm sure no woman could play the violin quite like I heard it played this morning."

"Of course, if you say so that settles the matter," said Mrs. Mendham. Mrs. Jehoram was the autocratic authority in Siddermorton upon all questions of art, music and belles-lettres. Her late husband had been a minor poet. Then Mrs. Mendham added a judicial "Still—"

"Do you know," said Mrs. Jehoram, "I'm half inclined to believe the dear Vicar's story."

"How *good* of you, Jessie," said Mrs. Mendham.

"But really, I don't think he *could* have had any one in the Vicarage before that afternoon. I feel sure we should have heard of it. I don't see how a strange cat could come within four miles of Siddermorton without the report coming round to us. The people here gossip so. . . . ''

"I always distrust the Vicar," said Mrs. Mendham. "I know him."

"Yes. But the story is plausible. If this Mr. Angel were someone very clever and eccentric—"

"He would have to be *very* eccentric to dress as he did. There are degrees and limits, dear."

"But kilts," said Mrs. Jehoram.

"Are all very well in the Highlands . . . ."

Mrs. Jehoram's eyes had rested upon a black speck creeping slowly across a patch of yellowish-green up the hill.

"There he goes," said Mrs. Jehoram, rising, "across the cornfield. I'm sure that's him. I can see the hump. Unless it's a man with a sack. Bless me, Minnie! here's an opera glass. How convenient for peeping at the Vicarage! . . . Yes, it's the man. He is a man. With *such* a sweet face."

Very unselfishly she allowed her hostess to share the opera glass. For a minute there was a rustling silence.

"His dress," said Mrs. Mendham, "is *quite* respectable now."

"Quite," said Mrs. Jehoram.

Pause.

"He looks cross!"

"And his coat is dusty."

"He walks steadily enough," said Mrs. Mendham, "or one might think . . . This hot weather. . . ."

Another pause.

"You see, dear," said Mrs. Jehoram, putting down the lorgnette. "What I was going to say was, that possibly he might be a genius in disguise."

"If you can call next door to nothing a disguise. "

"No doubt it was eccentric. But I've seen children in little blouses, not at all unlike him. So many clever people *are* peculiar in their dress and manners. A genius may steal a horse where a bank-clerk may not look over the hedge. Very possibly he's quite well known and laughing at our Arcadian simplicity. And really it wasn't so improper as some of these New Women bicycling costumes. I saw one in one of the Illustrated Papers only a few days ago—the *New Budget* I think—quite tights, you know, dear. No—I cling to the genius theory. Especially after the playing. I'm sure the creature is original. Perhaps very amusing. In fact, I intend to ask the Vicar to introduce me."

"My dear!" cried Mrs. Mendham.

"I'm resolute," said Mrs. Jehoram.

"I'm afraid you're rash," said Mrs. Mendham. "Geniuses and people of that kind are all very well in London. But here—at the Vicarage."

"We are going to educate the folks. I love originality. At any rate I mean to see him."

"Take care you don't see too much of him," said Mrs. Mendham. "I've heard the fashion is quite changing. I understand that some of the very best people have decided that genius is not to be encouraged any more. These recent scandals. . . ."

"Only in literature, I can assure you, dear. In music . . . ."

"Nothing you can say, my dear," said Mrs. Mendham, going off at a tangent, "will convince me that that person's costume was not extremely suggestive and improper."

A Trivial Incident
XXXII

THE ANGEL CAME thoughtfully by the hedge across the field towards the Vicarage. The rays of the setting sun shone on his shoulders, and touched the Vicarage with gold, and blazed like fire in all the windows. By the gate, bathed in the sunlight, stood little Delia, the waiting maid. She stood watching him under her hand. It suddenly came into the Angel's mind that she, at least, was beautiful, and not only beautiful but alive and warm.

She opened the gate for him and stood aside. She was sorry for him, for her elder sister was a cripple. He bowed to her, as he would have done to any woman, and for just one moment looked into her face. She looked back at him and something leapt within her.

The Angel made an irresolute movement.

"Your eyes are very beautiful," he said quietly, with a remote wonder in his voice.

"Oh, sir!" she said, starting back. The Angel's expression changed to perplexity. He went on up the pathway between the Vicar's flower-beds, and she stood with the gate held open in her hand, staring after him. Just under the rose-twined veranda he turned and looked at her.

She still stared at him for a moment, and then with a queer gesture turned round with her back to him, shutting the gate as she did so, and seemed to be looking down the valley towards the church tower.

The Warp and the Woof of Things
XXXIII

AT THE DINNER table the Angel told the Vicar the more striking of his day's adventures.

"The strange thing," said the Angel, "is the readiness of you Human Beings— the zest, with which you inflict pain. Those boys pelting me this morning—"

"Seemed to enjoy it," said the Vicar. "I know."

"Yet they don't like pain," said the Angel.

"No," said the Vicar; "*they* don't like it."

"Then," said the Angel, "I saw some beautiful plants rising with a spike of leaves, two this way and two that, and when I caressed one it caused the most uncomfortable—"

"Stinging nettle!" said the Vicar.

"At any rate a new sort of pain. And another plant with a head like a coronet, and richly decorated leaves, spiked and jagged—"

"A thistle, possibly."

"And in your garden, the beautiful, sweet-smelling plant—"

"The sweet briar," said the Vicar. "I remember."

"And that pink flower that sprang out of the box—"

"Out of the box?" said the Vicar.

"Last night," said the Angel, "that went climbing up the curtains— Flame!"

"Oh!—the matches and the candles! Yes," said the Vicar.

"Then the animals. A dog today behaved most disagreeably—. And these boys, and the way in which people speak—. Everyone seems anxious—willing at any rate—to give this Pain. Everyone seems busy giving pain—''

"Or avoiding it," said the Vicar, pushing his dinner away before him. "Yes— of course. It's fighting everywhere. The whole living world is a battle-field— the whole world. We are driven by Pain. Here. How it lies on the surface! This Angel sees it in a day!''

"But why does everyone—everything—want to give pain?" asked the Angel.

"It is not so in the Angelic Land?" said the Vicar.

"No," said the Angel. "Why is it so here?"

The Vicar wiped his lips with his napkin slowly. "It *is* so," he said. "Pain," said he still more slowly, "is the warp and the woof of this life. Do you know," he said, after a pause, "it is almost impossible for me to imagine . . . a world without pain. . . . And yet, as you played this morning—

"But this world is different. It is the very reverse of an Angelic world. Indeed, a number of people—excellent religious people—have been so impressed by the universality of pain that they think, after death, things will be even worse for a great many of us. It seems to me an excessive view. But it's a deep question. Almost beyond one's power of discussion—''

And incontinently the Vicar plumped into an impromptu dissertation upon "Necessity," how things were so because they were so, how one *had* to do this and that. "Even our food," said the Vicar. "What?" said the Angel. "Is not obtained without inflicting Pain," said the Vicar.

The Angel's face went so white that the Vicar checked himself suddenly. Or he was just on the very verge of a concise explanation of the antecedents of a leg of lamb. There was a pause.

"By-the-bye," said the Angel, suddenly. "Have you been pithed? Like the common people.''

The Angel's Debut
XXXIV

WHEN LADY HAMMERGALLOW made up her mind, things happened as she resolved. And though the Vicar made a spasmodic protest, she carried out her purpose and got audience, Angel, and violin together, at Siddermorton House before the week was out. "A genius the Vicar has discovered," she said; so with eminent foresight putting any possibility of blame for a failure on the Vicar's shoulders. "The dear Vicar tells me," she would say, and proceed to marvelous anecdotes of the Angel's cleverness with his instrument. But she was quite in love with her idea—she had always had a secret desire to play the patroness to obscure talent. Hitherto it had not turned out to be talent when it came to the test.

"It would be such a good thing for him," she said. "His hair is long already, and with that high color he would be beautiful, simply beautiful on a platform. The Vicar's clothes fitting him so badly makes him look quite like a fashionable pianist already. And the scandal of his birth—not told, of course, but whispered— would be—quite an Inducement—when he gets to London, that is.''

The Vicar had the most horrible sensations as the day approached. He spent hours trying to explain the situation to the Angel, other hours trying to imagine what people would think, still worse hours trying to anticipate the Angel's behavior. Hitherto the Angel had always played for his own satisfaction. The Vicar would startle him every now and then by rushing upon him with some new point of etiquette that had just occurred to him. As for instance: "It's very important where you put your hat, you know. Don't put it on a chair, whatever you do. Hold it until you get your tea, you know, and then—let me see—then put it down somewhere, you know." The journey to Siddermorton House was accomplished without misadventure, but at the moment of introduction the Vicar had a spasm of horrible misgivings. He had forgotten to explain introductions. The Angel's naïve amusement was evident, but nothing very terrible happened.

"Rummy looking greaser," said Mr. Rathbone Slater, who devoted considerable attention to costume. "Wants grooming. No manners. Grinned when he saw me shaking hands. Did it *chic* enough, I thought."

One trivial misadventure occurred. When Lady Hammergallow welcomed the Angel she looked at him through her glasses. The apparent size of her eyes startled him. His surprise and his quick attempt to peer over the brims was only too evident. But the Vicar had warned him of the ear trumpet.

The Angel's incapacity to sit on anything but a music stool appeared to excite some interest among the ladies, but led to no remarks. They regarded it perhaps as the affectation of a budding professional. He was remiss with the teacups and scattered the crumbs of his cake abroad. (You must remember he was quite an amateur at eating.) He crossed his legs. He fumbled over the hat business after vainly trying to catch the Vicar's eye. The eldest Miss Papaver tried to talk to him about continental watering places and cigarettes, and formed a low opinion of his intelligence.

The Angel was surprised by the production of an easel and several books of music, and a little unnerved at first by the sight of Lady Hammergallow sitting with her head on one side, watching him with those magnified eyes through her gilt glasses.

Mrs. Jehoram came up to him before he began to play and asked him the Name of the Charming Piece he was playing the other afternoon. The Angel said it had no name, and Mrs. Jehoram thought music ought never to have any names and wanted to know who it was by, and when the Angel told her he played it out of his head, she said he must be Quite a Genius and looked open (and indisputably fascinating) admiration at him. The Curate from Iping Hanger (who was professionally a Kelt and who played the piano and talked color and music with an air of racial superiority) watched him jealously.

The Vicar, who was presently captured and set down next to Lady Hammergallow, kept an anxious eye ever Angelward while she told him particulars of the incomes made by violinists—particulars which, for the most part, she invented as she went along. She had been a little ruffled by the incident of the glasses, but had decided that it came within the limits of permissible originality.

So figure to yourself the Green Saloon at Siddermorton Park; an Angel thinly disguised in clerical vestments and with a violin in his hands, standing by the grand piano, and a respectable gathering of quiet nice people, nicely dressed, grouped about the room. Anticipatory gabble—one hears scattered fragments of conversation.

"He is *incog.*"; said the very eldest Miss Papaver to Mrs. Pirbright. "Isn't it quaint and delicious. Jessica Jehoram says she saw him at Vienna, but she can't remember the name. The Vicar knows all about him, but he is so close—"

"How hot and uncomfortable the dear Vicar is looking," said Mrs. Pirbright. "I've noticed it before when he sits next to Lady Hammergallow. She simply will *not* respect his cloth. She goes on—"

"His tie is all askew," said the very eldest Miss Papaver, "and his hair! It really hardly looks as though he had brushed it all day."

"Seems a foreign sort of chap. Affected. All very well in a drawing-room," said George Harringay, sitting apart with the younger Miss Pirbright. "But for my part give me a masculine man and a feminine woman. What do you think?"

"Oh!—I think so too," said the younger Miss Pirbright

"Guineas and guineas," said Lady Hammergallow. "I've heard that some of them keep quite stylish establishments. You would scarcely credit it—"

"I love music, Mr. Angel, I adore it. It stirs something in me. I can scarcely describe it," said Mrs. Jehoram. "Who is it says that delicious antithesis: Life without music is brutality; music without life is— Dear me! perhaps you remember? Music without life—it's Ruskin I think?"

"I'm sorry that I do not," said the Angel. "I have read very few books."

"How charming of you!" said Mrs. Jehoram. "I wish I didn't. I sympathize with you profoundly. I would do the same, only we poor women—I suppose it's originality we lack—And down here one is driven to the most desperate proceedings—"

"He's certainly very *pretty*. But the ultimate test of a man is his strength," said George Harringay. "What do you think?"

"Oh!—I think so too," said the younger Miss Pirbright.

"It's the effeminate man who makes the masculine woman. When the glory of a man is his hair, what's a woman to do? And when men go running about with beautiful hectic dabs—"

"Oh George! You are so dreadfully satirical today," said the younger Miss Pirbright. "I'm *sure* it isn't paint."

"I'm really not his guardian, my dear Lady Hammergallow. Of course it's very kind indeed of you to take such an interest—"

"Are you really going to improvise?" said Mrs. Jehoram in a state of cooing delight.

"*SSsh!*" said the curate from Iping Hanger.

Then the Angel began to play, looking straight before him as he did so, thinking of the wonderful things of the Angelic Land, and yet insensibly letting the sadness he was beginning to feel, steal over the fantasia he was playing. When he forgot his company the music was strange and sweet; when the sense of his surroundings floated into his mind the music grew capricious and grotesque. But so great was the hold of the Angelic music upon the Vicar that his anxieties fell from him at once, so soon as the Angel began to play. Mrs. Jehoram sat and looked rapt and sympathetic as hard as she could (though the music was puzzling at times) and tried to catch the Angel's eye. He really had a wonderfully mobile face, and the tenderest shades of expression! And Mrs. Jehoram was a judge. George Harringay looked bored, until the younger Miss Pirbright, who adored him, put out her mousy little shoe to touch his manly boot, and then he turned his face to catch the feminine delicacy of her coquettish eye, and was comforted. The very eldest Miss Papaver and Mrs. Pirbright sat quite still and looked churchy for nearly four minutes.

Then said the eldest Miss Papaver in a whisper, "I always Enjoy violin music so much." And Mrs. Pirbright answered, "We get so little Nice music down here." And Miss Papaver said, "He plays Very nicely." And Mrs. Pirbright, "Such a Delicate Touch!" And Miss Papaver, "Does Willie keep up his lessons?" and so to a whispered conversation.

The Curate from Iping Hanger sat (he felt) in full view of the company. He had one hand curled round his ear, and his eyes hard and staring fixedly at the pedestal of the Hammergallow Sèvres vase. He supplied, by the movements of his mouth, a kind of critical guide to any of the company who were disposed to avail themselves of it. It was a generous way he had. His aspect was severely judicial, tempered by starts of evident disapproval and guarded appreciation. The Vicar leaned back in his chair and stared at the Angel's face, and was presently rapt away in a wonderful dream. Lady Hammergallow, with quick jerky movements of the head and a low but insistent rustling, surveyed and tried to judge of the effect of the Angelic playing. Mr. Rathbone-Slater stared very solemnly into his hat and looked very miserable, and Mrs. Rathbone-Slater made mental memoranda of Mrs. Jehoram's sleeves. And the air about them all was heavy with exquisite music—for all that had ears to hear.

"Scarcely affected enough," whispered Lady Hammergallow hoarsely, suddenly poking the Vicar in the ribs. The Vicar came out of Dreamland suddenly. "Eigh?" shouted the Vicar, startled, coming up with a jump. "Sssh!" said the Curate from Iping Hanger, and everyone looked shocked at the brutal insensibility of Hilyer. "So unusual of the Vicar," said the very eldest Miss Papaver, "to do things like that!" The Angel went on playing.

The Curate from Iping Hanger began making mesmeric movements with his index finger, and as the thing proceeded Mr. Rathbone-Slater got amazingly limp. He solemnly turned his hat round and altered his view. The Vicar lapsed from an uneasy discomfort into dreamland again. Lady Hammergallow rustled a great deal, and presently found a way of making her chair creak. And at last the thing came to an end. Lady Hammergallow exclaimed "De—licious!" though she had never heard a note, and began clapping her hands. At that everyone clapped except Mr. Rathbone-Slater, who rapped his hat brim instead. The Curate from Iping Hanger clapped with a judicial air.

"So I said *(clap, clap, clap)*, if you cannot cook the food my way *(clap, clap, clap)* you must *go*," said Mrs. Pirbright, clapping vigorously. "(This music is a delightful treat.)"

"(It is. I always *revel* in music,)" said the very eldest Miss Papaver. "And did she improve after that?"

"Not a bit of it," said Mrs. Pirbright.

The Vicar woke up again and stared round the saloon. Did other people see these visions, or were they confined to him alone? Surely they must all see . . . and have a wonderful command of their feelings. It was incredible that such music should not affect them. "He's a trifle *gauche*," said Lady Hammergallow, jumping upon the Vicar's attention. "He neither bows nor smiles. He must cultivate oddities like that. Every successful executant is more or less *gauche*."

"Did you really make that up yourself?" said Mrs. Jehoram, sparkling her eyes at him, "as you went along. Really, it is *wonderful!* Nothing less than wonderful."

"A little amateurish," said the Curate from Iping Hanger to Mr. Rathbone-Slater. "A great gift, undoubtedly, but a certain lack of sustained training. There were one or two little things . . . I would like to talk to him."

"His trousers look like concertinas," said Mr. Rathbone-Slater. "He ought to be told *that*. It's scarcely decent."

"Can you do Imitations, Mr. Angel?" said Lady Hammergallow.

"Oh *do*, do some Imitations!" said Mrs. Jehoram. "I adore Imitations."

"It was a fantastic thing," said the Curate of Iping Hanger to the Vicar of Siddermorton, waving his long indisputably musical hands as he spoke; "a little involved, to my mind. I have heard it before somewhere—I forget where. He has genius undoubtedly, but occasionally he is—loose. There is a certain deadly precision wanting. There are years of discipline yet.''

"I *don't* admire these complicated pieces of music," said George Harringay. "I have simple tastes, I'm afraid. There seems to me no *tune* in it. There's nothing I like so much as simple music. Tune, simplicity is the need of the age, in my opinion. We are so over subtle. Everything is far-fetched. Home grown thoughts and 'Home, Sweet Home' for me. What do you think?''

"Oh! I think so—*quite*," said the younger Miss Pirbright.

"Well, Amy, chattering to George as usual?" said Mrs. Pirbright, across the room.

As usual, Ma!" said the younger Miss Pirbright, glancing round with a bright smile at Miss Papaver, and turning again so as not to lose the next utterance from George.

"I wonder if you and Mr. Angel could manage a duet?" said Lady Hammergallow to the Curate from Iping Hanger, who was looking preternaturally gloomy.

"I'm sure I should be delighted," said the Curate from Iping Hanger, brightening up.

"Duets!" said the Angel; "the two of us. Then he can play. I understood—the Vicar told me—''

"Mr. Wilmerdings is an accomplished pianist," interrupted the Vicar.

"But the Imitations?" said Mrs. Jehoram, who detested Wildermings.

"Imitations!" said the Angel.

"A pig squeaking, a cock crowing, you know," said Mr. Rathbone-Slater, and added lower, "Best fun you can get out of a fiddle—*my* opinion.''

"I really don't understand," said the Angel. "A pig crowing!"

"You don't like Imitations," said Mrs. Jehoram.

"Nor do I—really. I accept the snub. I think they degrade. . . .''

"Perhaps afterwards Mr. Angel will Relent," said Lady Hammergallow, when Mrs. Pirbright had explained the matter to her. She could scarcely credit her ear-trumpet. When she asked for Imitations she was accustomed to get Imitations.

Mr. Wilmerdings had seated himself at the piano, and had turned to a familiar pile of music in the recess. "What do you think of that Barcarole thing of Spohr's?" he said over his shoulder. "I suppose you know it?" The Angel looked bewildered.

He opened the folio before the Angel.

"What an odd kind of book!" said the Angel. "What do all those crazy dots mean?" (At that the Vicar's blood ran cold.)

"What dots?" said the Curate.

"There!" said the Angel with incriminating finger.

"Oh *come*!" said the Curate.

There was one of those swift, short silences that mean so much in a social gathering.

Then the eldest Miss Papaver turned upon the Vicar. "Does not Mr. Angel play from ordinary. . . . Music—from the ordinary notation?''

"I have never heard," said the Vicar, getting red now after the first shock of horror. "I have really never seen. . . .''

The Angel felt the situation was strained, though what was straining it he could not understand. He became aware of a doubtful, an unfriendly look upon the faces that regarded him. "Impossible!" he heard Mrs. Pirbright say; "after that *beautiful* music." The eldest Miss Papaver went to Lady Hammergallow at once, and began to explain into her ear-trumpet that Mr. Angel did not wish to play with Mr. Wilmerdings, and alleged an ignorance of written music.

"He cannot play from Notes!" said Lady Hammergallow in a voice of measured horror. "Non—sense!"

"Notes!" said the Angel perplexed. "Are these notes?"

"It's carrying the joke too far—simply because he doesn't want to play with Wilmerdings," said Mr. Rathbone-Slater to George Harringay.

There was an expectant pause. The Angel perceived he had to be ashamed of himself. He was ashamed of himself.

"Then," said Lady Hammergallow, throwing her head back and speaking with deliberate indignation, as she rustled forward, "if you cannot play with Mr. Wilmerdings I am afraid I cannot ask you to play again." She made it sound like an ultimatum. Her glasses in her hand quivered violently with indignation. The Angel was now human enough to appreciate the fact that he was crushed.

"What is it?" said little Lucy Rustchuck in the further bay.

"He's refused to play with old Wilmerdings," said Tommy Rathbone-Slater. "What a lark! The old girl's purple. She thinks heaps of that ass, Wilmerdings."

"Perhaps, Mr. Wilmerdings, you will favor us with that delicious Polonaise of Chopin's," said Lady Hammergallow. Everybody else was hushed. The indignation of Lady Hammergallow inspired much the same silence as a coming earthquake or an eclipse. Mr. Wilmerdings perceived he would be doing a real social service to begin at once, and (be it entered to his credit now that his account draws near its settlement) he did.

"If a man pretend to practice an Art," said George Harringay, "he ought at least to have the conscience to study the elements of it. What do you . . ."

"Oh! I think so too," said the younger Miss Pirbright.

The Vicar felt that the heavens had fallen. He sat crumpled up in his chair, a shattered man. Lady Hammergallow sat down next to him without appearing to see him. She was breathing heavily, but her face was terribly calm. Everyone sat down. Was the Angel grossly ignorant or only grossly impertinent? The Angel was vaguely aware of some frightful offense, aware that in some mysterious way he had ceased to be the center of the gathering. He saw reproachful despair in the Vicar's eye. He drifted slowly towards the window in the recess and sat down on the little octagonal Moorish stool by the side of Mrs. Jehoram. And under the circumstances he appreciated at more than its proper value Mrs. Jehoram's kindly smile. He put down the violin in the window seat.

XXXV

MRS. JEHORAM AND the Angel (apart)—Mr. Wilmerdings playing.

"I have so longed for a quiet word with you," said Mrs. Jehoram in a low tone. "To tell you how delightful I found your playing."

"I am glad it pleased you," said the Angel.

"Pleased is scarcely the word," said Mrs. Jehoram. "I was moved—profoundly. These others did not understand . . . I was glad you did not play with him."

The Angel looked at the mechanism called Wilmerdings, and felt glad too. (The Angelic conception of duets is a kind of conversation upon violins.) But he said nothing.

"I worship music," said Mrs. Jehoram. "I know nothing about it technically, but there is something in it—a longing, a wish . . ."

The Angel stared at her face. She met his eyes.

"You understand," she said. "I see you understand." He was certainly a very nice boy, sentimentally precocious perhaps, and with deliciously liquid eyes.

There was an interval of Chopin (Op. 40) played with immense precision.

Mrs. Jehoram had a sweet face still, in shadow, with the light falling round her golden hair, and a curious theory flashed across the Angel's mind. The perceptible powder only supported his view of something infinitely bright and lovable caught, tarnished, coarsened, coated over.

"Do you," said the Angel in a low tone. "Are you. . . . separated from. . . . *your* world?"

"As you are?" whispered Mrs. Jehoram.

"This is so—cold," said the Angel. "So harsh!" He meant the whole world.

"I feel it too," said Mrs. Jehoram, referring to Siddermorton Home.

"There are those who cannot live without sympathy," she said after a sympathetic pause. "And times when one feels alone in the world. Fighting a battle against it all. Laughing, flirting, hiding the pain of it. . . ."

"And hoping," said the Angel with a wonderful glance.—"Yes."

Mrs. Jehoram (who was an epicure of flirtations) felt the Angel was more than redeeming the promise of his appearance. (Indisputably he worshipped her.) "Do *you* look for sympathy?" she said. "Or have you found it?"

"I think," said the Angel, very softly, leaning forward, "I think I have found it."

Interval of Chopin Op. 40. The very eldest Miss Papaver and Mrs. Pirbright whispering. Lady Hammergallow (glasses up) looking down the saloon with an unfriendly expression at the Angel. Mrs. Jehoram and the Angel exchanging deep and significant glances.

"Her name," said the Angel (Mrs. Jehoram made a movement) "is Delia. She is. . . ."

"Delia!" said Mrs. Jehoram sharply, slowly realizing a terrible misunderstanding. "A fanciful name. . . . Why! . . . . No! Not that little housemaid at the Vicarage—? . . . .

The Polonaise terminated with a flourish. The Angel was quite surprised at the change in Mrs. Jehoram's expression.

"I *never* did!" said Mrs. Jehoram recovering. "To make me your confidant in an intrigue with a servant. Really Mr. Angel it's possible to be too original. . . ."

Then suddenly their colloquy was interrupted.

XXXVI

THIS SECTION IS (so far as my memory goes) the shortest in the book.

But the enormity of the offense necessitates the separation of this section from all other sections.

The Vicar, you must understand, had done his best to inculcate the recognized differentiae of a gentleman. "Never allow a lady to carry anything," said the Vicar. "Say, 'permit me' and relieve her." "Always stand until every lady is seated." "Always rise and open a door for a lady . . . ." and so forth. (All men who have elder sisters know that code.)

And the Angel (who had failed to relieve Lady Hammergallow of her teacup) danced forward with astonishing dexterity (leaving Mrs. Jehoram in the window seat) and with an elegant "permit me" rescued the tea-tray from Lady Hammergallow's pretty parlor-maid and vanished officiously in front of her. The Vicar rose to his feet with an inarticulate cry.

XXXVII

"HE'S DRUNK!" SAID Mr. Rathbone-Slater, breaking a terrific silence. "That's the matter with *him*."

Mrs. Jehoram laughed hysterically.

The Vicar stood up, motionless, staring. "Oh! I *forgot* to explain servants to him!" said the Vicar to himself in a swift outbreak of remorse. "I thought he *did* understand servants."

"Really, Mr. Hilyer!" said Lady Hammergallow, evidently exercising enormous self-control and speaking in panting spasms. "Really, Mr. Hilyer!—Your genius is *too* terrible. I must, I really *must,* ask you to take him home."

So to the dialogue in the corridor of alarmed maid-servant and well-meaning (but shockingly *gauche)* Angel—appears the Vicar, his botryoidal little face crimson, gaunt despair in his eyes, and his necktie under his left ear.

"Come," he said—struggling with emotion.

"Come away. . . . I . . . I am disgraced forever."

And the Angel stared for a second at him and obeyed—meekly, perceiving himself in the presence of unknown but evidently terrible forces.

And so began and ended the Angel's social career.

In the informal indignation meeting that followed, Lady Hammergallow took the (informal) chair. "I feel humiliated," she said. "The Vicar assured me he was an exquisite player. I never imagined. . . ."

"He was drunk," said Mr. Rathbone-Slater. "You could tell it from the way he fumbled with his tea."

"Such a *fiasco!*" said Mrs. Mergle.

"The Vicar assured me," said Lady Hammergallow. " 'The man I have staying with me is a musical genius,' he said. His very words."

"His ears must be burning anyhow," said Tommy Rathbone-Slater.

"I was trying to keep him Quiet," said Mrs. Jehoram. "By humoring him. And do you know the things he said to me—there!"

"The thing he played," said Mr. Wilmerdings, "—I must confess I did not like to charge him to his face. But really! It was merely *drifting.*"

"Just fooling with a fiddle, eigh?" said George Harringay. "Well I thought it was beyond me. So much of your fine music is—"

"Oh, *George!*" said the younger Miss Pirbright.

"The Vicar was a bit on too—to judge by his tie," said Mr. Rathbone-Slater. "It's a dashed rummy go. Did you notice how he fussed after the genius?"

"One has to be so very careful," said the very eldest Miss Papaver.

"He told me he is in love with the Vicar's housemaid!" said Mrs. Jehoram. "I almost laughed in his face."

"The Vicar ought *never* to have brought him here," said Mrs. Rathbone-Slater with decision.

The Trouble of the Barbed Wire

XXXVIII

SO, INGLORIOUSLY, ENDED the Angel's first and last appearance in Society. Vicar and Angel returned to the Vicarage; crestfallen black figures in the bright sunlight, going dejectedly. The Angel, deeply pained that the Vicar was pained. The Vicar, dishevelled and desperate, intercalating spasmodic remorse and ap-

prehension with broken explanations of the Theory of Etiquette. "They do *not* understand," said the Vicar over and over again. "They will all be so very much aggrieved. I do not know what to say to them. It is all so confused, so perplexing." And at the gate of the Vicarage, at the very spot where Delia had first seemed beautiful, stood Horrocks the village constable, awaiting them. He held coiled up about his hand certain short lengths of barbed wire.

"Good evening, Horrocks," said the Vicar as the constable held the gate open.

"Evenin', Sir," said Horrocks, and added in a kind of mysterious undertone, "*Could* I speak to you a minute, Sir?"

"Certainly," said the Vicar. The Angel walked on thoughtfully to the house, and meeting Delia in the hall stopped her and cross-examined her at length over differences between Servants and Ladies.

"You'll excuse my taking the liberty, Sir," said Horrocks, "but there's trouble brewin' for that crippled gent you got stayin' here."

"Bless me!" said the Vicar. "You don't say so!"

"Sir John Gotch, Sir. He's very angry indeed, Sir. His language, Sir—. But I felt bound to tell you, Sir. He's certain set on taking out a summons on account of that there barbed wire. Certain set, Sir, he is."

"Sir John Gotch!" said the Vicar. "Wire! I don't understand."

"He asked me to find out who did it. Course I've had to do my duty, Sir. Naturally a disagreeable one."

"Barbed wire! Duty! I don't understand you, Horrocks."

"I'm afraid, Sir, there's no denying the evidence. I've made careful enquiries, Sir." And forthwith the constable began telling the Vicar of a new and terrible outrage committed by the Angelic visitor.

But we need not follow that explanation in detail—or the subsequent confession. (For my own part I think there is nothing more tedious than dialogue). It gave the Vicar a new view of the Angelic character, a vignette of the Angelic indignation. A shady lane, sun-mottled, sweet hedges full of honeysuckle and vetch on either side, and a little girl gathering flowers, forgetful of the barbed wire which, all along the Sidderford Road, fenced in the dignity of Sir John Gotch from "bounders" and the detested "million." Then suddenly a gashed hand, a bitter outcry, and the Angel sympathetic, comforting, inquisitive. Explanations sob-set, and then— altogether novel phenomenon in the Angelic career—*passion*. A furious onslaught upon the barbed wire of Sir John Gotch, barbed wire recklessly handled, slashed, bent and broken. Yet the Angel acted without personal malice—saw in the thing only an ugly and vicious plant that trailed insidiously among its fellows. Finally the Angel's explanations gave the Vicar a picture of the Angel alone amidst his destruction, trembling and amazed at the sudden force, not himself, that had sprung up within him, and set him striking and cutting. Amazed, too, at the crimson blood that trickled down his fingers.

"It is still more horrible," said the Angel when the Vicar explained the artificial nature of the thing. "If I had seen the man who put this silly-cruel stuff there to hurt little children, I know I should have tried to inflict pain upon him. I have never felt like this before. I am indeed becoming tainted and colored altogether by the wickedness of this world."

"To think, too, that you men should be so foolish as to uphold the laws that let a man do such spiteful things. Yes—I know; you will say it has to be so. For some remoter reason. That is a thing that only makes me angrier. Why cannot an act rest on its own merits? . . . As it does in the Angelic Land."

That was the incident the history of which the Vicar now gradually learned,

getting the bare outline from Horrocks, the color and emotion subsequently from the Angel. The thing had happened the day before the musical festival at Siddermorton House.

"Have you told Sir John who did it?" asked the Vicar. "And are you sure?"

"Quite sure, Sir. There can be no doubting it was your gentleman, Sir. I've not told Sir John yet, Sir. But I shall have to tell Sir John this evening. Meaning no offense to you, Sir, as I hopes you'll see. It's my duty, Sir. Besides which—"

"Of course," said the Vicar, hastily. "Certainly it's your duty. And what will Sir John do?"

"He's dreadful set against the person who did it—destroying property like that—and sort of slapping his arrangements in the face."

Pause. Horrocks made a movement. The Vicar, tie almost at the back of his neck now, a most unusual thing for him, stared blankly at his toes.

"I thought I'd tell you, Sir," said Horrocks.

"Yes," said the Vicar. "Thanks, Horrocks, thanks!" He scratched the back of his head. "You might perhaps . . . I think it's the best way . . . Quite sure Mr. Angel did it?"

"Sherlock 'Omes, Sir, couldn't be cocksurer."

"Then I'd better give you a little note to the Squire."

XXXIX

THE VICAR'S TABLE-TALK at dinner that night, after the Angel had stated his case, was full of grim explanations, prisons, madness.

"It's too late to tell the truth about you now," said the Vicar. "Besides, that's impossible. I really do not know what to say. We must face our circumstances, I suppose. I am so undecided—so torn. It's the two worlds. If your Angelic world were only a dream, or if *this* world were only a dream—or if I could believe either or both dreams, it would be all right with me. But here is a real Angel and a real summons—how to reconcile them I do not know. I must talk to Gotch. . . . But he won't understand. Nobody will understand. . . ."

"I am putting you to terrible inconvenience, I am afraid. My appalling unworldliness—"

"It's not you," said the Vicar. "It's not you. I perceive you have brought something strange and beautiful into my life. It's not you. It's myself. If I had more faith either way. If I could believe entirely in this world, and call you an Abnormal Phenomenon, as Crump does. But no. Terrestrial Angelic, Angelic Terrestrial. . . . See-Saw."

"Still, Gotch is certain to be disagreeable, *most* disagreeable. He always is. It puts me into his hands. He is a bad moral influence, I know. Drinking. Gambling. Worse. Still, one must render unto Cæsar the things that are Cæsar's. And he is against Disestablishment. . . ."

Then the Vicar would revert to the social collapse of the afternoon. "You are so very fundamental, you know," he said—several times.

The Angel went to his own room puzzled but very depressed. Every day the world had frowned darker upon him and his angelic ways. He could see how the trouble affected the Vicar, yet he could not imagine how he could avert it. It was all so strange and unreasonable. Twice again, too, he had been pelted out of the village.

He found the violin lying on his bed where he had laid it before dinner. And taking it up he began to play to comfort himself. But now he played no delicious vision of the Angelic Land. The iron of the world was entering into his soul. For a week now he had known pain and rejection, suspicion and hatred; a strange new spirit of revolt was growing up in his heart. He played a melody, still sweet and tender as those of the Angelic Land, but charged with a new note, the note of human sorrow and effort, now swelling into something like defiance, dying now into a plaintive sadness. He played softly, playing to himself to comfort himself, but the Vicar heard, and all his finite bothers were swallowed up in a hazy melancholy, a melancholy that was quite remote from sorrow. And besides the Vicar, the Angel had another hearer of whom neither Angel nor Vicar was thinking.

Delia

XL

SHE WAS ONLY four or five yards away from the Angel in the westward gable. The diamond-paned window of her little white room was open. She knelt on her box of japanned tin, and rested her chin on her hands, her elbows on the windowsill. The young moon hung over the pine trees, and its light, cool and colorless, lay softly upon the silent-sleeping world. Its light fell upon her white face, and discovered new depths in her dreaming eyes. Her soft lips fell apart and showed the little white teeth.

Delia was thinking, vaguely, wonderfully, as girls will think. It was feeling rather than thinking; clouds of beautiful translucent emotion drove across the clear sky of her mind, taking shape that changed and vanished. She had all that wonderful emotional tenderness, that subtle exquisite desire for self-sacrifice, which exists so inexplicably in a girl's heart, exists it seems only to be presently trampled under foot by the grim and gross humors of daily life, to be ploughed in again roughly and remorselessly, as the farmer ploughs in the clover that has sprung up in the soil. She had been looking out at the tranquillity of the moonlight long before the Angel began to play,—waiting; then suddenly the quiet, motionless beauty of silver and shadow was suffused with tender music.

She did not move, but her lips closed and her eyes grew even softer. She had been thinking before of the strange glory that had suddenly flashed out about the stooping hunchback when he spoke to her in the sunset; of that and of a dozen other glances, chance turns, even once the touching of her hand. That afternoon he had spoken to her, asking strange questions. Now the music seemed to bring his very face before her, his look of half-curious solicitude, peering into her face, into her eyes, into her and through her, deep down into her soul. He seemed now to be speaking directly to her, telling her of his solitude and trouble. Oh! that regret, that longing! For he was in trouble. And how could a servant-girl help him, this soft-spoken gentleman who carried himself so kindly, who played so sweetly. The music was so sweet and keen, it came so near to the thought of her heart, that presently one hand tightened on the other, and the tears came streaming down her face.

As Crump would tell you, people do not do that kind of thing unless there is something wrong with the nervous system. But then, from the scientific point of view, being in love is a pathological condition.

I am painfully aware of the objectionable nature of my story here. I have even thought of wilfully perverting the truth to propitiate the Lady Reader. But I could not. The story has been too much for me. I do the thing with my eyes open. Delia must remain what she really was—a servant girl. I know that to give a mere servant girl, or at least an English servant girl, the refined feelings of a human being, to present her as speaking with anything but an intolerable confusion of aspirates, places me outside the pale of respectable writers. Association with servants, even in thought, is dangerous in these days. I can only plead (pleading vainly, I know), that Delia was a very exceptional servant girl. Possibly, if one enquired, it might be found that her parentage was upper middle-class—that she was made of the finer upper middle-class clay. And (this perhaps may avail me better) I will promise that in some future work I will redress the balance, and the patient reader shall have the recognized article, enormous feet and hands, systematic aspiration of vowels and elimination of aspirates, no figure (only middle-class girls have figures—the thing is beyond a servant-girl's means), a fringe (by agreement), and a cheerful readiness to dispose of her self-respect for half-a-crown. That is the accepted English servant, the typical English woman (when stripped of money and accomplishments) as she appears in the works of contemporary writers. But Delia somehow was different. I can only regret the circumstance—it was altogether beyond my control.

Doctor Crump Acts
XLI

EARLY THE NEXT morning the Angel went down through the village, and climbing the fence, waded through the waist-high reeds that fringe the Sidder. He was going to Bandram Bay to take a nearer view of the sea, which one could just see on a clear day from the higher parts of Siddermorton Park. And suddenly he came upon Crump sitting on a log and smoking. (Crump always smoked exactly two ounces per week—and he always smoked it in the open air.)

"Hullo!" said Crump, in his healthiest tone. "How's the wing?"

"Very well," said the Angel. "The pain's gone."

"I suppose you know you are trespassing?"

"Trespassing!" said the Angel.

"I suppose you don't know what that means," said Crump.

"I don't," said the Angel.

"I must congratulate you. I don't know how long you will last, but you are keeping it up remarkably well. I thought at first you were a mattoid, but you're so amazingly consistent. Your attitude of entire ignorance of the elementary facts of Life is really a very amusing pose. You make slips of course, but very few. But surely we two understand one another."

He smiled at the Angel. "You would beat Sherlock Holmes. I wonder who you really are."

The Angel smiled back, with eyebrows raised and hands extended. "It's impossible for you to know who I am. Your eyes are blind, your ears deaf, your soul dark, to all that is wonderful about me. It's no good my telling that I fell into your world."

The Doctor waved his pipe. "Not that, please. I don't want to pry if you have your reasons for keeping quiet. Only I would like you to think of Hilyer's mental health. He really believes this story."

The Angel shrugged his dwindling wings.

"You did not know him before this affair. He's changed tremendously. He used to be neat and comfortable. For the last fortnight he's been hazy, with a far-away look in his eyes. He preached last Sunday without his cuff links, and something wrong with his tie, and he took for his text, 'Eye hath not seen nor ear heard.' He really believes all this nonsense about the Angel-land. The man is verging on monomania!''

''You *will* see things from your own standpoint,'' said the Angel.

''Everyone must. At any rate, I think it jolly regrettable to see this poor old fellow hypnotized, as you certainly have hypnotized him. I don't know where you come from nor who you are, but I warn you I'm not going to see the old boy made a fool of much longer.''

''But he's not being made a fool of. He's simply beginning to dream of a world outside his knowledge—''

''It won't do,'' said Crump. ''I'm not one of the dupe class. You are either of two things—a lunatic at large (which I don't believe), or a knave. Nothing else is possible. I think I know a little of this world, whatever I do of yours. Very well. If you don't leave Hillyer alone I shall communicate with the police, and either clap you into a prison, if you go back on your story, or into a madhouse if you don't. It's stretching a point, but I swear I'd certify you insane tomorrow to get you out of the village. It's not only the Vicar. As you know. I hope that's plain. Now what have you to say?''

With an affectation of great calm, the Doctor took out his penknife and began to dig the blade into his pipe bowl. His pipe had gone out during this last speech.

For a moment neither spoke. The Angel looked about him with a face that grew pale. The Doctor extracted a plug of tobacco from his pipe and flung it away, shut his penknife and put it in his waistcoat pocket. He had not meant to speak quite so emphatically, but speech always warmed him.

''Prison,'' said the Angel. ''Madhouse! Let me see.'' Then he remembered the Vicar's explanation. ''Not that!'' he said. He approached Crump with eyes dilated and hands outstretched.

''I knew *you* would know what those things meant—at any rate. Sit down,'' said Crump, indicating the tree trunk beside him by a movement of the head.

The Angel, shivering, sat down on the tree trunk and stared at the Doctor.

Crump was getting out his pouch. ''You are a strange man,'' said the Angel. ''Your beliefs are like—a steel trap.''

''They are,'' said Crump—flattered.

''But I tell you—I assure you the thing is so—I know nothing, or at least remember nothing of anything I knew of this world before I found myself in the darkness of night on the moorland above Sidderford.''

''Where did you learn the language then?''

''I don't know. Only I tell you—But I haven't an atom of the sort of proof that would convince you.''

''And you really,'' said Crump, suddenly coming round upon him and looking into his eyes; ''You really believe you were eternally in a kind of glorious heaven before then?''

''I do,'' said the Angel.

''Pshaw!'' said Crump, and lit his pipe. He sat smoking, elbow on knee, for some time, and the Angel sat and watched him. Then his face grew less troubled.

''It is just possible,'' he said to himself rather than to the Angel, and began another piece of silence.

''You see;'' he said, when that was finished. ''There is such a thing as double personality. . . . A man sometimes forgets who he is and thinks he is someone else. Leaves home, friends, and everything, and leads a double life. There was a case in *Nature* only a month or so ago. The man was sometimes English and right-handed, and sometimes Welsh and left-handed. When he was English he knew no Welsh, when he was Welsh he knew no English. . . . H'm.''

He turned suddenly on the Angel and said "Home!'' He fancied he might revive in the Angel some latent memory of his lost youth. He went on "Dadda, Pappa, Daddy, Mammy, Pappy, Father, Dad, Governor, Old Boy, Mother, dear Mother, Ma, Mumsy. . . . No good? What are you laughing at?''

"Nothing,'' said the Angel. "You surprised me a little,—that is all. A week ago I should have been puzzled by that vocabulary.''

For a minute Crump rebuked the Angel silently out of the corner of his eye.

"You have such an ingenuous face. You almost force me to believe you. You are certainly not an ordinary lunatic. Your mind—except for your isolation from the past—seems balanced enough. I wish Nordau or Lombroso or some of these *Saltpetriere* men could have a look at you. Down here one gets no practice worth speaking about in mental cases. There's one idiot—and he's just a damned idiot of an idiot—; all the rest are thoroughly sane people.''

"Possibly that accounts for their behavior,'' said the Angel thoughtfully.

"But to consider your general position here,'' said Crump, ignoring his comment, "I really regard you as a bad influence here. These fancies are contagious. It is not simply the Vicar. There is a man named Shine has caught the fad, and he has been in the drink for a week, off and on, and offering to fight anyone who says you are not an Angel. Then a man over at Sidderford is, I hear, affected with a kind of religious mania on the same tack. These things spread. There ought to be a quarantine in mischievous ideas. And I have heard another story. . . .''

"But what can I do?'' said the Angel. "Suppose I am (quite unintentionally) doing mischief. . . .''

"You can leave the village,'' said Crump.

"Then I shall only go into another village.''

"That's not my affair,'' said Crump. "Go where you like. Only go. Leave these three people, the Vicar, Shine, the little servant girl, whose heads are all spinning with galaxies of Angels. . . .''

"But,'' said the Angel. "Face your world! I tell you I can't. And leave Delia! I don't understand. . . . I do not know how to set about getting Work and Food and Shelter. And I am growing afraid of human beings. . . .''

"Fancies, fancies,'' said Crump, watching him, "mania..''

"It's no good my persisting in worrying you,'' he said suddenly, "but certainly the situation is impossible as it stands.'' He stood up with a jerk.

"Good-morning, Mr.—Angel,'' he said, "the long and the short of it is—I say it as the medical adviser of this parish—you are an unhealthy influence. We can't have you. You must go.''

He turned, and went striding through the grass towards the roadway, leaving the Angel sitting disconsolately on the tree trunk. "An unhealthy influence,'' said the Angel slowly, staring blankly in front of him, and trying to realize what it meant.

Sir John Gotch Acts

XLII

SIR JOHN GOTCH was a little man with scrubby hair, a small, thin nose sticking out of a face crackled with wrinkles, tight brown gaiters, and a riding whip. "I've come, you see,'' he said, as Mrs. Hinijer closed the door.

"Thank you," said the Vicar, "I'm obliged to you. I'm really obliged to you."

"Glad to be of any service to you," said Sir John Gotch. (Angular attitude.)

"This business," said the Vicar, "this unfortunate business of the barbed wire—is really, you know, a most unfortunate business."

Sir John Gotch became decidedly more angular in his attitude. "It is," he said.

"This Mr. Angel being my guest—"

"No. reason why he should cut my wire," said Sir John Gotch, briefly.

"None whatever."

"May I ask *who* this Mr. Angel is?" asked Sir John Gotch with the abruptness of long premeditation.

The Vicar's fingers jumped to his chin. What *was* the good of talking to a man like Sir John Gotch about Angels?

"To tell you the exact truth," said the Vicar, "there is a little secret—"

"Lady Hammergallow told me as much."

The Vicar's face suddenly became bright red.

"Do you know," said Sir John, with scarcely a pause, "he's been going about this village preaching Socialism?"

"Good heavens!" said the Vicar, *"No!"*

"He has. He has been buttonholing every yokel he came across, and asking them why they had to work, while we—I and you, you know—did nothing. He has been saying we ought to, educate every man up to your level and mine—out of the rates, I suppose, as usual. He has been suggesting that we—I and you, you know—keep these people down—pith 'em."

"Dear me!" said the Vicar, "I had no idea."

"He has done this wire-cutting as a demonstration, I tell you, as a Socialistic demonstration. If we don't come down on him pretty sharply, I tell you, we shall have the palings down in Flinders Lane next, and the next thing will be ricks afire, and every damned (I beg your pardon, Vicar, I know I'm too fond of that word), every blessed pheasant's egg in the parish smashed. I know these—"

"A Socialist," said the Vicar, quite put out, "I had *no* idea."

"You see why I am inclined to push matters against our gentleman though he *is* your guest. It seems to me he has been taking advantage of your paternal—"

"Oh, *not* paternal!" said the Vicar. "Really—"

"(I beg your pardon, Vicar—it was a slip.) Of your kindness, to go mischief-making everywhere, setting class against class, and the poor man against his bread and butter."

The Vicar's fingers were at his chin again.

"So there's one of two things," said Sir John Gotch. "Either that Guest of yours leaves the parish, or—I take proceedings. That's final."

The Vicar's mouth was all askew.

"That's the position," said Sir John, jumping to his feet, "if it were not for you, I should take proceedings at once. As it is—am I to take proceedings or no?"

"You see," said the Vicar in horrible perplexity.

"Well?"

"Arrangements have to be made."

"He's a mischief-making idler . . . I know the breed. But I'll give you a week—"

"Thank you," said the Vicar. "I understand your position. I perceive the situation is getting intolerable. . . ."

"Sorry to give you this bother, of course," said Sir John.

"A week," said the Vicar.

"A week," said Sir John, leaving.

The Vicar returned, after accompanying Gotch out, and for a long time he remained sitting before the desk in his study, plunged in thought. "A week!" he said, after an immense silence. "Here is an Angel, a glorious Angel, who has quickened my soul to beauty and delight, who has opened my eyes to Wonderland, and something more than Wonderland, . . . and I have promised to get rid of him in a week! What are we men made of? . . . How *can* I tell him?"

He began to walk up and down the room, then he went into the dining-room, and stood staring blankly out at the cornfield. The table was already laid for lunch. Presently he turned, still dreaming, and almost mechanically helped himself to a glass of sherry.

The Sea Cliff
XLIII

THE ANGEL LAY upon the summit of the cliff above Bandram Bay, and stared out at the glittering sea. Sheer from under his elbows fell the cliff, five hundred and seven feet of it down to the datum line, and the sea-birds eddied and soared below him. The upper part of the cliff was a greenish chalky rock, the lower two-thirds a warm red, marbled with gypsum bands, and from half-a-dozen places spurted jets of water, to fall in long cascades down its face. The swell frothed white on the flinty beach, and the water beyond where the shadows of an outstanding rock lay, was green and purple in a thousand tints and marked with streaks and flakes of foam. The air was full of sunlight and the tinkling of the little waterfalls and the slow soughing of the seas below. Now and then a butterfly flickered over the face of the cliff, and a multitude of sea birds perched and flew hither and thither.

The Angel lay with his crippled, shrivelled wings humped upon his back, watching the gulls and jackdaws and rooks, circling in the sunlight, soaring, eddying, sweeping down to the water or upward into the dazzling blue of the sky. Long the Angel lay there and watched them going to and fro on outspread wings. He watched, and as he watched them he remembered with infinite longing the rivers of starlight and the sweetness of the land from which he came. And a gull came gliding overhead, swiftly and easily, with its broad wings spreading white and fair against the blue. And suddenly a shadow came into the Angel's eyes, the sunlight left them, he thought of his own crippled pinions, and put his face upon his arm and wept.

A woman who was walking along the footpath across the Cliff Field saw only a twisted hunchback dressed in the Vicar of Siddermorton's cast-off clothes, sprawling foolishly at the edge of the cliff and with his forehead on his arm. She looked at him and looked again. "The silly creature has gone to sleep," she said, and though she had a heavy basket to carry, came towards him with an idea of waking him up. But as she drew near she saw his shoulders heave and heard the sound of his sobbing.

She stood still a minute, and her features twitched into a kind of grin. Then treading softly she turned and went back towards the pathway. " 'Tis so hard to think of anything to say," she said. "Poor afflicted soul!"

Presently the Angel ceased sobbing, and stared with a tear-stained face at the beach below him.

"This world," he said, "wraps me round and swallows me up. My wings grow shrivelled and useless. Soon I shall be nothing more than a crippled man, and I shall age, and bow myself to pain, and die. . . . I am miserable. And I am alone."

Then he rested his chin on his hands upon the edge of the cliff, and began to think of Delia's face with the light in her eyes. The Angel felt a curious desire to go to her and tell her of his withered wings. To place his arms about her and weep for the land he had lost. "Delia!" he said to himself very softly. And presently a cloud drove in front of the sun.

Mrs. Hinijer Acts
XLIV

MRS. HINIJER SURPRISED the Vicar by tapping at his study door after tea. "Begging your pardon, Sir," said Mrs. Hinijer. "But might I make so bold as to speak to you for a moment?"

"Certainly, Mrs. Hinijer," said the Vicar, little dreaming of the blow that was coming. He held a letter in his hand, a very strange and disagreeable letter from his bishop, a letter that irritated and distressed him, criticizing in the strongest language the guests he chose to entertain in his own house. Only a popular bishop living in a democratic age, a bishop who was still half a pedagogue, could have written such a letter.

Mrs. Hinijer coughed behind her hand and struggled with some respiratory disorganization. The Vicar felt apprehensive. Usually in their interviews he was the most disconcerted. Invariably so when the interview ended.

"Well?" he said.

"May I make so bold, sir, as to arst when Mr. Angel is a-going?" (Cough.)

The Vicar started. "To ask when Mr. Angel is going?" he repeated slowly to gain time. *"Another!"*

"I'm sorry, sir. But I've been used to waitin' on gentlefolks, sir; and you'd hardly imagine how it feels quite to wait on such as 'im."

"Such as . . . *'im!* Do I understand you, Mrs. Hinijer, that you don't like Mr. Angel?"

"You see, sir, before I came to you, sir, I was at Lord Dundoller's seventeen years, and you, sir—if you will excuse me—are a perfect gentleman yourself, sir—though in the Church. And then . . ."

"Dear, dear!" said the Vicar. "And don't you regard Mr. Angel as a gentleman?"

"I'm sorry to 'ave to say it, sir."

"But what . . . ? Dear me! Surely!"

"I'm sorry to 'ave to say it, sir. But when a party goes turning vegetarian suddenly and putting out all the cooking, and hasn't no proper luggage of his own, and borry's shirts and socks from his 'ost, and don't know no better than to try his knife at peas (as I seed my very self), and goes talking in odd corners to the housemaids, and folds up his napkin after meals, and eats with his fingers at minced veal, and plays the fiddle in the middle of the night keeping everybody awake, and stares and grins at his elders a-getting upstairs, and generally misconducts himself with things that I can scarcely tell you all, one can't help thinking, sir. Thought is free, sir, and one can't help coming to one's own conclusions. Besides which, there is talk all over the village about him—what with one thing and another. I know a gentleman when I sees a gentleman, and I know a gentleman when I don't see a gentleman, and me, and Susan, and George, we've talked it over, being the upper servants, so to speak, and experienced, and leaving out that girl Delia, who I only hope won't come to any harm through him, and depend upon it, sir, that Mr. Angel ain't what you think he is, sir, and the sooner he leaves this house the better."

Mrs. Hinijer ceased abruptly and stood panting but stern, and with her eyes grimly fixed on the Vicar's face.

"*Really,* Mrs. Hinijer!" said the Vicar, and then, "Oh *Lord!*"

"What *have* I done?" said the Vicar, suddenly starting up and appealing to the inexorable fates. "What HAVE I done?"

"There's no knowing," said Mrs. Hinijer. "Though a deal of talk in the village."

"*Bother!*" said the Vicar, going and staring out of the window. Then he turned. "Look here, Mrs. Hinijer! Mr. Angel will be leaving this house in the course of a week. Is that enough?"

"Quite," said Mrs. Hinijer. "And I feel sure, sir . . ."

The Vicar's eyes fell with unwonted eloquence upon the door.

The Angel in Trouble
XLV

"THE FACT IS," said the Vicar, "this is no world for Angels."

The blinds had not been drawn, and the twilight outer world under an overcast sky seemed unspeakably grey and cold. The Angel sat at table in dejected silence. His inevitable departure had been proclaimed. Since his presence hurt people and made the Vicar wretched he acquiesced in the justice of the decision, but what would happen to him after his plunge he could not imagine. Something very disagreeable certainly.

"There is the violin," said the Vicar. "Only after our experience—"

"I must get you clothes—a general outfit.— Dear me! you don't understand railway traveling!. And coinage! Taking lodgings! Eatinghouses!— I must come up at least and see you settled. Get work for you. But an Angel in London! Working for his living! That grey cold wilderness of people! What *will* become of you?— If I had one friend in the world I could trust to believe me!"

"I ought not to be sending you away—"

"Do not trouble overmuch for me, my friend," said the Angel. "At least this life of yours ends. And there are things in it. There is something in this life of yours— Your care for me! I thought there was nothing beautiful at all in life—"

"And I have betrayed you!" said the Vicar, with a sudden wave of remorse. "Why did I not face them all—say, 'This is the best of life'? What do these everyday things matter?"

He stopped suddenly. "What *do* they matter?" he said.

"I have only come into your life to trouble it," said the Angel.

"Don't say that," said the Vicar. "You have come into my life to awaken me. I have been dreaming—dreaming. Dreaming this was necessary and that. Dreaming that this narrow prison was the world. And the dream still hangs about me and troubles me. That is all. Even your departure—. Am I not dreaming that you must go?''

When he was in bed that night the mystical aspect of the case came still more forcibly before the Vicar. He lay awake and had the most horrible visions of his sweet and delicate visitor drifting through this unsympathetic world and happening upon the cruellest misadventures. His guest *was* an Angel assuredly. He tried to go over the whole story of the past eight days again. He thought of the hot afternoon, the shot fired out of sheer surprise, the fluttering iridescent wings, the beautiful saffron-robed figure upon the ground. How wonderful that had seemed to him! Then his mind turned to the things he had heard of the other world, to the dreams the violin had conjured up, to the vague, fluctuating, wonderful cities of the Angelic Land. He tried to recall the forms of the buildings, the shapes of the fruits upon the trees, the aspect of the winged shapes that traversed its ways. They grew from a memory into a present reality, grew every moment just a little more vivid and his troubles a little less immediate; and so, softly and quietly, the Vicar slipped out of his troubles and perplexities into the Land of Dreams.

XLVI

DELIA SAT WITH her window open, hoping to hear the Angel play. But that night there was to be no playing. The sky was overcast, yet not so thickly but that the moon was visible. High up a broken cloud-lace drove across the sky, and now the moon was a hazy patch of light, and now it was darkened, and now rode clear and bright and sharply outlined against the blue gulf of night. And presently she heard the door into the garden opening, and a figure came out under the drifting pallor of the moonlight.

It was the Angel. But he wore once more the saffron robe in the place of his formless overcoat. In the uncertain light this garment had only a colorless shimmer, and his wings behind him seemed a leaden grey. He began taking short runs, flapping his wings and leaping, going to and fro amidst the drifting patches of light and the shadows of the trees. Delia watched him in amazement. He gave a despondent cry, leaping higher. His shriveled wings flashed and fell. A thicker patch in the cloud-film made everything obscure. He seemed to spring five or six feet from the ground and fall clumsily. She saw him in the dimness crouching on the ground and then she heard him sobbing.

''He's hurt!'' said Delia, pressing her lips together hard and staring. ''I ought to help him.''

She hesitated, then stood up and flitted swiftly towards the door, went slipping quietly downstairs and out into the moonlight. The Angel still lay upon the lawn, and sobbed for utter wretchedness.

''Oh! what is the matter?'' said Delia, stooping over him and touching his head timidly.

The Angel ceased sobbing, sat up abruptly, and stared at her. He saw her face, moonlit, and soft with pity. ''What is the matter?'' she whispered. ''Are you hurt?''

The Angel stared about him, and his eyes came to rest on her face. ''Delia!'' he whispered.

''Are you hurt?'' said Delia.

''My wings,'' said the Angel. ''I cannot use my wings.''

Delia did not understand, but she realized that it was something very dreadful. "It is dark, it is cold," whispered the Angel; "I cannot use my wings."

It hurt her unaccountably to see the tears on his face. She did not know what to do.

"Pity me, Delia," said the Angel, suddenly extending his arms towards her; "pity me."

Impulsively she knelt down and took his face between her hands. "I do not know," she said; "but I am sorry. I am sorry for you, with all my heart."

The Angel said not a word. He was looking at her little face in the bright moonlight, with an expression of uncomprehending wonder in his eyes. "This strange world!" he said.

She suddenly withdrew her hands. A cloud drove over the moon. "What can I do to help you?" she whispered. "I would do anything to help you."

He still held her at arm's length, perplexity replacing misery in his face. "This strange world!" he repeated.

Both whispered, she kneeling, he sitting, in the fluctuating moonlight and darkness of the lawn.

"Delia!" said Mrs. Hinijer, suddenly projecting from her window; "Delia, is that you?"

They both looked up at her in consternation.

"Come in at once, Delia," said Mrs. Hinijer. "If that Mr. Angel was a gentleman (which he isn't), he'd feel ashamed of hisself. And you an orphan too!"

The Last Day of the Visit
XLVII

ON THE MORNING of the next day the Angel, after he had breakfasted, went out towards the moor, and Mrs. Hinijer had an interview with the Vicar. What happened need not concern us now. The Vicar was visibly disconcerted. "He *must* go," he said; "certainly he must go," and straightway he forgot the particular accusation in the general trouble. He spent the morning in hazy meditation, interspersed by a spasmodic study of Skiff and Waterlow's price list, and the catalogue of the Medical, Scholastic, and Clerical Stores. A schedule grew slowly on a sheet of paper that lay on the desk before him. He cut out a self-measurement form from the tailoring department of the Stores and pinned it to the study curtains. This was the kind of document he was making:

"*1 Black Melton Frock Coat. patts? £3, 10s.*

"*? Trousers. 2 pairs or one.*

"*1 Cheviot Tweed Suit (write for patterns. Self-meas.?)*"

The Vicar spent some time studying a pleasing array of model gentlemen. They were all very nice-looking, but he found it hard to imagine the Angel so transfigured. For, although six days had passed, the Angel remained without any suit of his own. The Vicar had vacillated between a project of driving the Angel into Portbroddock and getting him measured for a suit, and his absolute horror of the insinuating manners of the tailor he employed. He knew that tailor would demand an exhaustive explanation. Besides which, one never knew when the Angel might leave. So the six days had passed, and the Angel had grown steadily in the wisdom of this world and shrouded his brightness still in the ample retirement of the Vicar's newest clothes.

"1 Soft Felt Hat, No. G. 7 (say), 8s 6d.

"1 Silk Hat, 14s 6d. Hatbox?"

("I suppose he ought to have a silk hat," said the Vicar; "it's the correct thing up there. Shape No. 3 seems best suited to his style. But it's dreadful to think of him all alone in that great city. Everyone will misunderstand him, and he will misunderstand everybody. However, I suppose it *must* be. Where was I?)"

"1 Toothbrush. 1 Brush and Comb. Razor?

"1/2 doz. Shirts (? measure his neck), 6s ea.

"Socks? Pants?

"2 suits Pajamas. Price? Say 15s.

"1 doz. Collars ('The Life Guardsman'), 8s.

"Braces. Oxon Patent Versatile, 1s 11 1/2d" ("But how will he get them on?" said the Vicar.)

"1 Rubber Stamp, T. Angel, and Marking Ink in box complete, 9d.

("Those washerwomen are certain to steal all his things.")

"1 Single-bladed Penknife with Corkscrew, say 1s 6d.

"N.B.—Don't forget Cuff Links, Collar Stud, &c." (The Vicar loved "&c.", it gave things such a precise and business-like air.)

"1 Leather Portmanteau (had better see these)."

And so forth—meanderingly. It kept the Vicar busy until lunch time, though his heart ached.

The Angel did not return to lunch. This was not so very remarkable—once before he had missed the midday meal. Yet, considering how short was the time they would have together now, he might perhaps have come back. Doubtless he had excellent reasons, though, for his absence. The Vicar made an indifferent lunch. In the afternoon he rested in his usual manner, and did a little more to the list of requirements. He did not begin to feel nervous about the Angel till tea-time. He waited, perhaps, half an hour before he took tea. "Odd," said the Vicar, feeling still more lonely as he drank his tea.

As the time for dinner crept on and no Angel appeared the Vicar's imagination began to trouble him. "He will come in to dinner, surely," said the Vicar, caressing his chin, and beginning to fret about the house upon inconsiderable errands, as his habit was when anything occurred to break his routine. The sun set, a gorgeous spectacle, amidst tumbled masses of purple cloud. The gold and red faded into twilight; the evening star gathered her robe of light together from out the brightness of the sky in the West. Breaking the silence of evening that crept over the outer world, a corncrake began his whirring chant. The Vicar's face grew troubled; twice he went and stared at the darkening hillside, and then fretted back to the house again. Mrs. Hinijer served dinner. "Your dinner's ready," she announced for the second time, with a reproachful intonation. "Yes, yes," said the Vicar, fussing off upstairs.

He came down and went into his study and lit his reading lamp, a patent affair with an incandescent wick, dropping the match into his wastepaper basket without stopping to see if it was extinguished. Then he fretted into the diningroom and began a desultory attack on the cooling dinner . . .

(Dear Reader, the time is almost ripe to say farewell to this little Vicar of ours.)

XLVIII

Sir John Gotch (still smarting over the business of the barbed wire) was riding along one of the grassy ways through the preserves by the Sidder, when he saw, strolling slowly through the trees beyond the undergrowth, the one particular human being he did not want to see.

"I'm damned," said Sir John Gotch, with immense emphasis; "if this isn't altogether too much."

He raised himself in the stirrups. "Hi!" he shouted. "You there!"

The Angel turned smiling.

"Get out of this wood!" said Sir John Gotch.

"*Why?*" said the Angel.

"I'm—," said Sir John Gotch, meditating some cataclysmal expletive. But he could think of nothing more than "damned." "Get out of this wood," he said.

The Angel's smile vanished. "Why should I get out of this wood?" he said and stood still.

Neither spoke for a full half minute perhaps, and then Sir John Gotch dropped out of his saddle and stood by the horse.

(Now you must remember—lest the Angelic Hosts be discredited hereby— that this Angel had been breathing the poisonous air of this Struggle for Existence of ours for more than a week. It was not only his wings and the brightness of his face that suffered. He had eaten and slept and learnt the lesson of pain— had traveled so far on the road to humanity. All the length of his Visit he had been meeting more and more of the harshness and conflict of this world, and losing touch with the glorious altitudes of his own.)

"You won't go, eigh!" said Gotch, and began to lead his horse through the bushes towards the Angel. The Angel stood, all his muscles tight and his nerves quivering, watching his antagonist approach.

"Get out of this wood," said Gotch, stopping three yards away, his face white with rage, his bridle in one hand and his riding whip in the other.

Strange floods of emotion were running through the Angel. "Who are you," he said, in a low quivering voice; "who am I—that you should order me out of this place? What has the World done that men like you . . ."

"You're the fool who cut my barbed wire," said Gotch, threatening, "If you want to know!"

"*Your* barbed wire," said the Angel. "Was that your barbed wire? Are you the man who put down that barbed wire? What right have you . . ."

"Don't you go talking Socialist rot," said Gotch in short gasps. "This wood's mine, and I've a right to protect it how I can. I know your kind of muck. Talking rot and stirring up discontent. And if you don't get out of it jolly sharp . . ."

"*Well!*" said the Angel, a brimming reservoir of unaccountable energy.

"Get out of this damned wood!" said Gotch, flashing into the bully out of sheer alarm at the light in the Angel's face.

He made one step towards him, with the whip raised, and then something happened that neither he nor the Angel properly understood. The Angel seemed to leap into the air, a pair of grey wings flashed out at the Squire, he saw a face bearing down upon him, full of the wild beauty of passionate anger. His riding whip was torn out of his hand. His horse reared behind him, pulled him over, gained his bridle and fled.

The whip cut across his face as he fell back, stung across his face again as he sat on the ground. He saw the Angel, radiant with anger, in the act to strike again. Gotch flung up his hands, pitched himself forward to save his eyes, and rolled on the ground under the pitiless fury of the blows that rained down upon him.

"You brute," cried the Angel, striking wherever he saw flesh to feel. "You bestial thing of pride and lies! You who have overshadowed the souls of other men. You shallow fool with your horses and dogs! To lift your face against any living thing! Learn! Learn! Learn!"

Gotch began screaming for help. Twice he tried to clamber to his feet, got to his knees, and went headlong again under the ferocious anger of the Angel. Presently he made a strange noise in his throat, and ceased even to writhe under his punishment.

Then suddenly the Angel awakened from his wrath, and found himself standing, panting and trembling, one foot on a motionless figure, under the green stillness of the sunlit woods.

He stared about him, then down at his feet where, among the tangled dead leaves, the hair was matted with blood. The whip dropped from his hands, the hot color fled from his face. *"Pain!"* he said. "Why does he lie so still?"

He took his foot off Gotch's shoulder, bent down towards the prostrate figure, stood listening, knelt—shook him. "Awake!" said the Angel. Then still more softly, *"Awake!"*

He remained listening some minutes or more, stood up sharply, and looked round him at the silent trees. A feeling of profound horror descended upon him, wrapped him round about. With an abrupt gesture he turned. "What has happened to me?" he said, in an awe-stricken whisper.

He started back from the motionless figure. *"Dead!"* he said suddenly, and turning, panic stricken, fled headlong through the wood.

XLIX

IT WAS SOME minutes after the footsteps of the Angel had died away in the distance that Gotch raised himself on his hand. "By Jove!" he said. "Crump's right."

"Cut at the head, too!"

He put his hand to his face and felt the two weals running across it, hot and fat. "I'll think twice before I lift my hand against a lunatic again," said Sir John Gotch.

"He may be a person of weak intellect, but I'm damned if he hasn't a pretty strong arm. *Phew!* He's cut a bit clean off the top of my ear with that infernal lash."

"That infernal horse will go galloping to the house in the approved dramatic style. Little Madam'll be scared out of her wits. And I . . . I shall have to explain how it all happened. While she vivisects me with questions.

"I'm a jolly good mind to have spring guns and man-traps put in this preserve. Confound the Law!"

L

BUT THE ANGEL, thinking that Gotch was dead, went wandering off in a passion of remorse and fear through the brakes and copses along the Sidder. You can scarcely imagine how appalled he was at this last and overwhelming proof of his encroaching humanity. All the darkness, passion and pain of life seemed closing in upon him, inexorably, becoming part of him, chaining him to all that a week ago he had found strange and pitiful in men.

"Truly, this is no world for an Angel!" said the Angel. "It is a World of War, a World of Pain, a World of Death. Anger comes upon one . . . I who knew not pain and anger, stand here with blood stains on my hands. I have fallen. To come into this world is to fall. One must hunger and thirst and be tormented with a thousand desires. One must fight for foothold, be angry and strike—"

He lifted up his hands to Heaven, the ultimate bitterness of helpless remorse in his face, and then flung them down with a gesture of despair. The prison walls of this narrow passionate life seemed creeping in upon him, certainly and steadily, to crush him presently altogether. He felt what all we poor mortals have to feel sooner or later—the pitiless force of the Things that Must Be, not only without us but (where the real trouble lies) within, all the inevitable tormenting of one's high resolves, those inevitable seasons when the better self is forgotten. But with us it is a gentle descent, made by imperceptible degrees over a long space of years; with him it was the horrible discovery of one short week. He felt he was being crippled, caked over, blinded, stupefied in the wrappings of this life, he felt as a man might feel who has taken some horrible poison, and feels destruction spreading within him.

He took no account of hunger or fatigue or the flight of time. On and on he went, avoiding houses and roads, turning away from the sight and sound of a human being in a wordless desperate argument with Fate. His thoughts did not flow but stood banked back in inarticulate remonstrance against his degradation. Chance directed his footsteps homeward and, at last, after nightfall, he found himself faint and weary and wretched, stumbling along over the moor at the back of Siddermorton. He heard the rats run and squeal in the heather, and once a noiseless big bird came out of the darkness, passed, and vanished again. And he saw without noticing it a dull red glow in the sky before him.

LI

BUT WHEN HE came over the brow of the moor, a vivid light sprang up before him and refused to be ignored. He came on down the hill and speedily saw more distinctly what the glare was. It came from darting and trembling tongues of fire, golden and red, that shot from the windows and a hole in the roof of the Vicarage. A cluster of black heads, all the village in fact, except the fire-brigade—who were down at Aylmer's Cottage trying to find the key of the machine-house—came out in silhouette against the blaze. There was a roaring sound, and a humming of voices, and presently a furious outcry. There was a shouting of "No! No!"—"Come back!" and an inarticulate roar.

He began to run towards the burning house. He stumbled and almost fell, but he ran on. He found black figures running about him. The flaring fire blew gustily this way and that, and he smelt the smell of burning.

"She went in," said one voice, "she went in."

"The mad girl!" said another.

"Stand back! Stand back!" cried others.

He found himself thrusting through an excited swaying crowd, all staring at the flames, and with the red reflection in their eyes.

"Stand back!" said a laborer, clutching him.

"What is it?" said the Angel. "What does this mean?"

"There's a girl in the house, and she can't get out!"

"Went in after a fiddle," said another.

" 'Tas hopeless," he heard someone else say.

"I was standing near her. I heerd her. Says she: 'I *can* get his fiddle.' I heerd her—Just like that! 'I *can* get his fiddle.' "

For a moment the Angel stood staring. Then in a flash he saw it all, saw this grim little world of battle and cruelty, transfigured in a splendor that outshone the Angelic Land, suffused suddenly and insupportably glorious with the wonderful light of Love and Self-Sacrifice. He gave a strange cry, and before anyone could stop him, was running towards the burning building. There were cries of "The Hunchback! The Fowener!"

The Vicar, whose scalded hand was being tied up, turned his head, and he and Crump saw the Angel, a black outline against the intense, red glare of the doorway. It was the sensation of the tenth of a second, yet both men could not have remembered that transitory attitude more vividly had it been a picture they had studied for hours together. Then the Angel was hidden by something massive (no one knew what) that fell, incandescent, across the doorway.

LII

THERE WAS A cry of "Delia" and no more. But suddenly the flames spurted out in a blinding glare that shot upward to an immense height, a blinding brilliance broken by a thousand flickering gleams like the waving of swords. And a gust of sparks, flashing in a thousand colors, whirled up and vanished. Just then, and for a moment by some strange accident, a rush of music, like the swell of an organ, wove into the roaring or the flames.

The whole village standing in black knots heard the sound, except Gaffer Siddons who is deaf—strange and beautiful it was, and then gone again. Lumpy Durgan, the idiot boy from Sidderford, said it began and ended like the opening and shutting of a door.

But little Hetty Penzance had a pretty fancy of two figures with wings, that flashed up and vanished among the flames.

(And after that it was she began to pine for the things she saw in her dreams, and was abstracted and strange. It grieved her mother sorely at the time. She grew fragile, as though she was fading out of the world, and her eyes had a strange, far-away look. She talked of angels and rainbow colors and golden wings, and was forever singing an unmeaning fragment of an air that nobody knew. Until Crump took her in hand and cured her with fattening dietary, syrup of hypophosphites and cod liver oil.)

The Epilogue

AND THERE THE story of the Wonderful Visit ends. The Epilogue is in the mouth of Mrs. Mendham. There stand two little white crosses in the Siddermorton churchyard, near together, where the brambles come clambering over the stone wall. One is inscribed Thomas Angel and the other Delia Hardy, and the dates of the deaths are the same. Really there is nothing beneath them but the ashes of the Vicar's stuffed ostrich. (You will remember the Vicar had his ornithological side.) I noticed them when Mrs. Mendham was showing me the new De la Beche monument. (Mendham has been Vicar since Hilyer died.) "The granite came from somewhere in Scotland," said Mrs. Mendham, "and cost ever so much—I forget how much—but a wonderful lot! It's quite the talk of the village."

"Mother," said Cissie Mendham, "you are stepping on a grave."

"Dear me!" said Mrs. Mendham, "How heedless of me! And the cripple's grave too. But really you've no idea how much this monument cost them."

"These two people, by the bye," said Mrs. Mendham, "were killed when the old Vicarage was burned. It's rather a strange story. He was a curious person, a hunchbacked fiddler, who came from nobody knows where, and imposed upon the late Vicar to a frightful extent. He played in a pretentious way by ear, and we found out afterwards that he did not know a note of music—not a note. He was exposed before quite a lot of people. Among other things, he seems to have been 'carrying on,' as people say, with one of the servants, a sly little drab. . . . But Mendham had better tell you all about it. The man was half-witted and curiously deformed. It's strange the fancies girls have."

She looked sharply at Cissie, and Cissie blushed to the eyes.

"She was left in the house and he rushed into the flames in an attempt to save her. Quite romantic—isn't it? He was rather clever with the fiddle in his uneducated way.

"All the poor Vicar's stuffed skins were burned at the same time. It was almost all he cared for. He never really got over the blow. He came to stop with us—for there wasn't another house available in the village. But he never seemed happy. He seemed all shaken. I never saw a man so changed. I tried to stir him up, but it was no good—no good at all. He had the queerest delusions about angels and that kind of thing. It made him odd company at times. He would say he heard music, and stare quite stupidly at nothing for hours together. He got quite careless about his dress. . . . He died within a twelvemonth of the fire."

KIPPS

The Story of a Simple Soul

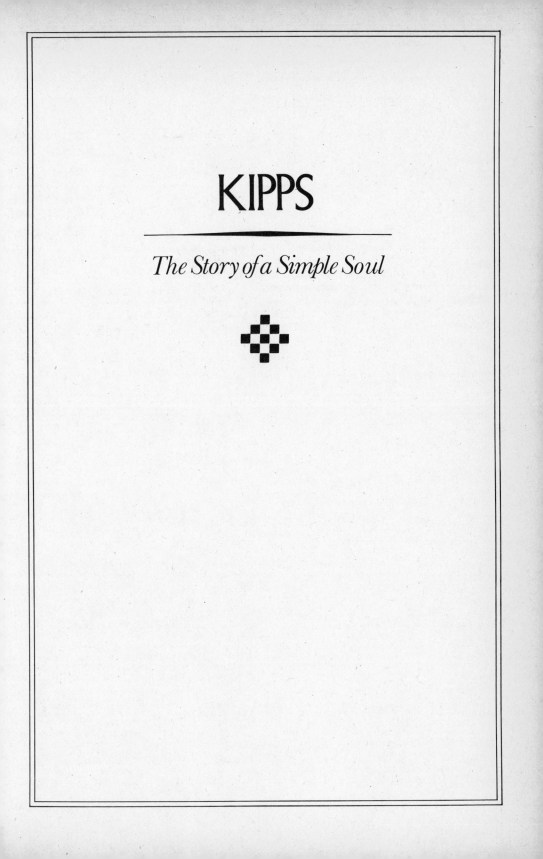

"THOSE individuals who have led secluded or isolated lives, or have hitherto moved in other spheres than those wherein well-bred people move, will gather all the information necessary from these pages to render them thoroughly conversant with the manners and amenities of society."

"MANNERS AND RULES OF GOOD SOCIETY,"
By a Member of the Aristocracy.

BOOK I
The Making of Kipps

CHAPTER I

The Little Shop at New Romney

1

UNTIL HE WAS nearly arrived at manhood, it did not become clear to Kipps how it was that he had come into the care of an aunt and uncle instead of having a father and mother like other little boys. He had vague memories of a somewhere else, a dim room, a window looking down on white buildings, and of a someone else who talked to forgotten people and who was his mother. He could not recall her features very distinctly, but he remembered with extreme definition a white dress she wore, with a pattern of little sprigs of flowers and little bows upon it, and a girdle of straight-ribbed white ribbon about the waist. Linked with this, he knew not how, were clouded, half-obliterated recollections of scenes in which there was weeping, weeping in which he was inscrutably moved to join. Some terrible tall man with a loud voice played a part in these scenes, and, either before or after them, there were impressions of looking for interminable periods out of the window of railway trains in the company of these two people.

He knew, though he could not remember that he had ever been told, that a certain faded wistful face that looked at him from a plush and gilt framed daguerreotype above the mantel of the "sitting-room" was the face of his mother. But that knowledge did not touch his dim memories with any elucidation. In that photograph she was a girlish figure, leaning against a photographer's stile, and with all the self-conscious shrinking natural to that position. She had curly hair and a face far younger and prettier than any other mother in his experience. She swung a Dolly Varden hat by the string, and looked with obedient respectful eyes on the photographer-gentleman who had commanded the pose. She was very slight and pretty. But the phantom mother that haunted his memory so elusively was not like that, though he could not remember how she differed. Perhaps she was older or a little less shrinking, or, it may be, only dressed in a different way. . . .

It is clear she handed him over to his aunt and uncle at New Romney with explicit directions and a certain endowment. One gathers she had something of that fine sense of social distinctions that subsequently played so large a part in Kipps' career. He was not to go to a "common" school, she provided, but to a certain seminary in Hastings, that was not only a "middle-class academy" with mortar-boards and every evidence of a higher social tone, but also remarkably cheap. She seems to have been animated by the desire to do her best for Kipps even at a certain sacrifice of herself, as though Kipps were in some way a superior sort of person. She sent pocket-money to him from time to time for a year or more after Hastings had begun for him, but her face he never saw in the days of his lucid memory.

His aunt and uncle were already high on the hill of life when first he came to them. They had married for comfort in the evening or, at any rate, in the late afternoon of their days. They were at first no more than vague figures in the background of proximate realities, such realities as familiar chairs and tables, quiet to ride and drive, the newel of the staircase, kitchen furniture, pieces of firewood, the boiler tap, old newspapers, the cat, the High Street, the back yard, and the flat fields that are always so near in that little town. He knew all the stones in the yard individually, the creeper in the corner, the dustbin and the mossy wall, better than many men know the faces of their wives. There was a corner under the ironing-board which, by means of a shawl, could be made, under propitious gods, a very decent cubby-house, a corner that served him for several years as the indisputable hub of the world, and the stringy places in the carpet, the knots upon the dresser, and the several corners of the rag hearthrug his uncle had made, became essential parts of his mental foundations. The shop he did not know so thoroughly; it was a forbidden region to him, yet somehow he managed to know it very well.

His aunt and uncle were, as it were, the immediate gods of this world, and, like the gods of the world of old, occasionally descended right into it, with arbitrary injunctions and disproportionate punishments. And, unhappily, one rose to their Olympian level at meals. Then one had to say one's "grace," hold one's spoon and fork in mad, unnatural ways called "properly," and refrain from eating even nice sweet things "too fast." If he "gobbled" there was trouble, and at the slightest *abandon* with knife, fork, and spoon his aunt rapped his knuckles, albeit his uncle always finished up his gravy with his knife. Sometimes, moreover, his uncle would come pipe in hand out of a sedentary remoteness in the most disconcerting way when a little boy was doing the most natural and attractive things, with "Drat and drabbit that young rascal! What's he a-doing of now?" and his aunt would appear at door or window to interrupt interesting conversation with children who were upon unknown grounds considered "low" and undesirable, and call him in. The pleasantest little noises, however softly you did them, drumming on tea-trays, trumpeting your fists, whistling on keys, ringing chimes with a couple of pails, or playing tunes on the window-panes, brought down the gods in anger. Yet what noise is fainter than your finger on the window—gently done? Sometimes, however, these gods gave him broken toys out of the shop, and then one loved them better—for the shop they kept was, among other things, a toy-shop. (The other things included books to read and books to give away, and local photographs; it had some pretensions to be a china-shop and the fascia spoke of glass; it was also a stationer's-shop with a touch of haberdashery about it, and in the windows and odd corners were mats and terra-cotta dishes and milking-stools for painting, and there was a hint of picture-frames, and fire-screens, and fishing-tackle, and air-guns, and bathing-suits, and tents—various things, indeed, but all cruelly attractive to a small boy's fingers.) Once his aunt gave him a trumpet if he would *promise* faithfully not to blow it, and afterwards took it away again. And his aunt made him say his catechism, and something she certainly called the "Colic for the Day," every Sunday in the year.

As the two grew old as he grew up, and as his impression of them modified insensibly from year to year, it seemed to him at last that they had always been as they were when in his adolescent days his impression of things grew fixed; his aunt he thought of as always lean, rather worried looking, and prone to a certain obliquity of cap, and his uncle massive, many-chinned, and careless about his buttons. They neither visited nor received visitors. They were always very suspicious about their neighbors and other people generally; they feared the "low" and they hated and despised the "stuck up," and so they "kept themselves *to* themselves," according to the English ideal. Consequently little Kipps had no playmates, except through the sin of disobedience. By inherent nature he had a sociable disposition. When he was in the High Street he made a point of saying "Hello!" to passing cyclists, and he would put his tongue out at the Quodling children whenever their nursemaid was not looking. And he began a friendship with Sid Pornick, the son of the haberdasher next door, that, with wide intermissions, was destined to last his lifetime through.

Pornick the haberdasher, I may say at once, was, according to old Kipps, a "blaring jackass"; he was a teetotaller, a "nyar, nyar, 'im-singing Methodis," and altogether distasteful and detrimental, he and his together, to true Kipps ideals so far as little Kipps could gather them. This Pornick certainly possessed an enormous voice, and he annoyed old Kipps greatly by calling "You-Arn" and "Siddee" up and down his house. He annoyed old Kipps by private choral services on Sunday, all his family, "nyar, nyar"-ing; and by mushroom culture, by behaving as though the pilaster between the two shops was common property, by making a noise of hammering in the afternoon when old Kipps wished to be quiet after his midday meal, by going up and down uncarpeted stairs in his boots, by having a black beard, by attempting to be friendly, and by—all that sort of thing. In fact, he annoyed old Kipps. He annoyed him especially with his shop-door mat. Old Kipps never beat his mat, preferring to let sleeping dust lie, and, seeking a motive for a foolish proceeding, he held that Pornick waited until there was a suitable wind in order that the dust disengaged in that operation might defile his neighbor's shop. These issues would frequently develop into loud and vehement quarrels, and on one occasion came so near to violence as to be subsequently described by Pornick (who read his newspaper) as a "Disgraceful Frackass." On that occasion he certainly went into his own shop with extreme celerity.

But it was through one of these quarrels that the friendship of little Kipps and Sid Pornick came about. The two small boys found themselves one day looking through the gate at the doctor's goats together; they exchanged a few contradictions about which goat could fight which, and then young Kipps was moved to remark that Sid's father was a "blaring jackass." Sid said he wasn't, and Kipps repeated that he was, and quoted his authority. Then Sid, flying off at a tangent rather alarmingly, said he could fight young Kipps with one hand, an assertion young Kipps with a secret want of confidence denied. There were some vain repetitions, and the incident might have ended there, but happily a sporting butcher boy chanced on the controversy at this stage, and insisted upon seeing fair play.

The two small boys, under his pressing encouragement, did at last button up their jackets, square, and fight an edifying drawn battle until it seemed good to the butcher boy to go on with Mrs. Holyer's mutton. Then, according to his directions and under his experienced stage management, they shook hands and made it up. Subsequently, a little tear-stained perhaps, but flushed with the butcher boy's approval ("tough little kids"), and with cold stones down their necks as he advised, they sat side by side on the doctor's gate, projecting very much behind, staunching an honorable bloodshed, and expressing respect for one another. Each had a bloody nose and a black eye—three days later they matched to a shade—neither had given in, and, though this was tacit, neither wanted any more.

It was an excellent beginning. After this first encounter the attributes of their parents and their own relative value in battle never rose between them, and if anything was wanted to complete the warmth of their regard it was found in a joint dislike of the eldest Quodling. The eldest Quodling lisped, had a silly sort of straw hat and a large pink face (all covered over with self-satisfaction), and he went to the National school with a green-baize bag—a contemptible thing to do. They called him names and threw stones at him, and when he replied by threatenings ("Look 'ere, young Art Kipth, you better *thtoppit!*") they were moved to attack, and put him to flight.

And after that they broke the head of Ann Pornick's doll, so that she went home weeping loudly—a wicked and endearing proceeding. Sid was whacked, but, as he explained, he wore a newspaper tactically adjusted during the transaction, and really it didn't hurt him at all. . . . And Mrs. Pornick put her head out of the shop door suddenly and threatened Kipps as he passed.

2

"Cavendish Academy," the school that had won the limited choice of Kipps' vanished mother, was established in a battered private house in the part of Hastings remotest from the sea; it was called an Academy for Young Gentlemen, and many of the young gentlemen had parents in "India," and other unverifiable places. Others were the sons of credulous widows anxious, as Kipps' mother had been, to get something a little "superior" to a board school education as cheaply as possible, and others, again, were sent to demonstrate the dignity of their parents and guardians. And of course there were boys from France.

Its "principal" was a lean long creature of indifferent digestion and temper, who proclaimed himself on a gilt-lettered board in his front area, George Garden Woodrow, F.S.Sc., letters indicating that he had paid certain guineas for a bogus diploma. A bleak whitewashed outhouse constituted his schoolroom, and the scholastic quality of its carved and worn desks and forms was enhanced by a slippery blackboard and two large yellow out-of-date maps—one of Africa and the other of Wiltshire—that he had picked up cheap at a sale. There were other maps and globes in his study, where he interviewed inquiring parents, but these his pupils never saw. And in a glass cupboard in the passage were several shillingsworth of test-tubes and chemicals, a tripod, a glass retort, and a damaged Bunsen burner, manifesting that the "Scientific laboratory" mentioned in the prospectus was no idle boast.

This prospectus, which was in dignified but incorrect English, laid particular stress on the sound preparation for a commercial career given in the Academy, but the army, navy, and civil service were glanced at in an ambiguous sentence. There was something vague in the prospectus about "examinational successes"— though Woodrow, of course, disapproved of "cram"—and a declaration that the curriculum included "art," "modern foreign languages," and "a sound technical and scientific training." Then came insistence upon the "moral well-being" of the pupils, and an emphatic boast of the excellence of the religious instruction, "so often neglected nowadays even in schools of wide repute." "That's bound to fetch 'em," Mr. Woodrow had remarked when he drew up the prospectus. And in conjunction with the mortar-boards it certainly did. Attention was directed to the "motherly" care of Mrs. Woodrow, in reality a small partially effaced woman with a plaintive face and a mind above cookery, and the prospectus concluded with a phrase intentionally vague, "Fare unrestricted, and our own milk and produce."

The memories Kipps carried from that school into after-life were set in an atmosphere of stuffiness and mental muddle, and included countless pictures of sitting on creaking forms bored and idle; of blot licking and the taste of ink; of torn books with covers that set one's teeth on edge; of the slimy surface of the labored slates; of furtive marble-playing, whispered story-telling, and of pinches, blows, and a thousand such petty annoyances being perpetually "passed on" according to the custom of the place; of standing up in class and being hit suddenly and unreasonably for imaginary misbehavior; of Mr. Woodrow's raving days, when a scarcely sane injustice prevailed; of the cold vacuity of the hour of preparation before the bread-and-butter breakfast; and of horrible headaches and queer, unprecedented internal feelings, resulting from Mrs. Woodrow's motherly rather than intelligent cookery. There were dreary walks when the boys marched two by two, all dressed in the mortar-board caps that so impressed the widowed mothers; there were dismal half-holidays when the weather was wet, and the spirit of evil temper and evil imagination had the pent boys to work its will on; there were unfair dishonorable fights, and miserable defeats and victories; there was bullying and being bullied. A coward boy Kipps particularly afflicted, until at last he was goaded to revolt by incessant persecution, and smote Kipps to tolerance with whirling fists. There were memories of sleeping three in a bed; of the dense leathery smell of the schoolroom when one returned thither after ten minutes' play; of a playground of mud and incidental sharp flints. And there was much furtive foul language.

"Our Sundays are our happiest days," was one of Woodrow's formulae with the inquiring parent, but Kipps was not called in evidence. They were to him terrible gaps of inanity, no work, no play—a drear expanse of time with the mystery of church twice and plum-duff once in the middle. The afternoon was given up to furtive relaxations, among which "Torture Chamber" games with the less agreeable weaker boys figured. It was from the difference between this day and common days that Kipps derived his first definite conceptions of the nature of God and heaven. His instinct was to evade any closer acquaintance as long as he could.

The solid work varied, according to the prevailing mood of Mr. Woodrow. Sometimes that was a despondent lethargy, copy-books were distributed or sums were "set," or the great mystery of book-keeping was declared in being, and beneath these superficial activities lengthy conversations and interminable guessing games with marbles went on, while Mr. Woodrow sat inanimate at his desk heedless of school affairs, staring in front of him at unseen things. At times his face was utterly inane; at times it had an expression of stagnant amazement, as if he saw before his eyes with pitiless clearness the dishonor and mischief of his being. . . .

At other times the F.S.Sc. roused himself to action, and would stand up a wavering class and teach it, goading it with bitter mockery and blows through a chapter of Ahn's "First French Course; or, France and the French," or a dialogue about a traveler's washing or the parts of an opera-house. His own knowledge of French had been obtained years ago in another English private school, and he had refreshed it by occasional weeks of loafing and mean adventure in Dieppe. He would sometimes in their lessons hit upon some reminiscence of these brighter days, and then he would laugh inexplicably and repeat French phrases of an unfamiliar type.

Among the commoner exercises he prescribed the learning of longer passages of poetry from a "Potry Book," which he would delegate an elder boy to "hear"; and there was reading aloud from the Holy Bible, verse by verse—it was none of your "godless" schools!—so that you counted the verses up to your turn and then gave yourself to conversation; and sometimes one read from a cheap History of this land. They did, as Kipps retorted, "loads of catechism." Also there was much learning of geographical names and lists, and sometimes Woodrow, in an outbreak of energy, would see these names were actually found in a map. And once, just once, there was a chemistry lesson—a lesson of indescribable excitement—glass things of the strangest shape, a smell like bad eggs, something bubbling in something, a smash and stench, and Mr. Woodrow saying quite distinctly—they threshed it out in the dormitory afterwards—"Damn!" Followed by the whole school being kept in, with extraordinary severities, for an hour. . . .

But interspersed with the memories of this grey routine were certain patches of brilliant color, the Holidays, his holidays, which, in spite of the feud between their seniors, he spent as much as possible with Sid Pornick, the son of the irascible black-bearded haberdasher next door. They seemed to be memories of a different world. There were glorious days of "mucking about" along the beach, the siege of unresisting Martello towers, the incessant interest of the mystery and motion of windmills, the windy excursions with boarded feet over the yielding shingle to Dungeness lighthouse—Sid Pornick and he far adrift from reality, smugglers and armed men from the moment they left Great Stone behind them—wanderings in the hedgeless reedy march, long excursions reaching even to Hythe where the machine guns of the Empire are forever whirling and tapping, and to Rye and Winchelsea perched like dream-cities on their little hills. The sky in these memories was the blazing hemisphere of the marsh heavens in summer, or its wintry tumult of sky and sea; and there were wrecks, real wrecks, in it (near Dymchurch pitched high and blackened and rotting were the ribs of a fishing-smack, flung aside like an empty basket when the sea had devoured its crew), and there was bathing all naked in the sea, bathing to one's armpits, and even trying to swim in the warm sea-water (spite of his aunt's prohibition) and (with her indulgence) the rare eating of dinner from a paper parcel miles away from home. Toke and cold ground-rice puddin' with plums it used to be— there is no better food at all. And for the background, in the place of Woodrow's mean and fretting rule, were his aunt's spare but frequently quite amiable figure— for though she insisted on his repeating the English Church catechism every Sunday, she had an easy way over dinners that one wanted to take abroad—and his uncle, corpulent and irascible, but sedentary and easily escaped. And freedom!

The holidays were indeed very different from school. They were free, they were spacious, and though he never knew it in these words—they had an element of beauty. In his memory of his boyhood they shone like strips of stained-glass window in a dreary waste of scholastic wall, they grew brighter and brighter as they grew remoter. There came a time at last and moods when he could look back to them with a feeling akin to tears.

The last of these windows was the brightest, and instead of the kaleidoscopic effects of its predecessors its glory was a single figure. For in the last of his holidays before the Moloch of Retail Trade got hold of him, Kipps made his first tentative essays at the mysterious shrine of Love. Very tentative they were, for he had become a boy of subdued passions, and potential rather than actual affectionateness.

And the object of these first stirrings of the great desire was no other than Ann Pornick, the head of whose doll he and Sid had broken long ago, and rejoiced over long ago, in the days when he had yet to learn the meaning of a heart.

3

Negotiations were already on foot to make Kipps into a draper before he discovered the lights that lurked in Ann Pornick's eyes. School was over, absolutely over, and it was chiefly present to him that he was never to go to school again. It was high summer. The "breaking up" of school had been hilarious; and the excellent maxim, "Last Day's Pay Day," had been observed by him with a scrupulous attention to his honor. He had punched the heads of all his enemies, wrung wrists and kicked shins; he had distributed all his unfinished copybooks, all his school books, his collection of marbles, and his mortar-board cap among such as loved him; and he had secretly written in obscure pages of their books "remember Art Kipps." He had also split the anemic Woodrow's cane, carved his own name deeply in several places about the premises, and broken the scullery window. He had told everybody so often that he was to learn to be a sea captain, that he had come almost to believe the thing himself. And now he was home, and school was at an end for him for evermore.

He was up before six on the day of his return, and out in the hot sunlight of the yard. He set himself to whistle a peculiarly penetrating arrangement of three notes, supposed by the boys of the Hastings Academy and himself and Sid Pornick, for no earthly reason whatever, to be the original Huron war-cry. As he did this he feigned not to be doing it, because of the hatred between his uncle and the Pornicks, but to be examining with respect and admiration a new wing of the dustbin recently erected by his uncle—a pretense that would not have deceived a nestling tomtit.

Presently there came a familiar echo from the Pornick hunting-ground. Then Kipps began to sing, "Ar pars eight tra-la, in the lane be'ind the church." To which an unseen person answered, "Ar pars eight it is, in the lane be'ind the church." The "tra-la" was considered to render this sentence incomprehensible to the uninitiated. In order to conceal their operations still more securely, both parties to this duet then gave vent to a vocalization of the Huron war-cry again, and after a lingering repetition of the last and shrillest note, dispersed severally, as became boys in the enjoyment of holidays, to light the house fires for the day.

Half-past eight found Kipps sitting on the sunlit gate at the top of the long lane that runs towards the sea, clashing his boots in a slow rhythm, and whistling with great violence all that he knew of an excruciatingly pathetic air. There appeared along by the churchyard wall a girl in a short frock, brown-haired, quick-colored, and with dark blue eyes. She had grown so that she was a little taller than Kipps, and her color had improved. He scarcely remembered her, so changed was she since last holidays—if, indeed, he had seen her during his last holidays, a thing he could not clearly recollect.

Some vague emotion arose at the sight of her. He stopped whistling and regarded her, oddly tongue-tied.

"He can't come," said Ann, advancing boldly. "Not yet."

"What—not Sid?"

"No. Father's made him dust all his boxes again."

"What for?"

"I dunno. Father's in a stew's morning."

"Oh!"

Pause. Kipps looked at her, and then was unable to look at her again. She regarded him with interest. "You left school?" she remarked, after a pause.

"Yes."

"So's Sid."

The conversation languished. Ann put her hands on the top of the gate, and began a stationary hopping, a sort of ineffectual gymnastic experiment.

"Can you run?" she said presently.

"Run you any day," said Kipps.

"Gimme a start?"

"Where for?" said Kipps.

Ann considered, and indicated a tree. She walked towards it and turned. "Gimme to here?" she called. Kipps, standing now and touching the gate, smiled to express conscious superiority. "Further!" he said.

"Here?"

"Bit more!" said Kipps; and then, repenting of his magnanimity, said "Orf!" suddenly, and so recovered his lost concession.

They arrived abreast at the tree, flushed and out of breath. "Tie!" said Ann, throwing her hair back from her face with her hand. "I won," panted Kipps. They disputed firmly, but quite politely. "Run it again, then," said Kipps. "*I* don't mind."

They returned towards the gate.

"You don't run bad," said Kipps, temperately, expressing sincere admiration. "I'm pretty good, you know."

Ann sent her hair back by an expert toss of the head. "You give me a start," she allowed.

They became aware of Sid approaching them. "You better look out, young Ann," said Sid, with that irreverent want of sympathy usual in brothers. "You been out nearly 'arf-'our. Nothing ain't been done upstairs. Father said he didn't know where you was, but when he did he'd warm y'r young ear."

Ann prepared to go.

"How about that race?" asked Kipps.

"Lor!" cried Sid, quite shocked. "You ain't been racing *her!*"

Ann swung herself around the end of the gate with her eyes on Kipps, and then turned away suddenly and ran off down the lane. Kipps' eyes tried to go after her, and came back to Sid's.

"I give her a lot of start," said Kipps, apologetically, "It wasn't a proper race." And so the subject was dismissed. But Kipps was *distrait* for some seconds perhaps, and the mischief had begun in him.

4

They proceeded to the question of how two accomplished Hurons might most satisfactorily spend the morning. Manifestly their line lay straight along the lane to the sea. "There's a new wreck," said Sid, "and my!—don't it stink just!"

"Stink?"

"Fair make you sick. It's rotten wheat."

They fell to talking of wrecks, and so came to ironclads and wars and such-like manly matters. Halfway to the wreck Kipps made a casual irrelevant remark.

"Your sister ain't a bad sort," he said off-handedly.

"I clout her a lot," said Sidney, modestly; and, after a pause, the talk reverted to more suitable topics.

The new wreck was full of rotting grain, and stank abominably, even as Sid had said. This was excellent. They had it all to themselves. They took possession of it in force, at Sid's suggestion, and had speedily to defend it against enormous numbers of imaginary "natives," who were at last driven off by loud shouts of *bang, bang,* and vigorous thrusting and shoving of sticks. Then, also at Sid's direction, they sailed with it into the midst of a combined French, German, and Russian fleet, demolishing the combination unassisted, and having descended to the beach, clambered up the side and cut out their own vessel in brilliant style, they underwent a magnificent shipwreck (with vocalized thunder) and floated "water-logged"—so Sid insisted—upon an exhausted sea.

These things drove Ann out of mind for a time. But at last, as they drifted without food or water upon a stagnant ocean, haggard-eyed, chins between their hands, looking in vain for a sail, she came to mind again abruptly.

"It's rather nice 'aving sisters," remarked one perishing mariner.

Sid turned round and regarded him thoughtfully.

"Not it!" he said.

"No?"

"Not a bit of it."

He grinned confidentially. "Know too much," he said, and afterwards "get out of things."

He resumed his gloomy scrutiny of the hopeless horizon. Presently he fell spitting jerkily between his teeth, as he had read was the way with such ripe manhood as chews its quid.

"Sisters," he said, "is rot. That's what sisters are. Girls if you like, but sisters—*No!*"

"But ain't sisters girls?"

"N-eaow!" said Sid, with unspeakable scorn; and Kipps answered, "Of course. I didn't mean— I wasn't thinking of that."

"You got a girl?" asked Sid, spitting very cleverly again.

Kipps admitted his deficiency. He felt compunction.

"You don't know who *my* girl is, Art Kipps, I bet."

"Who *is,* then?" asked Kipps, still chiefly occupied by his own poverty.

"Ah!"

Kipps let a moment elapse before he did his duty. "Tell us!"

Sid eyed him and hesitated.

"Secret?" he said.

"Secret."

"Dying solemn?"

"Dying solemn!" Kipps' self-concentration passed into curiosity.

Sid administered a terrible oath.

Sid adhered lovingly to his facts. "It begins with a Nem," he said, doling it out parsimoniously.

"M-A-U-D," he spelled, with a stern eye on Kipps. "C-H-A-R-T-E-R-I-S."

Now, Maud Charteris was a young person of eighteen and the daughter of the vicar of St. Bavon's—besides which she had a bicycle—so that as her name unfolded the face of Kipps lengthened with respect. "Get out," he gasped incredulously. "She ain't your girl, Sid Pornick."

"She is!" answered Sid, stoutly.

"What—truth?"

"Truth."

Kipps scrutinized his face. "Reely?"

Sid touched wood, whistled, and repeated a binding doggerel with great solemnity.

Kipps still struggled with the amazing new light on the world about him. "D'you mean—she knows?"

Sid flushed deeply, and his aspect became stern and gloomy. He resumed his wistful scrutiny of the sunlit sea. "I'd die for that girl, Art Kipps," he said presently; and Kipps did not press a question he felt to be ill-timed. "I'd do anything she asked me to do," said Sid; "just anything. If she was to ask me to chuck myself into the sea." He met Kipps' eye. "I *would*," he said.

They were pensive for a space, and then Sid began to discourse in fragments of Love, a theme upon which Kipps had already in a furtive way meditated a little, but which, apart from badinage, he had never yet heard talked about in the light of day. Of course, many and various aspects of life had come to light in the muffled exchange of knowledge that went on under the shadow of Woodrow, but this of Sentimental Love was not among them. Sid, who was a boy with an imagination, having once broached this topic, opened his heart, or, at any rate, a new chamber of his heart, to Kipps, and found no fault with Kipps for a lack of return. He produced a thumbed novelette that had played a part in his sentimental awakening; he proffered it to Kipps, and confessed there was a character in it, a baronet, singularly like himself. This baronet was a person of volcanic passions, which he concealed beneath a demeanor of "icy cynicism." The utmost expression he permitted himself was to grit his teeth, and, now his attention was called to it, Kipps remarked that Sid also had a habit of gritting his teeth, and, indeed, had had all the morning. They read for a time, and presently Sid talked again. The conception of love Sid made evident, was compact of devotion and much spirited fighting and a touch of mystery, but through all that cloud of talk there floated before Kipps a face that was flushed and hair that was tossed aside.

So they budded, sitting on the blackening old wreck in which men had lived and died, looking out to sea, talking of that other sea upon which they must presently embark. . . .

They ceased to talk, and Sid read; but Kipps, falling behind with the reading, and not wishing to admit that he read slowlier than Sid, whose education was of the inferior Elementary School brand, lapsed into meditation.

"I *would* like to 'ave a girl," said Kipps.

"I mean just to talk to, and all that. . . ."

A floating sack distracted them at last from this obscure topic. They abandoned the wreck, and followed the new interest a mile along the beach, bombarding it with stones until it came to land. They had inclined to a view that it would contain romantic mysteries, but it was simply an ill-preserved kitten—too much even for them. And at last they were drawn dinnerward, and went home hungry and pensive side by side.

5

But Kipps' imagination had been warmed by that talk of love, and in the afternoon when he saw Ann Pornick in the High Street and said "Hello!" it was a different "hello" from that of their previous intercourse. And when they had passed they both looked back and caught each other doing so. Yes, he *did* want a girl badly. . . .

Afterwards he was distracted by a traction engine going through the town, and his aunt had got some sprats for supper. When he was in bed, however, sentiment came upon him again in a torrent quite abruptly and abundantly, and he put his head under the pillow and whispered very softly, "I love Ann Pornick," as a sort of supplementary devotion.

In his subsequent dreams he ran races with Ann, and they lived in a wreck together, and always her face was flushed and her hair about her face. They just lived in a wreck and ran races, and were very, very fond of one another. And their favorite food was rock chocolate, dates, such as one buys off barrows, and sprats—fried sprats. . . .

In the morning he could hear Ann singing in the scullery next door. He listened to her for some time, and it was clear to him that he must put things before her.

Towards dusk that evening they chanced on one another out by the gate by the church, but though there was much in his mind, it stopped there with a resolute shyness until he and Ann were out of breath catching cockchafers and were sitting on that gate of theirs again. Ann sat up upon the gate, dark against vast masses of flaming crimson and darkling purple, and her eyes looked at Kipps from a shadowed face. There came a stillness between them, and quite abruptly he was moved to tell his love.

"Ann," he said, "I *do* like you. I wish you was my girl. . . .

"I say, Ann. Will you *be* my girl?"

Ann made no pretence of astonishment. She weighed the proposal for a moment with her eyes on Kipps. "If you like, Artie," she said lightly. *"I* don't mind if I am."

"All right," said Kipps, breathless with excitement, "then you are."

"All right," said Ann.

Something seemed to fall between them, they no longer looked openly at one another. "Lor!" cried Ann, suddenly, "see that one!" and jumped down and darted after a cockchafer that had boomed within a yard of her face. And with that they were girl and boy again. . . .

They avoided their new relationship painfully.

They did not recur to it for several days, though they met twice. Both felt that there remained something before this great experience was to be regarded as complete; but there was an infinite diffidence about the next step. Kipps talked in fragments of all sorts of matters, telling particularly of the great things that were being done to make a man and a draper of him; how he had two new pairs of trousers and a black coat and four new shirts. And all the while his imagination was urging him to that unknown next step, and when he was alone and in the dark he became even an enterprising wooer. It became evident to him that it would be nice to take Ann by the hand; even the decorous novelettes Sid affected egged him on to that greater nearness of intimacy.

Then a great idea came to him, in a paragraph called "Lover's Tokens" that he read in a torn fragment of *Tit Bits*. It fell in to the measure of his courage— a divided sixpence! He secured his aunt's best scissors, fished a sixpence out of his jejune tin money-box, and jabbed his finger in a varied series of attempts to get it in half. When they met again the sixpence was still undivided. He had not intended to mention the matter to her at that stage, but it came up spontaneously. He endeavored to explain the theory of broken sixpences and his unexpected failure to break one.

"But what you break it for?" said Ann. "It's no good if it's broke."

"It's a Token," said Kipps.

"Like—?"

"Oh, you keep half and I keep half, and when we're sep'rated, you look at your half and I look at mine—see? Then we think of each other."

"Oh!" said Ann, and appeared to assimilate this information.

"Only, *I* can't get it in 'arf nohow," said Kipps.

They discussed this difficulty for some time without illumination. Then Ann had a happy thought.

"Tell you what," she said, starting away from him abruptly and laying a hand on his arm, "you let *me* 'ave it, Artie. I know where father keeps his file."

Kipps handed her the sixpence, and they came upon a pause. "I'll easy do it," said Ann.

In considering the sixpence side by side, his head had come near her cheek. Quite abruptly he was moved to take his next step into the unknown mysteries of love.

"Ann," he said, and gulped at his temerity, "I *do* love you. Straight. I'd do anything for you, Ann. Reely—I would."

He paused for breath. She answered nothing, but she was no doubt enjoying herself. He came yet closer to her, his shoulder touched hers. "Ann, I wish you'd—"

He stopped.

"What?" said Ann.

"Ann—lemme kiss you."

Things seemed to hang for a space; his tone, the drop of his courage made the thing incredible as he spoke. Kipps was not of that bold order of wooers who impose conditions.

Ann perceived that she was not prepared for kissing after all. Kissing, she said, was silly, and when Kipps would have displayed a belated enterprise she flung away from him. He essayed argument. He stood afar off as it were—the better part of a yard—and said she *might* let him kiss her, and then that he didn't see what good it was for her to be his girl if he couldn't kiss her. . . .

She repeated that kissing was silly. A certain estrangement took them homeward. They arrived in the dusky High Street not exactly together, and not exactly apart, but straggling. They had not kissed, but all the guilt of kissing was between them. When Kipps saw the portly contours of his uncle standing dimly in the shop doorway his footsteps faltered, and the space between our young couple increased. Above, the window over Pornick's shop was open, and Mrs. Pornick was visible, taking the air. Kipps assumed an expression of extreme innocence. He found himself face to face with his uncle's advanced outposts of waistcoat buttons.

"Where ye bin, my boy?"

"Bin for a walk, uncle."

"Not along of that brat of Pornick's?"

"Along of who?"

"That gell"—indicating Ann with his pipe.

"Oh no, uncle!"—very faintly.

"Run in, my boy." Old Kipps stood aside, with an oblique glance upward, and his nephew brushed clumsily by him and vanished out of sight of the street into the vague obscurity of the little shop. The door closed behind old Kipps with a nervous jangle of its bell, and he set himself to light the single oil-lamp that illuminated his shop at nights. It was an operation requiring care and watching, or else it flared and "smelt." Often it smelt after all. Kipps, for some reason, found the dusky living-room with his aunt in it too populous for his feelings, and went upstairs.

"That brat of Pornick's!" It seemed to him that a horrible catastrophe had occurred. He felt he had identified himself inextricably with his uncle and cut himself off from her forever by saying "Oh no!" At supper he was so visibly depressed that his aunt asked him if he wasn't feeling well. Under this imminent threat of medicine he assumed an unnatural cheerfulness. . . .

He lay awake for nearly half an hour that night groaning because things had all gone wrong, because Ann wouldn't let him kiss her, and because his uncle had called her a brat. It seemed to Kipps almost as though he himself had called her a brat. . . .

There came an interval during which Ann was altogether inaccessible. One, two, three days passed and he did not see her. Sid he met several times; they went fishing, and twice they bathed, but though Sid lent and received back two further love stories, they talked no more of love. They kept themselves in accord however, agreeing that the most flagrantly sentimental story was "proper." Kipps was always wanting to speak of Ann, and never daring to do so. He saw her on Sunday evening going off to chapel. She was more beautiful than ever in her Sunday clothes, but she pretended not to see him because her mother was with her. But he thought she pretended not to see him because she had given him up forever. Brat!—who could be expected ever to forgive that? He abandoned himself to despair, he ceased even to haunt the places where she might be found. . . .

With paralyzing unexpectedness came the end.

Mr. Shalford, the draper at Folkestone to whom he was to be bound apprentice, had expressed a wish to "shape the lad a bit" before the autumn sale. Kipps became aware that his box was being packed, and gathered the full truth of things on the evening before his departure. He became feverishly eager to see Ann just once more. He made silly and needless excuses to go out into the yard, he walked three times across the street without any excuse at all to look up at the Pornick windows. Still she was hidden. He grew desperate. It was within half an hour of his departure that he came on Sid.

"Hello!" he said, "I'm orf!"

"Business?"

"Yes."

Pause.

"I say, Sid. You going 'ome?"

"Straight now."

"D'you mind—. Ask Ann about that."

"About what?"

"She'll know."

And Sid said he would. But even that, it seemed, failed to evoke Ann.

At last the Folkestone 'bus rumbled up, and he ascended. His aunt stood in the doorway to see him off. His uncle assisted with the box and portmanteau. Only furtively could he glance up at the Pornick windows, and still it seemed Ann hardened her heart against him. "Get up!" said the driver, and the hoofs began to clatter. No—she would not come out even to see him off. The 'bus was in motion, and old Kipps was going back into his shop. Kipps stared in front of him, assuring himself that he did not care.

He heard a door slam, and instantly craned out his neck to look back. He knew that slam so well. Behold! out of the haberdasher's door a small untidy figure in homely pink print had shot resolutely into the road and was sprinting in pursuit. In a dozen seconds she was abreast of the 'bus. At the sight of her Kipps' heart began to beat very quickly, but he made no immediate motion of recognition.

"Artie!" she cried breathlessly. "Artie! Artie! You know! I got *that!*"

The 'bus was already quickening its pace and leaving her behind again, when Kipps realized what "that" meant. He became animated, he gasped, and gathered his courage together and mumbled an incoherent request to the driver to "stop jest a jiff for sunthin'." The driver grunted, as the disparity of their years demanded, and then the 'bus had pulled up and Ann was below.

She leaped up upon the wheel. Kipps looked down into Ann's face, and it was foreshortened and resolute. He met her eyes just for one second as their hands touched. He was not a reader of eyes. Something passed quickly from hand to hand, something that the driver, alert at the corner of his eye, was not allowed to see. Kipps hadn't a word to say, and all she said was, "I done it, smorning." It was like a blank space in which something pregnant should have been written and wasn't. Then she dropped down, and the 'bus moved forward.

After the lapse of about ten seconds, it occurred to him to stand and wave his new bowler hat at her over the corner of the 'bus top, and to shout hoarsely, "Goo'-bye, Ann! Don' forget me—while I'm away!"

She stood in the road looking after him, and presently she waved her hand.

He remained standing unstably, his bright flushed face looking back at her and his hair fluffing in the wind, and he waved his hat until at last the bend of the road hid her from his eyes. Then he turned about and sat down, and presently he began to put the half-sixpence he held clenched in his hand into his trouser-pocket. He looked sideways at the driver to judge how much he had seen.

Then he fell a thinking. He resolved that, come what might, when he came back to New Romney at Christmas, he would, by hook or by crook, kiss Ann.

Then everything would be perfect and right, and he would be perfectly happy.

CHAPTER II

The Emporium

1

WHEN KIPPS LEFT New Romney, with a small yellow tin box, a still smaller portmanteau, a new umbrella, and a keepsake half-sixpence, to become a draper, he was a youngster of fourteen, thin, with whimsical drakes'-tails at the pole of his head, smallish features, and eyes that were sometimes very light and sometimes very dark, gifts those of his birth; and by the nature of his training he was indistinct in his speech, confused in his mind, and retreating in his manners. Inexorable fate had appointed him to serve his country in commerce, and the same national bias towards private enterprise and leaving bad alone, which had left his general education to Mr. Woodrow, now indentured him firmly into the hands of Mr. Shalford of the Folkestone Drapery Bazaar. Apprenticeship is still the recognized English way to the distributing branch of the social service. If Mr. Kipps had been so unfortunate as to have been born a German he might have been educated in an elaborate and costly special school ("over-educated—crammed up"—old Kipps) to fit him for his end—such being their pedagogic way. He might—. But why make unpatriotic reflections in a novel? There was nothing pedagogic about Mr. Shalford.

He was an irascible, energetic little man with hairy hands, for the most part under his coat-tails, a long shiny bald head, a pointed aquiline nose a little askew, and a neatly trimmed beard. He walked lightly and with a confident jerk, and he was given to humming. He had added to exceptional business "push," bankruptcy under the old dispensation, and judicious matrimony. His establishment was now one of the most considerable in Folkestone, and he insisted on every inch of frontage by alternate stripes of green and yellow down the houses over the shops. His shops were numbered 3, 5, and 7 on the street, and on his billheads 3 to 7. He encountered the abashed and awestricken Kipps with the praises of his System and himself. He spread himself out behind his desk with a grip on the lapel of his coat and made Kipps a sort of speech. "We expect y'r to work, y'r know, and we expect y'r to study our interests," explained Mr. Shalford, in the regal and commercial plural. "Our System here is the best system y'r could have. I made it, and I ought to know. I began at the very bottom of the ladder when I was fourteen, and there isn't a step in it I don't know. Not a step. Mr. Booch in the desk will give y'r the card of rules and fines. Jest wait a minute." He pretended to be busy with some dusty memoranda under a paper-weight, while Kipps stood in a sort of paralysis of awe regarding his new master's oval baldness. "Two thous'n three forty-seven pounds," whispered Mr. Shalford, audibly, feigning forgetfulness of Kipps. Clearly a place of great transactions!

Mr. Shalford rose, and, handing Kipps a blotting-pad and an inkpot to carry, mere symbols of servitude, for he made no use of them, emerged into a count-inghouse where three clerks had been feverishly busy ever since his door-handle had turned. "Booch," said Mr. Shalford, " 'ave y'r copy of the Rules?" and a downtrodden, shabby little old man, with a ruler in one hand and a quill pen in his mouth, silently held out a small book with green and yellow covers, mainly devoted, as Kipps presently discovered, to a voracious system of Fines. He became acutely aware that his hands were full and that everybody was staring at him. He hesitated a moment before putting the inkpot down to free a hand.

"Mustn't fumble like *that*," said Mr. Shalford as Kipps pocketed the Rules. "Won't do here. Come along, come along," cocked his coat-tails high, as a lady might hold up her dress, and led the way into the shop.

A vast interminable place it seemed to Kipps, with unending shining counters and innumerable faultlessly dressed young men and, presently, Houri-like young women staring at him. Here there was a long vista of gloves dangling from overhead rods, there ribbons and baby linen. A short young lady in black mittens was making out the account of a customer, and was clearly confused in her addition by Shalford's eagle eye.

A thick-set young man with a bald head and a round, very wise face, who was profoundly absorbed in adjusting all the empty chairs down the counter to absolutely equal distances, awoke out of his preoccupation and answered respectfully to a few Napoleonic and quite unnecessary remarks from his employer. Kipps was told that this young man's name was Mr. Buggins, and that he was to do whatever Mr. Buggins told him to do.

They came round a corner into a new smell, which was destined to be the smell of Kipps' life for many years, the vague distinctive smell of Manchester goods. A fat man with a large nose jumped—actually jumped—at their appearance, and began to fold a pattern of damask in front of him exactly like an automaton that is suddenly set going. "Carshot, see to this boy tomorrow," said the master. "See he don't fumble. Smart'n 'im up."

"Yussir," said Carshot fatly, glanced at Kipps, and resumed his pattern-folding with extreme zeal.

"Whatever Mr. Carshot says y'r to do, ye *do*," said Mr. Shalford, trotting onward; and Carshot blew out his face with an appearance of relief.

They crossed a large room full of the strangest things Kipps had ever seen. Lady-like figures, surmounted by black wooden knobs in the place of the refined heads one might have reasonably expected, stood about with a lifelike air of conscious fashion. "Costume Room," said Shalford. Two voices engaged in some sort of argument—"I can assure you, Miss Mergle, you are entirely mistaken—entirely, in supposing I should do anything so unwomanly,"—sank abruptly, and they discovered two young ladies, taller and fairer than any of the other young ladies, and with black trains to their dresses, who were engaged in writing at a little table. Whatever they told him to do Kipps gathered he was to do. He was also, he understood, to do whatever Carshot and Booch told him to do. And there were also Buggins and Mr. Shalford. And not to forget or fumble!

They descended into a cellar called "The Warehouse," and Kipps had an optical illusion of errand-boys fighting. Some aerial voice said "Teddy!" and the illusion passed. He looked again, and saw quite clearly that they were packing parcels, and always would be, and that the last thing in the world that they would or could possibly do was to fight. Yet he gathered from the remarks Mr. Shalford addressed to their busy backs that they had been fighting—no doubt at some past period of their lives.

Emerging in the shop again among a litter of toys and what are called "fancy articles," Shalford withdrew a hand from beneath his coat-tails to indicate an overhead change carrier. He entered into elaborate calculations to show how many minutes in one year were saved thereby, and lost himself among the figures. "Seven tums eight seven nine—was it? Or seven eight nine? Now, *now!* Why, when I was a boy your age I c'd do a sum like that as soon as hear it. We'll soon get y'r into better shape than that. Make you Fishent. Well, y'r must take my word it comes to pounds and pounds saved in the year—pounds and pounds. System! System everywhere. Fishency." He went on murmuring "Fishency" and "System" at intervals for some time. They passed into a yard, and Mr. Shalford waved his hand to his three delivery vans, all striped green and yellow— "uniform—green , yell'r—System." All over the premises were pinned absurd little cards, "This door locked after 7:30. By order, Edwin Shalford," and the like.

Mr. Shalford always wrote "By Order," though it conveyed no earthly meaning to him. He was one of those people who collect technicalities upon them as the Reduvius bug collects dirt. He was the sort of man who is not only ignorant but absolutely incapable of English. When he wanted to say he had a sixpenny-ha'penny longcloth to sell, he put it thus to startled customers: "Can DO you one, six-half, if y' like." He always omitted pronouns and articles and so forth; it seemed to him the very essence of the efficiently business-like. His only preposition was "as" or the compound "as per." He abbreviated every word he could; he would have considered himself the laughingstock of Wood Street if he had chanced to spell *socks* in any way but "sox." But, on the other hand, if he saved words here he wasted them there; he never acknowledged an order that was not an esteemed favor, nor sent a pattern without begging to submit it. He never stipulated for so many months' credit, but bought in November "as Jan." It was not only words he abbreviated in his London communications. In paying his wholesalers his "System" admitted of a constant error in the discount of a penny or twopence, and it "facilitated business," he alleged, to ignore odd pence in the cheques he wrote. His ledger clerk was so struck with the beauty of this part of the System that he started a private one on his own account with the stamp-box that never came to Shalford's knowledge.

This admirable British merchant would glow with a particular pride of intellect when writing his London orders.

"Ah! do y'r think *you'll* ever be able to write London orders?" he would say with honest pride to Kipps, waiting impatiently long after closing-time to take these triumphs of commercial efficiency to post, and so end the interminable day.

Kipps shook his head, anxious for Mr. Shalford to get on.

"Now, here, f'example, I've written—see? 'I piece 1 in. cott blk elas 1 / or'; what do I mean by that *or*—eh? d'ye know?"

Kipps promptly hadn't the faintest idea.

"And then, '2 ea silk net as per patts herewith'; *ea*—eh?"

"Dunno, sir."

It was not Mr. Shalford's way to explain things. "Dear, dear! Pity you couldn't get some c'mercial education at your school. 'Stid of all this lit'ry stuff. Well, my boy, if y'r not a bit sharper, y'll never write London orders, *that's* pretty plain. Jest stick stamps on all those letters, and mind y'r stick 'em right way up, and try and profit a little more by the opportunities your aunt and uncle have provided ye. Can't say *what'll* happen t'ye if ye don't."

And Kipps, tired, hungry, and belated, set about stamping with vigor and dispatch.

"Lick the *envelope*," said Mr. Shalford, "lick the *envelope*," as though he grudged the youngster the postage-stamp gum. "It's the little things mount up," he would say; and indeed that was his philosophy of life—to hustle and save, always to hustle and save. His political creed linked Reform, which meant nothing, with Peace and Economy, which meant a sweated expenditure, and his conception of a satisfactory municipal life was to "keep down the rates." Even his religion was to save his soul, and to preach a similar cheeseparing to the world.

2

The indentures that bound Kipps to Mr. Shalford were antique and complex; they insisted on the latter gentleman's parental privileges, they forbade Kipps to dice and game, they made him over, body and soul, to Mr. Shalford for seven long years, the crucial years of his life. In return there were vague stipulations about teaching the whole art and mystery of the trade to him, but as there was no penalty attached to negligence, Mr. Shalford, being a sound practical business man, considered this a mere rhetorical flourish, and set himself assiduously to get as much out of Kipps and to put as little into him as he could in the seven years of their intercourse.

What he put into Kipps was chiefly bread and margarine, infusions of chicory and tea-dust, colonial meat by contract at threepence a pound, potatoes by the sack, and watered beer. If, however, Kipps chose to buy any supplementary material for growth, Mr. Shalford had the generosity to place his kitchen resources at his disposal free—if the fire chanced to be going. He was also allowed to share a bedroom with eight other young men, and to sleep in a bed which, except in very severe weather, could be made, with the help of his overcoat and private underlinen, not to mention newspapers, quite sufficiently warm for any reasonable soul. In addition, Kipps was taught the list of fines, and how to tie up parcels, to know where goods were kept in Mr. Shalford's systematized shop, to hold his hands extended upon the counter, and to repeat such phrases as "What can I have the pleasure—?" "No trouble, I 'ssure you," and the like; to block, fold, and measure materials of all sorts, to lift his hat from his head when he passed Mr. Shalford abroad, and to practice a servile obedience to a large number of people. But he was not, of course, taught the "cost" mark of the goods he sold, nor anything of the method of buying such goods. Nor was his attention directed to the unfamiliar social habits and fashions to which his trade ministered. The use of half the goods he saw sold and was presently to assist in selling he did not understand; materials for hangings, cretonnes, chintzes, and the like; serviettes, and all the bright hard whitewear of a well-ordered house; pleasant dress materials, linings, stiffenings; they were to him from first to last no more than things, heavy and difficult to handle in bulk, that one folded up, unfolded, cut into lengths, and saw dwindle and pass away out into that mysterious happy world in which the Customer dwells. Kipps hurried from piling linen table-cloths, that were, collectively, as heavy as lead, to eat off oil-cloth in a gas-lit dining-room underground, and he dreamed of combing endless blankets beneath his overcoat, spare undershirt, and three newspapers. So he had at least the chance of learning the beginnings of philosophy.

In return for these benefits he worked so that he commonly went to bed exhausted and footsore. His round began at half-past six in the morning, when he would descend, unwashed and shirtless, in old clothes and a scarf, and dust boxes and yawn, and take down wrappers and clean the windows until eight. Then in half an hour he would complete his toilet, and take an austere breakfast of bread and margarine and what only an Imperial Englishman would admit to be coffee, after which refreshment he ascended to the shop for the labors of the day. Commonly these began with a mighty running to and fro with planks and boxes and goods for Carshot the window-dresser, who, whether he worked well or ill, nagged persistently, by reason of a chronic indigestion, until the window was done. Sometimes the costume window had to be dressed, and then Kipps staggered down the whole length of the shop from the costume-room with one after another of those ladylike shapes grasped firmly but shamefully each about her single ankle of wood. Such days as there was no window-dressing there was a mighty carrying and lifting of blocks and bales of goods into piles and stacks. After this there were terrible exercises, at first almost despairfully difficult; certain sorts of goods that came in folded had to be rolled upon rollers, and for the most part refused absolutely to be rolled, at any rate by Kipps; certain other sorts of goods that came from the wholesalers rolled had to be measured and folded, and folding makes young apprentices wish they were dead. All of it, too, quite avoidable trouble, you know, that is not avoided because of the cheapness of the genteeler sorts of labor and the dearness of forethought in the world. And then consignments of new goods had to be marked off and packed into paper parcels, and Carshot packed like conjuring tricks, and Kipps packed like a boy with tastes in some other direction—not ascertained. And always Carshot nagged—.

He had a curious formula of appeal to his visceral economy that the refinement of our times and the earnest entreaties of my friends oblige me to render by an etiolated paraphrase.

"My Heart and Liver! I never see such a boy," so I will present Carshot's refrain; and even when he was within a foot or so of the customer's face, the disciplined ear of Kipps would still at times develop a featureless intercalary murmur into—well, "My Heart and Liver!"

There came a blessed interval when Kipps was sent abroad "matching." This consisted chiefly in supplying unexpected defects in buttons, ribbon, lining, and so forth in the dressmaking department. He was given a written paper of orders with patterns pinned thereto and discharged into the sunshine and interest of the street. Then until he thought it wise to return and stand the racket of his delay, he was a free man, clear of all reproach.

He made remarkable discoveries in topography, as, for example, that the most convenient way from the establishment of Mr. Adolphus Davis to the establishment of Messrs. Plummer, Roddis and Tyrrell, two of his principal places of call, is not, as is generally supposed, down the Sandgate road but up the Sandgate road, round by West Terrace and along the Leas to the lift, watch the lift up and down *twice,* but not longer, because that wouldn't do, back along the Leas, watch the Harbor for a short time, and then round by the churchyard, and so (hurrying) into Church Street and Rendezvous Street. But on some exceptionally fine days the route lay through Radnor Park to the pond where little boys sail ships and there are interesting swans.

He would return to find the shop settling down to the business of serving customers. And now he had to stand by to furnish any help that was necessary to the seniors who served, to carry parcels and bills about the shop, to clear away "stuff" after each engagement, to hold up curtains until his arms ached, and, what was more difficult than all, to do nothing and not stare disconcertingly at customers when there was nothing for him to do. He plumbed an abyss of boredom, or stood a mere carcass with his mind far away, fighting the enemies of the empire, or steering a dream-ship perilously into unknown seas. To be recalled sharply to our higher civilization by some bustling senior's "Nar then, Kipps. *Look* alive! Ketch 'old. (My Heart and Liver!)"

At half-past seven o'clock—except on late nights—a feverish activity of "straightening up" began, and when the last shutter was up outside, Kipps, with the speed of an arrow leaving a bow, would start hanging wrappers over the fixtures and over the piles of wares upon the counters, preparatory to a vigorous scattering of wet sawdust and the sweeping out of the shop.

Sometimes people would stay long after the shop was closed. "They don't mind a bit at Shalford's," these ladies used to say, and while they loitered it was forbidden to touch a wrapper or take any measures to conclude the day until the doors closed behind them.

Mr. Kipps would watch these later customers from the shadow of a stack of goods, and death and disfigurement was the least he wished for them. Rarely much later than nine, a supper of bread and cheese and watered beer awaited him downstairs, and, that consumed, the rest of the day was entirely at his disposal for reading, recreation, and the improvement of his mind. . . .

The front door was locked at half-past ten, and the gas in the dormitory extinguished at eleven.

3

On Sundays he was obliged to go to church once, and commonly he went twice, for there was nothing else to do. He sat in the free seats at the back; he was too shy to sing, and not always clever enough to keep his place in the Prayer-book, and he rarely listened to the sermon. But he had developed a sort of idea that going to church had a tendency to alleviate life. His aunt wanted to have him confirmed, but he evaded this ceremony for some years.

In the intervals between services he walked about Folkestone with an air of looking for something. Folkestone was not so interesting on Sundays as on week-days, because the shops were shut; but, on the other hand, there was a sort of confusing brilliance along the front of the Leas in the afternoon. Sometimes the apprentice next above him would condescend to go with him; but when the apprentice next but one above him condescended to go with the apprentice next above him, then Kipps, being habited as yet in ready-made clothes without tails, and unsuitable, therefore, to appear in such company, went alone.

Sometimes he would strike out into the country—still as if looking for something he missed—but the rope of meal-times haled him home again, and sometimes he would invest the major portion of the weekly allowance of a shilling that old Booch handed out to him, in a sacred concert on the pier. He would sometimes walk up and down the Leas between twenty and thirty times after supper, desiring much the courage to speak to some other person in the multitude similarly employed. Almost invariably he ended his Sunday footsore.

He never read a book, there were none for him to read, and besides, in spite of Mr. Woodrow's guidance through a cheap and cheaply annotated edition of the "Tempest" (English Literature), he had no taste that way; he never read any newspapers except, occasionally, *Tit-Bits* or a ha'penny "comic." His chief intellectual stimulus was an occasional argey-bargey that sprang up between Carshot and Buggins at dinner. Kipps listened as if to unparalleled wisdom and wit, and treasured all the gems of repartee in his heart against the time when he too should be a Buggins and have the chance and courage for speech.

At times there came breaks in this routine—sale-times, darkened by extra toil and work past midnight, but brightened by a sprat supper and some shillings in the way of "premiums." And every year—not now and then, but every year— Mr. Shalford, with parenthetic admiration of his own generosity and glancing comparisons with the austerer days when *he* was apprenticed, conceded Kipps no less than ten days holiday—ten whole days every year! Many a poor soul at Portland might well envy the fortunate Kipps. Insatiable heart of man! but how those days were grudged and counted as they snatched themselves away from him one after another!

Once a year came stock-taking, and at intervals gusts of "marking off" goods newly arrived. Then the splendors of Mr. Shalford's being shone with oppressive brilliancy. "System!" he would say, "system! Come! *'ussel!'*" and issue sharp, confusing, contradictory orders very quickly. Carshot trotted about, confused, perspiring, his big nose up in the air, his little eye on Mr. Shalford, his forehead crinkled, his lips always going to the formula, "Oh, my Heart and Liver!" The smart junior and the second apprentice vied with one another in obsequious alacrity. The smart junior aspired to Carshot's position, and that made him almost violently subservient to Shalford. They all snapped at Kipps. Kipps held the blotting-pad and the safety inkpot and a box of tickets, and ran and fetched things. If he put the ink down before he went to fetch things Mr. Shalford usually knocked it over, and if he took it away Mr. Shalford wanted it before he returned. "You make my tooth ache, Kipps," Mr. Shalford would say. "You gimme n'ralgia. You got no more System in you than a bad potato." And at the times when Kipps carried off the inkpot Mr. Shalford would become purple in the face, and jab round with his dry pen at imaginary inkpots and swear, and Carshot would stand and vociferate, and the smart junior would run to the corner of the department and vociferate, and the second apprentice would pursue Kipps, vociferating, "Look Alive, Kipps! Look Alive! Ink, Man! Ink!"

A vague self-disgust that shaped itself as an intense hate of Shalford and all his fellow-creatures filled the soul of Kipps during these periods of storm and stress. He felt that the whole business was unjust and idiotic, but the why and the wherefore was too much for his unfortunate brain. His mind was a welter. One desire, the desire to dodge some at least of a pelting storm of disagreeable comment, guided him through a fumbling performance of his duties. His disgust was infinite! It was not decreased by the inflamed ankles and sore feet that form a normal incident in the business of making an English draper, and the senior apprentice, Minton, a gaunt sullen-faced youngster with close-cropped wiry black hair, a loose ugly mouth, and a moustache like a smudge of ink, directed his attention to deeper aspects of the question and sealed his misery.

"When you get too old to work they chuck you away," said Minton. "Lor! you find old drapers everywhere—tramps, beggars, dock laborers, 'bus conductor— Quod. Anywhere but in a crib."

"Don't they get shops of their own?"

"Lord! *'Ow* are they to get shops of their own? They 'aven't any Capital! How's a draper's shopman to save up five hundred pounds even? I tell you it can't be done. You got to stick to Cribs until it's over. I tell you we're in a blessed drain-pipe, and we've got to crawl along it till we die."

The idea that fermented perpetually in the mind of Minton was to "hit the little beggar slap in the eye"—the little beggar being Mr. Shalford—"and see how his blessed System met that."

This threat filled Kipps with splendid anticipations whenever Shalford went marking off in Minton's department. He would look at Minton and look at Shalford and decide where he would best like Shalford hit. . . . But for reasons known to himself Shalford never pished and tushed with Minton as he did at the harmless Carshot, and this interesting experiment upon the System was never attempted.

4

There were times when Kipps would lie awake, all others in the dormitory asleep and snoring, and think dismally of the outlook Minton pictured. Dimly he perceived the thing that had happened to him, how the great stupid machine of retail trade had caught his life into its wheels, a vast, irresistible force which he had neither strength of will nor knowledge to escape. This was to be his life until his days should end. No adventures, no glory, no change, no freedom. Neither—though the force of that came home to him later—might he dream of effectual love and marriage. And there was a terrible something called the "swap," or "the key of the street," and "crib hunting," of which the talk was scanty but sufficient. Night after night he would resolve to enlist, to run away to sea, to set fire to the warehouse or drown himself, and morning after morning he rose up and hurried downstairs in fear of a sixpenny fine. He would compare his dismal round of servile drudgery with those windy, sunlit days at Littlestone, those windows of happiness shining ever brighter as they receded. The little figure of Ann seemed in all these windows now.

She, too, had happened on evil things. When Kipps went home for the first Christmas after he was bound, that great suspended resolve of his to kiss her flared up to hot determination, and he hurried out and whistled in the yard. There was a silence, and then old Kipps appeared behind him.

"It's no good your whistling there, my boy," said old Kipps in a loud clear tone, designed to be audible over the wall. "They've cleared out all you 'ad any truck with. *She's* gone as help to Ashford, my boy. *Help!* Slavey is what we used to call 'em, but times are changed. Wonder they didn't say lady-'elp while they was about it. It 'ud be like 'em."

And Sid—? Sid had gone too. "Arrand boy or somethink," said old Kipps. "To one of these here brasted bicycle shops."

"Has 'e!'' said Kipps, with a feeling that he had been gripped about the chest; and he turned quickly and went indoors.

Old Kipps, still supposing him present, went on to further observations of an anti-Pornick tendency. . . .

When Kipps got upstairs, safe in his own bedroom, he sat down on the bed and stared at nothing. They were caught—they were all caught. All life took on the hue of one perpetual dismal Monday morning. The Hurons were scattered, the wrecks and the beach had passed away from him, the sun of those warm evenings at Littlestone had set forevermore. . . .

The only pleasure left for the brief remainder of his holiday after that was to think he was not in the shop. Even that was transient. Two more days, one more day, half a day. When he went back there were one or two very dismal nights indeed. He went so far as to write home some vague intimation of his feelings about business and his prospects, quoting Minton, but Mrs. Kipps answered him, "Did he want the Pornicks to say he wasn't good enough to be a draper?" This dreadful possibility was of course conclusive in the matter. "No"; he resolved they should not say he failed at that.

He derived much help from a "manly" sermon delivered in an enormous voice by a large, fat, sun-red clergyman, just home from a colonial bishopric he had resigned on the plea of ill-health, exhorting him that whatever his hand found to do, he was to do with all his might, and the revision of his catechism preparatory to his confirmation reminded him that it behooved him to do his duty in that state of life into which it had pleased God to call him.

After a time the sorrows of Kipps grew less acute, and, save for a miracle, the brief tragedy of his life was over. He subdued himself to his position even as his church required of him, seeing, moreover, no way out of it.

The earliest mitigation of his lot was that his soles and ankles became indurated to the perpetual standing. The next was an unexpected weekly whiff of freedom that came every Thursday. Mr. Shalford, after a brave stand for what he called "Innyvishal lib'ty" and the "Idea of my System," a stand which, he explained, he made chiefly on patriotic grounds, was at last, under pressure of certain of his customers, compelled to fall in line with the rest of the local Early Closing Association, and Mr. Kipps could emerge in daylight and go where he listed for long, long hours. Moreover, Minton, the pessimist, reached the end of his appointed time and left—to enlist in a cavalry regiment, and go about this planet leading an insubordinate but interesting life that ended at last in an intimate, vivid, and really, you know, by no means painful or tragic night grapple in the Terah Valley. In a little while Kipps cleaned windows no longer; he was serving customers (of the less important sort) and taking goods out on approval, and presently he was third apprentice, and his moustache was visible, and there were three apprentices whom he might legally snub and cuff. But one was (most dishonestly) too big to cuff, in spite of his greener years.

5

There came still other distractions, the natural distractions of adolescence, to take his mind off the inevitable. His costume, for example, began to interest him more; he began to realize himself as a visible object, to find an interest in the costume-room mirrors and the eyes of the girl-apprentices.

In this he was helped by counsel and example. Pearce, his immediate senior, was by way of being what was called a Masher, and preached his cult. During slack times grave discussions about collars, ties, the cut of trouser-legs, and the proper shape of a boot toe, were held in the Manchester department. In due course Kipps went to a tailor, and his short jacket was replaced by a morning coat with tails. Stirred by this, he purchased at his own expense three stand-up collars to replace his former turn-down ones. They were nearly three inches high, higher than those Pearce wore, and they made his neck quite sore, and left a red mark under his ears. . . . So equipped, he found himself fit company even for this fashionable apprentice, who had now succeeded Minton in his seniority.

Most potent help of all in the business of forgetting his cosmic disaster was this, that so soon as he was in tail-coats, the young ladies of the establishment began to discover that he was no longer a "horrid little boy." Hitherto they had tossed heads at him and kept him in his place. Now they discovered that he was a "nice boy," which is next door at least to being a "feller," and in some ways even preferable. It is painful to record that his fidelity to Ann failed at their first onset. I am fully sensible how entirely better this story would be, from a sentimental point of view, if he had remained true to that early love. Only then it would have been a different story altogether. And at least Kipps was thus far true, that with none of these later loves was there any of that particular quality that linked Ann's flushed face and warmth and the inner things of life so inseparably together. Though they were not without emotions of various sorts.

It was one of the young ladies in the costume-room who first showed by her manner that he was a visible object and capable of exciting interest. She talked to him, she encouraged him to talk to her, she lent him a book she possessed, and darned a sock for him and said she would be his elder sister. She allowed him to escort her to church with a great air of having induced him to go. Then she investigated his eternal welfare, overcame a certain affectation of virile indifference to religion, and extorted a promise that he would undergo "confirmation." This excited the other young lady in the costumes, her natural rival, and she set herself with great charm and subtlety to the capture of the ripening heart of Kipps. She took a more worldly line. She went for a walk with him to the pier on Sunday afternoon, and explained to him how a gentleman must always walk "outside" a lady on a pavement, and how all gentlemen wore or, at least, carried gloves, and generally the broad beginnings of the British social ideal. Afterwards the ladies exchanged "words" upon Sabbatical grounds. In this way was the *toga virilis* bestowed on Kipps, and he became recognized as a suitable object for that Platonic Eros whose blunted darts devastate even the very highest class establishments. In this way, too, did that pervading ambition of the British young man to be, if not a "gentleman," at least mistakably like one, take root in his heart.

He took to these new interests with a quite natural and personal zest. He became initiated into the mysteries of "flirting" and—at a slightly later stage and with some leading hints from Pearce, who was of a communicative disposition in these matters—of the milder forms of "spooning." Very soon he was engaged. Before two years were out he had been engaged six times, and was beginning to be rather a desperate fellow, so far as he could make out. Desperate, but quite gentlemanly, be it understood, and without let or hindrance to the fact that he was in four brief lessons "prepared" by a distant-mannered and gloomy young curate, and "confirmed" a member of the Established Church.

The engagements in drapery establishments do not necessarily involve a subsequent marriage. They are essentially more refined, less coarsely practical, and altogether less binding than the engagements of the vulgar rich. These young ladies do not like not to be engaged, it is so unnatural, and Mr. Kipps was as

easy to get engaged to as one could wish. There are, from the young lady's
point of view, many conveniences in being engaged. You get an escort for
church and walks, and so forth. It is not quite the thing to walk abroad with a
"feller," much more to "spoon" with him, when he is neither one's *fiancé* nor
an adopted brother; it is considered either a little fast or else as savoring of the
"walking-out" habits of the servant girls. Now, such is the sweetness of human
charity, that the shop young lady in England has just the same horror of doing
anything that savors of the servant girl as the lady journalist, let us say, has of
anything savoring of the shop-girl, or the really quite nice young lady has of
anything savoring of any sort of girl who has gone down into the economic
battlefield to earn herself a living. . . . But the very deepest of these affairs was
still among the shallow places of love, at best it was paddling where it is decreed
that men must sink or swim. Of the deep and dangerous places, and of the huge
buoyant lift of its waves, he tasted nothing. Affairs of clothes and vanities they
were, jealousies about a thing said, flatteries and mutual boastings, climaxes in
the answering grasp of hands, the temerarious use of Christian names, culminations
in a walk, or a near confidence, or a little pressure more or less. Close sitting
on a seat after twilight with some little fondling was, indeed, the boldest of
lover's adventures, the utmost limit of his enterprises in the service of that stark
Great Lady who is daughter of Uranus and the sea. The "young ladies" who
reigned in his heart came and went like people in an omnibus; there was the
vehicle, so to speak, upon the road, and they entered and left it without any
cataclysm of emotion. For all that, this development of the sex interest was
continuously very interesting to Kipps, and kept him going as much as anything
through all these servile years. . . .

6

For a tailpiece to this chapter one may vignette a specimen minute.

It is a bright Sunday afternoon; the scene is a secluded little seat halfway
down the front of the Leas, and Kipps is four years older than when he parted
from Ann. There is a quite perceptible down upon his upper lip, and his costume
is just as tremendous a "mash" as lies within his means. His collar is so high
that it scars his inaggressive jaw-bone, and his hat has a curly brim, his tie shows
taste, his trousers are modestly brilliant, and his boots have light cloth uppers
and button at the side. He jabs at the gravel before him with a cheap cane and
glances sideways at Flo Bates, the young lady from the cash desk. She is wearing
a brilliant blouse and a gaily trimmed hat. There is an air of fashion about her
that might disappear under the analysis of a woman of the world, but which is
quite sufficient to make Kipps very proud to be distinguished as her particular
"feller," and to be allowed at temperate intervals to use her Christian name.

The conversation is light and gay in the modern style, and Flo keeps on
smiling, good temper being her special charm.

"Ye see, you done mean what *I* mean," he is saying.

"Well, what do *you* mean?"

"Not what you mean!"

"Well, tell me."

"Ah! That's another story."

Pause. They look meaningly at one another.

"You *are* a one for being roundabout," says the lady.

"Well, you're not so plain, you know."

"Not plain?"

"No."

"You don't mean to say I'm roundabout?"

"No. I mean to say— Though—" Pause.

"Well?"

"You're not a bit plain—you're" (his voice jumps up to a squeak) "pretty. See?"

"Oh, get *out!*"—her voice lifts also—with pleasure.

She strikes him with her glove, then glances suddenly at a ring upon her finger. Her smile disappears momentarily. Another pause. Eyes meet and the smile returns.

"I wish I knew—" says Kipps.

"Knew—?"

"Where you got that ring."

She lifts the hand with the ring until her eyes just show (very prettily) over it. "You'd just *like* to know," she says slowly, and smiles still more brightly with the sense of successful effect.

"I dessay I could guess."

"I dessay you couldn't."

"Couldn't I?"

"No!"

"Guess it in three."

"Not the name."

"Ah!"

"*Ah!*"

"Well, anyhow, lemme look at it."

He looks at it. Pause. Giggles, slight struggle, and a slap on Kipps' coat-sleeve. A passer-by appears down the path and she hastily withdraws her hand.

She glances at the face of the approaching man. They maintain a bashful silence until he has passed . . .

CHAPTER III

The Woodcarving Class

1

THOUGH THESE SERVICES to Venus Epipontia, and these studies in the art of dress, did much to distract his thoughts and mitigate his earlier miseries, it would be mere optimism to present Kipps as altogether happy. A vague dissatisfaction with life drifted about him, and every now and again enveloped him like a sea-fog. During these periods it was grayly evident that there was something, something vital in life, lacking. For no earthly reason that Kipps could discover, he was haunted by a suspicion that life was going wrong, or had already gone wrong in some irrevocable way. The ripening self-consciousness of adolescence developed this into a clearly felt insufficiency. It was all very well to carry gloves, open doors, never say "Miss" to a girl, and walk "outside," but were there not other things, conceivably even deeper things, before the complete thing was attained? For example, certain matters of knowledge. He perceived great bogs of ignorance about him, fumbling traps, where other people, it was alleged, *real* gentlemen and ladies, for example, and the clergy, had knowledge and assurance, bogs which it was sometimes difficult to elude. A girl arrived in the millinery department who could, she said, *speak* French and German. She snubbed certain advances, and a realization of inferiority blistered Kipps. But he tried to pass the thing off as a joke by saying "Parlez-vous Francey" whenever he met her, and inducing the junior apprentice to say the same.

He even made some dim half-secret experiments towards remedying the deficiencies he suspected. He spent five shillings on five serial numbers of a Home Educator, and bought (and even thought of reading) a Shakespeare and a Bacon's "Advancement of Learning," and the poems of Herrick from a chap who was hard up. He battled with Shakespeare all one Sunday afternoon, and found the "English Literature," with which Mr. Woodrow had equipped him, had vanished down some crack in his mind. He had no doubt it was very splendid stuff, but he couldn't quite make out what it was all about. There was an occult meaning, he knew, in literature, and he had forgotten it. Moreover, he discovered one day, while taunting the junior apprentice with ignorance, that his "rivers of England" had also slipped his memory, and he laboriously restored that fabric of rote learning: "Ty Wear Tees 'Umber—"

I suppose some such phase of discontent is a normal thing in every adolescence. The ripening mind seeks something upon which its will may crystallize, upon which its discursive emotions, growing more abundant with each year of life, may concentrate. For many, though not for all, it takes a religious direction; but in those particular years the mental atmosphere of Folkestone was exceptionally free from any revivalistic disturbance that might have reached Kipps' mental being. Sometimes they fall in love. I have known this uneasiness end in different cases in a vow to read one book (not a novel) every week, to read the Bible through in a year, to pass in the Honors division of the London Matriculation examination, to become an accomplished chemist, and never more to tell a lie. It led Kipps finally into Technical Education, as we understand it in the south of England.

It was in the last year of his apprenticeship that he had pursued his researches after that missing qualification into the Folkestone Young Men's Association, where Mr. Chester Coote prevailed. Mr. Chester Coote was a young man of semi-independent means, who inherited a share in a house agency, read Mrs. Humphry Ward, and took an interest in social work. He was a whitish-faced young man, with a prominent nose, pale blue eyes, and a quivering quality in his voice. He was very active upon committees; he was very prominent and useful on all social occasions, in evidence upon platforms, and upon all those semi-public occasions when the Great descend. He lived with an only sister. To Kipps and his kind in the Young Men's Association he read a stimulating paper on "Self-Help." He said it was the noblest of all our distinctive English characteristics, and he was very much down upon the "over-educated" Germans. At the close a young German hairdresser made a few commendatory remarks which developed somehow into an oration on Hanoverian politics. As he became excited he became guttural and obscure; the meeting sniggered cheerfully at such ridiculous English, and Kipps was so much amused that he forgot a private project to ask this Chester Coote how he might set about a little Self-Help on his own private account in such narrow margins of time as the System of Mr. Shalford spared him. But afterwards in the night-time it came to him again.

It was a few months later, and after his apprenticeship was over, and Mr. Shalford had with depreciatory observations taken him on as an Improver at twenty pounds a year, that this question was revived by a casual article on Technical Education in a morning paper that a commercial traveler left behind him. It played the *rôle* of the word in season. Something in the nature of conversion, a faint sort of concentration of purpose, really occurred in him then. The article was written with penetrating vehemence, and it stimulated him to the pitch of inquiring about the local Science and Art Classes; and after he had told everybody in the shop about it, and taken the advice of all who supported his desperate resolution, he joined. At first he attended the class in Freehand, that being the subject taught on early closing night, and he had already made some progress in that extraordinary routine of reproducing freehand "copies," which for two generations had passed with English people for instruction in art when the dates of the classes were changed. Thereby, just as the March winds were blowing, he was precipitated into the Woodcarving class, and his mind diverted first to this useful and broadening pursuit, and then to its teacher.

2

The class in woodcarving was an extremely select class, conducted at that time by a young lady named Walshingham; and as this young lady was destined by Fortune to teach Kipps a great deal more than woodcarving, it will be well if the reader gets the picture of her correctly in mind. She was only a year or so older than he was, she had a pale intellectual face, dark gray eyes and black hair, which she wore over her forehead in an original and striking way that she had adapted from a picture by Rossetti in the South Kensington Museum. She was slender so that without ungainliness she had an effect of being tall, and her hands were shapely and white when they came into contrast with hands much exercised in rolling and blocking. She dressed in those loose and pleasant forms and those soft and tempered shades that arose in England in the socialistic-esthetic epoch, and remain to this day among us as the badge of those who read Turgenev's novels, scorn current fiction, and think on higher planes. I think she was as beautiful as most beautiful people, and to Kipps she was altogether beautiful. She had, Kipps learned, matriculated at London University, an astounding feat to his imagination, and the masterly way in which she demonstrated how to prod and worry honest pieces of wood into useless and unedifying patterns in relief, extorted his utmost admiration.

At first when Kipps had learned he was to be taught by a "girl" he was inclined to resent it, the more so as Buggins had recently been very strong on the gross injustice of feminine employment. "We have to keep wives," said Buggins (though, as a matter of fact, he did not keep even one), "and how are we to do it with a lot of girls coming in to take the work out of our mouths?" Afterwards Kipps, in conjunction with Pearce, looked at it from another point of view, and thought it would be rather a "lark." Finally, when he saw her, and saw her teaching and coming nearer to him with an impressive deliberation, he was breathless with awe and the quality of her dark slender femininity.

The class consisted of two girls and a maiden lady of riper years, friends of Miss Walshingham's, and anxious rather to support her in an interesting experiment than to become really expert woodcarvers; an elderly, oldish young man with spectacles, and a black beard, who never spoke to anyone, and who was evidently too short-sighted to see his work as a whole; a small boy, who was understood to have a "gift" for woodcarving; and a lodging-house keeper, who "took classes" every winter, she told Mr. Kipps, as though they were a tonic, and "found they did her good." And occasionally Mr. Chester Coote—refined and gentlemanly—would come into the class, with or without papers, ostensibly on committee business, but in reality to talk to the less attractive of the two girl-students, and sometimes a brother of Miss Walshingham's, a slender dark young man with a pale face and fluctuating resemblances to the young Napoleon, would arrive just at the end of the class-time to see his sister home.

All these personages impressed Kipps with a sense of inferiority that in the case of Miss Walshingham became positively abysmal. The ideas and knowledge they appeared to have, their personal capacity and freedom, opened a new world to his imagination. These people came and went with a sense of absolute assurance, against an overwhelming background of plaster casts, diagrams and tables, benches and a blackboard, a background that seemed to him to be saturated with recondite knowledge and the occult and jealously guarded tips and secrets that constitute Art and the Higher Life. They went home, he imagined, to homes where the piano was played with distinction and freedom, and books littered the tables and foreign languages were habitually used. They had complicated meals no doubt. They "knew etiquette," and how to avoid all the errors for which Kipps bought penny manuals—"What to Avoid," "Common Errors in Speaking," and the like. He knew nothing about it all, nothing whatever; he was a creature of the outer darkness blinking in an unsuspected light.

He heard them speak easily and freely to one another of examinations, of books and paintings, of "last year's Academy"—a little contemptuously—and once just at the end of the class-time Mr. Chester Coote and young Walshingham and the two girls argued about something or other called, he fancied, "Vagner," or "Vargner"—they seemed to say it both ways—and which presently shaped itself more definitely as the name of a man who made up music. (Carshot and Buggins weren't in it with them.) Young Walshingham, it appeared, said something or other that was an "epigram," and they all applauded him. Kipps, I say, felt himself a creature of outer darkness, an inexcusable intruder in an altitudinous world. When the epigram happened he first of all smiled to pretend he understood, and instantly suppressed the smile to show he did not listen. Then he became extremely hot and uncomfortable, though nobody had noticed either phase.

It was clear his only chance of concealing his bottomless baseness was to hold his tongue, and meanwhile he chipped with earnest care and abased his soul before the very shadow of Miss Walshingham. She used to come and direct and advise him, with, he felt, an effort to conceal the scorn she had for him, and indeed it is true that at first she thought of him chiefly as the clumsy young man with the red ears.

And as soon as he emerged from the first effect of pure and awe-stricken humility—he was greatly helped to emerge from that condition to a perception of human equality by the need the lodging-house keeper was under to talk while she worked, and as she didn't like Miss Walshingham and her friends very much, and the young man with spectacles was deaf, she naturally talked to Kipps—he perceived that he was in a state of adoration for Miss Walshingham that it seemed almost a blasphemous familiarity to speak of as being in love.

This state, you must understand, had nothing to do with "flirting" or "spooning" and that superficial passion that flashes from eye to eye upon the Leas and Pier—absolutely nothing. That he knew from the first. Her rather pallid, intellectual young face beneath those somber clouds of hair put her in a class apart; towards her the thought of "attentions" paled and vanished. To approach such a being, to perform sacrifices and to perish obviously for her, seemed the limit he might aspire to, he or any man. For if his love was abasement, at any rate it had this much of manliness that it covered all his sex. It had not yet come to Kipps to acknowledge any man as his better in his heart of hearts. When one does that the game is played, and one grows old indeed.

The rest of his sentimental interests vanished altogether in this great illumination.

He meditated about her when he was blocking cretonne, her image was before his eyes at teatime, and blotted out the more immediate faces and made him silent and preoccupied and so careless in his bearing that the junior apprentice, sitting beside him, mocked at and parodied his enormous bites of bread and butter unreproved. He became conspicuously less popular on the "fancy" side, the "costumes" was chilly with him and the "millinery" cutting. But he did not care. An intermittent correspondence with Flo Bates, that had gone on since she left Mr. Shalford's desk for a position at Tunbridge, "nearer home," and which had roused Kipps in its earlier stages to unparalleled heights of epistolary effort, died out altogether by reason of his neglect. He heard with scarcely a pang that, as a consequence perhaps of his neglect, Flo was "carrying on with a chap who managed a farm."

Every Thursday he jabbed and gouged at his wood, jabbing and gouging intersecting circles and diamond traceries, and that labored inane which our mad world calls ornament, and he watched Miss Walshingham furtively whenever she turned away. The circles, in consequence, were jabbed crooked, and his panels, losing their symmetry, became comparatively pleasing to the untrained eye—and once he jabbed his finger. He would cheerfully have jabbed all his fingers if he could have found some means of using the opening to express himself of the vague emotions that possessed him. But he shirked conversation just as earnestly as he desired it; he feared that profound general ignorance of his might appear.

3

There came a time when she could not open one of the class-room windows. The man with the black beard pored over his chipping heedlessly. . . .

It did not take Kipps a moment to grasp his opportunity. He dropped his gouge and stepped forward. "Lem *me*," he said. . . .

He could not open the window either!

"Oh, please don't trouble," she said.

" 'Sno trouble," he gasped.

Still the sash stuck. He felt his manhood was at stake. He gathered himself together for a tremendous effort, and the pane broke with a snap, and he thrust his hand into the void beyond.

"*There!*" said Miss Walshingham, and the glass fell ringing into the courtyard below.

Then Kipps made to bring his hand back and felt the keen touch of the edge of the broken glass at his wrist. He turned dolefully. "I'm tremendously sorry," he said, in answer to the accusation in Miss Walshingham's eyes. "I didn't think it would break like that"—as if he had expected it to break in some quite different and entirely more satisfactory manner. The boy with the gift for woodcarving, having stared at Kipps' face for a moment, became involved in a Laocoon struggle with a giggle.

"You've cut your wrist," said one of the girl friends, standing up and pointing. She was a pleasant-faced, greatly freckled girl, with a helpful disposition, and she said "You've cut your wrist" as brightly as if she had been a trained nurse.

Kipps looked down and saw a swift line of scarlet rush down his hand. He perceived the other man-student regarding this with magnified eyes. "You *have* cut your wrist," said Miss Walshingham; and Kipps regarded his damage with greater interest.

"He's cut his wrist," said the maiden lady to the lodging-house keeper, and seemed in doubt what a lady should do. "It's—" she hesitated at the word "bleeding," and nodded to the lodging-house keeper instead.

"Dreadfully," said the maiden lady, and tried to look and tried not to look at the same time.

"Of *course* he's cut his wrist," said the lodging-house keeper, momentarily quite annoyed at Kipps; and the other young lady, who thought Kipps rather common, went on quietly with her wood-cutting with an air of its being the proper thing to do—though nobody else seemed to know it.

"You must tie it up," said Miss Walshingham.

"We must tie it up," said the freckled girl.

"I 'adn't the slightest idea that window was going to break like that," said Kipps, with candor. "Nort the slightest."

He glanced again at the blood on his wrist, and it seemed to him that it was on the very point of dropping on the floor of that cultured class-room. So he very neatly licked it off, feeling at the same time for his handkerchief. "Oh, *don't!*" said Miss Walshingham as he did so, and the girl with the freckles made a movement of horror. The giggle got the better of the boy with the gift, and celebrated its triumph by unseemly noises, in spite of which it seemed to Kipps at the moment that the act that had made Miss Walshingham say "Oh, *don't!*" was rather a desperate and manly treatment of what was, after all, a creditable injury.

"It ought to be tied up," said the lodging-house keeper, holding her chisel upright in her hand. "It's a bad cut to bleed like that."

"We must tie it up," said the freckled girl, and hesitated in front of Kipps. "Have you got a handkerchief?" she said.

"I dunno 'ow I managed *not* to bring one," said Kipps. "I'm——. Not 'aving a cold, I suppose some 'ow I didn't think——!"

He checked a further flow of blood.

The girl with the freckles caught Miss Walshingham's eye and held it for a moment. Both glanced at Kipps' injury. The boy with the gift, who had reappeared with a chastened expression from some noisy pursuit beneath his desk, made the neglected motions of one who proffers shyly. Miss Walshingham, under the spell of the freckled girl's eye, produced a handkerchief. The voice of the maiden lady could be heard in the background: "I've been through all the technical education ambulance classes twice, and I know you go *so* if it's a vein, and *so* if it's an artery—at least you go *so* for one, and *so* for the other, whichever it may be—but . . ."

"If you will give me your hand," said the freckled girl; and proceeded, with Miss Walshingham's assistance, to bandage Kipps in a most businesslike way. Yes, they actually bandaged Kipps. They pulled up his cuffs—happily they were not a very frayed pair—and held his wrist and wrapped the soft handkerchief round it, and tightened the knot together. And Miss Walshingham's face, the face of that almost divine Over-human, came close to the face of Kipps.

"We're not hurting you, are we?" she said.

"Not a bit," said Kipps, as he would have said if they had been sawing his arm off.

"We're not experts, you know," said the freckled girl.

"I'm sure it's a dreadful cut," said Miss Walshingham.

"It ain't much, reelly," said Kipps; "and you're taking a lot of trouble. I'm sorry I broke that window. I can't think what I could have been doing."

"It isn't so much the cut at the time, it's the poisoning afterwards," came the voice of the maiden lady.

"Of course, I'm quite willing to pay for the window," panted Kipps, opulently.

"We must make it just as tight as possible to stop the bleeding," said the freckled girl.

"I don't think it's much, reelly," said Kipps. "I'm awful sorry I broke that window, though."

"Put your finger on the knot, dear," said the freckled girl.

"Eh?" said Kipps. "I mean—"

Both the young ladies became very intent on the knot, and Mr. Kipps was very red and very intent upon the two young ladies.

"Mortified, and had to be sawn off," said the maiden lady.

"Sawn off," said the lodging-house keeper.

"Sawn *right* off," said the maiden lady, and jabbed at her mangled design.

"There," said the freckled girl, "I think that ought to do. You're sure it's not too tight?"

"Not a bit," said Kipps.

He met Miss Walshingham's eyes and smiled to show how little he cared for wounds and pain. "It's only a little cut," he added.

The maiden lady appeared as an addition to their group. "You should have washed the wound, dear," she said. "I was just telling Miss Collis—" She peered through her glasses at the bandage. "That doesn't look *quite* right," she remarked critically. "You should have taken the ambulance classes. But I suppose it will have to do. Are you hurting?"

"Not a bit," said Kipps; and smiled at them all with the air of a brave soldier in hospital.

"I'm sure it *must* hurt," said Miss Walshingham.

"Anyhow, you're a very good patient," said the girl with the freckles.

Mr. Kipps became bright pink. "I'm only sorry I broke the window—that's all," he said. "But who would have thought it was going to break like that?"

Pause.

"I'm afraid you won't be able to go on carving tonight," said Miss Walshingham.

"I'll try," said Kipps. "It reelly doesn't hurt—not anything to matter."

Presently Miss Walshingham came to him, as he carved heroically with his hand bandaged in her handkerchief. There was a touch of novel interest in her eyes. "I'm afraid you're not getting on very fast," she said.

The freckled girl looked up and regarded Miss Walshingham.

"I'm doing a little, anyhow," said Kipps. "I don't want to waste any time. A feller like me hasn't much time to spare."

It struck the girls that there was a quality of modest disavowal about that "feller like me." It gave them light into this obscure person, and Miss Walshingham ventured to commend his work as "promising" and to ask whether he meant to follow it up. Kipps didn't "altogether know"—"things depended on so much," but if he was in Folkestone next winter he certainly should. It did not occur to Miss Walshingham at the time to ask why his progress in art depended upon his presence in Folkestone. There were some more questions and answers—they continued to talk to him for a little time even when Mr. Chester Coote had come into the room—and when at last the conversation had died out, it dawned upon Kipps just how much his cut wrist had done for him. . . .

He went to sleep that night revising that conversation for the twentieth time, treasuring this and expanding that, and inserting things he might have said to Miss Walshingham—things he might still say about himself—in relation, more or less explicit, to her. He wasn't quite sure if he wouldn't like his arm to mortify a bit, which would make him interesting, or to heal up absolutely, which would show the exceptional purity of his blood. . . .

4

The affair of the broken window happened late in April, and the class came to an end in May. In that interval there were several small incidents and great developments of emotion. I have done Kipps no justice if I have made it seem that his face was unsightly. It was, as the freckled girl pointed out to Helen Walshingham, an "interesting" face, and that aspect of him which presented chiefly erratic hair and glowing ears ceased to prevail.

They talked him over, and the freckled girl discovered there was something "wistful" in his manner. They detected a "natural delicacy," and the freckled girl set herself to draw him out from that time forth. The freckled girl was nineteen, and very wise and motherly and benevolent, and really she greatly preferred drawing out Kipps to woodcarving. It was quite evident to her that Kipps was in love with Helen Walshingham, and it struck her as a queer and romantic and pathetic and extremely interesting phenomenon. And as at that time she regarded Helen as "simply lovely," it seemed only right and proper that she should assist Kipps in his modest efforts to place himself in a state of absolute abandon upon her altar.

Under her sympathetic management the position of Kipps was presently defined quite clearly. He was unhappy in his position—misunderstood. He told her he "didn't seem to get on like" with customers, and she translated this for him as "too sensitive." The discontent with his fate in life, the dreadful feeling that Education was slipping by him, troubles that time and usage were glazing over a little, revived to their old acuteness but not to their old hopelessness. As a basis for sympathy, indeed, they were even a source of pleasure.

And one day at dinner it happened that Carshot and Buggins fell talking of "these here writers," and how Dickens had been a labeler of blacking, and Thackeray "an artis' who couldn't sell a drawing," and how Samuel Johnson had walked to London without any boots, having thrown away his only pair "out of pride." "It's Luck," said Buggins, "to a very large extent. They just happen to hit on something that catches on, and there you are!"

"Nice easy life they have of it, too," said Miss Mergle. "Write just an hour or so, and done for the day! Almost like gentlefolks."

"There's more work in it than you'd think," said Carshot, stooping to a mouthful.

"I wouldn't mind changing for all that," said Buggins. "I'd like to see one of these here authors marking off with Jimmy."

"I think they copy from each other a good deal," said Miss Mergle.

"Even then (chup, chup, chup)," said Carshot, "there's writing it out in their own hands."

They proceeded to enlarge upon the literary life, on its ease and dignity, on the social recognition accorded to those who led it, and on the ample gratifications their vanity achieved. "Pictures everywhere—never get a new suit without being photographed—almost like Royalty," said Miss Mergle. And all this talk impressed the imagination of Kipps very greatly. Here was a class that seemed to bridge the gulf. On the one hand essentially Low, but by factitious circumstances capable of entering upon these levels of social superiority to which all true Englishmen aspire, these levels from which one may tip a butler, scorn a tailor, and even commune with those who lead "men" into battle. "Almost like gentlefolks"—

that was it! He brooded over these things in the afternoon, until they blossomed into daydreams. Suppose, for example, he had chanced to write a book, a well-known book, under an assumed name, and yet kept on being a draper all the time. . . . Impossible, of course; but *suppose*—It made quite a long dream.

And at the next woodcarving class he let it be drawn from him that his real choice in life was to be a Nawther—"only one doesn't get a chance."

After this there were times when Kipps had that pleasant sense that comes of attracting interest. He was a mute inglorious Dickens, or at any rate something of the sort, and they were all taking him at that. The discovery of this indefinable "something in" him, the development of which was now painfully restricted and impossible, did much to bridge the gulf between himself and Miss Walshingham. He was unfortunate, he was futile, but he was not "common." Even now with help—? The two girls, and the freckled girl in particular, tried to "stir him up" to some effort to do his imputed potentialities justice. They were still young enough to believe that to nice and niceish members of the male sex—more especially when under the stimulus of feminine encouragement—nothing is finally impossible.

The freckled girl was, I say, the stage manager of this affair, but Miss Walshingham was the presiding divinity. A touch of proprietorship came in her eyes at times when she looked at him. He was hers—unconditionally—and she knew it.

To her directly, Kipps scarcely ever made a speech. The enterprising things that he was continually devising to say to her, he usually did not say, or said, with a suitable modification, to the girl with the freckles. And one day the girl with the freckles smote him to the heart. She said to him, looking across the class-room to where her friend reached a cast from the shelf, "I do think Helen Walshingham is sometimes the most lovely person in the world. Look at her now!"

Kipps gasped for a moment. The moment lengthened, and she regarded him as an intelligent young surgeon might regard an operation without anesthetics. "You're right," he said, and then looked at her with an entire abandonment of visage.

She colored under his glare of silent avowal, and he blushed brightly. "I think so too," he said hoarsely, cleared his throat, and, after a meditative moment, proceeded sacramentally with his woodcarving.

"You *are* wonderful," said the freckled girl to Miss Walshingham, *apropos* of nothing as they went on their way home together. "He simply adores you."

"But, my dear, what have I done?" said Helen.

"That's just it," said the freckled girl. "What *have* you done?"

And then with a terrible swiftness came the last class of the course to terminate this relationship altogether. Kipps was careless of dates, and the thing came upon him with an effect of abrupt surprise. Just as his petals were expanding so hopefully, "Finis," and the thing was at an end. But Kipps did not fully appreciate that the end was indeed and really and truly the end until he was back in the Emporium after the end was over.

The end began practically in the middle of the last class, when the freckled girl broached the topic of terminations. She developed the question of just how he was going on after the class ended. She hoped he would stick to certain resolutions of self-improvement he had breathed. She said quite honestly that he owed it to himself to develop his possibilities. He expressed firm resolve, but dwelled on difficulties. He had no books. She instructed him how to get books from the public library. He was to get a form of application for a ticket signed by a ratepayer, and he said "of course" when she said Mr. Shalford would do that, though all the time he knew perfectly well it would "never do" to ask Mr. Shalford for anything of the sort. She explained that she was going to North Wales for the summer, information he received without immediate regret. At intervals he expressed his intention of going on with woodcarving when the summer was over, and once he added, "if—"

She considered herself extremely delicate not to press for the completion of that "if—"

After that talk there was an interval of languid woodcarving and watching Miss Walshingham.

Then presently there came a bustle of packing, a great ceremony of handshaking all round by Miss Collis and the maiden lady of ripe years, and then Kipps found himself outside the class-room, on the landing with his two friends. It seemed to him he had only just learned that this was the last class of all. There came a little pause, and the freckled girl suddenly went back into the class-room, and left Kipps and Miss Walshingham alone together for the first time. Kipps was instantly breathless. She looked at his face with a glance that mingled sympathy and curiosity, and held out her white hand.

"Well, good-bye, Mr. Kipps," she said.

He took her hand and held it.

"I'd do anything," said Kipps, and had not the temerity to add "for you." He stopped awkwardly.

He shook her hand and said "Good-bye."

There was a little pause. "I hope you will have a pleasant holiday," she said.

"I shall come back to the class next year, anyhow," said Kipps, valiantly, and turned abruptly to the stairs.

"I hope you will," said Miss Walshingham.

He turned back towards her.

"Really?" he said.

"I hope everybody will come back."

"I will—anyhow," said Kipps. "You may count on that"; and he tried to make his tones significant.

They looked at one another through a little pause.

"Good-bye," she said.

Kipps lifted his hat.

She turned towards the class-room.

"Well?" said the freckled girl, coming back towards her.

"Nothing," said Helen. "At least—presently."

And she became very energetic about some scattered tools on a desk. The freckled girl went out and stood for a moment at the head of the stairs. When she came back she looked very hard at her friend. The incident struck her as important—wonderfully important. It was unassimilable, of course, and absurd, but there it was, the thing that is so cardinal to a girl, the emotion, the subservience, the crowning triumph of her sex. She could not help feeling that Helen took it on the whole a little too hardly.

CHAPTER IV

Chitterlow

1

THE HOUR OF the class on the following Thursday found Kipps in a state of nearly incredible despondency. He was sitting with his eyes on the reading-room clock, his chin resting on his fists, and his elbows on the accumulated comic papers, that were comic, alas! in vain. He paid no heed to the little man in spectacles glaring opposite to him, famishing for *Fun*. In this place it was he had sat night after night, each night more blissful than the last, waiting until it should be time to go to Her! And then—bliss! And now the hour had come and there was no class! There would be no class now until next October. It might be there would never be a class, so far as he was concerned, again.

It might be there would never be a class again, for Shalford, taking exception at a certain absent-mindedness that led to mistakes, and more particularly to the ticketing of several articles in Kipps' Manchester window upside down, had been "on to" him for the past few days in an exceedingly onerous manner. . .

He sighed profoundly, pushed the comic papers back—they were rent away from him instantly by the little man in spectacles—and tried the old engravings of Folkestone in the past that hung about the room. But these, too, failed to minister to his bruised heart. He wandered about the corridors for a time and watched the Library Indicator for awhile. Wonderful thing that! But it did not hold him for long. People came and laughed near him, and that jarred with him dreadfully. He went out of the building, and a beastly cheerful barrel-organ mocked him in the street. He was moved to a desperate resolve to go down to the beach. There, it might be, he would be alone. The sea might be rough—and attuned to him. It would certainly be dark.

"If I 'ad a penny I'm blest if I wouldn't go and chuck myself off the end of the pier. . . . *She'd* never miss me. . . ."

He followed a deepening vein of thought.

"Penny, though! It's tuppence," he said, after a space.

He went down Dover Street in a state of profound melancholia—at the pace and mood as it were of his own funeral procession—and he crossed at the corner of Tontine Street, heedless of all mundane things. And there it was that Fortune came upon him, in disguise and with a loud shout, the shout of a person endowed with an unusually rich, full voice, followed immediately by a violent blow in the back.

His hat was over his eyes, and an enormous weight rested on his shoulders, and something kicked him in the back of his calf.

Then he was on all fours in some mud that Fortune, in conjunction with the Folkestone corporation and in the pursuit of equally mysterious ends, had heaped together even lavishly for his reception.

He remained in that position for some seconds, awaiting further developments, and believing almost anything broken before his heart. Gathering at last that this temporary violence of things in general was over, and being perhaps assisted by a clutching hand, he arose, and found himself confronting a figure holding a bicycle and thrusting forward a dark face in anxious scrutiny.

"You aren't hurt, Matey?" gasped the figure.

"Was that *you* 'it me?" said Kipps.

"It's these handles, you know," said the figure, with an air of being a fellow-sufferer. "They're too *low*. And when I go to turn, if I don't remember, Bif!—and I'm *in* to something."

"Well—you give me a oner in the back—anyhow," said Kipps, taking stock of his damages.

"I was coming downhill, you know," explained the bicyclist. "These little Folkestone hills are a Fair Treat. It isn't as though I'd been on the level. I came rather a whop."

"You did *that*," said Kipps.

"I was back-pedalling for all I was worth, anyhow," said the bicyclist. "Not that I *am* worth much back-pedalling."

He glanced round and made a sudden movement almost as if to mount his machine. Then he turned as rapidly to Kipps again, who was now stooping down, pursuing the tale of his injuries.

"Here's the back of my trouser-leg all tore down," said Kipps, "and I believe I'm bleeding. You reely ought to be more careful—"

The stranger investigated the damage with a rapid movement. "Holy Smoke, so you are!" He laid a friendly hand on Kipps' arm. "I say—look here! Come up to my diggings and sew it up. I'm— Of course I'm to blame, and I say—" His voice sank to a confidential friendliness. "Here's a slop. Don't let on I ran you down. Haven't a lamp, you know. Might be a bit awkward, for *me*."

Kipps looked up towards the advancing policeman. The appeal to his generosity was not misplaced. He immediately took sides with his assailant. He stood as the representative of the law drew nearer. He assumed an air which he considered highly suggestive of an accident not having happened.

"All right," he said, "go on!"

"Right you are," said the cyclist, promptly, and led the way; and then, apparently with some idea of deception, called over his shoulder, "I'm tremendous glad to have met you, old chap.

"It really isn't a hundred yards," he said, after they had passed the policeman; "it's just round the corner."

"Of course," said Kipps, limping slightly. "I don't want to get a chap into trouble. Accidents *will* happen. Still—"

"Oh, *rather!* I believe you. Accidents *will* happen. Especially when you get *me* on a bicycle." He laughed. "You aren't the first I've run down, not by any manner of means! I don't think you can be hurt much either. It isn't as though I was scorching. You didn't see me coming. I was back-pedalling like anything. Only naturally it seems to you I must have been coming fast. And I did all I could to ease off the bump as I hit you. It was just the treadle, I think, came against your calf. But it was All Right of you about that policeman, you know. That was a Fair Bit of All Right. Under the Circs., if you'd told him I was riding, it might have been forty bob! Forty bob! I'd have had to tell 'em Time is Money just now for Mr. H. C.

"I shouldn't have blamed you either, you know. Most men, after a bump like that, might have been spiteful. The least I can do is to stand you a needle and thread. And a clothes' brush. It isn't everyone who'd have taken it like you.

"Scorching! Why, if I'd been scorching you'd have—coming as we did—you'd have been knocked silly.

"But, I tell you, the way you caught on about that show was something worth seeing. When I asked you—I didn't half expect it. Bif! Right off. Cool as a cucumber. Had your line at once. I tell you that there isn't many men would have acted as you have done, I *will* say that. You acted like a gentleman over that slop.''

Kipps' first sense of injury disappeared. He limped along a pace or so behind, making depreciatory noises in response to these flattering remarks, and taking stock of the very appreciative person who uttered them.

As they passed the lamps he was visible as a figure with a slight anterior plumpness, progressing buoyantly on knickerbockered legs, with quite enormous calves, legs that, contrasting with Kipps' own narrow practice, were even exuberantly turned out at the knees and toes. A cycling cap was worn very much on one side, and from beneath it protruded carelessly straight wisps of dark-red hair, and ever and again an ample nose came into momentary view round the corner. The muscular cheeks of this person and a certain generosity of chin he possessed were blue shaven, and he had no moustache. His carriage was spacious and confident, his gestures up and down the narrow, deserted back street they traversed were irresistibly suggestive of ownership; a succession of broadly gesticulating shadows were born squatting on his feet, and grew and took possession of the road and reunited at last with the shadows of the infinite, as lamp after lamp was passed. Kipps saw by the flickering light of one of them that they were in Little Fenchurch Street, and then they came round a corner sharply into a dark court and stopped at the door of a particularly ramshackle-looking little house, held up between two larger ones, like a drunken man between policemen.

The cyclist propped his machine carefully against the window, produced a key and blew down it sharply. ''The lock's a bit tricky,'' he said, and devoted himself for some moments to the task of opening the door. Some mechanical catastrophe ensued, and the door was open.

''You'd better wait here a bit while I get the lamp,'' he remarked to Kipps; ''very likely it isn't filled,'' and vanished into the blackness of the passage. ''Thank God for matches!'' he said; and Kipps had an impression of a passage in the transitory pink flare and the bicyclist disappearing into a further room. Kipps was so much interested by these things that for the time he forgot his injuries altogether.

An interval, and Kipps was dazzled by a pink-shaded kerosene lamp. ''You go in,'' said the red-haired man, ''and I'll bring in the bike,'' and for a moment Kipps was alone in the lamp-lit room. He took in rather vaguely the shabby ensemble of the little apartment, the round table covered with a torn, red, glass-stained cover on which the lamp stood, a mottled looking-glass over the fireplace, reflecting this, a disused gas-bracket, an extinct fire, a number of dusty postcards and memoranda stuck round the glass, a dusty, crowded paper-rack on the mantel with a number of cabinet photographs, a table littered with papers and cigarette ash, and a siphon of soda-water. Then the cyclist reappeared, and Kipps saw his blue-shaved, rather animated face, and bright, reddish-brown eyes for the first time. He was a man perhaps ten years older than Kipps, but his beardless face made them in a way contemporary.

''You behaved all right about that policeman, anyhow,'' he repeated as he came forward.

''I don't see 'ow else I could 'ave done,'' said Kipps, quite modestly. The cyclist scanned his guest for the first time, and decided upon hospitable details.

''We'd better let that mud dry a bit before we brush it. Whisky there is, good old Methusaleh, Canadian Rye; and there's some brandy that's all right. Which'll you have?''

''*I* dunno,'' said Kipps, taken by surprise; and then seeing no other course but acceptance, ''Well, whisky, then.''

"Right you are, old boy; and if you'll take my advice you'll take it neat. I may not be a particular judge of this sort of thing, but I do know old Methusaleh pretty well. Old Methusaleh—four stars. That's me! Good old Harry Chitterlow, and good old Methusaleh. Leave 'em together. Bif! He's gone!''

He laughed loudly, looked about him, hesitated, and retired, leaving Kipps in possession of the room, and free to make a more precise examination of its contents.

2

He particularly remarked the photographs that adorned the apartment. They were chiefly photographs of ladies, in one case in tights, which Kipps thought a "bit 'ot''; but one represented the bicyclist in the costume of some remote epoch. It did not take Kipps long to infer that the others were probably actresses and that his host was an actor, and the presence of the half of a large colored playbill seemed to confirm this. A note in an Oxford frame that was a little too large for it he presently demeaned himself to read. "Dear Mr. Chitterlow,'' it ran its brief course, "if, after all, you will send the play you spoke of, I will endeavor to read it,'' followed by a stylish but absolutely illegible signature, and across this was written in pencil, "What price Harry now?'' And in the shadow by the window was a rough and rather able sketch of the bicyclist in chalk on brown paper, calling particular attention to the curvature of the forward lines of his hull and calves and the jaunty carriage of his nose, and labeled unmistakably "Chitterlow.'' Kipps thought it "rather a take-off.'' The papers on the table by the siphon were in manuscript, Kipps observed, manuscript of a particularly convulsive and blottesque sort, and running obliquely across the page.

Presently he heard the metallic clamor as if of a series of irreparable breakages with which the lock of the front door discharged its function, and then Chitterlow reappeared, a little out of breath, and with a starry-labeled bottle in his large freckled hand.

"Sit down, old chap,'' he said, "sit down. I had to go out for it, after all. Wasn't a solitary bottle left. However, it's all right now we're here. No, don't sit on that chair, there's sheets of my play on that. That's the one—with the broken arm. I think this glass is clean, but, anyhow, wash it out with a squizz of siphon and shy it in the fireplace. Here, I'll do it! Lend it here!''

As he spoke Mr. Chitterlow produced a corkscrew from a table-drawer, attacked and overcame good old Methusaleh's cork in a style a bar-tender might envy, washed out two tumblers in his simple, effectual manner, and poured a couple of inches of the ancient fluid into each. Kipps took his tumbler, said "Thenks'' in an offhand way, and, after a momentary hesitation whether he should say "Here's to you!'' or not, put it to his lips without that ceremony. For a space fire in his throat occupied his attention to the exclusion of other matters, and then he discovered Mr. Chitterlow with an intensely bulldog pipe alight, seated on the opposite side of the empty fireplace, and pouring himself out a second dose of whisky.

"After all,'' said Mr. Chitterlow, with his eye on the bottle and a little smile wandering to hide amidst his larger features, "this accident might have been worse. I wanted someone to talk to a bit, and I didn't want to go to a pub, leastways not a Folkestone pub, because, as a matter of fact, I'd promised Mrs. Chitterlow, who's away, not to, for various reasons, though of course if I'd wanted to, I'm just that sort, I should have all the same—and here we are! It's curious how one runs up against people out bicycling!''

"Isn't it!" said Kipps, feeling that the time had come for him to say something.

"Here we are, sitting and talking like old friends, and half an hour ago we didn't know we existed. Leastways we didn't know each other existed. I might have passed you in the street perhaps, and you might have passed me, and how was I to tell that, put to the test, you would have behaved as decently as you have behaved. Only it happened otherwise, that's all. You're not smoking!'' he said. "Have a cigarette?''

Kipps made a confused reply that took the form of not minding if he did, and drank another sip of old Methusaleh in his confusion. He was able to follow the subsequent course of that sip for quite a long way. It was as though the old gentleman was brandishing a burning torch through his vitals, lighting him here and lighting him there, until at last his whole being was in a glow. Chitterlow produced a tobacco-pouch and cigarette-papers, and, with an interesting parenthesis that was a little difficult to follow about some lady, named Kitty something or other, who had taught him the art when he was as yet only what you might call a nice boy, made Kipps a cigarette, and, with a consideration that won Kipps' gratitude, suggested that, after all, he might find a little soda-water an improvement with the whisky. "Some people like it that way," said Chitterlow; and then with voluminous emphasis, *"I* don't.''

Emboldened by the weakened state of his enemy, Kipps promptly swallowed the rest of him, and had his glass at once hospitably replenished. He began to feel he was of a firmer consistency than he commonly believed, and turned his mind to what Chitterlow was saying with the resolve to play a larger part in the conversation than he had hitherto done. Also he smoked through his nose quite successfully, an art he had only very recently acquired.

Meanwhile, Chitterlow explained that he was a playwright, and the tongue of Kipps was unloosened to respond that he knew a chap, or rather one of their fellows knew a chap, or at least, to be perfectly correct, this fellow's brother did, who had written a play. In response to Chitterlow's inquiries, he could not recall the title of the play, nor where it had appeared, nor the name of the manager who produced it, though he thought the title was something about "Love's Ransom," or something like that.

"He made five 'undred pounds by it, though," said Kipps. "I know that.''

"That's nothing," said Chitterlow, with an air of experience that was extremely convincing. "Noth-ing. May seem a big sum to *you,* but *I* can assure you it's just what one gets any day. There's any amount of money, an-ny amount, in a good play.''

"I dessay," said Kipps, drinking.

"Any amount of money!''

Chitterlow began a series of illustrative instances. He was clearly a person of quite unequalled gift for monologue. It was as though some conversational dam had burst upon Kipps, and in a little while he was drifting along upon a copious rapid of talk about all sorts of theatrical things by one who knew all about them, and quite incapable of anticipating whither that rapid meant to carry him. Presently, somehow, they had got to anecdotes about well-known theatrical managers— little Teddy Bletherskite, artful old Chumps, and the magnificent Behemoth, "petted to death, you know, fair sickened, by all these society women.'' Chitterlow described various personal encounters with these personages, always with modest self-depreciation, and gave Kipps a very amusing imitation of old Chumps in a state of intoxication. Then he took two more stiff doses of old Methusaleh in rapid succession.

Kipps reduced the hither end of his cigarette to a pulp as he sat "dessaying" and "quite believing" Chitterlow in the sagest manner, and admiring the easy way in which he was getting on with this very novel and entertaining personage. He had another cigarette made for him, and then Chitterlow, assuming by insensible degrees more and more of the manner of a rich and successful playwright being interviewed by a young admirer, set himself to answer questions which sometimes Kipps asked, and sometimes Chitterlow, about the particulars and methods of his career. He undertook this self-imposed task with great earnestness and vigor, treating the matter, indeed, with such fulness that at times it seemed lost altogether under a thicket of parentheses, footnotes, and episodes that branched and budded from its stem. But it always emerged again, usually by way of illustration, to its own digressions. Practically it was a mass of material for the biography of a man who had been everywhere and done everything (including the Hon. Thomas Norgate, which was a Record), and in particular had acted with great distinction and profit (he dated various anecdotes, "when I was getting thirty, or forty, or fifty dollars a week") throughout America and the entire civilized world.

And as he talked on and on in that full, rich, satisfying voice he had, and as old Methusaleh, indisputably a most drunken old reprobate of a whisky, busied himself throughout Kipps, lighting lamp after lamp until the entire framework of the little draper was illuminated and glowing like some public building on a festival, behold Chitterlow, and Kipps with him, and the room in which they sat were transfigured! Chitterlow became in very truth that ripe full man of infinite experience and humor and genius, fellow of Shakespeare and Ibsen and Mæterlinck (three names he placed together quite modestly far above his own), and no longer ambiguously dressed in a sort of yachting costume with cycling knickerbockers, but elegantly if unconventionally attired, and the room ceased to be a small and shabby room in a Folkestone slum, and grew larger and more richly furnished, and the flyblown photographs were curious old pictures, and the rubbish on the walls the most rare and costly bric-à-brac, and the indisputable paraffin lamp a soft and splendid light. A certain youthful heat that to many minds might have weakened old Methusaleh's starry claim to a ripe antiquity vanished in that glamor; two burnt holes and a claimant darn in the table-cloth, moreover, became no more than the pleasing contradictions natural in the house of genius; and as for Kipps—Kipps was a bright young man of promise, distinguished by recent quick, courageous proceedings not too definitely insisted upon, and he had been rewarded by admission to a sanctum and confidences, for which the common prosperous, for which "society women" even, were notoriously sighing in vain. "Don't *want* them, my boy; they'd simply play old Harry with the Work, you know! Chaps outside, bank clerks and university fellows, think the life's all *that* sort of thing. Don't you believe 'em! Don't you believe 'em."

And then—!

"Boom . . . Boom . . . Boom . . . Boom . . ." right in the middle of a most entertaining digression on flats who join touring companies under the impression that they are actors, Kipps much amused at their flatness as exposed by Chitterlow.

"Lor!" said Kipps, like one who awakens, "that's not eleven!"

"Must be," said Chitterlow. "It was nearly ten when I got that whisky. It's early yet—"

"All the same, I must be going," said Kipps, and stood up. "Even now—may be. Fact is—I 'ad *no* idea. The 'ouse door shuts at 'arf-past ten, you know. I ought to 'ave thought before."

"Well, if you *must* go—! I tell you what. I'll come too. . . . Why! There's your leg, old man! Clean forgot it! You can't go through the streets like that. I'll sew up the tear. And meanwhile have another whisky."

"I ought to be getting on *now*," protested Kipps, feebly; and then Chitterlow was showing him how to kneel on a chair in order that the rent trouser leg should be attainable, and old Methusaleh on his third round was busy repairing the temporary eclipse of Kipps' arterial glow. Then suddenly Chitterlow was seized with laughter, and had to leave off sewing to tell Kipps that the scene wouldn't make a bad bit of business in a farcical comedy, and then he began to sketch out the farcical comedy, and that led him to a digression about another farcical comedy of which he had written a ripping opening scene which wouldn't take ten minutes to read. It had something in it that had never been done on the stage before, and was yet perfectly legitimate, namely, a man with a live beetle down the back of his neck trying to seem at his ease in a roomful of people. . . .

"*They* won't lock you out," he said, in a singularly reassuring tone, and began to read and act what he explained to be (not because he had written it, but simply because he knew it was so on account of his exceptional experience of the stage), and what Kipps also quite clearly saw to be, one of the best opening scenes that had ever been written.

When it was over, Kipps, who rarely swore, was inspired to say the scene was "damned fine" about six times over, whereupon, as if by way of recognition, Chitterlow took a simply enormous portion of the inspired antediluvian, declaring at the same time that he had rarely met a *"finer"* intelligence than Kipps' (stronger there might be, *that* he couldn't say with certainty as yet, seeing how little, after all, they had seen of each other, but a finer *never*), that it was a shame such a gallant and discriminating intelligence should be nightly either locked up or locked out at ten—well, ten-thirty, then—and that he had half a mind to recommend old somebody or other (apparently the editor of a London daily paper) to put on Kipps forthwith as a dramatic critic in the place of the current incapable.

"I don't think I've ever made up anything for print," said Kipps, "ever. I'd have a thundering good try, though, if ever I got a chance. I would that! I've written window tickets orfen enough. Made 'em up and everything. But that's different."

"You'd come to it all the fresher for not having done it before. And the way you picked up every point in that scene, my boy, was a Fair Treat! I tell you, you'd knock William Archer into fits. Not so literary, of course, you'd be, but I don't believe in literary critics any more than in literary playwrights. Plays *aren't* literature—that's just the point they miss. Plays are plays. No! That won't hamper you, anyhow. You're wasted down here, I tell you. Just as I was, before I took to acting. I'm hanged if I wouldn't like your opinion on these first two acts of that tragedy I'm on to. I haven't told you about that. It wouldn't take me more than an hour to read." . . .

3

Then, so far as he could subsequently remember, Kipps had "another," and then it would seem that, suddenly regardless of the tragedy, he insisted that he "really *must* be getting on," and from that point his memory became irregular. Certain things remained quite clearly, and as it is matter of common knowledge that intoxicated people forget what happens to them, it follows that he was not intoxicated. Chitterlow came with him, partly to see him home and partly for a freshener before turning in. Kipps recalled afterwards very distinctly how in Little Fenchurch Street he discovered that he could not walk straight, and also that Chitterlow's needle and thread in his still unmended trouser leg was making an annoying little noise on the pavement behind him. He tried to pick up the needle suddenly by surprise, and somehow tripped and fell, and then Chitterlow, laughing uproariously, helped him up. "It wasn't a bicycle this time, old boy," said Chitterlow, and that appeared to them both at the time as being a quite extraordinarily good joke indeed. They punched each other about on the strength of it.

For a time after that Kipps certainly pretended to be quite desperately drunk and unable to walk, and Chitterlow entered into the pretence and supported him. After that Kipps remembered being struck with the extremely laughable absurdity of going downhill to Tontine Street in order to go uphill again to the Emporium, and trying to get that idea into Chitterlow's head and being unable to do so on account of his own merriment and Chitterlow's evident intoxication; and his next memory after that was of the exterior of the Emporium, shut and darkened, and, as it were, frowning at him with all its stripes of yellow and green. The chilly way in which "SHALFORD" glittered in the moonlight printed itself with particular vividness on his mind. It appeared to Kipps that that establishment was closed to him forevermore. Those gilded letters, in spite of appearances, spelled FINIS for him and exile from Folkestone. He would never do woodcarving, never see Miss Walshingham again. Not that he had ever hoped to see her again. But this was the knife, this was final. He had stayed out, he had got drunk, there had been that row about the Manchester window dressing only three days ago. . . . In the retrospect he was quite sure that he was perfectly sober then and at bottom extremely unhappy, but he kept a brave face on the matter nevertheless, and declared stoutly he didn't care if he *was* locked out.

Whereupon Chitterlow slapped him on the back very hard and told him that was a "Bit of All-Right," and assured him that when he himself had been a clerk in Sheffield before he took to acting he had been locked out sometimes for six nights running.

"What's the result?" said Chitterlow. "I could go back to that place now, and they'd be glad to have me. . . . Glad to have me," he repeated, and then added, "That is to say, if they remember me—which isn't very likely."

Kipps asked a little weakly, "What am I to do?"

"Keep out," said Chitterlow. "You can't knock 'em up now—that would give you Right away. You'd better try and sneak in in the morning with the Cat. That'll do you. You'll probably get in all right in the morning if nobody gives you away."

Then for a time—perhaps as the result of that slap on the back—Kipps felt decidedly queer, and, acting on Chitterlow's advice, went for a bit of a freshener upon the Leas. After a time he threw off the temporary queerness, and found Chitterlow patting him on the shoulder and telling him that he'd be all right now in a minute and all the better for it—which he was. And the wind having dropped and the night being now a really very beautiful moonlight night indeed, and all before Kipps to spend as he liked, and with only a very little tendency to spin round now and again to mar its splendor, they set out to walk the whole length of the Leas to the Sandgate lift and back, and as they walked Chitterlow spoke first of moonlight transfiguring the sea and then of moonlight transfiguring faces, and so at last he came to the topic of Love, and upon that he dwelt a great while, and with a wealth of experience and illustrative anecdote that seemed remarkably pungent and material to Kipps. He forgot his lost Miss Walshingham and his outraged employer again. He became, as it were, a desperado by reflection.

Chitterlow had had adventures, a quite astonishing variety of adventures, in this direction; he was a man with a past, a really opulent past, and he certainly seemed to like to look back and see himself amidst its opulence.

He made no consecutive history, but he gave Kipps vivid momentary pictures of relations and entanglements. One moment he was in flight—only too worthily in flight—before the husband of a Malay woman in Cape Town. At the next he was having passionate complications with the daughter of a clergyman in York. Then he passed to a remarkable grouping at Seaford.

"They say you can't love two women at once," said Chitterlow. "But I tell you—" He gesticulated and raised his ample voice. "It's *Rot! Rot!*"

"*I* know that," said Kipps.

"Why, when I was in the smalls with Bessie Hopper's company there were Three." He laughed, and decided to add, "not counting Bessie, that is."

He set out to reveal Life as it is lived in touring companies, a quite amazing jungle of interwoven "affairs" it appeared to be, a mere amorous winepress for the crushing of hearts.

"People say this sort of thing's a nuisance and interferes with Work. I tell you it isn't. The Work couldn't go on without it. They *must* do it. They haven't the Temperament if they don't. If they hadn't the Temperament they wouldn't want to act; if they have—Bif!"

"You're right," said Kipps. "I see that."

Chitterlow proceeded to a close criticism of certain historical indiscretions of Mr. Clement Scott respecting the morals of the stage. Speaking in confidence, and not as one who addresses the public, he admitted regretfully the general truth of these comments. He proceeded to examine various typical instances that had almost forced themselves upon him personally, and with especial regard to the contrast between his own character towards women and that of the Hon. Thomas Norgate, with whom it appeared he had once been on terms of great intimacy. . . .

Kipps listened with emotion to these extraordinary recollections. They were wonderful to him, they were incredibly credible. This tumultuous passionate irregular course was the way life ran—except in high-class establishments! Such things happened in novels, in plays—only he had been fool enough not to understand they happened. His share in the conversation was now, indeed, no more than faint writing in the margin; Chitterlow was talking quite continuously. He expanded his magnificent voice into huge guffaws, he drew it together into a confidential intensity, it became drawlingly reminiscent, he was frank, frank with the effect of a revelation, reticent also with the effect of a revelation, a stupendously gesticulating moonlit black figure, wallowing in itself, preaching Adventure and the Flesh to Kipps. Yet withal shot with something of sentiment, with a sort of sentimental refinement very coarsely and egotistically done. The Times he had had!—even before he was as old as Kipps he had had innumerable Times.

Well, he said with a sudden transition, he had sown his wild oats—one had to sometime—and now, he fancied he had mentioned it earlier in the evening, he was happily married. She was, he indicated, a "born lady." Her father was a prominent lawyer, a solicitor in Kentish Town, "done a lot of public-house business"; her mother was second cousin to the wife of Abel Jones, the fashionable portrait painter—"almost Society people in a way." That didn't count with Chitterlow. He was no snob. What *did* count was that she possessed what he ventured to assert, without much fear of contradiction, was the very finest completely untrained contralto voice in all the world. ("But to hear it properly," said Chitterlow, "you want a Big Hall.") He became rather vague, and jerked his head about to indicate when and how he had entered matrimony. She was, it seemed, "away with her people." It was clear that Chitterlow did not get on with these people very well. It would seem they failed to appreciate his playwriting, regarding it as an unremunerative pursuit, whereas, as he and Kipps knew, wealth beyond the dreams of avarice would presently accrue. Only patience and persistence were needful.

He went off at a tangent to hospitality. Kipps must come down home with him. They couldn't wander about all night, with a bottle of the right sort pining at home for them. "You can sleep on the sofa. You won't be worried by broken springs, anyhow, for I took 'em all out myself two or three weeks ago. I don't see what they ever put 'em in for. It's a point I know about. I took particular notice of it when I was with Bessie Hopper. Three months we were, and all over England, North Wales, and the Isle of Man, and I never struck a sofa in diggings anywhere that hadn't a broken spring. Not once—all the time."

He added, almost absently, "It happens like that at times."

They descended the slant road towards Harbour Street and went on past the Pavilion Hotel.

4

They came into the presence of old Methusaleh again, and that worthy, under Chitterlow's direction, at once resumed the illumination of Kipps' interior with the conscientious thoroughness that distinguished him. Chitterlow took a tall portion to himself with an air of asbestos, lit the bulldog pipe again, and lapsed for a space into meditation, from which Kipps roused him by remarking that he expected "a nacter 'as a lot of ups and downs like, now and then."

At which Chitterlow seemed to bestir himself. "Ra-ther," he said. "And sometimes it's his own fault and sometimes it isn't. Usually it is. If it isn't one thing it's another. If it isn't the manager's wife it's bar-bragging. I tell you things happen at times. I'm a fatalist. The fact is, Character has you. You can't get away from it. You may think you do, but you don't."

He reflected for a moment. "It's that what makes tragedy. Psychology really. It's the Greek irony—Ibsen and—all that. Up to date."

He emitted this exhaustive summary of high-toned modern criticism as if he was repeating a lesson while thinking of something else; but it seemed to rouse him as it passed his lips, by including the name of Ibsen.

He became interested in telling Kipps, who was, indeed, open to any information whatever about this quite novel name, exactly where he thought Ibsen fell short, points where it happened that Ibsen was defective just where it chanced that he, Chitterlow, was strong. Of course, he had no desire to place himself in any way on an equality with Ibsen; still, the fact remained that his own experience in England and America and the colonies was altogether more extensive than Ibsen could have had. Ibsen had probably never seen "one decent bar scrap" in his life. That, of course, was not Ibsen's fault, or his own merit, but there the thing was. Genius, he knew, was supposed to be able to do anything or to do without anything; still, he was now inclined to doubt that. He had a play in hand that might perhaps not please William Archer—whose opinion, after all, he did not value as he valued Kipps' opinion—but which, he thought, was, at any rate, as well constructed as anything Ibsen ever did.

So with infinite deviousness Chitterlow came at last to his play. He decided he would not read it to Kipps, but tell him about it. This was the simpler, because much of it was still unwritten. He began to explain his plot. It was a complicated plot, and all about a nobleman who had seen everything and done everything and knew practically all that Chitterlow knew about women, that is to say, "all about women" and such-like matters. It warmed and excited Chitterlow. Presently he stood up to act a situation, which could not be explained. It was an extremely vivid situation.

Kipps applauded the situation vehemently. "Tha's dam fine," said the new dramatic critic, quite familiar with his part now, striking the table with his fist and almost upsetting his third portion (in the second series) of old Methusaleh. "Tha's *dam* fine, Chit'low!"

"You see it?" said Chitterlow, with the last vestiges of that incidental gloom disappearing. "Good old boy! I thought you'd see it. But it's just the sort of thing the literary critic can't see. However it's only a beginning—"

He replenished Kipps and proceeded with his exposition.

In a little while it was no longer necessary to give that over-advertised Ibsen the purely conventional precedence he had hitherto had. Kipps and Chitterlow were friends, and they could speak frankly and openly of things not usually admitted. "Any'ow," said Kipps, a little irrelevantly, and speaking over the brim of the replenishment, "what you read jus' now was dam fine. Nothing can't alter that."

He perceived a sort of faint buzzing vibration about things that was very nice and pleasant, and with a little care he had no difficulty whatever in putting his glass back on the table. Then he perceived Chitterlow was going on with the scenario, and then that old Methusaleh had almost entirely left his bottle. He was glad there was so little more Methusaleh to drink, because that would prevent his getting drunk. He knew that he was not now drunk, but he knew that he had had enough. He was one of those who always know when they have had enough. He tried to interrupt Chitterlow to tell him this, but he could not get a suitable opening. He doubted whether Chitterlow might not be one of those people who did not know when they had had enough. He discovered that he disapproved of Chitterlow. Highly. It seemed to him that Chitterlow went on and on like a river. For a time he was inexplicably and quite unjustly cross with Chitterlow, and wanted to say to him "you got the gift of the gab," but he only got so far as to say "the gift," and then Chitterlow thanked him and said he was better than Archer any day. So he eyed Chitterlow with a baleful eye until it dawned upon him that a most extraordinary thing was taking place. Chitterlow kept mentioning someone named Kipps. This presently began to perplex Kipps very gently. Dimly but decidedly he perceived this was wrong.

"Look 'ere," he said suddenly, *"what* Kipps?"

"This chap Kipps I'm telling you about."

"What chap Kipps you're telling which about?"

"I told you."

Kipps struggled with a difficulty in silence for a space. Then he reiterated firmly, *"What* chap Kipps?"

"This chap in my play—man who kisses the girl."

"Never kissed a girl," said Kipps, "leastways—" and subsided for a space. He could not remember whether he had kissed Ann or not—he knew he had meant to. Then suddenly, in a tone of great sadness, and addressing the hearth, he said, *"My* name's Kipps."

"Eh?" said Chitterlow.

"Kipps," said Kipps, smiling a little cynically.

"What about him?"

"He's me." He tapped his breastbone with his middle finger to indicate his essential self.

He leaned forward very gravely towards Chitterlow. "Look 'ere, Chit'low," he said. "You haven't no business putting my name into play. You mustn't do things like that. You'd lose me my crib, right away." And they had a little argument—so far as Kipps could remember. Chitterlow entered upon a general explanation of how he got his names. These he had, for the most part, got out of a newspaper that was still, he believed, "lying about." He even made to look for it, and while he was doing so Kipps went on with the argument, addressing himself more particularly to the photograph of the girl in tights. He said that at first her costume had not commended her to him, but now he perceived she had an extremely sensible face. He told her she would like Buggins if she met him, he could see she was just that sort. She would admit—all sensible people would admit—that using names in plays was wrong. You could, for example, have the law of him.

He became confidential. He explained that he was already in sufficient trouble for stopping out all night, without having his name put in plays. He was certain to be in the deuce of a row, the deuce of a row. Why had he done it? Why hadn't he gone at ten? Because one thing leads to another. One thing, he generalized, always does lead to another . . .

He was trying to tell her that he was utterly unworthy of Miss Walshingham, when Chitterlow gave up the search, and suddenly accused him of being drunk and talking "Rot—"

CHAPTER V

"Swapped!"

1

HE AWOKE ON the thoroughly comfortable sofa that had had all its springs removed, and although he had certainly not been intoxicated, he awoke with what Chitterlow pronounced to be, quite indisputably, a Head and a Mouth. He had slept in his clothes, and he felt stiff and uncomfortable all over, but the head and mouth insisted that he must not bother over little things like that. In the head was one large angular idea that it was physically painful to have there. If he moved his head, the angular idea shifted about in the most agonizing way. This idea was that he had lost his situation and was utterly ruined, and that it really mattered very little. Shalford was certain to hear of his escapade, and that, coupled with that row about the Manchester window—!

He raised himself into a sitting position under Chitterlow's urgent encouragement.

He submitted apathetically to his host's attentions. Chitterlow, who admitted being a "bit off it" himself and in need of an egg-cupful of brandy, just an egg-cupful neat, dealt with that Head and Mouth as a mother might deal with the fall of an only child. He compared it with other Heads and Mouths that he had met, and in particular to certain experienced by the Hon. Thomas Norgate. "Right up to the last," said Chitterlow, "he couldn't stand his liquor. It happens like that at times." And after Chitterlow had pumped on the young beginner's head and given him some anchovy paste piping hot on buttered toast, which he preferred to all the other remedies he had encountered, Kipps resumed his crumpled collar, brushed his clothes, tacked up his knee, and prepared to face Mr. Shalford and the reckoning for this wild unprecedented night—the first "night out" that ever he had taken.

Acting on Chitterlow's advice to have a bit of a freshener before returning to the Emporium, Kipps walked some way along the Leas and back, and then went down to a shop near the Harbour to get a cup of coffee. He found that extremely reinvigorating, and he went on up the High Street to face the inevitable terrors of the office, a faint touch of pride in his depravity tempering his extreme self-abasement. After all, it was not an unmanly headache; he had been out all night, and he had been drinking, and his physical disorder was there to witness the fact. If it wasn't for the thought of Shalford, he would have been even a proud man to discover himself at last in such a condition. But the thought of Shalford was very dreadful. He met two of the apprentices snatching a walk before shop began. At the sight of them he pulled his spirits together, put his hat back from his pallid brow, thrust his hands into his trousers pockets, and adopted an altogether more dissipated carriage; he met their innocent faces with a wan smile. Just for a moment he was glad that his patch at the knee was, after all, visible, and that some at least of the mud on his clothes had refused to move at Chitterlow's brushing. What wouldn't they think he had been up to? He passed them without speaking. He could imagine how they regarded his back. Then he recollected Mr. Shalford. . . .

The deuce of a row certainly, and perhaps—! He tried to think of plausible versions of the affair. He could explain he had been run down by rather a wild sort of fellow who was riding a bicycle, almost stunned for the moment (even now he felt the effects of the concussion in his head), and had been given whisky to restore him, and "the fact is, sir,"—with an upward inflection of the voice, an upward inflection of the eyebrows, and an air of its being the last thing one would have expected whisky to do, the manifestation indeed of a practically unique physiological weakness,—"it got into my '*ed*." . . .

Put like that it didn't look so bad.

He got to the Emporium a little before eight, and the housekeeper, with whom he was something of a favorite ("There's no harm in Mr. Kipps," she used to say), seemed to like him, if anything, better for having broken the rules, and gave him a piece of dry toast and a good hot cup of tea.

"I suppose the G. V.—" began Kipps.

"He knows," said the housekeeper.

He went down to shop a little before time, and presently Booch summoned him to the presence.

He emerged from the private office after an interval of ten minutes.

The junior clerk scrutinized his visage. Buggins put the frank question.

Kipps answered with one word.

"Swapped!" said Kipps.

2

Kipps leaned against the fixtures with his hands in his pockets and talked to the two apprentices under him.

"I don't care if I *am* swapped," said Kipps. "I been sick of Teddy and his System some time.

"I was a good mind to chuck it when my time was up," said Kipps. "Wish I 'ad now."

Afterwards Pearce came around, and Kipps repeated this.

"What's it for?" said Pearce. "That row about the window tickets?"

"No fear!" said Kipps, and sought to convey a perspective of splendid depravity. "I wasn't in las' night," he said, and made even Pearce, "man about town" Pearce, open his eyes.

"Why, where did you get to?" asked Pearce.

He conveyed that he had been "fair round the town." "With a Nactor chap I know.

"One can't *always* be living like a curit," he said.

"No fear," said Pearce, trying to play up to him.

But Kipps had the top place in that conversation.

"My lor!" said Kipps, when Pearce had gone, "but wasn't my mouth and 'ed bad this morning before I 'ad a pick-me-up!"

"Whad jer 'ave?"

"Anchovy on 'ot buttered toast. It's the very best pick-me-up there is. You trust me, Rodgers. I never take no other, and I don't advise you to. See?"

And when pressed for further particulars, he said again he had been "fair all *round* the town, with a Nactor chap" he knew. They asked curiously all he had done, and he said, "Well, what do *you* think?" And when they pressed for still further details, he said there were things little boys ought not to know, and laughed darkly, and found them some huckaback to roll.

And in this manner for a space did Kipps fend off the contemplation of the "key of the street" that Shalford had presented him.

3

This sort of thing was all very well when junior apprentices were about, but when Kipps was alone with himself it served him not at all. He was uncomfortable inside, and his skin was uncomfortable, and the Head and Mouth, palliated perhaps, but certainly not cured, were still with him. He felt, to tell the truth, nasty and dirty, and extremely disgusted with himself. To work was dreadful, and to stand still and think still more dreadful. His patched knee reproached him. These were the second best of his three pairs of trousers, and they had cost him thirteen and sixpence. Practically ruined they were. His dusting pair was unfit for shop, and he would have to degrade his best. When he was under inspection he affected the slouch of a desperado, but directly he found himself alone, this passed insensibly into the droop.

The financial aspect of things grew large before him. His whole capital in the world was the sum of five pounds in the Post Office Savings Bank, and four and sixpence cash. Besides, there would be two months' "screw." His little tin box upstairs was no longer big enough for his belongings, he would have to buy another, let alone that it was not calculated to make a good impression in a new "crib." Then there would be paper and stamps needed in some abundance for answering advertisements and railway fares when he went "crib hunting." He would have to write letters, and he never wrote letters. There was spelling, for example, to consider. Probably if nothing turned up before his month was up, he would have to go home to his Uncle and Aunt.

How would they take it? . . .

For the present, at any rate, he resolved not to write to them.

Such disagreeable things as this it was that lurked below the fair surface of Kipps' assertion, "I been wanting a change. If 'e 'adn't swapped me, I should very likely 'ave swapped 'im."

In the perplexed privacies of his own mind he could not understand how everything had happened. He had been the Victim of Fate, or at least of one as inexorable—Chitterlow. He tried to recall the successive steps that had culminated so disastrously. They were difficult to recall. . . .

Buggins that night abounded in counsel and reminiscence.

"Curious thing," said Buggins, "but every time I've had the swap I've never believed I should get another Crib—never. But I have," said Buggins. "Always. So don't lose heart, whatever you do.

"Whatever you do," said Buggins, "keep hold of your collars and cuffs— shirts if you can, but collars anyhow. Spout them last. And anyhow, it's summer! You won't want your coat. . . . You got a good umbrella. . . .

"You'll no more get a shop from New Romney than—anything. Go straight up to London, get the cheapest room you can find—and hang out. Don't eat too much. Many a chap's put his prospects in his stomach. Get a cup o' coffee and a slice—egg if you like—but remember you got to turn up at the Warehouse tidy. The best places *now*, I believe, are the old cabmen's eating houses. Keep your watch and chain as long as you can. . . .

"There's lots of shops going," said Buggins. "Lots!"

And added reflectively, "But not this time of year perhaps."

He began to recall his own researches. " 'Stonishing lot of chaps you see," lhe said. "All sorts. Look like Dukes some of 'em. High hat. Patent boots. Frock-coat. All there. All right for a West End crib. Others—Lord! It's a caution, Kipps. Boots been inked in some reading-rooms—*I* used to write in a Reading Room in Fleet Street, regular penny club—hat been wetted, collar frayed, tail-coat buttoned up, black chest-plaster tie—spread out. Shirt, you know, gone—" Buggins pointed upward with a pious expression.

"No shirt, I expect?"

"Eat it," said Buggins.

Kipps meditated. "I wonder where old Minton is," he said at last. "I often wondered about 'im."

4

It was the morning following Kipps' notice of dismissal that Miss Walshingham came into the shop. She came in with a dark, slender lady, rather faded, rather tightly dressed, whom Kipps was to know some day as her mother. He discovered them in the main shop, at the counter of the ribbon department. He had come to the opposite glove counter with some goods enclosed in a parcel that he had unpacked in his own department. The two ladies were both bent over a box of black ribbon.

He had a moment of tumultuous hesitations. The etiquette of the situation was incomprehensible. He put down his goods very quietly and stood, hands on counter, staring at these two ladies. Then, as Miss Walshingham sat back, the instinct of flight seized him. . . .

He returned to his Manchester shop wildly agitated. Directly he was out of sight of her he wanted to see her. He fretted up and down the counter, and addressed some snappish remarks to the apprentice in the window. He fumbled for a moment with a parcel, untied it needlessly, began to tie it up again, and then bolted back again into the main shop. He could hear his own heart beating.

The two ladies were standing in the manner of those who have completed their purchases and are waiting for their change. Mrs. Walshingham regarded some remnants with impersonal interest; Helen's eyes searched the shop. They distinctly lit up when they discovered Kipps.

He dropped his hands to the counter by habit, and stood for a moment regarding her awkwardly. What would she do? Would she cut him? She came across the shop to him.

"How are *you*, Mr. Kipps?" she said, in her clear distinct tones, and she held out her hand.

"Very well, thank you," said Kipps; "how are you?"

She said she had been buying some ribbon.

He became aware of Mrs. Walshingham very much surprised. This checked something allusive about the class, and he said instead that he supposed she was glad to be having her holidays now. She said she was, it gave her more time for reading and that sort of thing. He supposed that she would be going abroad, and she thought that perhaps they *would* go to Knocke or Bruges for a time.

Then came a pause, and Kipps' soul surged within him. He wanted to tell her he was leaving and would never see her again. He could find neither words nor voice to say it. The swift seconds passed. The girl in the ribbons was handing Mrs. Walshingham her change. "Well," said Miss Walshingham, "good-bye," and gave him her hand again.

Kipps bowed over her hand. His manners, his counter manners, were the easiest she had ever seen upon him. She turned to her mother. It was no good now, no good. Her mother! You couldn't say a thing like that before her mother! All was lost but politeness. Kipps rushed for the door. He stood at the door bowing with infinite gravity, and she smiled and nodded as she went out. She saw nothing of the struggle within him, nothing but a gratifying emotion. She smiled like a satisfied goddess as the incense ascends.

Mrs. Walshingham bowed stiffly and a little awkwardly.

He remained holding the door open for some seconds after they had passed out, then rushed suddenly to the back of the "costume" window to watch them go down the street. His hands tightened on the window-rack as he stared. Her mother appeared to be asking discreet questions. Helen's bearing suggested the offhand replies of a person who found the world a satisfactory place to live in. "Really, Mumsie, you cannot expect me to cut my own students dead," she was, in fact, saying. . . .

They vanished round Henderson's corner.

Gone! And he would never see her again—never!

It was as though someone had struck his heart with a whip. Never! Never! Never! And she didn't know! He turned back from the window, and the department, with its two apprentices, was impossible. The whole glaring world was insupportable.

He hesitated, and made a rush, head down, for the cellar that was his Manchester warehouse. Rogers asked him a question that he pretended not to hear.

The Manchester warehouse was a small cellar apart from the general basement of the building, and dimly lit by a small gas flare. He did not turn that up, but rushed for the darkest corner, where, on the lowest shelf, the Sale window-tickets were stored. He drew out the box of these with trembling hands and upset them on the floor, and so having made himself a justifiable excuse for being on the ground with his head well in the dark, he could let his poor bursting little heart have its way with him for a space.

And there he remained until the cry of "Kipps! Forward!" summoned him once more to face the world.

CHAPTER VI

The Unexpected

1

NOW IN THE slack of that same day, after the midday dinner and before the coming of the afternoon customers, this disastrous Chitterlow descended upon Kipps with the most amazing coincidence in the world. He did not call formally, entering and demanding Kipps, but privately, in a confidential and mysterious manner.

Kipps was first aware of him as a dark object bobbing about excitedly outside the hosiery window. He was stooping and craning and peering in the endeavor to see into the interior between and over the socks and stockings. Then he transferred his attention to the door, and after a hovering scrutiny, tried the baby-linen display. His movements and gestures suggested a suppressed excitement.

Seen by daylight, Chitterlow was not nearly such a magnificent figure as he had been by the subdued nocturnal lightings and beneath the glamor of his own interpretation. The lines were the same, indeed, but the texture was different. There was a quality about the yachting cap, an indefinable finality of dustiness, a shiny finish on all the salient surfaces of the reefer coat. The red hair and the profile, though still forcible and fine, were less in the quality of Michelangelo and more in that of the merely picturesque. But it was a bright brown eye still that sought amidst the interstices of the baby-linen.

Kipps was by no means anxious to interview Chitterlow again. If he had felt sure that Chitterlow would not enter the shop, he would have hid in the warehouse until the danger was past, but he had no idea of Chitterlow's limitations. He decided to keep up the shop in the shadows until Chitterlow reached the side window of the Manchester department, and then to go outside as if to inspect the condition of the window and explain to him that things were unfavorable to immediate intercourse. He might tell him he had already lost his situation. . . .

"Ullo, Chit'low," he said, emerging.

"Very man I want to see," said Chitterlow, shaking with vigor. "Very man I want to see." He laid a hand on Kipps' arm. "How *old* are you, Kipps?"

"One and twenty," said Kipps. "Why?"

"Talk about coincidences! And your name, now? Wait a minute." He held out a finger. "*Is* it Arthur?"

"Yes," said Kipps.

"You're the man," said Chitterlow.

"What man?"

"It's about the thickest coincidence I ever struck," said Chitterlow, plunging his extensive hand into his breast-coat pocket. "Half a jiff and I'll tell you your mother's Christian name." He laughed and struggled with his coat for a space, produced a washing-book and two pencils, which he deposited in his side pocket, then in one capacious handful, a bent but by no means finally disabled cigar, the rubber proboscis of a bicycle pump, some twine and a lady's purse, and finally a small pocket-book, and from this, after dropping and recovering several visiting-cards, he extracted a carelessly torn piece of newspaper. "Euphemia," he read, and brought his face close to Kipps'. "Eh?" He laughed noisily. "It's about as fair a Bit of All Right as anyone *could* have—outside a coincidence play. Don't say her name wasn't Euphemia, Kipps, and spoil the whole blessed show.''

"Whose name—Euphemia?" asked Kipps.

"Your mother's."

"Lemme see what it says on the paper."

Chitterlow handed him the fragment and turned away. "You may say what you like," he said, addressing a vast deep laugh to the street generally.

Kipps attempted to read. "WADDY or KIPPS. If Arthur Waddy or Arthur Kipps, the son of Margaret Euphemia Kipps, who—"

Chitterlow's finger swept over the print. "I went down the column, and every blessed name that seemed to fit my play I took. I don't believe in made-up names. As I told you. I'm all with Zola in that. Documents whenever you can. I like 'em hot and real. See? Who was Waddy?"

"Never heard his name."

"Not Waddy?"

"No!"

Kipps tried to read again, and abandoned the attempt. "What does it mean?" he said. "I don't understand."

"It means," said Chitterlow, with a momentary note of lucid exposition, "so far as I can make out, that you're going to strike it Rich. Never mind about the Waddy—that's a detail. What does it usually mean? You'll hear of something to your advantage—very well. I took that newspaper up to get my names by the merest chance. Directly I saw it again and read that—I knew it was you. I believe in coincidences. People say they don't happen. *I* say they do. Everything's a coincidence. Seen properly. Here you are. Here's one! Incredible? Not a bit of it! See? It's you! Kipps! Waddy be damned! It's a Mascot. There's luck in my play. Bif! You're there. *I'm* there. Fair *in* it! Snap!" And he discharged his fingers like a pistol. "Never you mind about the 'Waddy.' "

"Eh?" said Kipps, with a nervous eye on Chitterlow's fingers.

"You're all right," said Chitterlow, "you may bet the seat of your only breeches on that! Don't you worry about the Waddy—that's as clear as day. You're about as right side up as a billiard ball . . . whatever you do. Don't stand there gaping, man! Read the paper if you don't believe me. Read it!"

He shook it under Kipps' nose.

Kipps became aware of the second apprentice watching them from the shop. His air of perplexity gave place to a more confident bearing.

"—'who was born at East Grinstead.' I certainly was born there. I've 'eard my Aunt say—"

"I knew it," said Chitterlow, taking hold of one edge of the paper and bringing his face close alongside Kipps'.

"—on September the first, eighteen hundred and seventy-eight—"

"That's all right," said Chitterlow. "It's all, all right, and all you have to do is to write to Watson and Bean and get it—"

"Get what?"

"Whatever it is."

Kipps sought his moustache. "You'd write?" he asked.

"Ra-ther."

"But what d'you think it is?"

"That's the fun of it!" said Chitterlow, taking three steps in some as yet uninvented dance. "That's where the joke comes in. It may be anything—it may be a million. If so! Where does little Harry come in? Eh?"

Kipps was trembling slightly. "But—" he said, and thought. "If you was me—" he began. "About that Waddy—?"

He glanced up and saw the second apprentice disappear with amazing swiftness from behind the goods in the window.

"What?" asked Chitterlow, but he never had an answer.

"Lor! There's the guv'nor!" said Kipps, and made a prompt dive for the door.

He dashed in, only to discover that Shalford, with the junior apprentice in attendance, had come to mark off remnants of Kipps' cotton dresses, and was demanding him. "Hullo, Kipps," he said, "outside—?"

"Seein' if the window was straight, sir," said Kipps.

"Umph!" said Shalford.

For a space Kipps was too busily employed to think at all of Chitterlow or the crumpled bit of paper in his trouser pocket. He was, however, painfully aware of a suddenly disconnected excitement at large in the street. There came one awful moment when Chitterlow's nose loomed interrogatively over the ground glass of the department door, and his bright little red-brown eye sought for the reason of Kipps' disappearance, and then it became evident that he saw the high light of Shalford's baldness, and grasped the situation and went away. And then Kipps (with that advertisement in his pocket) was able to come back to the business in hand.

He became aware that Shalford had asked a question. "Yessir, nosir, rightsir. I'm sorting up zephyrs tomorrow, sir," said Kipps.

Presently he had a moment to himself again, and, taking up a safe position behind a newly unpacked pile of summer lace curtains, he straightened out the piece of paper and re-perused it. It was a little perplexing. That "Arthur Waddy or Arthur Kipps"—did that imply two persons or one? He would ask Pearce or Buggins. Only—

It had always been impressed upon him that there was something demanding secrecy about his mother.

"Don't you answer no questions about your mother," his aunt had been wont to say. "Tell them you don't know, whatever it is they ask you."

"Now, this—?"

Kipps' face became portentously careful, and he tugged at his moustache, such as it was, hard.

He had always represented his father as being a "gentleman farmer." "It didn't pay," he used to say, with a picture in his own mind of a penny magazine aristocrat prematurely worn out by worry. "I'm a Norfan, both sides," he would explain, with the air of one who had seen trouble. He said he lived with his uncle and aunt, but he did not say that they kept a toy-shop, and to tell anyone that his uncle had been a butler—*a servant!*—would have seemed the maddest of indiscretions. Almost all the assistants in the Emporium were equally reticent and vague, so great is their horror of "Lowness" of any sort. To ask about this "Waddy or Kipps" would upset all these little fictions. He was not, as a matter of fact, perfectly clear about his real status in the world (he was not, as a matter of fact, perfectly clear about anything), but he knew that there was a quality about his status that was—detrimental.

Under the circumstances—?

It occurred to him that it would save a lot of trouble to destroy the advertisement there and then.

In which case he would have to explain to Chitterlow!

"Eng!" said Mr. Kipps.

"Kipps!" cried Carshot, who was shopwalking. "Kipps Forward!"

He thrust back the crumpled paper into his pocket, and sallied forth to the customer.

"I want," said the customer, looking vaguely about her through glasses, "a little bit of something to cover a little stool I have. Anything would do—a remnant or anything."

The matter of the advertisement remained in abeyance for half an hour, and at the end the little stool was still a candidate for covering, and Kipps had a thoroughly representative collection of the textile fabrics in his department to clear away. He was so angry about the little stool that the crumpled advertisement lay for a space in his pocket, absolutely forgotten.

2

Kipps sat on his tin box under the gas-bracket that evening, and looked up the name Euphemia, and learned what it meant in the "Inquire Within About Everything" that constituted Buggins' reference library. He hoped Buggins, according to his habit, would ask him what he was looking for, but Buggins was busy turning out his week's washing. "Two collars," said Buggins, "half pair socks, two dickeys. Shirt? . . . M'm. There ought to be another collar somewhere."

"Euphemia," said Kipps at last, unable altogether to keep to himself this suspicion of a high origin that floated so delightfully about him, "Eu-phemia; it isn't a name *common* people would give to a girl, is it?"

"It isn't the name any decent people would give to a girl," said Buggins, "common or not."

"Lor!" said Kipps. "Why?"

"It's giving girls names like that," said Buggins, "that nine times out of ten makes 'em go wrong. It unsettles 'em. If ever I was to have a girl, if ever I was to have a dozen girls, I'd call 'em all Jane. Every one of 'em. You couldn't have a better name than that. Euphemia indeed! What next? . . . Good Lord! . . . That isn't one of my collars there, is it, under your bed?"

Kipps got him the collar.

"I don't see no great 'arm in Euphemia," he said as he did so.

After that he became restless. "I'm a good mind to write that letter," he said; and then, finding Buggins preoccupied wrapping his washing up in the "1/2 sox," added to himself, "a thundering good mind."

So he got his penny bottle of ink, borrowed the pen from Buggins, and with no very serious difficulty in spelling or composition, did as he had resolved.

He came back into the bedroom about an hour afterwards, a little out of breath and pale. "Where you been?" said Buggins, who was now reading the *Daily World Manager,* which came to him in rotation from Carshot.

"Out to post some letters," said Kipps, hanging up his hat.

"Crib hunting?"

"Mostly," said Kipps.

"Rather," he added with a nervous laugh; "what else?"

Buggins went on reading. Kipps sat on his bed and regarded the back of the *Daily World Manager* thoughtfully.

"Buggins," he said at last.

Buggins lowered his paper and looked.

"I say, Buggins, what do these here advertisements mean that say so-and-so will hear of something greatly to his advantage?"

"Missin' people," said Buggins, making to resume reading.

"How d'yer mean?" asked Kipps. "Money left, and that sort of thing?"

Buggins shook his head. "Debts," he said, "more often than not."

"But that ain't to his advantage."

"They put that to get 'old of 'em," said Buggins. "Often it's wives."

"What you mean?"

"Deserted wives try and get their husbands back that way."

"I suppose it *is* legacies sometimes, eh? Perhaps, if someone was left a hundred pounds by someone—"

"Hardly ever," said Buggins.

"Well, 'ow—?" began Kipps, and hesitated.

Buggins resumed reading. He was very much excited by a leader on Indian affairs. "By Jove!" he said, "it won't do to give these here Blacks votes."

"No fear," said Kipps.

"They're different altogether," said Buggins. "They 'aven't the sound sense of Englishmen, and they 'aven't the character. There's a sort of tricky dishonesty about 'em—false witness and all that—of which an Englishman has no idea. Outside their courts of law—it's a pos'tive fact, Kipps—there's witnesses waitin' to be 'ired. Reg'lar trade. Touch their 'ats as you go in. Englishmen 'ave no idea, I tell you—not ord'nary Englishmen. It's in their blood. They're too timid to be honest. Too slavish. They aren't used to being free like we are, and if you gave 'em freedom they wouldn't make a proper use of it. Now, *we*—Oh, *Damn!*"

For the gas had suddenly gone out, and Buggins had the whole column of Society Club Chat still to read.

Buggins could talk of nothing after that but Shalford's meanness in turning off the gas, and after being extremely satirical about their employer, undressed in the dark, hit his bare toe against a box, and subsided, after unseemly ejaculations, into silent ill-temper.

Though Kipps tried to get to sleep before the affair of the letter he had just posted resumed possession of his mind, he could not do so. He went over the whole thing again, quite exhaustively.

Now that his first terror was abating, he couldn't quite determine whether he was glad or sorry that he had posted that letter. If it *should* happen to be a hundred pounds!

It *must* be a hundred pounds!

If it was he could hold out for a year, for a couple of years even, before he got a Crib.

Even if it was fifty pounds—!

Buggins was already breathing regularly when Kipps spoke again. *"Buggins,"* he said.

Buggins pretended to be asleep, and thickened his regular breathing (a little too hastily) to a snore.

"I say, Buggins," said Kipps, after an interval.

"What's up now?" said Buggins, unamiably.

"S'pose *you* saw an advertisement in a paper, with your name in it, see, asking you to come and see someone, like, so as to hear of something very much to your—"

"Hide," said Buggins, shortly.

"But—"

"I'd hide."

"Er?"

"Goo'-night, o' man," said Buggins, with convincing earnestness. Kipps lay still for a long time, then blew profoundly, turned over and stared at the other side of the dark.

He had been a fool to post that letter!

Lord! *Hadn't* he been a fool!

3

It was just five days and a half after the light had been turned out while Buggins was reading, that a young man with a white face, and eyes bright and wide open, emerged from a side road upon the Leas front. He was dressed in his best clothes, and, although the weather was fine, he carried his umbrella, just as if he had been to church. He hesitated, and turned to the right. He scanned each house narrowly as he passed it, and presently came to an abrupt stop. "Hughenden," said the gateposts in firm black letters, and the fanlight in gold repeated "Hughenden." It was a stucco house, fit to take your breath away, and its balcony was painted a beautiful sea green, enlivened with gilding. He stood looking up at it.

"Gollys!" he said at last in an awe-stricken whisper.

It had rich-looking crimson curtains to all the lower windows, and brass-railed blinds above. There was a splendid tropical plant in a large artistic pot in the drawing-room window. There was a splendid bronzed knocker (ring also) and two bells—one marked "servants."

"Gollys! *Servants*, eh?"

He walked past away from it with his eyes regarding it, and then turned and came back. He passed through a further indecision, and finally drifted away to the sea front, and sat down on a seat a little way along the Leas and put his arm over the back and regarded "Hughenden." He whistled an air very softly to himself, put his head first on one side and then on the other. Then for a space he scowled fixedly at it.

A very stout old gentleman with a very red face and very protuberant eyes sat down beside Kipps, removed a Panama hat of the most abandoned desperado cut, and mopped his brow and blew. Then he began mopping the inside of his hat. Kipps watched him for a space, wondering how much he might have a year, and where he bought his hat. Then "Hughenden" reasserted itself.

An impulse overwhelmed him. "I say," he said, leaning forward to the old gentleman.

The old gentleman started and stared.

"*What* did you say?" he asked fiercely.

"You wouldn't think," said Kipps, indicating with his forefinger, "that that 'ouse there belongs to me."

The old gentleman twisted his neck round to look at "Hughenden." Then he came back to Kipps, looked at his mean little garments with apoplectic intensity, and blew at him by way of reply.

"It does," said Kipps, a little less confidently.

"Don't be a Fool," said the old gentleman, and put his hat on and wiped out the corners of his eyes. "It's hot enough," panted the old gentleman, indignantly, "without Fools." Kipps looked from the old gentleman to the house, and back to the old gentleman. The old gentleman looked at Kipps, and snorted and looked out to sea, and again, snorting very contemptuously, at Kipps.

"Mean to say it doesn't belong to me?" said Kipps.

The old gentleman just glanced over his shoulder at the house in dispute, and then fell to pretending Kipps didn't exist. "It's been lef' me this very morning," said Kipps. "It ain't the only one that's been lef' me, neither."

"Aw!" said the old gentleman, like one who is sorely tried. He seemed to expect the passers-by presently to remove Kipps.

"It 'as," said Kipps. He made no further remark to the old gentleman for a space, but looked with a little less certitude at the house. . . .

"I got—" he said, and stopped.

"It's no good telling you if you don't believe," he said.

The old gentleman, after a struggle with himself, decided not to have a fit. "Try that game on with me," he panted. "Give you in charge."

"What game?"

"Wasn't born yesterday," said the old gentleman, and blew. "Besides," he added, "*Look* at you!

"I know you," said the old gentleman, and coughed shortly, and nodded to the horizon, and coughed again.

Kipps looked dubiously from the house to the old gentleman, and back to the house. Their conversation, he gathered, was over.

Presently he got up and went slowly across the grass to its stucco portal again. He stood, and his mouth shaped the precious word, "Hughenden." It was all *right!* He looked over his shoulder as if in appeal to the old gentleman, then turned and went his way. The old gentleman was so evidently past all reason!

He hung for a moment some distance along the parade, as though some invisible string was pulling him back. When he could no longer see the house from the pavement he went out into the road. Then with an effort he snapped the string.

He went on down a quiet side street, unbuttoned his coat furtively, took out three bank-notes in an envelope, looked at them, and replaced them. Then he fished up five new sovereigns from his trouser pocket and examined them. To such a confidence had his exact resemblance to his dead mother's portrait carried Messrs. Watson and Bean.

It was right enough.

It really was *all* right.

He replaced the coins with grave precaution, and went his way with a sudden briskness. It was all right—he had it now—he was a rich man at large. He went up a street and round a corner and along another street, and started towards the Pavilion, and changed his mind and came round back, resolved to go straight to the Emporium and tell them all.

He was aware of someone crossing a road far off ahead of him, someone curiously relevant to his present extraordinary state of mind. It was Chitterlow. Of course, it was Chitterlow who had told him first of the whole thing! The playwright was marching buoyantly along a cross-street. His nose was in the air, the yachting-cap was on the back of his head, and the large freckled hand grasped two novels from the library, a morning newspaper, a new hat done up in paper, and a lady's net bag full of onions and tomatoes. . . .

He passed out of sight behind the wine-merchant's at the corner, as Kipps decided to hurry forward and tell him of the amazing change in the Order of the Universe that had just occurred.

Kipps uttered a feeble shout, arrested as it began, and waved his umbrella. Then he set off at a smart pace in pursuit. He came round the corner, and Chitterlow had gone; he hurried to the next, and there was no Chitterlow; he turned back unavailingly, and his eyes sought some other possible corner. His hand fluttered to his mouth, and he stood for a space on the pavement edge, staring about him. No good!

But the sight of Chitterlow was a wholesome thing, it connected events together, joined him on again to the past at a new point, and that was what he so badly needed. . . .

It was all right—all right.

He became suddenly very anxious to tell everybody at the Emporium, absolutely everybody, all about it. That was what wanted doing. He felt that telling was the thing to make this business real. He gripped his umbrella about the middle, and walked very eagerly.

He entered the Emporium through the Manchester department. He flung open the door (over whose ground glass he had so recently, in infinite apprehension, watched the nose of Chitterlow), and discovered the second apprentice and Pearce in conversation. Pearce was prodding his hollow tooth with a pin and talking in fragments about the distinctive characteristics of Good Style.

Kipps came up in front of the counter.

"I say," he said. "What d'yer think?"

"What?" said Pearce over the pin.

"Guess."

"You've slipped out because Teddy's in London."

"Something more."

"What?"

"Been left a fortune."

"Garn!"

"I 'ave."

"Get out!"

"Straight. I been lef' twelve 'undred pounds—twelve 'undred pounds a year!"

He moved towards the little door out of the department into the house, moving, as heralds say, *regardant passant*. Pearce stood with mouth wide open and pin poised in air. "No!" he said at last.

"It's right," said Kipps, "and I'm going."

And he fell over the doormat into the house.

4

It happened that Mr. Shalford was in London buying summer sale goods, and, no doubt, also interviewing aspirants to succeed Kipps.

So that there was positively nothing to hinder a wild rush of rumor from end to end of the Emporium. All the masculine members began their report with the same formula. "Heard about Kipps?"

The new girl in the cash desk had had it from Pearce, and had dashed out into the fancy shop to be the first with the news on the fancy side. Kipps had been left a thousand pounds a year—twelve thousand pounds a year. Kipps had been left twelve hundred thousand pounds. The figures were uncertain, but the essential facts they had correct. Kipps had gone upstairs. Kipps was packing his box. He said he wouldn't stop another day in the old Emporium not for a thousand pounds! It was said that he was singing ribaldry about old Shalford.

He had come down! He was in the counting-house. There was a general movement thither. (Poor old Buggins had a customer, and couldn't make out what the deuce it was all about! Completely out of it, was Buggins.)

There was a sound of running to and fro, and voices saying this, that, and the other thing about Kipps. Ring-a-dinger, ring-a-dinger went the dinner-bell, all unheeded. The whole of the Emporium was suddenly bright-eyed, excited, hungry to tell somebody, to find at any cost somebody who didn't know, and be first to tell them, "Kipps has been left thirty—forty—fifty thousand pounds!"

"What!" cried the senior porter, "Him!" and ran up to the counting-house as eagerly as though Kipps had broken his neck.

"One of our chaps just been left sixty thousand pounds," said the first apprentice, returning after a great absence, to his customer.

"Unexpectedly?" said the customer.

"Quite," said the first apprentice. . . .

"I'm sure if Anyone deserves it, it's Mr. Kipps," said Miss Mergle; and her train rustled as she hurried to the counting-house.

There stood Kipps amidst a pelting shower of congratulations. His face was flushed, and his hair disordered. He still clutched his hat and best umbrella in his left hand. His right hand was anyone's to shake rather than his own. (Ring-a-dinger, ring-a-dinger ding, ding, ding, dang you!" went the neglected dinner-bell.)

"Good old Kipps!" said Pearce, shaking. "Good old Kipps!"

Booch rubbed one anemic hand upon the other. "You're sure it's all right, Mr. Kipps?" he said in the background.

"I'm sure we all congratulate him," said Miss Mergle.

"Great Scott!" said the new young lady in the glove department. "Twelve hundred a year! Great Scott! You aren't thinking of marrying anyone, are you, Mr. Kipps?"

"Three pounds five and ninepence a day," said Mr. Booch, working in his head almost miraculously. . . .

Everyone, it seemed, was saying how glad they were it was Kipps, except the junior apprentice, upon whom—he being the only son of a widow, and used to having the best of everything as a right—an intolerable envy, a sense of unbearable wrong, had cast its gloomy shade. All the rest were quite honestly and simply glad—gladder, perhaps, at that time than Kipps, because they were not so overpowered. . . .

Kipps went downstairs to dinner, emitting fragmentary disconnected statements. "Never expected anything of the sort. . . . When this here old Bean told me, you could have knocked me down with a feather. . . . He says, 'You ben lef' money.' Even then I didn't expect it'd be more'n a hundred pounds, perhaps. Something like that."

With the sitting down to dinner and the handing of plates, the excitement assumed a more orderly quality. The housekeeper emitted congratulations as she carved, and the maidservant became dangerous to clothes with the plates—she held them anyhow; one expected to see one upside-down, even—she found Kipps so fascinating to look at. Everyone was the brisker and hungrier for the news (except the junior apprentice), and the housekeeper carved with unusual liberality. It was High Old Times there under the gaslight, High Old Times. "I'm sure if Anyone deserves it," said Miss Mergle—"pass the salt, please—it's Mr. Kipps."

The babble died away a little as Carshot began barking across the table at Kipps. "You'll be a bit of a Swell, Kipps," he said. "You won't hardly know yourself."

"Quite the gentleman," said Miss Mergle.

"Many real gentlemen's families," said the housekeeper, "have to do with less."

"See you on the Leas," said Carshot. "My—!" He met the housekeeper's eye. She had spoken about that expression before. "My eye!" he said, tamely, lest words should mar the day.

"You'll go to London, I reckon," said Pearce. "You'll be a man about town. We shall see you mashing 'em, with violets in your button'ole, down the Burlington Arcade."

"One of these West End Flats. That'd be *my* style," said Pearce. "And a first class club."

"Aren't these Clubs a bit 'ard to get into?" asked Kipps, open-eyed over a mouthful of potato.

"No fear. Not for Money," said Pearce. And the girl in the laces, who had acquired a cynical view of Modern Society from the fearless exposures of Miss Marie Corelli, said, "Money goes everywhere nowadays, Mr. Kipps."

But Carshot showed the true British strain.

"If I was Kipps," he said, pausing momentarily for a knifeful of gravy, "I should go to the Rockies and shoot bears."

"I'd certainly 'ave a run over to Boulogne," said Pearce, "and look about a bit. I'm going to do that next Easter myself, anyhow—see if I don't."

"Go to Oireland, Mr. Kipps," came the soft insistence of Biddy Murphy, who managed the big work-room, flushed and shining in the Irish way as she spoke. "Go to Oireland. Ut's the loveliest country in the world. Outside currs. Fishin', shootin', huntin'. An' pretty gals! Eh! You should see the Lakes of Killarney, Mr. Kipps!" And she expressed ecstasy by a facial pantomime, and smacked her lips.

And presently they crowned the event.

It was Pearce who said, "Kipps, you ought to stand Sham!"

And it was Carshot who found the more poetical word "Champagne."

"Rather!" said Kipps, hilariously; and the rest was a question of detail and willing emissaries. "Here it comes!" they said, as the apprentice came down the staircase. "How about the shop?" said someone. "Oh, *hang* the shop!" said Carshot; and made gruntulous demands for a corkscrew with a thing to cut the wire. Pearce, the dog! had a wire-cutter in his pocket-knife. How Shalford would have stared at the gold-tipped bottles if he had chanced to take an early train! Bang went the corks, and bang! Gluck, gluck, gluck, and sizzle!

When Kipps found them all standing about him under the gas-flare, saying almost solemnly "Kipps!" with tumblers upheld, "Have it in tumblers," Carshot had said, "have it in tumblers. It isn't a wine like you have in glasses. Not like port and sherry. It cheers you up, but you don't get drunk. It isn't hardly stronger than lemonade. They drink it at dinner, some of 'em, every day."

"What! At three and six a bottle!" said the housekeeper, incredulously.

"*They* don't stick at *that*," said Carshot. "Not the champagne sort."

The housekeeper pursed her lips and shook her head. . . . .

When Kipps, I say, found them all standing up to toast him in that manner, there came such a feeling in his throat and face that for the life of him he scarcely knew for a moment whether he was not going to cry. "Kipps!" they all said, with kindly eyes. It was very good of them, and hard there wasn't a stroke of luck for them all!

But the sight of upturned chins and glasses pulled him together again. . . . .

They did him honor. Unenviously and freely they did him honor.

For example, Carshot, being subsequently engaged in serving cretonne, and desiring to push a number of rejected blocks up the counter in order to have space for measuring, swept them by a powerful and ill-calculated movement of the arm, with a noise like thunder, partly onto the floor, and partly onto the foot of the still gloomily preoccupied junior apprentice. And Buggins, whose place it was to shopwalk while Carshot served, shopwalked with quite unparalleled dignity, dangling a new season's sunshade with a crooked handle on one finger. He arrested each customer who came down the shop with a grave and penetrating look. "Showing very tractive line new sheasons sunshade," he would remark; and after a suitable pause, " 'Markable thing, one our 'sistant leg'sy twelve 'undred a year. Very tractive. Nothing more to-day, mum? No!" And he would then go and hold the door open for them with perfect decorum, and with the sunshade dangling elegantly from his left hand. . . .

And the second apprentice, serving a customer with cheap ticking, and being asked suddenly if it was strong, answered remarkably—

"Oo, *no,* mum! Strong! Why, it ain't 'ardly stronger than lemonade." . . .

The head porter, moreover, was filled with a virtuous resolve to break the record as a lightning packer, and make up for lost time. Mr. Swaffenham of the Sandgate Riviera, for example, who was going out to dinner that night at seven, received at half-past six, instead of the urgently needed dress shirt he expected, a corset specially adapted to the needs of persons inclined to embonpoint. A parcel of summer underclothing selected by the elder Miss Waldershawe was somehow distributed in the form of gratis additions throughout a number of parcels of a less intimate nature, and a box of millinery on approval to Lady Pamshort (at Wampachs) was enriched by the addition of the junior porter's cap. . . .

These little things, slight in themselves, witness perhaps none the less eloquently to the unselfish exhilaration felt throughout the Emporium at the extraordinary and unexpected enrichment of Mr. Kipps.

5

The bus that plies between New Romney and Folkestone is painted a British red, and inscribed on either side with the word "Tip-top" in gold amidst voluptuous scrolls. It is a slow and portly bus; even as a young bus it must have been slow and portly. Below it swings a sort of hold, hung by chains between the wheels, and in the summer time the top has garden seats. The front over those two dauntless unhurrying horses rises in tiers like a theater; there is first a seat for the driver and his company, and above that a seat, and above that, unless my memory plays me false, a seat. You sit in a sort of composition by some Italian painter—a celestial group of you. There are days when this bus goes, and days when it doesn't go—you have to find out. And so you get to New Romney. So you will continue to get to New Romney for many years, for the light railway concession along the coast is happily in the South Eastern Railway Company's keeping, and the peace of the marsh is kept inviolate save for the bicycle bells of such as Kipps and I. This bus it was, this ruddy, venerable and, under God's mercy, immortal bus, that came down the Folkestone hill with unflinching deliberation, and trundled through Sandgate and Hythe, and out into the windy spaces of the Marsh, with Kipps and all his fortunes on its brow.

You figure him there. He sat on the nighest seat diametrically above the driver, and his head was spinning and spinning with champagne and this stupendous Tomfoolery of Luck; and his heart was swelling, swelling indeed at times as though it would burst him, and his face towards the sunlight was transfigured. He said never a word, but ever and again, as he thought of this or that, he laughed. He seemed full of chuckles for a time, detached and independent chuckles, chuckles that rose and burst on him like bubbles in a wine. . . . He held a banjo scepter-fashion and resting on his knee. He had always wanted a banjo, now he had got one at Melchior's, while he was waiting for the bus.

There sat beside him a young servant, who was sucking peppermint, and a little boy with a sniff whose flitting eyes showed him curious to know why ever and again Kipps laughed, and beside the driver were two young men in gaiters talking about "tegs." And there sat Kipps, all unsuspected, twelve hundred a year, as it were, except for the protrusion of the banjo, disguised as a common young man. And the young man in gaiters to the left of the driver eyed Kipps and his banjo, and especially his banjo, ever and again, as if he found it and him, with his rapt face, an insoluble enigma. And many a King has ridden into a conquered city with a lesser sense of splendor than Kipps.

Their shadows grew long behind them, and their faces were transfigured in gold as they rumbled on towards the splendid west. The sun set before they had passed Dymchurch, and as they came lumbering into New Romney past the windmill the dusk had come.

The driver handed down the banjo and the portmanteau, and Kipps having paid him, "That's aw right," he said to the change, as a gentleman should, turned about, and ran the portmanteau smartly into old Kipps, whom the sound of the stopping of the bus had brought to the door of the shop in an aggressive mood and with his mouth full of supper.

" 'Ullo Uncle; didn't see you," said Kipps.

"Blunderin' ninny," said old Kipps. "What's brought *you* here? Ain't early closing, is it? Not Toosday?"

"Got some news for you, Uncle," said Kipps, dropping the portmanteau.

"Ain't lost your situation, 'ave you? What's that you got there? I'm blowed if it ain't a banjo. Goolord! Spendin' your money on banjoes! Don't put down your portmanty there—anyhow. Right in the way of everybody. I'm blowed if ever I saw such a boy as you've got lately. Here! Molly! And look here! What you got a portmanty for? Why! Goolord! You ain't *really* lost your place, 'ave you?"

"Somethin's happened," said Kipps, slightly dashed. "It's all right, Uncle. I'll tell you in a minute."

Old Kipps took the banjo as his nephew picked up the portmanteau again.

The living-room door opened quickly, showing a table equipped with elaborate simplicity of supper, and Mrs. Kipps appeared.

"If it ain't young Artie!" she said. "Why, whatever's brought *you* 'ome?"

" 'Ullo, Aunt," said Artie. "I'm coming in. I got somethin' to tell you. I've 'ad a bit of luck."

He wouldn't tell them all at once. He staggered with the portmanteau round the corner of the counter, set a bundle of children's tin pails into clattering oscillation, and entered the little room. He deposited his luggage in the corner beside the tall clock, and turned to his Aunt and Uncle again. His aunt regarded him doubtfully; the yellow light from the little lamp on the table escaped above the shade, and lit her forehead and the tip of her nose. It would be all right in a minute. He wouldn't tell them all at once. Old Kipps stood in the shop door with the banjo in his hand, breathing noisily. "The fact is, Aunt, I've 'ad a bit of Luck."

"You ain't been backin' gordless 'orses, Artie?" she asked.

"No fear."

"It's a draw he's been in," said Old Kipps, still panting from the impact of the portmanteau, "it's a dratted draw. Jest look here, Molly. He's won this 'ere trashy banjer and throwd up his situation on the strength of it—that's what he's done. Goin' about singing. Dash and plunge. Jest the very fault poor Pheamy always 'ad. Blunder right in, and no one mustn't stop 'er!''

"You ain't thrown up your place, Artie, 'ave you?'' said Mrs. Kipps.

Kipps perceived his opportunity. "I 'ave,'' he said; "I've throwed it up.''

"What for?'' said Old Kipps.

"So's to learn the banjo!''

"Goo *Lord!'* '' said Old Kipps, in horror to find himself verified.

"I'm going about playing,'' said Kipps, with a giggle. "Goin' to black my face, Aunt, and sing on the beach. I'm going to 'ave a most tremenjous lark and earn any amount of money—you see. Twenty six fousand pounds I'm going to earn just as easy as nothing!''

"Kipps,'' said Mrs. Kipps, "he's been drinking!''

They regarded their nephew across the supper table with long faces. Kipps exploded with laughter, and broke out again when his aunt shook her head very sadly at him. Then suddenly he fell grave. He felt he could keep it up no longer. "It's all right, Aunt. Reely. I ain't mad, and I ain't been drinking. I been lef' money. I been left twenty-six fousand pounds.''

Pause.

"And you thrown up your place?'' said Old Kipps.

"Yes,'' said Kipps. "Rather!''

"And bort this banjer, put on your best noo trousers, and come right on 'ere?''

"Well,'' said Mrs. Kipps, "*I*—never—did!''

"These ain't my noo trousers, Aunt,'' said Kipps, regretfully. "My noo trousers wasn't done.''

"I shouldn't ha' thought that *even you* could ha' been such a fool as that,'' said Old Kipps.

Pause.

"It's *all* right,'' said Kipps, a little disconcerted by their distrustful solemnity. "It's all right—reely! Twenny-six thousan' pounds. And a 'ouse.''

Old Kipps pursed his lips and shook his head.

"A 'ouse on the Leas. I could have gone there. Only I didn't. I didn't care to. I didn't know what to say. I wanted to come and tell you.''

"How d'yer know the 'ouse—''

"They told me.''

"Well,'' said Old Kipps, and nodded his head portentously towards his nephew, with the corners of his mouth pulled down in a strikingly discouraging way. "Well, you *are* a young Gaby.''

"I didn't *think* it of you, Artie!'' said Mrs. Kipps.

"Wadjer mean?'' asked Kipps, faintly, looking from one to the other with a withered face.

Old Kipps closed the shop door. "They been 'avin' a lark with you,'' said Old Kipps, in a mournful undertone. "That's what I mean, my boy. They jest been seein' what a Gaby like you 'ud do.''

"I dessay that young Quodling was in it,'' said Mrs. Kipps. " 'E's jest that sort.''

(For Quodling of the green-baize bag had grown up to be a fearful dog, the terror of New Romney.)

"It's somebody after your place very likely,'' said Old Kipps.

Kipps looked from one skeptical reproving face to the other, and round him at the familar shabby little room, with his familiar cheap portmanteau on the mended chair, and that banjo amidst the supper-things like some irrevocable deed. Could he be rich indeed? Could it be that these things had really happened? Or had some insane fancy whirled him hither?

Still—perhaps a hundred pounds—

"But," he said. "It's all right, reely, Uncle. You don't think—? I 'ad a letter."

"Got up," said Old Kipps.

"But I answered it and went to a norfis."

Old Kipps felt staggered for a moment, but he shook his head and chins sagely from side to side. As the memory of old Bean and Shalford's revived, the confidence of Kipps came back to him.

"I saw an old gent, Uncle—perfect gentleman. And 'e told me all about it. Mos' respectable 'e was. Said 'is name was Watson and Bean—leastways 'e was Bean. Said it was lef' me"—Kipps suddenly dived into his breast pocket—"by my Grandfather—"

The old people started.

Old Kipps uttered an exclamation and wheeled round towards the mantelshelf, above which the daguerreotype of his lost younger sister smiled its fading smile upon the world.

"Waddy, 'is name was," said Kipps, with his hand still deep in his pocket. "It was 'is son was my father—"

"Waddy!" said Old Kipps.

"Waddy!" said Mrs. Kipps.

"She'd never say," said Old Kipps.

There was a long silence.

Kipps fumbled with a letter, a crumpled advertisement and three bank-notes. He hesitated between these items.

"Why! That young chap what was arsting questions—" said Old Kipps, and regarded his wife with an eye of amazement.

"Must 'ave been," said Mrs. Kipps.

"Must 'ave been," said Old Kipps.

"James," said Mrs. Kipps, in an awe-stricken voice. "After all—perhaps—It's true!"

"'*Ow* much did you say?" asked Old Kipps. " 'Ow much did you say 'e'd lef' you, me b'y?"

It was thrilling, though not quite in the way Kipps had expected. He answered almost meekly across the meager supper-things, with his documentary evidence in his hand—

"Twelve 'undred pounds. Proximately, he said. Twelve 'undred pounds a year. 'E made 'is will jest before 'e died—not more'n a month ago. When 'e was dying, 'e seemed to change like, Mr. Bean said. 'E'd never forgiven 'is son, never—not till then. 'Is son 'ad died in Australia, years and years ago, and *then* 'e 'adn't forgiven 'im. You know—'is son what was my father. But jest when 'e was ill and dying 'e seemed to get worried like, and longing for someone of 'is own. And 'e told Mr. Bean it was 'im that had prevented them marrying. So 'e thought. That's 'ow it all come about. . . ."

6

At last Kipps' flaring candle went up the narrow uncarpeted staircase to the little attic that had been his shelter and refuge during all the days of his childhood and youth. His head was whirling. He had been advised, he had been warned, he had been flattered and congratulated, he had been given whisky and hot water and lemon and sugar, and his health had been drunk in the same. He had also eaten two Welsh rarebits—an unusual supper. His Uncle was chiefly for his going into Parliament, his Aunt was consumed with a great anxiety. "I'm afraid he'll go and marry beneath 'im."

"Y'ought to 'ave a bit o' shootin' somewheer," said Old Kipps.

"It's your *duty* to marry into a county family, Artie—remember that."

"There's lots of young noblemen'll be glad to 'eng onto you," said Old Kipps. "You mark my words. And borry your money. And then good day to ye."

"I got to be precious careful," said Kipps. "Mr. Bean said that."

"And you got to be precious careful of this old Bean," said Old Kipps. "We may be out of the world in Noo Romney, but I've 'eard a bit about solicitors for all that. You keep your eye on old Bean, me b'y.

" 'Ow do we know what 'e's up to, with your money, even now?" said Old Kipps, pursuing this uncomfortable topic.

" 'E *looked* very respectable," said Kipps.

Kipps undressed with great deliberation and with vast gaps of pensive margin. Twenty-six thousand pounds!

His aunt's solicitude had brought back certain matters into the foreground that his "Twelve 'undred a year!" had for a time driven away altogether. His thoughts went back to the woodcarving class. Twelve Hundred a Year. He sat on the edge of the bed in profound meditation, and his boots fell "whop" and "whop" upon the floor, with a long interval between each "whop." Twenty-six thousand pounds. "By Gum!" He dropped the remainder of his costume about him on the floor, got into bed, pulled the patchwork quilt over him, and put his head on the pillow that had been first to hear of Ann Pornick's accession to his heart. But he did not think of Ann Pornick now.

It was about everything in the world except Ann Pornick that he seemed to be trying to think of—simultaneously. All the vivid happenings of the day came and went in his overtaxed brain—"that old Bean" explaining and explaining, the fat man who wouldn't believe, an overpowering smell of peppermint, the banjo, Miss Mergle saying he deserved it, Chitterlow vanishing round a corner, the wisdom and advice and warnings of his Aunt and Uncle. She was afraid he would marry beneath him, *was* she? She didn't know. . . .

His brain made an excursion into the woodcarving class and presented Kipps with the picture of himself amazing that class by a modest yet clearly audible remark, "I been left twenty-six thousand pounds." Then he told them all quietly but firmly that he had always loved Miss Walshingham—always, and so he had brought all his twenty-six thousand pounds with him to give to her there and then. He wanted nothing in return. . . . Yes, he wanted nothing in return. He would give it to her all in an envelope and go. Of course he would keep the banjo—and a little present for his Aunt and Uncle—and a new suit perhaps— and one or two other things she would not miss. He went off at a tangent. He might buy a motor-car, he might buy one of these here things that will play you a piano—that would make old Buggins sit up! He could pretend he had learned to play—he might buy a bicycle and a cyclist suit. . . .

A terrific multitude of plans of what he might do, and in particular of what he might buy, came crowding into his brain, and he did not so much fall asleep as pass into a disorder of dreams in which he was driving a four-horse Tip-Top coach down Sandgate Hill ("I shall have to be precious careful"), wearing innumerable suits of clothes, and through some terrible accident wearing them all wrong. Consequently, he was being laughed at. The coach vanished in the interest of the costume. He was wearing golfing suits and a silk hat. This passed into a nightmare that he was promenading on the Leas in a Highland costume, with a kilt that kept shrinking, and Shalford was following him with three policemen. "He's my assistant," Shalford kept repeating; "he's escaped. He's an escaped Improver. Keep by him, and in a minute you'll have to run him in. I know 'em. We say they wash, but they won't." . . . He could feel the kilt creeping up his legs. He would have tugged at it to pull it down, only his arms were paralyzed. He had an impression of giddy crises. He uttered a shriek of despair. *"Now!"* said Shalford. He woke in horror, his quilt had slipped off the bed.

He had a fancy he had just been called, that he had somehow overslept himself and missed going down for dusting. Then he perceived it was still night, and light by reason of the moonlight, and that he was no longer in the Emporium. He wondered where he could be. He had a curious fancy that the world had been swept and rolled up like a carpet, and that he was nowhere. It occurred to him that perhaps he was mad. "Buggins!" he said. There was no answer, not even the defensive snore. No room, no Buggins, nothing!

Then he remembered better. He sat on the edge of his bed for some time. Could anyone have seen his face, they would have seen it white, and drawn with staring eyes. Then he groaned weakly. "Twenty-six thousand pounds!" he whispered.

Just then it presented itself in an almost horribly overwhelming mass.

He remade his bed and returned to it. He was still dreadfully wakeful. It was suddenly clear to him that he need never trouble to get up punctually at seven again. That fact shone out upon him like a star through clouds. He was free to lie in bed as long as he liked, get up when he liked, go where he liked; have eggs every morning for breakfast, or rashers, or bloater-paste, or . . . Also he was going to astonish Miss Walshingham. . . .

Astonish her and astonish her. . . .

He was awakened by a thrush singing in the fresh dawn. The whole room was flooded with warm golden sunshine. "I say!" said the thrush. "I say! I say! Twelve 'undred a year! Twelve 'Undred a Year! Twelve 'UNDRED a Year! I say! I say! I say!"

He sat up in bed and rubbed the sleep from his eyes with his knuckles. Then he jumped out of bed and began dressing very eagerly. He did not want to lose any time in beginning the new life.

BOOK II
Mr. Coote the Chaperon

CHAPTER I

The New Conditions

1

THERE COMES A gentlemanly figure into these events, and for a space takes a leading part therein, a Good Influence, a refined and amiable figure, Mr. Chester Coote. You must figure him as about to enter our story, walking with a curious rectitude of bearing through the evening dusk towards the Public Library, erect, large-headed—he had a great big head, full of the suggestion of a powerful mind well under control—with a large official-looking envelope in his white and knuckly hand. In the other he carries a gold-handled cane. He wears a silken gray jacket suit, buttoned up, and anon he coughs behind the official envelope. He has a prominent nose, slaty gray eyes, and a certain heaviness about the mouth. His mouth hangs breathing open, with a slight protrusion of the lower jaw. His straw hat is pulled down a little in front, and he looks each person he passes in the eye, and, directly his look is answered, looks away.

Thus Mr. Chester Coote, as he was on the evening when he came upon Kipps. He was a local house-agent, and a most active and gentlemanly person, a conscious gentleman, equally aware of society and the serious side of life. From amateur theatricals of a nice refined sort to science classes, few things were able to get along without him. He supplied a fine full bass, a little flat and quavery perhaps, but very abundant, to the St. Stylites' choir. . . .

He goes on towards the Public Library, lifts the envelope in salutation to a passing curate, smiles and enters. . . .

It was in the Public Library that he came upon Kipps.

By that time Kipps had been rich a week or more, and the change in his circumstances was visible upon his person. He was wearing a new suit of drab flannels, a Panama hat, and a red tie for the first time, and he carried a silver-mounted stick with a tortoiseshell handle. He felt extraordinarily different, perhaps more different than he really was, from the meek Improver of a week ago. He felt as he felt Dukes must feel, yet at bottom he was still modest. He was leaning on his stick and regarding the indicator with a respect that never palled. He faced round to meet Mr. Coote's overflowing smile.

"What are you doang hea?" asked Mr. Chester Coote.

Kipps was momentarily abashed. "Oh," he said slowly, and then, "Mooching round a bit."

That Coote should address him with this easy familiarity was a fresh reminder of his enhanced social position. "Jest mooching round," he said. "I been back in Folkestone free days now. At my 'ouse, you know."

"Ah!" said Mr. Coote. "I haven't yet had an opportunity of congratulating you on your good fortune."

Kipps held out his hand. "It was the cleanest surprise that ever was," he said. "When Mr. Bean told me of it—you could have knocked me down with a feather."

"It must mean a tremendous change for you."

"0-o. Rather. Change? Why, I'm like the chap in the song they sing, I don't 'ardly know where I are. *You* know."

"An extraordinary change," said Mr. Coote. "I can quite believe it. Are you stopping in Folkestone?"

"For a bit. I got a 'ouse, you know. What my gran'father 'ad. I'm stopping there. His housekeeper was kep' on. Fancy—being in the same town and everything!"

"Precisely," said Mr. Coote. "That's it," and coughed like a sheep behind four straight fingers.

"Mr. Bean got me to come back to see to things. Else I was out in New Romney, where my Uncle and Aunt live. But it's a Lark coming back. In a way . . ."

The conversation hung for a moment.

"Are you getting a book?" asked Coote.

"Well, I 'aven't got a ticket yet. But I shall get one all right, and have a go in at reading. I've often wanted to. Rather. I was just 'aving a look at this Indicator. First-class idea. Tells you all you want to know."

"It's simple," said Coote, and coughed again, keeping his eyes fixed on Kipps. For a moment they hung, evidently disinclined to part. Then Kipps jumped at an idea he had cherished for a day or more—not particularly in relation to Coote, but in relation to anyone.

"You doing anything?" he asked.

"Just called with a papah about the classes."

"Because— Would you care to come up and look at my 'ouse and 'ave a smoke and a chat—eh?" He made indicative back jerks of the head, and was smitten with a horrible doubt whether possibly this invitation might not be some hideous breach of etiquette. Was it, for example, the correct hour? "I'd be awfully glad if you would," he added.

Mr. Coote begged for a moment while he handed the official-looking envelope to the librarian, and then declared himself quite at Kipps' service. They muddled a moment over precedence at each door they went through, and so emerged to the street.

"It feels awful rum to me at first, all this," said Kipps. " 'Aving a 'ouse of my own—and all that. It's strange, you know. 'Aving all day. Reely I don't 'ardly know what to do with my time.

"D'ju smoke?" he said suddenly, proffering a magnificent gold-decorated, pigskin cigarette-case, which he produced from nothing, almost as though it was some sort of trick. Coote hesitated and declined, and then with great liberality, "Don't let me hinder you . . ."

They walked a little way in silence, Kipps being chiefly concerned to affect ease in his new clothes and keeping a wary eye on Coote. "It's rather a big windfall," said Coote, presently. "It yields you an income—?"

"Twelve 'undred a year," said Kipps. "Bit over—if anything."

"Do you think of living in Folkestone?"

"Don't know 'ardly yet. I *may*. Then again, I may not. I got a furnished 'ouse, but I may let it."

"Your plans are undecided?"

"That's jest it," said Kipps.

"Very beautiful sunset it was tonight," said Coote, and Kipps said, "Wasn't it?" and they began to talk of the merits of sunsets. Did Kipps paint? Not since he was a boy. He didn't believe he could now. Coote said his sister was a painter, and Kipps received this intimation with respect. Coote sometimes wished he could find time to paint himself, but one couldn't do everything, and Kipps said that was "jest it."

They came out presently upon the end of the Leas, and looked down to where the squat, dark masses of the harbor and harbor station, gemmed with pinpoint lights, crouched against the twilit gray of the sea. "If one could do *that*," said Coote; and Kipps was inspired to throw his head back, cock it on one side, regard the harbor with one eye shut and say that it would take some doing. Then Coote said something about "Abend," which Kipps judged to be in a foreign language, and got over by lighting another cigarette from his by no means completed first one. "You're right—*puff, puff.*"

He felt that so far he had held up his end of the conversation in a very creditable manner, but that extreme discretion was advisable.

They turned away, and Coote remarked that the sea was good for crossing, and asked Kipps if he had been over the water very much. Kipps said he hadn't been—"much," but he thought very likely he'd have a run over to Boulogne soon; and Coote proceeded to talk of the charms of foreign travel, mentioning quite a number of unheard-of places by name. He had been to them! Kipps remained on the defensive, but behind his defenses his heart sank. It was all very well to pretend, but presently it was bound to come out. *He* didn't know anything of all this. . . .

So they drew near the house. At his own gate Kipps became extremely nervous. It was a fine impressive door. He knocked neither a single knock nor a double, but about one and a half—an apologetic half. They were admitted by an irreproachable housemaid with a steady eye, before which Kipps cringed dreadfully. He hung up his hat and fell about over hall chairs and things. "There's a fire in the study, Mary?" he had the audacity to ask, though evidently he knew, and led the way upstairs panting. He tried to shut the door, and discovered the housemaid behind him coming to light his lamp. This enfeebled him further. He said nothing until the door closed behind her. Meanwhile, to show his *sangfroid,* he hummed and flitted towards the window and here and there.

Coote went to the big hearthrug and turned and surveyed his host. His hand went to the back of his head and patted his occiput—a gesture frequent with him.

" 'Ere we are," said Kipps, hands in his pockets, and glancing round him.

It was a gaunt, Victorian room, with a heavy, dirty cornice, and the ceiling enriched by the radiant plaster ornament of an obliterated gas chandelier. It held two large glass-fronted bookcases, one of which was surmounted by a stuffed terrier encased in glass. There was a mirror over the mantel, and hangings and curtains of magnificent crimson patternings. On the mantel were a huge black clock of classical design, vases in the Burslem Etruscan style, spills and toothpicks in large receptacles of carved rock, large lava ash-trays, and an exceptionally big box of matches. The fender was very great and brassy. In a favorable position under the window was a spacious rosewood writing-desk, and all the chairs and other furniture were of rosewood and well stuffed.

"This," said Kipps, in something near an undertone, "was the o' gentleman's study—my grandfather that was. 'E used to sit at that desk and write."

"Books?"

"No. Letters to the *Times* and things like that. 'E's got 'em all cut out—stuck in a book. . . . Leastways he *'ad*. It's in that bookcase. . . . Won't you sit down?"

Coote did, blowing very slightly, and Kipps secured his vacated position on the extensive black-skin rug. He spread out his legs compass fashion, and tried to appear at his ease. The rug, the fender, the mantel and mirror, conspired with great success to make him look a trivial and intrusive little creature amidst their commonplace hauteur, and his own shadow on the opposite wall seemed to think everything a great lark, and mocked and made tremendous fun of him. . . .

2

For a space Kipps played a defensive game, and Coote drew the lines of the conversation. They kept away from the theme of Kipps' change of fortune, and Coote made remarks upon local and social affairs. "You must take an interest in these things now," was as much as he said in the way of personalities. But it speedily became evident that he was a person of wide and commanding social relationships. He spoke of "society" being mixed in the neighborhood, and of the difficulty of getting people to work together and "do" things; they were cliquish. Incidentally he alluded quite familiarly to men with military titles, and once even to someone with a title, a Lady Punnet. Not snobbishly, you understand, nor deliberately, but quite in passing. He had, it appeared, talked to Lady Punnet about private theatricals! In connection with the Hospitals. She had been unreasonable, and he had put her right—gently, of course, but firmly. "If you stand up to these people," said Coote, "they like you all the better." It was also very evident he was at his ease with the clergy; "my friend Mr. Densemore—a curate, you know, and rather curious, the Reverend *and* Honourable." Coote grew visibly in Kipps' eyes as he said these things; he became, not only the exponent of "Vagner or Vargner," the man whose sister had painted a picture to be exhibited at the Royal Academy, the type of the hidden thing called culture, but a delegate, as it were, or at least an intermediary from that great world "up there," where there were men-servants, where there were titles, where people dressed for dinner, drank wine at meals, wine costing very often as much as three and sixpence the bottle, and followed through a maze of etiquette, the most stupendous practices. . . .

Coote sat back in the armchair smoking luxuriously and expanding pleasantly with the delightful sense of *savoir faire;* Kipps sat forward, his elbows on his chair arm, alert, and his head a little on one side. You figure him as looking little and cheap, and feeling smaller and cheaper amidst his new surroundings. But it was a most stimulating and interesting conversation. And soon it became less general, and more serious and intimate. Coote spoke of people who had got on, and of people who hadn't; of people who seemed to be in everything, and people who seemed to be out of everything; and then he came round to Kipps.

"You'll have a good time," he said abruptly, with a smile that would have interested a dentist.

"I dunno," said Kipps.

"There's mistakes, of course."

"That's jest it."

Coote lit a new cigarette. "One can't help being interested in what you will do,'' he remarked. "Of course—for a young man of spirit, come suddenly into wealth—there's temptations.''

"I got to go careful,'' said Kipps. "'O' Bean told me that at the very first.''

Coote went on to speak of pitfalls, of Betting, of Bad Companions. "I know,'' said Kipps, "I know.'' "There's Doubt again,'' said Coote. "I know a young fellow—a solicitor—handsome, gifted. And yet, you know—utterly sceptical. Practically altogether a Sceptic.''

"Lor!'' said Kipps, "not a Natheist?''

"I fear so,'' said Coote. "Really, you know, an awfully fine young fellow— Gifted! But full of this dreadful Modern Spirit—Cynical! All this Overman stuff. Nietzsche and all that. . . . I wish I could do something for him.''

"Ah!'' said Kipps, and knocked the ash off his cigarette. "I know a chap— one of our apprentices he was—once. Always scoffing. . . . He lef'.''

He paused. "Never wrote for his refs,'' he said, in the deep tone proper to a moral tragedy; and then, after a pause, "Enlisted!''

"Ah!'' said Coote.

"And often,'' he said, after a pause, "it's just the most spirited chaps, just the chaps one likes best, who Go Wrong.''

"It's temptation,'' Kipps remarked.

He glanced at Coote, leaned forward, knocked the ash from his cigarette into the mighty fender. "That's jest it,'' he said, "you get tempted. Before you know where you are.''

"Modern life,'' said Coote, "is so—complex. It isn't everyone is Strong. Half the young fellows who go wrong aren't really bad.''

"That's jest it,'' said Kipps.

"One gets a tone from one's surroundings—''

"That's exactly it,'' said Kipps.

He meditated. "*I* picked up with a chap,'' he said. "A Nacter. Leastways, he writes plays. Clever feller. But—''

He implied extensive moral obloquy by a movement of his head. "Of course it's seeing life,'' he added.

Coote pretended to understand the full implications of Kipps' remark. "Is it *worth* it?'' he asked.

"That's jest it,'' said Kipps.

He decided to give some more. "One gets talking,'' he said. "Then it's ' 'ave a drink!' Old Methusaleh three stars—and where *are* you? *I* been drunk,'' he said, in a tone of profound humility, and added, "lots of times.''

"Tt—tt,'' said Coote.

"Dozens of times,'' said Kipps, smiling sadly; and added, "Lately.''

His imagination became active and seductive. "One thing leads to another. Cards, p'raps. Girls—''

"I know,'' said Coote, "I know.''

Kipps regarded the fire, and flushed slightly. He borrowed a sentence that Chitterlow had recently used. "One can't tell tales out of school,'' he said.

"I can imagine it,'' said Coote.

Kipps looked with a confidential expression into Coote's face. "It was bad enough when money was limited,'' he remarked. "But now''—he spoke with raised eyebrows—"I got to steady down.''

"You *must*,'' said Coote, protruding his lips into a sort of whistling concern for a moment.

"I must,'' said Kipps, nodding his head slowly, with raised eyebrows. He looked at his cigarette end and threw it into the fender. He was beginning to think he was holding his own in this conversation rather well after all.

Kipps was never a good liar. He was the first to break silence. "I don't mean to say I been reely bad or reely bad drunk. A 'eadache, perhaps—three or four times, say. But there it is!"

"I have never tasted alcohol in my life," said Coote, with an immense frankness, "never!"

"No?"

"Never. I don't feel *I* should be likely to get drunk at all,—it isn't that. And I don't go so far as to say even that in small quantities—at meals—it does one harm. But if I take it, someone else who doesn't know where to stop—you see?"

"That's jest it," said Kipps, with admiring eyes.

"I smoke," admitted Coote. "One doesn't want to be a Pharisee."

It struck Kipps what a tremendously Good chap this Coote was, not only tremendously clever and educated and a gentleman, and one knowing Lady Punnet, but Good. He seemed to be giving all his time and thought to doing good things to other people. A great desire to confide certain things to him arose. At first Kipps hesitated whether he should confide an equal desire for Benevolent activities or for further Depravity—either was in his mind. He rather affected the pose of the Good Intentioned Dog. Then suddenly his impulses took quite a different turn—fell, indeed, into what was a far more serious rut in his mind. It seemed to him Coote might be able to do for him something he very much wanted done.

"Companionship accounts for so much," said Coote.

"That's jest it," said Kipps. "Of course, you know, in my new position— That's just the difficulty."

He plunged boldly at his most secret trouble. He knew that he wanted refinement—culture. It was all very well—but he knew. But how was one to get it? He knew no one, knew no people— He rested on the broken sentence. The shop chaps were all very well, very good chaps and all that, but not what one wanted. "I feel be'ind," said Kipps. "I feel out of it. And consequently I feel it's no good. And then if temptation comes along—"

"Exactly," said Coote.

Kipps spoke of his respect for Miss Walshingham and her freckled friend. He contrived not to look too self-conscious. "You know, I'd like to talk to people like that, but I can't. A chap's afraid of giving himself away."

"Of course," said Coote, "of course."

"I went to a middle-class school, you know. You mustn't fancy I'm one of these here board-school chaps, but you know it reely wasn't a first-class affair. Leastways he didn't take pains with us. If you didn't want to learn you needn't— I don't believe it was *much* better than one of these here national schools. We wore mortar-boards o' course. But what's *that?*

"I'm a regular fish out of water with this money. When I got it—it's a week ago—reely I thought I'd got everything I wanted. But I dunno what to *do*."

His voice went up into a squeak. "Practically," he said, "it's no good shuttin' my eyes to things—I'm a gentleman."

Coote indicated a serious assent.

"And there's the responsibilities of a gentleman," he remarked.

"That's jest it," said Kipps.

"There's calling on people," said Kipps. "If you want to go on knowing Someone you knew before, like. People that's refined." He laughed nervously. "I'm a regular fish out of water," he said, with expectant eyes on Coote.

But Coote only nodded for him to go on.

"This actor chap," he meditated, "is a good sort of chap. But 'e isn't what *I* call a gentleman. I got to 'old myself in with 'im. 'E'd make me go it wild in no time. 'E's pretty near the on'y chap I know. Except the shop chaps. They've come round to 'ave supper once already and a bit of a sing-song afterwards. I sang. I got a banjo, you know, and I vamp a bit. Vamping—you know. Haven't got far in the book—'Ow to Vamp—but still I'm getting on. Jolly, of course, in a way, but what does it *lead* to? . . . Besides that, there's my Aunt and Uncle. *They're* very good old people—very—jest a bit interfering p'r'aps and thinking one isn't grown up, but Right enough. Only— It isn't what I *want*. I feel I've got be'ind with everything. I want to make it up again. I want to get with educated people who know 'ow to do things—in the regular proper way."

His beautiful modesty awakened nothing but benevolence in the mind of Chester Coote.

"If I had someone like you," said Kipps, "that I knew regular like—"

From that point their course ran swift and easy. "If I *could* be of any use to you," said Coote. . . .

"But you're so busy, and all that."

"Not *too* busy. You know, your case is a very interesting one. It was partly that made me speak to you and draw you out. Here you are with all this money and no experience, a spirited young chap—"

"That's jest it," said Kipps.

"I thought I'd see what you were made of, and I must confess I've rarely talked to anyone that I've found quite so interesting as you have been—"

"I seem able to say things to you, like, somehow," said Kipps.

"I'm glad. I'm tremendously glad."

"I want a Friend. That's it—straight."

"My dear chap, if I—"

"Yes; but—"

"*I* want a Friend too."

"Reely?"

"Yes. You know, my dear Kipps—if I may call you that."

"Go on," said Kipps.

"I'm rather a lonely dog myself. *This* tonight— I've not had anyone I've spoken to so freely of my Work for months."

"No?"

"Yes. And, my dear chap, if I can do anything to guide or help you—"

Coote displayed all his teeth in a kindly tremulous smile, and his eyes were shiny. "Shake 'ands," said Kipps, deeply moved; and he and Coote rose and clasped with mutual emotion.

"It's reely too good of you," said Kipps.

"Whatever I can do I will," said Coote.

And so their compact was made. From that moment they were Friends—intimate, confidential, high-thinking, *sotto-voce* friends. All the rest of their talk (and it inclined to be interminable) was an expansion of that. For that night Kipps wallowed in self-abandonment, and Coote behaved as one who had received a great trust. That sinister passion for pedagogy to which the Good-Intentioned are so fatally liable, that passion of infinite presumption that permits one weak human being to arrogate the direction of another weak human being's affairs, had Coote in its grip. He was to be a sort of lay confessor and director of Kipps; he was to help Kipps in a thousand ways; he was, in fact, to chaperon Kipps into the higher and better sort of English life. He was to tell him his faults, advise him about the right thing to do—

"It's all these things I don't know," said Kipps. "I don't know, for instance, what's the right sort of dress to wear—I don't even know if I'm dressed right now—"

"All these things"—Coote stuck out his lips and nodded rapidly to show he understood—"trust me for that," he said; "trust me."

As the evening wore on Coote's manner changed, became more and more the manner of a proprietor. He began to take up his *rôle,* to survey Kipps with a new, with a critical affection. It was evident the thing fell in with his ideas. "It will be awfully interesting," he said. "You know, Kipps, you're really good stuff." (Every sentence now he said "Kipps," or "my dear Kipps," with a curiously authoritative intonation.)

"I know," said Kipps, "only there's such a lot of things I don't seem to be up to some'ow. That's where the trouble comes in."

They talked and talked, and now Kipps was talking freely. They rambled over all sorts of things. Among others Kipps' character was dealt with at length. Kipps gave valuable lights on it. "When I'm reely excited," he said, "I don't seem to care *what* I do. I'm like that." And again, "I don't like to do anything under'and. I *must* speak out. . . ."

He picked a piece of cotton from his knee, the fire grimaced behind his back, and his shadow on the wall and ceiling was disrespectfully convulsed.

3

Kipps went to bed at last with an impression of important things settled, and he lay awake for quite a long time. He felt he was lucky. He had known—in fact Buggins and Carshot and Pearce had made it very clear indeed—that his status in life had changed, and that stupendous adaptations had to be achieved; but how they were to be effected had driven that adaptation into the incredible. Here in the simplest, easiest way was the adapter. The thing had become possible. Not, of course, easy, but possible.

There was much to learn, sheer intellectual toil, methods of address, bowing, an enormous complexity of laws. One broken, you are an outcast. How, for example, would one encounter Lady Punnet? It was quite possible some day he might really have to do that. Coote might introduce him. "Lord!" he said aloud to the darkness between grinning and dismay. He figured himself going into the Emporium, to buy a tie, for example, and there in the face of Buggins, Carshot, Pearce, and the rest of them, meeting "my friend, Lady Punnet!" It might not end with Lady Punnet! His imagination plunged and bolted with him, galloped, took wings and soared to romantic, to poetical altitudes. . . .

Suppose some day one met Royalty. By accident, say! He soared to that! After all—twelve hundred a year is a lift, a tremendous lift. How did one address Royalty? "Your Majesty's Goodness" it would be, no doubt—something like that—and on the knees. He became impersonal. Over a thousand a year made him an Esquire, didn't it? He thought that was it. In which case, wouldn't he have to be presented at court? Velvet breeches, like you wear cycling, and a sword! What a curious place a court must be! Kneeling and bowing; and what was it Miss Mergle used to talk about? Of course!—ladies with long trains walking about backward. Everybody walked about backward at court he knew, when not actually on their knees. Perhaps, though, some people regular stood up to the King! Talked to him, just as one might talk to Buggins, say. Cheek, of course! Dukes, it might be, did that—by permission? Millionaires? . . .

From such thoughts this free citizen of our Crowned Republic passed insensibly into dreams—turgid dreams of that vast ascent which constitutes the true-born Briton's social scheme, which terminates with retrogressive progression and a bending back.

4

The next morning he came down to breakfast looking grave—a man with much before him in the world.

Kipps made a very special thing of his breakfast. Daily once hopeless dreams came true then. It had been customary in the Emporium to supplement Shalford's generous, indeed unlimited, supply of bread and butter-substitute by private purchases, and this had given Kipps very broad artistic conceptions of what the meal might be. Now there would be a cutlet or so or a mutton chop—this splendor Buggins had reported from the great London clubs—haddock, kipper, whiting or fish-balls, eggs, boiled or scrambled, or eggs and bacon, kidney also frequently, and sometimes liver. Amidst a garland of such themes, sausages, black and white puddings, bubble-and-squeak, fried cabbage and scallops, came and went. Always as camp followers came potted meat in all varieties, cold bacon, German sausage, brawn, marmalade, and two sorts of jam; and when he had finished these he would sit among his plates and smoke a cigarette, and look at all these dishes crowded round him with beatific approval. It was his principal meal. He was sitting with his cigarette regarding his apartment with the complacency begotten of a generous plan of feeding successfully realized, when newspapers and post arrived.

There were several things by the post, tradesmen's circulars and cards, and two pathetic begging letters—his luck had got into the papers—and there was a letter from a literary man and a book to enforce his request for 10/- to put down Socialism. The book made it very clear that prompt action on the part of property owners was becoming urgent, if property was to last out the year. Kipps dipped in it, and was seriously perturbed. And there was a letter from old Kipps, saying it was difficult to leave the shop and come over and see him again just yet, but that he had been to a sale at Lydd the previous day, and bought a few good old books and things it would be difficult to find the equal of in Folkestone. "They don't know the value of these things out here," wrote old Kipps, "but you may depend upon it they are valuable," and a brief financial statement followed. "There is an engraving someone might come along and offer you a lot of money for one of these days. Depend upon it, these old things are about the best investment you could make. . . ."

Old Kipps had long been addicted to sales, and his nephew's good fortune had converted what had once been but a looking and a craving—he had rarely even bid for anything in the old days, except the garden tools or the kitchen gallipots or things like that, things one gets for sixpence and finds a use for—into a very active pleasure. Sage and penetrating inspection, a certain mystery of bearing, tactical bids and Purchase—Purchase!—the old man had had a good time.

While Kipps was re-reading the begging letters, and wishing he had the sound, clear commonsense of Buggins to help him a little, the Parcels Post brought along the box from his uncle. It was a large, insecure-looking case, held together by a few still loyal nails, and by what the British War Office would have recognized at once as an Army Corps of string,—rags, and odds and ends tied together. Kipps unpacked it with a table knife, assisted at a critical point by the poker, and found a number of books and other objects of an antique type.

There were three bound volumes of early issues of *Chambers's Journal,* a copy of Punch's Pocket Book for 1875, Sturm's Reflections, an early version of Gill's Geography (slightly torn), an illustrated work on Spinal Curvature, an early edition of Kirke's Human Physiology, "The Scottish Chiefs," and a little volume on the Language of Flowers. There was a fine steel engraving, oak-framed, and with some rusty spots, done in the Colossal style and representing the Handwriting on the Wall. There were also a copper kettle, a pair of candle-snuffers, a brass shoe-horn, a tea-caddy to lock, two decanters (one stoppered), and what was probably a portion of an eighteenth-century child's rattle. Kipps examined these objects one by one, and wished he knew more about them. Turning over the pages of the "Physiology" again, he came upon a striking plate, in which a youth of agreeable profile displayed his interior in an unstinted manner to the startled eye. It was a new view of humanity altogether for Kipps, and it arrested his mind. "Chubes," he whispered. "Chubes!"

This anatomized figure made him forget for a space that he was "practically a gentleman" altogether, and he was still surveying its extraordinary complications when another reminder of a world quite outside those spheres of ordered gentility into which his dreams had carried him overnight arrived (following the servant) in the person of Chitterlow.

5

"Ul-*lo!*" said Kipps, rising.

"Not busy?" said Chitterlow, enveloping Kipps' hand for a moment in one of his own, and tossing the yachting-cap upon the monumental carved oak sideboard.

"Only a bit of reading," said Kipps.

"Reading, eh?" Chitterlow cocked the red eye at the books and other properties for a moment, and then, "I've been expecting you round again one night."

"I been coming round," said Kipps; "on'y there's a chap 'ere—I was coming round last night, on'y I met 'im."

He walked to the hearthrug. Chitterlow drifted round the room for a time, glancing at things as he talked. "I've altered that play tremendously since I saw you," he said. "Pulled it all to pieces."

"What play's that, Chit'low?"

"The one we were talking about. You know. You said something—I don't know if you meant it—about buying half of it. Not the tragedy. I wouldn't sell my own twin brother a share in that. That's my investment. That's my Serious Work. No! I mean that new farce I've been on to. Thing with the business about a beetle."

"Oo yes," said Kipps. "*I* remember."

"I thought you would. Said you'd take a fourth share for a hundred pounds. *You* know."

"I seem to remember something—"

"Well, it's all different. Every bit of it. I'll tell you. You remember what you said about a butterfly. You got confused, you know—Old Meth. Kept calling the beetle a butterfly, and that set me off. I've made it quite different. Quite different. Instead of Popplewaddle—thundering good farce-name that, you know, for all that it came from a Visitors' List—instead of Popplewaddle getting a beetle down his neck and rushing about, I've made him a collector—collects butterflies, and this one you know's a rare one. Comes in at window, centre!'' Chitterlow began to illustrate with appropriate gestures. "Pop rushes about after it. Forget he mustn't let on he's in the house. After that— Tells 'em. Rare butterfly, worth lots of money. Some are, you know. Everyone's on to it after that. Butterfly can't get out of room; every time it comes out to have a try, rush and scurry. Well, I've worked on that. Only—''

He came very close to Kipps. He held up one hand horizontally and tapped it in a striking and confidential manner with the fingers of the other. "Something else,'' he said. "That's given me a Real Ibsenish Touch—like the Wild Duck. You know that woman—I've made her lighter—and she sees it. When they're chasing the butterfly the third time, she's on! She looks. 'That's me!' she says. Bif! Pestered Butterfly. *She's* the Pestered Butterfly. It's legitimate. Much more legitimate than the Wild Duck—where there isn't a duck!

"Knock 'em! The very title ought to knock 'em. I've been working like a horse at it. . . . You'll have a gold-mine in that quarter share, Kipps. . . . *I* don't mind. It's suited me to sell it, and suited you to buy. Bif!''

Chitterlow interrupted his discourse to ask, "You haven't any brandy in the house, have you? Not to drink, you know. But I want just an eggcupful to pull me steady. My liver's a bit queer. . . . It doesn't matter if you haven't. Not a bit. I'm like that. Yes, whisky'll do. Better!''

Kipps hesitated for a moment, then turned and fumbled in the cupboard of his sideboard. Presently he disinterred a bottle of whisky and placed it on the table. Then he put out first one bottle of soda-water, and, after the hesitation of a moment, another. Chitterlow picked up the bottle and read the label. "Good old Methusaleh,'' he said. Kipps handed him the corkscrew, and then his hand fluttered up to his mouth. "I'll have to ring now,'' he said, "to get glasses.'' He hesitated for a moment before doing so, leaning doubtfully, as it were, towards the bell.

When the housemaid appeared, he was standing on the hearthrug with his legs wide apart, with the bearing of a desperate fellow. And after they had both had whiskies, "You know a decent whisky,'' Chitterlow remarked, and took another, "just to drink.'' Kipps produced cigarettes, and the conversation flowed again.

Chitterlow paced the room. He was, he explained, taking a day off; that was why he had come round to see Kipps. Whenever he thought of any extensive change in a play he was writing, he always took a day off. In the end it saved time to do so. It prevented his starting rashly upon work that might have to be re-written. There was no good in doing work when you might have to do it over again, none whatever.

Presently they were descending the steps by the Parade *en route* for the Warren, with Chitterlow doing the talking and going with a dancing drop from step to step. . . .

They had a great walk, not a long one, but a great one. They went up by the Sanatorium, and over the East Cliff and into that queer little wilderness of slippery and tumbling clay and rock under the chalk cliffs—a wilderness of thorn and bramble, wild rose and wayfaring tree, that adds so greatly to Folkestone's charm. They traversed its intricacies and clambered up to the crest of the cliffs at last by a precipitous path that Chitterlow endowed in some mysterious way with suggestions of Alpine adventure. Every now and then he would glance aside at sea and cliffs with a fresh boyishness of imagination that brought back New Romney and the stranded wrecks to Kipps' memory; but mostly he talked of his great obsession of plays and playwriting, and that empty absurdity that is so serious to his kind, his Art. That was a thing that needed a monstrous lot of explaining. Along they went, sometimes abreast, sometimes in single file, up the little paths and down the little paths, and in among the bushes and out along the edge above the beach; and Kipps went along trying ever and again to get an insignificant word in edgeways, and the gestures of Chitterlow flew wide and far, and his great voice rose and fell, and he said this and he said that, and he biffed and banged into the circumambient Inane.

It was assumed that they were embarked upon no more trivial enterprise than the Reform of the British Stage, and Kipps found himself classed with many opulent and even royal and noble amateurs—the Honorable Thomas Norgate came in here—who had interested themselves in the practical realization of high ideals about the Drama. Only he had a finer understanding of these things, and instead of being preyed upon by the common professional—"and they *are* a lot," said Chitterlow; "I haven't toured for nothing"—he would have Chitterlow. Kipps gathered few details. It was clear he had bought the quarter of a farcical comedy—practically a gold-mine—and it would appear it would be a good thing to buy the half. A suggestion, or the suggestion of a suggestion, floated out that he should buy the whole play and produce it forthwith. It seemed he was to produce the play upon a royalty system of a new sort, whatever a royalty system of any sort might be. Then there was some doubt, after all, whether that farcical comedy was in itself sufficient to revolutionize the present lamentable state of the British Drama. Better, perhaps, for such a purpose was that tragedy—as yet unfinished—which was to display all that Chitterlow knew about women, and which was to center about a Russian nobleman embodying the fundamental Chitterlow personality. Then it became clearer that Kipps was to produce several plays. Kipps was to produce a great number of plays. Kipps was to found a National Theatre. . . .

It is probable that Kipps would have expressed some sort of disavowal, if he had known how to express it. Occasionally his face assumed an expression of whistling meditation, but that was as far as he got towards protest.

In the clutch of Chitterlow and the Incalculable, Kipps came round to the house in Fenchurch Street, and was there made to participate in the midday meal. He came to the house forgetting certain confidences, and was reminded of the existence of a Mrs. Chitterlow (with the finest completely untrained contralto voice in England) by her appearance. She had an air of being older than Chitterlow, although probably she wasn't, and her hair was a reddish brown, streaked with gold. She was dressed in one of those complaisant garments that are dressing-gowns, or tea-gowns, or bathing wraps, or rather original evening robes, according to the exigencies of the moment—from the first Kipps was aware that she possessed a warm and rounded neck, and her well-moulded arms came and vanished from the sleeves—and she had large, expressive brown eyes, that he discovered ever and again fixed in an enigmatical manner upon his own.

A simple but sufficient meal had been distributed with careless spontaneity over the little round table in the room with the photographs and looking-glass, and when a plate had, by Chitterlow's direction, been taken from under the marmalade in the cupboard, and the kitchen fork and a knife that was not loose in its handle had been found for Kipps, they began and made a tumultuous repast. Chitterlow ate with quiet enormity, but it did not interfere with the flow of his talk. He introduced Kipps to his wife very briefly; she had obviously heard of Kipps before, and he made it vaguely evident that the production of the comedy was the thing chiefly settled. His reach extended over the table, and he troubled nobody. When Mrs. Chitterlow, who for a little while seemed socially self-conscious, reproved him for taking a potato with a jab of his fork, he answered, "Well, you shouldn't have married a man of Genius," and from a subsequent remark it was perfectly clear that Chitterlow's standing in this respect was made no secret of in his household.

They drank old Methusaleh and syphon soda, and there was no clearing away; they just sat among the plates and things, and Mrs. Chitterlow took her husband's tobacco-pouch and made a cigarette and smoked, and blew smoke, and looked at Kipps with her large brown eyes. Kipps had seen cigarettes smoked by ladies before, "for fun," but this was real smoking. It frightened him rather. He felt he must not encourage this lady—at any rate, in Chitterlow's presence.

They became very cheerful after the repast, and as there was now no waste to deplore, such as one experiences in the windy open air, Chitterlow gave his voice full vent. He fell to praising Kipps very highly and loudly. He said he had known Kipps was the right sort, he had seen it from the first, almost before he got up out of the mud on that memorable night. "You can," he said, "sometimes. That was why—" He stopped, but he seemed on the verge of explaining that it was his certainty of Kipps being the right sort had led him to confer this great Fortune upon him. He left that impression. He threw out a number of long sentences and material for sentences of a highly philosophical and incoherent character about Coincidences. It became evident he considered dramatic criticism in a perilously low condition. . . .

About four Kipps found himself stranded, as it were, by a receding Chitterlow on a seat upon the Leas.

He was chiefly aware that Chitterlow was an overwhelming personality. He puffed his cheeks and blew.

No doubt this was seeing life, but had he particularly wanted to see life that day? In a way Chitterlow had interrupted him. The day he had designed for himself was altogether different from this. He had been going to read through a precious little volume called "Don't" that Coote had sent round for him—a book of invaluable hints, a summary of British deportment, that had only the one defect of being at points a little out of date.

That reminded him he had intended to perform a difficult exercise called an Afternoon Call upon the Cootes, as a preliminary to doing it in deadly earnest upon the Walshinghams. It was no good today, anyhow, now.

He came back to Chitterlow. He would have to explain to Chitterlow he was taking too much for granted—he would have to do that. It was so difficult to do in Chitterlow's presence, though; in his absence it was easy enough. This half-share, and taking a theater and all of it, was going too far.

The quarter share was right enough, he supposed, but even that—! A hundred pounds! What wealth is there left in the world after one has paid out a hundred pounds from it?

He had to recall that, in a sense, Chitterlow had indeed brought him his fortune before he could face even that.

You must not think too hardly of him. To Kipps, you see, there was as yet no such thing as proportion in these matters. A hundred pounds went to his horizon. A hundred pounds seemed to him just exactly as big as any other large sum of money.

CHAPTER II

The Walshinghams

1

THE COOTES LIVED in a little house in Bouverie Square, with a tangle of Virginia creeper up the veranda.

Kipps had been troubled in his mind about knocking double or single—it is these things show what a man is made of—but happily there was a bell.

A queer little maid with a big cap admitted Kipps, and took him through a bead curtain and a door into a little drawing-room, with a black and gold piano, a glazed bookcase, a Moorish cozy corner, and a draped looking-glass over-mantel, bright with Regent Street ornaments and photographs of various intellectual lights. A number of cards of invitation to meetings and the match list of a Band of Hope cricket club were stuck into the looking-glass frame, with Coote's name as a Vice-President. There was a bust of Beethoven over the bookcase, and the walls were thick with conscientiously executed but carelessly selected "views" in oil and water colors and gilt frames. At the end of the room, facing the light, was a portrait that struck Kipps at first as being Coote in spectacles and feminine costume, and that he afterwards decided must be Coote's mother. Then the original appeared, and he discovered that it was Coote's elder and only sister, who kept house for him. She wore her hair in a knob behind, and the sight of the knob suggested to Kipps an explanation for a frequent gesture of Coote's, a patting exploratory movement to the back of his head. And then it occurred to him that this was quite an absurd idea altogether.

She said, "Mr. Kipps, I believe," and Kipps laughed pleasantly, and said, "That's it!" and then she told him that "Chester" had gone down to the art school to see about sending off some drawings or other, and that he would be back soon. Then she asked Kipps if he painted, and showed him the pictures on the wall. Kipps asked her where each one was "of," and when she showed him some of the Leas slopes, he said he never would have recognized them. He said it was funny how things looked in a picture very often. "But they're awfully *good*," he said. "Did you do them?" He would look at them with his neck arched like a swan's, his head back and on one side, and then suddenly peer closely into them. "They *are* good. I wish I could paint." "That's what Chester says," she answered. "I tell him he has better things to do." Kipps seemed to get on very well with her.

Then Coote came in, and they left her and went upstairs together, and had a good talk about reading and the Rules of Life. Or rather Coote talked, and the praises of thought and reading were in his mouth. . . .

You must figure Coote's study, a little bedroom put to studious uses, and over the mantel an array of things he had been led to believe indicative of culture and refinement—an autotype of Rossetti's "Annunciation," an autotype of Watts' "Minotaur," a Swiss carved pipe with many joints and a photograph of Amiens Cathedral (these two the spoils of travel), a phrenological bust, and some broken fossils from the Warren. A rotating bookshelf carried the *Encyclopædia Britannica* (tenth edition), and on the top of it a large official-looking, age-grubby envelope, bearing the mystic words, "On His Majesty's Service," a number or so of the *Bookman,* and a box of cigarettes were lying. A table under the window bore a little microscope, some dust in a saucer, some grimy glass slips, and broken cover glasses, for Coote had "gone in for" biology a little. The longer side of the room was given over to bookshelves, neatly edged with pinked American cloth, and with an array of books—no worse an array of books than you find in any public library; an almost haphazard accumulation of obsolete classics, contemporary successes, the Hundred Best Books (including Samuel Warren's "Ten Thousand a Year"), old school-books, directories, the Times Atlas, Ruskin in bulk, Tennyson complete in one volume, Longfellow, Charles Kingsley, Smiles, a guide-book or so, several medical pamphlets, odd magazine numbers, and much indescribable rubbish—in fact, a compendium of the contemporary British mind. And in front of this array stood Kipps, ill-taught and untrained, respectful, awe-stricken, and, for the moment at any rate, willing to learn, while Coote, the exemplary Coote, talked to him of reading and the virtue in books.

"Nothing enlarges the mind," said Coote, "like Travel and Books. . . . And they're both so easy nowadays, and so cheap!"

"I've often wanted to 'ave a good go in at reading," Kipps replied.

"You'd hardly believe," Coote said, "how much you can get out of books. Provided you avoid trashy reading, that is. You ought to make a rule, Kipps, and read one Serious Book a week. Of course we can Learn even from Novels, Nace Novels that is, but it isn't the same thing as serious reading. I made a rule, One Serious Book and One Novel—no more. There's some of the Serious Books I've been reading lately—on that table: 'Sartor Resartus,' Mrs. Twaddletome's 'Pond Life,' 'The Scottish Chiefs,' 'Life and Letters of Dean Farrar.' . . ."

2

There came at last the sound of a gong, and Kipps descended to tea in that state of nervous apprehension at the difficulties of eating and drinking that his Aunt's knuckle rappings had implanted in him forever. Over Coote's shoulder he became aware of a fourth person in the Moorish cozy corner, and he turned, leaving incomplete something incoherent he was saying to Miss Coote about his modest respect and desire for literature, to discover this fourth person was Miss Helen Walshingham, hatless, and looking very much at home.

She rose at once with an extended hand to meet his hesitation.

"You're stopping in Folkestone, Mr. Kipps?"

" 'Ere on a bit of business," said Kipps. "I thought you was away in Bruges."

"That's later," said Miss Walshingham. "We're stopping until my brother's holiday begins, and we're trying to let our house. Where are you staying in Folkestone?"

"I got a 'ouse of mine—on the Leas."

"I've heard all about your good fortune—this afternoon."

"Isn't it a Go!" said Kipps. "I 'aven't nearly got to believe it's reely 'appened yet. When that—Mr. Bean told me of it, you could 'ave knocked me down with a feather. . . . It's a tremenjous change for me."

He discovered Miss Coote was asking him whether he took milk and sugar. "*I* don't mind," said Kipps. "Jest as you like."

Coote became active, handing tea and bread-and-butter. It was thinly cut, and the bread was rather new, and the half of the slice that Kipps took fell upon the floor. He had been holding it by the edge, for he was not used to this migratory method of taking tea without plates or table. This little incident ruled him out of the conversation for a time, and when he came to attend to it again, they were talking about something or other prodigious—a performer of some sort— that was coming, called, it seemed, "Padrooski!" So Kipps, who had dropped quietly into a chair, ate his bread-and-butter, said "no, thank you" to any more, and by this discreet restraint got more freedom with his cup and saucer.

Apart from the confusion natural to tea, he was in a state of tremulous excitement on account of the presence of Miss Walshingham. He glanced from Miss Coote to her brother, and then at Helen. He regarded her over the top of his cup as he drank. Here she was, solid and real. It was wonderful. He remarked, as he had done at times before, the easy flow of the dark hair back from her brow over her ears, the shapeliness of the white hands that came out from her simple white cuffs, the delicate penciling of her brow.

Presently she turned her face to him almost suddenly, and smiled with the easiest assurance of friendship.

"You will go, I suppose?" she said, and added, "to the Recital."

"If I'm in Folkestone I shall," said Kipps, clearing away a little hoarseness. "I don't *know* much about music, but what I do know I like."

"I'm sure you'll like Paderewski," she said.

"If you do," he said, "I dessay I shall."

He found Coote very kindly taking his cup.

"Do you think of living in Folkestone?" asked Miss Coote, in a tone of proprietorship from the hearthrug.

"No," said Kipps, "that's jest it—I hardly know." He also said that he wanted to look round a bit before doing anything. "There's so much to consider," said Coote, smoothing the back of his head.

"I may go back to New Romney for a bit," said Kipps. "I got an Uncle and Aunt there. I reely don't know."

Helen regarded him thoughtfully for a moment.

"You must come and see us," she said, "before we go to Bruges."

"Oh, rather!" said Kipps. "If I may."

"Yes, do," she said, and suddenly stood up before Kipps could formulate an inquiry when he should call.

"You're sure you can spare that drawing-board?" she said to Miss Coote; and the conversation passed out of range.

And when he had said "Good-bye" to Miss Walshingham, and she had repeated her invitation to call, he went upstairs again with Coote to look out certain initiatory books they had had under discussion. And then Kipps, blowing very resolutely, went back to his own place, bearing in his arm (1) "Sesame and Lilies," (2) "Sir George Tressady," (3) an anonymous book on "Vitality" that Coote particularly esteemed. And having got to his own sitting-room, he opened "Sesame and Lilies" and read with ruthless determination for some time.

3

Presently he leaned back and gave himself up to the business of trying to imagine just exactly what Miss Walshingham could have thought of him when she saw him. Doubts about the precise effect of the gray flannel suit began to trouble him. He turned to the mirror over the mantel, and then got into a chair to study the hang of the trousers. It looked all right. Luckily she had not seen the Panama hat. He knew he had the brim turned up wrong, but he could not find out which way the brim was right. However, that she had not seen. He might, perhaps, ask at the shop where he bought it.

He meditated for awhile on his reflected face—doubtful whether he liked it or not—and then got down again and flitted across to the sideboard where there lay two little books, one in a cheap magnificent cover of red and gold, and the other in green canvas. The former was called, as its cover witnessed, "Manners and Rules of Good Society, by a Member of the Aristocracy," and after the cover had indulged in a band of gilded decoration, light-hearted, but natural under the circumstances, it added, "TWENTY-FIRST EDITION." The second was that admirable classic, "The Art of Conversing." Kipps returned with these to his seat, placed the two before him, opened the latter with a sigh, and flattened it under his hand.

Then with knitted brows he began to read onward from a mark, his lips moving.

"Having thus acquired possession of an idea, the little ship should not be abruptly launched into deep waters, but should be first permitted to glide gently and smoothly into the shallows; that is to say, the conversation should not be commenced by broadly and roundly stating a fact, or didactically expressing an opinion, as the subject would be thus virtually or summarily disposed of, or perhaps be met with a 'Really' or 'Indeed,' or some equally brief monosyllabic reply. If an opposite opinion were held by the person to whom the remark were addressed, he might not, if a stranger, care to express it in the form of a direct contradiction or actual dissent. To glide imperceptibly into conversation is the object to be attained—"

At this point Mr. Kipps rubbed his fingers through his hair with an expression of some perplexity, and went back to the beginning.

4

When Kipps made his call on the Walshinghams, it all happened so differently from the "Manners and Rules" prescription ("Paying Calls") that he was quite lost from the very outset. Instead of the footman or maidservant proper in these cases, Miss Walshingham opened the door to him herself. "I'm so glad you've come," she said, with one of her rare smiles.

She stood aside for him to enter the rather narrow passage.

"I thought I'd call," he said, retaining his hat and stick.

She closed the door and led the way to a little drawing-room, which impressed Kipps as being smaller and less emphatically colored than that of the Cootes, and in which, at first, only a copper bowl of white poppies upon the brown tablecloth caught his particular attention.

"You won't think it unconventional to come in, Mr. Kipps, will you?" she remarked. "Mother is out."

"I don't mind," he said, smiling amiably, "if you don't."

She walked round the table and stood regarding him across it, with that same look between speculative curiosity and appreciation that he remembered from the last of the art-class meetings.

"I wondered whether you would call or whether you wouldn't before you left Folkestone."

"I'm not leaving Folkestone for a bit, and any'ow I should have called on you."

"Mother will be sorry she was out. I've told her about you, and she wants, I know, to meet you."

"I saw 'er—if that was 'er—in the shop," said Kipps.

"Yes—you did, didn't you? . . . She has gone out to make some duty calls, and I didn't go. I had something to write. I write a little, you know."

"Reely!" said Kipps.

"It's nothing much," she said, "and it comes to nothing." She glanced at a little desk near the window, on which there lay some paper. "One must do something." She broke off abruptly. "Have you seen our outlook?" she asked, and walked to the window, and Kipps came and stood beside her. "We look on the Square. It might be worse, you know. That out-porter's truck there is horrid—and the railings, but it's better than staring one's social replica in the face, isn't it? It's pleasant in early spring—bright green laid on with a dry brush—and it's pleasant in autumn."

"I like it," said Kipps. "That laylock there is pretty, isn't it?"

"Children come and pick it at times," she remarked.

"I dessay they do," said Kipps.

He rested on his hat and stick and looked appreciatively out of the window, and she glanced at him for one swift moment. A suggestion that might have come from the "Art of Conversing" came into his head. "Have you a garden?" he said.

She shrugged her shoulders. "Only a little one," she said, and then, "Perhaps you would like to see it."

"I like gardening," said Kipps, with memories of a pennyworth of nasturtiums he had once trained over his uncle's dustbin.

She led the way with a certain relief.

They emerged through a four-seasons' colored glass door to a little iron verandah, that led by iron steps to a minute walled garden. There was just room for a patch of turf and a flower-bed; one sturdy variegated Euonymus grew in the corner. But the early June flowers, the big narcissus, snow upon the mountains, and a fine show of yellow wallflowers, shone gay.

"That's our garden," said Helen. "It's not a very big one, is it?"

"I like it," said Kipps.

"It's small," she said, "but this is the day of small things."

Kipps didn't follow that.

"If you were writing when I came," he remarked, "I'm interrupting you."

She turned round with her back to the railing and rested leaning on her hands. "I had finished," she said. "I couldn't get on."

"Were you making up something?" asked Kipps.

There was a little interval before she smiled. "I try—quite vainly—to write stories," she said. "One must do something. I don't know whether I shall ever do any good—at that—anyhow. It seems so hopeless. And, of course—one must study the popular taste. But now my brother has gone to London—I get a lot of leisure."

"I seen your brother, 'aven't I?"

"He came to the class once or twice. Very probably you have. He's gone to London to pass his examinations and become a solicitor. And then I suppose he'll have a chance. Not much, perhaps, even then. But he's luckier than I am."

"You got your classes and things."

"They ought to satisfy me. But they don't. I suppose I'm ambitious. We both are. And we hadn't much of a spring-board." She glanced over her shoulder at the cramped little garden with an air of reference in her gesture.

"I should think you could do anything if you wanted to?" said Kipps.

"As a matter of fact, I can't do anything I want to."

"You done a good deal."

"What?"

"Well, didn't you pass one of these here University things?"

"Oh, I matriculated!"

"I should think I was no end of a swell if *I* did—I know that."

"Mr. Kipps, do you know how many people matriculate into London University every year?"

"How many, then?"

"Between two and three thousand."

"Well, just think how many don't!"

Her smile came again and broke into a laugh. "Oh, *they* don't count," she said; and then realizing that might penetrate Kipps if he was left with it, she hurried on to, "The fact is, I'm a discontented person, Mr. Kipps. Folkestone, you know, is a Sea Front, and it values people by sheer vulgar prosperity. We're not prosperous, and we live in a back street. We have to live here because this is our house. It's a mercy we haven't to 'let.' One feels one hasn't opportunities. If one had, I suppose one wouldn't use them. Still—"

Kipps felt he was being taken tremendously into her confidence. "That's jest it," he said.

He leaned forward on his stick and said very earnestly, "I believe you could do anything you wanted to, if you tried."

She threw out her hands in disavowal.

"I *know*," said he, very sagely, and nodding his head. "I watched you once or twice when you were teaching that woodcarving class."

For some reason this made her laugh—a rather pleasant laugh, and that made Kipps feel a very witty and successful person. "It's very evident," she said, "that you're one of those rare people who believe in me, Mr. Kipps," to which he answered, "Oo, I *do!*" and then suddenly they became aware of Mrs. Walshingham coming along the passage. In another moment she appeared through the four-seasons' door, bonneted and ladylike and a little faded, exactly as Kipps had seen her in the shop. Kipps felt a certain apprehension at her appearance, in spite of the reassurances he had had from Coote.

"Mr. Kipps has called on us," said Helen; and Mrs. Walshingham said it was very, very kind of him, and added that new people didn't call on them very much nowadays. There was nothing of the scandalized surprise Kipps had seen in the shop; she had heard, perhaps, he was a gentleman now. In the shop he had thought her rather jaded and haughty, but he had scarcely taken her hand, which responded to his touch with a friendly pressure, before he knew how mistaken he had been. She then told her daughter that someone called Mrs. Wace had been out, and turned to Kipps again to ask him if he had had tea. Kipps said he had not, and Helen moved towards some mysterious interior. "But, *I* say," said Kipps, "don't you on my account—"

Helen vanished, and he found himself alone with Mrs. Walshingham. Which, of course, made him breathless and Boreas-looking for a moment.

"You were one of Helen's pupils in the woodcarving class?" asked Mrs. Walshingham, regarding him with the quiet watchfulness proper to her position.

"Yes," said Kipps; "that's 'ow I 'ad the pleasure—"

"She took a great interest in her woodcarving class. She is so energetic, you know, and it gives her an Outlet."

"I thought she taught something splendid."

"Everyone says she did very well. Helen, I think, would do anything well that she undertook to do. She's so very clever. And she throws herself into things so."

She untied her bonnet-strings with a pleasant informality.

"She has told me all about her class. She used to be full of it. And about your cut hand."

"Lor!" said Kipps; "fancy telling that!"

"Oh yes. And how brave you were!"

(Though, indeed, Helen's chief detail had been his remarkable expedient for checking bloodshed.)

Kipps became bright pink. "She said you didn't seem to feel it a bit."

Kipps felt he would have to spend weeks over "The Art of Conversing."

While he still hung fire, Helen returned with the apparatus for afternoon tea upon a tray.

"Do you mind pulling out the table?" asked Mrs. Walshingham.

That again was very homelike. Kipps put down his hat and stick in the corner, and amidst an iron thunder pulled out a little rusty, green-painted, iron table, and then in the easiest manner followed Helen in to get chairs.

So soon as he had got rid of his teacup—he refused all food, of course, and they were merciful—he became wonderfully at his ease. Presently he was talking. He talked quite modestly and simply about his changed condition, and his difficulties and plans. He spread what indeed had an air of being all his simple little soul before their eyes. In a little while his clipped defective accent had become less perceptible to their ears, and they began to realize, as the girl with the freckles had long since realized, that there were passable aspects of Kipps. He confided, he submitted, and for both of them he had the realest, the most seductively flattering undertone of awe and reverence.

He remained about two hours, having forgotten how terribly incorrect it is to stay at such a length. They did not mind at all.

CHAPTER III

Engaged

1

WITHIN TWO MONTHS, within a matter of three-and-fifty days, Kipps had clambered to the battlements of Heart's Desire.

It all became possible by the Walshinghams—it would seem at Coote's instigation—deciding, after all, not to spend the holidays at Bruges. Instead they remained in Folkestone, and this happy chance gave Kipps just all those opportunities of which he stood in need.

His crowning day was at Lympne, and long before the summer warmth began to break, while, indeed, August still flamed on high. They had organized—no one seemed to know who suggested it first—a water party on the still reaches of the old military canal at Hythe, and they were to picnic by the brick bridge, and afterwards to clamber to Lympne Castle. The host of the gathering, it was understood very clearly, was Kipps.

They went a merry party. The canal was weedy, with only a few inches of water at the shallows, and so they went in three canoes. Kipps had learned to paddle—it had been his first athletic accomplishment; and his second—with the last three or four of ten private lessons still to come—was to be cycling. But Kipps did not paddle at all badly; muscles hardened by lifting pieces of cretonne could cut a respectable figure by the side of Coote's exertions, and the girl with the freckles, the girl who understood him, came in his canoe. They raced the Walshinghams, brother and sister; and Coote, in a liquefying state and blowing mightily, but still persistent, and always quite polite and considerate, toiled behind with Mrs. Walshingham. She could not be expected to paddle (though, of course, she "offered"), and she reclined upon specially adjusted cushions under a black-and-white sunshade, and watched Kipps and her daughter, and feared at intervals that Coote was getting hot.

They were all more or less in holiday costume; the eyes of the girls looked out under the shade of wide-brimmed hats; even the freckled girl was unexpectedly pretty, and Helen, swinging sunlit to her paddle, gave Kipps, almost for the first time, the suggestion of a graceful body. Kipps was arrayed in the completest boating costume, and when his fashionable Panama was discarded and his hair blown into disorder, he became, in his white flannels, as sightly as most young men. His complexion was a notable asset.

Things favored him, the day favored him, everyone favored him. Young Walshingham, the girl with the freckles, Coote, and Mrs. Walshingham, were playing up to him in the most benevolent way, and between the landing-place and Lympne, Fortune, to crown their efforts, had placed a small convenient field entirely at the disposal of an adolescent bull. Not a big, real, resolute bull, but, on the other hand, no calf; a young bull, at the same stage of emotional development as Kipps, "where the brook and river meet." Detachedly our party drifted towards him.

When they landed, young Walshingham, with the simple directness of a brother, abandoned his sister to Kipps and secured the freckled girl, leaving Coote to carry Mrs. Walshingham's light wool wrap. He started at once in order to put an effectual distance between himself and his companion on the one hand, and a certain pervasive chaperonage that went with Coote, on the other. Young Walshingham, I think I have said, was dark, with a Napoleonic profile, and it was natural for him therefore to be a bold thinker and an epigrammatic speaker, and he had long ago discovered great possibilities of appreciation in the freckled girl. He was in a very happy frame that day because he had just been intrusted with the management of Kipps' affairs (old Bean inexplicably dismissed), and that was not a bad beginning for a solicitor of only a few months' standing; and, moreover, he had been reading Nietzsche, and he thought that in all probability he was the Non-Moral Overman referred to by that writer. He wore fairly large-sized hats. He wanted to expand the theme of the Non-Moral Overman in the ear of the freckled girl, to say it over, so to speak, and in order to seclude his exposition they went aside from the direct path and trespassed through a coppice, avoiding the youthful bull. They escaped to these higher themes but narrowly, for Coote and Mrs. Walshingham, subtle chaperones both, and each indisposed, for excellent reasons, to encumber Kipps and Helen, were hot upon their heels. These two kept the direct route to the stile of the bull's field, and the sight of the animal at once awakened Coote's innate aversion to brutality in any shape or form. He said the stiles were too high, and that they could do better by going round by the hedge, and Mrs. Walshingham, nothing loth, agreed.

This left the way clear for Kipps and Helen, and they encountered the bull. Helen did not observe the bull; Kipps did; but that afternoon, at any rate, he was equal to facing a lion. And the bull really came at them. It was not an affair of the bull-ring exactly, no desperate rushes and gorings, but he came; he regarded them with a large, wicked, bluish eye, opened a mouth below his moistly glistening nose, and booed, at any rate, if he did not exactly bellow, and he shook his head wickedly, and showed that tossing was in his mind. Helen was frightened, without any loss of dignity, and Kipps went extremely white. But he was perfectly calm, and he seemed to her to have lost the last vestiges of his accent and his social shakiness. He directed her to walk quietly towards the stile and made an oblique advance towards the bull.

"You be orf!" he said. . . .

When Helen was well over the stile, Kipps withdrew in good order. He got over the stile under cover of a feint, and the thing was done—a small thing, no doubt, but just enough to remove from Helen's mind an incorrect deduction, that a man who was so terribly afraid of a teacup as Kipps must necessarily be abjectly afraid of everything else in the world. In her moment of reaction she went, perhaps, too far in the opposite direction. Hitherto Kipps had always had a certain flimsiness of effect for her. Now suddenly he was discovered solid. He was discovered possible in many new ways. Here, after all, was the sort of back a woman can get behind! . . .

As they went past the turf-crowned mass of Portus Lemanus, up the steep slopes towards the castle on the crest, the thing was almost manifest in her eyes.

2

Everyone who stays in Folkestone goes sooner or later to Lympne. The castle became a farmhouse, and the farmhouse, itself now ripe and venerable, wears the walls of the castle as a little man wears a big man's coat. The kindliest of farm ladies entertains a perpetual stream of visitors, and shows you her vast mangle and her big kitchen, and takes you out upon the sunniest little terrace-garden in all the world, and you look down the sheep-dotted slopes, to where, beside the canal and under the trees, the crumbled memories of Rome sleep for ever. One climbs the Keep, up a tortuous spiral of stone, worn now to the pitch of perforation, and there one is lifted to the center of far more than a hemisphere of view. Away below one's feet, almost at the bottom of the hill, the Marsh begins and spreads and spreads in a mighty crescent that sweeps about the sea, the Marsh dotted with the church towers of forgotten medieval towns, and breaking at last into the low blue hills by Winchelsea and Hastings; east hangs France between the sea and sky; and round the north, bounding the wide perspectives of farms and houses and woods, the Downs, with their hangers and chalk-pits, sustain the passing shadows of the sailing clouds.

And here it was, high out of the world of every day, and in the presence of spacious beauty, that Kipps and Helen found themselves agreeably alone. All six, it had seemed, had been coming for the Keep; but Mrs. Walshingham had hesitated at the horrid little stairs, and then suddenly felt faint, and so she and the freckled girl had remained below, walking up and down in the shadow of the house; and Coote had remembered they were all out of cigarettes, and had taken off young Walshingham into the village. There had been shouting to explain between ground and parapet, and then Helen and Kipps turned again to the view and commended it, and fell silent.

Helen sat fearlessly in an embrasure, and Kipps stood beside her.

"I've always been fond of scenery," Kipps repeated, after an interval.

Then he went off at a tangent. "D'you reely think that was right what Coote was saying?"

She looked interrogation.

"About my name."

"Being really C-U-Y-P-S? I have my doubts. I thought at first— What makes Mr. Coote add an 'S' to Cuyp?"

"*I* dunno," said Kipps, foiled. "I was jest thinking. . . ."

She shot one wary glance at him, and then turned her eyes to the sea.

Kipps was out for a space. He had intended to lead from this question to the general question of surnames and change of names: it had seemed a light and witty way of saying something he had in mind, and suddenly he perceived that this was an unutterably vulgar and silly project. The hitch about that "S" had saved him. He regarded her profile for a moment, framed in weather-beaten stone, and backed by the blue elements.

He dropped the question of his name out of existence, and spoke again of the view. "When I see scenery—and things that—that are beautiful, it makes me feel—"

She looked at him suddenly, and saw him fumbling for his words.

"Silly like," he said.

She took him in with her glance, the old look of proprietorship it was, touched with a certain warmth. She spoke in a voice as unambiguous as her eyes. "You needn't," she said. "You know, Mr. Kipps, you hold yourself too cheap."

Her eyes and words smote him with amazement. He stared at her like a man who awakens. She looked down.

"You mean—" he said; and then, "Don't you hold me cheap?"

She glanced up again and shook her head.

"But—for instance—you don't think of me—as an equal like."

"Why not?"

"Oo! But, reely—"

His heart beat very fast.

"If I thought—" he said; and then, "You know so much."

"That's nothing," she said.

Then for a long time, as it seemed to them, both kept silence—a silence that said and accomplished many things.

"I know what I am," he said at length. . . . "If I thought it was possible. . . . If I thought *you*. . . . I believe I could do anything—"

He stopped, and she sat downcast and strikingly still.

"Miss Walshingham," he said, "is it possible that you . . . could care for me enough to—to 'elp me? Miss Walshingham, do you care for me at all?"

It seemed she was never going to answer. She looked up at him. "I think," she said, "you are the most generous—look at what you have done for my brother!—the most generous and the most modest of—men. And this afternoon—I thought you were the bravest."

She turned her head, glanced down, waved her hand to someone on the terrace below, and stood up.

"Mother is signalling," she said. "We must go down."

Kipps became polite and deferential by habit, but his mind was a tumult that had nothing to do with that.

He moved before her towards the little door that opened on the winding stairs—"always precede a lady down or upstairs"—and then, on the second step, he turned resolutely. "But—" he said, looking up out of the shadow, flannel clad and singularly like a man.

She looked down on him, with her hand upon the stone lintel.

He held out his hand as if to help her. "Can you tell me?" he said. "You must know—"

"What?"

"If you care for me?"

She did not answer for a long time. It was as if everything in the world was drawn to the breaking-point, and in a minute must certainly break.

"Yes," she said at last, "I know."

Abruptly, by some impalpable sign, he knew what the answer would be, and he remained still.

She bent down over him and softened to her wonderful smile.

"Promise me," she insisted.

He promised with his still face.

"If *I* do not hold you cheap, you will never hold yourself cheap."

"If you do not hold me cheap! You mean—?"

She bent down quite close to him. "I hold you," she said, and then whispered, *"dear."*

"Me?"

She laughed aloud.

He was astonished beyond measure. He stipulated lest there might yet be some misconception. "You will marry me?"

She was laughing, inundated by the sense of bountiful power, of possession and success. He looked quite a nice little man to have. "Yes," she laughed. "What else could I mean?" and, "Yes."

He felt as a praying hermit might have felt, snatched from the midst of his quiet devotions, his modest sackcloth and ashes, and hurled neck and crop over the glittering gates of Paradise, smack among the iridescent wings, the bright-eyed Cherubim. He felt like some lowly and righteous man dynamited into Bliss. . . .

His hand tightened on the rope that steadies one upon the stairs of stone. He was for kissing her hand and did not.

He said not a word more. He turned about, and, with something very like a scared expression on his face, led the way into the obscurity of their descent. . . .

3

Everyone seemed to understand. Nothing was said, nothing was explained; the merest touch of the eyes sufficed. As they clustered in the castle gateway, Coote, Kipps remembered afterwards, laid hold of his arm as if by chance, and pressed it. It was quite evident he knew. His eyes, his nose, shone with benevolent congratulation; shone, too, with the sense of a good thing conducted to its climax. Mrs. Walshingham, who had seemed a little fatigued by the hill, recovered, and was even obviously stirred by affection for her daughter. There was in passing a motherly caress. She asked Kipps to give her his arm in walking down the steep. Kipps in a sort of dream obeyed. He found himself trying to attend to her, and soon he was attending.

She and Kipps talked like sober responsible people and went slowly, while the others drifted down the hill together a loose little group of four. He wondered momentarily what they would talk about, and then sank into his conversation with Mrs. Walshingham. He conversed, as it were, out of his superficial personality, and his inner self lay stunned in unsuspected depths within. It had an air of being an interesting and friendly talk, almost their first long talk together. Hitherto he had had a sort of fear of Mrs. Walshingham as of a person possibly satirical, but she proved a soul of sense and sentiment, and Kipps, for all his abstraction, got on with her unexpectedly well. They talked a little upon scenery and the inevitable melancholy attaching to old ruins and the thought of vanished generations.

"Perhaps they jousted here," said Mrs. Walshingham.

"They was up to all sorts of things," said Kipps; and then the two came round to Helen. She spoke of her daughter's literary ambitions. "She will do something, I feel sure. You know, Mr. Kipps, it's a great responsibility to a mother to feel her daughter is—exceptionally clever."

"I dessay it is," said Kipps. "There's no mistake about that."

She spoke, too, of her son—almost like Helen's twin—alike yet different. She made Kipps feel quite fatherly. "They are so quick, so artistic," she said, "so full of ideas. Almost they frighten me. One feels they need opportunities— as other people need air."

She spoke of Helen's writing. "Even when she was quite a little dot she wrote verse."

(Kipps, sensation.)

"Her father had just the same tastes—" Mrs. Walshingham turned a little beam of half-pathetic reminiscence on the past. "He was more artist than business man. That was the trouble. . . . He was misled by his partner, and when the crash came everyone blamed him. . . . Well, it doesn't do to dwell on horrid things . . . especially today. There are bright days, Mr. Kipps, and dark days. And mine have not always been bright."

Kipps presented a face of Coote-like sympathy.

She diverged to talk of flowers, and Kipps' mind was filled with the picture of Helen bending down towards him in the Keep. . . .

They spread the tea under the trees before the little inn, and at a certain moment Kipps became aware that everyone in the party was simultaneously and furtively glancing at him. There might have been a certain tension had it not been first of all for Coote and his tact, and afterwards for a number of wasps. Coote was resolved to make this memorable day pass off well, and displayed an almost boisterous sense of fun. Then young Walshingham began talking of the Roman remains below Lympne, intending to lead up to the Overman. "These old Roman chaps—" he said; and then the wasps arrived. They killed three in the jam alone.

Kipps killed wasps, as it were in a dream, and handed things to the wrong people, and maintained a thin surface of ordinary intelligence with the utmost difficulty. At times he became aware—aware with an extraordinary vividness— of Helen. Helen was carefully not looking at him, and behaving with amazing coolness and ease. But just for that one time there was the faintest suggestion of pink beneath the ivory of her cheeks. . . .

Tacitly the others conceded to Kipps the right to paddle back with Helen; he helped her into the canoe and took his paddle, and, paddling slowly, dropped behind the others. And now his inner self stirred again. He said nothing to her. How could he ever say anything to her again? She spoke to him at rare intervals about reflections and flowers and the trees, and he nodded in reply. But his mind moved very slowly forward now from the point at which it had fallen stunned in the Lympne Keep, moving forward to the beginnings of realization. As yet he did not say even in the recesses of his heart that she was his! But he perceived that the goddess had come from her altar, amazingly, and had taken him by the hand!

The sky was a vast splendor, and then close to them were the dark protecting trees, and the shining, smooth still water. He was an erect black outline to her; he plied his paddle with no unskillful gesture; the water broke to snaky silver and glittered far behind his strokes. Indeed, he did not seem so bad to her. Youth calls to youth the wide world through, and her soul rose in triumph over his subjection. And behind him was money and opportunity, freedom and London, a great background of seductively indistinct hopes. To him her face was a warm dimness. In truth he could not see her eyes, but it seemed to his love-witched brain he did, and that they shone out at him like dusky stars.

All the world that evening was no more than a shadowy frame of darkling sky and water and dipping boughs about Helen. He seemed to see through things with an extraordinary clearness; she was revealed to him certainly, as the cause and essence of it all.

He was, indeed, at his Heart's Desire. It was one of those times when there seems to be no future, when Time has stopped and we are at the end. Kipps that evening could not have imagined a tomorrow; all that his imagination had pointed towards was attained. His mind stood still, and took the moments as they came.

4

About nine that night Coote came round to Kipps' new apartment in the Upper Sandgate Road—the house on the Leas had been let furnished—and Kipps made an effort towards realization. He was discovered sitting at the open window and without a lamp—quite still. Coote was deeply moved, and he pressed Kipps' palm and laid a knobby white hand on his shoulder, and displayed the sort of tenderness becoming in a crisis. Kipps, too, was moved that night, and treated Coote like a very dear brother.

"She's splendid," said Coote, coming to it abruptly.

"Isn't she?" said Kipps.

"I couldn't help noticing her face," said Coote. . . . "You know, my dear Kipps, this is better than a legacy."

"I don't deserve it," said Kipps.

"You can't say that."

"I don't. I can't 'ardly believe it. I can't believe it at all. No!"

There followed an expressive stillness.

"It's wonderful," said Kipps. "It takes me like that."

Coote made a faint blowing noise, and so again they came for a time on silence.

"And it began—before your money?"

"When I was in 'er class," said Kipps, solemnly.

Coote, speaking out of a darkness which he was illuminating strangely with efforts to strike a match, said it was beautiful. He could not have *wished* Kipps a better fortune. . . .

He lit a cigarette, and Kipps was moved to do the same, with a sacramental expression.

Presently speech flowed more freely.

Coote began to praise Helen, and her mother and brother; he talked of when "it" might be; he presented the thing as concrete and credible. "It's a county family, you know," he said. "She is connected, you know, with the Beauprés family—you know Lord Beauprés."

"No!" said Kipps, "reely!"

"Distantly, of course," said Coote. "Still—"

He smiled a smile that glimmered in the twilight.

"It's too much," said Kipps, overcome. "It's so all like that."

Coote exhaled. For a time Kipps listened to Helen's praises and matured a point of view.

"I say, Coote," he said. "What ought I to do now?"

"What do you mean?" said Coote.

"I mean about calling on 'er and all that."

He reflected. "Naturally I want to do it all right."

"Of course," said Coote.

"It would be awful to go and do something now—all wrong."

Coote's cigarette glowed as he meditated. "You must call, of course," he decided. "You'll have to speak to Mrs. Walshingham."

" 'Ow?" said Kipps.

"Tell her you mean to marry her daughter."

"I dessay she knows," said Kipps, with defensive penetration.

Coote's head was visible, shaking itself judicially.

"Then there's the ring," said Kipps. "What 'ave I to do about that?"

"What ring do you mean?"

" 'Ngagement Ring. There isn't anything at all about that in 'Manners and Rules of Good Society'—not a word."

"Of course you must get something—tasteful. Yes."

"What sort of ring?"

"Something nace. They'll show you in the shop."

"O' course. I s'pose I got to take it to 'er, eh? Put it on 'er finger."

"Oh no! Send it. Much better."

"Ah!" said Kipps for the first time with a note of relief.

"Then 'ow about this call?—on Mrs. Walshingham I mean. 'Ow ought one to go?"

"Rather a ceremonial occasion," reflected Coote.

"Wadyer mean? Frock-coat?"

"I *think* so," said Coote, with discrimination.

"Light trousers, and all that?"

"Yes."

"Rose?"

"I think it might run to a buttonhole."

The curtain that hung over the future became less opaque to the eyes of Kipps. Tomorrow, and then other days, became perceptible at least as existing. Frock-coat, silk hat, and a rose! With a certain solemnity he contemplated himself in the process of slow transformation into an English gentleman, Arthur Cuyps, frock-coated on occasions of ceremony, the familiar acquaintance of Lady Punnet, the recognized wooer of a distant connection of the Earl of Beauprés.

Something like awe at the magnitude of his own fortunes came upon him. He felt the world was opening out like a magic flower in a transformation scene at the touch of this wand of gold. And Helen, nestling beautiful in the red heart of the flower. Only ten weeks ago he had been no more than the shabbiest of improvers and shamefully dismissed for dissipation, the mere soil-buried seed, as it were, of these glories. He resolved the engagement ring should be of expressively excessive quality and appearance, in fact the very best they had.

"Ought I to send 'er flowers?" he speculated.

"Not necessarily," said Coote. "Though, of course, it's an attention. . . . ."

Kipps meditated on flowers.

"When you see her," said Coote, "you'll have to ask her to name the day."

Kipps started. "That won't be just yet a bit, will it?"

"Don't know any reason for delay."

"Oo, but—a year say."

"Rather a long taime," said Coote.

"Is it?" said Kipps, turning his head sharply. "But—"

There was quite a long pause.

"I say!" he said at last, and in an altered voice, "you'll 'ave to 'elp me about the wedding."

"Only too happy!" said Coote.

"O' course," said Kipps, "I didn't think—" He changed his line of thought. "Coote," he asked, "wot's a 'tate-eh-tate?'"

"A 'tate-ah-tay,'" said Coote, improvingly, "is a conversation alone together."

"Lor!" said Kipps, "but I thought— It says *strictly* we oughtn't to enjoy a tater-tay, not sit together, walk together, ride together, or meet during any part of the day. That don't leave much time for meeting, does it?"

"The book says that?" asked Coote.

"I jest learnt it by 'eart before you came. I thought that was a bit rum, but I s'pose it's all right."

"You won't find Mrs. Walshingham so strict as all that," said Coote. "I think that's a bit extreme. They'd only do that now in very strict old aristocratic families. Besides, the Walshinghams are so modern—advanced you might say. I expect you'll get plenty of chances of talking together."

"There's a tremendous lot to think about," said Kipps, blowing a profound sigh. "D'you mean—p'raps we might be married in a few months or so."

"You'll *have* to be," said Coote. "Why not? . . ."

Midnight found Kipps alone, looking a little tired, and turning over the leaves of the red-covered text-book with a studious expression. He paused for a moment at page 233, his eye caught by the words—

"FOR AN UNCLE OR AUNT BY MARRIAGE the period is six weeks black with jet trimmings."

"No," said Kipps, after a vigorous mental effort. "That's not it." The pages rustled again. He stopped and flattened out the little book decisively at the beginning of the chapter on "Weddings."

He became pensive. He stared at the lamp-wick. "I suppose I ought to go over and tell them," he said at last.

5

Kipps called on Mrs. Walshingham attired in the proper costume for Ceremonial Occasions in the Day. He carried a silk hat, and he wore a deep-skirted frock-coat; his boots were patent leather, and his trousers a dark gray. He had generous white cuffs with gold links, and his gray gloves, one thumb of which had burst when he put them on, he held loosely in his hand. He carried a small umbrella, rolled to an exquisite tightness. A sense of singular correctness pervaded his being and warred with the enormity of the occasion for possession of his soul. Anon he touched his silk cravat. The world smelled of his rosebud.

He seated himself on a newly re-covered chintz armchair, and stuck out the elbow of the arm that held his hat.

"I know," said Mrs. Walshingham, "I know everything," and helped him out most amazingly. She deepened the impression he had already received of her sense and refinement. She displayed an amount of tenderness that touched him.

"This is a great thing," she said, "to a mother," and her hand rested for a moment on his impeccable coat-sleeve.

"A daughter, Arthur," she explained, "is so much more than a son."

Marriage, she said, was a lottery, and without love and toleration—there was much unhappiness. Her life had not always been bright—there had been dark days and bright days. She smiled rather sweetly. "This is a bright one," she said.

She said very kind and flattering things to Kipps, and she thanked him for his goodness to her son. ("That wasn't anything," said Kipps.) And then she expanded upon the theme of her two children. "Both so accomplished," she said, "so clever. I call them my Twin Jewels."

She was repeating a remark she had made at Lympne, that she always said her children needed opportunities as other people needed air, when she was abruptly arrested by the entry of Helen. They hung on a pause, Helen perhaps surprised by Kipps' week-day magnificence. Then she advanced with outstretched hand.

Both the young people were shy. "I jest called round," began Kipps, and became uncertain how to end.

"Won't you have some tea?" asked Helen.

She walked to the window, looked at the familiar out-porter's barrow, turned, surveyed Kipps for a moment ambiguously, said "I will get some tea," and so departed again.

Mrs. Walshingham and Kipps looked at one another, and the lady smiled indulgently. "You two young people mustn't be shy of each other," said Mrs. Walshingham, which damaged Kipps considerably.

She was explaining how sensitive Helen always had been, even about quite little things, when the servant appeared with the tea-things; and then Helen followed, and, taking up a secure position behind the little bamboo tea-table, broke the ice with officious teacup clattering. Then she introduced the topic of a forthcoming open-air performance of *As You Like It,* and steered past the worst of the awkwardness. They discussed stage illusion. "I mus' say," said Kipps, "I don't quite like a play in a theayter. It seems sort of unreal some'ow."

"But most plays are written for the stage," said Helen, looking at the sugar.

"I know," admitted Kipps.

They got through tea. "Well," said Kipps, and rose.

"You mustn't go yet," said Mrs. Walshingham, rising and taking his hand. "I'm sure you two must have heaps to say to each other"; and so she escaped towards the door.

6

Among other projects that seemed almost equally correct to Kipps at that exalted moment was one of embracing Helen with ardor so soon as the door closed behind her mother, and one of headlong flight through the open window. Then he remembered he ought to hold the door open for Mrs. Walshingham, and turned from that duty to find Helen still standing, beautifully inaccessible, behind the tea-things. He closed the door and advanced towards her with his arms akimbo and his hands upon his coat skirts. Then feeling angular, he moved his right hand to his moustache. Anyhow, he was dressed all right. Somewhere at the back of his mind, dim and mingled with doubt and surprise, appeared the perception that he felt now quite differently towards her, that something between them had been blown from Lympne Keep to the four winds of heaven. . . .

She regarded him with an eye of critical proprietorship.

"Mother has been making up to you," she said, smiling slightly.

She added, "It was nice of you to come round to see her."

They stood through a brief pause, as though each had expected something different in the other, and was a little perplexed at its not being there. Kipps found he was at the corner of the brown-covered table, and he picked up a little flexible book that lay upon it to occupy his mind.

"I bought you a ring today," he said, bending the book and speaking for the sake of saying something, and then he moved to genuine speech. "You know," he said, "I can't 'ardly believe it."

Her face relaxed slightly again. "No?" she said, and may have breathed, "Nor I."

"No," he went on. "It's as though everything 'ad changed. More even than when I got that money. 'Ere we are going to marry. It's like being someone else. What I feel is—"

He turned a flushed and earnest face to her. He seemed to come alive to her with one natural gesture. "I don't *know* things. I'm not good enough. I'm not refined. The more you see of me, the more you'll find me out."

"But I'm going to help you."

"You'll 'ave to 'elp me a fearful lot."

She walked to the window, glanced out of it, made up her mind, turned and came towards him, with her hands clasped behind her back.

"All these things that trouble you are very little things. If you don't mind— if you will let me tell you things—"

"I wish you would."

"Then I will."

"They're little things to you, but they aren't to me."

"It all depends, if you don't mind being told."

"By you?"

"I don't expect you to be told by strangers."

"Oo!" said Kipps, expressing much.

"You know, there are just a few little things— For instance, you know, you are careless with your pronunciation. . . . You don't mind my telling you?"

"I like it," said Kipps.

"There's aitches."

"I know," said Kipps, and then endorsingly, "I been told. Fact is, I know a chap, a Nacter, *he's* told me. He's told me, and he's going to give me a lesson or so."

"I'm glad of that. It only requires a little care."

"Of course, on the stage they got to look out. They take regular lessons."

"Of course," said Helen, a little absently.

"I dessay I shall soon get into it," said Kipps.

"And then there's dress," said Helen, taking up her thread again.

Kipps became pink, but he remained respectfully attentive.

"You don't mind?" she said.

"Oo no."

"You mustn't be too—too dressy. It's possible to be over conventional, over elaborate. It makes you look like a shop . . . like a common well-off person. There's a sort of easiness that is better. A real gentleman looks right, without looking as though he had tried to be right."

"Jest as though 'e'd put on what came first?" said the pupil, in a faded voice.

"Not exactly that, but a sort of ease."

Kipps nodded his head intelligently. In his heart he was kicking his silk hat about the room in an ecstasy of disappointment.

"And you must accustom yourself to be more at your ease when you are with people," said Helen. "You've only got to forget yourself a little and not be anxious—"

"I'll try," said Kipps, looking rather hard at the teapot. "I'll do my best to try."

"I know you will," she said; and laid a hand for an instant upon his shoulder and withdrew it.

He did not perceive her caress. "One has to learn," he said. His attention was distracted by the strenuous efforts that were going on in the back of his head to translate "I say, didn't you ought to name the day?" into easy as well as elegant English, a struggle that was still undecided when the time came for them to part. . . .

He sat for a long time at the open window of his sitting-room with an intent face, recapitulating that interview. His eyes rested at last almost reproachfully on the silk hat beside him. " 'Ow *is* one to know?" he asked. His attention was caught by a rubbed place in the nap, and, still thoughtful, he rolled up his handkerchief skillfully into a soft ball and began to smooth this down.

His expression changed slowly.

" 'Ow the Juice is one to know?" he said, putting down the hat with some emphasis.

He rose up, went across the room to the sideboard, and, standing there, opened and began to read in "Manners and Rules."

CHAPTER IV

The Bicycle Manufacturer

1

SO KIPPS EMBARKED upon his engagement, steeled himself to the high enterprise of marrying above his breeding. The next morning found him dressing with a certain quiet severity of movement, and it seemed to his landlady's housemaid that he was unusually dignified at breakfast. He meditated profoundly over his kipper and his kidney and bacon. He was going to New Romney to tell the old people what had happened and where he stood. And the love of Helen had also given him courage to do what Buggins had once suggested to him as a thing he would do were he in Kipps' place, and that was to hire a motor-car for the afternoon. He had an early cold lunch, and then, with an air of quiet resolution, assumed a cap and coat he had purchased to this end, and, thus equipped, strolled round, blowing slightly, to the motor-shop. The transaction was unexpectedly easy, and within the hour, Kipps, spectacled and wrapped about, was tootling through Dymchurch.

They came to a stop smartly and neatly outside the little toy-shop. "Make that thing 'oot a bit, will you?" said Kipps. "Yes. That's it." "Whup," said the motor-car. "Whurrup." Both his Aunt and Uncle came out on the pavement. "Why, it's Artie!" cried his Aunt; and Kipps had a moment of triumph.

He descended to hand-claspings, removed wraps and spectacles, and the motor-driver retired to take "an hour off." Old Kipps surveyed the machinery and disconcerted Kipps for a moment by asking him, in a knowing tone, what they asked him for a thing like that. The two men stood inspecting the machine and impressing the neighbors for a time, and then they strolled through the shop into the little parlor for a drink.

"They ain't settled," old Kipps had said at the neighbors. "They ain't got no further than experiments. There's a bit of take-in about each. You take my advice and wait, me boy, even if it's a year or two before you buy one for your own use."

(Though Kipps had said nothing of doing anything of the sort.)

" 'Ow d'you like that whisky I sent?" asked Kipps, dodging the old familiar bunch of children's pails.

Old Kipps became tactful. "It's very good whisky, my boy," said old Kipps. "I 'aven't the slightest doubt it's a very good whisky, and cost you a tidy price. But—dashed if it soots me! They put this here Foozle Ile in it, my boy, and it ketches me jest 'ere." He indicated his center of figure. "Gives me the heartburn," he said, and shook his head rather sadly.

"It's a very good whisky," said Kipps. "It's what the actor-manager chaps drink in London, I 'appen to know."

"I dessay they do, my boy," said old Kipps, "but then they've 'ad their livers burnt out—and I 'aven't. They ain't dellicat like me. My stummik always *'as* been extry-dellicat. Sometimes it's almost been as though nothing would lay on it. But that's in passing. I liked those segars. You can send me some more of them segars. . . ."

You cannot lead a conversation straight from the gastric consequences of Foozle Ile to Love, and so Kipps, after a friendly inspection of a rare old engraving after Morland (perfect except for a hole kicked through the center) that his Uncle had recently purchased by private haggle, came to the topic of the old people's removal.

At the outset of Kipps' great fortunes there had been much talk of some permanent provision for them. It had been conceded they were to be provided for comfortably, and the phrase "retire from business" had been very much in the air. Kipps had pictured an ideal cottage with a creeper always in exuberant flower about the door, where the sun shone forever, and the wind never blew, and a perpetual welcome hovered in the doorway. It was an agreeable dream, but when it came to the point of deciding upon this particular cottage or that, and on this particular house or that, Kipps was surprised by an unexpected clinging to the little home, which he had always understood to be the worst of all possible houses.

"We don't want to move in a 'urry," said Mrs. Kipps.

"When we want to move, we want to move for life. I've had enough moving about in my time," said old Kipps.

"We can do here a bit more now we done here so long," said Mrs. Kipps.

"You lemme look about a bit *fust,*" said old Kipps.

And in looking about old Kipps found perhaps a finer joy than any mere possession could have given. He would shut his shop more or less effectually against the intrusion of customers, and toddle abroad seeking new matter for his dream; no house was too small and none too large for his knowing inquiries. Occupied houses took his fancy more than vacant ones, and he would remark, "You won't be a-livin' 'ere forever, even if you think you will," when irate householders protested against the unsolicited examination of their more intimate premises. . . .

Remarkable difficulties arose, of a totally unexpected sort.

"If we 'ave a larger 'ouse," said Mrs. Kipps, with sudden bitterness, "we shall want a servant, and I don't want no gells in the place larfin' at me, sniggerin' and larfin' and prancin' and trapesin', lardy da!

"If we 'ave a smaller 'ouse," said Mrs. Kipps, "there won't be room to swing a cat."

Room to swing a cat, it seemed, was absolutely essential. It was an infrequent but indispensable operation.

"When we *do* move," said old Kipps, "if we could get a bit of shootin'—

"I don't want to sell off all this here stock for nothin'," said old Kipps. "It's took years to 'cumulate. I put a ticket in the winder sayin' 'sellin' orf,' but it 'asn't brought nothing like a roosh. One of these 'ere dratted visitors, pretendin' to want an air-gun, was all we 'ad in yesterday. Jest an excuse for spyin' round, and then go away and larf at you. Nothanky to everything, it didn't matter what. . . . That's 'ow *I* look at it, Artie."

They pursued meandering fancies about the topic of their future settlement for a space, and Kipps became more and more hopeless of any proper conversational opening that would lead to his great announcement, and more and more uncertain how such an opening should be taken. Once, indeed, old Kipps, anxious to get away from this dangerous subject of removals, began, "And what are you a-doin' of in Folkestone? I shall have to come over and see you one of these days," but before Kipps could get in upon that, his Uncle had passed into a general exposition of the proper treatment of landladies and their humbugging cheating ways, and so the opportunity vanished. It seemed to Kipps the only thing to do was to go out into the town for a stroll, compose an effectual opening at leisure, and then come back and discharge it at them in its consecutive completeness. And even out-of-doors and alone he found his mind distracted by irrelevant thoughts.

2

His steps led him out of the High Street towards the church, and he leaned for a time over the gate that had once been the winning-post of his race with Ann Pornick, and presently found himself in a sitting position on the top rail. He had to get things smooth again, he knew; his mind was like a mirror of water after a breeze. The image of Helen and his great future was broken and mingled into fragmentary reflections of remoter things, of the good name of Old Methusaleh Three Stars, of long-dormant memories the High Street saw fit, by some trick of light and atmosphere, to arouse that afternoon. . . .

Abruptly a fine full voice from under his elbow shouted, "What-o, Art!" and behold Sid Pornick was back in his world, leaning over the gate beside him, and holding out a friendly hand.

He was oddly changed, and yet oddly like the Sid that Kipps had known. He had the old broad face and mouth, abundantly freckled, the same short nose, and the same blunt chin, the same odd suggestion of his sister Ann without a touch of her beauty; but he had quite a new voice, loud, and a little hard, and his upper lip carried a stiff and very fair moustache.

Kipps shook hands. "I was jest thinking of *you,* Sid," he said, "jest this very moment, and wondering if ever I should see you again—ever. And 'ere you are!"

"One likes a look round at times," said Sid. "How are *you,* old chap?"

"All right," said Kipps. "I just been lef'—"

"You aren't changed much," interrupted Sid.

"Ent I?" said Kipps, foiled.

"I knew your back directly I came round the corner. Spite of that 'at you got on. Hang it, I said, that's Art Kipps or the devil. And so it was."

Kipps made a movement of his neck as if he would look at his back and judge. Then he looked Sid in the face. "You got a moustache, Sid," he said.

"I s'pose you're having your holidays?" said Sid.

"Well, partly. But I just been lef'—"

"*I'm* taking a bit of a holiday," Sid went on. "But the fact is, I have to give *myself* holidays nowadays. I've set up for myself."

"Not down here?"

"No fear! I'm not a turnip. I've started in Hammersmith, manufacturing." Sid spoke offhand, as though there was no such thing as pride.

"Not drapery?"

"No fear! Engineer. Manufacture bicycles." He clapped his hand to his breast pocket and produced a number of pink handbills. He handed one to Kipps, and prevented him reading it by explanations and explanatory dabs of a pointing finger. "That's our make—my make, to be exact—the Red Flag—see? I got a transfer with my name—Pantocrat tires, eight pounds—yes, *there*—Clinchers ten, Dunlops eleven, Ladies' one pound more—that's the lady's. Best machine at a democratic price in London. No guineas and no discounts—honest trade. I build 'em—to order. I've built," he reflected, looking away seaward, "seventeen. Counting orders in 'and. . . .

"Come down to look at the old place a bit," said Sid. "Mother likes it at times."

"Thought you'd all gone away—"

"What! after my father's death? No! My mother's come back, and she's living at Muggett's cottages. The sea-air suits 'er. She likes the old place better than Hammersmith . . . and I can afford it. Got an old crony or so here. . . . Gossip . . . have tea. . . . S'pose *you* ain't married, Kipps?"

Kipps shook his head. "I—" he began.

"*I* am," said Sid. "Married these two years, and got a nipper. Proper little chap."

Kipps got his word in at last. "I got engaged day before yesterday," he said.

"Ah!" said Sid, airily. "That's all right. Who's the fortunate lady?"

Kipps tried to speak in an offhand way. He stuck his hands in his pockets as he spoke. "She's a solicitor's daughter," he said, "in Folkestone. Rather'r nice set. County family. Related to the Earl of Beauprés—"

"Steady on!" cried Sid.

"You see, I've 'ad a bit of luck, Sid. Been lef' money."

Sid's eye traveled instinctively to mark Kipps' garments. "How much?" he asked.

" 'Bout twelve 'undred a year," said Kipps, more offhandedly than ever.

"Lord!" said Sid, with a note of positive dismay, and stepped back a pace or two.

"My granfaver it was," said Kipps, trying hard to be calm and simple. " 'Ardly knew I '*ad* a granfaver. And then—bang! When o' Bean, the solicitor, told me of it, you could 'ave knocked me down—"

" '*Ow* much?" demanded Sid, with a sharp note in his voice.

"Twelve 'undred pound a year—proximately, that is." . . .

Sid's attempt at genial unenvious congratulation did not last a minute. He shook hands with an unreal heartiness, and said he was jolly glad. "It's a blooming stroke of Luck," he said.

"It's a bloomin' stroke of Luck," he repeated, "that's what it is," with the smile fading from his face. "Of course, better you 'ave it than me, o' chap. So I don't envy you, anyhow. *I* couldn't keep it if I did 'ave it."

" 'Ow's that?" said Kipps, a little hipped by Sid's patent chagrin.

"I'm a Socialist, you see," said Sid. "I don't 'old with Wealth. What *is*

Wealth? Labor robbed out of the poor. At most it's only yours in trust. Leastways, that's 'ow *I* should take it.''

He reflected. ''The Present distribution of Wealth,'' he said, and stopped.

Then he let himself go, with unmasked bitterness. ''It's no sense at all. It's jest damn foolishness. Who's going to work and care in a muddle like this? Here first you do—something anyhow—of the world's work and it pays you hardly anything, and then it invites you to do nothing, nothing whatever, and pays you twelve hundred pounds a year. Who's going to respect laws and customs when they come to damn silliness like that?''

He repeated, ''Twelve hundred pounds a year!''

At the sight of Kipps' face he relented slightly.

''It's not you I'm thinking of, o' man; it's the system. Better you than most people. Still—''

He laid both hands on the gate and repeated to himself, ''Twelve 'undred a year. . . . Gee-whizz, Kipps! You'll be a swell!''

''I sha'n't,'' said Kipps, with imperfect conviction. ''No fear.''

''You can't 'ave money like that and not swell out. You'll soon be too big to speak to—'ow do they put it?—a mere mechanic like me.''

''No fear, Siddee,'' said Kipps, with conviction. ''I ain't that sort.''

''Ah!'' said Sid, with a sort of unwilling skepticism, ''money'll be too much for you. Besides—you're caught by a swell already.''

'' 'Ow d'yer mean?''

''That girl you're going to marry. Masterman says—''

''Oo's Masterman?''

''Rare good chap, I know—takes my first-floor front room. Masterman says it's always the wife pitches the key. Always. There's no social differences—till women come in.''

''Ah?'' said Kipps, profoundly. ''You don't know.''

Sid shook his head. ''Fancy!'' he reflected, ''Art Kipps! . . . Twelve 'Undred a Year!''

Kipps tried to bridge that opening gulf. ''Remember the Hurons, Sid?''

''Rather,'' said Sid.

''Remember that wreck?''

''I can smell it now—sort of sour smell.''

Kipps was silent for a moment, with reminiscent eyes on Sid's still troubled face.

''I say, Sid, 'ow's Ann?''

''*She's* all right,'' said Sid.

''Where is she now?''

''In a place . . . Ashford.''

''Oh!''

Sid's face had become a shade sulkier than before.

''The fact is,'' he said, ''we don't get on very well together. *I* don't hold with service. We're common people, I suppose, but I don't like it. I don't see why a sister of mine should wait at other people's tables. No. Not even if they got Twelve 'Undred a Year.''

Kipps tried to change the point of application. ''Remember 'ow you came out once when we were racing here? . . . She didn't run bad for a girl.''

And his own words raised an image brighter than he could have supposed, so bright it seemed to breathe before him, and did not fade altogether, even when he was back in Folkestone an hour or so later.

But Sid was not to be deflected from that other rankling theme by any reminiscences of Ann.

"I wonder what you will do with all that money," he speculated. "I wonder if you will do any good at all. I wonder what you *could* do. You should hear Masterman. He'd tell you things. Suppose it came to me; what should I do? It's no good giving it back to the State as things are. Start an Owenite profit-sharing factory perhaps. Or a new Socialist paper. We want a new Socialist paper."

He tried to drown his personal chagrin in elaborate exemplary suggestions. . . .

3

"I must be gettin' onto my motor," said Kipps at last, having to a large extent heard him out.

"What! Got a motor?"

"No!" said Kipps, apologetically. "Only jobbed for the day."

" 'Ow much?"

"Five pounds."

"Keep five families for a week! Good Lord!" That seemed to crown Sid's disgust.

Yet drawn by a sort of fascination, he came with Kipps and assisted at the mounting of the motor. He was pleased to note it was not the most modern of motors, but that was the only grain of comfort. Kipps mounted at once, after one violent agitation of the little shop-door to set the bell ajangle and warn his Uncle and Aunt. Sid assisted with the great fur-lined overcoat and examined the spectacles.

"Good-bye, o' chap!" said Kipps.

"Good-bye, o' chap!" said Sid.

The old people came out to say good-bye.

Old Kipps was radiant with triumph. " 'Pon my sammy, Artie! I'm a goo' mind to come with you," he shouted; and then, "I got something you might take with you!"

He dodged back into the shop and returned with the perforated engraving after Morland.

"You stick to this, my boy," he said. "You get it repaired by someone who knows. It's the most vallyble thing I got you so far—you take my word."

"Warrup!" said the motor, and tuff, tuff, tuff, and backed and snorted, while old Kipps danced about on the pavement as if foreseeing complex catastrophes, and told the driver, "That's all right."

He waved his stout stick to his receding nephew. Then he turned to Sid. "Now, if you could make something like that, young Pornick, you *might* blow a bit!"

"I'll make a doocid sight better than *that* before I done," said Sid, hands deep in his pockets.

"Not *you*," said old Kipps.

The motor set up a prolonged sobbing moan and vanished round the corner. Sid stood motionless for a space, unheeding some further remark from old Kipps. The young mechanic had just discovered that to have manufactured seventeen bicycles, including orders in hand, is not so big a thing as he had supposed, and such discoveries try one's manhood. . . .

"Oh, well!" said Sid, at last, and turned his face towards his mother's cottage. She had got a hot teacake for him, and she was a little hurt that he was dark and preoccupied as he consumed it. He had always been such a boy for teacake, and then when one went out specially and got him one—!

He did not tell her—he did not tell anyone—he had seen young Kipps. He did not want to talk about Kipps for a bit to anyone at all.

CHAPTER V

The Pupil Lover

1

WHEN KIPPS CAME to reflect upon his afternoon's work, he had his first inkling of certain comprehensive incompatibilities lying about the course of true love in his particular case. He had felt without understanding the incongruity between the announcement he had failed to make and the circle of ideas of his Aunt and Uncle. It was this rather than the want of a specific intention that had silenced him, the perception that when he traveled from Folkestone to New Romney he traveled from an atmosphere where his engagement to Helen was sane and excellent to an atmosphere where it was only to be regarded with incredulous suspicion. Coupled and associated with this jar was his sense of the altered behavior of Sid Pornick, the evident shock to that ancient alliance caused by the fact of his enrichment, the touch of hostility in his "You'll soon be swelled too big to speak to a poor mechanic like me." Kipps was unprepared for the unpleasant truth—that the path of social advancement is, and must be, strewn with broken friendships. This first protrusion of that fact caused a painful confusion in his mind. It was speedily to protrude in a far more serious fashion in relation to the "hands" from the Emporium, and Chitterlow.

From the day at Lympne Castle his relations with Helen had entered upon a new footing. He had prayed for Helen as good souls pray for heaven, with as little understanding of what it was he prayed for. And now that period of standing humbly in the shadows before the shrine was over, and the goddess, her veil of mystery flung aside, had come down to him and taken hold of him, a good strong firm hold, and walked by his side. . . . She liked him. What was singular was, that very soon she had kissed him thrice, whimsically upon the brow, and he had never kissed her at all. He could not analyze his feelings, only he knew the world was wonderfully changed about them; but the truth was that, though he still worshipped and feared her, though his pride in his engagement was ridiculously vast, he loved her now no more. That subtle something, woven of the most delicate strands of self-love and tenderness and desire, had vanished imperceptibly, and was gone now forever. But that she did not suspect in him, nor, as a matter of fact, did he.

She took him in hand in perfect good faith. She told him things about his accent; she told him things about his bearing, about his costume and his way of looking at things. She thrust the blade of her intelligence into the tenderest corners of Kipps' secret vanity; she slashed his most intimate pride to bleeding tatters. He sought very diligently to anticipate some at least of these informing thrusts by making great use of Coote. But the unanticipated made a brave number . . .

She found his simple willingness a very lovable thing.

Indeed, she liked him more and more. There was a touch of motherliness in her feelings towards him. But his upbringing and his associations had been, she diagnosed, "awful." At New Romney she glanced but little—that was remote. But in her inventory—she went over him as one might go over a newly taken house, with impartial thoroughness—she discovered more proximate influences, surprising intimations of nocturnal "sing-songs,"—she pictured it as almost shocking that Kipps should sing to the banjo—much low-grade wisdom treasured from a person called Buggins—"Who *is* Buggins?" said Helen—vague figures of indisputable vulgarity—Pearce and Carshot—and more particularly a very terrible social phenomenon—Chitterlow.

Chitterlow blazed upon them with unheralded oppressive brilliance, the first time they were abroad together.

They were going along the front of the Leas to see a school-play in Sandgate—at the last moment Mrs. Walshingham had been unable to come with them—when Chitterlow loomed up into the new world. He was wearing the suit of striped flannel and the straw hat that had followed Kipps' payment in advance for his course in elocution, his hands were deep in his side-pockets and animated the corners of his jacket, and his attentive gaze at the passing loungers, the faint smile under his boldly drawn nose, showed him engaged in studying character—no doubt for some forthcoming play.

"What HO!" said he, at the sight of Kipps, and swept off the straw hat with so ample a clutch of his great flat hand that it suggested to Helen's startled mind a conjuror about to palm a halfpenny.

"Ello, Chitt'low," said Kipps, a little awkwardly, and not saluting.

Chitterlow hesitated. "Half a mo', my boy," he said, and arrested Kipps by extending a large hand over his chest. "Excuse me, my dear," he said, bowing like a Russian count by way of apology to Helen, and with a smile that would have killed at a hundred yards. He effected a semi-confidential grouping of himself and Kipps, while Helen stood in white amazement.

"About that play," he said.

" 'Ow about it?" asked Kipps, acutely aware of Helen.

"It's all right," said Chitterlow. "There's a strong smell of syndicate in the air, I may tell you. Strong."

"That's aw right," said Kipps.

"You needn't tell everybody," said Chitterlow, with a transitory confidential hand to his mouth, which pointed the application of the "everybody" just a trifle too strongly. "But I think it's coming off. However— I mustn't detain you now. So long. You'll come round, eh?"

"Right you are," said Kipps.

"Tonight?"

"At eight."

And then, and more in the manner of a Russian prince than any common count, Chitterlow bowed and withdrew. Just for a moment he allowed a conquering eye to challenge Helen's, and noted her for a girl of quality . . .

There was a silence between our lovers for a space.

"That," said Kipps, with an allusive movement of the head, "was Chitt'low."

"Is he—a friend of yours?"

"In a way. . . . You see, I met 'im. Leastways 'e met me. Run into me with a bicycle, 'e did, and so we got talking together."

He tried to appear at his ease. The young lady scrutinized his profile.

"What is he?"

" 'E's a Nacter chap," said Kipps. "Leastways 'e writes plays."

"And sells them?"

"Partly."

"Whom to?"

"Different people. Shares he sells. . . . It's all right, reely—I meant to tell you about him before."

Helen looked over her shoulder to catch a view of Chitterlow's retreating aspect. It did not compel her complete confidence.

She turned to her lover, and said in a tone of quiet authority, "You must tell me all about Chitterlow. Now."

The explanation began. . . .

The School Play came almost as a relief to Kipps. In the flusterment of going in he could almost forget, for a time, his Laocoon struggle to explain, and in the intervals he did his best to keep forgetting. But Helen, with a gentle insistence, resumed the explanation of Chitterlow as they returned towards Folkestone.

Chitterlow was confoundedly difficult to explain. You could hardly imagine!

There was an almost motherly anxiety in Helen's manner, blended with the resolution of a schoolmistress to get to the bottom of the affair. Kipps' ears were soon quite brightly red.

"Have you seen one of his plays?"

" 'E's tole me about one."

"But on the stage."

"No. He 'asn't 'ad any on the stage yet. That's all coming. . . ."

"Promise me," she said in conclusion, "you won't do anything without consulting me."

And, of course, Kipps promised. "Oo no!"

They went on their way in silence.

"One can't know everybody," said Helen in general.

"Of course," said Kipps, "in a sort of way it was him that helped me to my money." And he indicated in a confused manner the story of the advertisement. "I don't like to drop 'im all at once," he added.

Helen was silent for a space, and when she spoke she went off at a tangent. "We shall live in London—soon," she remarked. "It's only while we are here."

It was the first intimation she gave him of their post-nuptial prospects.

"We shall have a nice little flat somewhere, not too far west, and there we shall build up a circle of our own."

2

All that declining summer Kipps was the pupil lover. He made an extraordinarily open secret of his desire for self-improvement; indeed Helen had to hint once or twice that his modest frankness was excessive, and all this new circle of friends did, each after his or her manner, everything that was possible to supplement Helen's efforts and help him to ease and skill in the more cultivated circles to which he had come. Coote was still the chief teacher, the tutor—there are so many little difficulties that a man may take to another man that he would not care to propound to the woman he loves—but they were all, so to speak, upon the staff. Even the freckled girl said to him once in a pleasant way, "You mustn't say 'contre temps,' you must say 'contraytom,' " when he borrowed that expression from "Manners and Rules," and she tried, at his own suggestion, to give him clear ideas upon the subject of "as" and "has." A certain confusion between these words was becoming evident, the firstfruits of a lesson from Chitterlow on the aspirate. Hitherto he had discarded that dangerous letter almost altogether, but now he would pull up at words beginning with "h" and draw a sawing breath—rather like a startled kitten—and then aspirate with vigor.

Said Kipps one day, "*As* 'e?—I should say, ah— Has 'e? Ye know I got a lot of difficulty over them two words, which is which?"

"Well, 'as' is a conjunction, and 'has' is a verb."

"I know," said Kipps, "but when is 'has' a conjunction and when is 'as' a verb?"

"Well," said the freckled girl, preparing to be very lucid. "It's *has* when it means one has, meaning having, but if it isn't it's *as*. As, for instance, one says 'e—I mean *he*—He has. But one says 'as he has.' "

"I see," said Kipps. "So I ought to say 'as 'e'?"

"No, if you are asking a question you say *has* 'e—I mean he—'as he?" She blushed quite brightly, but still clung to her air of lucidity.

"I see," said Kipps. He was about to say something further, but he desisted. "I got it much clearer now. *Has* 'e? *Has* 'e as. Yes."

"If you remember about having."

"Oo, I will," said Kipps. . . .

Miss Coote specialized in Kipps' artistic development. She had early formed an opinion that he had considerable artistic sensibility; his remarks on her work had struck her as decidedly intelligent, and whenever he called round to see them she would show him some work of art—now an illustrated book, now perhaps a color print of a Botticelli, now the Hundred Best Paintings, now "Academy Pictures," now a German art handbook, and now some magazine of furniture and design. "I know you like these things," she used to say, and Kipps said "Oo I *do*." He soon acquired a little armory of appreciative sayings. When presently the Walshinghams took him up to the Arts and Crafts, his deportment was intelligent in the extreme. For a time he kept a wary silence and suddenly pitched upon a color print. "That's rather nace," he said to Mrs. Walshingham. "That lill' thing. There." He always said things like that by preference to the mother rather than the daughter unless he was perfectly sure.

He quite took to Mrs. Walshingham. He was impressed by her conspicuous tact and refinement; it seemed to him that the ladylike could go no further. She was always dressed with a delicate fussiness that was never disarranged, and even a sort of faded quality about her hair, and face, and bearing, and emotions, contributed to her effect. Kipps was not a big man, and commonly he did not feel a big man, but with Mrs. Walshingham he always felt enormous and distended, as though he was a navvy who had taken some disagreeable poison which puffed him up inside his skin as a preliminary to bursting. He felt, too, as though he had been rolled in clay and his hair dressed with gum. And he felt that his voice was strident and his accent like somebody swinging a crowded pig's-pail in a free and careless manner. All this increased and enforced his respect for her. Her hand, which flitted often and again to his hand and arm, was singularly well shaped and cool. "Arthur" she called him from the very beginning.

She did not so much positively teach and tell him as tactfully guide and infect him. Her conversation was not so much didactic as exemplary. She would say, "I *do* like people to do" so and so. She would tell him anecdotes of nice things done, of gentlemanly feats of graceful consideration; she would record her neat observations of people in trains and omnibuses, how, for example, a man had passed her change to the conductor, "quite a common man he looked," but he had lifted his hat. She stamped Kipps so deeply with the hat-raising habit that he would uncover if he found himself in the same railway-ticket office with a lady, and so stand ceremoniously until the difficulties of change drove him to an apologetic provisional oblique resumption of his headgear. . . . And robbing these things of any air of personal application, she threw about them an abundant talk about her two children—she called them her Twin Jewels quite frequently—about their gifts, their temperaments, their ambition, their need of opportunity. They needed opportunity, she would say, as other people needed air. . . .

In his conversations with her Kipps always assumed—and she seemed to assume—that she was to join that home in London Helen foreshadowed; but he was surprised one day to gather that this was not to be the case. "It wouldn't do," said Helen, with decision. "We want to make a circle of our own."

"But won't she be a bit lonely down here?" asked Kipps.

"There's the Waces, and Mrs. Prebble, and Mrs. Bindon Botting, and—lots of people she knows." And Helen dismissed this possibility. . . .

Young Walshingham's share in the educational syndicate was smaller. But he shone out when they went to London on that Arts and Crafts expedition. Then this rising man of affairs showed Kipps how to buy the more theatrical weeklies for consumption in the train, how to buy and what to buy in the way of cigarettes with gold tips and shilling cigars, and how to order hock for lunch and sparkling Moselle for dinner, how to calculate the fare of a hansom cab—penny a minute while he goes—how to look intelligently at an hotel tape, and how to sit still in a train like a thoughtful man instead of talking like a fool and giving yourself away. And he, too, would glance at the good time coming when they were to be in London for good and all.

That prospect expanded and developed particulars. It presently took up a large part of Helen's conversation. Her conversations with Kipps were never of a grossly sentimental sort; there was a shyness of speech in that matter with both of them; but these new adumbrations were at least as interesting, and not so directly disagreeable, as the clear-cut intimations of personal defect that for a time had so greatly chastened Kipps' delight in her presence. The future presented itself with an almost perfect frankness as a joint campaign of Mrs. Walshingham's Twin Jewels upon the Great World, with Kipps in the capacity of baggage and supply. They would still be dreadfully poor, of course—this amazed Kipps, but he said nothing—until "Brudderkins" began to succeed; but if they were clever and lucky they might do a great deal.

When Helen spoke of London a brooding look, as of one who contemplates a distant country, came into her eyes. Already it seemed they had the nucleus of a set. Brudderkins was a member of the Theatrical Judges, an excellent and influential little club of journalists and literary people, and he knew Shimer and Stargate and Whiffle of the "Red Dragon," and besides these were the Revels. They knew the Revels quite well. Sidney Revel, before his rapid rise to prominence as a writer of epigrammatic essays that were quite above the ordinary public, had been an assistant master at one of the best Folkestone schools. Brudderkins had brought him home to tea several times, and it was he had first suggested Helen should try and write. "It's perfectly easy," Sidney had said. He had been writing occasional things for the evening papers and for the weekly reviews even at that time. Then he had gone up to London, and had almost unavoidably become a dramatic critic. Those brilliant essays had followed, and then "Red Hearts a Beating," the romance that had made him. It was a tale of spirited adventure, full of youth and beauty and naïve passion and generous devotion, bold, as the *Bookman* said, and frank in places, but never in the slightest degree morbid. He had met and married an American widow with quite a lot of money, and they had made a very distinct place for themselves, Kipps learned, in the literary and artistic society of London. Helen seemed to dwell on the Revels a great deal; it was her exemplary story, and when she spoke of Sidney—she often called him Sidney—she would become thoughtful. She spoke most of him, naturally, because she had still to meet Mrs. Revel. . . . Certainly they would be in the world in no time, even if the distant connection with the Beauprés family came to nothing.

Kipps gathered that with his marriage and the movement to London they were to undergo that subtle change of name Coote had first adumbrated. They were to become "Cuyps," Mr. and Mrs. Cuyps. Or was it Cuyp?

"It'll be rum at first," said Kipps.

"I dessay I shall soon get into it," he said. . . .

So in their several ways they all contributed to enlarge and refine and exercise the intelligence of Kipps. And behind all these other influences, and as it were presiding over and correcting these influences, was Kipps' nearest friend, Coote, a sort of master of the ceremonies. You figure his face, blowing slightly with solicitude, his slate-colored, projecting, but not unkindly eye intent upon our hero. The thing, he thought, was going off admirably. He studied Kipps' character immensely. He would discuss him with his sister, with Mrs. Walshingham, with the freckled girl, with anyone who would stand it. "He is an interesting character," he would say, "likeable—a sort of gentleman by instinct. He takes to all these things. He improves every day. He'll soon get Sang Froid. We took him up just in time. He wants now— Well— Next year, perhaps, if there is a good Extension Literature course he might go in for it. He wants to go in for something like that."

"He's going in for his bicycle now," said Mrs. Walshingham.

"That's all right for summer," said Coote, "but he wants to go in for some serious intellectual interest, something to take him out of himself a little more. Savoir Faire and self-forgetfulness is more than half the secret of Sang Froid." . . .

3

The world, as Coote presented it, was in part an endorsement, in part an amplification, and in part a rectification of the world of Kipps—the world that derived from the old couple in New Romney and had been developed in the Emporium; the world, in fact, of common British life. There was the same subtle sense of social gradation that had moved Mrs. Kipps to prohibit intercourse with laborers' children, the same dread of anything "common" that had kept the personal quality of Mr. Shalford's establishment so high. But now a certain disagreeable doubt about Kipps' own position was removed, and he stood with Coote inside the sphere of gentlemen assured. Within the sphere of gentlemen there are distinctions of rank indeed, but none of class; there are the Big People, and the modest, refined, gentlemanly little people, like Coote, who may even dabble in the professions and counterless trades; there are lords and magnificences, and there are gentlefolk who have to manage—but they can all call on one another, they preserve a general equality of deportment throughout, they constitute that great state within the state—Society.

"But reely," said the Pupil, "not what you call being in Society?"

"Yes," said Coote. "Of course, down here, one doesn't see much of it, but there's local society. It has the same rules."

"Calling and all that?"

"Precisely," said Coote.

Kipps thought, whistled a bar, and suddenly broached a question of conscience.

"I often wonder," he said, "whether I oughtn't to dress for dinner—when I'm alone 'ere."

Coote protruded his lips and reflected. "Not full dress," he adjudicated; "that would be a little excessive. But you should *change,* you know. Put on a mess jacket, and that sort of thing—easy dress. That is what *I* should do, certainly, if I wasn't in harness—and poor."

He coughed modestly, and patted his hair behind.

And after that the washing-bill of Kipps quadrupled, and he was to be seen at times by the bandstand with his light summer overcoat unbuttoned, to give a glimpse of his nice white tie. He and Coote would be smoking the gold-tipped cigarettes young Walshingham had prescribed as "chic," and appreciating the music highly. "That's—puff—a very nice bit," Kipps would say; or better, "That's nace." And at the first grunts of the loyal anthem up they stood with religiously uplifted hats. Whatever else you might call them, you could never call them disloyal.

The boundary of Society was admittedly very close to Coote and Kipps, and a leading solicitude of the true gentleman was to detect clearly those "beneath" him, and to behave towards them in a proper spirit. "It's jest there it's so 'ard for me," said Kipps. He had to cultivate a certain "distance" to acquire altogether the art of checking the presumption of bounders and old friends. It was difficult, Coote admitted.

"I got mixed up with this lot 'ere," said Kipps. "That's what's so harkward— I mean awkward."

"You could give them a hint," said Coote.

" 'Ow?"

"Oh—the occasion will suggest something."

The occasion came one early-closing night, when Kipps was sitting in a canopy chair near the bandstand with his summer overcoat fully open, and a new Gibus pulled slightly forward over his brow, waiting for Coote. They were to hear the band for an hour, and then go down to assist Miss Coote and the freckled girl in trying over some Beethoven duets, if they remembered them, that is, sufficiently well. And as Kipps lounged back in his chair and occupied his mind with his favorite amusement on such evenings, which consisted chiefly in supposing that everyone about him was wondering who he was, came a rude rap at the canvas back and the voice of Pearce.

"It's nice to be a gentleman," said Pearce, and swung a penny chair into position, while Buggins appeared smiling agreeably on the other side, and leaned upon his stick. *He was smoking a common briar pipe!*

The real ladies, very fashionably dressed, and sitting close at hand, glanced quickly at Pearce, and then away again, and it was evident *their* wonder was at an end.

"He's all right," said Buggins, removing his pipe and surveying Kipps.

"Ello, Buggins!" said Kipps, not too cordially. " 'Ow goes it?"

"All right. Holidays next week. If you don't look out, Kipps, I shall be on the Continong before you. Eh?"

"You going t' Boologne?"

"Ra-ther. Parley vous Francey. You bet."

"I shall 'ave a bit of a run over there one of these days," said Kipps.

There came a pause. Pearce applied the top of his stick to his mouth for a space, and regarded Kipps. Then he glanced at the people about them.

"I say, Kipps," he said in a distinct loud voice, "see 'er Ladyship lately?"

Kipps perceived the audience was to be impressed, but he responded half-heartedly. "No, I 'aven't," he said.

"She was along of Sir William the other night," said Pearce, still loud and clear, "and she asked to be remembered to you."

It seemed to Kipps that one of the two ladies smiled faintly, and said something to the other, and then certainly they glanced at Pearce. Kipps flushed scarlet. *"Did* she?" he answered.

Buggins laughed good-humoredly over his pipe.

"Sir William suffers a lot from his gout," Pearce continued unabashed.

(Buggins much amused with his pipe between his teeth.)

Kipps became aware of Coote at hand.

Coote nodded rather distantly to Pearce. "Hope I haven't kept you waiting, Kipps," he said.

"I kep' a chair for you," said Kipps, and removed a guardian foot.

"But you've got your friends," said Coote.

"Oh, *we* don't mind," said Pearce, cordially, "the more the merrier"; and, "Why don't you get a chair, Buggins?" Buggins shook his head in a sort of aside to Pearce, and Coote coughed behind his hand.

"Been kep' late at business?" asked Pearce.

Coote turned quite pale, and pretended not to hear. His eyes sought in space for a time, and with a convulsive movement he recognized a distant acquaintance and raised his hat.

Pearce had also become a little pale. He addressed himself to Kipps in an undertone.

"Mr. Coote, isn't he?" he asked.

Coote addressed himself to Kipps directly and exclusively. His manner had the calm of extreme tension.

"I'm rather late," he said. "I think we ought almost to be going on *now.*"

Kipps stood up. "That's all right," he said.

"Which way are you going?" said Pearce, standing also, and brushing some crumbs of cigarette ash from his sleeve.

For a moment Coote was breathless. "Thank you," he said, and gasped. Then he delivered the necessary blow, "I don't think we're in need of your society, you know," and turned away.

Kipps found himself falling over chairs and things in the wake of Coote, and then they were clear of the crowd.

For a space Coote said nothing; then he remarked abruptly, and quite angrily for him, "I think that was *awful* Cheek!"

Kipps made no reply. . . .

The whole thing was an interesting little object-lesson in "distance," and it stuck in the front of Kipps' mind for a long time. He had particularly vivid the face of Pearce with an expression between astonishment and anger. He felt as though he had struck Pearce in the face under circumstances that gave Pearce no power to reply. He did not attend very much to the duets, and even forgot at the end of one of them to say how perfectly lovely it was.

4

But you must not imagine that the national ideal of a gentleman, as Coote developed it, was all a matter of deportment and selectness, a mere isolation from debasing associations. There is a Serious Side, a deeper aspect of the true True Gentleman. But it is not vocal. The True Gentleman does not wear his heart on his sleeve. For example, he is deeply religious, as Coote was, as Mrs. Walshingham was; but outside the walls of a church it never appears, except perhaps now and then in a pause, in a profound look, in a sudden avoidance. In quite a little while Kipps also had learned the pause, the profound look, the sudden avoidance, that final refinement of spirituality, impressionistic piety.

And the True Gentleman is patriotic also. When one saw Coote lifting his hat to the National Anthem, then perhaps one got a glimpse of what patriotic emotions, what worship, the polish of a gentleman may hide. Or singing out his deep notes against the Hosts of Midian, in the St. Stylites' choir; then indeed you plumbed his spiritual side.

> *Christian, dost thou heed them*
> *On the holy ground,*
> *How the hosts of Mid-i-an*
> *Prowl and prowl around?*
> *Christian, up and smai-it them . . .*

But these were but gleams. For the rest, Religion, Nationality, Passion, Finance, Politics, much more so those cardinal issues Birth and Death, the True Gentleman skirted about, and became facially rigid towards, and ceased to speak, and panted and blew.

"One doesn't talk of that sort of thing," Coote would say, with a gesture of the knuckly hand.

"O' course," Kipps would reply, with an equal significance.

Profundities. Deep, as it were, blowing to deep.

One does not talk, but on the other hand one is punctilious to do. Action speaks. Kipps—in spite of the fact that the Walshinghams were more than a little lax—Kipps, who had formerly flitted Sunday after Sunday from one Folkestone church to another, had now a sitting of his own, paid for duly, at Saint Stylites. There he was to be seen, always at the surplice evening service, and sometimes of a morning, dressed with a sober precision, and with an eye on Coote in the chancel. No difficulties now about finding the place in his book. He became a communicant again—he had lapsed soon after his confirmation when the young lady in the costume-room who was his adopted sister left the Emporium—and he would sometimes go round to the Vestry for Coote, after the service. One evening he was introduced to the Hon. and Rev. Densmore. He was much too confused to say anything, and the noble cleric had nothing to say, but they were introduced. . . .

No! You must not imagine that the national ideal of a gentleman is without its "serious side," without even its stern and uncompromising side. The imagination, no doubt, refuses to see Coote displaying extraordinary refinements of courage upon the stricken field, but in the walks of peace there is sometimes sore need of sternness. Charitable as one may be, one must admit there are people who *do* things—impossible things; people who place themselves "out of it" in countless ways; people, moreover, who are by a sort of predestination out of it from the beginning; and against these Society has invented a terrible protection for its Cootery—the Cut. The cut is no joke for anyone. It is excommunication. You may be cut by an individual, you may be cut by a set, or you may be—and this is so tragic that beautiful romances have been written about it—"Cut by the County." One figures Coote discharging this last duty and cutting somebody— Coote, erect and pale, never speaking, going past with eyes of pitiless slate, lower jaw protruding a little, face pursed up and cold and stiff. . . .

It never dawned upon Kipps that he would one day have to face this terrible front, to be to Coote not only as one dead, but as one gone more than a stage or so in decay, cut and passed, banned and outcast forever. It never dawned upon either of them.

Yet so it was to be!

One cannot hide any longer that all this fine progress of Kipps is doomed to end in collapse. So far, indeed, you have seen him ascend. You have seen him becoming more refined and careful day by day, more carefully dressed, less clumsy in the uses of social life. You have seen the gulf widening between himself and his former low associates. I have brought you at last to the vision of him, faultlessly dressed and posed, in an atmosphere of candlelight and chanting, in his own sitting, his own sitting! in one of the most fashionable churches in Folkestone. . . . I have refrained from the lightest touch upon the tragic note that must now creep into my tale. Yet the net of his low connections has been about his feet, and, moreover, there was something interwoven in his being. . . .

CHAPTER VI

Discords

1

ONE DAY Kipps set out upon his newly mastered bicycle to New Romney, to break the news of his engagement to his Uncle and Aunt—positively. He was now a finished cyclist, but as yet an unseasoned one; the south-west wind, even in its summer guise, as one meets it in the Marsh, is the equivalent of a reasonable hill, and ever and again he got off and refreshed himself by a spell of walking. He was walking just outside New Romney, preparatory to his triumphal entry (one hand off), when abruptly he came upon Ann Pornick.

It chanced he was thinking about her at the time. He had been thinking curious things; whether, after all, the atmosphere of New Romney and the Marsh had not some difference, some faint impalpable quality that was missing in the great and fashionable world of Folkestone behind there on the hill. Here there was a homeliness, a familiarity. He had noted as he passed that old Mr. Cliffordown's gate had been mended with a fresh piece of string. In Folkestone he didn't take notice, and he didn't care if they built three hundred houses. Come to think of it, that was odd. It was fine and grand to have twelve hundred a year; it was fine to go about on trams and omnibuses and think not a person aboard was as rich as oneself; it was fine to buy and order this and that and never have any work to do, and to be engaged to a girl distantly related to the Earl of Beauprés; but yet there had been a zest in the old time out here, a rare zest in the holidays, in sunlight, on the sea beach, and in the High Street, that failed from these new things. He thought of those bright windows of holiday that had seemed so glorious to him in the retrospect from his apprentice days. It was strange that now, amidst his present splendors, they were glorious still!

All those things were over now—perhaps that was it! Something had happened to the world, and the old light had been turned out. He himself was changed, and Sid was changed, terribly changed, and Ann, no doubt, was changed.

He thought of her with the hair blown about her flushed cheeks as they stood together after their race. . . .

Certainly she must be changed, and all the magic she had been fraught with to the very hem of her short petticoats gone, no doubt, forever. And as he thought that, or before and while he thought it—for he came to all these things in his own vague and stumbling way—he looked up, and there was Ann!

She was seven years older, and greatly altered; yet for the moment it seemed to him that she had not changed at all. "Ann!" he said; and she, with a lifting note, "It's Art Kipps!"

Then he became aware of changes—improvements. She was as pretty as she had promised to be, her blue eyes as dark as his memory of them, and with a quick, high color; but now Kipps by several inches was the taller again. She was dressed in a simple gray dress, that showed her very clearly as a straight and healthy little woman, and her hat was Sundayfied, with pink flowers. She looked soft and warm and welcoming. Her face was alight to Kipps with her artless gladness at their encounter.

"It's Art Kipps!" she said.

"Rather," said Kipps.

"You got your holidays?"

It flashed upon Kipps that Sid had not told her of his great fortune. Much regretful meditation upon Sid's behavior had convinced him that he himself was to blame for exasperating boastfulness in that affair, and this time he took care not to err in that direction. So he erred in the other.

"I'm taking a bit of a 'oliday," he said.

"So'm I," said Ann.

"You been for a walk?" asked Kipps.

Ann showed him a bunch of wayside flowers.

"It's a long time since I seen you, Ann. Why, 'ow long must it be? Seven—eight years nearly."

"It don't do to count," said Ann.

"It don't look like it," said Kipps, with the slightest emphasis.

"You got a moustache," said Ann, smelling her flowers and looking at him over them, not without admiration.

Kipps blushed. . . .

Presently they came to the bifurcation of the roads.

"I'm going down this way to mother's cottage," said Ann.

"I'll come a bit your way, if I may."

In New Romney social distinctions that are primary realities in Folkestone are absolutely non-existent, and it seemed quite permissible for him to walk with Ann, for all that she was no more than a servant. They talked with remarkable ease to one another, they slipped into a vein of intimate reminiscence in the easiest manner. In a little while Kipps was amazed to find Ann and himself at this—

"You r'member that half-sixpence? What we cut togevver?"

"Yes?"

"I got it still."

She hesitated. "Funny, wasn't it?" she said, and then, "You got yours, Artie?"

"Rather," said Kipps. "What do *you* think?" and wondered in his heart of hearts why he had never looked at that sixpence for so long.

Ann smiled at him frankly.

"I didn't expect you'd keep it," she said. "I thought often—it was silly to keep mine.

"Besides," she reflected, "it didn't mean anything really."

She glanced at him as she spoke and met his eye.

"Oh, didn't it!" said Kipps, a little late with his response, and realizing his infidelity to Helen even as he spoke.

"It didn't mean much anyhow," said Ann. "You still in the drapery?"

"I'm living at Folkestone," began Kipps, and decided that that sufficed. "Didn't Sid tell you he met me?"

"No! Here?"

"Yes. The other day. 'Bout a week or more ago."

"That was before I came."

"Ah, that was it," said Kipps.

" 'E's got on," said Ann. "Got 'is own shop now, Artie."

" 'E tole me."

They found themselves outside Muggett's cottages. "You going in?" said Kipps.

"I s'pose so," said Ann.

They both hung upon the pause. Ann took a plunge.

"D'you often come to New Romney?" she asked.

"I ride over a bit at times," said Kipps.

Another pause. Ann held out her hand.

"I'm glad I seen you," she said.

Extraordinary impulses arose in neglected parts of Kipps' being. "Ann," he said, and stopped.

"Yes," said she, and was bright to him.

They looked at one another.

All, and more than all, of those first emotions of his adolescence had come back to him. Her presence banished a multitude of countervailing considerations. It was Ann more than ever. She stood breathing close to him with her soft-looking lips a little apart and gladness in her eyes.

"I'm awful glad to see you again," he said; "it brings back old times."

"Doesn't it?"

Another pause. He would have liked to have had a long talk to her, to have gone for a walk with her or something, to have drawn nearer to her in any conceivable way, and above all to have had some more of the appreciation that shone in her eyes, but a vestige of Folkestone, still clinging to him, told him it "wouldn't do." "Well," he said, "I must be getting on," and turned away reluctantly, with a will under compulsion. . . .

When he looked back from the corner she was still at the gate. She was perhaps a little disconcerted by his retreat. He felt that. He hesitated for a moment, half turned, stood, and suddenly did great things with his hat. That hat! The wonderful hat of our civilization! . . .

In another minute he was engaged in a singularly absent-minded conversation with his Uncle about the usual topics.

His Uncle was very anxious to buy him a few upright clocks as an investment for subsequent sale. And there was also some very nice globes, one terrestrial and the other celestial, in a shop at Lydd that would look well in a drawing-room, and inevitably increase in value. . . . Kipps either did or did not agree to this purchase, he was unable to recollect.

The south-west wind perhaps helped him back; at any rate he found himself through Dymchurch without having noticed the place. There came an odd effect as he drew near Hythe. The hills on the left and the trees on the right seemed to draw together and close in upon him until his way was straight and narrow. He could not turn round on that treacherous half-tamed machine, but he knew that behind him, he knew so well, spread the wide vast flatness of the Marsh shining under the afternoon sky. In some way this was material to his thoughts. And as he rode through Hythe he came upon the idea that there was a considerable amount of incompatibility between the existence of one who was practically a gentleman and of Ann.

In the neighborhood of Seabrook he began to think he had, in some subtle way, lowered himself by walking along by the side of Ann. . . . After all, she was only a servant.

Ann!

She called out all the least gentlemanly instincts of his nature. There had been a moment in their conversation when he had quite distinctly thought it would really be an extremely nice thing for someone to kiss her lips. . . . There was something warming about Ann—at least for Kipps. She impressed him as having, sometime during their vast interval of separation, contrived to make herself in some distinctive way his.

Fancy keeping that half-sixpence all this time!

It was the most flattering thing that ever happened to Kipps.

2

He found himself presently sitting over "The Art of Conversing," lost in the strangest musings. He got up, walked about, became stagnant at the window for a space, roused himself, and by way of something lighter tried "Sesame and Lilies." From that too his attention wandered. He sat back. Anon he smiled, anon sighed. He arose, pulled his keys from his pocket, looked at them, decided, and went upstairs. He opened the little yellow box that had been the nucleus of all his possessions in the world, and took out a small "Escritoire," the very humblest sort of present, and opened it—kneeling. And there in the corner was a little packet of paper, sealed as a last defense against any prying invader with red sealing-wax. It had gone untouched for years. He held this little packet between finger and thumb for a moment, regarding it, and then put down the escritoire and broke the seal. . . .

As he was getting into bed that night he remembered something for the first time!

"Dash it!" he said. "Deshed if I told 'em *this* time. . . . *Well!*

"I shall 'ave to go over to New Romney again!"

He got into bed, and remained sitting pensively on the pillow for a space.

"Rum world," he reflected, after a vast interval.

Then he recalled that she had noticed his moustache. He embarked upon a sea of egotistical musing.

He imagined himself telling Ann how rich he was. What a surprise that would be for her!

Finally he sighed profoundly, blew out his candle, and snuggled down, and in a little while he was asleep. . . .

But the next morning, and at intervals afterwards, he found himself thinking of Ann,—Ann the bright, the desirable, the welcoming, and with an extraordinary streakiness he wanted quite badly to go, and then as badly not to go, over to New Romney again.

Sitting on the Leas in the afternoon, he had an idea. "I ought to 'ave told 'er, I suppose, about my being engaged.

"Ann!"

All sorts of dreams and impressions that had gone clean out of his mental existence came back to him, changed and brought up-to-date to fit her altered presence. He thought of how he had gone back to New Romney for his Christmas holidays, determined to kiss her, and of the awful blankness of the discovery that she had gone away.

It seemed incredible now, and yet not wholly incredible, that he had cried real tears for her,—how many years was it ago?

3

Daily I should thank my Maker that He did not delegate to me the Censorship of the world of men. I should temper a fierce injustice with a spasmodic indecision, that would prolong rather than mitigate the bitterness of the Day. For human dignity, for all conscious human superiority I should lack the beginnings of charity; for bishops, prosperous schoolmasters, judges, and all large respect-pampered souls. And more especially bishops, towards whom I bear an atavistic Viking grudge, dreaming not infrequently and with invariable zest of galleys and landings, and well-known living ornaments of the episcopal bench sprinting inland on twinkling gaiters before my thirsty blade—all these people, I say, I should treat below their deserts; but, on the other hand, for such as Kipps— There the exasperating indecisions would come in. The Judgment would be arrested at Kipps. Everyone and everything would wait. The balance would sway and sway, and whenever it heeled towards an adverse decision, my finger would set it swaying again. Kings, warriors, statesmen, brilliant women, "personalities" panting with indignation, headline humanity in general, would stand undamned, unheeded, or be damned in the most casual manner for their importunity, while my eye went about for anything possible that could be said on behalf of Kipps. . . . Albeit I fear nothing can save him from condemnation upon this present score, that within two days he was talking to Ann again.

One seeks excuses. Overnight there had been an encounter of Chitterlow and young Walshingham in his presence that had certainly warped his standards. They had called within a few minutes of each other, and the two, swayed by virile attentions to Old Methuselah Three Stars, had talked against each other, over and at the hospitable presence of Kipps. Walshingham had seemed to win at the beginning, but finally Chitterlow had made a magnificent display of vociferation and swept him out of existence. At the beginning Chitterlow had opened upon the great profits of playwrights, and young Walshingham had capped him at once with a cynical but impressive display of knowledge of the High Finance. If Chitterlow boasted his thousands, young Walshingham boasted his hundreds of thousands, and was for a space left in sole possession of the stage, juggling with the wealth of nations. He was going on by way of Financial Politics to the Overman, before Chitterlow recovered from his first check, and came back to victory. "Talking of Women," said Chitterlow, coming in abruptly upon some things not generally known, beyond Walshingham's more immediate circle, about a recently departed Empire-builder; "Talking of Women and the way they Get at a man—"

(Though, as a matter of fact, they had been talking of the Corruption of Society by Speculation.)

Upon this new topic Chitterlow was soon manifestly invincible. He knew so much, he had known so many. Young Walshingham did his best with epigrams and reservations, but even to Kipps it was evident that this was a book-learned depravity. One felt Walshingham had never known the inner realities of passion. But Chitterlow convinced and amazed. He had run away with girls, he had been run away with by girls, he had been in love with several at a time—"not counting Bessie"—he had loved and lost, he had loved and refrained, and he had loved and failed. He threw remarkable lights upon the moral state of America—in which country he had toured with great success. He set his talk to the tune of one of Mr. Kipling's best-known songs. He told an incident of simple romantic passion, a delirious dream of love and beauty in a Saturday to Monday steamboat trip up the Hudson, and tagged his end with "I learnt about women from 'er!" After that he adopted the refrain, and then lapsed into the praises of Kipling. "Little Kipling," said Chitterlow, with the familiarity of affection, *"he* knows," and broke into quotation—

> *I've taken my fun where I've found it;*
> *I've rogued and I've ranged in my time;*
> *I've 'ad my picking of sweet'earts,*
> *An' four of the lot was Prime.*

(These things, I say, affect the moral standards of the best of us.)
"I'd have liked to have written that," said Chitterlow. "That's Life, that is! But go and put it on the Stage, put even a bit of the Realities of Life on the Stage and see what they'll do to you! Only Kipling could venture on a job like that. That Poem KNOCKED me! I won't say Kipling hasn't knocked me before and since, but that was a Fair Knock Out. And yet—you know—there's one thing in it . . . this—

> *I've taken my fun where I've found it,*
> *And now I must pay for my fun,*
> *For the more you 'ave known o' the others,*
> *The less will you settle to one.*

Well. In my case anyhow—I don't know how much that proves, seeing I'm exceptional in so many things and there's no good denying it—but so far as I'm concerned—I tell you two, but, of course, you needn't let it go any farther— I've been perfectly faithful to Muriel ever since I married her—ever since. . . . Not once. Not even by accident have I ever said or done anything in the slightest—" His little brown eye became pensive after this flattering intimacy, and the gorgeous draperies of his abundant voice fell into graver folds. *"I learnt about women from 'er,"* he said impressively.

"Yes," said Walshingham, getting into the hinder spaces of that splendid pause, "a man must know about women. And the only sound way of learning is the experimental method."

"If you want to know about the experimental method, my boy," said Chitterlow, resuming. . . .

So they talked. *Ex pede Herculem,* as Coote, that cultivated polyglot, would have put it. And in the small hours Kipps went to bed, with his brain whirling with words and whisky, and sat for an unconscionable time upon his bed edge, musing sadly upon the unmanly monogamy that had cast its shadow upon his career, musing with his thoughts pointing round more and more certainly to the possibility of at least duplicity with Ann.

4

For some days he had been refraining with some insistence from going off to New Romney again. . . .

I do not know if this may count in palliation of his misconduct. Men, real Strong-Souled, Healthy Men, should be, I suppose, impervious to conversational atmospheres, but I have never claimed for Kipps a place at these high levels. The fact remains, that next day he spent the afternoon with Ann, and found no scruple in displaying himself a budding lover.

He had met her in the High Street, had stopped her, and almost on the spur of the moment had boldly proposed a walk, "for the sake of old times."

"*I* don't mind," said Ann.

Her consent almost frightened Kipps. His imagination had not carried him to that. "It would be a lark," said Kipps, and looked up the street and down. "Now?" he said.

"I don't mind a bit, Artie. I was just going for a walk along towards St. Mary's."

"Let's go that way be'ind the church," said Kipps; and presently they found themselves drifting seaward in a mood of pleasant commonplace. For awhile they talked of Sid. It went clean out of Kipps' head, at that early stage even, that Ann was a "girl" according to the exposition of Chitterlow, and for a time he remembered only that she was Ann. But afterwards, with the reek of that talk in his head, he lapsed a little from that personal relation. They came out upon the beach and sat down in a tumbled pebbly place where a meager grass and patches of sea poppy were growing, and Kipps reclined on his elbow and tossed pebbles in his hand, and Ann sat up, sunlit, regarding him. They talked in fragments. They exhausted Sid, they exhausted Ann, and Kipps was chary of his riches.

He declined to a faint love-making. "I got that 'arf-sixpence still," he said. "Reely?"

That changed the key. "I always kept mine, some'ow," said Ann; and there was a pause.

They spoke of how often they had thought of each other during those intervening years. Kipps may have been untruthful, but Ann perhaps was not. "I met people here and there," said Ann; "but I never met anyone quite like you, Artie."

"It's jolly our meeting again, anyhow," said Kipps. "Look at that ship out there. She's pretty close in. . . ."

He had a dull period, became, indeed, almost pensive, and then he was enterprising for awhile. He tossed up his pebbles so that, as if by accident, they fell on Ann's hand. Then, very penitently, he stroked the place. That would have led to all sorts of coquetries on the part of Flo Bates, for example, but it disconcerted and checked Kipps to find Ann made no objection, smiled pleasantly down on him, with eyes half shut because of the sun. She was taking things very much for granted.

He began to talk, and Chitterlow standards resuming possession of him, he said he had never forgotten her.

"I never forgotten you either, Artie," she said. "Funny, 'sn't it?"

It impressed Kipps also as funny.

He became reminiscent, and suddenly a warm summer's evening came back to him. "Remember them cockchafers, Ann?" he said. But the reality of the evening he recalled was not the chase of cockchafers. The great reality that had suddenly arisen between them was that he had never kissed Ann in his life. He looked up, and there were her lips.

He had wanted to very badly, and his memory leaped and annihilated an interval. That old resolution came back to him, and all sorts of new resolutions passed out of mind. And he had learned something since those boyish days. This time he did not ask. He went on talking, his nerves began very faintly to quiver, and his mind grew bright.

Presently, having satisfied himself that there was no one to see, he sat up beside her, and remarked upon the clearness of the air, and how close Dungeness seemed to them. Then they came upon a pause again.

"Ann," he whispered, and put an arm that quivered about her.

She was mute and unresisting, and, as he was to remember, solemn.

He turned her face towards him and kissed her lips, and she kissed him back again—kisses frank and tender as a child's.

5

It was curious that in the retrospect he did not find nearly the satisfaction in this infidelity he had imagined was there. It was no doubt desperately doggish, doggish to an almost Chitterlowesque degree, to recline on the beach at Littlestone with a "girl," to make love to her and to achieve the triumph of kissing her, when he was engaged to another "girl" at Folkestone; but somehow these two people were not "girls," they were Ann and Helen. Particularly Helen declined to be considered as a "girl." And there was something in Ann's quietly friendly eyes, in her frank smile, in the naïve pressure of her hand, there was something undefended and welcoming that imparted a flavor to the business upon which he had not counted. He had learned about women from her. That refrain ran through his mind and deflected his thoughts, but, as a matter of fact, he had learned about nothing but himself.

He wanted very much to see Ann some more and explain— He did not clearly know what it was he wanted to explain.

He did not clearly know anything. It is the last achievement of the intelligence to get all of one's life into one coherent scheme, and Kipps was only in a measure more aware of himself as a whole than is a tree. His existence was an affair of dissolving and recurring moods. When he thought of Helen or Ann, or any of his friends, he thought sometimes of this aspect and sometimes of that—and often one aspect was finally incongruous with another. He loved Helen, he revered Helen. He was also beginning to hate her with some intensity. When he thought of that expedition to Lympne, profound, vague, beautiful emotions flooded his being; when he thought of paying calls with her perforce, or of her latest comment on his bearing, he found himself rebelliously composing fierce and pungent insults, couched in the vernacular. But Ann, whom he had seen so much less of, was a simpler memory. She was pretty, she was almost softly feminine, and she was possible to his imagination just exactly where Helen was impossible. More than anything else, she carried the charm of respect for him, the slightest glance of her eyes was balm for his perpetually wounded self-conceit.

Chance suggestions it was set the tune of his thoughts, and his state of health and repletion gave the color. Yet somehow he had this at least almost clear in his mind, that to have gone to see Ann a second time, to have implied that she had been in possession of his thoughts through all this interval, and, above all, to have kissed her, was shabby and wrong. Only unhappily this much of lucidity had come now just a few hours after it was needed.

6

Four days after this it was that Kipps got up so late. He got up late, cut his chin while shaving, kicked a slipper into his sponge bath, and said "Dash!"

Perhaps you know these intolerable mornings, dear Reader, when you seem to have neither the heart nor the strength to rise, and your nervous adjustments are all wrong and your fingers thumbs, and you hate the very birds for singing. You feel inadequate to any demand whatever. Often such awakenings follow a poor night's rest, and commonly they mean indiscriminate eating, or those subtle mental influences old Kipps ascribed to "Foozle Ile" in the system, or worry. And with Kipps—albeit Chitterlow had again been his guest overnight—assuredly worry had played a leading *rôle*. Troubles had been gathering upon him for days, there had been a sort of concentration of these hosts of Midian overnight, and in the gray small hours Kipps had held his review.

The predominating trouble marched under this banner—

MR. KIPPS.

MRS. BINDON BOTTING

At Home,

Thursday, September 16th.

Anagrams, 4 to 6:30.   R.S.V.P.

---

a banner that was the facsimile of a card upon his looking-glass in the room below. And in relation to this terribly significant document, things had come to a pass with Helen, that he would only describe in his own expressive idiom as "words."

It had long been a smoldering issue between them that Kipps was not availing himself with any energy or freedom of the opportunities he had of social exercises, much less was he seeking additional opportunities. He had, it was evident, a peculiar dread of that universal afternoon enjoyment, the Call, and Helen made it unambiguously evident that this dread was "silly" and had to be overcome. His first display of this unmanly weakness occurred at the Cootes' on the day before he kissed Ann. They were all there, chatting very pleasantly, when the little servant with the big cap announced the younger Miss Wace.

Whereupon Kipps manifested a lively horror and rose partially from his chair. "O Gum!" he protested. "Carn't I go upstairs?"

Then he sank back, for it was too late. Very probably the younger Miss Wace had heard him as she came in.

Helen said nothing of that, though her manner may have shown her surprise, but afterwards she told Kipps he must get used to seeing people, and suggested that he should pay a series of calls with Mrs. Walshingham and herself. Kipps gave a reluctant assent at the time, and afterwards displayed a talent for evasion that she had not expected in him. At last she did succeed in securing him for a call upon Miss Punchafer of Radnor Park—a particularly easy call, because, Miss Punchafer being so deaf, one could say practically what one liked—and then outside the gate he shirked again. "I can't go in," he said, in a faded voice.

"You must," said Helen, beautiful as ever, but even more than a little hard and forbidding.

"I can't."

He produced his handkerchief hastily, thrust it to his face, and regarded her over it with rounded hostile eyes.

"Possible," he said in a hoarse, strange voice out of the handkerchief. "Nozzez bleedin'." . . .

But that was the end of his power of resistance, and when the rally for the Anagram Tea occurred, she bore down his feeble protests altogether. She insisted. She said frankly, "I am going to give you a good talking to about this"; and she did. . . .

From Coote he gathered something of the nature of Anagrams and Anagram parties. An anagram, Coote explained, was a word spelled the same way as another, only differently arranged; as, for instance, T.O.C.O.E. would be an anagram for his own name Coote.

"T.O.C.O.E.," repeated Kipps, very carefully.

"Or T.O.E.C.O.," said Coote.

"Or T.O.E.C.O.," said Kipps, assisting his poor head by nodding it at each letter.

"Toe Company like," he said, in his efforts to comprehend.

When Kipps was clear what an anagram meant, Coote came to the second heading, the Tea. Kipps gathered there might be from thirty to sixty people present, and that each one would have an anagram pinned on. "They give you a card to put your guesses on, rather like a dence programme, and then, you know, you go round and guess," said Coote. "It's rather good fun."

"Oo, rather!" said Kipps, with simulated gusto.

"It shakes everybody up together," said Coote.

Kipps smiled and nodded. . . .

In the small hours all his painful meditations were threaded by the vision of that Anagram Tea; it kept marching to and fro and in and out of his other troubles, from thirty to sixty people, mostly ladies and callers, and a great number of the letters of the alphabet, and more particularly P.I.K.P.S. and T.O.E.C.O., and he was trying to make one word out of the whole interminable procession. . . .

This word, as he finally gave it with some emphasis to the silence of the night, was, *"Demn!"*

Then wreathed as it were in this lettered procession was the figure of Helen as she had appeared at the moment of "words"; her face a little hard, a little irritated, a little disappointed. He imagined himself going round and guessing under her eye. . . .

He tried to think of other things, without lapsing upon a still deeper uneasiness that was decorated with yellow sea-poppies, and the figures of Buggins, Pearce, and Carshot, three murdered friendships, rose reproachfully in the stillness and changed horrible apprehensions into unspeakable remorse. Last night had been their customary night for the banjo, and Kipps, with a certain tremulous uncertainty, had put Old Methuselah amidst a retinue of glasses on the table and opened a box of choice cigars. In vain. They were in no need, it seemed, of *his* society. But instead Chitterlow had come, anxious to know if it was all right about that syndicate plan. He had declined anything but a very weak whisky-and-soda, "just to drink," at least until business was settled, and had then opened the whole affair with an effect of great orderliness to Kipps. Soon he was taking another whisky by sheer inadvertency, and the complex fabric of his conversation was running more easily from the broad loom of his mind. Into that pattern had interwoven a narrative of extensive alterations in the Pestered Butterfly—the neck-and-beetle business was to be restored—the story of a grave difference of opinion with Mrs. Chitterlow, where and how to live after the play had succeeded, the reasons why the Hon. Thomas Norgate had never financed a syndicate, and much matter also about the syndicate now under discussion. But if the current of their conversation had been vortical and crowded, the outcome was perfectly clear. Kipps was to be the chief participator in the syndicate, and his contribution was to be two thousand pounds. Kipps groaned and rolled over, and found Helen again, as it were, on the other side. "Promise me," she had said, "you won't do anything without consulting me."

Kipps at once rolled back to his former position, and for a space lay quite still. He felt like a very young rabbit in a trap.

Then suddenly, with extraordinary distinctness, his heart cried out for Ann, and he saw her as he had seen her at New Romney, sitting amidst the yellow sea-poppies with the sunlight on her face. His heart called out for her in the darkness as one calls for rescue. He knew, as though he had known it always, that he loved Helen no more. He wanted Ann, he wanted to hold her and be held by her, to kiss her again and again, to turn his back forever on all these other things. . . .

He rose late, but this terrible discovery was still there, undispelled by cockcrow or the day. He rose in a shattered condition, and he cut himself while shaving, but at last he got into his dining-room, and could pull the bell for the hot constituents of his multifarious breakfast. And then he turned to his letters. There were two real letters in addition to the customary electric-belt advertisement, continental lottery circular, and betting tout's card. One was in a slight mourning envelope, and addressed in an unfamiliar hand. This he opened first, and discovered a note—

MRS. RAYMOND WACE
requests the pleasure of
MR. KIPPS'
Company at Dinner
on Tuesday, Sept. 21st, at 8 o'clock.

R.S.V.P.

With a hasty movement Kipps turned his mind to the second letter. It was an unusually long one from his Uncle, and ran as follows:—

"MY DEAR NEPHEW,

We are considerably startled by your letter though expecting something of the sort and disposed to hope for the best. If the young lady is a relation to the Earl of Beaupres well and good but take care you are not being imposed upon for there are many who will be glad enough to snap you up now your circumstances are altered. I waited on the old Earl once while in service and he was remarkably close with his tips and suffered from corns. A hasty old gent and hard to please—I daresay he has forgotten me altogether—and anyhow there is no need to rake up bygones. Tomorrow is bus day and as you say the young lady is living near by we shall shut up shop for there is really nothing doing now what with all the visitors bringing everything with them down to their very children's pails and say how de do to her and give her a bit of a kiss and encouragement if we think her suitable—she will be pleased to see your old uncle. We wish we could have had a look at her first but still there is not much mischief done and hoping that all will turn out well yet I am
          Your affectionate Uncle
          EDWARD GEORGE KIPPS"

"My heartburn still very bad. I shall bring over a few bits of rhubub I picked up, a sort you won't get in Folkestone and if possible a good bunch of flowers for the young lady."

"Comin' over today," said Kipps, standing helplessly with the letter in his hand.

"Ow the Juice—?"

"I carn't."

"Kiss 'er!"

A terrible anticipation of that gathering framed itself in his mind, a hideous impossible disaster.

"I carn't even face 'er—!"

His voice went up to a note of despair. "And it's too late to telegrarf and stop 'em!"

7

About twenty minutes after this, an out-porter in Castle Hill Avenue was accosted by a young man with a pale, desperate face, an exquisitely rolled umbrella, and a heavy Gladstone bag.

"Carry this to the station, will you?" said the young man. "I want to ketch the nex' train to London. . . . You'll 'ave to look sharp; I 'even't very much time."

CHAPTER VII

London

1

LONDON WAS KIPPS' third world. There were, no doubt, other worlds, but Kipps knew only these three; firstly, New Romney and the Emporium, constituting his primary world, his world of origin, which also contained Ann; secondly, the world of culture and refinement, the world of which Coote was chaperon, and into which Kipps was presently to marry, a world, it was fast becoming evident, absolutely incompatible with the first; and thirdly, a world still to a large extent unexplored, London. London presented itself as a place of great gray spaces and incredible multitudes of people, centering about Charing Cross station and the Royal Grand Hotel, and containing at unexpected arbitrary points shops of the most amazing sort, statuary, squares, restaurants—where it was possible for clever people like Walshingham to order a lunch item by item to the waiters' evident respect and sympathy—exhibitions of incredible things—the Walshinghams had taken him to the Arts and Crafts and to a Picture Gallery—and theaters. London, moreover, is rendered habitable by hansom cabs. Young Walshingham was a natural cab-taker; he was an all-round, large-minded young man, and he had in the course of their two days' stay taken Kipps into no less than nine, so that Kipps was singularly not afraid of these vehicles. He knew that wherever you were, so soon as you were thoroughly lost, you said "Hi!" to a cab, and then "Royal Grend Hotel." Day and night these trusty conveyances are returning the strayed Londoner back to his point of departure, and were it not for their activity, in a little while the whole population, so vast and incomprehensible is the intricate complexity of this great city, would be hopelessly lost forever. At any rate, that is how the thing presented itself to Kipps, and I have heard much the same from visitors from America.

His train was composed of corridor carriages, and he forgot his troubles for a time in the wonders of this modern substitute for railway compartments. He went from the non-smoking to the smoking carriage, and smoked a cigarette, and strayed from his second-class carriage to a first and back. But presently Black Care got aboard the train and came and sat beside him. The exhilaration of escape had evaporated now, and he was presented with a terrible picture of his Aunt and Uncle arriving at his lodgings and finding him fled. He had left a hasty message that he was called away suddenly on business, ''ver' important business,'' and they were to be sumptuously entertained. His immediate motive had been his passionate dread of an encounter between these excellent but unrefined old people and the Walshinghams, but now that end was secured, he could see how thwarted and exasperated they would be.

How to explain to them?

He ought never to have written to tell them!

He ought to have got married, and told them afterwards.

He ought to have consulted Helen.

"Promise me," she had said.

"Oh, *desh!*" said Kipps, and got up and walked back into the smoking-car and began to consume cigarettes.

Suppose, after all, they found out the Walshinghams' address and went there!

At Charing Cross, however, were distractions again. He took a cab in an entirely Walshingham manner, and was pleased to note the enhanced respect of the cabman when he mentioned the Royal Grand. He followed Walshingham's routine on their previous visit with perfect success. They were very nice in the office, and gave him an excellent room at fourteen shillings the night.

He went up and spent a considerable time examining the furniture of his room, scrutinizing himself in its various mirrors, and sitting on the edge of the bed whistling. It was a vast and splendid apartment, and cheap at fourteen shillings. But finding the figure of Ann inclined to resume possession of his mind, he roused himself and descended by the staircase, after a momentary hesitation before the lift. He had thought of lunch, but he drifted into the great drawing-room, and read a guide to the Hotels of Europe for a space, until a doubt whether he was entitled to use this palatial apartment without extra charge arose in his mind. He would have liked something to eat very much now, but his inbred terror of the table was strong. He did at last get by a porter in uniform towards the dining-room, but at the sight of a number of waiters and tables with remarkable complications of knives and glasses, terror seized him, and he backed out again with a mumbled remark to the waiter in the doorway about this not being the way.

He hovered in the hall and lounge until he thought the presiding porter regarded him with suspicion, and then went up to his room again by the staircase, got his hat and umbrella, and struck out boldly across the courtyard. He would go to a restaurant instead.

He had a moment of elation in the gateway. He felt all the Strand must notice him as he emerged through the great gate of the hotel. "One of these here rich swells," they would say. "Don't they go it just!" A cabman touched his hat. "No fear," said Kipps, pleasantly. . . .

Then he remembered he was hungry again.

Yet he decided he was in no great hurry for lunch, in spite of an internal protest, and turned eastward along the Strand in a leisurely manner. He would find a place to suit him soon enough. He tried to remember the sort of things Walshingham had ordered. Before all things he didn't want to go into a place and look like a fool. Some of these places rook you dreadful, besides making fun of you. There was a place near Essex Street where there was a window brightly full of chops, tomatoes, and lettuce. He stopped at this and reflected for a time, and then it occurred to him that you were expected to buy these things raw and cook them at home. Anyhow, there was sufficient doubt in the matter to stop him. He drifted on to a neat window with champagne bottles, a dish of asparagus, and a framed menu of a two-shilling lunch. He was about to enter, when fortunately he perceived two waiters looking at him over the back screen of the window with a most ironical expression, and he sheered off at once. There was a wonderful smell of hot food halfway down Fleet Street, and a nice-looking tavern with several doors, but he could not decide which door. His nerve was going under the strain.

He hesitated at Farringdon Street, and drifted up to St. Paul's and round the churchyard, full chiefly of dead bargains in the shop windows, to Cheapside. But now Kipps was getting demoralized, and each house of refreshment seemed to promise still more complicated obstacles to food. He didn't know how you went in, and what was the correct thing to do with your hat; he didn't know what you said to the waiter, or what you called the different things; he was convinced absolutely he would "fumble," as Shalford would have said, and look like a fool. Somebody might laugh at him! The hungrier he got, the more unendurable was the thought that anyone should laugh at him. For a time he considered an extraordinary expedient to account for his ignorance. He would go in and pretend to be a foreigner, and not know English. Then they might understand. . . . Presently he had drifted into a part of London where there did not seem to be any refreshment places at all.

"Oh, *desh!*" said Kipps, in a sort of agony of indecisiveness. "The very nex' place I see, in I go."

The next place was a fried-fish shop in a little side street, where there were also sausages on a gas-lit grill.

He would have gone in, but suddenly a new scruple came to him, that he was too well dressed for the company he could see dimly through the steam sitting at the counter and eating with a sort of nonchalant speed.

2

He was half minded to resort to a hansom and brave the terrors of the dining-room of the Royal Grand—they wouldn't know why he had gone out really—when the only person he knew in London appeared (as the only person one does know will do in London) and slapped him on the shoulder. Kipps was hovering at a window at a few yards from the fish shop pretending to examine some really strikingly cheap pink baby-linen, and trying to settle finally about those sausages. "Hullo, Kipps!" cried Sid, "spending the millions?"

Kipps turned and was glad to perceive no lingering vestige of the chagrin that had been so painful at New Romney. Sid looked grave and important, and he wore a quite new silk hat that gave a commercial touch to a generally socialistic costume. For the moment the sight of Sid uplifted Kipps wonderfully. He saw him as a friend and helper, and only presently did it come clearly into his mind that this was the brother of Ann.

He made amiable noises.

"I've just been up this way," Sid explained, "buying a second-hand 'namelling stove . . . I'm going to 'namel myself."

"Lor!" said Kipps.

"Yes. Do me a lot of good. Let the customer choose his color. See? What brings *you* up?"

Kipps had a momentary vision of his foiled Uncle and Aunt. "Jest a bit of a change," he said.

Sid came to a swift decision. "Come down to my little show. I got someone I'd like to see talking to you."

Even then Kipps did not think of Ann in this connection.

"Well," he said, trying to invent an excuse on the spur of the moment. "Fact is," he explained, "I was jest looking round to get a bit of lunch."

"Dinner we call it," said Sid. "But that's all right. You can't get anything to eat hereabout. If you're not too haughty to do a bit of slumming, there's some mutton spoiling for me now—"

The word mutton affected Kipps greatly.

"It won't take us 'arf an hour," said Sid, and Kipps was carried.

He discovered another means of London locomotion in the Underground Railway, and recovered his self-possession in that interest. "You don't mind going third?" asked Sid; and Kipps said, "Nort a *bit* of it." They were silent in the train for a time, on account of strangers in the carriage, and then Sid began to explain who it was he wanted Kipps to meet. "It's a chap named Masterman,—do you no end of good.

"He occupies our first-floor front room, you know. It isn't so much for gain I let as company. We don't *want* the whole 'ouse, that's one thing, and another is I knew the man before. Met him at our Sociological, and after a bit he said he wasn't comfortable where he was. That's how it came about. He's a first-class chap—first class. Science! You should see his books!

"Properly he's a sort of journalist. He's written a lot of things, but he's been too ill lately to do very much. Poetry he's written, all sorts. He writes for the *Commonweal* sometimes, and sometimes he reviews books. 'E's got 'eaps of books—'eaps. Besides selling a lot.

"He knows a regular lot of people, and all sorts of things. He's been a dentist, and he's a qualified chemist, and I seen 'im often reading German and French. Taught 'imself. He was here—"

Sid indicated South Kensington, which had come opportunely outside the carriage windows, with a nod of his head, "—three years. Studying science. But you'll see 'im. When he really gets to talking—he *pours* it out."

"Ah!" said Kipps, nodding sympathetically, with his two hands on his umbrella knob.

"He'll do big things some day," said Sid. "He's written a book on science already. 'Physiography,' it's called. 'Elementary Physiography!' Some day he'll write an Advanced—when he gets time."

He let this soak into Kipps.

"I can't introduce you to lords and swells," he went on, "but I *can* show you a Famous Man, that's going to be. I *can* do that. Leastways— Unless—"

Sid hesitated.

"He's got a frightful cough," he said.

"He won't care to talk to me," weighed Kipps.

"That's all right; *he* won't mind. He's fond of talking. He'd talk to anyone," said Sid, reassuringly, and added a perplexing bit of Londonized Latin. "He doesn't *pute* anything, *non alienum*. You know."

"*I* know," said Kipps, intelligently, over his umbrella knob, though of course that was altogether untrue.

3

Kipps found Sid's shop a practical-looking establishment, stocked with the most remarkable collection of bicycles and pieces of bicycle that he had ever beheld. "My hiring stock," said Sid, with a wave to this ironmongery; "and there's the best machine at a democratic price in London, The Red Flag, built by *me*. See?"

He indicated a graceful gray brown framework in the window. "And there's my stock of accessories—store prices.

"Go in for motors a bit," added Sid.

"Mutton?" said Kipps, not hearing him distinctly.

"Motors I *said*. . . . 'Owever, Mutton Department 'ere"; and he opened a door that had a curtain-guarded window in its upper panel, to reveal a little room with red walls and green furniture, with a white-clothed table and the generous promise of a meal. "Fanny!" he shouted. "Here's Art Kipps."

A bright-eyed young woman of five or six and twenty in a pink print appeared, a little flushed from cooking, and wiped a hand on an apron and shook hands and smiled and said it would all be ready in a minute. She went on to say she had heard of Kipps and his luck, and meanwhile Sid vanished to draw the beer, and returned with two glasses for himself and Kipps.

"Drink that," said Sid; and Kipps felt all the better for it.

"I give Mr. Masterman '*is* upstairs a hour ago," said Mrs. Sid. "I didn't think 'e ought to wait."

A rapid succession of brisk movements on the part of everyone and they were all four at dinner—the fourth person being Master Walt Whitman Pornick, a cheerful young gentleman of one and a half, who was given a spoon to hammer on the table with, to keep him quiet, and who got "Kipps" right at the first effort and kept it all through the meal, combining it first with this previous acquisition and then that. "Peacock Kipps," said Master Walt, at which there was great laughter, and also "More Mutton Kipps."

"He's a regular oner," said Mrs. Sid, "for catching up words. You can't say a word but what 'e's on to it."

There were no serviettes and less ceremony, and Kipps thought he had never enjoyed a meal so much. Everyone was a little excited by the meeting and chatting and disposed to laugh, and things went easily from the very beginning. If there was a pause, Master Walt filled it in. Mrs. Sid, who tempered her enormous admiration for Sid's intellect and his socialism and his severe business methods by a motherly sense of her sex and seniority, spoke of them both as "you boys," and dilated—when she was not urging Kipps to have some more of this or that—on the disparity between herself and her husband.

"Shouldn't ha' thought there was a year between you," said Kipps; "you seem jest a match."

"*I*'m *his* match anyhow," said Mrs. Sid, and no epigram of young Walshingham's was ever better received.

"Match," said young Walt, coming in on the tail of the joke and getting a round for himself.

Any sense of superior fortune had long vanished from Kipps' mind, and he found himself looking at host and hostess with enormous respect. Really old Sid was a wonderful chap, here in his own house at two-and-twenty, carving his own mutton and lording it over wife and child. No legacies needed by him! And Mrs. Sid, so kind and bright and hearty! And the child, old Sid's child! Old Sid had jumped round a bit. It needed the sense of his fortune at the back of his mind to keep Kipps from feeling abject. He resolved he'd buy young Walt something tremendous in toys at the very first opportunity.

"Drop more beer, Art?"

"Right you are, old man."

"Cut Mr. Kipps a bit more bread, Sid."

"Can't I pass *you* a bit? . . ."

Sid was all right, Sid was; there was no mistake about that.

It was growing up in his mind that Sid was the brother of Ann, but he said nothing about her, for excellent reasons. After all, Sid's irritation at her name when they had met in New Romney seemed to show a certain separation. They didn't tell each other much. . . . He didn't know how things might be between Ann and Mrs. Sid either.

Still, for all that, Sid was Ann's brother.

The furniture of the room did not assert itself very much above the cheerful business of the table, but Kipps was impressed with the idea that it was pretty. There was a dresser at the end with a number of gay plates and a mug or so, a Labor Day poster by Walter Crane on the wall, and through the glass and over the blind of the shop door one had a glimpse of the bright-color advertisement cards of bicycle dealers, and a shelf-ful of boxes labeled The Paragon Bell, The Scarum Bell, and The Patent Omi! Horn. . . .

It seemed incredible that he had been in Folkestone that morning, that even now his Aunt and Uncle—!

B-r-r-r. It didn't do to think of his Aunt and Uncle.

4

When Sid repeated his invitation to come and see Masterman, Kipps, now flushed with beer and Irish stew, said he didn't mind if he did, and after a preliminary shout from Sid that was answered by a voice and a cough, the two went upstairs.

"Masterman's a rare one," said Sid over his arm and in an undertone. "You should hear him speak at a meeting. . . . If he's in form, that is."

He rapped and went into a large untidy room.

"This is Kipps," he said. "You know. The chap I told you of. With twelve 'undred a year."

Masterman sat gnawing an empty pipe, and as close to the fire as though it was alight and the season midwinter. Kipps concentrated upon him for a space, and only later took in something of the frowsy furniture, the little bed half behind and evidently supposed to be wholly behind a careless screen, the spittoon by the fender, the remains of a dinner on the chest of drawers, and the scattered books and papers. Masterman's face showed him a man of forty or more, with curious hollows at the side of his forehead and about his eyes. His eyes were very bright, there was a spot of red in his cheeks, and the wiry black moustache under his short red nose had been trimmed with scissors into a sort of brush along his upper lip. His teeth were darkened ruins. His jacket collar was turned up about a knitted white neck-wrap, and his sleeves betrayed no cuffs. He did not rise to greet Kipps, but he held out a thin wristed hand and pointed with the other to a bedroom armchair.

"Glad to see you," he said. "Sit down and make yourself at home. Will you smoke?"

Kipps said he would, and produced his store. He was about to take one, and then with a civil afterthought handed the packet first to Masterman and Sid. Masterman pretended surprise to find his pipe out before he took one. There was an interlude of matches. Sid pushed the end of the screen out of his way, sat down on the bed thus frankly admitted, and prepared, with a certain quiet satisfaction of manner, to witness Masterman's treatment of Kipps.

"And how does it feel to have twelve hundred a year?" asked Masterman, holding his cigarette to his nose tip in a curious manner.

"It's rum," confided Kipps, after a reflective interval. "It feels juiced rum."

"I've never felt it," said Masterman.

"It takes a bit of getting into," said Kipps. "I can tell you that."

Masterman smoked and regarded Kipps with curious eyes.

"I expect it does," he said presently.

"And has it made you perfectly happy?" he asked abruptly.

"I couldn't 'ardly say *that*," said Kipps.

Masterman smiled. "No," he said. "Has it made you much happier?"

"It did at first."

"Yes. But you got used to it. How long, for example, did the real delirious excitement last?"

"Oo, *that!* Perhaps a week," said Kipps.

Masterman nodded his head. "That's what discourages *me* from amassing wealth," he said to Sid. "You adjust yourself. It doesn't last. I've always had an inkling of that, and it's interesting to get it confirmed. I shall go on sponging for a bit longer on *you,* I think."

"You don't," said Sid. "No fear."

"Twenty-four thousand pounds," said Masterman, and blew a cloud of smoke. "Lord! Doesn't it worry you?"

"It is a bit worrying at times. . . . Things 'appen."

"Going to marry?"

"Yes."

"H'm. Lady, I guess, of a superior social position?"

"Rather," said Kipps. "Cousin to the Earl of Beauprés."

Masterman readjusted his long body with an air of having accumulated all the facts he needed. He snuggled his shoulder-blades down into the chair and raised his angular knees. "I doubt," he said, flicking cigarette ash into the atmosphere, "if any great gain or loss of money does—as things are at present—make more than the slightest difference in one's happiness. It ought to—if money was what it ought to be, the token given for service, one ought to get an increase in power and happiness for every pound one got. But the plain fact is, the times are out of joint, and money—money, like everything else—is a deception and a disappointment."

He turned his face to Kipps and enforced his next words with the index-finger of his lean lank hand. "If I thought otherwise," he said, "I should exert myself to get some. But—if one sees things clearly one is so discouraged. So confoundedly discouraged. . . . When you first got your money you thought that it meant you might buy just anything you fancied?"

"It was a bit that way," said Kipps.

"And you found you couldn't. You found that for all sorts of things it was a question of where to buy and how to buy, and what you didn't know how to buy with your money, straight away this world planted something else upon you."

"I got rather done over a banjo first day," said Kipps. "Leastways, my uncle says so."

"Exactly," said Masterman.

Sid began to speak from the bed. "That's all very well, Masterman," he said, "but after all money *is* Power, you know. You can do all sorts of things—"

"I'm talking of happiness," said Masterman. "You can do all sorts of things with a loaded gun in the Hammersmith Broadway, but nothing—practically—that will make you or anyone else very happy. Nothing. Power's a different matter altogether. As for happiness, you want a world in order before money or property or any of those things have any real value, and this world, I tell you, is hopelessly out of joint. Man is a social animal with a mind nowadays that goes round the globe, and a community cannot be happy in one part and unhappy in another. It's all or nothing, no patching any more forever. It is the standing mistake of the world not to understand that. Consequently people think there is a class or order somewhere just above them or just below them, or a country or place somewhere that is really safe and happy. . . . The fact is, Society is one body, and it is either well or ill. That's the law. This society we live in is ill. It's a fractious, feverish invalid, gouty, greedy, ill-nourished. You can't have a happy left leg with neuralgia, or a happy throat with a broken leg. That's my position, and that's the knowledge you'll come to. I'm so satisfied of it that I sit here and wait for my end quite calmly, sure that I can't better things by bothering—in my time and so far as I am concerned that is. I'm not even greedy any more—my egotism's at the bottom of a pond with a philosophical brick round its neck. The world is ill, my time is short, and my strength is small. I'm as happy here as anywhere."

He coughed, was silent for a moment, then brought the index-finger round to Kipps again. "You've had the opportunity of sampling two grades of society, and you don't find the new people you're among much better or any happier than the old?"

"No," said Kipps, reflectively. "No. I 'aven't seen it quite like that before, but— No. They're not."

"And you might go all up the scale and down the scale and find the same thing. Man's a gregarious beast, a gregarious beast, and no money will buy you out of your own time—any more than out of your own skin. All the way up and all the way down the scale there's the same discontent. No one is quite sure where they stand, and everyone's fretting. The herd's uneasy and feverish. All the old tradition goes or has gone, and there's no one to make a new tradition. Where are your nobles now? Where are your gentlemen? They vanished directly the peasant found out he wasn't happy and ceased to be a peasant. There's big men and little men mixed up together, and that's all. None of us know where we are. Your cads in a bank-holiday train, and your cads on a two-thousand-pound motor, except for a difference in scale, there's not a pin to choose between them. Your smart society is as low and vulgar and uncomfortable for a balanced soul as a gin palace, no more and no less; there's no place or level of honor or fine living left in the world, so what's the good of climbing?"

" 'Ear, 'ear," said Sid.

"It's true," said Kipps.

"*I* don't climb," said Masterman, and accepted Kipps' silent offer of another cigarette.

"No," he said. "This world is out of joint. It's broken up, and I doubt if it'll heal. I doubt very much if it'll heal. We're in the beginning of the Sickness of the World."

He rolled his cigarette in his lean fingers and repeated with satisfaction, "The Sickness of the World."

"It's we've got to make it better," said Sid, and looked at Kipps.

"Ah, Sid's an optimist," said Masterman.

"So you are, most times," said Sid.

Kipps lit another cigarette with an air of intelligent participation.

"Frankly," said Masterman, recrossing his legs and expelling a jet of smoke luxuriously, "frankly, I think this civilization of ours is on the topple."

"There's Socialism," said Sid.

"There's no imagination to make use of it."

"We've got to *make* one," said Sid.

"In a couple of centuries, perhaps," said Masterman. "But meanwhile we're going to have a pretty acute attack of universal confusion. Universal confusion. Like one of those crushes when men are killed and maimed for no reason at all, going into a meeting or crowding for a train. Commercial and Industrial Stresses. Political Exploitation. Tariff Wars. Revolutions. All the bloodshed that will come of some fools calling half the white world yellow. These things alter the attitude of everybody to everybody. Everybody's going to feel 'em. Every fool in the world panting and shoving. We're all going to be as happy and comfortable as a household during a removal. What else can we expect?"

Kipps was moved to speak, but not in answer to Masterman's inquiry. "I've never rightly got the 'eng of this Socialism," he said. "What's it going to do, like?"

They had been imagining that he had some elementary idea in the matter, but as soon as he had made it clear that he hadn't, Sid plunged at exposition, and in a little while Masterman, abandoning his pose of the detached man ready to die, joined in. At first he joined in only to correct Sid's version, but afterwards he took control. His manner changed. He sat up and rested his elbow on his knees, and his cheek flushed a little. He expanded his case against property and the property class with such vigor that Kipps was completely carried away, and never thought of asking for a clear vision of the thing that would fill the void this abolition might create. For a time he quite forgot his own private opulence. And it was as if something had been lit in Masterman. His languor passed. He enforced his words by gestures of his long thin hands. And as he passed swiftly from point to point of his argument, it was evident he grew angry.

"Today," he said, "the world is ruled by rich men; they may do almost anything they like with the world. And what are they doing? Laying it waste!"

"Hear, hear!" said Sid, very sternly.

Masterman stood up, gaunt and long, thrust his hands in his pockets, and turned his back to the fireplace.

"Collectively, the rich today have neither heart nor imagination. No! They own machinery, they have knowledge and instruments and powers beyond all previous dreaming, and what are they doing with them? Think what they are doing with them, Kipps, and think what they might do. God gives them a power like the motor-car, and all they can do with it is to go careering about the roads in goggled masks, killing children and making machinery hateful to the soul of man! ('True,' said Sid, 'true.') God gives them means of communication, power unparalleled of every sort, time, and absolute liberty! They waste it all in folly! Here under their feet (and Kipps' eyes followed the direction of a lean index finger to the hearthrug), under their accursed wheels, the great mass of men festers and breeds in darkness, darkness those others make by standing in the light. The darkness breeds and breeds. It knows no better. . . . Unless you can crawl or pander or rob you must stay in the stew you are born in. And those rich beasts above claw and clutch as though they had nothing! They grudge us our schools, they grudge us a gleam of light and air, they cheat us, and then seek to forget us. . . . There is no rule, no guidance, only accidents and happy flukes. . . . Our multitudes of poverty increase, and this crew of rulers makes no provision, foresees nothing, anticipates nothing!''

He paused, and made a step, and stood over Kipps in a white heat of anger. Kipps nodded in a noncommittal manner, and looked hard and rather gloomily at his host's slipper as he talked.

''It isn't as though they had something to show for the waste they make of us, Kipps. They haven't. They are ugly and cowardly and mean. Look at their women! Painted, dyed, and drugged, hiding their ugly shapes under a load of dress! There isn't a woman in the swim of society at the present time who wouldn't sell herself body and soul, who wouldn't lick the boots of a Jew or marry a nigger, rather than live decently on a hundred a year! On what would be wealth for you or me! They know it. They know we know it. . . . No one believes in them. No one believes in nobility any more. Nobody believes in kingship any more. Nobody believes there is justice in the law. . . . But people have habits, people go on in the old grooves, as long as there's work, as long as there's weekly money. . . . It won't last, Kipps.''

He coughed and paused. ''Wait for the lean years,'' he cried. ''Wait for the lean years.'' And suddenly he fell into a struggle with his cough, and spat a gout of blood. ''It's nothing,'' he said to Kipps' note of startled horror.

He went on talking, and the protests of his cough interlaced with his words, and Sid beamed in an ecstasy of painful admiration.

''Look at the fraud they have let life become, the miserable mockery of the hope of one's youth. What have *I* had? I found myself at thirteen being forced into a factory like a rabbit into a chloroformed box. Thirteen!—when *their* children are babies. But even a child of that age could see what it meant, that Hell of a factory! Monotony and toil and contempt and dishonor! And then death. So I fought—at thirteen!''

Minton's ''crawling up a drainpipe till you die'' echoed in Kipps' mind, but Masterman, instead of Minton's growl, spoke in a high indignant tenor.

''I got out at last—somehow,'' he said quietly, suddenly plumping back in his chair. He went on after a pause. ''For a bit. Some of us get out by luck, some by cunning, and crawl onto the grass, exhausted and crippled, to die. That's a poor man's success, Kipps. Most of us don't get out at all. I worked all day, and studied half the night, and here I am with the common consequences. Beaten! And never once have I had a fair chance, never once!'' His lean clenched fist flew out in a gust of tremulous anger. ''These Skunks shut up all the university scholarships at nineteen for fear of men like me. And then—do *nothing*. . . . We're wasted for nothing. By the time I'd learnt something the doors were locked. I thought knowledge would do it—I did think that! I've fought for knowledge as other men fight for bread. I've starved for knowledge. I've turned my back on women; I've done even that. I've burst my accursed lung. . . .'' His voice rose with impotent anger. ''I'm a better man than any ten princes alive. And I'm beaten and wasted. I've been crushed, trampled, and defiled by a drove of hogs. I'm no use to myself or the world. I've thrown my life away to make myself too good for use in this hucksters' scramble. If I had gone in for business, if I had gone in for plotting to cheat my fellow-men. . . . Ah well! It's too late. It's too late for that, anyhow. It's too late for anything now! And I couldn't have done it. . . . And over in New York now there's a pet of society making a corner in wheat!

"By God!" he cried hoarsely, with a clutch of the lean hand. "By God! if I had his throat! Even now! I might do something for the world."

He glared at Kipps, his face flushed deep, his sunken eyes glowing with passion, and then suddenly he changed altogether.

There was a sound of tea-things rattling upon a tray outside the door, and Sid rose to open it.

"All of which amounts to this," said Masterman, suddenly quiet again and talking against time. "The world is out of joint, and there isn't a soul alive who isn't half waste or more. You'll find it the same with you in the end, wherever your luck may take you. . . . I suppose you won't mind my having another cigarette?"

He took Kipps' cigarette with a hand that trembled so violently it almost missed its object, and stood up, with something of guilt in his manner, as Mrs. Sid came into the room.

Her eye met his, and marked the flush upon his face.

"Been talking Socialism?" said Mrs. Sid, a little severely.

5

Six o'clock that day found Kipps drifting eastward along the southward margin of Rotten Row. You figure him a small respectably attired person going slowly through a sometimes immensely difficult and always immense world. At times he becomes pensive, and whistles softly; at times he looks about him. There are a few riders in the Row; a carriage flashes by every now and then along the roadway, and among the great rhododendrons and laurels and upon the green sward there are a few groups and isolated people dressed—in the style Kipps adopted to call upon the Walshinghams when first he was engaged. Amid the complicated confusion of Kipps' mind was a regret that he had not worn his other things. . . .

Presently he perceived that he would like to sit down; a green chair tempted him. He hesitated at it, took possession of it, and leaned back and crossed one leg over the other.

He rubbed his under lip with his umbrella handle, and reflected upon Masterman and his denunciation of the world.

"Bit orf 'is 'ead, poor chap," said Kipps; and added, "I wonder—"

He thought intently for a space.

"I wonder what 'e meant by the lean years." . . .

The world seemed a very solid and prosperous concern just here, and well out of reach of Masterman's dying clutch. And yet—

It was curious he should have been reminded of Minton.

His mind turned to a far more important matter. Just at the end Sid had said to him, "Seen Ann?" and as he was about to answer, "You'll see a bit more of her now. She's got a place in Folkestone."

It had brought him back from any concern about the world being out of joint or anything of that sort.

Ann!

One might run against her any day.

He tugged at his little moustache.

He would like to run against Ann very much. . . .

And it would be juiced awkward if he did!

In Folkestone! It was a jolly sight too close. . . .

Then at the thought that he might run against Ann in his beautiful evening dress on the way to the band, he fluttered into a momentary dream, that jumped abruptly into a nightmare.

Suppose he met her when he was out with Helen! "Oh, Lor!" said Kipps. Life had developed a new complication that would go on and go on. For some time he wished with the utmost fervor that he had not kissed Ann, that he had not gone to New Romney the second time. He marveled at his amazing forgetfulness of Helen on that occasion. Helen took possession of his mind. He would have to write to Helen, an easy offhand letter to say he had come to London for a day or so. He tried to imagine her reading it. He would write just such another letter to the old people, and say he had had to come up on business. That might do for *them* all right, but Helen was different. She would insist on explanations.

He wished he could never go back to Folkestone again. That would about settle the whole affair.

A passing group attracted his attention, two faultlessly dressed gentlemen and a radiantly expensive lady. They were talking, no doubt, very brilliantly. His eyes followed them. The lady tapped the arm of the left-hand gentleman with a daintily tinted glove. Swells! No end. . . .

His soul looked out upon life in general as a very small nestling might peep out of its nest. What an extraordinary thing life was to be sure, and what a remarkable variety of people there were in it!

He lit a cigarette, and speculated upon that receding group of three, and blew smoke and watched them. They seemed to do it all right. Probably they all had incomes of very much over twelve hundred a year. Perhaps not. Probably they none of them suspected as they went past that he too was a gentleman of independent means, dressed as he was without distinction. Of course things were easier for them. They were brought up always to dress well and do the right thing from their very earliest years; they started clear of all his perplexities; they had never got mixed up with all sorts of different people who didn't go together. If, for example, that lady there got engaged to that gentleman, she would be quite safe from any encounter with a corpulent, osculatory Uncle, or Chitterlow, or the dangerously significant eye of Pearce.

His thoughts came round to Helen.

When they were married and Cuyps, or Cuyp—Coote had failed to justify his "*s*"—and in that West-end flat, and shaken free of all these low-class associations, would he and she parade here of an afternoon dressed like that? It would be rather fine to do so. If one's dress was all right.

Helen!

She was difficult to understand at times.

He blew extensive clouds of cigarette smoke.

There would be teas, there would be dinners, there would be calls— Of course he would get into the way of it.

But Anagrams were a bit stiff to begin with!

It was beastly confusing at first to know when to use your fork at dinner, and all that. Still—

He felt an extraordinary doubt whether he would get into the way of it. He was interested for a space by a girl and groom on horseback, and then he came back to his personal preoccupations.

He would have to write to Helen. What could he say to explain his absence from the Anagram Tea? She had been pretty clear she wanted him to come. He recalled her resolute face without any great tenderness. He *knew* he would look like a silly ass at that confounded tea! Suppose he shirked it and went back in time for the dinner! Dinners were beastly difficult too, but not so bad as anagrams.

The very first thing that might happen when he got back to Folkestone would be to run against Ann. Suppose, after all, he did meet Ann when he was with Helen!

What queer encounters were possible in the world!

Thank goodness, they were going to live in London!

But that brought him round to Chitterlow. The Chitterlows would be coming to London too. If they didn't get money they'd come after it; they weren't the sort of people to be choked off easily, and if they did, they'd come to London to produce their play. He tried to imagine some seemly social occasion invaded by Chitterlow and his rhetoric, by his torrential thunder of self-assertion, the whole company flattened thereunder like wheat under a hurricane.

Confound and hang Chitterlow! Yet somehow, sometime, one would have to settle accounts with him! And there was Sid! Sid was Ann's brother. He realized with sudden horror the social indiscretion of accepting Sid's invitation to dinner.

Sid wasn't the sort of chap one could snub or cut, and besides—Ann's brother! He didn't want to cut him; it would be worse than cutting Buggins and Pearce— a sight worse. And after that lunch! It would be next thing to cutting Ann herself. And even as to Ann!

Suppose he was with Helen or Coote! . . .

"Oh, Blow!" he said at last, and then viciously, *"Blow!"* and so rose and flung away his cigarette end and pursued his reluctant dubitating way towards the really quite uncongenial splendors of the Royal Grand. . . .

And it is vulgarly imagined that to have money is to have no troubles at all!

6

Kipps endured splendor at the Royal Grand Hotel for three nights and days, and then he retreated in disorder. The Royal Grand defeated and overcame and routed Kipps not of intention, but by sheer royal grandeur, grandeur combined with an organization for his comfort carried to excess. On his return he came upon a difficulty, he had lost his circular piece of cardboard with the number of his room, and he drifted about the hall and passages in a state of perplexity for some time, until he thought all the porters and officials in gold lace caps must be watching him, and jesting to one another about him. Finally, in a quiet corner down below near the hairdresser's shop, he found a kindly-looking personage in bottle green, to whom he broached his difficulty. "I say," he said, with a pleasant smile, "I can't find my room nohow." The personage in bottle green, instead of laughing in a nasty way, as he might well have done, became extremely helpful, showed Kipps what to do, got his key, and conducted him by lift and passage to his chamber. Kipps tipped him half a crown.

Safe in his room, Kipps pulled himself together for dinner. He had learned enough from young Walshingham to bring his dress clothes, and now he began to assume them. Unfortunately in the excitement of his flight from his Aunt and Uncle he had forgotten to put in his other boots, and he was some time deciding between his purple cloth slippers with a golden marigold and the prospect of cleaning the boots he was wearing with the towel, but finally, being a little footsore, he took the slippers.

Afterwards, when he saw the porters and waiters and the other guests catch sight of the slippers, he was sorry he had not chosen the boots. However, to make up for any want of style at that end, he had his crush hat under his arm.

He found the dining-room without excessive trouble. It was a vast and splendidly decorated place, and a number of people, evidently quite *au fait,* were dining there at little tables lit with electric red-shaded candles, gentlemen in evening dress, and ladies with dazzling astonishing necks. Kipps had never seen evening dress in full vigor before, and he doubted his eyes. And there were also people not in evening dress, who no doubt wondered what noble family Kipps represented. There was a band in a decorated recess, and the band looked collectively at the purple slippers, and so lost any chance they may have had of a donation so far as Kipps was concerned. The chief drawback to this magnificent place was the excessive space of floor that had to be crossed before you got your purple slippers hidden under a table.

He selected a little table—not the one where a rather impudent-looking waiter held a chair, but another—sat down, and, finding his gibus in his hand, decided after a moment of thought to rise slightly and sit on it. (It was discovered in his abandoned chair at a late hour by a supper-party and restored to him next day.)

He put the napkin carefully on one side, selected his soup without difficulty, "Clear please," but he was rather floored by the presentation of a quite splendidly bound wine-card. He turned it over, discovered a section devoted to whisky, and had a bright idea.

" 'Ere," he said to the waiter, with an encouraging movement of the head; and then in a confidential manner, "You 'aven't any Old Methuselah Three Stars, 'ave you?"

The waiter went away to inquire, and Kipps went on with his soup with an enhanced self-respect. Finally, Old Methuselah being unattainable, he ordered a claret from about the middle of the list. "Let's 'ave some of this," he said. He knew claret was a good sort of wine.

"A half bottle?" said the waiter.

"Right you are," said Kipps.

He felt he was getting on. He leaned back after his soup, a man of the world, and then slowly brought his eyes round to the ladies in evening dress on his right. . . .

He couldn't have thought it!

They were scorchers. Jest a bit of black velvet over the shoulders!

He looked again. One of them was laughing with a glass of wine half raised— wicked-looking woman she was; the other, the black velvet one, was eating bits of bread with nervous quickness and talking fast.

He wished old Buggins could see them.

He found a waiter regarding him and blushed deeply. He did not look again for some time, and became confused about his knife and fork over the fish. Presently he remarked a lady in pink to the left of him eating the fish with an entirely different implement.

It was over the *vol au vent* that he began to go to pieces. He took a knife to it; then saw the lady in pink was using a fork only, and hastily put down his knife, with a considerable amount of rich creaminess on the blade, upon the cloth. Then he found that a fork in his inexperienced hand was an instrument of chase rather than capture. His ears became violently red, and then he looked up to discover the lady in pink glancing at him, and then smiling, as she spoke to the man beside her.

He hated the lady in pink very much.

He stabbed a large piece of the *vol au vent* at last, and was too glad of his luck not to make a mouthful of it. But it was an extensive fragment, and pieces escaped him. Shirt-front! "Desh it!" he said, and had resort to his spoon. His waiter went and spoke to two other waiters, no doubt jeering at him. He became very fierce suddenly. " 'Ere!'' he said, gesticulating; and then, "Clear this away!"

The entire dinner-party on his right, the party of the ladies in advanced evening dress, looked at him. . . . He felt that everyone was watching him and making fun of him, and the injustice of this angered him. After all, they had had every advantage he hadn't. And then, when they got him there doing his best, what must they do but glance and sneer and nudge one another. He tried to catch them at it, and then took refuge in a second glass of wine.

Suddenly and extraordinarily he found himself a Socialist. He did not care how close it was to the lean years when all these things would end.

Mutton came with peas. He arrested the hand of the waiter. "No peas," he said. He knew something of the danger and difficulty of eating peas. Then, when the peas went away, he was embittered again. . . . Echoes of Masterman's burning rhetoric began to reverberate in his mind. Nice lot of people these were to laugh at anyone! Women half undressed— It was that made him so beastly uncomfortable. How could one eat one's dinner with people about him like that? Nice lot they were. He was glad he wasn't one of them anyhow. Yes, they might look. He resolved, if they looked at him again, he would ask one of the men who he was staring at. His perturbed and angry face would have concerned anyone. The band, by an unfortunate accident, was playing truculent military music. The mental change Kipps underwent was, in its way, what psychologists call a conversion. In a few moments all Kipps' ideals were changed. He who had been "practically a gentleman," the sedulous pupil of Coote, the punctilious raiser of hats, was instantly a rebel, an outcast, the hater of everything "stuck up," the foe of Society and the social order of today. Here they were among the profits of their robbery, these people who might do anything with the world. . . .

"No thenks," he said to a dish.

He addressed a scornful eye at the shoulders of the lady to his left.

Presently he was refusing another dish. He didn't like it—fussed-up food! Probably cooked by some foreigner. He finished up his wine and his bread. . . .

"No, thenks."

"No, thenks." . . .

He discovered the eye of a diner fixed curiously upon his flushed face. He responded with a glare. Couldn't he go without things if he liked?

"What's this?" said Kipps, to a great green cone.

"Ice," said the waiter.

"I'll 'ave some," said Kipps.

He seized fork and spoon and assailed the bombe. It cut rather stiffly. "Come up!" said Kipps, with concentrated bitterness, and the truncated summit of the bombe flew suddenly, traveling eastward with remarkable velocity. Flop, it went upon the floor a yard away, and for awhile time seemed empty.

At the adjacent table they were laughing altogether.

Shy the rest of the bombe at them?

Flight?

At any rate, a dignified withdrawal.

"No!" said Kipps, "no more," arresting the polite attempt of the waiter to serve him with another piece. He had a vague idea he might carry off the affair as though he meant the ice to go on the floor—not liking ice, for example, and being annoyed at the badness of his dinner. He put both hands on the table, thrust back his chair, disengaged a purple slipper from his napkin, and rose. He stepped carefully over the prostrate ice, kicked the napkin under the table, thrust his hands deep into his pockets, and marched out—shaking the dust of the place as it were from his feet. He left behind him a melting fragment of ice upon the floor, his gibus hat, warm and compressed in his chair, and, in addition, every social ambition he had ever entertained in the world.

7

Kipps went back to Folkestone in time for the Anagram Tea. But you must not imagine that the change of heart that came to him in the dining-room of the Royal Grand Hotel involved any change of attitude towards this promised social and intellectual treat. He went back because the Royal Grand was too much for him.

Outwardly calm, or at most a little flushed and ruffled, inwardly Kipps was a horrible, tormented battleground of scruples, doubts, shames, and self-assertions during those days of silent, desperate grappling with the big hotel. He did not intend the monstrosity should beat him without a struggle; but at last he had sullenly to admit himself overcome. The odds were terrific. On the one hand himself—with, among other things, only one pair of boots; on the other a vast wilderness of rooms, covering several acres, and with over a thousand people, staff and visitors, all chiefly occupied in looking queerly at Kipps, in laughing at him behind his back, in watching for difficult corners at which to confront and perplex him and inflict humiliations upon him. For example, the hotel scored over its electric light. After the dinner the chambermaid, a hard, unsympathetic young woman with a superior manner, was summoned by a bell Kipps had rung under the impression the button was the electric-light switch. "Look 'ere," said Kipps, rubbing a shin that had suffered during his search in the dark, "why aren't there any candles or matches?" The hotel explained and scored heavily.

"It isn't everyone is up to these things," said Kipps.

"No, it isn't," said the chambermaid with ill-concealed scorn, and slammed the door at him.

"S'pose I ought to have tipped her," said Kipps.

After that Kipps cleaned his boots with a pocket-handkerchief and went for a long walk, and got home in a hansom; but the hotel scored again by his not putting out his boots, and so having to clean them again in the morning. The hotel also snubbed him by bringing him hot water when he was fully dressed and looking surprised at his collar, but he got a breakfast, I must admit, with scarcely any difficulty.

After that the hotel scored heavily by the fact that there are twenty-four hours in the day and Kipps had nothing to do in any of them. He was a little footsore from his previous day's pedestrianism, and he could make up his mind for no long excursions. He flitted in and out of the hotel several times, and it was the polite porter who touched his hat every time that first set Kipps tipping.

"What 'e wants is a tip," said Kipps.

So at the next opportunity he gave the man an unexpected shilling, and, having once put his hand in his pocket, there was no reason why he should not go on. He bought a newspaper at the bookstall and tipped the boy the rest of the shilling, and then went up by the lift and tipped the man sixpence, leaving his newspaper inadvertently in the lift. He met his chambermaid in the passage and gave her half a crown. He resolved to demonstrate his position to the entire establishment in this way. He didn't like the place; he disapproved of it politically, socially, morally; but he resolved no taint of meanness should disfigure his sojourn in its luxurious halls. He went down by the lift (tipping again), and, being accosted by a waiter with his gibus, tipped the finder half a crown. He had a vague sense that he was making a flank movement upon the hotel and buying over its staff. They would regard him as a "character"; they would get to like him. He found his stock of small silver diminishing and replenished it at a desk in the hall. He tipped a man in bottle green, who looked like the man who had shown him his room the day before; and then he saw a visitor eyeing him, and doubted whether he was in this instance doing right. Finally he went out and took chance buses to their destinations, and wandered a little in remote wonderful suburbs, and returned. He lunched at a chop-house in Islington, and found himself back in the Royal Grand, now unmistakably footsore and London-weary, about three. He was attracted to the drawing-room by a neat placard about afternoon tea.

It occurred to him that the campaign of tipping upon which he had embarked was, perhaps after all, a mistake. He was confirmed in this by observing that the hotel officials were watching him, not respectfully, but with a sort of amused wonder, as if to see whom he would tip next. However, if he backed out now, they would think him an awful fool. Everyone wasn't so rich as he was. It was his way to tip. Still—

He grew more certain the hotel had scored again.

He pretended to be lost in thought, and so drifted by, and, having put hat and umbrella in the cloakroom, went into the drawing-room for afternoon tea.

There he did get what for a time he held to be a point in his favor. The room was large and quiet at first, and he sat back restfully until it occurred to him that his attitude brought his extremely dusty boots too prominently into the light, so instead he sat up, and then people of the upper and upper middle classes began to come and group themselves about him and have tea likewise, and so revive the class animosities of the previous day.

Presently a fluffy fair-haired lady came into prominent existence a few yards away. She was talking to a respectful low-voiced clergyman, whom she was possibly entertaining at tea. "No," she said; "dear Lady Jane wouldn't like that!"

"Mumble, mumble, mumble," from the clergyman.

"Poor dear Lady Jane was always so sensitive," the voice of the lady sang out clear and emphatic.

A fat, hairless, important-looking man joined this group, took a chair and planted it firmly with its back in the face of Kipps, a thing that offended Kipps mightily. "Are you telling him," gurgled the fat, hairless man, "about dear Lady Jane's affliction?" A young couple, lady brilliantly attired, and the man in a magnificently cut frock-coat, arranged themselves to the right, also with an air of exclusion towards Kipps. "I've told him," said the gentleman in a flat abundant voice. "My!" said the young lady with an American smile. No doubt they all thought Kipps was out of it. A great desire to assert himself in some way surged up in his heart. He felt he would like to cut in on the conversation in some dramatic way. A monologue, something in the manner of Masterman? At any rate, abandoning that as impossible, he would like to appear self-centered and at ease. His eye, wandering over the black surfaces of a noble architectural mass close by, discovered a slot and an enameled plaque of directions.

It was some sort of musical box!

It occurred to Kipps that he would like some music, that to inaugurate some would show him a man of taste and at his ease at the same time. He rose, read over a list of tunes, selected one haphazard, pressed his sixpence—it was sixpence!— home, and prepared for a confidential refined little melody.

Considering the high social tone of the Royal Grand, it was really a very loud instrument indeed. It gave vent to three deafening brays, and so burst the dam of silence that had long pent it in. It seemed to be chiefly full of the great-uncles of trumpets, megalo-trombones, and railway brakes. It made sounds like shunting trains. It did not so much begin as blow up your counterscarp and rush forward to storm under cover of melodious shrapnel. It had not so much an air as a *ricochette*. The music had in short the inimitable quality of Sousa. It swept down upon the friend of Lady Jane and carried away something socially striking into the eternal night of the unheard; the American girl to the left of it was borne off shrieking. "HIGH cockalorum Tootltootle tootle loo. HIGH cockalorum tootle loo. BUMP, bump, bump—BUMP,"—Native American music, full of native American notes, full of the spirit of western college yells and election howls, joyous exorbitant music from the gigantic nursery of the Future, bearing the hearer along upon its torrential succession of sounds, as if he was in a cask on Niagara. Whiroo! Yah, Have at you! The Strenuous Life! Yaha! Stop! A Reprieve! A Reprieve! No! Bang! Bump!

Everybody looked round, conversation ceased and gave place to gestures.

The friend of Lady Jane became terribly agitated.

"Can't it be stopped?" she vociferated, pointing a gloved finger and saying something to the waiter about "that dreadful young man."

"Ought not to be working," said the clerical friend of Lady Jane.

The waiter shook his head at the fat, hairless gentleman.

People began to move away. Kipps leaned back luxurious, and then tapped with a half-crown to pay.

He paid, tipped like a gentleman, rose with an easy gesture, and strolled towards the door. His retreat evidently completed the indignation of the friend of Lady Jane, and from the door he could still discern her gestures as asking, "Can't it be stopped?" The music followed him into the passage and pursued him to the lift, and only died away completely in the quiet of his own room, and afterwards from his window he saw the friend of Lady Jane and her party having their tea carried out to a little table in the court.

Certainly that was a point to him. But it was his only score; all the rest of the game lay in the hands of the upper classes and the big hotel. And presently he was doubting whether even this was really a point. It seemed a trifle vulgar, come to think it over, to interrupt people when they were talking.

He saw a clerk peering at him from the office, and suddenly it occurred to him that the place might get back at him tremendously over the bill.

They would probably take it out of him by charging pounds and pounds.

Suppose they charged more than he had!

The clerk had a particularly nasty face, just the face to take advantage of a vacillating Kipps.

He became aware of a man in a cap touching it, and produced his shilling automatically, but the strain was beginning to tell. It was a deuce and all of an expense—this tipping.

If the hotel chose to stick it on to the bill something tremendous, what was Kipps to do? Refuse to pay? Make a row?

If he did he couldn't fight all these men in bottle green. . . .

He went out about seven and walked for a long time, and dined at last upon a chop in the Euston Road; then he walked along to the Edgeware Road and sat and rested in the Metropolitan Music Hall for a time, until a trapeze performance unnerved him, and finally he came back to bed. He tipped the lift-man sixpence and wished him good night. In the silent watches of the night he reviewed the tale of the day's tipping, went over the horrors of the previous night's dinner, and heard again the triumphant bray of the harmonicon devil released from its long imprisonment. Everyone would be told about him tomorrow. He couldn't go on! He admitted his defeat. Never in their whole lives had any of these people seen such a Fool as he! Ugh! . . .

His method of announcing his withdrawal to the clerk was touched with bitterness.

"I'm going to get out of this," said Kipps, blowing windily. "Let's see what you got on my bill."

"One breakfast?" asked the clerk.

"Do I *look* as if I'd ate two?" . . .

At his departure Kipps, with a hot face, convulsive gestures, and an embittered heart, tipped everyone who did not promptly and actively resist, including an absent-minded South African diamond merchant who was waiting in the hall for his wife. He paid his cabman a four-shilling piece at Charing Cross, having no smaller change, and wished he could burn him alive. Then in a sudden reaction of economy he refused the proffered help of a porter, and carried his bag quite violently to the train.

CHAPTER VIII

Kipps Enters Society

1

SUBMISSION TO INEXORABLE Fate took Kipps to the Anagram Tea.

At any rate he would meet Helen there in the presence of other people, and be able to carry off the worst of the difficulty of explaining his little jaunt to London. He had not seen her since his last portentous visit to New Romney. He was engaged to her, he would have to marry her, and the sooner he faced her again the better. Before wild plans of turning socialist, defying the world and repudiating all calling forever, his heart, on second thoughts, sank. He felt Helen would never permit anything of the sort. As for the Anagrams, he could do no more than his best, and that he was resolved to do. What had happened at the Royal Grand, what had happened at New Romney, he must bury in his memory and begin again at the reconstruction of his social position. Ann, Buggins, Chitterlow—all these, seen in the matter-of-fact light of the Folkestone corridor train, stood just as they stood before—people of an inferior social position, who had to be eliminated from his world. It was a bother about Ann, a bother and a pity. His mind rested so for a space on Ann until the memory of those Anagrams drew him away. If he could see Coote that evening he might, he thought, be able to arrange some sort of connivance about the anagrams, and his mind was chiefly busy sketching proposals for such an arrangement. It would not, of course, be ungentlemanly cheating, but only a little mystification. Coote, very probably, might drop him a hint of the solution of one or two of the things—not enough to win a prize, but enough to cover his shame. Or failing that, he might take a humorous, quizzical line, and pretend he was pretending to be very stupid. There were plenty of ways out of it if one kept a sharp lookout. . . .

The costume Kipps wore to the Anagram Tea was designed as a compromise between the strict letter of high fashion and seaside laxity—a sort of easy semi-state for afternoon. Helen's first reproof had always lingered in his mind. He wore a frock-coat, but mitigated it by a Panama hat of romantic shape with a black band, gray gloves, but, for relaxation, brown button boots. The only other man besides the clergy present—a new doctor with an attractive wife—was in full afternoon dress. Coote was not there.

Kipps was a little pale, but quite self-possessed, as he approached Mrs. Bindon Botting's door. He took a turn while some people went in, and then faced it manfully. The door opened and revealed—Ann!

In the background, through a draped doorway, behind a big fern in a great art pot, the elder Miss Botting was visible talking to two guests; the auditory background was a froth of feminine voices. . . .

Our two young people were much too amazed to give one another any formula of greeting, though they had parted warmly enough. Each was already in a state of extreme tension to meet the demands of this great and unprecedented occasion— an Anagram Tea. "Lor!" said Ann, her sole remark; and then the sense of Miss Botting's eye ruled her straight again. She became very pale, but she took his hat mechanically, and he was already removing his gloves. "Ann," he said in a low tone, and then "Fency!"

The eldest Miss Botting knew Kipps was the sort of guest who requires nursing, and she came forward vocalizing charm. She said it was "awfully jolly of him to come—awfully jolly. It was awfully difficult to get any good men!"

She handed Kipps forward, mumbling and in a dazed condition, to the drawing-room, and there he encountered Helen, looking unfamiliar in an unfamiliar hat. It was as if he had not met her for years.

She astonished him. She didn't seem to mind in the least his going to London. She held out a shapely hand, and smiled encouragingly. "You've faced the anagrams?" she said.

The second Miss Botting accosted them, a number of oblong pieces of paper in her hand, mysteriously inscribed. "Take an anagram," she said; "take an anagram," and boldly pinned one of these brief documents to Kipps' lapel. The letters were "Cypshi," and Kipps from the very beginning suspected this was an anagram for Cuyps. She also left a thing like a long dance program, from which dangled a little pencil, in his hand. He found himself being introduced to people, and then he was in a corner with the short lady in a big bonnet, who was pelting him with gritty little bits of small talk, that were gone before you could take hold of them and reply.

"Very hot," said this lady. "Very hot indeed——hot all the summer—remarkable year—all the years remarkable now—don't know what we're coming to. Don't you think so, Mr. Kipps?"

"Oo rather," said Kipps, and wondered if Ann was still in the hall. Ann!

He ought not to have stared at her like a stuck fish, and pretended not to know her. That couldn't be right. But what *was* right?

The lady in the big bonnet proceeded to a second discharge. "Hope you're fond of anagrams, Mr. Kipps—difficult exercise—still, one must do something to bring people together—better than Ludo, anyhow. Don't you think so, Mr. Kipps?"

Ann fluttered past the open door. Her eyes met his in amazed inquiry. Something had got dislocated in the world for both of them. . . .

He ought to have told her he was engaged. He ought to have explained things to her. Perhaps, even now, he might be able to drop her a hint.

"Don't you think so, Mr. Kipps?"

"Oo rather," said Kipps for the third time.

A lady with a tired smile, who was labeled conspicuously "Wogdelenk," drifted towards Kipps' interlocutor, and the two fell into conversation. Kipps found himself socially aground. He looked about him. Helen was talking to a curate and laughing. Kipps was overcome by a vague desire to speak to Ann. He was for sidling doorward.

"What are *you*, please?" said an extraordinarily bold, tall girl, and arrested him while she took down "Cypshi."

"I'm sure I don't know what it means," she explained. "I'm Sir Bubh. Don't you think anagrams are something chronic?"

Kipps made stockish noises, and the young lady suddenly became the nucleus of a party of excited friends who were forming a syndicate to guess, and barred his escape. She took no further notice of him. He found himself jammed against an occasional table and listening to the conversation of Mrs. "Wogdelenk" and his lady with the big bonnet.

"She packed her two beauties off together," said the lady in the big bonnet. "Time enough, too. Don't think much of this girl she's got as housemaid now. Pretty, of course, but there's no occasion for a housemaid to be pretty—none whatever. And she doesn't look particularly up to her work either. Kind of 'mazed expression."

"You never can tell," said the lady labeled "Wogdelenk"; "you never can tell. My wretches are big enough, Heaven knows, and do they work? Not a bit of it! . . ."

Kipps felt dreadfully out of it with regard to all these people, and dreadfully in it with Ann.

He scanned the back of the big bonnet, and concluded it was an extremely ugly bonnet indeed. It got jerking forward as each short, dry sentence was snapped off at the end, and a plume of osprey on it jerked excessively. "She hasn't guessed even one!" followed by a shriek of girlish merriment, came from the group about the tall, bold girl. They'd shriek at him presently, perhaps! Beyond thinking his own anagram might be Cuyps, he hadn't a notion. What a chatter they were all making! It was just like a summer sale! Just the sort of people who'd give a lot of trouble and swap you! And suddenly the smoldering fires of rebellion leaped to flame again. These were a rotten lot of people, and the anagrams were rotten nonsense, and he (Kipp) had been a rotten fool to come. There was Helen away there still laughing with her curate. Pity she couldn't marry a curate, and leave him (Kipps) alone! Then he'd know what to do. He disliked the whole gathering, collectively and in detail. Why were they all trying to make him one of themselves? He perceived unexpected ugliness everywhere about him. There were two great pins jabbed through the tall girl's hat, and the swirls of her hair below the brim, with the minutest piece of tape tie-up showing, did not repay close examination. Mrs. "Wogdelenk" wore a sort of mumps bandage of lace, and there was another lady perfectly dazzling with beads and jewels and bits of trimming. They were all flaps and angles and flounces, these women. Not one of them looked as neat and decent a shape as Ann's clean, trim little figure. Echoes of Masterman woke up in him again. Ladies indeed! Here were all these chattering people, with money, with leisure, with every chance in the world, and all they could do was to crowd like this into a couple of rooms and jabber nonsense about anagrams.

"Could Cypshi really mean Cuyps?" floated like a dissolving wreath of mist across his mind.

Abruptly resolution stood armed in his heart. He was going to get out of this!

" 'Scuse me," he said, and began to wade neck-deep through the bubbling tea-party.

He was going to get out of it all!

He found himself close by Helen. "I'm orf," he said, but she gave him the briefest glance. She did not appear to hear him. "Still Mr. Spratlingdown, you *must* admit there's a limit even to conformity," she was saying. . . .

He was in a curtained archway, and Ann was before him, carrying a tray supporting several small sugarbowls.

He was moved to speech. *"What* a Lot!" he said, and then mysteriously, "I'm engaged to *her."* He indicated Helen's new hat, and became aware of a skirt he had stepped upon.

Ann stared at him helplessly, borne past in the grip of incomprehensible imperatives.

Why shouldn't they talk together?

He was in a small room, and then at the foot of the staircase in the hall. He heard the rustle of a dress, and what was conceivably his hostess was upon him.

"But you're not going, Mr. Kipps?" she said.

"I must," he said. "I got to."

"But, Mr. Kipps!"

"I must," he said. "I'm not well."

"But before the guessing! Without any tea!"

Ann appeared and hovered behind him.

"I got to go," said Kipps.

If he parleyed with her Helen might awake to his desperate attempt.

"Of course, if you *must* go."

"It's something I've forgotten," said Kipps, beginning to feel regrets. "Reely I must."

Mrs. Botting turned with a certain offended dignity, and Ann, in a state of flushed calm that evidently concealed much, came forward to open the door.

"I'm very sorry," he said, "I'm very sorry," half to his hostess and half to her, and was swept past her by superior social forces—like a drowning man in a mill-race—and into the Upper Sandgate Road. He half turned upon the step, and then slam went the door. . . .

He retreated along the Leas, a thing of shame and perplexity, Mrs. Botting's aggrieved astonishment uppermost in his mind. . . .

Something—reinforced by the glances of the people he was passing—pressed its way to his attention through the tumultuous disorder of his mind.

He became aware that he was still wearing his little placard with the letters "Cypshi."

"Desh it!" he said, clutching off this abomination. In another moment its several letters, their task accomplished, were scattering gleefully before the breeze down the front of the Leas.

2

Kipps was dressed for Mrs. Wace's dinner half an hour before it was time to start, and he sat waiting until Coote should come to take him round. "Manners and Rules of Good Society" lay beside him neglected. He had read the polished prose of the Member of the Aristocracy on page 96 as far as—

> "the acceptance of an invitation is in the eyes of
> "diners out, a binding obligation which only ill-
> "health, family bereavement, or some all-important
> "reason justifies its being set on one side or other-
> wise evaded"—

and then he had lapsed into gloomy thoughts.

That afternoon he had had a serious talk with Helen.

He had tried to express something of the change of heart that had happened to him. But to broach the real state of the matter had been altogether too terrible for him. He had sought a minor issue. "I don't like all this Society," he had said.

"But you must *see* people," said Helen.

"Yes, but— It's the sort of people you see." He nerved himself. "I didn't think much of that lot at the Enegram Tea."

"You have to see all sorts of people if you want to see the world," said Helen.

Kipps was silent for a space, and a little short of breath.

"My dear Arthur," she began almost kindly, "I shouldn't ask you to go to these affairs if I didn't think it good for you, should I?"

Kipps acquiesced in silence.

"You will find the benefit of it all when we get to London. You learn to swim in a tank before you go out into the sea. These people here are good enough to learn upon. They're stiff and rather silly, and dreadfully narrow, and not an idea in a dozen of them, but it really doesn't matter at all. You'll soon get Savoir Faire."

He made to speak again, and found his powers of verbal expression lacking. Instead he blew a sigh.

"You'll get used to it all very soon," said Helen, helpfully. . . .

As he sat meditating over that interview, and over the vistas of London that opened before him, on the little flat and teas and occasions, and the constant presence of Brudderkins and all the bright prospect of his new and better life, and how he could never see Ann any more, the housemaid entered with a little package, a small, square envelope for "Arthur Kipps, Esquire."

"A young woman left this, sir," said the housemaid, a little severely.

"Eh?" said Kipps. "What young woman?" and then suddenly began to understand.

"She looked an ordinary young woman," said the housemaid, coldly.

"Ah!" said Kipps. *"That's* orlright."

He waited till the door had closed behind the girl, staring at the envelope in his hand, and then, with a curious feeling of increasing tension, tore it open. As he did so, some quicker sense than sight or touch told him its contents. It was Ann's half-sixpence. And besides, not a word!

Then she must have heard him—!

He was standing with the envelope in his hand when Coote became audible without.

Coote appeared in evening dress, a clean and radiant Coote, with large greenish white gloves, and a particularly large white tie edged with black. "For a third cousin," he presently explained. "Nace, isn't it?" He could see Kipps was pale and disturbed, and put this down to the approaching social trial. "You keep your nerve up, Kipps, my dear chap, and you'll be all right," said Coote, with a big brotherly glove on Kipps' sleeve.

3

The dinner came to a crisis so far as Kipps' emotions were concerned with Mrs. Bindon Botting's talk about servants, but before that there had been several things of greater or smaller magnitude to perturb and disarrange his social front. One little matter that was mildly insurgent throughout the entire meal was, if I may be permitted to mention so intimate a matter, the behavior of his left brace.

The webbing—which was of a cheerful scarlet silk—had slipped away from its buckle, fastened, no doubt, in agitation, and had developed a strong tendency to place itself obliquely, in the manner rather of an official decoration, athwart his spotless front. It first asserted itself before they went in to dinner. He replaced this ornament by a dexterous thrust when no one was looking, and thereafter the suppression of this novel innovation upon the stereotyped somberness of evening dress became a standing preoccupation. On the whole he was inclined to think his first horror excessive; at any rate, no one remarked upon it. However, you imagine him constantly throughout the evening with one eye and one hand, whatever the rest of him might be doing, predominantly concerned with the weak corner.

But this, I say, was a little matter. What exercised him much more was to discover Helen, quite terribly in evening dress.

The young lady had let her imagination rove Londonward, and this costume was perhaps an anticipation of that clever little flat, not too far west, which was to become the center of so delightful a literary and artistic set. It was, of all the feminine costumes present, most distinctly an evening dress. One was advised Miss Walshingham had arms and shoulders of a type by no means despicable; one was advised Miss Walshingham was capable not only of dignity but charm, even a certain glow of charm. It was, you know, her first evening dress, a tribute paid by Walshingham finance to her brightening future. Had she wanted keeping in countenance, she would have had to have fallen back upon her hostess, who was resplendent in black and steel. The other ladies had to a certain extent compromised. Mrs. Walshingham had dressed with just a refined little V, and Mrs. Bindon Botting, except for her dear mottled arms, confided scarcely more of her plump charm to the world. The elder Miss Botting stopped short of shoulders, and so did Miss Wace. But Helen didn't. She was—had Kipps had eyes to see it—a quite beautiful human figure; she knew it, and she met him with a radiant smile that had forgotten all the little difference of the afternoon. But to Kipps her appearance was the last release. With that she had become as remote, as foreign, as incredible as a wife and mate, as though the Cnidian Venus herself, in all her simple elegance, was, before witnesses, declared to be his. If, indeed, she had ever been credible as a wife and mate!

She ascribed his confusion to modest reverence, and, having blazed smiling upon him for a moment, turned a shapely shoulder towards him and exchanged a remark with Mrs. Bindon Botting. Ann's poor little half-sixpence came against Kipps' fingers in his pocket, and he clutched at it suddenly as though it was a talisman. Then he abandoned it to suppress his Order of the Brace. He was affected by a cough. "Miss Wace tells me Mr. Revel is coming," Mrs. Botting was saying.

"Isn't it delightful?" said Helen. "We saw him last night. He's stopped on his way to Paris. He's going to meet his wife there."

Kipps' eyes rested for a moment on Helen's dazzling deltoid, and then went inquiringly, accusingly, almost, to Coote's face. Where in the presence of this terrible emergence was the gospel of suppression now? that Furtive treatment of Religion and Politics, and Birth and Death, and Bathing and Babies and "all those things," which constitute your True Gentleman? He had been too modest even to discuss this question with his Mentor, but surely, surely this quintessence of all that is good and nice could regard these unsolicited confidences only in one way. With something between relief and the confirmation of his worst fears he perceived, by a sort of twitching of the exceptionally abundant muscles about Coote's lower jaw, in a certain deliberate avoidance of one particular direction by those pale but resolute gray eyes, by the almost convulsive grip of the ample, greenish-white gloves behind him, a grip broken at times for controlling pats at the black-bordered tie and the back of that spacious head, and by a slight but increasing disposition to cough, that *Coote did not approve!*

To Kipps Helen had once supplied a delicately beautiful dream, a thing of romance and unsubstantial mystery. But this was her final materialization, and the last thin wreath of glamor about her was dispelled. In some way (he had forgotten how, and it was perfectly incomprehensible) he was bound to this dark, solid and determined young person, whose shadow and suggestion he had once loved. He had to go through with the thing as a gentleman should. Still—

And when he was sacrificing Ann!

He wouldn't stand this sort of thing, whatever else he stood. . . . Should he say something about her dress to her—tomorrow?

He could put his foot down firmly. He could say, "Look 'ere. I don't care. I ain't going to stand it. See?"

She'd say something unexpected of course. She always did say something unexpected.

Suppose for once he overrode what she said, and simply repeated his point.

He found these thoughts battling with certain conversational aggressions from Mrs. Wace, and then Revel arrived and took the center of the stage.

The author of that brilliant romance, "Red Hearts a-Beating," was a less imposing man than Kipps had anticipated, but he speedily effaced that disappointment by his predominating manners. Although he lived habitually in the vivid world of London, his collar and tie were in no way remarkable, and he was neither brilliantly handsome, nor curly, nor long-haired. His personal appearance suggested armchairs rather than the equestrian exercises and amorous toyings and passionate intensities of his masterpiece; he was inclined to be fat, with whitish flesh, muddy-colored straight hair; he had a rather shapeless and truncated nose, and his chin was asymmetrical. One eye was more inclined to stare than the other. He might have been esteemed a little undistinguished-looking were it not for his beeswaxed moustache, which came amidst his features with a pleasing note of incongruity, and the whimsical wrinkles above and about his greater eye. His regard sought and found Helen's as he entered the room, and they shook hands presently with an air of intimacy Kipps, for no clear reason, found objectionable. He saw them clasp their hands, heard Coote's characteristic cough—a sound rather more like a very, very old sheep a quarter of a mile away being blown to pieces by a small charge of gunpowder than anything else in the world—did some confused beginnings of a thought, and then they were all going in to dinner, and Helen's shining bare arm lay along his sleeve. Kipps was in no state for conversation. She glanced at him, and, though he did not know it, very slightly pressed his elbow. He struggled with strange respiratory dislocations. Before them went Coote, discoursing in amiable reverberations to Mrs. Walshingham, and at the head of the procession was Mrs. Bindon Botting, talking fast and brightly beside the erect military figure of little Mr. Wace. (He was not a soldier really, but he had caught a martinet bearing by living so close to Shorncliffe.) Revel came last, in charge of Mrs. Wace's queenly black and steel, politely admiring in a flute-like cultivated voice the mellow wall-paper of the staircase. Kipps marveled at everybody's self-possession.

From the earliest spoonful of soup it became evident that Revel considered himself responsible for the table-talk. And before the soup was over it was almost as manifest that Mrs. Bindon Botting inclined to consider his sense of responsibility excessive. In her circle Mrs. Bindon Botting was esteemed an agreeable rattle, her manner and appearance were conspicuously vivacious for one so plump, and she had an almost Irish facility for humorous description. She would keep people amused all through an afternoon call with the story of how her jobbing gardener had got himself married and what his home was like, or how her favorite butt, Mr. Stigson Warder, had all his unfortunate children taught almost every conceivable instrument because they had the phrenological bump of music abnormally large. The family itself was also abnormally large. "They got to trombones, my dear!" she would say, with her voice coming to a climax. Usually her friends conspired to draw her out, but on this occasion they neglected to do so, a thing that militated against her keen desire to shine in Revel's eyes. After a time she perceived that the only thing for her to do was to cut in on the talk, on her own account, and this she began to do. She made several ineffectual snatches at the general attention, and then Revel drifted towards a topic she regarded as particularly her own—the ordering of households.

They came to the thing through talk about localities. "We are leaving our house in The Boltons," said Revel, "and taking a little place at Wimbledon, and I think of having rooms in Dane's Inn. It will be more convenient in many ways. My wife is furiously addicted to golf and exercise of all sorts, and I like to sit about in clubs—I haven't the strength necessary for these hygienic proceedings—and the old arrangement suited neither of us. And besides, no one could imagine the demoralization the domestics of West London have undergone during the last three years."

"It's the same everywhere," said Mrs. Bindon Botting.

"Very possibly it is. A friend of mine calls it the servile tradition in decay, and regards it all as a most hopeful phenomenon—"

"He ought to have had my last two criminals," said Mrs. Bindon Botting.

She turned to Mrs. Wace, while Revel came again a little too late with a "Possibly—"

"And I haven't told you, my dear," she said, speaking with voluble rapidity, "I'm in trouble again."

"That last girl?"

"The last girl. Before I can get a cook, my hard-won housemaid"—she paused—"chucks it."

"Panic?" asked young Walshingham.

"Mysterious grief! Everything merry as a marriage-bell until my Anagram Tea! Then in the evening a portentous rigor of bearing, a word or so from my Aunt, and immediately—Floods of Tears and Notice!" For a moment her eye rested thoughtfully on Kipps as she said, "Is there anything heart-rending about Anagrams?"

"I find them so," said Revel. "I—"

But Mrs. Bindon Botting got away again. "For a time it made me quite uneasy—"

Kipps jabbed his lip with his fork rather painfully, and was recalled from a fascinated glare at Mrs. Botting to the immediate facts of dinner.

"—whether anagrams might not have offended the good domestic's Moral Code—you never can tell. We made inquiries. No. No. No. She *must* go, and that's all!"

"One perceives," said Revel, "in these disorders, dimly and distantly, the last dying glow of the age of Romance. Let us suppose, Mrs. Botting, let us at least try to suppose—it is Love."

Kipps clattered with his knife and fork.

"It's love," said Mrs. Botting; "what else can it be? Beneath the orderly humdrum of our lives these romances are going on, until at last they bust up and give Notice and upset our humdrum altogether. Some fatal, wonderful soldier—"

"The passions of the common or house-domestic—" began Revel, and recovered possession of the table.

Upon the troubled disorder of Kipps' table manners there had supervened a quietness, an unusual calm. For once in his life he had distinctly made up his mind on his own account. He listened no more to Revel. He put down his knife and fork and refused everything that followed. Coote regarded him with tactful concern, and Helen flushed a little.

4

About half-past nine that night there came a violent pull at the bell of Mrs. Bindon Botting, and a young man in a dress-suit and a gibus and other marks of exalted social position stood without. Athwart his white expanse of breast lay a ruddy bar of patterned silk that gave him a singular distinction and minimized the glow of a few small stains of Burgundy. His gibus was thrust back, and exposed a disorder of hair that suggested a reckless desperation. He had, in fact, burned his boats and refused to join the ladies. Coote, in the subsequent conversation, had protested quietly, "You're going on all right, you know," to which Kipps had answered he didn't care a "Eng" about that, and so, after a brief tussle with Walshingham's detaining arm, had got away. "I got something to do," he said. " 'Ome." And here he was—panting an extraordinary resolve. The door opened, revealing the pleasantly furnished hall of Mrs. Bindon Botting, lit by rose-tinted lights, and in the center of the picture, neat and pretty in black and white, stood Ann. At the sight of Kipps her color vanished.

"Ann," said Kipps, "I want to speak to you. I got something to say to you right away. See? I'm—"

"This ain't the door to speak to me at," said Ann.

"But, Ann! It's something special."

"You spoke enough," said Ann.

"Ann!"

"Besides, that's my door, down there. Basement. If I was caught talking at *this* door—!"

"But, Ann, *I'm*—"

"Basement after nine. Them's my hours. I'm a servant, and likely to keep one. If you're calling here, what name, please? But you got your friends and I got mine, and you mustn't go talking to *me*."

"But, Ann, I want to ask you—"

Someone appeared in the hall behind Ann. "Not here," said Ann. "Don't know anyone of that name," and incontinently slammed the door in his face.

"What was that, Ann?" said Mrs. Bindon Botting's invalid Aunt.

"Ge'm a little intoxicated, Ma'am—asking for the wrong name, Ma'am."

"What name did he want?" asked the lady, doubtfully.

"No name that *we* know, Ma'am," said Ann, hustling along the hall towards the kitchen stairs.

"I hope you weren't too short with him, Ann."

"No shorter than he deserved, considering 'ow he be'aved," said Ann, with her bosom heaving.

And Mrs. Bindon Botting's invalid Aunt, perceiving suddenly that this call had some relation to Ann's private and sentimental trouble, turned, after one moment of hesitating scrutiny, away.

She was an extremely sympathetic lady was Mrs. Bindon Botting's invalid Aunt; she took an interest in the servants, imposed piety, extorted confessions and followed human nature, blushing and lying defensively to its reluctantly revealed recesses; but Ann's sense of privacy was strong, and her manner, under drawing-out and encouragement, sometimes even alarming. . . .

So the poor old lady went upstairs again.

5

The basement door opened, and Kipps came into the kitchen. He was flushed and panting.

He struggled for speech.

" 'Ere,'' he said, and held out two half-sixpences.

Ann stood behind the kitchen table—face pale and eyes round, and now—and it simplified Kipps very much—he could see she had indeed been crying.

"Well?'' she said.

"Don't you see?''

Ann moved her head slightly.

"I kep' it all these years.''

"You kep' it too long.''

His mouth closed and his flush died away. He looked at her. The amulet, it seemed, had failed to work.

"Ann!'' he said.

"Well?''

"Ann.''

The conversation still hung fire.

"Ann,'' he said; made a movement with his hands that suggested appeal and advanced a step.

Ann shook her head more definitely, and became defensive.

"Look here, Ann,'' said Kipps. "I been a fool.''

They stared into each other's miserable eyes.

"Ann,'' he said. "I want to marry you.''

Ann clutched the table edge. "You can't,'' she said faintly.

He made as if to approach her round the table, and she took a step that restored their distance.

"I must,'' he said.

"You can't.''

"I must. You *got* to marry me, Ann.''

"You can't go marrying everybody. You got to marry '*er.*''

"I sha'n't.''

Ann shook her head. "You're engaged to that girl. Lady, rather. You can't be engaged to me.''

"I don't want to be engaged to you. I *been* engaged. I want to be married to you. See? Right away.''

Ann turned a shade paler. "But what d'you mean?'' she asked.

"Come right off to London and marry me. Now.''

"What d'you mean?''

Kipps became extremely lucid and earnest.

"I mean, come right off and marry me now before anyone else can. See?''

"In London?"

"In London."

They stared at one another again. They took things for granted in the most amazing way.

"I couldn't," said Ann. "For one thing, my month's not up for mor'n free weeks yet."

They hung before that for a moment as though it was insurmountable.

"Look 'ere, Ann! Arst to go. Arst to go!"

"*She* wouldn't," said Ann.

"Then come without arsting," said Kipps.

"She'd keep my box—"

"She won't."

"She will."

"She won't."

"You don't know 'er."

"Well, desh 'er—let 'er! LET 'ER! Who cares? I'll buy you a 'undred boxes if you'll come."

"It wouldn't be right towards Her."

"It isn't Her you got to think about, Ann. It's me."

"And you 'aven't treated me properly," she said. "You 'aven't treated me properly, Artie. You didn't ought to 'ave—"

"I didn't say I 'ad," he interrupted, "did I? Ann," he appealed, "I didn't come to arguefy. I'm all wrong. I never said I wasn't. It's yes or no. Me or not. . . . I been a fool. There! See? I been a fool. Ain't that enough? I got myself all tied up with everyone and made a fool of myself all round. . . ."

He pleaded, "It isn't as if we didn't care for one another, Ann."

She seemed impassive, and he resumed his discourse.

"I thought I wasn't likely ever to see you again, Ann. I reely did. It isn't as though I was seein' you all the time. I didn't know what I wanted, and I went and be'aved like a fool—jest as anyone might. I know what I want, and I know what I don't want now.

"Ann!"

"Well?"

"Will you come? . . . Will you come? . . ."

Silence.

"If you don't answer me, Ann—I'm desprit—if you don't answer me now, if you don't say you'll come, I'll go right out now—"

He turned doorward passionately as he spoke, with his threat incomplete.

"I'll go," he said. "I 'aven't a friend in the world! I been and throwed everything away. I don't know why I done things and why I 'aven't. All I know is I can't stand nothing in the world any more." He choked. "The pier," he said.

He fumbled with the door-latch, grumbling some inarticulate self-pity, as if he sought a handle, and then he had it open.

Clearly he was going.

"Artie!" said Ann, sharply.

He turned about, and the two hung white and tense.

"I'll do it," said Ann.

His face began to work, he shut the door and came a step back to her, staring; his face became pitiful, and then suddenly they moved together. "Artie!" she cried, "don't go!" and held out her arms, weeping.

They clung close to one another. . . .

"Oh, I *been* so mis'bel!" cried Kipps, clinging to this lifebuoy; and suddenly his emotion, having no further serious work in hand, burst its way to a loud *boohoo!* His fashionable and expensive gibus flopped off, and fell and rolled and lay neglected on the floor.

"I been so mis'bel," said Kipps, giving himself vent. "Oh, I *been* so mis'bel, Ann!"

"Be quiet," said Ann, holding his poor blubbering head tightly to her heaving shoulder, herself all a-quiver; "be quiet. She's there! Listenin'. She'll 'ear you, Artie, on the stairs. . . ."

6

Ann's last words when, an hour later, they parted—Mrs. and Miss Bindon Botting having returned very audibly upstairs—deserve a section to themselves.

"I wouldn't do this for everyone, mind you," whispered Ann.

CHAPTER IX

The Labyrinthodon

1

YOU IMAGINE THEM fleeing through our complex and difficult social system as it were for life, first on foot and severally to the Folkestone Central Station, then in a first-class carriage, with Kipps' bag as sole chaperon to Charing Cross, and then in a four-wheeler, a long, rumbling, palpitating, slow flight through the multitudinous swarming London streets to Sid. Kipps kept peeping out of the window. "It's the next corner after this, I believe," he would say. For he had a sort of feeling that at Sid's he would be immune from the hottest pursuit. He paid the cabman in a manner adequate to the occasion, and turned to his prospective brother-in-law. "Me and Ann," he said, "we're going to marry."

"But I thought—" began Sid.

Kipps motioned him towards explanations in the shop. . . .

"It's no good my arguing with you," said Sid, smiling delightedly as the case unfolded. "You done it now." And Masterman, being apprised of the nature of the affair, descended slowly in a state of flushed congratulation.

"I thought you might find the Higher Life a bit difficult," said Masterman, projecting a bony hand. "But I never thought you'd have the originality to clear out. . . . Won't the young lady of the superior classes swear! Never mind—it doesn't matter anyhow.

"You were starting a climb," he said at dinner, "that doesn't lead anywhere. You would have clambered from one refinement of vulgarity to another, and never got to any satisfactory top. There isn't a top. It's a squirrel's cage. Things are out of joint, and the only top there is is a lot of blazing card-playing women and betting men, seasoned with archbishops and officials and all that sort of glossy pandering Tosh. . . . You'd have hung on, a disconsolate, dismal little figure, somewhere up the ladder, far below even the motor-car class, while your wife larked about, or fretted because she wasn't a bit higher than she was. . . . I found it all out long ago. I've seen women of that sort. And I don't climb any more."

"I often thought about what you said last time I saw you," said Kipps.

"I wonder what I said," said Masterman, in parenthesis. "Anyhow, you're doing the right and sane thing, and that's a rare spectacle. You're going to marry your equal, and you're going to take your own line, quite independently of what people up there, or people down there, think you ought or ought not to do. That's about the only course one can take nowadays, with everything getting more muddled and upside-down every day. Make your own little world and your own house first of all; keep that right side up whatever you do, and marry your mate. . . . That, I suppose, is what *I* should do—if *I* had a mate. . . . But people of my sort, luckily for the world, don't get made in pairs. No!

"Besides— However—" And abruptly, taking advantage of an interruption by Master Walt, he lapsed into thought.

Presently he came out of his musings.

"After all," he said, "there's Hope."

"What about?" said Sid.

"Everything," said Masterman.

"Where there's life there's hope," said Mrs. Sid. "But none of you aren't eating anything like you ought to."

Masterman lifted his glass.

"Here's to Hope!" he said, "the Light of the World!"

Sid beamed at Kipps, as who should say, "You don't meet a character like *this* every dinner-time."

"Here's to Hope!" repeated Masterman. "The best thing one can have. Hope of life— Yes."

He imposed his moment of magnificent self-pity on them all. Even young Walt was impressed.

2

They spent the days before their marriage in a number of agreeable excursions together. One day they went to Kew by steamboat, and admired the house full of paintings of flowers extremely; and one day they went early to have a good long day at the Crystal Palace, and enjoyed themselves very much indeed. They got there so early that nothing was open inside; all the stalls were wrappered up, and all the minor exhibitions locked and barred. They seemed the minutest creatures even to themselves in that enormous empty aisle, and their echoing footsteps indecently loud. They contemplated realistic groups of plaster savages, and Ann thought they'd be queer people to have about. She was glad there were none in this country. They meditated upon replicas of classical statuary without excessive comment. Kipps said, at large, it must have been a queer world then; but Ann very properly doubted if they really went about like that. But the place at that early hour was really lonely. One began to fancy things. So they went out into the October sunshine of the mighty terraces, and wandered amidst miles of stucco tanks, and about those quiet Gargantuan grounds. A great gray emptiness it was, and it seemed marvelous to them, but not nearly so marvelous as it might have seemed. "I never see a finer place, never," said Kipps, turning to survey the entirety of the enormous glass front with Paxton's vast image in the center.

"What it must 'ave cost to build!" said Ann, and left her sentence eloquently incomplete.

Presently they came to a region of caves and waterways, and amidst these waterways strange reminders of the possibilities of the Creator. They passed under an arch made of a whale's jaw, and discovered amidst herbage, browsing or standing unoccupied and staring as if amazed at themselves, huge effigies of iguanodons, and deinotheria, and mastodons and such-like cattle gloriously done in green and gold.

"They got everything," said Kipps. "Earl's Court isn't a patch on it."

His mind was very greatly exercised by these monsters, and he hovered about them and returned to them. "You'd wonder 'ow they ever got enough to eat," he said several times.

3

It was later in the day, and upon a seat in the presence of the green and gold Labyrinthodon that looms so splendidly above the lake, that the Kippses fell into talk about their future. They had made a sufficient lunch in the palace, they had seen pictures and no end of remarkable things, and that and the amber sunlight made a mood for them, quiet and philosophical—a haven mood. Kipps broke a contemplative silence with an abrupt allusion to one principal preoccupation. "I shall offer an 'pology, and I shall offer 'er brother damages. If she likes to bring an action for Breach after that, well,—I done all I can. . . . They can't get much out of reading my letters in court, because I didn't write none. I dessay a thousan' or two'll settle all that, anyhow. I ain't much worried about that. That don't worry me very much, Ann—No."

And then, "It's a lark our marrying.

"It's curious 'ow things come about. If I 'adn't run against you, where should I 'ave been now—eh? . . . Even after we met I didn't seem to see it like—not marrying you, I mean—until that night I came. I didn't—reely."

"I didn't neither," said Ann, with thoughtful eyes on the water.

For a time Kipps' mind was occupied by the prettiness of her thinking face. A faint tremulous network of lights, reflected from the ripples of a passing duck, played subtly over her cheek and faded away.

Ann reflected. "I s'pose things *'ad* to be," she said.

Kipps mused. "It's curious 'ow ever I got on to be engaged to 'er."

"She wasn't suited to you," said Ann.

"Suited? No fear! That's jest it. 'Ow did it come about?"

"I expect she led you on," said Ann.

Kipps was half minded to assent. Then he had a twinge of conscience. "It wasn't that, Ann," he said. "It's curious. I don't know what it was, but it wasn't that. I don't recollect. . . . No. . . . Life's jolly rum; that's one thing, any'ow. And I suppose I'm a rum sort of feller. I get excited sometimes, and then I don't seem to care *what* I do. That's about what it was, reely. Still—"

They meditated, Kipps with his arms folded and pulling at his scanty moustache. Presently a faint smile came over his face.

"We'll get a nice little 'ouse out Ithe way."

"It's 'omelier than Folkestone," said Ann.

"Jest a nice *little* 'ouse," said Kipps. "There's Hughenden, of course. But that's let. Besides being miles too big. And I wouldn't live in Folkestone again some'ow—not for anything."

"I'd like to 'ave a 'ouse of my own," said Ann. "I've often thought, being in service, 'ow much I'd like to manage a 'ouse of my own."

"You'd know all about what the servants was up to, anyhow," said Kipps, amused.

"Servants! We don't want no servants," said Ann, startled.

"You'll 'ave to 'ave a servant," said Kipps. "If it's only to do the 'eavy work of the 'ouse."

"What! and not be able 'ardly to go into my own kitchen?" said Ann.

"You ought to 'ave a servant," said Kipps.

"One could easy 'ave a woman in for anything that's 'eavy," said Ann. "Besides— If I 'ad one of the girls one sees about nowadays, I should want to be taking the broom out of 'er 'and and do it all over myself. I'd manage better without 'er."

"We ought to 'ave one servant, anyhow," said Kipps, "else 'ow should we manage if we wanted to go out together or anything like that?"

"I might get a *young* girl," said Ann, "and bring 'er up in my own way."

Kipps left the matter at that and came back to the house.

"There's little 'ouses going into Hythe just the sort we want, not too big and not too small. We'll 'ave a kitching and a dining-room and a little room to sit in of a night."

"It mustn't be a 'ouse with a basement," said Ann.

"What's a basement?"

"It's a downstairs, where there's not 'arf enough light and everything got to be carried—up and down, up and down, all day—coals and everything. And it's got to 'ave a water-tap and sink and things upstairs. You'd 'ardly believe, Artie, if you 'adn't been in service, 'ow cruel and silly some 'ouses are built— you'd think they 'ad a spite against servants the way the stairs are made."

"We won't 'ave one of that sort," said Kipps. . . . "We'll 'ave a quiet little life. Now go out a bit—now come 'ome again. Read a book, perhaps, if we got nothing else to do. 'Ave old Buggins in for an evening at times. 'Ave Sid down. There's bicycles—"

"I don't fancy myself on a bicycle," said Ann.

" 'Ave a trailer," said Kipps, "and sit like a lady. I'd take you out to New Romney easy as anything, jest to see the old people."

"I wouldn't mind that," said Ann.

"We'll jest 'ave a sensible little 'ouse, and sensible things. No art or anything of that sort, nothing stuck-up or anything, but jest sensible. We'll be as right as anything, Ann."

"No socialism," said Ann, starting a lurking doubt.

"No socialism," said Kipps, "just sensible—that's all."

"I dessay it's all right for them that understand it, Artie, but I don't agree with this socialism."

"I don't neither, reely," said Kipps. "I can't argue about it, but it don't seem real like to me. All the same, Masterman's a clever fellow, Ann."

"I didn't like 'im at first, Artie, but I do now—in a way. You don't understand 'im all at once."

" 'E's so clever," said Kipps. " 'Arf the time I can't make out what 'e's up to. 'E's the cleverest chap I ever met. I never 'eard such talking. 'E ought to write a book. . . . It's a rum world, Ann, when a chap like that isn't 'ardly able to earn a living."

"It's 'is 'ealth," said Ann.

"I expect it is," said Kipps, and ceased to talk for a little while.

"We shall be 'appy in that little 'ouse, Ann, don't y' think?"

She met his eyes and nodded.

"I seem to see it," said Kipps, "sort of cosy like. 'Bout teatime and muffins, kettle on the 'ob, cat on the 'earth-rug—we must get a cat, Ann—and *you* there. Eh?"

They regarded each other with appreciative eyes, and Kipps became irrelevant.

"I don't believe, Ann," he said, "I 'aven't kissed you not for 'arf an hour. Leastways, not since we was in those caves."

For kissing had already ceased to be a matter of thrilling adventure for them.

Ann shook her head. "You be sensible and go on talking ahout Mr. Masterman," she said. . . .

But Kipps had wandered to something else. "I like the way your 'air turns back jest there," he said, with an indicative finger. "It was like that, I remember, when you was a girl. Sort of wavy. I've often thought of it. . . . Member when we raced that time—out be'ind the church?"

Then for a time they sat idly, each following out agreeable meditations.

"It's rum," said Kipps.

"What's rum?"

" 'Ow everything's 'appened," said Kipps. "Who'd 'ave thought of our being 'ere like this six weeks ago? . . . Who'd 'ave thought of my ever 'aving any money?"

His eyes went to the big Labyrinthodon. He looked first carelessly and then suddenly with a growing interest in its vast face. "I'm deshed," he murmured. Ann became interested. He laid a hand on her arm and pointed. Ann scrutinized the Labyrinthodon, and then came round to Kipps' face in mute interrogation.

"Don't you see it?" said Kipps.

"See what?"

" 'E's *jest* like old Coote."

"It's extinct," said Ann, not clearly apprehending.

"I dessay 'e is. But 'e's jest like old Coote, all the same for that."

Kipps meditated on the monstrous shapes in sight. "I wonder 'ow all these old entediluvium animals *got* extinct," he asked. "No one couldn't possibly 'ave killed 'em."

"Why, *I* know that!" said Ann. "They was overtook by the Flood. . . ."

Kipps meditated for awhile. "But I thought they had to take two of everything there was—"

"Within reason they 'ad," said Ann. . . .

The Kippses left it at that.

The great green and gold Labyrinthodon took no notice of their conversation. It gazed with its wonderful eyes over their heads into the infinite—inflexibly calm. It might indeed have been Coote himself there, Coote the unassuming, cutting them dead.

There was something about its serenity that suggested patience, suggested the indifference of a power that waits. In the end this quality, dimly apprehended, made the Kippses uneasy, and after awhile they got up and, glancing backward, went their way.

4

And in due course these two simple souls married, and Venus Urania, the Goddess of Wedded Love, who is indeed a very great and noble and kindly goddess, bent down and blessed their union.

BOOK III
Kippses

CHAPTER I

The Housing Problem

1

HONEYMOONS AND ALL things come to an end, and you see at last Mr. and Mrs. Arthur Kipps descending upon the Hythe platform—coming to Hythe to find that nice *little* house, to realize that bright dream of a home they had first talked about in the grounds of the Crystal Palace. They are a valiant couple, you perceive, but small, and the world is a large, incongruous system of complex and difficult things. Kipps wears a gray suit, with a wing poke collar and a neat, smart tie. Mrs. Kipps is the same bright and healthy little girl-woman you saw in the marsh, not an inch has been added to her stature in all my voluminous narrative. Only now she wears a hat.

It is a hat very unlike the hats she used to wear on her Sundays out—a flourishing hat, with feathers and a buckle and bows and things. The price of that hat would take many people's breath away—it cost two guineas! Kipps chose it. Kipps paid for it. They left the shop with flushed cheeks and smarting eyes, glad to be out of range of the condescending saleswoman.

"Artie," said Ann, "you didn't ought to 'ave—"

That was all. And, you know, the hat didn't suit Ann a bit. Her clothes did not suit her at all. The simple, cheap, clean brightness of her former style had given place not only to this hat, but to several other things in the same key. And out from among these things looked her pretty face, the face of a wise little child—an artless wonder struggling through a preposterous dignity.

They had bought that hat one day when they had gone to see the shops in Bond Street. Kipps had looked at the passers-by, and it had suddenly occurred to him that Ann was dowdy. He had noted the hat of a very proud-looking lady passing in an electric brougham, and had resolved to get Ann the nearest thing to that.

The railway porters perceived some subtle incongruity in Ann, so did the knot of cabmen in the station doorway, the two golfers, and the lady with daughters, who had also got out of the train. And Kipps, a little pale, blowing a little, not in complete possession of himself, knew that they noticed her and him. And Ann— It is hard to say just what Ann observed of these things.

" 'Ere!" said Kipps to a cabman, and regretted too late a vanished "H."

"I got a trunk up there," he said to a ticket-inspector, "marked A. K."

"Ask a porter," said the inspector, turning his back.

"Demn!" said Kipps, not altogether inaudibly.

2

It is all very well to sit in the sunshine and talk of the house you will have, and another altogether to achieve it. We English—all the world indeed today— live in a strange atmosphere of neglected great issues, of insistent, triumphant petty things; we are given up to the fine littlenesses of intercourse; table manners and small correctitudes are the substance of our lives. You do not escape these things for long, even by so catastrophic a proceeding as flying to London with a young lady of no wealth and inferior social position. The mists of noble emotion swirl and pass, and there you are, divorced from all your deities, and grazing in the meadows under the Argus eyes of the social system, the innumerable mean judgments you feel raining upon you, upon your clothes and bearing, upon your pretensions and movements.

Our world today is a meanly conceived one—it is only an added meanness to conceal that fact. For one consequence, it has very few nice little houses. Such things do not come for the asking; they are not to be bought with money during ignoble times. Its houses are built on the ground of monstrously rich, shabbily extortionate landowners, by poor, parsimonious, greedy people in a mood of elbowing competition. What can you expect from such ridiculous conditions? To go house-hunting is to spy out the nakedness of this pretentious world, to see what our civilization amounts to when you take away curtains and flounces and carpets, and all the fluster and distraction of people and fittings. It is to see mean plans meanly executed for mean ends, the conventions torn aside, the secrets stripped, the substance underlying all such Chester Cootery, soiled and worn and left.

So you see our poor dear Kippses going to and fro, in Hythe, in Sandgate, in Ashford, and Canterbury and Deal and Dover—at last even in Folkestone— with "orders to view," pink and green and white and yellow orders to view, and labeled keys in Kipps' hand, and frowns and perplexity upon their faces. . . .

They did not clearly know what they wanted, but whatever it was they saw, they knew they did not want that. Always they found a confusing multitude of houses they could not take, and none they could. Their dreams began to turn mainly on empty, abandoned-looking rooms, with unfaded patches of paper to mark the place of vanished pictures, and doors that had lost their keys. They saw rooms floored with boards that yawned apart and were splintered, skirtings eloquent of the industrious mouse, kitchens with a dead black-beetle in the empty cupboard, and a hideous variety of coal-holes and dark cupboards under the stairs. They stuck their little heads through roof trap-doors, and gazed at disorganized ball-taps, at the black filthiness of unstopped roofs. There were occasions when it seemed to them that they must be the victims of an elaborate conspiracy of house agents, so bleak and cheerless is a second-hand empty house in comparison with the humblest of inhabited dwellings.

Commonly the houses were too big. They had huge windows that demanded vast curtains in mitigation, countless bedrooms, acreage of stone steps to be cleaned, kitchens that made Ann protest. She had come so far towards a proper conception of Kipps' social position as to admit the prospect of one servant. "But lor!" she would say, "you'd want a man-servant in this 'ouse." When the houses were not too big, then they were almost always the product of speculative building, of that multitudinous hasty building for the extravagant swarm of new births that was the essential disaster of the nineteenth century.

The new houses Ann refused as damp, and even the youngest of those that had been in use showed remarkable signs of a sickly constitution—the plaster flaked away, the floors gaped, the paper moulded and peeled, the doors dropped, the bricks were scaled, and the railings rusted; Nature, in the form of spiders, earwigs, cockroaches, mice, rats, fungi, and remarkable smells, was already fighting her way back. . . .

And the plan was invariably inconvenient, invariably. All the houses they saw had a common quality for which she could find no word, but for which the proper word is "incivility." "They build these 'ouses," she said, "as though girls wasn't 'uman beings." Sid's social democracy had got into her blood, perhaps, and anyhow they went about discovering the most remarkable inconsiderateness in the contemporary house. "There's kitching stairs to go up, Artie!" Ann would say. "Some poor girl's got to go up and down, up and down, and be tired out, jest because they haven't the sense to leave enough space to give their steps a proper rise—and no water upstairs anywhere—every drop got to be carried! It's 'ouses like this wear girls out.

"It's 'aving 'ouses built by men, I believe, makes all the work and trouble," said Ann. . . .

The Kippses, you see, thought they were looking for a reasonably simple little contemporary house, but indeed they were looking either for dreamland or 1975 A.D., or thereabouts, and it hadn't come.

3

But it was a foolish thing of Kipps to begin building a house.

He did that out of an extraordinary animosity for house-agents he had conceived.

Everybody hates house-agents, just as everybody loves sailors. It is, no doubt, a very wicked and unjust hatred, but the business of a novelist is not ethical principle, but facts. Everybody hates house-agents because they have everybody at a disadvantage. All other callings have a certain amount of give and take, the house-agent simply takes. All other callings want you; your solicitor is afraid you may change him, your doctor cannot go too far, your novelist—if only you knew it—is mutely abject towards your unspoken wishes; and as for your tradespeople, milkmen will fight outside your front door for you, and greengrocers call in tears if you discard them suddenly; but who ever heard of a house-agent struggling to serve anyone? You want a house; you go to him; you, disheveled and angry from travel, anxious, inquiring; he calm, clean, inactive, reticent, quietly doing nothing. You beg him to reduce rents, whitewash ceilings, produce other houses, combine the summer-house of No. 6 with the conservatory of No. 4—much he cares! You want to dispose of a house; then he is just the same—serene, indifferent. On one occasion I remember he was picking his teeth all the time he answered me. Competition is a mockery among house-agents; they are all alike; you cannot wound them by going to the opposite office, you cannot dismiss them, you can at most dismiss yourself. They are invulnerably placed behind mahogany and brass, too far usually even for a sudden swift lunge with an umbrella; to throw away the keys they lend you instead of returning them is larceny, and punishable as such. . . .

It was a house-agent in Dover who finally decided Kipps to build. Kipps, with a certain faltering in his voice, had delivered his ultimatum—no basement, not more than eight rooms, hot and cold water upstairs, coal-cellar in the house, but with intervening doors to keep dust from the scullery and so forth. He stood blowing. "You'll have to build a house," said the house-agent, sighing wearily, "if you want all that." It was rather for the sake of effective answer than with any intention at the time that Kipps mumbled, "That's about what I shall do—this goes on."

Whereupon the house-agent smiled. He smiled!

When Kipps came to turn the thing over in his mind, he was surprised to find quite a considerable intention had germinated and was growing up in him. After all, lots of people *have* built houses. How could there be so many if they hadn't? Suppose he "reely" did! Then he would go to the house-agent and say, " 'Ere, while you been getting me a sootable 'ouse, blowed if I 'aven't built one!" Go round to all of them—all the house-agents in Folkestone, in Dover, Ashford, Canterbury, Margate, Ramsgate, saying that—! Perhaps then they might be sorry. It was in the small hours that he awoke to a realization that he had made up his mind in the matter.

"Ann," he said, "Ann," and also used the sharp of his elbow.

Ann was at last awakened to the pitch of an indistinct inquiry what was the matter.

"I'm going to build a house, Ann."

"Eh?" said Ann, suddenly, as if awake.

"Build a house."

Ann said something incoherent about he'd better wait until the morning before he did anything of the sort, and immediately with a fine trustfulness went fast asleep again.

But Kipps lay awake for a long while building his house, and in the morning at breakfast he made his meaning clear. He had smarted under the indignities of house-agents long enough, and this seemed to promise revenge—a fine revenge. "And, you know, we might reely make rather a nice little 'ouse out of it—like we want."

So resolved, it became possible for them to take a house for a year, with a basement, no service lift, blackleading to do everywhere, no water upstairs, no bathroom, vast sash windows to be cleaned from the sill, stone steps with a twist and open to the rain, into the coal-cellar, insufficient cupboards, unpaved path to the dustbin, no fireplace to the servant's bedroom, no end of splintery wood to scrub—in fact, a very typical English middle-class house. And having added to this house some furniture, and a languid young person with unauthentic golden hair named Gwendolen, who was engaged to a sergeant-major and had formerly been in an hotel, having "moved in" and spent some sleepless nights, varied by nocturnal explorations in search of burglars, because of the strangeness of being in a house for which they were personally responsible, Kipps settled down for a time and turned himself with considerable resolution to the project of building a home.

4

At first Kipps gathered advice, finding an initial difficulty in how to begin. He went into a builder's shop at Seabrook one day and told the lady in charge that he wanted a house built. He was breathless, but quite determined, and he was prepared to give his order there and then; but she temporized with him, and said her husband was out, and he left without giving his name. Also he went and talked to a man in a cart, who was pointed out to him by a workman as the builder of a new house near Saltwood, but he found him first skeptical, and then overpoweringly sarcastic. "I suppose you build a 'ouse every 'oliday," he said, and turned from Kipps with every symptom of contempt.

Afterwards Carshot told alarming stories about builders, and shook Kipps' expressed resolution a good deal, and then Pearce raised the question whether one ought to go in the first instance to a builder at all, and not rather to an architect. Pearce knew a man at Ashford whose brother was an architect, and as it is always better in these matters to get someone you know, the Kippses decided, before Pearce had gone, and Carshot's warnings had resumed their sway, to apply to him. They did so—rather dubiously.

The architect, who was brother of Pearce's friend, appeared as a small, alert individual with a black bag and a cylindrical silk hat, and he sat at the dining-room table, with his hat and his bag exactly equidistant right and left of him, and maintained a demeanor of impressive woodenness, while Kipps, on the hearthrug, with a quaking sense of gigantic enterprise, vacillated answers to his inquiries. Ann held a watching brief for herself, in a position she had chosen as suitable to the occasion, beside the corner of the carved oak sideboard. They felt, in a sense, at bay.

The architect began by asking for the site, and seemed a little discomposed to discover this had still to be found. "I thought of building just anywhere," said Kipps. "I 'aven't made up my mind about that yet." The architect remarked that he would have preferred to see the site in order to know where to put what he called his "ugly side," but it was quite possible, of course, to plan a house "in the air," on the level, "simply with back and front assumed"—if they would like to do that. Kipps flushed slightly, and secretly hoping it would make no great difference in the fees, said a little doubtfully that he thought that would be all right.

The architect then marked off, as it were, the first section of his subject, with a single dry cough, opened his bag, took out a spring tape measure, some hard biscuits, a metal flask, a new pair of dogskin gloves, a clockwork motor-car partially wrapped in paper, a bunch of violets, a paper of small brass screws, and finally a large distended notebook; he replaced the other objects carefully, opened his notebook, put a pencil to his lips and said, "And what accommodation will you require?" To which Ann, who had followed his every movement with the closest attention and a deepening dread, replied with the violent suddenness of one who has lain in wait, "Cubbuds!"

"Anyhow," she added, catching her husband's eye.

The architect wrote it down.

"And how many rooms?" he said, coming to secondary matters.

The young people regarded one another. It was dreadfully like giving an order.

"How many bedrooms, for example?" asked the architect.

"One?" suggested Kipps, inclined now to minimize at any cost.

"There's Gwendolen!" said Ann.

"Visitors, perhaps," said the architect; and temperately, "You never know."

"Two p'r'aps?" said Kipps. "We don't want no more than a *little* 'ouse, you know."

"But the merest shooting-box—" said the architect. . . .

They got to six, he beat them steadily from bedroom to bedroom, the word "nursery" played across their imaginative skies—he mentioned it as the remotest possibility—and then six being reluctantly conceded, Ann came forward to the table, sat down, and delivered herself of one of her prepared conditions. " 'Ot and cold water," she said, "laid on to each room—any'ow."

It was an idea long since acquired from Sid.

"Yes," said Kipps, on the hearthrug, " 'ot and cold water laid on to each bedroom—we've settled on that."

It was the first intimation to the architect that he had to deal with a couple of exceptional originality, and as he had spent the previous afternoon in finding three large houses in *The Builder,* which he intended to combine into an original and copyright design of his own, he naturally struggled against these novel requirements. He enlarged on the extreme expensiveness of plumbing, on the extreme expensiveness of everything not already arranged for in his scheme, and only when Ann declared she'd as soon not have the house as not have her requirements, and Kipps, blenching the while, had said he didn't mind what a thing cost him so long as he got what he wanted, did he allow a kindred originality of his own to appear beneath the acquired professionalism of his methods. He dismissed their previous talk with his paragraphic cough. "Of course," he said, "if you don't mind being unconventional—"

He explained that he had been thinking of a Queen Anne style of architecture (Ann, directly she heard her name, shook her head at Kipps in an aside) so far as the exterior went. For his own part, he said, he liked to have the exterior of a house in a style, not priggishly in a style, but mixed, with one style uppermost, and the gables and dormers and casements of the Queen Anne style, with a little roughcast and sham timbering here and there, and perhaps a bit of an overhang, diversified a house and made it interesting. The advantages of what he called a Queen Anne style was that it had such a variety of features. . . . Still, if they were prepared to be unconventional, it could be done. A number of houses were now built in the unconventional style, and were often very pretty. In the unconventional style one frequently had what perhaps he might call Internal Features—for example, an old English oak staircase and gallery. White roughcast and green paint were a good deal favored in houses of this type.

He indicated that this excursus on style was finished by a momentary use of his cough, and reopened his notebook, which he had closed to wave about in a moment of descriptive enthusiasm while expatiating on the unbridled wealth of External Features associated with Queen Anne. "Six bedrooms," he said, moistening his pencil. "One with barred windows, suitable for a nursery if required."

Kipps endorsed this huskily and reluctantly.

There followed a most interesting discussion upon house-building, in which Kipps played a minor part. They passed from bedrooms to the kitchen and scullery, and there Ann displayed an intelligent exactingness that won the expressed admiration of the architect. They were particularly novel upon the position of the coal-cellar, which Ann held to be altogether too low in the ordinary house, necessitating much heavy carrying. They dismissed as impracticable the idea of having coal-cellar and kitchen at the top of the house, because that would involve carrying all the coal through the house, and therewith much subsequent cleaning, and for a time they dealt with a conception of a coal-cellar on the ground floor with a light staircase running up outside to an exterior shoot. "It might be made a Feature," said the architect a little doubtfully, jotting down a note of it. "It would be apt to get black, you know."

Thence they passed to the alternative of service lifts, and then, by an inspiration of the architect's, to the possibilities of gas-heating. Kipps did a complicated verbal fugue on the theme, "gas-heating heats the air," with variable aspirates; he became very red, and was lost to the discussion altogether for a time, though his lips kept silently moving.

Subsequently the architect wrote to say that he found in his notebook very full and explicit directions for bow windows to all rooms, for bedrooms, for water supply, lift, height of stairs and absence of twists therein, for a well-ventilated kitchen twenty feet square, with two dressers and a large box window-seat, for scullery and outhouses and offices, but nothing whatever about drawing-room, dining-room, library, or study, or approximate cost, and he awaited further instructions. He presumed there would be a breakfast-room, dining-room, drawing-room, and study for Mr. Kipps—at least that was his conception—and the young couple discussed this matter long and ardently.

Ann was distinctly restrictive in this direction. "I don't see what you want a drawin'-room and a dinin' *and* a kitchin for. If we was going to let in summer—well and good. But we're not going to let. Consequently we don't want so many rooms. Then there's a 'all. What use is a 'all? It only makes work. And a study!"

Kipps had been humming and stroking his moustache since he had read the architect's letter. "I think I'd like a little bit of a study—not a big one, of course, but one with a desk and bookshelves, like there was in Hughenden. I'd like that."

It was only after they had talked to the architect again, and seen how scandalized he was at the idea of not having a drawing-room, that they consented to that Internal Feature. They consented to please him. "But we shan't never use it," said Ann.

Kipps had his way about a study. "When I get that study," said Kipps, "I shall do a bit of reading I've long wanted to do. I shall make a habit of going in there and reading something an hour every day. There's Shakespeare and a lot of things a man like me ought to read. Besides, we got to 'ave *somewhere* to put the Encyclopædia. I've always thought a study was about what I've wanted all along. You can't 'elp reading if you got a study. If you 'aven't, there's nothing for it, so far's *I* can see, but treshy novels."

He looked down at Ann, and was surprised to see a joyless thoughtfulness upon her face.

"Fency, Ann!" he said not too buoyantly, " 'aving a little 'ouse of our own!"

"It won't be a little 'ouse," said Ann, "not with all them rooms."

5

Any lingering doubt in that matter was dispelled when it came to plans.

The architect drew three sets of plans on a transparent bluish sort of paper that smelt abominably. He painted them very nicely; brick-red and ginger, and arsenic green and a leaden sort of blue, and brought them over to show our young people. The first set were very simple, with practically no External Features—"a plain style," he said it was—but it looked a big sort of house, nevertheless; the second had such extras as a conservatory, bow windows of various sorts, one roughcast gable and one half-timbered ditto in plaster, and a sort of overhung verandah, and was much more imposing; and the third was quite fungoid with External Features, and honeycombed with Internal ones; it was, he said, "practically a mansion," and altogether a very noble fruit of the creative mind of man. It was, he admitted, perhaps almost too good for Hythe; his art had run away with him and produced a modern mansion in the "best Folkestone style"; it had a central hall with a staircase, a Moorish gallery, and a Tudor stained-glass window, crenelated battlements to the leading over the portico, an octagonal bulge with octagonal bay windows, surmounted by an Oriental dome of metal, lines of yellow bricks to break up the red and many other richnesses and attractions. It was the sort of house, ornate and in its dignified way voluptuous, that a city magnate might build, but it seemed excessive to the Kippses. The first plan had seven bedrooms, the second eight, the third eleven; they had, the architect explained, "worked in" as if they were pebbles in a mountaineer's boot.

"They're big 'ouses," said Ann, directly the elevations were unrolled.

Kipps listened to the architect, with round eyes and an exuberant caution in his manner, anxious not to commit himself further than he had done to the enterprise, and the architect pointed out the Features and other objects of interest with the scalpel belonging to a pocket manicure set that he carried. Ann watched Kipps' face, and communicated with him furtively over the architect's head. *"Not so big,"* said Ann's lips.

"It's a bit big for what I meant," said Kipps, with a reassuring eye on Ann.

"You won't think it big when you see it up," said the architect; "you take my word for that."

"We don't want no more than six bedrooms," said Kipps.

"Make this one a box-room, then," said the architect.

A feeling of impotence silenced Kipps for a time.

"Now which," said the architect, spreading them out, "is it to be?"

He flattened down the plans of the most ornate mansion to show it to better effect.

Kipps wanted to know how much each would cost "at the outside," which led to much alarmed signaling from Ann. But the architect could estimate only in the most general way.

They were not really committed to anything when the architect went away; Kipps had promised to think it over—that was all.

"We can't 'ave that 'ouse," said Ann.

"They're miles too big—all of them," agreed Kipps.

"You'd want— Four servants wouldn't be 'ardly enough," said Ann.

Kipps went to the hearthrug and spread himself. His tone was almost offhand. "Nex' time 'e comes," said Kipps, "I'll 'splain to him. It isn't at all the sort of thing we want. It's—it's a misunderstanding. You got no occasion to be anxious 'bout it, Ann."

"I don't see much good reely in building an 'ouse at all," said Ann.

"Oo, we *got* to build a 'ouse now we begun," said Kipps. "But now supposin' we 'ad—"

He spread out the most modest of the three plans and scratched his cheek.

6

It was unfortunate that old Kipps came over the next day.

Old Kipps always produced peculiar states of mind in his nephew—a rash assertiveness, a disposition towards display unlike his usual self. There had been great difficulty in reconciling both these old people to the Pornick *mésalliance,* and at times the controversy echoed in old Kipps' expressed thoughts. This perhaps it was, and no ignoble vanity, that set the note of florid successfulness going in Kipps' conversation whenever his uncle appeared. Mrs. Kipps was as a matter of fact, not reconciled at all; she had declined all invitations to come over on the bus, and was a taciturn hostess on the one occasion when the young people called at the toy-shop *en route* for Mrs. Pornick. She displayed a tendency to sniff that was clearly due to pride rather than catarrh, and, except for telling Ann she hoped she would not feel too "stuck up" about her marriage, confined her conversation to her nephew or the infinite. The call was a brief one, and made up chiefly of pauses, no refreshment was offered or asked for, and Ann departed with a singularly high color. For some reason she would not call at the toy-shop a second time when they found themselves again in New Romney.

But old Kipps, having adventured over and tried the table of the new *ménage* and found it to his taste, showed many signs of softening towards Ann. He came again, and then again. He would come over by the bus, and, except when his mouth was absolutely full, he would give his nephew one solid and continuous mass of advice of the most subtle and disturbing description until it was time to toddle back to the High Street for the afternoon bus. He would walk with him to the sea front, and commence *pourparlers* with boatmen for the purchase of one of their boats—"You ought to keep a boat of your own," he said—though Kipps was a singularly poor sailor—or he would pursue a plan that was forming in his mind in which he should own and manage what he called "weekly" property in the less conspicuous streets of Hythe. The cream of that was to be a weekly collection of rents in person, the nearest approach to feudal splendor left in this democratized country. He gave no hint of the source of the capital he designed for this investment, and at times it would appear he intended it as an occupation for his nephew rather than himself.

But there remained something in his manner towards Ann—in the glances of scrutiny he gave her unawares, that kept Kipps alertly expansive whenever he was about; and in all sorts of ways. It was on account of old Kipps, for example, that our Kipps plunged one day—a golden plunge—and brought home a box of cummerbundy ninepenny cigars, and substituted blue label old Methusaleh Four Stars for the common and generally satisfactory white brand.

"Some of this is whisky, my boy," said old Kipps, when he tasted it, smacking critical lips. . . .

"Saw a lot of young officery fellers coming along," said old Kipps. "You ought to join the volunteers, my boy, and get to know a few."

"I dessay I shall," said Kipps. "Later."

"They'd make you an officer, you know, 'n no time. They want officers," said old Kipps. "It isn't everyone can afford it. They'd be regular glad to 'ave you. . . . Ain't bort a dog yet?"

"Not yet, Uncle. 'Ave a segar?"

"Nor a moty car?"

"Not yet, Uncle."

"There's no 'urry about that. And don't get one of these 'ere trashy cheap ones when you do get it, my boy. Get one as'll last a lifetime. . . . I'm surprised you don't 'ire a bit more."

"Ann don't seem to fency a moty car," said Kipps.

"Ah," said old Kipps, "I expect not," and glanced a comment at the door. "She ain't used to going out," he said. "More at 'ome indoors."

"Fact is," said Kipps, hastily, "we're thinking of building a 'ouse."

"I wouldn't do that, my boy," began old Kipps; but his nephew was routing in the cheffonier drawer amidst the plans. He got them in time to check some further comment on Ann. "Um," said the old gentleman, a little impressed by the extraordinary odor and the unusual transparency of the tracing-paper Kipps put into his hands. "Thinking of building a 'ouse, are you?"

Kipps began with the most modest of the three projects.

Old Kipps read slowly through his silver-rimmed spectacles, "Plan of a 'ouse for Arthur Kipps, Esquire. Um."

He didn't warm to the project all at once, and Ann drifted into the room to find him still scrutinizing the architect's proposals a little doubtfully.

"We couldn't find a decent 'ouse anywhere," said Kipps, leaning against the table and assuming an offhand note. "I didn't see why we shouldn't run up one for ourselves." Old Kipps could not help liking the tone of that.

"We thought we might see—" said Ann.

"It's a spekerlation, of course," said old Kipps, and held the plan at a distance of two feet or more from his glasses and frowned. "This isn't exactly the 'ouse I should expect you to 'ave thought of though," he said. "Practically it's a villa. It's the sort of 'ouse a bank clerk might 'ave. 'Tisn't what I should call a gentleman's 'ouse, Artie."

"It's plain, of course," said Kipps, standing beside his Uncle and looking down at this plan, which certainly did seem a little less magnificent now than it had at the first encounter.

"You mustn't 'ave it too plain," said old Kipps.

"If it's comfortable—" Ann hazarded.

Old Kipps glanced at her over his spectacles. "You ain't comfortable, my gel, in this world, not if you don't live up to your position,"—so putting compactly into contemporary English that fine old phrase *noblesse oblige*. "A 'ouse of this sort is what a retired tradesman might 'ave, or some little whipper-snapper of a s'licitor. But *you*—"

"Course that isn't the o'ny plan," said Kipps, and tried the middle one.

But it was the third one won over old Kipps. "Now that's a *'ouse*, my boy," he said at the sight of it.

Ann came and stood just behind her husband's shoulder, while old Kipps expanded upon the desirability of the larger scheme. "You ought to 'ave a billiard-room," he said; "I don't see that, but all the rest's about right! A lot of these 'ere officers 'ere 'ud be glad of a game of billiards. . . .

"What's all these dots?" said old Kipps.

"S'rubbery," said Kipps. "Flow'ing s'rubs."

"There's eleven bedrooms in that 'ouse," said Ann. "It's a bit of a lot, ain't it, Uncle?"

"You'll want 'em, my girl. As you get on you'll be 'aving visitors. Friends of your 'usband's, p'r'aps, from the School of Musketry—what you want 'im to get on with. You can't never tell."

"If we 'ave a great s'rubbery," Ann ventured, "we shall 'ave to keep a gardener."

"If you don't 'ave a s'rubbery," said old Kipps, with a note of patient reasoning, " 'ow are you to prevent every jackanapes that goes by starin' into your drorin'-room winder—p'r'aps when you get someone a bit special to entertain?"

"We ain't *used* to a s'rubbery," said Ann, mulishly, "we get on very well 'ere."

"It isn't what you're used to," said old Kipps, "it's what you ought to 'ave *now*." And with that Ann dropped out of the discussion.

"Study and lib'ry," old Kipps read. "That's right. I see a Tantalus the other day over Brookland, the very thing for a gentleman's study. I'll try and get over and bid for it. . . ."

By bus time old Kipps was quite enthusiastic about the house-building, and it seemed to be definitely settled that the largest plan was the one decided upon.

But Ann had said nothing further in the matter.

7

When Kipps returned from seeing his Uncle into the bus—there always seemed a certain doubt whether that portly figure would go into the little red "Tip-top" box—he found Ann still standing by the table, looking with an expression of comprehensive disapproval at the three plans.

"There don't seem much the matter with Uncle," said Kipps, assuming the hearthrug, "spite of 'is 'eartburn. 'E 'opped up them steps like a bird."

Ann remained staring at the plans.

"You don't like them plans?" hazarded Kipps.

"No; I don't, Artie."

"We got to build somethin' now."

"But— It's a gentleman's 'ouse, Artie!"

"It's—it's a decent size, o' course."

Kipps took a flirting look at the drawing and went to the window.

"Look at the cleanin'. Free servants'll be lost in that 'ouse, Artie."

"We must *'ave* servants," said Kipps.

Ann looked despondently at the future residence.

"We got to keep up our position any'ow," said Kipps, turning towards her. "It stands to reason, Ann, we got a position. Very well! I can't 'ave you scrubbin' floors. You got to 'ave a servant, and you got to manage a 'ouse. You wouldn't 'ave me ashamed—"

Ann opened her lips and did not speak.

"What?" asked Kipps.

"Nothing," said Ann, "only I did want it to be a *little* 'ouse, Artie. I wanted it to be a 'andy little 'ouse, jest for us."

Kipps' face was suddenly flushed and obstinate. He took up the curiously smelling tracings again. "I'm not a-going to be looked down upon," he said. "It's not only Uncle I'm thinking of!"

Ann stared at him.

Kipps went on. "I won't 'ave that young Walshingham, f'r instance, sneering and sniffing at me. Making out as if we was all wrong. I see 'im yesterday. . . . Nor Coote neether. I'm as good—we're as good—whatever's 'appened."

Silence, and the rustle of plans.

He looked up and saw Ann's eyes bright with tears. For a moment the two stared at one another.

"We'll 'ave the big 'ouse," said Ann, with a gulp. "I didn't think of that, Artie."

Her aspect was fierce and resolute, and she struggled with emotion. "We'll 'ave the big 'ouse," she repeated. "They sha'n't say I dragged you down wiv me—none of them sha'n't say that. I've thought— I've always been afraid of that."

Kipps looked again at the plan, and suddenly the grand house had become very grand indeed. He blew.

"No, Artie. None of them sha'n't say that," and, with something blind in her motions, Ann tried to turn the plan round to her. . . .

After all, Kipps thought, there might be something to say for the milder project. . . . But he had gone so far that now he did not know how to say it.

And so the plans went out to the builders, and in a little while Kipps was committed to two thousand five hundred pounds' worth of building. But then, you know, he had an income of twelve hundred a year.

8

It is extraordinary what minor difficulties cluster about house-building.

"I say, Ann," remarked Kipps one day. "We shall 'ave to call this little 'ouse by a name. I was thinking of Ome Cottage. But I dunno whether Ome

Cottage is quite the thing like. All these little fisherman's places are called Cottages.''

"I like 'Cottage,' " said Ann.

"It's got eleven bedrooms, y' see," said Kipps. I don't see 'ow you call it a cottage with more bedrooms than four. Prop'ly speaking, it's a Large Villa. Prop'ly it's almost a Big 'Ouse. Leastways a 'Ouse.''

"Well," said Ann, "if you must call it Villa—Home Villa. . . . I wish it wasn't.''

Kipps meditated.

" 'Ow about Eureka Villa?" he said, raising his voice.

"What's Eureka?''

"It's a name," he said. "There used to be Eureka Dress Fasteners. There's lots of names, come to think of it, to be got out of a shop. There's Pyjama Villa. I remember that in the hosiery. No, come to think, that wouldn't do. But Maraposa—sort of oatmeal cloth, that was. . . . No! Eureka's better.''

Ann meditated. "It seems silly like to 'ave a name that don't mean much.''

"Perhaps it does," said Kipps. "Though it's what people 'ave to do.''

He became meditative. "I got it!" he cried.

"Not Oreeka!" said Ann.

"No! There used to be a 'ouse at Hastings opposite our school—quite a big 'ouse it was—St. Ann's. Now *that*—''

"No," said Mrs. Kipps, with decision. "Thanking you kindly, but I don't have no butcher-boys making game of me. . . .''

They consulted Carshot, who suggested, after some days of reflection, Waddycombe, as a graceful reminder of Kipps' grandfather; old Kipps, who was for "Upton Manor House," where he had once been second footman; Buggins, who favored either a stern, simple number, "Number One"—if there were no other houses there, or something patriotic, as "Empire Villa"; and Pearce, who inclined to "Sandringham"; but in spite of all this help they were still undecided, when amidst violent perturbations of the soul, and after the most complex and difficult hagglings, wranglings, fears, muddles, and goings to and fro, Kipps became the joyless owner of a freehold plot of three-eighths of an acre, and saw the turf being wheeled away from the site that should one day be his home.

CHAPTER II

The Callers

1

THE KIPPSES SAT at their midday dinner-table amidst the vestiges of rhubarb pie, and discussed two postcards the one o'clock post had brought. It was a rare bright moment of sunshine in a wet and windy day in the March that followed their marriage. Kipps was attired in a suit of brown, with a tie of fashionable green, while Ann wore one of those picturesque loose robes that are usually associated with sandals and advanced ideas. But there weren't any sandals on Ann or any advanced ideas, and the robe had come quite recently through the counsels of Mrs. Sid. Pornick. "It's Art-like," said Kipps, but giving way. "It's more comfortable," said Ann. The room looked out by French windows upon a little patch of green and the Hythe parade. The parade was all shiny wet with rain, and the green-gray sea tumbled and tumbled between parade and sky.

The Kipps' furniture, except for certain chromolithographs of Kipps' incidental choice, that struck a quiet note amidst the wall-paper, had been tactfully forced by an expert salesman, and it was in a style of mediocre elegance. There was a sideboard of carved oak that had only one fault—it reminded Kipps at times of woodcarving, and its panel of beveled glass now reflected the back of his head. On its shelf were two books from Parsons' Library, each with a "place" marked by a slip of paper; neither of the Kippses could have told you the title of either book they read, much less the author's name. There was an ebonized overmantel set with phials and pots of brilliant color, each duplicated by looking-glass, and bearing also a pair of Chinese jars made in Birmingham, a wedding-present from Mr. and Mrs. Sidney Pornick, and several sumptuous Japanese fans. And there was a Turkey carpet of great richness. In addition to these modern exploits of Messrs. Bunt and Bubble, there were two inactive tall clocks, whose extreme dilapidation appealed to the connoisseur; a terrestrial and a celestial globe, the latter deeply indented; a number of good old iron-moulded and dusty books; and a stuffed owl, wanting one (easily replaceable) glass eye, obtained by the exertions of Uncle Kipps. The table equipage was as much as possible like Mrs. Bindon Botting's, only more costly, and in addition there were green and crimson wine-glasses—though the Kippses never drank wine. . . .

Kipps turned to the more legible of his two postcards again.

" 'Unavoidably prevented from seein' me today,' 'e says. I like 'is cheek. After I give 'im 'is start and everything.''

He blew.

" 'E certainly treats you a bit orf 'and,'' said Ann.

Kipps gave vent to his dislike of young Walshingham. "He's getting too big for 'is britches,'' he said. "I'm beginning to wish she *'ad* brought an action for breach. Ever since *'e* said she wouldn't, 'e's seemed to think I've got no right to spend my own money.''

" 'E's never liked your building the 'ouse,'' said Ann.

Kipps displayed wrath. "What the goodness 'as it got to do wiv 'im?''

"Overman, indeed!'' he added; "Overmantel! . . . 'E trys that on with me— I'll tell 'im something 'e won't like.''

He took up the second card. "Dashed if I can read a word of it. I can jest make out Chit'low at the end, and that's all.''

He scrutinized it. "It's like someone in a fit writing. This here might be W-H-A-T—*what*. P-R-I-C-E—*I* got it! What price Harry now? It was a sort of saying of 'is. I expect 'e's either done something or not done something towards starting that play, Ann.''

"I expect that's about it,'' said Ann.

Kipps grunted with effort. "I can't read the rest,'' he said at last, "nohow.''

A thoroughly annoying post. He pitched the card on the table, stood up and went to the window, where Ann, after a momentary reconnaissance at Chitterlow's hieroglyphics, came to join him.

"Wonder what I shall do this afternoon,'' said Kipps, with his hands deep in his pockets.

He produced and lit a cigarette.

"Go for a walk, I s'pose,'' said Ann.

"I *been* for a walk this morning.''

"S'pose I must go for another,'' he added, after an interval.

They regarded the windy waste of sea for a space.

"Wonder why it is 'e won't see me,'' said Kipps, returning to the problem of young Walshingham. "It's all lies about 'is being too busy.''

Ann offered no solution.

"Rain again!" said Kipps—as the lash of the little drops stung the window.

"Oo, bother!" said Kipps, "you got to do something. Look 'ere, Ann! I'll go orf for a reg'lar tramp through the rain, up by Saltwood, round by Newington, over the camp, and so round and back, and see 'ow they're getting on about the 'ouse. See? And look 'ere!—you get Gwendolen to go out a bit before I come back. If it's still rainy, she can easy go round and see 'er sister. Then we'll 'ave a bit of tea, with teacake—all buttery—see? Toce it ourselves p'r'aps. Eh?"

"I dessay I can find something to do in the 'ouse," said Ann, considering. "You'll take your mackintosh and leggings, I s'pose? You'll get wet without your mackintosh over those roads."

"Right-O," said Kipps; and went to ask Gwendolen for his brown leggings and his other pair of boots.

2

Things conspired to demoralize Kipps that afternoon.

When he got outside the house everything looked so wet under the drive of the south-wester that he abandoned the prospect of the clay lanes towards Newington altogether, and turned east to Folkestone along the Seabrook digue. His mackintosh flapped about him, the rain stung his cheek; for a time he felt a hardy man. And then as abruptly the rain ceased and the wind fell, and before he was through Sandgate High Street it was a bright spring day. And there was Kipps in his mackintosh and squeaky leggings, looking like a fool!

Inertia carried him another mile to the Leas, and there the whole world was pretending there had never been such a thing as rain—ever. There wasn't a cloud in the sky; except for an occasional puddle, the asphalt paths looked as dry as a bone. A smartly dressed man, in one of those overcoats that look like ordinary cloth, and are really most deceitfully and unfairly waterproof, passed him and glanced at the stiff folds of his mackintosh. "Demn!" said Kipps. His mackintosh swished against his leggings, his leggings piped and whistled over his boot-tops.

"Why do I never get anything right?" Kipps asked of a bright implacable universe.

Nice old ladies passed him, refined people with tidy umbrellas, bright, beautiful, supercilious-looking children. Of course, the right thing for such a day as this was a light overcoat and an umbrella. A child might have known that. He had them at home, but how could one explain that? He decided to turn down by the Harvey monument and escape through Clifton Gardens towards the hills. And thereby he came upon Coote.

He already felt the most abject and propitiatory of social outcasts when he came upon Coote, and Coote finished him. He passed within a yard of Coote. Coote was coming along towards the Leas, and when Kipps saw him his legs hesitated about their office, and he seemed to himself to stagger about all over the footpath. At the sight of him Coote started visibly. Then a sort of *rigor vitae* passed through his frame, his jaw protruded, and errant bubbles of air seemed to escape and run about beneath his loose skin. (Seemed, I say,—I am perfectly well aware that there is really connective tissue in Coote, as in all of us, to prevent anything of the sort.) His eyes fixed themselves on the horizon and glazed. As he went by Kipps could hear his even, resolute breathing. He went by, and Kipps staggered on into a universe of dead cats and dustheaps, rind and ashes—*cut!*

It was part of the inexorable decrees of Providence that almost immediately afterwards the residuum of Kipps had to pass a very, very long and observant-looking girls' school.

Kipps recovered consciousness again on the road between Shorncliffe station and Cheriton, though he cannot remember, indeed to this day he has never attempted to remember, how he got there. And he was back at certain thoughts suggested by his last night's novel-reading, that linked up directly with the pariah-like emotions of these last encounters. The novel lay at home upon the cheffonier; it was one about society and politics—there is no need whatever to give the title or name the author—written with a heavy-handed thoroughness that overrode any possibility of resistance on the part of the Kipps' mind. It had crushed all his poor edifice of ideals, his dreams of a sensible, unassuming existence, of snugness, of not caring what people said and all the rest of it, to dust; it had reinstated, squarely and strongly again, the only proper conception of English social life. There was a character in the book, who trifled with Art, who was addicted to reading French novels, who dressed in a loose careless way, who was a sorrow to his dignified, silvery-haired, politico-religious mother, and met the admonitions of bishops with a front of brass. He treated a "nice girl," to whom they had got him engaged, badly; he married beneath him—some low thing or other. And sank. . . .

Kipps could not escape the application of the case. He was enabled to see how this sort of thing looked to decent people; he was enabled to gauge the measure of the penalties due. His mind went from that to the frozen marble of Coote's visage.

He deserved it! . . .

That day of remorse! Later it found him upon the site of his building operations and surveying the disorder of preparation in a mood near to despair, his mackintosh over his arm.

Hardly anyone was at work that day—no doubt the builders were having him in some obscure manner—and the whole place seemed a dismal and depressing litter. The builder's shed, black-lettered WILKINS, BUILDER, HYTHE, looked like a stranded thing amidst a cast-up disorder of wheelbarrows and wheeling planks, and earth, and sand, and bricks. The foundations of the walls were trenches full of damp concrete, drying in patches; the rooms—it was incredible they could ever be rooms—were shaped out as squares and oblongs of coarse wet grass and sorrel. They looked absurdly small—dishonestly small. What could you expect? Of course the builders were having him, building too small, building all wrong, using bad materials! Old Kipps had told him a wrinkle or two. The builders were having him, young Walshingham was having him, everybody was having him! They were having him and laughing at him because they didn't respect him. They didn't respect him because he couldn't do things right. Who could respect him? . . .

He was an outcast, he had no place in the society of mankind. He had had his chance in the world and turned his back on it. He had "behaved badly"—that was the phrase. . . .

Here a great house was presently to arise—a house to be paid for, a house neither he nor Ann could manage—with eleven bedrooms, and four disrespectful servants having them all the time!

How had it all happened exactly?

This was the end of his great fortune! What a chance he had had! If he had really carried out his first intentions and stuck to things, how much better everything might have been! If he had got a tutor—that had been in his mind originally—a special sort of tutor, to show him everything right. A tutor for gentlemen of neglected education. If he had read more and attended better to what Coote had said. . . .

Coote, who had just cut him! . . .

Eleven bedrooms! What had possessed him? No one would ever come to see them; no one would ever have anything to do with them. Even his Aunt cut him! His Uncle treated him with a half-contemptuous sufferance. He had not a friend worth counting in the world! Buggins, Carshot, Pearce—shop assistants! The Pornicks—a low socialist lot! He stood among his foundations like a lonely figure among ruins; he stood among the ruins of his future, and owned himself a foolish and mistaken man. He saw himself and Ann living out their shameful lives in this great crazy place—as it would be—with everybody laughing secretly at them, and the eleven bedrooms and nobody approaching them—nobody nice and right that is—forever. And Ann!

What was the matter with Ann? She'd given up going for walks lately, got touchy and tearful, been fitful with her food. Just when she didn't ought to. It was all a part of the judgment upon wrong-doing; it was all part of the social penalties that Juggernaut of a novel had brought home to his mind.

3

He let himself in with his latch-key. He went moodily into the dining-room and got out the plans to look at them. He had a vague hope that there would prove to be only ten bedrooms. But he found there were still eleven. He became aware of Ann standing over him. "Look 'ere, Artie!" said Ann.

He looked up and found her holding a number of white oblongs.

His eyebrows rose.

"It's Callers," said Ann.

He put his plans aside slowly, and took and read the cards in silence, with a sort of solemnity. Callers! Then perhaps he wasn't to be left out of the world after all. Mrs. G. Porrett Smith; Miss Porrett Smith; Miss Mabel Porrett Smith; and two smaller cards of the Rev. G. Porrett Smith. "Lor!" he said. *"Clergy!"*

"There was a lady," said Ann, "and two growed-up gels—all dressed up!"

"And *'im?"*

"There wasn't no 'im."

"Not—?" He held out the little card.

"No. There was a lady and two young ladies."

"But—these cards! What they go and leave these two little cards with the Rev. G. Smith on for? Not if 'e wasn't with 'em."

" 'E wasn't with 'em."

"Not a little chap—dodgin' about be'ind the others? And didn't come in?"

"I didn't see no gentleman with them at all," said Ann.

"Rum!" said Kipps. A half-forgotten experience came back to him. "I know," he said, waving the reverend gentleman's card, " 'e give 'em the slip; that's what he'd done. Gone off while they was rapping before you let 'em in. It's a fair call any'ow." He felt a momentary base satisfaction at his absence. "What did they talk about, Ann?"

There was a pause. "I didn't let 'em in," said Ann.

He looked up suddenly and perceived that something unusual was the matter with Ann. Her face was flushed, her eyes were red and hard.

"Didn't let 'em in?"

"No! They didn't come in at all."

He was too astonished for words.

"I answered the door," said Ann. "I'd been upstairs, 'namelling the floor. 'Ow was I to think about Callers, Artie? We ain't never 'ad Callers, all the time we been 'ere. I'd sent Gwendolen out for a bref of fresh air, and there I was upstairs, 'namelling that floor she done so bad, so's to get it done before she came back. I thought I'd 'namel that floor and then get tea, and 'ave it quiet with you, toce and all, before she came back. 'Ow was I to think about Callers?''

She paused. "Well," said Kipps, "what then?"

"They came and rapped. 'Ow was I to know? I thought it was a tradesman or something. Never took my apron off, never wiped the 'namel off my 'ands—nothing. There they was!''

She paused again. She was getting to the disagreeable part.

"Wad they say?" said Kipps.

"She says, 'Is Mrs. Kipps at home?' See? To me."

"Yes."

"And me all painty and no cap on and nothing, neither missis nor servant like. There, Artie, I could 'a sunk through the floor with shame, I really could. I could 'ardly get my voice. I couldn't think of nothing to say but just 'Not at 'Ome,' and out of 'abit like I 'eld the tray. And they give me the cards and went, and 'ow I shall ever look that lady in the face again I don't know. . . . And that's all about it, Artie! They looked me up and down, they did, and then I shut the door on 'em.''

"Goo!" said Kipps.

Ann went and poked the fire needlessly with a passion-quivering hand.

"I wouldn't 'ave 'ad that 'appen for five pounds," said Kipps. "Clergyman and all!''

Ann dropped the poker into the fender with some *éclat,* and stood up and looked at her hot face in the glass. Kipps' disappointment grew. "You did ought to 'ave known better than that, Ann! You reely did."

He sat forward, cards in hand, with a deepening sense of social disaster. The plates were laid upon the table, toast sheltered under a cover at mid-fender, the teapot warmed beside it, and the kettle, just lifted from the hob, sang amidst the coals. Ann glanced at him for a moment, then stooped with the kettle-holder to wet the tea.

"Tcha!" said Kipps, with his mental state developing.

"I don't see it's any use getting in a state about it now," said Ann.

"Don't you! I do. See? 'Ere's these people, good people, want to 'ssociate with us, and 'ere you go and slap 'em in the face!''

"I didn't slap 'em in the face."

"You do—practically. You slams the door in their face, and that's all we see of 'em ever! I wouldn't 'ave 'ad this 'appen not for a ten-pound note."

He rounded his regrets with a grunt. For awhile there was silence, save for the little stir of Ann's few movements preparing tea.

"Tea, Artie," said Ann, handing him a cup.

Kipps took it.

"I put sugar *once,*" said Ann.

"Oo, dash it! Oo cares?" said Kipps, taking an extraordinarily large additional lump with fury-quivering fingers, and putting his cup, with a slight excess of force, on the recess cupboard. "Oo cares?"

"I wouldn't 'ave 'ad that 'appen," he said, bidding steadily against accomplished things, "for twenty pounds."

He gloomed in silence through a long minute or so.

Then Ann said the fatal thing that exploded him. "Artie!" she said.

"What?"

"There's But-tud Toce down there! By your foot!"

There was a pause, husband and wife regarded one another.

"Buttud Toce indeed!" he said. "You go and mess up them callers, and then you try and stuff me up with Buttud Toce! Buttud Toce indeed! 'Ere's our first chance of knowing anyone that's at all fit to 'sociate with— Look 'ere, Ann! Tell you what it is—you got to return that call."

"Return that call!"

"Yes—you got to return that call. That's what you got to do! I know—" He waved his arm vaguely towards the miscellany of books in the recess. "It's in 'Manners and Rools of Good S'ity.' You got to find jest 'ow many cards to leave, and you got to go and leave 'em. See?"

Ann's face expressed terror. "But, Artie! 'Ow *can* I?"

" 'Ow *can* you? 'Ow *could* you? You got to do it, any'ow. They won't know you—not in your Bond Street 'At! If they do, they won't say nothing."

His voice assumed a note of entreaty. "You mus', Ann."

"I can't."

"You mus'."

"I can't, and I won't. Anything in reason I'll do, but face those people again I can't—after what 'as 'appened."

"You won't?"

"No!" . . .

"So there they go—orf! And we never see them again! And so it goes on! So it goes on! We don't know nobody, and we *sha'n't* know anybody! And you won't put yourself out not a little bit, or take the trouble to find out anything 'ow it ought to be done."

Terrible pause.

"I never ought to 'ave married you, Artie, that's the troof."

"Oh, *don't* go into that!"

"I never ought to 'ave married you, Artie. I'm not equal to the position. If you 'adn't said you'd drown yourself—" She choked.

"I don' see why you shouldn't *try*, Ann— *I've* improved. Why don't you? 'Stead of which you go sending out the servant and 'namelling floors, and then when visitors come—"

" 'Ow was *I* to know about y'r old visitors?" cried Ann in a wail, and suddenly got up and fled from amidst their ruined tea, the tea of which "toce, all buttery," was to be the crown and glory.

Kipps watched her with a momentary consternation.Then he hardened his heart. "Ought to 'ave known better," he said, "goin' on like that!" He remained for a space rubbing his knees and muttering. He emitted scornfully, "I carn't, an' I won't." He saw her as the source of all his shames.

Presently, quite mechanically, he stooped down and lifted the flowery china cover. "Ter dash 'er Buttud Toce!" he shouted at the sight of it, and clapped the cover down again hard. . . .

When Gwendolen came back she perceived things were in a slightly unusual poise. Kipps sat by the fire in a rigid attitude, reading a casually selected volume of the *Encyclopaedia Britannica,* and Ann was upstairs and inaccessible—to reappear at a later stage with reddened eyes. Before the fire, and still in a perfectly assimilable condition, was what was evidently an untouched supply of richly buttered toast under a cracked cover.

"They've 'ad a bit of a tiff," said Gwendolen, attending to her duties in the kitchen with her outdoor hat still on, and her mouth full. "They're rummuns—if ever! My eye!"

And she took another piece of Ann's generously buttered toast.

4

The Kippses spoke no more that day to one another.

The squabble about cards and buttered toast was as serious to them as the most rational of differences. It was all rational to them. Their sense of wrong burned within them; their sense of what was owing to themselves, the duty of implacability, the obstinacy of pride. In the small hours Kipps lay awake at the nadir of unhappiness, and came near groaning. He saw life as an extraordinarily desolating muddle; his futile house, his social discredit, his bad behavior to Helen, his low marriage with Ann. . . .

He became aware of something irregular in Ann's breathing. . . .

He listened. She was awake, and quietly and privately sobbing! . . .

He hardened his heart, resolutely he hardened his heart. And presently Ann lay still.

5

The stupid little tragedies of these clipped and limited lives!

As I think of them lying unhappily there in the darkness, my vision pierces the night. See what I can see! Above them, brooding over them, I tell you there is a monster, a lumpish monster, like some great clumsy griffin thing, like the Crystal Palace labyrinthodon, like Coote, like the leaden goddess of the Dunciad, like some fat, proud flunkey, like pride, like indolence, like all that is darkening and heavy and obstructive in life. It is matter and darkness, it is the anti-soul, it is the ruling power of this land, Stupidity. My Kippses live in its shadow. Shalford and his apprenticeship system, the Hastings Academy, the ideas of Coote, the ideas of the old Kippses, all the ideas that have made Kipps what he is,—all these are a part of its shadow. But for that monster they might not be groping among false ideas to hurt one another so sorely; but for that, the glowing promise of childhood and youth might have had a happier fruition; thought might have awakened in them to meet the thought of the world, the quickening sunshine of literature pierced to the substance of their souls; their lives might not have been divorced, as now they are divorced, from the apprehension of beauty that we favored ones are given,—the vision of the Grail that makes life fine forever. I have laughed, and I laugh at these two people; I have sought to make you laugh. . . .

But I see through the darkness the souls of my Kippses as they are, as little pink strips of quivering living stuff, as things like the bodies of little, ill-nourished, ailing, ignorant children—children who feel pain, who are naughty and muddled and suffer, and do not understand why. And the claw of this Beast rests upon them!

CHAPTER III

Terminations

1

NEXT MORNING CAME a remarkable telegram from Folkestone. "Please come at once,—urgent,—Walshingham," said the telegram, and Kipps, after an agitated but still ample breakfast, departed. . . .

When he returned his face was very white, and his countenance disordered. He let himself in with his latch-key and came into the dining-room, where Ann sat, affecting to work at a little thing she called a bib. She heard his hat fall in the hall before he entered, as though he had missed the peg. "I got something to tell you, Ann," he said, disregarding their overnight quarrel, and went to the hearthrug, and took hold of the mantel and stared at Ann as though the sight of her was novel.

"Well?" said Ann, not looking up, and working a little faster.

" 'E's gone!"

Ann looked up sharply, and her hands stopped. *"Who's* gone?" For the first time she perceived Kipps' pallor.

"Young Walshingham—I saw 'er, and she tole me."

"Gone! What d'you mean?"

"Cleared out! Gone off for good!"

"What for?"

"For 'is 'ealth," said Kipps, with sudden bitterness. " 'E's been speckylating. He's speckylated our money, and 'e's speckylated their money, and now 'e's took 'is 'ook. That's all about it, Ann."

"You mean—?"

"I mean 'e's orf, and our twenty-four fousand's orf too! And 'ere we are! Smashed up! That's all about it, Ann." He panted.

Ann had no vocabulary for such an occasion. "Oh, Lor!" she said, and sat still.

Kipps came about and stuck his hands deeply in his trouser pockets. "Speckylated every penny—lorst it all—and gorn. . . ."

Even his lips were white.

"You mean we ain't got nothin' left, Artie?"

"Not a penny! Not a bloomin' penny, Ann. No!"

A gust of passion whirled across the soul of Kipps. He flung out a knuckly fist. "If I 'ad 'im 'ere," he said, "I'd—I'd—I'd wring 'is neck for 'im. I'd—I'd—" His voice rose to a shout. He thought of Gwendolen in the kitchen, and fell to, "Ugh!"

"But, Artie," said Ann, trying to grasp it, "d'you mean to say he's took our money?"

"Speckylated it!" said Kipps, with an illustrative flourish of the arm that failed to illustrate. "Bort things dear and sold 'em cheap, and played the 'ankey-pankey jackass with everything we got. That's what I mean 'e's done, Ann." He repeated this last sentence with the addition of violent adverbs.

"D'you mean to say our money's *gone,* Artie?"

"Ter-dash it, *Yes,* Ann!" swore Kipps, exploding in a shout. "Ain't I tellin' you?"

He was immediately sorry. "I didn't mean to 'oller at you, Ann," he said, "but I'm all shook up. I don't 'ardly know what I'm sayin'. Ev'ry penny. . . ."

"But, Artie—"

Kipps grunted. He went to the window and stared for a moment at a sunlit sea. "Gord!" he swore.

"I mean," he said, coming back to Ann, and with an air of exasperation, "that's he's 'bezzled and 'ooked it. That's what I mean, Ann."

Ann put down the bib. "But wot are we going to *do,* Artie?"

Kipps indicated ignorance, wrath, and despair with one comprehensive gesture of his hands. He caught an ornament from the mantel and replaced it. "I'm going to bang about," he said, "if I ain't precious careful."

"You saw *'er,* you say?"

"Yes."

"What did she say 'xactly?" said Ann.

"Told me to see a s'licitor—tole me to get someone to 'elp me at once. She was there in black—like she used to be, and speaking cool and careful like. 'Elen! . . . She's precious 'ard, is 'Elen. She looked at me straight. 'It's my fault,' she said. 'I ought to 'ave warned you. . . . Only under the circumstances it was a little difficult.' Straight as anything. I didn't 'ardly say anything to 'er. I didn't seem to begin to take it in until she was showing me out. I 'adn't anything to say. Jest as well, perhaps. She talked—like a Call a'most. She said—what *was* it she said about her mother?—'My mother's overcome with grief,' she said, 'so naturally everything comes on me.' "

"And she told you to get someone to 'elp you?"

"Yes. I been to old Bean."

"O' Bean?"

"Yes. What I took my business away from!"

"What did he say?"

"He was a bit off 'and at first, but then 'e come round. He couldn't tell me anything till 'e knew the facts. What I know of young Walshingham, there won't be much 'elp in the facts. No!"

He reflected for a space. "It's a Smash-up, Ann. More likely than not, Ann—'e's left us over'ead in debt. We got to get out of it just 'ow we can. . . .

"We got to begin again," he went on. " *'Ow,* I don't know. All the way 'ome—my 'ead's been going. We got to get a living some'ow or other. 'Aving time to ourselves, and a bit of money to spend, and no hurry and worry; it's all over forever, Ann. We was fools, Ann. We didn't know our benefits. We been caught. Gord! . . . Gord!"

He was on the verge of "banging about" again.

They heard a jingle in the passage, the large, soft impact of a servant's indoor boots. As if she were a part, a mitigatory part of Fate, came Gwendolen to lay the midday meal. Kipps displayed self-control forthwith. Ann picked up the bib again and bent over it, and the Kippses bore themselves gloomily perhaps, but not despairfully, while their dependant was in the room. She spread the cloth and put out the cutlery with a slow inaccuracy, and Kipps, after a whisper to himself, went again to the window. Ann got up and put away her work methodically in the cheffonier.

"When I think," said Kipps, as soon as the door closed again behind Gwendolen—"when I think of the 'ole people, and 'aving to tell 'em of it all, I want to smesh my 'ead against the nearest wall. Smesh my silly brains out! And Buggins—Buggins, what I'd 'arf promised to start in a lill' outfitting shop in Rendezvous Street. . . ."

Gwendolen returned and restored dignity.

The midday meal spread itself slowly before them. Gwendolen, after her custom, left the door open, and Kipps closed it carefully before sitting down.

He stood for a moment, regarding the meal doubtfully.

"I don't feel as if I could swaller a moufful," he said.

"You got to eat," said Ann. . . .

For a time they said little, and once swallowing was achieved, ate on with a sort of melancholy appetite. Each was now busy thinking.

"After all," said Kipps, presently, "whatever 'appens, they can' turn us out or sell us up before nex' quarter day. I'm pretty sure about that."

"Sell us up!" said Ann.

"I dessay we're bankrup'," said Kipps, trying to say it easily, and helping himself with a trembling hand to unnecessary potatoes.

Then a long silence. Ann ceased to eat, and there were silent tears.

"More potatoes, Artie?" choked Ann.

"I couldn't," said Kipps. "No."

He pushed back his plate, which was indeed replete with potatoes, got up and walked about the room. Even the dinner-table looked distraught and unusual.

"What to do, I *don't* know," he said.

"Oh, *Lord!*" he ejaculated, and picked up and slapped down a book.

Then his eye fell upon another postcard that had come from Chitterlow by the morning's post, and which now lay by him on the mantelshelf. He took it up, glanced at its imperfectly legible message, and put it down.

"Delayed!" he said scornfully. "Not prodooced in the smalls. Or is it smells 'e says? 'Ow can one understand that? Any'ow, 'e's 'umbugging again. Somefing about the Strand. No! . . . Well, 'e's 'ad all the money 'e'll ever get out of me! . . . I'm done."

He seemed to find a momentary relief in the dramatic effect of his announcement. He came near to a swagger of despair upon the hearthrug, and then suddenly came and sat down next to Ann, and rested his chin on the knuckles of his two clenched hands.

"I been a fool, Ann," he said in a gloomy monotone. "I been a brasted fool. But it's 'ard on us, all the same. It's 'ard."

" 'Ow was you to know?" said Ann.

"I ought to 'ave known. I did in a sort of way know. And 'ere we are! I wouldn't care so much if it was myself, but it's *you,* Ann! 'Ere we are! Regular smashed up! And you—" He checked at an unspeakable aggravation of their disaster. "I knew 'e wasn't to be depended upon, and there I left it! And you got to pay. . . . What's to 'appen to us all, I don't know."

He thrust out his chin and glared at fate.

" 'Ow do you know 'e's speckylated everything?" said Ann, after a silent survey of him.

" 'E 'as," said Kipps, irritably, holding firm to disaster.

"She say so?"

"She don't know, of course; but you depend upon it, that's it. She told me she knew something was on, and when she found 'im gone and a note lef' for her, she knew it was up with 'im. 'E went by the night boat. She wrote that telegrarf off to me straight away."

Ann surveyed his features with tender perplexed eyes; she had never seen him so white and drawn before, and her hand rested an inch or so away from his arm. The actual loss was still, as it were, afar from her. The immediate thing was his enormous distress.

" 'Ow do you know—?" she said, and stopped. It would irritate him too much. Kipps' imagination was going headlong.

"Sold up!" he emitted presently, and Ann flinched.

"Going back to work, day after day. I can't stand it, Ann, I can't. And you—"

"It don't do to think of it," said Ann.

Presently he came upon a resolve. "I keep on thinking of it, and thinking of it, and what's to be done, and what's to be done. I sha'n't be any good 'ome s'arfernoon. It keeps on going round and round in my 'ead, and round and round. I better go for a walk or something. I'd be no comfort to you, Ann. I should want to 'owl and 'ammer things if I 'ung about 'ome. My fingers 'r all atwitch. I shall keep on thinking 'ow I might 'ave stopped it, and callin' myself a fool. . . ."

He looked at her between pleading and shame. It seemed like deserting her.

Ann regarded him with tear-dimmed eyes.

"You'd better do what's good for you, Artie," she said. . . . *"I'll* be best cleaning. It's no use sending off Gwendolen before her month, and the top room wants turning out." She added with a sort of grim humor, "May as well turn it out now while I got it."

"I *better* go for a walk," said Kipps. . . .

And presently our poor exploded Kipps was marching out to bear his sudden misery. Habit turned him up the road toward his growing house, and then suddenly he perceived his direction—"Oh, Lor!"—and turned aside and went up the steep way to the hill-crest and the Sandling Road, and over the line by that tree-embowered Junction, and athwart the wide fields towards Postling—a little black marching figure—and so up the Downs and over the hills, whither he had never gone before. . . .

2

He came back long after dark, and Ann met him in the passage.

"Where you been, Artie?" she asked, with a strained note in her voice.

"I been walking and walking—trying to tire myself out. All the time I been thinking, what shall I do? Trying to fix something up, all out of nothing."

"I didn't know you meant to be out all this time."

Kipps was gripped by compunction. . . .

"I can't think what we ought to do," he said presently.

"You can't do anything much, Artie, not till you hear from Mr. Bean."

"No. I can't do anything much. That's jest it. And all this time I keep feelin' if I don't do something the top of my 'ead'll bust. . . . Been trying to make up advertisements 'arf the time I been out—'bout finding a place; good salesman and stockkeeper, good Manchester dresses, window-dressing—Lor! Fancy that all beginning again! . . . If you went to stay with Sid a bit— If I sent every penny I got to you— I dunno! I dunno!"

When they had gone to bed there was an elaborate attempt to get to sleep. . . . In one of their great waking pauses Kipps remarked in a muffled tone, "I didn't mean to frighten you, Ann, being out so late. I kep' on walking and walking, and some'ow it seemed to do me good. I went out to the 'ill-top ever so far beyond Stanford, and sat there ever so long, and it seemed to make me better. Jest looking over the marsh like, and seeing the sun set. . . ."

"Very likely," said Ann, after a long interval, "it isn't so bad as you think it is, Artie."

"It's bad," said Kipps.

"Very likely, after all, it isn't quite so bad. If there's only a little—"

There came another long silence.

"Ann," said Kipps, in the quiet darkness.

"Yes," said Ann.

"Ann," said Kipps, and stopped as though he had hastily shut a door upon speech.

"I kep' thinking," he said, trying again—"I kep' thinking, after all, I been cross to you and a fool about things—about them cards, Ann—but"—his voice shook to pieces—"we 'ave been 'appy, Ann . . . some'ow . . . togever."

And with that he and then she fell into a passion of weeping.

They clung very tightly together—closer than they had been since ever the first brightness of their married days turned to the gray of common life again. . . .

All the disaster in the world could not prevent their going to sleep at last, with their poor little troubled heads close together on one pillow. There was nothing more to be done; there was nothing more to be thought. Time might go on with his mischiefs, but for a little while at least they still had one another.

3

Kipps returned from his second interview with Mr. Bean in a state of strange excitement. He let himself in with his latch-key and slammed the door. "Ann!" he shouted, in an unusual note: "Ann!"

Ann replied distantly.

"Something to tell you," said Kipps; "something noo!"

Ann appeared apprehensive from the kitchen.

"Ann," he said, going before her into the little dining-room, for his news was too dignified for the passage, "very likely, Ann, o' Bean says, we shall 'ave—" He decided to prolong the suspense. "Guess!"

"I can't, Artie."

"Think of a lot of money!"

"A 'undred pounds p'r'aps?"

He spoke with immense deliberation. "Over a fousand pounds!"

Ann stared and said nothing, only went a shade whiter.

"Over," he said. "A'most certainly over."

He shut the dining-room door and came forward hastily, for Ann, it was clear, meant to take this mitigation of their disaster with a complete abandonment of her self-control. She came near flopping; she fell into his arms.

"Artie," she got to at last, and began to weep, clinging tightly to him.

"Pretty near certain," said Kipps, holding her. "A fousand pounds!"

"I *said*, Artie," she wailed on his shoulder with the note of accumulated wrongs, "very likely it wasn't so bad. . . ."

"There's things," he said, when presently he came to particulars, " 'e couldn't touch. The noo place! It's freehold and paid for, and with the bit of building on it, there's five or six 'undred pounds p'r'aps—say worf free 'undred for safety. We can't be sold up to finish it, like we thought. O' Bean says we can very likely sell it and get money. 'E says you often get a chance to sell a 'ouse lesson 'arf done, specially free'old. *Very* likely 'e says. Then there's Hughenden. Hughenden 'asn't been mortgaged not for more than 'arf its value. There's a 'undred or so to be got on that, and the furniture, and the rent for the summer still coming in. 'E says there's very likely other things. A fousand pounds; that's what 'e said. 'E said it might even be more. . . ."

They were sitting now at the table.

"It alters everything," said Ann.

"I been thinking that, Ann, all the way 'ome. I came in the motor-car. First ride I've had since the Smash. We needn't send off Gwendolen; leastways, not till *after*. You know. We needn't turn out of 'ere—not for a long time. What we been doing for the o' people we can go on doing a'most as much. And your mother! . . . I wanted to 'oller, coming along. I pretty near run coming down the road by the Hotel."

"Oh, I *am* glad we can stop 'ere and be comfortable a bit," said Ann. "I *am* glad for that."

"I pretty near told the driver on the motor—only 'e was the sort won't talk. . . . You see, Ann, we'll be able to start a shop, we'll be able to get *into* something like. All about our 'aving to go back to places and that—all that doesn't matter any more."

For awhile they abandoned themselves to ejaculating transports. Then they fell talking to shape an idea to themselves of the new prospect that opened before them.

"We must start a sort of shop," said Kipps, whose imagination had been working. "It'll 'ave to be a shop."

"Drapery?" said Ann.

"You want such a lot of capital for the drapery; mor'n a thousand pounds you want by a long way—to start it anything like proper."

"Well, outfitting. Like Buggins was going to do."

Kipps glanced at that for a moment, because the idea had not occurred to him. Then he came back to his prepossession.

"Well, I thought of something else, Ann," he said. "You see, I've always thought a little bookshop— It isn't like the drapery—'aving to be learnt. I thought, even before this Smash Up, 'ow I'd like to 'ave something to do, instead of always 'aving 'olidays always like we 'ave been 'aving."

She reflected.

"You don't know *much* about books, do you, Artie?"

"You don't want to." He illustrated. "I noticed when we used to go to that Lib'ry at Folkestone, ladies weren't anything like what they was in a draper's— if you 'aven't got *just* what they want, it's 'Oh no!' and out they go. But in a bookshop it's different. One book's very like another—after all, what is it? Something to read and done with. It's not a thing that matters like print dresses or serviettes—where you either like 'em or don't, and people judge you by. They take what you give 'em in books and lib'ries, and glad to be told *what* to. See 'ow we was—up at that lib'ry. . . ."

He paused. "You see, Ann—

"Well, I read 'n 'dvertisement the other day— I been asking Mr. Bean. It said—five 'undred pounds."

"What did?"

"Branches," said Kipps.

Ann failed to understand. "It's a sort of thing that gets up bookshops all over the country," said Kipps. "I didn't tell you, but I arst about it a bit. On'y I dropped it again. Before this Smash I mean. I'd thought I'd like to keep a shop for a lark, on'y then I thought it silly. Besides, it 'ud 'ave been beneath me."

He blushed vividly. "It was a sort of projek of mine, Ann.

"On'y it wouldn't 'ave done," he added.

It was a tortuous journey when the Kippses set out to explain anything to each other. But through a maze of fragmentary elucidations and questions, their minds did presently begin to approximate to a picture of a compact, bright little shop, as a framework for themselves.

"I thought of it one day when I was in Folkestone. I thought of it one day when I was looking in at a window. I see a chap dressin' a window, and he was whistlin', reg'lar light-hearted. . . . I thought—I'd like to keep a bookshop any'ow, jest for something to do. And when people weren't about, then you could sit and read the books. See? It wouldn't be 'arf bad. . . ."

They mused, each with elbows on table and knuckles to lips, looking with speculative eyes at each other.

"Very likely we'll be 'appier than we should 'ave been with more money," said Kipps, presently.

"We wasn't 'ardly suited—" reflected Ann, and left her sentence incomplete.

"Fish out of water like," said Kipps. . . .

"You won't 'ave to return that call now," said Kipps, opening a new branch of the question. "That's one good thing."

"Lor!" said Ann, "no more I sha'n't!"

"I don't s'pose they'd want you to even if you did—with things as they are."

A certain added brightness came into Ann's face. "Nobody won't be able to come leaving cards on us, Artie, now, any more. We are out of *that!*"

"There isn't no necessity for us to be Stuck Up," said Kipps, "any more forever! 'Ere we are, Ann, common people, with jest no position at all, as you might say, to keep up. No se'v'nts not if you don't like. No dressin' better than other people. If it wasn't we been robbed—dashed if I'd care a rap about losing that money. I b'lieve"—his face shone with the rare pleasure of paradox—"I reely b'lieve, Ann, it'll prove a savin' in the end."

4

The remarkable advertisement which had fired Kipps' imagination with this dream of a bookshop opened out in the most alluring way. It was one little facet in a comprehensive scheme of transatlantic origin, which was to make our old-world methods of bookselling "sit up," and it displayed an imaginative briskness, a lucidity and promise that aroused the profoundest skepticism in the mind of Mr. Bean. To Kipps' renewed investigations it presented itself in an expository illustrated pamphlet (far too well printed, Mr. Bean thought, for a reputable undertaking) of the most convincing sort. Mr. Bean would not let him sink his capital in shares in its projected company that was to make all things new in the world of books, but he could not prevent Kipps becoming one of their associated booksellers. And so, when presently it became apparent that an Epoch was not to be made, and the "Associated Booksellers' Trading Union (Limited)" receded and dissolved and liquidated (a few drops) and vanished and went away to talk about something else, Kipps remained floating undamaged in this interestingly uncertain universe as an independent bookseller.

Except that it failed, the Associated Booksellers' Trading Union had all the stigmata of success. Its fault, perhaps, was that it had them all instead of only one or two. It was to buy wholesale for all its members and associates and exchange stock, having a common books-in-stock list and a common lending library, and it was to provide a uniform registered shop-front to signify all these things to the intelligent passer-by. Except that it was controlled by buoyant young Overmen, with a touch of genius in their arithmetic, it was, I say, a most plausible and hopeful project. Kipps went several times to London, and an agent came to Hythe, Mr. Bean made some timely interventions, and then behind a veil of planks and an announcement in the High Street, the uniform registered shop-front came rapidly into being. "Associated Booksellers' Trading Union," said this shop-front, in a refined artistic lettering that bookbuyers were going to value, as wise men over forty value the proper label for Berncasteler Doctor, and then, "Arthur Kipps."

Next to starting a haberdasher's shop, I doubt if Kipps could have been more truly happy than during those weeks of preparation.

There is, of course, nothing on earth, and I doubt at times if there is a joy in heaven, like starting a small haberdasher's shop. Imagine, for example, having a drawerful of tapes (one whole piece most exquisitely blocked of every possible width of tape), or again, an army of neat, large packages, each displaying one sample of hooks and eyes. Think of your cottons, your drawer of colored silks, the little, less, least of the compartments and thin packets of your needle-drawer! Poor princes and wretched gentlefolk, mysteriously above retail trade, may taste only the faint unsatisfactory shadow of these delights with trays of stamps or butterflies. I write, of course, for those to whom these things appeal; there are clods alive who see nothing, or next to nothing, in spools of mercerized cotton and endless bands of paper-set pins. I write for the wise, and as I write I wonder that Kipps resisted haberdashery. He did. Yet even starting a bookshop is at least twenty times as interesting as building your own house to your own design in unlimited space and time, or any possible thing people with indisputable social position and sound securities can possibly find to do. Upon that I rest.

You figure Kipps "going to have a look to see how the little shop is getting on," the shop that is not to be a loss and a spending of money, but a gain. He does not walk too fast towards it; as he comes into view of it his paces slacken and his head goes to one side. He crosses to the pavement opposite in order to inspect the fascia better, already his name is adumbrated in faint white lines; stops in the middle of the road and scrutinizes imaginary details, for the benefit of his future next-door neighbor, the curiosity-shop man, and so at last, in. . . . A smell of paint and of the shavings of imperfectly seasoned pinewood! The shop is already glazed, and a carpenter is busy over the fittings for adjustable shelves in the side windows. A painter is busy on the fixtures round about (shelving above and drawers below), which are to accommodate most of the stock, and the counter—the counter and desk are done. Kipps goes inside the desk, the desk which is to be the strategic center of the shop, brushes away some sawdust, and draws out the marvelous till; here gold is to be, here silver, here copper—notes locked up in a cash-box in the well below. Then he leans his elbows on the desk, rests his chin on his fist and fills the shelves with imaginary stock; books beyond reading. Every day a man who cares to wash his hands and read uncut pages artfully may have his cake and eat it, among that stock. Under the counter to the right paper and string are to lurk, ready to leap up and embrace goods sold; on the table to the left, art publications—whatever they may prove to be. He maps it out, serves an imaginary customer, receives a dream seven-and-sixpence, packs, bows out. He wonders how it was he ever came to fancy a shop a disagreeable place.

"It's different," he says at last, after musing on that difficulty, "being your own."

It *is* different. . . .

Or, again, you figure Kipps with something of the air of a young sacristan, handling his brightly virginal account books, and looking and looking again, and then still looking, at an unparalleled specimen of copperplate engraving, ruled money below, and above bearing the words, "In Account with ARTHUR

KIPPS (loud flourishes), The Booksellers' Trading Union" (temperate decoration). You figure Ann sitting and stitching at one point of the circumference of the light of the lamp, stitching queer little garments for some unknown stranger, and over against her sits Kipps. Before him is one of those engraved memorandum forms, a moist pad, wet with some thick and greasy, greenish purple ink, that is also spreading quietly but steadily over his fingers, a cross-nibbed pen for first-aid surgical assistance to the patient in his hand, a dating rubber stamp. At intervals he brings down this latter with great care and emphasis upon the paper, and when he lifts it there appears a beautiful oval design, of which "Paid, Arthur Kipps, The Associated Booksellers' Trading Union," and a date, are the essential ingredients, stamped in purple ink.

Anon he turns his attention to a box of small, round yellow labels, declaring "This book was bought from the Associated Booksellers' Trading Union." He licks one with deliberate care, sticks it on the paper before him and defaces it with great solemnity. "I can do it, Ann," he says, looking up brightly. For the Associated Booksellers' Trading Union, among other brilliant notions and inspirations, devised an ingenious system of taking back its books again in part payment for new ones within a specified period. When it failed all sorts of people were left with these unredeemed pledges in hand.

5

Amidst all this bustle and interest, all this going to and fro before they "moved in" to the High Street, came the great crisis that hung over the Kippses, and one morning in the small hours Ann's child was born. . . .

Kipps was coming to manhood swiftly now. The once rabbit-like soul that had been so amazed by the discovery of "chubes" in the human interior and so shocked by the sight of a woman's shoulder-blades, that had found shame and anguish in a mislaid Gibus and terror in an Anagram Tea, was at last facing the greater realities. He came suddenly upon the master thing in life—birth. He passed through hours of listening, hours of impotent fear in the night and in the dawn, and then there was put into his arms something most wonderful, a weak and wailing creature, incredibly, heart-stirringly soft and pitiful, with minute appealing hands that it wrung his heart to see. He held it in his arms and touched its tender cheek as if he feared his lips might injure it. And this marvel was his Son!

And there was Ann, with a greater strangeness and a greater familiarity in her quality than he had ever found before. There were little beads of perspiration on her temples and her lips, and her face was flushed, not pale, as he had feared to see it. She had the look of one who emerges from some strenuous and invigorating act. He bent down and kissed her, and he had no words to say. She wasn't to speak much yet, but she stroked his arm with her hand and had to tell him one thing.

"He's over nine pounds, Artie," she whispered. "Bessie's— Bessie's wasn't no more than eight."

To have given Kipps a pound of triumph over Sid seemed to her almost to justify Nunc Dimittis. She watched his face for a moment, then closed her eyes in a kind of blissful exhaustion as the nurse, with something motherly in her manner, pushed Kipps out of the room.

6

Kipps was far too much preoccupied with his own life to worry about the further exploits of Chitterlow. The man had got his two thousand; on the whole Kipps was glad he had had it rather than young Walshingham, and there was an end to the matter. As for the complicated transaction he achieved and proclaimed by mainly illegible and always incomprehensible postcards, they were like passing voices heard in the street as one goes about one's urgent concerns. Kipps put them aside, and they got in between the pages of the stock and were lost for ever, and sold in with the goods to customers, who puzzled over them mightily.

Then one morning as our bookseller was dusting round before breakfast, Chitterlow returned, appeared suddenly in the shop doorway.

It was the most unexpected thing in the world. The man was in evening dress, evening dress in that singularly crumpled state it assumes after the hour of dawn, and above his disheveled red hair a smallish Gibus hat tilted remarkably forward. He opened the door and stood tall and spread, with one vast white glove flung out, as if to display how burst a glove might be, his eyes bright, such wrinkling of brow and mouth as only an experienced actor can produce, and a singular radiance of emotion upon his whole being—an altogether astonishing spectacle.

The bell jangled for a bit, and then gave it up and was silent. For a long long second everything was quietly attentive. Kipps was amazed to his uttermost; had he had ten times the capacity, he would still have been fully amazed. "It's Chit'low!" he said at last, standing duster in hand.

But he doubted whether it was not a dream.

"Tzit!" gasped that most extraordinary person, still in an incredibly expanded attitude, and then with a slight forward jerk of the starry split glove, "Bif!"

He could say no more. The tremendous speech he had had ready vanished from his mind. Kipps stared at his facial changes, vaguely conscious of the truth of the teachings of Nisbet and Lombroso concerning men of genius.

Then suddenly Chitterlow's features were convulsed, the histrionic fell from him like a garment, and he was weeping. He said something indistinct about "Old Kipps! *Good* old Kipps! Oh, old Kipps!" and somehow he managed to mix a chuckle and a sob in the most remarkable way. He emerged from somewhere near the middle of his original attitude, a merely life-size creature. "My play, boohoo!" he sobbed, clutching at his friend's arm. "My play, Kipps! (sob). You know?"

"Well?" cried Kipps, with his heart sinking in sympathy. "It ain't—?"

"No," howled Chitterlow. "No. It's a Success! My dear chap! my dear boy! Oh! It's a—Bu—boohoo!—a Big Success!" He turned away and wiped streaming tears with the back of his hand. He walked a pace or so and turned. He sat down on one of the specially designed artistic chairs of the Associated Booksellers' Trading Union and produced an exiguous lady's handkerchief, extraordinarily belaced. He choked. "*My* play," and covered his face here and there.

He made an unsuccessful effort to control himself, and shrank for a space to the dimensions of a small and pathetic creature. His great nose suddenly came through a careless place in the handkerchief.

"I'm knocked," he said in a muffled voice, and so remained for a space—wonderful—veiled.

He made a gallant effort to wipe his tears away. "I had to tell you," he said gulping.

"Be all right in a minute," he added, "Calm!" and sat still. . . .

Kipps stared in commiseration of such success. Then he heard footsteps, and went quickly to the house doorway. "Jest a minute," he said. "Don't go in the shop, Ann, for a minute. It's Chitterlow. He's a bit essited. But he'll be better in a minute. It's knocked him over a bit. You see"—his voice sank to a hushed note as one who announces death—" 'e's made a success with his play."

He pushed her back, lest she should see the scandal of another male's tears. . . .

Soon Chitterlow felt better, but for a little while his manner was even alarmingly subdued. "I *had* to come and tell you," he said. "I *had* to astonish someone. Muriel—she'll be first-rate, of course. But she's over at Dymchurch." He blew his nose with enormous noise, and emerged instantly, a merely garrulous optimist.

"I expect she'll be precious glad."

"She doesn't know yet, my dear boy. She's at Dymchurch—with a friend. She's seen some of my first nights before. . . . Better out of it. . . . I'm going to her now. I've been up all night—talking to the Boys and all that. I'm a bit off it just for a bit. But—it Knocked 'em. It Knocked everybody."

He stared at the floor and went on in a monotone. "They laughed a bit at the beginning—but nothing like a settled laugh—not until the second act—you know—the chap with the beetle down his neck. Little Chisholme did that bit to rights. Then they began—*to* rights." His voice warmed and increased. "Laughing! It made *me* laugh! We jumped 'em into the third act before they had time to cool. Everybody was on it. I never saw a first night go so fast. Laugh, laugh, laugh, LAUGH, LAUGH, LAUGH" (he howled the last repetition with stupendous violence). "Everything they laughed at. They laughed at things that we hadn't meant to be funny—not for one moment. Bif! Bizz! Curtain. A Fair Knock Out! . . . I went on—but I didn't say a word. Chisholme did the patter. Shouting! It was like walking under Niagara—going across that stage. It was like never having seen an audience before. . . .

"Then afterwards—the Boys!"

His emotion held him for a space. "Dear old Boys!" he murmured.

His word multiplied, his importance increased. In a little while he was restored to something of his old self. He was enormously excited. He seemed unable to sit down anywhere. He came into the breakfast-room so soon as Kipps was sure of him, shook hands with Mrs. Kipps parenthetically, sat down and immediately got up again. He went to the bassinet in the corner and looked absent-mindedly at Kipps junior, and said he was glad if only for the youngster's sake. He immediately resumed the thread of his discourse. . . . He drank a cup of coffee noisily and walked up and down the room talking, while they attempted breakfast amidst the gale of his excitement. The infant slept marvelously through it all.

"You won't mind my not sitting down, Mrs. Kipps—I couldn't sit down for anyone, or I'd do it for you. It's you I'm thinking of more than anyone, you and Muriel, and all Old Pals and Good Friends. It means wealth, it means money—hundreds and thousands. . . . If you'd heard 'em, *you'd know*."

He was silent through a portentous moment, while topics battled for him, and finally he burst and talked of them all together. It was like the rush of water when a dam bursts and washes out a fair-sized provincial town; all sorts of things floated along on the swirl. For example, he was discussing his future behavior. "I'm glad it's come now. Not before. I've had my lesson. I shall be very discreet now, trust me. We've learnt the value of money." He discussed the possibility of a country house, of taking a Martello tower as a swimming-box (as one might say a shooting-box), of living in Venice because of its artistic associations and scenic possibilities, of a flat in Westminster or a house in the West End. He also raised the question of giving up smoking and drinking, and what classes of drink were especially noxious to a man of his constitution. But discourses on all this did not prevent a parenthetical computation of the probable profits on the supposition of a thousand nights here and in America, nor did it ignore the share Kipps was to have, nor the gladness with which Chitterlow would pay that share, nor the surprise and regret with which he had learned, through an indirect source which awakened many associations, of the turpitude of young Walshingham, nor the distaste Chitterlow had always felt for young Walshingham, and men of his type. An excursus upon Napoleon had got into the torrent somehow, and kept bobbing up and down. The whole thing was thrown into the form of a single complex sentence, with parenthetical and subordinate clauses fitting one into the other like Chinese boxes, and from first to last it never even had an air of approaching anything in the remotest degree partaking of the nature of a full stop.

Into this deluge came the *Daily News,* like the gleam of light in Watts' picture, the waters were assuaged while its sheet was opened, and it had a column, a whole column, of praise. Chitterlow held the paper, and Kipps read over his left hand, and Ann under his right. It made the affair more real to Kipps; it seemed even to confirm Chitterlow against lurking doubts he had been concealing. But it took him away. He departed in a whirl, to secure a copy of every morning paper, every blessed rag there is, and take them all to Dymchurch and Muriel forthwith. It had been the send-off the Boys had given him that had prevented his doing as much at Charing Cross—let alone that he only caught it by the skin of his teeth. . . . Besides which, the bookstall wasn't open. His white face, lit by a vast excitement, bid them a tremendous farewell, and he departed through the sunlight, with his buoyant walk, buoyant almost to the tottering pitch. His hair, as one got it sunlit in the street, seemed to have grown in the night.

They saw him stop a newsboy.

"Every blessed rag," floated to them on the notes of that gorgeous voice.

The newsboy too had happened on luck. Something like a faint cheer from the newsboy came down the air to terminate that transaction.

Chitterlow went on his way swinging a great budget of papers, a figure of merited success. The newsboy recovered from his emotion with a jerk, examined something in his hand again, transferred it to his pocket, watched Chitterlow for a space, and then in a sort of hushed silence resumed his daily routine. . . .

Ann and Kipps regarded that receding happiness in silence, until it vanished round the bend of the road.

"I *am* glad," said Ann at last, speaking with a little sigh.

"So'm I," said Kipps, with emphasis. "For if ever a feller 'as worked and waited—it's 'im. . . ."

They went back through the shop rather thoughtfully, and, after a peep at the sleeping baby, resumed their interrupted breakfast. "If ever a feller 'as worked and waited, it's 'im," said Kipps, cutting bread.

"Very likely it's true," said Ann, a little wistfully.

"What's true?"

"About all that money coming."

Kipps meditated. "I don't see why it shouldn't be," he decided, and handed Ann a piece of bread on the tip of his knife.

"But we'll keep on the shop," he said, after an interval for further reflection, "all the same. . . . I 'aven't much trust in money after the things we've seen."

7

That was two years ago, and, as the whole world knows, the "Pestered Butterfly" is running still. It *was* true. It has made the fortune of a once declining little theater in the Strand; night after night the great beetle scene draws happy tears from a house packed to repletion, and Kipps—for all that Chitterlow is not what one might call a business man—is almost as rich as he was in the beginning. People in Australia, people in Lancashire, Scotland, Ireland, in New Orleans, in Jamaica, in New York and Montreal, have crowded through doorways to Kipps' enrichment, lured by the hitherto unsuspected humors of the entomological drama. Wealth rises like an exhalation all over our little planet, and condenses, or at least some of it does, in the pockets of Kipps.

"It's rum," said Kipps.

He sat in the little kitchen out behind the bookshop and philosophized and smiled while Ann gave Arthur Waddy Kipps his evening tub before the fire. Kipps was always present at this ceremony, unless customers prevented; there was something in the mixture of the odors of tobacco, soap, and domesticity that charmed him unspeakably.

"Chukerdee, o' man," he said affably, wagging his pipe at his son, and thought incidentally, after the manner of all parents, that very few children could have so straight and clean a body.

"Dadda's got a cheque," said Arthur Waddy Kipps, emerging for a moment from the towel.

" 'E gets 'old of everything," said Ann. "You can't say a word—"

"Dadda got a cheque," this marvelous child repeated.

"Yes, o' man, I got a cheque. And it's got to go into a bank for you, against when you got to go to school. See? So's you'll grow up knowing your way about a bit."

"Dadda's got a cheque," said the wonder son, and then gave his mind to making mighty splashes with his foot. Every time he splashed, laughter overcame him, and he had to be held up for fear he should tumble out of the tub in his merriment. Finally he was toweled to his toe-tips, wrapped up in warm flannel, and kissed and carried off to bed by Ann's cousin and lady help, Emma. And then after Ann had carried away the bath into the scullery, she returned to find her husband with his pipe extinct and the cheque still in his hand.

"Two fousand pounds," he said. "It's dashed rum. Wot 'ave *I* done to get two fousand pounds, Ann?"

"What 'aven't you—not to?" said Ann.

He reflected upon this view of the case.

"I sha'n't never give up this shop," he said at last.

"We're very 'appy 'ere," said Ann.

"Not if I 'ad *fifty* fousand pounds."

"No fear," said Ann.

"You got a shop," said Kipps, "and you come along in a year's time and there it is. But money—look 'ow it comes and goes! There's no sense in money. You may kill yourself trying to get it, and then it comes when you aren't looking. There's my 'riginal money! Where is it now? Gone! And it's took young Walshingham with it, and 'e's gone too. It's like playing skittles. Long comes the ball, right and left you fly, and there it is rolling away and not changed a bit. No sense in it. 'E's gone, and she's gone—gone off with that chap Revel, that sat with me at dinner. Married man! And Chit'low rich! Lor!—what a fine place that Gerrik Club is to be sure, where I 'ad lunch wiv' 'im! Better'n *any* 'otel. Footmen in powder they got—not waiters, Ann,—footmen! 'E's rich and me rich—in a sort of way. . . . Don't seem much sense in it, Ann—'owever you look at it.'' He shook his head.

"I know one thing,'' said Kipps.

"What?''

"I'm going to put it in jest as many different banks as I can. See? Fifty 'ere, fifty there. 'Posit. I'm not going to 'nvest it—no fear.''

"It's only frowing money away,'' said Ann.

"I'm 'arf a mind to bury some of it under the shop. Only I expect one 'ud always be coming down at nights to make sure it was there. . . . I don't seem to trust anyone—not with money.'' He put the cheque on the table corner and smiled and tapped his pipe on the grate, with his eyes on that wonderful document. "S'pose old Bean started orf,'' he reflected. . . . "One thing,—'e *is* a bit lame.''

" 'E wouldn't,'' said Ann; "not 'im.''

"I was only joking like.'' He stood up, put his pipe among the candlesticks on the mantel, took up the cheque and began folding it carefully to put it back in his pocket-book.

A little bell jangled.

"Shop!'' said Kipps. "That's right. Keep a shop and the shop'll keep you. That's 'ow I look at it, Ann.''

He drove his pocket-book securely into his breast-pocket before he opened the living-room door. . . .

But whether indeed it is the bookshop that keeps Kipps, or whether it is Kipps who keeps the bookshop, is just one of those commercial mysteries people of my unarithmetical temperament are never able to solve. They do very well, the dears, anyhow, thank Heaven!

The bookshop of Kipps is on the left-hand side of the Hythe High Street coming from Folkestone, between the yard of the livery-stable and the shop window full of old silver and such-like things—it is quite easy to find—and there you may see him for yourself and speak to him and buy this book of him if you like. He has it in stock I know. Very delicately I've seen to that. His name is not Kipps, of course, you must understand that; but everything else is exactly as I have told you. You can talk to him about books, about politics, about going to Boulogne, about life, and the ups and downs of life. Perhaps he will quote you Buggins—from whom, by-the-bye, one can now buy everything a gentleman's wardrobe should contain at the little shop in Rendezvous Street, Folkestone. If you are fortunate enough to find Kipps in a good mood, he may even let you know how he inherited a fortune "once.'' "Run froo it,'' he'll say with a not unhappy smile. "Got another afterwards—speckylating in plays. Needn't keep this shop if I didn't like. But it's something to do. . . .''

Or he may be even more intimate. "I seen some things,'' he said to me once. "Raver! Life! Why, once I—I *loped!* I did—reely!''

(Of course you will not tell Kipps that he *is* "Kipps,'' or that I have put him in this book. He hasn't the remotest suspicion of that. And, you know, you never can tell how people are going to take that sort of thing. I am an old and trusted customer now, and for many amiable reasons I should prefer that things remained exactly on their present footing.)

8

One early-closing evening in July they left the baby to the servant cousin, and Kipps took Ann for a row on the Hythe canal. The sun set in a mighty blaze, and left a world warm, and very still. The twilight came. And there was the water, shining bright, and the sky a deepening blue, and the great trees that dipped their boughs towards the water, exactly as it had been when he paddled home with Helen, when her eyes had seemed to him like dusky stars. He had ceased from rowing and rested on his oars, and suddenly he was touched by the wonder of life—the strangeness that is a presence stood again by his side.

Out of the darknesses beneath the shallow weedy stream of his being rose a question, a question that looked up dimly and never reached the surface. It was the question of the wonder of the beauty, the purposeless, inconsecutive beauty, that falls so strangely among the happenings and memories of life. It never reached the surface of his mind, it never took to itself substance or form; it looked up merely as the phantom of a face might look, out of deep waters, and sank again into nothingness.

"Artie," said Ann.

He woke up and pulled a stroke. "What?" he said.

"Penny for your thoughts, Artie."

He considered.

"I reely don't think I was thinking of anything," he said at last, with a smile. "No."

He still rested on his oars.

"I expect," he said, "I was thinking jest what a Rum Go everything is. I expect it was something like that."

"Queer old Artie!"

"Ain't I? I don't suppose there ever was a chap quite like me before."

He reflected for just another minute.

"Oo!—I dunno," he said at last, and roused himself to pull.

THE WIFE
OF
SIR ISAAC HARMAN

CHAPTER THE FIRST

Introduces Lady Harman

1

THE MOTOR-CAR ENTERED a little white gate, came to a porch under a thick wig of jasmine, and stopped. The chauffeur indicated by a movement of the head that this at last was it. A tall young woman with a big soft mouth, great masses of blue-black hair on either side of a broad, low forehead, and eyes of so dark a brown you might have thought them black, drooped forward and surveyed the house with a mixture of keen appreciation and that gentle apprehension which is the shadow of desire in unassuming natures. . . .

The little house with the white-framed windows looked at her with a sleepy wakefulness from under its blinds, and made no sign. Beyond the corner was a glimpse of lawn, a rank of delphiniums, and the sound of a wheelbarrow.

"Clarence!" the lady called again.

Clarence, with an air of exceeding his duties, decided to hear, descended slowly, and came to the door.

"Very likely—if you were to look for a bell, Clarence. . . ."

Clarence regarded the porch with a hostile air, made no secret that he thought it a fool of a porch, seemed on the point of disobedience, and submitted. His gestures suggested a belief that he would next be asked to boil eggs or do the boots. He found a bell and rang it with the needless violence of a man who has no special knowledge of ringing bells. How was *he* to know? he was a chauffeur. The bell did not so much ring as explode and swamp the place. Sounds of ringing came from all the windows, and even out of the chimneys. It seemed as if once set ringing that bell would never cease. . . .

Clarence went to the hood of his machine, and presented his stooping back in a defensive manner against anyone who might come out. He wasn't a footman, anyhow. He'd rung that bell all right, and now he must see to his engine.

"He's rung so *loud!*" said the lady weakly—apparently to God.

The door behind the neat white pillars opened, and a little red-nosed woman, in a cap she had evidently put on without a proper glass, appeared. She surveyed the car and its occupant with disfavor over her also very oblique spectacles.

The lady waved a pink paper to her, a house-agent's order to view. "Is this Black Strands?" she shouted.

The little woman advanced slowly with her eyes fixed malevolently on the pink paper. She seemed to be stalking it.

"This *is* Black Strands?" repeated the tall lady. "I should be so sorry if I disturbed you—if it isn't; ringing the bell like that—and all. You can't think—"

"This is Black *Strand*," said the little old woman with a note of deep reproach, and suddenly ceased to look over her glasses and looked through them. She looked no kindlier through them, and her eye seemed much larger. She was now regarding the lady in the car, though with a sustained alertness towards the pink paper. "I suppose," she said, "you've come to see over the place?"

"If it doesn't disturb anyone; if it is quite convenient—"

"Mr. Brumley is *hout*," said the little old woman. "And if you got an order to view, you got an order to view."

"If you think I might."

The lady stood up in the car, a tall and graceful figure of doubt and desire and glossy black fur. "I'm sure it looks a very charming house."

"It's *clean*," said the little old woman, "from top to toe. Look as you may."

"I'm sure it is," said the tall lady, and put aside her great fur coat from her lithe, slender, red-clad body. (She was permitted by a sudden civility of Clarence's to descend.) "Why! the windows," she said, pausing on the step, "are like crystal."

"These very 'ands," said the little old woman, and glanced up at the windows the lady had praised. The little old woman's initial sternness wrinkled and softened as the skin of a windfall does after a day or so upon the ground. She half turned in the doorway and made a sudden vergerlike gesture. "We enter," she said, "by the 'all. . . . Them's Mr. Brumley's 'ats and sticks. Every 'at or cap 'as a stick, and every stick 'as a 'at *or* cap, and on the 'all table is the gloves corresponding. On the right is the door leading to the kitching, on the left is the large droring-room which Mr. Brumley 'as took as 'is study." Her voice fell to lowlier things. "The other door beyond is a small lavatory 'aving a basing for washing 'ands."

"It's a perfectly delightful hall," said the lady. "So low and wide-looking. And everything so bright—and lovely. Those long, Italian pictures! And how charming that broad outlook upon the garden beyond!"

"You'll think it charminger when you see the garding," said the little old woman. "It was Mrs. Brumley's especial delight. Much of it—with 'er own 'ands."

"We now enter the droring-room," she proceeded, and flinging open the door to the right was received with an indistinct cry suggestive of the words, "Oh, *damn* it!" The stout medium-sized gentleman in an artistic green-gray Norfolk suit, from whom the cry proceeded, was kneeling on the floor close to the wide-open window, and he was engaged in lacing up a boot. He had a round, ruddy, rather handsome, amiable face with a sort of bang of brown hair coming over one temple, and a large silk bow under his chin and a little towards one ear, such as artists and artistic men of letters affect. His profile was regular and fine, his eyes expressive, his mouth, a very passable mouth. His features expressed at first only the naïve horror of a shy man unveiled.

Intelligent appreciation supervened.

There was a crowded moment of rapid mutual inspection. The lady's attitude was that of the enthusiastic house-explorer arrested in full flight, falling swiftly towards apology and retreat. (It was a frightfully attractive room, too, full of the brightest color, and with a big white cast of a statue—a Venus!—in the window.) She backed over the threshold again.

"I thought you was out by that window, sir," said the little old woman intimately, and was nearly shutting the door between them and all the beginnings of this story.

But the voice of the gentleman arrested and wedged open the closing door.

"I—Are you looking at the house?" he said. "I say! Just a moment, Mrs. Rabbit."

He came down the length of the room with a slight flicking noise due to the scandalized excitement of his abandoned laces. The lady was reminded of her not so very distant schooldays, when it would have been considered a suitable answer to such a question as his to reply, "No, I am walking down Piccadilly on my hands." But instead she waved that pink paper again. "The agents," she said. "Recommended—specially. So sorry if I intrude. I ought, I know, to have written first; but I came on an impulse."

By this time the gentleman in the artistic tie, who had also the artistic eye for such matters, had discovered that the lady was young, delightfully slender, either pretty or beautiful, he could scarcely tell which, and very, very well dressed. "I am glad," he said, with remarkable decision, "that I was not out. *I* will show you the house."

" 'Ow *can* you, sir?" intervened the little old woman.

"Oh! show a house! Why not?"

"The kitchings—you don't understand the range, sir—it's beyond you. And upstairs. You can't show a lady upstairs."

The gentleman reflected upon these difficulties.

"Well, I'm going to show her all I can show her anyhow. And after that, Mrs. Rabbit, you shall come in. You needn't wait."

"I'm thinking," said Mrs. Rabbit, folding stiff little arms and regarding him sternly. "You won't be much good after tea, you know, if you don't get your afternoon's exercise."

"Rendez-vous in the kitchen, Mrs. Rabbit," said Mr. Brumley, firmly, and Mrs. Rabbit after a moment of mute struggle disappeared discontentedly.

"I do not want to be the least bit a bother," said the lady. "I'm intruding, I know, without the least bit of notice. I *do* hope I'm not disturbing you—" she seemed to make an effort to stop at that, and failed and added—"the least bit. Do please tell me if I am."

"Not at all," said Mr. Brumley. "I hate my afternoon's walk as a prisoner hates the treadmill."

"She's such a nice old creature."

"She's been a mother—and several aunts—to us ever since my wife died. She was the first servant we ever had.

"All this house," he explained to his visitor's questioning eyes, "was my wife's creation. It was a little featureless agent's house on the edge of these pinewoods. She saw something in the shape of the rooms—and that central hall. We've enlarged it of course. Twice. This was two rooms, that is why there is a step down in the center."

"That window and window-seat—"

"That was her addition," said Mr. Brumley. "All this room is—replete—with her personality." He hesitated, and explained further. "When we prepared this house—we expected to be better off—than we subsequently became—and she could let herself go. Much is from Holland and Italy."

"And that beautiful old writing-desk with the little single rose in a glass!"

"She put it there. She even in a sense put the flower there. It is renewed of course. By Mrs. Rabbit. She trained Mrs. Rabbit."

He sighed slightly, apparently at some thought of Mrs. Rabbit.

"You—you write—" the lady stopped, and then diverted a question that she perhaps considered too blunt, "there?"

"Largely. I am—a sort of author. Perhaps you know my books. Not very important books—but people sometimes read them."

The rose-pink of the lady's cheek deepened by a shade. Within her pretty head, her mind rushed to and fro saying "Brumley? Brumley?" Then she had a saving gleam. "Are you *George* Brumley?" she asked,—"*the* George Brumley?"

"My name *is* George Brumley," he said, with a proud modesty. "Perhaps you know my little Euphemia books? They are still the most read."

The lady made a faint, dishonest assent-like noise; and her rose-pink deepened another shade. But her interlocutor was not watching her very closely just then.

"Euphemia was my wife," he said, "at least, my wife gave her to me—a kind of exhalation. *This*"— his voice fell with a genuine respect for literary associations—"was Euphemia's home.

"I still," he continued, "go on. I go on writing about Euphemia. I have to. In this house. With my tradition. . . . But it is becoming painful—painful. Curiously more painful now than at the beginning. And I want to go. I want at last to make a break. That is why I am letting or selling the house. . . . There will be no more Euphemia."

His voice fell to silence.

The lady surveyed the long low clear room so cleverly prepared for life, with its white wall, its Dutch clock, its Dutch dresser, its pretty seats about the open fireplace, its cleverly placed bureau, its suntrap at the garden end; she could feel the rich intention of living in its every arrangement and a sense of uncertainty in things struck home to her. She seemed to see a woman, a woman like herself—only very, very much cleverer—flitting about the room and making it. And then this woman had vanished—nowhither. Leaving this gentleman—sadly left— in the care of Mrs. Rabbit.

"And she is dead?" she said with a softness in her dark eyes and a fall in her voice that was quite natural and very pretty.

"She died," said Mr. Brumley, "three years and a half ago." He reflected. "Almost exactly."

He paused and she filled the pause with feeling.

He became suddenly very brave and brisk and businesslike. He led the way back into the hall and made explanations. "It is not so much a hall as a hall living-room. We use that end, except when we go out upon the veranda beyond, as our dining-room. The door to the right is the kitchen."

The lady's attention was caught again by the bright long eventful pictures that had already pleased her. "They are copies of two of Carpaccio's St. George series in Venice," he said. "We bought them together there. But no doubt you've seen the originals. In a little old place with a custodian and rather dark. One of those corners—so full of that delightful out-of-the-wayishness which is so characteristic, I think, of Venice. I don't know if you found that in Venice?"

"I've never been abroad," said the lady. "Never. I should love to go. I suppose you and your wife went—ever so much."

He had a transitory wonder that so fine a lady should be untravelled, but his eagerness to display his backgrounds prevented him thinking that out at the time. "Two or three times," he said, "before our little boy came to us. And always returning with something for this place. Look!" he went on, stepped across an exquisite little brick court to a lawn of soft emerald and turning back upon the house. "That Della Robbia plaque we lugged all the way back from Florence with us, and that stone bird-bath is from Siena."

"How bright it is!" murmured the lady after a brief still appreciation. "Delightfully bright. As though it would shine even if the sun didn't." And she abandoned herself to the rapture of seeing a house and garden that were for once better even than the agent's superlatives. And within her grasp if she chose—within her grasp.

She made the garden melodious with soft appreciative sounds. She had a small voice for her size but quite a charming one, a little live bird of a voice, bright and sweet. It was a clear unruffled afternoon; even the unseen wheelbarrow had very sensibly ceased to creak and seemed to be somewhere listening. . . .

Only one trivial matter marred their easy explorations;—his boots remained unlaced. No propitious moment came when he could stoop and lace them. He was not a dexterous man with eyelets, and stooping made him grunt and his head swim. He hoped these trailing imperfections went unmarked. He tried subtly to lead this charming lady about and at the same time walk a little behind her. She on her part could not determine whether he would be displeased or not if she noticed this slight embarrassment and asked him to set it right. They were quite long leather laces and they flew about with a sturdy negligence of anything but their own offensive contentment, like a gross man who whistles a vulgar tune as he goes round some ancient church; flick, flock, they went, and flip, flap, enjoying themselves, and sometimes he trod on one and halted in his steps, and sometimes for a moment she felt her foot tether him. But man is the adaptable animal and presently they both became more used to these inconveniences and more mechanical in their efforts to avoid them. They treated those laces then exactly as nice people would treat that gross man; a minimum of polite attention and all the rest pointedly directed away from him. . . .

The garden was full of things that people dream about doing in their gardens and mostly never do. There was a rose garden all blooming in chorus, and with pillar-roses and arches that were not so much growths as overflowing cornucopias of roses, and a neat orchard with shapely trees white-painted to their exact middles, a stone wall bearing clematis and a clothesline so gay with Mr. Brumley's blue and white flannel shirts that it seemed an essential part of the design. And then there was a great border of herbaceous perennials backed by delphiniums and monkshood already in flower and budding hollyhocks rising to their duty; a border that reared its blaze of color against a hill-slope dark with pines. There was no hedge whatever to this delightful garden. It seemed to go straight into the pinewoods; only an invisible netting marked its limits and fended off the industrious curiosity of the rabbits.

"This strip of wood is ours right up to the crest," he said, "and from the crest one has a view. One has two views. If you would care—?"

The lady made it clear that she was there to see all she could. She radiated her appetite to see. He carried a fur stole for her over his arm and flicked the way up the hill. Flip, flap, flop. She followed demurely.

"This is the only view I care to show you now," he said at the crest. "There was a better one beyond there. But—it has been defiled. . . . Those hills! I knew you would like them. The space of it! And . . . yet—. This view—lacks the shining ponds. There are wonderful distant ponds. After all I must show you the other! But you see there is the high-road, and the high-road has produced an abomination. Along here we go. Now. Don't look down please." His gesture covered the foreground. "Look right over the nearer things into the distance. There!"

The lady regarded the wide view with serene appreciation. "I don't see," she said, "that it's in any way ruined. It's perfect."

"You don't see! Ah! you look right over. You look high. I wish I could too. But that screaming board! I wish the man's crusts would choke him."

And indeed quite close at hand, where the road curved about below them, the statement that Staminal Bread, the True Staff of Life, was sold only by the International Bread Shops, was flung out with a vigor of yellow and Prussian blue that made the landscape tame.

His finger directed her questioning eye.

"*Oh!*" said the lady suddenly, as one who is convicted of a stupidity and colored slightly.

"In the morning of course it is worse. The sun comes directly on to it. Then really and truly it blots out everything."

The lady stood quite silent for a little time, with her eyes on the distant ponds. Then he perceived that she was blushing. She turned to her interlocutor as a puzzled pupil might turn to a teacher.

"It really is very good bread," she said. "They make it— Oh! most carefully. With the germ in. And one has to tell people."

Her point of view surprised him. He had expected nothing but a docile sympathy. "But to tell people *here!*" he said.

"Yes, I suppose one oughtn't to tell them here."

"Man does not live by bread alone."

She gave the faintest assent.

"This is the work of one pushful, shoving creature, a man named Harman. Imagine him! Imagine what he must be! Don't you feel his soul defiling us?— this summit of a stupendous pile of—dough, thinking of nothing but his miserable monstrous profits, seeing nothing in the delight of life, the beauty of the world but something that attracts attention, draws eyes, something that gives him his horrible opportunity of getting ahead of all his poor little competitors and inserting— *this!* It's the quintessence of all that is wrong with the world;—squalid, shameless huckstering!" He flew off at a tangent. "Four or five years ago they made this landscape disease,—a knight!"

He looked at her for a sympathetic indignation, and then suddenly something snapped in his brain and he understood. There wasn't an instant between absolute innocence and absolute knowledge.

"You see," she said as responsive as though he had cried out sharply at the horror in his mind, "Sir Isaac is my husband. Naturally . . . I ought to have given you my name to begin with. It was silly . . ."

Mr. Brumley gave one wild glance at the board, but indeed there was not a word to be said in its mitigation. It was the crude advertisement of a crude pretentious thing crudely sold. "My dear lady!" he said in his largest style, "I am desolated! But I have said it! It isn't a pretty board."

A memory of epithets pricked him. "You must forgive—a certain touch of— rhetoric."

He turned about as if to dismiss the board altogether, but she remained with her brows very faintly knit, surveying the cause of his offense.

"It isn't a *pretty* board," she said. "I've wondered at times. . . . It isn't."

"I implore you to forget that outbreak—mere petulance—because, I suppose, of a peculiar liking for that particular view. There are—associations—"

"I've wondered lately," she continued, holding on to her own thoughts, "what people *did* think of them. And it's curious—to hear—"

For a moment neither spoke, she surveyed the board and he the tall ease of her pose. And he was thinking she must surely be the most beautiful woman he had ever encountered. The whole country might be covered with boards if it gave us such women as this. He felt the urgent need of some phrase, to pull the situation out of this pit into which it had fallen. He was a little unready, his faculties all as it were neglecting his needs and crowding to the windows to stare, and meanwhile she spoke again, with something of the frankness of one who thinks aloud.

"You see," she said, "one *doesn't* hear. One thinks perhaps—And there it is. When one marries very young one is apt to take so much for granted. And afterwards—"

She was wonderfully expressive in her inexpressiveness, he thought, but found as yet no saving phrase. Her thought continued to drop from her. "One sees them so much that at last one doesn't see them."

She turned away to survey the little house again; it was visible in bright strips between the red-scarred pine stems. She looked at it chin up, with a still approval—but she was the slenderest loveliness, and with such a dignity!—and she spoke at length as though the board had never existed. "It's like a little piece of another world; so bright and so—perfect."

There was the phantom of a sigh in her voice.

"I think you'll be charmed by our rockery," he said. "It was one of our particular efforts. Every time we two went abroad we came back with something, stonecrop or Alpine or some little bulb from the wayside."

"How can you leave it!"

He was leaving it because it bored him to death. But so intricate is the human mind that it was with perfect sincerity he answered: "It will be a tremendous wrench. . . . I have to go."

"And you've written most of your books here and lived here!"

The note of sympathy in her voice gave him a sudden suspicion that she imagined his departure due to poverty. Now to be poor as an author is to be unpopular, and he valued his popularity—with the better sort of people. He hastened to explain. "I have to go, because here, you see, here, neither for me nor my little son, is it Life. It's a place of memories, a place of accomplished beauty. My son already breaks away,—a preparatory school at Margate. Healthier, better, for us to break altogether I feel, wrench though it may. It's full for us at least—a new tenant would be different of course—but for *us* it's full of associations we can't alter, can't for the life of us change. Nothing you see goes on. And life you know *is* change—change and going on."

He paused impressively on his generalization.

"But you will want—You will want to hand it over to—to sympathetic people of course. People," she faltered, "who will understand."

Mr. Brumley took an immense stride—conversationally. "I am certain there is no one I would more readily see in that house than yourself," he said.

"But—" she protested. "And besides, you don't know me!"

"One knows some things at once, and I am as sure you would—understand—as if I had known you twenty years. It may seem absurd to you, but when I looked up just now and saw you for the first time, I thought—this, this is the tenant. This is her house. . . . Not a doubt. That is why I did not go for my walk—came round with you."

"You really think you would like us to have that house?" she said. "*Still?*"

"No one better," said Mr. Brumley.

"After the board?"

"After a hundred boards, I let the house to you. . . ."

"My husband of course will be the tenant," reflected Lady Harman.

She seemed to brighten again by an effort: "I have always wanted something like this, that wasn't gorgeous, that wasn't mean. I can't *make* things. It isn't everyone—can *make* a place. . . .''

2

Mr. Brumley found their subsequent conversation the fullest realization of his extremest hopes. Behind his amiable speeches, which soon grew altogether easy and confident again, a hundred imps of vanity were patting his back for the intuition, the swift decision that had abandoned his walk so promptly. In some extraordinary way the incident of the board became impossible; it hadn't happened, he felt, or it had happened differently. Anyhow there was no time to think that over now. He guided the lady to the two little greenhouses, made her note the opening glow of the great autumnal border and brought her to the rock garden. She stooped and loved and almost kissed the soft healthy cushions of pampered saxifrage: she appreciated the cleverness of the moss-bed—where there were droseras; she knelt to the gentians; she had a kindly word for that bank-holiday corner where London Pride still belatedly rejoiced; she cried out at the delicate Iceland poppies that thrust up between the stones of the rough pavement; and so in the most amiable accord they came to the raised seat in the heart of it all, and sat down and took in the whole effect of the place, and backing of woods, the lush borders, the neat lawn, the still neater orchard, the pergola, the nearer delicacies among the stones, and the gable, the shining white rough-cast of the walls, the casement windows, the projecting upper story, the carefully sought-out old tiles of the roof. And everything bathed in that caressing sunshine which does not scorch nor burn but gilds and warms deliciously, that summer sunshine which only northward islands know.

Recovering from his first astonishment and his first misadventure, Mr. Brumley was soon himself again, talkative, interesting, subtly and gently aggressive. For once one may use a hackneyed phrase without the slightest exaggeration; he was charmed. . . .

He was one of those very natural-minded men with active imaginations who find women the most interesting things in a full and interesting universe. He was an entirely good man and almost professionally on the side of goodness, his pen was a pillar of the home and he was hostile and even actively hostile to all those influences that would undermine and change—anything; but he did find women attractive. He watched them and thought about them, he loved to be with them, he would take great pains to please and interest them, and his mind was frequently dreaming quite actively of them, of championing them, saying wonderful and impressive things to them, having great friendships with them, adoring them and being adored by them. At times he had to ride this interest on the curb. At times the vigor of its urgencies made him inconsistent and secretive. . . . Comparatively his own sex was a matter of indifference to him. Indeed he was a very normal man. Even such abstractions as Goodness and Justice had rich feminine figures in his mind, and when he sat down to write criticism at his desk, that pretty little slut of a Delphic Sibyl presided over his activities.

So that it was a cultivated as well as an attentive eye that studied the movements of Lady Harman and an experienced ear that weighed the words and cadences of her entirely inadequate and extremely expressive share in their conversation. He had enjoyed the social advantages of a popular and presentable man of letters, and he had met a variety of ladies; but he had never yet met anyone at all like Lady Harman. She was pretty and quite young and fresh; he doubted if she was as much as four-and-twenty; she was as simple-mannered as though she was ever so much younger than that, and dignified as though she was ever so much older; and she had a sort of luster of wealth about her—. One met it sometimes in young richly married Jewesses, but though she was very dark she wasn't at all of that type; he was inclined to think she must be Welsh. This manifest spending of great lots of money on the richest, finest and fluffiest things was the only aspect of her that sustained the parvenu idea; and it wasn't in any way carried out by her manners, which were as modest and silent and inaggressive as the very best can be. Personally he liked opulence, he responded to countless-guinea furs. . . .

Soon there was a neat little history in his mind that was reasonably near the truth, of a hard-up professional family, fatherless perhaps, of a mercenary marriage at seventeen or so—and this. . . .

And while Mr. Brumley's observant and speculative faculties were thus active, his voice was busily engaged. With the accumulated artistry of years he was developing his pose. He did it almost subconsciously. He flung out hint and impulsive confidence and casual statement with the careless assurance of the accustomed performer, until by nearly imperceptible degrees that finished picture of the two young lovers, happy, artistic, a little Bohemian and one of them doomed to die, making their home together in an atmosphere of sunny gaiety, came into being in her mind. . . .

"It must have been beautiful to have begun life like that," she said in a voice that was a sigh, and it flashed joyfully across Mr. Brumley's mind that this wonderful person could envy his Euphemia.

"Yes," he said, "at least we had our Spring."

"To be together," said the lady, "and—so beautifully poor. . . ."

There is a phase in every relationship when one must generalize if one is to go further. A certain practice in this kind of talk with ladies blunted the finer sensibilities of Mr. Brumley. At any rate he was able to produce this sentence without a qualm. "Life," he said, "is sometimes a very extraordinary thing."

Lady Harman reflected upon this statement and then responded with an air of remembered moments: "Isn't it."

"One loses the most precious things," said Mr. Brumley, "and one loses them and it seems as though one couldn't go on. And one goes on."

"And one finds oneself, " said Lady Harman, "without all sorts of precious things—" And she stopped, transparently realizing that she was saying too much.

"There is a sort of vitality about life," said Mr. Brumley, and stopped as if on the verge of profundities.

"I suppose one hopes," said Lady Harman. "And one doesn't think. And things happen."

"Things happen," assented Mr. Brumley.

For a little while their minds rested upon this thought, as chasing butterflies might rest together on a flower.

"And so I am going to leave this," Mr. Brumley resumed. "I am going up there to London for a time with my boy. Then perhaps we may travel—Germany, Italy, perhaps—in his holidays. It is beginning again, I feel with him. But then even we two must drift apart. I can't deny him a public school sooner or later. His own road. . . ."

"It will be lonely for you," sympathized the lady.

"I have my work," said Mr. Brumley with a sort of valiant sadness.

"Yes, I suppose your work—"

She left an eloquent gap.

"There, of course, one's fortunate," said Mr. Brumley.

"I wish," said Lady Harman, with a sudden frankness and a little quickening of her color, "that I had some work. Something—that was my own."

"But you have— There are social duties. There must be all sorts of things."

"There are—all sorts of things. I suppose I'm ungrateful. I have my children."

"You have children, Lady Harman!"

"I've *four*."

He was really astonished. "Your *own?*"

She turned her fawn's eyes on his with a sudden wonder at his meaning. "My own!" she said with the faintest tinge of astonished laughter in her voice. "What else could they be?"

"I thought— I thought you might have stepchildren."

"Oh! of course! No! I'm their mother;—all four of them. They're mine as far as that goes. Anyhow."

And her eye questioned him again for his intentions.

But his thought ran along its own path. "You see," he said, "there is something about you—so freshly beginning life. So like—Spring."

"You thought I was too young! I'm nearly six-and-twenty! But all the same,—though they're mine,—*still*— Why shouldn't a woman have work in the world, Mr. Brumley? In spite of all that."

"But surely—that's the most beautiful work in the world that anyone could possibly have."

Lady Harman reflected. She seemed to hesitate on the verge of some answer and not to say it.

"You see," she said, "it may have been different with you. . . . When one has a lot of nurses, and not very much authority."

She colored deeply and broke back from the impending revelations.

"No," she said, "I would like some work of my own."

3

At this point their conversation was interrupted by the lady's chauffeur in a manner that struck Mr. Brumley as extraordinary, but which the tall lady evidently regarded as the most natural thing in the world.

Mr. Clarence appeared walking across the lawn towards them, surveying the charms of as obviously a charming garden as one could have, with the disdain and hostility natural to a chauffeur. He did not so much touch his cap as indicate that it was within reach, and that he could if he pleased touch it. "It's time you were going, my lady," he said. "Sir Isaac will be coming back by the five-twelve, and there'll be a nice to-do if you ain't at home and me at the station and everything in order again."

Manifestly an abnormal expedition.

"Must we start at once, Clarence?" asked the lady consulting a bracelet watch. "You surely won't take two hours—"

"I can give you fifteen minutes more, my lady," said Clarence, "provided I may let her out and take my corners just exactly in my own way."

"And I must give you tea," said Mr. Brumley, rising to his feet. "And there is the kitchen."

"And upstairs! I'm afraid, Clarence, for this occasion only you must—what is it?—let her out."

"And no 'Oh Clarence!' my lady?"

She ignored that.

"I'll tell Mrs. Rabbit at once," said Mr. Brumley, and started to run and trod in some complicated way on one of his loose laces and was precipitated down the rockery steps. "Oh!" cried the lady. "Mind!" and clasped her hands.

He made a sound exactly like the word "damnation" as he fell, but he didn't so much get up as bounce up, apparently in the brightest of tempers, and laughed, held out two earthy hands for sympathy with a mock rueful grimace, and went on, earthy-green at the knees and a little more carefully towards the house. Clarence, having halted to drink deep satisfaction from this disaster, made his way along a nearly parallel path towards the kitchen, leaving his lady to follow as she chose to the house.

"*You'll* take a cup of tea?" called Mr. Brumley.

"Oh! *I'll* take a cup all right," said Clarence in the kindly voice of one who addresses an amusing inferior. . . .

Mrs. Rabbit had already got the tea-things out upon the cane table in the pretty veranda, and took it ill that she should be supposed not to have thought of these preparations.

Mr. Brumley disappeared for a few minutes into the house.

He returned with a conscious relief on his face, clean hands, brushed knees, and his boots securely laced. He found Lady Harman already pouring out tea.

"You see," she said, to excuse this pleasant enterprise on her part, "my husband has to be met at the station with the car. . . . And of course he has no idea—"

She left what it was of which Sir Isaac had no idea to the groping speculations of Mr. Brumley.

4

That evening Mr. Brumley was quite unable to work. His mind was full of this beautiful dark lady who had come so unexpectedly into his world.

Perhaps there are such things as premonitions. At any rate he had an altogether disproportionate sense of the significance of the afternoon's adventure,—which after all was a very small adventure indeed. A mere talk. His mind refused to leave her, her black furry slenderness, her dark trustful eyes, the sweet firmness of her perfect lips, her appealing simplicity that was yet somehow compatible with the completest self-possession. He went over the incident of the board again and again, scraping his memory for any lurking crumb of detail as a starving man might scrape an insufficient plate. Her dignity, her gracious frank forgiveness; no queen alive in these days could have touched her. . . . But it wasn't a mere elaborate admiration. There was something about her, about the quality of their meeting.

Most people know that sort of intimation. This person, it says, so fine, so brave, so distant still in so many splendid and impressive qualities, is yet in ways as yet undefined and unexplored, subtly and abundantly—for *you.* It was that made all her novelty and distinction and high quality and beauty so dominating among Mr. Brumley's thoughts. Without that his interest might have been almost entirely—academic. But there was woven all through her the hints of an imaginable alliance, with *us,* with the things that are Brumley, with all that makes beautiful little cottages and resents advertisements in lovely places, with us as against something over there lurking behind that board, something else, something out of which she came. He vaguely adumbrated what it was out of which she came. A closed narrow life—with horrid vast enviable quantities of money. A life, could one use the word *vulgar?*—so that Carpaccio, Della Robbia, old furniture, a garden unostentatiously perfect, and the atmosphere of *belles-lettres,* seemed things of another more desirable world. (She had never been abroad.) A world, too, that would be so willing, so happy to enfold her, furs, funds, freshness— everything.

And all this was somehow animated by the stirring warmth in the June weather, for spring raised the sap in Mr. Brumley as well as in his trees, had been a restless time for him all his life. This spring particularly had sensitized him, and now a light had shone.

He was so unable to work that for twenty minutes he sat over a pleasant little essay on Shakespeare's garden that by means of a concordance and his natural aptitude he was writing for the book of the National Shakespeare Theatre, without adding a single fancy to its elegant playfulness. Then he decided he needed his afternoon's walk after all, and he took cap and stick and went out, and presently found himself surveying that yellow and blue board and seeing it from an entirely new point of view. . . .

It seemed to him that he hadn't made the best use of his conversational opportunities, and for a time this troubled him. . . .

Towards the twilight he was walking along the path that runs through the heather along the edge of the rusty dark ironstone lake opposite the pinewoods. He spoke his thoughts aloud to the discreet bat that flitted about him. "I wonder," he said, "whether I shall ever set eyes on her again. . . ."

In the small hours when he ought to have been fast asleep he decided she would certainly take the house, and that he would see her again quite a number of times. A long tangle of unavoidable detail for discussion might be improvised by an ingenious man. And the rest of that waking interval passed in such inventions, which became more and more vague and magnificent and familiar as Mr. Brumley lapsed into slumber again. . . .

Next day the garden essay was still neglected, and he wrote a pretty vague little song about an earthly mourner and a fresh presence that set him thinking of the story of Persephone and how she passed in the springtime up from the shadows again, blessing as she passed. . . .

He pulled himself together about midday, cycled over to Gorshott for lunch at the clubhouse and a round with Horace Toomer in the afternoon, re-read the poem after tea, decided it was poor, tore it up and got himself down to his little fantasy about Shakespeare's Garden for a good two hours before supper. It was a sketch of that fortunate poet (whose definitive immortality is now being assured by an influential committee) walking around his Stratford garden with his daughter, quoting himself copiously with an accuracy and inappropriateness that reflected more credit upon his heart than upon his head, and saying in addition many distinctively Brumley things. When Mrs. Rabbit, with a solicitude acquired from the late Mrs. Brumley, asked him how he had got on with his work—the sight of verse on his paper had made her anxious—he could answer quite truthfully, "Like a house afire."

CHAPTER THE SECOND

The Personality of Sir Isaac

1

IT IS TO be remarked that two facts, usually esteemed as supremely important in the life of a woman, do not seem to have affected Mr. Brumley's state of mind nearly so much as quite trivial personal details about Lady Harman. The first of these facts was the existence of the lady's four children, and the second, Sir Isaac.

Mr. Brumley did not think very much of either of these two facts; if he had they would have spoiled the portrait in his mind; and when he did think of them it was chiefly to think how remarkably little they were necessary to that picture's completeness.

He spent some little time however trying to recall exactly what it was she had said about her children. He couldn't now succeed in reproducing her words, if indeed it had been by anything so explicit as words that she had conveyed to him that she didn't feel her children were altogether hers. "Incidental results of the collapse of her girlhood," tried Mr. Brumley, "when she married Harman."

Expensive nurses, governesses—the best that money without prestige or training could buy. And then probably a mother-in-law.

And as for Harman—?

There Mr. Brumley's mind desisted for sheer lack of material. Given this lady and that board and his general impression of Harman's refreshment and confectionery activity—the data were insufficient. A commonplace man no doubt, a tradesman, energetic perhaps and certainly a little brassy, successful by the chances of that economic revolution which everywhere replaces the isolated shop by the syndicated enterprise, irrationally conceited about it; a man perhaps ultimately to be pitied—with this young goddess finding herself. . . . Mr. Brumley's mind sat down comfortably to the more congenial theme of a young goddess finding herself, and it was only very gradually in the course of several days that the personality of Sir Isaac began to assume its proper importance in the scheme of his imaginings.

2

In the afternoon as he went around the links with Horace Toomer he got some definite lights upon Sir Isaac.

His mind was so full of Lady Harman that he couldn't but talk of her visit. "I've a possible tenant for my cottage," he said as he and Toomer, full of the sunny contentment of English gentlemen who had played a proper game in a proper manner, strolled back towards the clubhouse. "That man Harman."

"Not the International Stores and Staminal Bread man."

"Yes. Odd. Considering my hatred of his board."

"He ought to pay—anyhow," said Toomer. "They say he has a pretty wife and keeps her shut up."

"She came," said Brumley, neglecting to add the trifling fact that she had come alone.

"Pretty?"

"Charming, I thought."

"He's jealous of her. Someone was saying that the chauffeur has orders not to take her into London—only for trips in the country. They live in a big ugly house I'm told on Putney Hill. Did she in any way *look*—as though—?''

"Not in the least. If she isn't an absolutely straight young woman I've never set eyes on one."

"*He,*" said Toomer, "is a disgusting creature."

"Morally?"

"No, but—generally. Spends his life ruining little tradesmen, for the fun of the thing. He's three parts an invalid with some obscure kidney disease. Sometimes he spends whole days in bed, drinking Contrexéville Water and planning the bankruptcy of decent men. . . . So the party made a knight of him."

"A party must have funds, Toomer."

"He didn't pay nearly enough. Blapton is an idiot with the honors. When it isn't Mrs. Blapton. What can you expect when ▬▬▬ ▬▬▬▬''

(But here Toomer became libellous.)

Toomer was an interesting type. He had a disagreeable disposition profoundly modified by a public school and university training. Two antagonistic forces made him. He was the spirit of scurrility incarnate, that was, as people say, innate; and by virtue of those molding forces he was doing his best to be an English gentleman. That mysterious impulse which compels the young male to make objectionable imputations against seemly lives and to write rare inelegant words upon clean and decent things burned almost intolerably within him, and equally powerful now was the gross craving he had acquired for personal association with all that is prominent, all that is successful, all that is of good report. He had found his resultant in the censorious defense of established things. He conducted the *British Critic,* attacking with a merciless energy all that was new, all that was critical, all those fresh and noble tentatives that admit of unsavory interpretations, and when the urgent Yahoo in him carried him below the pretentious dignity of his accustomed organ he would squirt out his bitterness in a little sham facetious bookstall volume with a bright cover and quaint woodcuts, in which just as many prominent people as possible were mentioned by name and a sauce of general absurdity could be employed to cover and, if need be, excuse particular libels. So he managed to relieve himself and get along. Harman was just on the borderline of the class he considered himself free to revile. Harman was an outsider and aggressive and new, one of Mrs. Blapton's knights, and of no particular weight in society; so far he was fair game; but he was not so new as he had been, he was almost through with the running of the Toomer gauntlet, he had a tremendous lot of money and it was with a modified vehemence that the distinguished journalist and humorist expatiated on his offensiveness to Mr. Brumley. He talked in a gentle, rather weary voice, that came through a moustache like a fringe of light tobacco.

"Personally I've little against the man. A wife too young for him and jealously guarded, but that's all to his credit. Nowadays. If it wasn't for his blatancy in his business. . . . And the knighthood. . . . I suppose he can't resist taking anything he can get. Bread made by wholesale and distributed like a newspaper can't, I feel, be the same thing as the loaf of your honest old-fashioned baker— each loaf made with individual attention—out of wholesome English flour— hand-ground—with a personal touch for each customer. Still, everything drifts on to these hugger-mugger large enterprises; Chicago spreads over the world. One thing goes after another, tobacco, tea, bacon, drugs, bookselling. Decent homes destroyed right and left. Not Harman's affair, I suppose. The girls in his London tea-shops have of course to supplement their wages by prostitution— probably don't object to that nowadays considering the novels we have. And his effect on the landscape— Until they stopped him he was trying very hard to get Shakespeare's Cliff at Dover. He did for a time have the Toad Rock at Tunbridge. Still''—something like a sigh escaped from Toomer,—''his private life appears to be almost as blameless as anybody's can be. . . . Thanks no doubt to his defective health. I made the most careful enquiries when his knighthood was first discussed. Someone has to. Before his marriage he seems to have lived at home with his mother. At Highbury. Very quietly and inexpensively.''

''Then he's not the conventional vulgarian?''

''Much more of the Rockefeller type. Bad health, great concentration, organizing power. . . . Applied of course to a narrower range of business. . . . I'm glad I'm not a small confectioner in a town he wants to take up.''

''He's—hard?''

''Merciless. Hasn't the beginnings of an idea of fair play. . . . None at all. . . . No human give or take. . . . Are you going to have tea here, or are you walking back now?''

3

It was fully a week before Mr. Brumley heard anything more of Lady Harman. He began to fear that this shining furry presence would glorify Black Strand no more. Then came a telegram that filled him with the liveliest anticipations. It was worded: ''Coming see cottage Saturday afternoon Harman. . . .''

On Saturday morning Mr. Brumley dressed with an apparent ease and unusual care. . . .

He worked rather discursively before lunch. His mind was busy picking up the ends of their previous conversation and going on with them to all sorts of bright knots, bows and elegant cats' cradling. He planned openings that might give her tempting opportunities of confidences if she wished to confide, and artless remarks and questions that would make for self-betrayal if she didn't. And he thought of her, he thought of her imaginatively, this secluded rare thing so happily come to him, who was so young, so frank and fresh and so unhappily married (he was sure) to a husband at least happily mortal. Yes, dear Reader, even on that opening morning Mr. Brumley's imagination, trained very largely upon Victorian literature and *belles-lettres,* leaped forward to the very ending of this story. . . . We, of course, do nothing of the sort, our lot is to follow a more pedestrian route. . . . He lapsed into a vague series of meditations, slower perhaps but essentially similar, after his temperate palatable lunch.

He was apprised of the arrival of his visitor by the sudden indignant yaup followed by the general subdued uproar of a motor-car outside the front door, even before Clarence, this time amazingly prompt, assaulted the bell. Then the whole house was like that poem by Edgar Allan Poe, one magnificent texture of clangor.

At the first toot of the horn Mr. Brumley had moved swiftly into the bay, and screened partly by the life-size Venus of Milo that stood in the bay window, and partly by the artistic curtains, surveyed the glittering vehicle. He was first aware of a vast fur coat enclosing a lean gray-headed obstinate-looking man with a diabetic complexion who was fumbling with the door of the car and preventing Clarence's assistance. Mr. Brumley was able to remark that the gentleman's nose projected to a sharpened point, and that his thin-lipped mouth was all awry and had a kind of habitual compression, the while that his eyes sought eagerly for the other occupant of the car. She was unaccountably invisible. Could it be that that hood really concealed her? Could it be . . . ?

The white-faced gentleman descended, relieved himself tediously of the vast fur coat, handed it to Clarence and turned to the house. Reverentially Clarence placed the coat within the automobile and closed the door. Still the protesting mind of Mr. Brumley refused to believe! . . .

He heard the house-door open and Mrs. Rabbit in colloquy with a flat masculine voice. He heard his own name demanded and conceded. Then a silence, not the faintest suggestion of a feminine rustle, and then the sound of Mrs. Rabbit at the door-handle. Conviction stormed the last fastness of the disappointed author's mind.

"Oh *damn!*" he shouted with extreme fervor.

He had never imagined it was possible that Sir Isaac could come alone.

4

But the house had to be let, and it had to be let to Sir Isaac Harman. In another moment an amiable though distinguished man of letters was in the hall interviewing the great *entrepreneur*.

The latter gentleman was perhaps three inches shorter than Mr. Brumley, his hair was gray-shot brown, his face clean-shaven, his features had a thin irregularity, and he was dressed in a neat brown suit with a necktie very exactly matching it. "Sir Isaac Harman?" said Mr. Brumley with a note of gratification.

"That's it," said Sir Isaac. He appeared to be nervous and a little out of breath. "Come," he said, "just to look over it. Just to see it. Probably too small, but if it doesn't put you out—"

He blew out the skin of his face about his mouth a little.

"Delighted to see you anyhow," said Mr. Brumley, filling the world of unspoken things with singularly lurid curses.

"This. Nice little hall,—very," said Sir Isaac. "Pretty, that bit at the end. Many rooms are there?"

Mr. Brumley answered inexactly and meditated a desperate resignation of the whole job to Mrs. Rabbit. Then he made an effort and began to explain.

"That clock," said Sir Isaac interrupting in the dining-room, "is a fake."

Mr. Brumley made silent interrogations.

"Been there myself," said Sir Isaac. "They sell those brass fittings in Ho'bun."

They went upstairs together. When Mr. Brumley wasn't explaining or pointing out, Sir Isaac made a kind of whistling between his clenched teeth. "This bathroom wants refitting anyhow," he said abruptly. "I daresay Lady Harman would like that room with the bay—but it's all—small. It's really quite pretty; you've done it cleverly, but—the size of it! I'd have to throw out a wing. And that you know might spoil the style. That roof,—a gardener's cottage? . . . I thought it might be. What's this other thing here? Old barn. Empty? That might expand a bit. Couldn't do only just this anyhow."

He walked in front of Mr. Brumley downstairs and still emitting that faint whistle led the way into the garden. He seemed to regard Mr. Brumley merely as a source of answers to his questions, and a seller in process of preparation for an offer. It was clear he meant to make an offer. "It's not the house I should buy if I was alone in this," he said, "but Lady Harman's taken a fancy somehow. And it might be adapted. . . ."

From first to last Mr. Brumley never said a single word about Euphemia and the young matrimony and all the other memories this house enshrined. He felt instinctively that it would not affect Sir Isaac one way or the other. He tried simply to seem indifferent to whether Sir Isaac bought the place or not. He tried to make it appear almost as if houses like this often happened to him, and interested him only in the most incidental manner. They had their proper price, he tried to convey, which of course no gentleman would underbid.

In the exquisite garden Sir Isaac said: "One might make a very pretty little garden of this—if one opened it out a bit."

And of the sunken rock-garden: "That might be dangerous of a dark night."

"I suppose," he said, indicating the hill of pines behind, "one could buy or lease some of that. If one wanted to throw it into the place and open out more.

"From my point of view," he said, "it isn't a house. It's—" He sought in his mind for an expression—"a Cottage Ornay."

This history declines to record either what Mr. Brumley said or what he did not say.

Sir Isaac surveyed the house thoughtfully for some moments from the turf edging of the great herbaceous border.

"How far," he asked, "is it from the nearest railway station? . . ."

Mr. Brumley gave details.

"Four miles. And an infrequent service? Nothing in any way suburban? Better to motor into Guildford and get the Express. H'm . . . And what sort of people do we get about here?"

Mr. Brumley sketched.

"Mildly horsey. That's not bad. No officers about? . . . Nothing nearer than Aldershot . . . That's eleven miles, is it? H'm. I suppose there aren't any *literary* people about here, musicians or that kind of thing, no advanced people of that sort?"

"Not when I've gone," said Mr. Brumley, with the faintest flavor of humor.

Sir Isaac stared at him for a moment with eyes vacantly thoughtful.

"It mightn't be so bad," said Sir Isaac, and whistled a little between his teeth.

Mr. Brumley was suddenly minded to take his visitor to see the view and the effect of his board upon it. But he spoke merely of the view and left Sir Isaac to discover the board or not as he thought fit. As they ascended among the trees, the visitor was manifestly seized by some strange emotion, his face became very white, he gasped and blew for breath, he felt for his face with a nervous hand.

"Four thousand," he said suddenly. "An outside price."

"A minimum," said Mr. Brumley, with a slight quickening of the pulse.

"You won't get three eight," gasped Sir Isaac.

"Not a business man, but my agent tells me—" panted Mr. Brumley.

"Three eight," said Sir Isaac.

"We're just coming to the view," said Mr. Brumley. "Just coming to the view."

"Practically got to rebuild the house," said Sir Isaac.

"There!" said Mr. Brumley, and waved an arm widely.

Sir Isaac regarded the prospect with a dissatisfied face. His pallor had given place to a shiny, flushed appearance, his nose, his ears, and his cheeks were pink. He blew his face out, and seemed to be studying the landscape for defects. "This might be built over at any time," he complained.

Mr. Brumley was reassuring.

For a brief interval Sir Isaac's eyes explored the countryside vaguely, then his expression seemed to concentrate and run together to a point. "H'm," he said.

"That board," he remarked, "quite wrong there."

"*Well!*" said Mr. Brumley, too surprised for coherent speech.

"Quite," said Sir Isaac Harman. "Don't you see what's the matter?"

Mr. Brumley refrained from an eloquent response.

"They ought to be," Sir Isaac went on, "white and a sort of green. Like the County Council notices on Hampstead Heath. So as to blend. . . . You see, an ad. that hits too hard is worse than no ad. at all. It leaves a dislike. . . . Advertisements ought to blend. It ought to seem as though all this view were saying it. Not just that board. Now suppose we had a shade of very light brown, a kind of light khaki—"

He turned a speculative eye on Mr. Brumley as if he sought for the effect of this latter suggestion on him.

"If the whole board was invisible—" said Mr. Brumley.

Sir Isaac considered it. "Just the letters showing, " he said. "No,—that would be going too far in the other direction."

He made a faint sucking noise with his lips and teeth as he surveyed the landscape and weighed this important matter. . . .

"Queer how one gets ideas," he said at last, turning away. "It was my wife told me about that board."

He stopped to survey the house from the exact point of view his wife had taken nine days before. "I wouldn't give this place a second thought," said Sir Isaac, "if it wasn't for Lady Harman."

He confided. "*She* wants a weekend cottage. But *I* don't see why it *should* be a weekend cottage. I don't see why it shouldn't be made into a nice little country house. Compact, of course. By using up that barn."

He inhaled three bars of a tune. "London," he explained, "doesn't suit Lady Harman."

"Health?" asked Mr. Brumley, all alert.

"It isn't her health exactly," Sir Isaac dropped out. "You see—she's a young woman. She gets ideas.

"You know," he continued, "I'd like to have a look at that barn again. If we develop that—and a sort of corridor across where the shrubs are—and ran out offices. . . ."

5

Mr. Brumley's mind was still vigorously struggling with the flaming implications of Sir Isaac's remark that Lady Harman "got ideas," and Sir Isaac was gently whistling his way towards an offer of three thousand nine hundred when they came down out of the pines into the path along the edge of the herbaceous border. And then Mr. Brumley became aware of an effect away between the white-stemmed trees towards the house as if the Cambridge boat-race crew was indulging in a vigorous scrimmage. Drawing nearer this resolved itself into the fluent contours of Lady Beach-Mandarin, dressed in sky-blue and with a black summer straw hat larger than ever and trimmed effusively with marguerites.

"Here," said Sir Isaac, "can't I get off? You've got a friend."

"You must have some tea," said Mr. Brumley, who wanted to suggest that they should agree to Sir Isaac's figure of three thousand eight hundred, but not as pounds but guineas. It seemed to him a suggestion that might prove insidiously attractive. "It's a charming lady, my friend Lady Beach-Mandarin. She'll be delighted—"

"I don't think I can," said Sir Isaac. "Not in the habit—social occasions."

His face expressed a panic terror of this gallant full-rigged lady ahead of them.

"But you see now," said Mr. Brumley, with a detaining grip, "it's unavoidable."

And the next moment Sir Isaac was mumbling his appreciations of the introduction.

I must admit that Lady Beach-Mandarin was almost as much to meet as one can meet in a single human being, a broad abundant billowing personality with a taste for brims, streamers, pennants, panniers, loose sleeves, sweeping gestures, top notes and the like that made her altogether less like a woman than an occasion of public rejoicing. Even her large blue eyes projected, her chin and brows and nose all seemed racing up to the front of her as if excited by the clarion notes of her abundant voice, and the pinkness of her complexion was as exuberant as her manners. Exuberance—it was her word. She had evidently been a big, bouncing, bright gaminesque girl at fifteen, and very amusing and very much admired; she had liked the rôle and she had not so much grown older as suffered enlargement—a very considerable enlargement.

"Ah!" she cried, "and so I've caught you at home, Mr. Brumley! And, poor dear, you're at my mercy." And she shook both his hands with both of hers.

That was before Mr. Brumley introduced Sir Isaac, a thing he did so soon as he could get one of his hands loose and wave a surviving digit or so at that gentleman.

"You see, Sir Isaac," she said, taking him in, in the most generous way; "I and Mr. Brumley are old friends. We knew each other of yore. We have our jokes."

Sir Isaac seemed to feel the need of speech but got no further than a useful all-round noise.

"And one of them is that when I want him to do the least little thing for me he hides away! Always. By a sort of instinct. It's such a Small thing, Sir Isaac."

Sir Isaac was understood to say vaguely that they always did. But he had become very indistinct.

"Aren't I always at your service?" protested Mr. Brumley with a responsive playfulness. "And I don't even know what it is you want."

Lady Beach-Mandarin, addressing herself exclusively to Sir Isaac, began a tale of a Shakespeare Bazaar she was holding in an adjacent village, and how she knew Mr. Brumley (naughty man) meant to refuse to give her autographed copies of his littlest book for the Book Stall she was organizing. Mr. Brumley confuted her gaily and generously. So discoursing they made their way to the veranda where Lady Harman had so lately "poured."

Sir Isaac was borne along upon the lady's stream of words in a state of mulish reluctance, nodding, saying "Of course " and similar phrases, and wishing he was out of it all with an extreme manifestness. He drank his tea with unmistakable discomfort, and twice inserted into the conversation an entirely irrelevant remark that he had to be going. But Lady Beach-Mandarin had her purposes with him and crushed these quivering tentatives.

Lady Beach-Mandarin had of course like everybody else at that time her own independent movement in the great national effort to create an official British Theatre upon the basis of William Shakespeare, and she saw in the as yet unenlisted resources of Sir Isaac strong possibilities of reinforcement of her own particular contribution to the great Work. He was manifestly shy and sulky and disposed to bolt at the earliest possible moment, and so she set herself now with a swift and concentrated combination of fascination and urgency to commit him to participations. She flattered and cajoled and bribed. She was convinced that even to be called upon by Lady Beach-Mandarin is no light privilege for these new commercial people, and so she made no secret of her intention of decorating the hall of his large but undistinguished house in Putney, with her redeeming pasteboard. She appealed to the instances of Venice and Florence to show that "such men as you, Sir Isaac," who control commerce and industry, have always been the guardians and patrons of art. And who more worthy of patronage than William Shakespeare? Also she said that men of such enormous wealth as his owed something to their national tradition. "You have to pay your footing, Sir Isaac," she said with impressive vagueness.

"Putting it in round figures," said Sir Isaac, suddenly and with a white gleam of animosity in his face, the animosity of a trapped animal at the sight of its captors, "What does coming on your Committee mean, Lady Beach-Mandarin?"

"It's your name we want," said the lady, "but I'm sure you'd not be ungenerous. The tribute success owes the arts."

"A hundred?" he threw out,—his ears red.

"Guineas," breathed Lady Beach-Mandarin with a lofty sweetness of consent.

He stood up hastily as if to escape further exaction, and the lady rose too.

"And you'll let me call on Lady Harman," she said, honestly doing her part in the bargain.

"Can't keep the car waiting," was what Brumley could distinguish in his reply.

"I expect you have a perfectly splendid car, Sir Isaac," said Lady Beach-Mandarin, drawing him out. "Quite the modernest thing."

Sir Isaac replied with the reluctance of an Income Tax Return that it was a forty-five Rolls Royce, good of course but nothing amazing.

"We must see it," she said, and turned his retreat into a procession.

She admired the car, she admired the color of the car, she admired the lamps of the car and the door of the car and the little fittings of the car. She admired the horn. She admired the twist of the horn. She admired Clarence and the uniform of Clarence and she admired and coveted the great fur coat that he held ready for his employer. (But if she had it, she said, she would wear the splendid fur outside to show every little bit of it.) And when the car at last moved forward and tooted—she admired the note—and vanished softly and swiftly through the gates, she was left in the porch with Mr. Brumley still by sheer inertia admiring and envying. She admired Sir Isaac's car number Z 900. (Such an easy one to remember!) Then she stopped abruptly, as one might discover that the water in the bathroom was running to waste and turn it off.

She had a cynicism as exuberant as the rest of her.

"Well," she said, with a contented sigh and an entire flattening of her tone, "I laid it on pretty thick that time. . . . I wonder if he'll send me that hundred guineas or whether I shall have to remind him of it. . . ." Her manner changed again to that of a gigantic gamin. "I mean to have that money," she said with bright determination and round eyes. . . .

She reflected and other thoughts came to her. "Plutocracy," she said, "*is* perfectly detestable, don't you think so, Mr. Brumley?" . . . And then, "I can't *imagine* how a man who deals in bread and confectionery can manage to go about so completely half-baked."

"He's a very remarkable type," said Mr. Brumley.

He became urgent: "I do hope, dear Lady Beach-Mandarin, you will contrive to call on Lady Harman. She is—in relation to *that*—quite the most interesting woman I have seen."

6

Presently as they paced the croquet lawn together, the preoccupation of Mr. Brumley's mind drew their conversation back to Lady Harman.

"I wish," he repeated, "you would go and see these people. She's not at all what you might infer from him."

"What could one infer about a wife from a man like that? Except that she'd have a lot to put up with."

"You know,—she's a beautiful person, tall, slender, dark. . . ."

Lady Beach-Mandarin turned her full blue eye upon him.

"*Now!*" she said archly.

"I'm interested in the incongruity."

Lady Beach-Mandarin's reply was silent and singular. She compressed her lips very tightly, fixed her eye firmly on Mr. Brumley's, lifted her finger to the level of her left eyelash, and then shook it at him very deliberately five times. Then with a little sigh and a sudden and complete restoration of manner she remarked that never in any year before had she seen peonies quite so splendid. "I've a peculiar sympathy with peonies," she said. "They're so exactly my style."

CHAPTER THE THIRD

Lady Harman at Home

1

EXACTLY THREE WEEKS after that first encounter between Lady Beach-Mandarin and Sir Isaac Harman, Mr. Brumley found himself one of a luncheon party at that lady's house in Temperley Square and talking very freely and indiscreetly about the Harmans.

Lady Beach-Mandarin always had her luncheons in a family way at a large round table so that nobody could get out of her range, and she insisted upon conversation being general, except for her mother who was impenetrably deaf and the Swiss governess of her only daughter Phyllis who was incomprehensible in any European tongue. The mother was incalculably old and had been a friend of Victor Hugo and Alfred de Musset; she maintained an intermittent monologue about the private lives of those great figures; nobody paid the slightest attention to her but one felt she enriched the table with an undertow of literary associations. A small dark stealthy butler and a convulsive boy with hair (apparently) taking the place of eyes waited. On this occasion Lady Beach-Mandarin had gathered together two cousins, maiden ladies from Perth, wearing valiant hats, Toomer the wit and censor, and Miss Sharsper the novelist (whom Toomer detested), a gentleman named Roper whom she had invited under a misapprehension that he was the Arctic Roper, and Mr. Brumley. She had tried Mr. Roper with questions about penguins, seals, cold and darkness, icebergs and glaciers, Captain Scott, Doctor Cook and the shape of the earth, and all in vain, and feeling at last that something was wrong, she demanded abruptly whether Mr. Brumley had sold his house.

"I'm selling it," said Mr. Brumley, "by almost imperceptible degrees."

"He haggles?"

"Haggles and higgles. He higgles passionately. He goes white and breaks into a cold perspiration. He wants me now to include the gardener's tools—in whatever price we agree upon."

"A rich man like that ought to be easy and generous," said Lady Beach-Mandarin.

"Then he wouldn't be a rich man like that," said Mr. Toomer.

"But doesn't it distress you highly, Mr. Brumley," one of the Perth ladies asked, "to be leaving Euphemia's Home to strangers? The man may go altering it."

"That—that weighs with me very much," said Mr. Brumley, recalled to his professions. "There—I put my trust in Lady Harman."

"You've seen her again?" asked Lady Beach-Mandarin.

"Yes. She came with him—a few days ago. That couple interests me more and more. So little akin."

"There's eighteen years between them," said Toomer.

"It's one of those cases," began Mr. Brumley with a note of scientific detachment, "where one is really tempted to be ultra-feminist. It's clear, he uses every advantage. He's her owner, her keeper, her obstinate insensitive little tyrant. . . . And yet there's a sort of effect, as though nothing was decided. . . . As if she was only just growing up."

"They've been married six or seven years," said Toomer. "She was just eighteen."

"They went over the house together and whenever she spoke he contradicted her with a sort of vicious playfulness. Tried to poke clumsy fun at her. Called her 'Lady Harman.' Only it was quite evident that what she said stuck in his mind. . . . Very queer—interesting people."

"I wouldn't have anyone allowed to marry until they were five-and-twenty," said Lady Beach-Mandarin.

"Sweet seventeen sometimes contrives to be very marriageable," said the gentleman named Roper.

"Sweet seventeen must contrive to wait," said Lady Beach-Mandarin. "Sweet fourteen has to—and when I was fourteen—I was Ardent! There's no earthly objection to a little harmless flirtation of course. It's the marrying."

"You'd conduce to romance," said Miss Sharsper, "anyhow. Eighteen won't bear restriction and everyone would begin by eloping—illegally."

"I'd put them back," said Lady Beach-Mandarin. "Oh! remorselessly."

Mr. Roper, who was more and more manifestly not the Arctic one, remarked that she would "give the girls no end of an adolescence. . . ."

Mr. Brumley did not attend very closely to the subsequent conversation. His mind had gone back to Black Strand and the second visit that Lady Harman, this time under her natural and proper protection, had paid him. A little thread from the old lady's discourse drifted by him. She had scented marriage in the air and she was saying, "of course they ought to have let Victor Hugo marry over and over again. He would have made it all so beautiful. He could throw a Splendour over—over almost anything." Mr. Brumley sank out of attention altogether. It was so difficult to express his sense of Lady Harman as a captive, enclosed but unsubdued. She had been as open and shining as a celandine flower in the sunshine on that first invasion, but on the second it had been like overcast weather and her starry petals had been shut and still. She hadn't been in the least subdued or effaced, but closed, inaccessible to conversational bees, that astonishing honey of trust and easy friendship had been hidden in a dignified impenetrable reserve. She had had the effect of being not so much specially shut against Mr. Brumley as habitually shut against her husband, as a protection against his continual clumsy mental interferences. And once when Sir Isaac had made a sudden allusion to price Mr. Brumley had glanced at her and met her eyes. . . .

"Of course," he said, coming up to the conversational surface again, "a woman like that is bound to fight her way out."

"Queen Mary!" cried Miss Sharsper. "Fight her way out!"

"Queen Mary!" said Mr. Brumley, "No!— Lady Harman."

"*I* was talking of Queen Mary," said Miss Sharsper.

"And Mr. Brumley was thinking of Lady Harman!" cried Lady Beach-Mandarin.

"Well," said Mr. Brumley, "I confess I do think about her. She seems to me to be so typical in many ways of—of everything that is weak in the feminine position. As a type—yes, she's perfect."

"I've never seen this lady," said Miss Sharsper. "Is she beautiful?"

"I've not seen her myself yet," said Lady Beach-Mandarin. "She's Mr. Brumley's particular discovery."

"You haven't called?" he asked with a faint reproach.

"But I've been going to—oh! tremendously. And you revive all my curiosity. Why shouldn't some of us this very afternoon—?"

She caught at her own passing idea and held it. "Let's Go," she cried. "Let's visit the wife of this Ogre, the last of the women in captivity. We'll take the big car and make a party and call *en masse.*"

Mr. Toomer protested he had no morbid curiosities.

"But you, Susan?"

Miss Sharsper declared she would *love* to come. Wasn't it her business to study out-of-the-way types? Mr. Roper produced a knowing sort of engagement— "I'm provided for already, Lady Beach-Mandarin," he said, and the cousins from Perth had to do some shopping.

"Then we three will be the expedition," said the hostess. "And afterwards if we survive we'll tell you our adventures. It's a house on Putney Hill, isn't it, where this Christian maiden, so to speak, is held captive? I've had her in my mind, but I've always intended to call with Agatha Alimony; she's so inspiring to down-trodden women."

"Not exactly down-trodden," said Mr. Brumley, "not down-trodden. That's what's so curious about it."

"And what shall we do when we get there?" cried Lady Beach-Mandarin. "I feel we ought to do something more than call. Can't we carry her off right away, Mr. Brumley? I want to go right in to her and say 'Look here! I'm on your side. Your husband's a tyrant. I'm help and rescue. I'm all that a woman ought to be—fine and large. Come out from under that unworthy man's heel!' "

"Suppose she isn't at all the sort of person you seem to think she is," said Miss Sharsper. "And suppose she came!"

"Suppose she didn't," reflected Mr. Roper.

"I seem to see your flight," said Mr. Toomer. "And the newspaper placards and head-lines. 'Lady Beach-Mandarin elopes with the wife of an eminent confectioner. She is stopped at the landing stage by the staff of the Dover Branch establishment. Recapture of the fugitive after a hot struggle. Brumley, the eminent *littérateur,* stunned by a spent bun. . . . ' "

"We're all talking great nonsense," said Lady Beach-Mandarin. "But anyhow we'll make our call. And *I* know!—I'll make her accept an invitation to lunch without him."

"If she won't?" threw out Mr. Roper.

"I *will*," said Lady Beach-Mandarin with roguish determination. "And if I can't—"

"Not ask him too!" protested Mr. Brumley.

"Why not get her to come to your Social Friends meeting?" said Miss Sharsper.

2

When Mr. Brumley found himself fairly launched upon this expedition he had the grace to feel compunction. The Harmans, he perceived, had inadvertently made him the confidant of their domestic discords and to betray them to these others savored after all of treachery. And besides much as he had craved to see Lady Harman again, he now realized he didn't in the least want to see her in association with the exuberant volubility of Lady Beach-Mandarin and the hard professional observation, so remarkably like the ferrule of an umbrella being poked with a noiseless persistence into one's eye, of Miss Sharsper. And as he thought these afterthoughts Lady Beach-Mandarin's chauffeur darted and dodged and threaded his way with an alacrity that was almost distressing to Putney.

They ran over the ghost of Swinburne, at the foot of Putney Hill,—or perhaps it was only the rhythm of the engine changed for a moment, and in a couple of minutes more they were outside the Harman residence. "Here we are!" said Lady Beach-Mandarin, more capaciously gaminesque than ever. "We've done it now."

Mr. Brumley had an impression of a big house in the distended stately-homes-of-England style and very necessarily and abundantly covered by creepers and then he was assisting the ladies to descend and the three of them were waiting clustered in the ample Victorian doorway. For some little interval there came no answer to the bell Mr. Brumley had rung, but all three of them had a sense of hurried, furtive and noiseless readjustments in progress behind the big and bossy oak door. Then it opened and a very large egg-shaped butler with sandy whiskers appeared and looked down himself at them. There was something paternal about this man, his professional deference was touched by the sense of ultimate responsibility. He seemed to consider for a moment whether he should permit Lady Harman to be in, before he conceded that she was.

They were ushered through a hall that resembled most of the halls in the world, it was dominated by a handsome oak staircase and scarcely gave Miss Sharsper a point, and then across a creation of the Victorian architect, a massive kind of conservatory with classical touches—there was an impluvium in the center and there were arches hung with manifestly costly Syrian rugs, into a large apartment looking through four French windows upon a veranda and a large floriferous garden. At a sideways glance it seemed a very pleasant garden indeed. The room itself was like the rooms of so many prosperous people nowadays; it had an effect of being sedulously and yet irrelevantly over-furnished. It had none of the large vulgarity that Mr. Brumley would have considered proper to a wealthy caterer, but it confessed a compilation of "pieces" very carefully authenticated. Some of them were rather splendid "pieces"; three big bureaus burly and brassy dominated it; there was a Queen Anne cabinet, some exquisite colored engravings, an ormolu mirror and a couple of large French vases that set Miss Sharsper, who had a keen eye for this traffic, confusedly cataloguing. And a little incongruously in the midst of this exhibit, stood Lady Harman, as if she was trying to conceal the fact that she too was a visitor, in a creamy white dress and dark and defensive and yet entirely unabashed.

The great butler gave his large vague impression of Lady Beach-Mandarin's name, and stood aside and withdrew.

"I've heard so much of you," said Lady Beach-Mandarin advancing with hand upraised. "I had to call. Mr. Brumley—"

"Lady Beach-Mandarin met Sir Isaac at Black Strand," Mr. Brumley intervened to explain.

Miss Sharsper was as it were introduced by default.

"My vividest anticipations outdone," said Lady Beach-Mandarin, squeezing Lady Harman's fingers with enthusiasm. "And what a charming garden you have, and what a delightful situation! Such air! And on the very verge of London, high, on this delightful *literary* hill, and ready at any moment to swoop in that enviable great car of yours. I suppose you come a great deal into London, Lady Harman?"

"No," reflected Lady Harman, "not very much." She seemed to weigh the accuracy of this very carefully. "No," she added in confirmation.

"But you should, you ought to; it's your duty. You've no right to hide away fro us. I was telling Sir Isaac. We look to him, we look to you. You've no right to bury your talents away from us; you who are rich and young and brilliant and beautiful—

"But if I go on I shall begin to flatter you," said Lady Beach-Mandarin with a delicious smile. "I've begun upon Sir Isaac already. I've made him promise a hundred guineas and his name to the Shakespeare Dinners Society,—nothing he didn't mention eaten (*you* know) and all the profits to the National movement—and I want your name too. I know you'll let us have your name too. Grant me that, and I'll subside into the ordinariest of callers."

"But surely; isn't his name enough?" asked Lady Harman.

"Without yours, it's only half a name!" cried Lady Beach-Mandarin. "If it were a *business* thing—! Different of course. But on my list, I'm like dear old Queen Victoria you know, the wives must come too."

"In that case," hesitated Lady Harman. . . . "But really I think Sir Isaac—"

She stopped. And then Mr. Brumley had a psychic experience. It seemed to him as he stood observing Lady Harman with an entirely unnecessary and unpremeditated intentness, that for the briefest interval her attention flashed over Lady Beach-Mandarin's shoulder to the end veranda window; and following her glance, he saw—and then he did not see—the arrested figure, the white face of Sir Isaac, bearing an expression in which anger and horror were extraordinarily intermingled. If it was Sir Isaac he dodged back with amazing dexterity; if it was a phantom of the living it vanished with an air of doing that. Without came the sound of a flower-pot upset and a faint expletive. Mr. Brumley looked very quickly at Lady Beach-Mandarin, who was entirely unconscious of anything but her own uncoiling and enveloping eloquence, and as quickly at Miss Sharsper. But Miss Sharsper was examining a blackish bureau through her glasses as though she were looking for birthmarks and meant if she could find one to claim the piece as her own long-lost connection. With a mild but gratifying sense of exclusive complicity Mr. Brumley reverted to Lady Harman's entire self-possession.

"But, dear Lady Harman, it's entirely unnecessary you should consult him,—entirely," Lady Beach-Mandarin was saying.

"I'm sure," said Mr. Brumley with a sense that somehow he had to intervene, "that Sir Isaac would not possibly object. I'm sure that if Lady Harman consults him—"

The sandy-whiskered butler appeared hovering.

"Shall I place the tea-things in the garden, me lady?" he asked, in the tone of one who knows the answer.

"Oh *please* in the garden!" cried Lady Beach-Mandarin. "Please! And how delightful to *have* a garden, a London garden, in which one *can* have tea. Without being smothered in blacks. The southwest wind. The dear *English* wind. All your blacks come to *us,* you know."

She led the way upon the veranda. "Such a wonderful garden! The space, the breadth! Why! you must have Acres!"

She surveyed the garden—comprehensively; her eye rested for a moment on a distant patch of black that ducked suddenly into a group of lilacs. "Is dear Sir Isaac at home?" she asked.

"He's very uncertain," said Lady Harman, with a quiet readiness that pleased Mr. Brumley. "Yes, Snagsby, please, under the big cypress. And tell my mother and sister."

Lady Beach-Mandarin having paused a moment or so upon the veranda admiring the garden as a whole, now prepared to go into details. She gathered her ample skirts together and advanced into the midst of the large lawn, with very much of the effect of a fleet of captive balloons dragging their anchors. Mr. Brumley followed, as it were in attendance upon her and Lady Harman. Miss Sharsper, after one last hasty glance at the room, rather like the last hasty glance of a still unprepared schoolboy at his book, came behind with her powers of observation strainingly alert.

Mr. Brumley was aware of a brief mute struggle between the two ladies of title. It was clear that Lady Harman would have had them go to the left, to where down a vista of pillar roses a single large specimen cypress sounded a faint but recognizable Italian note, and he did his loyal best to support her, but Lady Beach-Mandarin's attraction to that distant clump of lilac on the right was equally great and much more powerful. She flowed, a great and audible tide of socially influential womanhood, across the green spaces of the garden, and drew the others with her. And it seemed to Mr. Brumley—not that he believed his eyes—that beyond those lilacs something ran out, something black that crouched close to the ground and went very swiftly. It flashed like an arrow across a further space of flower-bed, dropped to the ground, became two agitatedly receding boot soles and was gone. Had it ever been? He glanced at Lady Harman, but she was looking back with the naïve anxiety of a hostess to her cypress,— at Lady Beach-Mandarin, but she was proliferating compliments and decorative scrolls and flourishes like the engraved frontispiece to a seventeenth-century book.

"I know I'm inordinately curious," said Lady Beach-Mandarin, "but gardens are my Joy. I want to go into every corner of this. Peep into everything. And I feel somehow"—and here she urged a smile on Lady Harman's attention—"that I shan't begin to know *you,* until I know all your environment."

She turned the flank of the lilacs as she said these words and advanced in echelon with a stately swiftness upon the laurels beyond.

Lady Harman said there was nothing beyond but sycamores and the fence, but Lady Beach-Mandarin would press on through a narrow path that pierced the laurel hedge, in order, she said, that she might turn back and get the whole effect of the grounds.

And so it was they discovered the mushroom shed.

"A mushroom shed!" cried Lady Beach-Mandarin. "And if we look in— shall we see hosts and regiments of mushrooms? I must—I must."

"I *think* it is locked," said Lady Harman.

Mr. Brumley darted forward; tried the door and turned quickly. "It's locked," he said and barred Lady Beach-Mandarin's advance.

"And besides," said Lady Harman, "there's no mushrooms there. They won't come up. It's one of my husband's—annoyances."

Lady Beach-Mandarin had turned around and now surveyed the house. "What a splendid idea," she cried, "that wisteria! All mixed with the laburnum. I don't think I have ever seen such a charming combination of blossoms!"

The whole movement of the party swept about and faced cypress-ward. Away there the sandy-whiskered butler and a footman and basket chairs and a tea-table, with a shining white cloth, and two ladies were now grouping themselves. . . .

But the mind of Mr. Brumley gave little heed to these things. His mind was full of a wonder, and the wonder was this, that the mushroom shed had behaved like a living thing. The door of the mushroom shed was not locked and in that matter he had told a lie. The door of the mushroom shed had been unlocked quite recently and the key and padlock had been dropped upon the ground. And when he had tried to open the mushroom shed it had first of all yielded to his hand and then it had closed again with great strength—exactly as a living mussel will behave if one takes it unawares. But in addition to this passionate contraction the mushroom shed had sworn in a hoarse whisper and breathed hard, which is more than your mussel can do. . . .

3

Mr. Brumley's interest in Lady Harman was to be almost too crowded by detail before that impulsive call was over. Superposed upon the mystery of the mushroom shed was the vivid illumination of Lady Harman by her mother and sister. They had an effect of having reluctantly become her social inferiors for her own good; the mother—her name he learned was Mrs. Sawbridge—had all Lady Harman's tall slenderness, but otherwise resembled her only in the poise of her neck and an occasional gesture; she was fair and with a kind of ignoble and premeditated refinement in her speech and manner. She was dressed with the restraint of a prolonged and attenuated widowhood, in a rich and complicatedly quiet dress of mauve and gray. She was obviously a transitory visitor and not so much taking the opulence about her and particularly the great butler for granted as pointedly and persistently ignoring it in an effort to seem to take it for granted. The sister, on the other hand, had Lady Harman's pale darkness but none of her fineness of line. She missed altogether that quality of fineness. Her darkness was done with a quite perceptible heaviness, her dignity passed into solidity and her profile was, with an entire want of hesitation, handsome. She was evidently the elder by a space of some years and she was dressed with severity in gray.

These two ladies seemed to Mr. Brumley to offer a certain resistance of spirit to the effusion of Lady Beach-Mandarin, rather as two small anchored vessels might resist the onset of a great and foaming tide, but after a time it was clear they admired her greatly. His attention was, however, a little distracted from them by the fact that he was the sole representative of the more serviceable sex among five women and so in duty bound to stand by Lady Harman and assist with various handings and offerings. The tea equipage was silver and not only magnificent but, as certain quick movements of Miss Sharsper's eyes and nose at its appearance betrayed, very genuine and old.

Lady Beach-Mandarin having praised the house and garden all over again to Mrs. Sawbridge, and having praised the cypress and envied the tea things, resumed her efforts to secure the immediate establishment of permanent social relations with Lady Harman. She reverted to the question of the Shakespeare Dinners Society and now with a kind of large skilfulness involved Mrs. Sawbridge in her appeal. "Won't *you* come on our Committee?" said Lady Beach-Mandarin.

Mrs. Sawbridge gave a pinched smile and said she was only staying in London for quite a little time, and when pressed admitted that there seemed no need whatever for consulting Sir Isaac upon so obviously foregone a conclusion as Lady Harman's public adhesion to the great movement.

"I shall put his hundred guineas down to Sir Isaac and Lady Harman," said Lady Beach-Mandarin with an air of conclusion, "and now I want to know, dear Lady Harman, whether we can't have *you* on our Committee of administration. We want—just one other woman to complete us."

Lady Harman could only parry with doubts of her ability.

"You ought to go on, Ella," said Miss Sawbridge suddenly, speaking for the first time and in a manner richly suggestive of great principles at stake.

"Ella," thought the curious mind of Mr. Brumley. "And is that Eleanor now or Ellen or—is there any other name that gives one Ella? Simply Ella?"

"But what should I have to do?" fenced Lady Harman, resisting but obviously attracted.

Lady Beach-Mandarin invented a lengthy paraphrase for prompt acquiescences.

"I shall be chairwoman," she crowned it with. "I can so easily *see you through* as they say."

"Ella doesn't go out half enough," said Miss Sawbridge suddenly to Miss Sharsper, who was regarding her with furtive intensity—as if she was surreptitiously counting her features.

Miss Sharsper caught in mid-observation started and collected her mind. "One ought to go out," she said. "Certainly."

"And independently," said Miss Sawbridge, with meaning.

"Oh independently!" assented Miss Sharsper. It was evident she would now have to watch her chance and begin counting all over again from the beginning.

Mr. Brumley had an impression that Mrs. Sawbridge had said something quite confidential in his ear. He turned perplexed.

"Such charming weather," the lady repeated in the tone of one who doesn't wish so pleasant a little secret to be too generally discussed.

"Never known a better summer," agreed Mr. Brumley.

And then all these minor eddies were submerged in Lady Beach-Mandarin's advance towards her next step, an invitation to lunch. "There," said she, "I'm not Victorian. I always separate husbands and wives—by at least a week. You must come alone."

It was clear to Mr. Brumley that Lady Harman wanted to come alone—and was going to accept, and equally clear that she and her mother and sister regarded this as a very daring thing to do. And when that was settled Lady Beach-Mandarin went on to the altogether easier topic of her Social Friends, a society of smart and influential women; who devoted a certain fragment of time every week to befriending respectable girls employed in London, in a briskly amiable manner, having them to special teas, having them to special evenings with special light refreshments, knowing their names as far as possible and asking about their relations, and generally making them feel that Society was being very frank and amiable to them and had an eye on them and meant them well, and was better for them than socialism and radicalism and revolutionary ideas. To this also Lady Harman it seemed was to come. It had an effect to Mr. Brumley's imagination as if the painted scene of that lady's life was suddenly bursting out into open doors—everywhere.

"Many of them are *quite* ladylike," echoed Mrs. Sawbridge suddenly, picking up the whole thing instantly and speaking over her tea cup in that quasi-confidential tone of hers to Mr. Brumley.

"Of course they are mostly quite dreadfully Sweated," said Lady Beach-Mandarin. "Especially in the confectionery—" She thought of her position in time. "In the inferior class of confectioners' establishments," she said and then hurried on to: "Of course when you come to lunch,—Agatha Alimony. I'm most anxious for you and her to meet."

"Is that *the* Agatha Alimony?" asked Miss Sawbridge abruptly.

"The one and only," said Lady Beach-Mandarin, flashing a smile at her. "And what a marvel she is! I do so want you to know her, Lady Harman. She'd be a Revelation to you. . . ."

Everything had gone wonderfully so far. "And now," said Lady Beach-Mandarin, thrusting forward a face of almost exaggerated motherliness and with an unwonted tenderness suffusing her voice, "show me the Chicks."

There was a brief interrogative pause.

"Your Chicks," expanded Lady Beach-Mandarin, on the verge of crooning. "Your *little* Chicks."

"*Oh!*" cried Lady Harman understanding. "The children."

"Lucky woman!" cried Lady Beach-Mandarin. "Yes."

"One hasn't begun to be friends," she added, "until one has seen—them. . . ."

"So *true*," Mrs. Sawbridge confided to Mr. Brumley with a look that almost languished. . . .

"Certainly," said Mr. Brumley, "rather."

He was a little distraught because he had just seen Sir Isaac step forward in a crouching attitude from beyond the edge of the lilacs, peer at the tea-table with a serpent-like intentness and then dart back convulsively into cover. . . .

If Lady Beach-Mandarin saw him Mr. Brumley felt that anything might happen.

4

Lady Beach-Mandarin always let herself go about children.

It would be unjust to the general richness of Lady Beach-Mandarin to say that she excelled herself on this occasion. On all occasions Lady Beach-Mandarin excelled herself. But never had Mr. Brumley noted quite so vividly Lady Beach-Mandarin's habitual self-surpassingness. She helped him, he felt, to understand better those stories of great waves that sweep in from the ocean and swamp islands and devastate whole littorals. She poured into the Harman nursery and filled every corner of it. She rose to unprecedented heights therein. It seemed to him at moments that they ought to make marks on the walls, like the marks one sees on the houses in the lower valley of the Main to record the more memorable floods. "The dears!" she cried: "the *little* things!" before the nursery door was fairly opened.

(There should have been a line for that at once on the jamb just below the lintel.)

The nursery revealed itself as a large airy white and green apartment entirely free from old furniture and done rather in the style of an aesthetically designed hospital, with a tremendously humorous decorative frieze of cocks and puppies and very bright-colored prints on the walls. The dwarfish furniture was specially designed in green-stained wood and the floor was of cork carpet diversified by white furry rugs. The hospital quality was enhanced by the uniformed and disciplined appearance of the middle-aged and reliable head nurse and her subdued but intelligent subordinate.

Three sturdy little girls, with a year step between each of them, stood up to receive Lady Beach-Mandarin's invasion; an indeterminate baby sprawled regardless of its dignity on a rug. "Aah!" cried Lady Beach-Mandarin, advancing in open order. "Come and be hugged, you dears! Come and be hugged!" Before she knelt down and enveloped their shrinking little persons Mr. Brumley was able to observe that they were pretty little things, but not the beautiful children he could have imagined from Lady Harman. Peeping through their infantile delicacy, hints all too manifest of Sir Isaac's characteristically pointed nose gave Mr. Brumley a peculiar—a eugenic, qualm.

He glanced at Lady Harman and she was standing over the ecstasies of her tremendous visitor, polite, attentive—with an entirely unemotional speculation in her eyes. Miss Sawbridge, stirred by the great waves of violent philoprogenitive enthusiasm that circled out from Lady Beach-Mandarin, had caught up the baby and was hugging it and addressing it in terms of humorous rapture, and the nurse and her assistant were keeping respectful but wary eyes upon the handling of their four charges. Miss Sharsper was taking in the children's characteristics with a quick expertness. Mrs. Sawbridge stood a little in the background and caught Mr. Brumley's eye and proffered a smile of sympathetic tolerance.

Mr. Brumley was moved by a ridiculous impulse, which he just succeeded in suppressing, to say to Mrs. Sawbridge, "Yes, I admit it looks very well. But the essential point, you know, is that it isn't so. . . ."

That it wasn't so, indeed, entirely dominated his impression of that nursery. There was Lady Beach-Mandarin winning Lady Harman's heart by every rule of the game, rejoicing effusively in those crowning triumphs of a woman's being, there was Miss Sawbridge vociferous in support and Mrs. Sawbridge almost offering to join hands in rapturous benediction, and there was Lady Harman wearing her laurels, not indeed with indifference but with a curious detachment. One might imagine her genuinely anxious to understand why Lady Beach-Mandarin was in such a stupendous ebullition. One might have supposed her a mere cold-hearted intellectual if it wasn't that something in her warm beauty absolutely forbade any such interpretation. There came to Mr. Brumley again a thought that had occurred to him first when Sir Isaac and Lady Harman had come together to Black Strand, which was that life had happened to this woman before she was ready for it, that her mind some years after her body was now coming to womanhood, was teeming with curiosity about all she had hitherto accepted, about Sir Isaac, about her children and all her circumstances. . . .

There was a recapitulation of the invitations, a renewed offering of outlooks and vistas and Agatha Alimony. "You'll not forget," insisted Lady Beach-Mandarin. "You'll not afterwards throw us over."

"No," said Lady Harman, with that soft determination of hers. "I'll certainly come."

"I'm so sorry, so very sorry, not to have seen Sir Isaac," Lady Beach-Mandarin insisted.

The raid had accomplished its every object and was drifting doorward. For a moment Lady Beach-Mandarin desisted from Lady Harman and threw her whole being into an eddying effort to submerge the already subjugated Mrs. Sawbridge. Miss Sawbridge was behind up the oak staircase explaining Sir Isaac's interest in furniture-buying to Miss Sharsper. Mr. Brumley had his one moment with Lady Harman.

"I gather," he said, and abandoned that sentence.

"I hope," he said, "that you will have my little house down there. I like to think of *you*—walking in my garden."

"I shall love that garden," she said. "But I shall feel unworthy."

"There are a hundred little things I want to tell you—about it."

Then all the others seemed to come into focus again, and with a quick mutual understanding—Mr. Brumley was certain of its mutuality—they said no more to one another. He was entirely satisfied he had said enough. He had conveyed just everything that was needed to excuse and explain and justify his presence in that company. . . . Upon a big table in the hall he noticed that a silk hat and an umbrella had appeared since their arrival. He glanced at Miss Sharsper but she was keenly occupied with the table legs. He began to breathe freely again when the partings were over and he could get back into the automobile. "Toot," said the horn and he made a last grave salutation to the slender white figure on the steps. The great butler stood at the side of the entrance and a step or so below her, with the air of a man who has completed a difficult task. A small attentive valet hovered out of the shadows behind.

5

(A fragment of the conversation in Lady Beach-Mandarin's returning automobile may be recorded in a parenthesis here.

"But did you see Sir Isaac?" she cried, abruptly.

"Sir Isaac?" defended the startled Mr. Brumley. "Where?"

"He was dodging about in the garden all the time."

"Dodging about the garden! . . . I saw a sort of gardener—"

"I'm sure I saw Him," said Lady Beach-Mandarin. "Positive. He hid away in the mushroom shed. The one you found locked."

"But my *dear* Lady Beach-Mandarin!" protested Mr. Brumley with the air of one who listens to preposterous suggestions. "What can make you think—?"

"Oh I *know* I saw him," said Lady Beach-Mandarin. "I know. He seemed all over the place. Like a Boy Scout. Didn't you see him too, Susan?"

Miss Sharsper was roused from deep preoccupation. "What, dear?" she asked. "See Sir Isaac?"

"Sir Isaac?"

"Dodging about the garden when we went through it."

The novelist reflected. "I didn't notice," she said. "I was busy observing things.")

6

Lady Beach-Mandarin's car passed through the open gates and was swallowed up in the dusty stream of traffic down Putney Hill; the great butler withdrew, the little manservant vanished, Mrs. Sawbridge and her elder daughter had hovered and now receded from the back of the hall; Lady Harman remained standing thoughtfully in the large Bulwer-Lyttonesque doorway of her house. Her face expressed a vague expectation. She waited to be addressed from behind.

Then she became aware of the figure of her husband standing before her. He had come out of the laurels in front. His pale face was livid with anger, his hair dishevelled, there was garden mold and greenness upon his knees and upon his extended hands.

She was startled out of her quiet defensiveness. "Why, Isaac!" she cried. "Where have you been?"

It enraged him further to be asked so obviously unnecessary a question. He forgot his knightly chivalry.

"What the Devil do you mean," he cried, "by chasing me all round the garden?"

"Chasing you? All round the garden?"

"You heard me breaking my shins on that infernal flowerpot you put for me, and out you shot with all your pack of old women and chased me round the garden. What do you mean by it?"

"I didn't think you were in the garden."

"Any Fool could have told I was in the garden. Any Fool might have known I was in the garden. If I wasn't in the garden, then where the Devil was I? Eh? Where else could I be? Of course I was in the garden, and what you wanted was to hunt me down and make a fool of me. And look at me! Look, I say! Look at my hands!"

Lady Harman regarded the lord of her being and hesitated before she answered. She knew what she had to say would enrage him, but she had come to a point in their relationship when a husband's good temper is no longer a supreme consideration. "You've had plenty of time to wash them," she said.

"Yes," he shouted. "And instead I kept 'em to show you. I stayed out here to see the last of that crew for fear I might run against 'em in the house. Of all the infernal old women—"

His lips were providentially deprived of speech. He conveyed his inability to express his estimate of Lady Beach-Mandarin by a gesture of despair.

"If—if anyone calls and I am at home I have to receive them," said Lady Harman, after a moment's deliberation.

"Receiving them's one thing. Making a Fool of yourself—"

His voice was rising.

"Isaac," said Lady Harman, leaning forward and then in a low penetrating whisper, "*Snagsby!*"

(It was the name of the great butler.)

"*Damn* Snagsby!" hissed Sir Isaac, but dropping his voice and drawing near to her. What his voice lost in height it gained in intensity. "What I say is this, Ella, you oughtn't to have brought that old woman out into the garden at all—"

"She insisted on coming."

"You ought to have snubbed her. You ought to have done—anything. How the Devil was I to get away, once she was through the veranda? There I was! *Bagged!*"

"You could have come forward."

"What! And meet *her!*"

"*I* had to meet her."

Sir Isaac felt that his rage was being frittered away upon details. "If you hadn't gone fooling about looking at houses," he said, and now he stood very close to her and spoke with a confidential intensity, "you wouldn't have got that Holy Terror on our track, see? And now—here we are!"

He walked past her into the hall, and the little manservant suddenly materialized in the middle of the space and came forward to brush him obsequiously. Lady Harman regarded that proceeding for some moments in a preoccupied manner and then passed slowly into the classical conservatory. She felt that in view of her engagements the discussion of Lady Beach-Mandarin was only just beginning.

7

She reopened it herself in the long drawing-room into which they both drifted after Sir Isaac had washed the mold from his hands. She went to a French window, gathered courage, it seemed, by a brief contemplation of the garden, and turned with a little effort.

"I don't agree," she said, "with you about Lady Beach-Mandarin."

Sir Isaac appeared surprised. He had assumed the incident was closed. "*How?*" he asked compactly.

"I don't agree," said Lady Harman. "She seems friendly and jolly."

"She's a Holy Terror," said Sir Isaac. "I've seen her twice, Lady Harman."

"A call of that kind," his wife went on, "—when there are cards left and so on—has to be returned."

"You won't," said Sir Isaac.

Lady Harman took a blind-tassel in her hand,—she felt she had to hold on to something. "In any case," she said, "I should have to do that."

"In any case?"

She nodded. "It would be ridiculous not to. We— It is why we know so few people—because we don't return calls. . . ."

Sir Isaac paused before answering. "We don't *want* to know a lot of people," he said. "And, besides— Why! anybody could make us go running about all over London calling on them, by just coming and calling on us. No sense in it. She's come and she's gone, and there's an end of it."

"No," said Lady Harman, gripping her tassel more firmly. "I shall have to return that call."

"I tell you, you won't."

"It isn't only a call," said Lady Harman. "You see, I promised to go there to lunch."

"Lunch!"

"And to go to a meeting with her."

"Go to a meeting!"

"— of a society called the Social Friends. And something else. Oh! to go to the committee meetings of her Shakespeare Dinners Movement."

"I've heard of that."

"She said you supported it—or else of course . . ."

Sir Isaac restrained himself with difficulty.

"Well," he said at last, "you'd better write and tell her you can't do any of these things; that's all."

He thrust his hands into his trousers pockets and walked to the French window next to the one in which she stood, with an air of having settled this business completely, and being now free for the tranquil contemplation of horticulture. But Lady Harman had still something to say.

"I am going to *all* these things," she said. "I said I would, and I will."

He didn't seem immediately to hear her. He made the little noise with his teeth that was habitual to him. Then he came towards her. "This is your infernal sister," he said.

Lady Harman reflected. "No," she decided. "It's myself."

"I might have known when we asked her here," said Sir Isaac with an habitual disregard of her judgments that was beginning to irritate her more and more.

"You can't take on all these people. They're not the sort of people we want to know."

"I want to know them," said Lady Harman.

"I don't."

"I find them interesting," Lady Harman said. "And I've promised."

"Well you oughtn't to have promised without consulting me."

Her reply was the material of much subsequent reflection on the part of Sir Isaac. There was something in her manner. . . .

"You see, Isaac," she said, "you kept so out of the way. . . ."

In the pause that followed her words, Mrs. Sawbridge appeared from the garden smiling with a determined amiability, and bearing a great bunch of the best roses (which Sir Isaac hated to have picked) in her hands.

CHAPTER THE FOURTH

The Beginnings of Lady Harman

1

LADY HARMAN HAD been married when she was just eighteen.

Mrs. Sawbridge was the widow of a solicitor who had been killed in a railway collision while his affairs, as she put it, were unsettled; and she had brought up her two daughters in a villa at Penge upon very little money, in a state of genteel protest. Ellen was the younger. She had been a sturdy dark-eyed doll-dragging little thing and had then shot up very rapidly. She had gone to a boarding-school at Wimbledon because Mrs. Sawbridge thought the Penge day-school had made Georgina opinionated and unladylike, besides developing her muscular system to an unrefined degree. The Wimbledon school was on less progressive lines, and anyhow Ellen grew taller and more feminine than her sister and by seventeen was already womanly, dignified and intensely admired by a number of schoolmates and a large circle of their cousins and brothers. She was generally very good and only now and then broke out with a venturesome enterprise that hurt nobody. She got out of a skylight, for example, and perambulated the roof in the moonshine to see how it felt and did one or two other little things of a similar kind. Otherwise her conduct was admirable and her temper in those days was always contagiously good. That attractiveness which Mr. Brumley felt, was already very manifest, and a little hindered her in the attainment of other distinctions. Most of her lessons were done for her by willing slaves, and they were happy slaves because she abounded in rewarding kindnesses; but on the other hand the study of English literature and music was almost forced upon her by the zeal of the two visiting Professors of these subjects.

And at seventeen, which is the age when girls most despise the boyishness of young men, she met Sir Isaac and filled him with an invincible covetousness. . . .

2

The school at Wimbledon was a large, hushed, faded place presided over by a lady of hidden motives and great exterior calm named Miss Beeton Clavier. She was handsome without any improper attractiveness, an Associate in Arts of St. Andrew's University and a cousin of Mr. Blenker of the *Old Country Gazette*. She was assisted by several resident mistresses and two very carefully married visiting masters for music and Shakespeare, and playground and shrubbery and tennis-lawn were all quite effectively hidden from the high-road. The curriculum included Latin Grammar—nobody ever got to the reading of books in that formidable tongue—French by an English lady who had been in France, Hanoverian German by an irascible native, the more seemly aspects of English history and literature, arithmetic, algebra, political economy and drawing. There was no hockey played within the precincts, science was taught without the clumsy apparatus or objectionable diagrams that are now so common, and stress was laid upon the carriage of the young ladies and the iniquity of speaking in raised voices. Miss Beeton Clavier deprecated the modern "craze for examinations," and released from such pressure her staff did not so much give courses of lessons as circle in a thorough-looking and patient manner about their subjects. This turn-spit quality was reflected in the school idiom; one did not learn algebra or Latin or so-forth, one *did* algebra, one was *put into* Latin. . . .

The girls went through this system of exercises and occupations, evasively and as it were *sotto voce,* making friends, making enemies, making love to one another, following instincts that urged them to find out something about life— in spite of the most earnest discouragement. . . . None of them believed for a moment that the school was preparing them for life. Most of them regarded it as a long inexplicable passage of blank, gray occupations through which they had to pass. Beyond was the sunshine.

Ellen gathered what came to her. She realized a certain beauty in music in spite of the biographies of great musicians, the technical enthusiasms and the general professionalism of her teacher; the literature master directed her attention to memoirs and through these she caught gleams of understanding when the characters of history did for brief intervals cease to be rigidly dignified and institutional like Miss Beeton Clavier and became human—like schoolfellows. And one little spectacled mistress, who wore art dresses and adorned her classroom with flowers, took a great fancy to her, talked to her with much vagueness and emotion of High Aims, and lent her with an impressive furtiveness the works of Emerson and Shelley and a pamphlet by Bernard Shaw. It was a little difficult to understand what these writers were driving at, they were so dreadfully clever, but it was clear they reflected criticism upon the silences of her mother and the rigidities of Miss Beeton Clavier.

In that suppressed and evasive life beneath the outer forms and procedures of school and home, there came glimmerings of something that seemed charged with the promise of holding everything together, the key, religion. She was attracted to religion, much more attracted than she would confess even to herself, but every circumstance in her training dissuaded her from a free approach. Her mother treated religion with a reverence that was almost indistinguishable from huffiness. She never named the deity and she did not like the mention of His name: she threw a spell of indelicacy over religious topics that Ellen never thoroughly cast off. She put God among objectionable topics—albeit a sublime one. Miss Beeton Clavier sustained this remarkable suggestion. When she read prayers in school she did so with the balanced impartiality of one who offers no comment. She seemed pained as she read and finished with a sigh. Whatever she intended to convey, she conveyed that even if the divinity was not all He should be, if, indeed, He was a person almost primitive, having neither the restraint nor the self-obliteration of a refined gentlewoman, no word of it should ever pass her lips. And so Ellen as a girl never let her mind go quite easily into this reconciling core of life, and talked of it only very rarely and shyly with a few chosen coevals. It wasn't very profitable talk. They had a guilty feeling, they laughed a little uneasily, they displayed a fatal proclivity to stab the swelling gravity of their souls with some forced and silly jest and so tumble back to ground again before they rose too high. . . .

Yet great possibilities of faith and devotion stirred already in the girl's heart. She thought little of God by day, but had a strange sense of Him in the starlight; never under the moonlight—that was in no sense divine—but in the stirring darkness of the stars. And it is remarkable that after a course of astronomical enlightenment by a visiting master and descriptions of masses and distances, incredible aching distances, then even more than ever she seemed to feel God among the stars. . . .

A fatal accident to a schoolfellow turned her mind for a time to the dark stillnesses of death. The accident happened away in Wales during the summer holidays; she saw nothing of it, she only knew of its consequence. Hitherto she had assumed it was the function of girls to grow up and go out from the gray intermediate state of school work into freedoms and realities beyond. Death happened, she was aware, to young people, but not she had thought to the people one knew. This termination came with a shock. The girl was no great personal loss to Ellen, they had belonged to different sets and classes, but the conception of her as lying very very still forever was a haunting one. Ellen felt she did not want to be still forevermore in a confined space, with life and sunshine going on all about her and above her, and it quickened her growing appetite for living to think that she might presently have to be like that. How stifled one would feel!

It couldn't be like that.

She began to speculate about that future life upon which religion insists so much and communicates so little. Was it perhaps in other planets, under those wonderful, many-mooned, silver-banded skies? She perceived more and more a kind of absurdity in the existence all about her. Was all this world a mere make-believe, and would Miss Beeton Clavier and everyone about her presently cast aside a veil? Manifestly there was a veil. She had a very natural disposition to doubt whether the actual circumstances of her life were real. Her mother for instance was so lacking in blood and fire, so very like the stiff paper wrapping of something else. But if these things were not real, what was real? What might she not presently do? What might she not presently be? Perhaps death had something to do with that. Was death perhaps no more than the flinging off of grotesque outer garments by the newly arrived guests at the feast of living? She had that feeling that there might be a feast of living.

These preoccupations were a jealously guarded secret, but they gave her a quality of slight detachment that added a dreaming dignity to her dark tall charm.

There were moments of fine, deep excitement that somehow linked themselves in her mind with these thoughts as being set over against the things of every-day. These too were moments quite different and separate in quality from delight, from the keen appreciation of flowers or sunshine or little vividly living things. Daylight seemed to blind her to them, as they blinded her to starshine. They too had a quality of reference to things large and remote, distances, unknown mysteries of light and matter, the thought of mountains, cool white wildernesses and driving snowstorms, or great periods of time. Such were the luminous transfigurations that would come to her at the evening service in church.

The school used to sit in the gallery over against the organist, and for a year and more Ellen had the place at the corner from which she could look down the hazy candle-lit vista of the nave and see the congregation as ranks and ranks of dim faces and vaguely apprehended clothes, ranks that rose with a peculiar deep and spacious rustle to sing, and sang with a massiveness of effect she knew in no other music. Certain hymns in particular seemed to bear her up and carry her into another larger, more wonderful world: "Heart's Abode, Celestial Salem" for example, a world of luminous spiritualized sensuousness. Of such a quality she thought the Heavenly City must surely be, away there and away. But this persuasion differed from those other mystical intimations in its detachment from any sense of the divinity. And remarkably mixed up with it and yet not belonging to it, antagonistic and kindred like a silver dagger stuck through a mystically illuminated parchment, was the angelic figure of a tall fair boy in a surplice who stood out amidst the choir below and sang, it seemed to her, alone.

She herself on these occasions of exaltation would be far too deeply moved to sing. She was inundated by a swimming sense of boundaries nearly transcended, as though she was upon the threshold of a different life altogether, the real enduring life, and as though if she could only maintain herself long enough in this shimmering exaltation she would get right over; things would happen, things that would draw her into that music and magic and prevent her ever returning to everyday life again. There one would walk through music between great candles under eternal stars, hand-in-hand with a tall white figure. But nothing ever did happen to make her cross that boundary; the hymn ceased, the "Amen" died away, as if a curtain fell. The congregation subsided. Reluctantly she would sink back into her seat. . . .

But all through the sermon, to which she never gave the slightest attention, her mind would feel mute and stilled, and she used to come out of church silent and preoccupied, returning unwillingly to the commonplaces of life. . . .

3

Ellen met Sir Isaac—in the days before he was Sir Isaac—at the house of a school friend with whom she was staying at Hythe, and afterwards her mother and sister came down and joined her for a fortnight at a Folkstone boarding house. Mr. Harman had caught a chill while inspecting his North Wales branches and had come down with his mother to recuperate. He and his mother occupied a suite of rooms in the most imposing hotel upon the Leas. Ellen's friend's people were partners in a big flour firm and had a pleasant new esthetic white and green house of roughcast and slates in the pretty country beyond the Hythe golf links, and Ellen's friend's father was deeply anxious to develop amiable arrangements with Mr. Harman. There was much tennis, much croquet, much cycling to the Hythe sea-wall and bathing from little tents and sitting about in the sunshine, and Mr. Harman had his first automobile with him—they were still something of a novelty in those days—and was urgent to take picnic parties to large lonely places on the downs.

There were only two young men in that circle, one was engaged to Ellen's friend's sister, and the other was bound to a young woman remote in Italy; neither was strikingly attractive and both regarded Harman with that awe tempered by undignified furtive derision which wealth and business capacity so often inspire in the young male. At first he was quiet and simply looked at her, as it seemed anyone might look, then she perceived he looked at her intently and continuously, and was persistently close to her and seemed always to be trying to do things to please her and attract her attention. And then from the general behavior of the women about her, her mother and Mrs. Harman and her friend's mother and her friend's sister, rather than from any one specific thing they said, it grew upon her consciousness that this important and fabulously wealthy person, who was also it seemed to her so modest and quiet and touchingly benevolent, was in love with her.

"Your daughter," said Mrs. Harman repeatedly to Mrs. Sawbridge, "is charming, perfectly charming."

"She's *such* a child," said Mrs. Sawbridge repeatedly in reply.

And she told Ellen's friend's mother apropos of Ellen's friend's engagement that she wanted all her daughters to marry for love, she didn't care what the man had so long as they loved each other, and meanwhile she took the utmost care that Isaac had undisputed access to the girl, was watchfully ready to fend off anyone else, made her take everything he offered and praised him quietly and steadily to her. She pointed out how modest and unassuming he was, in spite of the fact that he was "controlling an immense business" and in his own particular trade "a perfect Napoleon."

"For all one sees to the contrary he might be just a private gentleman. And he feeds thousands and thousands of people. . . ."

"Sooner or later," said Mrs. Harman, "I suppose Isaac will marry. He's been such a good son to me that I shall feel it dreadfully, and yet, you know, I wish I could see him settled. Then *I* shall settle—in a little house of my own somewhere. Just a little place. I don't believe in coming too much between son and daughter-in-law. . . ."

Harman's natural avidity was tempered by a proper modesty. He thought Ellen so lovely and so infinitely desirable—and indeed she was—that it seemed incredible to him that he could ever get her. And yet he had got most of the things in life he had really and urgently wanted. His doubts gave his love-making an eager, lavish and pathetic delicacy. He watched her minutely in an agony of appreciation. He felt ready to give or promise anything.

She was greatly flattered by his devotion and she liked the surprises and presents he heaped upon her extremely. Also she was sorry for him beyond measure. In the deep recesses of her heart was an oleographic ideal of a large brave young man with blue eyes, a wave in his fair hair, a wonderful tenor voice and—she could not help it, she tried to look away and not think of it—a broad chest. With him she intended to climb mountains. So clearly she could not marry Mr. Harman. And because of that she tried to be very kind indeed to him, and when he faltered that she could not possibly care for him, she reassured him so vaguely as to fill him with wild gusts of hope and herself with a sense of pledges. He told her one day between two sets of tennis—which he played with a certain tricky skill—that he felt that the very highest happiness he could ever attain would be to die at her feet. Presently her pity and her sense of responsibility had become so large and deep that the dream hero with the blue eyes was largely overlaid and hidden by them.

Then, at first a little indirectly and then urgently and with a voice upon the edge of tears, Harman implored her to marry him. She had never before in the whole course of her life seen a grown-up person on the very verge of tears. She felt that the release of such deep fountains as that must be averted at any cost. She felt that for a mere schoolgirl like herself, a backward schoolgirl who had never really mastered quadratics, to cause these immense and tragic distresses was abominable. She was sure her former headmistress would disapprove very highly of her. "I will make you a queen," said Harman, "I will give all my life to your happiness."

She believed he would.

She refused him for the second time but with a weakening certainty in a little white summer-house that gave a glimpse of the sea between green and wooded hills. She sat and stared at the sea after he had left her, through a mist of tears; so pitiful did he seem. He had beaten his poor fists on the stone table and then caught up her hand, kissed it and rushed out. . . . She had not dreamt that love could hurt like that.

And all that night—that is to say for a full hour before her wet eyelashes closed in slumber—she was sleepless with remorse for the misery she was causing him.

The third time when he said with suicidal conviction that he could not live without her, she burst into tears of pity and yielded. And instantly, amazingly, with the famished swiftness of a springing panther he caught her body into his arms and kissed her on the lips. . . .

4

They were married with every circumstance of splendor, with very expensive music, and portraits in the illustrated newspapers and a great glitter of favors and carriages. The bridegroom was most thoughtful and generous about the Sawbridge side of the preparations. Only one thing was a little perplexing. In spite of his impassioned impatience he delayed the wedding. Full of dark hints and a portentous secret, he delayed the wedding for twenty-five whole days in order that it should follow immediately upon the publication of the birthday honors list. And then they understood.

"You will be Lady Harman," he exulted; "*Lady* Harman. I would have given double. . . . I have had to back the *Old Country Gazette* and I don't care a rap. I'd have done anything. I'd have bought the rotten thing outright. . . . Lady Harman!"

He remained loverlike until the very eve of their marriage. Then suddenly it seemed to her that all the people she cared for in the world were pushing her away from them towards him, giving her up, handing her over. He became—possessive. His abjection changed to pride. She perceived that she was going to be left tremendously alone with him, with an effect, as if she had stepped off a terrace on to what she believed to be land and had abruptly descended into very deep water. . . .

And while she was still feeling quite surprised by everything and extremely doubtful whether she wanted to go any further with this business, which was manifestly far more serious, out of all proportion more serious, than anything that had ever happened to her before—and *unpleasant,* abounding indeed in crumpling indignities and horrible nervous stresses, it dawned upon her that she was presently to be that strange, grown-up and preoccupied thing, a mother, and that girlhood and youth and vigorous games, mountains and swimming and running and leaping were over for her as far as she could see forever. . . .

Both the prospective grandmothers became wonderfully kind and helpful and intimate, preparing with gusto and an agreeable sense of delegated responsibility for the child that was to give them all the pride of maternity again and none of its inconveniences.

CHAPTER THE FIFTH

The World According to Sir Isaac

1

HER MARRIAGE HAD carried Ellen out of the narrow world of home and school into another that had seemed at first vastly larger, if only on account of its freedom from the perpetual achievement of small economies. Hitherto the urgent necessity of these had filled life with irksome precautions and clipped the wings of every dream. This new life into which Sir Isaac led her by the hand promised not only that release but more light, more color, more movement, more people. There was to be at any rate so much in the way of rewards and compensation for her pity of him.

She found the establishment at Putney ready for her. Sir Isaac had not consulted her about it, it had been his secret, he had prepared it for her with meticulous care as a surprise. They returned from a honeymoon in Skye in which the attentions of Sir Isaac and the comforts of a first-class hotel had obscured a marvelous background of somber mountain and wide stretches of shining sea. Sir Isaac had been very fond and insistent and inseparable, and she was doing her best to conceal a strange distressful jangling of her nerves which she now feared might presently dispose her to scream. Sir Isaac had been goodness itself, but how she craved now for solitude! She was under the impression now that they were going to his mother's house in Highbury. Then she thought he would have to go away to business for part of the day at any rate, and she could creep into some corner and begin to think of all that had happened to her in these short summer months.

They were met at Euston by his motor-car. "*Home,*" said Sir Isaac, with a little gleam of excitement, when the more immediate luggage was aboard.

As they hummed through the West-End afternoon Ellen became aware that he was whistling through his teeth. It was his invariable indication of mental activity, and her attention came drifting back from her idle contemplation of the shoppers and strollers of Piccadilly to link this already alarming symptom with the perplexing fact that they were manifestly traveling west.

"But this," she said presently, "is Knightsbridge."

"Goes to Kensington," he replied with attempted indifference.

"But your mother doesn't live this way."

"*We* do," said Sir Isaac, shining at every point of his face.

"But," she halted. "Isaac!—where are we going?"

"Home," he said.

"You've not taken a house?"

"Bought it."

"But,—it won't be ready!"

"I've seen to that."

"Servants!" she cried in dismay.

"That's all right." His face broke into an excited smile. His little eyes danced and shone. "Everything," he said.

"But the servants!" she said.

"You'll see," he said. "There's a butler—and everything."

"A butler!" He could now no longer restrain himself. "I was weeks," he said, "getting it ready. Weeks and weeks. . . . It's a house. . . . I'd had my eye on it before ever I met you. It's a real *good* house, Elly. . . ."

The fortunate girl-wife went on through Brompton to Walham Green with a stunned feeling. So women have felt in tumbrils. A nightmare of butlers, a galaxy of possible butlers, filled her soul.

No one was quite so big and formidable as Snagsby, towering up to receive her, upon the steps of the home her husband was so amazingly giving her.

The reader has already been privileged to see something of this house in the company of Lady Beach-Mandarin. At the top of the steps stood Mrs. Crumble, the new and highly recommended cook-housekeeper in her best black silk flounced and expanded, and behind her peeped several neat maids in caps and aprons. A little valet-like under-butler appeared and tried to balance Snagsby by hovering two steps above him on the opposite side of the Victorian medieval porch.

Assisted officiously by Snagsby and amidst the deferential unhelpful gestures of the under-butler, Sir Isaac handed his wife out of the car. "Everything all right, Snagsby?" he asked brusquely if a little breathless.

"Everything in order, Sir Isaac."

"And here;—this is her ladyship."

"I 'ope her ladyship 'ad a pleasant journey to 'er new 'ome. I'm sure if I may presume, Sir Isaac, we shall all be very glad to serve her ladyship."

(Like all well-trained English servants, Snagsby always dropped as many h's as he could when conversing with his superiors. He did this as a mark of respect and to prevent social confusion, just as he was always careful to wear a slightly misfitting dress coat and fold his trousers so that they creased at the sides and had a wide flat effect in front.)

Lady Harman bowed a little shyly to his good wishes and was then led up to Mrs. Crumble, in a stiff black silk, who curtseyed with a submissive amiability to her new mistress. "I'm sure, me lady," she said. "I'm sure—"

There was a little pause. "Here they are, you see, right and ready," said Sir Isaac, and then with an inspiration, "Got any tea for us, Snagsby?"

Snagsby addressing his mistress inquired if he should serve tea in the garden or the drawing-room, and Sir Isaac decided for the garden.

"There's another hall beyond this," he said, and took his wife's arm, leaving Mrs. Crumble still bowing amiably before the hall table. And every time she bowed she rustled richly. . . .

"It's quite a big garden," said Sir Isaac.

2

And so the woman who had been a girl three weeks ago, this tall, dark-eyed, slightly perplexed and very young-looking lady, was introduced to the home that had been made for her. She went about it with an alarmed sense of strange responsibilities, not in the least feeling that anything was being given to her. And Sir Isaac led her from point to point full of the pride and joy of new possession—for it was his first own house as well as hers—rejoicing over it and exacting gratitude.

"It's all right, isn't it?" he asked looking up at her.

"It's wonderful. I'd no idea."

"See," he said, indicating a great brass bowl of perennial sunflowers on the landing, "your favorite flower!"

"My favorite flower?"

"You said it was—in that book. Perennial sunflower."

She was perplexed and then remembered.

She understood now why he had said downstairs, when she had glanced at a big photographic enlargement of a portrait of Doctor Barnardo, "your favorite hero in real life."

He had brought her at Hythe one day a popular Victorian device, a confession album, in which she had had to write down on a neat rose-tinted page, her favorite author, her favorite flower, her favorite color, her favorite hero in real life, her "pet aversion," and quite a number of such particulars of her subjective existence. She had filled this page in a haphazard manner late one night, and she was disconcerted to find how thoroughly her careless replies had come home to roost. She had put down "pink" as her favorite color because the page she was writing upon suggested it, and the paper of the room was pale pink, the curtains strong pink with a pattern of paler pink and tied with large pink bows, and the lamp shades, the bedspread, the pillow-cases, the carpet, the chairs, the very crockery—everything but the omnipresent perennial sunflowers—was pink. Confronted with this realization, she understood that pink was the least agreeable of all possible hues for a bedroom. She perceived she had to live now in a chromatic range between rather underdone mutton and salmon. She had said that her favorite musical composers were Bach and Beethoven; she really meant it, and a bust of Beethoven materialized that statement, but she had made Doctor Barnardo her favorite hero in real life because his name also began with a B and she had heard someone say somewhere that he was a very good man. The predominance of George Eliot's pensive rather than delightful countenance in her bedroom and the array of all that lady's works in a lusciously tooled pink leather, was due to her equally reckless choice of a favorite author. She had said too that Nelson was her favorite historical character, but Sir Isaac with a delicate jealousy had preferred to have this heroic but regrettably immoral personality represented in his home only by an engraving of the Battle of Copenhagen. . . .

She stood surveying this room, and her husband watched her eagerly. She was, he felt, impressed at last! . . .

Certainly she had never seen such a bedroom in her life. By comparison even with the largest of the hotel apartments they had occupied it was vast; it had writing-tables and a dainty bookcase and a blushing sofa, and dressing-tables and a bureau and a rose-red screen and three large windows. Her thoughts went back to the narrow little bedroom at Penge with which she had hitherto been so entirely content. Her own few little books, a photograph or so,—they'd never dare to come here, even if she dared to bring them.

"Here," said Sir Isaac, flinging open a white door, "is your dressing-room."

She was chiefly aware of a huge white bath standing on a marble slab under a window of crinkled pink-stained glass, and of a wide space of tiled floor with white fur rugs.

"And here," he said, opening a panel that was covered by wallpaper, "is *my* door."

"Yes," he said to the question in her eyes, "that's my room. You got this one—for your own. It's how people do now. People of our position. . . . There's no lock."

He shut the door slowly again and surveyed the splendors he had made with infinite satisfaction.

"All right?" he said, "isn't it?" . . . He turned to the pearl for which the casket was made, and slipped an arm about her waist. His arm tightened.

"Got a kiss for me, Elly?" he whispered.

At this moment, a gong almost worthy of Snagsby summoned them to tea. It came booming in to them with a vast officious arrogance that brooked no denial. It made one understand the imperatives of the Last Trump, albeit with a greater dignity. . . . There was a little awkward pause.

"I'm so dirty and trainy," she said, disengaging herself from his arm. "And we ought to go to tea."

3

The same exceptional aptitude of Sir Isaac for detailed administration that had relieved his wife from the need of furnishing and arranging a home, made the birth of her children and the organization of her nursery an almost detached affair for her. Sir Isaac went about in a preoccupied way, whistling between his teeth and planning with expert advice the equipment of an ideal nursery, and her mother and his mother became as it were voluminous clouds of uncommunicative wisdom and precaution. In addition the conversation of Miss Crump, the extremely skilled and costly nurse, who arrived a full Advent before the child, fresh from the birth of a viscount, did much to generalize whatever had remained individual of this thing that was happening. With so much intelligence focused, there seemed to Lady Harman no particular reason why she should not do her best to think as little as possible about the impending affair, which meant for her, she now understood quite clearly, more and more discomfort culminating in an agony. The summer promised to be warm, and Sir Isaac took a furnished house for the great event in the hills behind Torquay. The maternal instinct is not a magic thing, it has to be evoked and developed, and I decline to believe it is indicative of any peculiar unwomanliness in Lady Harman that when at last she beheld her newly-born daughter in the hands of the experts, she moaned druggishly, "Oh! please take it away. Oh! Take it—away. Anywhere—anywhere."

It was very red and wrinkled and aged-looking and, except when it opened its mouth to cry, extraordinarily like its father. This resemblance disappeared—along with a crop of darkish red hair—in the course of a day or two, but it left a lurking dislike to its proximity in her mind long after it had become an entirely infantile and engaging baby.

4

Those early years of their marriage were the happiest period of Sir Isaac's life.

He seemed to have everything that man could desire. He was still only just forty at his marriage; he had made for himself a position altogether dominant in the world of confectionery and popular refreshment, he had won a title, he had a home after his own heart, a beautiful young wife, and presently delightful children in his own image, and it was only after some years of contentment and serenity and with a certain incredulity that he discovered that something in his wife, something almost in the nature of discontent with her lot, was undermining and threatening all the comfort and beauty of his life.

Sir Isaac was one of those men whom modern England delights to honor, a man of unpretentious acquisitiveness, devoted to business and distracted by no aesthetic or intellectual interests. He was the only son of his mother, the widow of a bankrupt steam-miller, and he had been a delicate child to rear. He left Mr. Gambard's college at Ealing after passing the second-class examination of the College of Preceptors at the age of sixteen, to go into a tea-office as clerk without a salary, a post he presently abandoned for a clerkship in the office of a large refreshment catering firm. He attracted the attention of his employers by suggesting various administrative economies, and he was already drawing a salary of two hundred and fifty pounds a year when he was twenty-one. Many young men would have rested satisfied with so rapid an advancement, and would have devoted themselves to the amusements that are now considered so permissible to youth, but young Harman was made of sterner stuff, and it only spurred him to further efforts. He contrived to save a considerable proportion of his salary for some years, and at the age of twenty-seven he started, in association with a firm of flour millers, the International Bread and Cake Stores, which spread rapidly over the country. They were not in any sense of the word "International," but in a search for inflated and inflating adjectives this word attracted him most, and the success of the enterprise justified his choice. Originally conceived as a syndicated system of baker's shops running a specially gritty and nutritious line of bread, the Staminal Bread, in addition to the ordinary descriptions, it rapidly developed a catering side, and in a little time there were few centers of clerkly employment in London or the Midlands where an International could not be found supplying the midday scone or poached egg, washed down by a cup of tea, or coffee, or lemonade. It meant hard work for Isaac Harman. It drew lines on his cheeks, sharpened his always rather pointed nose to an extreme efficiency, grayed his hair, and gave an acquired firmness to his rather retreating mouth. All his time was given to the details of this development; always he was inspecting premises, selecting and dismissing managers, making codes of rules and fines for his growing army of employees, organizing and reorganizing his central offices and his central bakeries, hunting up cheaper and cheaper supplies of eggs and flour, and milk and ham, devising advertisements and agency developments. He had something of an artist's passion in these things; he went about, a little bent and peaky, calculating and planning and hissing through his teeth, and feeling not only that he was getting on, but that he was getting on in the most exemplary way. Manifestly, anybody in his line of business who wanted to be leisurely, or to be generous, who possessed any broader interests than the shop, who troubled to think about the nation or the race or any of the deeper mysteries of life, was bound to go down before him. He dealt privately with every appetite— until his marriage no human being could have suspected him of any appetite but business—he disposed of every distracting impulse with unobtrusive decision; and even his political inclination towards Radicalism sprang chiefly from an irritation with the legal advantages of landlordism natural to a man who is frequently leasing shops.

At school Sir Isaac had not been a particularly prominent figure; his disposition at cricket to block and to bowl "sneaks" and "twisters" under-arm had raised his average rather than his reputation; he had evaded fights and dramatic situations, and protected himself upon occasions of unavoidable violence by punching with his white knuckles held in a peculiar and vicious manner. He had always been a little insensitive to those graces of style, in action if not in art, which appeal so strongly to the commoner sort of English mind; he played first for safety, and that assured, for the uttermost advantage. These tendencies became more marked with maturity. When he took up tennis for his health's sake he developed at once an ungracious service that had to be killed like vermin; he developed an instinct for the deadest ball available, and his returns close up to the net were like assassinations. Indeed, he was inherently incapable of any vision beyond the express prohibitions and permissions of the rules of the games he played, or beyond the laws and institutions under which he lived. His idea of generosity was the undocumented and unqualified purchase of a person by payments made in the form of a gift.

And this being the quality of Sir Isaac's mind, it followed that his interpretations of the relationship of marriage were simple and strict. A woman, he knew, had to be wooed to be won, but when she was won, she was won. He did not understand wooing after that was settled. There was the bargain and her surrender. He on his side had to keep her, dress her, be kind to her, give her the appearances of pride and authority, and in return he had his rights and his privileges and undefined powers of control. That you know, by the existing rules, is the reality of marriage where there are no settlements and no private property of the wife's. That is to say, it is the reality of marriage in ninety-nine cases out of the hundred. And it would have shocked Sir Isaac extremely, and as a matter of fact it did shock him, for anyone to suggest the slightest revision of so entirely advantageous an arrangement. He was confident of his good intentions, and resolved to the best of his ability to make his wife the happiest of living creatures, subject only to reasonable acquiescences and general good behavior.

Never before had he cared for anything so much as he did for her—not even for the International Bread and Cake Stores. He gloated upon her. She distracted him from business. He resolved from the outset to surround her with every luxury and permit her no desire that he had not already anticipated. Even her mother and Georgina, whom he thought extremely unnecessary persons, were frequent visitors to his house. His solicitude for her was so great that she found it difficult even to see her doctor except in his presence. And he bought her a pearl necklace that cost six hundred pounds. He was, in fact, one of those complete husbands who grow rare in these decadent days.

The social circle to which Sir Isaac introduced his wife was not a very extensive one. The business misadventures of his father had naturally deprived his mother of most of her friends; he had made only acquaintances at school, and his subsequent concentration upon business had permitted very few intimacies. Renewed prosperity had produced a certain revival of cousins, but Mrs. Harman, established in a pleasant house at Highbury, had received their attentions with a well-merited stiffness. His chief associates were his various business allies, and these and their wives and families formed the nucleus of the new world to which Ellen was gradually and temperately introduced. There were a few local callers, but Putney is now too deeply merged with London for this practice of the countryside to have any great effect upon a newcomer's visiting circle.

Perhaps Mr. Charterson might claim to be Sir Isaac's chief friend at the time of that gentleman's marriage. Transactions in sugar had brought them together originally. He was Sir Isaac's best man, and the new knight entertained a feeling of something very like admiration for him. Moreover, Mr. Charterson had very large ears, more particularly was the left one large, extraordinarily large and projecting upper teeth, which he sought vainly to hide beneath an extravagant moustache, and a harsh voice, characteristics that did much to allay the anxieties natural to a newly married man. Mr. Charterson was moreover adequately married to a large, attentive, enterprising, swarthy wife, and possessed a splendid house in Belgravia. Not quite so self-made as Sir Isaac, he was still sufficiently self-made to take a very keen interest in his own social advancement and in social advancement generally, and it was through him that Sir Isaac's attention had been first directed to those developing relations with politics that arise as a business grows to greatness. "I'm for Parliament," said Charterson. "Sugar's in politics, and I'm after it. You'd better come too, Harman. Those chaps up there, they'll play jiggery-pokery with sugar if we aren't careful. And it won't be only sugar, Harman!"

Pressed to expand this latter sentence, he pointed out to his friend that "any amount of interfering with employment" was in the air—"any amount."

"And besides," said Mr. Charterson, "men like us have a stake in the country, Harman. We're getting biggish people. We ought to do our share. I don't see the fun of leaving everything to the landlords and the lawyers. Men of our sort have got to make ourselves felt. We want a business government. Of course—one pays. So long as I get a voice in calling the tune I don't mind paying the piper a bit. There's going to be a lot of interference with trade. All this social legislation. And there's what you were saying the other day about these leases. . . ."

"I'm not much of a talker," said Harman. "I don't see myself gassing in the House."

"Oh! I don't mean going into Parliament," said Charterson. "That's for some of us, perhaps. . . . But come into the party, make yourself felt."

Under Charterson's stimulation it was that Harman joined the National Liberal Club, and presently went on to the Climax, and through him he came to know something of that inner traffic of arrangements and bargains which does so much to keep a great historical party together and maintain its vitality. For a time he was largely overshadowed by the sturdy Radicalism of Charterson, but presently as he understood this interesting game better, he embarked upon a line of his own. Charterson wanted a seat, and presently got it; his maiden speech on the Sugar Bounties won a compliment from Mr. Evesham; and Harman, who would have piloted a monoplane sooner than address the House, decided to be one of those silent influences that work outside our national assembly. He came to the help of an embarrassed Liberal weekly, and then, in a Fleet Street crisis, undertook the larger share of backing the *Old Country Gazette,* that important social and intellectual party organ. His knighthood followed almost automatically.

Such political developments introduced a second element into the intermittent social relations of the Harman household. Before his knighthood and marriage Sir Isaac had participated in various public banquets and private parties and little dinners in the vaults of the House and elsewhere, arising out of his political intentions, and with the appearance of a Lady Harman there came a certain urgency on the part of those who maintain in a state of hectic dullness the social activities of the great Liberal party. Horatio Blenker, Sir Isaac's editor, showed a disposition to be socially very helpful, and after Mrs. Blenker had called in a state of worldly instructiveness, there was a little dinner at the Blenkers' to introduce young Lady Harman to the great political world. It was the first dinner-party of her life, and she found it dazzling rather than really agreeable.

She felt very slender and young and rather unclothed about the arms and neck, in spite of the six hundred pound pearl necklace that had been given to her just as she stood before the mirror in her white-and-gold dinner dress ready to start. She had to look down at that dress ever and again and at her shining arms to remind herself that she wasn't still in school-girl clothes, and it seemed to her there was not another woman in the room who was not fairly entitled to send her off to bed at any moment. She had been a little nervous about the details of the dinner, but there was nothing strange or difficult but caviar, and in that case she waited for someone else to begin. The Chartersons were there, which was very reassuring, and the abundant flowers on the table were a sort of protection. The man on her right was very nice, gently voluble, and evidently quite deaf, so that she had merely to make kind respectful faces at him. He talked to her most of the time, and described the peasant costumes in Marken and Walcheren. And Mr. Blenker, with a fine appreciation of Sir Isaac's watchful temperament and his own magnetism, spoke to her three times and never looked at her once all through the entertainment.

A few weeks later they went to dinner at the Chartersons', and then she gave a dinner, which was arranged very skilfully by Sir Isaac and Snagsby and the cook-housekeeper, with a little outside help, and then came a big party reception at Lady Barleypound's, a multitudinous miscellaneous assembly in which the obviously wealthy rubbed shoulders with the obviously virtuous and the not quite so obviously clever. It was a great orgy of standing about and seeing the various Blenkers and the Cramptons and the Weston Massinghays and the Daytons and Mrs. Millingham with her quivering lorgnette and her last tame genius and Lewis, and indeed all the Tapirs and Tadpoles of Liberalism, being tremendously active and influential and important throughout the evening. The house struck Ellen as being very splendid, the great staircase particularly so, and never before had she seen a great multitude of people in evening dress. Lady Barleypound in the golden parlor at the head of the stairs shook hands automatically, lest it would seem in some amiable dream, Mrs. Blapton and a daughter rustled across the gathering in a hasty vindictive manner and vanished, and a number of handsome, glittering, dark-eyed, splendidly dressed women kept together in groups and were tremendously but occultly amused. The various Blenkers seemed everywhere, Horatio in particular with his large fluent person and his luminous tenor was like a shop-walker taking customers to the departments: one felt he was weaving all these immiscibles together into one great wise Liberal purpose, and that he deserved quite wonderful things from the party; he even introduced five or six people to Lady Harman, looking sternly over her head and restraining his charm as he did so on account of Sir Isaac's feelings. The people he brought up to her were not very interesting people, she thought, but then that was perhaps due to her own dreadful ignorance of politics.

Lady Harman ceased even to dip into the vortex of London society after March, and in June she went with her mother and a skilled nurse to that beautiful furnished house Sir Isaac had found near Torquay, in preparation for the birth of their first little daughter.

5

It seemed to her husband that it was both unreasonable and ungrateful of her to become a tearful young woman after their union, and for a phase of some months she certainly was a tearful young woman, but his mother made it clear to him that this was quite a correct and permissible phase for her, as she was, and so he expressed his impatience with temperance, and presently she was able to pull herself together and begin to readjust herself to a universe that had seemed for a time almost too shattered for endurance. She resumed the process of growing up that her marriage had for a time so vividly interrupted, and if her school-days were truncated and the college phase omitted, she had at any rate a very considerable amount of fundamental experience to replace these now customary completions.

Three little girls she brought into the world in the first three years of her married life, then after a brief interval of indifferent health she had a fourth girl baby of a physique quite obviously inferior to its predecessors, and then, after— and perhaps as a consequence of—much whispered conversation of the two mothers-in-law, protests and tactful explanation on the part of the elderly and trustworthy family doctor and remarks of an extraordinary breadth (and made at table too, almost before the door had closed on Snagsby!) from Ellen's elder sister, there came a less reproductive phase. . . .

But by that time Lady Harman had acquired the habit of reading and the habit of thinking over what she read, and from that it is an easy step to thinking over oneself and the circumstances of one's own life. The one thing trains for the other.

Now the chief circumstance in the life of Lady Harman was Sir Isaac. Indeed as she grew to a clear consciousness of herself and her position, it seemed to her he was not so much a circumstance as a circumvallation. There wasn't a direction in which she could turn without immediately running up against him. He had taken possession of her extremely. And from her first resignation to this as an inevitable fact she had come, she hardly knew how, to a renewed disposition to regard this large and various universe beyond him and outside of him, with something of the same slight adventurousness she had felt before he so comprehensively happened to her. After her first phase of despair she had really done her best to honor the bargain she had rather unwittingly made and to love and to devote herself and be a loyal and happy wife to this clutching, hard-breathing little man who had got her, and it was the insatiable excesses of his demands quite as much as any outer influence that made her realize the impossibility of such a concentration.

His was a supremely acquisitive and possessive character, so that he insulted her utmost subjugations by an obtrusive suspicion and jealousy, he was jealous of her childish worship of her dead father, jealous of her disposition to go to church, jealous of the poet Wordsworth because she liked to read his sonnets, jealous because she loved great music, jealous when she wanted to go out; if she seemed passionless and she seemed more and more passionless he was jealous, and the slightest gleam of any warmth of temperament filled him with a vile and furious dread of dishonoring possibilities. And the utmost resolution to believe in him could not hide from her forever the fact that his love manifested itself almost wholly as a parade of ownership and a desire, without kindliness, without any self-forgetfulness. All his devotion, his self-abjection, had been the mere qualms of a craving, the flush of eager courtship. Do as she would to overcome these realizations, forces within her stronger than herself, primordial forces with the welfare of all life in their keeping, cried out upon the meanness of his face, the ugly pointed nose and the thin compressed lips, the weak neck, the clammy hands, the ungainly nervous gestures, the tuneless whistling between the clenched teeth. He would not let her forget a single detail. Whenever she tried to look at any created thing, he thrust himself, like one of his own open-air advertisements, athwart the attraction.

As she grew up to an achieved womanhood—and it was even a physical growing-up, for she added more than an inch of stature after her marriage—her life became more and more consciously like a fencing match in which her vision flashed over his head and under his arms and this side of him and that, while with a toiling industry he fought to intercept it. And from the complete acceptance of her matrimonial submission, she passed on by almost insensible degrees towards a conception of her life as a struggle, that seemed at first entirely lonely and unsupported, to exist—*against* him.

In every novel as in every picture there must be an immense simplification, and so I tell the story of Lady Harman's changing attitude without any of those tangled leapings-forward or harkings-back, those moods and counter moods and relapses which made up the necessary course of her mind. But sometimes she was here and sometimes she was there, sometimes quite back to the beginning an obedient, scrupulously loyal and up-looking young wife, sometimes a wife concealing the humiliation of an unhappy choice in a spurious satisfaction and affection. And mixed up with widening spaces of criticism and dissatisfaction and hostility there were, you must understand, moments of real iking for this outrageous little man and streaks of an absurd maternal tenderness for him. They had been too close together to avoid that. She had a woman's affection of ownership too, and disliked to see him despised or bettered or untidy; even those ridiculous muddy hands had given her a twinge of solicitude. . . .

And all the while she was trying to see the universe also, the great background of their two little lives, and to think what it might mean for her over and above their too obliterating relationship.

6

It would be like counting the bacteria of an infection to trace how ideas of insubordination came drifting into Sir Isaac's Paradise. The epidemic is in the air. There is no Tempter nowadays, no definitive apple. The disturbing force has grown subtler, blows in now like a draft, creeps and gathers like the dust,— a disseminated serpent. Sir Isaac brought home his young, beautiful and rather crumpled and astonished Eve and by all his standards he was entitled to be happy ever afterwards. He knew of one danger, but against that he was very watchful. Never once for six long years did she have a private duologue with another male. But Mudie and Sir Jesse Boot sent parcels to the house unchecked, the newspaper drifted in not even censored: the nurses who guided Ellen through the essential incidents of a feminine career talked of something called a "movement." And there was Georgina. . . .

The thing they wanted they called the Vote, but that demand so hollow, so eyeless, had all the terrifying effect of a mask. Behind that mask was a formless invincible discontent with the lot of womanhood. It wanted,—it was not clear what it wanted, but whatever it wanted, all the domestic instincts of mankind were against admitting there was anything it could want. That remarkable agitation had already worked up to the thunderous pitch, there had been demonstrations at Public Meetings, scenes in the Ladies' Gallery and something like rioting in Parliament Square before ever it occurred to Sir Isaac that this was a disturbance that touched his home. He had supposed suffragettes were ladies of all too certain an age with red noses and spectacles and a masculine style of costume, who wished to be hugged by policemen. He said as much rather knowingly and wickedly to Charterson. He could not understand any woman not coveting the privileges of Lady Harman. And then one day while Georgina and her mother were visiting them, as he was looking over the letters at the breakfast table according to his custom before giving them out, he discovered two identical newspaper packets addressed to his wife and his sister-in-law, and upon them were these words printed very plainly, "Votes for Women."

"Good Lord!" he cried. "What's this? It oughtn't to be allowed." And he pitched the papers at the wastepaper basket under the sideboard.

"I'll thank you," said Georgina, "not to throw away our *Votes for Women*. We subscribe to that."

"Eh?" cried Sir Isaac.

"We're subscribers. Snagsby, just give us those papers." (A difficult moment for Snagsby.) He picked up the papers and looked at Sir Isaac.

"Put 'em down there," said Sir Isaac, waving to the sideboard and then in an ensuing silence handed two letters of no importance to his mother-in-law.

His face was pale and he was breathless. Snagsby with an obvious tactfulness retired.

Sir Isaac watched the door close.

His remark pointedly ignored Georgina.

"What you been thinking about, Elly," he asked, "subscribing to *that* thing?"

"I wanted to read it."

"But you don't hold with all that Rubbish—"

"*Rubbish!*" said Georgina, helping herself to marmalade.

"Well, rot then, if you like," said Sir Isaac, unamiably and panting.

With that as Snagsby afterwards put it—for the battle raged so fiercely as to go on even when he presently returned to the room—"the fat was in the fire." The Harman breakfast-table was caught up into the Great Controversy with heat and fury like a tree that is overtaken by a forest fire. It burned for weeks, and smoldered still when the first white heats had abated. I will not record the arguments of either side, they were abominably bad and you have heard them all time after time; I do not think that whatever side you have taken in this matter you would find much to please you in Sir Isaac's goadings or Georgina's repartees. Sir Isaac would ask if women were prepared to go as soldiers and Georgina would enquire how many years of service he had done or horrify her mother by manifest allusion to the agonies and dangers of maternity,—things like that. It gave a new interest to breakfast for Snagsby; and the peculiarly ladylike qualities of Mrs. Sawbridge, a gift for silent, pallid stiffness, a disposition, tactful but unsuccessful, to "change the subject," an air of being about to leave the room in disdain, had never shone with such baleful splendor. Our interest here is rather with the effect of these remarkable disputes, which echoed in Sir Isaac's private talk long after Georgina had gone again, upon Lady Harman. He could not leave this topic of feminine emancipation alone, once it had been set going, and though Ellen would always preface her remarks by, "Of course Georgina goes too far," he worried her slowly into a series of definite insurgent positions. Sir Isaac's attacks on Georgina certainly brought out a good deal of absurdity in her positions, and Georgina at times left Sir Isaac without a leg to stand on, and the net result of their disputes as of most human controversies was not conviction for the hearer but release. Her mind escaped between them, and went exploring for itself through the great gaps they had made in the simple obedient assumptions of her girlhood. That question originally put in Paradise, "Why shouldn't we?" came into her mind and stayed there. It is a question that marks a definite stage in the departure from innocence. Things that had seemed opaque and immutable appeared translucent and questionable. She began to read more and more in order to learn things and get a light upon things, and less and less to pass the time. Ideas came to her that seemed at first strange altogether and then grotesquely justifiable and then crept to a sort of acceptance by familiarity. And a disturbing intermittent sense of a general responsibility increased and increased in her.

You will understand this sense of responsibility which was growing up in Lady Harman's mind if you have felt it yourself, but if you have not then you may find it a little difficult to understand. You see it comes, when it comes at all, out of a phase of disillusionment. All children, I suppose, begin by taking for granted the rightness of things in general, the soundness of accepted standards, and many people are at least so happy that they never really grow out of this assumption. They go to the grave with an unbroken confidence that somewhere behind all the immediate injustices and disorders of life, behind the antics of politics, the rigidities of institutions, the pressure of custom and the vagaries of law, there is wisdom and purpose and adequate provision, they never lose that faith in the human household they acquired among the directed securities of home. But for more of us and more there comes a dissolution of these assurances; there comes illumination as the day comes into a candle-lit uncurtained room. The warm lights that once rounded off our world so completely are betrayed for what they are, smoky and guttering candles. Beyond what once seemed a casket of dutiful security is now a limitless and indifferent universe. Ours is the wisdom or there is no wisdom; ours is the decision or there is no decision. That burden is upon each of us in the measure of our capacity. The talent has been given us and we may not bury it.

7

And as we reckon up the disturbing influences that were stirring Lady Harman out of that life of acquiescences to which women are perhaps even more naturally disposed than men, we may pick out the conversation of Susan Burnet as something a little apart from the others, as something with a peculiar barbed pointedness of its own that was yet in other respects very representative of a multitude of nudges and nips and pricks and indications that life was giving Lady Harman's awaking mind. Susan Burnet was a woman who came to renovate and generally do up the Putney curtains and furniture and loose covers every spring; she was Mrs. Crumble's discovery, she was sturdy and short and she had open blue eyes and an engaging simplicity of manner that attracted Lady Harman from the outset. She was stuck away in one of the spare bedrooms and there she was available for anyone, so long, she explained, as they didn't fluster her when she was cutting out, with a flow of conversation that not even a mouth full of pins seemed to interrupt. And Lady Harman would go and watch Susan Burnet by the hour together and think what an enviably independent young woman she was, and listen with interest and something between horror and admiration to the various impressions of life she had gathered during a hardy and adventurous career.

Their early conversations were about Susan Burnet's business and the general condition of things in that world of upholsterers' young women in which Susan had lived until she perceived the possibilities of a "connexion," and set up for herself. And the condition of things in that world, as Susan described it, brought home to Lady Harman just how sheltered and limited her own upbringing had been. "It isn't right," said Susan, "the way they send girls out with fellers into empty houses. Naturally the men get persecuting them. They don't seem hardly able to help it, some of them, and I will say this for them, that a lot of the girls go more than half way with them, leading them on. Still there's a sort of man won't leave you alone. One I used to be sent out with and a married man too he was, Oh!—he used to give me a time. Why I've bit his hands before now, bit hard, before he'd leave go of me. It's my opinion the married men are worse than the single. Bolder they are. I pushed him over a scuttle once and he hit his head against a bookcase. I was fair frightened of him. 'You little devil,' he says; 'I'll be even with you yet. . . .' Oh! I've been called worse things than that. . . . Of course a respectable girl gets through with it, but it's trying and to some it's a sort of temptation. . . ."

"I should have thought," reflected Lady Harman, "you could have told someone."

"It's queer," said Susan; "but it never seemed to me the sort of thing a girl ought to go telling. It's a kind of private thing. And besides, it isn't exactly easy to tell. . . . I suppose the Firm didn't want to be worried by complaints and disputes about that sort of thing. And it isn't always easy to say just which of the two is to blame.''

"But how old are the girls they send out?" asked Lady Harman.

"Some's as young as seventeen or eighteen. It all depends on the sort of work that's wanted to be done. . . ."

"Of course a lot of them have to marry. . . ."

This lurid little picture of vivid happenings in unoccupied houses and particularly of the prim, industrious, capable Susan Burnet, biting aggressive wrists, stuck in Lady Harman's imagination. She seemed to be looking into hitherto unsuspected pits of simple and violent living just beneath her feet. Susan told some upholsteress love tales, real love tales, with a warmth and honesty of passion in them that seemed at once dreadful and fine to Lady Harman's underfed imagination. Under encouragement Susan expanded the picture, beyond these mere glimpses of workshop and piece-work and furtive lust. It appeared that she was practically the head of her family; there was a mother who had specialized in ill-health, a sister of defective ability who stayed at home, a brother in South Africa who was very good and sent home money, and three younger sisters growing up. And father,—she evaded the subject of father at first. Then presently Lady Harman had some glimpses of an earlier phase in Susan Burnet's life "before any of us were earning money." Father appeared as a kindly, ineffectual, insolvent figure struggling to conduct a baker's and confectioner's business in Walthamstow, mother was already specializing, there were various brothers and sisters being born and dying. "How many were there of you altogether?" asked Lady Harman.

"Thirteen there was. Father always used to laugh and say he'd had a fair baker's dozen. There was Luke to begin with—"

Susan began to count on her fingers and recite braces of scriptural names.

She could only make up her tale to twelve. She became perplexed. Then she remembered. "Of course!" she cried: "there was Nicodemus. He was still-born. I *always* forget Nicodemus, poor little chap! But he came—was it sixth or seventh?—seventh after Anna."

She gave some glimpses of her father and then there was a collapse of which she fought shy. Lady Harman was too delicate to press her to talk of that.

But one day in the afternoon Susan's tongue ran.

She was telling how first she went to work before she was twelve.

"But I thought the board schools—" said Lady Harman.

"I had to go before the committee," said Susan. "I had to go before the committee and ask to be let go to work. There they was, sitting round a table in a great big room, and they was as kind as anything, one old gentleman with a great white beard, he was as kind as could be. 'Don't you be frightened, my dear,' he says. 'You tell us why you want to go out working.' 'Well,' I says, '*somebody's* got to earn something,' and that made them laugh in a sort of fatherly way, and after that there wasn't any difficulty. You see it was after Father's Inquest, and everybody was disposed to be kind to us. 'Pity they can't all go instead of this educational Tommy Rot,' the old gentleman says. 'You learn to work, my dear'—and I did. . . ."

She paused.

"Father's inquest?" said Lady Harman.

Susan seemed to brace herself to the occasion. "Father," she said, "was drowned. I know—I hadn't told you that before. He was drowned in the Lea. It's always been a distress and humiliation to us there had to be an Inquest. And they threw out things. . . . It's why we moved to Haggerston. It's the worst that ever happened to us in all our lives. Far worse. Worse than having the things sold or the children with scarlet fever and having to burn everything. . . . I don't like to talk about it. I can't help it but I don't. . . .

"I don't know why I talk to you as I do, Lady Harman, but I don't seem to mind talking to you. I don't suppose I've opened my mouth to anyone about it, not for years—except to one dear friend I've got—her who persuaded me to be a church member. But what I've always said and what I will always say is this, that I don't believe any evil of Father, I don't believe, I won't ever believe he took his life. I won't even believe he was in drink. I don't know how he got in the river, but I'm certain it wasn't so. He was a weak man, was Father, I've never denied he was a weak man. But a harder working man than he was never lived. He worried, anyone would have worried seeing the worries he had. The shop wasn't paying as it was; often we never tasted meat for weeks together, and then there came one of these Internationals, giving overweight and under-selling. . . ."

"One of these Internationals?"

"Yes, I don't suppose you've ever heard of them. They're in the poorer neighborhoods chiefly. They sell teas and things mostly now but they began as bakers' shops and what they did was to come into a place and undersell until all the old shops were ruined and shut up. That was what they tried to do and Father hadn't no more chance amongst them than a mouse in a trap. . . . It was just like being run over. All the trade that stayed with us after a bit was Bad Debts. You can't blame people I suppose for going where they get more and pay less, and it wasn't till we'd all gone right away to Haggerston that they altered things and put the prices up again. Of course Father lost heart and all that. He didn't know what to do, he'd sunk all he had in the shop; he just sat and moped about. Really,—he was pitiful. He wasn't able to sleep; he used to get up at nights and go about downstairs. Mother says she found him once sweeping out the bakehouse at two o'clock in the morning. He got it into his head that getting up like that would help him. But I don't believe and I won't believe he wouldn't have seen it through if he could. Not to my dying day will I believe that. . . ."

Lady Harman reflected. "But couldn't he have got work again—as a baker?"

"It's hard after you've had a shop. You see all the younger men've come on. They know the new ways. And a man who's had a shop and failed, he's lost heart. And these stores setting up make everything drivinger. They do things a different way. They make it harder for everyone."

Both Lady Harman and Susan Burnet reflected in silence for a few seconds upon the International Stores. The sewing woman was the first to speak.

"Things like that," she said, "didn't ought to be. One shop didn't ought to be allowed to set out to ruin another. It isn't fair trading, it's a sort of murder. It oughtn't to be allowed. How was father to know? . . ."

"There's got to be competition," said Lady Harman.

"I don't call that competition," said Susan Burnet.

"But,—I suppose they give people cheaper bread."

"They do for a time. Then when they've killed you they do what they like. . . . Luke—he's one of those who'll say anything—well, he used to say it was a regular Monopoly. But it's hard on people who've set out to live honest and respectable and bring up a family plain and decent to be pushed out of the way like that."

"I suppose it is," said Lady Harman.

"What was father to *do?*" said Susan, and turned to Sir Isaac's armchair from which this discourse had distracted her.

And then suddenly, in a voice thick with rage, she burst out: "And then Alice must needs go and take their money. That's what sticks in *my* throat."

Still on her knees she faced about to Lady Harman.

"Alice goes into one of their Ho'burn branches as a waitress, do what I could to prevent her. It makes one mad to think of it. Time after time I've said to her, 'Alice,' I've said, 'sooner than touch their dirty money I'd starve in the street.' And she goes! She says it's all nonsense of me to bear a spite. Laughs at me! 'Alice,' I told her, 'it's a wonder the spirit of poor father don't rise up against you.' And she laughs. Calls that bearing a spite. . . . Of course she was little when it happened. She can't remember, not as I remember. . . ."

Lady Harman reflected for a time. "I suppose you don't know," she began, addressing Susan's industrious back; "you don't know who—who owns these International Stores?"

"I suppose it's some company," said Susan. "I don't see that it lets them off—being in a company."

8

We have done much in the last few years to destroy the severe limitations of Victorian delicacy, and all of us, from princesses and prime-ministers' wives downward, talk of topics that would have been considered quite gravely improper in the nineteenth century. Nevertheless, some topics have, if anything, become more indelicate than they were, and this is especially true of the discussion of income, of any discussion that tends, however remotely, to inquire, Who is it at the base of everything who really pays in blood and muscle and involuntary submissions for *your* freedom and magnificence? This, indeed, is almost the ultimate surviving indecency. So that it was with considerable private shame and discomfort that Lady Harman pursued even in her privacy the train of thought that Susan Burnet had set going. It had been conveyed into her mind long ago, and it had settled down there and grown into a sort of security, that the International Bread and Cake Stores were a very important contribution to Progress, and that Sir Isaac, outside the gates of his home, was a very useful and beneficial personage, and richly meriting a baronetcy. She hadn't particularly analyzed this persuasion, but she supposed him engaged in a kind of daily repetition, but upon modern scientific lines, of the miracle of the loaves and fishes, feeding a great multitude that would otherwise have gone hungry. She knew, too, from the advertisements that flowered about her path through life, that this bread in question was exceptionally clean and hygienic; whole front pages of the *Daily Messenger,* headed the "Fauna of Small Bakehouses," and adorned with a bordering of *Blatta orientalis,* the common cockroach, had taught her that, and she knew that Sir Isaac's passion for purity had also led to the *Old Country Gazette*'s spirited and successful campaign for a nonparty measure securing additional bakehouse regulation and inspection. And her impression had been that the growing and developing refreshment side of the concern was almost a public charity; Sir Isaac gave, he said, a larger, heavier scone, a bigger pat of butter, a more elegant teapot, ham more finely cut and less questionable pork-pies than any other system of syndicated tea-shops. She supposed that whenever he sat late at night going over schemes and papers, or when he went off for days together to Cardiff or Glasgow or Dublin, or such-like centers, or when he became preoccupied at dinner and whistled thoughtfully through his teeth, he was planning to increase the amount or diminish the cost of tea and cocoa-drenched farinaceous food in the stomachs of that section of our national adolescence which goes out daily into the streets of our great cities to be fed. And she knew his vans and catering were indispensable to the British Army upon its maneuvers. . . .

Now the smashing up of the Burnet family by the International Stores was disagreeably not in the picture of these suppositions. And the remarkable thing is that this one little tragedy wouldn't for a moment allow itself to be regarded as an exceptional accident in an otherwise fair vast development. It remained obstinately a specimen—of the other side of the great syndication.

It was just as if she had been doubting subconsciously all along. . . . In the silence of the night she lay awake and tried to make herself believe that the Burnet case was just a unique overlooked disaster, that it needed only to come to Sir Isaac's attention to be met by the fullest reparation. . . .

After all she did not bring it to Sir Isaac's attention.

But one morning, while this phase of new doubts was still lively in her mind, Sir Isaac told her he was going down to Brighton, and then along the coast road in a car to Portsmouth, to pay a few surprise visits, and see how the machine was working. He would be away a night, an unusual breach in his habits.

"Are you thinking of any new branches, Isaac?"

"I may have a look at Arundel."

"Isaac." She paused to frame her question carefully. "I suppose there are some shops at Arundel now."

"I've got to see to that."

"If you open—I suppose the old shops get hurt. What becomes of the people if they do get hurt?"

"That's *their* look-out," said Sir Isaac.

"Isn't it bad for them?"

"Progress is Progress, Elly."

"It *is* bad for them. I suppose— Wouldn't it be sometimes kinder if you took over the old shop—made a sort of partner of him, or something?"

Sir Isaac shook his head. "I want younger men," he said. "You can't get a move on the older hands."

"But, then, it's rather bad— I suppose these little men you shut up,—some of them must have families."

"You're theorizing a bit this morning, Elly," said Sir Isaac, looking up over his coffee cup.

"I've been thinking—about these little people."

"Someone's been talking to you about my shops," said Sir Isaac, and stuck out an index finger. "If that's Georgina—"

"It isn't Georgina," said Lady Harman, but she had it very clear in her mind that she must not say who it was.

"You can't make a business without squeezing somebody," said Sir Isaac. "It's easy enough to make a row about any concern that grows a bit. Some people would like to have every business tied down to a maximum turnover and so much a year profit. I daresay you've been hearing of these articles in *The London Lion*. Pretty stuff it is, too. This fuss about the little shopkeepers; that's a new racket. I've had all that row about the waitresses before, and the yarn about the Normandy eggs, and all that, but I don't see that you need go reading it against me, and bringing it up at the breakfast-table. A business is a business, it isn't a charity, and I'd like to know where you and I would be if we didn't run the concern on business lines. . . . Why, that *London Lion* fellow came to me with the first two of those articles before the thing began. I could have had the whole thing stopped if I liked, if I'd chosen to take the back page of his beastly cover. That shows the stuff the whole thing is made of. That shows you.

Why!—he's just a blackmailer, that's what he is. Much he cares for my waitresses if he can get the dibs. Little shopkeepers, indeed! I know 'em! Nice martyrs they are! There isn't one wouldn't *skin* all the others if he got half a chance. . . ."

Sir Isaac gave way to an extraordinary fit of nagging anger. He got up and stood upon the hearthrug to deliver his soul the better. It was an altogether unexpected and illuminating outbreak. He was flushed with guilt. The more angry and eloquent he became, the more profoundly thoughtful grew the attentive lady at the head of his table. . . .

When at last Sir Isaac had gone off in the car to Victoria, Lady Harman rang for Snagsby. "Isn't there a paper," she asked, "called *The London Lion?*"

"It isn't one I think your ladyship would like," said Snagsby, gently but firmly.

"I know. But I want to see it. I want copies of all the issues in which there have been articles upon the International Stores."

"They're thoroughly volgar, me lady," said Snagsby, with a large dissuasive smile.

"I want you to go out into London and get them now."

Snagsby hesitated and went. Within five minutes he reappeared with a handful of buff-covered papers.

"There 'appened to be copies in the pantry, me lady," he said. "We can't imagine 'ow they got there; someone must have brought them in, but 'ere they are quite at your service, me lady." He paused for a discreet moment. Something indescribably confidential came into his manner. "I doubt if Sir Isaac will quite like to 'ave them left about, me lady—after you done with them."

She was in a mood of discovery. She sat in the room that was all furnished in pink (her favorite color) and read a bitter, malicious, coarsely written and yet insidiously credible account of her husband's business methods. Something within herself seemed to answer, "But didn't you know this all along?" That large conviction that her wealth and position were but the culmination of a great and honorable social service, a conviction that had been her tacit comfort during much distasteful loyalty seemed to shrivel and fade. No doubt the writer was a thwarted blackmailer; even her accustomed mind could distinguish a twang of some such vicious quality in his sentences; but that did not alter the realities he exhibited and exaggerated. There was a description of how Sir Isaac pounced on his managers that was manifestly derived from a manager he had dismissed. It was dreadfully like him. Convincingly like him. There was a statement of the wages he paid his girl assistants and long extracts from his codes of rules and schedules of fines. . . .

When she put down the paper she was suddenly afflicted by a vivid vision of Susan Burnet's father, losing heart and not knowing what to do. She had an unreasonable feeling that Susan Burnet's father must have been a small, kindly, furry, bunnyish, little man. Of course there had to be progress and the survival of the fittest. She found herself weighing what she imagined Susan Burnet's father to be like, against the ferrety face, stooping shoulders and scheming whistle of Sir Isaac.

There were times now when she saw her husband with an extreme distinctness.

9

As this cold and bracing realization that all was not right with her position, with Sir Isaac's business procedure and the world generally, took possession of Lady Harman's thoughts there came also with it and arising out of it quite a series of new moods and dispositions. At times she was very full of the desire "to do something," something that would, as it were, satisfy and assuage this growing uneasiness of responsibility in her mind. At times her consuming wish was not to assuage but escape from this urgency. It worried her and made her feel helpless, and she wanted beyond anything else to get back to that child's world where all experiences are adventurous and everything is finally right. She felt, I think, that it was a little unfair to her that this something within her should be calling upon her to take all sorts of things gravely—hadn't she been a good wife and brought four children into the world . . . ?

I am setting down here as clearly as possible what wasn't by any means clear in Lady Harman's mind. I am giving you side by side phases that never came side by side in her thoughts but which followed and ousted and obliterated one another. She had moods of triviality. She had moods of magnificence. She had moods of intense secret hostility to her urgent little husband, and moods of genial tolerance for everything there was in her life. She had moods, and don't we all have moods?—of skepticism and cynicism, much profounder than the conventions and limitations of novel-writing permit us to tell here. And for hardly any of these moods had she terms and recognitions. . . .

It isn't a natural thing to keep on worrying about the morality of one's material prosperity. These are proclivities superinduced by modern conditions of the conscience. There is a natural resistance in every healthy human being to such distressful heart-searchings. Strong instincts battled in Lady Harman against this intermittent sense of responsibility that was beginning to worry her. An immense lot of her was for simply running away from these troublesome considerations, for covering herself up from them, for distraction.

And about this time she happened upon "Elizabeth and her German Garden," and was very greatly delighted and stimulated by that little sister of Montaigne. She was charmed by the book's fresh gaiety, by its gallant resolve to set off all the good things there are in this world, the sunshine and flowers and laughter, against the limitations and thwartings and disappointments of life. For a time it seemed to her that these brave consolations were solutions, and she was stirred by an imitative passion. How stupid had she not been to let life and Sir Isaac overcome her! She felt that she must make herself like Elizabeth, exactly like Elizabeth; she tried forthwith, and a certain difficulty she found, a certain deadness, she ascribed to the square modernity of her house and something in the Putney air. The house was too large, it dominated the garden and controlled her. She felt she must get away to some place that was chiefly exterior, in the sunshine, far from towns and struggling, straining, angry and despairing humanity, from syndicated shops and all the embarrassing challenges of life. Somehow there it would be possible to keep Sir Isaac at arm's length; and the ghost of Susan Burnet's father could be left behind to haunt the square rooms of the London house. And there she would live, horticultural, bookish, whimsical, witty, defiant, happily careless.

And it was this particular conception of evasion that had set her careering about the countryside in her car, looking for conceivable houses of refuge from this dark novelty of social and personal care, and that had driven her into the low long room of Black Strand and the presence of Mr. Brumley.

Of what ensued and the appearance and influence of Lady Beach-Mandarin and how it led among other things to a lunch invitation from that lady the reader has already been informed.

CHAPTER THE SIXTH

The Adventurous Afternoon

1

YOU WILL PERHAPS remember that before I fell into this extensive digression about Lady Harman's upbringing, we had got to the entry of Mrs. Sawbridge into the house bearing a plunder of Sir Isaac's best roses. She interrupted a conversation of some importance. Those roses at this point are still unwithered and fragrant, and moreover they are arranged according to Mrs. Sawbridge's ideas of elegance about Sir Isaac's home. . . . And Sir Isaac, when that conversation could be renewed, categorically forbade Lady Harman to go to Lady Beach-Mandarin's lunch and Lady Harman went to Lady Beach-Mandarin's lunch.

She had some peculiar difficulties in getting to that lunch.

It is necessary to tell certain particulars. They are particulars that will distress the delicacy of Mrs. Sawbridge unspeakably if ever she chances to read this book. But a story has to be told. You see Sir Isaac Harman had never considered it advisable to give his wife a private allowance. Whatever she wished to have, he maintained, she could have. The bill would afterwards be paid by his cheque on the first day of the month following the receipt of the bill. He found a generous pleasure in writing these cheques, and Lady Harman was magnificently housed, fed and adorned. Moreover, whenever she chose to ask for money he gave her money, usually double of what she demanded,—and often a kiss or so into the bargain. But after he had forbidden her to go to Lady Beach-Mandarin's so grave an estrangement ensued that she could not ask him for money. A door closed between them. And the crisis had come at an unfortunate moment. She possessed the sum of five shillings and eightpence.

She perceived quite early that this shortness of money would greatly embarrass the rebellion she contemplated. She was exceptionally ignorant of most worldly things, but she knew there was never yet a campaign without a war chest. She felt entitled to money. . . .

She planned several times to make a demand for replenishment with a haughty dignity; the haughty dignity was easy enough to achieve, but the demand was not. A sensitive dread of her mother's sympathetic curiosity barred all thoughts of borrowing in that direction,—she and her mother "never discussed money matters." She did not want to get Georgina into further trouble. And besides, Georgina was in Devonshire.

Even to get to Lady Beach-Mandarin's became difficult under these circumstances. She knew that Clarence, though he would take her into the country quite freely, had been instructed, on account of Sir Isaac's expressed dread of any accident happening to her while alone, not to plunge with her into the vortex of London traffic. Only under direct orders from Sir Isaac would Clarence take her down Putney Hill; though she might go up and away—to anywhere. She knew nothing of pawnshops or any associated methods of getting cash advances, and the possibility of using the telephone to hire an automobile never occurred to her. But she was fully resolved to go. She had one advantage in the fact that Sir Isaac didn't know the precise date of the disputed engagement. When that arrived she spent a restless morning and dressed herself at last with great care. She instructed Peters, her maid, who participated in these preparations with a mild astonishment, that she was going out to lunch, asked her to inform Mrs.

Sawbridge of the fact and, outwardly serene, made a bolt for it down the staircase and across the hall. The great butler appeared; she had never observed how like a large note of interrogation his forward contours could be.

"I shall be out to lunch, Snagsby," she said, and went past him into the sunshine.

She left a discreetly astonished Snagsby behind her.

("Now where are we going out to lunch?" said Snagsby presently to Peters.

"I've never known her so particular with her clothes," said the maid.

"Never before—not in the same way; it's something new and special to this affair," Snagsby reflected, "I wonder now if Sir Isaac. . . ."

"One can't help observing things," said the maid, after a pause. "Mute though we be.")

Lady Harman had the whole five and eightpence with her. She had managed to keep it intact in her jewel case, declaring she had no change when any small demands were made on her.

With an exhilaration so great that she wanted sorely to laugh aloud she walked out through her big open gates and into the general publicity of Putney Hill. Why had she not done as much years ago? How long she had been, working up to this obvious thing! She hadn't been out in such complete possession of herself since she had been a schoolgirl. She held up a beautifully gloved hand to a private motor-car going downhill and then to an engaged taxi going up, and then with a slightly dashed feeling, picked up her skirt and walked observantly downhill. Her reason dispelled a transitory impression that these two vehicles were on Sir Isaac's side against her.

There was quite a nice taxi on the rank at the bottom of the hill. The driver, a pleasant-looking young man in a white cap, seemed to have been waiting for her in particular; he met her timid invitation halfway and came across the road to her and jumped down and opened the door. He took her instructions as though they were after his own heart, and right in front of her as she sat was a kind of tin cornucopia full of artificial flowers that seemed like a particular attention to her. His fare was two and eightpence and she gave him four shillings. He seemed quite gratified by her largesse, his manner implied he had always thought as much of her, from first to last their relations had been those of sunny contentment, and it was only as she ascended the steps of Lady Beach-Mandarin's portico, that it occurred to her that she now had insufficient money for an automobile to take her home. But there were railways and buses and all sorts of possibilities; the day was an adventure; and she entered the drawing-room with a brow that was beautifully unruffled. She wanted to laugh still; it animated her eyes and lips with the pleasantest little stir you can imagine.

"A-a-a-a-a-h!" cried Lady Beach-Mandarin in a high note, and threw out—it had an effect of being quite a number of arms—as though she was one of those brass Indian goddesses one sees.

Lady Harman felt taken in at once to all that capacious bosom involved and contained. . . .

2

It was quite an amusing lunch. But any lunch would have been amusing to Lady Harman in the excitement of her first act of deliberate disobedience. She had never been out to lunch alone in all her life before; she experienced a kind of scared happiness, she felt like someone at Lourdes who has just thrown away crutches. She was seated between a pink young man with an eyeglass whose place was labelled "Bertie Trevor" and who was otherwise unexplained, and Mr. Brumley. She was quite glad to see Mr. Brumley again, and no doubt her eyes showed it. She had hoped to see him. Miss Sharsper was sitting nearly opposite to her, a real live novelist pecking observations out of life as a hen pecks seeds amidst scenery, and next beyond was a large-headed inattentive fluffy person who was Mr. Keystone the well-known critic. And there was Agatha Alimony under a rustling vast hat of green-black cock's feathers next to Sir Markham Crosby, with whom she had been having an abusive controversy in the *Times* and to whom quite elaborately she wouldn't speak, and there was Lady Viping with her lorgnette and Adolphus Blenker, Horatio's younger and if possible more gentlemanly brother—Horatio of the *Old Country Gazette* that is—sole reminder that there was such a person as Sir Isaac in the world. Lady Beach-Mandarin's mother and the Swiss governess and the tall but retarded daughter, Phyllis, completed the party. The reception was lively and cheering; Lady Beach-Mandarin enfolded her guests in generosities and kept them all astir like a sea-swell under a squadron, and she introduced Lady Harman to Miss Alimony by public proclamation right across the room because there were two lavish tables of bric-à-brac, a marble bust of old Beach-Mandarin and most of the rest of the party in the way. And at the table conversation was like throwing bread, you never knew whom you might hit or who might hit you. (But Lady Beach-Mandarin produced an effect of throwing whole loaves.) Bertie Trevor was one of those dancing young men who talk to a woman as though they were giving a dog biscuits, and mostly it was Mr. Brumley who did such talking as reached Lady Harman's ear.

Mr. Brumley was in very good form that day. He had contrived to remind her of all their Black Strand talk while they were still eating *Petites Bouchées à la Reine.* "Have you found that work yet?" he asked and carried her mind to the core of her situation. Then they were snatched up into a general discussion of Bazaars. Sir Markham spoke of a great bazaar that was to be held on behalf of one of the many Shakespeare Theatre movements that were then so prevalent. Was Lady Beach-Mandarin implicated? Was anyone? He told of novel features in contemplation. He generalized about bazaars and, with an air of having forgotten the presence of Miss Alimony, glanced at the Suffrage Bazaar—it was a season of bazaars. He thought poorly of the Suffrage Bazaar. The hostess intervened promptly with anecdotes of her own cynical daring as a Bazaar-seller, Miss Sharsper offered fragments of a reminiscence about signing one of her own books for a Bookstall, Blenker told a well-known Bazaar anecdote brightly and well, and the impending skirmish was averted.

While the Bazaar talk still whacked to and fro about the table Mr. Brumley got at Lady Harman's ear again. "Rather tantalizing these meetings at table," he said. "It's like trying to talk while you swim in a rough sea. . . ."

Then Lady Beach-Mandarin intervened with demands for support for her own particular Bazaar project and they were eating salad before there was a chance of another word between them. "I must confess that when I want to talk to people I like to get them alone," said Mr. Brumley, and gave form to thoughts that were already on the verge of crystallization in her own mind. She had been recalling that she had liked his voice before, noting something very kindly and thoughtful and brotherly about his right profile and thinking how much an hour's talk with him would help to clear up her ideas.

"But it's so difficult to get one alone," said Lady Harman, and suddenly an idea of the utmost daring and impropriety flashed into her mind. She was on the verge of speaking it forthwith and then didn't, she met something in his eye that answered her own and then Lady Beach-Mandarin was foaming over them like a dam-burst over an American town.

"What do *you* think, Mr. Brumley?" demanded Lady Beach-Mandarin. "?"

"About Sir Markham's newspaper symposium. They asked him what allowance he gave his wife. Sent a prepaid reply telegram."

"But he hasn't got a wife!"

"They don't stick at a little thing like that," said Sir Markham grimly.

"I think a husband and wife ought to have everything in common like the early Christians," said Lady Beach-Mandarin. "*We* always did," and so got the discussion afloat again off the sandbank of Mr. Brumley's inattention.

It was quite a good discussion and Lady Harman contributed an exceptionally alert and intelligent silence. Sir Markham distrusted Lady Beach-Mandarin's communism and thought that anyhow it wouldn't do for a financier or business man. He favored an allowance. "So did Sir Joshua," said the widow Viping. This roused Agatha Alimony. "Allowance indeed!" she cried. "Is a wife to be on no better footing than a daughter? The whole question of a wife's financial autonomy needs reconsidering. . . ."

Adolphus Blenker became learned and lucid upon Pin-money and dowry and the customs of savage tribes, and Mr. Brumley helped with corroboration. . . .

Mr. Brumley managed to say just one other thing to Lady Harman before the lunch was over. It struck her for a moment as being irrelevant. "The gardens at Hampton Court," he said, "are delightful just now. Have you seen them? Autumnal fires. All the September perennials lifting their spears in their last great chorus. It's the *Götterdämmerung* of the year."

She was going out of the room before she appreciated his possible intention.

Lady Beach-Mandarin delegated Sir Markham to preside over the men's cigars and bounced and slapped her four ladies upstairs to the drawing-room. Her mother disappeared and so did Phyllis and the governess. Lady Harman heard a large aside to Lady Viping: "Isn't she perfectly lovely?" glanced to discover the lorgnette in appreciative action, and then found herself drifting into a secluded window-seat and a duologue with Miss Agatha Alimony. Miss Alimony was one of that large and increasing number of dusky, gray-eyed ladies who go through life with an air of darkly incomprehensible significance. She led off Lady Harman as though she took her away to reveal unheard-of mysteries and her voice was a contralto undertone that she emphasized in some inexplicable way by the magnetic use of her eyes. Her hat of cock's feathers which rustled like familiar spirits greatly augmented the profundity of her effect. As she spoke she glanced guardedly at the other ladies at the end of the room and from first to last she seemed undecided in her own mind whether she was a conspirator or a prophetess. She had heard of Lady Harman before, she had been longing impatiently to talk to her all through the lunch. "You are just what we want," said Agatha. "What who want?" asked Lady Harman, struggling against the hypnotic influence of her interlocutor. "*We*," said Miss Agatha, "the Cause. The G. S. W. S.

"We want just such people as you," she repeated, and began in panting rhetorical sentences to urge the militant cause.

For her it was manifestly a struggle against "the Men." Miss Alimony had no doubts of her sex. It had nothing to learn, nothing to be forgiven, it was compact of obscured and persecuted marvels, it needed only revelation. "They know Nothing," she said of the antagonist males, bringing deep notes out of the melodious caverns of her voice; "they know *Nothing* of the Deeper Secrets of Woman's Nature." Her discourse of a general feminine insurrection fell in very closely with the spirit of Lady Harman's private revolt. "We want the Vote," said Agatha, "and we want the Vote because the Vote means Autonomy. And then—"

She paused voluminously. She had already used that word "Autonomy" at the lunch table and it came to her hearer to supply a long-felt want. Now she poured meanings into it, and Lady Harman with each addition realized more clearly that it was still a roomy sack for more. "A woman should be absolute mistress of herself," said Miss Alimony, "absolute mistress of her person. She should be free to develop—"

Germinating phrases these were in Lady Harman's ear.

She wanted to know about the Suffrage movement from someone less generously impatient than Georgina, for Georgina always lost her temper about it and to put it fairly *ranted*, this at any rate was serene and confident, and she asked tentative ill-formed questions and felt her way among Miss Alimony's profundities. She had her doubts, her instinctive doubts about this campaign of violence, she doubted its wisdom, she doubted its rightness, and she perceived, but she found it difficult to express her perception, that Miss Alimony wasn't so much answering her objections as trying to swamp her with exalted emotion. And if there was any flaw whatever in her attention to Miss Alimony's stirring talk, it was because she was keeping a little look-out in the tail of her eye for the reappearance of the men, and more particularly for the reappearance of Mr. Brumley with whom she had a peculiar feeling of uncompleted relations. And at last the men came and she caught his glance and saw that her feeling was reciprocated.

She was presently torn from Agatha, who gasped with pain at the parting and pursued her with a sedulous gaze as a doctor might watch an injected patient, she parted with Lady Beach-Mandarin with a vast splash of enthusiasm and mutual invitations, and Lady Viping came and pressed her to come to dinner and rapped her elbow with her lorgnette to emphasize her invitation. And Lady Harman after a still moment for reflection athwart which the word Autonomy flickered, accepted this invitation also.

3

Mr. Brumley hovered for a few moments in the hall conversing with Lady Beach-Mandarin's butler, whom he had known for some years and helped about a small investment, and who was now being abjectly polite and grateful to him for his attention. It gave Mr. Brumley a nice feudal feeling to establish and maintain such relationships. The furry-eyed boy fumbled with the sticks and umbrellas in the background and wondered if he too would ever climb to these levels of respectful gilt-tipped friendliness. Mr. Brumley hovered the more readily because he knew Lady Harman was with the looking-glass in the little parlor behind the dining-room on her way to the outer world. At last she emerged. It was instantly manifest to Mr. Brumley that she had expected to find him there. She smiled frankly at him, with the faintest admission of complicity in her smile.

"Taxi, milady?" said the butler.

She seemed to reflect. "No, I will walk." She hesitated over a glove button. "Mr. Brumley, is there a Tube station near here?"

"Not two minutes. But can't I perhaps take you in a taxi?"

"I'd rather walk."

"I will show you—"

He found himself most agreeably walking off with her.

Still more agreeable things were to follow for Mr. Brumley.

She appeared to meditate upon a sudden idea. She disregarded some conversational opening of his that he forgot in the instant. "Mr. Brumley," she said, "I didn't intend to go directly home."

"I'm altogether at your service," said Mr. Brumley.

"At least," said Lady Harman with that careful truthfulness of hers, "it occurred to me during lunch that I wouldn't go directly home."

Mr. Brumley reined in an imagination that threatened to bolt with him.

"I want," said Lady Harman, "to go to Kensington Gardens, I think. This can't be far from Kensington Gardens—and I want to sit there on a green chair and—meditate—and afterwards I want to find a tube railway or something that will take me back to Putney. There is really no need for me to go directly home. . . . It's very stupid of me but I don't know my way about London as a rational creature should do. So will you take me and put me in a green chair and—tell me how afterwards I can find the Tube and get home? Do you mind?"

"All my time, so long as you want it, is at your service," said Mr. Brumley with convincing earnestness. "And it's not five minutes to the gardens. And afterwards a taxi-cab—"

"No," said Lady Harman mindful of her one-and-eightpence, "I prefer a tube. But that we can talk about later. You're sure, Mr. Brumley, I'm not invading your time?"

"I wish you could see into my mind," said Mr. Brumley.

She became almost barefaced. "It is so true," she said, "that at lunch one can't really talk to anyone. And I've so wanted to talk to you. Ever since we met before."

Mr. Brumley conveyed an unfeigned delight.

"Since then," said Lady Harman, "I've read your *Euphemia* books." Then after a little unskilful pause, "again." Then she blushed and added, "I *had* read one of them, you know, before."

"Exactly," he said with an infinite helpfulness.

"And you seem so sympathetic, so understanding. I feel that all sorts of things that are muddled in my mind would come clear if I could have a really Good Talk. To you. . . ."

They were now through the gates approaching the Albert Memorial. Mr. Brumley was filled with an idea so desirable that it made him fear to suggest it.

"Of course we can talk very comfortably here," he said, "under these great trees. But I do so wish—Have you seen those great borders at Hampton Court? The whole place is glowing, and in such sunshine as this— A taxi—will take us there under the hour. If you are free until half-past five."

Why shouldn't she?

The proposal seemed so outrageous to all the world of Lady Harman that in her present mood she felt it was her duty in the cause of womanhood to nerve herself and accept it. . . .

"I mustn't be later than half-past five."

"We could snatch a glimpse of it all and be back before then."

"In that case— It would be very agreeable."

(*Why shouldn't she?* It would no doubt make Sir Isaac furiously angry—if he heard of it. But it was the sort of thing other women of her class did; didn't all the novels testify? She had a perfect right—

And besides, Mr. Brumley was so entirely harmless.)

4

It had been Lady Harman's clear intention to have a luminous and illuminating discussion of the peculiar difficulties and perplexities of her position with Mr. Brumley. Since their first encounter this idea had grown up in her mind. She was one of those women who turn instinctively to men and away from women for counsel. There was to her perception something wise and kindly and reassuring in him; she felt that he had lived and suffered and understood and that he was ready to help other people to live; his heart she knew from his published works was buried with his dead Euphemia, and he seemed as near a thing to a brother and a friend as she was ever likely to meet. She wanted to tell him all this and then to broach her teeming and tangled difficulties, about her own permissible freedoms, about her social responsibilities, about Sir Isaac's business. But now as their taxi dodged through the traffic of Kensington High Street and went on its way past Olympia and so out westwards, she found it extremely difficult to fix her mind upon the large propositions with which it had been her intention to open. Do as she would to feel that this was a momentous occasion, she could not suppress, she could not ignore an obstinate and entirely undignified persuasion that she was having a tremendous lark. The passing vehicles, various motors, omnibuses, vans, carriages, the thronging pedestrians, the shops and houses, were all so distractingly interesting that at last she had to put it fairly to herself whether she hadn't better resign herself to the sensations of the present and reserve that sustained discussion for an interval she foresaw as inevitable on some comfortable seat under great trees at Hampton Court. You cannot talk well and penetratingly about fundamental things when you are in a not too well-hung taxi which is racing to get ahead of a vast red motor-omnibus. . . .

With a certain discretion Mr. Brumley had instructed the chauffeur to cross the river not at Putney but at Hammersmith, and so they went by Barnes station and up a still almost rural lane into Richmond Park, and there suddenly they were among big trees and bracken and red deer and it might have been a hundred miles from London streets. Mr. Brumley directed the driver to make a detour that gave them quite all the best of the park.

The mind of Mr. Brumley was also agreeably excited and dispersed on this occasion. It was an occasion of which he had been dreaming very frequently of late, he had invented quite remarkable dialogues during those dreams, and now he too was conversationally inadequate and with a similar feeling of unexpected adventure. He was now no more ready to go to the roots of things than Lady Harman. He talked on the way down chiefly of the route they were following, of the changes in the London traffic due to motor traction and of the charm and amenity of Richmond Park. And it was only after they had arrived at Hampton Court and dismissed the taxi and spent some time upon the borders, that they came at last to a seat under a grove beside a long piece of water bearing water lilies, and sat down and made a beginning with the Good Talk. Then indeed she tried to gather together the heads of her perplexity and Mr. Brumley did his best to do justice to the confidence she reposed in him. . . .

It wasn't at all the conversation he had dreamed of; it was halting, it was inconclusive, it was full of a vague dissatisfaction.

The roots of this dissatisfaction lay perhaps more than anything else in her inattention to him—how shall I say it?—as *Him*. Hints have been conveyed to the reader already that for Mr. Brumley the universe was largely a setting, a tangle, a maze, a quest enshrining at the heart of it and adumbrating everywhere, a mystical Her, and his experience of this world had pointed him very definitely to the conclusion that for that large other half of mankind which is woman, the quality of things was reciprocal and centered, for all the appearances and pretenses of other interests, in—Him. And he was disposed to believe that the other things in life, not merely the pomp and glories but the faiths and ambitions and devotions, were all demonstrably little more than posings and dressings of this great duality. A large part of his own interests and of the interests of the women he knew best, was the sustained and in some cases recurrent discovery and elaboration of lights and glimpses of Him or Her as the case might be, in various definite individuals; and it was a surprise to him, it perplexed him to find that this lovely person, so beautifully equipped for those mutual researches which constituted, he felt, the heart of life, was yet completely in her manner unaware of this primary sincerity and looking quite simply, as it were, over him and through him at such things as the ethics of the baking, confectionery and refreshment trade and the limits of individual responsibility in these matters. The conclusion that she was "unawakened" was inevitable.

The dream of "awakening" this Sleeping Beauty associated itself in a logical sequence with his interpretations. I do not say that such thoughts were clear in Mr. Brumley's mind, they were not, but into this shape the forms of his thoughts fell. Such things dimly felt below the clear level of consciousness were in him. And they gave his attempt to take up and answer the question that perplexed her, something of the quality of an attempt to clothe and serve hidden purposes. It could not but be evident to him that the effort of Lady Harman to free herself a little from her husband's circumvallation and to disentangle herself a little from the realities of his commercial life, might lead to such a liberation as would leave her like a nascent element ready to recombine. And it was entirely in the vein of this drift of thought in him that he should resolve upon an assiduous proximity against that moment of release and awakening. . . .

I do not do Mr. Brumley as the human lover justice if I lead you to suppose that he plotted thus clearly and calculatingly. Yet all this was in his mind. All this was in Mr. Brumley, but it wasn't Mr. Brumley. Presented with it as a portrait of his mind, he would have denied it indignantly—and, knowing it was there, have grown a little flushed in his denials. Quite equally in his mind was a simple desire to please her, to do what she wished, to help her because she wanted help. And a quite keen desire to be clean and honest about her and everything connected with her, for his own sake as well as for her sake—for the sake of the relationship. . . .

So you have Mr. Brumley on the green seat under the great trees at Hampton Court, in his neat London clothes, his quite becoming silk-hat, above his neatly handsome and intelligent profile, with his gloves in his hand and one arm over the seat back, going now very earnestly and thoughtfully into the question of the social benefit of the International Bread and Cake Stores and whether it was possible for her to "do anything" to repair any wrongs that might have arisen out of that organization, and you will understand why there is a little flush in his cheek and why his sentences are a trifle disconnected and tentative and why his eye wanders now to the soft raven tresses about Lady Harman's ear, now to the sweet movement of her speaking lips and now to the gracious droop of her pose as she sits forward, elbow upon crossed knee and chin on glove, and jabs her parasol at the ground in her unaccustomed efforts to explain and discuss the difficulties of her position.

And you will understand too why it is that he doesn't deal with the question before him so simply and impartially as he seems to do. Obscuring this extremely interesting problem of a woman growing to man-like sense of responsibility in her social consequences, is the dramatic proclivity that makes him see all this merely as something which must necessarily weaken Lady Harman's loyalty and qualify her submission to Sir Isaac, that makes him want to utilize it and develop it in that direction. . . .

5

Moreover so complex is the thought of man, there was also another stream of mental activity flowing in the darker recesses of Mr. Brumley's mind. Unobtrusively he was trying to count the money in his pockets and make certain estimates.

It had been his intention to replenish his sovereign purse that afternoon at his club and he was only reminded of this abandoned plan when he paid off his taxi at the gates of Hampton Court. The fare was nine and tenpence and the only piece of gold he had was a half-sovereign. But there was a handful of loose silver in his trouser pocket and so the fare and tip were manageable. "Will you be going back, sir?" asked the driver.

And Mr. Brumley reflected too briefly and committed a fatal error. "No," he said with his mind upon that loose silver. "We shall go back by train."

Now it is the custom with taxi-cabs that take people to such outlying and remote places as Hampton Court, to be paid off and to wait loyally until their original passengers return. Thereby the little machine is restrained from ticking out twopences which should go in the main to the absent proprietor, and a feeling of mutuality is established between the driver and his fare. But of course this cab being released presently found another passenger and went away. . . .

I have written in vain if I have not conveyed to you that Mr. Brumley was a gentleman of great and cultivated delicacy, that he liked the seemly and handsome side of things and dreaded the appearance of any flaw upon his prosperity as only a man trained in an English public school can do. It was intolerable to think of any hitch in this happy excursion which was to establish he knew not what confidence between himself and Lady Harman. From first to last he felt it had to go with an air—and what was the first class fare from Hampton Court to Putney—which latter station he believed was on the line from Hampton Court to London—and could one possibly pretend it was unnecessary to have tea? And so while Lady Harman talked about her husband's business—"our business" she called it—and shrank from ever saying anything more about the more intimate question she had most in mind, the limits to a wife's obedience, Mr. Brumley listened with these financial solicitudes showing through his expression and giving it a quality of intensity that she found remarkably reassuring. And once or twice they made him miss points in her remarks that forced him back upon that very inferior substitute for the apt answer, a judicious "Um."

(It would be quite impossible to go without tea, he decided. He himself wanted tea quite badly. He would think better when he had had some tea. . . .)

The crisis came at tea. They had tea at the inn upon the green that struck Mr. Brumley as being most likely to be cheap and which he pretended to choose for some trivial charm about the windows. And it wasn't cheap, and when at last Mr. Brumley was faced by the little slip of the bill and could draw his money from his pocket and look at it, he knew the worst and the worst was worse than he had expected. The bill was five shillings (Should he dispute it? Too ugly altogether, a dispute with a probably ironical waiter!) and the money in his hand amounted to four shillings and sixpence.

He acted surprise with the waiter's eye upon him. (Should he ask for credit? They might be frightfully disagreeable in such a cockney resort as this.) "Tut, tut," said Mr. Brumley, and then—a little late for it—resorted to and discovered the emptiness of his sovereign purse. He realized that this was out of the picture at this stage, felt his ears and nose and cheeks grow hot and pink. The waiter's colleague across the room became interested in the proceedings.

"I had no idea," said Mr. Brumley, which was a premeditated falsehood.

"Is anything the matter?" asked Lady Harman with a sisterly interest.

"My dear Lady Harman, I find myself— Ridiculous position. Might I borrow half a sovereign?"

He felt sure that the two waiters exchanged glances. He looked at them,—a mistake again—and got hotter.

"Oh!" said Lady Harman and regarded him with frank amusement in her eyes. The thing struck her at first in the light of a joke. "I've only got one-and-eightpence. I didn't expect—"

She blushed as beautifully as ever. Then she produced a small but plutocratic-looking purse and handed it to him.

"Most remarkable—inconvenient," said Mr. Brumley, opening the precious thing and extracting a shilling. "That will do," he said and dismissed the waiter with a tip of sixpence. Then with the open purse still in his hand, he spent much of his reaining strength trying to look amused and unembarrassed, feeling all the time that with his flushed face and in view of all the circumstances of the case he must be really looking very silly and fluffy.

"It's really most inconvenient," he remarked.

"I never thought of the—of this. It was silly of me," said Lady Harman.

"Oh no! Oh dear no! The silliness I can assure you is all mine. I can't tell you how entirely apologetic— Ridiculous fix. And after I had persuaded you to come here."

"Still we were able to pay," she consoled him.

"But you have to get home!"

She hadn't so far thought of that. It brought Sir Isaac suddenly into the picture. "By half-past five," she said with just the faintest flavor of interrogation.

Mr. Brumley looked at his watch. It was ten minutes to five.

"Waiter," he said, "how do the trains run from here to Putney?"

"I don't *think,* sir, that we have any trains from here to Putney—"

An A.B.C. Railway Guide was found and Mr. Brumley learned for the first time that Putney and Hampton Court are upon two distinct and separate and, as far as he could judge by the timetable, mutually hostile branches of the South Western Railway, and that at the earliest they could not get to Putney before six o'clock.

Mr. Brumley was extremely disconcerted. He perceived that he ought to have kept his taxi. It amounted almost to a debt of honor to deliver this lady secure and untarnished at her house within the next hour. But this reflection did not in the least degree assist him to carry it out and as a matter of fact Mr. Brumley became flurried and did not carry it out. He was not used to being without money, it unnerved him, and he gave way to a kind of hectic *savoir faire.* He demanded a taxi of the waiter. He tried to evolve a taxi by will power alone. He went out with Lady Harman and back towards the gates of Hampton Court to look for taxis. Then it occurred to him that they might be losing the 5:25 up. So they hurried over the bridge of the station.

He had a vague notion that he would be able to get tickets on credit at the booking office if he presented his visiting card. But the clerk in charge seemed to find something uncongenial in his proposal. He did not seem to like what he saw of Mr. Brumley through his little square window and Mr. Brumley found something slighting and unpleasant in his manner. It was one of those little temperamental jars which happen to men of delicate sensibilities and Mr. Brumley tried to be reassuringly overbearing in his manner and then lost his temper and was threatening and so wasted precious moments what time Lady Harman waited on the platform, with a certain shadow of doubt falling upon her confidence in him, and watched the five-twenty-five gather itself together and start Londonward. Mr. Brumley came out of the ticket office resolved to travel without tickets and carry things through with a high hand just as it became impossible to do so by that train, and then I regret to say he returned for some further haughty passages with the ticket clerk upon the duty of public servants to point out such oversights as his, that led to repartee and did nothing to help Lady Harman on her homeward way.

Then he discovered a current timetable and learned that now even were all the ticket difficulties overridden he could not get Lady Harman to Putney before twenty minutes past seven, so completely is the South Western Railway not organized for conveying people from Hampton Court to Putney. He explained this as well as he could to Lady Harman, and then led her out of the station in another last desperate search for a taxi.

"We can always come back for that next train," he said. "It doesn't go for half an hour."

"I cannot blame myself sufficiently," he said for the eighth or ninth time. . . .

It was already well past a quarter to six before Mr. Brumley bethought himself of the London County Council tramcars that run from the palace gates. Along these an ample four-pennyworth was surely possibie and at the end would be taxis— There *must* be taxis. The tram took them—but oh! how slowly it seemed!— to Hammersmith by a devious route through interminable roads and streets, and long before they reached that spot twilight had passed into darkness, and all the streets and shops were flowering into light and the sense of night and lateness was very strong. After they were seated in the tram a certain interval of silence came between them and then Lady Harman laughed and Mr. Brumley laughed— there was no longer any need for him to be energetic and fussy—and they began to have that feeling of adventurous amusement which comes on the further side of desperation. But beneath the temporary elation Lady Harman was a prey to grave anxieties and Mr. Brumley could not help thinking he had made a tremendous ass of himself in that ticket clerk dispute. . . .

At Hammersmith they got out, two quite penniless travellers, and after some anxious moments found a taxi. It took them to Putney Hill. Lady Harman descended at the outer gates of her home and walked up the drive in the darkness while Mr. Brumley went on to his club and solvency again. It was five minutes past eight when he entered the hall of his club. . . .

6

It had been Lady Harman's original intention to come home before four, to have tea with her mother and to inform her husband when he returned from the city of her entirely dignified and correct disobedience to his absurd prohibitions. Then he would have bullied at a disadvantage, she would have announced her intention of dining with Lady Viping and making the various calls and expeditions for which she had arranged and all would have gone well. But you see how far accident and a spirit of enterprise may take a lady from so worthy a plan, and when at last she returned to the Victorian baronial home in Putney it was very nearly eight and the house blazed with crisis from pantry to nursery. Even the elder three little girls, who were accustomed to be kissed goodnight by their "boofer muvver," were still awake and—catching the subtle influence of the atmosphere of dismay about them—in tears. The very under-housemaids were saying: "Where *ever* can her ladyship 'ave got to?"

Sir Isaac had come home that day at an unusually early hour and with a peculiar pinched expression that filled even Snagsby with apprehensive alertness. Sir Isaac had in fact returned in a state of quite unwonted venom. He had come home early because he wished to vent it upon Ellen, and her absence filled him with something of that sensation one has when one puts out a foot for the floor and instead a step drops one down—it seems abysmally.

"But where's she gone, Snagsby?"

"Her ladyship *said* to lunch, Sir Isaac," said Snagsby.

"Good gracious! Where?"

"Her ladyship didn't *say,* Sir Isaac."

"But where? Where the devil—?"

"I have—'ave no means whatever of knowing, Sir Isaac."

He had a defensive inspiration.

"Perhaps Mrs. Sawbridge, Sir Isaac. . . ."

Mrs. Sawbridge was enjoying the sunshine upon the lawn. She sat in the most comfortable garden chair, held a white sunshade overhead, had the last new novel by Mrs. Humphry Ward upon her lap, and was engaged in trying not to wonder where her daughter might be. She beheld with a distinct blenching of the spirit Sir Isaac advancing towards her. She wondered more than ever where Ellen might be.

"Here!" cried her son-in-law. "Where's Ellen gone?"

Mrs. Sawbridge with an affected off-handedness was sure she hadn't the faintest idea.

"Then you *ought* to have," said Isaac. "She ought to be at home."

Mrs. Sawbridge's only reply was to bridle slightly.

"Where's she got to? Where's she gone? Haven't you any idea at all?"

"I was not favored by Ellen's confidence," said Mrs. Sawbridge.

"But you *ought* to know," cried Sir Isaac. "She's your daughter. Don't you know anything of *either* of your daughters? I suppose you don't care where they are, either of them, or what mischief they're up to. Here's a man—comes home early to his tea—and no wife! After hearing all I've done at the club."

Mrs. Sawbridge stood up in order to be more dignified than a seated position permitted.

"It is scarcely my business, Sir Isaac," she said, "to know of the movements of your wife."

"Nor Georgina's apparently either. Good God! I'd have given a hundred pounds that this shouldn't have happened!"

"If you must speak to me, Sir Isaac, will you please kindly refrain from—from the deity—"

"Oh! shut it!" said Sir Isaac, blazing up to violent rudeness. "Why! Don't you know, haven't you an idea? The infernal foolery! Those tickets. She got those women— Look here, if you go walking away with your nose in the air before I've done— Look here! Mrs. Sawbridge, you listen to me— Georgina. I'm speaking of Georgina."

The lady was walking now swiftly and stiffly towards the house, her face very pale and drawn, and Sir Isaac hurrying beside her in a white fury of expostulation. "I tell you," he cried, "Georgina—"

There was something maddeningly incurious about her. He couldn't understand why she didn't even pause to hear what Georgina had done and what he had to say about it. A person so wrapped up in her personal and private dignity makes a man want to throw stones. Perhaps she knew of Georgina's misdeeds. Perhaps she sympathized. . . .

A sense of the house windows checked his pursuit of her ear. "Then go," he said to her retreating back. "*Go!* I don't care if you go for good. I don't care if you go altogether. If *you* hadn't had the upbringing of these two girls—"

She was manifestly out of earshot and in full yet almost queenly flight for the house. He wanted to say things about her. *To* someone. He was already saying things to the garden generally. What does one marry a wife for? His mind came round to Ellen again. Where had she got to? Even if she had gone out to lunch, it was time she was back. He went to his study and rang for Snagsby.

"Lady Harman back yet?" he asked grimly.

"No, Sir Isaac."

"Why isn't she back?"

Snagsby did his best. "Perhaps, Sir Isaac, her ladyship has experienced—'as hexperienced a naxident."

Sir Isaac stared at that idea for a moment. Then he thought, 'Someone would have telephoned.' "No," he said, "she's out. That's where she is. And I suppose I can wait here, as well as I can until she chooses to come home. Degenerate foolish nonsense. . . !"

He whistled between his teeth like an escape of steam. Snagsby, after the due pause of attentiveness, bowed respectfully and withdrew. . . .

He had barely time to give a brief outline of the interview to the pantry before a violent ringing summoned him again. Sir Isaac wished to speak to Peters, Lady Harman's maid. He wanted to know where Lady Harman had gone; this being impossible, he wanted to know where Lady Harman had seemed to be going.

"Her Ladyship *seemed* to be going out to lunch, Sir Isaac," said Peters, her meek face irradiated by helpful intelligence.

"Oh *get* out!" said Sir Isaac. "*Get* out!"

"Yes, Sir Isaac," said Peters and obeyed. . . .

"He's in a rare bait about her," said Peters to Snagsby downstairs.

"I'm inclined to think her ladyship will catch it pretty hot," said Snagsby.

"He can't *know* anything," said Peters.

"What about?" asked Snagsby.

"Oh, *I* don't know," said Peters. "Don't ask *me* about her. . . ."

About ten minutes later Sir Isaac was heard to break a little china figure of the goddess Kwannon, that had stood upon his study mantel-shelf. The fragments were found afterwards in the fireplace. . . .

The desire for self-expression may become overwhelming. After Sir Isaac had talked to himself about Georgina and Lady Harman for some time in his study, he was seized with a great longing to pour some of this spirited stuff into the entirely unsympathetic ear of Mrs. Sawbridge. So he went about the house and garden looking for her, and being at last obliged to enquire about her, learned from a scared defensive housemaid whom he cornered suddenly in the conservatory, that she had retired to her own room. He went and rapped at her door but after one muffled "Who's that?" he could get no further response.

"I want to tell you about Georgina," he said.

He tried the handle but the discreet lady within had turned the key upon her dignity.

"I want," he shouted, "to tell you about Georgina. . . . GEORGINA! Oh *damn!*"

Silence.

Tea awaited him downstairs. He hovered about the drawing-room, making noises between his teeth.

"Snagsby," said Sir Isaac, "just tell Mrs. Sawbridge I shall be obliged if she will come down to tea."

"Mrs. Sawbridge 'as a *'ead*ache, Sir Isaac," said Mr. Snagsby with extreme blandness. "She asked me to acquaint you. She 'as ordered tea in 'er own apartment."

For a moment Sir Isaac was baffled. Then he had an inspiration. "Just get me the *Times,* Snagsby," he said.

He took the paper and unfolded it until a particular paragraph was thrown into extreme prominence. This he lined about with his fountain pen and wrote above it with a quivering hand, "These women's tickets were got by Georgina under false pretences from me." He handed the paper thus prepared back to Snagsby. "Just take this paper to Mrs. Sawbridge," he said, "and ask her what she thinks of it?"

But Mrs. Sawbridge tacitly declined this proposal for a correspondence *viâ* Snagsby.

7

There was no excuse for Georgina.

Georgina had obtained tickets from Sir Isaac for the great party reception at Barleypound House, under the shallow pretext that she wanted them for "two spinsters from the country," for whose good behavior she would answer, and she had handed them over to that organization of disorder which swayed her mind. The historical outrage upon Mr. Blapton was the consequence.

Two desperate and misguided emissaries had gone to the great reception, dressed and behaving as much as possible like helpful Liberal women; they had made their way towards the brilliant group of leading Liberals of which Mr. Blapton was the center, assuming an almost Whig-like expression and bearing to mask the fires within, and had then suddenly accosted him. It was one of those great occasions when the rank and file of the popular party is privileged to look upon Court dress. The ministers and great people had come on from Buckingham Palace in their lace and legs. Scarlet and feathers, splendid trains and mysterious ribbons and stars, gave an agreeable intimation of all that it means to be in office to the dazzled wives and daughters of the party stalwarts and fired the ambition of innumerable earnest but earnestly competitive young men. It opened the eyes of the Labour leaders to the higher possibilities of Parliament. And then suddenly came a stir, a rush, a cry of "Tear off his epaulettes!" and outrage was afoot. And two quite nice-looking young women!

It is unhappily not necessary to describe the scene that followed. Mr. Blapton made a brave fight for his epaulettes, fighting chiefly with his cocked hat, which was bent double in the struggle. Mrs. Blapton gave all the assistance true womanliness could offer and, in fact, she boxed the ears of one of his assailants very soundly. The intruders were rescued in an extremely torn and draggled condition from the indignant statesmen who had fallen upon them by tardy but decisive police. . . .

Such scenes sprinkle the recent history of England with green and purple patches and the interest of this particular one for us is only because of Georgina's share in it. That was brought home to Sir Isaac, very suddenly and disagreeably, while he was lunching at the Climax Club with Sir Robert Charterson. A man named Gobbin, an art critic or something of that sort, one of those flimsy literary people who mar the solid worth of so many great clubs, a man with a lot of hair and the sort of loose tie that so often seems to be less of a tie than a detachment from all decent restraints, told him. Charterson was holding forth upon the outrage.

"That won't suit Sir Isaac, Sir Robert," said Gobbin presuming on his proximity.

Sir Isaac tried to give him a sort of look one gives to an unsatisfactory clerk.

"They went ther with Sir Isaac's tickets," said Gobbin.

"They *never*—!"

"Horatio Blenker was looking for you in the hall. Haven't you seen him? After all the care they took. The poor man's almost in tears."

"They never had tickets of mine!" cried Sir Isaac stoutly and indignantly.

And then the thought of Georgina came like a blow upon his heart. . . .

In his flurry he went on denying. . . .

The subsequent conversation in the smoking-room was as red-eared and disagreeable for Sir Isaac as any conversation could be. "But how *could* such a thing have happened?" he asked in a voice that sounded bleached to him. "How could such a thing have come about?" Their eyes were dreadful. Did they guess? Could they guess? Conscience within him was going up and down shouting out, "Georgina, your sister-in-law, Georgina," so loudly that he felt the whole smoking-room must be hearing it. . . .

8

As Lady Harman came up through the darkness of the drive to her home, she was already regretting very deeply that she had not been content to talk to Mr. Brumley in Kensington Gardens instead of accepting his picturesque suggestion of Hampton Court. There was an unpleasant waif-like feeling about this return. She was reminded of pictures published in the interests of Doctor Barnardo's philanthropies,—Dr. Barnardo her favorite hero in real life,—in which wistful little outcasts creep longingly towards brightly lit but otherwise respectable homes. It wasn't at all the sort of feeling she would have chosen if she had had a choice of feelings. She was tired and dusty and as she came into the hall the bright light was blinding. Snagsby took her wrap. "Sir Isaac, me lady, 'as been enquiring for your ladyship," he communicated.

Sir Isaac appeared on the staircase.

"Good gracious, Elly!" he shouted. "Where you been?"

Lady Harman decided against an immediate reply. "I shall be ready for dinner in half an hour," she told Snagsby and went past him to the stairs.

Sir Isaac awaited her. "Where you been?" he repeated as she came up to him.

A housemaid on the staircase and the second nursemaid on the nursery landing above shared Sir Isaac's eagerness to hear her answer. But they did not hear her answer, for Lady Harman with a movement that was all too reminiscent of her mother's in the garden, swept past him towards the door of her own room. He followed her and shut the door on the thwarted listeners.

"Here!" he said, with a connubial absence of restraint. "Where the devil you been? What the deuce do you think you've been getting up to?"

She had been calculating her answers since the moment she had realized that she was to return home at a disadvantage. (It is not my business to blame her for a certain disingenuousness; it is my business simply to record it.) "I went out to lunch at Lady Beach-Mandarin's," she said. "I told you I meant to."

"Lunch!" he cried. "Why, it's eight!"

"I met—some people. I met Agatha Alimony. I have a perfect right to go out to lunch—"

"You met a nice crew I'll bet. But that don't account for your being out to eight, does it? With all the confounded household doing as it pleases!"

"I went on—to see the borders at Hampton Court."

"With *her?*"

"*Yes,*" said Lady Harman. . . .

It wasn't what she had meant to happen. It was an inglorious declension from her contemplated pose of dignified assertion. She was impelled to do her utmost to get away from this lie she had uttered at once, to eliminate Agatha from the argument by an emphatic generalization. "I've a perfect right," she said, suddenly nearly breathless, "to go to Hampton Court with anyone I please, talk about anything I like and stay there as long as I think fit."

He squeezed his thin lips together for a silent moment and then retorted. "You've got nothing of the sort, nothing of the sort. You've got to do your duty like everybody else in the world, and your duty is to be in this house controlling it—and not gossiping about London just where any silly fancy takes you."

"I don't think that *is* my duty," said Lady Harman after a slight pause to collect her forces.

"Of *course* it's your duty. You know it's your duty. You know perfectly well. It's only these rotten, silly, degenerate, decadent fools who've got ideas into you—" The sentence staggered under its load of adjectives like a camel under the last straw and collapsed. "*See?*" he said.

Lady Harman knitted her brows.

"I do my duty," she began.

But Sir Isaac was now resolved upon eloquence. His mind was full with the accumulations of an extremely long and bitter afternoon and urgent to discharge. He began to answer her and then a passion of rage flooded him. Suddenly he wanted to shout and use abusive expressions and it seemed to him there was nothing to prevent his shouting and using abusive expressions. So he did. "Call this your duty," he said, "gadding about with some infernal old suffragette—"

He paused to gather force. He had never quite let himself go to his wife before; he had never before quite let himself go to anyone. He had always been in every crisis just a little too timid to let himself go. But a wife is privileged. He sought strength and found it in words from which he had hitherto abstained. It was not a discourse to which print could do justice; it flickered from issue to issue. He touched upon Georgina, upon the stiffness of Mrs. Sawbridge's manner, upon the neurotic weakness of Georgina's unmarried state, upon the general decay of feminine virtue in the community, upon the laxity of modern literature, upon the dependent state of Lady Harman, upon the unfairness of their relations which gave her every luxury while he spent his days in arduous toil, upon the shame and annoyance in the eyes of his servants that her unexplained absence had caused him.

He emphasized his speech by gestures. He thrust out one rather large ill-shaped hand at her with two vibrating fingers extended. His ears became red, his nose red, his eyes seemed red and all about these points his face was wrathful white. His hair rose up into stiff scared listening ends. He had his rights, he had some *little* claim to consideration surely, he might be just nobody but he wasn't going to stand this much anyhow. He gave her fair warning. What was she, what did she know of the world into which she wanted to rush? He lapsed into views of Lady Beach-Mandarin—unfavorable views. I wish Lady Beach-Mandarin could have heard him. . . .

Ever and again Lady Harman sought to speak. This incessant voice confused and baffled her; she had a just attentive mind at bottom and down there was a most weakening feeling that there must indeed be some misdeed in her to evoke so impassioned a storm. She had a curious and disconcerting sense of responsibility for his dancing exasperation, she felt she was to blame for it, just as years ago she had felt she was to blame for his tears when he had urged her so desperately to marry him. Some irrational instinct made her want to allay him. It is the supreme feminine weakness, that wish to allay. But she was also clinging desperately to her resolution to proclaim her other forthcoming engagements. Her will hung on to that as a man hangs on to a mountain path in a thunderburst. She stood gripping her dressing-table and ever and again trying to speak. But whenever she did so Sir Isaac lifted a hand and cried almost threateningly: "You hear me out, Elly! You hear me out!" and went on a little faster. . . .

(Limburger in his curious *"Sexuelle Unterschiede der Seele,"* points out as a probably universal distinction between the sexes that when a man scolds a woman, if only he scolds loudly enough and long enough, conviction of sin is aroused, while in the reverse case the result is merely a murderous impulse. This he further says is not understood by women, who hope by scolding to produce the similar effect upon men that they themselves would experience. The passage is illustrated by figures of ducking stools and followed by some carefully analyzed statistics of connubial crime in Berlin in the years 1901–2. But in this matter let the student compare the achievement of Paulina in *The Winter's Tale* and reflect upon his own life. And moreover it is difficult to estimate how far the twinges of conscience that Lady Harman was feeling were not due to an entirely different cause, the falsification of her position by the lie she had just told Sir Isaac.)

And presently upon this noisy scene in the great pink bedroom, with Sir Isaac walking about and standing and turning and gesticulating and Lady Harman clinging on to her dressing-table, and painfully divided between her new connections, her sense of guilty deception and the deep instinctive responsibilities of a woman's nature, came, like one of those rows of dots that are now so frequent and so helpful in the art of fiction, the surging, deep, assuaging note of Snagsby's gong: Booooooom. Boom. Boooooom. . . .

"Damn it!" cried Sir Isaac, smiting at the air with both fists clenched and speaking as though this was Ellen's crowning misdeed, "and we aren't even dressed for dinner!"

9

Dinner had something of the stiffness of court ceremonial.

Mrs. Sawbridge, perhaps erring on the side of discretion, had consumed a little soup and a wing of chicken in her own room. Sir Isaac was down first and his wife found him grimly astride before the great dining-room fire awaiting her. She had had her dark hair dressed with extreme simplicity and had slipped on a blue velvet tea-gown, but she had been delayed by a visit to the nursery, where the children were now flushed and uneasily asleep.

Husband and wife took their places at the genuine Sheraton dining-table— one of the very best pieces Sir Isaac had ever picked up—and were waited on with a hushed, scared dexterity by Snagsby and the footman.

Lady Harman and her husband exchanged no remarks during the meal; Sir Isaac was a little noisy with his soup as became a man who controls honest indignation, and once he complained briefly in a slightly hoarse voice to Snagsby about the state of one of the rolls. Between the courses he leaned back in his chair and made faint sounds with his teeth. These were the only breach of the velvety quiet. Lady Harman was surprised to discover herself hungry, but she ate with thoughtful dignity and gave her mind to the attempted digestion of the confusing interview she had just been through.

It was a very indigestible interview.

On the whole her heart hardened again. With nourishment and silence her spirit recovered a little from its abasement, and her resolution to assert her freedom to go hither and thither and think as she chose renewed itself. She tried to plan some way of making her declaration so that she would not again be overwhelmed by a torrent of response. Should she speak to him at the end of dinner? Should she speak to him while Snagsby was in the room? But he might behave badly even with Snagsby in the room and she could not bear to think of him behaving badly to her in the presence of Snagsby. She glanced at him over the genuine old silver bowl of roses in the middle of the table—all the roses were good *new* sorts—and tried to estimate how he might behave under various methods of declaration.

The dinner followed its appointed ritual to the dessert. Came the wine and Snagsby placed the cigars and a little silver lamp beside his master.

She rose slowly with a speech upon her lips. Sir Isaac remained seated looking up at her with a mitigated fury in his little red-brown eyes.

The speech receded from her lips again.

"I think," she said after a strained pause, "I will go and see how mother is now."

"She's only shamming," said Sir Isaac belatedly to her back as she went out of the room.

She found her mother in a wrap before her fire and made her dutiful enquiries.

"It's only quite a *slight* headache," Mrs. Sawbridge confessed. "But Isaac was so upset about Georgina and about"—she flinched—"about—everything, that I thought it better to be out of the way."

"What exactly has Georgina done?"

"It's in the paper, dear. On the table there."

Ellen studied the *Times*.

"Georgina got them the tickets," Mrs. Sawbridge explained. "I wish she hadn't. It was so—so unnecessary of her."

There was a little pause as Lady Harman read. She put down the paper and asked her mother if she could do anything for her.

"I—I suppose it's all Right, dear, now?" Mrs. Sawbridge asked.

"Quite," said her daughter. "You're sure I can do nothing for you, mummy?"

"I'm kept so in the dark about things."

"It's quite all right now, mummy."

"He went on—dreadfully."

"It was annoying—of Georgina."

"It makes my position so difficult. I do wish he wouldn't want to speak to me—about all these things. . . . Georgina treats me like a Perfect Nonentity and then he comes— It's so inconsiderate. Starting Disputes. Do you know, dear, I really think—if I were to go for a little time to Bournemouth—?"

Her daughter seemed to find something attractive in the idea. She came to the hearthrug and regarded her mother with maternal eyes.

"Don't you *worry* about things, mummy," she said.

"Mrs. Bleckhorn told me of such a nice quiet boarding-house, almost looking on the sea. . . . One would be safe from Insult there. You know—" her voice broke for a moment, "he was Insulting, he *meant* to be Insulting. I'm—Upset. I've been thinking over it ever since."

10

Lady Harman came out upon the landing. She felt absolutely without backing in the world. (If only she hadn't told a lie!) Then with an effort she directed her course downstairs to the dining-room.

(The lie had been necessary. It was only a detail. It mustn't blind her to the real issue.)

She entered softly and found her husband standing before the fire plunged in gloomy thoughts. Upon the marble mantel-shelf behind him was a little glass; he had been sipping port in spite of the express prohibition of his doctor and the wine had reddened the veins of his eyes and variegated the normal pallor of his countenance with little flushed areas. "Hel-lo," he said looking up suddenly as she closed the door behind her.

For a moment there was something in their two expressions like that on the faces of men about to box.

"I want you to understand," she said, and then; "The way you behaved—"

There was an uncontrollable break in her voice. She had a dreadful feeling that she might be going to cry. She made a great effort to be cold and clear.

"I don't think you have a right—just because I am your wife—to control every moment of my time. In fact you haven't. And I have a right to make engagements. . . . I want you to know I am going to an afternoon meeting at Lady Beach-Mandarin's. Next week. And I have promised to go to Miss Alimony's to tea."

"Go on," he encouraged grimly.

"I am going to Lady Viping's to dinner, too; she asked me and I accepted. Later."

She stopped.

He seemed to deliberate. Then suddenly he thrust out a face of pinched determination.

"You *won't*, my lady," he said. "You bet your life you won't. *No!* So *now* then!"

And then gripping his hands more tightly behind him, he made a step towards her.

"You're losing your bearings, Lady Harman," he said, speaking with much intensity in a low earnest voice. "You don't seem to be remembering where you are. You come and you tell me you're going to do this and that. Don't you know, Lady Harman, that it's your wifely duty to obey, to do as I say, to behave as I wish?" He brought out a lean index finger to emphasize his remarks. "And I am going to make you do it!" he said.

"I've a perfect right," she repeated.

He went on, regardless of her words. "What do you think you can do, Lady Harman? You're going to all these places—how? Not in *my* motor-car, not with *my* money. You've not a thing that isn't mine, that *I* haven't given you. And if you're going to have a lot of friends I haven't got, where're they coming to see you? Not in *my* house! I'll chuck 'em out if I find 'em. I won't have 'em. I'll turn 'em out. See?"

"I'm not a slave."

"You're a wife—and a wife's got to do what her husband wishes. You can't have two heads on a horse. And in *this* horse—this house I mean, the head's— *me!*"

"I'm not a slave and I won't be a slave."

"You're a wife and you'll stick to the bargain you made when you married me. I'm ready in reason to give you anything you want—if you do your duty as a wife should. Why!—I spoil you. But this going about on your own, this highty-flighty go-as-you-please,—no man on earth who's worth calling a man will stand it. I'm not going to begin to stand it. . . . You try it on. You try it, Lady Harman. . . . You'll come to your senses soon enough. See? You start trying it on now—straight away. We'll make an experiment. We'll watch how it goes. Only don't expect me to give you any money, don't expect me to help your struggling family, don't expect me to alter my arrangements because of you. Let's keep apart for a bit and you go your way and I'll go mine. And we'll see who's sick of it first, we'll see who wants to cry off."

"I came down here," said Lady Harman, "to give you a reasonable notice—"

"And you found *I* could reason too," interrupted Sir Isaac in a kind of miniature shout, "you found I could reason too!"

"You think— Reason! I *won't*," said Lady Harman, and found herself in tears. By an enormous effort she recovered something of her dignity and withdrew. He made no effort to open the door, but stood a little hunchbacked and with a sense of rhetorical victory surveying her retreat.

11

After Lady Harman's maid had left her that night, she sat for some time in a low easy chair before her fire, trying at first to collect together into one situation all the events of the day and then lapsing into that state of mind which is not so much thinking as resting in the attitude of thought. Presently, in a vaguely conceived future, she would go to bed. She was stunned by the immense dimensions of the row her simple act of defiance had evoked.

And then came an incredible incident, so incredible that next day she still had great difficulty in deciding whether it was an actuality or a dream. She heard a little very familiar sound. It was the last sound she would have expected to hear and she turned sharply when she heard it. The paper-covered door in the wall of her husband's apartment opened softly, paused, opened some more and his little undignified head appeared. His hair was already tumbled from his pillow.

He regarded her steadfastly for some moments with an expression between shame and curiosity and smoldering rage, and then allowed his body, clad now in purple-striped pajamas, to follow his head into her room. He advanced guiltily.

"Elly," he whispered. "Elly!"

She caught her dressing-gown about her and stood up.

"What is it, Isaac?" she asked, feeling curiously abashed at this invasion.

"Elly," he said, still in that furtive undertone. "*Make it up!*"

"I want my freedom," she said, after a little pause.

"Don't be *silly*, Elly," he whispered in a tone of remonstrance and advancing slowly towards her. "Make it up. Chuck all these ideas."

She shook her head.

"We've got to get along together. You can't go going about just anywhere. We've got—we've got to be reasonable."

He halted, three paces away from her. His eyes weren't sorrowful eyes, or friendly eyes; they were just shiftily eager eyes. "Look here," he said. "It's all nonsense. . . . Elly, old girl; let's—let's make it up."

She looked at him and it dawned upon her that she had always imagined herself to be afraid of him and that indeed she wasn't. She shook her head obstinately.

"It isn't reasonable," he said. "Here, we've been the happiest of people— Anything in reason I'll let you have." He paused with an effect of making an offer.

"I want my autonomy," she said.

"Autonomy!" he echoed. "Autonomy! What's autonomy? Autonomy!"

This strange word seemed first to hold him in distressful suspense and then to infuriate him.

"I come in here to make it up," he said, with a voice charged with griefs, "after all you've done, and you go and you talk of autonomy!"

His feelings passed beyond words. An extremity of viciousness flashed into his face. He gave vent to a snarl of exasperation, "Ya-ap!" he said, he raised his clenched fists and seemed on the verge of assault, and then with a gesture between fury and despair, he wheeled about and the purple-striped pajamas danced in passionate retreat from her room.

"Autonomy! . . . ."

A slam, a noise of assaulted furniture, and then silence.

Lady Harman stood for some moments regarding the paper-covered door that had closed behind him. Then she bared her white forearm and pinched it—hard.

It wasn't a dream! This thing had happened.

12

At a quarter to three in the morning, Lady Harman was surprised to find herself wide awake. It was exactly a quarter to three when she touched the stud of the ingenious little silver apparatus upon the table beside her bed which reflected a luminous clock-face upon the ceiling. And her mind was no longer resting in the attitude of thought but extraordinarily active. It was active, but as she presently began to realize it was not progressing. It was spinning violently round and round the frenzied figure of a little man in purple-striped pajamas retreating from her presence, whirling away from her like something blown before a gale. That seemed to her to symbolize the completeness of the breach the day had made between her husband and herself.

She felt as a statesman might feel who had inadvertently—while conducting some trivial negotiations—declared war.

She was profoundly alarmed. She perceived ahead of her abundant possibilities of disagreeable things. And she wasn't by any means as convinced of the righteousness of her cause as a happy warrior should be. She had a natural disposition towards truthfulness and it worried her mind that while she was struggling to assert her right to these common social freedoms she should be tacitly admitting a kind of justice in her husband's objections by concealing the fact that her afternoon's companion was a man. She tried not to recognize the existence of a doubt, but deep down in her mind there did indeed lurk a weakening uncertainty about the right of a woman to free conversation with any man but her own. Her reason disowned that uncertainty with scorn. But it wouldn't go away for all her reason. She went about in her mind doing her utmost to cut that doubt dead. . . .

She tried to go back to the beginning and think it all out. And as she was not used to thinking things out, the effort took the form of an imaginary explanation to Mr. Brumley of the difficulties of her position. She framed phrases. "You see, Mr. Brumley," she imagined herself to be saying, "I want to do my duty as a wife, I have to do my duty as a wife. But it's so hard to say just where duty leaves off and being a mere slave begins. I cannot believe that *blind* obedience is any woman's duty. A woman needs—autonomy." Then her mind went off for a time to wrestle with the exact meaning of autonomy, an issue that had not arisen hitherto in her mind. . . . And as she planned out such elucidations, there grew more and more distinct in her mind a kind of idealized Mr. Brumley, very grave, very attentive, wonderfully understanding, saying illuminating helpful tonic things, that made everything clear, everything almost easy. She wanted someone of that quality so badly. The night would have been unendurable if she could not have imagined Mr. Brumley of that quality. And imagining him of that quality her heart yearned for him. She felt that she had been terribly inexpressive that afternoon, she had shirked points, misstated points, and yet he had been marvelously understanding. Ever and again his words had seemed to pierce right through what she had been saying to what she had been thinking. And she recalled with peculiar comfort a kind of abstracted calculating look that had come at times into his eyes, as though his thoughts were going ever so much deeper and ever so much further than her blundering questionings could possibly have taken them. He weighed every word, he had a guarded way of saying "Um. . . ."

Her thoughts came back to the dancing little figure in purple-striped pajamas. She had a scared sense of irrevocable breaches. What would he do tomorrow? What should she do tomorrow? Would he speak to her at breakfast or should she speak first to him? . . . She wished she had some money. If she could have foreseen all this she would have got some money before she began. . . .

So her mind went on round and round and the dawn was breaking before she slept again.

13

Mr. Brumley, also, slept little that night. He was wakefully mournful, recalling each ungraceful incident of the afternoon's failure in turn and more particularly his dispute with the ticket clerk, and thinking over all the things he might have done—if only he hadn't done the things he had done. He had made an atrocious mess of things. He felt he had hopelessly shattered the fair fabric of impressions of him that Lady Harman had been building up, that image of a wise humane capable man to whom a woman would gladly turn; he had been flurried, he had been incompetent, he had been ridiculously incompetent, and it seemed to him that life was a string of desolating inadequacies and that he would never smile again.

The probable reception of Lady Harman by her husband never came within his imaginative scope. Nor did the problems of social responsibility that Lady

Harman had been trying to put to him exercise him very greatly. The personal disillusionment was too strong for that.

About half-past four a faint ray of comfort came with the consideration that after all a certain practical incapacity is part of the ensemble of a literary artist, and then he found himself wondering what flowers of wisdom Montaigne might not have culled from such a day's experience; he began an imitative essay in his head and he fell asleep upon this at last at about ten minutes past five in the morning.

There were better things than this in the composition of Mr. Brumley, we shall have to go deep into these reserves before we have done with him, but when he had so recently barked the shins of his self-esteem they had no chance at all.

CHAPTER THE SEVENTH

Lady Harman Learns About Herself

1

SO IT WAS that the great and long incubated quarrel between Lady Harman and her husband broke into active hostilities.

In spite of my ill-concealed bias in favor of Lady Harman I have to confess that she began this conflict rashly, planlessly, with no equipment and no definite end. Particularly I would emphasize that she had no definite end. She had wanted merely to establish a right to go out by herself occasionally, exercise a certain choice of friends, take on in fact the privileges of a grown-up person, and in asserting that she had never anticipated that the participation of the household would be invoked, or that a general breach might open between herself and her husband. It had seemed just a definite little point at issue, but at Sir Isaac's angry touch a dozen other matters that had seemed safely remote, matters she had never yet quite properly thought about, had been drawn into controversy. It was not only that he drew in things from outside; he evoked things within herself. She discovered she was disposed to fight not simply to establish certain liberties for herself but also—which had certainly not been in her mind before—to keep her husband away from herself. Something latent in the situation had surprised her with this effect. It had arisen out of the quarrel like a sharpshooter out of an ambuscade. Her right to go out alone had now only the value of a mere pretext for far more extensive independence. The ultimate extent of these independences, she still dared not comtemplate.

She was more than a little scared. She wasn't prepared for so wide a revision of her life as this involved. She wasn't at all sure of the rightfulness of her position. Her conception of the marriage contract at that time was liberal towards her husband. After all, didn't she owe obedience? Didn't she owe him a subordinate's cooperation? Didn't she in fact owe him the whole marriage service contract? When she thought of the figure of him in his purple-striped pajamas dancing in a paroxysm of exasperation, that sense of responsibility which was one of her innate characteristics reproached her. She had a curious persuasion that she must be dreadfully to blame for provoking so ridiculous, so extravagant an outbreak. . . .

2

She heard him getting up tumultuously and when she came down,—after a brief interview with her mother who was still keeping her room,—she found him sitting at the breakfast-table eating toast and marmalade in a greedy malignant manner. The tentative propitiations of his proposal to make things up had entirely disappeared, he was evidently in a far profounder rage with her than he had been overnight. Snagsby too, that seemly domestic barometer, looked extraordinarily hushed and grave. She made a greeting-like noise and Sir Isaac scrunched "morning" up amongst a crowded fierce mouthful of toast. She helped herself to tea and bacon and looking up presently discovered his eye fixed upon her with an expression of ferocious hatred. . . .

He went off in the big car, she supposed to London, about ten and she helped her mother to pack and depart by a train a little after midday. She made a clumsy excuse for not giving that crisp little trifle of financial assistance she was accustomed to, and Mrs. Sawbridge was anxiously tactful about the disappointment. They paid a visit of inspection and farewell to the nursery before the departure. Then Lady Harman was left until lunch to resume her meditation upon this unprecedented breach that had opened between her husband and herself. She was presently moved to write a little note to Lady Beach-Mandarin expressing her intention of attending a meeting of the Social Friends and asking whether the date was the following Wednesday or Thursday. She found three penny stamps in the bureau at which she wrote and this served to remind her of her penniless condition. She spent some time thinking out the possible consequences of that. How after all was she going to do things, with not a penny in the world to do them with?

Lady Harman was not only instinctively truthful but also almost morbidly honorable. In other words, she was simple-minded. The idea of a community of goods between husband and wife had never established itself in her mind, she took all Sir Isaac's presents in the spirit in which he gave them, presents she felt they were on trust, and so it was that with a six-hundred pound pearl necklace, a diamond tiara, bracelets, lockets, rings, chains and pendants of the most costly kind—there had been a particularly beautiful bracelet when Millicent was born, a necklace on account of Florence, a fan painted by Charles Conder for Annette and a richly splendid set of old Spanish jewelry—yellow sapphires set in gold—to express Sir Isaac's gratitude for the baby—with all sorts of purses, bags, boxes, trinkets and garments, with a bedroom and morning-room rich in admirable loot, and with endless tradespeople willing to give her credit it didn't for some time occur to her that there was any possible means of getting pocket-money except by direct demand from Sir Isaac. She surveyed her balance of two penny stamps and even about these she felt a certain lack of negotiable facility.

She thought indeed that she might perhaps borrow money, but there again her paralyzing honesty made her recoil from the prospect of uncertain repayment. And besides, from whom could she borrow? . . .

It was on the evening of the second day that a chance remark from Peters turned her mind to the extensive possibilities of liquidation that lay close at hand. She was discussing her dinner dress with Peters, she wanted something very plain and high and unattractive, and Peters, who disapproved of this tendency and was all for female wiles and propitiations, fell into an admiration of the pearl necklace. She thought perhaps by so doing she might induce Lady Harman to wear it, and if she wore it Sir Isaac might be a little propitiated, and if Sir

Isaac was a little propitiated it would be much more comfortable for Snagsby and herself and everyone. She was reminded of a story of a lady who sold one and substituted imitation pearls, no one the wiser, and she told this to her mistress out of sheer garrulousness. "But if no one found out," said Lady Harman, "how do you know?"

"Not till her death, me lady," said Peters, brushing, "when all things are revealed. Her husband, they say, made it a present of to another lady and the other lady, me lady, had it valued. . . ."

Once the idea had got into Lady Harman's head it stayed there very obstinately. She surveyed the things on the table before her with a slightly lifted eyebrow. At first she thought the idea of disposing of them an entirely dishonorable idea, and if she couldn't get it out of her head again at least she made it stand in a corner. And while it stood in a corner she began putting a price for the first time in her life first upon this coruscating object and then that. Then somehow she found herself thinking more and more whether among all these glittering possessions there wasn't something that she might fairly regard as absolutely her own. There were for example her engagement ring and, still more debatable, certain other pre-nuptial trinkets Sir Isaac had given her. Then there were things given her on her successive birthdays. A birthday present of all presents is surely one's very own? But selling is an extreme exercise of ownership. Since those early schooldays when she had carried on an unprofitable traffic in stamps she had never sold anything—unless we are to reckon that for once and for all she had sold herself.

Concurrently with these insidious speculations Lady Harman found herself trying to imagine how one sold jewels. She tried to sound Peters by taking up the story of the necklace again. But Peters was uninforming. "But where," asked Lady Harman, "could such a thing be done?"

"There are places, me lady," said Peters.

"But where?"

"In the West End, me lady. The West End is full of places—for things of that sort. There's scarcely anything you can't do there, me lady—if only you know how."

That was really all that Peters could impart.

"How *does* one sell jewels?" Lady Harman became so interested in this side of her perplexities that she did a little lose sight of those subtler problems of integrity that had at first engaged her. Do jewellers buy jewels as well as sell them? And then it came into her head that there were such things as pawnshops. By the time she had thought about pawnshops and tried to imagine one, her original complete veto upon any idea of selling had got lost to sight altogether. Instead there was a growing conviction that if ever she sold anything it would be a certain sapphire and diamond ring which she didn't like and never wore that Sir Isaac had given her as a birthday present two years ago. But of course she would never dream of selling anything; at the utmost she need but pawn. She reflected and decided that on the whole it would be wiser not to ask Peters how one pawned. It occurred to her to consult the *Encyclopaedia Britannica* on the subject, but though she learned that the Chinese pawnshops must not charge more than three percent per annum, that King Edward the Third pawned his jewels in 1338 and that Father Bernardino di Feltre who set up pawnshops in Assisi and Padua and Pavia was afterward canonized, she failed to get any very clear idea of the exact ritual of the process. And then suddenly she remembered that she knew a finished expert in pawnshop work in the person of Susan Burnet. Susan could tell her everything. She found some curtains in the study that needed replacement, consulted Mrs. Crumble and, with a view to economizing her own resources, made that lady send off an urgent letter to Susan bidding her come forthwith.

3

It has been said that Fate is a plagiarist. Lady Harman's Fate at any rate at this juncture behaved like a benevolent plagiarist who was also a little old-fashioned. This phase of speechless hostility was complicated by the fact that two of the children fell ill, or at least seemed for a couple of days to be falling ill. By all the rules of British sentiment, this ought to have brought about a headlong reconciliation at the tumbled bedside. It did nothing of the sort; it merely wove fresh perplexities into the tangled skein of her thoughts.

On the day after her participation in that forbidden lunch Millicent, her eldest daughter, was discovered with a temperature of a hundred and one, and then Annette, the third, followed suit with a hundred. This carried Lady Harman post haste to the nursery, where to an unprecedented degree she took command. Latterly she had begun to mistrust the physique of her children and to doubt whether the trained efficiency of Mrs. Harblow the nurse wasn't becoming a little blunted at the edges by continual use. And the tremendous quarrel she had afoot made her keenly resolved not to let anything go wrong in the nursery and less disposed than she usually was to leave things to her husband's servants. She interviewed the doctor herself, arranged for the isolation of the two flushed and cross little girls, saw to the toys and amusements which she discovered had become a little flattened and disused by the servants' imperatives of tidying up and putting away, and spent the greater part of the next two days between the night and day nurseries.

She was a little surprised to find how readily she did this and how easily the once entirely authoritative Mrs. Harblow submitted. It was much the same surprise that growing young people feel when they reach some shelf that has hitherto been inaccessible. The crisis soon passed. At his first visit the doctor was a little doubtful whether the Harman nursery wasn't under the sway of measles, which were then raging in a particularly virulent form in London; the next day he inclined to the view that the trouble was merely a feverish cold, and before night this second view was justified by the disappearance of the "temperatures" and a complete return to normal conditions.

But as for that hushed reconciliation in the fevered presence of the almost sacrificial offspring, it didn't happen. Sir Isaac merely thrust aside the stiff silences behind which he masked his rage to remark: "This is what happens when wimmen go gadding about!"

That much and glaring eyes and compressed lips and emphasizing fingers and then he had gone again.

Indeed rather than healing their widening breach this crisis did much to spread it into strange new regions. It brought Lady Harman to the very verge of realizing how much of instinct and how much of duty held her the servant of the children she had brought into the world, and how little there mingled with that any of those factors of pride and admiration that go to the making of heroic maternal love. She knew what is expected of a mother, the exalted and lyrical devotion, and it was with something approaching terror that she perceived that certain things in these children of hers she *hated*. It was her business she knew to love them blindly; she lay awake at night in infinite dismay realizing she did nothing of the sort. Their weakness held her more than anything else, the invincible pathos of their little limbs in discomfort so that she was ready to die she felt to give them ease. But so she would have been held, she was assured, by the little children of anybody if they had fallen with sufficient helplessness into her care.

Just how much she didn't really like her children she presently realized when in the feeble irascibility of their sickness they fell quarrelling. They became— horrid. Millicent and Annette being imprisoned in their beds it seemed good to Florence when she came back from the morning's walk, to annex and hide a selection of their best toys. She didn't take them and play with them, she hid them with an industrious earnestness in a box window-seat that was regarded as peculiarly hers, staggering with armfuls across the nursery floor. Then Millicent by some equally mysterious agency divined what was afoot and set up a clamor for a valued set of doll's furniture, which immediately provoked a similar outcry from little Annette for her Teddy Bear. Followed woe and uproar. The invalids insisted upon having every single toy they possessed brought in and put upon their beds; Florence was first disingenuous and then surrendered her loot with passionate howlings. The Teddy Bear was rescued from Baby after a violent struggle in which one furry hind leg was nearly twisted off. It jars upon the philoprogenitive sentiment of our time to tell of these things and still more to record that all four, stirred by possessive passion to the profoundest depths of their beings, betrayed to an unprecedented degree in their little sharp noses, their flushed faces, their earnest eyes, their dutiful likeness to Sir Isaac. He peeped from under Millicent's daintily knitted brows and gestured with Florence's dimpled fists. It was as if God had tried to make him into four cherubim and as if in spite of everything he was working through.

Lady Harman toiled to pacify these disorders, gently, attentively, and with a faint dismay in her dark eyes. She bribed and entreated and marveled at mental textures so unlike her own. Baby was squared with a brand new Teddy Bear, a rare sort, a white one, which Snagsby went and purchased in the Putney High Street and brought home in his arms, conferring such a luster upon the deed that the lower orders, the very street-boys, watched him with reverence as he passed. Annette went to sleep amidst a discomfort of small treasures and woke stormily when Mrs. Harblow tried to remove some of the spikier ones. And Lady Harman went back to her large pink bedroom and meditated for a long time upon these things and tried to remember whether in her own less crowded childhood with Georgina, either of them had been quite so inhumanly hard and grasping as these feverish little mites in her nursery. She tried to think she had been, she tried to think that all children were such little distressed lumps of embittered individuality, and she did what she could to overcome the queer feeling that this particular clutch of offspring had been foisted upon her and weren't at all the children she could now imagine and desire,—gentle children, sweet-spirited children. . . .

4

Susan Burnet arrived in a gusty mood and brought new matter for Lady Harman's ever broadening consideration of the wifely position. Susan, led by a newspaper placard, had discovered Sir Isaac's relations to the International Bread and Cake Stores.

"At first I thought I wouldn't come," said Susan. "I really did. I couldn't hardly believe it. And then I thought, 'it isn't *her*. It can't be *her!*' But I'd never have dreamt before that I could have been brought to set foot in the house of the man who drove poor father to ruin and despair. . . . You've been so kind to me. . . ."

Susan's simple right-down mind stopped for a moment with something very like a sob, baffled by the contradictions of the situation.

"So I came," she said, with a forced bright smile.

"I'm glad you came," said Lady Harman. "I wanted to see you. And you know, Susan, I know very little—very little indeed—of Sir Isaac's business."

"I quite believe it, my lady. I've never for one moment thought *you*— I don't know how to say it, my lady."

"And indeed I'm not," said Lady Harman, taking it as said.

"I knew you weren't," said Susan, relieved to be so understood.

And the two women looked perplexedly at one another over the neglected curtains Susan had come to "see to," and shyness just snatched back Lady Harman from her impulse to give Susan a sisterly kiss. Nevertheless Susan who was full of wise intuitions felt that kiss that was never given, and in the remote world of unacted deeds returned it with effusion.

"But it's hard," said Susan, "to find one's own second sister mixed up in a strike, and that's what it's come to last week. They've struck, all the International waitresses have struck, and last night in Piccadilly they were standing on the curb and picketing and her among them. With a crowd cheering. . . . And me ready to give my right hand to keep that girl respectable!"

And with a volubility that was at once tumultuous and effective, Susan sketched in the broad outlines of the crisis that threatened the dividends and popularity of the International Bread and Cake Stores. The unsatisfied demands of that bright journalistic enterprise, *The London Lion,* lay near the roots of the trouble. *The London Lion* had stirred it up. But it was only too evident that *The London Lion* had merely given a voice and form and cohesion to long smoldering discontents.

Susan's account of the matter had that impartiality which comes from intellectual incoherence, she hadn't so much a judgment upon the whole as a warring mosaic of judgments. It was talking upon Post Impressionist lines, talking in the manner of Picasso. She had the firmest conviction that to strike against employment, however ill-paid or badly conditioned, was a disgraceful combination of folly, ingratitude and general wickedness, and she had an equally strong persuasion that the treatment of the employees of the International Bread and Cake Stores was such as no reasonably spirited person ought to stand. She blamed her sister extremely and sympathized with her profoundly, and she put it all down in turn to *The London Lion,* to Sir Isaac, and to a small round-faced person called Babs Wheeler, who appeared to be the strike leader and seemed always to be standing on tables in the branches, or clambering up to the lions in Trafalgar Square, or being cheered in the streets.

But there could be no mistaking the quality of Sir Isaac's "International" organization as Susan's dabs of speech shaped it out. It was indeed what we all of us see everywhere about us, the work of the base energetic mind, raw and untrained, in possession of the keen instruments of civilization, the peasant mind allied and blended with the Ghetto mind, grasping and acquisitive, clever as a Norman peasant or a Jew pedlar is clever, and beyond that outrageously stupid and ugly. It was a new view and yet the old familiar view of her husband, but now she saw him not as little eager eyes, a sharp nose, gaunt gestures and a leaden complexion, but as shops and stores and rules and cash registers and harsh advertisements and a driving merciless hurry to get—to get anything and everything, money, monopoly, power, prominence, whatever any other human being seemed to admire or seemed to find desirable, a lust rather than a living soul. Now that her eyes were at last opened Lady Harman, who had seen too little heretofore, now saw too much; she saw all that she had not seen, with an excess of vision, monstrous, caricatured. Susan had already dabbed in the disaster of Sir Isaac's unorganized competitors going to the wall—for charity or the state to neglect or bandage as it might chance—the figure of that poor little "Father," moping hopelessly before his "accident" symbolized that; and now she gave in vivid splotches of allusion, glimpses of the business machine that had replaced those shattered enterprises and carried Sir Isaac to the squalid glory of a Liberal honors list,—the carefully balanced antagonisms and jealousies of the girls and the manageresses, those manageresses who had been obliged to invest little bunches of savings as guarantees and who had to account for every crumb and particle of food stock that came to the branch, and the hunt for cases and inefficiency by the inspectors, who had somehow to justify a salary of two hundred a year, not to mention a percentage of the fines they inflicted.

"There's all that business of the margarine," said Susan. "Every branch gets its butter under weight,— the water squeezes out,—and every branch has over weight margarine. Of course the rules say that mixing's forbidden and if they get caught they go, but they got to pay-in for that butter, and it's setting a snare for their feet. People who've never thought to cheat, when they get it like that, day after day, they cheat, my lady. . . . And the girls get left food for rations. There's always trouble, it's against what the rules say, but they get it. Of course it's against the rules, but what can a manageress do?—if the waste doesn't fall on them, it falls on her. She's tied there with her savings. . . . Such driving, my lady, it's against the very spirit of God. It makes scoffers point. It makes people despise law and order. There's Luke, he gets bitterer and bitterer; he says that it's in the Word we mustn't muzzle the ox that treadeth out the corn, but these Stores, he says, they'd muzzle the ox and keep it hungry and make it work a little machine, he says, whenever it put down its head in the hope of finding a scrap. . . ."

So Susan, bright-eyed, flushed and voluble, pleading the cause of that vague greatness in humanity that would love, that would loiter, that would think, that would if it could give us art, delight and beauty, that turns blindly and stumblingly towards joy, towards intervals, towards the mysterious things of the spirit, against all this sordid strenuousness, this driving destructive association of hard-fisted peasant soul and Ghetto greed, this fool's "efficiency," that rules our world today.

Then Susan lunged for a time at the waitress life her sister led. "She has 'er 'ome with us, but some—they haven't homes."

"They make a fuss about all this White Slave Traffic," said Susan, "but if ever there were white slaves it's the girls who work for a living and keep themselves respectable. And nobody wants to make an example of the men who get rich out of *them*. . . ."

And after some hearsay about the pressure in the bake-houses and the accidents to the van-men, who worked on a speeding-up system that Sir Isaac had adopted from an American business specialist, Susan's mental discharge poured out into the particulars of the waitresses' strike and her sister's share in that. "She *would* go into it," said Susan, "she let herself be drawn in. I asked her never to take the place. Better Service, I said, a thousand times. I begged her, I could have begged her on my bended knees. . . ."

The immediate cause of the strike it seemed was the exceptional disagreeableness of one of the London district managers. "He takes advantage of his position," repeated Susan with face aflame, and Lady Harman was already too wise about Susan's possibilities to urge her towards particulars. . . .

Now as Lady Harman listened to all this confused effective picturing of the great catering business which was the other side of her husband and which she had taken on trust so long, she had in her heart a quite unreasonable feeling of shame that she should listen at all, a shyness, as though she was prying, as though this really did not concern her. She knew she had to listen and still she felt beyond her proper jurisdiction. It is against instinct, it is with an enormous reluctance that women are bringing their quick emotions, their flashing unstable intelligences, their essential romanticism, their inevitable profound generosity into the world of politics and business. If only they could continue believing that all that side of life is grave and wise and admirably managed for them they would. It is not in a day or a generation that we shall un-specialize women. It is a wrench nearly as violent as birth for them to face out into the bleak realization that the man who goes out for them into business, into affairs, and returns so comfortably loaded with housings and wrappings and trappings and toys, isn't, as a matter of fact, engaged in benign creativeness while he is getting these desirable things.

5

Lady Harman's mind was so greatly exercised by Susan Burnet's voluminous confidences that it was only when she returned to her own morning room that she recalled the pawning problem. She went back to Sir Isaac's study and found Susan with all her measurements taken and on the very edge of departure.

"Oh Susan!" she said.

She found the matter a little difficult to broach. Susan remained in an attitude of respectful expectation.

"I wanted to ask you," said Lady Harman and then broke off to shut the door. Susan's interest increased.

"You know, Susan," said Lady Harman with an air of talking about commonplace things, "Sir Isaac is very rich and—of course—very generous. . . . But sometimes one feels, one wants a little money of one's own."

"I think I can understand that, my lady," said Susan.

"I knew you would," said Lady Harman and then with a brightness that was slightly forced, "I can't always get money of my own. It's difficult—sometimes."

And then blushing vividly: "I've got lots of *things*. . . . Susan, have you ever pawned anything?"

And so she broached it.

"Not since I got fairly into work," said Susan; "I wouldn't have it. But when I was little we were always pawning things. Why! we've pawned kettles! . . ."

She flashed three reminiscences.

Meanwhile Lady Harman produced a little glittering object and held it between finger and thumb. "If I went into a pawnshop near here," she said, "it would seem so odd. . . . This ring, Susan, must be worth thirty or forty pounds. And it seems so silly when I have it that I should really be wanting money. . . ."

Susan displayed a peculiar reluctance to handle the ring. "I've never," she said, "pawned anything valuable—not valuable like that. Suppose—suppose they wanted to know how I had come by it."

"It's more than Alice earns in a year," she said. "It's—" she eyed the glittering treasure; "it's a queer thing for me to have."

A certain embarrassment arose between them. Lady Harman's need of money became more apparent. "I'll do it for you," said Susan, "indeed I'll do it. But— There's one thing—"

Her face flushed hotly. "It isn't that I want to make difficulties. But people in our position—we aren't like people in your position. It's awkward sometimes to explain things. You've got a good character, but people don't know it. You can't be too careful. It isn't sufficient—just to be honest. If I take that— If you were just to give me a little note—in your handwriting—on your paper—just asking me—I don't suppose I need show it to anyone. . . ."

"I'll write the note," said Lady Harman. A new set of uncomfortable ideas was dawning upon her. "But Susan— You don't mean that anyone, anyone who's really honest—might get into trouble?"

"You can't be too careful," said Susan, manifestly resolved not to give our highly civilized state half a chance with her.

6

The problem of Sir Isaac and just what he was doing and what he thought he was doing and what he meant to do increased in importance in Lady Harman's mind as the days passed by. He had an air of being malignantly up to something and she could not imagine what this something could be. He spoke to her very little but he looked at her a great deal. He had more and more of the quality of a premeditated imminent explosion. . . .

One morning she was standing quite still in the drawing-room thinking over this now almost oppressive problem of why the situation did not develop further with him, when she became aware of a thin flat unusual book upon the small side table near the great armchair at the side of the fire. He had been reading that overnight and it lay obliquely—it might almost have been left out for her.

She picked it up. It was *The Taming of the Shrew* in that excellent folio edition of Henley's which makes each play a comfortable thin book apart. A curiosity to learn what it was had drawn her husband to English Literature made her turn over the pages. *The Taming of the Shrew* was a play she knew very slightly. For the Harmans, though deeply implicated like most other rich and striving people in plans for honoring the immortal William, like most other people found scanty leisure to read him.

As she turned over the pages a pencil mark caught her eye. Thence words were underlined and further accentuated by a deeply scored line in the margin.

> *But for my bonny Kate, she must with me.*
> *Nay; look not big, nor stamp, nor stare, nor fret;*
> *I will be master of what is mine own:*
> *She is my goods, my chattels; she is my house,*
> *She is my household stuff, my field, my barn,*
> *My horse, my ox, my ass, my any thing:*
> *And here she stands, touch her whoever dare;*
> *I'll bring mine action on the proudest He,*
> *That stops my way in Padua.*

With a slightly heightened color Lady Harman read on and presently found another page slashed with Sir Isaac's approval. . . .

Her face became thoughtful. Did he mean to attempt—Petruchio? He could never dare. There were servants, there were the people one met, the world. . . . He would never dare. . . .

What a strange play it was! Shakespeare of course was wonderfully wise, the crown of English wisdom, the culminating English mind,—or else one might almost find something a little stupid and clumsy. . . . Did women nowadays really feel like these Elizabethan wives who talked—like girls, very forward girls indeed, but girls of sixteen? . . .

She read the culminating speech of Katherine and now she had so forgotten Sir Isaac she scarcely noted the pencil line that endorsed the immortal words.

> Thy husband is thy Lord, thy Life, thy Keeper,
> Thy Head, thy Sovereign; one who cares for thee,
> And for thy maintenance commits his body
> To painful labor both by sea and land,
> To watch the night in storms, the day in cold,
> While thou liest warm at home, secure and safe;
> And craves no other tribute at thy hands
> But love, fair looks, and true obedience;
> Too little payment for so great a debt.
> Such duty as the Subject owes the Prince,
> Even such a woman oweth to her husband;
> And when she is froward, peevish, sullen, sour,
> And not obedient to his honest will,
> What is she but a foul contending Rebel
> And graceless traitor to her loving Lord?
> I am ashamed that women are so simple
> To offer war, where they should kneel for peace;

> * * * * * * *

> My mind has been as big as one of yours,
> My heat as great; my reason, haply, more,
> To bandy word for word and frown for frown.
> But now I see our lances are but straws;
> Our strength is weak, our weakness past compare,
> Seeming that most which we indeed least are. . . .

She wasn't indignant. Something in these lines took hold of her protesting imagination.

She knew that so she could have spoken of a man.

But that man,—she apprehended him as vaguely as an Anglican bishop apprehends God. He was obscured altogether by shadows; he had only one known characteristic, that he was totally unlike Sir Isaac. And the play was false she felt in giving this speech to a broken woman. Such things are not said by broken women. Broken women do no more than cheat and lie. But so a woman might speak out of her unconquered wilfulness, as a queen might give her lover a kingdom out of the fullness of her heart.

7

The evening after his wife had had this glimpse into Sir Isaac's mental processes he telephoned that Charterson and Horatio Blenker were coming home to dinner with him. Neither Lady Charterson nor Mrs. Blenker were to be present; it was to be a business conversation and not a social occasion, and Lady Harman he desired should wear her black and gold with just a touch of crimson in her hair. Charterson wanted a word or two with the flexible Horatio on sugar at the London docks, and Sir Isaac had some vague ideas that a turn might be given to the public judgment upon the waitresses' strike, by a couple of Horatio's thoughtful yet gentlemanly articles. And in addition Charterson seemed to have something else upon his mind; he did not tell as much to Sir Isaac but he was weighing the possibilities of securing a controlling share in the *Daily Spirit,* which simply didn't know at present where it was upon the sugar business, and of installing Horatio's brother, Adolphus, as its editor. He wanted to form some idea from Horatio of what Adolphus might expect before he approached Adolphus.

Lady Harman wore the touch of crimson in her hair as her husband had desired, and the table was decorated simply with a big silver bowl of crimson roses. A slight shade of apprehension in Sir Isaac's face changed to approval at the sight of her obedience. After all perhaps she was beginning to see the commonsense of her position.

Charterson struck her as looking larger, but then whenever she saw him he struck her as looking larger. He enveloped her hand in a large amiable paw for a minute and asked after the children with gusto. The large teeth beneath his discursive moustache gave him the effect of a perennial smile to which his asymmetrical ears added a touch of waggery. He always betrayed a fatherly feeling towards her as became a man who was married to a handsome wife old enough to be her mother. Even when he asked about the children he did it with something of the amused knowingness of assured seniority, as if indeed he knew all sorts of things about the children that she couldn't as yet even begin to imagine. And though he confined his serious conversation to the two other men, he would ever and again show himself mindful of her and throw her some friendly enquiry, some quizzically puzzling remark. Blenker as usual treated her as if she were an only very indistinctly visible presence to whom an effusive yet inattentive politeness was due. He was clearly nervous almost to the pitch of jumpiness. He knew he was to be spoken to about the sugar business directly he saw Charterson, and he hated being spoken to about the sugar business. He had his code of honor. Of course one had to make concessions to one's proprietors, but he could not help feeling that if only they would consent to see his really quite obvious gentlemanliness more clearly it would be better for the paper, better for the party, better for them, far better for himself. He wasn't altogether a fool about that sugar; he knew how things lay. They ought to trust him more. His nervousness betrayed itself in many little ways. He crumbled his bread constantly until, thanks to Snagsby's assiduous replacement, he had made quite a pile of crumbs, he dropped his glasses in the soup—a fine occasion for Snagsby's *sangfroid*—and he forgot not to use a fish knife with the fish as Lady Grove directs and tried when he discovered his error to replace it furtively on the table cloth. Moreover he kept on patting the glasses on his nose—after Snagsby had whisked his soup plate away, rescued, wiped and returned them to him—until that feature glowed modestly at such excesses of attention, and the soup and sauces and things bothered his fine blond moustache unusually. So that Mr. Blenker what with the glasses, the napkin, the food and the things seemed as restless as a young sparrow. Lady Harman did her duties as hostess in the quiet key of her somber dress, and until the conversation drew her out into unexpected questionings she answered rather than talked, and she did not look at her husband once throughout the meal.

At first the talk was very largely Charterson. He had no intention of coming to business with Blenker until Lady Harman had given place to the port and the man's nerves were steadier. He spoke of this and that in the large discursive way men use in clubs, and it was past the fish before the conversation settled down upon the topic of business organization and Sir Isaac, a little warmed by champagne, came out of the uneasily apprehensive taciturnity into which he had fallen in the presence of his wife. Horatio Blenker was keenly interested in the idealization of commercial syndication, he had been greatly stirred by a book of Mr. Gerald Stanley Lee's called *Inspired Millionaires* which set out to show just what magnificent airs rich men might give themselves, and he had done his best to catch its tone and to find *Inspired Millionaires* in Sir Isaac and Charterson and to bring it to their notice and to the notice of the readers of the *Old Country Gazette*. He felt that if only Sir Isaac and Charterson would see getting rich as a Great Creative Act it would raise their tone and his tone and the tone of the *Old Country Gazette* tremendously. It wouldn't of course materially alter the methods or policy of the paper but it would make them all feel nobler, and Blenker was of that finer clay that does honestly want to feel nobler. He hated pessimism and all that criticism and self-examination that makes weak men pessimistic, he wanted to help weak men and be helped himself, he was all for that school of optimism that would have each dunghill was a well-upholstered throne, and his nervous, starry contributions to the talk were like patches of water ranunculuses trying to flower in the overflow of a sewer.

Because you know it is idle to pretend that the talk of Charterson and Sir Isaac wasn't a heavy flow of base ideas; they hadn't even the wit to sham very much about their social significance. They cared no more for the growth, the stamina, the spirit of the people whose lives they dominated than a rat cares for the stability of the house it gnaws. They *wanted* a broken-spirited people. They were in such relations wilfully and offensively stupid, and I do not see why we people who read and write books should pay this stupidity merely because it is prevalent even the mild tribute of an ironical civility. Charterson talked of the gathering trouble that might lead to a strike of the transport workers in London docks, and what he had to say, he said,—he repeated it several times—was, "*Let* them strike. We're ready. The sooner they strike the better. Devonport's a Man and this time we'll *beat* 'em. . . ."

He expanded generally on strikes. "It's a question practically whether we are to manage our own businesses or whether we're to have them managed for us. *Managed* I say! . . ."

"They know nothing of course of the details of organization," said Blenker, shining with intelligence and looking quickly first to the right and then to the left. "Nothing."

Sir Isaac broke out into confirmatory matter. There was an idea in his head that this talk might open his wife's eyes to some sense of the magnitude of his commercial life, to the wonder of its scale and quality. He compared notes with Charterson upon a speeding-up system for delivery vans invented by an American specialist and it made Blenker flush with admiration and turn as if for sympathy to Lady Harman to realize how a modification in a tail-board might mean a yearly saving in wages of many thousand pounds. "The sort of thing they don't understand," he said. And then Sir Isaac told of some of his own little devices. He had recently taken to having the returns of percentage increase and decrease from his various districts printed on postcards and circulated monthly among the district managers, postcards endorsed with such stimulating comments in red type as "Well done Cardiff!" or "What ails Portsmouth?"—the results had been amazingly good; "neck and neck work," he said, "everywhere"—and thence they passed to the question of confidential reports and surprise inspectors. Thereby they came to the rights and wrongs of the waitress strike.

And then it was that Lady Harman began to take a share in the conversation. She interjected a question. "Yes," she said suddenly and her interruption was so unexpected that all three men turned their eyes to her. "But how much do the girls get a week?"

"I thought," she said to some confused explanations by Blenker and Charterson, "that gratuities were forbidden."

Blenker further explained that most of the girls of the class Sir Isaac was careful to employ lived at home. Their income was "supplementary."

"But what happens to the others who don't live at home, Mr. Blenker?" she asked.

"Very small minority," said Mr. Blenker reassuring himself about his glasses.

"But what do they do?"

Charterson couldn't imagine whether she was going on in this way out of sheer ignorance or not.

"Sometimes their fines make big unexpected holes in their week's pay," she said.

Sir Isaac made some indistinct remark about "utter nonsense."

"It seems to me to be driving them straight upon the streets."

The phrase was Susan's. Its full significance wasn't at that time very clear to Lady Harman and it was only when she had uttered it that she realized from Horatio Blenker's convulsive start just what a blow she had delivered at that table. His glasses came off again. He caught them and thrust them back, he seemed to be holding his nose on, holding his face on, preserving those carefully arranged features of himself from hideous revelations; his free hand made weak movements with his dinner napkin. He seemed to be holding it in reserve against the ultimate failure of his face. Charterson surveyed her through an immense pause open-mouthed; then he turned his large now frozen amiability upon his host. "These are Awful questions," he gasped, "rather beyond Us don't you think?" and then magnificently; "Harman, things are looking pretty Queer in the Far East again. I'm told there are chances—of revolution—even in Pekin. . . ."

Lady Harman became aware of Snagsby's arm and his steady well-trained breathing beside her as, tenderly almost but with a regretful disapproval, he removed her plate. . . .

8

If Lady Harman had failed to remark at the time the deep impression her words had made upon her hearers, she would have learned it later from the extraordinary wrath in which Sir Isaac, as soon as his guests had departed, visited her. He was so angry he broke the seal of silence he had set upon his lips. He came raging into the pink bedroom through the paper-covered door as if they were back upon their old intimate footing. He brought a flavor of cigars and manly refreshment with him, his shirt front was a little splashed and crumpled and his white face was variegated with flushed patches.

"What ever d'you mean," he cried, "by making a fool of me in front of those fellers? . . . What's my business got to do with you?"

Lady Harman was too unready for a reply.

"I ask you what's my business got to do with you? It's *my* affair, *my* side. You got no more right to go shoving your spoke into that than—anything. See? What do *you* know of the rights and wrongs of business? How can *you* tell what's right and what isn't right? And the things you came out with—the things you came out with! Why Charterson—after you'd gone Charterson said, she doesn't know, she can't know what she's talking about! A decent woman! a *lady!* talking of driving girls on the street. You ought to be ashamed of yourself!

You aren't fit to show your face. . . . It's these damned papers and pamphlets, all this blear-eyed stuff, these decadent novels and things putting narsty thoughts, *narsty dirty* thoughts into decent women's heads. It ought to be rammed back down their throats, it ought to be put a stop to!''

Sir Isaac suddenly gave way to woe. ''What have I *done?*'' he cried, ''what have I done? Here's everything going so well! We might be the happiest of couples! We're rich, we got everything we want. . . . And then you go harboring these ideas, fooling about with rotten people, taking up with Socialism— Yes, I tell you—Socialism!''

His moment of pathos ended. ''NO?'' he shouted in an enormous voice.

He became white and grim. He emphasized his next words with a shaken finger.

''It's got to end, my lady. It's going to end sooner than you expect. That's all! . . .''

He paused at the papered door. He had a popular craving for a vivid curtain and this he felt was just a little too mild.

''It's going to end,'' he repeated and then with great violence, with almost alcoholic violence, with the round eyes and shouting voice and shaken fist and blaspheming violence of a sordid, thrifty peasant enraged, ''it's going to end a Damned Sight sooner than you expect.''

CHAPTER THE EIGHTH

Sir Isaac as Petruchio

1

TWICE HAD SIR ISAAC come near to betraying the rapid and extensive preparations for the subjugation of his wife, that he hid behind his silences. He hoped that their estrangement might be healed by a certain display of strength and decision. He still refused to let himself believe that all this trouble that had arisen between them, this sullen insistence upon unbecoming freedoms of intercourse and move-ment, this questioning spirit and a gaucherie of manner that might almost be mistaken for an aversion from his person, were due to any essential evil in her nature; he clung almost passionately to the alternative that she was the victim of those gathering forces of discontent, of that interpretation which can only be described as decadent and that veracity which can only be called immodest, that darken the intellectual skies of our time, a sweet thing he held her still though touched by corruption, a prey to ''idees,'' ''idees'' imparted from the poisoned mind of her sister, imbibed from the carelessly edited columns of newspapers, from all too laxly censored plays, from ''blear-eyed'' books—how he thanked the Archbishop of York for that clever expressive epithet!—from the careless talk of rashly admitted guests, from the very atmosphere of London. And it had grown clearer and clearer to him that his duty to himself and the world and her was to remove her to a purer, simpler air, beyond the range of these infections, to isolate her and tranquillize her and so win her back again to that acquiescence, that entirely hopeless submissiveness that had made her so sweet and dear a companion for him in the earlier years of their married life. Long before Lady Beach-Mandarin's crucial luncheon, his deliberate foreseeing mind had been planning such a retreat. Black Strand even at his first visit had appeared to him in the light of a great opportunity, and the crisis of their quarrel did but release that same torrential energy which had carried him to a position of Napoleonic predominance in the world of baking, light catering and confectionery, into the channels of a scheme already very definitely formed in his mind.

His first proceeding after the long hours of sleepless passion that had followed his wife's Hampton Court escapade, had been to place himself in communication with Mr. Brumley. He learned at Mr. Brumley's club that that gentleman had slept there overnight and had started but a quarter of an hour before, back to Black Strand. Sir Isaac in hot pursuit and gathering force and assistance in mid flight reached Black Strand by midday.

It was with a certain twinge of the conscience that Mr. Brumley perceived his visitor, but it speedily became clear that Sir Isaac had no knowledge of the guilty circumstances of the day before. He had come to buy Black Strand—incontinently, that was all. He was going, it became clear at once, to buy it with all its fittings and furnishings as it stood, lock, stock and barrel. Mr. Brumley, concealing that wild elation, that sense of a joyous rebirth, that only the liquidation of nearly all one's possessions can give, was firm but not excessive. Sir Isaac haggled as a wave breaks and then gave in and presently they were making a memorandum upon the pretty writing-desk beneath the traditional rose Euphemia had established there when Mr. Brumley was young and already successful.

This done, and it was done in less than fifteen minutes, Sir Isaac produced a rather crumpled young architect from the motor-car as a conjurer might produce a rabbit from a hat, a builder from Aleham appeared astonishingly in a dog-cart—he had been summoned by telegram—and Sir Isaac began there and then to discuss alterations, enlargements and, more particularly, with a view to his nursery requirements, the conversion of the empty barn into a nursery wing and its connection with the house by a corridor across the shrubbery.

"It will take you three months," said the builder from Aleham. "And the worst time of the year coming."

"It won't take three weeks—if I have to bring down a young army from London to do it," said Sir Isaac.

"But such a thing as plastering—"

"We won't have plastering."

"There's canvas and paper, of course," said the young architect.

"There's canvas and paper," said Sir Isaac. "And those new patent building units, so far as the corridor goes. I've seen the ads."

"We can whitewash 'em. They won't show much," said the young architect.

"Oh if you do things in *that* way," said the builder from Aleham with bitter resignation. . . .

2

The morning dawned at last when the surprise was ripe. It was four days after Susan's visit, and she was due again on the morrow with the money that would enable her employer to go to Lady Viping's now imminent dinner. Lady Harman had had to cut the Social Friends' meeting altogether, but the day before the surprise Agatha Alimony had come to tea in her jobbed car, and they had gone together to the committee meeting of the Shakespeare Dinner Society. Sir Isaac had ignored that defiance, and it was an unusually confident and quite unsuspicious woman who descended in a warm October sunshine to the surprise. In the breakfast-room she discovered an awe-stricken Snagsby standing with his plate-basket before her husband, and her husband wearing strange unusual tweeds and gaiters,—buttoned gaiters, and standing a-straddle,—unusually a-straddle, on the hearthrug.

"That's enough, Snagsby," said Sir Isaac, at her entrance. "Bring it all."

She met Snagsby's eye, and it was portentous.

Latterly Snagsby's eye had lost the assurance of his former days. She had noted it before, she noted it now more than ever; as though he was losing confidence, as though he was beginning to doubt, as though the world he had once seemed to rule grew insecure beneath his feet. For a moment she met his eye; it might have been a warning he conveyed, it might have been an appeal for sympathy, and then he had gone. She looked at the table. Sir Isaac had breakfasted acutely.

In silence, among the wreckage and with a certain wonder growing, Lady Harman attended to her needs.

Sir Isaac cleared his throat.

She became aware that he had spoken. "What did you say, Isaac?" she asked, looking up. He seemed to have widened his straddle almost dangerously, and he spoke with a certain conscious forcefulness.

"We're going to move out of this house, Elly," he said. "We're going down into the country right away."

She sat back in her chair and regarded his pinched and determined visage.

"What do you mean?" she asked.

"I've bought that house of Brumley's,—Black Strand. We're going to move down there—*now*. I've told the servants. . . . When you've done your breakfast, you'd better get Peters to pack your things. The big car's going to be ready at half-past ten."

Lady Harman reflected.

"Tomorrow evening," she said, "I was going out to dinner at Lady Viping's."

"Not my affair—seemingly," said Sir Isaac with irony. "Well, the car's going to be ready at half-past ten."

"But that dinner—!"

"We'll think about it when the time comes."

Husband and wife regarded each other.

"I've had about enough of London," said Sir Isaac. "So we're going to shift the scenery. See?"

Lady Harman felt that one might adduce good arguments against this course if only one knew of them.

Sir Isaac had a bright idea. He rang.

"Snagsby," he said, "just tell Peters to pack up Lady Harman's things. . . ."

"*Well!*" said Lady Harman, as the door closed on Snagsby. Her mind was full of confused protest, but she had again that entirely feminine and demoralizing conviction that if she tried to express it she would weep or stumble into some such emotional disaster. If now she went upstairs and told Peters *not* to pack—!

Sir Isaac walked slowly to the window, and stood for a time staring out into the garden.

Extraordinary bumpings began overhead in Sir Isaac's room. No doubt somebody was packing something. . . .

Lady Harman realized with a deepening humiliation that she dared not dispute before the servants, and that he could. "But the children—" she said at last.

"I've told Mrs. Harblow," he said, over his shoulder. "Told her it was a bit of a surprise." He turned, with a momentary lapse into something like humor. "You see," he said, "it *is* a bit of a surprise."

"But what are you going to do with this house?"

"Lock it all up for a bit. . . . I don't see any sense in living where we aren't happy. Perhaps down there we shall manage better. . . ."

It emerged from the confusion of Lady Harman's mind that perhaps she had better go to the nursery, and see how things were getting on there. Sir Isaac watched her departure with a slightly dubious eye, made little noises with his teeth for a time, and then went towards the telephone.

In the hall she found two strange young men in green aprons assisting the under-butler to remove the hats and overcoats and such-like personal material into a motor-van outside. She heard two of the housemaids scurrying upstairs. "'Arf an hour," said one, "isn't what I call a proper time to pack a box in."

In the nursery the children were disputing furiously what toys were to be taken into the country.

Lady Harman was a very greatly astonished woman. The surprise had been entirely successful.

3

It has been said, I think, by Limburger, in his already cited work, that nothing so excites and prevails with woman as rapid and extensive violence, sparing and yet centering upon herself, and certainly it has to be recorded that, so far from being merely indignant, and otherwise a helplessly pathetic spectacle, Lady Harman found, though perhaps she did not go quite so far as to admit to herself that she found, this vehement flight from the social, moral, and intellectual contaminations of London an experience not merely stimulating but entertaining. It lifted her delicate eyebrows. Something, it may have been a sense of her own comparative immobility amid this sudden extraordinary bustle of her home, put it into her head that so it was long ago that Lot must have bundled together his removable domesticities.

She made one attempt at protest. "Isaac," she said, "isn't all this rather ridiculous—"

"Don't speak to me!" he answered, waving her off. "Don't speak to me! You should have spoken before, Elly. *Now,*—things are happening."

The image of Black Strand as, after all, a very pleasant place indeed returned to her. She adjudicated upon the nursery difficulties, and then went in a dreamlike state of mind to preside over her own more personal packing. She found Peters exercising all that indecisive helplessness which is characteristic of ladies' maids the whole world over.

It was from Peters she learned that the entire household, men and maids together, was to be hurled into Surrey. "Aren't they all rather surprised?" asked Lady Harman.

"Yes, m'm," said Peters on her knees, "but of course if the drains is wrong the sooner we all go the better."

(So that was what he had told them.)

A vibration and a noise of purring machinery outside drew the lady to the window, and she discovered that at least four of the large motor-vans from the International Stores were to cooperate in the trek. There they were waiting, massive and uniform. And then she saw Snagsby in his alpaca jacket *running* towards the house from the gates. Of course he was running only very slightly indeed, but still he was running, and the expression of distress upon his face convinced her that he was being urged to unusual and indeed unsuitable tasks under the immediate personal supervision of Sir Isaac. . . . Then from round the corner appeared the under-butler or at least the legs of him going very fast, under a pile of shirt boxes and things belonging to Sir Isaac. He dumped them into the nearest van and heaved a deep sigh and returned houseward after a remorseful glance at the windows.

A violent outcry from baby, who, with more than her customary violence was making her customary morning protest against being clad, recalled Lady Harman from the contemplation of these exterior activities. . . .

The journey to Black Strand was not accomplished without misadventure; there was a puncture near Farnham, and as Clarence with a leisurely assurance entertained himself with the Stepney, they were passed first by the second car with the nursery contingent, which went by in a shrill chorus, crying, "We-e-e shall get there first, *We-e-e* shall get there first," and then by a large hired car all agog with housemaids and Mrs. Crumble and with Snagsby, as round and distressed as the full moon, and the under-butler, cramped and keen beside the driver. There followed the leading International Stores car, and then the Stepney was on and they could hasten in pursuit. . . .

And at last they came to Black Strand, and when they saw Black Strand it seemed to Lady Harman that the place had blown out a huge inflamed red cheek and lost its pleasant balance altogether. "*Oh!*" she cried.

It was the old barn flushed by the strain of adaptation to a new use, its comfortable old wall ruptured by half a dozen brilliant new windows, a light red chimney stack at one end. From it a vividly artistic corridor ran to the house and the rest of the shrubbery was all trampled and littered with sheds, bricks, poles and material generally. Black Strand had left the hands of the dilettante school and was in the grip of those vigorous molding forces that are shaping our civilization today.

The jasmine wig over the porch had suffered a strenuous clipping; the door might have just come out of prison. In the hall the Carpaccio copies still glowed, but there were dust sheets over most of the furniture and a plumber was moving his things out with that eleventh hour reluctance so characteristic of plumbers. Mrs. Rabbit, a little tearful, and dressed for departure very respectably in black was giving the youngest and least experienced housemaid a faithful history of Mr. Brumley's earlier period. " 'Appy we all was," said Mrs. Rabbit, "as Birds in a Nest."

Through the windows two of the Putney gardeners were busy replacing Mr. Brumley's doubtful roses by recognized sorts, the *right* sorts. . . .

"I've been doing all I can to make it ready for you," said Sir Isaac at his wife's ear, bringing a curious reminiscence of the first home-coming to Putney into her mind.

<h1 style="text-align:center">4</h1>

"And now," said Sir Isaac with evident premeditation and a certain deliberate amiability, "now we got down here, now we got away a bit from all those London things with nobody to cut in between us, me and you can have a bit of a talk, Elly, and see what it's all about."

They had lunched together in the little hall-dining room,—the children had had a noisily cheerful picnic in the kitchen with Mrs. Harblow, and now Lady Harman was standing at the window surveying the ravages of rose replacement.

She turned towards him. "Yes," she said. "I think—I think we can't go on like this."

"*I* can't," said Sir Isaac, "anyhow."

He too came and stared at the rose planting.

"If we were to go up there—among the pine woods"—he pointed with his head at the dark background of Euphemia's herbaceous borders—"we shouldn't hear quite so much of this hammering. . . ."

Husband and wife walked slowly in the afternoon sunlight across the still beautiful garden. Each was gravely aware of an embarrassed incapacity for the task they had set themselves. They were going to talk things over. Never in their lives had they really talked to each other clearly and honestly about anything. Indeed it is scarcely too much to say that neither had ever talked about anything to anyone. She was too young, her mind was now growing up in her and feeling its way to conscious expression, and he had never before wanted to express himself. He did now want to express himself. For behind his rant and fury Sir Isaac had been thinking very hard indeed during the last three weeks about his life and her life and their relations; he had never thought so much about anything except his business economics. So far he had either joked at her, talked "silly" to her, made, as they say, "remarks," or vociferated. That had been the sum of their mental intercourse, as indeed it is the sum of the intercourse of most married couples. His attempt to state his case to her had so far always flared into rhetorical outbreaks. But he was discontented with these rhetorical outbreaks. His dispositions to fall into them made him rather like a nervous sepia that cannot keep its ink sac quiet while it is sitting for its portrait. In the earnestness of his attempt at self-display he vanished in his own outpourings.

He wanted now to reason with her simply and persuasively. He wanted to say quietly impressive and convincing things in a low tone of voice and make her abandon every possible view except his view. He walked now slowly meditating the task before him, making a faint thoughtful noise with his teeth, his head sunken in the collar of the motor overcoat he wore because of a slight cold he had caught. And he had to be careful about colds because of his constitutional defect. She too felt she had much to say. Much too she had in her mind that she couldn't say, because this strange quarrel had opened unanticipated things for her; she had found and considered repugnances in her nature she had never dared to glance at hitherto. . . .

Sir Isaac began rather haltingly when they had reached a sandy, ant-infested path that ran slantingly up among the trees. He affected a certain perplexity. He said he did not understand what it was his wife was "after," what she "thought she was doing" in "making all this trouble"; he wanted to know just what it was she wanted, how she thought they ought to live, just what she considered his rights were as her husband and just what she considered were her duties as his wife—if, that is, she considered she had any duties. To these enquiries Lady Harman made no very definite reply; their estrangement instead of clearing her mind had on the whole perplexed it more, by making her realize the height and depth and extent of her possible separation from him. She replied therefore with an unsatisfactory vagueness; she said she wanted to feel that she possessed herself, that she was no longer a child, that she thought she had a right to read what she chose, see what people she liked, go out a little by herself, have a certain independence—she hesitated, "have a certain definite allowance of my own."

"Have I ever refused you money?" cried Sir Isaac protesting.

"It isn't that," said Lady Harman; "it's the feeling—"

"The feeling of being able to—defy—anything I say," said Sir Isaac with a note of bitterness. "As if I didn't understand!"

It was beyond Lady Harman's powers to express just how that wasn't the precise statement of the case.

Sir Isaac, reverting to his tone of almost elaborate reasonableness, expanded his view that it was impossible for husband and wife to have two different sets of friends;—let alone every other consideration, he explained, it wasn't convenient for them not to be about together, and as for reading or thinking what she chose he had never made any objection to anything unless it was "decadent rot" that any decent man would object to his womanfolk seeing, rot she couldn't understand the drift of—fortunately. Blear-eyed humbug. . . . He checked himself on the verge of an almost archiepiscopal outbreak in order to be patiently reasonable again. He was prepared to concede that it would be very nice if Lady Harman could be a good wife and also an entirely independent person, very nice, but the point was—his tone verged on the ironical—that she couldn't be two entirely different people at the same time.

"But you have your friends," she said, "you go away alone—"

"That's different," said Sir Isaac with a momentary note of annoyance. "It's business. It isn't that I want to."

Lady Harman had a feeling that they were neither of them gaining any ground. She blamed herself for her lack of lucidity. She began again, taking up the matter at a fresh point. She said that her life at present wasn't full, that it was only half a life, that it was just home and marriage and nothing else; he had his business, he went out into the world, he had politics and—"all sorts of things"; she hadn't these interests; she had nothing in the place of them—

Sir Isaac closed this opening rather abruptly by telling her that she should count herself lucky she hadn't, and again the conversation was suspended for a time.

"But I want to know about these things," she said.

Sir Isaac took that musingly.

"There's things go on," she said; "outside home. There's social work, there's interests— Am I never to take any part—in that?"

Sir Isaac still reflected.

"There's one thing," he said at last, "I want to know. We'd better have it out—*now*."

But he hesitated for a time.

"Elly!" he blundered, "you aren't—you aren't getting somehow—not fond of me?"

She made no immediate reply.

"Look here!" he said in an altered voice. "Elly! there isn't something below all this? There isn't something been going on that I don't know?"

Her eyes with a certain terror in their depths questioned him.

"Something," he said, and his face was deadly white—"*Some other man, Elly?*"

She was suddenly crimson, a flaming indignation.

"Isaac!" she said, "what do you *mean?* How can you *ask* me such a thing?"

"If it's that!" said Sir Isaac, his face suddenly full of malignant force, "I'll— But I'd *kill* you. . . ."

"If it isn't that," he went on searching his mind; "why should a woman get restless? Why should she want to go away from her husband, go meeting other people, go gadding about? If a woman's satisfied, she's satisfied. She doesn't harbor fancies. . . . All this grumbling and unrest. Natural for your sister, but why should you? You've got everything a woman needs, husband, children, a perfectly splendid home, clothes, good jewels and plenty of them, respect! Why should you want to go out after things? It's mere spoilt-childishness. Of course you want to wander out—and if there isn't a man—"

He caught her wrist suddenly. "There isn't a man?" he demanded.

"Isaac!" she protested in horror.

"Then there'll be one. You think I'm a fool, you think I don't know anything all these literary and society people know. I *do* know. I know that a man and a woman have got to stick together, and if you go straying—you may think you're straying after the moon or social work or anything—but there's a strange man waiting round the corner for every woman and a strange woman for every man. Think *I've* had no temptations? . . . Oh! I *know, I know.* What's life or anything but that? and it's just because we've not gone on having more children, just because we listened to all those fools who said you were overdoing it, that all this fretting and grumbling began. We've got on to the wrong track, Elly, and we've got to get back to plain wholesome ways of living. See? That's what I've come down here for and what I mean to do. We've got to save ourselves. I've been too—too modern and all that. I'm going to be a husband as a husband should. I'm going to protect you from these idees—protect you from your own self. . . . And that's about where we stand, Elly, as I make it out."

He paused with the effect of having delivered himself of long premeditated things.

Lady Harman essayed to speak. But she found that directly she set herself to speak she sobbed and began weeping. She choked for a moment. Then she determined she would go on, and if she must cry, she must cry. She couldn't let a disposition to tears seal her in silence forever.

"It isn't," she said, "what I expected—of life. It isn't—"

"It's what life is," Sir Isaac cut in.

"When I think," she sobbed, "of what I've lost—"

"*Lost!*" cried Sir Isaac. "Lost! Oh come now, Elly, I like that. What!—*lost.* Hang it! You got to look facts in the face. You can't deny— Marrying like this,—you made a jolly good thing of it."

"But the beautiful things, the noble things!"

"*What's* beautiful?" cried Sir Isaac in protesting scorn. "*What's* noble? ROT! Doing your duty if you like and being sensible, that's noble and beautiful, but not fretting about and running yourself into danger. You've got to have a sense of humor, Elly, in this life—" He created a quotation. "As you make your bed—so shall you lie."

For an interval neither of them spoke. They crested the hill, and came into view of that advertisement board she had first seen in Mr. Brumley's company. She halted, and he went a step further and halted too. He recalled his ideas about the board. He had meant to have them all altered but other things had driven it from his mind. . . .

"Then you mean to imprison me here," said Lady Harman to his back. He turned about.

"It isn't much like a prison. I'm asking you to stay here—and be what a wife *should* be."

"I'm to have no money."

"That's—that depends entirely on yourself. You know that well enough."

She looked at him gravely.

"I won't stand it," she said at last with a gentle deliberation.

She spoke so softly that he doubted his hearing. "*What?*" he asked sharply.

"I won't stand it," she repeated. "No."

"But—what can you do?"

"I don't know," she said, after a moment of grave consideration.

For some moments his mind hunted among possibilities.

"It's me that's standing it," he said. He came closely up to her. He seemed on the verge of rhetoric. He pressed his thin white lips together. "Standing it! when we might be so happy," he snapped, and shrugged his shoulders and turned with an expression of mournful resolution towards the house again. She followed slowly.

He felt that he had done all that a patient and reasonable husband could do. *Now*—things must take their course.

5

The imprisonment of Lady Harman at Black Strand lasted just one day short of a fortnight.

For all that time except for such interludes as the urgent needs of the strike demanded, Sir Isaac devoted himself to the siege. He did all he could to make her realize how restrainedly he used the powers the law vests in a husband, how little he forced upon her the facts of marital authority and wifely duty. At times he sulked, at times he affected a cold dignity, and at times a virile anger swayed him at her unsubmissive silences. He gave her little peace in that struggle, a struggle that came to the edge of physical conflict. There were moments when it seemed to her that nothing remained but that good old-fashioned connubial institution, the tussle for the upper hand, when with a feminine horror she felt violence shouldering her shoulder or contracting ready to grip her wrist. Against violence she doubted her strength, was filled with a desolating sense of yielding nerve and domitable muscle. But just short of violence Sir Isaac's spirit failed him. He would glower and bluster, half threaten, and retreat. It might come to that at last but at present it had not come to that.

She could not understand why she had neither message nor sign from Susan Burnet, but she hid that anxiety and disappointment under her general dignity.

She spent as much time with the children as she could, and until Sir Isaac locked up the piano she played, and was surprised to find far more in Chopin than she had ever suspected in the days when she had acquired a passable dexterity of execution. She found, indeed, the most curious things in Chopin, emotional phrases, that stirred and perplexed and yet pleased her. . . .

The weather was very fine and open that year. A golden sunshine from October passed on into November and Lady Harman spent many of these days amidst the pretty things the builder from Aleham had been too hurried to desecrate, dump, burn upon, and flatten into indistinguishable mire, after the established custom of builders in gardens since the world began. She would sit in the rockery where she had sat with Mr. Brumley and recall that momentous conversation, and she would wander up the pinewood slopes behind, and she would spend long musing intervals among Euphemia's perennials, thinking sometimes, and sometimes not so much thinking as feeling the warm tendernesses of nature and the perplexing difficulties of human life. With an amused amazement Lady Harman reflected as she walked about the pretty borders and the little patches of lawn and orchard that in this very place she was to have realized an imitation of the immortal "Elizabeth" and have been wise, witty, gay, defiant, gallant and entirely successful with her "Man of Wrath." Evidently there was some temperamental difference, or something in her situation, that altered the values of the affair. It was clearly a different sort of man for one thing. She didn't feel a bit gay, and her profound and deepening indignation with the alternative to this stagnation was tainted by a sense of weakness and incapacity.

She came very near surrender several times. There were afternoons of belated ripened warmth, a kind of summer that had been long in the bottle, with a certain lassitude in the air and a blue haze among the trees, that made her feel the folly of all resistances to fate. Why, after all, shouldn't she take life as she found it, that is to say, as Sir Isaac was prepared to give it to her? He wasn't really so bad, she told herself. The children—their noses were certainly a little sharp, but there might be worse children. The next might take after herself more. Who was she to turn upon her appointed life and declare it wasn't good enough? Whatever happened the world was still full of generous and beautiful things, trees, flowers, sunset and sunrise, music and mist and morning dew. . . . And as for this matter of the sweated workers, the harshness of the business, the ungracious competition, suppose if instead of fighting her husband with her weak powers, she persuaded him. She tried to imagine just exactly how he might be persuaded. . . .

She looked up and discovered with an extraordinary amazement Mr. Brumley with eager gestures and a flushed and excited visage hurrying towards her across the croquet lawn.

6

Lady Viping's dinner-party had been kept waiting exactly thirty-five minutes for Lady Harman. Sir Isaac, with a certain excess of zeal, had intercepted the hasty note his wife had written to account for her probable absence. The party was to have centered entirely upon Lady Harman, it consisted either of people who knew her already, or of people who were to have been specially privileged to know her, and Lady Viping telephoned twice to Putney before she abandoned hope. "It's disconnected," she said, returning in despair from her second struggle with the great public service. "They can't get a reply."

"It's that little wretch," said Lady Beach-Mandarin. "He hasn't let her come. *I* know him."

"It's like losing a front tooth," said Lady Viping, surveying her table as she entered the dining-room.

"But surely—she would have written," said Mr. Brumley, troubled and disappointed, regarding an aching gap to the left of his chair, a gap upon which a pathetic little card bearing Lady Harman's name still lay obliquely.

Naturally the talk tended to center upon the Harmans. And naturally Lady Beach-Mandarin was very bold and outspoken and called Sir Isaac quite a number of vivid things. She also aired her views of the marriage of the future, which involved a very stringent treatment of husbands indeed. "Half his property and half his income," said Lady Beach-Mandarin, "paid into her separate banking account."

"But," protested Mr. Brumley, "would men marry under those conditions?"

"Men will marry anyhow," said Lady Beach-Mandarin, "under *any* conditions."

"Exactly Sir Joshua's opinion," said Lady Viping.

All the ladies at the table concurred and only one cheerful bachelor barrister dissented. The other men became gloomy and betrayed a distaste for this general question. Even Mr. Brumley felt a curious faint terror and had for a moment a glimpse of the possibilities that might lie behind the Vote. Lady Beach-Mandarin went bouncing back to the particular instance. At present, she said, witness Lady Harman, women were slaves, pampered slaves if you will, but slaves. As things were now there was nothing to keep a man from locking up his wife, opening all her letters, dressing her in sack-cloth, separating her from her children. Most men, of course, didn't do such things, they were amenable to public opinion, but Sir Isaac was a jealous little Ogre. He was a gnome who had carried off a princess. . . .

She threw out projects for assailing the Ogre. She would descend tomorrow morning upon the Putney house, a living flamboyant writ of Habeas Corpus. Mr. Brumley, who had been putting two and two together, was abruptly moved to tell of the sale of Black Strand. "They may be there," he said.

"He's carried her off," cried Lady Beach-Mandarin on a top note. "It might be the eighteenth century for all he cares. But if it's Black Strand,—I'll go to Black Strand. . . ."

But she had to talk about it for a week before she actually made her raid, and then, with an instinctive need for an audience, she took with her a certain Miss Garradice, one of those mute, emotional nervous spinsters who drift detachedly, with quick sudden movements, glittering eyeglasses, and a pent-up imminent look, about our social system. There is something about this type of womanhood— it is hard to say—almost as though they were the bottled souls of departed buccaneers grown somehow virginal. She came with Lady Beach-Mandarin quietly, almost humorosly, and yet it was as if the pirate glittered dimly visible through the polished glass of her erect exterior.

"Here we are!" said Lady Beach-Mandarin, staring astonished at the once familiar porch. "Now for it!"

She descended and assailed the bell herself and Miss Garradice stood beside her with the light of combat in her eyes and glasses and cheeks.

"Shall I offer to take her for a drive!"

"*Let's*," said Miss Garradice in an enthusiastic whisper. "*Right away! Forever.*"

"*I will*," said Lady Beach-Mandarin, and nodded desperately.

She was on the point of ringing again when Snagsby appeared.

He stood with a large obstructiveness in the doorway. "Lady 'Arman, my lady," he said with a well-trained deliberation, "is not a Tome."

"Not at home!" queried Lady Beach-Mandarin.

"Not a Tome, my lady," repeated Snagsby invincibly.

"But—when will she be at home?"

"I can't say, my lady."

"Is Sir Isaac—?"

"Sir Isaac, my lady, is not a Tome. Nobody is a Tome, my lady."

"But we've come from London!" said Lady Beach-Mandarin.

"I'm very sorry, my lady."

"You see, I want my friend to see this house and garden."

Snagsby was visibly disconcerted. "I 'ave no instructions, my lady," he tried.

"Oh, but Lady Harman would never object—"

Snagsby's confusion increased. He seemed to be wanting to keep his face to the visitors and at the same time glance over his shoulder. "I will," he considered, "I will enquire, my lady." He backed a little, and seemed inclined to close the door upon them. Lady Beach-Mandarin was too quick for him. She got herself well into the open doorway. "And of whom are you going to enquire?"

A large distress betrayed itself in Snagsby's eye. "The 'ousekeeper," he attempted. "It falls to the 'ousekeeper, my lady."

Lady Beach-Mandarin turned her face to Miss Garradice, shining in support. "Stuff and nonsense," she said, "of course we shall come in." And with a wonderful movement that was at once powerful and perfectly lady-like this intrepid woman—"butted" is not the word—collided herself with Snagsby and hurled him backward into the hall. Miss Garradice followed closely behind and at once extended herself in open order on Lady Beach-Mandarin's right. "Go and enquire," said Lady Beach-Mandarin with a sweeping gesture of her arm. "Go and enquire."

For a moment Snagsby surveyed the invasion with horror and then fled precipitately into the recesses of the house.

"Of *course* they're at home!" said Lady Beach-Mandarin. "Fancy that— that—that *navigable*—trying to shut the door on us!"

For a moment the two brightly excited ladies surveyed each other and then Lady Beach-Mandarin, with a quickness of movement wonderful in one so abundant, began to open first one and then another of the various doors that opened into the long hall-living room. At a peculiar little cry from Miss Garradice she turned from a contemplation of the long low study in which so much of the Euphemia books had been written, to discover Sir Isaac behind her, closely followed by an agonized Snagsby.

"A-a-a-a-h!" she cried, with both hands extended, "and so you've come in, Sir Isaac! That's perfectly delightful. This is my friend Miss Garradice, who's *dying* to see anything you've left of poor Euphemia's garden. And *how* is dear Lady Harman?"

For some crucial moments Sir Isaac was unable to speak and regarded his visitors with an expression that was unpretendingly criminal.

Then he found speech. "You can't," he said. "It—can't be managed." He shook his head; his lips were whitely compressed.

"But all the way from London, Sir Isaac!"

"Lady Harman's ill," lied Sir Isaac. "She mustn't be disturbed. Everything has to be kept quiet. See? Not even shouting. Not even ordinarily raised voices. A voice like yours—might kill her. That's why Snagsby here said we were not at home. We aren't at home—not to anyone."

Lady Beach-Mandarin was baffled.

"Snagsby," said Sir Isaac, "open that door."

"But can't I see her—just for a moment?"

Sir Isaac's malignity had softened a little at the prospect of victory. "Absolutely impossible," he said. "Everything disturbs her, every tiny thing. You—You'd be certain to."

Lady Beach-Mandarin looked at her companion and it was manifest that she was at the end of her resources. Miss Garradice after the fashion of highly strung spinsters suddenly felt disappointed in her leader. It wasn't, her silence intimated, for her to offer suggestions.

The ladies were defeated. When at last that stiff interval ended their dresses rustled doorward, and Sir Isaac broke out into the civilities of a victor. . . .

It was only when they were a mile away from Black Strand that fluent speech returned to Lady Beach-Mandarin. "The little—Crippen," she said. "He's got her locked up in some cellar. . . . Horrid little face he has! He looked like a rat at bay."

"I think perhaps if we'd done *differently*," said Miss Garradice in a tone of critical irresponsibility.

"I'll write to her. That's what I'll do," said Lady Beach-Mandarin contemplating her next step. "I'm really—concerned. And didn't you feel—something sinister? That butler-man's expression—a kind of round horror."

That very evening she told it all—it was almost the trial trip of the story—to Mr. Brumley. . . .

Sir Isaac watched their departure furtively from the study window and then ran out to the garden. He went right through into the pine woods beyond and presently, far away up the slopes, he saw his wife loitering down towards him, a gracious white tallness touched by a ray of sunlight—and without a suspicion of how nearly rescue had come to her.

7

So you see under what excitement Mr. Brumley came down to Black Strand. Luck was with him at first and he forced the defense with ridiculous ease.

"Lady Harman, sir, is not a Tome," said Snagsby.

"Ah!" said Mr. Brumley, with all the assurance of a former proprietor, "then I'll just have a look round the garden," and was through the green door in the wall and round the barn end before Snagsby's mind could function. That unfortunate man went as far as the green door in pursuit and then with a gesture of despair retreated to the pantry and began cleaning all his silver to calm his agonized spirit. He could pretend perhaps that Mr. Brumley had never rung at the front door at all. If not—

Moreover Mr. Brumley had the good fortune to find Lady Harman quite unattended and pensive upon the little seat that Euphemia had placed for the better seeing of her herbaceous borders.

"Lady Harman!" he said rather breathlessly, taking both her hands with an unwonted assurance and then sitting down beside her, "I am so glad to see you. I came down to see you—to see if I couldn't be of any service to you."

"It's so kind of you to come," she said, and her dark eyes said as much or more. She glanced round and he too glanced round for Sir Isaac.

"You see," he said. "I don't know. . . . I don't want to be impertinent. . . . But I feel—if I can be of any service to you. . . . I feel perhaps you want help here. I don't want to seem to be taking advantage of a situation. Or making unwarrantable assumptions. But I want to assure you—I would willingly die— if only I could do anything. . . . Ever since I first saw you."

He said all this in a distracted way, with his eyes going about the garden for the possible apparition of Sir Isaac, and all the time his sense of possible observers made him assume an attitude as though he was engaged in the smallest of small talk. Her color quickened at the import of his words, and emotion, very rich and abundant emotion, its various factors not altogether untouched perhaps by the spirit of laughter, lit her eyes. She doubted a little what he was saying and yet she had anticipated that somehow, someday, in quite other circumstances, Mr. Brumley might break into some such strain.

"You see," he went on with a quality of appeal in his eyes, "there's so little time to say things—without possible interruption. I feel you are in difficulties and I want to make you understand— We— Every beautiful woman, I suppose, has a sort of right to a certain sort of man. I want to tell you—I'm not really presuming to make love to you—but I want to tell you I am altogether yours, altogether at your service. I've had sleepless nights. All this time I've been thinking about you. I'm quite clear, I haven't a doubt, I'll do anything for you, without reward, without return, I'll be your devoted brother, anything, if only you'll make use of me. . . ."

Her color quickened. She looked around and still no one appeared. "It's so kind of you to come like this," she said. "You say things— But I *have* felt that you wanted to be brotherly. . . ."

"Whatever I *can* be," assured Mr. Brumley.

"My situation here," she said, her dark frankness of gaze meeting his troubled eyes. "It's so strange and difficult. I don't know what to do. I don't know— what I *want* to do. . . ."

"In London," said Mr. Brumley, "they think—they say—you have been taken off—brought down here—to a sort of captivity."

"I *have*," admitted Lady Harman with a note of recalled astonishment in her voice.

"If I can help you to escape—!"

"But where can I escape?"

And one must admit that it is a little difficult to indicate a correct refuge for a lady who finds her home intolerable. Of course there was Mrs. Sawbridge, but Lady Harman felt that her mother's disposition to lock herself into her bedroom at the slightest provocation made her a weak support for a defensive fight, and in addition that boarding-house at Bournemouth did not attract her. Yet what other wall in all the world was there for Lady Harman to set her back against? During the last few days Mr. Brumley's mind had been busy with the details of impassioned elopements conducted in the most exalted spirit, but now in the actual presence of the lady these projects did in the most remarkable manner vanish.

"Couldn't you," he said at last, "go somewhere?" And then with an air of being meticulously explicit, "I mean, isn't there somewhere, where you might safely go?"

(And in his dreams he had been crossing high passes with her; he had halted suddenly and stayed her mule. In his dream because he was a man of letters and a poet it was always a mule, never a *train de luxe*. "Look," he had said, "below there,— *Italy!*—the country you have never seen before.")

"There's nowhere," she answered.

"Now *where?*" asked Mr. Brumley, "and how?" with the tone and something of the gesture of one who racks his mind. "If you only trust yourself to me— Oh! Lady Harman, if I dared ask it—"

He became aware of Sir Isaac walking across the lawn towards them. . . .

The two men greeted each other with a reasonable cordiality. "I wanted to see how you were getting on down here," said Mr. Brumley, "and whether there was anything I could do for you."

"We're getting on all right," said Sir Isaac with no manifest glow of gratitude.

"You've altered the old barn—tremendously."

"Come and see it," said Sir Isaac. "It's a wing."

Mr. Brumley remained seated. "It was the first thing that struck me, Lady Harman. This evidence of Sir Isaac's energy."

"Come and look over it," Sir Isaac persisted.

Mr. Brumley and Lady Harman rose together.

"One's enough to show him that," said Sir Isaac.

"I was telling Lady Harman how much we missed her at Lady Viping's, Sir Isaac."

"It was on account of the drains," Sir Isaac explained. "You can't—it's foolhardy to stay a day when the drains are wrong, dinners or no dinners."

"You know *I* was extremely sorry not to come to Lady Viping's. I hope you'll tell her. I wrote."

But Mr. Brumley didn't remember clearly enough to make any use of that.

"Everybody naturally *is* sorry on an occasion of that sort," said Sir Isaac. "But you come and see what we've done in that barn. In three weeks. They couldn't have got it together in three months ten years ago. It's—system."

Mr. Brumley still tried to cling to Lady Harman.

"Have you been interested in this building?" he asked.

"I still don't understand the system of the corridor," she said, rising a little belatedly to the occasion. "I *will* come."

Sir Isaac regarded her for a moment with a dubious expression and then began to explain the new method of building with large prepared units and shaped pieces of reinforced concrete instead of separate bricks that Messrs. Prothero & Cuthbertson had organized and which had enabled him to create this artistic corridor so simply. It was a rather uncomfortable three-cornered conversation. Sir Isaac addressed his exposition exclusively to Mr. Brumley and Mr. Brumley made repeated ineffectual attempts to bring Lady Harman, and Lady Harman made repeated ineffectual attempts to bring herself, into a position in the conversation.

Their eyes met, the glow of Mr. Brumley's declarations remained with them, but neither dared risk any phrase that might arouse Sir Isaac's suspicions or escape his acuteness. And when they had gone through the new additions pretty thoroughly—the plumbers were still busy with the barn bath-room— Sir Isaac asked Mr. Brumley if there was anything more he would like to see. In the slight pause that ensued Lady Harman suggested tea. But tea gave them no opportunity of resuming their interrupted conversation, and as Sir Isaac's invincible determination to shadow his visitor until he was well off the premises became more and more unmistakable,—he made it quite ungraciously unmistakable,—Mr. Brumley's inventiveness failed. One thing came to him suddenly, but it led to nothing of any service to him.

"But I heard you were dangerously ill, Lady Harman!" he cried. "Lady Beach-Mandarin called here—"

"But when?" asked Lady Harman, astonished over the tea-things.

"But you *know* she called!" said Mr. Brumley and looked in affected reproach at Sir Isaac.

"I've not been ill at all!"

"Sir Isaac told her."

"Told her I was ill!"

"Dangerously ill. That you couldn't bear to be disturbed."

"But *when*, Mr. Brumley?"

"Three days ago."

They both looked at Sir Isaac who was sitting on the music stool and eating a piece of tea-cake with a preoccupied air. He swallowed and then spoke thoughtfully—in a tone of detached observation. Nothing but a slight reddening of the eyes betrayed any unusual feeling in him.

"It's my opinion," he said, "that that old lady—Lady Beach-Mandarin I mean—doesn't know what she's saying half the time. She says—oh! remarkable things. Saying *that* for example!"

"But did she call on me?"

"She called. I'm surprised you didn't hear. And she was all in a flurry for going on. . . . Did you come down, Mr. Brumley, to see if Lady Harman was ill?"

"That weighed with me."

"Well,—you see she isn't," said Sir Isaac and brushed a stray crumb from his coat. . . .

Mr. Brumley was at last impelled gateward and Sir Isaac saw him as far as the high-road.

"Good-bye!" cried Mr. Brumley with excessive amiability.

Sir Isaac with soundless lips made a good-bye like gesture.

"And now," said Sir Isaac to himself with extreme bitterness, "now to see about getting a dog."

"Bull mastiff?" said Sir Isaac developing his idea as he went back to Lady Harman. "Or perhaps a Thoroughly Vicious collie?"

"How did that chap get in?" he demanded. "What had he got to say to you?"

"He came in—to look at the garden," said Lady Harman. "And of course he wanted to know if I had been well—because of Lady Viping's party. And I suppose because of what you told Lady Beach-Mandarin."

Sir Isaac grunted doubtfully. He thought of Snagsby and of all the instructions he had given Snagsby. He turned about and went off swiftly and earnestly to find Snagsby. . . .

Snagsby lied. But Sir Isaac was able to tell from the agitated way in which he was cleaning his perfectly clean silver at that unseasonable hour that the wretched man was lying.

8

Quite a number of words came to the lips of Mr. Brumley as he went unwillingly along the pleasant country road that led from Black Strand to the railway station. But the word he ultimately said showed how strongly the habits of the gentlemanly *littérateur* prevailed in him. It was the one inevitable word for his mood,— "Baffled!"

Close upon its utterance came the weak irritation of the impotent man. "What the *devil?*" cried Mr. Brumley.

Some critical spirit within him asked him urgently why he was going to the station, what he thought he was doing, what he thought he had done, and what he thought he was going to do. To all of which questions Mr. Brumley perceived he had no adequate reply.

Earlier in the day he had been inspired by a vague yet splendid dream of large masterful liberations achieved. He had intended to be very disinterested, very noble, very firm, and so far as Sir Isaac was concerned, a trifle overbearing. You know now what he said and did. "Of course if we could have talked for a little longer," he said. From the stormy dissatisfaction of his retreat this one small idea crystallized, that he had not talked enough without disturbance to Lady Harman. The thing he had to do was to talk to her some more. To go on with what he had been saying. That thought arrested his steps. On that hypothesis there was no reason whatever why he should go on to the station and London. Instead— He stopped short, saw a convenient gate ahead, went to it, seated himself upon its topmost rail and attempted a calm survey of the situation. He had somehow to continue that conversation with Lady Harman.

Was it impossible to do that by going back to the front door of Black Strand? His instinct was against that course. He knew that if he went back now openly he would see nobody but Sir Isaac or his butler. He must therefore not go back openly. He must go round now and into the pine-woods at the back of Black Strand; thence he must watch the garden and find his opportunity of speaking to the imprisoned lady. There was something at once attractively romantic and repellently youthful about this course of action. Mr. Brumley looked at his watch, then he surveyed the blue clear sky overhead, with just one warm tinted wisp of cloud. It would be dark in an hour and it was probable that Lady Harman had already gone indoors for the day. Might it be possible after dark to approach the house? No one surely knew the garden so well as he.

Of course this sort of thing is always going on in romances; in the stories of that last great survivor of the Stevensonian tradition, H. B. Marriot Watson, the heroes are always creeping through woods, tapping at windows, and scaling house-walls, but Mr. Brumley as he sat on his gate became very sensible of his own extreme inexperience in such adventures. And yet anything seemed in his present mood better than going back to London.

Suppose he tried his luck!

He knew of course the lie of the land about Black Strand very well indeed and his harmless literary social standing gave him a certain freedom of trespass. He dropped from his gate on the inner side and taking a bridle path through a pine-wood was presently out upon the moorland behind his former home. He struck the high-road that led past the Staminal Bread Board and was just about to clamber over the barbed wire on his left and make his way through the trees to the crest that commanded the Black Strand garden when he perceived a man in a velveteen coat and gaiters strolling towards him. He decided not to leave the road until he was free from observation. The man was a stranger, an almost conventional gamekeeper, and he endorsed Mr. Brumley's remark upon the charmingness of the day with guarded want of enthusiasm. Mr. Brumley went on for some few minutes, then halted, assured himself that the stranger was well out of sight and returned at once towards the point where high-roads were to be left and adventure begun. But he was still some yards away when he became aware of that velveteen-coated figure approaching again. "Damn!" said Mr. Brumley and slacked his eager paces. This time he expressed a view that the weather was extremely mild. "Very," said the man in velveteen with a certain lack of respect in his manner.

It was no good turning back again. Mr. Brumley went on slowly, affected to botanize, watched the man out of sight and immediately made a dash for the pine-woods, taking the barbed wire in a manner extremely detrimental to his left trouser leg. He made his way obliquely up through the trees to the crest from which he had so often surveyed the shining ponds of Aleham. There he paused to peer back for that gamekeeper—whom he supposed in spite of reason to be stalking him—to recover his breath and to consider his further plans. The sunset was very fine that night, a great red sun was sinking towards acutely outlined hill-crests, the lower nearer distances were veiled in lavender mists and three of the ponds shone like the fragments of a shattered pink topaz. But Mr. Brumley had no eye for landscape. . . .

About two hours after nightfall Mr. Brumley reached the railway station. His trousers and the elbow of his coat bore witness to a second transit of the barbed-wire fence in the darkness, he had manifestly walked into a boggy place and had some difficulty in recovering firm ground and he had also been sliding in a recumbent position down a bank of moist ferruginous sand. Moreover he had cut the palm of his left hand. There was a new strange station-master who regarded him without that respect to which he had grown accustomed. He received the information that the winter train service had been altered and that he would have to wait forty-five minutes for the next train to London with the resignation of a man already chastened by misfortune and fatigue. He went into the waiting-room and after a vain search for the poker—the new stationmaster evidently kept it in a different place—sat down in front of an irritatingly dull fire banked up with slack, and nursed his damaged hand and meditated on his future plans.

His plans were still exactly in the state in which they had been when Sir Isaac parted from him at the gate of Black Strand. They remained in the same state for two whole days. Throughout all that distressing period his general intention of some magnificent intervention on behalf of Lady Harman remained unchanged, it produced a number of moving visions of flights at incredible speeds in (recklessly hired) motor-cars of colossal power,—most of the purchase money for Black Strand was still uninvested at his bank—of impassioned interviews with various people, of a divorce court with a hardened judge congratulating the manifestly quite formal co-respondent on the moral beauty of his behavior, but it evolved no sort of concrete practicable detail upon which any kind of action might be taken. And during this period of indecision Mr. Brumley was hunted through London by a feverish unrest. When he was in his little flat in Pont Street he was urged to go to his club, when he got to his club he was urged to go anywhere else, he called on the most improbable people and as soon as possible fled forth again, he even went to the British Museum and ordered out a lot of books on matrimonial law. Long before that great machine had disgorged them for him he absconded and this neglected, this widowed pile of volumes still standing to his account only came back to his mind in the middle of the night suddenly and disturbingly while he was trying to remember the exact words he had used in his brief conversation with Lady Harman. . . .

9

Two days after Mr. Brumley's visit Susan Burnet reached Black Strand. She too had been baffled for a while. For some week or more she couldn't discover the whereabouts of Lady Harman and lived in the profoundest perplexity. She had brought back her curtains to the Putney house in a large but luggable bundle, they were all made and ready to put up, and she found the place closed and locked, in the charge of a caretaker whose primary duty it was to answer no questions. It needed several days of thought and amazement, and a vast amount of "I wonder," and "I just would like to know," before it occurred to Susan that if she wrote to Lady Harman at the Putney address the letter might be forwarded. And even then she almost wrecked the entire enterprise by mentioning the money, and it was by a quite exceptional inspiration that she thought after all it was wiser not to say that but to state that she had finished the curtains and done everything (underlined) that Lady Harman had desired. Sir Isaac read it and tossed it over to his wife. "Make her send her bill," he remarked.

Whereupon Lady Harman set Mrs. Crumble in motion to bring Susan down to Black Strand. This wasn't quite easy because as Mrs. Crumble pointed out they hadn't the slightest use for Susan's curtains there, and Lady Harman had to find the morning light quite intolerable in her bedroom—she always slept with window wide open and curtains drawn back—to create a suitable demand for Susan's services. But at last Susan came, too humbly invisible for Sir Isaac's attention, and directly she found Lady Harman alone in the room with her, she produced a pawn ticket and twenty pounds. "I 'ad to give all sorts of particulars," she said. "It was a job. But I did it. . . ."

The day was big with opportunity, for Sir Isaac had been unable to conceal the fact that he had to spend the morning in London. He had gone up in the big car and his wife was alone, and so, with Susan upstairs still deftly measuring for totally unnecessary hangings, Lady Harman was able to add a fur stole and a muff and some gloves to her tweed gardening costume, walk unchallenged into the garden and from the garden into the wood and up the hillside and over the crest and down to the high-road and past that great advertisement of Staminal Bread and so for four palpitating miles, to the railway station and the outer world.

She had the good fortune to find a train imminent,—the twelve-seventeen.

She took a first-class ticket for London and got into a compartment with another woman because she felt it would be safer.

10

Lady Harman reached Miss Alimony's flat at half-past three in the afternoon. She had lunched rather belatedly and uncomfortably in the Waterloo Refreshment Room and she had found out that Miss Alimony was at home 'through the telephone. "I want to see you urgently," she said, and Miss Alimony received her in that spirit. She was hatless but she had a great cloud of dark fuzzy hair above the gray profundity of her eyes and she wore an artistic tea-gown that in spite of a certain looseness at neck and sleeve emphasized the fine lines of her admirable figure. Her flat was furnished chiefly with books and rich oriental hangings and vast cushions and great bowls of scented flowers. On the mantel-shelf was the crystal that amused her lighter moments and above it hung a circular allegory by Florence Swinstead, very rich in color, the Awakening of Woman, in a heavy gold frame. Miss Alimony conducted her guest to an armchair, knelt flexibly on the hearthrug before her, took up a small and elegant poker with a brass handle and a spear-shaped service end of iron and poked the fire.

The service end came out from the handle and fell into the grate. "It always does that," said Miss Alimony charmingly. "But never mind." She warmed both hands at the blaze. "Tell me all about it," she said, softly.

Lady Harman felt she would rather have been told all about it. But perhaps that would follow.

"You see," she said, "I find— My married life—"

She halted. It *was* very difficult to tell.

"Everyone," said Agatha, giving a fine firelit profile, and remaining gravely thoughtful through a little pause.

"Do you mind," she asked abruptly, "if I smoke?"

When she had completed her effect with a delicately flavored cigarette, she encouraged Lady Harman to proceed.

This Lady Harman did in a manner do. She said her husband left her no freedom of mind or movement, gave her no possession of herself, wanted to control her reading and thinking. "He insists—" she said.

"Yes," said Miss Agatha sternly blowing aside her cigarette smoke. "They all insist."

"He insists," said Lady Harman, "on seeing all my letters, choosing all my friends. I have no control over my house or my servants, no money except what he gives me."

"In fact you are property."

"I'm simply property."

"A harem of one. And all *that* is within the provisions of the law!"

"How any woman can marry!" said Miss Agatha, after a little interval. "I sometimes think that is where the true strike of the sex ought to begin. If none of us married! If we said all of us, 'No,—definitely—we refuse this bargain! It is a manmade contract. We have had no voice in it. We decline.' Perhaps it will come to that. And I knew that you, you with that quiet beautiful penetration in your eyes would come to see it like that. The first task, after the vote is won, will be the revision of that contract. The very first task of our Women States-men. . . ."

She ceased and revived her smoldering cigarette and mused blinking through the smoke. She seemed for a time almost lost to the presence of her guest in a great daydream of womanstatecraft.

"And so," she said, "you've come, as they all come,—to join us."

"*Well,*" said Lady Harman in a tone that made Agatha turn eyes of surprise upon her.

"Of course," continued Lady Harman, "I suppose—I shall join you; but as a matter of fact you see, what I've done today has been to come right away. . . . You see I am still in my garden tweeds. . . . There it was down there, a sort of stale mate. . . ."

Agatha sat up on her heels.

"But my dear!" she said, "you don't mean you've run away?"

"Yes,—I've run away."

"But—run away!"

"I sold a ring and got some money and here I am!"

"But—what are you going to do?"

"I don't know. I thought you perhaps—might advise."

"But—a man like your husband! He'll pursue you!"

"If he knows where I am, he will," said Lady Harman.

"He'll make a scandal. My dear! are you wise? Tell me, tell me exactly, *why* have you run away? I didn't understand at all—that you had run away."

"Because," began Lady Harman and flushed hotly. "It was impossible," she said.

Miss Alimony regarded her deeply. "I wonder," she said.

"I feel," said Lady Harman, "if I stayed, if I gave in— I mean after—after I had once—rebelled. Then I should just be—a wife—ruled, ordered—"

"It wasn't your place to give in," said Miss Alimony and added one of those parliament touches that creep more and more into feminine phraseology; "I agree to that—*nemine contradicente.* But—I *wonder.* . . ."

She began a second cigarette and thought in profile again.

"I think, perhaps, I haven't explained, clearly, how things are," said Lady Harman, and commenced a rather more explicit statement of her case. She felt she had not conveyed and she wanted to convey to Miss Alimony that her rebellion was not simply a desire for personal freedom and autonomy, that she desired these things because she was becoming more and more aware of large affairs outside her home life in which she ought to be not simply interested but concerned, that she had been not merely watching the workings of the business that made her wealthy, but reading books about socialism, about social welfare that had stirred her profoundly. . . . "But he won't even allow me to know of such things," she said. . . .

Miss Alimony listened a little abstractedly.

Suddenly she interrupted. "Tell me," she said, "one thing. . . . I confess," she explained, "I've no business to ask. But if I'm to advise— If my advice is to be worth anything. . . ."

"Yes?" asked Lady Harman.

"Is there— Is there someone else?"

"Someone else?" Lady Harman was crimson.

"On *your* side!"

"Someone else on my side?"

"I mean—someone. A man perhaps? Some man that you care for? More than you do for your husband? . . ."

"*I can't imagine,*" whispered Lady Harman, "*anything—*" And left her sentence unfinished. Her breath had gone. Her indignation was profound.

"Then I can't understand why you should find it so important to come away."

Lady Harman could offer no elucidation.

"You see," said Miss Alimony, with an air of expert knowledge, "our case against our opponents is just exactly their great case against us. They say to us when we ask for the Vote, 'the Woman's Place is the Home.' 'Precisely,' we answer, 'the Woman's Place *is* the Home. *Give* us our Homes!' Now *your* place is your home—with your children. That's where you have to fight your battle. Running away—for you it's simply running away."

"But— If I stay I shall be beaten." Lady Harman surveyed her hostess with a certain dismay. "Do you understand, Agatha? I *can't* go back."

"But my dear! What else can you do? What had you thought?"

"You see," said Lady Harman, after a little struggle with that childish quality in her nerves that might, if it wasn't controlled, make her eyes brim. "You see, I didn't expect you quite to take this view. I thought perhaps you might be disposed— If I could have stayed with you here, only for a little time, I could have got some work or something—"

"It's so dreadful," said Miss Alimony, sitting far back with the relaxation of infinite regrets. "It's dreadful."

"Of course if you don't see it as I do—"

"I can't," said Miss Alimony. "I can't."

She turned suddenly upon her visitor and grasped her knees with her shapely hands. "Oh let me implore you! Don't run away. Please for my sake, for all our sakes, for the sake of Womanhood, don't run away! Stay at your post. You mustn't run away. You must *not*. If you do, you admit everything. Everything. You must fight in your home. It's *your* home. That is the great principle you must grasp,—it's not his. It's there your duty lies. And there are your children— *your* children, your little ones! Think if you go—there may be a fearful fuss— proceedings. Lawyers—a search. Very probably he will take all sorts of proceedings. It will be a Matrimonial Case. How can I be associated with that? We mustn't mix up Women's Freedom with Matrimonial Cases. Impossible! We *dare* not! A woman leaving her husband! Think of the weapon it gives our enemies. If once other things complicate the Vote,—the Vote is lost. After all our self-denial, after all our sacrifices. . . . You see! Don't you *see?* . . .

"*Fight!*" she summarized after an eloquent interval.

"You mean," said Lady Harman,—"you think I ought to go back."

Miss Alimony paused to get her full effect. "*Yes*," she said in a profound whisper and endorsed it, "Oh so much so!—yes."

"Now?"

"Instantly."

For an interval neither lady spoke. It was the visitor at last who broke the tension.

"Do you think," she asked in a small voice and with the hesitation of one whom no refusal can surprise; "you could give me a cup of tea?"

Miss Alimony rose with a sigh and a slow unfolding rustle. "I forgot," she said. "My little maid is out."

Lady Harman left alone sat for a time staring at the fire with her eyes rather wide and her eyebrows raised as though she mutely confided to it her infinite astonishment. This was the last thing she had expected. She would have to go to some hotel. Can a woman stay alone at an hotel? Her heart sank. Inflexible forces seemed to be pointing her back to home—and Sir Isaac. He would be a very triumphant Sir Isaac, and she'd not have much heart left in her. . . . "I *won't* go back," she whispered to herself. "Whatever happens I *won't* go back. . . ."

Then she became aware of the evening newspaper Miss Alimony had been reading. The headline, "Suffrage Raid on Regent Street," caught her eye. A queer little idea came into her head. It grew with tremendous rapidity. She put out a hand and took up the paper and read.

She had plenty of time to read because her hostess not only got the tea herself but went during that process to her bedroom and put on one of those hats that have contributed so much to remove the stigma of dowdiness from the suffrage cause, as an outward and visible sign that she was presently ceasing to be at home. . . .

Lady Harman found an odd fact in the report before her. "One of the most difficult things to buy at the present time in the West End of London," it ran, "is a hammer. . . ."

Then a little further: "The magistrate said it was impossible to make discriminations in this affair. All the defendants must have a month's imprisonment. . . ."

When Miss Alimony returned Lady Harman put down the paper almost guiltily.

Afterwards Miss Alimony recalled that guilty start, and the still more guilty start that had happened, when presently she went out of the room again and returned with a lamp, for the winter twilight was upon them. Afterwards, too, she was to learn what had become of the service end of her small poker, the little iron club, which she missed almost as soon as Lady Harman had gone. . . .

Lady Harman had taken that grubby but convenient little instrument and hidden it in her muff, and she had gone straight out of Miss Alimony's flat to the Post Office at the corner of Jago Street, and there, with one simple effective impact, had smashed a ground-glass window, the property of His Majesty King George the Fifth. And having done so, she had called the attention of a youthful policeman, fresh from Yorkshire, to her offense, and after a slight struggle with his incredulity and a visit to the window in question, had escorted him to the South Hampsmith police-station, and had there made him charge her. And on the way she explained to him with a newfound lucidity why it was that women should have votes.

And all this she did from the moment of percussion onward, in a mood of exaltation entirely strange to her, but, as she was astonished to find, by no means disagreeable. She found afterwards that she only remembered very indistinctly her selection of the window and her preparations for the fatal blow, but that the effect of the actual breakage remained extraordinarily vivid upon her memory. She saw with extreme distinctness both as it was before and after the breakage, first as a rather irregular gray surface, shining in the oblique light of a street lamp, and giving pale phantom reflections of things in the street, and then as it was after her blow. It was all visual impression in her memory; she could not recollect afterwards if there had been any noise at all. Where there had been nothing but a milky dinginess a thin-armed, irregluar star had flashed into being, and a large triangular piece at its center, after what seemed an interminable indecision, had slid, first covertly downward, and then fallen forward at her feet and shivered into a hundred fragments. . . .

Lady Harman realized that a tremendous thing had been done—irrevocably. She stared at her achievement open-mouthed. The creative lump of iron dropped from her hand. She had a momentary doubt whether she had really wanted to break that window at all; and then she understood that this business had to be seen through, and seen through with neatness and dignity; and that wisp of regret vanished absolutely in her concentration upon these immediate needs.

11

Some day, when the arts of the writer and illustrator are more closely blended than they are today, it will be possible to tell of all that followed this blow, with an approach to its actual effect. Here there should stand a page showing simply and plainly the lower half of the window of the Jago Street Post Office, a dark, rather grimy pane, reflecting the light of a street lamp—and *broken*. Below the pane would come a band of evilly painted woodwork, a corner of letter-box, a foot or so of brickwork, and then the pavement with a dropped lump of iron. That would be the sole content of this page, and the next page would be the same, but very slightly fainter, and across it would be printed a dim sentence or so of explanation. The page following that would show the same picture again, but now several lines of type would be visible, and then, as one turned over, the smashed window would fade a little, and the printed narrative, still darkened and dominated by it, would nevertheless resume. One would read on how Lady Harman returned to convince the incredulous young Yorkshireman of her feat, how a man with a barrow-load of bananas volunteered comments, and how she went in custody, but with the extremest dignity, to the police-station. Then, with some difficulty, because that imposed picture would still prevail over the letterpress, and because it would be in small type, one would learn how she was bailed out by Lady Beach-Mandarin, who was clearly the woman she ought to have gone to in the first place, and who gave up a dinner with a duchess to entertain her, and how Sir Isaac, being too torn by his feelings to come near her spent the evening in a frantic attempt to keep the whole business out of the papers. He could not manage it. The magistrate was friendly next morning, but inelegant in his friendly expedients; he remanded Lady Harman until her mental condition could be inquired into, but among her fellow-defendants—there had been quite an epidemic of window-smashing that evening—Lady Harman shone preeminently sane. She said she had broken this window because she was assured that nothing would convince people of the great dissatisfaction of women with their conditions except such desperate acts, and when she was reminded of her four daughters she said it was precisely the thought of how they too would grow up to womanhood that had made her strike her blow. The statements were rather the outcome of her evening with Lady Beach-Mandarin than her own unaided discoveries, but she had honestly assimilated them, and she expressed them with a certain simple dignity.

Sir Isaac made a pathetic appearance before the court, and Lady Harman was shocked to see how worn he was with distress at her scandalous behavior. He looked a broken man. That curious sense of personal responsibility, which had slumbered throughout the Black Strand struggle, came back to her in a flood, and she had to grip the edge of the dock tightly to maintain her self-control. Unaccustomed as he was to public speaking, Sir Isaac said in a low, sorrow-laden voice, he had provided himself with a written statement dissociating himself from the views his wife's rash action might seem to imply, and expressing his own opinions upon woman's suffrage and the relations of the sexes generally, with especial reference to contemporary literature. He had been writing it most of the night. He was not, however, permitted to read this, and he then made an unstudied appeal for the consideration and mercy of the court. He said Lady Harman had always been a good mother and a faithful wife; she had been influenced by misleading people and bad books and publications, the true significance of which she did not understand, and if only the court would regard this first offense leniently he was ready to take his wife away and give any guarantee that might be specified that it should not recur. The magistrate was sympathetic and kindly, but he pointed out that this window-breaking had to be stamped out, and that it could only be stamped out by refusing any such exception as Sir Isaac desired. And so Sir Isaac left the court widowed for a month, a married man without a wife, and terribly distressed.

All this and more one might tell in detail, and how she went to her cell, and the long tedium of her imprisonment, and how deeply Snagsby felt the disgrace, and how Miss Alimony claimed her as a convert to the magic of her persuasions, and many such matters—there is no real restraint upon a novelist fully resolved to be English and Gothic and unclassical except obscure and inexplicable instincts. But these obscure and inexplicable instincts are at times imperative, and on this occasion they insist that here must come a break, a pause, in the presence of this radiating gap in the Postmaster-General's glass, and the phenomenon of this gentle and beautiful lady, the mother of four children, grasping in her gloved hand, and with a certain amateurishness, a lumpish poker-end of iron.

We make the pause by ending the chapter here and by resuming the story at a fresh point—with an account of various curious phases in the mental development of Mr. Brumley.

CHAPTER THE NINTH

Mr. Brumley Is Troubled by Difficult Ideas

1

THEN AS THAT picture of a post office pane, smashed and with a large hole knocked clean through it, fades at last upon the reader's consciousness, let another and a kindred spectacle replace it. It is the carefully cleaned and cherished window of Mr. Brumley's mind, square and tidy and as it were "frosted" against an excess of light, and in that also we have now to record the most jagged all and devastating fractures.

Little did Mr. Brumley reckon when first he looked up from his laces at Black Strand, how completely that pretty young woman in the dark furs was destined to shatter all the assumptions that had served his life.

But you have already had occasion to remark a change in Mr. Brumley's bearing and attitude that carries him far from the kindly and humorous conservatism of his earlier work. You have shared Lady Harman's astonishment at the ardor of his few stolen words in the garden, an astonishment that not only grew but flowered in the silences of her captivity, and you know something of the romantic impulses, more at least than she did, that gave his appearance at the little local railway station so belated and so disreputable a flavor. In the chilly ill-flavored solitude of her prison cell and with a mind quickened by meagre and distasteful fare, Lady Harman had ample leisure to reflect upon many things, she had already fully acquainted herself with the greater proportion of Mr. Brumley's published works, and she found the utmost difficulty in reconciling the flushed impassioned quality of his few words of appeal, with the moral assumptions of his published opinions. On the whole she was inclined to think that her memory had a little distorted what he had said. In this however she was mistaken; Mr. Brumley had really been proposing an elopement and he was now entirely preoccupied with the idea of rescuing, obtaining and possessing Lady Harman for himself as soon as the law released her.

One may doubt whether this extensive change from a humorous conservatism to a primitive and dangerous romanticism is to be ascribed entirely to the personal charm, great as it no doubt was, of Lady Harman; rather did her tall soft dark presence come to release a long accumulating store of discontent and unrest beneath the polished surfaces of Mr. Brumley's mind. Things had been stirring in him for some time; the latter Euphemia books had lacked much of the freshness of their precursors and he had found it increasingly hard, he knew not why, to keep up the lightness, the geniality, the friendly badinage of successful and accepted things, the sunny disregard of the grim and unamiable aspects of existence, that were the essential merits of that Optimistic Period of our literature in which Mr. Brumley had begun his career. With every justification in the world Mr. Brumley had set out to be an optimist, even in the *Granta* his work had been distinguished by its gay yet steadfast superficiality, and his early success, his rapid popularity, had done much to turn this early disposition into a professional attitude. He had determined that for all his life he would write for comfortable untroubled people in the character of a light-spirited, comfortable, untroubled person, and that each year should have its book of connubial humor, its travel in picturesque places, its fun and its sunshine, like roses budding in succession on a stem. He did his utmost to conceal from himself the melancholy realization that the third and the fourth roses were far less wonderful than the first and the second, and that by continuing the descending series a rose might be attained at last that was almost unattractive, but he was already beginning to suspect that he was getting less animated and a little irritable when Euphemia very gently and gracefully but very firmly and rather enigmatically died, and after an interval of tender and tenderly expressed regrets he found himself, in spite of the most strenuous efforts to keep bright and kindly and optimistic in the best style, dull and getting duller—he could disguise the thing no longer. And he weighed more. Six—eight—eleven pounds more. He took a flat in London, dined and lunched out lightly but frequently, sought the sympathetic friendship of several charming ladies, and involved himself deeply in the affairs of the Academic Committee. Indeed he made a quite valiant struggle to feel that optimism was just where it always had been and everything all right and very bright with him and with the world about him. He did not go under without a struggle. But as Max Beerbohm's caricature—the 1908 one I mean—brought out all too plainly, there was in his very animation, something of the alert liveliness of the hunted man. Do what he would he had a terrible irrational feeling that things, as yet scarce imagined things, were after him and would have him. Even as he makes his point, even as he gesticulates airily, with his rather distinctively North European nose Beerbohmically enlarged and his sensitive nostril in the air, he seems to be looking at something he does not want to look at, something conceivably pursuing, out of the corner of his eye.

The thing that was assailing Mr. Brumley and making his old established humor and tenderness seem dull and opaque and giving this new uneasy quality to his expression was of course precisely the thing that Sir Isaac meant when he talked about "idees" and their disturbing influence upon all the once assured tranquilities and predominances of Putney life. It was criticism breaking bounds.

As a basis and substance for the tissue of whimsically expressed happiness and confident appreciation of the good things of life, which Mr. Brumley had set before himself as his agreeable—and it was to be hoped popular and profitable— life-task, certain assumptions had been necessary. They were assumptions he had been very willing to make and which were being made in the most exemplary way by the writers who were succeeding all about him at the commencement of his career. And these assumptions had had such an air then of being quite trustworthy, as being certain to wash and wear! Already nowadays it is difficult to get them stated; they have become incredible while still too near to justify the incredibility that attaches to history. It was assumed, for example, that in the institutions, customs and culture of the middle Victorian period, humanity had, so far as the broad lines of things are concerned, achieved its goal. There were of course still bad men and women—individually—and classes one had to recognize as "lower," but all the main things were right, general ideas were right; the law was right, institutions were right, Consols and British Railway Debentures were right and were going to keep right forever. The Abolition of Slavery in America had been the last great act which had inaugurated this millennium. Except for individual instances the tragic intensities of life were over now and done with; there was no more need for heroes and martyrs; for the generality of humanity the phase of genial comedy had begun. There might be improvements and refinements ahead, but social, political and economic arrangement were now in their main outlines settled for good and all; nothing better was possible and it was the agreeable task of the artist and the man of letters to assist and celebrate this establishment. There was to be much editing of Shakespeare and Charles Lamb, much delightful humor and costume romance, and an Academy of refined Fine Writers would presently establish belles-lettres on the reputable official basis, write *finis* to creative force and undertake the task of stereotyping the language. Literature was to have its once terrible ferments reduced to the quality of a helpful pepsin. Ideas were dead—or domesticated. The last wild idea, in an impoverished and pitiful condition, had been hunted down and killed in the mobbing of, "The Woman Who Did." For a little time the world did actually watch a phase of English writing that dared nothing, penetrated nothing, suppressed everything and aspired at most to Charm, creep like a transitory patch of sunlight across a storm-rent universe. And vanish. . . .

At no time was it a perfectly easy task to pretend that the crazy makeshifts of our legal and political systems, the staggering accidents of economic relationship, the festering disorder of contemporary philosophy and religious teaching, the cruel and stupid bed of King Og that is our last word in sexual adjustment, really constituted a noble and enduring sanity, and it became less and less so with the acute disillusionments that arose out of the Boer War. The first decade of the twentieth century was for the English a decade of badly sprained optimism. Our Empire was nearly beaten by a handful of farmers amidst the jeering contempt of the whole world—and we felt it acutely for several years. We began to question ourselves. Mr. Brumley found his gay but entirely respectable irresponsibility harder and harder to keep up as that decade wore on. And close upon the South African trouble came that extraordinary new discontent of women with a woman's lot which we have been observing as it reached and troubled the life of Lady Harman. Women who had hitherto so passively made the bulk of that reading public which sustained Mr. Brumley and his kind—they wanted something else!

And behind and beneath these immediately disconcerting things still more sinister hintings and questioning were beginning to pluck at contentment. In 1899 nobody would have dreamed of asking and in 1909 even Mr. Brumley was asking, "Are things going on much longer?" A hundred little incidents conspired to suggest that a Christianity that had, to put it mildly, shirked the Darwinian challenge, had no longer the palliating influence demanded of a national religion, and that down there in the deep levels of labor where they built railways to carry Mr. Brumley's food and earn him dividends, where they made engines and instruments and textiles and drains for his little needs, there was a new, less bounded discontent, a grimmer spirit, something that one tried in vain to believe was only the work of "agitators," something that was to be pacified no longer by the thin pretenses of liberalism, something that might lead ultimately—optimism scarcely dared to ask whither. . . .

Mr. Brumley did his best to resist the influence of these darkening ideas. He tried to keep it up that everything was going well and that most of these shadows and complaints were the mischief of a few incurably restless personalities. He tried to keep it up that to belong to the working class was a thoroughly jolly thing—for those who were used to it. He declared that all who wanted to alter our laws or our ideas about property or our methods of production were envious and base and all who wanted any change between the sexes, foolish or vicious. He tried to go on disposing of socialists, agitators, feminists, women's suffragists, educationists and every sort of reformer with a good-humored contempt. And he found an increasing difficulty in keeping his contempt sufficiently good-humored. Instead of laughing down at folly and failure, he had moments when he felt that he was rather laughing up—a little wryly—at monstrous things impending. And since ideas are things of atmosphere and the spirit, insidious wolves of the soul, they crept up to him and gnawed the insides out of him even as he posed as their manful antagonist.

Insensibly Mr. Brumley moved with his times. It is the necessary first phase in the break-up of any system of unsound assumptions that a number of its votaries should presently set about padding its cutting corners and relieving the harsh pressure of its injustices by exuberances of humor and sentimentality. Mr. Brumley became charitable and romantic,—orthodox still but charitable and romantic. He was all for smashing with the generalization, but now in the particular instance he was more and more for forgiveness. One finds creeping into the later Euphemia books a Bret-Harte-like doctrine that a great number of bad women are really good and a persuasion in the 'Raffles' key that a large proportion of criminals are really very picturesque and admirable fellows. One wonders how far Mr. Brumley's less ostensible life was softening in harmony with this exterior change, this tender twilight of principle. He wouldn't as yet face the sterner fact that most people who are condemned by society, whether they are condemned justly or not, are by the very gregariousness of man's nature debased, and that a law or custom that stamps you as bad makes you bad. A great state should have high and humane and considerate laws nobly planned, nobly administered and needing none of these shabby little qualifications *sotto voce*. To find goodness in the sinner and justification in the outcast is to condemn the law, but as yet Mr. Brumley's heart failed where his intelligence pointed towards that conclusion. He hadn't the courage to revise his assumptions about right and wrong to that extent; he just allowed them to get soft and sloppy. He waded, where there should be firm ground. He waded towards wallowing. This is a perilous way of living and the sad little end of Euphemia, flushed and coughing, left him no doubt in many ways still more exposed to the temptations of the sentimental byway and the emotional gloss. Happily this is a book about Lady Harman and not an exhaustive monograph upon Mr. Brumley. We will at least leave him the refuge of a few shadows.

Occasionally he would write an important signed review for the *Twentieth Century* or the *Hebdomadal Review,* and on one such occasion he took in hand several studies of contemporary conditions by various "New Witnesses," "Young Liberals," *New Age* rebels and associated insurgent authors. He intended to be rather kindly with them, rather disillusioned, quite sympathetic but essentially conventional and conservative and sane. He sat at a little desk near the drooping Venus, under the benediction of Euphemia's posthumous rose, and turned over the pages of one of the least familiar of the group. The stuff was written with a crude force that at times became almost distinguished, but with a bitterness that he felt he must reprove. And suddenly he came upon a passionate tirade against the present period. It made him nibble softly with his lips at the top of his fountain pen as he read.

"We live," said the writer, "in a second Byzantine age, in one of those multitudinous accumulations of secondary interests, of secondary activities and conventions and colossal intricate insignificances, that lie like dust heaps in the path of the historian. The true history of such periods is written in bank books and check counterfoils and burnt to save individual reputations; it sneaks along under a thousand pretences, it finds its molelike food and safety in the dirt; its outer forms remain for posterity, a huge débris of unfathomable riddles."

"Hm!" said Mr. Brumley. "He slings it out. And what's this?"

"A civilization arrested and decayed, waiting through long inglorious ages of unscheduled crime, unchallenged social injustice, senseless luxury, mercenary politics and universal vulgarity and weakness, for the long overdue scavenging of the Turk."

"I wonder where the children pick up such language," whispered Mr. Brumley with a smile.

But presently he had pushed the book away and was thinking over this novel and unpleasant idea that perhaps after all his age didn't matter as some ages have mattered and as he had hitherto always supposed it did matter. Byzantine, with the gold of life stolen and the swans changed to geese? Of course always there had been a certain qualification upon heroes, even Cæsar had needed a wreath, but at any rate the age of Cæsar had mattered. Kings no doubt might be more kingly and the issues of life plainer and nobler, but this had been true of every age. He tried to weigh values against values, our past against our present, temperately and sanely. Our art might perhaps be keener for beauty than it seemed to be, but still—it flourished. And our science at least was wonderful—wonderful. There certainly this young detractor of existing things went astray. What was there in Byzantium to parallel with the electric light, the electric tram, wireless telegraphy, aseptic surgery? Of course this about "unchallenged social injustice" was nonsense. Rant. Why! we were challenging social injustice at every general election—plainly and openly. And crime! What could the man mean about unscheduled crime? Mere words! There was of course a good deal of luxury, but not *wicked* luxury, and to compare our high-minded and constructive politics with the mere conflict of unscrupulous adventurers about that semi-oriental throne! It was nonsense!

"This young man must be spanked," said Mr. Brumley and, throwing aside an open illustrated paper in which a full-length portrait of Sir Edward Carson faced a picture of the King and Queen in their robes sitting side by side under a canopy at the Coronation Durbar, he prepared himself to write in an extremely salutary manner about the follies of the younger generation, and incidentally to justify his period and his professional contentment.

2

One is reminded of those houses into which the white ants have eaten their way; outwardly still fair and solid, they crumble at the touch of a hand. And now you will begin to understand those changes of bearing that so perplexed Lady Harman, that sudden insurgence of flushed half-furtive passion in the garden, through the thin pretences of a liberal friendship. His hollow honor had been gripped and had given way.

He had begun so well. At first Lady Harman had occupied his mind in the properest way. She was another man's wife and sacred—according to all honorable standards, and what he wanted was merely to see more of her, talk to her, interest her in himself, share whatever was available outside her connubial obligations,— and think as little of Sir Isaac as possible.

How quickly the imaginative temperament of Mr. Brumley enlarged that to include a critical hostility to Sir Isaac, we have already recorded. Lady Harman was no longer simply a charming, suppressed young wife, crying out for attentive development; she became an ill-treated beautiful woman—misunderstood. Still scrupulously respecting his own standards, Mr. Brumley embarked upon the dangerous business of inventing just how Sir Isaac might be outraging them, and once his imagination had started to hunt in that field, it speedily brought in enough matter for a fine state of moral indignation, a white heat of not altogether justifiable chivalry. Assisted by Lady Beach-Mandarin Mr. Brumley had soon converted the little millionaire into a matrimonial ogre to keep an anxious lover very painfully awake at nights. Because by that time and quite insensibly he had become an anxious lover—with all the gaps in the thread of realities that would have made him that, quite generously filled up from the world of reverie.

Moral indignation is jealousy with a halo. It is the peculiar snare of the perplexed orthodox, and soon Mr. Brumley was in a state of nearly unendurable moral indignation with Sir Isaac for a hundred exaggerations of what he was and of what conceivably he might have done to his silent yet manifestly unsuitably mated wife. And now that romantic streak which is as I have said the first certain symptom of decay in a system of moral assumptions began to show itself in Mr. Brumley's thoughts and conversation. "A marriage like that," said Mr. Brumley to Lady Beach-Mandarin, "isn't a marriage. It flouts the True Ideal of Marriage. It's slavery—following a kidnapping. . . ."

But this is a wide step from the happy optimism of the Cambridge days. What becomes of the sanctity of marriage and the institution of the family when respectable gentlemen talk of something called "True Marriage," as non-existent in relation to a lady who is already the mother of four children? I record this lapsing of Mr. Brumley into romanticism without either sympathy or mitigation. The children, it presently became apparent, were not "true" children. "Forced upon her," said Mr. Brumley. "It makes one ill to think of it!" It certainly very nearly made him ill. And as if these exercises in distinction had inflamed his conscience Mr. Brumley wrote two articles in the *Hebdomadal* denouncing impure literature, decadence, immorality, various recent scandalous instances, and the suffragettes, declaring that woman's place was the home and that "in a pure and exalted monogamy lies the sole unitary basis for a civilized state." The most remarkable thing about this article is an omission. That Sir Isaac's monogamy with any other instances that might be akin to it was not pure and exalted, and that it needed—shall we call it readjustment? is a view that in this article Mr. Brumley conspicuously doesn't display. It's as if for a moment, pen in hand, he had eddied back to his old absolute positions. . . .

In a very little while Mr. Brumley and Lady Beach-Mandarin had almost persuaded each other that Sir Isaac was applying physical torture to his proudly silent wife, and Mr. Brumley was no longer dreaming and glancing at but steadily facing the possibility of a pure-minded and handsomely done elopement to "free" Lady Harman, that would be followed in due course by a marriage, a "true marriage" on a level of understanding far above any ordinary respectable wedding, amidst universal sympathy and admiration and the presence of all the very best people. In these anticipations he did rather remarkably overlook the absence of any sign of participation on the part of Lady Harman in his own impassioned personal feelings, and he overlooked still more remarkably as possible objections to his line of conduct, Millicent, Florence, Annette and Baby. These omissions no doubt simplified but also greatly falsified his outlook.

This proposal that all the best people shall applaud the higher rightness that was to be revealed in his projected elopement, is in the very essence of the romantic attitude. All other people are still to remain under the law. There is to be nothing revolutionary. But with exceptional persons under exceptional conditions—

Mr. Brumley stated his case over and over again to his utmost satisfaction, and always at great moral altitudes and with a kind of transcendent orthodoxy. The more difficult any aspect of the affair appeared from the orthodox standpoint the more valiantly Mr. Brumley soared; if it came to his living with Lady Harman for a time before they could be properly married amidst picturesque foreign scenery in a little *casa* by the side of a stream, then the water in that stream was to be quite the purest water conceivable and the scenery and associations as morally faultless as a view that had passed the exacting requirements of Mr. John Ruskin. And Mr. Brumley was very clear in his mind that what he proposed to do was entirely different in quality even if it was similar in form from anything that anyone else had ever done who had ever before made a scandal or appeared in the divorce court. This is always the way in such cases—always. The scandal was to be a noble scandal, a proud scandal, one of those instances of heroical love that turn aside misdemeanors—admittedly misdemeanors—into edifying marvels.

This was the state of mind to which Mr. Brumley had attained when he made his ineffectual raid upon Black Strand, and you will remark about it, if you are interested in the changes in people's ideas that are going on today, that although he was prepared to make the most extensive glosses in this particular instance upon the commonly accepted rules of what is right and proper, he was not for a moment prepared to accord the terrible gift of an independent responsibility to Lady Harman. In that direction lay regions that Mr. Brumley had still to explore. Lady Harman he considered was married wrongly and disastrously and this he held to be essentially the fault of Sir Isaac—with perhaps some slight blame attaching to Lady Harman's mother. The only path of escape he could conceive as yet for Lady Harman lay through the chivalry of some other man. That a woman could possibly rebel against one man without the sympathy and moral maintenance of another was still outside the range of Mr. Brumley's understanding. It is still outside the range of most men's understandings—and of a great many women's. If he generalized at all from these persuasions it was in the direction that in the interest of "true marriage" there should be greater facilities for divorce and also a kind of respectable-ization of divorce. Then these "false marriages" might be rectified without suffering. The reasons for divorce he felt should be extended to include things not generally reprehensible, and chivalrous people coming into court should be protected from the indelicate publicity of free reporting. . . .

3

Mr. Brumley was still contemplating rather inconclusively the possibility of a long and intimate talk leading up to and preparing for an elopement with Lady Harman, when he read of her Jago Street escapade and of her impending appearance at the South Hampsmith police court. He was astonished. The more he contemplated the thing the greater became his astonishment.

Even at the first impact he realized that the line she had taken wasn't quite in the picture with the line he had proposed for her. He felt—left out. He felt as though a door had slammed between himself and affairs to which he had supposed himself essential. He could not understand why she had done this thing instead of coming straight to his flat and making use of all that chivalrous service she surely knew was at her disposal. This self-reliance, this direct dealing with the world, seemed to him, even in the height of his concern, unwomanly, a deeper injury to his own abandoned assumptions than any he had contemplated. He felt it needed explanation, and he hurried to secure an elbowed unsavory corner in the back of the court in order to hear her defense. He had to wait through long stuffy spaces of time before she appeared. There were half a dozen other window smashers,—plain or at least untidy-looking young women. The magistrate told them they were silly and the soul of Mr. Brumley acquiesced. One tried to make a speech, and it was such a poor speech—squeaky. . . .

When at last Lady Harman entered the box—the strangest place it seemed for her—he tried to emerge from the jostling crowd about him into visibility, to catch her eye, to give her the support of his devoted presence. Twice at least she glanced in his direction but gave no sign of seeing him. He was surprised that she could look without fear or detestation, indeed once with a gesture of solicitude, at Sir Isaac. She was astonishingly serene. There seemed to be just the faintest shadow of a smile about her lips as the stipendiary explained the impossibility of giving her anything less than a month. An uneasy object like the smashed remains of a colossal box of bonbons that was riding out a gale, down in the middle of the court, turned round at last completely and revealed itself as the hat of Lady Beach-Mandarin, but though Mr. Brumley waved his hand he could not even make that lady aware of his presence. A powerful rude criminal-looking man who stood in front of him and smelt grossly of stables, would not give him a fair chance of showing himself, and developed a strong personal hostility to him on account of his alleged "shoving about." It would not he felt be of the slightest help to Lady Harman for him to involve himself in a personal struggle with a powerful and powerfully flavored criminal.

It was all very dreadful.

After the proceedings were over and Lady Harman had been led away into captivity, he went out and took a taxi in an agitated distraught manner to Lady Beach-Mandarin's house.

"She meant," said Lady Beach-Mandarin, "to have a month's holiday from him and think things out. And she's got it."

Perhaps that was it. Mr. Brumley could not tell, and he spent some days in that state of perplexity which, like the weariness that heralds a cold, marks so often the onset of a new series of ideas. . . .

Why hadn't she come to him? Had he after all rather overloaded his memory of her real self with imaginative accessories? Had she really understood what he had been saying to her in the garden? Afterwards when he had met her eyes as he and she went over the new wing with Sir Isaac she had so manifestly—and, when one came to think of it, so tranquilly—seemed to understand. . . .

It was such an extraordinary thing to go smashing a window like that—when there he was at hand ready to help her. She knew his address? Did she? For a moment Mr. Brumley cherished that wild surmise. Was that perhaps it? But surely she could have looked in the Telephone Directory or Who's Who. . . .

But if that was the truth of the matter she would have looked and behaved differently in court—quite differently. She would have been looking for him. She would have seen him. . . .

It was queer too to recall what she had said in court about her daughters. . . .

Could it be, he had a frightful qualm, that after all—he wasn't the man? How little he knew of her really. . . .

"This wretched agitation," said Mr. Brumley, trying to flounder away anyhow from these disconcerting riddles; "it seems to unbalance them all."

But he found it impossible to believe that Lady Harman was seriously unbalanced.

4

And if Mr. Brumley's system of romantically distorted moral assumptions was shattered by Lady Harman's impersonal blow at a post office window when all the rules seemed to require her to fly from the oppression of one man to the chivalry of another, what words can convey the devastating effect upon him of her conduct after her release? To that crisis he had been looking forward continually; to record the variety of his expectations would fill a large volume, but throughout them all prevailed one general idea, that when she came out of prison her struggle with her husband would be resumed, and that this would give Mr. Brumley such extraordinary opportunities of displaying his devotion that her response, which he was now beginning to suspect might be more reluctant than his earlier dreams had assumed, was ultimately inevitable. In all these dreams and meditations that response figured as the crown. He had to win and possess Lady Harman. The idea had taken hold of his busy yet rather pointless life, had become his directing object. He was full of schemes for presently arresting and captivating her imagination. He was already convinced that she cared for him; he had to inflame interest and fan liking into the fire of passion. And with a mind so occupied, Mr. Brumley wrote this and that and went about his affairs. He spent two days and a night at Margate visiting his son at his preparatory school, and he found much material for musing in the question of just how the high romantic affairs ahead of him would affect this delicately intelligent boy. For a time perhaps he might misjudge his father. . . . He spent a week-end with Lady Viping and stayed on until Wednesday and then he came back to London. His plans were still unformed when the day came for Lady Harman's release, and indeed beyond an idea that he would have her met at the prison gates by an enormous bunch of snowy-white and crimson chrysanthemums he had nothing really concrete at all in his mind.

She had, however, been released stealthily a day before her time, and this is what she had done. She had asked that—of all improbable people!—Sir Isaac's mother should meet her, the biggest car had come to the prison gates, and she had gone straight down with Mrs. Harman to her husband—who had taken a chill and was in bed drinking Contrexéville water—at Black Strand.

As these facts shaped themselves in answer to the blanched inquiries of Mr. Brumley his amazement grew. He began to realize that there must have been a correspondence during her incarceration, that all sorts of things had been happening while he had been dreaming, and when he went round to Lady Beach-Mandarin, who was just packing up to be the life and soul of a winter-sports party at a nice non-Lunnite hotel at Lenzerheide, he learned particulars that chilled him to the marrow. "They've made it up," said Lady Beach-Mandarin.

"But how?" gasped Mr. Brumley, with his soul in infinite distress. "But how?"

"The Ogre, it seems, has come to see that bullying on't do. He's given in tremendously. He's let her have her way with the waitress strike and she's going to have an allowance of her own and all kinds of things. It's settled. It's his mother and that man Charterson talked him over. You know—his mother came to me—as her friend. For advice. Wanted to find out what sort of things we might have been putting in her head. She said so. A curious old thing—vulgar

but—*wise*. I liked her. He's her darling—and she just knows what he is. . . .
He doesn't like it but he's taken his dose. The thought of her going to prison
again—! He's let her do anything rather than that. . . ."

"And she's gone to him!"

"Naturally," said Lady Beach-Mandarin with what he felt to be deliberate
brutality. Surely she must have understood—

"But the waitress strike—what has it got to do with the waitress strike?"

"She cared—tremendously."

"*Did* she?"

"Tremendously. And they all go back and the system of inspection is being
altered, and he's even forgiven Babs Wheeler. It made him ill to do it but he
did."

"And she's gone back to him."

"Like Godiva," said Lady Beach-Mandarin with that sweeping allusiveness
that was part of her complicated charm.

5

For three days Mr. Brumley was so staggered by these things that it did not
occur to him that it was quite possible for him to see Lady Harman for himself
and find out just how things stood. He remained in London with an imagination
dazed. And as it was the Christmas season and as George Edmund in a rather
expectant holiday state had now come up from Margate, Mr. Brumley went in
succession to the Hippodrome, to Peter Pan and to an exhibition at Olympia,
assisted at an afternoon display of the kinemacolor at La Scala Theatre, visited
Hamley's and lunched George Edmund once at the Criterion and twice at the
Climax Club, while thinking of nothing in all the world but the incalculable
strangeness of women. George Edmund thought him a very passive leadable
parent indeed, less querulous about money matters and altogether much improved.
The glitter and color of these various entertainments reflected themselves upon
the surface of that deep flood of meditation, hook-armed wooden-legged pirates,
intelligent elephants, ingenious but extremely expensive toys, flickering processions,
comic turns, snatches of popular music and George Edmund's way of eating an
orange, pictured themselves on his mind confusedly without in any way deflecting
its course. Then on the fourth day he roused himself, gave George Edmund ten
shillings to get himself a cutlet at the Café Royal and do the cinematographs
round and about the West End, and so released reached Aleham in time for a
temperate lunch. He chartered the Aleham car to take him to Black Strand and
arrived there about a quarter past three, in a great effort to feel himself a matter-
of-course visitor.

It ought to be possible to record that Mr. Brumley's mind was full of the
intensest sense of Lady Harman during that journey and of nothing else, but as
a matter of fact his mind was now curiously detached and reflective, the tensions
and expectation of the past month and the astonishment of the last few days had
worked themselves out and left him as it were the passive instrument of the
purpose of his more impassioned moods. This distressed lover approached Black
Strand in a condition of philosophical lassitude.

The road from Aleham to Black Strand is a picturesque old English road,
needlessly winding and badly graded, wriggling across a healthy wilderness with
occasional pine-woods. Something in that familiar landscape—for his life had
run through it since first he and Euphemia on a tandem bicycle and altogether
very young had sought their ideal home in the South of England—set his mind

swinging and generalizing. How freshly youthful he and Euphemia had been when first he came along that road, how crude, how full of happy expectations of success; it had been as bright and it was now as completely gone as the sunsets they had seen together.

How great a thing life is! How much greater than any single romance, or any individual affection! Since those days he had grown, he had succeeded, he had suffered in a reasonable way of course, still he could recall with a kind of satisfaction tears and deep week-long moods of hopeless melancholy—and he had changed. And now dominating this landscape, filling him with new emotions and desires and perplexing intimations of ignorance and limitations he had never suspected in his youth, was this second figure of a woman. She was different from Euphemia. With Euphemia everything had been so simple and easy; until that slight fading, that fatigue of entire success and satisfaction, of the concluding years. He and Euphemia had always kept it up that they had no thought in the world except for one another. . . . Yet if that had been true, why hadn't he died when she did? He hadn't died—with remarkable elasticity. Clearly in his case there had been these unexplored, unsuspected hinterlands of possibility towards which Lady Harman seemed now to be directing him. It came to him that afternoon as an entirely fresh thought that there might also have been something in Euphemia beyond their simple, so charmingly treated relationship. He began to recall moments when Euphemia had said perplexing little things, had looked at him with an expression that was unexpected, had been—difficult. . . .

I write of Mr. Brumley to tell you things about him and not to explain him. It may be that the appetite for thorough good talks with people grows upon one, but at any rate it did occur to Mr. Brumley on his way to talk to Lady Harman, it occurred to him as a thing distressingly irrevocable that he could now never have a thorough good talk with Euphemia about certain neglected things between them. It would have helped him so much. . . .

His eyes rested as he thought of these things upon the familiar purple hill crests, patched that afternoon with the lingering traces of a recent snowstorm, the heather slopes, the dark mysterious woods, the patches of vivid green where a damp and marshy meadow or so broke the moorland surface. Today in spite of the sun there was a bright blue-white line of frost to the northward of every hedge and bank, the trees were dripping down the white edgings of the morning into the pine-needle mud at their feet; he had seen it so like this before; years hence he might see it all like this again; all this great breezy countryside had taken upon itself a quality of endurance, as though it would still be real and essential in his mind when Lady Harman had altogether passed again. It would be real when he himself had passed away, and in other costumes and other vehicles fresh Euphemias and new crude George Brumleys would come along, feeling in the ultimate bright new wisdom of youth that it was all for them—a subservient scenery, when really it was entirely indifferent in its careless permanence to all their hopes and fancies. . . .

6

Mr. Brumley's thoughts on the permanence of landscape and the mutability of human affairs were more than a little dashed when he came within sight of Black Strand and perceived that once cosily beautiful little home clipped and extended, its shrubbery wrecked and the old barn now pierced with windows and adorned—for its new chimneys were not working very well—by several efficient novelties in chimney cowls. Up the slopes behind Sir Isaac had extended his boundaries, and had been felling trees and levelling a couple of tennis courts for next summer.

Something was being done to the porch, and the jasmine had been cleared away altogether. Mr. Brumley could not quite understand what was in progress; Sir Isaac he learned afterwards had found a wonderful bargain in a real genuine Georgian portal of great dignity and simplicity in Aleham, and he was going to improve Black Strand by transferring it thither—with the utmost precaution and every piece numbered—from its original situation. Mr. Brumley stood among the preparatory débris of this and rang a quietly resolute electric bell, which was answered no longer by Mrs. Rabbit but by the ample presence of Snagsby.

Snagsby in that doorway had something of the preposterous effect of a very large face beneath a very small hat. He had to Mr. Brumley's eyes a restored look, as though his self-confidence had been thoroughly done up since their last encounter. Bygones were bygones. Mr. Brumley was admitted as one is admitted to any normal home. He was shown into the little study-drawing-room with the stepped floor, which had been so largely the scene of his life with Euphemia, and he was left there for the better part of a quarter of an hour before his hostess appeared.

The room had been changed very little. Euphemia's solitary rose had gone, and instead there were several bowls of beaten silver scattered about, each filled with great chrysanthemums from London. Sir Isaac's jackdaw acquisitiveness had also overcrowded the corner beyond the fireplace with a very fine and genuine Queen Anne cabinet; there were a novel by Elizabeth Robins and two or three feminist and socialist works lying on the table which would certainly not have been visible, though they might have been in the house, during the Brumley régime. Otherwise things were very much as they always had been.

A room like this, thought Mr. Brumley among much other mental driftage, is like a heart,—so long as it exists it must be furnished and tenanted. No matter what has been, however bright and sweet and tender, the spaces still cry aloud to be filled again. The very essence of life is its insatiability. How complete all this had seemed in the moment when first he and Euphemia had arranged it. And indeed how complete life had seemed altogether at seven-and-twenty. Every year since then he had been learning—or at any rate unlearning. Until at last he was beginning to realize he had still everything to learn. . . .

The door opened and the tall dark figure of Lady Harman stood for a moment in the doorway before she stepped down into the room.

She had always the same effect upon him, the effect of being suddenly remembered. When he was away from her he was always sure that she was a beautiful woman, and when he saw her again he was always astonished to see how little he had borne her beauty in mind. For a moment they regarded one another silently. Then she closed the door behind her and came towards him.

All Mr. Brumley's philosophizing had vanished at the sight of her. His spirit was reborn within him. He thought of her and of his effect upon her, vividly, and of nothing else in the world.

She was paler he thought beneath her dusky hair, a little thinner and graver. . . .

There was something in her manner as she advanced towards him that told him he mattered to her, that his coming there was something that moved her imagination as well as his own. With an almost impulsive movement she held out both her hands to him, and with an inspiration as sudden he took them and kissed them. When he had done so he was ashamed of his temerity; he looked up to meet in her dark eyes the scared shyness of a fallow deer. She suddenly remembered to withdraw her hands, and it became manifest to both of them that the incident must never have happened. She went to the window, stood almost awkwardly for a moment looking out of it, then turned. She put her hands on the back of the chair and stood holding it.

"I knew you would come to see me," she said.

"I've been very anxious about you," he said, and on that their minds rested through a little silence.

"You see," he explained, "I didn't know what was happening to you. Or what you were doing."

"After asking your advice," she said.

"Exactly."

"I don't know why I broke that window. Except I think that I wanted to get away."

"But why didn't you come to me?"

"I didn't know where you were. And besides—I didn't somehow want to come to you."

"But wasn't it wretched in prison? Wasn't it miserably cold? I used to think of you of nights in some wretched ill-aired cell. . . . You. . . ."

"It *was* cold," she admitted. "But it was very good for me. It was quiet. The first few days seemed endless; then they began to go by quickly. Quite quickly at last. And I came to think. In the day there was a little stool where one sat. I used to sit on that and brood and try to think things out—all sorts of things I've never had the chance to think about before."

"Yes," said Mr. Brumley.

"All this," she said.

"And it has brought you back here!" he said, with something of the tone of one who has a right to enquire, with some flavor too of reproach.

"You see," she said after a little pause, "during that time it was possible to come to understandings. Neither I nor my husband had understood the other. In that interval it was possible—to explain.

"Yes. You see, Mr. Brumley, we—we both misunderstood. It was just because of that and because I had no one who seemed able to advise me that I turned to you. A novelist always seems so wise in these things. He seems to know so many lives. One can talk to you as one can scarcely talk to anyone; you are a sort of doctor—in these matters. And it was necessary—that my husband should realize that I had grown up and that I should have time to think just how one's duty and one's—freedom have to be fitted together. . . . And my husband is ill. He has been ill, rather short of breath—the doctor thinks it is asthma—for some time, and all the agitation of this business has upset him and made him worse. He is upstairs now—asleep. Of course if I had thought I should make him ill I could never have done any of this. But it's done now and here I am, Mr. Brumley, back in my place. With all sorts of things changed. Put right. . . ."

"I see," said Mr. Brumley stupidly.

Her speech was like the falling of an opaque curtain upon some romantic spectacle. She stood there, almost defensively behind her chair as she made it. There was a quality of premeditation in her words, yet something in her voice and bearing made him feel that she knew just how it covered up and extinguished his dreams and impulses. He heard her out and then suddenly his spirit rebelled against her decision. "No!" he cried.

She waited for him to go on.

"You see," he said, "I thought that it was just that you wanted to get away— That this life was intolerable— That you were— Forgive me if I seem to be going beyond—going beyond what I ought to be thinking about you. Only, why should I pretend? I care, I care for you tremendously. And it seemed to me that you didn't love your husband, that you were enslaved and miserable. I would have done anything to help you—anything in the world, Lady Harman. I know— it may sound ridiculous—there have been times when I would have faced death to feel you were happy and free. I thought all that, I felt all that,—and then— then you come back here. You seem not to have minded. As though I had misunderstood. . . ."

He paused and his face was alive with an unwonted sincerity. His self-consciousness had for a moment fallen from him.

"I know," she said, "it *was* like that. I knew you cared. That is why I have so wanted to talk to you. It looked like that. . . ."

She pressed her lips together in that old familiar hunt for words and phrases.

"I didn't understand, Mr. Brumley, all there was in my husband or all there was in myself. I just saw his hardness and his—his hardness in business. It's become so different now. You see, I forgot he has bad health. He's ill; I suppose he was getting ill then. Instead of explaining himself—he was—excited and— unwise. And now—"

"Now I suppose he has—explained," said Mr. Brumley slowly and with infinite distaste. "Lady Harman, *what* has he explained?"

"It isn't so much that he has explained, Mr. Brumley," said Lady Harman, "as that things have explained themselves."

"But how, Lady Harman? How?"

"I mean about my being a mere girl, almost a child when I married him. Naturally he wanted to take charge of everything and leave nothing to me. And quite as naturally he didn't notice that now I am a woman, grown up altogether. And it's been necessary to do things. And naturally, Mr. Brumley, they shocked and upset him. But he sees now so clearly, he wrote to me, such a fair letter— an unusual letter—quite different from when he talks—it surprised me, telling me he wanted me to feel free, that he meant to make me—to arrange things that is, so that I should feel free and more able to go about as I pleased. It was a *generous* letter, Mr. Brumley. Generous about all sorts of affairs that there had been between us. He said things, quite kind things, not like the things he has ever said before—"

She stopped short and then began again.

"You know, Mr. Brumley, it's so hard to tell things without telling other things that somehow are difficult to tell. Yet if I don't tell you them, you won't know them and then you won't be able to understand in the least how things are with us."

Her eyes appealed to him.

"Tell me," he said, "whatever you think fit."

"When one has been afraid of anyone and felt they were ever so much stronger and cruel and hard than one is and one suddenly finds they aren't. It alters everything."

He nodded, watching her.

Her voice fell nearly to a whisper. "Mr. Brumley," she said, "when I came back to him—you know he was in bed here—instead of scolding me—he *cried*. He cried like a vexed child. He put his face into the pillow—just misery. . . . I'd never seen him cry—at least only once—long ago. . . ."

Mr. Brumley looked at her flushed and tender face and it seemed to him that indeed he could die for her quite easily.

"I saw how hard I had been," she said. "In prison I'd thought of that, I'd thought women mustn't be hard, whatever happens to them. And when I saw him like that I knew at once how true that was. . . . He begged me to be a good wife to him. No!— he just said, 'Be a wife to me,' not even a good wife—and then he cried. . . .''

For a moment or so Mr. Brumley didn't respond. "I see," he said at last. "Yes."

"And there were the children—such helpless little things. In the prison I worried about them. I thought of things for them. I've come to feel—they are left too much to nurses and strangers. . . . And then you see he has agreed to nearly everything I had wanted. It wasn't only the personal things—I was anxious about those silly girls—the strikers. I didn't want them to be badly treated. It distressed me to think of them. I don't think you know how it distressed me. And he—he gave way upon all that. He says I may talk to him about the business, about the way we do our business—the kindness of it I mean. And this is why I am back here. Where else *could* I be?"

"No," said Mr. Brumley still with the utmost reluctance. "I see. Only—"

He paused downcast and she waited for him to speak.

"Only it isn't what I expected, Lady Harman. I didn't think that matters could be settled by such arrangements. It's sane, I know, it's comfortable and kindly. But I thought—Oh! I thought of different things, quite different things from all this. I thought of you who are so beautiful caught in a loveless passionless world. I thought of the things there might be for you, the beautiful and wonderful things of which you are deprived. . . . Never mind what I thought! Never mind! You've made your choice. But I thought that you didn't love, that you couldn't love— this man. It seemed to me that you felt too—that to live as you are doing—with him—was a profanity. Something—I'd give everything I have, everything I am, to save you from. Because—because I care. . . . I misunderstood you. I suppose you can—do what you are doing."

He jumped to his feet as he spoke and walked three paces away and turned to utter his last sentences. She too stood up.

"Mr. Brumley," she said weakly, "I don't understand. What do you mean? I have to do what I am doing. He—he is my husband."

He made a gesture of impatience. "Do you understand nothing of *love?*" he cried.

She pressed her lips together and remained still and silent, dark against the casement window.

There came a sound of tapping from the room above. Three taps and again three taps.

Lady Harman made a little gesture as though she would put this sound aside.

"Love," she said at last. "It comes to some people. It happens. It happens to young people. . . . But when one is married—"

Her voice fell almost to a whisper. "One must not think of it," she said. "One must think of one's husband and one's duty. Life cannot begin again, Mr. Brumley."

The taps were repeated, a little more urgently.

"That is my husband," she said.

She hesitated through a little pause. "Mr. Brumley," she said, "I want friendship so badly, I want someone to be my friend. I don't want to think of things—disturbing things—things I have lost—things that are spoilt. *That*—that which you spoke of; what has it to do with me?"

She interrupted him as he was about to speak.

"Be my friend. Don't talk to me of impossible things. Love! Mr. Brumley, what has a married woman to do with love? I never think of it. I never read of it. I want to do my duty. I want to do my duty by him and by my children and by all the people I am bound to. I want to help people, weak people, people who suffer. I want to help him to help them. I want to stop being an idle, useless, spending woman. . . .''

She made a little gesture of appeal with her hands.

"Oh!" he sighed, and then, "You know if I can help you— Rather than distress you—"

Her manner changed. It became confidential and urgent.

"Mr. Brumley," she said, "I must go up to my husband. He will be impatient. And when I tell him you are here he will want to see you. . . . You will come up and see him?"

Mr. Brumley sought to convey the struggle within him by his pose.

"I will do what you wish, Lady Harman," he said, with an almost theatrical sigh.

He closed the door after her and was alone in his former study once more. He walked slowly to his old writing-desk and sat down in his familiar seat. Presently he heard her footfalls across the room above. Mr. Brumley's mind under the stress of the unfamiliar and the unexpected was now lapsing rapidly towards the theatrical. "My *God!*" said Mr. Brumley.

He addressed that friendly memorable room in tones that mingled amazement and wrong. "He is her husband!" he said, and then: "The power of words!" . . .

<h1 style="text-align:center">7</h1>

It seemed to Mr. Brumley's now entirely disordered mind that Sir Isaac, propped up with cushions upon a sofa in the upstairs sitting-room, white-faced, wary and very short of breath, was like Proprietorship enthroned. Everything about him referred deferentially to him. Even his wife dropped at once into the position of a beautiful satellite. His illness, he assured his visitor with a thin-lipped emphasis, was "quite temporary, quite the sort of thing that might happen to anyone." He had had a queer little benumbing of one leg, "just a trifle of nerve fag did it," and the slight asthma that came and went in his life had taken advantage of his condition to come again with a little beyond its usual aggressiveness. "Elly is going to take me off to Marienbad next week or the week after," he said. "I shall have a cure and she'll have a treat, and we shall come back as fit as fiddles." The incidents of the past month were to be put on a facetious footing it appeared. "It's a mercy they didn't crop her hair," he said, apropos of nothing and with an air of dry humor. No further allusion was made to Lady Harman's incarceration.

He was dressed in a lama wool bedroom suit and his resting leg was covered by a very splendid and beautiful fur rug. All Euphemia's best and gayest cushions sustained his back. The furniture had been completely rearranged for his comfort and convenience. Close to his hand was a little table with carefully selected remedies and aids and helps and stimulants, and the latest and best of the light fiction of the day was tossed about between the table, the couch and the floor. At the foot of the couch Euphemia's bedroom writing-table had been placed, and over this there were scattered traces of the stenographer who had assisted him to wipe off the day's correspondence. Three black cylinders and other appliances in the corner witnessed that his slight difficulty in breathing could be relieved by oxygen, and his eyes were regaled by a great abundance of London flowers at every available point in the room. Of course there were grapes, fabulous looking grapes.

Everything conspired to give Sir Isaac and his ownership the center of the picture. Mr. Brumley had been brought upstairs to him, and the tea table, with scarcely a reference to anyone else, was arranged by Snagsby conveniently to his hand. And Sir Isaac himself had a confidence—the assurance of a man who has been shaken and has recovered. Whatever tears he had ever shed had served their purpose and were forgotten. "Elly" was his and the house was his and everything about him was his—he laid his hand upon her once when she came near him, his possessiveness was so gross—and the strained suspicion of his last meeting with Mr. Brumley was replaced·now by a sage and wizened triumph over anticipated and arrested dangers.

Their party was joined by Sir Isaac's mother, and the sight of her sturdy, swarthy, and rather dignified presence flashed the thought into Mr. Brumley's mind that Sir Isaac's father must have been a very blond and very nosey person indeed. She was homely and practical and contributed very usefully to a conversation that remained a trifle fragmentary and faintly uncomfortable to the end.

Mr. Brumley avoided as much as he could looking at Lady Harman, because he knew Sir Isaac was alert for that, but he was acutely aware of her presence dispensing the tea and moving about the room, being a good wife. It was his first impression of Lady Harman as a good wife and he disliked the spectacle extremely. The conversation hovered chiefly about Marienbad, drifted away and came back again. Mrs. Harman made several confidences that provoked the betrayal of a strain of irritability in Sir Isaac's condition. "We're all looking forward to this Marienbad expedition," she said. "I do hope it will turn out well. Neither of them have ever been abroad before—and there's the difficulty of the languages."

"Ow," snarled Sir Isaac, with a glance at his mother that was almost vicious and a lapse into Cockney intonations and phrases that witnessed how her presence recalled his youth, "It'll *go* all right, mother. *You* needn't fret."

"Of course they'll have a courier to see to their things, and go train de luxe and all that," Mrs. Harman explained with a certain gusto. "But still it's an adventure, with him not well, and both as I say more like children than grown-up people."

Sir Isaac intervened with a crushing clumsiness to divert this strain of explanation, with questions about the quality of the soil in the wood where the ground was to be cleared and levelled for his tennis lawns.

Mr. Brumley did his best to behave as a man of the world should. He made intelligent replies about the sand, he threw out obvious but serviceable advice upon travel upon the continent of Europe, and he tried not to think that this was the way of living into which the sweetest, tenderest, most beautiful woman in the world had been trapped. He avoided looking at her until he felt it was becoming conspicuous, a negative stare. Why had she come back again? Fragmentary phrases she had used downstairs came drifting through his mind. "I never think of it. I never read of it." And she so made for beautiful love and a beautiful life! He recalled Lady Beach-Mandarin's absurdly apt, absurdly inept, "like Godiva," and was suddenly impelled to raise the question of those strikers.

"Your trouble with your waitresses is over, Sir Isaac?"

Sir Isaac finished a cup of tea audibly and glanced at his wife. "I never meant to be hard on them," he said, putting down his cup. "Never. The trouble blew up suddenly. One can't be all over a big business everywhere all at once, more particularly if one is worried about other things. As soon as I had time to look into it I put things right. There was misunderstandings on both sides."

He glanced up again at Lady Harman. (She was standing behind Mr. Brumley so that he could not see her but—did their eyes meet?)

"As soon as we are back from Marienbad," Sir Isaac volunteered, "Lady Harman and I are going into all that business thoroughly."

Mr. Brumley concealed his intense aversion for this association under a tone of intelligent interest. "Into—I don't quite understand—what business?"

"Women employees in London—Hostels—all that kind of thing. Bit more sensible than suffragetting, eh, Elly?"

"Very interesting," said Mr. Brumley with a hollow cordiality, "very."

"Done on business lines, mind you," said Sir Isaac, looking suddenly very sharp and keen, "done on proper business lines, there's no end of a change possible. And it's a perfectly legitimate outgrowth from such popular catering as ours. It interests me."

He made a little whistling noise with his teeth at the end of this speech.

"I didn't know Lady Harman was disposed to take up such things," he said. "Or I'd have gone into them before."

"He's going into them now," said Mrs. Harman, "heart and soul. Why! we have to take his temperature over it, to see he doesn't work himself up into a fever." Her manner became reasonable and confidential. She spoke to Mr. Brumley as if her son was slightly deaf. "It's better than his fretting," she said. . . .

8

Mr. Brumley returned to London in a state of extreme mental and emotional unrest. The sight of Lady Harman had restored all his passion for her, the all too manifest fact that she was receding beyond his reach stirred him with unavailing impulses towards some impossible extremity of effort. She had filled his mind so much that he could not endure the thought of living without hope of her. But what hope was there of her? And he was jealous, detestably jealous, so jealous that in that direction he did not dare to let his mind go. He sawed at the bit and brought it back, or he would have had to writhe about the carriage. His thoughts ran furiously all over the place to avoid that pit. And now he found himself flashing at moments into wild and hopeless rebellion against the institution of marriage, of which he had hitherto sought always to be the dignified and smiling champion against the innovator, the over-critical and the young. He had never rebelled before. He was so astonished at the violence of his own objection that he lapsed from defiance to an incredulous examination of his own novel attitude. "It's not *true* marriage I object to," he told himself. "It's this marriage like a rat trap, alluring and scarcely unavoidable, so that in we all go, and then with no escape—unless you tear yourself to rags. No escape. . . ."

It came to him that there was at least one way out for Lady Harman: *Sir Isaac might die!* . . .

He pulled himself up presently, astonished and dismayed at the activities of his own imagination. Among other things he had wondered if by any chance Lady Harman had ever allowed her mind to travel in this same post-mortem direction. At times surely the thing must have shone upon her as a possibility, a hope. From that he had branched off to a more general speculation. How many people were there in the world, nice people, kind people, moral and delicate-minded people, to whom the death of another person means release from that inflexible barrier—possibilities of secretly desired happiness, the realization of crushed and forbidden dreams? He had a vision of human society, like the vision of a night landscape seen suddenly in a lightning flash, as of people caught by couples in traps and quietly hoping for one another's deaths. "Good Heavens!" said Mr. Brumley, "what are we coming to," and got up in his railway compartment—he had it to himself—and walked up and down its narrow limits until a jolt over a point made him suddenly sit down again. "Most marriages are happy," said Mr. Brumley, like a man who has fallen into a river and scrambles back to safety. "One mustn't judge by the exceptional cases. . . .

"Though of course there are—a good many—exceptional cases." . . .

He folded his arms, crossed his legs, frowned and reasoned with himself,— resolved to dismiss post-mortem speculations—absolutely.

He was not going to quarrel with the institution of marriage. That was going too far. He had never been able to see the beginnings of reason in sexual anarchy, never. It is against the very order of things. Man is a marrying animal just as much as he was a fire-making animal; he goes in pairs like mantel ornaments; it is as natural for him to marry and to exact and keep good faith—if need be with a savage jealousy, as it is for him to have lobes to his ears and hair under his armpits. These things jar with the dream perhaps; the gods on painted ceilings have no such ties, acting beautifully by their very nature; and here on the floor of the world one had them and one had to make the best of them. . . . Are we making the best of them? Mr. Brumley was off again. That last thought opened the way to speculative wildernesses, and into these Mr. Brumley went wandering with a novel desperate enterprise to find a kind of marriage that would suit him.

He began to reform the marriage laws. He did his utmost not to think especially of Lady Harman and himself while he was doing so. He would just take up the whole question and deal with it in a temperate reasonable way. It was so necessary to be reasonable and temperate in these questions—and not to think of death as a solution. Marriages to begin with were too easy to make and too difficult to break; countless girls—Lady Harman was only a type—were married long before they could know the beginnings of their own minds. We wanted to delay marriage— until the middle twenties, say. Why not? Or if by the infirmities of humanity one must have marriage before then, there ought to be some especial opportunity of rescinding it later. (Lady Harman ought to have been able to rescind her marriage.) What ought to be the marriageable age in a civilized community? When the mind was settled into its general system of opinions Mr. Brumley thought, and then lapsed into a speculation whether the mind didn't keep changing and developing all through life; Lady Harman's was certainly still doing so. . . . This pointed to logical consequences of an undesirable sort. . . .

(Some little mind-slide occurred just at this point and he found himself thinking that perhaps Sir Isaac might last for years and years, might even outlive a wife exhausted by nursing. And anyhow to wait for death! To leave the thing one loved in the embrace of the moribund!)

He wrenched his thoughts back as quickly as possible to a disinterested reform of the marriage laws. What had he decided so far? Only for more deliberation and a riper age in marrying. Surely that should appeal even to the most orthodox. But that alone would not eliminate mistakes and deceptions altogether. (Sir Isaac's skin had a peculiar, unhealthy look.) There ought in addition to be the widest facilities for divorce possible. Mr. Brumley tried to draw up a schedule in his head of the grounds for divorce that a really civilized community would entertain. But there are practical difficulties. Marriage is not simply a sexual union, it is an economic one of a peculiarly inseparable sort,—and there are the children. And jealousy! Of course so far as economics went, a kind of marriage settlement might meet most of the difficulties, and as for the children, Mr.

Brumley was no longer in that mood of enthusiastic devotion to children that had made the birth of George Edmund so tremendous an event. Children, alone, afforded no reason for indissoluble lifelong union. Face the thing frankly. How long was it absolutely necessary for people to keep a home together for their children? The prosperous classes, the best classes in the community, packed the little creatures off to school at the age of nine or ten. One might overdo—we were overdoing in our writing nowadays this—philoprogenitive enthusiasm. . . .

He found himself thinking of George Meredith's idea of Ten Year Marriages. . . .

His mind recoiled to Sir Isaac's pillowed-up possession. What flimsy stuff all this talk of altered marriage was! These things did not even touch the essentials of the matter. He thought of Sir Isaac's thin lips and wary knowing eyes. What possible divorce law could the wit of man devise that would release a desired woman from that—grip? Marriage was covetousness made law. As well ask such a man to sell all his goods and give to the poor as expect the Sir Isaacs of this world to relax the matrimonial subjugation of the wife. Our social order is built on jealousy, sustained by jealousy, and those brave schemes we evolve in our studies for the release of women from ownership,—and for that matter for the release of men too,—they will not stand the dusty heat of the marketplace for a moment, they wilt under the first fierce breath of reality. Marriage and property are the twin children of man's individualistic nature; only on these terms can he be drawn into societies. . . .

Mr. Brumley found his little scheme for novelties in marriage and divorce lying dead and for the most part stillborn in his mind; himself in despair. To set to work to alter marriage in any essential point was, he realized, as if an ant should start to climb a thousand feet of cliff. This great institution rose upon his imagination like some insurmountable sierra, blue and somber, between himself and the life of Lady Harman and all that he desired. There might be a certain amount of tinkering with matrimonial law in the next few years, of petty tinkering that would abolish a few pretences and give ease to a few amiable people, but if he were to come back to life a thousand years hence he felt he would still find the ancient gigantic barrier, crossed perhaps by a dangerous road, pierced perhaps by a narrow tunnel or so, but in all its great essentials the same, between himself and Lady Harman. It wasn't that it was rational, it wasn't that it was justifiable, but it was one with the blood in one's veins and the rain-cloud in the sky, a necessity in the nature of present things. Before mankind emerged from the valley of these restraints—if ever they did emerge—thousands of generations must follow one another, there must be tens of thousands of years of struggle and thought and trial, in the teeth of prevalent habit and opinion—and primordial instincts. A new humanity. . . .

His heart sank to hopelessness.

Meanwhile? Meanwhile we had to live our lives.

He began to see a certain justification for the hidden cults that run beneath the fair appearances of life, those social secrecies by which people—how could one put it?—people who do not agree with established institutions, people, at any rate not merely egoistic and jealous as the crowd is egoistic and jealous, hide and help one another to mitigate the inflexible austerities of the great unreason.

Yes, Mr. Brumley had got to a phrase of that quality for the undiscriminating imperatives of the fundamental social institution. You see how a particular situation may undermine the assumptions of a mind originally devoted to uncritical acceptances. He still insisted it was a necessary great unreason, absolutely necessary—for the mass of people, a part of them, a natural expression of them, but he could imagine the possibility—of "understandings." . . . Mr. Brumley was very vague about those understandings, those mysteries of the exalted that were to filch happiness from the destroying grasp of the crude and jealous. He had to be vague. For secret and noble are ideas like oil and water; you may fling them together with all the force of your will but in a little while they will separate again.

For a time this dream of an impossible secrecy was uppermost in Mr. Brumley's meditations. It came into his head with the effect of a discovery that always among the unclimbable barriers of this supreme institution there had been,— caves. He had been reading Anatole France recently and the lady of *Le Lys Rouge* came into his thoughts. There was something in common between Lady Harman and the Countess Martin, they were tall and dark and dignified, and Lady Harman was one of those rare women who could have carried the magnificent name of Thérèse. And there in the setting of Paris and Florence was a whole microcosm of love, real but illicit, carried out as it were secretly and tactfully, beneath the great shadow of the cliff. But he found it difficult to imagine Lady Harman in that. Or Sir Isaac playing Count Martin's part. . . .

How different were those Frenchwomen, with their afternoons vacant except for love, their detachment, their lovers, those secret, convenient, romantically furnished flats, that compact explicit business of *l'amour!* He had indeed some moments of regret that Lady Harman wouldn't go into that picture, She was different—if only in her simplicity. There was something about these others that put them whole worlds apart from her, who was held so tethered from all furtive adventure by her filmy tentacles of responsibility, her ties and strands of relationship, her essential delicacy. That momentary vision of Ellen as the Countess Martin broke up into absurdities directly he looked at it fully and steadfastly. From thinking of the two women as similar types he passed into thinking of them as opposites; Thérèse, hard, clear, sensuous, secretive, trained by a brilliant tradition in the technique of connubial betrayal, was the very antithesis of Ellen's vague but invincible veracity and openness. Not for nothing had Anatole France made his heroine the daughter of a grasping financial adventurer. . . .

Of course the cave is a part of the mountain. . . .

His mind drifted away to still more general speculations, and always he was trying not to see the figure of Sir Isaac, grimly and yet meanly resolute—in possession. Always too like some open-mouthed yokel at a fair who knows nothing of the insult chalked upon his back, he disregarded how he himself coveted and desired and would if he could have gripped. He forgot his own watchful attention to Euphemia in the past, nor did he think what he might have been if Lady Harman had been his wife. It needed the chill veracities of the small hours to bring him to that. He thought now of crude egotism as having Sir Isaac's hands and Sir Isaac's eyes and Sir Isaac's position. He forgot any egotism he himself was betraying.

All the paths of enlightenment he thought of, led to Lady Harman.

9

That evening George Edmund, who had come home with his mind aglitter with cinematograph impressions, found his father a patient but inattentive listener. For indeed Mr. Brumley was not listening at all; he was thinking and thinking. He made noises like "Ah!" and "Um," at George Edmund and patted the boy's shoulder kindly and repeated words unintelligently, such as, "Red Indians, eh!" or "Came out of the water backwards! My eye!"

Sometimes he made what George Edmund regarded as quite footling comments. Still George Edmund had to tell someone and there was no one else to tell. So George Edmund went on talking and Mr. Brumley went on thinking.

10

Mr. Brumley could not sleep at all until it was nearly five. His intelligence seemed to be making up at last for years of speculative restraint. In a world for the most part given up to slumber Mr. Brumley may be imagined as clambering hand over fist in the silences, feverishly and wonderfully overtaking his age. In the morning he got up pallid and he shaved badly, but he was a generation ahead of his own Euphemia series, and the school of charm and quiet humor and of letting things slide with a kind of elegant donnishness, had lost him forever. . . .

And among all sorts of things that had come to him in that vast gulf of nocturnal thinking was some vivid self-examination. At last he got to that. He had been dragged down to very elemental things indeed by the manifest completeness of Lady Harman's return to her husband. He had had at last to look at himself starkly for the male he was, to go beneath the gentlemanly airs, the refined and elegant virilities of his habitual poses. Either this thing was unendurable—there were certainly moments when it came near to being unendurable—or it was not. On the whole and excepting mere momentary paroxysms it was not, and so he had to recognize and he did recognize with the greatest amazement that there could be something else besides sexual attraction and maneuvering and possession between a beautiful woman and a man like himself. He loved Lady Harman, he loved her, he now began to realize just how much, and she could defeat him and reject him as a conceivable lover, turn that aside as a thing impossible, shame him as the romantic school would count shame and still command him with her confident eyes and her friendly extended hands. He admitted he suffered, let us rather say he claimed to suffer the heated torments of a passionate nature, but he perceived like fresh air and sunrise coming by blind updrawn and opened window into a fetid chamber, that also he loved her with a clean and bodiless love, was anxious to help her, was anxious now—it was a new thing—to understand her, to reassure her, to give unrequited what once he had sought rather to seem to give in view of an imagined exchange.

He perceived too in these still hours how little he had understood her hitherto. He had been blinded,—obsessed. He had been seeing her and himself and the whole world far too much as a display of the eternal dualism of sex, the incessant pursuit. Now with his sexual imaginings newly humbled and hopeless, with a realization of her own tremendous minimization of that fundamental of romance, he began to see all that there was in her personality and their possible relations outside that. He saw how gravely and deeply serious was her fine philanthropy, how honest and simple and impersonal her desire for knowledge and understandings. There is the brain of her at least, he thought, far out of Sir Isaac's reach. She wasn't abased by her surrenders, their simplicity exalted her, showed her innocent and himself a flushed and congested soul. He perceived now with the astonishment of a man newly awakened just how the great obsession of sex had dominated him—for how many years? Since his early undergraduate days. Had he anything to put beside her own fine detachment? Had he ever since his manhood touched philosophy, touched a social question, thought of anything human, thought of art, or literature or belief, without a glancing reference of the whole question to the uses of this eternal hunt? During that time had he ever talked to a girl or woman with an unembarrassed sincerity? He stripped his pretences bare; the answer was no. His very refinements had been no more than indicative fig-leaves. His conservatism and morality had been a mere dalliance with interests that too brutal a simplicity might have exhausted prematurely. And indeed hadn't the whole period of literature that had produced him been, in its straining purity and refinement, as it were one glowing, one illuminated fig-leaf, a vast conspiracy to keep certain matters always in mind by conspicuously covering them away? But this wonderful woman—it seemed—she hadn't them in mind! She shamed him if only by her trustful unsuspiciousness of the ancient selfish game of Him and Her that he had been so ardently playing. . . . He idealized and worshipped this clean blindness. He abased himself before it.

"No," cried Mr. Brumley suddenly in the silence of the night, "I will rise again. I will rise again by love out of these morasses. . . . She shall be my goddess and by virtue of her I will end this incessant irrational craving for women. . . . I will be her friend and her faithful friend."

He lay still for a time and then he said in a whisper very humbly: "*God help me.*"

He set himself in those still hours which are so endless and so profitable to men in their middle years, to think how he might make himself the perfect lover instead of a mere plotter for desire, and how he might purge himself from covetousness and possessiveness and learn to serve.

And if very speedily his initial sincerity was tinged again with egotism and if he drowsed at last into a portrait of himself as beautifully and admirably self-sacrificial, you must not sneer too readily at him, for so God has made the soul of Mr. Brumley and otherwise it could not do.

CHAPTER THE TENTH

Lady Harman Comes Out

1

THE TREATY BETWEEN Lady Harman and her husband which was to be her Great Charter, the constitutional basis of her freedoms throughout the rest of her married life, had many practical defects. The chief of these was that it was largely undocumented; it had been made piecemeal, in various ways, at different times and for the most part indirectly through diverse intermediaries. Charterson had introduced large vaguenesses by simply displaying more of his teeth at crucial moments; Mrs. Harman had conveyed things by hugging and weeping that were afterwards discovered to be indistinct; Sir Isaac writing from a bed of sickness had frequently been totally illegible. One cannot therefore detail the clauses of this agreement or give its provisions with any great precision; one can simply intimate the kind of understanding that had had an air of being arrived at. The working interpretations were still to come.

Before anything else it was manifestly conceded by Lady Harman that she would not run away again, and still more manifest that she undertook to break no more windows or do anything that might lead to a second police court scandal. And she was to be a true and faithful wife and comfort, as a wife should be, to Sir Isaac. In return for that consideration and to ensure its continuance Sir Isaac came great distances from his former assumption of a matrimonial absolutism. She was to be granted all sorts of small autonomies,—the word autonomy was carefully avoided throughout but its spirit was omnipresent.

She was in particular to have a banking account for her dress and personal expenditure into which Sir Isaac would cause to be paid a hundred pounds monthly and it was to be private to herself alone until he chose to go through the cashed checks and counterfoils. She was to be free to come and go as she saw fit, subject to a punctual appearance at meals, the comfort and dignity of Sir Isaac and such specific engagements as she might make with him. She might have her own friends, but there the contract became a little misty; a time was to come when Sir Isaac was to betray a conviction that the only proper friends that a woman can have are women. There were also non-corroborated assurances as to the privacy of her correspondence. The second Rolls-Royce car was to be entirely at her service, and Clarence was to be immediately supplemented by a new and more deferential man, and as soon as possible assisted to another situation and replaced. She was to have a voice in the further furnishing of Black Strand and in the arrangement of its garden. She was to read what she chose and think what she liked within her head without too minute or suspicious an examination by Sir Isaac, and short of flat contradiction at his own table she was to be free to express her own opinions in any manner becoming a lady. But more particularly if she found her ideas infringing upon the management or influence of the International Bread and Cake Stores, she was to convey her objections and ideas in the first instance privately and confidentially to Sir Isaac.

Upon this point he displayed a remarkable and creditable sensitiveness. His pride in that organization was if possible greater than his original pride in his wife, and probably nothing in all the jarring of their relationship had hurt him more than her accessibility to hostile criticism and the dinner-table conversation with Charterson and Blenker that had betrayed this fact. He began to talk about it directly she returned to him. His protestations and explanations were copious and heartfelt. It was perhaps the chief discovery made by Lady Harman at this period of reconstruction that her husband's business side was not to be explained completely as a highly energetic and elaborate avarice. He was no doubt acquisitive and retentive and mean-spirited, but these were merely the ugly aspects of a disposition that involved many other factors. He was also incurably a schemer. He liked to fit things together, to dove-tail arrangements, to devise economies, to spread ingeniously into new fields, he had a love of organization and contrivance as disinterested as an artist's love for the possibilities of his medium. He would rather have made a profit of ten percent out of a subtly planned shop than thirty by an unforeseen accident. He wouldn't have cheated to get money for the world. He knew he was better at figuring out expenditures and receipts than most people and he was as touchy about his reputation for this kind of cleverness as any poet or painter for his fame. Now that he had awakened to the idea that his wife was capable of looking into and possibly even understanding his business, he was passionately anxious to show her just how wonderfully he had done it all, and when he perceived she was in her large, unskilled, helpless way, intensely concerned for all the vast multitude of incompetent or partially competent young women who floundered about in badly paid employment in our great cities, he grasped at once at the opportunity of recovering her lost interest and respect by doing some brilliant feats of contrivance in that direction. Why shouldn't he? He had long observed with a certain envy the admirable advertisement such firms as Lever and Cadbury and Burroughs & Wellcome gained from their ostentatiously able and generous treatment of their workpeople, and it seemed to him conceivable that in the end it might not be at all detrimental to his prosperity to put his hand to this long neglected piece of social work. The Babs Wheeler business had been a real injury in every way to the International Bread and Cake Stores and even if he didn't ultimately go to all the lengths his wife seemed to contemplate, he was resolved at any rate that an affair of that kind should not occur again. The expedition to Marienbad took with it a secretary who was also a stenographer. A particularly smart young inspector and Graper, the staff manager, had brisk four-day holidays once or twice for consultation purposes; Sir Isaac's rabbit-like architect was in attendance for a week and the Harmans returned to Putney with the first vivid greens of late March,—for the Putney Hill house was to be reopened and Black Strand reserved now for week-end and summer use—with plans already drawn out for four residential Hostels in London primarily for the girl waitresses of the International Stores who might have no homes or homes at an inconvenient distance, and, secondarily, if any vacant accommodation remained over, for any other employed young women of the same class. . . .

2

Lady Harman came back to England from the pine-woods and bright order and regimen and foreign novelty of their Bohemian Kur-Ort, in a state of renewed perplexity. Already that undocumented Magna Charta was manifestly not working upon the lines she had anticipated. The glosses Sir Isaac put upon it were extensive and remarkable and invariably in the direction of restricting her liberties and resuming controls she had supposed abandoned.

Marienbad had done wonders for him; his slight limp had disappeared, his nervous energy was all restored; except for a certain increase in his natural irritability and occasional panting fits, he seemed as well as he had ever been. At the end of their time at the Kur he was even going for walks. Once he went halfway up the Podhorn on foot. And with every increment in his strength his aggressiveness increased, his recognition of her new freedoms was less cordial and her sense of contrition and responsibility diminished. Moreover, as the scheme of those Hostels, which had played so large a part in her conception of their reconciliation, grew more and more definite, she perceived more and more that it was not certainly that fine and humanizing thing she had presumed it would be. She began to feel more and more that it might be merely an extension of Harman methods to cheap boarding-houses for young people. But faced with a mass of detailed concrete projects and invited to suggest modifications she was able to realize for the first time how vague, how ignorant and incompetent her wishes had been, how much she had to understand and how much she had to discover before she could meet Sir Isaac with his "I'm doing it all for you, Elly. If you don't like it, you tell me what you don't like and I'll alter it. But just vague doubting! One can't do anything with vague doubting."

She felt that once back in England out of this picturesque toylike German world she would be able to grasp realities again and deal with these things. She wanted advice, she wanted to hear what people said of her ideas. She would also, she imagined, begin to avail herself of those conceded liberties which their isolation together abroad and her husband's constant need of her presence had so far prevented her from tasting. She had an idea that Susan Burnet might prove suggestive about the Hostels.

And moreover, if now and then she could have a good talk with someone understanding and intelligent, someone she could trust, someone who cared enough for her to think with her and for her. . . .

3

We have traced thus far the emergence of Lady Harman from that state of dutiful subjection and social irresponsibility which was the lot of woman in the past to that limited, ill-defined and quite unsecured freedom which is her present condition. And now we have to give an outline of the ideas of herself and her uses and what she had to do, which were forming themselves in her mind. She had made a determinatin of herself, which carried her along the lines of her natural predisposition, to duty, to service. There she displayed that acceptance of responsibility which is so much more often a feminine than a masculine habit of thinking. But she brought to the achievement of this determination a discriminating integrity of mind that is more frequently masculine than feminine. She wanted to know clearly what she was undertaking and how far its consequences would reach and how it was related to other things.

Her confused reading during the last few years and her own observation and such leakages of fact into her life as the talk of Susan Burnet, had all contributed to her realization that the world was full of needless discomfort and hardships and failure, due to great imperfectly apprehended injustices and maladjustments in the social system, and recently it had been borne in upon her, upon the barbed point of *The London Lion* and the quick tongue of Susan, that if any particular class of people was more answerable than any other for these evils, it was the people of leisure and freedom like herself, who had time to think, and the directing organizing people like her husband, who had power to change. She was called upon to do something, at times the call became urgent, and she could not feel any assurance which it was of the many vague and conflicting suggestions that came drifting to her that she had to do. Her idea of Hostels for the International waitresses had been wrung out of her prematurely during her earlier discussions with her husband. She did not feel that it was anything more than a partial remedy for a special evil. She wanted something more general than that, something comprehensive enough to answer completely so wide a question as "What ought I to be doing with all my life?" In the honest simplicity of her nature she wanted to find an answer to that. Out of the confusion of voices about us she hoped to be able to disentangle directions for her life. Already she had been reading voraciously: while she was still at Marienbad she had written to Mr. Brumley and he had sent her books and papers, advanced and radical in many cases, that she might know, "What are people thinking?"

Many phrases from her earlier discussions with Sir Isaac stuck in her mind in a curiously stimulating way and came back to her as she read. She recalled him, for instance, with his face white and his eyes red and his flat hand sawing at her, saying: "I dessay I'm all wrong, I dessay I don't know anything about anything and all those chaps you read, Bernud Shaw, and Gosworthy, and all the rest of them are wonderfully clever; but you tell me, Elly, what they say we've got to do! You tell me that. You go and ask some of those chaps just what they want a man like me to do. . . . They'll ask me to endow a theatre or run a club for novelists or advertise the lot of them in the windows of my International Stores or something. And that's about all it comes to. You go and see if I'm not right. They grumble and they grumble; I don't say there's not a lot to grumble at, but give me something they'll back themselves for all they're worth as good to get done. . . . That's where I don't agree with all these idees. They're Wind, Elly, Weak wind at that."

It is distressing to record how difficult it was for Lady Harman to form even the beginnings of a disproof of that. Her life through all this second phase of mitigated autonomy was an intermittent pilgrimage in search of that disproof. She could not believe that things as they were, this mass of hardships, cruelties, insufficiencies and heartburnings were the ultimate wisdom and possibility of human life, yet when she went from them to the projects that would replace or change them she seemed to pass from things of overwhelming solidity to matters more thin and flimsy than the twittering of sparrows on the gutter. So soon as she returned to London she started upon her search for a solution; she supplemented Mr. Brumley's hunt for books with her own efforts, she went to meetings— sometimes Sir Isaac took her, once or twice she was escorted by Mr. Brumley, and presently her grave interest and her personal charm had gathered about her a circle of companionable friends. She tried to talk to people and made great efforts to hear people who seemed authoritative and wise and leaderlike, talking.

There were many interruptions to this research, but she persevered. Quite early she had an illness that ended in a miscarriage, an accident for which she was by no means inconsolable, and before she had completely recovered from that Sir Isaac fell ill again, the first of a series of relapses that necessitated further foreign travel—always in elaborately comfortable trains with maid, courier, valet, and secretary, to some warm and indolent southward place. And few people knew how uncertain her liberties were. Sir Isaac was the victim of an increasing irritability, at times he had irrational outbursts of distrust that would culminate in passionate outbreaks and scenes that were truncated by an almost suffocating breathlessness. On several occasions he was on the verge of quarrelling violently with her visitors, and he would suddenly oblige her to break engagements, pour abuse upon her and bring matters back to the very verge of her first revolt. And then he would break her down by pitiful appeals. The cylinders of oxygen would be resorted to, and he would emerge from the crisis, rather rueful, tamed and quiet for the time.

He was her chief disturbance. Her children were healthy children and fell in with the routines of governess and tutor that their wealth provided. She saw them often, she noted their increasing resemblance to their father, she did her best to soften the natural secretiveness and aggressiveness of their manners, she watched their teachers and intervened whenever the influences about them seemed to her to need intervention, she dressed them and gave them presents and tried to believe she loved them, and as Sir Isaac's illness increased she took a larger and larger share in the direction of the household. . . .

Through all these occupations and interruptions and immediacies she went trying to comprehend and at times almost believing she comprehended life, and then the whole spectacle of this modern world of which she was a part would seem to break up again into a multitude of warring and discordant fragments having no conceivable common aim or solution. Those moments of unifying faith and confidence, that glowed so bravely and never endured, were at once tantalizing and sustaining. She could never believe but that ultimately she would not grasp and hold—something. . . .

Many people met her and liked her and sought to know more of her; Lady Beach-Mandarin and Lady Viping were happy to be her social sponsors, the Blenkers and the Chartersons met her out and woke up cautiously to this new possibility; her emergence was rapid in spite of the various delays and interruptions I have mentioned and she was soon in a position to realize just how little one meets when one meets a number of people and how little one hears when one has much conversation. Her mind was presently crowded with confused impressions of pleasant men evading her agreeably and making out of her gravities an opportunity for bright sayings, and of women being vaguely solemn and quite indefinite.

She went into the circle of movements, was tried over by Mrs. Hubert Plessington, she questioned this and that promoter of constructive schemes, and instead of mental meat she was asked to come upon committees and sounded for subscriptions. On several occasions, escorted by Mr. Brumley—some instinct made her conceal or minimize his share in these expeditions to her husband—she went as inconspicuously as possible to the backs of public meetings in which she understood great questions were being discussed or great changes inaugurated. Some public figures she even followed up for a time, distrusting her first impressions.

She became familiar with the manners and bearing of our platform class, with the solemn dummy-like chairman or chairwoman, saying a few words, the alert secretary or organizer, the prominent figures sitting with an air of grave responsibility, generously acting an intelligent attention to others until the moment came for them themselves to deliver. Then with an ill-concealed relief some would come to the footlights, some leap up in their places with a tenoring eagerness, some would be facetious and some speak with neuralgic effort, some were impertinent, some propitiatory, some dull, but all were—disappointing, disappointing. God was not in any of them. A platform is no setting for the shy processes of an honest human mind,—we are all strained to artificiality in the excessive glare of attention that beats upon us there. One does not exhibit opinions at a meeting, one acts them, the very truth must rouge its cheeks and blacken its eyebrows to tell, and to Lady Harman it was the acting chiefly and the make-up that was visible. They didn't grip her, they didn't lift her, they failed to convince her even of their own belief in what they supported.

4

But occasionally among the multitude of conversations that gave her nothing, there would come some talk that illuminated and for the time almost reconciled her to the effort and the loss of time and distraction her social expeditions involved. One evening at one of Lady Tarville's carelessly compiled parties she encountered Edgar Wilkins the novelist and got the most suggestive glimpses of his attitude towards himself and towards the world of intellectual ferment to which he belonged. She had been taken down by an amiable but entirely uninteresting permanent official who when the time came turned his stereotyped talk over to the other side of him with a quiet mechanical indifference, and she was left for a little while in silence until Wilkins had disengaged himself.

He was a flushed man with untidy hair, and he opened at once with an appeal to her sympathies.

"Oh! Bother!" he said. "I say,—I've eaten that mutton. I didn't notice. One eats too much at these affairs. One doesn't notice at the time and then afterwards one finds out."

She was a little surprised at his gambit and could think of nothing but a kindly murmur.

"Detestable thing," he said; "my body."

"But surely not," she tried and felt as she said it that was a trifle bold.

"You're all right," he said making her aware he saw her. "But I've this thing that wheezes and fattens at the slightest excuse and—it encumbers me— bothers me to take exercise. . . . But I can hardly expect you to be interested in my troubles, can I?"

He made an all too manifest attempt to read her name on the slip of card that lay before her among the flowers and as manifestly succeeded. "We people who write and paint and all that sort of thing are a breed of insatiable egotists, Lady Harman. With the least excuse. Don't you think so?"

"Not—not exceptionally," she said.

"Exceptionally," he insisted.

"It isn't my impression," she said. "You're—franker."

"But someone was telling me—you've been taking impressions of us lately. I mean all of us people who go flapping ideas about in the air. Somebody—was it Lady Beach-Mandarin?—was saying you'd come out looking for Intellectual Heroes—and found Bernard Shaw. . . . But what could you have expected?"

"I've been trying to find out and understand what people are thinking. I want ideas."

"It's disheartening, isn't it?"

"It's—perplexing sometimes."

"You go to meetings, and try to get to the bottom of Movements, and you want to meet and know the people who write the wonderful things? Get at the wonderful core of it?"

"One feels there are things going on."

"Great illuminating things."

"Well—yes."

"And when you see those great Thinkers and Teachers and Guides and Brave Spirits and High Brows generally—"

He laughed and stopped just in time on the very verge of taking pheasant.

"Oh, take it away," he cried sharply.

"We've all been through that illusion, Lady Harman," he went on.

"But I don't like to think— Aren't Great Men after all—great?"

"In their ways, in their places—Yes. But not if you go up to them and look at them. Not at the dinner table, not in their beds. . . . What a time of disillusionment you must have had!

"You see, Lady Harman," he said, leaning back from his empty plate, inclining himself confidentially to her ear and speaking in a privy tone; "it's in the very nature of things that we—if I may put myself into the list—we ideologists, should be rather exceptionally loose and untrustworthy and disappointing men. Rotters—to speak plain contemporary English. If you come to think of it, it has to be so."

"But—" she protested.

He met her eye firmly. "It has to be."

"Why?"

"The very qualities that make literature entertaining, vigorous, inspiring, revealing, wonderful, beautiful and—all that sort of thing, make its producers—if you will forgive the word again—rotters."

She smiled and lifted her eyebrows protestingly.

"Sensitive nervous tissue," he said with a finger up to emphasize his words. "Quick responsiveness to stimulus, a vivid, almost uncontrollable, expressiveness; that's what you want in your literary man."

"Yes," said Lady Harman following cautiously. "Yes, I suppose it is."

"Can you suppose for a moment that these things conduce to self-control, to reserve, to consistency, to any of the qualities of a trustworthy man? . . . Of course you can't. And so we *aren't* trustworthy, we *aren't* consistent. Our virtues are our vices. . . . *My* life," said Mr. Wilkins still more confidentially, "won't bear examination. But that's by the way. It need not concern us now."

"But Mr. Brumley?" she asked on the spur of the moment.

"I'm not talking of him," said Wilkins with careless cruelty. "He's restrained. I mean the really imaginative people, the people with vision, the people who let themselves go. You see now why they are rotten, why they must be rotten. (No! No! take it away. I'm talking.) I feel so strongly about this, about the natural and necessary disreputableness of everybody who produces reputable writing—and for the matter of that, art generally—that I set my face steadily against all these attempts that keep on cropping up to make Figures of us. We aren't Figures, Lady Harman; it isn't our line. Of all the detestable aspects of the Victorian period surely that disposition to make Figures of its artists and literary men was the most detestable. Respectable Figures—Examples to the young. The suppressions, the coverings up that had to go on, the white-washing of Dickens,—who was more than a bit of a rip, you know, the concealment of Thackeray's mistresses. Did you know he had mistresses? Oh rather! And so on. It's like that bust of Jove—or Bacchus was it?—they pass off as Plato, who probably looked like any other literary Grub. That's why I won't have anything to do with these Academic developments that my friend Brumley—Do you know him by the way?—goes in for. He's the third man down— You *do* know him. And he's giving up the Academic Committee, is he? I'm glad he's seen it at last. What *is* the good of trying to have an Academy and all that, and put us in uniform and make out we are Somebodies, and respectable enough to be shaken hands with by George and Mary, when as a matter of fact we are, by our very nature, a collection of miscellaneous scandals— We *must* be. Bacon, Shakespeare, Byron, Shelley—all the stars. . . . No, Johnson wasn't a star, he was a character by Boswell. . . . Oh! great things come out of us, no doubt, our arts are the vehicles of wonder and hope, the world is dead without these things we produce, but that's no reason why—why the mushroom-bed should follow the mushrooms into the soup, is it? Perfectly fair image. (No, take it away.)"

He paused and then jumped in again as she was on the point of speaking.

"And you see even if our temperaments didn't lead inevitably to our—dipping rather, we should still have to—*dip*. Asking a writer or a poet to be seemly and Academic and so on, is like asking an eminent surgeon to be stringently decent. It's—you see, it's incompatible. Now a king or a butler or a family solicitor—if you like."

He paused again.

Lady Harman had been following him with an attentive reluctance.

"But what are we to do," she asked, "we people who are puzzled by life, who want guidance and ideas and—help, if—if all the people we look to for ideas are—"

"Bad characters."

"Well,—it's your theory, you know—bad characters?"

Wilkins answered with the air of one who carefully disentangles a complex but quite solvable problem. "It doesn't follow," he said, "that because a man is a bad character he's not to be trusted in matters where character—as we commonly use the word—doesn't come in. These sensitives, these—would you mind if I were to call myself an Æolian Harp?—these Æolian Harps; they can't help responding to the winds of heaven. Well,—listen to them. Don't follow them, don't worship them, don't even honor them, but listen to them. Don't let anyone stop them from saying and painting and writing and singing what they want to. Freedom, canvas and attention, those are the proper honors for the artist, the poet and the philosopher. Listen to the noise they make, watch the stuff they produce, and presently you will find certain things among the multitude of things that are said and shown and put out and published, something—light in *your* darkness—a writer for you, something for you. Nobody can have a greater contempt for artists and writers and poets and philosophers than I, oh! a squalid crew they are, mean, jealous, pugnacious, disgraceful in love, *disgraceful*—but out of it all comes the greatest serenest thing, the mind of the world, Literature. Nasty little midges, yes,—but fireflies—carrying light for the darkness.''

His face was suddenly lit by enthusiasm and she wondered that she could have thought it rather heavy and commonplace. He stopped abruptly and glanced beyond her at her other neighbor who seemed on the verge of turning to them again. ''If I go on,'' he said with a voice suddenly dropped, ''I shall talk loud.''

''You know,'' said Lady Harman, in a halty undertone, ''you—you are too hard upon—upon clever people, but it is true. I mean it is true in a way. . . .''

''Go on, I understand exactly what you are saying.''

''I mean, there *are* ideas. It's just that, that is so—so— I mean they seem never to be just there and always to be present.''

''Like God. Never in the flesh—now. A spirit everywhere. You think exactly as I do, Lady Harman. It is just that. This is a great time, so great that there is no chance for great men. Every chance for great work. And we're doing it. There is a wind—blowing out of heaven. And when beautiful people like yourself come into things—''

''I try to understand,'' she said. ''I want to understand. I want—I want not to miss life.''

He was on the verge of saying something further and then his eyes wandered down the table and he stopped short.

He ended his talk as he had begun it with ''Bother! Lady Tarvrille, Lady Harman, is trying to catch your eye.''

Lady Harman turned her face to her hostess and answered her smile. Wilkins caught at his chair and stood up.

''It would have been jolly to have talked some more,'' he said.

''I hope we shall.''

''Well!'' said Wilkins, with a sudden hardness in his eyes and she was swept away from him.

She found no chance of talking to him upstairs, Sir Isaac came for her early; but she went in hope of another meeting.

It did not come. For a time that expectation gave dinners and luncheon parties a quite appreciable attraction. Then she told Agatha Alimony. ''I've never met him but that once,'' she said.

''One doesn't meet him now,'' said Agatha, deeply.

''But why?''

Deep significance came into Miss Alimony's eyes. ''My dear,'' she whispered, and glanced about them. ''Don't you *know?*''

Lady Harman was a radiant innocence.

And then Miss Alimony began in impressive undertones, with awful omissions like pits of darkness and with such richly embroidered details as serious spinsters enjoy, adding, indeed, two quite new things that came to her mind as the tale unfolded, and, naming no names and giving no chances of verification or reply, handed on the fearful and at that time extremely popular story of the awful wickedness of Wilkins the author.

Upon reflection Lady Harman perceived that this explained all sorts of things in their conversation and particularly the flash of hardness at the end.

Even then, things must have been hanging over him. . . .

5

And while Lady Harman was making these meritorious and industrious attempts to grasp the significance of life and to get some clear idea of her social duty, the developments of those Hostels she had started—she now felt so prematurely—was going on. There were times when she tried not to think of them, turned her back on them, fled from them, and times when they and what she ought to do about them and what they ought to be and what they ought not to be, filled her mind to the exclusion of every other topic. Rigorously and persistently Sir Isaac insisted they were hers, asked her counsel, demanded her appreciation, presented as it were his recurring bill for them.

Five of them were being built, not four but five. There was to be one, the largest, in a conspicuous position in Bloomsbury near the British Museum, one in a conspicuous position looking out upon Parliament Hill, one conspicuously placed upon the Waterloo Road near St. George's Circus, one at Sydenham, and one in the Kensington Road which was designed to catch the eye of people going to and fro to the various exhibitions at Olympia.

In Sir Isaac's study at Putney there was a huge and rather splendid-looking morocco portfolio on a stand, and this portfolio bore in excellent gold lettering the words, International Bread and Cake Hostels. It was her husband's peculiar pleasure after dinner to take her to turn over this with him; he would sit pencil in hand, while she, poised at his request upon the arm of his chair, would endorse a multitude of admirable modifications and suggestions. These hostels were to be done—indeed they were being done—by Sir Isaac's tame architect, and the interlacing yellow and mauve tiles, and the Doulton ware moldings that were already familiar to the public as the uniform of the Stores, were to be used upon the façades of the new institutions. They were to be boldly labeled

INTERNATIONAL HOSTELS

right across the front.

The plans revealed in every case a site depth as great as the frontage, and the utmost ingenuity had been used to utilize as much space as possible. "Every room we get in," said Sir Isaac, "adds one to the denominator in the cost;" and carried his wife back to her schooldays. At last she had found sense in fractions. There was to be a series of convenient and spacious rooms on the ground floor, a refectory, which might be cleared and used for meetings—"dances," said Lady Harman. "Hardly the sort of thing we want 'em to get up to," said Sir Isaac—various offices, the matron's apartments—"We ought to begin thinking about matrons," said Sir Isaac;—a bureau, a reading-room and a library—"We can pick good, serious stuff for them," said Sir Isaac, "instead of their filling their heads with trash"—one or two work-rooms with tables for cutting out and sewing; this last was an idea of Susan Burnet's. Upstairs there was to be a beehive of bedrooms, floor above floor, and each floor as low as the building regulations permitted. There were to be long dormitories with cubicles at three-and-sixpence a week—make your own beds—and separate rooms at prices ranging from four-and-sixpence to seven-and-sixpence. Every three cubicles and every bedroom had lavatory basins with hot and cold water; there were pull-out drawers under the beds and a built-in chest of drawers, a hanging cupboard, a looking-glass and a radiator in each cubicle, and each floor had a box-room. It was ship-shape.

"A girl can get this cubicle for three-and-six a week," said Sir Isaac, tapping the drawing before him with his pencil. "She can get her breakfast with a bit of bacon or a sausage for two shillings a week, and she can get her high tea, with cold meat, good potted salmon, shrimp paste, jam and cetera, for three-and-six a week. Say her bus fares and lunch out mean another four shillings. That means she can get along on about twelve-and-six a week, comfortable, read the papers, have a book out of the library. . . . There's nothing like it to be got now for twice the money. The sort of thing they have now is one room, dingy, badly fitted, extra for coals.

"That's the answer to your problem, Elly," he said. "There we are. Every girl who doesn't live at home can live here—with a matron to keep her eye on her. . . . And properly run, Elly, properly run the thing's going to pay two or three percent,—let alone the advertisement for the Stores.

"We can easily make these Hostels obligatory on all our girls who don't live at their own homes," he said. "That ought to keep them off the streets, if anything can. I don't see how even Miss Babs Wheeler can have the face to strike against that.

"And then we can arrange with some of the big firms, drapers' shops and all that sort of thing near each hostel, to take over most of our other cubicle space. A lot of them—overflow.

"Of course we'll have to make sure the girls get in at night." He reached out for a ground floor plan of the Bloomsbury establishment which was to be the first built. "If," he said, "we were to have a sort of porter's lodge with a book—and make 'em ring a bell after eleven say—just here. . . ."

He took out a silver pencil case and got to work.

Lady Harman's expression as she leaned over him became thoughtful.

There were points about this project that gave her the greatest misgivings; that matron, keeping her eye on the girls, that carefully selected library, the porter's bell, these casual allusions to "discipline" that set her thinking of scraps of the Babs Wheeler controversy. There was a regularity, an austerity about this project that chilled her, she hardly knew why. Her own vague intentions had been an amiable, hospitable, agreeably cheap establishment to which the homeless feminine employees in London could resort freely and cheerfully, and it was only very slowly that she perceived that her husband was by no means convinced of the spontaneity of their coming. He seemed always glancing at methods for compelling them to come in and oppressions when that compulsion had succeeded. There had already hovered over several of these anticipatory evenings, his very manifest intention to have very carefully planned "Rules." She felt there lay ahead of them much possibility for divergence of opinion about these "Rules." She foresaw a certain narrowness and hardness. She herself had made her fight against the characteristics of Sir Isaac and—perhaps she was lacking in that aristocratic feeling which comes so naturally to most successful middle-class people in England—she could not believe that what she had found bad and suffocating for herself could be agreeable and helpful for her poorer sisters.

It occurred to her to try the effect of the scheme upon Susan Burnet. Susan had such a knack of seeing things from unexpected angles. She contrived certain operations upon the study blinds, and then broached the business to Susan casually in the course of an enquiry into the welfare of the Burnet family.

Susan was evidently prejudiced against the idea.

"Yes," said Susan after various explanations and exhibitions, "but where's the home in it?"

"The whole thing is a home."

"Barracks *I* call it," said Susan. "Nobody ever felt at home in a room colored up like that—and no curtains, nor vallances, nor toilet covers, nor anywhere where a girl can hang a photograph or anything. What girl's going to feel at home in a strange place like that?"

"They ought to be able to hang up photographs," said Lady Harman, making a mental note of it.

"And of course there'll be all sorts of Rules."

"*Some* rules."

"Homes, real homes don't have Rules. And I daresay—Fines."

"No, there shan't be any Fines," said Lady Harman quickly. "I'll see to that."

"You got to back up rules somehow—once you got 'em," said Susan. "And when you get a crowd, and no father and mother, and no proper family feeling, I suppose there's got to be Rules."

Lady Harman pointed out various advantages of the project.

"I'm not saying it isn't cheap and healthy and social," said Susan, "and if it isn't too strict I expect you'll get plenty of girls to come to it, but at the best it's an Institution, Lady Harman. It's going to be an Institution. That's what it's going to be."

She held the front elevation of the Bloomsbury Hostel in her hand and reflected.

"Of course for my part, I'd rather lodge with nice struggling believing Christian people anywhere than go into a place like that. It's the feeling of freedom, of being yourself and on your own. Even if the water wasn't laid on and I had to fetch it myself. . . . If girls were paid properly there wouldn't be any need of such places, none at all. It's the poverty makes 'em what they are. . . . And after all, somebody's got to lose the lodgers if this place gets them. Suppose this sort of thing grows up all over the place, it'll just be the story of the little bakers and little grocers and all those people over again. Why in London there are thousands of people just keep a home together by letting two or three rooms or boarding someone—and it stands to reason, they'll have to take less or lose the lodgers if this kind of thing's going to be done. Nobody isn't going to build a Hostel for them."

"No," said Lady Harman, "I never thought of them."

"Lots of 'em haven't anything in the world but their bits of furniture and their lease and there they are stuck and tied. There's Aunt Hannah, Father's sister, she's like that. Sleeps in the basement and works and slaves, and often I've had to lend her ten shillings to pay the rent with, through her not being full. This sort of place isn't going to do much good to her."

Lady Harman surveyed the plan rather blankly. "I suppose it isn't."

"And then if you manage this sort of place easy and attractive, it's going to draw girls away from their homes. There's girls like Alice who'd do anything to get a bit of extra money to put on their backs and seem to think of nothing but chattering and laughing and going about. Such a place like this would be fine fun for Alice; in when she liked and out when she liked, and none of us to ask her questions. She'd be just the sort to go, and mother, who's had the upbringing of her, how's she to make up for Alice's ten shillings what she pays in every week? There's lots like Alice. She's not bad isn't Alice, she's a good girl and a good-hearted girl; I will say that for her, but she's shallow, say what you like she's shallow, she's got no thought and she's wild for pleasure, and sometimes it seems to me that that's as bad as being bad for all the good it does to anyone else in the world, and so I tell her. But of course she hasn't seen things as I've seen them and doesn't feel as I do about all these things. . . ."

Thus Susan.

Her discourse so puzzled Lady Harman that she bethought herself of Mr. Brumley and called in his only too readily accorded advice. She asked him to tea on a day when she knew unofficially that Sir Isaac would be away, she showed him the plans and sketched their probable development. Then with that charming confidence of hers in his knowledge and ability she put her doubts and fears before him. What did he really think of these places? What did he think of Susan Burnet's idea of ruined lodginghouse keepers? "I used to think our stores were good things," she said. "Is this likely to be a good thing at all?"

Mr. Brumley said "Um" a great number of times and realized that he was a humbug. He fenced with her and affected sagacity for a time and suddenly he threw down his defences and confessed he knew as little of the business as she did. "But I see it is a complex question and—it's an interesting one too. May I enquire into it for you? I think I might be able to hunt up a few particulars. . . ."

He went away in a glow of resolution.

Georgina was about the only intimate who regarded the new development without misgiving.

"You think you're going to do all sorts of things with these Hostels, Ella," she said, "but as a matter of fact they're bound to become just exactly what we've always wanted."

"And what may that be?" asked Mrs. Sawbridge over her macramé work.

"Strongholds for a garrison of suffragettes," said Georgina with the light of the Great Insane Movement in her eyes and a ringing note in her voice. "Fort Chabrols for women."

6

For some months in a negative and occasionally almost negligent fashion Mr. Brumley had been living up to his impassioned resolve to be an unselfish lover of Lady Harman. He had been rather at loose ends intellectually, deprived of his old assumptions and habitual attitudes and rather chaotic in the matter of his new convictions. He had given most of his productive hours to the writing of a novel which was to be an entire departure from the Euphemia tradition. The more he got on with this, the more clearly he realized that it was essentially insignificant. When he re-read what he had written he was surprised by crudities where he had intended sincerities and rhetoric where the scheme had demanded passion. What was the matter with him? He was stirred that Lady Harman should send for him, and his inability to deal with her perplexities deepened his realization of the ignorance and superficiality he had so long masked even from himself beneath the tricks and pretensions of a gay skepticism. He went away fully resolved to grapple with the entire Hostel question, and he put the patched and tortured manuscript of the new novel aside with a certain satisfaction to do this.

The more he reflected upon the nature of this study he proposed for himself the more it attracted him. It was some such reality as this he had been wanting. He could presently doubt whether he would ever go back to his novel-writing again, or at least to the sort of novel-writing he had been doing hitherto. To invent stories to save middle-aged prosperous middle-class people from the distresses of thinking, is surely no work for a self-respecting man. Stevenson in the very deeps of that dishonorable traffic had realized as much and likened himself to a *fille de joie,* and Haggard, of the same school and period, had abandoned blood and thunder at the climax of his success for the honest study of agricultural conditions. The newer successes were turning out work, less and less conventional and agreeable and more and more stiffened with facts and sincerities. . . . He would show Lady Harman that a certain debonair quality he had always affected, wasn't incompatible with a powerful grasp of general conditions. . . . And she wanted this done. Suppose he did it in a way that made him necessary to her. Suppose he did it very well.

He set to work, and understanding as you do a certain quality of the chameleon in Mr. Brumley's moral nature, you will understand that he worked through a considerable variety of moods. Sometimes he worked with disinterested passion and sometimes he was greatly sustained by this thought that here was something that would weave him in with the gravities of her life and give him perhaps a new inlet to intimacy. And presently a third thing came to his help, and that was the discovery that the questions arising out of this attempt to realize the importance of those Hostels, were in themselves very fascinating questions for an intelligent person.

Because before you have done with the business of the modern employee, you must, if you are an intelligent person, have taken a view of the whole vast process of social reorganization that began with the development of factory labor and big towns, and which is even now scarcely advanced enough for us to see its general trend. For a time Mr. Brumley did not realize the magnitude of the thing he was looking at; when he did, theories sprouted in his mind like mushrooms and he babbled with mental excitement. He came in a state of the utmost lucidity to explain his theories to Lady Harman, and they struck that lady at the time as being the most illuminating suggestions she had ever encountered. They threw an appearance of order, of process, over a world of trade and employment and competition that had hitherto seemed too complex and mysterious for any understanding.

"You see," said Mr. Brumley—they had met that day in Kensington Gardens and they were sitting side by side upon green chairs near the frozen writings of Physical Energy—"You see, if I may lecture a little, putting the thing as simply as possible, the world has been filling up new spaces ever since the discovery of America; all the period from then to about 1870, let us say, was a period of rapid increase of population in response to new opportunities of living and new fulnesses of life in every direction. During that time, four hundred years of it roughly, there was a huge development of family life; to marry and rear a quite considerable family became the chief business of everybody, celibacy grew rare, monasteries and nunneries which had abounded vanished like things dissolving in a flood and even the priests became Protestant against celibacy and took unto themselves wives and had huge families. The natural checks upon increase, famine and pestilence, were lifted by more systematized communication and by scientific discovery; and altogether and as a consequence the world now has probably three or four times the human population it ever carried before. Everywhere in that period the family prevailed again, the prospering multiplying household; it was a return to the family, to the reproductive social grouping of early barbaric life, and naturally all the thought of the modern world which has emerged since the fifteenth century falls into this form. So I see it, Lady Harman. The generation of our grandfathers in the opening nineteenth century had two shaping ideas, two forms of thought, the family and progress, not realizing that that very progress which had suddenly reopened the doors of opportunity for the family that had revived the ancient injunction to increase and multiply and replenish the earth, might presently close that door again and declare the world was filled. But that is what is happening now. The doors close. That immense swarming

and multiplying of little people is over, and the forces of social organization
have been coming into play now, more and more for a century and a half, to
produce new wholesale ways of doing things, new great organizations, organizations
that invade the autonomous family more and more, and are perhaps destined
ultimately to destroy it altogether and supersede it. At least it is so I make my
reading of history in these matters."

"Yes," said Lady Harman, with knitted brows, "Yes," and wondered privately
whether it would be possible to get from that opening to the matter of her Hostels
before it was time for her to return for Sir Isaac's tea.

Mr. Brumley continued to talk with his eyes fixed as it were upon his thoughts.
"These things, Lady Harman, go on at different paces in different regions. I
will not trouble you with a discussion of that, or of emigration, of any of the
details of the vast proliferation that preceded the present phase. Suffice it, that
now all the tendency is back towards restraints upon increase, to an increasing
celibacy, to a fall in the birth rate and in the average size of families, to—to a
release of women from an entire devotion to a numerous offspring, and so at
last to the supersession of those little family units that for four centuries have
made up the substance of social life and determined nearly all our moral and
sentimental attitudes. The autonomy of the family is being steadily destroyed,
and it is being replaced by the autonomy of the individual in relation to some
syndicated economic effort."

"I think," said Lady Harman slowly, arresting him by a gesture, "if you
could make that about autonomy a little clearer. . . ."

Mr. Brumley did. He went on to point out with the lucidity of a University
Extension lecturer what he meant by these singular phrases. She listened intelligently
but with effort. He was much too intent upon getting the thing expressed to his
own satisfaction to notice any absurdity in his preoccupation with these theories
about the population of the world in the face of her immediate practical difficulties.
He declared that the onset of this new phase in human life, the modern phase,
wherein there was apparently to be no more "proliferating," but instead a settling
down of population towards a stable equilibrium, became apparent first with the
expropriation of the English peasantry and the birth of the factory system and
machine production. "Since that time one can trace a steady substitution of
wholesale and collective methods for household and family methods. It has gone
far with us now. Instead of the woman drawing water from a well, the pipes
and taps of the water company. Instead of the home-made rushlight, the electric
lamp. Instead of home-spun, ready-made clothes. Instead of home-brewed, the
brewer's cask. Instead of home-baked, first the little baker and then, clean and
punctual, the International Bread and Cake Stores. Instead of the child learning
at its mother's knee, the compulsory elementary school. Flats take the place of
separate houses. Instead of the little holding, the big farm, and instead of the
children working at home, the factory. Everywhere synthesis. Everywhere the
little independent proprietor gives place to the company and the company to the
trust. You follow all this, Lady Harman?"

"Go on," she said, encouraged by that transitory glimpse of the Stores in his
discourse.

"Now London—and England generally—had its period of expansion and got
on to the beginnings at least of this period of synthesis that is following it,
sooner than any other country in the world; and because it was the first to reach
the new stage it developed the characteristics of the new stage with a stronger
flavor of the old than did such later growths of civilization as New York or
Bombay or Berlin. That is why London and our British big cities generally are

congestions of little houses, little homes, while the newer great cities run to apartments and flats. We hadn't grasped the logical consequences of what we were in for so completely as the people abroad did who caught it later, and that is why, as we began to develop our new floating population of mainly celibate employees and childless people, they had mostly to go into lodgings, they went into the homes that were intended for families as accessories to the family, and they were able to go in because the families were no longer so numerous as they used to be. London is still largely a city of landladies and lodgings, and in no other part of the world is there so big a population of lodgers. And this business of your Hostels is nothing more nor less than the beginning of the end of that. Just as the great refreshment caterers have mopped up the ancient multitude of coffee-houses and squalid little special feeding arrangements of the days of Tittlebat Titmouse and Dick Swiveller, so now your Hostels are going to mop up the lodging-house system of London. Of course there are other and kindred movements. Naturally. The Y.W.C.A., the Y.M.C.A., the London Girls Club Union and so forth are all doing kindred work.''

''But what, Mr. Brumley, what is to become of the landladies?'' asked Lady Harman.

Mr. Brumley was checked in mid theory.

''I hadn't thought of the landladies,'' he said, after a short pause.

''They worry me,'' said Lady Harman.

''Um,'' said Mr. Brumley, thrown out.

''Do you know the other day I went into Chelsea, where there are whole streets of lodgings, and—I suppose it was wrong of me, but I went and pretended to be looking for rooms for a girl clerk I knew, and I saw—Oh!no end of rooms. And such poor old women, such dingy, worked-out, broken old women, with a kind of fearful sharpness, so eager, so dreadfully eager to get that girl clerk who didn't exist. . . .''

She looked at him with an expression of pained enquiry.

''That,'' said Mr. Brumley, ''that I think is a question, so to speak, for the social ambulance. If perhaps I might go on— That particular difficulty we might consider later. I think I was talking of the general synthesis.''

''Yes,'' said Lady Harman. ''And what is it exactly that is to take the place of these isolated little homes and these dreary little lodgings? Here are we, my husband and I, rushing in with this new thing, just as he rushed in with his stores thirty years ago and overset little bakers and confectioners and refreshment dealers by the hundred. Some of them—poor dears—they— I don't like to think. And it wasn't a good thing he made after all,—only a hard sort of thing. He made all those shops of his—with the girls who strike and say they are sweated and driven. . . . And now here we are making a kind of barrack place for people to live in!''

She expressed the rest of her ideas with a gesture of the hands.

''I admit the process has its dangers,'' said Mr. Brumley. ''It's like the supersession of the small holdings by the *latifundia* in Italy. But that's just where our great opportunity comes in. These synthetic phases have occurred before in the world's history and their history is a history of lost opportunities. . . . But need ours be?''

She had a feeling as though something had slipped through her fingers.

''I feel,'' she said, ''that it is more important to me than anything else in life, that these Hostels, anyhow, which are springing so rapidly from a chance suggestion of mine, shouldn't be lost opportunities.''

"Exactly," said Mr. Brumley, with the gesture of one who recovers a thread. "That is just what I am driving at."

The fingers of his extended hand felt in the warm afternoon air for a moment, and then he said "Ah!" in a tone of recovery while she waited respectfully for the resumed thread.

"You see," he said, "I regard this process of synthesis, this substitution of wholesale and collective methods for homely and individual ones as, under existing conditions, inevitable—inevitable. It's the phase we live in, it's to this we have to adapt ourselves. It is as little under your control or mine as the movement of the sun through the zodiac. Practically, that is. And what we have to do is not, I think, to sigh for lost homes and the age of gold and spade husbandry, and pigs and hens in the home, and so on, but to make this new synthetic life tolerable for the mass of men and women, hopeful for the mass of men and women, a thing developing and ascending. That's where your Hostels come in, Lady Harman; that's where they're so important. They're a pioneer movement. If they succeed—and things in Sir Isaac's hands have a way of succeeding at any rate to the paying point—then there'll be a headlong rush of imitations, imitating your good features, imitating your bad features, deepening a groove. . . . You see my point?"

"Yes," she said. "It makes me—more afraid than ever."

"But hopeful," said Mr. Brumley, presuming to lay his hand for an instant on her arm. "It's big enough to be inspiring."

"But I'm afraid," she said.

"It's laying down the lines of a new social life—no less. And what makes it so strange, so typical, too, of the way social forces work nowadays, is that your husband, who has all the instinctive insistence upon every right and restriction of the family relation in his private life, who is narrowly, passionately *for* the home in his own case, who hates all books and discussion that seem to touch it, should in his business activities be striking this tremendous new blow at the ancient organization. For that, you see, is what it amounts to."

"Yes," said Lady Harman slowly. "Yes. Of course, he doesn't know. . . ."

Mr. Brumley was silent for a little while. "You see," he resumed, "at the worst this new social life may become a sort of slavery in barracks; at the best—it might become something very wonderful. My mind's been busy now for days thinking just how wonderful the new life might be. Instead of the old bickering, crowded family home, a new home of comrades. . . ."

He made another pause, and his thoughts ran off upon a fresh track.

"In looking up all these things I came upon a queer little literature of pamphlets and so forth, dealing with the case of the shop assistants. They have a great grievance in what they call the living-in system. The employers herd them in dormitories over the shops, and usually feed them by gaslight in the basements; they fine them and keep an almost intolerable grip upon them; make them go to bed at half-past ten, make them go to church on Sundays,—all sorts of petty tyrannies. The assistants are passionately against this, but they've got no power to strike. Where could they go if they struck? Into the street. Only people who live out and have homes of their own to sulk in *can* strike. Naturally, therefore, as a preliminary to any other improvement in the shop assistant's life, these young people want to live out. Practically that's an impossible demand at present, because they couldn't get lodgings and live out with any decency at all on what it costs their employers to lodge and feed them *in*. Well, here you see a curious possibility for your Hostels. You open the prospect of a living-out system for shop assistants. But just in the degree in which you choose to interfere with them, regulate them, bully and deal with them wholesale through their employers, do you make the new living-out method approximate to the living-in. *That's* a curious side development, isn't it?''

Lady Harman appreciated that.

''That's only the beginning of the business. There's something more these Hostels might touch. . .''

Mr. Brumley gathered himself together for the new aspect. ''There's marriage,'' he said.

''One of the most interesting and unsatisfactory aspects of the life of the employee today—and you know the employee is now in the majority in the adult population—is this. You see, we hold them celibate. We hold them celibate for a longer and longer period; the average age at marriage rises steadily; and so long as they remain celibate we are prepared with some sort of ideas about the future development of their social life, clubs, hostels, living-in, and so forth. But at present we haven't any ideas at all about the adaptation of the natural pairing instinct to the new state of affairs. Ultimately the employee marries; they hold out as long as they possibly can, but ultimately they have to. They have to, even in the face of an economic system that holds out no prospects of anything but insecurity and an increasing chance of trouble and disaster to the employee's family group. What happens is that they drop back into a distressful, crippled, insecure imitation of the old family life as one had it in what I might call the multiplying periods of history. They start a home,—they dream of a cottage, but they drift to a lodging, and usually it isn't the best sort of lodging, for landladies hate wives and the other lodgers detest babies. Often the young couple doesn't have babies. You see, they are more intelligent than peasants, and intelligence and fecundity vary reciprocally,'' said Mr. Brumley.

''You mean?'' interrupted Lady Harman softly.

''There is a world-wide fall in the birthrate. People don't have the families they did.''

''Yes,'' said Lady Harman. ''I understand now.''

''And the more prosperous or the more sanguine take these suburban little houses, these hutches that make such places as Hendon nightmares of monotony, or go into ridiculous jerry-built sham cottages in some Garden Suburb, where each young wife does her own housework and pretends to like it. They have a sort of happiness for a time, I suppose; the woman stops all outside work, the man, very much handicapped, goes on competing against single men. Then— nothing more happens. Except difficulties. The world goes dull and gray for them. They look about for a lodger, perhaps. Have you read Gissing's *Paying Guest?* . . .''

''I suppose,'' said Lady Harman, ''I suppose it is like that. One tries not to think it is so.''

''One needn't let oneself believe that dullness is unhappiness,'' said Mr. Brumley. ''I don't want to paint things sadder than they are. But it's not a fine life, it's not a full life, that life in a Neo-Malthusian suburban hutch.''

''Neo—?'' asked Lady Harman.

''A mere phrase,'' said Mr. Brumley hastily. ''The extraordinary thing is that, until you set me looking into these things with your questions, I've always taken this sort of thing for granted, as though it couldn't be otherwise. Now I seem to see with a kind of freshness. I'm astounded at the muddle of it, the waste and aimlessness of it. And here again it is, Lady Harman, that I think your opportunity comes in. With these Hostels as they might be projected now, you seem to have the possibility of a modernized, more collective and civilized family life than the old close congestion of the single home, and I see no reason at all why you shouldn't carry that collective life on to the married stage. As things are now these little communities don't go beyond the pairing—and out they drift to find the homestead they will never possess. What has been borne in upon me more and more forcibly as I have gone through your—your nest of problems, is the idea that the new social—association, that has so extensively replaced the old family group, might be carried on right through life, that it might work in with all sorts of other discontents and bad adjustments. . . . The life of the women in these little childless or one-or-two-child homes is more unsatisfactory even than the man's.''

Mr. Brumley's face flushed with enthusiasm and he wagged a finger to emphasize his words. ''Why not make Hostels, Lady Harman, for married couples? Why not try that experiment so many people have talked about of the conjoint kitchen and refectory, the conjoint nursery, the collective social life, so that the children who are single children or at best children in small families of two or three, may have the advantages of playfellows, and the young mothers still, if they choose, continue to have a social existence and go on with their professional or business, work? That's the next step your Hostels might take . . . Incidentally you see this opens a way to a life of relative freedom for the woman who is married. . . . I don't know if you have read Mrs. Stetson. Yes, Charlotte Perkins Gilman Stetson. . . . Yes, *Woman and Economics,* that's the book.

''I know,'' Mr. Brumley went on, ''I seem to be opening out your project like a concertina, but I want you to see just how my thoughts have been going about all this. I want you to realize I haven't been idle during these last few weeks. I know it's a far cry from what the Hostels are to all these ideas of what they might begin to be, I know the difficulties in your way—all sorts of difficulties. But when I think just how you stand at the very center of the molding forces in these changes. . . .''

He dropped into an eloquent silence.

Lady Harman looked thoughtfully at the sunlight under the trees.

''You think,'' she said, ''that it comes to as much as all this.''

''More,'' said Mr. Brumley.

''I was frightened before. *Now*— You make me feel as though someone had put the wheel of a motor car in my hand, started it and told me to steer. . . .''

7

Lady Harman went home from that talk in a taxi, and on the way she passed the building operations in Kensington Road. A few weeks ago it had been a mere dusty field of operation for the house-wreckers; now its walls were already rising to the second story. She realized how swiftly nowadays the search for wisdom can be outstripped by reinforced concrete.

8

It was only by slow degrees and rather in the absence of a more commanding interest than through any invincible quality in their appeal to her mind that these Hostels became in the next three years the grave occupation of Lady Harman's thoughts and energies. She yielded to them reluctantly. For a long time she wanted to look over them and past them and discover something—she did not know what—something high and domineering to which it would be easy to give herself. It was difficult to give herself to the Hostels. In that Mr. Brumley, actuated by a mixture of more or less admirable motives, did his best to assist her. These Hostels alone he thought could give them something upon which they could meet, give them a common interest and him a method of service and companionship. It threw the qualities of duty and justification over their more or less furtive meetings, their little expeditions together, their quiet frequent association.

Together they made studies of the Girls' Clubs which are scattered about London, supplementary homes that have in such places as Walworth and Soho worked small miracles of civilization. These institutions appealed to a lower social level than the one their Hostels were to touch, but they had been organized by capable and understanding minds and Lady Harman found in one or two of their evening dances and in the lunch she shared one morning with a row of cheerful young factory girls from Soho just that quality of concrete realization for which her mind hungered. Then Mr. Brumley took her once or twice for evening walks, just when the stream of workers is going home; he battled his way with her along the footpath of Charing Cross Railway Bridge from the Waterloo side, they swam in the mild evening sunshine of September against a trampling torrent of bobbing heads, and afterwards they had tea together in one of the International Stores near the Strand, where Mr. Brumley made an unsuccessful attempt to draw out the waitress on the subject of Babs Wheeler and the recent strike. The young woman might have talked freely to a man alone or freely to Lady Harman alone but the combination of the two made her shy. The bridge experience led to several other expeditions, to see home-going on the tube, at the big railway termini, on the train—and once they followed up the process to Streatham and saw how the people pour out of the train at last and scatter—until at last they are just isolated individuals running up steps, diving into basements. And then it occurred to Mr. Brumley that he knew someone who would take them over "Gerrard," that huge telephone exchange, and there Lady Harman saw how the National Telephone Company, as it was in those days, had a care for its staff, the pleasant club rooms, the rest room, and stood in that queer rendezvous of messages, where the "Hello" girl sits all day, wearing a strange metallic apparatus over ear and mouth, watching small lights that wink significantly at her and perpetually pulling out and slipping in and releasing little flexible strings that seem to have a resilient volition of their own. They hunted out Mrs. Barnet and heard her ideas about conjoint homes for spinsters in the Garden Suburb. And then they went over a Training College for elementary teachers and visited the Post Office and then came back to more unobtrusive contemplation, from the customer's little table, of the ministering personalities of the International Stores.

There were times when all these things seen, seemed to fall into an entirely explicable system under Mr. Brumley's exposition, when they seemed to be giving and most generously giving the clearest indications of what kind of thing the Hostels had to be, and times when this all vanished again and her mind became confused and perplexed. She tried to express just what it was she missed to Mr. Brumley. "One doesn't," she said, "see all of them and what one sees isn't what we have to do with. I mean we see them dressed up and respectable and busy and then they go home and the door shuts. It's the home that we are going to alter and replace—and what is it like?" Mr. Brumley took her for walks in Highbury and the newer parts of Hendon and over to Clapham. "I want to go inside those doors," she said.

"That's just what they won't let you do," said Mr. Brumley. "Nobody visits but relations—and prospective relations, and the only other social intercourse is over the garden wall. Perhaps I can find books—"

He got her novels by Edwin Pugh and Pett Ridge and Frank Swinnerton and George Gissing. They didn't seem to be attractive homes. And it seemed remarkable to her that no woman had ever given the woman's view of the small London home from the inside. . . .

She overcame her own finer scruples and invaded the Burnet household. Apart from fresh aspects of Susan's character in the capacity of a hostess she gained little light from that. She had never felt so completely outside a home in her life as she did when she was in the Burnets' parlor. The very tablecloth on which the tea was spread had an air of being new and protective of familiar things; the tea was manifestly quite unlike their customary tea, it was no more intimate than the confectioner's shop window from which it mostly came; the whole room was full of the muffled cries of things hastily covered up and specially put away. Vivid oblongs on the faded wallpaper betrayed even a rearrangement of the pictures. Susan's mother was a little dingy woman, wearing a very smart new cap to the best of her ability; she had an air of having been severely shaken up and admonished, and her general bearing confessed only too plainly how shattered those preparations had left her. She watched her capable daughter for cues. Susan's sisters displayed a disposition to keep their backs against something and at the earliest opportunity to get into the passage and leave Susan and her tremendous visitor alone but within earshot. They started convulsively when they were addressed and insisted on "your ladyship." Susan had told them not to but they would. When they supposed themselves to be unobserved they gave themselves up to the impassioned inspection of Lady Harman's costume. Luke had fled into the street, and in spite of various messages conveyed to him by the youngest sister he refused to enter until Lady Harman had gone again and was well out of the way. And Susan was no longer garrulous and at her ease; she had no pins in her mouth and that perhaps hampered her speech; she presided flushed and bright-eyed in a state of infectious nervous tension. Her politeness was awful. Never in all her life had Lady Harman felt her own lack of real conversational power so acutely. She couldn't think of a thing that mightn't be construed as an impertinence and that didn't remind her of district visiting. Yet perhaps she succeeded better than she supposed.

"What a family you have had!" she said to Mrs. Burnet. "I have four little girls, and I find them as much as we can manage."

"You're young yet, my ladyship," said Mrs. Burnet, "and they aren't always the blessings they seem to be. It's the rearing's the difficulty."

"They're all such healthy-looking—people."

"I wish we could get hold of Luke, my ladyship, and show you 'im. He's that sturdy. And yet when 'e was a little feller—"

She was launched for a time on those details that were always so dear to the mothers of the past order of things. Her little spate of reminiscences was the only interlude of naturalness in an afternoon of painfully constrained behavior. . . .

Lady Harman returned a trifle shamefacedly from this abortive dip into realities to Mr. Brumley's speculative assurance.

9

While Lady Harman was slowly accustoming her mind to this idea that the development of those Hostels was her appointed career in life, so far as a wife may have a career outside her connubial duties, and while she was getting insensibly to believe in Mr. Brumley's theory of their exemplary social importance, the Hostels themselves with a haste that she felt constantly was premature, were achieving a concrete existence. They were developing upon lines that here and there disregarded Mr. Brumley's ideas very widely; they gained in practicality what perhaps they lost in social value, through the entirely indirect relations between Mr. Brumley on the one hand and Sir Isaac on the other. For Sir Isaac manifestly did not consider and would have been altogether indisposed to consider Mr. Brumley as entitled to plan or suggest anything of the slightest importance in this affair, and whatever of Mr. Brumley reached that gentleman reached him in a very carefully transmitted form as Lady Harman's own unaided idea. Sir Isaac had sound Victorian ideas about the place of literature in life. If anyone had suggested to him that literature could supply ideas to practical men he would have had a choking fit, and he regarded Mr. Brumley's sedulous attentions to these hostel schemes with feelings, the kindlier elements of whose admixture was a belief that ultimately he would write some elegant and respectful approval of the established undertaking.

The entire admixture of Sir Isaac's feelings towards Mr. Brumley was by no means kindly. He disliked any man to come near Lady Harman, any man at all; he had a faint uneasiness even about waiters and hotel porters and the clergy. Of course he had agreed she should have friends of her own and he couldn't very well rescind that without something definite to go upon. But still this persistent follower kept him uneasy. He kept this uneasiness within bounds by reassuring himself upon the point of Lady Harman's virtuous obedience, and so reassured he was able to temper his distrust with a certain contempt. The man was in love with his wife; that was manifest enough, and dangled after her. . . . Let him dangle. What after all did he get for it? . . .

But occasionally he broke through this complacency, betrayed a fitful ingenious jealousy, interfered so that she missed appointments and had to break engagements. He was now more and more a being of pathological moods. The subtle changes of secretion that were hardening his arteries, tightening his breath and poisoning his blood, reflected themselves upon his spirit in an uncertainty of temper and exasperating fatigues and led to startling outbreaks. Then for a time he would readjust himself, become in his manner reasonable again, become accessible.

He was the medium through which this vision that was growing up in her mind of a reorganized social life, had to translate itself, as much as it could ever translate itself, into reality. He called these hostels her hostels, made her the approver of all he did, but he kept every particle of control in his own hands. All her ideas and desires had to be realized by him. And his attitudes varied with his moods; sometimes he was keenly interested in the work of organization and then he terrified her by his bias towards acute economies, sometimes he was resentful at the burden of the whole thing, sometimes he seemed to scent Brumley or at least some moral influence behind her mind and met her suggestions with a bitter resentment as though any suggestion must needs be a disloyalty to him. There was a remarkable outbreak upon her first tentative proposal that the hostel system might ultimately be extended to married couples.

He heard her with his lips pressing tighter and tighter together until they were yellow white and creased with a hundred wicked little horizontal creases. Then he interrupted her with silent gesticulations. Then words came.

"I never did, Elly," he said. "I never did. Reely—there are times when you ain't rational. Married couples who're assistants in shops and places!"

For a little while he sought some adequate expression of his point of view.

"Nice thing to go keeping a place for these chaps to have their cheap bits of skirt in," he said at last.

Then further: "If a man wants a girl let him work himself up until he can keep her. Married couples indeed!"

He began to expand the possibilities of the case with a quite unusual vividness. "Double beds in each cubicle, I suppose," he said, and played for a time about this fancy. . . . "Well, to hear such an idea from you of all people, Elly. I never did."

He couldn't leave it alone. He had to go on to the bitter end with the vision she had evoked in his mind. He was jealous, passionately jealous, it was only too manifest, of the possible happinesses of these young people. He was possessed by that instinctive hatred for the realized love of others which lies at the base of so much of our moral legislation. The bare thought—whole corridors of bridal chambers!—made his face white and his hand quiver. *His* young men and young women! The fires of a hundred Vigilance Committees blazed suddenly in his reddened eyes. He might have been a concentrated society for preventing the rapid multiplication of the unfit. The idea of facilitating early marriages was manifestly shameful to him, a disgraceful service to render, a job for Pandarus. What was she thinking of? Elly of all people! Elly who had been as innocent as driven snow before Georgina came interfering!

It ended in a fit of abuse and a panting seizure, and for a day or so he was too ill to resume the discussion, to do more than indicate a disgusted aloofness. . . .

And then it may be the obscure chemicals at work within him changed their phase of reaction. At any rate he mended, became gentler, was more loving to his wife than he had been for some time and astonished her by saying that if she wanted Hostels for married couples, it wasn't perhaps so entirely unreasonable. Selected cases, he stipulated, it would have to be and above a certain age limit, sober people. "It might even be a check on immorality," he said, "properly managed. . . ."

But that was as far as his acquiescence went and Lady Harman was destined to be a widow before she saw the foundation of any Hostel for young married couples in London.

10

The reinforced concrete rose steadily amidst Lady Harman's questionings and Mr. Brumley's speculations. The Harmans returned from a recuperative visit to Kissingen, to which Sir Isaac had gone because of a suspicion that his Marienbad specialist had failed to cure him completely in order to get him back again, to find the first of the five hostels nearly ripe for its opening. There had to be a manageress and a staff organized and neither Lady Harman nor Mr. Brumley were prepared for that sort of business. A number of abler people however had become aware of the opportunities of the new development and Mrs. Hubert Plessington, that busy publicist, got the Harmans to a helpful little dinner, before Lady Harman had the slightest suspicion of the needs that were now so urgent. There shone a neat compact widow, a Mrs. Pembrose, who had buried her husband some eighteen months ago after studying social questions with him with great éclat for ten happy years, and she had done settlement work and Girls' Club work and had perhaps more power of organization—given a suitable director to provide for her lack of creativeness, Mrs. Plessington told Sir Isaac, than any other woman in London. Afterwards Sir Isaac had an opportunity of talking to her; he discussed the suffrage movement with her and was pleased to find her views remarkably sympathetic with his own. She was, he declared, a sensible woman, anxious to hear a man out and capable, it was evident, of a detachment from feminist particularism rare in her sex at the present time. Lady Harman had seen less of the lady that evening, she was chiefly struck by her pallor, by a kind of animated silence about her, and by the deep impression her capabilities had made on Mr. Plessington, who had hitherto seemed to her to be altogether too over-worked in admiring his wife to perceive the points of any other human being. Afterwards Lady Harman was surprised to hear from one or two quite separate people that Mrs. Pembrose was the only possible person to act as general director of the new hostels. Lady Beach-Mandarin was so enthusiastic in the matter that she made a special call. "You've known her a long time?" said Lady Harman.

"Long enough to see what a chance she is!" said Lady Beach-Mandarin.

Lady Harman perceived equivocation. "Now how long is that really?" she said.

"Count not in years, nor yet in moments on a dial," said Lady Beach-Mandarin with a fine air of quotation. "I'm thinking of her quiet strength of character. Mrs. Plessington brought her round to see me the other afternoon."

"Did she talk to you?"

"I saw, my dear, I saw."

A vague aversion from Mrs. Pembrose was in some mysterious way strengthened in Lady Harman by this extraordinary convergence of testimony. When Sir Isaac mentioned the lady with a kind of forced casualness at breakfast as the only conceivable person for the work of initiation and organization that lay before them, Lady Harman determined to see more of her. With a quickened subtlety she asked her to tea. "I have heard so much of your knowledge of social questions and I want you to advise me about my work," she wrote, and then scribbled a note to Mr. Brumley to call and help her judgments.

Mrs. Pembrose appeared dressed in dove color with a near bonnetesque straw hat to match. She had a pale slightly freckled complexion, little hard blue-gray eyes with that sort of nose which redeems a squarish shape by a certain delicacy of structure; her chin was long and protruding and her voice had a wooden resonance and a ghost of a lisp. Her talk had a false consecutiveness due to the frequent use of the word "Yes." Her bearing was erect and her manner guardedly alert.

From the first she betrayed a conviction that Mr. Brumley was incidental and unnecessary and that her real interest lay with Sir Isaac. She might almost have been in possession of special information upon that point.

"Yes," she said, "I'm rather specially *up* in this sort of question. I worked side by side with my poor Frederick all his life, we were collaborators, and this question of the urban distributive employee was one of his special studies. Yes, he would have been tremendously interested in Sir Isaac's project."

"You know what we are doing?"

"Everyone is interested in Sir Isaac's enterprise. Naturally. Yes, I think I have a fairly good idea of what you mean to do. It's a great experiment."

"You think it is likely to answer?" said Mr. Brumley.

"In Sir Isaac's hands it is *very* likely to answer," said Mrs. Pembrose with her eye steadily on Lady Harman.

There was a little pause. "Yes, now you wrote of difficulties and drawing upon my experience. Of course just now I'm quite at Sir Isaac's disposal."

Lady Harman found herself thrust perforce into the rôle of her husband's spokeswoman. She asked Mrs. Pembrose if she knew the exact nature of the experiment they contemplated.

Mrs. Pembrose hadn't a doubt she knew. Of course for a long time and more especially in the Metropolis where the distances were so great and increasing so rapidly, there had been a gathering feeling not only in the catering trade, but in very many factory industries, against the daily journey to employment and home again. It was irksome and wasteful to everyone concerned, there was a geat loss in control, later hours of beginning, uncertain service. "Yes, my husband calculated the hours lost in London every week, hours that are neither work nor play, mere tiresome stuffy journeying. It made an enormous sum. It worked out at hundreds of working lives per week." Sir Isaac's project was to abolish all that, to bring his staff into line with the drapers and grocers who kept their assistants on the living-in system. . . .

"I thought people objected to the living-in system," said Mr. Brumley.

"There's an agitation against it on the part of a small Trade Union of Shop Assistants," said Mrs. Pembrose. "But they have no real alternative to propose."

"And this isn't Living In," said Mr. Brumley.

"Yes, I think you'll find it is," said Mrs. Pembrose with a nice little expert smile.

"Living-in isn't *quite* what we want," said Lady Harman slowly and with knitted brows, seeking a method of saying just what the difference was to be.

"Yes, not perhaps in the strictest sense," said Mrs. Pembrose giving her no chance, and went on to make fine distinctions. Strictly speaking, living-in meant sleeping over the shop and eating underneath it, and this hostel idea was an affair of a separate house and of occupants who would be assistants from a number of shops. "Yes, collectivism, if you like," said Mrs. Pembrose. But the word collectivism, she assured them, wouldn't frighten her, she was a collectivist, a socialist, as her husband had always been. The day was past when socialist could be used as a term of reproach. "Yes, instead of the individual employer of labor, we already begin to have the collective employer of labor, with a labor bureau—and so on. We share them. We no longer compete for them. It's the keynote of the time."

Mr. Brumley followed this with a lifted eyebrow. He was still new to these modern developments of collectivist ideas, this socialism of the employer.

The whole thing Mrs. Pembrose declared was a step forward in civilization, it was a step in the organization and discipline of labor. Of course the unruly and the insubordinate would cry out. But the benefits were plain enough, space, light, baths, association, reasonable recreations, opportunities for improvement—

"But freedom?" said Mr. Brumley.

Mrs. Pembrose inclined her head a little on one side, looked at him this time and smiled the expert smile again. "If you knew as much as I do of the difficulties of social work," she said, "you wouldn't be very much in love with freedom."

"But—it's the very substance of the soul!"

"You must permit me to differ," said Mrs. Pembrose, and for weeks afterwards Mr. Brumley was still seeking a proper polite retort to that difficult counterstroke. It was such a featureless reply. It was like having your nose punched suddenly by a man without a face.

They descended to a more particular treatment of the problems ahead. Mrs. Pembrose quoted certain precedents from the Girls' Club Union.

"The people Lady Harman contemplates—entertaining," said Mr. Brumley, "are of a slightly more self-respecting type than those young women."

"It's largely veneer," said Mrs. Pembrose. . . .

"Detestable little wretch," said Mr. Brumley when at last she had departed. He was very uncomfortable. "She's just the quintessence of all one fears and dreads about these new developments, she's perfect—in that way—self-confident, arrogant, instinctively aggressive, with a tremendous class contempt. There's a multitude of such people about who hate the employed classes, who *want* to see them broken in and subjugated. I suppose that kind of thing is in humanity. Every boys' school has louts of that kind, who love to torment fags for their own good, who spring upon a chance smut on the face of a little boy to scrub him painfully, who have a kind of lust to dominate under the pretence of improving. I remember— But never mind that now. Keep that woman out of things or your hostels work for the devil.''

"Yes," said Lady Harman. "Certainly she shall not—. No."

But there she reckoned without her husband.

"I've settled it," he said to her at dinner two nights later.

"What?"

"Mrs. Pembrose."

"You've not made her—?"

"Yes, I have. And I think we're very lucky to get her."

"But—Isaac! I don't want her!"

"You should have told me that before, Elly. I've made an agreement."

She suddenly wanted to cry. "But— You said I should manage these Hostels myself."

"So you shall, Elly. But we must have somebody. When we go abroad and all that and for all the sort of business stuff and looking after things that you can't do. We've *got* to have her. She's the only thing going of her sort."

"But—I don't like her."

"Well," cried Sir Isaac, "why in goodness couldn't you tell me that before, Elly? I've been and engaged her."

She sat pale-faced staring at him with wide open eyes in which tears of acute disappointment were shining. She did not dare another word because of her trick of weeping.

"It's all right, Elly," said Sir Isaac. "How touchy you are! Anything you want about these Hostels of yours, you've only got to tell me and it's done."

11

Lady Harman was still in a state of amazement at the altered prospects of her hostels when the day arrived for the formal opening of the first of these in Bloomsbury. They made a little public ceremony of it in spite of her reluctance, and Mr. Brumley had to witness things from out of the general crowd and realize just how completely he wasn't in it, in spite of all his efforts. Mrs. Pembrose was modestly conspicuous, like the unexpected in all human schemes. There were several reporters present, and Horatio Blenker who was going to make a loyal leader about it, to be followed by one or two special articles for the *Old Country Gazette*.

Horatio had procured Mrs. Blapton for the opening after some ineffectual angling for the Princess Adeline, and the thing was done at half-past three in the afternoon. In the bright early July sunshine outside the new building there was a crimson carpet down on the pavement and an awning above it, there was a great display of dog-daisies at the windows and on the steps leading up to the locked portals, an increasing number of invited people lurked shyly in the ground-floor rooms ready to come out by the back way and cluster expectantly when Mrs. Blapton arrived, Graper the staff manager and two assistants in dazzling silk hats seemed everywhere, the rabbit-like architect had tried to look doggish in a huge black silk tie and only looked more like a rabbit than ever, and there was a steady driftage of small boys and girls, nurses with perambulators, cab touts, airing grandfathers and similar unemployed people towards the promise of the awning, the carpet and the flowers. The square building in all its bravery of Doulton ware and yellow and mauve tiles and its great gilt inscription

INTERNATIONAL HOSTELS

above the windows of the second story seemed typical of all those modern forces that are now invading and dispelling the ancient residential peace of Bloomsbury.

Mrs. Blapton appeared only five minutes late, escorted by Bertie Trevor and her husband's spare secretary. Graper became so active at the sight of her that he seemed more like some beast out of the Apocalypse with seven hands and ten hats than a normal human being; he marshalled the significant figures into their places, the door was unlocked without serious difficulty, and Lady Harman found herself in the main corridor beside Mr. Trevor and a little behind Mrs. Blapton, engaged in being shown over the new creation. Sir Isaac (driven by Graper at his elbow) was in immediate attendance on the great political lady, and Mrs. Pembrose, already with an air of proprietorship, explained glibly on her other hand. Close behind Lady Harman came Lady Beach-Mandarin, expanding like an appreciative gas in a fine endeavor to nestle happily into the whole big place, and with her were Mrs. Hubert Plessington and Mr. Pope, one of those odd people who are called publicists because one must call them something, and who take chairs and political sides and are vice-presidents of everything and organize philanthropies, write letters to the papers and cannot let the occasion pass without saying a few words and generally prevent the institutions of this country from falling out of human attention. He was a little abstracted in his manner, every now and then his lips moved as he imagined a fresh turn to some classic platitude; anyone who knew him might have foretold the speech into which he presently broke. He did this in the refectory where there was a convenient step up at the end. Beginning with the customary confession of incontinence, "could not let the occasion pass," he declared that he would not detain them long, but he felt that everyone there would agree with him that they shared that day in no slight occasion, no mean enterprise, that here was one of the most promising, one of the most momentous, nay! he would go further and add with due deference to them all, one of the most pregnant of social experiments in modern social work. In the past he had himself—if he might for a moment allow a personal note to creep into his observations, he himself had not been unconnected with industrial development.— (Querulous voice, "Who the devil is that?" and whispered explanations on the part of Horatio Blenker; "Pope—very good man— East Purblow Experiment—Payment in Kind instead of Wages—Yes."). . . .

Lady Harman ceased to listen to Mr. Pope's strained but not unhappy tenor. She had heard him before, and she had heard his like endlessly. He was the larger moiety of every public meeting she had ever attended. She had ceased even to marvel at the dull self-satisfaction that possessed him. Today her capacity for marvelling was entirely taken up by the details of this extraordinary reality which had sprung from her dream of simple, kindly, beautiful homes for distressed and overworked young women; nothing in the whole of life had been so amazing since that lurid occasion when she had been the agonized vehicle for the entry of Miss Millicent Harman upon this terrestrial scene. It was all so entirely what she could never have thought possible. A few words from other speakers followed, Mrs. Blapton, with the young secretary at hand to prompt, said something, and Sir Isaac was poked forwards to say, "Thank you very much. It's all my wife's doing, really. . . . Oh dash it! Thank you very much.'' It had the effect of being the last vestige of some more elaborate piece of eloquence that had suddenly disintegrated in his mind.

"And now, Elly," he said, as their landaulette took them home, "you're beginning to have your hostels."

"Then they *are* my hostels?" she asked abruptly.

"Didn't I say they were?" The satisfaction of his face was qualified by that fatigued irritability that nowadays always followed any exertion or excitement.

"If I want things done? If I want things altered?"

"Of course you may, of course you may. What's the matter with you, Elly? What's been putting ideers into your head? You got to have a directress to the thing; you must have a woman of education who knows a bit about things to look after the matrons and so on. Very likely she isn't everything you want. She's the only one we could get, and I don't see—. Here I go and work hard for a year and more getting these things together to please you, and then suddenly you don't like 'em. There's a lot of the spoilt child in you, Elly—first and last. There they are. . . ."

They were silent for the rest of the journey to Putney, both being filled with incommunicable things.

12

And now Lady Harman began to share the trouble of all those who let their minds pass out of the circle of their immediate affections with any other desire save interest and pleasure. Assisted in this unhappy development by the sedulous suggestions of Mr. Brumley she had begun to offend against the most sacred law in our sensible British code, she was beginning to take herself and her hostels seriously, and think that it mattered how she worked for them and what they became. She tried to give all the attention her children's upbringing. her husband's ailments and the general demands of her household left free, to this complex, elusive, puzzling and worrying matter. Instead of thinking that these hostels were just old hostels and that you start them and put in a Mrs. Pembrose and feel very benevolent and happy and go away, she had come to realize partly by dint of her own conscientious thinking and partly through Mr. Brumley's strenuous resolve that she should not take Sir Isaac's gift horse without the most exhaustive examination of its quality, that this new work, like most new things in human life, was capable not only of admirable but of altogether detestable consequences, and that it rested with her far more than with any other human being to realize the former and avoid the latter. And directly one has got to this critical pose towards things, just as one ceases to be content with things anyhow and to want them precisely somehow, one begins to realize just how intractable, confused and disingenuous are human affairs. Mr. Brumley had made himself see and had made her see how inevitable these big wholesale ways of doing things, these organizations and close social cooperations, have become unless there is to be a social disintegration and set back, and he had also brought himself and her to realize how easily they may develop into a new servitude, how high and difficult is the way towards methods of association that will ensure freedom and permit people to live fine individual lives. Every step towards organization raises a crop of vices peculiar to itself, fresh developments of the egotism and greed and vanity of those into whose hands there falls control, fresh instances of that hostile pedantry which seems so natural to officials and managers, insurgencies and obstinacies and suspicions on the part of everyone. The poor lady had supposed that when one's intentions were obviously benevolent everyone helped. She only faced the realities of this task that she had not so much set for herself as had happened to her, after dreadful phases of disillusionment and dismay.

"These hostels," said Mr. Brumley in his most prophetic mood, "can be made free, fine things—or no—just as all the world of men we are living in, could be made a free, fine world. And it's our place to see they are that. It's just by being generous and giving ourselves, helping without enslaving, and giving without exacting gratitude, planning and protecting with infinite care, that we bring that world nearer. . . . Since I've known you I've come to know such things are possible. . . ."

The Bloomsbury hostel started upon its career with an embarrassing difficulty. The young women of the International Stores Refreshment Departments for whom these institutions were primarily intended displayed what looked extremely like a concerted indisposition to come in. They had been circularized and informed that henceforth, to ensure the "good social tone" of the staff, all girls not living at home with their parents or close relations would be expected to reside in the new hostels. There followed an attractive account of the advantages of the new establishment. In drawing up this circular with the advice of Mrs. Pembrose, Sir Isaac had overlooked the fact that his management was very imperfectly informed just where the girls did live, and that after its issue it was very improbable that it would be possible to find out this very necessary fact. But the girls seemed to be unaware of this ignorance at headquarters, Miss Babs Wheeler was beginning to feel a little bored by good behavior and crave for those dramatic cessations at the lunch hour, those speeches, with cheers, from a table top, those interviews with reporters, those flushed and eager councils of war and all the rest of that good old crisis feeling that had previously ended so happily. Mr. Graper came to his proprietor headlong, Mrs. Pembrose was summoned and together they contemplated the lamentable possibility of this great social benefit they had done the world being discredited at the outset by a strike of the proposed beneficiaries. Sir Isaac fell into a state of vindictiveness and was with difficulty restrained by Mr. Graper from immediately concluding the negotiations that were pending with three great Oxford Street firms that would have given over the hostels to their employees and closed them against the International girls forever.

Even Mrs. Pembrose couldn't follow Sir Isaac in that, and remarked: "As I understand it, the whole intention was to provide proper housing for our own people first and foremost."

"And haven't we provided it, *damn* them?" said Sir Isaac in white desperation. . . .

It was Lady Harman who steered the newly launched institutions through these first entanglements. It was her first important advantage in the struggle that had hitherto been going relentlessly against her. She now displayed her peculiar gift, a gift that indeed is unhappily all too rare among philanthropists, the gift of not being able to classify the people with whom she was dealing, but of continuing to regard them as a multitude of individualized souls as distinct and considerable as herself. That makes no doubt for slowness and "inefficiency" and complexity in organization, but it does make for understandings. And now, through a little talk with Susan Burnet about her sister's attitude upon the dispute, she was able to take the whole situation in the flank.

Like many people who are not easily clear, Lady Harman when she was clear acted with very considerable decision, which was perhaps none the less effective because of the large softnesses of her manner.

She surprised Sir Isaac by coming of her own accord into his study, where with an altogether novel disfavor he sat contemplating the detailed plans for the Sydenham Hostel. "I think I've found out what the trouble is," she said.

"What trouble?"

"About my hostel."

"How do you know?"

"I've been finding out what the girls are saying."

"They'd say anything."

"I don't think they're clever enough for that," said Lady Harman after consideration. She recovered her thread. "You see, Isaac, they've been frightened by the Rules. I didn't know you had printed a set of Rules."

"One must *have* rules, Elly."

"In the background," she decided. "But you see these Rules—were made conspicuous. They were printed in two colors on wall cards just exactly like that list of rules and scale of fines you had to withdraw—"

"I know," said Sir Isaac, shortly.

"It reminded the girls. And that circular that seems to threaten them if they don't give up their lodgings and come in. And the way the front is got up to look just exactly like one of the refreshment-room branches—it makes them feel it will be unhomelike, and that there will be a kind of repetition in the evening of all the discipline and regulations they have to put up with during the day."

"Have to put up with!" murmured Sir Isaac.

"I wish that had been thought of sooner. If we had made the places look a little more ordinary and called them Osborne House or something a little old-fashioned like that, something with a touch of the Old Queen about it and all that kind of thing."

"We can't go to the expense of taking down all those big gilt letters just to please the fancies of Miss Babs Wheeler."

"It's too late now to do that, perhaps. But we could do something, I think, to remove the suspicions—. . . I want, Isaac— I think—" She pulled herself together to announce her determination. "I think if I were to go to the girls and meet a delegation of them, and just talk to them plainly about what we mean by this hostel."

"*You* can't go making speeches."

"It would just be talking to them."

"It's such a Come Down," said Sir Isaac, after a momentary contemplation of the possibility.

For some time they talked without getting very far from these positions they had assumed. At last Sir Isaac shifted back upon his expert. "Can't we talk about it to Mrs. Pembrose? She knows more about this sort of business than we do."

"I'm not going to talk to Mrs. Pembrose," said Lady Harman, after a little interval. Some unusual quality in her quiet voice made Sir Isaac lift his eyes to her face for a moment.

So one Saturday afternoon, Lady Harman had a meeting with a roomful of recalcitrant girls at the Regent Street Refreshment Branch, which looked very odd to her with gray cotton wrappers over everything and its blinds down, and for the first time she came face to face with the people for whom almost in spite of herself she was working. It was a meeting summoned by the International Branch of the National Union of Waitresses and Miss Babs Wheeler and Mr. Graper were so to speak the north and south poles of the little group upon the improvised platform from which Lady Harman was to talk to the gathering. She would have liked the support of Mr. Brumley, but she couldn't contrive any unostentatious way of bringing him into the business without putting it upon a footing that would have involved the appearance of Sir Isaac and Mrs. Pembrose and—everybody. And essentially it wasn't to be everybody. It was to be a little talk.

Lady Harman rather liked the appearance of Miss Babs Wheeler, and met more than an answering approval in that insubordinate young woman's eye. Miss Wheeler was a minute swaggering person, much akimbo, with a little round blue-eyed innocent face that shone with delight at the lark of living. Her three companions who were in the lobby with her to receive and usher in Lady Harman seemed just as young, but they were relatively unilluminated except by their manifest devotion to their leader. They displayed rather than concealed their opinion of her as a "dear" and a "fair wonder." And the meeting generally it seemed to her was a gathering of very human young women, rather restless, then agog to see her and her clothes, and then somehow allayed by her appearance and quite amiably attentive to what she had to say. A majority were young girls dressed with the cheap smartness of the suburbs, the rest were for the most part older and dingier, and here and there were dotted young ladies of a remarkable and questionable smartness. In the front row, full of shy recognitions and a little disguised by an unfamiliar hat was Susan's sister Alice.

As Lady Harman had made up her mind that she was not going to deliver a speech she felt no diffidence in speaking. She was far too intent on her message to be embarrassed by any thought of the effect she was producing. She talked as she might have talked in one of her easier moods to Mr. Brumley. And as she talked it happened that Miss Babs Wheeler and quite a number of the other girls present watched her face and fell in love with her.

She began with her habitual prelude. "You see," she said, and stopped and began again. She wanted to tell them and with a clumsy simplicity she told them how these Hostels had arisen out of her desire that they should have something better than the uncomfortable lodgings in which they lived. They weren't a business enterprise, but they weren't any sort of charity. "And I wanted them to be the sort of place in which you would feel quite free. I hadn't any sort of intention of having you interfered with. I hate being interfered with myself, and I understand just as well as anyone can that you don't like it either. I wanted these Hostels to be the sort of place that you might perhaps after a time almost manage and run for yourselves. You might have a committee or something. . . . Only you know it isn't always easy to do as one wants. Things don't always go in this world as one wants them to go—particularly if one isn't clever." She lost herself for a moment at that point, and then went on to say she didn't like the new rules. They had been drawn up in a hurry and she had only read them after they were printed. All sorts of things in them—

She seemed to be losing her theme again, and Mr. Graper handed her the offending card, a big varnished wall placard, with eyelets and tape complete. She glanced at it. For example, she said, it wasn't her idea to have fines. (Great and long continued applause.) There was something she had always disliked about fines. (Renewed applause.) But these rules could easily be torn up. And as she said this and as the meeting broke into acquiescence again it occurred to her that there was the card of rules in her hands, and nothing could be simpler than to tear it up there and then. It resisted her for a moment, she compressed her lips and then she had it in halves. This tearing was so satisfactory to her that she tore it again and then again. As she tore it, she had a pleasant irrational feeling that she was tearing Mrs. Pembrose. Mr. Graper's face betrayed his shocked feelings, and the meeting which had become charged with a strong desire to show how entirely it approved of her, made a crowning attempt at applause. They hammered umbrellas on the floor, they clapped hands, they rattled chairs and gave a shrill cheer. A chair was broken.

"I wish," said Lady Harman when that storm had abated, "you'd come and look at the Hostel. Couldn't you come next Saturday afternoon? We could have a stand-up tea and you could see the place and then afterwards your committee and I—and my husband—could make out a real set of rules. . . ."

She went on for some little time longer, she appealed to them with all the strength of her honest purpose to help her to make this possible good thing a real good thing, not to suspect, not to be hard on her—"and my husband"— not to make a difficult thing impossible, it was so easy to do that, and when she finished she was in the happiest possession of her meeting. They came thronging round her with flushed faces and bright eyes, they wanted to come near her, wanted to touch her, wanted to assure her that for her they were quite prepared to live in any kind of place. For her. "You come and talk to us, Lady Harman," said one; "*we'll* show you."

"Nobody hasn't told us, Lady Harman, how these Hostels were *yours*."

"You come and talk to us again, Lady Harman." . . .

They didn't wait for the following Saturday. On Monday morning Mrs. Pembrose received thirty-seven applications to take up rooms.

13

For the next few years it was to be a matter of recurrent heart-searching for Lady Harman whether she had been profoundly wise or extremely foolish in tearing up that card of projected rules. At the time it seemed the most natural and obvious little action imaginable; it was long before she realized just how symbolical and determining a few movements of the hand and wrist can be. It fixed her line not so much for herself as for others. It put her definitely, much more definitely than her convictions warranted, on the side of freedom against discipline. For indeed her convictions like most of our convictions kept along a tortuous watershed between these two. It is only a few rare extravagant spirits who are wholly for the warp or wholly for the woof of human affairs.

The girls applauded and loved her. At one stroke she had acquired the terrible liability of partisans. They made her their champion and sanction; she was responsible for an endless succession of difficulties that flowered out of their interpretations of her act. These Hostels that had seemed passing out of her control, suddenly turned back upon her and took possession of her.

And they were never simple difficulties. Right and wrong refused to unravel for her; each side of every issue seemed to be so often in suicidal competition with its antagonist for the inferior case. If the forces of order and discipline showed themselves perennially harsh and narrow, it did not blind her perplexed eyes to the fact that the girls were frequently extremely naughty. She wished very often, she did so wish—they wouldn't be. They set out with a kind of eagerness for conflict.

Their very loyalty to her expressed itself not so much in any sustained attempt to make the hostels successful as in cheering inconveniently, in embarrassing declarations of a preference, in an ingenious and systematic rudeness to anyone suspected of imperfect devotion to her. The first comers into the Hostels were much more like the swelling inrush of a tide than, as Mrs. Pembrose would have preferred, like something laid on through a pipe, and when this lady wanted to go on with the old rules until Sir Isaac had approved of the new, the new arrivals went into the cutting-out room and manifested. Lady Harman had to be telephoned for to allay the manifestation.

And then arose questions of deportment, trivial in themselves, but of the gravest moment for the welfare of the hostels. There was a phrase about "noisy or improper conduct" in the revised rules. Few people would suspect a corridor, ten feet wide and two hundred feet long, as a temptation to impropriety, but Mrs. Pembrose found it was so. The effect of the corridors upon undisciplined girls quite unaccustomed to corridors was for a time most undesirable. For example they were moved to *run* along them violently. They ran races along them, when they overtook they jostled, when they were overtaken they squealed. The average velocity in the corridors of the lady occupants of the Bloomsbury Hostel during the first fortnight of its existence was seven miles an hour. Was that violence? Was that impropriety? The building was all steel construction, but one *heard* even in the Head Matron's room. And then there was the effect of the rows and rows of windows opening out upon the square. The square had some pleasant old trees and it was attractive to look down into their upper branches, where the sparrows mobbed and chattered perpetually, and over them at the chimneys and turrets and sky signs of the London world. The girls looked. So far they were certainly within their rights. But they did not look modestly, they did not look discreetly. They looked out of wide-open windows, they even sat perilously and protrudingly on the window sills conversing across the façade from window to window, attracting attention, and once to Mrs. Pembrose's certain knowledge a man in the street joined in. It was on a Sunday morning, too, a Bloomsbury Sunday morning!

But graver things were to rouse the preventive prohibitionist in the soul of Mrs. Pembrose. There was the visiting of one another's rooms and cubicles. Most of these young people had never possessed or dreamed of possessing a pretty and presentable apartment to themselves, and the first effect of this was to produce a decorative outbreak, a vigorous framing of photographs and hammering of nails ("dust-gathering litter."—*Mrs. Pembrose*) and then—visiting. They visited at all hours and in all costumes; they sat in groups of three or four, one on the chair and the rest on the bed conversing into late hours,—entirely uncensored conversations too often accompanied by laughter. When Mrs. Pembrose took this to Lady Harman she found her extraordinarily blind to the conceivable evils of this free intercourse. "But Lady Harman!" said Mrs. Pembrose, with a note of horror, "some of them—kiss each other!"

"But if they're fond of each other," said Lady Harman. "I'm sure I don't see—"

And when the floor matrons were instructed to make little surprise visits up and down the corridors the girls who occupied rooms took to locking their doors— and Lady Harman seemed inclined to sustain their right to do that. The floor matrons did what they could to exercise authority, one or two were former department manageresses, two were ex-elementary teachers, crowded out by younger and more certificated rivals, one, and the most trustworthy one, Mrs. Pembrose found, was an ex-wardress from Holloway. The natural result of these secret talkings and conferrings in the rooms became apparent presently in some mild ragging and in the concoction of petty campaigns of annoyance designed to soften the manners of the more authoritative floor matrons. Here again were perplexing difficulties. If a particular floor matron has a clear commanding note in her voice, is it or is it not "violent and improper" to say "Haw!" in clear commanding tones whenever you suppose her to be within earshot? As for the door-locking Mrs. Pembrose settled that by carrying off all the keys.

Complaints and incidents drifted towards definite scenes and "situations." Both sides in this continuing conflict of dispositions were so definite, so intolerant, to the mind of the lady with the perplexed dark eyes who mediated. Her reason was so much with the matrons; her sympathies so much with the girls. She did not like the assured brevity of Mrs. Pembrose's judgments and decisions; she had an instinctive perception of the truth that all compact judgments upon human beings are unjust judgments. The human spirit is but poorly adapted either to rule or to be ruled, and the honesty of all the efforts of Mrs. Pembrose and her staffs—for soon the hostels at Sydenham and West Kensington were open— were marred not merely by arrogance but by an irritability, a real hostility to complexities and difficulties and resisters and troublesome characters. And it did not help the staff to a triumphant achievement of its duties that the girls had an exaggerated perception that Lady Harman's heart was on their side.

And presently the phrase "weeding out" crept into the talk of Mrs. Pembrose. Some of the girls were being marked as ringleaders, foci of mischief, characters it was desirable to "get rid of." Confronted with it Lady Harman perceived she was absolutely opposed to this idea of getting rid of anyone—unless it was Mrs. Pembrose. She liked her various people; she had no desire for a whittled success with a picked remnant of subdued and deferential employees. She put that to Mr. Brumley and Mr. Brumley was indignant and eloquent in his concurrence. A certain Mary Trunk, a dark young woman with a belief that it became her to have a sweet disorder in her hair, and a large blond girl named Lucy Baxandall seemed to be the chief among the bad influences of the Bloomsbury hostel, and they took it upon themselves to appeal to Lady Harman against Mrs. Pembrose. They couldn't, they complained, "do a Thing right for her. . . ."

So the tangle grew.

Presently Lady Harman had to go to the Riviera with Sir Isaac and when she came back Mary Trunk and Lucy Baxandall had vanished from both the International Hostel and the International Stores. She tried to find out why, and she was confronted by inadequate replies and enigmatical silences. "They decided to go," said Mrs. Pembrose, and dropped "fortunately" after that statement. She disavowed any exact knowledge of their motives. But she feared the worst. Susan Burnet was uninforming. Whatever had happened had failed to reach Alice Burnet's ears. Lady Harman could not very well hold a commission of enquiry into the matter, but she had an uneasy sense of a hidden campaign of dislodgment. And about the corridors and cubicles and club rooms there was she thought a difference, a discretion, a flavor of subjugation. . . .

CHAPTER THE ELEVENTH

The Last Crisis

1

IT WOULD BE quite easy for anyone with the knack of reserve to go on from this point with a history of Lady Harman that would present her as practically a pure philanthropist. For from these beginnings she was destined to proceed to more and more knowledge and understanding and clear purpose and capable work in this interesting process of collective regrouping, this process which may even at last justify Mr. Brumley's courageous interpretations and prove to be an early experiment in the beginning of a new social order. Perhaps someday there will be an official biography, another addition to the inscrutable records of British public lives, in which all these things will be set out with tact and dignity. Horatio Blenker or Adolphus Blenker may survive to be entrusted with this congenial task. She will be represented as a tall inanimate person pursuing one clear benevolent purpose in life from her very beginning, and Sir Isaac and her relations with Sir Isaac will be rescued from reality. The book will be illustrated by a number of carefully posed photographer's photographs of her, studies of the Putney house and perhaps an unappetizing woodcut of her early home at Penge. The aim of all British biography is to conceal. A great deal of what we have already told will certainly not figure in any such biography, and still more certainly will the things we have yet to tell be missing.

Lady Harman was indeed only by the force of circumstances and intermittently a pure philanthropist, and it is with the intercalary passages of less exalted humanity that we are here chiefly concerned. At times no doubt she did really come near to filling and fitting and becoming identical with that figure of the pure philanthropist which was her world-ward face, but for the most part that earnest and dignified figure concealed more or less extensive spaces of nothingness, while the errant soul of the woman within strayed into less exalted ways of thinking.

There were times when she was almost sure of herself—Mrs. Hubert Plessington could scarcely have been surer of herself, and times when the whole magnificent project of constructing a new urban social life out of those difficult hostels, a collective urban life that should be liberal and free, broke into grimacing pieces and was the most foolish of experiments. Her struggles with Mrs. Pembrose thereupon assumed a quality of mere bickering and she could even doubt whether Mrs. Pembrose wasn't justified in her attitude and wiser by her very want of generosity. She felt then something childish in the whole undertaking that otherwise escaped her, she was convicted of an absurd self-importance, she discovered herself an ignorant woman availing herself of her husband's power and wealth to attempt presumptuous experiments. In these moods of disillusionment, her mind went adrift and was driven to and fro from discontent to discontent; she would find herself taking soundings and seeking an anchorage upon the strangest, most unfamiliar shoals. And in her relations and conflicts with her husband there was a smoldering shame for her submissions to him that needed only a phase of fatigue to become acute. So long as she believed in her hostels and her mission that might be endured, but forced back upon her more personal life its hideousness stood unclothed. Mr. Brumley could sometimes reassure her by a rhetorical effort upon the score of her hostels, but most of her more intimate and inner life was not, for very plain reasons, to be shown to him. He was full of the intention of generous self-denials, but she had long since come to measure the limits of his self-denial. . . .

Mr. Brumley was a friend in whom smoldered a love, capable she knew quite clearly of tormented and tormenting jealousies. It would be difficult to tell, and she certainly could never have told how far she knew of this by instinct, how far it came out of rapid intuitions from things seen and heard. But she understood that she dared not let a single breath of encouragement, a hint of physical confidence, reach that banked-up glow. A sentinel discretion in her brain was always on the watch for that danger, and that restraint, that added deliberate inexpressiveness, kept them most apart, when most her spirit cried out for companionship.

The common quality of all these moods of lassitude was a desolating loneliness. She had at times a need that almost overwhelmed her to be intimate, to be comforted and taken up out of the bleak harsh disappointments and stresses of her customary life. At times after Sir Isaac had either been too unloving or too loving, or when the girls or the matrons had achieved some new tangle of mutual unreasonableness, or when her faith failed, she would lie in the darkness of her own room with her soul crying out for—how can one put it?—the touch of other soul-stuff. And perhaps it was the constant drift of Mr. Brumley's talk, the little suggestions that fell drop by drop into her mind from his, that disposed her to believe that this aching sense of solitude in the void was to be assuaged by love, by some marvel of close exaltation that one might reach through a lover. She had told Mr. Brumley long ago that she would never let herself think of love, she still maintained to him that attitude of resolute aloofness, but almost without noting what she did, she was tampering now in her solitude with the seals of that locked chamber. She became secretly curious about love. Perhaps there was something in it of which she knew nothing. She found herself drawn towards poetry, found a new attraction in romance; more and more did she dally with the idea that there was some unknown beauty in the world, something to which her eyes might presently open, something deeper and sweeter than anything she had ever known, close at hand, something to put all the world into proportion for her.

In a little while she no longer merely tampered with these seals, for quite silently the door had opened and she was craning in. This love it seemed to her might after all be so strange a thing that it goes unsuspected and yet fills the whole world of a human soul. An odd grotesque passage in a novel by Wilkins gave her that idea. He compared love to electricity, of all things in the world; that throbbing life amidst the atoms that we now draw upon for light, warmth, connection, the satisfaction of a thousand wants and the cure of a thousand ills. There it is and always has been in the life of man, and yet until a century ago it worked unsuspected, was known only for a disregarded oddity of amber, a crackling in frost-dry hair and thunder. . . .

And then she remembered how Mr. Brumley had once broken into a panegyric of love. "It makes life a different thing. It is like the home-coming of something lost. All this dispersed perplexing world *centers*. Think what true love means; to live always in the mind of another and to have that other living always in your mind. . . . Only there can be no restraints, no reserves, no admission of prior rights. One must feel *safe* of one's welcome and freedoms. . . ."

Wasn't it worth the risk of almost any breach of boundaries to get to such a light as that? . . .

She hid these musings from every human being, she was so shy with them, she hid them almost from herself. Rarely did they have their way with her and when they did, presently she would accuse herself of slackness and dismiss them and urge herself to fresh practicalities in her work. But her work was not always at hand, Sir Isaac's frequent relapses took her abroad to places where she found herself in the midst of beautiful scenery with little to do and little to distract her from these questionings. Then such thoughts would inundate her.

This feeling of the unsatisfactoriness of life, of incompleteness and solitariness, was not of that fixed sort that definitely indicates its demand. Under its oppression she tried the idea of love, but she also tried certain other ideas. Very often this vague appeal had the quality of a person, sometimes a person shrouded in night, a soundless whisper, the unseen lover who came to Psyche in the darkness. And sometimes that person became more distinct, less mystic and more companionable. Perhaps because imaginations have a way of following the line of least resistance, it took upon itself something of the form, something of the voice and bearing of Mr. Brumley. She recoiled from her own thoughts when she discovered herself wondering what manner of lover Mr. Brumley might make—if suddenly she lowered her defences, freed his suffocating pleading, took him to herself.

In my anxiety to draw Mr. Brumley as he was, I have perhaps a little neglected to show him as Lady Harman saw him. We have employed the inconsiderate verisimilitude of a novelist repudiating romance in his portrayal; towards her he kept a better face. He was at least a very honest lover and there was little disingenuousness in the flow of fine mental attitudes that met her; the thought and presence of her made him fine; as soon could he have turned his shady side towards the sun. And she was very ready and eager to credit him with generous qualities. We of his club and circle, a little assisted perhaps by Max Beerbohm's diabolical index finger, may have found and been not unwilling to find his face chiefly expressive of a kind of empty alertness; but when it was turned to her its quite pleasantly modelled features glowed and it was transfigured. So far as she was concerned, with Sir Isaac as foil, he was real enough and good enough for her. And by the virtue of that unlovely contrast even a certain ineffectiveness— became infinite delicacy. . . .

The thought of Mr. Brumley in that relation and to that extent of clearness came but rarely into her consciousness, and when it did it was almost immediately dismissed again. It was the most fugitive of proffered consolations. And it is to be remarked that it made its most successful apparitions when Mr. Brumley was far away, and by some weeks or months of separation a little blurred and forgotten. . . .

And sometimes this unrest of her spirit, this unhappiness turned her in quite another direction as it seemed and she had thoughts of religion. With a deepened shame she would go seeking into that other, that greater indelicacy, from which her upbringing had divorced her mind. She would even secretly pray. Greatly daring she fled on several occasions from her visitation of the hostels or slipped out of her home, and evading Mr. Brumley, went once to the Brompton Oratory, once or twice to the Westminster Cathedral and then having discovered Saint Paul's, to Saint Paul's in search of this nameless need. It was a need that no plain and ugly little place of worship would satisfy. It was a need that demanded choir and organ. She went to Saint Paul's haphazard when her mood and opportunity chanced together and there in the afternoons she found a wonder of great music and chanting voices, and she would kneel looking up into those divine shadows and perfect archings and feel for a time assuaged, wonderfully assuaged. Sometimes, there, she seemed to be upon the very verge of grasping that hidden reality which makes all things plain. Sometimes it seemed to her that this very indulgence was the hidden reality.

She could never be sure in her mind whether these secret worshippings helped or hampered her in her daily living. They helped her to a certain disregard of annoyances and indignities and so far they were good, but they also helped towards a more general indifference. She might have told these last experiences to Mr. Brumley if she had not felt them to be indescribable. They could not be half told. They had to be told completely or they were altogether untellable. So she had them hid, and at once accepted and distrusted the consolation they brought her, and went on with the duties and philanthropies that she had chosen as her task in the world.

2

One day in Lent—it was nearly three years after the opening of the first hostel— she went to Saint Paul's.

She was in a mood of great discouragement; the struggle between Mrs. Pembrose and the Bloomsbury girls had suddenly reopened in an acute form and Sir Isaac, who was sickening again after a period of better health, had become strangely restless and irritable and hostile to her. He had thwarted her unusually and taken the side of the matrons in a conflict in which Susan Burnet's sister Alice was now distinguished as the chief of the malcontents. The new trouble seemed to Lady Harman to be traceable in one direction to that ardent Unionist, Miss Babs Wheeler, under the spell of whose round-faced, blue-eyed, distraught personality Alice had altogether fallen. Miss Babs Wheeler was fighting for the Union; she herself lived at Highbury with her mother, and Alice was her chosen instrument in the hostels. The Union had always been a little against the ladylike instincts of many of the waitresses; they felt strikes were vulgar and impaired their social standing, and this feeling had been greatly strengthened by irruptions of large contingents of shop assistants from various department stores. The Bloomsbury Hostel in particular now accommodated a hundred refined and elegant hands— they ought rather to be called figures—from the great Oxford Street costume house of Eustace and Mills, young people with a tall sweeping movement and an elevation of chin that had become nearly instinctive, and a silent yet evident intention to find the International girls "low" at the slightest provocation. It is only too easy for poor humanity under the irritation of that tacit superiority to respond with just the provocation anticipated. What one must regretfully speak of as the vulgar section of the International girls had already put itself in the wrong by a number of aggressive acts before the case came to Lady Harman's attention. Mrs. Pembrose seized the occasion for weeding on a courageous scale, and Miss Alice Burnet and three of her dearest friends were invited to vacate their rooms "pending redecoration."

With only too much plausibility the threatened young women interpreted this as an expulsion, and declined to remove their boxes and personal belongings. Miss Babs Wheeler thereupon entered the Bloomsbury Hostel, and in the teeth of three express prohibitions from Mrs. Pembrose, went a little up the staircase and addressed a confused meeting in the central hall. There was loud and continuous cheering for Lady Harman at intervals during this incident. Thereupon Mrs. Pembrose demanded sweeping dismissals, not only from the Hostels but the shops as an alternative to her resignation, and Lady Harman found herself more perplexed than ever. . . .

Georgina Sawbridge had contrived to mingle herself in an entirely characteristic way in these troubles by listening for a brief period to an abstract of her sister's perplexities, then demanding to be made Director-General of the whole affair, refusing to believe this simple step impossible and retiring in great dudgeon to begin a series of letters of even more than sisterly bitterness. And Mr. Brumley when consulted had become dangerously sentimental. Under these circumstances Lady Harman's visit to Saint Paul's had much of the quality of a flight.

It was with an unwonted sense of refuge that she came from the sombre stress and roar of London without into the large hushed spaces of the cathedral. The door closed behind her—and all things changed. Here was meaning, coherence, unity. Here instead of a pelting confusion of movements and motives was a quiet concentration upon the little focus of light about the choir, the gentle complete dominance of a voice intoning. She slipped along the aisle and into the nave and made her way to a seat. How good this was! Outside she had felt large, awkwardly responsible, accessible to missiles, a distressed conspicuous thing; within this living peace she suddenly became no more than one of a tranquil hushed community of small black-clad Lenten people; she found a chair and knelt and felt she vanished even from her own consciousness. . . .

How beautiful was this place! She looked up presently at the great shadowy arcs far above her, so easy, so gracious that it seemed they had not so much been built by men as shaped by circling flights of angels. The service, a little clustering advance of voices unsustained by any organ, mingled in her mind with the many-pointed glow of candles. And then into this great dome of worship and beauty, like a bed of voices breaking into flower, like a springtime breeze of sound, came Allegri's Miserere. . . .

Her spirit clung to this mood of refuge. It seemed as though the disorderly, pugnacious, misunderstanding universe had opened and shown her luminous mysteries. She had a sense of penetration. All that conflict, that jar of purposes and motives, was merely superficial; she had left it behind her. For a time she had no sense of effort in keeping hold of this, only of attainment, she drifted happily upon the sweet sustaining sounds, and then—then the music ceased. She came back into herself. Close to her a seated man stirred and sighed. She tried to get back her hold upon that revelation but it had gone. Inexorably, opaque, impenetrable doors closed softly on her moment of vision. . . .

All about her was the stir of departure.

She walked out slowly into the cold March daylight, to the leaden grays, the hurrying black shapes, the chaotic afternoon traffic of London. She paused on the steps, still but half reawakened. A passing omnibus obtruded the familiar inscription, "International Stores for Staminal Bread."

She turned like one who remembers, to where her chauffeur stood waiting.

3

As her motor car, with a swift smoothness, carried her along the Embankment towards the lattice bar of Charing Cross bridge and the remoter towers of the Houses of Parliament, gray now and unsubstantial against the bright western sky, her mind came back slowly to her particular issues in life. But they were no longer the big exasperatingly important things that had seemed to hold her life by a hundred painful hooks before she went into the cathedral. They were small still under this dome of evening, small even by the measure of the gray buildings to the right of her and the warm lit river to her left, by the measure of the clustering dark barges, the teeming trams, the streaming crowds of people, the note of the human process that sounds so loud there. She felt small even to herself, for the touch of beauty saves us from our own personalities, makes Gods of us to our own littleness. She passed under the railway bridge at Charing Cross, watched the square cluster of Westminster's pinnacles rise above her until they were out of sight overhead, ran up the little incline and round into Parliament Square, and was presently out on the riverside embankment again with the great chimneys of Chelsea smoking athwart the evening gold. And thence with a sudden effect of skies shut and curtains drawn she came by devious ways to the Fulham Road and the crowding traffic of Putney Bridge and Putney High Street and so home.

Snagsby, assisted by a new under-butler, a lean white-faced young man with red hair, received her ceremoniously and hovered serviceably about her. On the hall table lay three or four visiting cards of no importance, some circulars and two letters. She threw the circulars into the basket placed for them and opened her first letter. It was from Georgina; it was on several sheets and it began, "I still cannot believe that you refuse to give me the opportunity the director-generalship of your hostels means to me. It is not as if you yourself had either the time or the abilities necessary for them yourself; you haven't, and there is something almost dog-in-the-manger-ish to my mind in the way in which you will not give me my chance, the chance I have always been longing for—''

At this point Lady Harman put down this letter for subsequent perusal and took its companion, which was addressed in an unfamiliar hand. It was from Alice Burnet and it was written in that sprawling hand and diffused style natural to a not very well educated person with a complicated story to tell in a state of unusual emotion. But the gist was in the first few sentences which announced that Alice had been evicted from the hostel. "I found my things on the pavement," wrote Alice.

Lady Harman became aware of Snagsby still hovering at hand.

"Mrs. Pembrose, my lady, came here this afternoon," he said, when he had secured her attention.

"Came here."

"She asked for you, my lady, and when I told her you were not at 'ome, she asked if she might see Sir Isaac."

"And did she?"

"Sir Issac saw her, my lady. They 'ad tea in the study."

"I wish I had been at home to see her," said Lady Harman, after a brief interval of reflection.

She took her two letters and turned to the staircase. They were still in her hand when presently she came into her husband's study. "I don't want a light," he said, as she put out her hand to the electric switch. His voice had a note of discontent, but he was sitting in the armchair against the window so that she could not see his features.

"How are you feeling this afternoon?" she asked.

"I'm feeling all right," he answered testily. He seemed to dislike inquiries after his health almost as much as he disliked neglect.

She came and stood by him and looked out from the dusk of the room into the garden darkening under a red-barred sky. "There is fresh trouble between Mrs. Pembrose and the girls," she said.

"She's been telling me about it."

"She's been here?"

"Pretty nearly an hour," said Sir Isaac.

Lady Harman tried to imagine that hour's interview on the spur of the moment and failed. She came to her immediate business. "I think," she said, "that she has been—high-handed. . . ."

"You would," said Sir Isaac after an interval.

His tone was hostile, so hostile that it startled her.

"Don't you?"

He shook his head. "My idees and your idees—or anyhow the idees you've got hold of—somewhere—somehow— I don't know where you *get* your idees. We haven't got the same idees, anyhow. You got to keep order in these places— anyhow. . . ."

She perceived that she was in face of a prepared position. "I don't think," she threw out, "that she does keep order. She represses—and irritates. She gets an idea that certain girls are against her. . . ."

"And you get an idea she's against certain girls. . . ."

"Practically she expels them. She has in fact just turned one out into the street."

"You got to expel 'em. You got to. You can't run these places on sugar and water. There's a sort of girl, a sort of man, who makes trouble. There's a sort makes strikes, makes mischief, gets up grievances. You got to get rid of 'em somehow. You got to be practical somewhere. You can't go running these places on a lot of littry idees and all that. It's no good."

The phrase "littry idees" held Lady Harman's attention for a moment. But she could not follow it up to its implications, because she wanted to get on with the issue she had in hand.

"I want to be consulted about these expulsions. Girl after girl has been sent away—"

Sir Isaac's silhouette was obstinate.

"She knows her business," he said.

He seemed to feel the need of a justification. "They shouldn't make trouble."

On that they rested for a little while in silence. She began to realize with a gathering emotion that this matter was far more crucial than she had supposed. She had been thinking only of the reinstatement of Alice Burnet, she hadn't yet estimated just what that overriding of Mrs. Pembrose might involve.

"I don't want to have any girl go until I have looked into her case. It's—It's vital."

"She says she can't run the show unless she has some power."

Neither spoke for some seconds. She had the feeling of hopeless vexation that might come to a child that has wandered into a trap. "I thought," she began. "These hostels—"

She stopped short.

Sir Isaac's hand tightened on the arm of his chair. "I started 'em to please you," he said. "I didn't start 'em to please your friends."

She turned her eyes quickly to his gray up-looking face.

"I didn't start them for you and that chap Brumley to play about with," he amplified. "And now you know about it, Elly."

The thing had found her unprepared. "As if—" she said at last.

"As if!" he mocked.

She stood quite still staring blankly at this unmanageable situation. He was the first to break silence. He lifted one hand and dropped it again with a dead impact on the arm of his chair. "I got the things," he said, "and there they are. Anyhow,—they got to be run in a proper way."

She made no immediate answer. She was seeking desperately for phrases that escaped her. "Do you think," she began at last. "Do you really think—?"

He stared out of the window. He answered in tones of excessive reasonableness: "I didn't start these hostels to be run by you and your—friend." He gave the sentence the quality of an ultimatum, an irreducible minimum.

"He's my friend," she explained, "only—because he does work—for the hostels."

Sir Isaac seemed for a moment to attempt to consider that. Then he relapsed upon his predetermined attitude. "God!" he exclaimed, "but I been a fool!"

She decided that that must be ignored.

"I care more for those hostels than I care for anything—anything else in the world," she told him. "I want them to work—I want them to succeed. . . . And then—"

He listened in skeptical silence.

"Mr. Brumley is nothing to me but a helper. He— How can you imagine, Isaac—? I! How can you dare? To suggest—!"

"Very well," said Sir Isaac and reflected and made his old familiar sound with his teeth. "Run the hostels without him, Elly," he propounded. "Then I'll believe."

She perceived that suddenly she was faced by a test or a bargain. In the background of her mind the figure of Mr. Brumley, as she had seen him last, in brown and with a tie rather to one side, protested vainly. She did what she could for him on the spur of the moment. "But," she said, "he's so helpful. He's so—harmless."

"That's as may be," said Sir Isaac and breathed heavily.

"How can one suddenly turn on a friend?"

"I don't see that you ever wanted a friend," said Sir Isaac.

"He's been so good. It isn't reasonable, Isaac. When anyone has—*slaved*."

"I don't say he isn't a good sort of chap," said Sir Isaac, with that same note of almost superhuman rationality, "only—he isn't going to run my hostels."

"But what do you mean, Isaac?"

"I mean you got to choose."

He waited as if he expected her to speak and then went on.

"What it comes to is this, Elly, I'm about sick of that chap. I'm sick of him." He paused for a moment because his breath was short. "If you go on with the hostels he's—Phew—got to mizzle. *Then*—I don't mind—if you want that girl Burnet brought back in triumph. . . . It'll make Mrs. Pembrose chuck the whole blessed show, you know, but I say—I don't mind. . . . Only in that case, I don't want to see or hear—or hear about—Phew—or hear about your Mr. Brumley again. And I don't want you to, either. . . . I'm being pretty reasonable and pretty patient over this, with people—people—talking right and left. Still,—there's a limit. . . . You've been going on—if I didn't know you were an innocent—in a way . . . I don't want to talk about that. There you are, Elly."

It seemed to her that she had always expected this to happen. But however much she had expected it to happen she was still quite unprepared with any course of action. She wanted with an equal want of limitation to keep both Mr. Brumley and her hostels.

"But Isaac," she said. "What do you suspect? What do you think? This friendship has been going on— How can I end it suddenly?"

"Don't you be too innocent, Elly. You know and I know perfectly well what there is between men and women. I don't make out I know—anything I don't know. I don't pretend you are anything but straight. Only—"

He suddenly gave way to his irritation. His self-control vanished. "Damn it!" he cried, and his panting breath quickened; "the thing's got to end. As if I didn't understand! As if I didn't understand!"

She would have protested again but his voice held her. "It's got to end. It's got to end. Of course you haven't done anything, of course you don't know anything or think of anything. . . . Only here I am ill. . . . *You* wouldn't be sorry if I got worse. . . . *You* can wait; you can. . . . All right! All right! And there you stand, irritating me—arguing. You know—it chokes me. . . . Got to end, I tell you. . . . Got to end. . . ."

He beat at the arms of his chair and then put a hand to his throat.

"Go away," he cried to her. "Go to hell!"

4

I cannot tell whether the reader is a person of swift decisions or one of the newer race of doubters; if he be the latter he will the better understand how Lady Harman did in the next two days make up her mind definitely and conclusively to two entirely opposed lines of action. She decided that her relations with Mr. Brumley, innocent as they were, must cease in the interests of the hostels and her struggle with Mrs. Pembrose, and she decided with quite equal certainty that her husband's sudden veto upon these relations was an intolerable tyranny that must be resisted with passionate indignation. Also she was surprised to find how difficult it was now to think of parting from Mr. Brumley. She made her way to these precarious conclusions and on from whichever it was to the other through a jungle of conflicting considerations and feelings. When she thought of Mrs. Pembrose and more particularly of the probable share of Mrs. Pembrose in her husband's objection to Mr. Brumley her indignation kindled. She perceived Mrs. Pembrose as a purely evil personality, as a spirit of espionage, distrust, calculated treachery and malignant intervention, as all that is evil in rule and officialism, and a vast wave of responsibility for all those difficult and feeble and likeable young women who elbowed and giggled and misunderstood and blundered and tried to live happily under the commanding stresses of Mrs. Pembrose's austerity carried her away. She had her duty to do to them and it overrode every other duty. If a certain separation from Mr. Brumley's assiduous aid was demanded, was it too great a sacrifice? And no sooner was that settled than the whole question reopened with her indignant demand why anyone at any price had the right to prohibit a friendship that she had so conscientiously kept innocent. If she gave way to this outrageous restriction today, what fresh limitations might not Sir Isaac impose tomorrow? And now, she was so embarrassed in her struggle by his health. She could not go to him and have things out with him, she could not directly defy him, because that might mean a suffocating seizure for him. . . .

It was entirely illogical, no doubt, but extremely natural for Lady Harman to decide that she must communicate her decision, whichever one it was, to Mr. Brumley in a personal interview. She wrote to him and arranged to meet and talk to him in Kew Gardens, and with a feeling of discretion went thither not in the automobile but in a taxi-cab. And so delicately now were her two irrevocable decisions balanced in her mind that twice on her way to Kew she swayed over from one to the other.

Arrived at the gardens she found herself quite disinclined to begin the announcement of either decision. She was quite exceptionally glad to see Mr. Brumley; he was dressed in a new suit of lighter brown that became him very well indeed, the day was warm and bright, a day of scyllas and daffodils and snow-upon-the-mountains and green-powdered trees and frank sunshine,—and the warmth of her feelings for her friend merged indistinguishably with the springtime stir and glow. They walked across the bright turf together in a state of unjustifiable happiness, purring little admirations at the ingenious elegance of creation at its best as gardeners set it out for our edification, and the whole tenor of Lady Harman's mind was to make this occasion an escape from the particular business that had brought her thither.

"We'll look for daffodils away there towards the river under the trees," said Mr. Brumley, and it seemed preposterous not to enjoy those daffodils at least before she broached the great issue between an irresistible force and an immovable post, that occupied her mental background.

Mr. Brumley was quite at his best that afternoon. He was happy, gay and deferential; he made her realize by his every tone and movement that if he had his choice of the whole world that afternoon and all its inhabitants and everything, there was no other place in which he would be, no other companion, no other occupation than this he had. He talked of spring and flowers, quoted poets and added the treasures of a well-stored mind to the amenities of the day. "It's good to take a holiday at times," he said, and after that it was more difficult than ever to talk about the trouble of the hostels.

She was able to do this at last while they were having tea in the little pavilion near the pagoda. It was the old pavilion, the one that Miss Alimony's suffragettes were afterwards to burn down in order to demonstrate the relentless logic of women. They did it in the same eventful week when Miss Alimony was, she declared, so nearly carried off by White Slave Traders (disguised as nurses but, fortunately for her, smelling of brandy) from the Brixton Temperance Bazaar. But in those simpler days the pavilion still existed; it was tended by agreeable waiters whose evening dress was mitigated by cheerful little straw hats, and an enormous multitude of valiant and smutty Cockney sparrows chirped and squeaked and begged and fluttered and fought, venturing to the very tables and feet of the visitors. And here, a little sobered from their first elation by much walking about and the presence of jam and watercress, Mr. Brumley and Lady Harman could think again of the work they were doing for the reconstitution of society upon collective lines.

She began to tell him of the conflict between Mrs. Pembrose and Alice Burnet that threatened the latter with extinction. She found it more convenient to talk at first as though the strands of decision were still all in her hands; afterwards she could go on to the peculiar complication of the situation through the unexpected weakening of her position in relation to Mrs. Pembrose. She described the particular of the new trouble, the perplexing issue between the "ladylike," for which as a feminine ideal there was so much to be said on the one hand and the "genial," which was also an admirable quality, on the other. "You see," she said, "it's very rude to cough at people and make noises, but then it's so difficult to explain to the others that it's equally rude to go past people and pretend not to see or hear them. Girls of that sort always seem so much more underbred when they are trying to be superior than when they are not; they get so stiff and—exasperating. And this keeping out of the Union because it isn't genteel, it's the very essence of the trouble with all these employees. We've discussed that so often. Those drapers' girls seem full of such cold, selfish, base, pretentious notions; much more full even than our refreshment girls. And then as if it wasn't all difficult enough comes Mrs. Pembrose and her wardresses doing all sorts of hard, clumsy things, and one can't tell them just how little they are qualified to judge good behavior. Their one idea of discipline is to speak to people as if they were servants and to be distant and crushing. And long before one can do anything come trouble and tart replies and reports of "gross impertinence" and expulsion. We keep on expelling girls. This is the fourth time girls have had to go. What is to become of them? I know this Burnet girl quite well as you know. She's just a human, kindly little woman. . . . She'll feel disgraced. . . . How can I let a thing like that occur?"

She spread her hands apart over the tea things.

Mr. Brumley held his chin in his hand and said "Um" and looked judicial, and admired Lady Harman very much, and tried to grasp the whole trouble and wring out a solution. He made some admirable generalizations about the development of a new social feeling in response to changed conditions, but apart from a remark that Mrs. Pembrose was all organization and no psychology, and quite the wrong person for her position, he said nothing in the slightest degree contributory to the particular drama under consideration. From that utterance, however, Lady Harman would no doubt have gone on to the slow, tentative but finally conclusive statement of the new difficulty that had arisen out of her husband's jealousy and to the discussion of the more fundamental decisions it forced upon her, if a peculiar blight had not fallen upon their conversation and robbed it at last of even an appearance of ease.

This blight crept upon their minds. . . . It began first with Mr. Brumley.

Mr. Brumley was rarely free from self-consciousness. Whenever he was in a restaurant or any such place of assembly, then whatever he did or whatever he said he had a kind of surplus attention, a quickening of the ears, a wandering of the eyes, to the groups and individuals round about him. And while he had seemed entirely occupied with Lady Harman, he had nevertheless been aware from the outset that a dingy and inappropriate-looking man in a bowler hat and a ready-made suit of gray, was listening to their conversation from an adjacent table.

This man had entered the pavilion oddly. He had seemed to dodge in and hesitate. Then he had chosen his table rather deliberately—and he kept looking, and trying not to seem to look.

That was not all. Mr. Brumley's expression was overcast by the effort to recall something. He sat elbows on table and leaned forward towards Lady Harman and at the blossom-laden trees outside the pavilion and trifled with two fingers on his lips and spoke between them in a voice that was speculative and confidential and muffled and mysterious. "Where have I seen our friend to the left before?"

She had been aware of his distraction for some time.

She glanced at the man and found nothing remarkable in him. She tried to go on with her explanations.

Mr. Brumley appeared attentive and then he said again: "But where have I seen him?"

And from that point their talk was blighted; the heart seemed to go out of her. Mr. Brumley she felt was no longer taking in what she was saying. At the time she couldn't in any way share his preoccupation. But what had been difficult before became hopeless and she could no longer feel that even presently she would be able to make him understand the peculiar alternatives before her. They drifted back by the great conservatory and the ornamental water, aripple with ducks and swans, to the gates where his taxi waited.

Even then it occurred to her that she ought to tell him something of the new situation. But now their time was running out, she would have to be concise, and what wife could ever say abruptly and offhand that frequent fact, "Oh, by the by, my husband is jealous of you"? Then she had an impulse to tell him simply, without any explanation at all, that for a time he must not meet her. And while she gathered herself together for that, his preoccupations intervened again.

He stood up in the open taxi-cab and looked back.

"That chap," he said, "is following us."

5

The effect of this futile interview upon Lady Harman was remarkable. She took to herself an absurd conviction that this inconclusiveness had been an achievement. Confronted by a dilemma, she had chosen neither horn and assumed an attitude of inoffensive defiance. Springs in England vary greatly in their character; some are easterly and quarrelsome, some are north-westerly and wetly disastrous, a bleak invasion from the ocean; some are but the broken beginnings of what are not so much years as stretches of meteorological indecision. This particular spring was essentially a south-westerly spring, good and friendly, showery but in the lightest way and so softly reassuring as to be gently hilarious.

It was a spring to get into the blood of anyone; it gave Lady Harman the feeling that Mrs. Pembrose would certainly be dealt with properly and without unreasonable delay by Heaven, and that meanwhile it was well to take the good things of existence as cheerfully as possible. The good things she took were very innocent things. Feeling unusually well and enjoying great drafts of spring air and sunshine were the chief. And she took them only for three brief days. She carried the children down to Black Strand to see her daffodils, and her daffodils surpassed expectation. There was a delirium of blackthorn in the new wild garden she had annexed from the woods and a close carpet of encouraged wild primroses. Even the Putney garden was full of happy surprises. The afternoon following her visit to Black Strand was so warm that she had tea with her family in great gaiety on the lawn under the cedar. Her offspring were unusually sweet that day, they had new blue cotton sunbonnets, and Baby and Annette at least succeeded in being pretty. And Millicent, under the new Swiss governess, had acquired, it seemed quite suddenly, a glib colloquial French that somehow reconciled one to the extreme thinness and shapelessness of her legs.

Then an amazing new fact broke into this gleam of irrational contentment, a shattering new fact. She found she was being watched. She discovered that dingy man in the gray suit following her.

The thing came upon her one afternoon. She was starting out for a talk with Georgina. She felt so well, so confident of the world that it was intolerable to think of Georgina harboring resentment; she resolved she would go and have things out with her and make it clear just how impossible it was to impose a Director-General upon her husband. She became aware of the man in gray as she walked down Putney Hill.

She recognized him at once. He was at the corner of Redfern Road and still unaware of her existence. He was leaning against the wall with the habituated pose of one who is frequently obliged to lean against walls for long periods of time, and he was conversing in an elucidatory manner with the elderly crossing-sweeper who still braves the motor-cars at that point. He became aware of her emergence with a start, he ceased to lean and became observant.

He was one of those men whose face suggests the word "muzzle," with an erect combative nose and a forward slant of the body from the rather inturned feet. He wore an observant bowler hat a little too small for him, and there was something about the tail of his jacket—as though he had been docked.

She passed at a stride to the acceptance of Mr. Brumley's hitherto incredible suspicion. Her pulses quickened. It came into her head to see how far this man would go in following her. She went on demurely down the hill leaving him quite unaware that she had seen him.

She was amazed, and after her first belief incredulous again. Could Isaac be going mad? At the corner she satisfied herself of the gray man's proximity and hailed a taxi-cab. The man in gray came nosing across to listen to her directions and hear where she was going.

"Please drive up the hill until I tell you," she said, "slowly"—and had the satisfaction, if one may call it a satisfaction, of seeing the gray man dive towards the taxi-cab rank. Then she gave herself up to hasty scheming.

She turned her taxi-cab abruptly when she was certain of being followed, went back into London, turned again and made for Westridge's great stores in Oxford Street. The gray man ticked up two pences in pursuit. All along the Brompton Road he pursued her with his nose like the jib of a ship.

She was excited and interested, and not nearly so shocked as she ought to have been. It didn't somehow jar as it ought to have jarred with her idea of Sir

Isaac. Watched by a detective! This then was the completion of the conditional freedom she had won by smashing that window. She might have known. . . .

She was astonished and indignant but not nearly so entirely indignant as a noble heroine should have been. She was certainly not nearly so queenly as Mrs. Sawbridge would have shown herself under such circumstances. It may have been due to some plebeian strain in her father's blood that over and above her proper indignation she was extremely interested. She wanted to know what manner of man it was whose nose was just appearing above the window edge of the taxi-cab behind. In her inexperienced inattention she had never yet thought it was possible that men could be hired to follow women.

She sat a little forward, thinking.

How far would he follow her and was it possible to shake him off? Or are such followers so expert that once upon a scent, they are like the Indian hunting dog, inevitable? She must see.

She paid off her taxi at Westridge's and, with the skill of her sex, observed him by the window reflection, counting the many doors of the establishment. Would he try to watch them all? There were also some round the corner. No, he was going to follow her in. She had a sudden desire, an unreasonable desire, perhaps an instinctive desire to see that man among baby-linen. It was in her power for a time to wreathe him with incongruous objects. This was the sort of fancy a woman must control. . . .

He stalked her with an unreal sang-froid. He ambushed behind a display of infants' socks. Driven to buy by a saleswoman he appeared to be demanding improbable varieties of infant's socks.

Are these watchers and trackers sometimes driven to buying things in shops? If so, strange items must figure in accounts of expenses. If he bought those socks, would they appear in Sir Isaac's bill? She felt a sudden craving for the sight of Sir Isaac's Private Detective Account. And as for the articles themselves, what became of them? She knew her husband well enough to feel sure that if he paid for anything he would insist upon having it. But where—where did he keep them? . . .

But now the man's back was turned; he was no doubt improvising paternity and an extreme fastidiousness in baby's footwear— Now for it!—through departments of deepening indelicacy to the lift!

But he had considered that possibility of embarrassment; he got round by some other way, he was just in time to hear the lift gate clash upon a calmly preoccupied lady, who still seemed as unaware of his existence as the sky.

He was running upstairs, when she descended again, without getting out; he stopped at the sight of her shooting past him, their eyes met and there was something appealing in his. He was very moist and his bowler was flagging. He had evidently started out in the morning with misconceptions about the weather. And it was clear he felt he had blundered in coming into Westridge's. Before she could get a taxi he was on the pavement behind her, hot but pursuing.

She sought in her mind for corner shops, with doors on this street and that. She exercised him upon Peter Robinson's and Debenham and Freebody's and then started for the monument. But on her way to the monument she thought of the moving staircase at Harrod's. If she went up and down on this, she wanted to know what he would do, would he run up and down the fixed flight? He did. Several times. And then she bethought herself of the Piccadilly tube; she got in at Brompton Road and got out at Down Street and then got in again and went to South Kensington and he darted in and out of adjacent carriages and got into lifts by curious retrograde movements, being apparently under the erroneous impression that his back was less characteristic than his face.

By this time he was evidently no longer unaware of her intelligent interest in his movements. It was clear too that he had received a false impression that she wanted to shake him off and that all the sleuth in him was aroused. He was dishevelled and breathing hard and getting a little close and coarse in his pursuit, but he was sticking to it with a puckered intensified resolution. He came up into the South Kensington air open-mouthed and sniffing curiously, but invincible.

She discovered suddenly that she did not like him at all and that she wanted to go home.

She took a taxi, and then away in the wilds of the Fulham Road she had her crowning idea. She stopped the cab at a dingy little furniture shop, paid the driver exorbitantly and instructed him to go right back to South Kensington station, buy her an evening paper and return for her. The pursuer drew up thirty yards away, fell into her trap, paid off his cab and feigned to be interested by a small window full of penny toys, cheap chocolate and cocoanut ice. She bought herself a brass door weight, paid for it hastily and posted herself just within the furniture-shop door.

Then you see her cab returned suddenly and she got in at once and left him stranded.

He made a desperate effort to get a motor omnibus. She saw him rushing across the traffic gesticulating. Then he collided with a boy with a basket on a bicycle—not so far as she could see injuriously, they seemed to leap at once into a crowd and an argument, and then he was hidden from her by a bend in the road.

6

For a little while her mind was full of fragments of speculation about this man. Was he a married man? Was he very much away from home? What did he earn? Were there ever disputes about his expenses? . . .

She must ask Isaac. For she was determined to go home and challenge her husband. She felt buoyed up by indignation and the consciousness of innocence. . . .

And then she felt an odd little doubt whether her innocence was quite so manifest as she supposed.

That doubt grew to uncomfortable proportions.

For two years she had been meeting Mr. Brumley as confidently as though they had been invisible beings, and now she had to rack her brains for just what might be mistaken, what might be misconstrued. There was nothing, she told herself, nothing, it was all as open as the day, and still her mind groped about for some forgotten circumstance, something gone almost out of memory that would bear misinterpretation. . . . How should she begin? "Isaac," she would say, "I am being followed about London." Suppose he denied his complicity! How could he deny his complicity?

The cab ran in through the gates of her home and stopped at the door. Snagsby came hurrying down the steps with a face of consternation. "Sir Isaac, my lady, has come home in a very sad state indeed."

Beyond Snagsby in the hall she came upon a lost-looking round-eyed Florence.

"Daddy's ill again," said Florence.

"You run to the nursery," said Lady Harman.

"I thought I might help," said Florence. "I don't want to play with the others."

"No, run away to the nursery."

"I want to see the ossygen let out," said Florence petulantly to her mother's unsympathetic back. "I *never* see the ossygen let out. Mum—my! . . ."

Lady Harman found her husband on the couch in his bedroom. He was propped up in a sitting position with every available cushion and pillow. His coat and waistcoat and collar had been taken off, and his shirt and vest torn open. The nearest doctor, Almsworth, was in attendance, but oxygen had not arrived, and Sir Isaac with an expression of bitter malignity upon his face was fighting desperately for breath. If anything his malignity deepened at the sight of his wife. "Damned climate," he gasped. "Wouldn't have come back—except for *your* foolery."

It seemed to help him to say that. He took a deep inhalation, pressed his lips tightly together, and nodded at her to confirm his words.

"If he's fanciful," said Almsworth. "If in any way your presence irritates him—"

"Let her stay," said Sir Isaac. "It—pleases her. . . ."

Almsworth's colleague entered with the long-desired oxygen cylinder.

7

And now every other interest in life was dominated, and every other issue postponed by the immense urgencies of Sir Isaac's illness. It had entered upon a new phase. It was manifest that he could no longer live in England, that he must go to some warm and kindly climate. There and with due precautions and observances Almsworth assured Lady Harman he might survive for many years— "an invalid, of course, but a capable one."

For some time the business of the International Stores had been preparing itself for this withdrawal. Sir Isaac had been entrusting his managers with increased responsibility and making things ready for the flotation of a company that would take the whole network of enterprises off his hands. Charterson was associated with him in this, and everything was sufficiently definite to be managed from any continental resort to which his doctors chose to send him. They chose to send him to Santa Margherita on the Ligurian coast near Rapallo and Porto Fino.

It was old Bergener of Marienbad who chose this place. Sir Isaac had wanted to go to Marienbad, his first resort abroad; he had a lively and indeed an exaggerated memory of his Kur there; his growing disposition to distrust had turned him against his London specialist, and he had caused Lady Harman to send gigantic telegrams of inquiry to old Bergener before he would be content. But Bergener would not have him at Marienbad; it wasn't the place, it was the wrong time of year, there was the very thing for them at the Regency Hotel at Santa Margherita, an entire dépendance in a beautiful garden right on the sea, admirably furnished and adapted in every way to Sir Isaac's peculiar needs. There, declared Doctor Bergener, with a proper attendant, due precaution, occasional oxygen and no excitement he would live indefinitely, that is to say eight or ten years. And attracted by the eight or ten years, which was three more than the London specialist offered, Sir Isaac finally gave in and consented to be taken to Santa Margherita.

He was to go as soon as possible, and he went in a special train and with an immense elaboration of attendance and comforts. They took with them a young doctor their specialist at Marienbad had recommended, a bright young Bavarian with a perfectly square blond head, an incurable frock coat, the manners of the less kindly type of hotel-porter and luggage which apparently consisted entirely of apparatus, an arsenal of strange-shaped shining black cases. He joined them in London and went right through with them. From Genoa at his request they obtained the services of a trained nurse, an amiable fluent-shaped woman who knew only Italian and German. For reasons that he declined to give, but which apparently had something to do with the suffrage agitation, he would have nothing to do with an English trained nurse. They had also a stenographer and typist for Sir Isaac's correspondence, and Lady Harman had a secretary, a young lady with glasses named Summersly Satchell who obviously reserved opinions of a harshly intellectual kind and had previously been in the service of the late Lady Mary Justin. She established unfriendly relations with the young doctor at an early date by attempting, he said, to learn German from him. Then there was a maid for Lady Harman, an assistant maid, and a valet-attendant for Sir Isaac. The rest of the service in the dépendance was supplied by the hotel management.

It took some weeks to assemble this expedition and transport it to its place of exile. Arrangements had to be made for closing the Putney house and establishing the children with Mrs. Harman at Black Strand. There was an exceptional amount of packing up to do, for this time Lady Harman felt she was not coming back— it might be for years. They were going out to warmth and sunlight for the rest of Sir Isaac's life.

He was entering upon the last phase in the slow disorganization of his secretions and the progressive hardening of his arterial tissues that had become his essential history. His appearance had altered much in the last few months; he had become visibly smaller, his face in particular had become sharp and little-featured. It was more and more necessary for him to sit up in order to breathe with comfort, he slept sitting up; and his senses were affected, he complained of strange tastes in his food, quarrelled with the cook and had fits of sickness. Sometimes, latterly, he had complained of strange sounds, like air whistling in water-pipes, he said, that had no existence outside his ears. Moreover, he was steadily more irritable and more suspicious and less able to control himself when angry. A long-hidden vein of vile and abusive language, hidden, perhaps, since the days of Mr. Gambard's college at Ealing, came to the surface. . . .

For some days after his seizure Lady Harman was glad to find in the stress of his necessities an excuse for disregarding altogether the crisis in the hostels and the perplexing problem of her relations to Mr. Brumley. She wrote two brief notes to the latter gentleman breaking appointments and pleading pressure of business. Then, at first during intervals of sleeplessness at night, and presently during the day, the danger and ugliness of her outlook began to trouble her. She was still, she perceived, being watched, but whether that was because her husband had failed to change whatever orders he had given, or because he was still keeping himself minutely informed of her movements, she could not tell. She was now constantly with him, and except for small spiteful outbreaks and occasional intervals of still and silent malignity, he tolerated and utilized her attentions. It was clear his jealousy of her rankled, a jealousy that made him even resentful at her health and ready to complain of any brightness of eye or vigour of movement. They had drifted far apart from the possibility of any real discussion of the hostels since that talk in the twilit study. To re-open that now or to complain of the shadowing pursuer who dogged her steps abroad would have been to precipitate Mr. Brumley's dismissal.

Even at the cost of letting things drift at the hostels for a time she wished to avoid that question. She would not see him, but she would not shut the door upon him. So far as the detective was concerned she could avoid discussion by pretending to be unaware of his existence, and as for the hostels—the hostels each day were left until the morrow.

She had learned many things since the days of her first rebellion, and she knew now that this matter of the man friend and nothing else in the world is the central issue in the emancipation of women. The difficulty of him is latent in every other restriction of which women complain. The complete emancipation of women will come with complete emancipation of humanity from jealousy—and no sooner. All other emancipations are shams until a woman may go about as freely with this man as with that, and nothing remains for emancipation when she can. In the innocence of her first revolt this question of friendship had seemed to Lady Harman the simplest, most reasonable of minor concessions, but that was simply because Mr. Brumley hadn't in those days been talking of love to her, nor she been peeping through that once locked door. Now she perceived how entirely Sir Isaac was by his standards justified.

And after all that was recognized she remained indisposed to give up Mr. Brumley.

Yet her sense of evil things happening in the hostels was a deepening distress. It troubled her so much that she took the disagreeable step of asking Mrs. Pembrose to meet her at the Bloomsbury Hostel and talk out the expulsions. She found that lady alertly defensive, entrenched behind expert knowledge and pretension generally. Her little blue eyes seemed harder than ever, the metallic resonance in her voice more marked, the lisp stronger. "Of course, Lady Harman, if you were to have some practical experience of control—" and "Three times I have given these girls every opportunity—*every* opportunity."

"It seems so hard to drive these girls out," repeated Lady Harman. "They're such human creatures."

"You have to think of the ones who remain. You must—think of the Institution as a Whole."

"I wonder," said Lady Harman, peering down into profundities for a moment. Below the great truth glimmered and vanished that Institutions were made for man and not man for Institutions.

"You see," she went on, rather to herself than to Mrs. Pembrose, "we shall be away now for a long time."

Mrs. Pembrose betrayed no excesses of grief.

"It's no good for me to interfere and then leave everything. . . ."

"That way spells utter disorganization," said Mrs. Pembrose .

"But I wish something could be done to lessen the harshness—to save the pride—of such a girl as Alice Burnet. Practically you tell her she isn't fit to associate with—the other girls."

"She's had her choice and warning after warning."

"I daresay she's—stiff. Oh!—she's difficult. But—being expelled is bitter."

"I've not *expelled* her—technically."

"She thinks she's expelled. . . ."

"You'd rather perhaps, Lady Harman, that *I* was expelled."

The dark lady lifted her eyes to the little bridling figure in front of her for a moment and dropped them again. She had had an unspeakable thought, that Mrs. Pembrose wasn't a gentlewoman, and that this sort of thing was a business for the gentle and for nobody else in the world. "I'm only anxious not to hurt anyone if I can help it," said Lady Harman.

She went on with her attempt to find some way of compromise with Mrs. Pembrose that should save the spirit of the new malcontents. She was much too concerned on account of the things that lay ahead of them to care for her own pride with Mrs. Pembrose. But that good lady had all the meager inflexibilities of her class and at last Lady Harman ceased.

She came out into the great hall of the handsome staircase, ushered by Mrs. Pembrose as a guest is ushered by a host. She looked at the spacious proportion of the architecture and thought of the hopes and imaginations she had allowed to center upon this place. It was to have been a glowing home of happy people, and over it all brooded the chill stillness of rules and regulations and methodical suppressions and tactful discouragement. It was an Institution, it had the empty orderliness of an Institution, Mrs. Pembrose had just called it an Institution, and so Susan Burnet had prophesied it would become five years or more ago. It was a dream subjugated to reality.

So it seemed to Lady Harman must all dreams be subjugated to reality, and the tossing spring greenery of the square, the sunshine, the tumult of sparrows and the confused sound of distant traffic, framed as it was in the hard dark outline of the entrance door, was as near as the promise of joy could ever come to her. "Caught and spoilt," that seemed to be the very essential of her life; just as it was of these Hostels, all the hopes, the imaginings, the sweet large anticipations, the generosities, and stirring warm desires. . . .

Perhaps Lady Harman had been a little over-working with her preparations for exile. Because as these unhappy thoughts passed through her mind she realized that she was likely to weep. It was extremely undesirable that Mrs. Pembrose should see her weeping.

But Mrs. Pembrose did see her weeping, saw her dark eyes swimming with uncontrollable tears, watched her walk past her and out, without a word or a gesture of farewell.

A kind of perplexity came upon the soul of Mrs. Pembrose. She watched the tall figure descend to her car and enter it and dispose itself gracefully and depart. . . .

"Hysterical," whispered Mrs. Pembrose at last and was greatly comforted.

"Childish," said Mrs. Pembrose sipping further consolation for an unwonted spiritual discomfort.

"Besides," said Mrs. Pembrose, "what else can one do?"

8

Sir Isaac was greatly fatigued by his long journey to Santa Margherita in spite of every expensive precaution to relieve him; but as soon as the effect of that wore off, his recovery under the system Bergener had prescribed was for a time remarkable. In a little while he was out of bed again and in an armchair. Then the young doctor began to talk of drives. They had no car with them, so he went into Genoa and spent an energetic day securing the sweetest-running automobile he could find and having it refitted for Sir Isaac's peculiar needs. In this they made a number of excursions through the hot beauty of the Italian afternoons, eastward to Genoa, westward to Sestri and northward towards Montallegro. Then they went up to the summit of the Monte de Porto Fino and Sir Isaac descended and walked about and looked at the view and praised Bergener. After that he was encouraged to visit the gracious old monastery that overhangs the road to Porto Fino.

At first Lady Harman did her duty of control and association with an apathetic resignation. This had to go on—for eight or ten years. Then her imagination began to stir again. There came a friendly letter from Mr. Brumley and she answered with a description of the color of the sea and the charm and wonder of its tideless shore. The three elder children wrote queer little letters and she answered them. She went into Rapallo and got herself a carriageful of Tauchnitz books. . . .

That visit to the monastery on the Porto Fino road was like a pleasant little glimpse into the brighter realities of the Middle Ages. The place, which is used as a home of rest for convalescent Carthusians, chanced to be quite empty and deserted; the Bavarian rang a jangling bell again and again and at last gained the attention of an old gardener working in the vineyard above, an unkempt, unshaven, ungainly creature dressed in scarce decent rags of brown, who was yet courteous-minded and, albeit crack-voiced, with his yellow-fanged mouth full of gracious polysyllables. He hobbled off to get a key and returned through the still heat of the cobbled yard outside the monastery gates, and took them into cool airy rooms and showed them clean and simple cells in shady corridors, and a delightful orangery, and led them to a beautiful terrace that looked out upon the glowing quivering sea. And he became very anxious to tell them something about "Francesco"; they could not understand him until the doctor caught "Battaglia" and "Pavia" and had an inspiration. Francis the First, he explained in clumsy but understandable English, slept here, when he was a prisoner of the Emperor and all was lost but honor. They looked at the slender pillars and graceful archings about them.

"Chust as it was now," the young doctor said, his imagination touched for a moment by mere unscientific things. . . .

They returned to their dépendance in a state of mutual contentment, Sir Isaac scarcely tired, and Lady Harman ran upstairs to change her dusty dress for a fresher muslin, while he went upon the doctor's arm to the balcony where tea was to be served to them.

She came down to find her world revolutionized.

On the table in the balcony the letters had been lying convenient to his chair and he—it may be without troubling to read the address, had seized the uppermost and torn it open.

He was holding that letter now a little crumpled in his hand.

She had walked close up to the table before she realized the change. The little eyes that met hers were afire with hatred, his lips were white and pressed together tightly, his nostrils were dilated in his struggle for breath. "I knew it," he gasped.

She clung to her dignity though she felt suddenly weak within. "That letter," she said, "was addressed to me."

There was a gleam of derision in his eyes.

"Look at it!" he said, and flung it towards her.

"My private letter!"

"Look at it!" he repeated.

"What right have you to open my letter?"

"Friendship!" he said. "Harmless friendship! Look what your—friend says!"

"Whatever there was in my letter—"

"Oh!" cried Sir Isaac. "Don't come *that* over me! Don't you try it! Oooh! phew—" He struggled for breath for a time. "He's so harmless. He's so helpful. He— Read it, you—"

He hesitated and then hurled a strange word at her.

She glanced at the letter on the table but made no movement to touch it. Then she saw that her husband's face was reddening and that his arm waved helplessly. His eyes, deprived abruptly of all the fury of conflict, implored assistance.

She darted to the French window that opened into the dining-room from the balcony. "Doctor Greve!" she cried. "Doctor Greve!"

Behind her the patient was making distressful sounds. "Doctor Greve," she screamed, and from above she heard the Bavarian shouting and then the noise of his coming down the stairs.

He shouted some direction in German as he ran past her. By an inspiration she guessed he wanted the nurse.

Miss Summersley Satchell appeared in the doorway and became helpful.

Then everyone in the house seemed to be converging upon the balcony.

It was an hour before Sir Isaac was in bed and sufficiently allayed for her to go to her own room. Then she thought of Mr. Brumley's letter, and recovered it from the table on the balcony where it had been left in the tumult of her husband's seizure.

It was twilight and the lights were on. She stood under one of them and read with two moths circling about her. . . .

Mr. Brumley had had a mood of impassioned declaration. He had alluded to his "last moments of happiness at Kew." He said he would rather kiss the hem of her garment than be the "lord of any other woman's life."

It was all so understandable—looked at in the proper light. It was all so impossible to explain. And why had she let it happen? Why had she let it happen?

9

The young doctor was a little puzzled and rather offended by Sir Isaac's relapse. He seemed to consider it incorrect and was on the whole disposed to blame Lady Harman. He might have had such a seizure, the young doctor said, later, but not now. He would be thrown back for some weeks, then he would begin to mend again and then whatever he said, whatever he did, Lady Harman must do nothing to contradict him. For a whole day Sir Isaac lay inert, in a cold sweat. He consented once to attempt eating, but sickness overcame him. He seemed so ill that all the young doctor's reassurances could not convince Lady Harman that he would recover. Then suddenly towards evening his arrested vitality was flowing again, the young doctor ceased to be anxious for his own assertions, the patient could sit up against a pile of pillows and breathe and attend to affairs. There was only one affair he really seemed anxious to attend to. His first thought when he realized his returning strength was of his wife. But the young doctor would not let him talk that night.

Next morning he seemed still stronger. He was restless and at last demanded Lady Harman again.

This time the young doctor transmitted the message .

She came to him forthwith and found him, white-faced and unfamiliar-looking, his hands gripping the quilt and his eyes burning with hatred.

"You thought I'd forgotten," was his greeting.

"Don't argue," signaled the doctor from the end of Sir Isaac's bed.

"I've been thinking it out," said Sir Isaac. "When you were thinking I was too ill to think. . . . I know better now."

He sucked in his lips and then went on. "You've got to send for old Crappen," he said. "I'm going to alter things. I had a plan. But that would have been letting you off too easy. See? So—you send for old Crappen."

"What do you mean to do?"

"Never you mind, my lady, never you mind. You send for old Crappen."

She waited for a moment. "Is that all you want me to do?"

"I'm going to make it all right about those Hostels. Don't you fear. You and your Hostels! You shan't *touch* those hostels ever again. Ever. Mrs. Pembrose go! Why! You ain't worthy to touch the heel of her shoe! Mrs. Pembrose!"

He gathered together all his forces and suddenly expelled with rousing force the word he had already applied to her on the day of the intercepted letter.

He found it seemed great satisfaction in the sound and taste of it. He repeated it thrice. "Zut," cried the doctor, "Sssh!"

Then Sir Isaac intimated his sense that calm was imperative. "You send for Crappen," he said with a quiet earnestness.

She had become now so used to terms of infamy during the last year or so, so accustomed to forgive them as part of his suffering, that she seemed not to hear the insult.

"Do you want him at once?" she asked. "Shall I telegraph?"

"Want him at once!" He dropped his voice to a whisper. "Yes, you fool—yes. Telegraph. (Phew.) Telegraph. . . . I mustn't get angry, you know. You—telegraph."

He became suddenly still. But his eyes were active with hate.

She glanced at the doctor, then moved to the door.

"I will send a telegram," she said, and left him still malignant.

She closed the door softly and walked down the long cool passage towards her own room. . . .

10

She had to be patient. She had to be patient. This sort of thing had to go on from crisis to crisis. It might go on for years. She could see no remedy and no escape.

What else was there to do but be patient? It was all amazingly unjust, but to be a married woman she was beginning to understand is to be outside justice. It is autocracy. She had once imagined otherwise, and most of her life had been the slow unlearning of that initial error. She had imagined that the hostels were hers simply because he had put it in that way. They had never been anything but his, and now it was manifest he would do what he liked with his own. The law takes no cognizance of the unwritten terms of a domestic reconciliation.

She sat down at the writing-table the hotel management had improvised for her.

She rested her chin on her hand and tried to think out her position. But what was there to think out, seeing that nature and law and custom have conspired together to put women altogether under the power of jealous and acquisitive men?

She drew the telegram form towards her.

She was going to write a telegram that she knew would bring Crappen headlong—to disinherit her absolutely. And—it suddenly struck her—her husband had trusted her to write it. She was going to do what he had trusted her to do. . . . But it was absurd.

She sat making patterns of little dots with her pencil point upon the telegram form, and there was a faint smile of amusement upon her lips.

It was absurd—and everything was absurd. What more was to be said or thought about it? This was the lot of woman. She had made her struggle, rebelled her little bit of rebellion. Most other women no doubt had done as much. It made no difference in the long run.

But it was hard to give up the hostels. She had been foolish of course, but she had not let them make her feel *real*. And she wasn't real. She was a wife—just *this*. . . .

She sighed and bestirred herself and began to write.

Then abruptly she stopped writing.

For three years her excuse for standing—everything, had been these hostels. If now the hostels were to be wrenched out of her hands, if at her husband's death she was to be stripped of every possession and left a helpless dependant on her own children, if for all her good behavior she was to be insulted by his frantic suspicions so long as he lived and then disgraced by his posthumous mistrust; was there any reason why she should go on standing anything any more? Away there in England was Mr. Brumley, *her* man, ready with service and devotion. . . .

It was a profoundly comforting thing to think of him there as hers. He was hers. He'd given so much and on the whole so well. If at last she were to go to him. . . .

Yet when she came to imagine the reality of the step that was in her mind, it took upon itself a chill and forbidding strangeness. It was like stepping out of a familiar house into empty space. What could it be like? To take some odd trunks with her, meet him somewhere, travel, travel through the evening, travel past nightfall? The bleak strangeness of that going out never to return!

Her imagination could give her no figure of Mr. Brumley as intimate, as habitual. She could as easily imagine his skeleton. He remained in all this queer speculation something friendly, something incidental, more than a trifle disembodied, entirely devoted of course in that hovering way—but hovering. . . .

And she wanted to be free. It wasn't Mr. Brumley she wanted; he was but a means—if indeed he was a means—to an end. The person she wanted, the person she had always wanted—was *herself*. Could Mr. Brumley give her that? Would Mr. Brumley give her that? Was it conceivable he would carry sacrifice to such a pitch as that? . . .

And what nonsense was this dream! Here was her husband needing her. And the children, whose inherent ungainliness, whose ungracious spirits demanded a perpetual palliation of culture and instilled deportment. What honest over-nurse was there for him or helper and guide and friend for them, if she withdrew? There was something undignified in a flight for mere happiness. There was something vindictive in flight from mere insult. To go, because she was disinherited, because her hostels were shattered,—No! And in short—she couldn't do it. . . .

If Sir Isaac wanted to disinherit her he must disinherit her. If he wanted to go on seizing and reading her letters, then he could. There was nothing in the whole scheme of things to stop him if he did not want to stop himself, nothing at all. She was caught. This was the lot of women. She was a *wife*. What else in honor was there but to be a wife up to the hilt? . . .

She finished writing her telegram.

11

Suddenly came a running in the passage outside, a rap at the door and the nurse entered, scared, voluble in Italian, but with gestures that translated her.

Lady Harman rose, realized the gravity and urgency of the moment and hurried with her along the passage. "Est-il mauvais?" the poor lady attempted, "Est-il—"

Oh! what words are there for "taken worse"?

The woman attempted English and failed. She resorted to her native Italian and exclaimed about the "povero signore." She conveyed a sense of pitiful extremities. Could it be he was in pain again? What was it? What was it? Ten minutes ago he had been so grimly angry.

At the door of the sick room the nurse laid a warning hand on the arm of Lady Harman and made an apprehensive gesture. They entered almost noiselessly.

The Bavarian doctor turned his face from the bed at their entrance. He was bending over Sir Isaac. He held up one hand as if to arrest them; his other was engaged with his patient. "No," he said. His attention went back to the sick man, and he remained very still in that position, leaving Lady Harman to note for the first time how broad and flat he was both between his shoulders and between his ears. Then his face came round slowly, he relinquished something heavy, stood up, held up a hand. "Zu spät," he whispered, as though he too was surprised. He sought in his mind for English and then found his phrase: "He has gone!"

"Gone?"

"In one instant."

"Dead?"

"So. In one instant."

On the bed lay Sir Isaac. His hand was thrust out as though he grasped at some invisible thing. His open eyes stared hard at his wife, and as she met his eyes he snored noisily in his nose and throat.

She looked from the doctor to the nurse. It seemed to her that both these people must be mad. Never had she seen anything less like death. "But he's not dead!" she protested, still standing in the middle of the room.

"It iss chust the air in his throat," the doctor said. "He went—so! In one instant as I was helping him."

He waited to see some symptom of feminine weakness. There was a quality in his bearing—as though this event did him credit.

"But—Isaac!"

It was astounding. The noise in his throat ceased. But he still stared at her. And then the nurse made a kind of assault upon Lady Harman, caught her— even if she didn't fall. It was no doubt the proper formula to collapse. Or to fling oneself upon the deceased. Lady Harman resisted this assistance, disentangled herself and remained amazed; the nurse a little disconcerted but still ready behind her.

"But," said Lady Harman slowly, not advancing and pointing incredulously at the unwinking stare that met her own, "is he dead? Is he really dead? Like that?"

The doctor's gesture to the nurse betrayed his sense of the fine quick scene this want of confidence had ruined. Under no circumstances in life did English people really seem to know how to behave or what was expected of them. He answered with something bordering upon irony. "Madam," he said, with a slight bow, "he is *really* det."

"But—like *that!*" cried Lady Harman.

"Like that," repeated the doctor.

She went three steps nearer and stopped, open-eyed, wonder-struck, her lips compressed.

12

For a time astonishment overwhelmed her mind. She did not think of Sir Isaac, she did not think of herself, her whole being was filled by this marvel of death and cessation. Like *that!*

Death!

Never before had she seen it. She had expected an extreme dignity, an almost ceremonial sinking back, a slow ebbing, but this was like a shot from a bow. It stunned her. And for some time she remained stunned, while the doctor and her secretary and the hotel people did all that they deemed seemly on this great occasion. She let them send her into another room; she watched with detached indifference a post-mortem consultation in whispers with a doctor from Rapallo. Then came a great closing of shutters. The nurse and her maid hovered about her, ready to assist her when the sorrowing began. But she had no sorrow. The long moments lengthened out, and he was still dead and she was still only amazement. It seemed part of the extraordinary, the perennial surprisingness of Sir Isaac that he should end in this way. Dead! She didn't feel for some hours that he had in any way ended. He had died with such emphasis that she felt now that he was capable of anything. What mightn't he do next? When she heard movements in the chamber of death it seemed to her that of all the people there, most probably it was he who made them. She would not have been amazed if he had suddenly appeared in the doorway of her room, anger-white and his hand quiveringly extended, spluttering some complaint.

He might have cried: "Here I am dead! And it's *you,* damn you—it's *you!*"

It was after distinct efforts, after repeated visits to the room in which he lay, that she began to realize that death was death, that death goes on, that there was no more any Sir Isaac, but only a still body he had left behind, that was being molded now into a stiff image of peace.

Then for a time she roused herself to some control of their proceedings. The doctor came to Lady Harman to ask her about the meals for the day, the hotel manager was in entanglements of tactful consideration, and then the nurse came for instructions upon some trivial matter. They had done what usage prescribes and now, in the absence of other direction, they appealed to her wishes. She remarked that everyone was going on tiptoe and speaking in undertones. . . .

She realized duties. What does one have to do when one's husband is dead? People would have to be told. She would begin by sending off telegrams to various people, to his mother, to her own, to his lawyer. She remembered she had already written a telegram—that very morning to Crappen. Should she still let the lawyer come out? He was her lawyer now. Perhaps he had better come, but instead of that telegram, which still lay upon the desk, she would wire the news of the death to him. . . .

Does one send to the papers? How does one send to the papers?

She took Miss Summersly Satchell who was hovering outside in the sunshine on the balcony, into her room, and sat pale and businesslike and very careful about details, while Miss Summersly Satchell offered practical advice and took notes and wrote telegrams and letters. . . .

There came a hush over everything as the day crept towards noon, and the widowed woman sat in her own room with an inactive mind, watching thin bars of sunlight burn their slow way across the floor. He was dead. It was going on now more steadfastly than ever. He was keeping dead. He was dead at last for good and her married life was over, that life that had always seemed the only possible life, and this stunning incident, this thing that was like the blinding of eyes or the bursting of eardrums, was to be the beginning of strange new experiences.

She was afraid at first at their possible strangeness. And then, you know, in spite of a weak protesting compunction she began to feel glad. . . .

She would not admit to herself that she was glad, that she was anything but a woman stunned, she maintained her still despondent attitude as long as she could, but gladness broke upon her soul as the day breaks, and a sense of release swam up to the horizons of her mind and rose upon her, flooding every ripple of her being, as the sun rises over water in a clear sky. Presently she could sit there no longer, she had to stand up. She walked to the closed Venetians to look out upon the world and checked herself upon the very verge of flinging them open. He was dead and it was all over forever. Of course!—it was all over! Her marriage was finished and done. Miss Satchell came to summon her to lunch. Throughout that meal Lady Harman maintained a somber bearing, and listened with attention to the young doctor's comments on the manner of Sir Isaac's going. And then,—it was impossible to go back to her room.

"My head aches," she said, "I must go down and sit by the sea," and her maid, a little shocked, brought her not only her sunshade, but needless wraps— as though a new-made widow must necessarily be very sensitive to the air. She would not let her maid come with her, she went down to the beach alone. She sat on some rocks near the very edge of the transparent water and fought her gladness for a time and presently yielded to it. He was dead. One thought filled her mind, for a while so filled her mind, that no other thought it seemed could follow it, it had an effect of being final; it so filled her mind that it filled the whole world; the broad sapphire distances of the sea, the lapping waves amidst the rocks at her feet, the blazing sun, the dark headland of Porto Fino and a small sailing boat that hung beyond came all within it like things enclosed within a golden globe. She forgot all the days of nursing and discomfort and pity behind her, all the duties and ceremonies before her, forgot all the details and circumstances of life in this one luminous realization. She was free at last. She was a free woman.

Never more would he make a sound or lift a finger against her life, never more would he contradict her or flout her; never more would he come peeping through that papered panel between his room and hers, never more could hateful and humiliating demands be made upon her as his right; no more strange distresses of the body nor raw discomfort of the nerves could trouble her—forever. And no more detectives, no more suspicions, no more accusations. That last blow he had meant to aim was frozen before it could strike her. And she would have the Hostels in her hands, secure and undisputed, she could deal as she liked with Mrs. Pembrose, take such advisers as she pleased. . . . She was free.

She found herself planning the regeneration of those difficult and disputed hostels, plans that were all colored by the sun and sky of Italy. The manacles had gone; her hands were free. She would make this her supreme occupation. She had learned her lesson now she felt, she knew something of the mingling of control and affectionate regard that was needed to weld the warring uneasy units of her new community. And she could do it, now as she was and unencumbered, she knew this power was in her. When everything seemed lost to her, suddenly it was all back in her hands. . . .

She discovered the golden serenity of her mind with a sudden astonishment and horror. She was amazed and shocked that she should be glad. She struggled against it and sought to subdue her spirit to a becoming grief. One should be sorrowful at death in any case, one should be grieved. She tried to think of Sir Isaac with affection, to recall touching generosities, to remember kind things and tender and sweet things and she could not do so. Nothing would come back but the white intensities of his face, nothing but his hatred, his suspicion and his pitiless mean mastery. From which she was freed.

She could not feel sorry. She did her utmost to feel sorry; presently when she went back into the dépendance, she had to check her feet to a regretful pace;

she dreaded the eyes of the hotel visitors she passed in the garden lest they should detect the liberation of her soul. But the hotel visitors being English were for the most part too preoccupied with manifestations of a sympathy that should be at once heart-felt and quite unobtrusive and altogether in the best possible taste, to have any attention free for the soul of Lady Harman.

The sense of her freedom came and went like the sunlight of a day in spring, though she attempted her utmost to remain overcast. After dinner that night she was invaded by a vision of the great open years before her, at first hopeful but growing at last to fear and a wild restlessness, so that in defiance of possible hotel opinion, she wandered out into the moonlight and remained for a long time standing by the boat landing, dreaming, recovering, drinking in the white serenities of sea and sky. There was no hurry now. She might stay there as long as she chose. She need account for herself to no one; she was free. She might go where she pleased, do what she pleased, there was no urgency anymore. . . .

There was Mr. Brumley. Mr. Brumley made a very little figure at first in the great prospect before her. . . . Then he grew larger in her thoughts. She recalled his devotions, his services, his self-control. It was good to have one understanding friend in this great limitless world. . . .

She would have to keep that friendship. . . .

But the glorious thing was freedom, to live untrammelled. . . .

Through the stillness a little breeze came stirring, and she awoke out of her dream and turned and faced the shuttered dépendance. A solitary dim light was showing on the veranda. All the rest of the building was a shapeless mass of gray. The long pale front of the hotel seen through a grove of orange trees was lit now at every other window with people going to bed. Beyond, a black hillside clambered up to the edge of the sky.

Far away out of the darknesses a man with a clear strong voice was singing to a tinkling accompaniment.

In the black orange trees swam and drifted a score of fireflies, and there was a distant clamor of nightingales when presently the unseen voice had done.

13

When she was in her room again she began to think of Sir Isaac and more particularly of that last fixed stare of his. . . .

She was impelled to go and see him, to see for herself that he was peaceful and no longer a figure of astonishment. She went slowly along the corridor and very softly into his room—it remained, she felt, his room. They had put candles about him, and the outline of his face, showing dimly through the linen that veiled it, was like the face of one who sleeps very peacefully. Very gently she uncovered it.

He was not simply still, he was immensely still. He was more still and white than the moonlight outside, remoter than moon or stars. . . . She stood surveying him.

He looked small and pinched and as though he had been very tired. Life was over for him, altogether over. Never had she seen anything that seemed so finished. Once, when she was a girl she had thought that death might be but the opening of a door upon a more generous feast of living than this cramped world could give, but now she knew, she saw, that death can be death.

Life was over. She felt she had never before realized the meaning of death. That beautiful night outside, and all the beautiful nights and days that were still to come and all the sweet and wonderful things of God's world could be nothing to him now forever. There was no dream in him that could ever live again, there was no desire, no hope in him.

And had he ever had his desire or his hope, or felt the intensities of life?

There was this beauty she had been discovering in the last few years, this mystery of love,—all that had been hidden from him.

She began to realize something sorrowful and pitiful in his quality, in his hardness, his narrowness, his bickering suspicions, his malignant refusals of all things generous and beautiful. He made her feel, as sometimes the children made her feel, the infinite pity of perversity and resistance to the bounties and kindliness of life.

The shadow of sorrow for him came to her at last.

Yet how obstinate he looked, the little frozen white thing that had been Sir Isaac Harman! And satisfied, wilfully satisfied; his lips were compressed and his mouth a little drawn in at the corners as if he would not betray any other feeling than content with the bargain he had made with life. She did not touch him; not for the world would she ever touch that cold waxen thing that had so lately clasped her life, but she stood for a long time by the side of his quiet, immersed in the wonder of death. . . .

He had been such a hard little man, such a pursuing little man, so unreasonable and difficult a master, and now—he was such a poor shrunken little man for all his obstinacy! She had never realized before that he was pitiful. . . . Had she perhaps feared him too much, disliked him too much to deal fairly with him? Could she have helped him? Was there anything she could have done that she had not done? Might she not at least have saved him his suspicion? Behind his rages, perhaps he had been wretched.

Could anyone else have helped him? If perhaps someone had loved him more than she had ever pretended to do—

How strange that she should be so intimately in this room—and still so alien. So alien that she could feel nothing but detached wonder at his infinite loss. . . . Alien,—that was what she had always been, a captured alien in this man's household,—a girl he had taken. Had he ever suspected how alien? The true mourner, poor woman! was even now, in charge of Cook's couriers and interpreters, coming by express from London, to see with her own eyes this last still phase of the son she had borne into the world and watched and sought to serve. She was his nearest; she indeed was the only near thing there had ever been in his life. Once at least he must have loved her? And even she had not been very near. No one had ever been very near his calculating suspicious heart. Had he ever said or thought any really sweet or tender thing—even about her? He had been generous to her in money matters, of course,—but out of a vast abundance. . . .

How good it was to have a friend! How good it was to have even one single friend! . . .

At the thought of his mother Lady Harman's mind began to drift slowly from this stiff culmination of life before her. Presently she replaced the white cloth upon his face and turned slowly away. Her imagination had taken up the question of how that poor old lady was to be met, how she was to be consoled, what was to be said to her. . . .

She began to plan arrangements. The room ought to be filled with flowers; Mrs. Harman would expect flowers, large heavy white flowers in great abundance. That would have to be seen to soon. One might get them in Rapallo. And afterwards,—they would have to take him to England, and have a fine great funeral, with every black circumstance his wealth and his position demanded. Mrs. Harman would need that, and so it must be done. Cabinet Ministers must follow him, members of Parliament, all Blenkerdom feeling self-consciously and, as far as possible, deeply, the Chartersons by way of friends, unfamiliar blood relations, a vast retinue of employees. . . .

How could one take him? Would he have to be embalmed? Embalming!— what a strange complement of death. She averted herself a little more from the quiet figure on the bed, and could not turn to it again. They might come here and do all sorts of things to it, mysterious, evil-seeming things with knives and drugs. . . .

She must not think of that. She must learn exactly what Mrs. Harman thought and desired. Her own apathy with regard to her husband had given way completely now to a desire to anticipate and meet Mrs. Harman's every conceivable wish.

CHAPTER THE TWELFTH

Love and a Serious Lady

1

THE NEWS OF Sir Isaac's death came quite unexpectedly to Mr. Brumley. He was at the Climax Club, and rather bored; he had had some tea and dry toast in the magazine room, and had been through the weeklies, and it was a particularly uninteresting week. Then he came down into the hall, looked idly at the latest bulletins upon the board, and read that "Sir Isaac Harman died suddenly this morning at Sta. Margherita, in Ligure, whither he had gone for rest and change."

He went on mechanically reading down the bulletin, leaving something of himself behind him that did not read on. Then he returned to that remarkable item and re-read it, and picked up that lost element of his being again.

He had awaited this event for so long, thought of it so often in such a great variety of relationships, dreamed of it, hoped for it, prayed for it, and tried not to think of it, that now it came to him in reality it seemed to have no substance or signficance whatever. He had exhausted the fact before it happened. Since first he had thought of it there had passed four long years, and in that time he had seen it from every aspect, exhausted every possibility. It had become a theoretical possibility, the basis of continually less confident, continually more unsubstantial day dreams. Constantly he had tried not to think of it, tried to assure himself of Sir Isaac's invalid immortality. And here it was!

The line above it concerned an overdue ship, the line below resumed a speech by Mr. Lloyd George. "He would challenge the honorable member to repeat his accusations—"

Mr. Brumley stood quite still before the mauve-colored print letters for some time, then went slowly across the hall into the breakfast-room, sat down in a chair by the fireplace, and fell into a kind of featureless thinking. Sir Isaac was dead, his wife was free, and the long waiting that had become a habit was at an end.

He had anticipated a wild elation, and for a while he was only sensible of change, a profound change. . . .

He began to feel glad that he had waited, that she had insisted upon patience, that there had been no disaster, no scandal between them. Now everything was clear for them. He had served his apprenticeship. They would be able to marry, and have no quarrel with the world.

He sat with his mind forming images of the prospect before him, images that were at first feeble and vague, and then, though still in a silly way, more concrete and definite. At first they were quite petty anticipations, of how he would have to tell people of his approaching marriage, of how he would break it to George Edmund that a new mother impended. He mused for some time upon the details of that. Should he take her down to George Edmund's school, and let the boy fall in love with her—he would certainly fall in love with her—before anything definite was said, or should he first go down alone and break the news? Each method had its own attractive possibilities of drama.

Then Mr. Brumley began to think of the letter he must write Lady Harman— a difficult letter. One does not rejoice at death. Already Mr. Brumley was beginning to feel a generous pity for the man he had done his utmost not to detest for so long. Poor Sir Isaac had lived like a blind thing in the sunlight, gathering and gathering, when the pride and pleasure of life is to administer and spend. . . . Mr. Brumley fell wondering just how she could be feeling now about her dead husband. She might be in a phase of quite real sorrow. Probably the last illness had tired and strained her. So that his letter would have to be very fine and tender and soothing, free from all harshness, free from any gladness— yet it would be hard not to let a little of his vast relief peep out. Always hitherto, except for one or two such passionate lapses as that which had precipitated the situation at Santa Margherita, his epistolary manner had been formal, his matter intellectual and philanthropic, for he had always known that no letter was absolutely safe from Sir Isaac's insatiable research. Should he still be formal, still write to "Dear Lady Harman," or suddenly break into a new warmth? Half an hour later he was sitting in the writing-room with some few flakes of torn paper on the carpet between his feet and the partially filled wastepaper basket, still meditating upon this difficult issue of the address.

The letter he achieved at last began, "My dear Lady," and went on to, "I do not know how to begin this letter—perhaps you will find it almost as difficult to receive. . . ."

In the small hours he woke to one of his habitual revulsions. Was that, he asked himself, the sort of letter a lover should write to the beloved on her release, on the sudden long prayed-for opening of a way to her, on the end of her shameful servitude and his humiliations? He began to recall the cold and stilted sentences of that difficult composition. The gentility of it! All his life he had been a prey to gentility, had cast himself free from it, only to relapse again in such fashion as this. Would he never be human and passionate and sincere? Of course he was glad, and she ought to be glad, that Sir Isaac, their enemy and their prison, was dead; it was for them to rejoice together. He turned out of bed at last, when he could lie still under these self-accusations no longer, and wrapped himself in his warm dressing-gown and began to write. He wrote in pencil. His fountain-pen was as usual on his night table, but pencil seemed the better medium, and he wrote a warm and glowing love-letter that was brought to an end at last by an almost passionate fit of sneezing. He could find no envelopes in his bedroom Davenport, and so he left that honest scrawl under a paper-weight, and went back to bed greatly comforted. He re-read it in the morning with emotion, and some slight misgivings that grew after he had despatched it. He went to lunch at his club contemplating a third letter that should be sane and fine and sweet, and that should rectify the confusing effect of those two previous efforts. He wrote this letter later in the afternoon.

The days seemed very long before the answer to his first letter came to him, and in that interval two more—aspects went to her. Her reply was very brief, and written in the large, firm, still girlishly clear hand that distinguished her.

"I was so glad of your letter. My life is so strange here, a kind of hushed life. The nights are extraordinarily beautiful, the moon very large and the little leaves on the trees still and black. We are coming back to England and the funeral will be from our Putney house."

That was all, but it gave Mr. Brumley an impression of her that was exceedingly vivid and close. He thought of her, shadowy and dusky in the moonlight until his soul swam with love for her; he had to get up and walk about; he whispered her name very softly to himself several times; he groaned gently, and at last he went to his little desk and wrote to her his sixth letter—quite a beautiful letter. He told her that he loved her, that he had always loved her since their first moment of meeting, and he tried to express just the wave of tenderness that inundated him at the thought of her away there in Italy. Once, he said, he had dreamed that he would be the first to take her to Italy. Perhaps someday they would yet be in Italy together.

2

It was only by insensible degrees that doubt crept into Mr. Brumley's assurances. He did not observe at once that none of the brief letters she wrote him responded to his second, the impassioned outbreak in pencil. And it seemed only in keeping with the modest reserves of womanhood that she should be restrained—she always had been restrained.

She asked him not to see her at once when she returned to England; she wanted, she said, "to see how things are," and that fell in very well with a certain delicacy in himself. The unburied body of Sir Isaac—it was now provisionally embalmed—was, through some inexplicable subtlety in his mind, a far greater barrier than the living man had ever been, and he wanted it out of the way. And everything settled. Then, indeed, they might meet.

Meanwhile he had a curious little private conflict of his own. He was trying not to think, day and night he was trying not to think, that Lady Harman was now a very rich woman. Yet some portions of his brain, and he had never suspected himself of such lawless regions, persisted in the most vulgar and outrageous suggestions, suggestions that made his soul blush; schemes, for example, of splendid foreign travel, of hotel staffs bowing, of a yacht in the Mediterranean, of motor cars, of a palatial flat in London, of a box at the opera, of artists patronized, of—most horrible!—a baronetcy. . . . The more authentic parts of Mr. Brumley cowered from and sought to escape these squalid dreams of magnificences. It shocked and terrified him to find such things could come out in him. He was like some pest-stricken patient, amazedly contemplating his first symptom. His better part denied, repudiated. Of course he would never touch, never even propose—or hint. . . . It was an aspect he had never once contemplated before Sir Isaac died. He could on his honor, and after searching his heart, say that. Yet in Pall Mall one afternoon, suddenly, he caught himself with a thought in his head so gross, so smug, that he uttered a faint cry and quickened his steps. . . . Benevolent stepfather!

These distresses begot a hope. Perhaps, after all, probably, there would be some settlement. . . . She might not be rich, not so very rich. . . . She might be tied up. . . .

He perceived in that lay his hope of salvation. Otherwise—oh, pitiful soul!— things were possible in him; he saw only too clearly what dreadful things were possible.

If only she were disinherited, if only he might take her, stripped of all these possessions that even in such glancing anticipations begot—this horrid indigestion of the imagination!

But then,—the Hostels? . . .

There he stumbled against an invincible riddle!

There was something dreadful about the way in which these considerations blotted out the essential fact of separations abolished, barriers lowered, the way to an honorable love made plain and open. . . .

The day of the funeral came at last, and Mr. Brumley tried not to think of it, paternally, at Margate. He fled from Sir Isaac's ultimate withdrawal. Blenker's obituary notice in the *Old Country Gazette* was a masterpiece of tactful eulogy, ostentatiously loyal, yet extremely not unmindful of the widowed proprietor, and of all the possible changes of ownership looming ahead. Mr. Brumley, reading it in the Londonward train, was greatly reminded of the Hostels. That was a riddle he didn't begin to solve. Of course, it was imperative the Hostels should continue—imperative. Now they might run them together, openly, side by side. But then, with such temptations to hitherto inconceivable vulgarities. And again, insidiously, those visions returned of two figures, manifestly opulent, grouped about a big motor car or standing together under a large subservient archway. . . .

There was a long letter from her at his flat, a long and amazing letter. It was so folded that his eye first caught the writing on the third page: "*never marry again. It is so clear that our work needs all my time and all my means.*" His eyebrows rose, his expression became consternation; his hands trembled a little as he turned the letter over to read it through. It was a deliberate letter. It began—

"*Dear Mr. Brumley, I could never have imagined how much there is to do after we are dead, and before we can be buried.*"

"Yes," said Mr. Brumley; "but what does this *mean?*"

"*There are so many surprises—*"

"It isn't clear."

"*In ourselves and the things about us.*"

"Of course, he would have made some complicated settlement. I might have known."

"*It is the strangest thing in the world to be a widow, much stranger than anyone could ever have supposed, to have no one to control one, no one to think of as coming before one, no one to answer to, to be free to plan one's life for oneself—*"

He stood with the letter in his hand after he had read it through, perplexed.

"I can't stand this," he said. "I want to know."

He went to his desk and wrote:—

"*My Dear, I want you to marry me.*"

What more was to be said? He hesitated with this brief challenge in his hand, was minded to telegraph it and thought of James's novel, *In the Cage*. Telegraph operators are only human after all. He determined upon a special messenger and rang up his quarter valet—he shared service in his flat—to despatch it.

The messenger boy got back from Putney that evening about half-past eight. He brought a reply in pencil.

"*My dear Friend,*" she wrote. "*You have been so good to me, so helpful. But I do not think that is possible. Forgive me. I want so badly to think and here I cannot think. I have never been able to think here. I am going down to Black Strand, and in a day or so I will write and we will talk. Be patient with me.*"

She signed her name "*Ellen*"; always before she had been "E. H."

"Yes," cried Mr. Brumley, "but I want to know!"

He fretted for an hour and went to the telephone.

Something was wrong with the telephone, it buzzed and went faint, and it would seem that at her end she was embarrassed. "I want to come to you now," he said. "Impossible," was the clearest word in her reply. Should he go in a state of virile resolution, force her hesitation as a man should? She might be involved there with Mrs. Harman, with all sorts of relatives and strange people. . . .

In the end he did not go.

3

He sat at his lunch alone next day at one of the little tables men choose when they shun company. But to the right of him was the table of the politicians, Adolphus Blenker and Pope of the East Purblow Experiment, and Sir Piper Nicolls, and Munk, the editor of the *Daily Rectification,* sage men all and deep in those mysterious manipulations and wire-pullings by which the Liberal Party organization was even then preparing for itself unusual distrust and dislike, and Horatio Blenker was tenoring away after his manner about a case of right and conscience, "Blenking like Winking" was how a silent member had put it once to Brumley in a gust of hostile criticism. "Practically if she marries again, she is a pauper," struck on Brumley's ears.

"Of course," said Mr. Brumley, and stopped eating.

"I don't know if you remember the particulars of the Astor case," began Munk. . . .

Never had Mr. Brumley come so frankly to eavesdropping. But he heard no more of Lady Harman. Munk had to quote the rights and wrongs of various American wills, and then Mr. Pope seized his opportunity. "At East Purblow," he went on, "in quite a number of instances we had to envisage this problem of the widow—"

Mr. Brumley pushed back his plate and strolled towards the desk.

It was exactly what he might have expected, what indeed had been at the back of his mind all along, and on the whole he was glad. Naturally she hesitated; naturally she wanted time to think, and as naturally it was impossible for her to tell him what it was she was thinking about.

They would marry. They must marry. Love has claims supreme over all other claims and he felt no doubt that for her his comparative poverty of two thousand a year would mean infinitely more happiness than she had ever known or could know with Sir Isaac's wealth. She was reluctant, of course, to become dependent upon him until he made it clear to her what infinite pleasure it would be for him to supply her needs. Should he write to her forthwith? He outlined a letter in his mind, a very fine and generous letter, good phrases came, and then he reflected that it would be difficult to explain to her just how he had learned of her peculiar situation. It would be far more seemly to wait either for a public announcement or for some intimation from her.

And then he began to realize that this meant the end of all their work at the Hostels. In his first satisfaction at escaping that possible great motor-car and all the superfluities of Sir Isaac's accumulation, he had forgotten that side of the business. . . .

When one came to think it over, the Hostels did complicate the problem. It was ingenious of Sir Isaac. . . .

It was infernally ingenious of Sir Isaac. . . .

He could not remain in the club for fear that somebody might presently come talking to him and interrupt his train of thought. He went out into the streets.

These Hostels upset everything.

What he had supposed to be a way of escape was really the mouth of a net. Whichever way they turned Sir Isaac crippled them. . . .

4

Mr. Brumley grew so angry that presently even the strangers in the street annoyed him. He turned his face homeward. He hated dilemmas; he wanted always to deny them, to thrust them aside, to take impossible third courses.

"For three years," shouted Mr. Brumley, free at last in his study to give way to his rage, "for three years I've been making her care for these things. And then—and then—they turn against me!"

A violent, incredibly undignified wrath against the dead man seized him. He threw books about the room. He cried out vile insults and mingled words of an unfortunate commonness with others of extreme rarity. He wanted to go off to Kensal Green and hammer at the grave there and tell the departed knight exactly what he thought of him. Then presently he became calmer, he lit a pipe, picked up the books from the floor, and meditated revenges upon Sir Isaac's memory. I deplore my task of recording these ungracious moments in Mr. Brumley's love history. I deplore the ease with which men pass from loving and serving women to an almost canine fight for them. It is the ugliest essential of romance. There is indeed much in the human heart that I deplore. But Mr. Brumley was exasperated by disappointment. He was sore, he was raw. Driven by an intolerable desire to explore every possibility of the situation, full indeed of an unholy vindictiveness, he went off next morning with strange questions to Maxwell Hartington.

He put the case as a general case.

"Lady Harman?" said Maxwell Hartington.

"No, not particularly Lady Harman. A general principle. What are people— what are women tied up in such a way to do?"

Precedents were quoted and possibilities weighed. Mr. Brumley was flushed, vague but persistent.

"Suppose," he said, "that they love each other passionately—and their work, whatever it may be, almost as passionately. Is there no way—?"

"He'll have a *dum casta* clause right enough," said Maxwell Hartington.

"*Dum—? Dum casta!* But, oh! anyhow *that's* out of the question—absolutely," said Mr. Brumley.

"Of course," said Maxwell Hartington, leaning back in his chair and rubbing the ball of his thumb into one eye. "Of course—nobody ever enforces these *dum casta* clauses. There isn't anyone to enforce them. Ever."— He paused and then went on, speaking apparently to the array of black tin boxes in the dingy fixtures before him. "Who's going to watch you? That's what I always ask in these cases. Unless the lady goes and does things right under the noses of these trustees they aren't going to bother. Even Sir Isaac I suppose hasn't provided funds for a private detective. Eh? You said something?"

"Nothing," said Mr. Brumley.

"Well, why should they start a perfectly rotten action like that," continued Maxwell Hartington, now addressing himself very earnestly to his client, "when they've only got to keep quiet and do their job and be comfortable? In these matters, Brumley, as in most matters affecting the relations of men and women, people can do absolutely what they like nowadays, absolutely, unless there's someone about ready to make a row. Then they can't do anything. It hardly matters if they don't do anything. A row's a row and damned disgraceful. If there isn't a row, nothing's disgraceful. Of course all these laws and regulations and institutions and arrangements are just ways of putting people at the mercy of blackmailers and jealous and violent persons. One's only got to be a lawyer for a bit to realize that. Still that's not *our* business. That's psychology. If there aren't any jealous and violent persons about, well, then no ordinary decent person is going to worry what you do. No decent person ever does. So far as I can gather the only barbarian in this case is the testator—now in Kensal Green. With additional precautions I suppose in the way of an artistic but thoroughly massive monument presently to be added—"

"He'd—turn in his grave."

"Let him. No trustees are obliged to take action on *that*. I don't suppose they'd know if he did. I've never known a trustee bother yet about post-mortem movements of any sort. If they did, we'd all be having Prayers for the Dead. Fancy having to consider the subsequent reflections of the testator!"

"Well anyhow," said Mr. Brumley, after a little pause, "such a breach, such a proceeding is out of the question—absolutely out of the question. It's unthinkable."

"Then why did you come here to ask me about it?" demanded Maxwell Hartington, beginning to rub the other eye in an audible and unpleasant manner.

5

When at last Mr. Brumley was face to face with Lady Harman again, a vast mephitic disorderly creation of anticipations, intentions, resolves, suspicions, provisional hypotheses, urgencies, vindications, and wild and whirling stuff generally vanished out of hi mind. There beside the raised seat in the midst of the little rock garden where they had talked together five years before, she stood waiting for him, this tall simple woman he had always adored since their first encounter, a little strange and shy now in her dead black uniform of widowhood, but with her honest eyes greeting him, her friendly hands held out to him. He would have kissed them but for the restraining presence of Snagsby who had brought him to her; as it was it seemed to him that the phantom of a kiss passed like a breath between them. He held her hands for a moment and relinquished them.

"It is so good to see you," he said, and they sat down side by side. "I am very glad to see you again."

Then for a little while they sat in silence.

Mr. Brumley had imagined and rehearsed this meeting in many different moods. Now, he found none of his premeditated phrases served him, and it was the lady who undertook the difficult opening.

"I could not see you before," she began. "I did not want to see anyone." She sought to explain. "I was strange. Even to myself. Suddenly—" She came to the point. "To find oneself free. . . . Mr. Brumley,—*it was wonderful!*"

He did not interrupt her and presently she went on again.

"You see," she said, "I have become a human being—owning myself. I had never thought what this change would be to me. . . . It has been—. It has been—like being born, when one hadn't realized before that one wasn't born. . . . Now—now I can act. I can do this and that. I used to feel as though I was on strings—with somebody able to pull. . . . There is no one now able to pull at me, no one able to thwart me. . . ."

Her dark eyes looked among the trees and Mr. Brumley watched her profile.

"It has been like falling out of a prison from which one never hoped to escape. I feel like a moth that has just come out of its case,—you know how they come out, wet and weak but—released. For a time I feel I can do nothing but sit in the sun."

"It's queer," she repeated, "how one tries to feel differently from what one really feels, how one tries to feel as one supposes people expect one to feel. At first I hardly dared look at myself. . . . I thought I ought to be sorrowful and helpless. . . . I am not in the least sorrowful or helpless. . . ."

"But," said Mr. Brumley, "are you so free?"

"Yes."

"Altogether?"

"As free now—as a man."

"But—people are saying in London—. Something about a will—."

Her lips closed. Her brows and eyes became troubled. She seemed to gather herself together for an effort and spoke at length, without looking at him. "Mr. Brumley," she said, "before I knew anything of the will—. On the very evening when Isaac died—. I knew—I would never marry again. Never."

Mr. Brumley did not stir. He remained regarding her with a mournful expression.

"I was sure of it then," she said, "I knew nothing about the will. I want you to understand that—clearly."

She said no more. The still pause lengthened. She forced herself to meet his eyes.

"I thought," he said after a silent scrutiny, and left her to imagine what he had thought. . . .

"But," he urged to her protracted silence, "you *care?*"

She turned her face away. She looked at the hand lying idle upon her crape-covered knee. "You are my dearest friend," she said very softly. "You are almost my only friend. But—. I can never go into marriage any more. . . ."

"My dear," he said, "the marriage you have known—."

"No," she said. "No sort of marriage."

Mr. Brumley heaved a profound sigh.

"Before I had been a widow twenty-four hours, I began to realize that I was an escaped woman. It wasn't the particular marriage. . . . It was any marriage. . . . All we women are tied. Most of us are willing to be tied perhaps, but only as people are willing to be tied to life-belts in a wreck—from fear from drowning. And now, I am just one of the free women, like the women who can earn large incomes, or the women who happen to own property. I've paid my penalties and my service is over. . . . I knew, of course, that you would ask me this. It isn't that I don't care for you, that I don't love your company and your help—and the love and the kindness. . . ."

"Only," he said, "although it is the one thing I desire, although it is the one return you can make me—. But whatever I have done—I have done willingly. . . .

"My dear!" cried Mr. Brumley, breaking out abruptly at a fresh point, "I want you to marry me. I want you to be mine, to be my dear close companion, the care of my life, the beauty in my life. . . . I can't frame sentences, my dear. You know, you know. . . . Since first I saw you, talked to you in this very garden. . . ."

"I don't forget a thing," she answered. "It has been my life as well as yours. Only—"

The grip of her hand tightened on the back of their seat. She seemed to be examining her thumb intently. Her voice sank to a whisper. "I won't marry you," she said.

6

Mr. Brumley leaned back, then he bent forward in a desperate attitude with his hands and arms thrust between his knees, then suddenly he recovered, stood up and then knelt with one knee upon the seat. "What are you going to do with me then?" he asked.

"I want you to go on being my friend."

"I can't."

"You can't?"

"No,—I've *hoped*."

And then with something almost querulous in his voice, he repeated, "My dear, I want you to marry me and I want now nothing else in the world."

She was silent for a moment. "Mr. Brumley," she said, looking up at him, "have you no thought for our Hostels?"

Mr. Brumley as I have said hated dilemmas. He started to his feet, a man stung. He stood in front of her and quivered extended hands at her. "What do such things matter," he cried, "when a man is in love?"

She shrank a little from him. "But," she asked, "haven't they always mattered?"

"Yes," he expostulated; "but these Hostels, these Hostels. . . . We've started them—isn't that good enough? We've set them going . . ."

"Do you know," she asked, "what would happen to the hostels if I were to marry?"

"They would go on," he said.

"They would go to a committee. Named. It would include Mrs. Pembrose. . . . Don't you see what would happen? He understood the case so well. . . ."

Mr. Brumley seemed suddenly shrunken. "He understood too well," he said.

He looked down at her soft eyes, at her drooping gracious form, and it seemed to him that indeed she was made for love and that it was unendurable that she should be content to think of friendship and freedom as the ultimate purposes of her life. . . .

7

Presently these two were walking in the pine-woods beyond the garden and Mr. Brumley was discoursing lamentably of love, this great glory that was denied them.

The shade of perplexity deepened in her dark eyes as she listened. Ever and again she seemed about to speak and then checked herself and let him talk on.

He spoke of the closeness of love and the deep excitement of love and how it filled the soul with pride and the world with wonder, and of the universal right of men and women to love. He told of his dreams and his patience, and of the stormy hopes that would not be suppressed when he heard that Sir Isaac was dead. And as he pictured to himself the lost delights at which he hinted, as he called back those covert expectations, he forgot that she had declared herself resolved upon freedom at any cost, and his rage against Sir Isaac, who had possessed and wasted all that he would have cherished so tenderly, grew to nearly uncontrollable proportions. "Here was your life," he said, "your beautiful life opening and full—full of such dear seeds of delight and wonder, calling for love, ready for love, and there came this *Clutch,* this Clutch that embodied all the narrow meanness of existence, and gripped and crumpled you and spoilt you. . . . For I tell you my dear you don't know; you don't begin to know. . . ."

He disregarded her shy eyes, giving way to his gathered wrath.

"And he conquers! This little monster of meanness, he conquers to the end—his dead hand, his dead desires, out of the grave they hold you! Always, always, it is Clutch that conquers; the master of life! I was a fool to dream, a fool to hope. I forgot. I thought only of you and I—that perhaps you and I—"

He did not heed her little sound of protest. He went on to a bitter denunciation of the rule of jealousy in the world, forgetting that the sufferer under that rule in this case was his own consuming jealousy. That was life. Life was jealousy. It was all made up of fierce graspings, fierce suspicions, fierce resentments; men preyed upon one another even as the beasts they came from; reason made its crushed way through their conflict, crippled and wounded by their blows at one another. The best men, the wisest, the best of mankind, the stars of human wisdom, were but half ineffectual angels carried on the shoulders and guided by the steps of beasts. One might dream of a better world of men, of civilizations and wisdom latent in our passion-strained minds, of calms and courage and great heroical conquests that might come, but they lay tens of thousands of years away and we had to live, we had to die, no more than a herd of beasts tormented by gleams of knowledge we could never possess, of happiness for which we had no soul. He grew more and more eloquent as these thoughts sprang and grew in his mind.

"Of course I am absurd," he cried. "All men are absurd. Man is the absurd animal. We have parted from primordial motives—lust and hate and hunger and fear, and from all the tragic greatness of uncontrollable fate and we, we've got nothing to replace them. We are comic—comic! Ours is the stage of comedy in life's history, half lit and blinded,—and we fumble. As absurd as a kitten with its poor little head in a bag. There's your soul of man! Mewing. We're all at it, the poets, the teachers. How can anyone hope to escape? Why should I escape? What am I that I should expect to be anything but a thwarted lover, a man mocked by his own attempts at service? Why should I expect to discover beauty and think that it won't be snatched away from me? All my life is comic—the story of this—this last absurdity could it make anything but a comic history? and yet within me my heart is weeping tears. The further one has gone, the deeper one wallows in the comic marsh. I am one of the newer kind of men, one of those men who cannot sit and hug their credit and their honor and their possessions and be content. I have seen the light of better things than that, and because of my vision, because of my vision and for no other reason I am the most ridiculous of men. Always I have tried to go out from myself to the world and give. Those early books of mine, those meretricious books in which I pretended all was so well with the world,—I did them because I wanted to give happiness and contentment and to be happy in the giving. And all the watchers and the grippers, the strong silent men and the calculating possessors of things, the masters of the world, they grinned at me. How I lied to please! But I tell you for all their grinning, in my very prostitution there was a better spirit than theirs in their successes. If I had to live over again—"

He left that hypothesis uncompleted.

"And now," he said, with a curious contrast between his voice and the exaltation of his sentiments, "now that I am to be your tormented, your emasculated lover to the very end of things, emasculated by laws I hate and customs I hate and vile foresights that I despise—"

He paused, his thread lost for a moment.

"Because," he said, "I'm going to do it. I'm going to do what I can. I'm going to be as you wish me to be, to help you, to serve you. . . . If you can't come to meet me, I'll meet you. I can't help but love you, I can't do without you. Never in my life have I subscribed willingly to the idea of renunciation. I've hated renunciation. But if there is no other course but renunciation, renunciation let it be. I'm bitter about this, bitter to the bottom of my soul, but at least I'll have you know I love you. Anyhow. . . ."

His voice broke. There were tears in his eyes.

And on the very crest of these magnificent capitulations his soul rebelled. He turned about so swiftly that for a sentence or so she did not realize the nature of his change. Her mind remained glowing with her distressed acceptance of his magnificent nobility.

"I can't," he said.

He flung off his surrenders as a savage might fling off a garment.

"When I think of his children," he said.

"When I think of the world filled by his children, the children you have borne him—and I—forbidden almost to touch your hand!"

And flying into a passion Mr. Brumley shouted "No!"

"Not even to touch your hand!

"I won't do it," he assured her. "I won't do it. If I cannot be your lover— I will go away. I will never see you again. I will do anything—anything, rather than suffer this degradation. I will go abroad. I will go to strange places. I will aviate. I will kill myself—or anything, but I won't endure this. I won't. You see, you ask too much, you demand more than flesh and blood can stand. I've done my best to bring myself to it and I can't. I won't have that—that—"

He waved his trembling fingers in the air. He was absolutely unable to find an epithet pointed enough and bitter enough to stab into the memory of the departed knight. He thought of him as marble, enthroned at Kensal Green, with a false dignity, a false serenity, and intolerable triumph. He wanted something, some monosyllable to expound and strip all that, some lung-filling sky-splitting monosyllable that one could shout. His failure increased his exasperation.

"I won't have him grinning, at me," he said at last. "And so, it's one thing or the other. There's no other choice. But I know your choice. I see your choice. It's good-bye—and why—why shouldn't I go now?"

He waved his arms about. He was pitifully ridiculous. His face puckered as an ill-treated little boy's might do. This time it wasn't just the pathetic twinge that had broken his voice before; he found himself to his own amazement on the verge of loud, undignified, childish weeping. He was weeping passionately and noisily; he was over the edge of it, and it was too late to snatch himself back. The shame which could not constrain him, overcame him. A preposterous upward gesture of the hands expressed his despair. And abruptly this unhappy man of letters turned from her and fled, the most grief-routed of creatures, whooping and sobbing along a narrow pathway through the trees.

8

He left behind him an exceedingly distressed and astonished lady. She had stood with her eyes opening wider and wider at this culminating exhibition.

"But Mr. Brumley!" she had cried at last. "Mr. Brumley!"

He did not seem to hear her. And now he was running and stumbling along very fast through the trees, so that in a few minutes he would be out of sight. Dismay came with the thought that he might presently go out of sight altogether.

For a moment she seemed to hesitate. Then with a swift decision and a firm large grasp of the hand, she gathered up her black skirts and set off after him along the narrow path. She ran. She ran lightly, with a soft rhythmic fluttering of white and black. The long crape bands she wore in Sir Isaac's honor streamed out behind her.

"But Mr. Brumley," she panted unheard. "Mister Brumley!"

He went from her fast, faster than she could follow, amidst the sun-dappled pine stems, and as he went he made noises between bellowing and soliloquy, heedless of any pursuit. All she could hear was a heart-wringing but inexpressive "Wa, wa, wooh, wa, woo," that burst from him ever and again. Through a more open space among the trees she fancied she was gaining upon him, and then as the pines came together again and were mingled with young spruces, she perceived that he drew away from her more and more. And he went round a curve and was hidden, and then visible again much further off, and then hidden—.

She attempted one last cry to him, but her breath failed her, and she dropped her pace to a panting walk.

Surely he would not go thus into the high road! It was unendurable to think of him rushing out into the high road—blind with sorrow—it might be into the very bonnet of a passing automobile.

She passed beyond the pines and scanned the path ahead as far as the stile. Then she saw him, lying where he had flung himself, face downward among the bluebells.

"Oh!" she whispered to herself, and put one hand to her heart and drew nearer.

She was flooded now with that passion of responsibility, with that wild irrational charity which pours out of the secret depths of a woman's stirred being.

She came up to him so lightly as to be noiseless. He did not move, and for a moment she remained looking at him.

Then she said once more, and very gently—

"Mr. Brumley."

He started, listened for a second, turned over, sat up and stared at her. His face was flushed and his hair extremely ruffled. And a slight moisture recalled his weeping.

"Mr. Brumley," she repeated, and suddenly there were tears of honest vexation in her voice and eyes. "You *know* I cannot do without you."

He rose to his knees, and never, it seemed to him, had she looked so beautiful. She was a little out of breath, her dusky hair was disordered, and there was an unwonted expression in her eyes, a strange mingling of indignation and tenderness. For a moment they stared unaffectedly at each other, each making discoveries.

"Oh!" he sighed at last; "whatever you please, my dear. Whatever you please. I'm going to do as you wish, if you wish it, and be your friend and forget all this"—he waved an arm—"loving."

There were signs of a recrudescence of grief, and, inarticulate as ever, she sank to her knees close beside him.

"Let us sit quietly among these hyacinths," said Mr. Brumley. "And then afterwards we will go back to the house and talk . . . talk about our Hostels."

He sat back and she remained kneeling.

"Of course," he said, "I'm yours—to do just as you will with. And we'll work—. I've been a bit of a stupid brute. We'll work. For all those people. It will be—oh! a big work, quite a big work. Big enough for us to thank God for. Only—."

The sight of her panting lips had filled him with a wild desire, that set every nerve aquivering, and yet for all that had a kind of moderation, a reasonableness. It was a sisterly thing he had in mind. He felt that if this one desire could be satisfied, then honor would be satisfied, that he would cease grudging Sir Isaac—anything. . . .

But for some moments he could not force himself to speak of this desire, so great was his fear of a refusal.

"There's one thing," he said, and all his being seemed aquiver.

He looked hard at the trampled bluebells about their feet. "Never once," he went on, "never once in all these years—have we two even—once—kissed. . . . It is such a little thing. . . . So much."

He stopped, breathless. He could say no more because of the beating of his heart. And he dared not look at her face. . . .

There was a swift, soft rustling as she moved. . . .

She crouched down upon him and, taking his shoulder in her hand, upset him neatly backwards, and, doing nothing by halves, had kissed the astonished Mr. Brumley full upon his mouth.

LOVE AND MR. LEWISHAM

The Story of a Very Young Couple

CHAPTER I

Introduces Mr. Lewisham

THE OPENING CHAPTER does not concern itself with Love—indeed that antagonist does not certainly appear until the third—and Mr. Lewisham is seen at his studies. It was ten years ago, and in those days he was assistant master in the Whortley Proprietary School, Whortley, Sussex, and his wages were forty pounds a year, out of which he had to afford fifteen shillings a week during term time to lodge with Mrs. Munday, at the little shop in the West Street. He was called "Mr." to distinguish him from the bigger boys, whose duty it was to learn, and it was a matter of stringent regulation that he should be addressed as "Sir."

He wore ready-made clothes, his black jacket of rigid line was dusted about the front and sleeves with scholastic chalk, and his face was downy and his moustache incipient. He was a passable-looking youngster of eighteen, fair-haired, indifferently barbered and with a quite unnecessary pair of glasses on his fairly prominent nose—he wore these to make himself look older, that discipline might be maintained. At the particular moment when this story begins he was in his bedroom. An attic it was, with lead-framed dormer windows, a slanting ceiling and a bulging wall, covered, as a number of torn places witnessed, with innumerable strata of florid old-fashioned paper.

To judge by the room Mr. Lewisham thought little of Love but much on Greatness. Over the head of the bed, for example, where good folks hang texts, these truths asserted themselves, written in a clear, bold, youthfully florid hand:— "Knowledge is Power," and "What man has done man can do,"—man in the second instance referring to Mr. Lewisham. Never for a moment were these things to be forgotten. Mr. Lewisham could see them afresh every morning as his head came through his shirt. And over the yellow-painted box upon which—for lack of shelves—Mr. Lewisham's library was arranged, was a "*Schema.*" (Why he should not have headed it "Scheme," the editor of the *Church Times,* who calls his miscellaneous notes "*Varia,*" is better able to say than I.) In this scheme, 1892 was indicated as the year in which Mr. Lewisham proposed to take his B.A. degree at the London University with "hons. in all subjects," and 1895 as the date of his "gold medal." Subsequently there were to be "pamphlets in the Liberal interest," and such like things duly dated. "Who would control others must first control himself," remarked the wall over the wash-hand stand, and behind the door against the Sunday trousers was a portrait of Carlyle.

These were no mere threats against the universe; operations had begun. Jostling Shakespeare, Emerson's Essays, and the penny Life of Confucius, there were battered and defaced school books, a number of the excellent manuals of the

Universal Correspondence Association, exercise books, ink (red and black) in penny bottles, and an india-rubber stamp with Mr. Lewisham's name. A trophy of bluish green South Kensington certificates for geometrical drawing, astronomy, physiology, physiography, and inorganic chemistry, adorned his further wall. And against the Carlyle portrait was a manuscript list of French irregular verbs.

Attached by a drawing-pin to the roof over the wash-hand stand, which—the room being an attic—sloped almost dangerously, dangled a Time-Table. Mr. Lewisham was to rise at five, and that this was no vain boasting, a cheap American alarm clock by the books on the box witnessed. The lumps of mellow chocolate on the papered ledge by the bedhead, indorsed that evidence. "French until eight," said the time-table curtly. Breakfast was to be eaten in twenty minutes; then twenty-five minutes of "literature" to be precise, learning extracts (preferably pompous) from the plays of William Shakespeare—and then to school and duty. The time-table further prescribed Latin Composition for the recess and the dinner hour ("literature," however, during the meal), and varied its injunctions for the rest of the twenty-four hours according to the day of the week. Not a moment for Satan and that "mischief still" of his. Only three-score and ten has the confidence, as well as the time, to be idle.

But just think of the admirable quality of such a scheme! Up and busy at five, with all the world about one horizontal, warm, dreamy-brained or stupidly hullish, if roused, roused only to grunt and sigh and roll over again into oblivion. By eight three hours' clear start, three hours' knowledge ahead of everyone. It takes, I have been told by an eminent scholar, about a thousand hours of sincere work to learn a language completely—after three or four languages much less—which gives you, even at the outset, one each a year before breakfast. The gift of tongues—picked up like mushrooms! Then that "literature"—an astonishing conception! In the afternoon mathematics and the sciences. Could anything be simpler or more magnificent? In six years Mr. Lewisham will have his five or six languages, a sound, all-round education, a habit of tremendous industry, and be still but four and twenty. He will already have honor in his university and ampler means. One realizes that those pamphlets in the Liberal interests will be no obscure platitudes. Where Mr. Lewisham will be at thirty stirs the imagination. There will be modifications of the Schema, of course, as experience widens. But the spirit of it—the spirit of it is a devouring flame!

He was sitting facing the diamond-framed window, writing, writing fast, on a second yellow box that was turned on end and empty, and the lid was open, and his knees were conveniently stuck into the cavity. The bed was strewn with books and copygraphed sheets of instructions from his remote correspondence tutors. Pursuant to the dangling time-table he was, you would have noticed, translating Latin into English.

Imperceptibly the speed of his writing diminished. "*Urit me Glyceroe nitor*" lay ahead and troubled him. "Urit me," he murmured, and his eyes traveled from his book out of window to the vicar's roof opposite and its ivied chimneys. His brows were knit at first and then relaxed. "*Urit me!*" He had put his pen into his mouth and glanced about for his dictionary. *Urare?*

Suddenly his expression changed. Movement dictionary-ward ceased. He was listening to a light tapping sound—it was a footfall—outside.

He stood up abruptly, and, stretching his neck, peered through his unnecessary glasses and the diamond panes down into the street. Looking acutely downward he could see a hat daintily trimmed with pinkish white blossom, the shoulder of a jacket, and just the tips of nose and chin. Certainly the stranger who sat under the gallery last Sunday next to the Frobishers. Then, too, he had seen her only obliquely. . . .

He watched her until she passed beyond the window frame. He strained to see impossibly round the corner. . . .

Then he started, frowned, took his pen from his mouth. "This wandering attention!" he said. "The slightest thing! Where was I? Tcha!" He made a noise with his teeth to express his irritation, sat down, and replaced his knees in the upturned box. "Urit me," he said, biting the end of his pen and looking for his dictionary.

It was a Wednesday half-holiday late in March, a spring day glorious in amber light, dazzling white clouds and the intensest blue, casting a powder of wonderful green hither and thither among the trees and rousing all the birds to tumultuous rejoicings, a rousing day, a clamatory insistent day, a veritable herald of summer. The stir of that anticipation was in the air, the warm earth was parting above the swelling seeds, and all the pine-woods were full of the minute crepitation of opening bud scales. And not only was the stir of Mother Nature's awakening in the earth and the air and the trees, but also in Mr. Lewisham's youthful blood, bidding him rouse himself to live—live in a sense quite other than that the Schema indicated.

He saw the dictionary peeping from under a paper, looked up "Urit me," appreciated the shining "nitor" of Glycera's shoulders, and so fell idle again to rouse himself abruptly.

"I *can't* fix my attention," said Mr. Lewisham. He took off the needless glasses, wiped them, and blinked his eyes. This confounded Horace and his stimulating epithets! A walk?

"I won't be beat," he said—incorrectly—replaced his glasses, brought his elbows down on either side of his box with resonant violence, and clutched the hair over his ears with both hands. . . .

In five minutes' time he found himself watching the swallows curving through the blue over the vicarage garden.

"Did ever man have such a bother with himself as me?" he asked vaguely but vehemently. "It's self-indulgence does it—sitting down's the beginning of laziness."

So he stood up to his work, and came into permanent view of the village street. "If she has gone round the corner by the post office, she will come in sight over the palings above the allotments," suggested the unexplored and undisciplined region of Mr. Lewisham's mind. . . .

She did not come into sight. Apparently she had not gone round by the post office after all. It made one wonder where she had gone. Did she go up through the town to the avenue on these occasions? . . . Then abruptly a cloud drove across the sunlight, the glowing street went cold and Mr. Lewisham's imagination submitted to control. So "*Mater saeva cupidinum,*" "The untameable mother of desires,"—Horace (Book II of the Odes) was the author appointed by the university for Mr. Lewisham's matriculation—was, after all, translated to its prophetic end.

Precisely as the church clock struck five Mr. Lewisham, with a punctuality that was indeed almost too prompt for a really earnest student, shut his Horace, took up his Shakespeare, and descended the narrow, curved, uncarpeted staircase that led from his garret to the living room in which he had his tea with his landlady, Mrs. Munday. That good lady was alone, and after a few civilities Mr. Lewisham opened his Shakespeare and read from a mark onward—that mark, by-the-bye, was in the middle of a scene—while he consumed mechanically a number of slices of bread and whort jam.

Mrs. Munday watched him over her spectacles and thought how bad so much reading must be for the eyes, until the tinkling of her shop-bell called her away to a customer. At twenty-five minutes to six he put the book back in the window-sill, dashed a few crumbs from his jacket, assumed a mortar-board cap that was lying on the tea-caddy, and went forth to his evening "preparation duty."

The West Street was empty and shining golden with the sunset. Its beauty seized upon him, and he forgot to repeat the passage from Henry VIII that should have occupied him down the street. Instead he was presently thinking of that insubordinate glance from his window and of little chins and nose-tips. His eyes became remote in their expression. . . .

The school door was opened by an obsequious little boy with "lines" to be examined.

Mr. Lewisham felt a curious change of atmosphere on his entry. The door slammed behind him. The hall with its insistent scholastic suggestions, its yellow marbled paper, its long rows of hat-pegs, its disreputable array of umbrellas, a broken mortar-board and a tattered and scattered *Principia*, seemed dim and dull in contrast with the luminous stir of the early March evening outside. An unusual sense of the grayness of a teacher's life, of the grayness indeed of the life of all studious souls, came and went in his mind. He took the "lines," written painfully over three pages of exercise book, and obliterated them with a huge G. E. L., scrawled monstrously across each page. He heard the familiar mingled noises of the playground drifting in to him through the open schoolroom door.

CHAPTER II

"As the Wind Blows"

A FLAW IN that pentagram of a time-table, that pentagram by which the demons of distraction were to be excluded from Mr. Lewisham's career to Greatness, was the absence of a clause forbidding study out of doors. It was the day after the trivial window peeping of the last chapter that this gap in the time-table became apparent, a day if possible more gracious and alluring than its predecessor, and at half-past twelve, instead of returning from the school directly to his lodging, Mr. Lewisham escaped through the omission and made his way— Horace in pocket—to the park gates and so to the avenue of ancient trees that encircles the broad Whortley domain. He dismissed a suspicion of his motive with perfect success. In the avenue—for the path is but little frequented—one might expect to read undisturbed. The open air, the erect attitude, are surely better than sitting in a stuffy, enervating bedroom. The open air is distinctly healthy, hardy, simple. . . .

The day was breezy, and there was a perpetual rustling, a going and coming in the budding trees.

The network of the beeches was full of golden sunlight, and all the lower branches were shot with horizontal dashes of new-born green.

> *"Tu, nisi ventis*
> *Debes ludibrium, cave,"*

was the appropriate matter of Mr. Lewisham's thoughts, and he was mechanically trying to keep the book open in three places at once, at the text, the notes, and the literal translation, while he turned up the vocabulary for *ludibrium*, when his attention, wandering dangerously near the top of the page, fell over the edge and escaped with incredible swiftness down the avenue. . . .

A girl wearing a straw hat adorned with white blossom, was advancing towards him. Her occupation, too, was literary. Indeed, she was so busy writing that evidently she did not perceive him.

Unreasonable emotions descended upon Mr. Lewisham—emotions that are unaccountable on the mere hypothesis of a casual meeting. Something was whispered; it sounded suspiciously like "It's her!" He advanced with his fingers in his book, ready to retreat to its pages if she looked up, and watched her over it. *Ludibrium* passed out of his universe. She was clearly unaware of his nearness, he thought, intent upon her writing, whatever that might be. He wondered what it might be. Her face, foreshortened by her downward regard, seemed infantile. Her fluttering skirt was short, and showed her shoes and ankles. He noted her graceful, easy steps. A figure of health and lightness it was, sunlit, and advancing towards him, something, as he afterwards recalled with a certain astonishment, quite outside the Schema.

Nearer she came and nearer, her eyes still downcast. He was full of vague, stupid promptings towards an uncalled-for intercourse. It was curious she did not see him. He began to expect almost painfully the moment when she would look up, though what there was to expect—! He thought of what she would see when she discovered him, and wondered where the tassel of his cap might be hanging—it sometimes occluded one eye. It was of course quite impossible to put up a hand and investigate. He was near trembling with excitement. His paces, acts which are usually automatic, became uncertain and difficult. One might have thought he had never passed a human being before. Still nearer, ten yards now, nine, eight. Would she go past without looking up? . . .

Then their eyes met.

She had hazel eyes, but Mr. Lewisham being quite an amateur about eyes, could find no words for them. She looked demurely into his face. She seemed to find nothing there. She glanced away from him among the trees, and passed, and nothing remained in front of him but an empty avenue, a sunlit, green-shot void.

The incident was over.

From far away the soughing of the breeze swept towards him, and in a moment all the twigs about him were quivering and rustling and the boughs creaking with a gust of wind. It seemed to urge him away from her. The faded dead leaves that had once been green and young sprang up, raced one another, leapt, danced and pirouetted, and then something large struck him on the neck, stayed for a startling moment, and drove past him up the avenue.

Something vividly white! A sheet of paper—the sheet upon which she had been writing!

For what seemed a long time he did not grasp the situation. He glanced over his shoulder and understood suddenly. His awkwardness vanished. Horace in hand, he gave chase, and in ten paces had secured the fugitive document. He turned towards her, flushed with triumph, the quarry in his hand. He had as he picked it up seen what was written, but the situation dominated him for the instant. He made a stride towards her, and only then understood what he had seen. Lines of a measured length and capitals! Could it really be—? He stopped. He looked again, eyebrows rising. He held it before him, staring now quite frankly. It had been written with a stylographic pen. Thus it ran:

"Come! Sharp's the word."
And then again,
"Come! Sharp's the word."
And then,
"Come! Sharp's the word."
"Come! Sharp's the word."

And so on all down the page, in a boyish hand uncommonly like Frobisher ii's.

Surely! "I say!" said Mr. Lewisham, struggling with the new aspect and forgetting all his manners in his surprise. . . . He remembered giving the imposition quite well:—Frobisher ii had repeated the exhortation just a little too loudly—had brought the thing upon himself. To find her doing this jarred oddly upon certain vague preconceptions he had formed of her. Somehow it seemed as if she had betrayed him. That of course was only for the instant.

She had come up with him now. "May I have my sheet of paper, please?" she said with a catching of her breath. She was a couple of inches less in height than he. Do you observe her half-open lips, said Mother Nature in a noiseless aside to Mr. Lewisham—a thing he afterwards recalled. In her eyes was a touch of apprehension.

"I say," he said, with protest still uppermost, "You oughtn't to do this."

"Do what?"

"This. Impositions. For my boys."

She raised her eyebrows, then knitted them momentarily, and looked at him. "Are *you* Mr. Lewisham?" she asked with an affectation of entire ignorance and discovery.

She knew him perfectly well, which was one reason why she was writing the imposition, but pretending not to know gave her something to say.

Mr. Lewisham nodded.

"Of all people! Then"—frankly—"you have just found me out."

"I am afraid I have," said Lewisham. "I am afraid I *have* found you out."

They looked at one another for the next move. She decided to plead in extenuation.

"Teddy Frobisher is my cousin. I know it's very wrong, but he seemed to have such a lot to do and to be in *such* trouble. And I had nothing to do. In fact, it was *I* who offered. . . ."

She stopped and looked at him. She seemed to consider her remark complete.

That meeting of the eyes had an oddly disconcerting quality. He tried to keep to the business of the imposition. "You ought not to have done that," he said, encountering her steadfastly.

She looked down and then into his face again. "No," she said, "I suppose I ought not to. I'm very sorry."

Her looking down and up again produced another unreasonable effect. It seemed to Lewisham that they were discussing something quite other than the topic of their conversation; a persuasion patently absurd and only to be accounted for by the general disorder of his faculties. He made a serious attempt to keep his footing of reproof.

"I should have detected the writing, you know."

"Of course you would. It was very wrong of me to persuade him. But I did—I assure you. He seemed in such trouble. And I thought—"

She made another break, and there was a faint deepening of color in her cheeks. Suddenly, stupidly, his own adolescent cheeks began to glow. It became necessary to banish that sense of a duplicate topic forthwith.

"I can assure you," he said, now very earnestly, "I never give a punishment, never, unless it is merited. I make that a rule. I—er—*always* make that a rule. I am very careful indeed."

"I am really sorry," she interrupted with frank contrition. "It *was* silly of me."

Lewisham felt unaccountably sorry she should have to apologize, and he spoke at once with the idea of checking the reddening of his face. "I don't think *that*," he said with a sort of belated alacrity. "Really, it was kind of you, you know—very kind of you indeed. And I know that—I can quite understand that—er—your kindness. . . ."

"Ran away with me. And now poor little Teddy will get into worse trouble for letting me. . . ."

"Oh no," said Mr. Lewisham, perceiving an opportunity and trying not to smile his appreciation of what he was saying. "I had no business to read this as I picked it up—absolutely no business. Consequently. . . ."

"You won't take any notice of it? Really!"

"Certainly not," said Mr. Lewisham.

Her face lit with a smile, and Mr. Lewisham's relaxed in sympathy. "It is nothing—it's the proper thing for me to do, you know."

"But so many people wouldn't do it. Schoolmasters are not usually so—chivalrous."

He was chivalrous! The phrase acted like a spur. He obeyed a foolish impulse.

"If you like—" he said.

"What?"

"He needn't do this. The Impot., I mean. I'll let him off."

"Really?"

"I can."

"It's awfully kind of you."

"I don't mind," he said. "It's nothing much. If you really think. . . ."

He was full of self-applause for this scandalous sacrifice of justice.

"It's awfully kind of you," she said.

"It's nothing, really," he explained, "nothing."

"Most people wouldn't—"

"I know."

Pause.

"It's all right," he said. "Really."

He would have given worlds for something more to say, something witty and original, but nothing came.

The pause lengthened. She glanced over her shoulder down the vacant avenue. This interview—this momentous series of things unsaid was coming to an end! She looked at him hesitatingly and smiled again. She held out her hand. No doubt that was the proper thing to do. He took it, searching a void, tumultuous mind in vain.

"It's awfully kind of you," she said again as she did so.

"It don't matter a bit," said Mr. Lewisham, and sought vainly for some other saying, some doorway remark into new topics. Her hand was cool and soft and firm, the most delightful thing to grasp, and this observation ousted all other things. He held it for a moment, but nothing would come.

They discovered themselves hand in hand. They both laughed and felt "silly." They shook hands in the manner of quite intimate friends, and snatched their hands away awkwardly. She turned, glanced timidly at him over her shoulder, and hesitated. "Good-bye," she said, and was suddenly walking from him.

He bowed to her receding bck, made a seventeenth-century sweep with his college cap, and then some hitherto unexplored regions of his mind flashed into revolt.

Hardly had she gone six paces when he was at her side again.

"I say," he said with a fearful sense of his temerity and raising his mortar-board awkwardly as though he was passing a funeral. "But that sheet of paper . . ."

"Yes," she said, surprised—quite naturally.

"May I have it?"

"Why?"

He felt a breathless pleasure, like that of sliding down a slope of snow. "I would like to have it."

She smiled and raised her eyebrows, but his excitement was now too great for smiling. "Look here!" she said, and displayed the sheet crumpled into a ball. She laughed—with a touch of effort.

"I don't mind that," said Mr. Lewisham laughing too. He captured the paper by an insistent gesture and smoothed it out with fingers that trembled.

"You don't mind?" he said.

"Mind what?"

"If I keep it?"

"Why should I?"

Pause. Their eyes met again. There was an odd constraint about both of them, a palpitating interval of silence.

"I really *must* be going," she said suddenly, breaking the spell by an effort. She turned about and left him with the crumpled piece of paper in the fist that held the book, the other hand lifting the mortar-board in a dignified salute again.

He watched her receding figure. His heart was beating with remarkable rapidity. How light, how living she seemed! Little round flakes of sunlight raced down her as she went. She walked fast, then slowly, looking sideways once or twice but not back, until she reached the park gates. Then she looked towards him, a remote, friendly little figure, made a gesture of farewell, and disappeared.

His face was flushed and his eyes bright. Curiously enough, he was out of breath. He stared for a long time at the vacant end of the avenue. Then he turned his eyes to his trophy gripped against the closed and forgotten Horace in his hand.

CHAPTER III

The Wonderful Discovery

ON SUNDAY IT was Lewisham's duty to accompany the boarders twice to church. The boys sat in the gallery above the choir, facing the organ loft and at right angles to the general congregation. It was a prominent position, and made him feel painfully conspicuous, except in moods of exceptional vanity, when he used to imagine that all these people were thinking how his forehead and his certificates accorded. He thought a lot in those days of his certificates and forehead, but little of his honest, healthy face beneath it. (To tell the truth there was nothing very wonderful about his forehead.) He rarely looked down the church, as he fancied to do so would be to meet the collective eye of the congregation regarding him. So that in the morning he was not able to see that the Frobishers' pew was empty until the litany.

But in the evening, on the way to church, the Frobishers and their guest crossed the market-square as his string of boys marched along the west side. And the guest was arrayed in a gay new dress, as if it was already Easter, and her face set in its dark hair came with a strange effect of mingled freshness and familiarity. She looked at him calmly! He felt very awkward and was for cutting his new acquaintance. Then hesitated, and raised his hat with a jerk as if to Mrs. Frobisher. Neither lady acknowledged his salute, which may possibly have been a little unexpected. Then young Siddons dropped his hymn-book, stooped to pick it up, and Lewisham almost fell over him. . . . He entered church in a mood of black despair.

But consolation of a sort came soon enough. As *she* took her seat she distinctly glanced up at the gallery, and afterwards as he knelt to pray, he peeped between his fingers and saw her looking up again. She was certainly not laughing at him.

In those days much of Lewisham's mind was still an unknown land to him. He believed among other things that he was always the same consistent intelligent human being, whereas under certain stimuli he became no longer reasonable and disciplined but a purely imaginative and emotional person. Music, for instance, carried him away, and particularly the effect of many voices in unison whirled him of from almost any state of mind to a fine massive emotionality. And the evening service at Whortley church—at the evening service surplices were worn— the chanting and singing, the vague brilliance of the numerous candle flames, the multitudinous unanimity of the congregation down there, kneeling, rising, thunderously responding invariably inebriated him. Inspired him, if you will, and turned the prose of his life into poetry. And Chance, coming to the aid of Dame Nature, dropped just the apt suggestion into his now highly responsive ear.

The second hymn was a simple and popular one, dealing with the theme of Faith, Hope and Charity, and having each verse ending with the word "Love." Conceive it, long drawn out and disarticulate—

> *Faith will van . . . ish in . . . to sight,*
> *Hope be emp . . . tied in deli . . . ight,*
> *Love in Heaven will shine more bri . . . ight*
> *There . . . fore give us Love.*

At the third repetition of the refrain, Lewisham looked down across the chancel and met her eyes for a brief instant. . . .

He stopped singing abruptly. Then the consciousness of the serried ranks of faces below there, came with almost overwhelming force upon him, and he dared not look at her again. He felt the blood rushing to his face.

Love! The greatest of these. The greatest of all things. Better than fame. Better than knowledge. So came the great discovery like a flood across his mind, pouring over it with the cadence of the hymn and sending a tide of pink in sympathy across his forehead. The rest of the service was phantasmagorial background to that great reality—a phantasmagorial background a little inclined to stare. He, Mr. Lewisham, was in Love.

"A . . . men." He was so preoccupied that he found the whole congregation subsiding into their seats, and himself still standing, rapt. He sat down spasmodically, with an impact that seemed to him to re-echo through the church.

As they came out of the porch into the thickening night, he seemed to see her everywhere. He fancied she had gone on in front, and he hurried up the boys in the hope of overtaking her. They pushed through the throng of dim people going homeward. Should he raise his hat to her again? . . . But it was

Susie Hopbrow in a light-colored dress—a raven in dove's plumage. He felt a curious mixture of relief and disappointment. He would see her no more that night.

He hurried from the school to his lodging. He wanted very urgently to be alone. He went upstairs to his little room and sat before the upturned box on which his Butler's Analogy was spread open. He did not go to the formality of lighting the candle. He leaned back and gazed blissfully at the solitary planet that hung over the vicarage garden.

He took out of his pocket a crumpled sheet of paper, smoothed and carefully refolded, covered with a writing not unlike that of Frobisher ii, and after some maidenly hesitation pressed this treasure to his lips. The Schema and the time-table hung in the darkness like the mere ghosts of themselves.

Mrs. Munday called him thrice to his supper.

He went out immediately after it was eaten and wandered under the stars until he came over the hill behind the town again, and clambered up the back to the stile in sight of the Frobishers' house. He selected the only lit window as hers. Behind the blind, Mrs. Frobisher, thirty-eight, was busy with her curl-papers— she used papers because they were better for the hair—and discussing certain neighbors in a fragmentary way with Mr. Frobisher, who was in bed. Presently she moved the candle to examine a faint discoloration of her complexion that rendered her uneasy.

Outside, Mr. Lewisham (eighteen) stood watching the orange oblong for the best part of half an hour, until it vanished and left the house black and blank. Then he sighed deeply and returned home in a very glorious mood indeed.

He awoke the next morning feeling extremely serious, but not clearly remembering the overnight occurrences. His eye fell on his clock. The time was six and he had not heard the alarm; as a matter of fact the alarm had not been wound up. He jumped out of bed at once and alighted upon his best trousers amorphously dropped on the floor instead of methodically cast over a chair. As he soaped his head he tried, according to his rules of revision, to remember the overnight reading. He could not for the life of him. The truth came to him as he was getting into his shirt. His head, struggling in its recesses, became motionless, the handless cuffs ceased to dangle for a minute. . . .

Then his head came through slowly with a surprised expression upon his face. He remembered. He remembered the thing as a bald discovery, and without a touch of emotion. With all the achromatic clearness, the unromantic colorlessness of the early morning. . . .

Yes. He had it now quite distinctly. There had been no overnight reading. He was in Love.

The proposition jarred with some vague thing in his mind. He stood staring for a space, and then began looking about absent-mindedly for his collar-stud. He paused in front of his Schema, regarding it.

CHAPTER IV

Raised Eyebrows

"WORK MUST BE done anyhow," said Mr. Lewisham.

But never had the extraordinary advantages of open-air study presented themselves so vividly. Before breakfast he took half an hour of open-air reading along the allotments lane near the Frobishers' house, after breakfast and before school he went through the avenue with a book, and returned from school to his lodgings circuitously through the avenue, and so back to the avenue for thirty minutes or so before afternoon school. When Mr. Lewisham was not looking over the top of his book during these periods of open-air study, then commonly he was glancing over his shoulder. And at last who should he see but—!

He saw her out of the corner of his eye, and he turned away at once, pretending not to have seen her. His whole being was suddenly irradiated with emotion. The hands holding his book gripped it very tightly. He did not glance back again, but walked slowly and steadfastly, reading an ode that he could not have translated to save his life, and listening acutely for her approach. And after an interminable time, as it seemed, came a faint footfall and the swish of skirts behind him.

He felt as though his head was directed forward by a clutch of iron.

"Mr. Lewisham," she said close to him, and he turned with a quality of movement that was almost convulsive. He raised his cap clumsily.

He took her extended hand by an afterthought, and held it until she withdrew it. "I am so glad to have met you," she said.

"So am I," said Lewisham simply.

They stood facing one another for an expressive moment, and then by a movement she indicated her intention to walk along the avenue with him. "I wanted so much," she said looking down at her feet, "to thank you for letting Teddy off, you know. That is why I wanted to see you." Lewisham took his first step beside her. "And it's odd, isn't it," she said looking up into his face, "that I should meet you here in just the same place. I believe . . . Yes. The very same place we met before."

Mr. Lewisham was tongue-tied.

"Do you often come here," she said.

"Well," he considered—and his voice was most unreasonably hoarse when he spoke—"No. No. . . . That is— at least not often. Now and then. In fact I like it rather for reading and that sort of thing. It's so quiet."

"I suppose you read a great deal?"

"When one teaches one has to."

"But you . . ."

"I'm rather fond of reading, certainly. Are you?"

"I *love* it."

Mr. Lewisham was glad she loved reading. He would have been disappointed had she answered differently. But she spoke with real fervor. She *loved* reading! It was pleasant. She would understand him a little perhaps. "Of course," she went on, "I'm not clever like some people are. And I have to read books as I get hold of them."

"So do I," said Mr. Lewisham, "for the matter of that. . . . Have you read . . . Carlyle?"

The conversation was now fairly under way. They were walking side by side beneath the swaying boughs. Mr. Lewisham's sensations were ecstatic, marred only by a dread of some casual boy coming upon them. She had not read *much* Carlyle. She had always wanted to, even from quite a little girl—she had heard so much about him. She knew he was a Really Great Writer, a *very* Great Writer indeed. All she *had* read of him she liked. She could say that. As much as she liked anything. And she had seen his house in Chelsea.

Lewisham, whose knowledge of London had been obtained by excursion trips on six or seven isolated days, was much impressed by this. It seemed to put her at once on a footing of intimacy with this imposing Personality. It had never occurred to him at all vividly that these Great Writers had real abiding places. She gave him a few descriptive touches that made the house suddenly real and distinctive to him. She lived quite near, she said, at least within walking distance, in Clapham. He instantly forgot the vague design of lending her his *"Sartor Resartus"* in his curiosity to learn more about her home. "Clapham—that's almost in London, isn't it?" he said.

"Quite," she said, but she volunteered no further information about her domestic circumstances. "I like London," she generalized, "and especially in winter." And she proceeded to praise London, its public libraries, its shops, the multitudes of people, the facilities for "doing what you like," the concerts one could go to, the theatres. (It seemed she moved in fairly good society.) "There's always something to see even if you only go out for a walk," she said, "and down here there's nothing to read but idle novels. And those not new."

Mr. Lewisham had regretfully to admit the lack of such culture and mental activity in Whortley. It made him feel terribly her inferior. He had only his bookishness and his certificates to set against it all—and she had seen Carlyle's house! "Down here," she said, "there's nothing to talk about but scandal." It was too true.

At the corner by the stile, beyond which the willows were splendid against the blue with silvery aments and golden pollen, they turned by mutual impulse and retraced their steps. "I've simply had no one to talk to down here," she said. "Not what *I* call talking."

"I hope," said Lewisham, making a resolute plunge, "perhaps while you are staying at Whortley . . ."

He paused perceptibly, and she, following his eyes, saw a voluminous black figure approaching. "We may," said Mr. Lewisham, resuming his remark, "chance to meet again, perhaps."

He had been about to challenge her to a deliberate meeting. A certain delightful tangle of paths that followed the bank of the river had been in his mind. But the apparition of Mr. George Bonover, headmaster of the Whortley Proprietary School, chilled him amazingly. Dame Nature no doubt had arranged the meeting of our young couple, but about Bonover she seems to have been culpably careless. She now receded illimitably, and Mr. Lewisham, with the most unpleasant feelings, found himself face to face with a typical representative of a social organization which objects very strongly *inter alia* to promiscuous conversation on the part of the young unmarried junior master.

"—chance to meet again, perhaps," said Mr. Lewisham, with a sudden lack of spirit.

"I hope so too," she said.

Pause. Mr. Bonover's features, and particularly a bushy pair of black eyebrows, were now very near, those eyebrows already raised, apparently to express a refined astonishment.

"Is this Mr. Bonover approaching?" she asked.

"Yes."

Prolonged pause.

Would he stop and accost them? At any rate this frightful silence must end. Mr. Lewisham sought in his mind for some remark wherewith to cover his employer's approach. He was surprised to find his mind a desert. He made a colossal effort. If they could only talk, if they could only seem at their ease! But this blank incapacity was eloquent of guilt. Ah!

"It's a lovely day, though," said Mr. Lewisham. "Isn't it?"

She agreed with him. "Isn't it?" she said.

And then Mr. Bonover passed, forehead tight reefed so to speak, and lips impressively compressed. Mr. Lewisham raised his mortar-board, and to his astonishment Mr. Bonover responded with a markedly formal salute—mock clerical hat sweeping circuitously—and the regard of a searching, disapproving eye, and so passed. Lewisham was overcome with astonishment at this improvement on the nod of their ordinary commerce. And so this terrible incident terminated for the time.

He felt a momentary gust of indignation. After all, why should Bonover or anyone interfere with his talking to a girl if he chose? And for all he knew they might have been properly introduced. By young Frobisher, say. Nevertheless, Lewisham's spring-tide mood relapsed into winter. He was, he felt, singularly stupid for the rest of their conversation, and the delightful feeling of enterprise that had hitherto inspired and astonished him when talking to her had shrivelled beyond contempt. He was glad—positively glad—when things came to an end.

At the park gates she held out her hand. "I'm afraid I have interrupted your reading," she said.

"Not a bit," said Mr. Lewisham warming slightly. "I don't know when I've enjoyed a conversation. . . ."

"It was—a breach of etiquette, I am afraid, my speaking to you, but I did so want to thank you. . . ."

"Don't mention it," said Mr. Lewisham, secretly impressed by the etiquette.

"Good-bye." He stood hesitating by the lodge, and then turned back up the avenue in order not to be seen to follow her too closely up the West Street.

And then, still walking away from her, he remembered that he had not lent her a book as he had planned, nor made any arrangement ever to meet her again. She might leave Whortley anywhen for the amenities of Clapham. He stopped and stood irresolute. Should he run after her? Then he recalled Bonover's enigmatical expression of face. He decided that to pursue her would be altogether too conspicuous. Yet . . . So he stood in inglorious hesitation, while the seconds passed.

He reached his lodging at last to find Mrs. Munday halfway through dinner.

"You get them books of yours," said Mrs. Munday, who took a motherly interest in him, "and you read and you read, and you take no account of time. And now you'll have to eat your dinner half cold and no time for it to settle proper before you goes off to school. It's ruination to a stummik—such ways."

"Oh, never mind my stomach, Mrs. Munday," said Lewisham, roused from a tangled and apparently gloomy meditation, "that's *my* affair." Quite crossly he spoke for him.

"I'd rather have a good sensible actin' stummik than a full head," said Mrs. Munday, "any day."

"I'm different, you see," snapped Mr. Lewisham, and relapsed into silence and gloom.

("Hoity toity!" said Mrs. Munday under her breath.)

CHAPTER V

Hesitations

MR. BONOVER, HAVING fully matured a Hint suitable for the occasion, dropped it in the afternoon, while Lewisham was superintending cricket practice. He made a few remarks about the prospects of the first eleven by way of introduction, and Lewisham agreed with him that Frobisher i looked like shaping very well this season.

A pause followed and the headmaster hummed. "By-the-bye," he said, as if making conversation and still watching the play "I, ah—understood that you, ah—were a *stranger* to Whortley."

"Yes," said Lewisham, "that's so."

"You have made friends in the neighborhood?"

Lewisham was troubled with a cough and his ears—those confounded ears—brightened. "Yes," he said, recovering. "Oh yes. Yes. I have."

"Local people, I presume."

"Well, no. Not exactly." The brightness spread from Lewisham's ears over his face.

"I saw you," said Bonover, "talking to a young lady in the avenue. Her face was somehow quite familiar to me. Who *was* she?"

Should he say she was a friend of the Frobishers? In that case Bonover, in his insidious amiable way might talk to the Frobisher parents and make things disagreeable for her. "She was," said Lewisham, flushing deeply with the stress on his honesty and dropping his voice to a mumble, "a . . . a . . . an old friend of my mother's. In fact, I met her once at Salisbury."

"Where?"

"Salisbury."

"And her name?"

"Smith," said Lewisham, a little hastily and repenting the lie even as it left his lips.

"Well *hit,* Harris!" shouted Bonover, and began to clap his hands. "Well *hit,* sir."

"Harris shapes very well," said Mr. Lewisham.

"Very," said Mr. Bonover. "And—what was it? Ah! I was just remarking the odd resemblances there are in the world. There is a Miss Henderson—or Henson—stopping with the Frobishers—in the very same town, in fact, the very picture of your Miss . . ."

"Smith," said Lewisham, meeting his eye and recovering the full crimson note of his first blush.

"It's odd," said Bonover, regarding him pensively.

"Very odd," mumbled Lewisham, cursing his own stupidity and looking away.

"*Very*—very odd," said Bonover.

"In fact," said Bonover, turning towards the schoolhouse, "I hardly expected it of you, Mr. Lewisham."

"Expected what, sir?"

But Mr. Bonover feigned to be already out of earshot.

"Damn!" said Mr. Lewisham. "Oh!—*damn!*"—a most objectionable expression and rare with him in those days. He had half a mind to follow the headmaster and ask him if he doubted his word. It was only too evident what the answer would be.

He stood for a minute undecided, then turned on his heel and marched homeward with savage steps. His muscles quivered as he walked, and his face twitched. The tumult of his mind settled at last into angry indignation.

"Confound him!" said Mr. Lewisham, arguing the matter out with the bedroom furniture. "Why the *devil* can't he mind his own business?"

"Mind your own business, sir!" shouted Mr. Lewisham at the wash-hand stand. "Confound you, sir, mind your own business!"

The wash-hand stand did.

"You overrate your power, sir," said Mr. Lewisham a little mollified. "Understand me! I am my own master out of school."

Nevertheless, for four days and some hours after Mr. Bonover's Hint, Mr. Lewisham so far observed its implications as to abandon open-air study and struggle with diminishing success to observe the spirit as well as the letter of his time table prescriptions. For the most part he fretted at accumulating tasks, did them with slipshod energy or looked out of window. The Career constituent insisted that to meet and talk to this girl again meant reproof, worry, interference with his work for his matriculation, the destruction of all "Discipline," and he saw the entire justice of the insistence. It was nonsense this being in love; there wasn't such a thing as love outside of trashy novelettes. And forthwith his mind went off at a tangent to her eyes under the shadow of her hat brim, and had to be lugged back by main force. On Thursday when he was returning from school he saw her far away down the street, and hurried in to avoid her, looking ostentatiously in the opposite direction. But that was a turning-point. Shame overtook him. On Friday his belief in love was warm and living again, and his heart full of remorse for laggard days.

On Saturday morning his preoccupation with her was so vivid that it distracted him even while he was teaching that most teachable subject, algebra, and by the end of the school hours the issue was decided and the Career in headlong rout. That afternoon he would go, whatever happened, and see her and speak to her again. The thought of Bonover arose only to be dismissed. And besides— Bonover took a siesta early in the afternoon.

Yes, he would go out and find her and speak to her. Nothing should stop him.

Once that decision was taken his imagination became riotous with things he might say, attitudes he might strike, and a multitude of vague fine dreams about her. He would say this, he would say that, his mind would do nothing but circle round this wonderful pose of lover. What a cur he had been to hide from her so long! What could he have been thinking about? How *could* he explain it to her, when the meeting really came? Suppose he was very frank—

He considered the limits of frankness. Would she believe he had not seen her on Thursday?—if he assured her that it was so?

And, most horrible, in the midst of all this came Bonover with a request that he would take "duty" in the cricket field instead of Dunkerley that afternoon. Dunkerley was the senior assistant master, Lewisham's sole colleague. The last vestige of disapprobation had vanished from Bonover's manner; asking a favor was his autocratic way of proffering the olive branch. But it came to Lewisham as a cruel imposition. For a fateful moment he trembled on the brink of acquiescence. In a flash came a vision of the long duty of the afternoon—she possibly packing for Clapham all the while. He turned white. Mr. Bonover watched his face.

"*No,*" said Lewisham bluntly, saying all he was sure of, and forthwith racking his unpracticed mind for an excuse. "I'm sorry I can't oblige you, but . . . my arrangements . . . I've made arrangements, in fact, for the afternoon."

Mr. Bonover's eyebrows went up at this obvious lie, and the glow of his suavity faded. "You see," he said, "Mrs. Bonover expects a friend this afternoon, and we rather want Mr. Dunkerley to make four at croquet. . . ."

"I'm sorry," said Mr. Lewisham, still resolute, and making a mental note that Bonover would be playing croquet.

"You don't play croquet by any chance?" asked Bonover.

"No," said Lewisham, "I haven't an idea."

"If Mr. Dunkerley had asked you? . . ." persisted Bonover, knowing Lewisham's respect for etiquette.

"Oh! it wasn't on that account," said Lewisham, and Bonover with eyebrows still raised and a general air of outraged astonishment left him standing there, white and stiff, and wondering at his extraordinary temerity.

CHAPTER VI

The Scandalous Ramble

As soon as school was dismissed Lewisham made a gaol-delivery of his outstanding impositions, and hurried back to his lodgings, to spend the time until his dinner was ready—Well? . . . It seems hardly fair, perhaps, to Lewisham to tell this; it is doubtful, indeed, whether a male novelist's duty to his sex should not restrain him, but, as the wall in the shadow by the diamond-framed window insisted, "*Magna est veritas et prevalebit.*" Mr. Lewisham brushed his hair with elaboration, and ruffled it picturesquely, tried the effect of all his ties and selected a white one, dusted his boots with an old pocket-handkerchief, changed his trousers because the week-day pair was minutely frayed at the heels, and inked the elbows of his coat where the stitches were a little white. And, to be still more intimate, he studied his callow appearance in the glass from various points of view, and decided that his nose might have been a little smaller with advantage. . . .

Directly after dinner he went out, and by the shortest path to the allotment lane, telling himself he did not care if he met Bonover forthwith in the street. He did not know precisely what he intended to do, but he was quite clear that he meant to see the girl he had met in the avenue. He knew he should see her. A sense of obstacles merely braced him and was pleasurable. He went up the stone steps out of the lane to the stile that overlooked the Frobishers, the stile from which he had watched the Frobisher bedroom. There he seated himself with his arms folded, in full view of the house.

That was at ten minutes to two. At twenty minutes to three he was still sitting there, but his hands were deep in his jacket pockets, and he was scowling and kicking his foot against the step with an impatient monotony. His needless glasses had been thrust into his waistcoat pocket—where they remained throughout the afternoon—and his cap was tilted a little back from his forehead and exposed a wisp of hair. One or two people had gone down the lane, and he had pretended not to see them, and a couple of hedge-sparrows chasing each other along the side of the sunlit, wind-rippled field had been his chief entertainment. It is unaccountable, no doubt, but he felt angry with her as the time crept on. His expression lowered.

He heard someone going by in the lane behind him. He would not look round—it annoyed him to think of people seeing him in this position. His once eminent discretion, though overthrown, still made muffled protests at the afternoon's enterprise. The feet down the lane stopped close at hand.

"Stare away," said Lewisham between his teeth. And then began mysterious noises, a violent rustle of hedge twigs, a something like a very light foot-tapping.

Curiosity boarded Lewisham and carried him after the briefest struggle. He looked round, and there she was, her back to him, reaching after the spiky blossoming blackthorn that crested the opposite hedge. Remarkable accident! She had not seen him!

In a moment Lewisham's legs were flying over the stile. He went down the steps in the bank with such impetus that it carried him up into the prickly bushes beside her. "Allow me," he said, too excited to see she was not astonished.

"Mr. Lewisham!" she said in feigned surprise, and stood away to give him room at the blackthorn.

"Which spike will you have?" he cried overjoyed. "The whitest? The highest? Any!"

"That piece," she chose haphazard, "with the black spike sticking out from it."

A mass of snowy blossom it was against the April sky, and Lewisham, struggling for it—it was by no means the most accessible—saw with fantastic satisfaction a lengthy scratch flash white on his hand, and turn to red.

"Higher up the lane," he said, descending triumphant and breathless, "there is blackthorn. . . . This cannot compare for a moment. . . ."

She laughed and looked at him as he stood there flushed, his eyes triumphant, with an unpremeditated approval. In church, in the gallery, with his face fore-shortened, he had been effective in a way, but this was different. "Show me," she said, though she knew this was the only place for blackthorn for a mile in either direction.

"I *knew* I should see you," he said, by way of answer. "I felt sure I should see you today."

"It was our last chance almost," she answered with as frank a quality of avowal. "I'm going home to London on Monday."

"I knew," he cried in triumph. "To Clapham?" he asked.

"Yes. I have got a situation. You did not know that I was a shorthand clerk and typewriter, did you? I am. I have just left the school, the Grogram School. And now there is an old gentleman who wants an amanuensis."

"So you know shorthand?" said he. "That accounts for the stylographic pen. Those lines were written. . . . I have them still."

She smiled and raised her eyebrows. "Here," said Mr. Lewisham tapping his breast-pocket.

"This lane," he said—their talk was curiously inconsecutive—"some way along this lane, over the hill and down, there is a gate, and that goes—I mean, it opens into the path that runs along the river bank. Have you been?"

"No," she said.

"It's the best walk about Whortley. It brings you out upon Immering Common. You *must*—before you go."

"*Now?*" she said with her eyes dancing.

"Why not?"

"I told Mrs. Frobisher I should be back by four," she said.

"It's a walk not to be lost."

"Very well," said she.

"The trees are all budding," said Mr. Lewisham, "the rushes are shooting, and all along the edge of the river there are millions of little white flowers floating on the water. *I* don't know the names of them, but they're fine. . . . May I carry that branch of blossom?"

As he took it their hands touched momentarily . . . and there came another of those significant gaps.

"Look at those clouds," said Lewisham abruptly remembering the remark he had been about to make and waving the white froth of blackthorn. "And look at the blue between them."

"It's perfectly splendid. Of all the fine weather the best has been kept for now. My last day. My very last day."

And off these two young people went together in a highly electrical state— to the infinite astonishment of Mrs. Frobisher, who was looking out of the attic window—stepping out manfully and finding the whole world lit and splendid for their entertainment. The things they discovered and told each other that afternoon down by the river!—that spring was wonderful, young leaves beautiful, bud scales astonishing things, and clouds dazzling and stately!—with an air of supreme originality! And their naïve astonishment to find one another in agreement upon these novel delights! It seemed to them quite outside the play of accident that they should have met each other.

They went by the path that runs among the trees along the river bank, and she must needs repent and wish to take the lower one, the towing path, before they had gone three hundred yards. So Lewisham had to find a place fit for her descent, where a friendly tree proffered its protruding roots as a convenient balustrade, and down she clambered with her hand in his.

Then a water-vole washing his whiskers gave occasion for a sudden touching of hands and the intimate confidence of whispers and silence together. After which Lewisham essayed to gather her a marsh mallow at the peril, as it was judged, of his life, and gained it together with a bootful of water. And at the gate by the black and shiny lock, where the path breaks away from the river, she overcame him by an unexpected feat, climbing gleefully to the top rail with the support of his hand, and leaping down, a figure of light and grace, to the ground.

They struck boldly across the meadows, which were gay with lady's smock, and he walked, by special request, between her and three matronly cows— feeling as Perseus might have done when he fended off the sea-monster. And so by the mill, and up a steep path to Immering Common. Across the meadows Lewisham had broached the subject of her occupation. "And are you really going away from here to be an amanuensis?" he said, and started her upon the theme of herself, a theme she treated with a specialist's enthusiasm. They dealt with it by the comparative method, and neither noticed the light was out of the sky until the soft feet of the advancing shower had stolen right upon them.

"Look!" said he. "Yonder! A shed," and they ran together. She ran laughing, and yet swiftly and lightly. He pulled her through the hedge by both hands, and released her skirt from an amorous bramble, and so they came into a little black shed in which a rusty harrow of gigantic proportions sheltered. He noted how she still kept her breath after that run.

She sat down on the harrow and hesitated. "I *must* take off my hat," she said, "that rain will spot it," and so he had a chance of admiring the sincerity of her curls—not that he had ever doubted them. She stooped over her hat, pocket-handkerchief in hand, daintily wiping off the silvery drops. He stood up at the opening of the shed and looked at the country outside through the veil of the soft vehemence of the April shower.

"There's room for two on this harrow," she said.

He made inarticulate sounds of refusal, and then came and sat down beside her, close beside her, so that he was almost touching her. He felt a fantastic desire to take her in his arms and kiss her, and overcame the madness by an effort. "I don't even know your name," he said, taking refuge from his whirling thoughts in conversation.

"Henderson," she said.

"*Miss* Henderson?"

She smiled in his face—hesitated. "Yes—*Miss* Henderson."

Her eyes, her atmosphere were wonderful. He had never felt quite the same sensation before, a strange excitement, almost like a faint echo of tears. He was for demanding her Christian name. For calling her "dear" and seeing what she would say. He plunged headlong into a rambling description of Bonover and how he had told a lie about her and called her Miss Smith, and so escaped this unaccountable emotional crisis. . . .

The whispering of the rain about them sank and died, and the sunlight struck vividly across the distant woods beyond Immering. Just then they had fallen on a silence again that was full of daring thoughts for Mr. Lewisham. He moved his arm suddenly and placed it so that it was behind her on the frame of the harrow.

"Let us go on now," she said abruptly. "The rain has stopped."

"That little path goes straight to Immering," said Mr. Lewisham.

"But, four o'clock?"

He drew out his watch and his eyebrows went up. It was already nearly a quarter past four.

"Is it past four?" she asked, and abruptly they were face to face with parting. That Lewisham had to take "duty" at half-past five seemed a thing utterly trivial. "Surely," he said, only slowly realizing what this parting meant. "But must you? I—I want to talk to you."

"Haven't you been talking to me?"

"It isn't that. Besides—no."

She stood looking at him. "I promised to be home by four," she said. "Mrs. Frobisher has tea. . . ."

"We may never have a chance to see one another again."

"Well?"

Lewisham suddenly turned very white.

"Don't leave me," he said, breaking a tense silence and with a sudden stress in his voice. "Don't leave me. Stop with me yet—for a little while. . . . You . . . You can lose your way."

"You seem to think," she said forcing a laugh, "that I live without eating and drinking."

"I have wanted to talk to you so much. The first time I saw you. . . . At first I dared not . . . I did not know you would let me talk. . . . And now, just as I am—happy, you are going."

He stopped abruptly. Her eyes were downcast. "No," she said, tracing a curve with the point of her shoe. "No. I am not going."

Lewisham restrained an impulse to shout. "You will come to Immering?" he cried, and as they went along the narrow path through the wet grass, he began to tell her with simple frankness how he cared for her company. "I would not change this," he said, casting about for an offer to reject, "for—anything in the world. . . . I shall not be back for duty. I don't care. I don't care what happens so long as we have this afternoon."

"Nor I," she said.

"Thank you for coming," he said in an outburst of gratitude. "Oh, thank you for coming," and held out his hand. She took it and pressed it, and so they went on hand in hand until the village street was reached. Their high resolve to play truant at all costs had begotten a wonderful sense of fellowship. "I can't call you Miss Henderson," he said. "You know I can't. You know . . . I must have your Christian name."

"Ethel," she told him.

"Ethel," he said and looked at her, gathering courage as he did so. "Ethel," he repeated. "It is a pretty name. But no name is quite pretty enough for you, Ethel . . . *dear*." . . .

The little shop in Immering lay back behind a garden full of wallflowers, and was kept by a very fat and very cheerful little woman, who insisted on regarding them as brother and sister, and calling them both "dearie." These points conceded she gave them an admirable tea of astonishing cheapness. Lewisham did not like the second condition very much, because it seemed to touch a little on his latest enterprise. But the tea and the bread and butter and the whort jam were like no food on earth. There were wallflowers, heavy scented, in a jug upon the table, and Ethel admired them, and when they set out again the little old lady insisted on her taking a bunch with her.

It was after they left Immering that this ramble, properly speaking, became scandalous. The sun was already a golden ball above the blue hills in the west— it turned our two young people into little figures of flame—and yet, instead of going homeward, they took the Wentworth road that plunges into the Forshaw woods. Behind them the moon, almost full, hung in the blue sky above the tree-tops, ghostly and indistinct, and slowly gathered to itself such light as the setting sun left for it in the sky.

Going out of Immering they began to talk of the future. And for the very young lover there is no future but the immediate future.

"You must write to me," he said, and she told him she wrote such *silly* letters. "But I shall have reams to write to you," he told her.

"How are you to write to me?" she asked, and they discussed a new obstacle between them. It would never do to write home—never. She was sure of that with an absolute assurance. "My mother—" she said and stopped.

That prohibition cut him, for at that time he had the makings of a voluminous letter-writer. Yet it was only what one might expect. The whole world was unpropitious—obdurate indeed. . . . A splendid isolation *à deux*.

Perhaps she might find some place where letters might be sent to her? Yet that seemed to her deceitful.

So these two young people wandered on, full of their discovery of love, and yet so full too of the shyness of adolescence that the word "Love" never passed their lips that day. Yet as they talked on, and the kindly dusk gathered about them, their speech and their hearts came very close together. But their speech would seem so threadbare, written down in cold blood, that I must not put it here. To them it was not threadbare.

When at last they came down the long road into Whortley, the silent trees were black as ink and the moonlight made her face pallid and wonderful, and her eyes shone like stars. She still carried the blackthorn from which most of the blossoms had fallen. The fragrant wallflowers were fragrant still. And far away, softened by the distance, the Whortley band, performing publicly outside the vicarage for the first time that year, was playing with unctuous slowness a sentimental air. I don't know if the reader remembers it, that favorite melody of the early eighties:—

> "Sweet dreamland faces, passing to and fro, (pum, pum)
> Bring back to Mem'ry days of long ago-o-o-oh."

was the essence of it, very slow and tender and with an accompaniment of pum, pum. Pathetically cheerful that pum, pum, hopelessly cheerful indeed against the dirge of the air, a dirge accentuated by sporadic vocalization. But to young people things come differently.

"I *love* music," she said.

"So do I," said he.

They came on down the steepness of West Street. They walked athwart the metallic and leathery tumult of sound into the light cast by the little circle of yellow lamps. Several people saw them and wondered what the boys and girls were coming to nowadays, and one eye-witness even subsequently described their carriage as "brazen." Mr. Lewisham was wearing his mortar-board cap of office—there was no mistaking him. They passed the Proprietary School and saw a yellow picture framed and glazed, of Mr. Bonover taking duty for his aberrant assistant master. And outside the Frobisher house at last they parted perforce.

"Good-bye," he said for the third time. "Good-bye, Ethel."

She hesitated. Then suddenly she darted towards him. He felt her hands upon his shoulders, her lips soft and warm upon his cheek, and before he could take hold of her she had eluded him, and had flitted into the shadow of the house. "Good-bye," came her sweet, clear voice out of the shadow, and while he yet hesitated an answer, the door opened.

He saw her, black in the doorway, heard some indistinct words, and then the door closed and he was alone in the moonlight, his cheek still glowing from her lips. . . .

So ended Mr. Lewisham's first day with Love.

CHAPTER VII

The Reckoning

AND AFTER THE day of Love came the days of Reckoning. Mr. Lewisham was astonished—overwhelmed almost—by that Reckoning, as it slowly and steadily unfolded itself. The wonderful emotions of Saturday carried him through Sunday, and he made it up with the neglected Schema by assuring it that She was his Inspiration, and that he would work for Her a thousand times better than he could possibly work for himself. That was certainly not true, and indeed he found himself wondering whither the interest had vanished out of his theological examination of Butler's Analogy. The Frobishers were not at church for either service. He speculated rather anxiously why?

Monday dawned coldly and clearly—a Herbert Spencer of a day—and he went to school sedulously assuring himself there was nothing to apprehend. Day boys were whispering in the morning apparently about him, and Frobisher ii was in great request. Lewisham overheard a fragment. "My mother *was* in a wax," said Frobisher ii.

At twelve came an interview with Bonover, and voices presently rising in angry altercation and audible to Senior-assistant Dunkerley through the closed study door. Then Lewisham walked across the schoolroom, staring straight before him, his cheeks very bright.

Thereby Dunkerley's mind was prepared for the news that came the next morning over the exercise books. "When?" said Dunkerley.

"End of next term," said Lewisham.

"About this girl that's been staying at the Frobishers?"

"Yes."

"She's a pretty bit of goods. But it will mess up your matric next June," said Dunkerley.

"That's what I'm sorry for."

"It's scarcely to be expected he'll give you leave to attend the exam. . . ."

"He won't," said Lewisham shortly, and opened his first exercise book. He found it difficult to talk.

"He's a greaser," said Dunkerley. "But there!—what can you expect from Durham?" For Bonover had only a Durham degree and Dunkerley, having none, inclined to be particular. Therewith Dunkerley lapsed into a sympathetic and busy rustling over his own pile of exercises. It was not until the heap had been reduced to a book or so that he spoke again—an elaborate point.

"Male and female created He them," said Dunkerley ticking his way down the page. "Which (tick, tick) was damned hard (tick, tick) on assistant masters."

He closed the book with a snap and flung it on the floor behind him. "You're lucky," he said. "I *did* think I should be first to get out of this scandalizing hole. You're lucky. It's always acting down here. Running on parents and guardians round every corner. That's what I object to in life in the country: it's so confoundedly artificial. *I* shall take jolly good care *I* get out of it just as soon as ever I can. You bet!"

"And work those patents?"

"Rather, my boy. Yes. Work those patents. The Patent Square Top Bottle! Lord! Once let me get to London. . . ."

"I think *I* shall have a shot at London," said Lewisham.

And then the experienced Dunkerley, being one of the kindest young men alive, forgot certain private ambitions of his own—he cherished dreams of amazing patents—and bethought him of agents. He proceeded to give a list of these necessary helpers of the assistant master at the gangway—Orellana, Gabbitas, The Lancaster Gate Agency, and the rest of them. He knew them all—intimately. He had been a "nix" eight years. "Of course that Kensington thing may come off," said Dunkerley, "but it's best not to wait. I tell you frankly—the chances are against you."

The "Kensington thing" was an application for admission to the Normal School of Science at South Kensington, which Lewisham had made in a sanguine moment. There being an inadequate supply of qualified science teachers in England, the Science and Art Department is wont to offer free instruction at its great central school and a guinea a week to select young pedagogues who will bind themselves to teach science after their training is over. Dunkerley had been in the habit of applying for several years, always in vain, and Lewisham had seen no harm in following his example. But then Dunkerley had no green-gray certificates.

So Lewisham spent all that "duty" left him of the next day composing a letter to copy out and send the several scholastic agencies. In this he gave a brief but appreciative sketch of his life, and enlarged upon his discipline and educational methods. At the end was a long and decorative schedule of his certificates and distinctions, beginning with a good-conduct prize at the age of eight. A considerable amount of time was required to recopy this document, but his modesty upheld him. After a careful consideration of the time-table, he set aside the midday hour for "Correspondence."

He found that his work in mathematics and classics was already some time in arrears, and a "test" he had sent to his correspondence Tutor during those troublous days after the meeting with Bonover in the Avenue, came back blottesquely indorsed: "Below Pass Standard." This last experience was so unprecedented and annoyed him so much that for a space he contemplated retorting with a sarcastic letter to the tutor. And then came the Easter recess, and he had to go home and tell his mother, with a careful suppression of details, that he was leaving Whortley. "Where you have been getting on so well!" cried his mother.

But that dear old lady had one consolation. She observed he had given up his glasses—he had forgotten to bring them with him—and her secret fear of grave optical troubles—that were being "kept" from her—was alleviated.

Sometimes he had moods of intense regret for the folly of that walk. One such came after the holidays, when the necessity of revising the dates of the Schema brought before his mind, for the first time quite clearly, the practical issue of this first struggle with all those mysterious and powerful influences the spring-time sets a-stirring. His dream of success and fame had been very real and dear to him, and the realization of the inevitable postponement of his long anticipated matriculation, the doorway to all the other great things, took him abruptly like an actual physical sensation in his chest.

He sprang up, pen in hand, in the midst of his corrections, and began pacing up and down the room. "What a fool I have been!" he cried. "What a fool I have been!"

He flung the pen on the floor and made a rush at an ill-drawn attempt upon a girl's face that adorned the end of his room, the visible witness of his slavery. He tore this down and sent the fragments of it scattering. . .

"Fool!"

It was a relief—a definite abandonment. He stared for a moment at the destruction he had made, and then went back to the revision of the time-table, with a mutter about "silly spooning."

That was one mood. The rarer one. He watched the posts with far more eagerness for the address to which he might write to her than for any reply to those reiterated letters of application, the writing of which now ousted Horace and the higher mathematics (Lewisham's term for conics) from his attention. Indeed he spent more time meditating the letter to her than even the schedule of his virtues had required.

Yet the letters of application were wonderful compositions; each had a new pen to itself and was for the first page at least in a handwriting far above even his usual high standard. And day after day passed and that particular letter he hoped for still did not come.

His moods were complicated by the fact that, in spite of his studied reticence on the subject, the reason of his departure did in an amazingly short time get "all over Whortley." It was understood that he had been discovered to be "fast," and Ethel's behavior was animadverted upon with complacent indignation—if the phrase may be allowed—by the ladies of the place. Pretty looks were too often a snare. One boy—his ear was warmed therefor—once called aloud "Ethel," as Lewisham went by. The curate, a curate of the pale-faced, large-knuckled, nervous sort, now passed him without acknowledgment of his existence. Mrs. Bonover took occasion to tell him that he was a "mere boy," and once Mrs. Frobisher sniffed quite threateningly at him when she passed him in the street. She did it so suddenly she made him jump.

This general disapproval inclined him at times to depression, but in certain moods he found it exhilarating, and several times he professed himself to Dunkerley not a little of a blade. In others, he told himself he bore it for *her* sake. Anyhow he had to bear it.

He began to find out too, how little the world feels the need of a young man of nineteen—he called himself nineteen, though he had several months of eighteen still to run—even though he adds prizes for good conduct, general improvement, and arithmetic, and advanced certificates signed by a distinguished engineer and headed with the Royal Arms, guaranteeing his knowledge of geometrical drawing, nautical astronomy, animal physiology, physiography, inorganic chemistry and building construction, to his youth and strength and energy. At first he had imagined headmasters clutching at the chance of him, and presently he found himself clutching eagerly at them. He began to put a certain urgency into his applications for vacant posts, an urgency that helped him not at all. The applications grew longer and longer until they ran to four sheets of note-paper—a pennyworth in fact. "I can assure you," he would write, "that you will find me a loyal and devoted assistant." Much in that strain. Dunkerley pointed out that Bonover's testimonial ignored the question of moral character and discipline in a marked manner, and Bonover refused to alter it. He was willing to do what he could to help Lewisham, in spite of the way he had been treated, but unfortunately his conscience . . .

Once or twice Lewisham misquoted the testimonial—to no purpose. And May was halfway through, and South Kensington was silent. The future was gray.

And in the depths of his doubt and disappointment came her letter. It was typewritten on thin paper. "Dear," she wrote simply, and it seemed to him the most sweet and wonderful of all possible modes of address, though as a matter of fact it was because she had forgotten his Christian name and afterwards forgotten the blank she had left for it.

"Dear, I could not write before because I have no room at home now where I can write a letter, and Mrs. Frobisher told my mother falsehoods about you. My mother has surprised me dreadfully—I did not think it of her. She told me nothing. But of that I must tell you in another letter. I am too angry to write about it now. Even now you cannot write back, for *you must not send letters here*. It would *never* do. But I think of you, dear,"—the "dear" had been erased and rewritten—"and I must write and tell you so, and of that nice walk we had, if I never write again. I am very busy now. My work is rather difficult and I am afraid I am a little stupid. It is hard to be interested in anything just because that is how you have to live, is it not? I daresay you sometimes feel the same of school. But I suppose everybody is doing things they don't like. I don't know when I shall come to Whortley again, if ever, but very likely you will be coming to London. Mrs. Frobisher said the most horrid things. It would be nice if you could come to London, because then perhaps you might see me. There is a big boys' school at Chelsea, and when I go by it every morning I wish you were there. Then you would come out in your cap and gown as I went by. Suppose some day I was to see you there suddenly!!"

So it ran, with singularly little information in it, and ended quite abruptly, "Good-bye, dear. Good-bye, dear," scribbled in pencil. And then, "Think of me sometimes."

Reading it, and especially that opening "dear," made Lewisham feel the strangest sensation in his throat and chest, almost as though he was going to cry. So he laughed instead and read it again, and went to and fro in his little room with his eyes bright and that precious writing held in his hand. That "dear" was just as if she had spoken—a voice suddenly heard. He thought of her farewell, clear and sweet, out of the shadow of the moonlit house.

But why that "If I never write again," and that abrupt ending? Of course he would think of her.

It was her only letter. In a little time its creases were worn through.

Early in June came a loneliness that suddenly changed into almost intolerable longing to see her. He had vague dreams of going to London, to Clapham, to find her. But you do not find people in Clapham as you do in Whortley. He spent an afternoon writing and re-writing a lengthy letter, against the day when her address should come. If it was to come. He prowled about the village disconsolately, and at last set off about seven and retraced by moonlight almost every step of that one memorable walk of theirs.

In the blackness of the shed he worked himself up to the pitch of talking as if she were present. And he said some fine brave things.

He found the little old lady of the wallflowers with a candle in her window, and drank a bottle of ginger beer with a sacramental air. The little old lady asked him, a trifle archly, after his sister, and he promised to bring her again some day. "I'll certainly bring her," he said. Talking to the little old lady somehow blunted his sense of desolation. And then home through the white indistinctness in a state of melancholy that became at last so fine as to be almost pleasurable.

The day after that mood a new "text" attracted and perplexed Mrs. Munday, an inscription at once mysterious and familiar, and this inscription was:

ART

It was in Old English lettering and evidently very carefully executed.

Where had she seen it before?

It quite dominated all the rest of the room at first, it flaunted like a flag of triumph over "discipline" and the time-table and the Schema. Once indeed it was taken down, but the day after it reappeared. Later a list of scholastic vacancies partially obscured it, and some pencil memoranda were written on the margin.

And when at last the time came for him to pack up and leave Whortley, he took it down and used it with several other suitable papers—the Schema and the time-table were its next-door neighbors—to line the bottom of the yellow box in which he packed his books; chiefly books for that matriculation that had now to be postponed.

CHAPTER VIII

The Career Prevails

THERE IS AN interval of two years and a half and the story resumes with a much maturer Mr. Lewisham, indeed no longer a youth, but a man, a legal man, at any rate, of one and twenty years. Its scene is no longer little Whortley embedded among its trees, ruddy banks, parks and common land, but the gray spaciousness of West London.

And it does not resume with Ethel at all. For that promised second letter never reached him, and though he spent many an afternoon during his first few months in London, wandering about Clapham, that arid waste of people, the meeting that he longed for never came. Until at last after the manner of youth, so gloriously recuperative in body, heart, and soul, he began to forget.

The quest of a "crib" had ended in the unexpected fruition of Dunkerley's blue paper. The green-blue certificates had, it seemed, a value beyond mural decoration, and when Lewisham was already despairing of any employment for the rest of his life, came a marvellous blue document from the Education Department promising inconceivable things. He was to go to London and be paid a guinea a week for listening to lectures—lectures beyond his most ambitious dreams! Among the names that swam before his eyes was Huxley—Huxley and then

Lockyer! What a chance to get! Is it any wonder that for three memorable years the Career prevailed with him?

You figure him on his way to the Normal School of Science at the opening of his third year of study there. (They call the place the Royal College of Science in these latter days.) He carried in his right hand a shiny black bag, well stuffed with text-books, notes, and apparatus for the forthcoming session; and in his left was a book that the bag had no place for, a book with gilt edges, and its binding very carefully protected by a brown paper cover.

The lapse of time had asserted itself upon his upper lip in an inaggressive but indisputable moustache, in an added inch or so of stature, and in his less conscious carriage. For he no longer felt that universal attention he believed in at eighteen; it was beginning to dawn on him indeed that quite a number of people were entirely indifferent to the fact of his existence. But if less conscious, his carriage was decidedly more confident—as of one with whom the world goes well.

His costume was—with one exception—a tempered black,—mourning put to hard uses and, "cutting up rusty." The mourning was for his mother, who had died more than a year before the date when this story resumes, and had left him property that capitalized at nearly a hundred pounds, a sum which Lewisham hoarded jealously in the Savings Bank, paying only for such essentials as university fees, and the books and instruments his brilliant career as a student demanded. For he was having a brilliant career, after all, in spite of the Whortley check, licking up paper certificates indeed like a devouring flame.

(Surveying him, Madam, your eye would inevitably have fallen to his collar— curiously shiny, a surface like wet gum. Although it has practically nothing to do with this story, I must, I know, dispose of that before I go on, or you will be inattentive. London has its mysteries, but this strange gloss on his linen! "Cheap laundresses always make your things blue," protests the lady. "It ought to have been blue-stained, generously frayed, and loose about the button, fretting his neck. But this gloss . . ." You would have looked nearer, and finally you would have touched—a charnel house surface, dank and cool! You see, Madam, the collar was a patent waterproof one. One of those you wash over night with a tooth-brush, and hang on the back of your chair to dry, and there you have it next morning, rejuvenesced. It was the only collar he had in the world, it saved threepence a week at least, and that, to a South Kensington "science teacher in training," living on the guinea a week allowed by a parental but parsimonious government, is a sum to consider. It had come to Lewisham as a great discovery. He had seen it first in a shop window full of indiarubber goods, and it lay at the bottom of a glass bowl in which goldfish drifted discontentedly to and fro. And he told himself that he rather liked that gloss.)

But the wearing of a bright red tie would have been unexpected—a bright red tie after the fashion of a South-Western railway guard's! The rest of him by no means dandiacal, even the vanity of glasses long since abandoned. You would have reflected. . . . Where had you seen a crowd—red ties abundant and in some way significant? The truth has to be told. Mr. Lewisham had become a Socialist!

That red tie was indeed but one outward and visible sign of much inward and spiritual development. Lewisham, in spite of the demands of a studious career, had read his Butler's Analogy through by this time, and some other books; he had argued, had had doubts, and called upon God for "Faith" in the silence of the night—"Faith" to be delivered immediately if Mr. Lewisham's patronage was valued, and which nevertheless was not so delivered. . . . And his conception of his destiny in this world was no longer an avenue of examinations to a remote

Bar and political eminence "in the Liberal interest (D. V.)" He had begun to realize certain aspects of our social order that Whortley did not demonstrate, begun to feel something of the dull stress deepening to absolute wretchedness and pain, which is the color of so much human life in modern London. One vivid contrast hung in his mind symbolical. On the one hand were the coalies of the Westbourne Park yards, on strike and gaunt and hungry, children begging in the black slush, and starving loungers outside a soup kitchen; and on the other, Westbourne Grove, two streets further, a blazing array of crowded shops, a stirring traffic of cabs and carriages, and such a spate of spending that a tired student in leaky boots and graceless clothes hurrying home was continually impeded in the whirl of skirts and parcels and sweetly pretty womanliness. No doubt the tired student's own inglorious sensations pointed the moral. But that was only one of a perpetually recurring series of vivid approximations.

Lewisham had a strong persuasion, an instinct it may be, that human beings should not be happy while others near them were wretched, and this gay glitter of prosperity had touched him with a sense of crime. He still believed people were responsible for their own lives; in those days he had still to gauge the possibilities of moral stupidity in himself and his fellow-men. He happened upon "Progress and Poverty" just then, and some casual numbers of the "Commonweal," and it was only too easy to accept the theory of cunning plotting capitalists and landowners, and faultless, righteous, martyr workers. He became a Socialist forthwith. The necessity to do something at once to manifest the new faith that was in him was naturally urgent. So he went out and (historical moment) bought that red tie!

"Blood color, please," said Lewisham meekly to the young lady at the counter.

"*What* color?" said the young lady at the counter, sharply.

"A bright scarlet, please," said Lewisham, blushing. And he spent the best part of the evening and much of his temper in finding out how to tie this into a neat bow. It was a plunge into novel handicraft—for previously he had been accustomed to made-up ties.

So it was that Lewisham proclaimed the Social Revolution. The first time that symbol went abroad a string of stalwart policemen were walking in single file along the Brompton Road. In the opposite direction marched Lewisham. He began to hum. He passed the policemen with a significant eye and humming the *Marseillaise*. . . .

But that was months ago, and by this time the red tie was a thing of use and wont.

He turned out of the Exhibition Road through a gateway of wrought iron, and entered the hall of the Normal School. The hall was crowded with students carrying books, bags, and boxes of instruments, students standing and chattering, students reading the framed and glazed notices of the Debating Society, students buying note-books, pencils, rubber, or drawing pins from the privileged stationer. There was a strong representation of new hands, the paying students, youths and young men in black coats and silk hats or tweed suits, the scholar contingent, youngsters of Lewisham's class, raw, shabby, discordant, grotesquely ill-dressed and awe-stricken; one Lewisham noticed with a sailor's peaked cap gold-decorated, and one with mittens and very genteel gray kid gloves; and Grummett the perennial Official of the Books was busy among them.

"Der Zozalist!" said a wit.

Lewisham pretended not to hear and blushed vividly. He often wished he did not blush quite so much, seeing he was a man of one and twenty. He looked studiously away from the Debating Society notice board, whereon "G. E. Lewisham on Socialism" was announced for the next Friday, and struggled through the hall to where the Book awaited his signature. Presently he was hailed by name, and then again. He could not get to the Book for a minute or so, because of the hand-shaking and clumsy friendly jests of his fellow-"men."

He was pointed out to a raw hand, by the raw hand's experienced fellow-townsman, as "that beast Lewisham—awful swat. He was second last year on the year's work. Frightful mugger. But all these swats have a touch of the beastly prig. Exams—Debating Society—more Exams. Don't seem to have ever heard of being alive. Never goes near a Music Hall from one year's end to the other."

Lewisham heard a shrill whistle, made a run for the lift and caught it just on the point of departure. The lift was unlit and full of black shadows; only the sapper who conducted it was distinct. As Lewisham peered doubtfully at the dim faces near him, a girl's voice addressed him by name.

"Is that you, Miss Heydinger?" he answered. "I didn't see. I hope you have had a pleasant vacation."

CHAPTER IX

Alice Heydinger

WHEN HE ARRIVED at the top of the building he stood aside for the only remaining passenger to step out before him. It was the Miss Heydinger who had addressed him, the owner of that gilt-edged book in the cover of brown paper. No one else had come all the way up from the ground floor. The rest of the load in the lift had emerged at the "astronomical" and "chemical" floors, but these two had both chosen "zoology" for their third year of study, and zoology lived in the attics. She stepped into the light, with a rare touch of color springing to her cheeks in spite of herself. Lewisham perceived an alteration in her dress. Perhaps she was looking for and noticed the transitory surprise in his face.

The previous session—their friendship was now nearly a year old—it had never once dawned upon him that she could possibly be pretty. The chief thing he had been able to recall with any definiteness during the vacation was, that her hair was not always tidy and that even when it chanced to be so, she was nervous about it; she distrusted it. He remembered her gesture while she talked, a patting exploration that verged on the exasperating. From that he went on to remember that its color was, on the whole, fair, a light brown. But he had forgotten her mouth, he had failed to name the color of her eyes. She wore glasses, it is true. And her dress was indefinite in his memory—an amorphous dinginess.

And yet he had seen a good deal of her. They were not in the same course, but he had made her acquaintance on the committee of the school Debating Society. Lewisham was just then discovering Socialism. That had afforded a basis of conversation—an incentive to intercourse. She seemed to find something rarely interesting in his peculiar view of things, and, as chance would have it, he met her accidentally quite a number of times, in the corridors of the schools, in the big Education Library, and in the Art Museum. After a time those meetings appear to have been no longer accidental.

Lewisham for the first time in his life began to fancy he had conversational powers. She resolved to stir up his ambitions—an easy task. She thought he had exceptional gifts and that she might serve to direct them; she certainly developed his vanity. She had matriculated at the London University and they took the

Intermediate Examination in Science together in July—she a little unwisely—which served, as almost anything will serve in such cases, as a further link between them. She failed, which in no way diminished Lewisham's regard for her. On the examination days they discoursed about Friendship in general, and things like that, down the Burlington Arcade during the lunch time,—Burlington Arcade undisguisedly amused by her learned dinginess and his red tie—and among other things that were said she reproached him for not reading poetry. When they parted in Piccadilly, after the examination, they agreed to write, about poetry and themselves, during the holidays, and then she lent him, with a touch of hesitation, Rossetti's poems. He began to forget what had at first been very evident to him, that she was two or three years older than he.

Lewisham spent the vacation with an unsympathetic but kindly uncle who was a plumber and builder. His uncle had a family of six, the eldest eleven, and Lewisham made himself agreeable and instructive. Moreover he worked hard for the culminating third year of his studies (in which he had decided to do great things) and he learned to ride the Ordinary Bicycle. He also thought about Miss Heydinger, and she, it would seem, thought about him.

He argued on social questions with his uncle, who was a prominent local Conservative. His uncle's controversial methods were coarse in the extreme. Socialists, he said, were thieves. The object of Socialism was to take away what a man earned and give it to "a lot of lazy scoundrels." Also rich people were necessary. "If there weren't well-off people, how d'ye think I'd get a livin'? Hey? And where'd *you* be then?" Socialism, his uncle assured him, was "got up" by agitators. "They get money out of young Gabies like you, and they spend it in champagne." And thereafter he met Mr. Lewisham's arguments with the word "Champagne" uttered in an irritating voice, followed by a luscious pantomime of drinking.

Naturally Lewisham felt a little lonely, and perhaps he laid stress upon it in his letters to Miss Heydinger. It came to light that she felt rather lonely too. They discussed the question of True as distinguished from Ordinary Friendship, and from that they passed to Goethe and Elective Affinities. He told her how he looked for her letters, and they became more frequent. Her letters were indisputably well written. Had he been a journalist with a knowledge of "*per thou.*" he would have known each for a day's work. After the practical plumber had been asking what he expected to make by this here science of his, re-reading her letters was balsamic. He liked Rossetti—the exquisite sense of separation in "The Blessed Damozel" touched him. But, on the whole, he was a little surprised at Miss Heydinger's taste in poetry. Rossetti was so sensuous . . . so florid. He had scarcely expected that sort of thing.

Altogether he had returned to the schools decidedly more interested in her than when they had parted. And the curious vague memories of her appearance as something a little frayed and careless, vanished at sight of her emerging from the darkness of the lift. Her hair was in order, as the light glanced through it it looked even pretty, and she wore a well-made, dark-green and black dress, loose-gathered as was the fashion in those days, that somehow gave a needed touch of warmth to her face. Her hat too was a change from the careless lumpishness of last year, a hat that, to a feminine mind, would have indicated design. It suited her—these things are past a male novelist's explaining.

"I have this book of yours, Miss Heydinger," he said.

"I am glad you have written that paper on Socialism," she replied, taking the brown-covered volume.

They walked along the little passage towards the biological laboratory side by side, and she stopped at the hat pegs to remove her hat. For that was the shameless way of the place, a girl student had to take her hat off publicly, and publicly assume the holland apron that was to protect her in the laboratory. Not even a looking-glass!

"I shall come and hear your paper," she said.

"I hope you will like it," said Lewisham at the door of the laboratory.

"And in the vacation I have been collecting evidence about ghosts—you remember our arguments. Though I did not tell you in my letters."

"I'm sorry you're still obdurate," said Lewisham. "I thought that was over."

"And have you read 'Looking Backward'?"

"I want to."

"I have it here with my other books, if you'd care for me to lend it to you. Wait till I reach my table. My hands are so full."

They entered the laboratory together, Lewisham holding the door open courtly-wise, Miss Heydinger taking a reassuring pat at her hair. Near the door was a group of four girls, which group Miss Heydinger joined, holding the brown-covered book as inconspicuously as possible. Three of them had been through the previous two years with her, and they greeted her by her Christian name. They had previously exchanged glances at her appearance in Lewisham's company.

A morose elderly young demonstrator brightened momentarily at the sight of Lewisham. "Well, we've got one of the decent ones anyhow," said the morose elderly young demonstrator, who was apparently taking an inventory, and then brightening at a fresh entry. "Ah! and here's Smithers."

CHAPTER X

In the Gallery of Old Iron

As ONE GOES into the South Kensington Art Museum from the Brompton Road, the Gallery of Old Iron is overhead to the right. But the way thither is exceedingly devious and not to be revealed to everybody, since the young people who pursue science and art thereabouts set a peculiar value on its seclusion. The gallery is long and narrow and dark, and set with iron gates, iron-bound chests, locks, bolts and bars, fantastic great keys, lamps, and the like, and over the balustrade one may lean and talk of one's finer feelings and regard Michelangelo horned Moses, or Trajan's Column (in plaster) rising gigantic out of the hall below and far above the level of the gallery. And here, on a Wednesday afternoon, were Lewisham and Miss Heydinger, the Wednesday afternoon immediately following that paper upon Socialism, that you saw announced on the notice board in the hall.

The paper had been an immense success, closely reasoned, delivered with a disciplined emotion, the redoubtable Smithers practically converted, the reply after the debate methodical and complete, and it may be there were symptoms of that febrile affection known to the vulgar as "swelled 'ed." Lewisham regarded Moses and spoke of his future. Miss Heydinger for the most part watched his face.

"And then?" said Miss Heydinger.

"One must bring these views prominently before people. I believe still in pamphlets. I have thought . . ." Lewisham paused, it is to be hoped through modesty.

"Yes?" said Miss Heydinger.

"Well—Luther, you know. There is room, I think, in Socialism, for a Luther."

"Yes," said Miss Heydinger, imagining it. "Yes—that would be a grand way."

So it seemed to many people in those days. But eminent reformers have been now for more than seven years going about the walls of the Social Jericho, blowing their own trumpets and shouting—with such small result beyond incidental displays of ill-temper within, that it is hard to recover the fine hopefulness of those departed days.

"Yes," said Miss Heydinger. "That would be a grand way."

Lewisham appreciated the quality of personal emotion in her voice. He turned his face towards her, and saw unstinted admiration in her eyes. "It would be a great thing to do," he said, and added, quite modestly, "if only one could do it."

"*You* could do it."

"You think I could?" Lewisham blushed vividly—with pleasure.

"I do. Certainly you could set out to do it. Even to fail hopelessly would be Great. Sometimes . . ."

She hesitated. He looked expectation. "I think sometimes it is greater even to fail than to succeed."

"I don't see that," said the proposed Luther, and his eyes went back to the Moses. She was about to speak and changed her mind.

Contemplative pause.

"And then, when a great number of people have heard of your views?" she said presently.

"Then I suppose we must form a party and . . . bring things about."

Another pause—full, no doubt, of elevated thoughts.

"I say," said Lewisham quite suddenly. "You do put—well—courage into a chap. I shouldn't have done that Socialism paper if it hadn't been for you." He turned round and stood leaning with his back to the Moses, and smiling at her. "You do help a fellow," he said.

That was one of the vivid moments of Miss Heydinger's life. She changed color a little. "Do I?" she said, standing straight and awkward and looking into his face. "I'm . . . glad."

"I haven't thanked you for your letters," said Lewisham. "And I've been thinking . . ."

"Yes?"

"We're first-rate friends, aren't we? The best of friends."

She held out her hand and drew a breath. "Yes," she said as they gripped. He hesitated whether to hold her hand. He looked into her eyes, and at that moment she would have given three quarters of the years she had still to live, to have had eyes and features that could have expressed her. Instead, she felt her face hard, the little muscles of her mouth twitching insubordinate, and fancied that her self-consciousness made her eyes dishonest.

"What I mean," said Lewisham, "is—that this will go on. We're always going to be friends, side by side."

"Always. Just as I am able to help you—I will help you. However I can help you, I will."

"We two," said Lewisham gripping her hand.

Her face lit. Her eyes were for a moment touched with the beauty of simple emotion. "We two," she said, and her lips trembled and her throat seemed to swell. She snatched her hand back suddenly and turned her face away. Abruptly she walked towards the end of the gallery, and he saw her fumbling for her handkerchief in the folds of the green and black dress.

She was going to cry!

It set Lewisham marvelling—this totally inappropriate emotion.

He followed her and stood by her. Why cry? He hoped no one would come into the little gallery until her handkerchief was put away. Nevertheless he felt vaguely flattered. She controlled herself, dashed her tears away, and smiled bravely at him with reddened eyes. "I'm sorry," she said, gulping.

"I am so glad," she explained.

"But we will fight together. We two. I *can* help you. I know I can help you. And there is such Work to be done in the world!"

"You are very good to help me," said Lewisham, quoting a phrase from what he had intended to say before he found out that he had a hold upon her emotions.

"No!

"Has it ever occurred to you," she said abruptly, "how little a woman can do alone in the world?"

"Or a man," he answered after a momentary meditation.

So it was Lewisham enrolled his first ally in the cause of the red tie—of the red tie and of the Greatness that was presently to come. His first ally; for hitherto—save for the indiscretion of his mural inscriptions—he had made a secret of his private ambitions. In that now half-forgotten love affair at Whortley even, he had, in spite of the considerable degree of intimacy attained, said absolutely nothing about his Career.

CHAPTER XI

Manifestations

MISS HEYDINGER DECLINED to disbelieve in the spirits of the dead, and this led to controversy in the laboratory over Tea. For the girl students, being in a majority that year, had organized Tea between four o'clock and the advent of the extinguishing policeman at five. And the men students were occasionally invited to Tea. But not more than two of them at a time really participated, because there were only two spare cups after that confounded Simmons broke the third.

Smithers, the square-headed student with the hard gray eyes, argued against the spirits of the dead with positive animosity, while Bletherley, who displayed an orange tie and lank hair in unshorn abundance, was vaguely open-minded. "What is love?" asked Bletherley, "surely that at any rate is immortal!" His remark was considered irrelevant and ignored.

Lewisham, as became the most promising student of the year, weighed the evidence—comprehensively under headings. He dismissed the mediumistic *séances* as trickery.

"Rot and imposture," said Smithers loudly, and with an oblique glance to see if his challenge reached its mark. Its mark was a grizzled little old man with a very small face and very big gray eyes, who had been standing listlessly at one of the laboratory windows until the discussion caught him. He wore a brown velvet jacket and was reputed to be enormously rich. His name was Lagune. He was not a regular attendant, but one of those casual outsiders who are admitted to laboratories that are not completely full. He was known to be an ardent spiritualist—it was even said that he had challenged Huxley to a public discussion on materialism, and he came to the biological lectures and worked intermittently, in order, he explained, to fight disbelief with its own weapons. He rose greedily to Smithers' controversial bait.

"I say *no!*" he said, calling down the narrow laboratory and following his voice. He spoke with the ghost of a lisp. "Pardon my interrupting, sir. The question interests me profoundly. I hope I don't intrude. Excuse me, sir. Make it personal. Am I a—fool, or an impostor?"

"Well," parried Smithers with all a South Kensington student's want of polish, "that's a bit personal."

"Assume, sir, that I am an honest observer."

"Well?"

"I have *seen* spirits, *heard* spirits, *felt* the touch of spirits." He opened his pale eyes very widely.

"Fool, then," said Smithers in an undertone which did not reach the ears of the spiritualist.

"You may have been deceived," paraphrased Lewisham.

"I can assure you . . . others can see, hear, feel. I have tested, sir. Tested! I have some scientific training and I have employed tests. Scientific and exhaustive tests! Every possible way. I ask you, sir—have you given the spirits a chance?"

"It is only paying guineas to humbugs," said Smithers.

"There you are! Prejudice! Here is a man denies the facts and consequently *won't* see them, won't go near them."

"But you wouldn't have every man in the three kingdoms, who disbelieved in spirits, attend *séances* before he should be allowed to deny?"

"Most assuredly yes. Most assuredly yes! He knows nothing about it till then."

The argument became heated. The little old gentleman was soon under way. He knew a person of the most extraordinary gifts, a medium . . .

"Paid?" asked Smithers.

"Would you muzzle the ox that treadeth out the corn?" said Lagune promptly. Smithers' derision was manifest.

"Would you distrust a balance because you bought it? Come and see." Lagune was now very excited and inclined to gesticulate and raise his voice. He invited the whole class incontinently to a series of special *séances*. "Not all at once—the spirits—new influences." But in sections. "I warn you we may get nothing. But the chances are . . . I would rejoice infinitely . . ."

So it came about that Lewisham consented to witness a spirit-raising. Miss Heydinger it was arranged should be there, and the skeptic Smithers, Lagune, his typewriter and the medium would complete the party. Afterwards there was to be another party for the others. Lewisham was glad he had the moral support of Smithers. "It's an evening wasted," said Smithers, who had gallantly resolved to make the running for Lewisham in the contest for the Forbes medal. "But I'll prove my case. You see if I don't." They were given an address in Chelsea.

The house, when Lewisham found it at last, proved a large one with such an air of mellowed dignity that he was abashed. He hung his hat up for himself beside a green-trimmed hat of straw in the wide, rich-toned hall. Through an open door he had a glimpse of a palatial study, book shelves bearing white busts, a huge writing-table lit by a green-shaded electric lamp and covered thickly with papers. The housemaid looked, he thought, with infinite disdain at the rusty mourning and flamboyant tie, and flounced about and led him upstairs.

She rapped, and there was a discussion within. "They're at it already, I believe," she said to Lewisham confidentially. "Mr. Lagune's always at it."

There were sounds of chairs being moved, Smithers' extensive voice making a suggestion and laughing nervously. Lagune appeared opening the door. His grizzled face seemed smaller and his big gray eyes larger than usual.

"We were just going to begin without you," he whispered. "Come along."

The room was furnished even more finely than the drawing-room of the Whortley Grammar School, hitherto the finest room (except certain of the State Apartments at Windsor) known to Lewisham. The furniture struck him in a general way as akin to that in the South Kensington Museum. His first impression was an appreciation of the vast social superiority of the chairs; it seemed impertinent to think of sitting on anything quite so quietly stately. He perceived Smithers standing with an air of bashful hostility against a bookcase. Then he was aware that Lagune was asking them all to sit down. Already seated at the table was the Medium, Chaffery, a benevolent-looking, faintly shabby gentleman with bushy iron-gray side-whiskers, a wide, thin-lipped mouth tucked in at the corners, and a chin like the toe of a boot. He regarded Lewisham critically and disconcertingly over gilt glasses. Miss Heydinger was quite at her ease and began talking at once. Lewisham's replies were less confident than they had been in the Gallery of Old Iron; indeed there was almost a reversal of their positions. She led and he was abashed. He felt obscurely that she had taken an advantage of him. He became aware of another girlish figure in a dark dress on his right.

Everyone moved towards the round table in the center of the room, on which lay a tambourine and a little green box. Lagune developed unsuspected lengths of knobby wrist and finger directing his guests to their seats. Lewisham was to sit next to him, between him and the Medium; beyond the Medium sat Smithers with Miss Heydinger on the other side of him, linked to Lagune by the typewriter. So skeptics compassed the Medium about. The company was already seated before Lewisham looked across Lagune and met the eyes of the girl next that gentleman. It was Ethel! The close green dress, the absence of a hat, and a certain loss of color made her seem less familiar, but did not prevent the instant recognition. And there was recognition in her eyes.

Immediately she looked away. At first his only emotion was surprise. He would have spoken but a little thing robbed him of speech. For a moment he was unable to remember her surname. Moreover, the strangeness of his surroundings made him undecided. He did not know what was the proper way to address her—and he still kept to the superstition of etiquette. Besides—to speak to her would involve a general explanation to all these people . . .

"Just leave a pin-point of gas, Mr. Smithers, please," said Lagune, and suddenly the one surviving jet of the gas chandelier was turned down and they were in darkness. The moment for recognition had passed.

The joining of hands was punctiliously verified, the circle was linked little finger to little finger. Lewisham's abstraction received a rebuke from Smithers. The Medium, speaking in an affable voice, premised that he could promise nothing, he had no "*directing*" power over manifestations. Thereafter ensued a silence. . . .

For a space Lewisham was inattentive to all that happened.

He sat in the breathing darkness, staring at the dim elusive shape that had presented that remembered face. His mind was astonishment mingled with annoyance. He had settled that this girl was lost to him forever. The spell of the old days of longing, of the afternoons that he had spent after his arrival in London, wandering through Clapham with a fading hope of meeting her, had not returned to him. But he was ashamed of his stupid silence, and irritated by the awkwardness of the situation. At one moment he was on the very verge of breaking the compact and saying "Miss Henderson" across the table. . . .

How was it he had forgotten that "Henderson?" He was still young enough to be surprised at forgetfulness.

Smithers coughed, one might imagine with a warning intention.

Lewisham, recalling his detective responsibility with an effort, peered about him, but the room was very dark. The silence was broken ever and again by deep sighs and a restless stirring from the Medium. Out of this mental confusion Lewisham's personal vanity was first to emerge. What did she think of him? Was she peering at him through the darkness even as he peered at her? Should he pretend to see her for the first time when the lights were restored? As the minutes lengthened it seemed as though the silence grew deeper and deeper. There was no fire in the room, and it looked, for lack of that glow, chilly. A curious skepticism arose in his mind as to whether he had actually seen Ethel or only mistaken someone else for her. He wanted the *séance* over in order that he might look at her again. The old days at Whortley came out of his memory with astonishing detail and yet astonishingly free from emotion. . . .

He became aware of a peculiar sensation down his back, that he tried to account for as a draught. . . .

Suddenly a beam of cold air came like a touch against his face, and made him shudder convulsively. Then he hoped that she had not marked his shudder. He thought of laughing a low laugh to show he was not afraid. Someone else shuddered too, and he perceived an extraordinarily vivid odor of violets. Lagune's finger communicated a nervous quivering.

What was happening?

The musical box somewhere on the table began playing a rather trivial, rather plaintive air that was strange to him. It seemed to deepen the silence about him, an accent on the expectant stillness, a thread of tinkling melody spanning an abyss.

Lewisham took himself in hand at this stage. What *was* happening? He must attend. Was he really watching as he should do? He had been wool-gathering. There were no such things as spirits, mediums were humbugs, and he was here to prove that sole remaining Gospel. But he must keep up with things—he was missing points. What was that scent of violets? And who had set the musical box going? The Medium of course: but how? He tried to recall whether he had heard a rustling or detected any movement before the music began. He could not recollect. Come! he must be more on the alert than this!

He became acutely desirous of a successful exposure. He figured the dramatic moment he had prepared with Smithers—Ethel a spectator. He peered suspiciously into the darkness.

Somebody shuddered again, someone opposite him this time. He felt Lagune's finger quiver still more palpably, and then suddenly the raps began, abruptly, all about him. *Rap!*—making him start violently. A swift percussive sound, tap, rap, dap, under the table, under the chair, in the air, round the cornices. The Medium groaned again and shuddered, and his nervous agitation passed sympathetically round the circle. The music seemed to fade to the vanishing point and grew louder again.

How was it done?

He heard Lagune's voice next him speaking with a peculiar quality of breathless reverence. "The alphabet?" he asked, "shall we—shall we use the alphabet?"

A forcible rap under the table.

"No!" interpreted the voice of the Medium.

The raps were continued everywhere.

Of course it was trickery. Lewisham endeavored to think what the mechanism was. He tried to determine whether he really had the Medium's little finger touching his. He peered at the dark shape next him. There was a violent rapping far away behind them with an almost metallic resonance. Then the raps ceased, and over the healing silence the little jet of melody from the musical box played alone. And after a moment that ceased also. . . .

The stillness was profound. Mr. Lewisham was now highly strung. Doubts assailed him suddenly, and an overwhelming apprehension, a sense of vast occurrences gathering above him. The darkness was a physical oppression. . . .

He started. Something had stirred on the table. There was the sharp ping of metal being struck. A number of little crepitating sounds like paper being smoothed. The sound of wind without the movement of air. A sense of a presence hovering over the table.

The excitement of Lagune communicated itself in convulsive tremblings; the Medium's hand quivered. In the darkness on the table something faintly luminous, a greenish-white patch, stirred and hopped slowly among the dim shapes.

The object, whatever it was, hopped higher, rose slowly in the air, expanded. Lewisham's attention followed this slavishly. It was ghostly—unaccountable—marvelous. For the moment he forgot even Ethel. Higher and higher this pallid luminosity rose overhead, and then he saw that it was a ghostly hand and arm, rising, rising. Slowly, deliberately it crossed the table, seemed to touch Lagune, who shivered. It moved slowly round and touched Lewisham. He gritted his teeth.

There was no mistaking the touch, firm and yet soft, of finger-tips. Almost simultaneously, Miss Heydinger cried out that something was smoothing her hair, and suddenly the musical box set off again with a reel. The faint oval of the tambourine rose, jangled, and Lewisham heard it pat Smithers in the face. It seemed to pass overhead. Immediately a table somewhere beyond the Medium began moving audibly on its castors.

It seemed impossible that the Medium, sitting so still beside him, could be doing all these things—grotesquely unmeaning though they might be. After all. . . .

The ghostly hand was hovering almost directly in front of Mr. Lewisham's eyes. It hung with a slight quivering. Ever and again its fingers flapped down and rose stiffly again.

Noise! A loud noise it seemed. Something moving? What was it he had to do?

Lewisham suddenly missed the Medium's little finger. He tried to recover it. He could not find it. He caught, held and lost an arm. There was an exclamation. A faint report. A curse close to him bitten in half by the quick effort to suppress it. Tzit! The little pin-point of light flew up with a hiss.

Lewisham, standing, saw a circle of blinking faces turned to the group of two this sizzling light revealed. Smithers was the chief figure of the group; he stood triumphant, one hand on the gas tap, the other gripping the Medium's wrist, and in the Medium's hand—the incriminatory tambourine.

"How's this, Lewisham," cried Smithers, with the shadows on his face jumping as the gas flared.

"*Caught!*" said Lewisham loudly, rising in his place and avoiding Ethel's eyes.

"What's this?" cried the Medium.

"Cheating," panted Smithers.

"Not so," cried the Medium. "When you turned up the light . . . put my hand up . . . caught tambourine . . . to save head."

"Mr. Smithers," cried Lagune. "Mr. Smithers, this is very wrong. This— shock—"

The tambourine fell noisily to the floor. The Medium's face changed, he groaned strangely and staggered back. Lagune cried out for a glass of water. Everyone looked at the man, expecting him to fall, save Lewisham. The thought of Ethel had flashed back into his mind. He turned to see how she took this exposure in which he was such a prominent actor. He saw her leaning over the table as if to pick up something that lay across it. She was not looking at him, she was looking at the Medium. Her face was set and white. Then, as if she felt his glance, her eyes met his.

She started back, stood erect, facing him with a strange hardness in her eyes.

In the moment Lewisham did not grasp the situation. He wanted to show that he was acting upon equal terms with Smithers in the exposure. For the moment her action simply directed his attention to the object towards which she had been leaning, a thing of shrivelled membrane, a pneumatic glove, lying on the table. This was evidently part of the mediumistic apparatus. He pounced and seized it.

"Look!" he said holding it towards Smithers. "Here is more! What is this?"

He perceived that the girl started. He saw Chaffery, the Medium, look instantly over Smithers' shoulders, saw his swift glance of reproach at the girl. Abruptly the situation appeared to Lewisham; he perceived her complicity. And he stood, still in the attitude of triumph, with the evidence against her in his hand! But his triumph had vanished.

"Ah!" cried Smithers, leaning across the table to secure it. "*Good* old Lewisham! . . . Now we *have* it. This is better than the tambourine."

His eyes shone with triumph. "Do you see, Mr. Lagune?" said Smithers. "The Medium held this in his teeth and blew it out. There's no denying this. This wasn't falling on your head, Mr. Medium, was it? *This*—this was the luminous hand!"

CHAPTER XII

Lewisham Is Unaccountable

THAT NIGHT, AS she went with him to Chelsea station, Miss Heydinger discovered an extraordinary moodiness in Lewisham. She had been vividly impressed by the scene in which they had just participated, she had for a time believed in the manifestations; the swift exposure had violently revolutionized her ideas. The details of the crisis were a little confused in her mind. She ranked Lewisham with Smithers in the scientific triumph of the evening. On the whole she felt elated. She had no objection to being confuted by Lewisham. But she was angry with the Medium. "It is dreadful," she said. "Living a lie! How can the world grow better, when sane, educated people use their sanity and enlightenment to darken others? It is dreadful!

"He was a horrible man—such an oily, dishonest voice. And the girl—I was sorry for her. She must have been oh!—bitterly ashamed, or why should she have burst out crying? That *did* distress me. Fancy crying like that! It was— yes—*abandon*. But what can one do?"

She paused. Lewisham was walking along, looking straight before him, lost in some grim argument with himself.

"It makes me think of Sludge the Medium," she said.

He made no answer.

She glanced at him suddenly. "Have you read Sludge the Medium?"

"Eigh?" he said, coming back out of infinity. "What? I beg your pardon. Sludge, the Medium? I thought his name was—it *was*—Chaffery."

He looked at her, clearly very anxious upon this question of fact.

"But I mean Browning's 'Sludge.' You know—the poem."

"No—I'm afraid I don't," said Lewisham.

"I must lend it to you," she said. "It's splendid. It goes to the very bottom of this business."

"Does it?"

"It never occurred to me before. But I see the point clearly now. If people, poor people, are offered money if phenomena happen, it's too much. They are *bound* to cheat. It's bribery—immorality!"

She talked in panting little sentences, because Lewisham was walking in heedless big strides. "I wonder how much—such people—could earn honestly."

Lewisham slowly became aware of the question at his ear. He hurried back from infinity. "How much they could earn honestly? I haven't the slightest idea."

He paused. "The whole of this business puzzles me," he said. "I want to think."

"It's frightfully complex, isn't it?" she said—a little staggered.

But the rest of the way to the station was silence. They parted with a handclasp they took a pride in—a little perfunctory so far as Lewisham was concerned on this occasion. She scrutinized his face as the train moved out of the station, and tried to account for his mood. He was staring before him at unknown things—as if he had already forgotten her.

He wanted to think! But two heads, she thought, were better than one in a matter of opinion. It troubled her to be so ignorant of his mental states. "How we are wrapped and swathed about—soul from soul!" she thought, staring out of the window at the dim things flying by outside.

Suddenly a fit of depression came upon her. She felt alone—absolutely alone—in a void world.

Presently she returned to external things. She became aware of two people in the next compartment eyeing her critically. Her hand went patting at her hair.

CHAPTER XIII

Lewisham Insists

ETHEL HENDERSON SAT at her machine before the window of Mr. Lagune's study, and stared blankly at the grays and blues of the November twilight. Her face was white, her eyelids were red from recent weeping, and her hands lay motionless in her lap. The door had just slammed behind Lagune.

"Heigh-ho!" she said. "I wish I was dead. Oh! I wish I was out of it all."

She became passive again. "I wonder what I have *done*," she said, "that I should be punished like this."

She certainly looked anything but a Fate-haunted soul, being indeed visibly and immediately a very pretty girl. Her head was shapely and covered with curly dark hair, and the eyebrows above her hazel eyes were clear and dark. Her lips were finely shaped, her mouth was not too small to be expressive, her chin small, and her neck white and full and pretty. There is no need to lay stress upon her nose—it sufficed. She was of a mediocre height, sturdy rather than slender, and her dress was of a pleasant, golden-brown material with the easy sleeves and graceful line of those aesthetic days. And she sat at her typewriter and wished she was dead and wondered what she had *done*.

The room was lined with bookshelves and conspicuous therein were a long row of foolish pretentious volumes, the "works" of Lagune—the witless, meandering imitation of philosophy that occupied his life. Along the cornices were busts of Plato, Socrates and Newton. Behind Ethel was the great man's desk with its green-shaded electric light, and littered with proofs and copies of *Hesperus*, "A Paper for Doubters," which, with her assistance, he edited, published, compiled, wrote, and (without her help) paid for and read. A pen, flung down forcibly, quivered erect with its one surviving nib in the blotting pad. Mr. Lagune had flung it down.

The collapse of the previous night had distressed him dreadfully, and ever and again before his retreat he had been breaking into passionate monologue. The ruin of a life-work, it was, no less. Surely she had known that Chaffery was a cheat. Had she not known? Silence. "After so many kindnesses—"

She interrupted him with a wailing "Oh, I know—I know."

But Lagune was remorseless and insisted she had betrayed him, worse—made him ridiculous! Look at the "work" he had undertaken at South Kensington—how could he go on with that now? How could he find the heart? When his own typewriter sacrificed him to her stepfather's trickery? "Trickery!"

The gesticulating hands became active, the gray eyes dilated with indignation, the piping voice eloquent.

"If he hadn't cheated you, someone else would," was Ethel's inadequate muttered retort, unheard by the seeker after phenomena.

It was perhaps not so bad as dismissal, but it certainly lasted longer. And at home was Chaffery, grimly malignant at her failure to secure that pneumatic glove. He had no right to blame her, he really had not; but a disturbed temper is apt to falsify the scales of justice. The tambourine, he insisted he could have explained by saying he put up his hand to catch it and protect his head directly Smithers moved. But the pneumatic glove there was no explaining. He had made a chance for her to secure it when he had pretended to faint. It was rubbish to say anyone could have been looking on the table then—rubbish.

Beside that significant wreck of a pen stood a little carriage clock in a case, and this suddenly lifted a slender voice and announced *five*. She turned round on her stool and sat staring at the clock. She smiled with the corners of her mouth down. "Home," she said, "and begin again. It's like battledore and shuttlecock. . . .

"I *was* silly. . . .

"I suppose I've brought it on myself. I ought to have picked it up, I suppose. I had time. . . .

"Cheats . . . just cheats.

"I never thought I should see him again. . . .

"He was ashamed, of course. . . He had his own friends."

For a space she sat still, staring blankly before her. She sighed, rubbed a knuckle in a reddened eye, rose.

She went into the hall where her hat, transfixed by a couple of hat pins, hung above her jacket, assumed these garments, and let herself out into the cold gray street.

She had hardly gone twenty yards from Lagune's door before she became aware of a man overtaking her and walking beside her. That kind of thing is a common enough experience to girls who go to and from work in London, and she had had perforce to learn many things since her adventurous Whortley days. She looked stiffly in front of her. The man deliberately got in her way so that she had to stop. She lifted eyes of indignant protest. It was Lewisham—and his face was white.

He hesitated awkwardly and then in silence held out his hand. She took it mechanically. He found his voice. "Miss Henderson," he said.

"What do you want?" she asked faintly.

"I don't know," he said. . . . "I want to talk to you."

"Yes?" Her heart was beating fast.

He found the thing unexpectedly difficult.

"May I—? Are you expecting—? Have you far to go? I would like to talk to you. There is a lot . . . ."

"I walk to Clapham," she said. "If you care . . . to come part of the way . . ."

She moved awkwardly. Lewisham took his place at her side. They walked side by side for a moment, their manner constrained, having so much to say that they could not find a word to begin upon.

"Have you forgotten Whortley?" he asked abruptly.

"No."

He glanced at her; her face was downcast. "Why did you never write?" he asked bitterly.

"I wrote."

"Again, I mean."

"I did—in July."

"I never had it."

"It came back."

"But Mrs. Munday . . ."

"I had forgotten her name. I sent it to the Grammar School."

Lewisham suppressed an exclamation.

"I am very sorry," she said.

They went on again in silence. "Last night," said Lewisham at length. "I have no business to ask. But—"

She took a long breath. "Mr. Lewisham," she said. "That man you saw—the Medium—was my stepfather."

"Well?"

"Isn't that enough?"

Lewisham paused. "No," he said.

There was another constrained silence. "No," he said less dubiously. "I don't care a rap what your stepfather is. Were *you* cheating?"

Her face turned white. Her mouth opened and closed. "Mr. Lewisham," she said deliberately, "you may not believe it, it may sound impossible, but on my honor . . . I did not know—I did not know for certain, that is—that my stepfather . . . ."

"Ah!" said Lewisham, leaping at conviction. "Then I was right . . ."

For a moment she stared at him, and then, "I *did* know," she said, suddenly beginning to cry. "How can I tell you? It is a lie. I *did* know. I *did* know all the time."

He stared at her in white astonishment. He fell behind her one step, and then in a stride came level again. Then, a silence, a silence that seemed it would never end. She had stopped crying, she was one huge suspense, not daring even to look at his face. And at last he spoke.

"No," he said slowly. "I don't mind even that. I don't care—even if it was that."

Abruptly they turned into the King's Road, with its roar of wheeled traffic and hurrying foot-passengers, and forthwith a crowd of boys with a broken-spirited Guy involved and separated them. In a busy highway of a night one must needs talk disconnectedly in shouted snatches or else hold one's peace. He glanced at her face and saw that it was set again. Presently she turned southward out of the tumult into a street of darkness and warm blinds, and they could go on talking again.

"I understand what you mean," said Lewisham. "I know I do. You knew but you did not want to know. It was like that."

But her mind had been active. "At the end of this road," she said, gulping a sob, "you must go back. It was kind of you to come, Mr. Lewisham. But you were ashamed—you are sure to be ashamed. My employer is a spiritualist, and my stepfather is a professional Medium, and my mother is a spiritualist. You were quite right not to speak to me last night. Quite. It was kind of you to come, but you must go back. Life is hard enough as it is . . . You must go back at the end of the road. Go back at the end of the road . . ."

Lewisham made no reply for a hundred yards. "I'm coming on to Clapham," he said.

They came to the end of the road in silence. Then at the curb corner she turned and faced him. "Go back," she whispered.

"No," he said obstinately, and they stood face to face at the cardinal point of their lives.

"Listen to me," said Lewisham. "It is hard to say what I feel. I don't know myself. . . . But I'm not going to lose you like this. I'm not going to let you slip a second time. I was awake about it all last night. I don't care where you are, what your people are, nor very much whether you've kept quite clear of this medium humbug. I don't. You will in future. Anyhow. I've had a day and night to think it over. I had to come and try to find you. It's you. I've never forgotten you. Never. I'm not going to be sent back like this."

"It can be no good for either of us," she said as resolute as he.

"I shan't leave you."

"But what is the good? . . ."

"I'm coming," said Lewisham, dogmatically.

And he came.

He asked her a question point blank and she would not answer him, and for some way they walked in grim silence. Presently she spoke with a twitching mouth. "I wish you would leave me," she said. "You are quite different from what I am. You felt that last night. You helped find us out. . . ."

"When first I came to London I used to wander about Clapham looking for you," said Lewisham, "week after week."

They had crossed the bridge and were in a narrow little street of shabby shops near Clapham Junction before they talked again. She kept her face averted and expressionless.

"I'm sorry," said Lewisham, with a sort of stiff civility, "if I seem to be forcing myself upon you. I don't want to pry into your affairs—if you don't wish me to. The sight of you has somehow brought back a lot of things. . . . I can't explain it. Perhaps—I had to come to find you—I kept on thinking of your face, of how you used to smile, how you jumped from the gate by the lock, and how we had tea . . . a lot of things."

He stopped again.

"A lot of things."

"If I may come," he said, and went unanswered. They crossed the wide streets by the Junction and went on towards the Common.

"I live down this road," she said stopping abruptly at a corner. "I would rather . . ."

"But I have said nothing."

She looked at him with her face white, unable to speak for a space. "It can do no good," she said. "I am mixed up with this. . . ."

She stopped.

He spoke deliberately. "I shall come," he said, "tomorrow night."

"No," she said.

"But I shall come."

"No," she whispered.

"I shall come." She could hide the gladness of her heart from herself no longer. She was frightened that he had come, but she was glad and she knew he knew that she was glad. She made no further protest. She held out her hand dumbly. And on the morrow she found him awaiting her even as he had said.

CHAPTER XIV

Mr. Lagune's Point of View

FOR THREE DAYS the Laboratory at South Kensington saw nothing of Lagune, and then he came back more invincibly voluble than ever. Everyone had expected him to return apostate, but he brought back an invigorated faith, a propaganda unashamed. From some source he had derived strength and conviction afresh. Even the rhetorical Smithers availed nothing. There was a joined battle over the insufficient tea-cups, and the elderly young assistant demonstrator hovered on the verge of the discussion, rejoicing, it is supposed, over the entanglements of Smithers. For at the outset Smithers displayed an overweening confidence and civility, and at the end his ears were red and his finer manners lost to him.

Lewisham, it was remarked by Miss Heydinger, made but a poor figure in this discussion. Once or twice he seemed about to address Lagune, and thought better of it with the words upon his lips.

Lagune's treatment of the exposure was light and vigorous. "The man Chaffery," he said, "has made a clean breast of it. His point of view—"

"Facts are facts," said Smithers.

"A fact is a synthesis of impressions," said Lagune, "but that you will learn when you are older. The thing is that we were at cross purposes. I told Chaffery you were beginners. He treated you as beginners—arranged a demonstration."

"It *was* a demonstration," said Smithers.

"Precisely. If it had not been for your interruptions . . ."

"Ah!"

"He forged elementary effects . . ."

"You can't but admit that."

"I don't attempt to deny it. But, as he explained—the thing is necessary—justifiable. Psychic phenomena are subtle, a certain training of the observation is necessary. A medium is a more subtle instrument than a balance or a borax bead, and see how long it is before you can get assured results with a borax bead! In the elementary class, in the introductory phase, conditions are too crude. . . ."

"For honesty."

"Wait a moment. *Is* it dishonest—rigging a demonstration?"

"Of course it is."

"Your professors do it."

"I deny that in toto," said Smithers, and repeated with satisfaction, "in toto."

"That's all right," said Lagune, "because I have the facts. Your chemical lecturers—you may go downstairs now and ask, if you disbelieve me—always cheat over the indestructibility of matter experiment—always. And then another—a physiography thing. You know the experiment I mean? To demonstrate the existence of the earth's rotation. They use—they use—"

"Foucault's pendulum," said Lewisham. "They use a rubber ball with a pinhole hidden in the hand, and blow the pendulum round the way it ought to go."

"But that's different," said Smithers.

"Wait a moment," said Lagune, and produced a piece of folded printed paper from his pocket. "Here is a review from *Nature* of the work of no less a person than Professor Greenhill. And see—a convenient pin is introduced in the apparatus for the demonstration of virtual velocities! Read it—if you doubt me. I suppose you doubt me."

Smithers abruptly abandoned his position of denial "in toto." "This isn't my point, Mr. Lagune; this isn't my point," he said. "These things that are done in the lecture theatre are not to prove facts, but to give ideas."

"So was my demonstration," said Lagune.

"We didn't understand it in that light."

"Nor does the ordinary person who goes to Science lectures understand it in that light. He is comforted by the thought that he is seeing things with his own eyes."

"Well, I don't care," said Smithers, "two wrongs don't make a right. To rig demonstrations is wrong."

"There I agree with you. I have spoken plainly with this man Chaffery. He's not a full-blown professor, you know, a highly salaried ornament of the rock of truth like your demonstration-rigging professors here, and so I can speak plainly to him without offense. He takes quite the view they would take. But I am more rigorous. I insist that there shall be no more of this. . . ."

"Next time—" said Smithers with irony.

"There will be no next time. I have done with elementary exhibitions. You must take the word of the trained observer—just as you do in the matter of chemical analysis."

"Do you mean you are going on with that chap when he's been caught cheating under your very nose?"

"Certainly. Why not?"

Smithers set out to explain why not, and happened on confusion. "I still believe the man has powers," said Lagune.

"Of deception," said Smithers.

"Those I must eliminate," said Lagune. "You might as well refuse to study electricity because it escaped through your body. All new science is elusive. No investigator in his senses would refuse to investigate a compound because it did unexpected things. Either this dissolves in acid or I have nothing more to do with it—eh? That's fine research!"

Then it was the last vestiges of Smithers' manners vanished. "I don't care *what* you say," said Smithers. "It's all rot—it's all just rot. Argue if you like—but have you convinced anybody? Put it to the vote?"

"That's democracy with a vengeance," said Lagune. "A general election of the truth half-yearly, eh?"

"That's simply wriggling out of it," said Smithers. "That hasn't anything to do with it at all."

Lagune, flushed but cheerful was on his way downstairs when Lewisham overtook him. He was pale and out of breath, but as the staircase invariably rendered Lagune breathless he did not remark the younger man's disturbance. "Interesting talk," panted Lewisham. "Very interesting talk, sir."

"I'm glad you found it so—very," said Lagune.

There was a pause, and then Lewisham plunged desperately. "There is a young lady—she is your typewriter. . . ."

He stopped from sheer loss of breath.

"Yes?" said Lagune.

"Is she a medium or anything of that sort?"

"Well," Lagune reflected. "She is not a medium, certainly. But—why do you ask?"

"Oh! . . . I wondered."

"You noticed her eyes, perhaps. She is the stepdaughter of that man Chaffery—, a queer character but indisputably mediumistic. It's odd the thing should have struck you. Curiously enough I myself have fancied she might be something of a psychic—judging from her face."

"A what?"

"A psychic—undeveloped of course. I have thought once or twice. Only a little while ago I was speaking to that man Chaffery about her."

"Were you?"

"Yes. He of course would like to see any latent powers developed. But it's a little difficult to begin, you know."

"You mean—she won't?"

"Not at present. She is a good girl, but in this matter she is—timid. There is often a sort of disinclination—a queer sort of feeling—one might almost call it modesty."

"I see," said Lewisham.

"One can override it usually. I don't despair."

"No," said Lewisham shortly. They were at the foot of the staircase now. He hesitated. "You've given me a lot to think about," he said with an attempt at an offhand manner. "The way you talked upstairs," and turned towards the book he had to sign.

"I'm glad you don't take up quite such an intolerant attitude as Mr. Smithers," said Lagune, "very glad. I must lend you a book or two. If your *cramming* here leaves you any time, that is."

"Thanks," said Lewisham shortly, and walked away from him. The studiously characteristic signature quivered and sprawled in an unfamiliar manner.

"I'm *damned* if he overrides it," said Lewisham, under his breath.

CHAPTER XV

Love in the Streets

LEWISHAM WAS NOT quite clear what course he meant to take in the high enterprise of foiling Lagune, and indeed he was anything but clear about the entire situation. His logical processes, his emotions and his imagination seemed playing some sort of snatching game with his will. Enormous things hung imminent, but it worked out to this, that he walked home with Ethel night after night for—to be exact—seven and sixty nights. Every week night through November and December, save once, when he had to go into the far East to buy himself an overcoat, he was waiting to walk with her home. A curious, inconclusive affair, that walk, to which he came nightly full of vague longings and which ended invariably under an odd shadow of disappointment. It began outside Lagune's most punctually at five, and ended—mysteriously—at the corner of a side road in Clapham, a road of little yellow houses with sunk basements and tawdry decorations of stone. Up that road she vanished night after night, into a gray mist and the shadow beyond a feeble yellow gas-lamp, and he would watch her vanish, and then sigh and turn back towards his lodgings.

They talked of this and that, their little superficial ideas about themselves, and of their circumstances and tastes, and always there was something, something that was with them unspoken, unacknowledged, which made all these things unreal and insincere.

Yet out of their talk he began to form vague ideas of the home from which she came. There was, of course, no servant, and the mother was something meandering, furtive, tearful in the face of troubles. Sometimes of an afternoon or evening she grew garrulous. "Mother does talk so—sometimes." She rarely went out of doors. Chaffery always rose late, and would sometimes go away for days together. He was mean, he allowed only a weekly twenty-five shillings for housekeeping and sometimes things grew unsatisfactory at the week end. There seemed to be little sympathy between mother and daughter; the widow had been flighty in a dingy fashion, and her marriage with her chief lodger Chaffery had led to unforgettable sayings. It was to facilitate this marriage that Ethel had been sent to Whortley, so that was counted a mitigated evil. But these were far-off things, remote and unreal down the long, ill-lit vista of the suburban street which swallowed up Ethel nightly. The walk, her warmth and light and motion close to him, her clear little voice, and the touch of her hand; that was reality.

The shadow of Chaffery and his deceptions lay indeed across all these things, sometimes faint, sometimes dark and present. Then Lewisham became insistent, his sentimental memories ceased, and he asked questions that verged on gulfs of doubt. Had she ever "helped"? She had not, she declared. Then she added that twice at home she had "sat down" to complete the circle. She would never help again. That she promised—if it needed promising. There had already been dreadful trouble at home about the exposure at Lagune's. Her mother had sided with her stepfather and joined in blaming her. But was she to blame?

"Of *course* you were not to blame," said Lewisham.

Lagune, he learned, had been unhappy and restless for the three days after the *séance*—indulging in wearisome monologue—with Ethel as sole auditor (at twenty-one shillings a week). Then he had decided to give Chaffery a sound lecture on his disastrous dishonesty. But it was Chaffery gave the lecture. Smithers, had he only known it, had been overthrown by a better brain than Lagune's, albeit it spoke through Lagune's treble.

Ethel did not like talking of Chaffery and these other things. "If you knew how sweet it was to forget it all," she would say, "to be just us two together for a little while." And, "What good *does* it do to keep on?" when Lewisham was pressing. Lewisham wanted very much to keep on at times, but the good of it was a little hard to demonstrate. So his knowledge of the situation remained imperfect and the weeks drifted by.

Wonderfully varied were those seven and sixty nights, as he came to remember in after life. There were nights of damp and drizzle, and then thick fogs, beautiful, isolating, gray-white veils, turning every yard of pavement into a private room. Grand indeed were these fogs, things to rejoice at mightily, since then it was no longer a thing for public scorn when two young people hurried along arm in arm, and one could do a thousand impudent, significant things with varying pressure and the fondling of a little hand (a hand in a greatly mended glove of cheap kid). Then indeed one seemed to be nearer that elusive something that threaded it all together. And the dangers of the street corners, the horses looming up suddenly out of the dark, the carters with lanterns at their horses' heads, the street lamps, blurred, smoky orange at one's nearest, and vanishing at twenty yards into dim haze, seemed to accentuate the infinite need of protection on the part of a delicate young lady who had already traversed three winters of fogs, thornily alone. Moreover, one could come right down the quiet street where she lived, half-way to the steps of her house, with a delightful sense of enterprise.

The fogs passed all too soon into a hard frost, into nights of starlight and presently moonlight, when the lamps looked hard, flashing like rows of yellow gems, and their reflections and the glare of the shop windows were sharp and frosty, and even the stars hard and bright, snapping noiselessly (if one may say so) instead of twinkling. A jacket trimmed with imitation Astrachan replaced Ethel's lighter coat, and a round cap of Astrachan her hat, and her eyes shone hard and bright, and her forehead was broad and white beneath it. It was exhilarating, but one got home too soon, and so the way from Chelsea to Clapham was lengthened, first into a loop of side streets, and then when the first pulverulent snows told that Christmas was at hand, into a new loop down King's Road, and once even through the Brompton Road and Sloane Street, where the shops were full of decorations and entertaining things.

And, under circumstances of infinite gravity, Mr. Lewisham secretly spent three-and-twenty shillings out of the vestiges of that hundred pounds, and bought Ethel a little gold ring set with pearls. With that there must needs be a ceremonial, and on the verge of the snowy, foggy Common she took off her glove and the ring was placed on her finger. Whereupon he was moved to kiss her—on the frost-pink knuckle next to an inky nail.

"It's silly of us," she said. "What can we do?—ever?"

"You wait," he said, and his tone was full of vague promises.

Afterwards he thought over those promises, and another evening went into the matter more fully, telling her of all the brilliant things that he held it was possible for a South Kensington student to do and be—of head-masterships, northern science schools, inspectorships, demonstratorships, yea, even professorships. And then, and then— to all of which she lent a willing and incredulous ear, finding in that dreaming a quality of fear as well as delight.

The putting on of the pearl-set ring was mere ceremonial, of course; she could not wear it either at Lagune's or at home, so instead she threaded it on a little white satin ribbon and wore it round her neck—"next her heart." He thought of it there warm "next her heart."

When he had bought the ring he had meant to save it for Christmas before he gave it to her. But the desire to see her pleasure had been too strong for him.

Christmas Eve, I know not by what deceit on her part, these young people spent together all day. Lagune was down with a touch of bronchitis and had given his typewriter a holiday. Perhaps she forgot to mention it at home. The Royal College was in vacation and Lewisham was free. He declined the plumber's invitation; "work" kept him in London, he said, though it meant a pound or more of added expenditure. These absurd young people walked sixteen miles that Christmas Eve, and parted warm and glowing. There had been a hard frost and a little snow, the sky was a colorless gray, icicles hung from the arms of the street lamps, and the pavements were patterned out with frond-like forms that were trodden into slides as the day grew older. The Thames they knew was a wonderful sight, but that they kept until last. They went first along the Brompton Road. . . .

And it is well that you should have the picture of them right; Lewisham in the ready-made overcoat, blue cloth and velvet collar, dirty tan gloves, red tie, and bowler hat; and Ethel in a two-year-old jacket and hat of curly Astrachan; both pink-cheeked from the keen air, shyly arm in arm occasionally, and very alert to miss no possible spectacle. The shops were varied and interesting along the Brompton Road, but nothing to compare with Piccadilly. There were windows in Piccadilly so full of costly little things, it took fifteen minutes to get them done, card shops, drapers' shops full of foolish, entertaining attractions. Lewisham, in spite of his old animosities, forgot to be severe on the Shopping Class, Ethel was so vastly entertained by all these pretty follies.

Then up Regent Street by the place where the sham diamonds are, and the place where the girls display their long hair, and the place where the little chickens run about in the window, and so into Oxford Street, Holborn, Ludgate Hill, St. Paul's Churchyard, to Leadenhall, and the markets where turkeys, geese, ducklings and chickens—turkeys predominant, however—hang in rows of a thousand at a time.

"I *must* buy you something," said Lewisham, resuming a topic.

"No, no," said Ethel with her eye down a vista of innumerable birds.

"But I *must*," said Lewisham. "You had better choose it, or I shall get something wrong." His mind ran on brooches and clasps.

"You mustn't waste your money, and besides, I have that ring."

But Lewisham insisted.

"Then—if you must—I am starving. Buy me something to eat."

An immense and memorable joke. Lewisham plunged recklessly—orientally—into an awe-inspiring place with mitred napkins. They lunched on cutlets—stripped the cutlets to the bone—and little crisp brown potatoes, and they drank between them a whole half bottle of—some white wine or other, Lewisham selected in an off-hand way from the list. Neither of them had ever taken wine at a meal before. One-and-ninepence it cost him, Sir, and the name of it was Capri! It was really very passable Capri—a manufactured product, no doubt, but warming and aromatic. Ethel was aghast at his magnificence and drank a glass and a half.

Then, very warm and comfortable, they went down by the Tower, and the Tower Bridge with its crest of snow, huge pendant icicles, and the ice blocks choked in its side arches, was seasonable seeing. And as they had had enough of shops and crowds they set off resolutely along the desolate Embankment homeward.

But indeed the Thames was a wonderful sight that year! ice-fringed along either shore, and with drift-ice in the middle reflecting a luminous scarlet from the broad red setting sun, and moving steadily, incessantly seaward. A swarm of mewing gulls went to and fro, and with them mingled pigeons and crows. The buildings on the Surrey side were dim and gray and very mysterious, the moored, ice-blocked barges silent and deserted, and here and there a lit window shone warm. The sun sank right out of sight into a bank of blue, and the Surrey side dissolved in mist save for a few insoluble spots of yellow light, that presently became many. And after our lovers had come under Charing Cross Bridge the Houses of Parliament rose before them at the end of a great crescent of golden lamps, blue and faint, halfway between the earth and sky. And the clock on the Tower was like a November sun.

It was a day without a flaw, or at most but the slightest speck. And that only came at the very end.

"Good-bye, dear," she said. "I have been very happy today."

His face came very close to hers. "Good-bye," he said, pressing her hand and looking into her eyes.

She glanced round, she drew nearer to him. "*Dearest* one," she whispered very softly, and then, " Good-bye."

Suddenly he became unaccountably petulant, he dropped her hand. "It's always like this. We are happy. *I* am happy. And then—then you are taken away. . . ."

There was a silence of mute interrogations.

"Dear," she whispered, "we must wait."

A moment's pause. "*Wait!*" he said, and broke off. He hesitated. "Good-bye," he said as though he was snapping a thread that held them together.

CHAPTER XVI

Miss Heydinger's Private Thoughts

THE WAY FROM Chelsea to Clapham and the way from South Kensington to Battersea, especially if the former is looped about a little to make it longer, come very near to each other. One night close upon Christmas two friends of Lewisham's passed him and Ethel. But Lewisham did not see them, because he was looking at Ethel's face.

"Did you see?" said the other girl, a little maliciously.

"Mr. Lewisham—wasn't it?" said Miss Heydinger in a perfectly indifferent tone.

Miss Heydinger sat in the room her younger sisters called her "Sanctum." Her Sanctum was only too evidently an intellectualized bedroom, and a cheap wall-paper of silvery roses peeped coquettishly from among her draped furniture. Her particular glories were the writing-desk in the middle and the microscope on the unsteady octagonal table under the window. There were bookshelves of workmanship patently feminine in their facile decoration and structural instability, and on them an array of glittering poets, Shelley, Rossetti, Keats, Browning, and odd volumes of Ruskin, South Place Sermons, Socialistic publications in torn paper covers, and above, science text-books and note-books in an oppressive abundance. The autotypes that hung about the room were eloquent of aesthetic ambitions and of a certain impermeability to implicit meanings. There was the Mirror of Venus by Burne Jones, Rossetti's Annunciation, Lippi's Annunciation, and the Love of Life and Love and Death of Watts. And among other photographs was one of last year's Debating Society Committee, Lewisham smiling a little weakly near the center, and Miss Heydinger out of focus in the right wing. And Miss Heydinger sat with her back to all these things, in her black horsehair armchair, staring into the fire, her eyes hot, and her chin on her hand.

"I might have guessed—before," she said. "Ever since that *séance*. It has been different . . ."

She smiled bitterly. "Some shop girl . . ."

She mused. "They are all alike, I suppose. They come back—a little damaged, as the woman says in 'Lady Windermere's Fan.' Perhaps he will. I wonder . . .

"Why should he be so deceitful? Why should he act to me? . . ."

"Pretty, pretty, pretty—that is our business. What man hesitates in the choice? He goes his own way, thinks his own thoughts, does his own work . . .

"His dissection is getting behind—one can see he takes scarcely any notes. . . ."

For a long time she was silent. Her face became more intent. She began to bite her thumb, at first slowly, then faster. She broke out at last into words again.

"The things he might do, the great things he might do. He is able, he is dogged, he is strong. And then comes a pretty face! Oh God! *Why* was I made with heart and brain?" She sprang to her feet, with her hands clenched and her face contorted. But she shed no tears.

Her attitude fell limp in a moment. One hand dropped by her side, the other rested on a fossil on the mantel-shelf, and she stared down into the red fire.

"To think of all we might have done! It maddens me!

"To work, and think, and learn. To hope and wait. To despise the petty arts of womanliness, to trust to the sanity of man. . . .

"To awake like the foolish virgins," she said, "and find the hour of life is past!"

Her face, her pose, softened into self-pity.

"Futility . . .

"It's no good. . . ." Her voice broke.

"I shall never be happy. . . ."

She saw the grandiose vision of the future she had cherished, suddenly rolled aside and vanishing, more and more splendid as it grew more and more remote—like a dream at the waking moment. The vision of her inevitable loneliness came to replace it, clear and acute. She saw herself alone and small in a huge desolation—infinitely pitiful, Lewisham callously receding. With "some shop girl." The tears came, came faster, until they were streaming down her face. She turned as if looking for something. She flung herself upon her knees before the little arm-chair, and began an incoherent sobbing prayer for the pity and comfort of God.

The next day one of the other girls in the biological course remarked to her friend that "Heydinger-dingery" had relapsed. Her friend glanced down the laboratory. "It's a bad relapse," she said. "Really . . . I couldn't . . . wear my hair like that."

She continued to regard Miss Heydinger with a critical eye. She was free to do this because Miss Heydinger was standing, lost in thought, staring at the December fog outside the laboratory windows. "She looks white," said the girl who had originally spoken. "I wonder if she works hard."

"It makes precious little difference if she does," said her friend. "I asked her yesterday what were the bones in the parietal segment, and she didn't know one. Not one."

The next day Miss Heydinger's place was vacant. She was ill—from overstudy—and her illness lasted to within three weeks of the terminal examination. Then she came back with a pallid face and a strenuous unavailing industry.

CHAPTER XVII

In the Raphael Gallery

IT WAS NEARLY three o'clock, and in the Biological Laboratory the lamps were all alight. The class was busy with razors cutting sections of the root of a fern to examine it microscopically. A certain silent frog-like boy, a private student who plays no further part in this story, was working intently, looking more like a frog than usual—his expression modest with a touch of effort. Behind Miss Heydinger, jaded and untidy in her early manner again, was a vacant seat, an abandoned microscope and scattered pencils and note-books.

On the door of the class-room was a list of those who had passed the Christmas examination. At the head of it was the name of the aforesaid frog-like boy; next to him came Smithers and one of the girls bracketed together. Lewisham ingloriously headed the second class, and Miss Heydinger's name did not appear—there was, the list asserted, "one failure." So the student pays for the finer emotions.

And in the spacious solitude of the museum gallery devoted to the Raphael cartoons, sat Lewisham, plunged in gloomy meditation. A negligent hand pulled thoughtfully at the indisputable moustache, with particular attention to such portions as were long enough to gnaw.

He was trying to see the situation clearly. As he was just smarting acutely under his defeat, this speaks little for the clearness of his mind. The shadow of that defeat lay across everything, blotted out the light of his pride, shaded his honor, threw everything into a new perspective. The rich prettiness of his love-making had fled to some remote quarter of his being. Against the frog-like youngster he felt a savage animosity. And Smithers had betrayed him. He was angry, bitterly angry with "swats" and "muggers" who spent their whole time grinding for these foolish chancy examinations. Nor had the practical examination been altogether fair, and one of the questions in the written portion was quite outside the lectures. Biver, Professor Biver, was an indiscriminating ass, he felt assured, and so too was Weeks, the demonstrator. But these obstacles could not blind his intelligence to the manifest cause of his overthrow, the waste of more than half his available evening, the best time for study in the twenty-four hours, day after day. And that was going on steadily, a perpetual leakage of time. Tonight he would go to meet her again, and begin to accumulate to himself ignominy in the second part of the course, the botanical section, also. And so, reluctantly rejecting one cloudy excuse after another, he clearly focussed the antagonism between his relations to Ethel and his immediate ambitions.

Things had come so easily to him for the last two years that he had taken his steady upward progress in life as assured. It had never occurred to him, when he went to intercept Ethel after that *séance*, that he went into any peril of that sort. Now he had had a sharp reminder. He began to shape a picture of the frog-like boy at home—he was a private student of the upper middle class—sitting in a convenient study with a writing-table, book-shelves and a shaded lamp—Lewisham worked at his chest of drawers, with his great coat on, and his feet in the lowest drawer wrapped in all his available linen—and in the midst of incredible conveniences the frog-like boy was working, working, working. Meanwhile Lewisham toiled through the foggy streets, Chelsea-ward, or, after he had left her, tramped homeward—full of foolish imaginings.

He began to think with bloodless lucidity of his entire relationship to Ethel. His softer emotions were in abeyance, but he told himself no lies. He cared for her, he loved to be with her and to talk to her and please her, but that was not all his desire. He thought of the bitter words of an orator at Hammersmith, who had complained that in our present civilization even the elemental need of marriage was denied. Virtue had become a vice. "We marry in fear and trembling, sex for a home is the woman's traffic, and the man comes to his heart's desire when his heart's desire is dead." The thing which had seemed a mere flourish, came back now with a terrible air of truth. Lewisham saw that it was a case of divergent ways. On the one hand that shining staircase to fame and power, that had been his dream from the very dawn of his adolescence, and on the other hand—Ethel.

And if he chose Ethel, even then, would he have his choice? What would come of it? A few walks more or less! She was hopelessly poor, he was hopelessly poor, and this cheat of a Medium was her stepfather! After all she was not well-educated, she did not understand his work and his aims. . . .

He suddenly perceived with absolute conviction that after the *séance* he should have gone home and forgotten her. Why had he felt that irresistible impulse to seek her out? Why had his imagination spun such a strange web of possibilities about her? He was involved now, foolishly involved. . . . All his future was a sacrifice to this transitory ghost of love-making in the streets. He pulled spitefully at his moustache.

His picture began to shape itself into Ethel, and her mysterious mother and the vague dexterous Chaffery holding him back, entangled in an impalpable net from that bright and glorious ascent to performance and distinction. Leaky boots and the splash of cabs for all his life as his portion! Already the Forbes Medal, the immediate step, was as good as lost. . . .

What on earth had he been thinking about? He fell foul of his upbringing. Men of the upper or middle classes were put up to these things by their parents; they were properly warned against involving themselves in this love nonsense before they were independent. It was much better. . . .

Everything was going. Not only his work—his scientific career, but the Debating Society, the political movement, all his work for Humanity. . . . Why not be resolute—even now? . . . Why not put the thing clearly and plainly to her? Or write? If he wrote now he could get the advantage of the evening at the Library. He must ask her to forego these walks home—at least until the next examination. *She* would understand. He had a qualm of doubt whether she would understand. . . . He grew angry at this possibility. But it was no good mincing matters. If once he began to consider her— Why should he consider her in that way? Simply because she was unreasonable!

Lewisham had a transitory gust of anger.

Yet that abandonment of the walks insisted on looking mean to him. And she would think it mean. Which was very much worse, somehow. *Why* mean? Why should she think it mean? He grew angry again.

The portly museum policeman who had been watching him furtively, wondering why a student should sit in front of the "Sacrifice of Lystra" and gnaw lips and nails and moustache, and scowl and glare at that masterpiece, saw him rise suddenly to his feet with an air of resolution, spin on his heel, and set off with a quick step out of the gallery. He looked neither to the right nor the left. He passed out of sight down the staircase.

"Gone to get some more moustache to eat, I suppose," said the policeman reflectively. . . .

"One 'ud think something had bit him."

After some pensive moments the policeman strolled along down the gallery and came to a stop opposite the cartoon.

"Figgers is a bit big for the houses," said the policeman, anxious to do impartial justice. "But that's Art. I lay 'e couldn't do anything . . . not arf so good."

CHAPTER XVIII

The Friends of Progress Meet

THE NIGHT NEXT but one after this meditation saw a new order in the world. A young lady dressed in an Astrachan-edged jacket and with a face of diminished cheerfulness marched from Chelsea to Clapham alone, and Lewisham sat in the flickering electric light of the Education Library, staring blankly over a business-like pile of books at unseen things.

The arrangement had not been effected without friction, the explanation had proved difficult. Evidently she did not appreciate the full seriousness of Lewisham's mediocre position in the list. "But you have *passed* all right," she said. Neither could she grasp the importance of evening study. "Of course I don't know," she said judicially, "but I thought you were learning all day." She calculated the time consumed by their walk as half an hour, "just one half hour," she forgot that he had to get to Chelsea and then to return to his lodgings. Her customary tenderness was veiled by an only too apparent resentment. First at him, and then when he protested, at Fate. "I suppose it *has* to be," she said. "Of course, it doesn't matter, I suppose, if we *don't* see each other quite so often," with a quiver of pale lips.

He had returned from the parting with an uneasy mind, and that evening had gone in the composition of a letter that was to make things clearer. But his scientific studies rendered his prose style "hard," and things he could whisper he could not write. His justification indeed did him no sort of justice. But her reception of it made her seem a very unreasonable person. He had some violent fluctuations. At times he was bitterly angry with her for her failure to see things as he did. He would wander about the museum conducting imaginary discussions with her and making even scathing remarks. At other times he had to summon all his powers of acrid discipline and all his memories of her resentful retorts, to keep himself from a headlong rush to Chelsea and unmanly capitulation.

And this new disposition of things endured for two weeks. It did not take Miss Heydinger all that time to discover that the disaster of the examination had wrought a change in Lewisham. She perceived those nightly walks were over. It was speedily evident to her that he was working with a kind of dogged fury; he came early, he went late. The wholesome freshness of his cheek paled. He was to be seen on each of the late nights amidst a pile of diagrams and text-books in one of the less draughty corners of the Educational Library, accumulating piles of memoranda. And nightly in the Students' "club" he wrote a letter addressed to a stationer's shop in Clapham, but that she did not see. For the most part these letters were brief, for Lewisham, South Kensington fashion, prided himself upon not being "literary," and some of the more despatch-like wounded a heart perhaps too hungry for tender words.

He did not meet Miss Heydinger's renewed advances with invariable kindness. Yet something of the old relations were presently restored. He would talk well to her for a time, and then snap like a dry twig. But the loaning of books was resumed, the subtle process of his aesthetic education that Miss Heydinger had devised. "Here is a book I promised you," she said one day, and he tried to remember the promise.

The book was a collection of Browning's Poems, and it contained "Sludge"; it also happened that it contained "The Statue and the Bust"—that stimulating lecture on half-hearted constraints. "Sludge" did not interest Lewisham, it was not at all his idea of a medium, but he read and re-read "The Statue and the Bust." It had the profoundest effect upon him. He went to sleep—he used to read his literature in bed because it was warmer there, and over literature nowadays it did not matter as it did with science if one dozed a little—with these lines stimulating his emotion:—

> "So weeks grew months, years; gleam by gleam
> The glory dropped from their youth and love,
> And both perceived they had dreamed a dream."

By way of fruit it may be to such seed, he dreamed a dream that night. It concerned Ethel, and at last they were a-marrying. He drew her to his arms. He bent to kiss her. And suddenly he saw her lips were shriveled and her eyes were dull, saw the wrinkles seaming her face! She was old! She was intolerably old! He woke in a kind of horror and lay awake and very dismal until dawn, thinking of their separation and of her solitary walk through the muddy streets, thinking of his position, the leeway he had lost and the chances there were against him in the battle of the world. He perceived the colorless truth; the Career was improbable, and that Ethel should be added to it was almost hopeless. Clearly the question was between these two. Or should he vacillate and lose both? And then his wretchedness gave place to that anger that comes of perpetually thwarted desires. . . .

It was on the day after this dream that he insulted Parkson so grossly. He insulted Parkson after a meeting of the "Friends of Progress" at Parkson's rooms.

No type of English student quite realizes the noble ideal of plain living and high thinking nowadays. Our admirable examination system admits of extremely little thinking at any level, high or low. But the Kensington student's living is at any rate insufficient, and he makes occasional signs of recognition towards the cosmic process.

One such sign was the periodic gathering of these "Friends of Progress," an association begotten of Lewisham's paper on Socialism. It was understood that strenuous things were to be done to make the world better, but so far no decisive action had been taken.

They met in Parkson's sitting-room, because Parkson was the only one of the Friends opulent enough to have a sitting-room, he being a Whitworth Scholar and in receipt of one hundred pounds a year. The Friends were of various ages, mostly very young. Several smoked and others held pipes which they had discontinued smoking—but there was nothing to drink, except coffee, because that was the extent of their means. Dunkerley, an assistant master in a suburban school, and Lewisham's former colleague at Whortley, attended these assemblies through the introduction of Lewisham. All the Friends wore red ties except Bletherley, who wore an orange one to show that he was aware of Art, and Dunkerley who wore a black one with blue specks, because assistant masters in small private schools have to keep up appearances. And their simple procedure was that each talked as much as the others would suffer.

Usually the self-proposed "Luther of Socialism"—ridiculous Lewisham!—had a thesis or so to maintain, but this night he was depressed and inattentive. He sat with his legs over the arm of his chair by way of indicating the state of his mind. He had a packet of Algerian cigarettes (twenty for five pence) and appeared chiefly concerned to smoke them all before the evening was out. Bletherley was going to discourse of "Woman under Socialism," and he brought a big American edition of Shelley's works and a volume of Tennyson with the "Princess," both bristling with paper tongues against his marked quotations. He was all for the abolition of "monopolies," and the *crèche* was to replace the family. He was unctuous when he was not pretty-pretty, and his views were evidently unpopular.

Parkson was a man from Lancashire, and a devout Quaker; his third and completing factor was Ruskin, with whose work and phraseology he was saturated. He listened to Bletherley with a marked disapproval, and opened a vigorous defense of that ancient tradition of loyalty that Bletherley had called the monopolist institution of marriage. "The pure and simple old theory—love and faithfulness," said Parkson, "suffices for me. If we are to smear our political movements with this sort of stuff . . ."

"Does it work?" interjected Lewisham, speaking for the first time.

"What work?"

"The pure and simple old theory. I know the theory. I believe in the theory. Bletherley's Shelley-witted. But it's theory. You meet the inevitable girl. The theory says you may meet her anywhen. You meet too young. You fall in love. You marry—in spite of obstacles. Love laughs at locksmiths. You have children. That's the theory. All very well for a man whose father can leave him five hundred a year. But how does it work for a shopman? . . . An assistant master like Dunkerley? Or . . . Me?"

"In these cases one must exercise restraint," said Parkson. "Have faith. A man that is worth having is worth waiting for."

"Worth growing old for?" said Lewisham.

"Chap ought to fight," said Dunkerley. "Don't see your difficulty, Lewisham. Struggle for existence keen, no doubt, tremendous in fact—still. In it—may as well struggle. Two—join forces—pool the luck. If I saw a girl I fancied so that I wanted to, I'd marry her tomorrow. And my market value is seventy *non res*."

Lewisham looked round at him eagerly, suddenly interested. "*Would* you?" he said. Dunkerley's face was slightly flushed.

"Like a shot. Why not?"

"But how are you to live?"

"That comes after. If . . ."

"I can't agree with you, Mr. Dunkerley," said Parkson. "I don't know if you have read Sesame and Lilies, but there you have, set forth far more fairly than any words of mine could do, an ideal of a woman's place . . ."

"All rot—Sesame and Lilies," interrupted Dunkerley. "Read bits. Couldn't stand it. Never *can* stand Ruskin. Too many prepositions. Tremendous English, no doubt, but not my style. Sort of thing a wholesale grocer's daughter might read to get refined. *We* can't afford to get refined."

"But would you really marry a girl . . . ?" began Lewisham, with an unprecedented admiration for Dunkerley in his eyes.

"Why not?"

"On—?" Lewisham hesitated.

"Forty pounds a year *res*. Whack! Yes."

A silent youngster began to speak, cleared an accumulated huskiness from his throat and said "Consider the girl."

"Why *marry*?" asked Bletherley, unregarded.

"You must admit you are asking a great thing when you want a girl . . ." began Parkson.

"Not so. When a girl's chosen a man, and he chooses her, her place is with him. What is the good of hankering. Mutual. Fight together."

"Good!" said Lewisham suddenly emotional. "You talk like a man, Dunkerley. I'm hanged if you don't."

"The place of Woman," insisted Parkson, "is the Home. And if there is no home—! I hold that, if need be, a man should toil seven years—as Jacob did for Rachel—ruling his passions, to make the home fitting and sweet for her . . ."

"Get the hutch for the pet animal," said Dunkerley, "No. I mean to marry a *woman*. Female sex always *has* been in the struggle for existence—no great damage so far—always will be. Tremendous idea—that struggle for existence. Only sensible theory you've got hold of, Lewisham. Woman who isn't fighting square side by side with a man—woman who's just kept and fed and petted is . . ." He hesitated.

A lad with a spotted face and a bulldog pipe between his teeth supplied a Biblical word.

"That's shag," said Dunkerley. "I was going to say 'a harem of one.' "

The youngster was puzzled for a moment. "I smoke Perique," he said.

"It will make you just as sick," said Dunkerley.

"Refinement's so beastly vulgar," was the belated answer of the smoker of Perique.

That was the interesting part of the evening to Lewisham. Parkson suddenly rose, got down "Sesame and Lilies," and insisted upon reading a lengthy mellifluous extract that went like a garden roller over the debate, and afterwards Bletherley became the center of a wrangle that left him grossly insulted and in a minority of one. The institution of marriage, so far as the South Kensington student is concerned, is in no immediate danger.

Parkson turned out with the rest of them at half-past ten, for a walk. The night was warm for February and the waxing moon bright. Parkson fixed himself upon Lewisham and Dunkerley, to Lewisham's intense annoyance—for he had a few intimate things he could have said to the man of Ideas that night. Dunkerley lived north, so that the three went up Exhibition Road to High Street Kensington. There they parted from Dunkerley and Lewisham and Parkson turned southward again for Lewisham's new lodging in Chelsea.

Parkson was one of those exponents of virtue for whom the discussion of sexual matters has an irresistible attraction. The meeting had left him eloquent. He had argued with Dunkerley to the verge of indelicacy, and now he poured out a vast and increasingly confidential flow of talk upon Lewisham. Lewisham was distraught. He walked as fast as he could. His sole object was to get rid of Parkson. Parkson's sole object was to tell him interesting secrets, about himself and a Certain Person with a mind of extraordinary Purity of whom Lewisham had heard before.

Ages passed.

Lewisham suddenly found himself being shown a photograph under a lamp. It represented an unsymmetrical face singularly void of expression, the upper part of an "art" dress, and a fringe of curls. He perceived he was being given to understand that this was a Paragon of Purity, and that she was the particular property of Parkson. Parkson was regarding him proudly and apparently awaiting his verdict.

Lewisham struggled with the truth. "It's an interesting face," he said.

"It is a face essentially beautiful," said Parkson quietly but firmly. "Do you notice the eyes, Lewisham?"

"Oh, yes," said Lewisham. "Yes. I see the eyes."

"They are . . . innocent. They are the eyes of a little child."

"Yes. They look that sort of eye. Very nice, old man. I congratulate you. Where does she live?"

"You never saw a face like that in London," said Parkson.

"*Never*," said Lewisham decisively.

"I would not show that to everyone," said Parkson. "You can scarcely judge all that pure-hearted, wonderful girl is to me." He returned the photograph solemnly to its envelope, regarding Lewisham with an air of one who has performed the ceremony of blood-brotherhood. Then taking Lewisham's arm affectionately—a thing Lewisham detested—he went on to a copious outpouring on Love—with illustrative anecdotes of the Paragon. It was just sufficiently cognate to the matter of Lewisham's thoughts to demand attention. Every now and then he had to answer, and he felt an idiotic desire—albeit he clearly perceived its idiocy—to reciprocate confidences. The necessity of fleeing Parkson became urgent—Lewisham's temper under these multitudinous stresses was going.

"Every man needs a Lode Star," said Parkson—and Lewisham swore under his breath.

Parkson's lodgings were now near at hand to the left, and it occurred to him this boredom would be soonest ended if he took Parkson home. Parkson consented mechanically, still discoursing.

"I have often seen you talking to Miss Heydinger," he said. "If you will pardon my saying it . . ."

"We are excellent friends," admitted Lewisham. "But here we are at your diggings."

Parkson stared at his "diggings." "There's Heaps I want to talk about. I'll come part of the way at any rate to Battersea. Your Miss Heydinger, I was saying . . ."

From that point onwards he made casual appeals to a supposed confidence between Lewisham and Miss Heydinger, each of which increased Lewisham's exasperation. "It will not be long before you also, Lewisham, will begin to know the infinite purification of a Pure Love. . . ." Then suddenly, with a vague idea of suppressing Parkson's unendurable chatter, as one motive at least, Lewisham rushed into the confidential.

"I know," he said. "You talk to me as though . . . I've marked out my destiny these three years." His confidential impulse died as he relieved it.

"You don't mean to say Miss Heydinger—?" asked Parkson.

"Oh, *damn* Miss Heydinger!" said Lewisham, and suddenly, abruptly, uncivilly, he turned away from Parkson at the end of the street and began walking away southward, leaving Parkson in mid-sentence at the crossing.

Parkson stared in astonishment at his receding back and ran after him to ask for the grounds of this sudden offense. Lewisham walked on for a space with Parkson trotting by his side. Then suddenly he turned. His face was quite white and he spoke in a tired voice.

"Parkson," he said, "you are a fool! . . . You have the face of a sheep, the manners of a buffalo, and the conversation of a bore. Pewrity indeed! . . . The girl whose photograph you showed me has eyes that don't match. She looks as loathsome as one would naturally expect. . . . I'm not joking now. . . . Go away!"

After that Lewisham went on his southward way alone. He did not go straight to his room in Chelsea, but spent some hours in a street in Battersea pacing to and fro in front of a possible house. His passion changed from savageness to a tender longing. If only he could see her tonight! He knew his own mind now.

Tomorrow he was resolved he would fling work to the dogs and meet her. The things Dunkerley had said had filled his mind with wonderful novel thoughts. If only he could see her now!

His wish was granted. At the corner of the street two figures passed him: one of these, a tall man in glasses and a quasi-clerical hat, with coat collar turned up under his gray side-whiskers, he recognized as Chaffery; the other he knew only too well. The pair passed him without seeing him, but for an instant the lamplight fell upon her face and showed it white and tired.

Lewisham stopped dead at the corner, staring in blank astonishment after these two figures as they receded into the haze under the lights. He was dumfounded. A clock struck slowly. It was midnight. Presently down the road came the slamming of their door.

Long after the echo died away he stood there. "She has been at a *séance;* she has broken her promise. She has been at a *séance,* she has broken her promise," sang in perpetual reiteration through his brain.

And then came the interpretation. "She has done it because I have left her. I might have told it from her letters. She has done it because she thinks I am not in earnest, that my love-making was just boyishness . . .

"I knew she would never understand."

CHAPTER XIX

Lewisham's Solution

THE NEXT MORNING Lewisham learned from Lagune that his intuition was correct, that Ethel had at last succumbed to pressure and consented to attempt thought-reading. "We made a good beginning," said Lagune rubbing his hands. "I am sure we shall do well with her. Certainly she has powers. I have always felt it in her face. She has powers."

"Was much . . . pressure necessary?" asked Lewisham by an effort.

"We had—considerable difficulty. Considerable. But of course—as I pointed out to her—it was scarcely possible for her to continue as my typewriter unless she was disposed to take an interest in my investigations—"

"You did that?"

"Had to. Fortunately Chaffery—it was his idea. I must admit—"

Lagune stopped astonished. Lewisham, after making an odd sort of movement with his hands, had turned round and was walking away down the laboratory. Lagune stared, confronted by a psychic phenomenon beyond his circle of ideas. "Odd!" he said at last, and began to unpack his bag. Ever and again he stopped and stared at Lewisham, who was now sitting in his own place and drumming on the table with both hands.

Presently Miss Heydinger came out of the specimen room and addressed a remark to the young man. He appeared to answer with considerable brevity. He then stood up, hesitated for a moment between the three doors of the laboratory, and walked out by that opening on the back staircase. Lagune did not see him again until the afternoon.

That night Ethel had Lewisham's company again on her way home and their voices were earnest. She did not go straight home, but instead they went up under the gas lamps to the vague spaces of Clapham Common to talk there at length. And the talk that night was a momentous one. "Why have you broken your promise?" he said.

Her excuses were vague and weak. "I thought you did not care so much as you did," she said. "And when you stopped these walks—nothing seemed to matter. Besides—it is not like *séances* with spirits . . ."

At first Lewisham was passionate and forcible. His anger at Lagune and Chaffery blinded him to her turpitude. He talked her defenses down. "It is cheating," he said. "Well—even if what *you* do is not cheating, it is delusion—unconscious cheating. Even if there is something in it, it is wrong. True or not, it is wrong. Why don't they thought-read each other? Why should they want you? Your mind is your own. It is sacred. To probe it!—I won't have it! I won't have it! At least you are mine to that extent. I can't think of you like that—bandaged. And that little fool pressing his hand on the back of your neck and asking questions. I won't have it! I would rather kill you than that."

"They don't do that!"

"I don't care! that is what it will come to. The bandage is the beginning. People must not get their living in that way anyhow. I've thought it out. Let them thought-read their daughters and hypnotize their aunts, and leave their typewriters alone."

"But what am I to do?"

"That's not it. There are things one must not suffer anyhow, whatever happens! Or else—one might be made to do anything. Honor! Just because we are poor—Let him dismiss you! *Let* him dismiss you. You can get another place—"

"Not at a guinea a week."

"Then take less."

"But I have to pay sixteen shillings every week."

"That doesn't matter."

She caught at a sob. "But to leave London—I can't do it. I can't."

"But how?—Leave London?" Lewisham's face changed.

"Oh! life is *hard,*" she said. "I can't. They—they wouldn't let me stop in London."

"What do you mean?"

She explained if Lagune dismissed her she was to go into the country to an aunt, a sister of Chaffery's who needed a companion. Chaffery insisted upon that. "Companion they call it. I shall be just a servant—she has no servant. My mother cries when I talk to her. She tells me she doesn't want me to go away from her. But she's afraid of him. 'Why don't you do what he wants?' she says."

She sat staring in front of her at the gathering night. She spoke again in an even tone.

"I hate telling you these things. It is you . . . If you didn't mind . . . But you make it all different. I could do it—if it wasn't for you. I was . . . I *was* helping . . . I had gone meaning to help if anything went wrong at Mr. Lagune's. Yes—that night. No . . . don't! It was too hard before to tell you. But I really did not feel it . . . until I saw you there. Then all at once I felt shabby and mean."

"Well?" said Lewisham.

"That's all. I may have done thought-reading, but I have never really cheated since—*never*. . . . If you knew how hard it is . . . ."

"I wish you had told me that before."

"I couldn't. Before you came it was different. He used to make fun of the people—used to imitate Lagune and make me laugh. It seemed a sort of joke." She stopped abruptly. "Why did you ever come on with me? I told you not to—you *know* I did."

She was near wailing. For a minute she was silent.

"I can't go to his sister's," she cried. "I may be a coward—but I can't."

Pause. And then Lewisham saw his solution straight and clear. Suddenly his secret desire had become his manifest duty.

"Look here," he said, not looking at her and pulling his moustache. "I won't have you doing any more of that damned cheating. You shan't soil yourself any more. And I won't have you leaving London."

"But what am I to do?" Her voice went up.

"Well—there is one thing you can do. If you dare."

"What is it?"

He made no answer for some seconds. Then he turned round and sat looking at her. Their eyes met. . . .

The gray of his mind began to color. Her face was white and she was looking at him, in fear and perplexity. A new tenderness for her sprang up in him—a new feeling. Hitherto he had loved and desired her sweetness and animation—but now she was white and weary-eyed. He felt as though he had forgotten her and suddenly remembered. A great longing came into his mind.

"But what is the other thing I can do?"

It was strangely hard to say. There came a peculiar sensation in his throat and facial muscles, a nervous stress between laughing and crying. All the world vanished before that great desire. And he was afraid she would not dare, that she would not take him seriously.

"What is it?" she said again.

"Don't you see that we can marry?" he said, with the flood of his resolution suddenly strong and steady. "Don't you see that is the only thing for us? The dead lane we are in! You must come out of your cheating, and I must come out of my . . . cramming. And we—we must marry."

He paused and then became eloquent. "The world is against us, against—us. To you it offers money to cheat—to be ignoble. For it *is* ignoble! It offers you no honest way, only a miserable drudgery. And it keeps you from me. And me too it bribes with the promise of success—if I will desert you . . . You don't know all . . . We may have to wait for years—we may have to wait forever, if we wait until life is safe. We may be separated. . . . We may lose one another altogether. . . . Let us fight against it. Why should we separate? Unless True Love is like the other things—an empty cant. This is the only way. We two—who belong to one another."

She looked at him, her face perplexed with this new idea, her heart beating very fast. "We are so young," she said. "And how are we to live? You get a guinea."

"I can get more—I can earn more. I have thought it out. I have been thinking of it these two days. I have been thinking what we could do. I have money."

"You have money?"

"Nearly a hundred pounds."

"But we are so young— And my mother . . ."

"We won't ask her. We will ask no one. This is *our* affair. Ethel! this is *our* affair. It is not a question of ways and means—even before this—I have thought . . . Dear one!—*don't* you love me?"

She did not grasp his emotional quality. She looked at him with puzzled eyes—still practical—making the suggestion arithmetical.

"I could typewrite if I had a machine. I have heard—"

"It's not a question of ways and means. Now. Ethel—I have longed—"

He stopped. She looked at his face, at his eyes now eager and eloquent with the things that never shaped themselves into words.

"*Dare* you come with me?" he whispered.

Suddenly the world opened out in reality to her as sometimes it had opened out to her in wistful dreams. And she quailed before it. She dropped her eyes from his. She became a fellow-conspirator. "But, how—?"

"I will think how. Trust me! Surely we know each other now— Think! We two—"

"But I have never thought—"

"I could get apartments for us both. It would be so easy. And think of it— think—of what life would be!"

"How can I?"

"You will come?"

She looked at him, startled. "You know," she said, "you must know I would like—I would love—"

"You will come."

"But dear—! Dear, if you *make* me—"

"Yes!" cried Lewisham triumphantly. "You will come." He glanced round and his voice dropped. "Oh! my dearest! my dearest! . . ."

His voice sank to an inaudible whisper. But his face was eloquent. Two garrulous, home-going clerks passed opportunely to remind him that his emotions were in a public place.

CHAPTER XX

The Career Is Suspended

ON THE WEDNESDAY afternoon following this—it was hard upon the botanical examination—Mr. Lewisham was observed by Smithers in the big Education Library reading in a volume of the British Encyclopaedia. Beside him were the current Whitaker's Almanac, an open note-book, a book from the Contemporary Science Series, and the Science and Art Department's Directory. Smithers, who had a profound sense of Lewisham's superiority in the art of obtaining facts of value in examinations, wondered for some minutes what valuable tip for a student in botany might be hidden in Whitaker, and on reaching his lodgings spent some time over the landlady's copy. But really Lewisham was not studying botany, but the art of marriage according to the best authorities. (The book from the Contemporary Science Series was Professor Letourneau's "Evolution of Marriage." It was interesting certainly, but of little immediate use.)

From Whitaker Lewisham learned that it would be possible at a cost of £2 6s. 1d. or £2 7s. 1d. (one of the items was ambiguous) to get married within the week—that charge being exclusive of vails—at the district registry office. He did little addition sums in the note-book. The church fees he found were variable, but for more personal reasons he rejected a marriage at church. Marriage by certificate at a registrar's involved an inconvenient delay. It would have to be £2 7s. 1. Vails—ten shillings, say.

Afterwards, without needless ostentation, he produced a cheque-book and a deposit-book, and proceeded to further arithmetic. He found that he was master of £61 4s. 7d. Not a hundred as he had said, but a fine big sum—men have started great businesses on less. It had been a hundred originally. Allowing five pounds for the marriage and moving, this would leave about £56. Plenty. No provision was made for flowers, carriages or the honeymoon. But there would be a typewriter to buy. Ethel was to do her share. . . .

"It will be a devilish close thing," said Lewisham with a quite unreasonable exultation. For, strangely enough, the affair was beginning to take on a flavor of adventure not at all unpleasant. He leaned back in his chair with the note-book closed in his hand. . . .

But there was much to see to that afternoon. First of all he had to discover the district superintendent registrar, and then to find a lodging whither he should take Ethel—their lodging, where they were to live together.

At the thought of that new life together that was drawing so near, she came into his head, vivid and near and warm. . . .

He recovered himself from a day dream. He became aware of a library attendant down the room leaning forward over his desk, gnawing the tip of a paper knife after the fashion of South Kensington library attendants, and staring at him curiously. It occurred to Lewisham that thought reading was one of the most possible things in the world. He blushed, rose clumsily and took the volume of the Encyclopaedia back to its shelf.

He found the selection of lodgings a difficult business. After his first essay he began to fancy himself a suspicious-looking character, and that perhaps hampered him. He had chosen the district southward of the Brompton Road. It had one disadvantage—he might blunder into a house with a fellow-student. . . . Not that it mattered vitally. But the fact is, it is rather unusual for married couples to live permanently in furnished lodgings in London. People who are too poor to take a house or a flat commonly find it best to take part of a house or unfurnished apartments. There are a hundred couples living in unfurnished rooms (with "the use of the kitchen") to one in furnished in London. The absence of furniture predicates a dangerous want of capital to the discreet landlady. The first landlady Lewisham interviewed didn't like ladies, they required such a lot of attendance, the second was of the same mind, the third told Mr. Lewisham he was "youngish to be married," the fourth said she only "did" for single "gents." The fifth was a young person with an arch manner, who liked to know all about people she took in, and subjected Lewisham to a searching cross-examination. When she had spitted him in a downright lie or so, she expressed an opinion that her rooms "would scarcely do," and bowed him amiably out.

He cooled his ears and cheeks by walking up and down the street for a space, and then tried again. This landlady was a terrible and pitiful person, so gray and dusty she was, and her face deep lined with dust and trouble and labor. She wore a dirty cap that was all askew. She took Lewisham up into a threadbare room on the first floor. "There's the use of a piano," she said, and indicated an instrument with a front of torn green silk. Lewisham opened the keyboard and evoked a vibration of broken strings. He took one further survey of the dismal place. "Eighteen shillings," he said. "Thank you . . . I'll let you know." The woman smiled with the corners of her mouth down, and without a word moved wearily towards the door. Lewisham felt a transient wonder at her hopeless position, but he did not pursue the inquiry.

The next landlady sufficed. She was a clean-looking German woman, rather smartly dressed; she had a fringe of flaxen curls and a voluble flow of words, for the most part recognizably English. With this she sketched out remarks. Fifteen shillings was her demand for a minute bedroom and a small sitting-room, separated by folding doors on the ground floor, and her personal services. Coals were to be "six-pence a kettle," she said—a pretty substitute for scuttle. She had not understood Lewisham to say he was married. But she had no hesitation.

"Aayteen shillin'," she said imperturbably. "Paid furs day ich wik . . . See?" Mr. Lewisham surveyed the rooms again. They looked clean, and the bonus tea vases, the rancid, gilt-framed oleographs, two toilet tidies used as ornaments, and the fact that the chest of drawers had been crowded out of the bedroom into the sitting-room, simply appealed to his sense of humor. "I'll take 'em from Saturday next," he said.

She was sure he would like them and proposed to give him his book forthwith. She mentioned casually that the previous lodger had been a captain and had stayed three years. (One never hears by any chance of lodgers stopping for a shorter period.) Something happened (German) and now he kept his carriage— apparently an outcome of his stay. She returned with a small penny account-book, a bottle of ink and an execrable pen, wrote Lewisham's name on the cover of this, and a receipt for eighteen shillings on the first page. She was evidently a person of considerable business aptitude. Lewisham paid, and the transaction terminated. "Szhure to be gomfortable," followed him comfortingly to the street.

Then he went on to Chelsea and interviewed a fatherly gentleman at the Vestry offices. The fatherly gentleman was chubby-faced and spectacled, and his manner was sympathetic but business-like. He "called back" each item of the interview. "And what can I do for you? You wish to be married! By license?"

"By license."

"By license!"

And so forth. He opened a book and made neat entries of the particulars. "The lady's age?"

" Twenty-one."

"A very suitable age. . . . for a lady."

He advised Lewisham to get a ring and said he would need two witnesses.

"*Well*—" hesitated Lewisham.

"There is always someone about," said the superintendent registrar. "And they are quite used to it."

Thursday and Friday Lewisham passed in exceedingly high spirits. No consciousness of the practical destruction of the Career seems to have troubled him at this time. Doubt had vanished from his universe for a space. He wanted to dance along the corridors. He felt curiously irresponsible and threw up an unpleasant sort of humor that pleased nobody. He wished Miss Heydinger many happy returns of the day, *apropos* of nothing, and he threw a bun across the refreshment room at Smithers and hit one of the Art School officials. Both were extremely silly things to do. In the first instance he was penitent immediately after the outrage, but in the second he added insult to injury by going across the room and asking in an offensively suspicious manner if anyone had seen his bun. He crawled under a table and found it at last, rather dusty but quite eatable, under the chair of a lady art student. He sat down by Smithers to eat it, while he argued with the Art official. The Art official said the manners of the Science students were getting unbearable, and threatened to bring the matter before the refreshment-room Committee. Lewisham said it was a pity to make such a fuss about a trivial thing, and proposed that the Art official should throw his lunch— steak and kidney pudding—across the room at him, Lewisham, and so get immediate satisfaction. He then apologized to the official and pointed out in extenuation that it was a very long and difficult shot he had attempted. The official then drank a crumb, or breathed some beer, or something of that sort, and the discussion terminated. In the afternoon, however, Lewisham, to his undying honor, felt acutely ashamed of himself. Miss Heydinger would not speak to him.

On Saturday morning he absented himself from the schools, pleading by post a slight indisposition, and took all his earthly goods to the booking office at Vauxhall Station. Chaffery's sister lived at Tongham, near Farnham, and Ethel, dismissed a week since by Lagune, had started that morning under her mother's maudlin supervision, to begin her new slavery. She was to alight either at Farnham or Woking, as opportunity arose, and to return to Vauxhall to meet him. So that Lewisham's vigil on the main platform was of indefinite duration.

At first he felt the exhilaration of a great adventure. Then, as he paced the long platform, came a philosophical mood, a sense of entire detachment from the world. He saw a bundle of uprooted plants beside the portmanteau of a fellow-passenger and it suggested a grotesque simile. His roots, his earthly possessions, were all downstairs in the booking-office. What a flimsy thing he was! A box of books and a trunk of clothes, some certificates and scraps of paper, an entry here and an entry there, a body not over strong—and the vast multitude of people about him—against him—the huge world in which he found himself! Did it matter anything to one human soul save her if he ceased to exist forthwith? And miles away perhaps she also was feeling little and lonely. . . .

Would she have trouble with her luggage? Suppose her aunt were to come to Farnham Junction to meet her? Suppose someone stole her purse? Suppose she came too late! The marriage was to take place at two. . . . Suppose she never came at all! After three trains in succession had disappointed him his vague feelings of dread gave place to a profound depression. . . .

But she came at last, and it was twenty-three minutes to two. He hurried her luggage downstairs, booked it with his own, and in another minute they were in a hansom—their first experience of that species of conveyance—on the way to the vestry-office. They had said scarcely anything to one another, save hasty directions from Lewisham, but their eyes were full of excitement, and under the apron of the cab their hands were gripped together.

The little old gentleman was business-like but kindly. They made their vows to him, to a little black-bearded clerk and a lady who took off an apron in the nether part of the building to attend. The little old gentleman made no long speeches. "You are young people," he said slowly, "and life together is a difficult thing. . . . Be kind to each other." He smiled a little sadly, and held out a friendly hand.

Ethel's eyes glistened and she found she could not speak.

CHAPTER XXI

Home!

THEN A FURTIVE payment of witnesses, and Lewisham was beside her. His face was radiant. A steady current of workers going home to their half-holiday rest poured along the street. On the steps before them lay a few grains of rice from some more public nuptials.

A critical little girl eyed our couple curiously and made some remark to her ragamuffin friend.

"Not them," said the ragamuffin friend. "They've only been askin' questions."

The ragamuffin friend was no judge of faces.

They walked back through the thronged streets to Vauxhall station, saying little to one another, and there Lewisham, assuming as indifferent a manner as he could command, recovered their possessions from the booking-office by means of two separate tickets and put them aboard a four-wheeler. His luggage went outside, but the little brown portmanteau containing Ethel's trousseau was small enough to go on the seat in front of them. You must figure a rather broken-down four-wheeler bearing the yellow-painted box and the experienced trunk and Mr. Lewisham and all his fortunes, a despondent fitful horse, and a threadbare venerable driver, blasphemous *sotto voce* and flagellant, in an ancient coat with capes. When our two young people found themselves in the cab again a certain stiffness of manner between them vanished and there was more squeezing of hands. "Ethel *Lewisham*," said Lewisham several times, and Ethel reciprocated with "Husbinder" and "Hubby dear," and took off her glove to look again in an ostentatious manner at a ring. And she kissed the ring.

They were resolved that their newly-married state should not appear, and with considerable ceremony it was arranged that he should treat her with off-hand brusqueness when they arrived at their lodging. The Teutonic landlady appeared in the passage with an amiable smile and the hope that they had had a pleasant journey, and became voluble with promises of comfort. Lewisham having assisted the slatternly general servant to carry in his boxes, paid the cabman a florin in a resolute manner and followed the ladies into the sitting-room.

Ethel answered Madam Gadow's inquiries with admirable self-possession, followed her through the folding-doors and displayed an intelligent interest in a new spring mattress. Presently the folding-doors were closed again. Lewisham hovered about the front room pulling his moustache and pretending to admire the oleographs, surprised to find himself trembling. . . .

The slatternly general servant reappeared with the chops and tinned salmon he had asked Madam Gadow to prepare for them. He went and stared out of the window, heard the door close behind the girl, and turned at a sound as Ethel appeared shyly through the folding-doors.

She was suddenly domestic. Hitherto he had seen her without a hat and jacket only on one indistinct dramatic occasion. Now she wore a little blouse of soft, dark red material, with a white froth about the wrists and that pretty neck of hers. And her hair was a new wonderland of curls and soft strands. How delicate she looked and sweet as she stood hesitating there. These gracious moments in life! He took two steps and held out his arms. She glanced at the closed door of the room and came flitting towards him. . . .

CHAPTER XXII

Epithalamy

FOR THREE INDELIBLE days Lewisham's existence was a fabric of fine emotions, life was too wonderful and beautiful for any doubts or forethought. To be with Ethel was perpetual delight—she astonished this sisterless youngster with a thousand feminine niceties and refinements. She shamed him for his strength and clumsiness. And the light in her eyes and the warmth in her heart that lit them!

Even to be away from her was a wonder and in its way delightful. He was no common Student, he was a man with a Secret Life. To part from her on Monday near South Kensington station and go up Exhibition Road among all the fellows who lived in sordid, lonely lodgings and were boys to his day-old experience! To neglect one's work and sit back and dream of meeting again! To slip off to the shady churchyard behind the Oratory when, or even a little before, the midday bell woke the great staircase to activity, and to meet a smiling face and hear a soft voice saying sweet foolish things! And after four another meeting and the walk home—their own home.

No little form now went from him and flitted past a gas lamp down a foggy vista, taking his desire with her. Never more was that to be. Lewisham's long hours in the laboratory were spent largely in a dreamy meditation, in—to tell the truth—the invention of foolish terms of endearment: "Dear Wife," "Dear Little Wife Thing," "Sweetest Dearest Little Wife," "Dillywings." A pretty employment! And these are quite a fair specimen of his originality during those wonderful days. A moment of heart-searching in that particular matter led to the discovery of hitherto undreamed-of kindred with Swift. For Lewisham, like Swift and most other people, had hit upon the Little Language. Indeed it was a very foolish time.

Such section cutting as he did that third day of his married life—and he did very little—was a thing to marvel at. Bindon, the botany professor, under the fresh shock of his performance, protested to a colleague in the grill room that never had a student been so foolishly overrated.

And Ethel too had a fine emotional time. She was mistress of a home—*their* home together. She shopped and was called "Ma'am" by respectful, good-looking shopmen; she designed meals and copied out papers of notes with a rich sense of helpfulness. And ever and again she would stop writing and sit dreaming. And for four bright weekdays she went to and fro to accompany and meet Lewisham and listen greedily to the latest fruits of his imagination.

The landlady was very polite and conversed entertainingly about the very extraordinary and dissolute servants that had fallen to her lot. And Ethel disguised her newly wedded state by a series of ingenious prevarications. She wrote a letter that Saturday evening to her mother—Lewisham had helped her to write it—making a sort of proclamation of her heroic departure and promising a speedy visit. They posted the letter so that it might not be delivered until Monday.

She was quite sure with Lewisham that only the possible dishonor of mediumship could have brought their marriage about—she sank the mutual attraction beyond even her own vision. There was more than a touch of magnificence, you perceive, about this affair.

It was Lewisham had persuaded her to delay that reassuring visit until Monday night. "One whole day of honeymoon," he insisted, was to be theirs. In his prenuptial meditations he had not clearly focussed the fact that even after marriage some sort of relations with Mr. and Mrs. Chaffery would still go on. Even now he was exceedingly disinclined to face that obvious necessity. He foresaw, in spite of a resolute attempt to ignore it, that there would be explanatory scenes of some little difficulty. But the prevailing magnificence carried him over this trouble.

"Let us at least have this little time for ourselves," he said, and that seemed to settle their position.

Save for its brevity and these intimations of future trouble it was a very fine time indeed. Their midday dinner together, for example—it was a little cold when at last they came to it on Saturday—was immense fun. There was no marked subsidence of appetite; they ate extremely well in spite of the meeting of their souls, and in spite of certain shiftings of chairs and hand claspings and similar delays. He really made the acquaintance of her hands then for the first time, plump white hands with short white fingers, and the engagement ring had come out of its tender hiding-place and acted as keeper to the wedding ring.

Their eyes were perpetually flitting about the room and coming back to mutual smiles. All their movements were faintly tremulous.

She professed to be vastly interested and amused by the room and its furniture and her position, and he was delighted by her delight. She was particularly entertained by the chest of drawers in the living room, and by Lewisham's witticisms at the toilet tidies and the oleographs.

And after the chops and the most of the tinned salmon and the very new loaf were gone they fell to with fine effect upon a tapioca pudding. Their talk was fragmentary. "Did you hear her call me *Madame? Mádáme*—so!" "And presently I must go out and do some shopping. There are all the things for Sunday and Monday morning to get. I must make a list. It will never do to let her know how little I know about things. . . . I wish I knew more."

At the time Lewisham regarded her confession of domestic ignorance as a fine basis for facetiousness. He developed a fresh line of thought, and condoled with her on the inglorious circumstances of their wedding. "No bridesmaids," he said, "no little children scattering flowers, no carriages, no policemen to guard the wedding presents, nothing proper—nothing right. Not even a white favor. Only you and I."

"Only you and I. *Oh!*"

"This is nonsense," said Lewisham, after an interval.

"And think what we lose in the way of speeches," he resumed. "Cannot you imagine the best man rising;—'Ladies and gentlemen—the health of the bride.' That is what the best man has to do isn't it?"

By way of answer she extended her hand.

"And do you know," he said, after that had received due recognition, "we have never been introduced!"

"Neither have we!" said Ethel. "Neither have we! We have never been introduced!"

For some inscrutable reason it delighted them both enormously to think that they had never been introduced. . . .

In the later afternoon Lewisham, having unpacked his books to a certain extent and so forth, was visible to all men, visibly in the highest spirits, carrying home Ethel's shopping. There were parcels and cones in blue and parcels in rough gray paper and a bag of confectionery, and out of one of the side pockets of that East-end overcoat the tail of a haddock protruded from its paper. Under such magnificent sanctions and amid such ignoble circumstances did this honeymoon begin.

On Sunday evening they went for a long rambling walk through the quiet streets, coming out at last into Hyde Park. The early spring night was mild and clear and the kindly moonlight was about them. They went to the bridge and looked down the Serpentine, with the little lights of Paddington yellow and remote. They stood there, dim little figures and very close together. They whispered and became silent.

Presently it seemed that something passed and Lewisham began talking in his magnificent vein. He likened the Serpentine to Life, and found Meaning in the dark banks of Kensington Gardens and the remote bright lights. "The long struggle," he said, "and the lights at the end,"—though he really did not know what he meant by the lights at the end. Neither did Ethel, though the emotion was indisputable. "We are Fighting the World," he said, finding great satisfaction in the thought. "All the world is against us—and we are fighting it all."

"We will not be beaten," said Ethel.

"How could we be beaten—together?" said Lewisham. "For you I would fight a dozen worlds."

It seemed a very sweet and noble thing to them under the sympathetic moonlight, almost indeed too easy for their courage, to be merely fighting the world.

"You 'aven't bin married ver' long," said Madam Gadow with an insinuating smile, when she re-admitted Ethel on Monday morning after Lewisham had been swallowed up by the Schools.

"No, I haven't *very* long," admitted Ethel.

"You are ver' 'appy," said Madam Gadow, and sighed.

"*I* was ver' 'appy," said Madam Gadow.

CHAPTER XXIII

Mr. Chaffery at Home

THE GOLDEN MISTS of delight lifted a little on Monday, when Mr. and Mrs. G. E. Lewisham went to call on his mother-in-law and Mr. Chaffery. Mrs. Lewisham went in evident apprehension, but clouds of glory still hung about Lewisham's head, and his manner was heroic. He wore a cotton shirt and linen collar, and a very nice black satin tie that Mrs. Lewisham had bought on her own responsibility during the day. She naturally wanted him to look all right.

Mrs. Chaffery appeared in the half light of the passage as the top of a grimy cap over Ethel's shoulder and two black sleeves about her neck. She emerged as a small, middle-aged woman, with a thin little nose between silver-rimmed spectacles, a weak mouth and perplexed eyes, a queer little dust-lined woman with the oddest resemblance to Ethel in her face. She was trembling visibly with nervous agitation.

She hesitated, peering, and then kissed Mr. Lewisham effusively. "And this is Mr. Lewisham!" she said as she did so.

She was the third thing feminine to kiss Lewisham since the promiscuous days of his babyhood. "I was so afraid—There!" She laughed hysterically.

"You'll excuse my saying that it's comforting to see you—honest like and young. Not but what Ethel . . . *He* has been something dreadful," said Mrs. Chaffery. "You didn't ought to have written about that mesmerizing. And of all letters that which Jane wrote—there! But he's waiting and listening—"

"Are we to go downstairs, Mums?" asked Ethel.

"He's waiting for you there," said Mrs. Chaffery. She held a dismal little oil lamp, and they descended a tenebrous spiral structure into an underground breakfast-room lit by gas that shone through a partially frosted globe with cut-glass stars. That descent had a distinctly depressing effect upon Lewisham. He went first. He took a deep breath at the door. What on earth was Chaffery going to say? Not that he cared, of course.

Chaffery was standing with his back to the fire, trimming his finger-nails with a pocket-knife. His gilt glasses were tilted forward so as to make an inflamed knob at the top of his long nose, and he regarded Mr. and Mrs. Lewisham over them with—Lewisham doubted his eyes for a moment—but it was positively a smile, an essentially waggish smile.

"You've come back," he said quite cheerfully over Lewisham to Ethel. There was a hint of falsetto in his voice.

"She has called to see her mother," said Lewisham. "You, I believe, are Mr. Chaffery?"

"I would like to know who the Deuce *you* are?" said Chaffery, suddenly tilting his head back so as to look through his glasses instead of over them, and laughing genially. "For thorough-going Cheek, I'm inclined to think you take the Cake. Are you the Mr. Lewisham to whom this misguided girl refers in her letter?"

"I am."

"Maggie," said Mr. Chaffery to Mrs. Chaffery, "there is a class of being upon whom delicacy is lost—to whom delicacy is practically unknown. Has your daughter got her marriage lines?"

"Mr. Chaffery!" said Lewisham, and Mrs. Chaffery exclaimed, "James! How *can* you?"

Chaffery shut his penknife with a click and slipped it into his vest-pocket. Then he looked up again, speaking in the same equal voice. "I presume we are civilized persons prepared to manage our affairs in a civilized way. My stepdaughter vanishes for two nights and returns with an alleged husband. I at least am not disposed to be careless about her legal position."

"You ought to know her better—" began Lewisham.

"Why argue about it?" said Chaffery gaily, pointing a lean finger at Ethel's gesture, "when she has 'em in her pocket? She may just as well show me now. I thought so. Don't be alarmed at my handling them. Fresh copies can always be got at the nominal price of two-and-seven. Thank you . . . Lewisham, George Edgar. One and twenty. And . . . You—one and twenty! I never did know your age, my dear, exactly, and now your mother won't say. Student! Thank you. I am greatly obliged. Indeed I am greatly relieved. And now, what have you got to say for yourselves in this remarkable affair?"

"You had a letter," said Lewisham.

"I had a letter of excuses—the personalities I overlook . . . Yes, sir—they were excuses. You young people wanted to marry—and you seized an occasion. You did not even refer to the fact that you wanted to marry in your letter. Pure modesty! But now you have come here married. It disorganizes this household, it inflicts endless bother on people, but never you mind that! I'm not blaming *you*. Nature's to blame! Neither of you know what you are in for yet. You will. You're married and that is the great essential thing. . . . (Ethel, my dear, just put your husband's hat and stick behind the door.) And you, sir, are so good as to disapprove of the way in which I earn my living?"

"Well," said Lewisham. "Yes—I'm bound to say I do."

"You are really *not* bound to say it. The modesty of inexperience would excuse you."

"Yes, but it isn't right—it isn't straight."

"Dogma," said Chaffery. "Dogma!"

"What do you mean by dogma?" asked Lewisham.

"I mean, dogma. But we must argue this out in comfort. It is our supper hour, and I'm not the man to fight against accomplished facts. We have intermarried. There it is. You must stop to supper—and you and I must thresh these things out. We've involved ourselves with each other and we've got to make the best of it. Your wife and mine will spread the board, and we will go on talking. Why not sit in that chair instead of leaning on the back? This is a home—*domus*—not a debating society—humble in spite of my manifest frauds. . . . That's better. And in the first place I hope—I do so hope"—Chaffery was suddenly very impressive—"that you're not a Dissenter."

"Eh!" said Lewisham, and then, "No! I am *not* a Dissenter."

"That's better," said Mr. Chaffery. "I'm glad of that. I was just a little afraid—. Something in your manner. I can't stand Dissenters. I've a peculiar dislike to Dissenters. To my mind it's the great drawback of this Clapham. You see . . . I have invariably found them deceitful—invariably."

He grimaced and dropped his glasses with a click against his waistcoat buttons. "I'm very glad of that," he said, replacing them. "The Dissenter, the Nonconformist Conscience, the Puritan, you know, the Vegetarian and Total Abstainer, and all that sort of thing, I cannot away with them. I have cleared my mind of cant and formulae. I've a nature essentially Hellenic. Have you ever read Matthew Arnold?"

"Beyond my scientific reading—"

"Ah! you *should* read Matthew Arnold—a mind of singular clarity. In him you would find a certain quality that is sometimes a little wanting in your scientific men. They are apt to be a little too phenomenal, you know, a little too objective. Now I seek after noumena. Noumena, Mr. Lewisham! If you follow me—?"

He paused, and his eyes behind the glasses were mildly interrogative. Ethel re-entered without her hat and jacket, and with a noisy square black tray, a white cloth, some plates and knives and glasses, and began to lay the table.

"*I* follow you," said Lewisham reddening. He had not the courage to admit ignorance of this remarkable word. "You state your case."

"I seek after *noumena*," repeated Chaffery with great satisfaction, and gesticulated with his hand, waving away everything but that. "I cannot do with surfaces and appearances. I am one of those nympholepts, you know, nympholepts . . . Must pursue the truth of things! the elusive fundamental . . . I make a rule, I never tell myself lies—never. There are few who can say that. To my mind—truth begins at home. And for the most part—stops there. Safest and seemliest! *you* know. With most men—with your typical Dissenter *par excellence*— it's always gadding abroad, calling on the neighbors. You see my point of view?"

He glanced at Lewisham, who was conscious of an unwonted opacity of mind. He became wary, as wary as he could manage to be on the spur of the moment.

"It's a little surprising, you know," he said very carefully, "if I may say so—and considering what happened—to hear *you* . . ."

"Speaking of truth? Not when you understand my position. Not when you see where I stand. That is what I am getting at. That is what I am naturally anxious to make clear to you now that we have intermarried, now that you are my step-son-in-law. You're young, you know, you're young, and you're hard and fast. Only years can give a mind *tone*—mitigate the varnish of education. I gather from this letter—and your face—that you are one of the party that participated in that little affair at Lagune's."

He stuck out a finger at a point he had just seen. "By-the-bye!—That accounts for Ethel," he said.

Ethel rapped down the mustard on the table. "It does," she said, but not very loudly.

"But you had met before?" said Chaffery.

"At Whortley," said Lewisham.

"I see," said Chaffery.

"I was in— I was one of those who arranged the exposure," said Lewisham. "And now you have raised the matter, I am bound to say—"

"I knew," interrupted Chaffery. "But what a shock that was for Lagune!" He looked down at his toes for a moment with the corners of his mouth tucked in. "The hand dodge wasn't bad, you know," he said with a queer sidelong smile.

Lewisham was very busy for a moment trying to get this remark in focus. "I don't see it in the same light as you do," he explained at last.

"Can't get away from your moral bias, eh?—Well, well. We'll go into all that. But apart from its moral merits—simply as an artistic trick—it was not bad."

"I don't know much about tricks—"

"So few who undertake exposures do. You admit you never heard or thought of that before—the bladder, I mean. Yet it's as obvious as tintacks that a medium who's hampered at his hands will do all he can with his teeth, and what *could* be so self-evident as a bladder under one's lapel? What could be? Yet I know psychic literature pretty well and it's never been suggested even! Never. It's a perpetual surprise to me how many things are *not* thought of by investigators. For one thing, they never count the odds against them, and that puts them wrong at the start. Look at it! I am by nature tricky. I spend all my leisure standing or sitting about and thinking up or practicing new little tricks, because it amuses me immensely to do so. The whole thing amuses me. Well—what is the result of these meditations? Take one thing:—I know eight and forty ways of making raps—of which at least ten are original. Ten original ways of making raps." His manner was very impressive. "And, some of them simply tremendous raps. There!"

A confirmatory rap exploded—as it seemed between Lewisham and Chaffery.

"*Eh?*" said Chaffery.

The mantelpiece opened a dropping fire, and the table went off under Lewisham's nose like a cracker.

"You see?" said Chaffery, putting his hands under the tail of his coat. The whole room seemed snapping its fingers at Lewisham for a space.

"Very well, and now take the other side. Take the severest test I ever tried. Two respectable professors of physics—not Newtons, you understand, but good, worthy, self-important professors of physics—a lady anxious to prove there's a life beyond the grave, a journalist who wants stuff to write—a person, that is, who gets his living by these researches just as I do—undertook to test me. Test *me!* . . . Of course they had their other work to do, professing physics, professing religion, organizing research, and so forth. At the outside they don't think an hour a day about it, and most of them had never cheated anybody in their existence, and couldn't, for example, travel without a ticket for a three-mile journey and not get caught, to save their lives. . . . Well—you see the odds?"

He paused. Lewisham appeared involved in some interior struggle.

"You know," explained Chaffery, "it was quite an accident you got me—quite. The thing slipped out of my mouth. Or your friend with the flat voice wouldn't have had a chance. Not a chance."

Lewisham spoke like a man who is lifting a weight. "All *this,* you know, is off the question. I'm not disputing your ability. But the thing is . . . it isn't right."

"We're coming to that," said Chaffery.

"It's evident we look at things in a different light."

"That's it. That's just what we've got to discuss. Exactly!"

"Cheating is cheating. You can't get away from that. That's simple enough."

"Wait till I've done with it," said Chaffery with a certain zest. "Of course it's imperative you should understand my position. It isn't as though I hadn't one. Ever since I read your letter I've been thinking over that. Really!—a justification! In a way you might almost say I had a mission. A sort of prophet. You really don't see the beginning of it yet."

"Oh, but hang it!" protested Lewisham.

"Ah! you're young, you're crude. My dear young man, you're only at the beginning of things. You really must concede a certain possibility of wider views to a man more than twice your age. But here's supper. For a little while at any rate we'll call a truce."

Ethel had come in again bearing an additional chair, and Mrs. Chaffery appeared behind her, crowning the preparations with a jug of small beer. The cloth, Lewisham observed, as he turned towards it, had several undarned holes and discolored places, and in the center stood a tarnished cruet which contained mustard, pepper, vinegar, and three ambiguous dried-up bottles. The bread was on an ample board with a pious rim, and an honest wedge of cheese loomed disproportionate on a little plate. Mr. and Mrs. Lewisham were seated facing one another, and Mrs. Chaffery sat in the broken chair because she understood its ways.

"This cheese is as nutritious and unattractive and indigestible as Science," remarked Chaffery, cutting and passing wedges. "But crush it—so—under your fork, add a little of this good Dorset butter, a dab of mustard, pepper—the pepper is very necessary—and some malt vinegar, and crush together. You get a compound called Crab and by no means disagreeable. So the wise deal with the facts of life, neither bolting nor rejecting, but adapting."

"As though pepper and mustard were not facts," said Lewisham, scoring his solitary point that evening.

Chaffery admitted the collapse of his image in very complimentary terms, and Lewisham could not avoid a glance across the table at Ethel. He remembered that Chaffery was a slippery scoundrel whose blame was better than his praise, immediately afterwards.

For a time the Crab engaged Chaffery, and the conversation languished. Mrs. Chaffery asked Ethel formal questions about their lodgings, and Ethel's answers were buoyant. "You must come and have tea one day," said Ethel, not waiting for Lewisham's endorsement, "and see it all."

Chaffery astonished Lewisham by suddenly displaying a complete acquaintance with his status as a South Kensington teacher in training. "I suppose you have some money beyond that guinea," said Chaffery off-handedly.

"Enough to go on with," said Lewisham reddening.

"And you look to them at South Kensington to do something for you—a hundred a year or so, when your scholarship is up?"

"Yes," said Lewisham a little reluctantly. "Yes. A hundred a year or so. That's the sort of idea. And there's lots of places beyond South Kensington, of course, even if they don't put me up there."

"I see," said Chaffery, "but it will be a pretty close shave for all that—one hundred a year. Well, well—there's many a deserving man has to do with less," and after a meditative pause he asked Lewisham to pass the beer.

"Hev you a mother living, Mr. Lewisham?" said Mrs. Chaffery suddenly, and pursued him through the tale of his connections. When he came to the plumber, Mrs. Chaffery remarked with an unexpected air of consequence, that most families have their poor relations. Then the air of consequence vanished again into the past from which it had arisen.

Supper finished, Chaffery poured the residuum of the beer into his glass, produced a Broseley clay of the longest sort, and invited Lewisham to smoke. "Honest smoking," said Chaffery, tapping the bowl of his clay, and added: "In this country—cigars—sound cigars—and honesty rarely meet."

Lewisham fumbled in his pocket for his Algerian cigarettes, and Chaffery having regarded them unfavorably through his glasses, took up the thread of his promised apologia. The ladies retired to wash up the supper things.

"You see," said Chaffery, opening abruptly so soon as the clay was drawing, "about this cheating—I do not find life such a simple matter as you do."

"*I* don't find life simple," said Lewisham, "but I do think there's a Right and a Wrong in things. And I don't think you have said anything so far to show that spiritualistic cheating is Right."

"Let us thresh the matter out," said Chaffery, crossing his legs, "let us thresh the matter out. Now"—he drew at his pipe—"I don't think you fully appreciate the importance of Illusion in life, the Essential Nature of Lies and Deception of the body politic. You are inclined to discredit one particular form of Imposture, because it is not generally admitted—carries a certain discredit, and—witness the heel edges of my trouser legs, witness yonder viands—small rewards."

"It's not that," said Lewisham.

"Now I am prepared to maintain," said Chaffery, proceeding with his proposition, "that Honesty is essentially an anarchistic and disintegrating force in society, that communities are held together and the progress of civilization made possible only by vigorous and sometimes even violent Lying; that the Social Contract is nothing more or less than a vast conspiracy of human beings to lie to and humbug themselves and one another for the general Good. Lies are the mortar that bind the savage individual man into the social masonry. There is the general thesis upon which I base my justification. My mediumship, I can assure you, is a particular instance of the general assertion. Were I not of a profoundly indolent, restless, adventurous nature, and horribly averse to writing, I would make a great book of this and live honored by every profound duffer in the world."

"But how are you going to prove it?"

"Prove it! It simply needs pointing out. Even now there are men—Bernard Shaw, Ibsen, and such like—who have seen bits of it in a new-gospel-grubbing sort of fashion. What is man? Lust and greed tempered by fear and an irrational vanity."

"I don't agree with that," said Mr. Lewisham.

"You will as you grow older," said Chaffery. "There's truths you have to grow into. But about this matter of Lies—let us look at the fabric of society, let us compare the savage. You will discover the only essential difference between savage and civilized is this: The former hasn't learned to shirk the truth of things, and the latter has. Take the most obvious difference—the clothing of the civilized man, his invention of decency. What *is* clothing? The concealment of essential facts. What is decorum? Suppression! I don't argue against decency and decorum, mind you, but there they are—essentials to civilization and essentially '*suppressio veri*.' And in the pockets of his clothes our citizen carries money. The pure savage has no money. To him a lump of metal is a lump of metal—possibly ornamental—no more. That's right. To any lucid-minded man it's the same or different only through the gross folly of his fellows. But to the common civilized man the universal exchangeability of this gold is a sacred and fundamental fact. Think of it! Why should it be? There isn't a why! I live in perpetual amazement at the gullibility of my fellow-creatures. Of a morning sometimes, I can assure you, I lie in bed fancying that people may have found out this swindle in the night, expect to hear a tumult downstairs and see your mother-in-law come rushing into the room with a rejected shilling from the milkman. 'What's this?' says he. 'This Muck for milk?' But it never happens. Never. If it did, if people suddenly cleared their minds of this cant of money, what would happen? The true nature of man would appear. I should whip out of bed, seize some weapon, and after the milkman forthwith. It's becoming to keep the peace, but it's necessary to have milk. The neighbors would come pouring out—also after milk. Milkman, suddenly enlightened, would start clattering up the street. After him! Clutch—tear! Got him! Over goes the cart! Fight if you like, but don't upset the can! . . . Don't you see it all—perfectly reasonable every bit of it. I should return, bruised and bloody, with the milk-can under my arm. Yes—*I* should have the milk-can—I should keep my eye on that. . . . But why go on? You of all men should know that life is a struggle for existence, a fight for food. Money is just the lie that mitigates our fury.''

"No," said Lewisham, "no! I'm not prepared to admit that."

"What *is* money?"

Mr. Lewisham dodged. "You state your case first," he said. "I really don't see what all this has to do with cheating at a *séance*."

"I weave my defense from this loom, though. Take some aggressively respectable sort of man—a bishop, for example."

"Well," said Lewisham, "I don't much hold with bishops."

"It doesn't matter. Take a professor of science, walking the earth. Remark his clothing, making a decent citizen out of him, concealing the fact that physically he is a flabby, pot-bellied degenerate. That is the first Lie of his being. No fringes round *his* trousers, my boy. Notice his hair, groomed and clipped, the tacit lie that its average length is half an inch, whereas in nature he would wave a few score yard-long hairs of ginger gray to the winds of heaven. Notice the smug suppressions of his face. In his mouth are Lies in the shape of false teeth. Then on the earth somewhere poor devils are toiling to get him meat and corn and wine. He is clothed in the lives of bent and thwarted weavers, his way is lit by phossy jaw, he eats from lead-glazed crockery—all his ways are paved with the lives of men. . . . Think of the chubby, comfortable creature! And, as Swift has it—to think that such a thing should deal in pride! . . . He pretends that his blessed little researches are in some way a fair return to these remote beings for their toil, their suffering; pretends that he and his parasitic career are payment for their thwarted desires. Imagine him bullying his gardener over some transplanted geraniums, the thick mist of lies they stand in, so that the man does not immediately, with the edge of a spade smite down his impertinence to the dust from which it rose. . . . And his case is the case of all comfortable lives. What a lie and sham all civility is, all good breeding, all culture and refinement, while one poor ragged wretch drags hungry on the earth!''

"But this is Socialism!" said Lewisham. "*I*—"

"No Ism," said Chaffery, raising his rich voice. "Only the ghastly truth of things—the truth that the warp and the woof of the world of men is Lying. Socialism is no remedy, no *ism* is a remedy; things are so.''

"I don't agree—" began Lewisham.

"Not with the hopelessness, because you are young, but with the description you do.''

"Well—within limits."

"You agree that most respectable positions in the world are tainted with the fraud of our social conditions. If they were not tainted with fraud they would not be respectable. Even your own position— Who gave you the right to marry and prosecute interesting scientific studies while other young men rot in mines?"

"I admit—"

"You can't help admitting. And here is my position. Since all ways of life are tainted with fraud, since to live and speak the truth is beyond human strength and courage—as one finds it—is it not better for a man that he engage in some straightforward comparatively harmless cheating, than if he risk his mental integrity in some ambiguous position and fall at last into self-deception and self-righteousness? That is the essential danger. That is the thing I always guard against. Heed that! It is the master sin. Self-righteousness.''

Mr. Lewisham pulled at his moustache.

"You begin to take me. And after all, these worthy people do not suffer so greatly. If I did not take their money some other impostor would. Their huge conceit of intelligence would breed perhaps some viler swindle than my facetious rappings. That's the line our doubting bishops take, and why shouldn't I? For example, these people might give it to Public Charities, minister to the fattened secretary, the prodigal younger son. After all, at worst, I am a sort of latter-day Robin Hood; I take from the rich according to their incomes. I don't give to the poor certainly, I don't get enough. But—there are other good works. Many a poor weakling have I comforted with Lies, great thumping, silly Lies, about the grave! Compare me with one of those rascals who disseminate phossy jaw and lead poisons, compare me with a millionaire who runs a music hall with an eye to feminine talent, or an underwriter, or the common stockbroker. Or any sort of lawyer. . . .

"There are bishops," said Chaffery, "who believe in Darwin and doubt Moses. Now, I hold myself better than they—analogous perhaps but better— for I do at least invent something of the tricks I play—I do do that.''

"That's all very well," began Lewisham.

"I might forgive them their dishonesty," said Chaffery, "but the stupidity of it, the mental self-abnegation—Lord! If a solicitor doesn't swindle in the proper shabby-magnificent way, they chuck him for unprofessional conduct." He paused. He became meditative, and smiled faintly.

"Now, some of *my* dodges," he said with a sudden change of voice, turning towards Lewisham, his eyes smiling over his glasses and an emphatic hand patting the table-cloth; "some of *my* dodges are *damned* ingenious, you know— *damned* ingenious—and well worth double the money they bring me—double."

He turned towards the fire again, pulling at his smoldering pipe and eyeing Lewisham over the corner of his glasses.

"One or two of my little things would make Maskelyne sit up," he said presently. "They would set that mechanical orchestra playing out of pure aston-ishment. I really must explain some of them to you—now we have intermarried."

It took Mr. Lewisham a minute or so to re-form the regiment of his mind, disordered by its headlong pursuit of Chaffery's flying arguments. "But on your principles you might do almost anything!" he said.

"Precisely!" said Chaffery.

"But—"

"It is rather a curious method," protested Chaffery, "to test one's principles of action by judging the resultant actions on some other principle, isn't it?''

Lewisham took a moment to think. "I suppose that is so," he said, in the manner of a man convinced against his will.

He perceived his logic insufficient. He suddenly thrust the delicacies of argument aside. Certain sentences he had brought ready for use in his mind came up and he delivered them abruptly. "Anyhow," he said, "I don't agree with this cheating. In spite of what you say, I hold to what I said in my letter. Ethel's connection with all these things is at an end. I shan't go out of my way to expose you, of course, but if it comes in my way I shall speak my mind of all these spiritualistic phenomena. It's just as well that we should know clearly where we are.''

"That is clearly understood, my dear step-son-in-law," said Chaffery. "Our present object is discussion."

"But Ethel—"

"Ethel is yours," said Chaffery. "Ethel is yours," he repeated after an interval, and added pensively—"to keep."

"But talking of Illusion," he resumed, dismissing the sordid with a sign of relief, "I sometimes think with Bishop Berkeley, that all experience is probably something quite different from reality. That consciousness is *essentially* hallucination. I here, and you, and our talk—it is all Illusion. Bring your Science to bear—what am I? A cloudy multitude of atoms, an infinite interplay of little cells. Is this hand that I hold out me? This head? Is the surface of my skin any more than a rude average boundary? You say it is my mind that is me? But consider the war of motives. Suppose I have an impulse that I resist—it is *I* resist it—the impulse is outside me, eh? But suppose that impulse carries me and I do the thing—that impulse is part of me, is it not? Ah! My brain reels at these mysteries! Lord! what flimsy fluctuating things we are—first this, then that, a thought, an impulse, a deed and a forgetting, and all the time madly cocksure we are ourselves. And as for you—you who have hardly learned to think for more than five or six short years, there you sit, assured, coherent, there you sit in all your inherited original sin—Hallucinatory Windlestraw!—judging and condemning. *You* know Right from Wrong! My boy, so did Adam and Eve . . . *so soon as they'd had dealings with the father of lies!*"

At the end of the evening whiskey and hot water were produced, and Chaffery, now in a mood of great urbanity, said he had rarely enjoyed anyone's conversation so much as Lewisham's, and insisted upon everyone having whiskey. Mrs. Chaffery and Ethel added sugar and lemon. Lewisham felt an instantaneous mild surprise at the sight of Ethel drinking grog.

At the door Mrs. Chaffery kissed Lewisham an effusive good-bye and told Ethel she really believed it was all for the best.

On the way home Lewisham was thoughtful and preoccupied. The problem of Chaffery assumed enormous proportions. At times indeed even that good man's own philosophical sketch of himself as a practical exponent of mental sincerity touched with humor and the artistic spirit, seemed plausible. Lagune was an undeniable ass, and conceivably psychic research was an incentive to trickery. Then he remembered the matter in his relation to Ethel. . . .

"Your stepfather is a little hard to follow," he said at last, sitting on the bed and taking off one boot. "He's dodgy—he's so confoundedly dodgy. One doesn't know where to take hold of him. He's got such a break he's clean bowled me again and again."

He thought for a space, and then removed his boot and sat with it on his knee. "Of course! . . . all that he said was wrong—quite wrong. Right is right and cheating is cheating, whatever you say about it."

"That's what I feel about him," said Ethel at the looking-glass. "That's exactly how it seems to me."

CHAPTER XXIV

The Campaign Opens

ON SATURDAY LEWISHAM was first through the folding doors. In a moment he reappeared with a document extended. Mrs. Lewisham stood arrested with her dress skirt in her hand, astonished at the astonishment on his face. "*I* say!" said Lewisham; "just look here!"

She looked at the book that he held open before her, and perceived that its vertical ruling betokened a sordid import, that its list of items in an illegible mixture of English and German was lengthy. "1 kettle of coals 6d." occurred regularly down that portentous array and buttoned it all together. It was Madam Gadow's first bill. Ethel took it out of his hand and examined it closer. It looked no smaller closer. The overcharges were scandalous. It was curious how the humor of calling a scuttle "kettle" had evaporated.

That document, I take it, was the end of Mr. Lewisham's informal honeymoon. It's advent was the snap of that bright Prince Rupert's drop; and in a moment—Dust. For a glorious week he had lived in the persuasion that life was made of love and mystery, and now he was reminded with singular clearness that it was begotten of a struggle for existence and the Will to Live. "Confounded imposition!" fumed Mr. Lewisham, and the breakfast table was novel and ominous, mutterings towards anger on the one hand and a certain consternation on the other. "I must give her a talking to this afternoon," said Lewisham at his watch, and after he had bundled his books into the shiny black bag, he gave the first of his kisses that was not a distinct and self-subsisting ceremony. It was usage and done in a hurry, and the door slammed as he went his way to the schools. Ethel was not coming that morning, because by special request and because she wanted to help him she was going to copy out some of his botanical notes which had fallen into arrears.

On his way to the schools Lewisham felt something suspiciously near a sinking of the heart. His pre-occupation was essentially arithmetical. The thing that engaged his mind to the exclusion of all other matters is best expressed in the recognized business form.

Dr.		£	s.	d.	Cr.		£	s.	d.
Cash in hand	Mr. L. ⎰	13	10	4½	By 'bus fares to South Kensington (late)........				2
	Mrs. L. ⎱		11	7	By 6 lunches at the Students' Club..			5	2½
......					By 2 packets of cigarettes (to smoke after dinner).............				6
At Bank		45	0	0	By marriage and elopement........		4	18	10
To Scholarship		1	1	0	By necessary subsequent additions to bride's trousseau............			16	1
					By housekeeping exs.	1	1	1	4½
					By "A few little things" bought by housekeeper......			15	3½
					By Madam Gadow for coal, lodging and attendance (as per account rendered)........		1	15	0
					By missing........				4
					By balance........		50	11	2
		£60.	3	11½			£60.	3	11½

From this it will be manifest to the most unbusinesslike that, disregarding the extraordinary expenditure on the marriage, and the by no means final "few little things" Ethel had bought, out-goings exceeded income by two pounds and more, and a brief excursion into arithmetic will demonstrate that in five and twenty weeks the balance of the account would be nothing.

But that guinea a week was not to go on for five and twenty weeks, but simply for fifteen, and then the net outgoings will be well over three guineas, reducing the "law" accorded our young couple to two and twenty weeks. These details are tiresome and disagreeable, no doubt, to the refined reader, but just imagine how much more disagreeable they were to Mr. Lewisham, trudging meditative to the schools. You will understand his slipping out of the laboratory, and betaking himself to the Educational Reading-room, and how it was that the observant Smithers, grinding his lecture notes against the now imminent second examination for the "Forbes," was presently perplexed to the center of his being by the spectacle of Lewisham, intent upon a pile of current periodicals, the *Educational Times,* the *Journal of Education,* the *Schoolmaster, Science and Art, The University Correspondent, Nature, The Athenaeum, The Academy,* and *The Author.*

Smithers remarked the appearance of a note-book, the jotting down of memoranda. He edged into the bay nearest Lewisham's table and approached him suddenly from the flank. "What are *you* after?" said Smithers in a noisy whisper and with a detective eye on the papers. He perceived Lewisham was scrutinizing the advertisement column, and his perplexity increased.

"Oh—nothing," said Lewisham blandly, with his hand falling casually over his memoranda, "what's your particular little game?"

"Nothing much," said Smithers, "just mooching round. You weren't at the meeting last Friday?"

He turned a chair, knelt on it, and began whispering over the back about Debating Society politics. Lewisham was inattentive and brief. What had he to do with these puerilities. At last Smithers went away foiled, and met Parkson by the entrance. Parkson, by-the-bye, had not spoken to Lewisham since their painful misunderstanding. He made a wide detour to his seat at the end table, and so, and by a singular rectitude of bearing and a dignified expression, showed himself aware of Lewisham's offensive presence.

Lewisham's investigations were two-fold. He wanted to discover some way of adding materially to that weekly guinea by his own exertions, and he wanted to learn the conditions of the market for typewriting. For himself he had a vague idea, an idea subsequently abandoned, that it was possible to get teaching work in evening classes during the month of March. But, except by reason of sudden death, no evening class in London changes its staff after September until July comes round again. Private tuition, moreover, offered many attractions to him, but no definite proposals. His ideas of his own possibilities were youthful, or he would not have spent time in noting the conditions of application for a vacant professorship in physics at the Melbourne University. He also made a note of the vacant editorship of a monthly magazine devoted to social questions. He would not have minded doing that sort of thing at all, though the proprietor might. There was also a vacant curatorship in the Museum of Eton College.

The typewriting business was less varied and more definite. Those were the days before the violent competition of the half-educated had brought things down to an impossible tenpence the thousand words, and the prevailing price was as high as one-and-six. Calculating that Ethel could do a thousand words in an hour and that she could work five or six hours in the day, it was evident that her contributions to the household expenses would be by no means despicable; thirty shillings a week perhaps. Lewisham was naturally elated at this discovery. He could find no advertisements of authors or others seeking typewriting, but he saw that a great number of typewriters advertised themselves in the literary papers. It was evident Ethel also must advertise. " 'Scientific phraseology a speciality' might be put," meditated Lewisham. He returned to his lodgings in a hopeful mood with quite a bundle of memoranda of possible employments. He spent five shillings in stamps on the way.

After lunch, Lewisham—a little short of breath—asked to see Madam Gadow. She came up in the most affable frame of mind; nothing could be further from the normal indignation of the British landlady. She was very voluble, gesticulatory and lucid, but unhappily bi-lingual, and at all the crucial points German. Mr. Lewisham's natural politeness restrained him from too close a pursuit across the boundary of the two imperial tongues. Quite half an hour's amicable discussion led at last to a reduction of sixpence, and all parties professed themselves satisfied with this result.

Madam Gadow was quite cool even at the end. Mr. Lewisham was flushed in the face, red-eared, and his hair slightly disordered, but that sixpence was at any rate an admission of the justice of his claim. "She was evidently trying it on," he said almost apologetically to Ethel. "It was absolutely necessary to present a firm front to her. I doubt if we shall have any trouble again. . . .

"Of course what she says about kitchen coals is perfectly just."

Then the young couple went for a walk in Kensington Gardens, and—the spring afternoon was so warm and pleasant—sat on two attractive green chairs near the band-stand, for which Lewisham had subsequently to pay twopence. They had what Ethel called a "serious talk." She was really wonderfully sensible and discussed the situation exhaustively. She was particularly insistent upon the importance of economy in her domestic disbursements and deplored her general ignorance very earnestly. It was decided that Lewisham should get a good elementary text-book of domestic economy for her private study. At home Mrs. Chaffery guided her house by the oracular items of "Inquire Within upon Everything," but Lewisham considered that work unscientific.

Ethel was also of opinion that much might be learned from the sixpenny ladies' papers—the penny ones had hardly begun in those days. She had bought such publications during seasons of affluence, but chiefly, as she now deplored, with an eye to the trimming of hats and such like vanities. The sooner the typewriter came the better. It occurred to Lewisham with unpleasant suddenness that he had not allowed for the purchase of a typewriter in his estimate of their resources. It brought their "law" down to twelve or thirteen weeks.

They spent the evening in writing and copying a number of letters, addressing envelopes and enclosing stamps. There were optimistic moments.

"Melbourne's a fine city," said Lewisham, "and we should have a glorious voyage out." He read the application for the Melbourne professorship out loud to her, just to see how it read, and she was greatly impressed by the list of his accomplishments and successes. "I did not know you knew *half* those things," she said, and became depressed at her relative illiteracy. It was natural, after such encouragement, to write to the scholastic agents in a tone of assured consequence.

The advertisement for typewriting in the *Athenaeum* troubled his conscience a little. After he had copied out his draft with its "Scientific phraseology a speciality," fine and large, he saw the notes she had written out for him. Her handwriting was still round and boyish, even as it had appeared in the Whortley avenue, but her punctuation was confined to the erratic comma and the dash, and there was a disposition to spell the imperfectly legible along the line of least resistance. However he dismissed that matter with a resolve to read over and correct anything in that way that she might have sent her to do. It would not be a bad idea, he thought parenthetically, if he himself read up some sound authority on the punctuation of sentences.

They sat at this business quite late, heedless of the examination in botany that came on the morrow. It was very bright and cozy in their little room with their fire burning, the gas lit and the curtains drawn, and the number of applications they had written made them hopeful. She was flushed and enthusiastic, now flitting about the room, now coming close to him and leaning over him to see what he had done. At Lewisham's request she got him the envelopes from the chest of drawers. "You *are* a help to a chap," said Lewisham, leaning back from the table. "I feel I could do anything for a girl like you—anything."

"*Really!*" she cried. "Really! Am I really a help?"

Lewisham's face and gesture were all assent. She gave a little cry of delight, stood for a moment, and then by way of practical demonstration of her unflinching helpfulness, hurried round the table towards him with arms extended. "You dear!" she cried.

Lewisham, partially embraced, pushed his chair back with his disengaged arm, so that she might sit on his knee. . . .

Who could doubt that she was a help?

CHAPTER XXV

The First Battle

LEWISHAM'S INQUIRIES FOR evening teaching and private tuition were essentially provisional measures. His proposals for a more permanent establishment displayed a certain defect in his sense of proportion. That Melbourne professorship, for example, was beyond his merits and there were aspects of things that would have affected the welcome of himself and his wife at Eton College. At the outset he was inclined to regard the South Kensington scholar as the intellectual salt of the earth, to overrate the abundance of "decent things" yielding from one hundred and fifty to three hundred a year, and to disregard the competition of such inferior enterprises as the universities of Oxford, Cambridge, and the literate North. But the scholastic agents to whom he went on the following Saturday did much in a quiet way to disabuse his mind.

Mr. Blendershin's chief assistant in the grimy little office in Oxford Street cleared up the matter so vigorously that Lewisham was angered. "Head Master of an endowed school, perhaps!" said Mr. Blendershin's chief assistant. "Lord!— why not a bishopric? I say,"—as Mr. Blendershin entered smoking an assertive cigar—"one and twenty, *no* degree, *no* games, two years' experience as junior—

wants a headmastership of an endowed school!'' He spoke so loudly that it was inevitable the selection of clients in the waiting-room should hear, and he pointed with his pen.

"Look here!'' said Lewisham hotly, "if I knew the ways of the market I shouldn't come to you.''

Mr. Blendershin stared at Lewisham for a moment. "What's he done in the way of certificates?'' asked Mr. Blendershin of the assistant.

The assistant read a list of 'ologies and 'ographies. "Fifty-resident,'' said Mr. Blendershin concisely—"that's *your* figure. Sixty, if you're lucky.''

"*What?*'' said Mr. Lewisham.

"Not enough for you?''

"Not nearly.''

"You can get a Cambridge graduate for eighty resident—and grateful,'' said Mr. Blendershin.

"But I don't want a resident post,'' said Lewisham.

"Precious few non-resident shops,'' said Mr. Blendershin. "Precious few. They want you for dormitory supervision—and they're afraid of your taking pups outside.''

"Not married by any chance?'' said the assistant suddenly, after an attentive study of Lewisham's face.

"Well—er.'' Lewisham met Mr. Blendershin's eye. "Yes,'' he said.

The assistant was briefly unprintable. "Lord! you'll have to keep that dark,'' said Mr. Blendershin. But you have got a tough bit of hoeing before you. If I was you I'd go on and get my degree now you're so near it. You'll stand a better chance.''

Pause.

"The fact is,'' said Lewisham slowly and looking at his boot toes, "I must be doing *something* while I am getting my degree.''

The assistant whistled softly.

"Might get you a visiting job, perhaps,'' said Mr. Blendershin speculatively. "Just read me those items again, Binks.'' He listened attentively. "Objects to religious teaching!—Eh?'' He stopped the reading by a gesture. "That's nonsense. You can't have everything, you know. Scratch that out. You won't get a place in any middle-class school in England if you object to religious teaching. It's the mothers—bless 'em! Say nothing about it. Don't believe—who does? There's hundreds like you, you know—hundreds. Parsons—all sorts. Say nothing about it—''

"But if I'm asked?''

"Church of England. Every man in this country who has not dissented belongs to the Church of England. It'll be hard enough to get you anything without that.''

"But—'' said Mr. Lewisham. "It's lying.''

"Legal fiction,'' said Mr. Blendershin. "Everyone understands. If you don't do that, my dear chap, we can't do anything for you. It's journalism, or London docks. Well, considering your experience—say docks.''

Lewisham's face flushed irregularly. He did not answer. He scowled and tugged at the still by no means ample moustache.

"Compromise, you know,'' said Mr. Blendershin, watching him kindly. "Compromise.''

For the first time in his life Lewisham faced the necessity of telling a lie in cold blood. He glissaded from the austere altitudes of his self-respect and his next words were already disingenuous.

"I won't promise to tell lies if I'm asked," he said aloud. "I can't do that."

"Scratch it out," said Blendershin to the clerk. "You needn't mention it. Then you don't say you can teach drawing."

"I can't," said Lewisham.

"You just give out the copies," said Blendershin, "and take care they don't see you draw, you know."

"But that's not teaching drawing—"

"It's what's understood by it in *this* country," said Blendershin. "Don't you go corrupting your mind with pedagogueries. They're the ruin of assistants. Put down drawing. Then there's shorthand—"

"Here, I say!" said Lewisham.

"There's shorthand, French, book-keeping, commercial geography, land measuring—"

"But I can't teach any of those things!"

"Look here," said Blendershin, and paused. "Has your wife or you a private income?"

"No," said Lewisham.

"Well?"

A pause of further moral descent, and a whack against an obstacle. "But they will find me out," said Lewisham.

Blendershin smiled. "It's not so much ability as willingness to teach, you know. And *they* won't find you out. The sort of schoolmaster we deal with can't find anything out. He can't teach any of these things himself—and consequently he doesn't believe they *can* be taught. Talk to him of pedagogics and he talks of practical experience. But he puts 'em on his prospectus, you know, and he wants 'em on his time-table. Some of these subjects— There's commercial geography, for instance. What *is* commercial geography?"

"Barilla," said the assistant biting the end of his pen, and added pensively, "*and* blethers."

"Fad," said Blendershin. "Just fad. Newspapers talk rot about commercial education, Duke of Devonshire catches on and talks ditto—pretends he thought it himself—much *he* cares—parents get hold of it—schoolmasters obliged to put something down, consequently assistants must. And that's the end of the matter!"

"*All* right," said Lewisham catching his breath in a faint sob of shame. "Stick 'em down. But mind—a non-resident place."

"Well," said Blendershin, "your science may pull you through. But I tell you it's hard. Some grant-earning grammar school may want that. And that's about all, I think. Make a note of the address. . . ."

The assistant made a noise, something between a whistle and the word "Fee." Blendershin glanced at Lewisham and nodded doubtfully.

"Fee for booking," said the assistant, "half a crown. Postage—in advance—half a crown."

But Lewisham remembered certain advice Dunkerley had given him in the old Whortley days. He hesitated. "No," he said. "I don't pay that. If you get me anything there's the commission—if you don't—"

"We lose," supplied the assistant.

"And you ought to," said Lewisham. "It's a fair game."

"Living in London?" asked Blendershin.

"Yes," said the clerk.

"That's all right," said Mr. Blendershin. "We won't say anything about the postage in that case. Of course it's the off season, and you mustn't expect anything at present very much. Sometimes there's a shift or so at Easter. . . . There's nothing more. . . . Afternoon. Anyone else, Binks?''

Messrs. Maskelyne, Smith and Thrums did a higher class of work than Blendershin, whose specialties were lower class private establishments and the cheaper sort of endowed schools. Indeed, so superior were Maskelyne, Smith and Thrums that they enraged Lewisham by refusing at first to put him on their books. He was interviewed briefly by a young man dressed and speaking with offensive precision, whose eye adhered rigidly to the waterproof collar throughout the interview.

''Hardly our line,'' he said, and pushed Lewisham a form to fill up. ''Mostly upper class and good preparatory schools here, you know.''

As Lewisham filled up the form with his multitudinous '' 'ologies'' and '' 'ographies,'' a youth of ducal appearance entered and greeted the precise young man in a friendly way. Lewisham, bending down to write, perceived that this professional rival wore a very long frock coat, patent leather boots, and the most beautiful gray trousers. His conceptions of competition enlarged. The precise young man by a motion of his eyes directed the newcomer's attention to Lewisham's waterproof collar, and was answered by raised eyebrows and a faint tightening of the mouth. ''That bounder at Castleford has answered me,'' said the newcomer in a fine rich voice. ''Is he any bally good?''

When the bounder at Castleford had been discussed Lewisham presented his paper, and the precise young man with his eye still fixed on the waterproof collar took the document in the manner of one who reaches across a gulf. ''I doubt if we shall be able to do anything for you,'' he said reassuringly. ''But an English mastership may chance to be vacant. Science doesn't count for much in *our* sort of schools, you know. Classics and good games—that's our sort of thing.''

''I see,'' said Lewisham.

''Good games, good form, you know, and all that sort of thing.''

''I see,'' said Lewisham.

''You don't happen to be a public-school boy?'' asked the precise young man.

''No,'' said Lewisham.

''Where were you educated?''

Lewisham's face grew hot. ''Does that matter?'' he asked with his eye on the exquisite gray trousering.

''In our sort of school—decidedly. It's a question of tone, you know.''

''I see,'' said Lewisham, beginning to realize new limitations. His immediate impulse was to escape the eye of the nicely dressed assistant master. ''You'll write, I suppose, if you have anything,'' he said, and the precise young man responded with alacrity to his doorward motion.

''Often get that kind of thing?'' asked the nicely dressed young man when Lewisham had departed.

''Rather. Not quite so bad as that, you know. That waterproof collar—did you notice it? Ugh! And—'I see.' And the scowl and the clumsiness of it. Of course *he* hasn't any decent clothes—he'd go to a new shop with one tin box! But that sort of thing—and board school teachers—they're getting everywhere! Only the other day—Rowton was here.''

''Not Rowton of Pinner?''

''Yes, Rowton of Pinner. And he asked right out for a board schoolmaster. He said, 'I want someone who can teach arithmetic.' ''

He laughed. The nicely dressed young man meditated over the handle of his cane. ''A bounder of that kind can't have a particularly nice time,'' he said, "anyhow. If he does get into a decent school, he must get tremendously cut by all the decent men."

"Too thick-skinned to mind that sort of thing, I fancy," said the scholastic agent. "He's a new type. This South Kensington place and the polytechnics are turning him out by the hundred. . . ."

Lewisham forgot his resentment at having to profess a religion he did not believe, in this new discovery of the scholastic importance of clothing. He went along with an eye to all the shop windows that afforded a view of his person. Indisputably his trousers *were* ungainly, flapping abominably over his boots and bagging terribly at the knees, and his boots were not only worn and ugly but extremely ill blacked. His wrists projected offensively from his coat sleeves, he perceived a huge asymmetry in the collar of his jacket, his red tie was askew and ill tied, and that waterproof collar! It was shiny, slightly discolored, suddenly clammy to the neck. What if he did happen to be well equipped for science teaching? That was nothing. He speculated on the cost of a complete outfit. It would be difficult to get such gray trousers as those he had seen for less than sixteen shillings, and he reckoned a frock coat at forty shillings at least—possibly even more. He knew good clothes were very expensive. He hesitated at Poole's door and turned away. The thing was out of the question. He crossed Leicester Square and went down Bedford Street disliking every well-dressed person he met.

Messrs. Danks & Wimborne inhabited a bank-like establishment near Chancery Lane, and without any conversation presented him with forms to fill up. Religion? asked the form. Lewisham paused and wrote "Church of England."

Thence he went to the College of Pedagogues in Holborn. The College of Pedagogues presented itself as a long-bearded, corpulent, comfortable person with a thin gold watch chain and fat hands. He wore gilt glasses and had a kindly confidential manner that did much to heal Lewisham's wounded feelings. The 'ologies and 'ographies were taken down with polite surprise at their number. "You ought to take one of our diplomas," said the stout man. "You would find no difficulty. No competition. And there are prizes—several prizes—in money."

Lewisham was not aware that the waterproof collar had found a sympathetic observer.

"We give courses of lectures, and have an examination in the theory and practice of education. It is the only examination in the theory and practice of education for men engaged in middle and upper class teaching in this country. Except the Teacher's Diploma. And so few come—not two hundred a year. Mostly governesses. The men prefer to teach by rule of thumb, you know. English characteristic—rule of thumb. It doesn't do to say anything of course— but there's bound to be—something happen—something a little disagreeable— somewhen, if things go on as they do. American schools keep on getting better— German too. What used to do won't do now. I tell this to you, you know, but it doesn't do to tell everyone. It doesn't do. It doesn't do to do anything. So much has to be considered. However . . . But you'd do well to get a diploma and make yourself efficient. Though that's looking ahead."

He spoke of looking ahead with an apologetic laugh as though it was an amiable weakness of his. He turned from such abstruse matters and furnished Lewisham with the particulars of the college diplomas, and proceeded to other possibilities. "There's private tuition," he said. "Would you mind a backward boy? Then we are occasionally asked for visiting masters. Mostly by girls' schools. But that's for older men—married men, you know."

"I am married," said Lewisham.

"*Eh?*" said the College of Pedagogues, startled.

"I *am* married," said Lewisham.

"Dear me," said the College of Pedagogues gravely, and regarding Mr. Lewisham over gold-rimmed glasses. "Dear me! And I am more than twice your age, and I am not married at all. One and twenty! Have you—have you been married long?"

"A few weeks," said Lewisham.

"That's very remarkable," said the College of Pedagogues. "Very interesting. . . . *Really!* Your wife must be a very courageous young person. . . . Excuse me! You know—. You will really have a hard fight for a position. However—it certainly makes you eligible for girls' schools; it does do that. To a certain extent, that is."

The evidently enhanced respect of the College of Pedagogues pleased Lewisham extremely. But his encounter with the Medical, Scholastic and Clerical Agency that holds by Waterloo Bridge was depressing again, and after that he set out to walk home. Long before he reached home he was tired, and his simple pride in being married and in active grapple with an unsympathetic world had passed. His surrender on the religious question had left a rankling bitterness behind it; the problem of the clothes was acutely painful. He was still far from a firm grasp of the fact that his market price was under rather than over one hundred pounds a year, but that persuasion was gaining ground in his mind.

The day was a grayish one, with a dull cold wind, and a nail in one of his boots took upon itself to be objectionable. Certain wild shots and disastrous lapses in his recent botanical examination, that he had managed to keep out of his mind hitherto, forced their way on his attention. For the first time since his marriage he harbored premonitions of failure.

When he got in he wanted to sit down at once in the little creaky chair by the fire, but Ethel came flitting from the newly bought typewriter with arms extended and prevented him. "Oh!—it *has* been dull," she said.

He missed the compliment. "*I* haven't had such a giddy time that you should grumble," he said, in a tone that was novel to her. He disengaged himself from her arms and sat down. He noticed the expression of her face.

"I'm rather tired," he said by way of apology. "And there's a confounded nail I must hammer down in my boot. It's tiring work hunting up these agents, but of course it's better to go and see them. How have you been getting on?"

"All right," she said regarding him. And then, "You *are* tired. We'll have some tea. And—let me take off your boot for you, dear. Yes—I will."

She rang the bell, bustled out of the room, called for tea at the staircase, came back, pulled out Madam Gadow's ungainly hassock and began unlacing his boot. Lewisham's mood changed. "You *are* a trump, Ethel," he said, "I'm hanged if you're not." As the laces flicked he bent forward and kissed her ear. The unlacing was suspended and there were reciprocal endearments. . . .

Presently he was sitting in his slippers, with a cup of tea in his hand, and Ethel, kneeling on the hearthrug with the firelight on her face, was telling him of an answer that had come that afternoon to her advertisement in the *Athenaeum*.

"That's good," said Lewisham.

"It's a novelist," she said with the light of pride in her eyes, and handed him the letter. "Lucas Holderness, the author of 'The Furnace of Sin' and other stories."

"That's first rate," said Lewisham with just a touch of envy, and bent forward to read by the firelight.

The letter was from an address in Judd Street, Euston Road, written on good paper and in a fair round hand such as one might imagine a novelist using. "Dear Madam," said the letter, "I propose to send you, by registered letter, the MS. of a three-volume novel. It is about 90,000 words—but you must count the exact number."

"How I shall count I don't know," said Ethel.

"I'll show you a way," said Lewisham. "There's no difficulty in that. You count the words on three or four pages, strike an average, and multiply."

"But of course, before doing so I must have a satisfactory guarantee that my confidence in putting my work in your hands will not be misplaced and that your execution is of the necessary high quality."

"Oh!" said Lewisham, "that's a bother."

"Accordingly I must ask you for references."

"That's a downright nuisance," said Lewisham. "I suppose that ass, Lagune . . . But what's this? 'Or, failing references, for a deposit . . .' That's reasonable, I suppose."

It was such a moderate deposit too—merely a guinea. Even had the doubt been stronger, the aspect of helpful hopeful little Ethel eager for work might well have thrust it aside. "Sending him a cheque will show him we have a banking account behind us," said Lewisham—his banking was still sufficiently recent for pride. "We will send him a cheque. That'll settle *him* all right."

That evening after the guinea cheque had been despatched, things were further brightened by the arrival of a letter of atrociously jellygraphed advices from Messrs. Danks & Wimborne. They all referred to resident vacancies for which Lewisham was manifestly unsuitable, nevertheless their arrival brought an encouraging assurance of things going on, of shifting and unstable places in the defences of the beleaguered world. Afterwards, with occasional endearments for Ethel, he set himself to a revision of his last year's note-books, for now the botany was finished, the advanced zoological course—the last lap, as it were, for the Forbes medal—was beginning. She got her best hat from the next room to make certain changes in the arrangement of its trimmings. She sat in the little chair, while Lewisham, with documents spread before him, sat at the table.

Presently she looked up from an experimental arrangement of her cornflowers, and discovered Lewisham, no longer reading, but staring blankly at the middle of the table-cloth, with an extraordinary misery in his eyes. She forgot the cornflowers and stared at him.

"Penny," she said after an interval.

Lewisham started and looked up. "*Eh?*"

"Why were you looking so miserable?" she asked.

"*Was* I looking miserable?"

"Yes. And *cross!*"

"I was thinking just then that I would like to boil a bishop or so in oil."

"My dear!"

"They know perfectly well the case against what they teach, they know it's neither madness nor wickedness nor any great harm to others, not to believe, they know perfectly well that a man may be as honest as the day, and right— right and decent in every way—and not believe in what they teach. And they know that it only wants the edge off a man's honor, for him to profess anything in the way of belief. Just anything. And they won't say so. I suppose they want the edge off every man's honor. If a man is well off they will truckle to him no end, though he laughs at all their teaching. They'll take gold plate from company promoters and rent from insanitary houses. But if a man is poor and doesn't profess to believe in what some of them scarcely believe themselves, they wouldn't lift a finger to help him against the ignorance of their followers. Your stepfather was right enough there. They know what's going on. They know that it means lying and humbug for any number of people, and they don't care. Why should they? *They've* got it down all right. They're spoilt and why shouldn't we be?''

Lewisham having selected the bishops as scapegoats for his turpitude, was inclined to ascribe even the nail in his boot to their agency.

Mrs. Lewisham looked puzzled. She realized his drift.

"You're not," she said, and dropped her voice, "an *infidel?*"

Lewisham nodded gloomily. "Aren't you?" he said.

"Oh no," said Mrs. Lewisham.

"But you don't go to church, you don't—"

"No, I don't," said Mrs. Lewisham; and then with more assurance. "But I'm not an infidel."

"Christian?"

"I suppose so."

"But a Christian— What do you believe?"

"Oh! to tell the truth, and do right, and not hurt or injure people and all that."

"That's not a Christian. A Christian is one who believes."

"It's what *I* mean by a Christian," said Mrs. Lewisham.

"Oh! at that rate anyone's a Christian," said Lewisham. "We all think it's right to do right and wrong to do wrong."

"But we don't all do it," said Mrs. Lewisham, taking up the cornflowers again.

"No," said Lewisham, a little taken aback by the feminine method of discussion. "We don't all do it—certainly." He stared at her for a moment—her head was a little on one side and her eyes on the cornflower—and his mind was full of a strange discovery. He seemed on the verge of speaking, and turned to his notebook again.

Very soon the center of the table-cloth resumed its sway.

The following day Mr. Lucas Holderness received his cheque for a guinea. Unhappily it was crossed. He meditated for some time and then took pen and ink and improved Lewisham's careless "one" to "five" and touched up his unticked figure one to correspond.

You perceive him, a lank, cadaverous, good-looking man with long black hair and a semi-clerical costume of quite painful rustiness. He made the emendations with grave carefulness. He took the cheque round to his grocer. His grocer looked at it suspiciously.

"You pay it in," said Mr. Lucas Holderness, "if you've any doubts about it. Pay it in. *I* don't know the man or what he is. He may be a swindler for all I can tell. *I* can't answer for him. Pay it in and see. Leave the change till then. I can wait. I'll call round in a few days' time."

"All right, wasn't it?" said Mr. Lucas Holderness in a casual tone two days later.

"Quite, sir," said his grocer with enhanced respect, and handed him his four pounds thirteen and sixpence change.

Mr. Lucas Holderness, who had been eyeing the grocer's stock with a curious intensity, immediately became animated and bought a tin of salmon. He went out of the shop with the rest of the money in his hand, for the pockets of his clothes were old and untrustworthy. At the baker's he bought a new roll.

He bit a huge piece of the roll directly he was out of the shop, and went on his way gnawing. It was so large a piece that his gnawing mouth was contorted into the ugliest shapes. He swallowed by an effort, stretching his neck each time. His eyes expressed an animal satisfaction. He turned the corner of Judd Street biting again at the roll, and the reader of this story, like the Lewishams, hears of him no more.

CHAPTER XXVI

The Glamour Fades

AFTER ALL, THE rosy love-making and marrying and Epithalamy are no more than the dawn of things, and to follow comes all the spacious interval of white laborious light. Try as we may to stay those delightful moments, they fade and pass remorselessly; there is no returning, no recovering, only—for the foolish—the vilest peep-shows and imitations in dens and darkened rooms. We go on—we grow. At least we age. Our young couple, emerging presently from an atmosphere of dusk and morning stars, found the sky gathering grayly overhead and saw one another for the first time clearly in the light of every-day.

It might perhaps witness better to Lewisham's refinement if one could tell only of a moderated and dignified cooling, of pathetic little concealments of disappointment and a decent maintenance of the sentimental atmosphere. And so at last daylight. But our young couple were too crude for that. The first intimations of their lack of identity have already been described, but it would be tedious and pitiful to tell of all the little intensifications, shade by shade, of the conflict of their individualities. They fell out, dear lady! they came to conflict of words. The stress of perpetual worry was upon them, of dwindling funds and the anxious search for work that would not come. And on Ethel lay long, vacant, lonely hours in dull surroundings. Differences arose from the most indifferent things; one night Lewisham lay awake in unfathomable amazement because she had convinced him she did not care a rap for the Welfare of Humanity, and deemed his Socialism a fancy and an indiscretion. And one Sunday afternoon they started for a walk under the pleasantest auspices, and returned flushed and angry, satire and retort flying free—on the score of the social conventions in Ethel's novelettes. For some inexplicable reason Lewisham saw fit to hate her novelettes very bitterly. These encounters indeed were mere skirmishes for the most part, and the silences and embarrassments that followed ended sooner or later in a "making up," tacit or definite, though once or twice this making up only re-opened the healing wound. And always each skirmish left its scar, effaced from yet another line of their lives the lingering tints of romantic color.

There came no work, no added income for either of them, saving two trifles, for five long months. Once Lewisham won twelve shillings in the prize competition of a penny weekly, and three times came infinitesimal portions of typewriting from a poet who had apparently seen the *Athenaeum* advertisement. His name was Edwin Peak Baynes and his handwriting was sprawling and unformed. He sent her several short lyrics on scraps of paper with instructions that he desired "three copies of each written beautifully in different styles" and "*not* fastened with metal fasteners but with silk thread of an appropriate color." Both of our young people were greatly exercised by these instructions. One fragment was called "Bird Song," one "Cloud Shadows," and one "Eryngium," but Lewisham thought they might be spoken of collectively as Bosh. By way of payment, this poet sent, in contravention of the postal regulations, half a sovereign stuck into a card, asking her to keep the balance against future occasions. In a little while, greatly altered copies of these lyrics were returned by the poet in person, with this enigmatical instruction written across the cover of each: "This style I like, only if possible more so."

Lewisham was out, but Ethel opened the door, so this endorsement was unnecessary. "He's really only a boy," said Ethel, describing the interview to Lewisham, who was curious. They both felt that the youthfulness of Edwin Peak Baynes detracted something from the reality of this employment.

From his marriage until the final examination in June, Lewisham's life had an odd amphibious quality. At home were Ethel and the perpetual aching pursuit of employment, the pelting irritations of Madame Gadow's persistent overcharges, and so forth, and amid such things he felt extraordinarily grown up; but intercalated with these experiences were those intervals at Kensington, scraps of his adolescence, as it were, lying amidst the new matter of his manhood, intervals during which he was simply an insubordinate and disappointing student with an increasing disposition to gossip. At South Kensington he dwelt with theories and ideals as a student should; at the little rooms in Chelsea—they grew very stuffy as the summer came on, and the accumulation of the penny novelettes Ethel favored made a litter—there was his particular private concrete situation, and ideals gave place to the real.

It was a strangely narrow world, he perceived dimly, in which his manhood opened. The only visitors were the Chafferys. Chaffery would come to share their supper, and won upon Lewisham in spite of his roguery by his incessantly entertaining monologue and by his expressed respect for and envy of Lewisham's scientific attainments. Moreover, as time went on Lewisham found himself more and more in sympathy with Chaffery's bitterness against those who order the world. It was good to hear him on bishops and that sort of people. He said what Lewisham wanted to say beautifully. Mrs. Chaffery was perpetually flitting— out of the house as Lewisham came home, a dim, black, nervous, untidy little figure. She came because Ethel, in spite of her expressed belief that love was "all in all," found married life a little dull and lonely while Lewisham was away. And she went hastily when he came, because of a certain irritability that the struggle against the world was developing. He told no one at Kensington about his marriage, at first because it was such a delicious secret and then for quite other reasons. So there was no overlapping. The two worlds began and ended sharply at the wrought-iron gates. But the day came when Lewisham passed those gates for the last time and his adolescence ended altogether.

In the final examination of the biological course, the examination that signalized the end of his income of a weekly guinea, he knew well enough that he had done badly. The evening of the last day's practical work found him belated, hot-headed, beaten, with ruffled hair and red ears. He sat to the last moment doggedly struggling to keep cool and to mount the ciliated funnel of an earthworm's nephridium. But ciliated funnels come not to those who have shirked the laboratory practice. He rose, surrendered his paper to the morose elderly young assistant demonstrator who had welcomed him so flatteringly eight months before, and walked down the laboratory to the door where the rest of his fellow-students clustered.

Smithers was talking loudly about the "twistiness" of the identification, and the youngster with the big ears was listening attentively.

"Here's Lewisham! How did *you* get on, Lewisham?" asked Smithers, not concealing his assurance.

"Horribly," said Lewisham shortly, and pushed past.

"Did you spot D?" clamored Smithers.

Lewisham pretended not to hear.

Miss Heydinger stood with her hat in her hand and looked at Lewisham's hot eyes. He was for walking past her, but something in her face penetrated even his disturbance. He stopped.

"Did you get out the nephridium?" he said as graciously as he could.

She shook her head. "Are you going downstairs?" she asked.

"Rather," said Lewisham with a vague intimation in his manner of the offense Smithers gave him.

He opened the glass door from the passage to the staircase. They went down one tier of that square spiral in silence.

"Are you coming up again next year," asked Miss Heydinger.

"No," said Lewisham. "No, I shall not come here again. Ever."

Pause. "What will you do?" she asked.

"I don't know. I have to get a living somehow. It's been bothering me all the session."

"I thought—" She stopped. "Will you go down to your uncle's again?" she said.

"No. I shall stop in London. It's no good going out of things into the country. And besides—I've quarrelled rather with my uncle."

"What do you think of doing?—teaching?"

"I suppose it will be teaching. I'm not sure. Anything that turns up."

"I see," she said.

They went on down in silence for a time.

"I suppose you will come up again?" he asked.

"I may try the botanical again—if they can find room. And, I was thinking—sometimes one hears of things. What is your address? So that if I heard of anything."

Lewisham stopped on the staircase and thought. "Of course," he said. He made no effort to give her the address, and she demanded it again at the foot of the stairs.

"That confounded nephridium—!" he said. "It has put everything out of my head."

They exchanged addresses on leaflets torn from Miss Heydinger's little note-book.

She waited at the Book in the hall while he signed his name. At the iron gates of the Schools she said: "I am going through Kensington Gardens."

He was now feeling irritated about the addresses, and he would not see the implicit invitation. "I am going towards Chelsea."

She hesitated a moment, looking at him—puzzled. "Good-bye then," she said.

"Good-bye," he answered, lifting his hat.

He crossed the Exhibition Road slowly with his packed glazed bag, now seamed with cracks, in his hand. He went thoughtfully down to the corner of the Cromwell Road and turned along that to the right so that he could see the red pile of the Science Schools rising fair and tall across the gardens of the Natural History Museum. He looked back towards it regretfully.

He was quite sure that he had failed in this last examination. He knew that any career as a scientific man was now closed to him forever. And he remembered now how he had come along this very road to that great building for the first time in his life, and all the hopes and resolves that had swelled within him as he had drawn near. That dream of incessant unswerving work! Where might he have reached if only he had had singleness of purpose to realize that purpose? . . .

And in these gardens it was that he and Smithers and Parkson had sat on a seat hard by the fossil tree and discoursed of Socialism together before the great paper was read. . . .

"Yes," he said, speaking aloud to himself, "yes—*that's* all over too. Everything's over."

Presently the corner of the Natural History Museum came between him and his receding Alma Mater. He sighed and turned his face towards the stuffy little rooms at Chelsea, and the still unconquered world.

CHAPTER XXVII

Concerning a Quarrel

IT WAS LATE in September that this particular quarrel occurred. Almost all the roseate tints seemed gone by this time, for the Lewishams had been married six months. Their financial affairs had changed from the catastrophic to the sordid; Lewisham had found work. An army crammer named Captain Vigours wanted someone energetic for his mathematical duffers and to teach geometrical drawing and what he was pleased to call "Sandhurst Science." He paid no less than two shillings an hour for his uncertain demands on Lewisham's time. Moreover, there was a class in lower mathematics beginning at Walham Green where Lewisham was to show his quality. Fifty shillings a week or more seemed credible—more might be hoped for. It was now merely a case of tiding over the interval until Vigours paid. And meanwhile the freshness of Ethel's blouses departed, and Lewisham refrained from the repair of his boot which had cracked across the toe.

The beginning of the quarrel was trivial enough. But by the end they got to generalities. Lewisham had begun the day in a bad temper and under the cloud of an overnight passage of arms—and a little incident that had nothing to do with their ostensible difference lent it a warmth of emotion quite beyond its merits. As he emerged through the folding doors he saw a letter lying among the sketchily laid breakfast things, and Ethel's attitude suggested the recoil of a quick movement; the letter suddenly dropped. Her eyes met his and she flushed. He sat down and took the letter—a trifle awkwardly perhaps. It was from Miss Heydinger. He hesitated with it half-way to his pocket, then decided to open it. It displayed an ample amount of reading, and he read. On the whole he thought it rather a dull sort of letter, but he did not allow this to appear. When it was read he put it carefully in his pocket.

That formally had nothing to do with the quarrel. The breakfast was already over when the quarrel began. Lewisham's morning was vacant, and he proposed to occupy it in the revision of certain notes bearing upon "Sandhurst Science." Unhappily the search for his note-book brought him into collision with the accumulation of Ethel's novelettes.

"These things are everywhere," he said after a gust of vehement handling. "I *wish* you'd tidy them up sometimes."

"They were tidy enough till you began to throw them about," Ethel pointed out.

"Confounded muck! it's only fit to be burnt," Lewisham remarked to the universe, and pitched one viciously into the corner.

"Well, you tried to write one, anyhow," said Ethel, recalling a certain "Mammoth" packet of note-paper that had come on an evil end before Lewisham found his industrial level. This reminiscence always irritated him exceedingly.

"Eh?" he said sharply.

"You tried to write one," repeated Ethel—a little unwillingly.

"You don't mean me to forget that."

"It's you reminded me."

He stared hostility for a space.

"Well, the things make a beastly litter anyhow, there isn't a tidy corner anywhere in the room. There never is."

"That's just the sort of thing you always say."

"Well—*is* there?"

"Yes, there is."

"*Where?*"

Ethel professed not to hear. But a devil had possession of Lewisham for a time. "It isn't as though you had anything else to do," he remarked, wounding dishonorably.

Ethel turned. "If I *put* those things away," she said with tremendous emphasis on the "*put,*" "you'd only say I'd hidden them. What *is* the good of trying to please you?"

The spirit of perversity suggested to Lewisham, "None apparently."

Ethel's cheeks glowed and her eyes were bright with unshed tears. Abruptly she abandoned the defensive and blurted out the thing that had been latent so long between them. Her voice took a note of passion. "Nothing I can do ever does please you, since that Miss Heydinger began to write to you."

There was a pause, a gap. Something like astonishment took them both. Hitherto it had been a convention that she knew nothing of the existence of Miss Heydinger. He saw a light. "How did you know?" he began, and perceived that line was impossible. He took the way of the natural man; he ejaculated an "Ugh!" of vast disgust, he raised his voice. "You *are* unreasonable!" he cried in angry remonstrance. "Fancy saying that! As though you ever tried to please me! Just as though it wasn't all the other way about!" He stopped—struck by a momentary perception of injustice. He plunged at the point he had shirked. "How did you know it *was* Miss Heydinger—?"

Ethel's voice took upon itself the quality of tears. "I wasn't *meant* to know, was I?" she said.

"But how?"

"I suppose you think it doesn't concern me? I suppose you think I'm made of stone."

"You mean—you think—?"

"Yes—I *do*."

For a brief interval Lewisham stared at the issue she had laid bare. He sought some crushing proposition, some line of convincing reasoning, with which to overwhelm and hide this new aspect of things. It would not come. He found himself fenced in on every side. A surging, irrational rage seized upon him.

"Jealousy!" he cried. "Jealousy! Just as though— Can't I have letters about things you don't understand—that you *won't* understand? If I asked you to read them you wouldn't— It's just because—"

"You never give me a *chance* to understand."

"Don't I?"

"No!"

"Why!—At first I was always trying. Socialism, religion—all those things.

But you don't care—you won't care. You won't have that I've thought over these things at all, that I care for these things! It wasn't any *good* to argue. You just care for me in a way—and all the rest of me—doesn't matter! And because I've got a friend . . ."

"Friend!"

"Yes—*friend!*"

"Why!—you hide her letters!"

"Because I tell you you wouldn't understand what they are about. But, pah! I won't argue. I *won't!* You're jealous and there's the end of the matter!"

"Well, who *wouldn't* be jealous?"

He stared at her as if he found the question hard to see. The theme was difficult—invincibly difficult. He surveyed the room for a diversion. The note-book he had disinterred from her novelettes lay upon the table and reminded him of his grievance of ruined hours. His rage exploded. He struck out abruptly towards fundamental things. He gesticulated forcibly. "This can't go on!" he cried, "this can't go on! How can I work? How can I do anything?"

He made three steps and stood in a clear space.

"I won't *stand* it—I won't go on at this! Quarrels—bickerings—discomfort. Look there! I meant to work this morning. I meant to look up notes! Instead of which you start a quarrel—"

The gross injustice raised Ethel's voice to an outcry. "*I* didn't start the quarrel—"

The only response to this was to shout, and Lewisham shouted. "You start a quarrel!" he repeated. "You make a shindy! You spring a dispute—jealousy!— on me! How can I do anything? How can one stop in a house like this? I shall go out. Look here!—I shall go out. I shall go to Kensington and work there!"

He perceived himself wordless, and Ethel was about to speak. He glared about him, seeking a prompt climax. Instant action was necessary. He perceived Huxley's *Vertebrata* upon the side-table. He clutched it, swayed it through a momentous arc, hurled it violently into the empty fireplace.

For a second he seemed to be seeking some other missile. He perceived his hat on the chest of drawers, seized it and strode tragically from the room.

He hesitated with the door half closed, then opened it wide and slammed it vehemently. Thereby the world was warned of the justice of his rage, and so he passed with credit into the street.

He went striding heedless of his direction through the streets dotted with intent people hurrying to work, and presently habit turned his feet towards the Brompton Road. The eastward trend of the morning traffic caught him. For a time, save for a rebellious ingredient of wonder at the back of his mind, he kept his anger white and pure. Why had he married her? was the text to which he clung. Why in the name of destiny had he married her? But anyhow he had said the decisive thing. He would not stand it! It must end. Things were intolerable and they must end. He meditated devastating things that he might presently say to her in pursuance of this resolution. He contemplated acts of cruelty. In such ways he would demonstrate clearly that he would not stand it. He was very careful to avoid inquiring what it was he would not stand.

How in the name of destiny had he come to marry her? The quality of his surroundings mingled in some way with the quality of his thoughts. The huge distended buildings of corrugated iron in which the Art Museum (of all places!) culminates, the truncated Oratory all askew to the street, seemed to have a similar quarrel with fate. How in the name of destiny? After such high prolusions!

He found that his thoughts had carried him past the lodge of the museum. He turned back irritably and went through the turnstile. He entered the museum and passed beneath the gallery of Old Iron on his way to the Education Library. The vacant array of tables, the bays of attendant books had a quality of refuge. . . .

So much for Lewisham in the morning. Long before midday all the vigor of his wrath was gone, all his passionate conviction of Ethel's unworthiness. Over a pile of neglected geological works he presented a face of gloom. His memory presented a picture of himself as noisy, overbearing, and unfair. What on earth had it all been about?

By two o'clock he was on his way to Vigours', and his mood was acute remorse. Of the transition there can be no telling in words, for thoughts are more subtle than words and emotions infinitely vaguer. But one thing at least is definite, that a memory returned.

It drifted in to him, through the glass roof of the Library far above. He did not perceive it as a memory at first, but as an irritating obstacle to attention. He struck the open pages of the book before him with his flat hand. "Damn that infernal hurdy-gurdy!" he whispered.

Presently he made a fretful movement and put his hands over his ears.

Then he thrust his books from him, got up, and wandered about the Library. The organ came to an abrupt end in the middle of a bar, and vanished in the circumambient silence of space.

Lewisham standing in a bay closed a book with a snap and returned to his seat.

Presently he found himself humming a languid tune, and thinking again of the quarrel that he had imagined banished from his mind. What in the name of destiny had it all been about? He had a curious sense that something had got loose, was sliding about in his mind. And as if by way of answer emerged a vision of Whortley—a singularly vivid vision. It was moonlight and a hillside, the little town lay lit and warm below, and the scene was set to music, a lugubriously sentimental air. For some reason this music had the quality of a barrel organ—though he knew that properly it came from a band—and it associated with itself a mystical formula of words, drawing words:—

> *"Sweet dreamland fa—ces passing to and fro,*
> *Bring back to mem'ry, days of long ago—oh!"*

This air not only reproduced the picture with graphic vividness, but it trailed after it an enormous cloud of irrational emotion, emotion that had but a moment before seemed gone forever from his being.

He recalled it all! He had come down that hillside and Ethel had been with him. . . .

Had he really felt like that about her?

"Pah!" he said suddenly and reverted to his books.

But the tune and the memory had won their footing, they were with him through his meager lunch of milk and scones—he had resolved at the outset he would not go back to her for the midday meal—and on his way to Vigours' they insisted on attention. It may be that lunching on scone and milk does in itself make for milder ways of thinking. A sense of extraordinary contradiction, of infinite perplexity, came to him.

"But then," he asked, "how the devil did we get to *this?*"

Which is indeed one of the fundamental questions of matrimony.

The morning tumults had given place to an almost scientific calm. Very soon he was grappling manfully with the question. There was no disputing it, they had quarrelled. Not once but several times lately they had quarrelled. It was real quarrelling;—they had stood up against one another, striking, watching to strike, seeking to wound. He tried to recall just how things had gone—what he had said and what she had replied. He could not do it. He had forgotten phrases and connections. It stood in his memory not as a sequence of events but as a collection of disconnected static sayings; each saying blunt, permanent, inconsecutive like a graven inscription. And of the scene there came only one picture—Ethel with a burning face and her eyes shining with tears.

The traffic of a cross street engaged him for a space. He emerged on the further side full of the vivid contrast of their changed relations. He made a last effort to indict her, to show that for the transition she was entirely to blame. She had quarrelled with him, she had quarrelled deliberately because she was jealous. She was jealous of Miss Heydinger because she was stupid. But now these accusations faded like smoke as he put them forth. But the picture of two little figures back there in the moonlit past did not fade. It was in the narrows of Kensington High Street that he abandoned her arraignment. It was beyond the Town Hall that he made the new step. Was it, after all, just possible that in some degree he himself rather was the chief person to blame?

It was instantly as if he had been aware of that all the time.

Once he had made that step, he moved swiftly. Not a hundred paces before the struggle was over, and he had plunged headlong into the blue abyss of remorse. And all these things that had been so dramatic and forcible, all the vivid brutal things he had said, stood no longer graven inscriptions but in letters of accusing flame. He tried to imagine he had not said them, that his memory played him a trick, tried to suppose he had said something similar perhaps but much less forcible. He attempted with almost equal futility to minimize his own wounds. His endeavor served only to measure the magnitude of his fall.

He had recovered everything now, he saw it all. He recalled Ethel, sunlit in the avenue, Ethel, white in the moonlight before they parted outside the Frobisher house, Ethel as she would come out of Lagune's house greeting him for their nightly walk, Ethel new wedded, as she came to him through the folding doors radiant in the splendor his emotions threw about her. And at last Ethel angry, dishevelled and tear-stained in that ill-lit, untidy little room. All to the cadence of a hurdy-gurdy tune! From that to this! How had it been possible to get from such an opalescent dawning to such a dismal day? What was it had gone? He and she were the same two persons who walked so brightly in his awakened memory; he and she who had lived so bitterly through the last few weeks of misery!

His mood sank for a space to the quality of groaning. He implicated her now at most as his partner in their failure—"What a mess we have made of things!" was his new motif. "What a mess!"

He knew love now for what it was, knew it for something more ancient and more imperative than reason. He knew now that he loved her, and his recent rage, his hostility, his condemnation of her seemed to him the reign of some exterior influence in his mind. He thought incredulously of the long decline in tenderness that had followed the first days of their delight in each other, the diminution of endearment, the first yielding to irritability, the evenings he had spent doggedly working, resisting all his sense of her presence. "One cannot always be love-making," he had said, and so—they were slipping apart. Then in countless little things he had not been patient, he had not been fair. He had wounded her by harshness, by unsympathetic criticism, above all by his absurd secrecy about Miss Heydinger's letters. Why on earth had he kept those letters from her? as though there was something to hide! What was there to hide? What possible antagonism could there be? Yet it was by such little things that their love was now like some once valued possession that had been in brutal hands, it was scratched and chipped and tarnished, it was on its way to being altogether destroyed. Her manner had changed towards him, a gulf was opening that he might never be able to close again.

"No, it *shall* not be!" he said, "it shall not be!"

But how to get back to the old footing? how to efface the things he had said, the things that had been done?

Could they get back?

For a moment he faced a new possibility. Suppose they could not get back! Suppose the mischief was done! Suppose that when he slammed the door behind him it locked, and was locked against him forever!

"But we *must!*" said Lewisham, "we must!"

He perceived clearly that this was no business of reasoned apologies. He must begin again, he must get back to emotion, he must thrust back the overwhelming pressure of every-day stresses and necessities that was crushing all the warmth and color from their lives. But how? How?

He must make love to her again. But how to begin—how to mark the change? There had been making-up before, sullen concessions and treaties. But this was different. He tried to imagine something he might say, some appeal that he might make. Everything he thought of was cold and hard, or pitiful and undignified, or theatrical and foolish. Suppose the door *was* closed! If already it was too late! In every direction he was confronted by the bristling memories of harsh things. He had a glimpse of how he must have changed in her eyes, and things became intolerable for him. For now he was assured he loved her still with all his heart.

And suddenly came a florist's window, and in the center of it a glorious heap of roses.

They caught his eye before they caught his mind. He saw white roses, virginal white, roses of cream and pink and crimson, the tints of flesh and pearl, rich, a mass of scented color, visible odors, and in the midst of them a note of sullen red. It was as it were the very color of his emotion. He stopped abruptly. He turned back to the window and stared frankly. It was gorgeous, he saw, but why so particularly did it appeal to him?

Then he perceived as though it was altogether self-evident what he had to do. This was what he wanted. This was the note he had to strike. Among other things because it would repudiate the accursed worship of pinching self-restraint that was one of the incessant stresses between them. They would come to her with a pure unexpectedness, they would flame upon her.

Then, after the roses, he would return.

Suddenly the gray trouble passed from his mind; he saw the world full of color again. He saw the scene he desired bright and clear, saw Ethel no longer bitter and weeping, but glad as once she had always seemed glad. His heart-beats quickened. It was giving had been needed, and he would give.

Some weak voice of indiscreet discretion squeaked and vanished. He had, he knew, a sovereign in his pocket. He went in.

He found himself in front of a formidable young lady in black, and unprepared with any formula. He had never bought flowers before. He looked about him for an inspiration. He pointed at the roses. "I want those roses," he said. . . .

He emerged again with only a few small silver coins remaining out of the sovereign he had changed. The roses were to go to Ethel, properly packed; they were to be delivered according to his express direction at six o'clock.

"Six o'clock," Lewisham had reiterated very earnestly.

"We quite understand," the young lady in black had said, and had pretended to be unable to conceal a smile. "We're *quite* accustomed to sending out flowers."

CHAPTER XXVIII

The Coming of the Roses

AND THE ROSES miscarried!

When Lewisham returned from Vigours' it was already nearly seven. He entered the house with a beating heart. He had expected to find Ethel excited, the roses displayed. But her face was white and jaded. He was so surprised by this that the greeting upon his lips died away. He was balked! He went into the sitting-room and there were no roses to be seen. Ethel came past him and stood with her back to him looking out of the window. The suspense was suddenly painful. . . .

He was obliged to ask, though he was certain of the answer, "Has nothing come?"

Ethel looked at him. "What did you think had come?"

"Oh! nothing."

She looked out of the window again. "No," she said slowly, "nothing has come."

He tried to think of something to say that might bridge the distance between them, but he could think of nothing. He must wait until the roses came. He took out his books and a gaunt hour passed to supper time. Supper was a chilly ceremonial set with necessary over-polite remarks. Disappointment and exasperation darkened Lewisham's soul. He began to feel angry with everything—even with her—he perceived she still judged him angry and that made him angry with her. He was resuming his books and she was helping Madam Gadow's servant to clear away, when they heard a rapping at the street door. "They have come at last," he said to himself brightening, and hesitated whether he should bolt or witness her reception of them. The servant was a nuisance. Then he heard Chaffery's voice, and whispered a soft "damn!" to himself.

The only thing to do now if the roses came was to slip out into the passage, intercept them and carry them into the bedroom by the door between that and the passage. It would be undesirable for Chaffery to witness that phase of sentiment. He might flash some dart of ridicule that would stick in their memory forever.

Lewisham tried to show that he did not want a visitor. But Chaffery was in high spirits and could have warmed a dozen cold welcomes. He sat down without any express invitation in the chair that he preferred.

Before Mr. and Mrs. Chaffery the Lewishams veiled whatever trouble might be between them beneath an insincere cordiality, and Chaffery was soon talking freely, unsuspicious of their crisis. He produced two cigars. "I had a wild moment," he said. 'For once,' said I, 'the honest shall smoke the admirable—or the admirable shall smoke the honest,' whichever you like best. Try one? No? Those austere principles of yours! There will be more pleasure then. But really, I would as soon you smoked it as I. For tonight I radiate benevolence."

He cut the cigar with care, he lit it with ceremony, waiting until nothing but honest wood was burning on the match, and for fully a minute he was silent, evolving huge puffs of smoke. And then he spoke again, punctuating his words by varied and beautiful spirals. "So far," he said, "I have only trifled with knavery."

As Lewisham said nothing he resumed after a pause.

"There are three sorts of men in the world, my boy, three and no more—and of women only one. There are happy men and there are knaves and fools. Hybrids I don't count. And to my mind knaves and fools are very much alike."

He paused again.

"I suppose they are," said Lewisham flatly, and frowned at the fireplace.

Chaffery eyed him. "I am talking wisdom. Tonight I am talking a particular brand of wisdom. I am broaching some of my oldest and finest, because—as you will find one day—this is a special occasion. And you are distrait!"

Lewisham looked up. "Birthday?" he said.

"You will see. But I was making golden observations about knaves and fools. I was early convinced of the absolute necessity of righteousness if a man is to be happy. I know it as surely as there is a sun in the heavens. Does that surprise you?"

"Well, it hardly squares—"

"No. I know. I will explain all that. But let me tell you the happy life. Let me give you that, as if I lay on my deathbed and this was a parting gift. In the first place, mental integrity. Prove all things, hold fast to that which is right. Let the world have no illusions for you, no surprises. Nature is full of cruel catastrophies, man is a physically degenerate ape, every appetite, every instinct, needs the curb; salvation is not in the nature of things but whatever salvation there may be is in the nature of man; face all these painful things. I hope you follow that?"

"Go on," said Lewisham, with the debating-society taste for a thesis prevailing for a minute over that matter of the roses.

"In youth, exercise and learning; in adolescence, ambition, and in early manhood, love—no footlight passion." Chaffery was very solemn and insistent, with a lean extended finger, upon this point.

"Then marriage, young and decent, and then children and stout honest work for them, work too for the State in which they live; a life of self-devotion, indeed, and for sunset a decent pride—that is the happy life. Rest assured that is the happy life; the life Natural Selection has been shaping for man since life began. So a man may go happy from the cradle to the grave—at least—passably happy. And to do this needs just three things—a sound body, a sound intelligence, and a sound will . . . A sound will."

Chaffery paused on the repetition.

"No other happiness endures. And when all men are wise, all men will seek that life. Fame! Wealth! Art!—the Red Indians worship lunatics, and we are still by way of respecting the milder sorts. But I say that all men who do not lead that happy life are knaves and fools. The physical cripple, you know, poor devil, I count a sort of bodily fool."

"Yes," weighed Lewisham, "I suppose he is."

"Now a fool fails of happiness because of his insufficient mind, he miscalculates, he stumbles and hobbles, some cant or claptrap whirls him away; he gets passion out of a book and a wife out of the stews, or he quarrels on a petty score; threats frighten him, vanity beguiles him, he fails by blindness. But the knave who is not a fool fails against the light. Many knaves are fools also—*most* are—but some are not. I know—I am a knave but no fool. The essence of your knave is that he lacks the will, the motive capacity to seek his own greater good. The knave abhors persistence. Strait is the way and narrow the gate; the knave cannot keep to it and the fool cannot find it.''

Lewisham lost something of what Chaffery was saying by reason of a rap outside. He rose, but Ethel was before him. He concealed his anxiety as well as he could, and was relieved when he heard the front door close again and her footsteps pass into the bedroom by the passage door. He reverted to Chaffery.

"Has it ever occurred to you," asked Chaffery, apparently apropos of nothing, "that intellectual conviction is no motive at all? Any more than a railway map will run a train a mile.''

"Eh?" said Lewisham. "Map—run a train a mile—of course, yes. No, it won't.''

"That is precisely my case," said Chaffery. "That is the case of your pure knave everywhere. We are not fools—because we know. But yonder runs the highway, windy, hard and austere, a sort of dry happiness that will endure; and here is the pleasant by-way—lush, my boy, lush, as the poets have it, and with its certain man-trap among the flowers . . .''

Ethel returned through the folding doors. She glanced at Lewisham, remained standing for awhile, sat down in the basket chair as if to resume some domestic needlework that lay upon the table, then rose and went back into the bedroom.

Chaffery proceeded to expatiate on the transitory nature of passion and all glorious and acute experiences. Whole passages of that discourse Lewisham did not hear, so intent was he upon those roses. Why had Ethel gone back into the bedroom? Was it possible—? Presently she returned, but she sat down so that he could not see her face.

"If there is one thing to set against the wholesome life it is adventure," Chaffery was saying. "But let every adventurer pray for an early death, for with adventure come wounds, and with wounds come sickness, and—except in romances—sickness affects the nervous system. Your nerve goes. Where are you then, my boy?''

"Ssh! what's that?" said Lewisham.

It was a rap at the house door. Heedless of the flow of golden wisdom, he went out at once and admitted a gentleman friend of Madam Gadow, who passed along the passage and vanished down the staircase. When he returned Chaffery was standing to go.

"I could have talked with you longer," he said, "but you have something on your mind, I see. I will not worry you by guessing what. Some day you will remember . . .'' He said no more but laid his hand on Lewisham's shoulder.

One might almost fancy he was offended at something.

At any other time Lewisham might have been propitiatory, but now he offered no apology. Chaffery turned to Ethel and looked at her curiously for a moment. "Good-bye," he said, holding out his hand to her.

On the doorstep Chaffery regarded Lewisham with the same curious look, and seemed to weigh some remark. "Good-bye," he said at last with something in his manner that kept Lewisham at the door for a moment looking after his stepfather's receding figure. But immediately the roses were uppermost again.

When he re-entered the living room he found Ethel sitting idly at her typewriter, playing with the keys. She got up at his return and sat down in the armchair with a novelette that hid her face. He stared at her, full of questions. After all, then, they had not come. He was intensely disappointed now, he was intensely angry with the ineffable young shop-woman in black. He looked at his watch and then again, he took a book and pretended to read and found himself composing a scathing speech of remonstrance to be delivered on the morrow at the flower-shop. He put his book down, went to his black bag, opened and closed it aimlessly. He glanced covertly at Ethel and found her looking covertly at him. He could not quite understand her expression.

He fidgeted into the bedroom and stopped as dead as a pointer.

He felt an extraordinary persuasion of the scent of roses. So strong did it seem that he glanced outside the room door, expecting to find a box there, mysteriously arrived. But there was no scent of roses in the passage.

Then he saw close by his foot an enigmatical pale object, and stooping, picked up the creamy petal of a rose. He stood with it in his hand, perplexed beyond measure. He perceived a slight disorder of the valence of the dressing-table and linked it with this petal by a swift intuition.

He made two steps, lifted the valence, and behold! there lay his roses crushed together!

He gasped like a man who plunges suddenly into cold water. He remained stooping with the valence raised.

Ethel appeared in the half doorway and her expression was unfamiliar. He stared at her white face.

"Why on earth did you put my roses here?" he asked.

She stared back at him. Her face reflected his astonishment.

"Why did you put my roses here?" he asked again.

"Your roses!" she cried. "What! Did *you* send those roses?"

CHAPTER XXIX

Thorns and Rose Petals

HE REMAINED STOOPING and staring up at her, realizing the implication of her words only very slowly.

Then it grew clear to him.

As she saw understanding dawning in his face, she uttered a cry of consternation. She came forward and sat down upon the little bedroom chair. She turned to him and began a sentence. "I," she said and stopped, with an impatient gesture of her hands.*"Oh!"*

He straightened himself and stood regarding her. The basket of roses lay overturned between them.

"You thought these came from someone else?" he said, trying to grasp this inversion of the universe.

She turned her eyes. "I did not know," she panted. "A trap. . . . Was it likely—they came from you?"

"You thought they came from someone else," he said.

"Yes," she said, "I did."

"Who?"

"Mr. Baynes."

"That boy!"

"Yes—that boy."

"Well!"

Lewisham looked about him—a man in the presence of the inconceivable.

"You mean to say you have been carrying on with that youngster behind my back?" he asked.

She opened her lips to speak and had no words to say.

His pallor increased until every tinge of color had left his face. He laughed and then set his teeth. Husband and wife looked at one another.

"I never dreamt," he said in even tones.

He sat down on the bed, thrusting his feet among the scattered roses with a sort of grim satisfaction. "I never dreamt," he repeated, and the flimsy basket kicked by his swinging foot hopped indignantly through the folding doors into the living-room and left a trail of blood-red petals.

They sat for perhaps two minutes and when he spoke again his voice was hoarse. He reverted to a former formula. "Look here," he said, and cleared his throat. "I don't know whether you think I'm going to stand this, but I'm not."

He looked at her. She sat staring in front of her, making no attempt to cope with disaster.

"When I say I'm not going to stand it," explained Lewisham, "I don't mean having a row or anything of that sort. One can quarrel and be disappointed over— other things—and still go on. But this is a different thing altogether.

"Of all dreams and illusions! . . . Think what I have lost in this accursed marriage. And *now* . . . You don't understand—you won't understand."

"Nor you," said Ethel, weeping but neither looking at him nor moving her hands from her lap where they lay helplessly. "*You* don't understand."

"I'm beginning to."

He sat in silence gathering force. "In one year," he said, "all my hopes, all my ambitions have gone. I know I have been cross and irritable—I know that. I've been pulled two ways. But . . . I bought you these roses."

She looked at the roses, and then at his white face, made an imperceptible movement towards him, and became impassive again.

"I do think one thing. I have found out you are shallow, you don't think, you can't feel things that I think and feel. I have been getting over that. But I did think you were loyal—"

"I *am* loyal," she cried.

"And you think—Bah!—you poke my roses under the table!"

Another portentous silence. Ethel stirred and he turned his eyes to watch what she was about to do. She produced her handkerchief and began to wipe her dry eyes rapidly, first one and then the other. Then she began sobbing. "I'm . . . as loyal as you . . . anyhow," she said.

For a moment Lewisham was aghast. Then he perceived he must ignore that argument.

"I would have stood it—I would have stood anything if you had been loyal— if I could have been sure of you. I am a fool, I know, but I would have stood the interruption of my work, the loss of any hope of a Career, if I had been sure you were loyal. I . . . I cared for you a great deal."

He stopped. He had suddenly perceived the pathetic. He took refuge in anger.

"And you have deceived me! How long, how much, I don't care. You have deceived me. And I tell you"—he began to gesticulate—"I'm not so much your slave and fool as to stand that! No woman shall make me *that* sort of fool, whatever else— so far as I am concerned, this ends things. This ends things. We are married—but I don't care if we were married five hundred times. I won't stop with a woman who takes flowers from another man—"

"I *didn't*," said Ethel.

Lewisham gave way to a transport of anger. He caught up a handful of roses and extended them, trembling. "What's *this?*" he asked. His finger bled from a thorn, as once it had bled from a blackthorn spray.

"I *didn't* take them," said Ethel. "I couldn't help it if they were sent."

"Ugh!" said Lewisham. "But what is the good of argument and denial? You took them in, you had them. You may have been cunning, but you have given yourself away. And our life and all this"—he waved an inclusive hand at Madam Gadow's furniture—"is at an end."

He looked at her and repeated with bitter satisfaction, "At an end."

She glanced at his face and his expression was remorseless. "I will not go on living with you," he said, lest there should be any mistake. "Our life is at an end."

Her eyes went from his face to the scattered roses. She remained staring at these. She was no longer weeping, and her face, save about the eyes, was white.

He presented it in another form. "I shall go away.

"We never ought to have married," he reflected. "But . . . I never expected *this!*"

"I didn't know," she cried out, lifting up her voice. "I *didn't* know. How could *I* help! *Oh!*"

She stopped and stared at him with hands clenched, her eyes haggard with despair.

Lewisham remained impenetrably malignant.

"I don't *want* to know," he said, answering her dumb appeal. "That settles everything. *That!*" He indicated the scattered flowers. "What does it matter to me what has happened or hasn't happened? Anyhow—oh! I don't mind. I'm glad. See? It settles things.

"The sooner we part the better. I shan't stop with you another night. I shall take my box and my portmanteau into that room and pack. I shall stop in there tonight, sleep in a chair or *think*. And tomorrow I shall settle up with Madam Gadow and go. You can go back . . . to your cheating."

He stopped for some seconds. She was deadly still. "You wanted to, and now you may. You wanted to, before I got work. You remember? You know your place is still open at Lagune's. I don't care. I tell you I don't care *that*. Not that! You may go your own way—and I shall go mine. See? And all this rot—this sham of living together when neither cares for the other—I don't care for you *now*, you know, so you needn't think it—will be over and done with. As for marriage—I don't care *that* for marriage—it can't make a sham and a blunder anything but a sham.

"It's a sham, and shams have to end, and that's the end of the matter."

He stood up resolutely. He kicked the scattered roses out of his way and dived beneath the bed for his portmanteau. Ethel neither spoke nor moved, but remained watching his movements. For a time the portmanteau refused to emerge, and he marred his stern resolution by a half audible "Come here—damn you!" He swung it into the living room and returned for his box. He proposed to pack in that room.

When he had taken all his personal possessions out of the bedroom, he closed the folding doors with an air of finality. He knew from the sounds that followed that she flung herself upon the bed, and that filled him with grim satisfaction.

He stood listening for a space, then set about packing methodically. The first rage of discovery had abated, he knew quite clearly that he was inflicting grievous punishment and that gratified him. There was also indeed a curious pleasure in the determination of a long and painful period of vague misunderstanding by this unexpected crisis. He was acutely conscious of the silence on the other side of the folding doors, he kept up a succession of deliberate little noises, beat books together and brushed clothes, to intimate the resolute prosecution of his preparations.

That was about nine o'clock. At eleven he was still busy. . . .

Darkness came suddenly upon him. It was Madam Gadow's economical habit to turn off all her gas at that hour unless she chanced to be entertaining friends.

He felt in his pocket for matches and he had none. He whispered curses. Against such emergencies he had bought a brass lamp and in the bedroom there were candles. Ethel had a candle alight, he could see the bright yellow line that appeared between the folding doors. He felt his way presently towards the mantel, receiving a blow in the ribs from a chair on the way, and went carefully amidst Madam Gadow's once amusing ornaments.

There were no matches on the mantel. Going to the chest of drawers he almost fell over his open portmanteau. He had a silent ecstacy of rage. Then he kicked against the basket in which the roses had come. He could find no matches on the chest of drawers.

Ethel must have the matches in the bedroom, but that was absolutely impossible. He might even have to ask her for them, for at times she pocketed matches . . . There was nothing for it but to stop packing. Not a sound came from the other room.

He decided he would sit down in the armchair and go to sleep. He crept very carefully to the chair and sat down. Another interval of listening and he closed his eyes and composed himself for slumber.

He began to think over his plans for the morrow. He imagined the scene with Madam Gadow, and then his departure to find bachelor lodgings once more. He debated in what direction he should go to get suitable lodgings. Possible difficulties with his luggage, possible annoyances of the search loomed gigantic. He felt greatly irritated at these minor difficulties. He wondered if Ethel also was packing. What particularly would she do? He listened but he could hear nothing. She was very still. She was really very still! What could she be doing? He forgot the bothers of the morrow in this new interest. Presently he rose very softly and listened. Then he sat down again impatiently. He tried to dismiss his curiosity about the silence by recapitulating the story of his wrongs.

He had some difficulty in fixing his mind upon this theme, but presently his memories were flowing freely. Only it was not wrongs now that he could recall. He was pestered by an absurd idea that he had again behaved unjustly to Ethel, that he had been headlong and malignant. He made strenuous efforts to recover his first heat of jealousy—in vain. Her remark that she had been as loyal as he, became an obstinate headline in his mind. Something arose within him that insisted upon Ethel's possible fate if he should leave her. What particularly would she do? He knew how much her character leaned upon his. Good Heavens! What might she not do?

By an effort he succeeded in fixing his mind on Baynes. That helped him back to the harsher footing. However hard things might be for her she deserved them. She deserved them!

Yet presently he slipped again, slipped back to the remorse and regrets of the morning time. He clutched at Baynes as a drowning man clutches at a rope, and recovered himself. For a time he meditated on Baynes. He had never seen the poet, so his imagination had scope. It appeared to him as an exasperating obstacle to a tragic avenging of his honor that Baynes was a mere boy—possibly even younger than himself.

The question, "What will become of Ethel?" rose to the surface again. He struggled against its possibilities. No! That was not it! That was her affair.

He felt inexorably kept to the path he had chosen, for all the waning of his rage. He had put his hand to the plough. "If you condone this," he told himself, "you might condone anything. There are things one *must* not stand." He tried to keep to that point of view,—assuming for the most part out of his imagination what it was he was not standing. A dim sense came to him of how much he was assuming. At any rate she must have flirted! . . . He resisted this reviving perception of justice as though it was some unspeakably disgraceful craving. He tried to imagine her with Baynes.

He determined he would go to sleep.

But his was a waking weariness. He tried counting. He tried to distract his thoughts from her by going over the atomic weights of the elements. . . .

He shivered, and realized that he was cold and sitting cramped on an uncomfortable horsehair chair. He had dozed. He glanced for the yellow line between the folding doors. It was still there but it seemed to quiver. He judged the candle must be flaring. He wondered why everything was so still.

Now why should he suddenly feel afraid.

He sat for a long time trying to hear some movement, his head craning forward in the darkness. . . .

A grotesque idea came into his head that all that had happened a very long time ago. He dismissed that. He contested an unreasonable persuasion that some irrevocable thing had passed. But why was everything so still?

He was invaded by a prevision of unendurable calamity.

Presently he rose and crept very slowly and with infinite precautions against noise, towards the folding doors. He stood listening with his ear near the yellow chink.

He could hear nothing, not even the measured breathing of a sleeper.

He perceived that the doors were not shut but slightly ajar. He pushed against the inner one very gently and opened it silently. Still there was no sound of Ethel. He opened the door still wider and peered into the room. The candle had burned down and was flaring in its socket. Ethel was lying half undressed upon the bed, and in her hand and close to her face was a rose.

He stood watching her, fearing to move. He listened hard and his face was very white. Even now he could not hear her breathing.

After all, it was probably all right. She was just asleep. He would slip back before she woke. If she found him—

He looked at her again. There was something in her face—

He came nearer, no longer heeding the sounds he made. He bent over her. Even now she did not seem to breathe.

He saw that her eyelashes were still wet, the pillow by her cheek was wet. Her white, tear-stained face hurt him. . . .

She was intolerably pitiful to him. He forgot everything but that and how he had wounded her that day. And then she stirred and murmured indistinctly a foolish name she had given him.

He forgot that they were going to part forever. He felt nothing but a great joy that she could stir and speak. His jealousy flashed out of being. He dropped upon his knees.

"Dear," he whispered. "Is it all right? I . . . I could not hear you breathing. I could not hear you breathing."

She started and was awake.

"I was in the other room," said Lewisham in a voice full of emotion. "Everything was so quiet. I was afraid—I did not know what had happened. Dear—Ethel dear. Is it all right?"

She sat up quickly and scrutinized his face. "Oh! let me tell you," she wailed.

"Do let me tell you. It's nothing. It's nothing. You wouldn't hear me. You wouldn't hear me. It wasn't fair—before you had heard me. . . ."

His arms tightened about her. "Dear," he said, "I knew it was nothing. I knew. I knew."

She spoke in sobbing sentences. "It was so simple. Mr. Baynes . . . something in his manner . . . I knew he might be silly . . . Only I did so want to help you." She paused. Just for one instant she saw one untellable indiscretion as it were in a lightning flash. A chance meeting it was, a "silly" thing or so said, a panic, retreat. She would have told it—had she known how. But she could not do it. She hesitated. She abolished it—untold. She went on: "And then, I thought he had sent the roses and I was frightened. . . . I was frightened."

"Dear one," said Lewisham. "Dear one! I have been cruel to you. I have been unjust. I understand. I do understand. Forgive me. Dearest—forgive me."

"I did so want to do something for you. It was all I could do—that little money. And then you were angry. I thought you didn't love me any more because I did not understand your work. . . . And that Miss Heydinger—Oh! it was hard."

"Dear one," said Lewisham, "I do not care your little finger for Miss Heydinger."

"I know how I hamper you. But if you will help me. Oh! I would work, I would study. I would do all I could to understand."

"Dear," whispered Lewisham. "*Dear.*"

"And to have *her*—"

"Dear," he vowed, "I have been a brute. I will end all that. I will end all that."

He took her suddenly into his arms and kissed her.

"Oh, I *know* I'm stupid," she said.

"You're not. It's I have been stupid. I have been unkind, unreasonable. All today— . . . I've been thinking about it. Dear! I don't care for anything—. It's *you*. If I have you nothing else matters. . . . Only I get hurried and cross. It's the work and being poor. Dear one, we *must* hold to each other. All today.— It's been dreadful . . ."

He stopped. They sat clinging to one another.

"I do love you," she said presently with her arms about him. "Oh! I do—*do*—love you."

He drew her closer to him.

He kissed her neck. She pressed him to her.

Their lips met.

The expiring candle streamed up into a tall flame, flickered, and was suddenly extinguished. The air was heavy with the scent of roses.

CHAPTER XXX

A Withdrawal

ON TUESDAY LEWISHAM returned from Vigours' at five—at half-past six he would go on to his science class at Walham Green—and discovered Mrs. Chaffery and Ethel in tears. He was fagged and rather anxious for some tea, but the news they had for him drove tea out of his head altogether.

"He's gone," said Ethel.

"Who's gone? What! Not Chaffery?"

Mrs. Chaffery, with a keen eye to Lewisham's behavior, nodded tearfully over an experienced handkerchief.

Lewisham grasped the essentials of the situation forthwith, and trembled on the brink of an expletive. Ethel handed him a letter.

For a moment Lewisham held this in his hand asking questions. Mrs. Chaffery had come upon it in the case of her eight-day clock when the time to wind it came round. Chaffery, it seemed, had not been home since Saturday night. The letter was an open one addressed to Lewisham, a long rambling would-be clever letter, oddly inferior in style to Chaffery's conversation. It had been written some hours before Chaffery's last visit; his talk then had been perhaps a sort of codicil.

"The inordinate stupidity of that man Lagune is driving me out of the country," Lewisham saw. "It has been at last a definite stumbling block—even a legal stumbling block, I fear. I am off. I skedaddle. I break ties. I shall miss our long refreshing chats—you had found me out and I could open my mind. I am sorry to part from Ethel also, but thank Heaven she has you to look to! And indeed they both have you to look to, though the 'both' may be a new light to you."

Lewisham growled, went from page 1 to page 3—conscious of their both looking to him now—even intensely—and discovered Chaffery in a practical vein.

"There is but little light and portable property in that house in Clapham that has escaped my lamentable improvidence, but there are one or two things; the iron-bound chest, the bureau with a broken hinge, and the large air pump, distinctly pawnable if only you can contrive to get them to a pawnshop. You have more Will power than I—I never could get the confounded things downstairs. That iron-bound box was originally mine, before I married your mother-in-law, so that I am not altogether regardless of your welfare and the necessity of giving some equivalent. Don't judge me too harshly."

Lewisham turned over sharply without finishing that page.

"My life at Clapham," continued the letter, "has irked me for some time, and to tell you the truth, the spectacle of your vigorous young happiness—you are having a very good time, you know, fighting the world—reminded me of the passing years. To be frank in self-criticism, there is more than a touch of the New Woman about me, and I feel I have still to live my own life. What a beautiful phrase that is—to live one's own life!—redolent of honest scorn for moral plagiarism. No *Imitatio Christi* in that. . . . I long to see more of men and cities. . . . I begin late, I know, to live my own life, bald as I am and gray-whiskered; but better late than never. Why should the educated girl have the monopoly of the game? And after all, the whiskers will dye. . . .

"There are things—I touch upon them lightly—that will presently astonish Lagune." Lewisham became more attentive. "I marvel at that man, grubbing hungry for marvels amidst the almost incredibly marvellous. What can be the nature of a man who gapes after Poltergeists with the miracle of his own silly existence (inconsequent, reasonless, unfathomably weird) nearer to him than breathing and closer than hands and feet. What is *he* for, that he should wonder at Poltergeists? I am astonished these by no means flimsy psychic phenomena do not turn upon their investigators, and that a Research Society of eminent illusions and hallucinations does not pursue Lagune with skeptical inquiries. Take his house—expose the alleged man of Chelsea! *A priori* they might argue that a thing so vain, so unmeaning, so strongly beset by cackle, could only be the diseased imagining of some hysterical phantom. Do *you* believe that such a thing as Lagune exists? I must own to the gravest doubts. But happily his banker is of a more credulous type than I. . . . Of all that Lagune will tell you soon enough.''

Lewisham read no more. ''I suppose he thought himself clever when he wrote that rot,'' said Lewisham bitterly, throwing the sheets forcibly athwart the table. ''The simple fact is, he's stolen, or forged, or something—and bolted.''

There was a pause. ''What will become of Mother?'' said Ethel.

Lewisham looked at Mother and thought for a moment. Then he glanced at Ethel.

''We're all in the same boat,'' said Lewisham.

''I don't want to give any trouble to a single human being,'' said Mrs. Chaffery.

''I think you might get a man his tea, Ethel,'' said Lewisham sitting down suddenly, ''anyhow.'' He drummed on the table with his fingers. ''I have to get to Walham Green by a quarter to seven.''

''We're all in the same boat,'' he repeated after an interval, and continued drumming. He was chiefly occupied by the curious fact that they were all in the same boat. What an extraordinary faculty he had for acquiring responsibility! He looked up suddenly and caught Mrs. Chaffery's tearful eye directed to Ethel and full of distressful interrogation, and his perplexity was suddenly changed to pity. ''It's all right, Mother,'' he said. ''I'm not going to be unreasonable. I'll stand by you.''

''Ah!'' said Mrs. Chaffery. ''As if I didn't know!'' and Ethel came and kissed him.

He seemed in imminent danger of universal embraces.

''I wish you'd let me have my tea,'' he said. And while he had his tea he asked Mrs. Chaffery questions and tried to get the new situation into focus.

But even at ten o'clock when he was returning hot and jaded from Walham Green he was still trying to get the situation into focus. There were vague ends and blank walls of interrogation in the matter, that perplexed him.

He knew that his supper would be only the prelude to an interminable ''talking over,'' and indeed he did not get to bed until nearly two. By that time a course of action was already agreed upon. Mrs. Chaffery was tied to the house in Clapham by a long lease and thither they must go. The ground floor and first floor were let unfurnished, and the rent of these practically paid the rent of the house. The Chafferys occupied basement and second floor. There was a bedroom on the second floor formerly let to the first floor tenants, that he and Ethel could occupy, and in this an old toilet table could be put for such studies as were to be prosecuted at home. Ethel could have her typewriter in the subterranean breakfast-room. Mrs. Chaffery and Ethel must do the catering and the bulk of the housework, and as soon as possible, since letting lodgings would not square with Lewisham's professional pride, they must get rid of the lease that bound them and take some smaller and more suburban residence. If they did that without leaving any address it might save their feelings from any return of the prodigal Chaffery.

Mrs. Chaffery's frequent and pathetic acknowledgments of Lewisham's goodness only partly relieved his disposition to a philosophical bitterness. And the practical issues were complicated by excursions upon the subject of Chaffery, what he might have done, and where he might have gone, and whether by any chance he might not return.

When at last Mrs. Chaffery, after a violent and tearful kissing and blessing of them both—they were ''good dear children'' she said—had departed, Mr. and Mrs. Lewisham returned into their sitting-room. Mrs. Lewisham's little face was enthusiastic. "You're a Trump," she said, extending the willing arms that were his reward. "I know," she said, "I know, and all tonight I have been loving you. Dear! Dear! Dear. . . ."

The next day Lewisham was too full of engagements to communicate with Lagune, but the following morning he called and found the psychic investigator busy with the proofs of *Hesperus*. He welcomed the young man cordially nevertheless, conceiving him charged with the questions that had been promised long ago—it was evident he knew nothing of Lewisham's marriage. Lewisham stated his case with some bluntness.

"He was last here on Saturday," said Lagune. "You have always been inclined to suspicion about him. Have you any grounds?"

"You'd better read this," said Lewisham, repressing a grim smile, and he handed Lagune Chaffery's letter.

He glanced at the little man ever and again to see if he had come to the personal portion and for the rest of the time occupied himself with an envious inventory of the writing appointments about him. No doubt the boy with the big ears had had the same sort of thing . . .

When Lagune came to the question of his real identity he blew out his cheeks in the most astonishing way but made no other sign.

"Dear, dear!" he said at last. "My bankers!"

He looked at Lewisham with the exaggerated mildness of his spectacled eye. "What do you think it means?" he asked. "Has he gone mad? We have been conducting some experiments involving—considerable mental strain. He and I and a lady. Hypnotic—"

"I should look at my cheque-book if I were you."

Lagune produced some keys and got out his cheque-book. He turned over the counterfoils. "There's nothing wrong here," he said, and handed the book to Lewisham.

"Um," said Lewisham. "I suppose this— I say, is *this* right?"

He handed back the book to Lagune, open at the blank counterfoil of a cheque that had been removed. Lagune stared and passed his hand over his forehead in a confused way. "I can't see this," he said.

Lewisham had never heard of post hypnotic suggestion and he stood incredulous. "You can't see that?" he said. "What nonsense!"

"I can't see it," repeated Lagune.

For some seconds Lewisham could not get away from stupid repetitions of his inquiry. Then he hit upon a collateral proof. "But look here! Can you see *this* counterfoil?"

"Plainly," said Lagune.

"Can you read the number?"

"Five thousand two hundred and seventy-nine."

"Well, and this?"

"Five thousand two hundred and eighty-one."

"Well—where's five thousand two hundred and eighty?"

Lagune began to look uncomfortable. "Surely," he said, "he has not— Will you read it out—the cheque, the counterfoil I mean, that I am unable to see."

"It's blank," said Lewisham with an irresistible grin.

"Surely," said Lagune, and the discomfort of his expression deepened. "Do you mind if I call in a servant to confirm—?"

Lewisham did not mind, and the same girl who had admitted him to the *séance* appeared. When she had given her evidence she went again. As she left the room by the door behind Lagune her eyes met Lewisham's, and she lifted her eyebrows, depressed her mouth and glanced at Lagune with a meaning expression.

"I'm afraid," said Lagune, "that I have been shabbily treated. Mr. Chaffery is a man of indisputable powers—indisputable powers; but I am afraid—I am very much afraid he has abused the conditions of the experiment. All this—and his insults—touch me rather nearly."

He paused. Lewisham rose. "Do you mind if you come again?" asked Lagune with gentle politeness.

Lewisham was surprised to find himself sorry.

"He was a man of extraordinary gifts," said Lagune. "I had come to rely upon him. . . . My cash balance has been rather heavy lately. How he came to know of that I am unable to say. Without supposing, that is, that he had very remarkable gifts."

When Lewisham saw Lagune again he learned the particulars of Chaffery's misdeed and the additional fact that the "lady" had also disappeared. "That's a good job," he remarked selfishly. "There's no chance of *his* coming back." He spent a moment trying to imagine the "lady"; he realized more vividly than he had ever done before the narrow range of his experience, the bounds of his imagination. These people also—with gray hair and truncated honor—had their emotions! Even it may be glowing! He came back to facts. Chaffery had induced Lagune when hypnotized to sign a blank cheque as an "autograph." "The strange thing is," explained Lagune, "it's doubtful if he's legally accountable. The law is so peculiar about hypnotism, and I certainly signed the cheque, you know."

The little man, in spite of his losses, was now almost cheerful again on account of a curious side issue. "You may say it is coincidence," he said, "you may call it a fluke, but I prefer to look for some other interpretation. Consider this. The amount of my balance is a secret between me and my bankers. He never had it from *me,* for I did not know it—I hadn't looked at my pass-book for months. But he drew it all in one cheque, within seventeen and sixpence of the total. And the total was over five hundred pounds!"

He seemed quite bright again as he culminated.

"Within seventeen and sixpence," he said. "Now how do you account for that, eh? Give me a materialistic explanation that will explain away all that. You can't. Neither can I."

"I think I can," said Lewisham.

"Well—what is it?"

Lewisham nodded towards a little drawer of the bureau. "Don't you think—perhaps"—a little ripple of laughter passed across his mind—"he had a skeleton key?"

Lagune's face lingered amusingly in Lewisham's mind as he returned to Clapham. But after a time that amusement passed away. He declined upon the extraordinary fact that Chaffery was his father-in-law, Mrs. Chaffery his mother-in-law, that these two and Ethel constituted his family, his clan, and that grimy graceless house up the Clapham hillside was to be his home. Home! His connection with these things as a point of worldly departure was as inexorable now as though he had been born to it. And a year ago, except for a fading reminiscence of Ethel, none of these people had existed for him. The ways of Destiny! The happenings of the last few months, foreshortened in perspective, seemed to have almost a pantomimic rapidity. The thing took him suddenly as being laughable; and he laughed.

His laugh marked an epoch. Never before had Lewisham laughed at any fix in which he had found himself. The enormous seriousness of adolescence was coming to an end; the days of his growing were numbered. It was a laugh of infinite admissions.

CHAPTER XXXI

In Battersea Park

NOW ALTHOUGH LEWISHAM had promised to bring things to a conclusion with Miss Heydinger, he did nothing in the matter for five weeks, he merely left that crucial letter of hers unanswered. In that time their removal from Madam Gadow's into the gaunt house at Clapham was accomplished—not without polyglot controversy—and the young couple settled themselves into the little room on the second floor even as they had arranged. And there it was that suddenly the world was changed—was astonishingly transfigured—by a whisper.

It was a whisper between sobs and tears, with Ethel's arms about him and Ethel's hair streaming down so that it hid her face from him. And he too had whispered, dismayed perhaps a little, and yet feeling a strange pride, a strange novel emotion, feeling altogether different from the things he had fancied he might feel when this thing that he had dreaded should come. Suddenly he perceived finality, the advent of the solution, the reconciliation of the conflict that had been waged so long. Hesitations were at an end;—he took his line.

Next day he wrote a note and two mornings later he started for his mathematical duffers an hour before it was absolutely necessary, and instead of going directly to Vigours', went over the bridge to Battersea Park. There waiting for him by a seat where once they had met before, he found Miss Heydinger pacing. They walked up and down side by side, speaking for a little while about indifferent topics, and then they came upon a pause . . .

"You have something to tell me?" said Miss Heydinger abruptly.

Lewisham changed color a little. "Oh yes," he said, "the fact is—." He affected ease. "Did I ever tell you I was married?"

"*Married?*"

"Yes."

"Married!"

"Yes," a little testily.

For a moment neither spoke. Lewisham stood without dignity staring at the dahlias of the London County Council, and Miss Heydinger stood regarding him.

"And that is what you have to tell me?"

Mr. Lewisham turned and met her eyes. "Yes!" he said. "That is what I have to tell you."

Pause. "Do you mind if I sit down," asked Miss Heydinger in an indifferent tone.

"There is a seat yonder," said Lewisham, "under the tree."

They walked to the seat in silence.

"Now," said Miss Heydinger, quietly. "Tell me whom you have married."

Lewisham answered sketchily. She asked him another question and another. He felt stupid and answered with a halting truthfulness.

"I might have known," she said, "I might have known. Only I would not know. Tell me some more. Tell me about her."

Lewisham did. The whole thing was abominably disagreeable to him, but it had to be done, he had promised Ethel it should be done. Presently Miss Heydinger had to be done, he had promised Ethel it should be done. Presently Miss Heydinger knew the main outline of his story, knew all his story except the emotion that made it credible. "And you were married—before the second examination?" she repeated.

"Yes," said Lewisham.

"But why did you not tell me of this before?" asked Miss Heydinger.

"I don't know," said Lewisham. "I wanted to—that day, in Kensington Gardens. But I didn't. I suppose I ought to have done so."

"I think you ought to have done so."

"Yes, I suppose I ought . . . But I didn't. Somehow—it has been hard. I didn't know what you would say. The thing seemed so rash, you know, and all that."

He paused blankly.

"I suppose you had to do it," said Miss Heydinger presently, with her eyes on his profile.

Lewisham began the second and more difficult part of his explanation. "There's been a difficulty," he said, "all the way along—I mean—about you, that is. It's a little difficult—. The fact is, my wife, you know—. She looks at things differently from what we do."

"We?"

"Yes—it's odd, of course. But she has seen your letters—"

"You didn't show her—?"

"No. But, I mean, she knows you write to me, and she knows you write about Socialism and Literature and—things we have in common—things she hasn't."

"You mean to say she doesn't understand these things?"

"She's not thought about them. I suppose there's a sort of difference in education—"

"And she objects—?"

"No," said Lewisham, lying promptly. "She doesn't *object* . . ."

"Well?" said Miss Heydinger, and her face was white.

"She feels that—. She feels—she does not say, of course, but I know she feels that it is something she ought to share. I know—how she cares for me. And it shames her—it reminds her—. Don't you see how it hurts her?"

"Yes. I see. So that even that little—." Miss Heydinger's breath seemed to catch and she was abruptly silent.

She spoke at last with an effort. "That it hurts *me*," she said, and grimaced and stopped again.

"No," said Lewisham, "that is not it." He hesitated. "I *knew* this would hurt you."

"You love her. You can sacrifice—"

"No. It is not that. But there is a difference. Hurting *her*—she would not understand. But you—somehow it seems a natural thing for me to come to you. I seem to look to you—. For her I am always making allowances—"

"You love her."

"I wonder if it *is* that makes the difference. Things are so complex. Love means anything—or nothing. I know you better than I do her, you know me better than she will ever do. I could tell you things I could not tell her. I could put all myself before you—almost—and know you would understand—. Only—"

"You love her."

"Yes," said Lewisham lamely and pulling at his moustache. "I suppose . . . that must be it."

For a space neither spoke. Then Miss Heydinger said *"Oh!"* with extraordinary emphasis.

"To think of this end to it all! That all your promise . . . What is it she gives that I could not have given?

"Even now! Why should I give up that much of you that is mine? If she could take it— But she cannot take it. If I let you go—you will do nothing. All this ambition, all these interests will dwindle and die, and she will not mind. She will not understand. She will think that she still has you. Why should she covet what she cannot possess? Why should she be given the thing that is mine—to throw aside?"

She did not look at Lewisham, but before her, her face a white misery.

"In a way—I had come to think of you as something belonging to me . . . I shall—still."

"There is one thing," said Lewisham after a pause, "it is a thing that has come to me once or twice lately. Don't you think that perhaps you over-estimate the things I might have done? I know we've talked of great things to do. But I've been struggling for half a year and more to get the sort of living almost anyone seems able to get. It has taken me all my time. One can't help thinking after that, perhaps the world is a stiffer sort of affair . . ."

"No," she said decisively. "You could have done great things.

"Even now," she said, "you may do great things—. If only I might see you sometimes, write to you sometimes—. You are so capable and—weak. You must have somebody—. That is your weakness. You fail in your belief. You must have support and belief—unstinted support and belief. Why could I not be that to you? It is all I want to be. At least—all I want to be now. Why need she know? It robs her of nothing. I want nothing—she has. But I know of my own strength too I can do nothing. I know that with you . . . It is only knowing hurts her. Why should she know?"

Mr. Lewisham looked at her doubtfully. That phantom greatness of his, it was that lit her eyes. In that instant at least he had no doubts of the possibility of his Career. But he knew that in some way the secret of his greatness and this admiration went together. Conceivably they were one and indivisible. Why indeed need Ethel know? His imagination ran over the things that might be done, the things that might happen, and touched swiftly upon complication, confusion, discovery.

"The thing is, I must simplify my life. I shall do nothing unless I simplify my life. Only people who are well off can be—complex. It is one thing or the other—"

He hesitated and suddenly had a vision of Ethel weeping as once he had seen her weep with the light on the tears in her eyes.

"No," he said almost brutally. "No. It's like this—. I can't do anything underhand. I mean—. I'm not so amazingly honest—now. But I've not that sort of mind. She would find me out. It would do no good and she would find me out. My life's too complex. I can't manage it and go straight. I—you've overrated me. And besides—. Things have happened. Something—." He hesitated and then snatched at his resolve. "I've got to simplify—and that's the plain fact of the case. I'm sorry, but it is so."

Miss Heydinger made no answer. Her silence astonished him. For nearly twenty seconds perhaps they sat without speaking. With a quick motion she stood up and at once he stood up before her. Her face was flushed, her eyes downcast.

"Good-bye," she said suddenly in a low tone and held out her hand.

"But," said Lewisham and stopped. Miss Heydinger's color left her.

"Good-bye," she said, looking him suddenly in the eyes and smiling awry. "There is no more to say, is there? Good-bye."

He took her hand. "I hope I didn't—"

"Good-bye," she said impatiently, and suddenly disengaged her hand and turned away from him. He made a step after her.

"Miss Heydinger," he said, but she did not stop. "Miss Heydinger." He realized that she did not want to answer him again. . . .

He remained motionless, watching her retreating figure. An extraordinary sense of loss came into his mind, a vague impulse to pursue her and pour out vague passionate protestations. . . .

Not once did she look back. She was already remote when he began hurrying after her. Once he was in motion he quickened his pace and gained upon her. He was within thirty yards of her as she drew near the gates.

His pace slackened. Suddenly he was afraid she might look back. She passed out of the gates, out of his sight. He stopped, looking where she had disappeared. He sighed and took the pathway to his left that led back to the bridge and Vigours.

Halfway across this bridge came another crisis of indecision. He stopped, hesitating. An impertinent thought obtruded. He looked at his watch and saw that he must hurry if he would catch the train for Earl's Court and Vigours. He said Vigours might go to the devil.

But in the end he caught his train.

CHAPTER XXXII

The Crowning Victory

THAT NIGHT ABOUT seven Ethel came into their room with a waste-paper basket she had bought for him, and found him sitting at the little toilet table at which he was to "write." The outlook was, for a London outlook, spacious, down a long slope of roofs towards the Junction, a huge sky of blue passing upward to the darkling zenith and downward into a hazy bristling mystery of roofs and chimneys, from which emerged signal lights and steam puffs, gliding chains of lit window carriages and the vague vistas of streets. She showed him the basket and put it beside him, and then her eye caught the yellow document in his hand. "What is that you have there?"

He held it out to her, "I found it—lining my yellow box. I had it at Whortley."

She took it and perceived a chronological scheme. It was headed "SCHEMA," there were memoranda in the margin, and all the dates had been altered by a hasty hand.

"Hasn't it got yellow?" she said.

That seemed to him the wrong thing for her to say. He stared at the document with a sudden accession of sympathy. There was an interval. He became aware of her hand upon his shoulder, that she was bending over him. "Dear," she whispered, with a strange change in the quality of her voice. He knew she was seeking to say something that was difficult to say.

"Yes?" he said presently.

"You are not grieving?"

"What about?"

"*This.*"

"No!"

"You are not—you are not even sorry?" she said.

"No—not even sorry."

"I can't understand that. It's so much—"

"I'm glad," he proclaimed. "*Glad*."

"But—the trouble—the expense—everything—and your work?"

"Yes," he said, "that's just it."

She looked at him doubtfully. He glanced up at her, and she questioned his eyes. He put his arm about her, and presently and almost absent-mindedly she obeyed his pressure and bent down and kissed him.

"It settles things," he said holding her. "It joins us. Don't you see? Before . . . But now it's different. It's something we have between us. It's something that . . . It's the link we needed. It will hold us together, cement us together. It will be our life. This will be my work now. The other . . ."

He faced a truth. "It was just . . . vanity!"

There was still a shade of doubt in her face, a wistfulness.

Presently she spoke.

"Dear," she said.

"Yes?"

She knitted her brows. "No!" she said. "I can't say it."

In the interval she came into a sitting position on his knees.

He kissed her hand, but her face remained grave, and she looked out upon the twilight. "I know I'm stupid," she said. "The things I say . . . aren't the things I feel."

He waited for her to say more.

"It's no good," she said.

He felt the onus of expression lay on him. He too found it a little difficult to put into words. "I think I understand," he said, and wrestled with the impalpable. The pause seemed long and yet not altogether vacant. She lapsed abruptly into the prosaic. She started from him.

"If I don't go down, Mother will get supper . . ."

At the door she stopped and turned a twilight face to him. For a moment they scrutinized one another. To her he was no more than a dim outline. Impulsively he held out his arms. . . .

Then at the sound of a movement downstairs she freed herself and hurried out. He heard her call "Mother! You're not to lay supper. You're to rest."

He listened to her footsteps until the kitchen had swallowed them up. Then he turned his eyes to the Schema again and for a moment it seemed but a little thing.

He picked it up in both hands and looked at it as if it was the writing of another man, and indeed it was the writing of another man. "Pamphlets in the Liberal Interest," he read, and smiled.

Presently a train of thought carried him off. His attitude relaxed a little, the Schema became for a time a mere symbol, a point of departure, and he stared out of the window at the darkling night. For a long time he sat pursuing thoughts that were half emotions, emotions that took upon themselves the shape and substance of ideas. The deepening current stirred at last among the roots of speech.

"Yes, it was vanity," he said. "A boy's vanity. For me—anyhow. I'm too two-sided . . . Two-sided? . . . Commonplace!

"Dreams like mine—abilities like mine. Yes—any man! And yet . . .—The things I meant to do!"

His thoughts went to his Socialism, to his red-hot ambition of world mending. He marveled at the vistas he had discovered since those days.

"Not for us— Not for us.

"We must perish in the wilderness.—Some day. Somewhen. But not for us. . . .

"Come to think, it is all the Child. The future is the Child. The Future. What are we—any of us—but servants or traitors to that? . . .

"Natural Selection—it follows . . . this way is happiness . . . must be. There can be no other."

He sighed. "To last a lifetime, that is.

"And yet—it is almost as if Life had played me a trick—promised so much—given so little! . . .

"No! One must not look at it in that way! That will not do! That will *not* do.

"Career! In itself it is a career—the most important career in the world. Father! Why should I want more?

"And . . . Ethel! No wonder she seemed shallow . . . She has been shallow. No wonder she was restless. Unfulfilled . . . What had she to do? She was drudge, she was toy . . .

"Yes. This is life. This alone is life! For this we were made and born. All these other things—all other things—they are only a sort of play . . .

"Play!"

His eyes came back to the Schema. His hands shifted to the opposite corner and he hesitated. The vision of that arranged Career, that ordered sequence of work and successes, distinctions and yet further distinctions, rose brightly from the symbol. Then he compressed his lips and tore the yellow sheet in half, tearing very deliberately. He doubled the halves and tore again, doubled again very carefully and neatly until the Schema was torn into numberless little pieces. With it he seemed to be tearing his past self.

"Play," he whispered after a long silence.

"It is the end of adolescence," he said, "the end of empty dreams. . . ."

He became very still, his hands resting on the table, his eyes staring out of the blue oblong of the window. The dwindling light gathered itself together and became a star.

He found he was still holding the torn fragments. He stretched out his hand and dropped them into that new waste paper basket Ethel had bought for him.

Two pieces fell outside the basket. He stooped, picked them up and put them carefully with their fellows.

SHORT STORIES

THE PLATTNER STORY

WHETHER THE STORY of Gottfried Plattner is to be credited or not, is a pretty question in the value of evidence. On the one hand, we have seven witnesses—to be perfectly exact, we have six and a half pairs of eyes, and one undeniable fact; and on the other we have—what is it?—prejudice, common sense, the inertia of opinion. Never were there seven more honest-seeming witnesses; never was there a more undeniable fact than the inversion of Gottfried Plattner's anatomical structure, and—never was there a more preposterous story than the one they have to tell! The most preposterous part of the story is the worthy Gottfried's contribution (for I count him as one of the seven). Heaven forbid that I should be led into giving countenance to superstition by a passion for impartiality, and so come to share the fate of Eusapia's patrons! Frankly, I believe there is something crooked about this business of Gottfried Plattner; but what that crooked factor is, I will admit as frankly, I do not know. I have been surprised at the credit accorded to the story in the most unexpected and authoritative quarters. The fairest way to the reader, however, will be for me to tell it without further comment.

Gottfried Plattner is, in spite of his name, a free-born Englishman. His father was an Alsatian who came to England in the Sixties, married a respectable English girl of unexceptionable antecedents, and died, after a wholesome and uneventful life (devoted, I understand, chiefly to the laying of parquet flooring), in 1887. Gottfried's age is seven-and-twenty. He is, by virtue of his heritage of three languages, Modern Languages Master in a small private school in the South of England. To the casual observer he is singularly like any other Modern Languages Master in any other small private school. His costume is neither very costly nor very fashionable, but, on the other hand, it is not markedly cheap or shabby; his complexion, like his height and his bearing, is inconspicuous. You would notice perhaps that, like the majority of people, his face was not absolutely symmetrical, his right eye a little larger than the left, and his jaw a trifle heavier on the right side. If you, as an ordinary careless person, were to bare his chest and feel his heart beating, you would probably find it quite like the heart of anyone else. But here you and the trained observer would part company. If you found his heart quite ordinary, the trained observer would find it quite otherwise. And once the thing was pointed out to you, you too would perceive the peculiarity easily enough. It is that Gottfried's heart beats on the right side of his body.

Now that is not the only singularity of Gottfried's structure, although it is the only one that would appeal to the untrained mind. Careful sounding of Gottfried's internal arrangements, by a well-known surgeon, seems to point to the fact that all the other unsymmetrical parts of his body are similarly misplaced. The right lobe of his liver is on the left side, the left on his right; while his lungs, too, are similarly contraposed. What is still more singular, unless Gottfried is a consummate actor we must believe that his right hand has recently become his left. Since the occurrences we are about to consider (as impartially as possible), he has found the utmost difficulty in writing except from right to left across the paper with his left hand. He cannot throw with his right hand, he is perplexed at meal times between knife and fork, and his ideas of the rule of the road—he is a cyclist—are still a dangerous confusion. And there is not a scrap of evidence to show that before these occurrences Gottfried was at all left-handed.

There is yet another wonderful fact in this preposterous business. Gottfried produces three photographs of himself. You have him at the age of five or six, thrusting fat legs at you from under a plaid frock, and scowling. In that photograph his left eye is a little larger than his right, and his jaw is a trifle heavier on the left side. This is the reverse of his present living conditions. The photograph of Gottfried at fourteen seems to contradict these facts, but that is because it is one of those cheap "Gem" photographs that were then in vogue, taken direct upon metal, and therefore reversing things just as a looking-glass would. The third photograph represents him at one-and-twenty, and confirms the record of the others. There seems here evidence of the strongest confirmatory character that Gottfried has exchanged his left side for his right. Yet how a human being can be so changed, short of a fantastic and pointless miracle, it is exceedingly hard to suggest.

In one way, of course, these facts might be explicable on the supposition that Plattner has undertaken an elaborate mystification on the strength of his heart's displacement. Photographs may be fudged, and left-handedness imitated. But the character of the man does not lend itself to any such theory. He is quiet, practical, unobtrusive, and thoroughly sane from the Nordau standpoint. He likes beer and smokes moderately, takes walking exercise daily, and has a healthily high estimate of the value of his teaching. He has a good but untrained tenor voice, and takes a pleasure in singing airs of a popular and cheerful character. He is fond, but not morbidly fond, of reading—chiefly fiction pervaded with a vaguely pious optimism,—sleeps well, and rarely dreams. He is, in fact, the very last person to evolve a fantastic fable. Indeed, so far from forcing this story upon the world, he has been singularly reticent on the matter. He meets inquirers with a certain engaging—bashfulness is almost the word, that disarms the most suspicious. He seems genuinely ashamed that anything so unusual has occurred to him.

It is to be regretted that Plattner's aversion to the idea of post-mortem dissection may postpone, perhaps forever, the positive proof that his entire body has had its left and right sides transposed. Upon that fact mainly the credibility of his story hangs. There is no way of taking a man and moving him about *in space,* as ordinary people understand space, that will result in our changing his sides. Whatever you do, his right is still his right, his left his left. You can do that with a perfectly thin and flat thing, of course. If you were to cut a figure out of paper, any figure with a right and left side, you could change its sides simply by lifting it up and turning it over. But with a solid it is different. Mathematical theorists tell us that the only way in which the right and left sides of a solid body can be changed is by taking that body clean out of space as we know it,— taking it out of ordinary existence, that is, and turning it somewhere outside space. This is a little abstruse, no doubt, but anyone with a slight knowledge of mathematical theory will assure the reader of its truth. To put the thing in technical language, the curious inversion of Plattner's right and left sides is proof that he has moved out of our space into what is called the Fourth Dimension, and that he has returned again to our world. Unless we choose to consider ourselves the victims of an elaborate and motiveless fabrication, we are almost bound to believe that this has occurred.

So much for the tangible facts. We come now to the account of the phenomena that attended his temporary disappearance from the world. It appears that in the Sussexville Proprietary School, Plattner not only discharged the duties of Modern Languages Master, but also taught chemistry, commercial geography, bookkeeping, shorthand, drawing, and any other additional subject to which the changing fancies of the boy's parents might direct attention. He knew little or nothing of these various subjects, but in secondary as distinguished from Board or elementary schools, knowledge in the teacher is, very properly, by no means so necessary as high moral character and gentlemanly tone. In chemistry he was particularly deficient, knowing, he says, nothing beyond the Three Gases (whatever the three gases may be). As, however, his pupils began by knowing nothing, and derived all their information from him, this caused him (or anyone) but little inconvenience for several terms. Then a little boy named Whibble joined the school, who had been educated, it seems, by some mischievous relative into an inquiring habit of mind. This little boy followed Plattner's lessons with marked and sustained interest, and in order to exhibit his zeal on the subject, brought at various times substances for Plattner to analyze. Plattner, flattered by this evidence of his power to awaken interest and trusting to the boy's ignorance, analyzed these and even made general statements as to their composition. Indeed he was so far stimulated by his pupil as to obtain a work upon analytical chemistry, and study it during his supervision of the evening's preparation. He was surprised to find chemistry quite an interesting subject.

So far the story is absolutely commonplace. But now the greenish powder comes upon the scene. The source of that greenish powder seems, unfortunately, lost. Master Whibble tells a tortuous story of finding it done up in a packet in a disused limekiln near the Downs. It would have been an excellent thing for Plattner, and possibly for Master Whibble's family, if a match could have been applied to that powder there and then. The young gentleman certainly did not bring it to school in a packet, but in a common eight-ounce graduated medicine bottle, plugged with masticated newspaper. He gave it to Plattner at the end of the afternoon school. Four boys had been detained after school prayers in order to complete some neglected tasks, and Plattner was supervising these in the small classroom in which the chemical teaching was conducted. The appliances for the practical teaching of chemistry in the Sussexville Proprietary School, as in most private schools in this country, are characterized by a severe simplicity. They are kept in a cupboard standing in a recess and having about the same capacity as a common traveling trunk. Plattner, being bored with his passive superintendence, seems to have welcomed the intervention of Whibble with his green powder as an agreeable diversion, and, unlocking this cupboard, proceeded at once with his analytical experiments. Whibble sat, luckily for himself, at a safe distance, regarding him. The four malefactors, feigning a profound absorption in their work, watched him furtively with the keenest interest. For even within the limits of the Three Gases, Plattner's practical chemistry was, I understand, temerarious.

They are practically unanimous in their account of Plattner's proceedings. He poured a little of the green powder into a test-tube, and tried the substance with water, hydrochloric acid, nitric acid, and sulphuric acid in succession. Getting no result, he emptied out a little heap—nearly half the bottleful, in fact—upon a slate and tried a match. He held the medicine bottle in his left hand. The stuff began to smoke and melt, and then—exploded with deafening violence and a blinding flash.

The five boys, seeing the flash and being prepared for catastrophes, ducked below their desks, and were none of them seriously hurt. The window was blown out into the playground, and the blackboard on its easel was upset. The slate was smashed to atoms. Some plaster fell from the ceiling. No other damage was done to the school edifice or appliances, and the boys at first, seeing nothing of Plattner, fancied he was knocked down and lying out of their sight below the desks. They jumped out of their places to go to his assistance, and were amazed to find the space empty. Being still confused by the sudden violence of the report, they hurried to the open door, under the impression that he must have been hurt, and have rushed out of the room. But Carson, the foremost, nearly collided in the doorway with the principal, Mr. Lidgett.

Mr. Lidgett is a corpulent, excitable man with one eye. The boys describe him as stumbling into the room mouthing some of those tempered expletives irritable schoolmasters accustom themselves to use—lest worse befall. "Wretched mumchancer!" he said. "Where's Mr. Plattner?" The boys are ageed on the very words ("Wobbler," "snivelling puppy," and "mumchancer" are, it seems, among the ordinary small change of Mr. Lidgett's scholastic commerce.)

Where's Mr. Plattner? That was a question that was to be repeated many times in the next few days. It really seemed as though that frantic hyperbole, "blown to atoms," had for once realized itself. There was not a visible particle of Plattner to be seen; not a drop of blood nor a stitch of clothing to be found. Apparently he had been blown clean out of existence and left not a wrack behind. Not so much as would cover a sixpenny piece, to quote a proverbial expression! The evidence of his absolute disappearance, as a consequence of that explosion, is indubitable.

It is not necessary to enlarge here upon the commotion excited in the Sussexville Proprietary School, and in Sussexville and elsewhere, by this event. It is quite possible, indeed, that some of the readers of these pages may recall the hearing of some remote and dying version of that excitement during the last summer holidays. Lidgett, it would seem, did everything in his power to supress and minimize the story. He instituted a penalty of twenty-five lines for any mention of Plattner's name among the boys, and stated in the schoolroom that he was clearly aware of his assistant's whereabouts. He was afraid, he explains, that the possibility of an explosion happening, in spite of the elaborate precautions taken to minimize the practical teaching of chemistry, might injure the reputation of the school; and so might any mysterious quality in Plattner's departure. Indeed, he did everything in his power to make the occurrence seem as ordinary as possible. In particular, he cross-examined the five eye-witnesses of the occurrence so searchingly that they began to doubt the plain evidence of their senses. But, in spite of these efforts, the tale, in a magnified and distorted state, made a nine days' wonder in the district, and several parents withdrew their sons on colorable pretexts. Not the least remarkable point in the matter is the fact that a large number of people in the neighborhood dreamed singularly vivid dreams of Plattner during the period of excitement before his return, and that these dreams had a curious uniformity. In almost all of them Plattner was seen, sometimes singly, sometimes in company, wandering about through a coruscating iridescence. In all cases his face was pale and distressed, and in some he gesticulated towards the dreamer. One or two of the boys, evidently under the influence of nightmare, fancied that Plattner approached them with remarkable swiftness, and seemed to look closely into their very eyes. Others fled with Plattner from the pursuit of vague and extraordinary creatures of a globular shape. But all these fancies were forgotten in inquiries and speculations when, on the Wednesday next but one after the Monday of the explosion, Plattner returned.

The circumstances of his return were as singular as those of his departure. So far as Mr. Lidgett's somewhat choleric outline can be filled in from Plattner's hesitating statements, it would appear that on Wednesday evening, towards the hour of sunset, the former gentleman, having dismissed evening preparation, was engaged in his garden, picking and eating strawberries, a fruit of which he is inordinately fond. It is a large old-fashioned garden, secured from observation, fortunately, by a high and ivy-covered red-brick wall. Just as he was stooping over a particularly prolific plant, there was a flash in the air and a heavy thud, and before he could look round, some heavy body struck him violently from behind. He was pitched forward, crushing the strawberries he held in his hand, and with such force that his silk hat—Mr. Lidgett adheres to the older ideas of scholastic costume—was driven violently down upon his forehead, and almost over one eye. This heavy missile, which slid over him sideways and collapsed into a sitting posture among the strawberry plants, proved to be our long-lost Mr. Gottfried Plattner, in an extremely dishevelled condition. He was collarless and hatless, his linen was dirty, and there was blood upon his hands. Mr. Lidgett was so indignant and surprised that he remained on all-fours, and with his hat jammed down on his eye, while he expostulated vehemently with Plattner for his disrespectful and unaccountable conduct.

This scarcely idyllic scene completes what I may call the exterior version of the Plattner story—its exoteric aspect. It is quite unnecessary to enter here into all the details of his dismissal by Mr. Lidgett. Such details, with the full names and dates and references, will be found in the larger report of these occurrences that was laid before the Society for the Investigation of Abnormal Phenomena. The singular transposition of Plattner's right and left sides was scarcely observed for the first day or so, and then first in connection with his disposition to write from right to left across the blackboard. He concealed rather than ostended this curious confirmatory circumstance, as he considered it would unfavorably affect his prospects in a new situation. The displacement of his heart was discovered some months after, when he was having a tooth extracted under anesthetics. He then, very unwillingly, allowed a cursory surgical examination to be made of himself, with a view to a brief account in the *Journal of Anatomy*. That exhausts the statement of the material facts; and we may now go on to consider Plattner's account of the matter.

But first let us clearly differentiate between the preceding portion of this story and what is to follow. All I have told thus far is established by such evidence as even a criminal lawyer would approve. Every one of the witnesses is still alive; the reader, if he have the leisure, may hunt the lads out tomorrow or even brave the terrors of the redoubtable Lidgett, and cross-examine and trap and test to his heart's content; Gottfried Plattner, himself, and his twisted heart and his three photographs are producible. It may be taken as proved that he did disappear for nine days as the consequence of an explosion; that he returned almost as violently, under circumstances in their nature annoying to Mr. Lidgett, whatever the details of those circumstances may be; and that he returned inverted, just as a reflection returns from a mirror. From the last fact, as I have already stated, it follows almost inevitably that Plattner, during those nine days, must have been in some state of existence altogether out of space. The evidence to these statements is, indeed, far stronger than that upon which most murderers are hanged. But for his own particular account of where he had been, with its confused explanations and well-nigh self-contradictory details, we have only Mr. Gottfried Plattner's word. I do not wish to discredit that, but I must point out—what so many writers upon obscure psychic phenomena fail to do—that we are passing here from the practically undeniable to that kind of matter which any reasonable man is entitled to believe or reject as he thinks proper. The previous statements render it plausible; its discordance with common experience tilts it towards the incredible. I would prefer not to sway the beam of the reader's judgment either way, but simply to tell the story as Plattner told it me.

He gave me his narrative, I may state, at my house at Chislehurst; and so soon as he had left me that evening, I went into my study and wrote down everything as I remembered it. Subsequently he was good enough to read over a type-written copy, so that its substantial correctness is undeniable.

He states that at the moment of the explosion he distinctly thought he was killed. He felt lifted off his feet and driven forcibly backward. It is a curious fact for psychologists that he thought clearly during his backward flight, and wondered whether he should hit the chemistry cupboard or the blackboard easel. His heels struck ground, and he staggered and fell heavily into a sitting position on something soft and firm. For a moment the concussion stunned him. He became aware at once of a vivid scent of singed hair, and he seemed to hear the voice of Lidgett asking for him. You will understand that for a time his mind was greatly confused.

At first he was distinctly under the impression that he was still in the classroom. He perceived quite distinctly the surprise of the boys and the entry of Mr. Lidgett. He is quite positive upon that score. He did not hear their remarks, but that he ascribed to the deafening effect of the experiment. Things about him seemed curiously dark and faint, but his mind explained that on the obvious but mistaken idea that the explosion had engendered a huge volume of dark smoke. Through the dimness the figures of Lidgett and the boys moved, as faint and silent as ghosts. Plattner's face still tingled with the stinging heat of the flash. He was, he says, "all muddled." His first definite thoughts seem to have been of his personal safety. He thought he was perhaps blinded and deafened. He felt his limbs and face in a gingerly manner. Then his perceptions grew clearer, and he was astonished to miss the old familiar desks and other schoolroom furniture about him. Only dim, uncertain, gray shapes stood in the place of these. Then came a thing that made him shout aloud, and awoke his stunned faculties to instant activity. *Two of the boys, gesticulating, walked one after the other clean through him!* Neither manifested the slightest consciousness of his presence. It is difficult to imagine the sensation he felt. They came against him, he says, with no more force than a wisp of mist.

Plattner's first thought after that was that he was dead. Having been brought up with thoroughly sound views in these matters, however, he was a little surprised to find his body still about him. His second conclusion was that he was not dead, but that the others were: that the explosion had destroyed the Sussexville Proprietary School and every soul in it except himself. But that, too, was scarcely satisfactory. He was thrown back upon astonished observation.

Everything about him was extraordinarily dark: at first it seemed to have an altogether ebony blackness. Overhead was a black firmament. The only touch of light in the scene was a faint greenish glow at the edge of the sky in one direction, which threw into prominence a horizon of undulating black hills. This, I say, was his impression at first. As his eye grew accustomed to the darkness, he began to distinguish a faint quality of differentiating greenish color in the circumambient night. Against this background the furniture and occupants of the classroom, it seems, stood out like phosphorescent spectres, faint and impalpable. He extended his hand, and thrust it without an effort through the wall of the room by the fireplace.

He describes himself as making a strenuous effort to attract attention. He shouted to Lidgett, and tried to seize the boys as they went to and fro. He only desisted from these attempts when Mrs. Lidgett, whom he as an Assistant Master naturally disliked, entered the room. He says the sensation of being in the world, and yet not a part of it, was an extraordinarily disagreeable one. He compared his feelings not inaptly to those of a cat watching a mouse through a window. Whenever he made a motion to communicate with the dim, familiar world about him, he found an invisible, incomprehensible barrier preventing intercourse.

He then turned his attention to his solid environment. He found the medicine bottle still unbroken in his hand, with the remainder of the green powder therein. He put this in his pocket, and began to feel about him. Apparently, he was sitting on a boulder of rock covered with a velvety moss. The dark country about him he was unable to see, the faint, misty picture of the schoolroom blotting it out, but he had a feeling (due perhaps to a cold wind) that he was near the crest of a hill, and that a steep valley fell away beneath his feet. The green glow along the edge of the sky seemed to be growing in extent and intensity. He stood up, rubbing his eyes.

It would seem that he made a few steps, going steeply downhill, and then stumbled, nearly fell, and sat down again upon a jagged mass of rock to watch the dawn. He became aware that the world about him was absolutely silent. It was as still as it was dark, and though there was a cold wind blowing up the hill-face, the rustle of grass, the soughing of the boughs that should have accompanied it, were absent. He could hear, therefore, if he could not see, that the hillside upon which he stood was rocky and desolate. The green grew brighter every moment, and as it did so a faint, transparent blood-red mingled with, but did not mitigate, the blackness of the sky overhead and the rocky desolations about him. Having regard to what follows, I am inclined to think that that redness may have been an optical effect due to contrast. Something black fluttered momentarily against the livid yellow-green of the lower sky, and then the thin and penetrating voice of a bell rose out of the black gulf below him. An oppressive expectation grew with the growing light.

It is probable that an hour or more elapsed while he sat there, the strange green light growing brighter every moment, and spreading slowly, in flamboyant fingers, upward towards the zenith. As it grew, the spectral vision of *our* world became relatively or absolutely fainter. Probably both, for the time must have been about that of our earthly sunset. So far as his vision of our world went, Plattner by his few steps downhill, had passed through the floor of the classroom, and was now, it seemed, sitting in mid-air in the larger schoolroom downstairs. He saw the boarders distinctly, but much more faintly than he had seen Lidgett. They were preparing their evening tasks, and he noticed with interest that several were cheating with their Euclid riders by means of a crib, a compilation whose existence he had hitherto never suspected. As the time passed they faded steadily, as steadily as the light of the green dawn increased.

Looking down into the valley, he saw that the light had crept far down its rocky sides, and that the profound blackness of the abyss was now broken by a minute green glow, like the light of a glow-worm. And almost immediately the limb of a huge heavenly body of blazing green rose over the basaltic undulations of the distant hills, and the monstrous hill-masses about him came out gaunt and desolate, in green light and deep, ruddy black shadows. He became aware of a vast number of ball-shaped objects drifting as thistledown drifts over the high ground. There were none of these nearer to him than the opposite side of the gorge. The bell below twanged quicker and quicker, with something like impatient insistence, and several lights moved hither and thither. The boys at work at their desks were now almost imperceptibly faint.

This extinction of our world, when the green sun of this other universe rose, is a curious point upon which Plattner insists. During the Other-World night it is difficult to move about, on account of the vividness with which the things of this world are visible. It becomes a riddle to explain why, if this is the case, we in this world catch no glimpse of the Other-World. It is due, perhaps, to the comparatively vivid illumination of this world of ours. Plattner describes the midday of the Other-World, at its brightest, as not being nearly so bright as this world at full moon, while its night is profoundly black. Consequently, the amount of light, even in an ordinary dark room, is sufficient to render the things of the Other-World invisible, on the same principle that faint phosphorescence is only visible in the profoundest darkness. I have tried, since he told me his story, to see something of the Other-World by sitting for a long space in a photographer's dark room at night. I have certainly seen indistinctly the form of greenish slopes and rocks, but only, I must admit, very indistinctly indeed. The reader may possibly be more successful. Plattner tells me that since his return he has seen and recognized places in the Other-World in his dreams, but this is probably due to his memory of these scenes. It seems quite possible that people with unusually keen eyesight may occasionally catch a glimpse of this strange Other-World about us.

However, this is a digression. As the green sun rose, a long street of black buildings became perceptible, though only darkly and indistinctly, in the gorge, and, after some hesitation, Plattner began to clamber down the precipitous descent towards them. The descent was long and exceedingly tedious, being so not only by the extraordinary steepness, but also by reason of the looseness of the boulders with which the whole face of the hill was strewn. The noise of his descent— now and then his heels struck fire from the rocks—seemed now the only sound in the universe, for the beating of the bell had ceased. As he drew nearer he perceived that the various edifices had a singular resemblance to tombs and mausoleums and monuments, saving only that they were all uniformly black instead of being white as most sepulchers are. And then he saw, crowding out of the largest building very much as people disperse from church, a number of pallid, rounded, pale-green figures. These scattered in several directions about the broad street of the place, some going through side alleys and reappearing upon the steepness of the hill, others entering some of the small black buildings which lined the way.

At the sight of these things drifting up towards him, Plattner stopped, staring. They were not walking, they were indeed limbless; and they had the appearance of human heads beneath which a tadpole-like body swung. He was too astonished at their strangeness, too full indeed of strangeness, to be seriously alarmed by them. They drove towards him, in front of the chill wind that was blowing uphill, much as soap-bubbles drive before a draught. And as he looked at the nearest of those approaching, he saw it was indeed a human head, albeit with singularly large eyes, and wearing such an expression of distress and anguish as he had never seen before upon mortal countenance. He was surprised to find that it did not turn to regard him, but seemed to be watching and following some unseen moving thing. For a moment he was puzzled, and then it occurred to him that this creature was watching with its enormous eyes something that was happening in the world he had just left. Nearer it came, and nearer, and he was too astonished to cry out. It made a very faint fretting sound as it came close to him. Then it struck his face with a gentle pat—its touch was very cold—and drove past him, and upward towards the crest of the hill.

An extraordinary conviction flashed across Plattner's mind that this head had a strong likeness to Lidgett. Then he turned his attention to the other heads that were now swarming thickly up the hillside. None made the slightest sign of recognition. One or two, indeed, came close to his head and almost followed the example of the first, but he dodged convulsively out of the way. Upon most of them he saw the same expression of unavailing regret he had seen upon the first, and heard the same faint sounds of wretchedness from them. One or two wept, and one rolling swiftly uphill wore an expression of diabolical rage. But others were cold, and several had a look of gratified interest in their eyes. One, at least, was almost in an ecstasy of happiness. Plattner does not remember that he recognised any more likenesses in those he saw at this time.

For several hours, perhaps, Plattner watched these strange things dispersing themselves over the hills, and not till long after they had ceased to issue from the clustering black buildings in the gorge did he resume his downward climb. The darkness about him increased so much that he had a difficulty in stepping true. Overhead the sky was now a bright pale green. He felt neither hunger nor thirst. Later, when he did, he found a chilly stream running down the center of the gorge, and the rare moss upon the boulders, when he tried it at last in desperation, was good to eat.

He groped about among the tombs that ran down the gorge, seeking vaguely for some clue to these inexplicable things. After a long time he came to the entrance of the big mausoleum-like building from which the heads had issued. In this he found a group of green lights burning upon a kind of basaltic altar, and a bell-rope from a belfry overhead hanging down into the center of the place. Round the wall ran a lettering of fire in a character unknown to him. While he was still wondering at the purport of these things, he heard the receding tramp of heavy feet echoing far down the street. He ran out into the darkness again, but he could see nothing. He had a mind to pull the bell-rope, and finally decided to follow the footsteps. But although he ran far, he never overtook them; and his shouting was of no avail. The gorge seemed to extend an interminable distance. It was as dark as earthly starlight throughout its length, while the ghastly green day lay along the upper edge of its precipices. There were none of the heads, now, below. They were all, it seemed, busily occupied along the upper slopes. Looking up, he saw them drifting hither and thither, some hovering stationary, some flying swiftly through the air. It reminded him, he said, of "big snowflakes"; only these were black and pale green.

In pursuing the firm, undeviating footsteps that he never overtook, in groping into new regions of this endless devil's dyke, in clambering up and down the pitiless heights, in wandering about the summits, and in watching the drifting faces, Plattner states that he spent the better part of seven or eight days. He did not keep count, he says. Though once or twice he found eyes watching him, he had word with no living soul. He slept among the rocks on the hillside. In the gorge things earthly were invisible, because, from the earthly standpoint, it was far underground. On the altitudes, so soon as the earthly day began, the world became visible to him. He found himself sometimes stumbling over the dark green rocks, or arresting himself on a precipitous brink, while all about him the green branches of the Sussexville lanes were swaying; or, again, he seemed to be walking through the Sussexville streets, or watching unseen the private business of some household. And then it was he discovered, that to almost every human being in our world there pertained some of these drifting heads; that everyone in the world is watched intermittently by these helpless disembodiments.

What are they—these Watchers of the Living? Plattner never learned. But two that presently found and followed him, were like his childhood's memory of his father and mother. Now and then other faces turned their eyes upon him: eyes like those of dead people who had swayed him, or injured him, or helped him in his youth and manhood. Whenever they looked at him, Plattner was overcome with a strange sense of responsibility. To his mother he ventured to speak; but she made no answer. She looked sadly, steadfastly, and tenderly—a little reproachfully, too, it seemed—into his eyes.

He simply tells this story: he does not endeavor to explain. We are left to surmise who these Watchers of the Living may be, or if they are indeed the Dead, why they should so closely and passionately watch a world they have left forever. It may be—indeed to my mind it seems just—that, when our life has closed, when evil or good is no longer a choice for us, we may still have to witness the working out of the train of consequences we have laid. If human souls continue after death, then surely human interests continue after death. But that is merely my own guess at the meaning of the things seen. Plattner offers no interpretation, for none was given him. It is well the reader should understand this clearly. Day after day, with his head reeling, he wandered about this green-lit world outside the world, weary and, towards the end, weak and hungry. By day—by our earthly day, that is—the ghostly vision of the old familiar scenery of Sussexville, all about him, irked and worried him. He could not see where to put his feet, and ever and again with a chilly touch one of these Watching Souls would come against his face. And after dark the multitude of these Watchers about him, and their intent distress, confused his mind beyond describing. A great longing to return to the earthly life that was so near and yet so remote consumed him. The unearthliness of things about him produced a positively painful mental distress. He was worried beyond describing by his own particular followers. He would shout at them to desist from staring at him, scold at them, hurry away from them. They were always mute and intent. Run as he might over the uneven ground, they followed his destinies.

On the ninth day, towards evening, Plattner heard the invisible footsteps approaching, far away down the gorge. He was then wandering over the broad crest of the same hill upon which he had fallen in his entry into this strange Other-World of his. He turned to hurry down into the gorge, feeling his way hastily, and was arrested by the sight of the thing that was happening in a room in a back street near the school. Both of the people in the room he knew by sight. The windows were open, the blinds up, and the setting sun shone clearly into it, so that it came out quite brightly at first, a vivid oblong of room, lying like a magic-lantern picture upon the black landscape and the livid green dawn. In addition to the sunlight, a candle had just been lit in the room.

On the bed lay a lank man, his ghastly white face terrible upon the tumbled pillow. His clenched hands were raised above his head. A little table beside the bed carried a few medicine bottles, some toast and water, and an empty glass. Every now and then the lank man's lips fell apart, to indicate a word he could not articulate. But the woman did not notice that he wanted anything, because she was busy turning out papers from an old-fashioned bureau in the opposite corner of the room. At first the picture was very vivid indeed, but as the green dawn behind it grew brighter and brighter, so it became fainter and more and more transparent.

As the echoing footsteps paced nearer and nearer, those footsteps that sound so loud in that Other-World and come so silently in this, Plattner perceived about him a great multitude of dim faces gathering together out of the darkness and watching the two people in the room. Never before had he seen so many of the Watchers of the Living. A multitude had eyes only for the sufferer in the room, another multitude, in infinite anguish, watched the woman as she hunted with greedy eyes for something she could not find. They crowded about Plattner, they came across his sight and buffeted his face, the noise of their unavailing regrets was all about him. He saw clearly only now and then. At other times the pictures quivered dimly, through the veil of green reflections upon their movements. In the room it must have been very still, and Plattner says the candle flame streamed up into a perfectly vertical line of smoke, but in his ears each footfall and its echoes beat like a clap of thunder. And the faces! Two more particularly, near the woman's: one a woman's also, white and clear-featured, a face which might have once been cold and hard but which was now softened by the touch of a wisdom strange to earth. The other might have been the woman's father. Both were evidently absorbed in the contemplation of some act of hateful meanness, so it seemed, which they could no longer guard against and prevent. Behind were others, teachers it may be who had taught ill, friends whose influence had failed. And over the man, too—a multitude, but none that seemed to be parents or teachers! Faces that might once have been coarse, now purged to strength by sorrow! And in the forefront one face, a girlish one, neither angry nor remorseful but merely patient and weary, and, as it seemed to Plattner, waiting for relief. His powers of description fail him at the memory of this multitude of ghastly countenances. They gathered on the stroke of the bell. He saw them all in the space of a second. It would seem that he was so worked upon by his excitement that quite involuntarily his restless fingers took the bottle of green powder out of his pocket and held it before him. But he does not remember that.

Abruptly the footsteps ceased. He waited for the next and there was silence, and then suddenly, cutting through the unexpected stillness like a keen, thin blade, came the first stroke of the bell. At that the multitudinous faces swayed to and fro, and a louder crying began all about him. The woman did not hear; she was burning something now in the candle flame. At the second stroke everything grew dim, and a breath of wind, icy cold, blew through the host of watchers. They swirled about him like an eddy of dead leaves in the spring, and at the third stroke something was extended through them to the bed. You have heard of a beam of light. This was like a beam of darkness, and looking again at it, Plattner saw that it was a shadowy arm and hand.

The green sun was now topping the black desolations of the horizon, and the vision of the room was very faint. Plattner could see that the white of the bed struggled, and was convulsed; and that the woman looked round over her shoulder at it, startled.

The cloud of watchers lifted high like a puff of green dust before the wind, and swept swiftly downwards towards the temple in the gorge. Then suddenly Plattner understood the meaning of the shadowy black arm that stretched across his shoulder and clutched its prey. He did not dare turn his head to see the Shadow behind the arm. With a violent effort, and covering his eyes, he set himself to run, made perhaps twenty strides, then slipped on a boulder and fell.

He fell forward on his hands; and the bottle smashed and exploded as he touched the ground.

In another moment he found himself, stunned and bleeding, sitting face to face with Lidgett in the old walled garden behind the school.

There the story of Plattner's experiences ends. I have resisted, I believe successfully, the natural disposition of a writer of fiction to dress up incidents of this sort. I have told the thing as far as possible in the order in which Plattner told it to me. I have carefully avoided any attempt at style, effect, or construction. It would have been easy, for instance, to have worked the scene of the death-bed into a kind of plot in which Plattner might have been involved. But quite apart from the objectionableness of falsifying a most extraordinary true story, any such trite devices would spoil, to my mind, the peculiar effect of this dark world, with its livid green illumination and its drifting Watchers of the Living, which, unseen and unapproachable to us, is yet lying all about us.

It remains to add, that a death did actually occur in Vincent Terrace, just beyond the school garden, and, so far as can be proved, at the moment of Plattner's return. Deceased was a rate-collector and insurance agent. His widow, who was much younger than himself, married last month a Mr. Whymper, a veterinary surgeon of Allbeeding. As the portion of this story given here has in various forms circulated orally in Sussexville, she has consented to my use of her name, on condition that I make it distinctly known that she emphatically contradicts every detail of Plattner's account of her husband's last moments. She burnt no will, she says, although Plattner never accused her of doing so: her husband made but one will, and that just after their marriage. Certainly, from a man who had never seen it, Plattner's account of the furniture of the room was curiously accurate.

One other thing, even at the risk of an irksome repetition, I must insist upon lest I seem to favor the credulous superstitious view. Plattner's absence from the world for nine days is, I think, proved. But that does not prove his story. It is quite conceivable that even outside space hallucinations may be possible. That, at least, the reader must bear distinctly in mind.

THE CRYSTAL EGG

THERE WAS, UNTIL a year ago, a little and very grimy-looking shop near Seven Dials, over which, in weather-worn yellow lettering, the name of "C. Cave, Naturalist and Dealer in Antiquities," was inscribed. The contents of its window were curiously varied. They comprised some elephant tusks and an imperfect set of chessmen, beads and weapons, a box of eyes, two skulls of tigers and one human, several moth-eaten stuffed monkeys (one holding a lamp), an old-fashioned cabinet, a fly-blown ostrich egg or so, some fishing-tackle, and an extraordinarily dirty, empty glass fish-tank. There was also, at the moment the story begins, a mass of crystal, worked into the shape of an egg and brilliantly polished. And at that two people, who stood outside the window, were looking, one of them a tall, thin clergyman, the other a black-bearded young man of dusky complexion and unobstrusive costume. The dusky young man spoke with eager gesticulation, and seemed anxious for his companion to purchase the article.

While they were there, Mr. Cave came into his shop, his beard still wagging with the bread and butter of his tea. When he saw these men and the object of their regard, his countenance fell. He glanced guiltily over his shoulder, and softly shut the door. He was a little old man, with pale face and peculiar watery blue eyes; his hair was a dirty gray, and he wore a shabby blue frockcoat, an ancient silk hat, and carpet slippers very much down at heel. He remained watching the two men as they talked. The clergyman went deep into his trouser pocket, examined a handful of money, and showed his teeth in an agreeable smile. Mr. Cave seemed still more depressed when they came into the shop.

The clergyman, without any ceremony, asked the price of the crystal egg. Mr. Cave glanced nervously towards the door leading into the parlor, and said five pounds. The clergyman protested that the price was high, to his companion as well as to Mr. Cave—it was, indeed, very much more than Mr. Cave had intended to ask, when he had stocked the article—and an attempt at bargaining ensued. Mr. Cave stepped to the shop-door, and held it open. "Five pounds is my price," he said, as though he wished to save himself the trouble of unprofitable discussion. As he did so, the upper portion of a woman's face appeared above the blind in the glass upper panel of the door leading into the parlor, and stared curiously at the two customers. "Five pounds is my price," said Mr. Cave, with a quiver in his voice.

The swarthy young man had so far remained a spectator, watching Cave keenly. Now he spoke. "Give him five pounds," he said. The clergyman glanced at him to see if he were in earnest, and, when he looked at Mr. Cave again, he saw that the latter's face was white. "It's a lot of money," said the clergyman, and, diving into his pocket, began counting his resources. He had little more than thirty shillings, and he appealed to his companion, with whom he seemed to be on terms of considerable intimacy. This gave Mr. Cave an opportunity of collecting his thoughts, and he began to explain in an agitated manner that the crystal was not, as a matter of fact, entirely free for sale. His two customers were naturally surprised at this, and inquired why he had not thought of that before he began to bargain. Mr. Cave became confused, but he stuck to his story, that the crystal was not in the market that afternoon, that a probable purchaser of it had already appeared. The two, treating this as an attempt to raise the price still further, made as if they would leave the shop. But at this point the parlor door opened, and the owner of the dark fringe and the little eyes appeared.

She was a coarse-featured, corpulent woman, younger and very much larger than Mr. Cave; she walked heavily, and her face was flushed. "That crystal *is* for sale," she said. "And five pounds is a good enough price for it. I can't think what you're about, Cave, not to take the gentleman's offer!"

Mr. Cave, greatly perturbed by the irruption, looked angrily at her over the rims of his spectacles, and, without excessive assurance, asserted his right to manage his business in his own way. An altercation began. The two customers watched the scene with interest and some amusement, occasionally assisting Mrs. Cave with suggestions. Mr. Cave, hard driven, persisted in a confused and impossible story of an enquiry for the crystal that morning, and his agitation became painful. But he stuck to his point with extraordinary persistence. It was the young Oriental who ended this curious controversy. He proposed that they should call again in the course of two days—so as to give the alleged enquirer a fair chance. "And then we must insist," said the clergyman. "Five pounds." Mrs. Cave took it on herself to apologize for her husband, explaining that he was sometimes "a little odd," and as the two customers left, the couple prepared for a free discussion of the incident in all its bearings.

Mrs. Cave talked to her husband with singular directness. The poor little man, quivering with emotion, muddled himself between his stories, maintaining on the one hand that he had another customer in view, and on the other asserting that the crystal was honestly worth ten guineas. "Why did you ask five pounds?" said his wife. *"Do* let me manage my business my own way!" said Mr. Cave.

Mr. Cave had living with him a step-daughter and a step-son, and at supper that night the transaction was re-discussed. None of them had a high opinion of Mr. Cave's business methods, and this action seemed a culminating folly.

"It's my opinion he's refused that crystal before," said the step-son, a loose-limbed lout of eighteen.

"But *Five Pounds!"* said the step-daughter, an argumentative young woman of six-and-twenty.

Mr. Cave's answers were wretched; he could only mumble weak assertions that he knew his own business best. They drove him from his half-eaten supper into the shop, to close it for the night, his ears aflame and tears of vexation behind his spectacles. "Why had he left the crystal in the window so long? The folly of it!" That was the trouble closest in his mind. For a time he could see no way of evading sale.

After supper his step-daughter and step-son smartened themselves up and went out and his wife retired upstairs to reflect upon the business aspects of the crystal, over a little sugar and lemon and so forth in hot water. Mr. Cave went into the shop, and stayed there until late, ostensibly to make ornamental rockeries for gold-fish cases but really for a private purpose that will be better explained later. The next day Mrs. Cave found that the crystal had been removed from the window, and was lying behind some second-hand books on angling. She replaced it in a conspicuous position. But she did not argue further about it, as a nervous headache disinclined her from debate. Mr. Cave was always disinclined. The day passed disagreeably. Mr. Cave was, if anything, more absent-minded than usual, and uncommonly irritable withal. In the afternoon, when his wife was taking her customary sleep, he removed the crystal from the window again.

The next day Mr. Cave had to deliver a consignment of dog-fish at one of the hospital schools, where they were needed for dissection. In his absence Mrs. Cave's mind reverted to the topic of the crystal, and the methods of expenditure suitable to a windfall of five pounds. She had already devised some very agreeable expedients, among others a dress of green silk for herself and a trip to Richmond, when a jangling of the front doorbell summoned her into the shop. The customer was an examination coach who came to complain of the non-delivery of certain frogs asked for the previous day. Mrs. Cave did not approve of this particular branch of Mr. Cave's business, and the gentleman, who had called in a somewhat aggressive mood, retired after a brief exchange of words—entirely civil so far as he was concerned. Mrs. Cave's eye then naturally turned to the window; for the sight of the crystal was an assurance of the five pounds and of her dreams. What was her surprise to find it gone!

She went to the place behind the locker on the counter, where she had discovered it the day before. It was not there; and she immediately began an eager search about the shop.

When Mr. Cave returned from his business with the dog-fish, about a quarter to two in the afternoon, he found the shop in some confusion, and his wife, extremely exasperated and on her knees behind the counter, routing among his taxidermic material. Her face came up hot and angry over the counter, as the jangling bell announced his return, and she forthwith accused him of "hiding it."

"Hid *what?"* asked Mr. Cave.

"The crystal!"

At that Mr. Cave, apparently much surprised, rushed to the window. "Isn't it here?" he said. "Great Heavens! What has become of it?"

Just then, Mr. Cave's step-son re-entered the shop from the inner room—he had come home a minute or so before Mr. Cave—and he was blaspheming freely. He was apprenticed to a second-hand furniture dealer down the road, but he had his meals at home, and he was naturally annoyed to find no dinner ready.

But, when he heard of the loss of the crystal, he forgot his meal, and his anger was diverted from his mother to his step-father. Their first idea, of course, was that he had hidden it. But Mr. Cave stoutly denied all knowledge of its fate—freely offering his bedabbled affidavit in the matter—and at last was worked up to the point of accusing, first, his wife and then his step-son of having taken it with a view to a private sale. So began an exceedingly acrimonious and emotional discussion, which ended for Mrs. Cave in a peculiar nervous condition midway between hysterics and amuck, and caused the step-son to be half-an-hour late at the furniture establishment in the afternoon. Mr. Cave took refuge from his wife's emotions in the shop.

In the evening the matter was resumed, with less passion and in a judicial spirit, under the presidency of the step-daughter. The supper passed unhappily and culminated in a painful scene. Mr. Cave gave way at last to extreme exasperation, and went out banging the front door violently. The rest of the family, having discussed him with the freedom his absence warranted, hunted the house from garret to cellar, hoping to light upon the crystal.

The next day the two customers called again. They were received by Mrs. Cave almost in tears. It transpired that no one *could* imagine all that she had stood from Cave at various times in her married pilgrimage. . . . She also gave a garbled account of the disappearance. The clergyman and the Oriental laughed silently at one another, and said it was very extraordinary. As Mrs. Cave seemed disposed to give them the complete history of his life they made to leave the shop. Thereupon Mrs. Cave, still clinging to hope, asked for the clergyman's address, so that, if she could get anything out of Cave, she might communicate it. The address was duly given, but apparently was afterwards mislaid. Mrs. Cave can remember nothing about it.

In the evening of that day, the Caves seem to have exhausted their emotions, and Mr. Cave, who had been out in the afternoon, supped in a gloomy isolation that contrasted pleasantly with the impassioned controversy of the previous days. For some time matters were very badly strained in the Cave household, but neither crystal nor customer reappeared.

Now, without mincing the matter, we must admit that Mr. Cave was a liar. He knew perfectly well where the crystal was. It was in the rooms of Mr. Jacoby Wace, Assistant Demonstrator at St. Catherine's Hospital, Westbourne Street. It stood on the sideboard partially covered by a black velvet cloth, and beside a decanter of American whisky. It is from Mr. Wace, indeed, that the particulars upon which this narrative is based were derived. Cave had taken off the thing to the hospital hidden in the dog-fish sack, and there had pressed the young investigator to keep it for him. Mr. Wace was a little dubious at first. His relationship to Cave was peculiar. He had a taste for singular characters, and he had more than once invited the old man to smoke and drink in his rooms, and to unfold his rather amusing views of life in general and of his wife in particular. Mr. Wace had encountered Mrs. Cave, too, on occasions when Mr. Cave was not at home to attend to him. He knew the constant interference to which Cave was subjected, and having weighed the story judicially, he decided to give the crystal a refuge. Mr. Cave promised to explain the reasons for his remarkable affection for the crystal more fully on a later occasion, but he spoke distinctly of seeing visions therein. He called on Mr. Wace the same evening.

He told a complicated story. The crystal he said had come into his possession with other oddments at the forced sale of another curiosity dealer's effects, and not knowing what its value might be, he had ticketed it at ten shillings. It had hung upon his hands at that price for some months, and he was thinking of "reducing the figure," when he made a singular discovery.

At that time his health was very bad—and it must be borne in mind that, throughout all this experience, his physical condition was one of ebb—and he was in considerable distress by reason of the negligence, the positive ill-treatment even, he received from his wife and step-children. His wife was vain, extravagant, unfeeling, and had a growing taste for private drinking; his step-daughter was mean and over-reaching; and his step-son had conceived a violent dislike for him, and lost no chance of showing it. The requirements of his business pressed heavily upon him, and Mr. Wace does not think that he was altogether free from occasional intemperance. He had begun life in a comfortable position, he was a man of fair education, and he suffered, for weeks at a stretch, from melancholia and insomnia. Afraid to disturb his family, he would slip quietly from his wife's side, when his thoughts became intolerable, and wander about the house. And about three o'clock one morning, late in August, chance directed him into the shop.

The dirty little place was impenetrably black except in one spot, where he perceived an unusual glow of light. Approaching this, he discovered it to be the crystal egg, which was standing on the corner of the counter towards the window. A thin ray smote through a crack in the shutters, impinged upon the object, and seemed as it were to fill its entire interior.

It occurred to Mr. Cave that this was not in accordance with the laws of optics as he had known them in his younger days. He could understand the rays being refracted by the crystal and coming to a focus in its interior, but this diffusion jarred with his physical conceptions. He approached the crystal nearly, peering into it and round it, with a transient revival of the scientific curiosity that in his youth had determined his choice of a calling. He was surprised to find the light not steady, but writhing within the substance of the egg, as though that object was a hollow sphere of some luminous vapor. In moving about to get different points of view, he suddenly found that he had come between it and the ray, and that the crystal none the less remained luminous. Greatly astonished, he lifted it out of the light ray and carried it to the darkest part of the shop. It remained bright for some four or five minutes, when it slowly faded and went out. He placed it in the thin streak of daylight, and its luminousness was almost immediately restored.

So far, at least, Mr. Wace was able to verify the remarkable story of Mr. Cave. He has himself repeatedly held this crystal in a ray of light (which had to be of a less diameter than one millimetre). And in a perfect darkness, such as could be produced by velvet wrapping, the crystal did undoubtedly appear very faintly phosphorescent. It would seem, however, that the luminousness was of some exceptional sort, and not equally visible to all eyes; for Mr. Harbinger—whose name will be familiar to the scientific reader in connection with the Pasteur Institute—was quite unable to see any light whatever. And Mr. Wace's own capacity for its appreciation was out of comparison inferior to that of Mr. Cave's. Even with Mr. Cave the power varied very considerably; his vision was most vivid during states of extreme weakness and fatigue.

Now from the outset this light in the crystal exercised an irresistible fascination upon Mr. Cave. And it says more for his loneliness of soul than a volume of pathetic writing could do, that he told no human being of his curious observations. He seems to have been living in such an atmosphere of petty spite that to admit the existence of a pleasure would have been to risk the loss of it. He found that as the dawn advanced, and the amount of diffused light increased, the crystal became to all appearance non-luminous. And for some time he was unable to see anything in it, except at nighttime, in dark corners of the shop.

But the use of an old velvet cloth, which he used as a background for a collection of minerals, occurred to him, and by doubling this, and putting it over his head and hands, he was able to get a sight of the luminous movement within the crystal even in the daytime. He was very cautious lest he should be thus discovered by his wife, and he practiced this occupation only in the afternoons, while she was asleep upstairs, and then circumspectly in a hollow under the counter. And one day, turning the crystal about in his hands, he saw something. It came and went like a flash, but it gave him the impression that the object had for a moment opened to him the view of a wide and spacious and strange country; and, turning it about, he did, just as the light faded, see the same vision again.

Now, it would be tedious and unnecessary to state all the phases of Mr. Cave's discovery from this point. Suffice that the effect was this: the crystal, being peered into at an angle of about 137 degrees from the direction of the illuminating ray, gave a clear and consistent picture of a wide and peculiar countryside. It was not dream-like at all; it produced a definite impression of reality, and the better the light the more real and solid it seemed. It was a moving picture: that is to say, certain objects moved in it, but slowly in an orderly manner like real things, and, according as the direction of the lighting and vision changed, the picture changed also. It must, indeed, have been like looking through an oval glass at a view, and turning the glass about to get at different aspects.

Mr. Cave's statements, Mr. Wace assures me, were extremely circumstantial, and entirely free from any of that emotional quality that taints hallucinatory impressions. But it must be remembered that all the efforts of Mr. Wace to see any similar clarity in the faint opalescence of the crystal were wholly unsuccessful, try as he would. The difference in intensity of the impressions received by the two men was very great, and it is quite conceivable that what was a view to Mr. Cave was a mere blurred nebulosity to Mr. Wace.

The view, as Mr. Cave described it, was invariably of an extensive plain, and he seemed always to be looking at it from a considerable height, as if from a tower or a mast. To the east and to the west the plain was bounded at a remote distance by vast reddish cliffs, which reminded him of those he had seen in some picture; but what the picture was Mr. Wace was unable to ascertain. These cliffs passed north and south—he could tell the points of the compass by the stars that were visible of a night—receding in an almost illimitable perspective and fading into the mists of the distance before they met. He was nearer the eastern set of cliffs, on the occasion of his first vision the sun was rising over them, and black against the sunlight and pale against their shadow appeared a multitude of soaring forms that Mr. Cave regarded as birds. A vast range of buildings spread below him; he seemed to be looking down upon them; and, as they approached the blurred and refracted edge of the picture, they became indistinct. There were also trees curious in shape, and in coloring, a deep mossy green and an exquisite gray, beside a wide and shining canal. And something great and brilliantly colored flew across the picture. But the first time Mr. Cave saw these pictures he saw only in flashes, his hands shook, his head moved, the vision came and went, and grew foggy and indistinct. And at first he had the greatest difficulty in finding the picture again once the direction of it was lost.

His next clear vision, which came about a week after the first, the interval having yielded nothing but tantalizing glimpses and some useful experience, showed him the view down the length of the valley. The view was different, but he had a curious persuasion, which his subsequent observations abundantly confirmed, that he was regarding this strange world from exactly the same spot, although he was looking in a different direction. The long façade of the great building, whose roof he had looked down upon before, was now receding in perspective. He recognized the roof. In the front of the façade was a terrace of massive proportions and extraordinary length, and down the middle of the terrace, at certain intervals, stood huge but very graceful masts, bearing small shiny objects which reflected the setting sun. The import of these small objects did not occur to Mr. Cave until some time after, as he was describing the scene to Mr. Wace. The terrace overhung a thicket of the most luxuriant and graceful vegetation, and beyond this was a wide grassy lawn on which certain broad creatures, in form like beetles but enormously larger, reposed. Beyond this again was a richly decorated causeway of pinkish stone; and beyond that, and lined with dense *red* weeds, and passing up the valley exactly parallel with the distant cliffs, was a broad and mirror-like expanse of water. The air seemed full of squadrons of great birds, manœuvring in stately curves; and across the river was a multitude of splendid buildings, richly colored and glittering with metallic tracery and facets, among a forest of moss-like and lichenous trees. And suddenly something flapped repeatedly across the vision, like the fluttering of a jeweled fan or the beating of a wing, and a face, or rather the upper part of a face with very large eyes, came as it were close to his own and as if on the other side of the crystal. Mr. Cave was so startled and so impressed by the absolute reality of these eyes, that he drew his head back from the crystal to look behind it. He had become so absorbed in watching that he was quite surprised to find himself in the cool darkness of his little shop, with its familiar odor of methyl, mustiness, and decay. And, as he blinked about him, the glowing crystal faded, and went out.

Such were the first general impressions of Mr. Cave. The story is curiously direct and circumstantial. From the outset, when the valley first flashed momentarily on his senses, his imagination was strangely affected, and, as he began to appreciate the details of the scene he saw, his wonder rose to the point of a passion. He went about his business listless and distraught, thinking only of the time when he should be able to return to his watching. And then a few weeks after his first sight of the valley came the two customers, the stress and excitement of their offer, and the narrow escape of the crystal from sale, as I have already told.

Now while the thing was Mr. Cave's secret, it remained a mere wonder, a thing to creep to covertly and peep at, as a child might peep upon a forbidden garden. But Mr. Wace has, for a young scientific investigator, a particularly lucid and consecutive habit of mind. Directly the crystal and its story came to him, and he had satisfied himself, by seeing the phosphorescence with his own eyes, that there really was a certain evidence for Mr. Cave's statements, he proceeded to develop the matter systematically. Mr. Cave was only too eager to come and feast his eyes on this wonderland he saw, and he came every night from half-past eight until half-past ten, and sometimes in Mr. Wace's absence, during the day. On Sunday afternoons, also, he came. From the outset Mr. Wace made copious notes, and it was due to his scientific method that the relation between the direction from which the initiating ray entered the crystal and the orientation of the picture was proved. And, by covering the crystal in a box perforated only with a small aperture to admit the exciting ray, and by substituting black holland for his buff blinds, he greatly improved the conditions of the observations; so that in a little while they were able to survey the valley in any direction they desired.

So having cleared the way, we may give a brief account of this visionary world within the crystal. The things were in all cases seen by Mr. Cave, and the method of working was invariably for him to watch the crystal and report what he saw, while Mr. Wace (who as a science student had learnt the trick of writing in the dark) wrote a brief note of his report. When the crystal faded, it was put into its box in the proper position and the electric light turned on. Mr. Wace asked questions, and suggested observations to clear up difficult points. Nothing, indeed, could have been less visionary and more matter-of-fact.

The attention of Mr. Cave had been speedily directed to the bird-like creatures he had seen so abundantly present in each of his earlier visions. His first impression was soon corrected, and he considered for a time that they might represent a diurnal species of bat. Then he thought, grotesquely enough, that they might be cherubs. Their heads were round, and curiously human, and it was the eyes of one of them that had so startled him on his second observation. They had broad, silvery wings, not feathered, but glistening almost as brilliantly as new-killed fish and with the same subtle play of color, and these wings were not built on the plan of bird-wing, or bat, Mr. Wace learned, but supported by curved ribs radiating from the body. (A sort of butterfly wing with curved ribs seems best to express their appearance.) The body was small, but fitted with two bunches of prehensile organs, like long tentacles, immediately under the mouth. Incredible as it appeared to Mr. Wace, the persuasion at last became irresistible, that it was these creatures which owned the great quasi-human buildings and the magnificent garden that made the broad valley so splendid. And Mr. Cave perceived that the buildings, with other peculiarities, had no doors, but that the great circular windows, which opened freely, gave the creatures egress, and entrance. They would alight upon their tentacles, fold their wings to a smallness almost rod-like, and hop into the interior. But among them was a multitude of smaller-winged creatures, like great dragon-flies and moths and flying beetles, and across the greensward brilliantly-colored gigantic ground-beetles crawled lazily to and fro. Moreover, on the causeways and terraces, large-headed creatures similar to the greater winged flies, but wingless, were visible, hopping busily upon their hand-like tangle of tentacles.

Allusion has already been made to the glittering objects upon masts that stood upon the terrace of the nearer building. It dawned upon Mr. Cave, after regarding one of these masts very fixedly on one particularly vivid day, that the glittering object there was a crystal exactly like that into which he peered. And a still more careful scrutiny convinced him that each one in a vista of nearly twenty carried a similar object.

Occasionally one of the large flying creatures would flutter up to one, and, folding its wings and coiling a number of its tentacles about the mast, would regard the crystal fixedly for a space,—sometimes for as long as fifteen minutes. And a series of observations, made at the suggestion of Mr. Wace, convinced both watchers that, so far as this visionary world was concerned, the crystal into which they peered actually stood at the summit of the end-most mast on the terrace, and that on one occasion at least one of these inhabitants of this other world had looked into Mr. Cave's face while he was making these observations.

So much for the essential facts of this very singular story. Unless we dismiss it all as the ingenious fabrication of Mr. Wace, we have to believe one of two things: either that Mr. Cave's crystal was in two worlds at once, and that, while it was carried about in one, it remained stationary in the other, which seems altogether absurd; or else that it had some peculiar relation of sympathy with another and exactly similar crystal in this other world, so that what was seen in the interior of the one in this world was, under suitable conditions, visible to an observer in the corresponding crystal in the other world; and *vice versa*. At present, indeed, we do not know of any way in which two crystals could so come *en rapport*, but nowadays we know enough to understand that the thing is not altogether impossible. This view of the crystals as *en rapport* was the supposition that occurred to Mr. Wace, and to me at least it seems extremely plausible. . . .

And where was this other world? On this, also, the alert intelligence of Mr. Wace speedily threw light. After sunset, the sky darkened rapidly—there was a very brief twilight interval indeed—and the stars shone out. They were recognizably the same as those we see, arranged in the same constellations. Mr. Cave recognized the Bear, the Pleiades, Aldebaran, and Sirius: so that the other world must be somewhere in the solar system, and, at the utmost, only a few hundreds of millions of miles from our own. Following up this clue, Mr. Wace learned that the midnight sky was a darker blue even than our mid-winter sky, and that the sun seemed a little smaller. *And there were two small moons!* "like our moon but smaller, and quite differently marked" one of which moved so rapidly that its motion was clearly visible as one regarded it. These moons were never high in the sky, but vanished as they rose: that is, every time they revolved they were eclipsed because they were so near their primary planet. And all this answers quite completely, although Mr. Cave did not know it, to what must be the condition of things on Mars.

Indeed, it seems an exceedingly plausible conclusion that peering into this crystal Mr. Cave did actually see the planet Mars and its inhabitants. And, if that be the case, then the evening star that shone so brilliantly in the sky of that distant vision, was neither more nor less than our own familiar earth.

For a time the Martians—if they were Martians—do not seem to have known of Mr. Cave's inspection. Once or twice one would come to peer, and go away very shortly to some other mast, as though the vision was unsatisfactory. During this time Mr. Cave was able to watch the proceedings of these winged people without being disturbed by their attentions, and, although his report is necessarily vague and fragmentary, it is nevertheless very suggestive. Imagine the impression of humanity a Martian observer would get who, after a difficult process of preparation and with considerable fatigue to the eyes, was able to peer at London from the steeple of St. Martin's Church for stretches, at longest, of four minutes at a time. Mr. Cave was unable to ascertain if the winged Martians were the same as the Martians who hopped about the causeways and terraces, and if the latter could put on wings at will. He several times saw certain clumsy bipeds, dimly suggestive of apes, white and partially translucent, feeding among certain of the lichenous trees, and once some of these fled before one of the hopping, round-headed Martians. The latter caught one in its tentacles, and then the picture faded suddenly and left Mr. Cave most tantalizingly in the dark. On another occasion a vast thing, that Mr. Cave thought at first was some gigantic insect, appeared advancing along the causeway beside the canal with extraordinary rapidity. As this drew nearer Mr. Cave perceived that it was a mechanism of shining metals and of extraordinary complexity. And then, when he looked again, it had passed out of sight.

After a time Mr. Wace aspired to attract the attention of the Martians, and the next time that the strange eyes of one of them appeared close to the crystal Mr. Cave cried out and sprang away, and they immediately turned on the light and began to gesticulate in a manner suggestive of signaling. But when at last Mr. Cave examined the crystal again the Martian had departed.

Thus far these observations had progressed in early November, and then Mr. Cave, feeling that the suspicions of his family about the crystal were allayed, began to take it to and fro with him in order that, as occasion arose in the daytime or night, he might comfort himself with what was fast becoming the most real thing in his existence.

In December Mr. Wace's work in connection with a forthcoming examination became heavy, the sittings were reluctantly suspended for a week, and for ten or eleven days—he is not quite sure which—he saw nothing of Cave. He then grew anxious to resume these investigations, and, the stress of his seasonal labors being abated, he went down to Seven Dials. At the corner he noticed a shutter before a bird fancier's window, and then another at a cobbler's. Mr. Cave's shop was closed.

He rapped and the door was opened by the step-son in black. He at once called Mrs. Cave, who was, Mr. Wace could not but observe, in cheap but ample widow's weeds of the most imposing pattern. Without any great surprise Mr. Wace learnt that Cave was dead and already buried. She was in tears, and her voice was a little thick. She had just returned from Highgate. Her mind seemed occupied with her own prospects and the honorable details of the obsequies, but Mr. Wace was at last able to learn the particulars of Cave's death. He had been found dead in his shop in the early morning, the day after his last visit to Mr. Wace, and the crystal had been clasped in his stone-cold hands. His face was smiling, said Mrs. Cave, and the velvet cloth from the minerals lay on the floor at his feet. He must have been dead five or six hours when he was found.

This came as a great shock to Wace, and he began to reproach himself bitterly for having neglected the plain symptoms of the old man's ill-health. But his chief thought was of the crystal. He approached that topic in a gingerly manner, because he knew Mrs. Cave's peculiarities. He was dumbfounded to learn that it was sold.

Mrs. Cave's first impulse, directly Cave's body had been taken upstairs, had been to write to the mad clergyman who had offered five pounds for the crystal, informing him of its recovery; but after a violent hunt in which her daughter joined her, they were convinced of the loss of his address. As they were without the means required to mourn and bury Cave in the elaborate style the dignity of an old Seven Dials inhabitant demands, they had appealed to a friendly fellow-tradesman in Great Portland Street. He had very kindly taken over a portion of the stock at a valuation. The valuation was his own and the crystal egg was included in one of the lots. Mr. Wace, after a few suitable consolatory observations, a little off-handedly proffered perhaps, hurried at once to Great Portland Street. But there he learned that the crystal egg had already been sold to a tall, dark man in gray. And there the material facts in this curious, and to me at least very suggestive story come abruptly to an end. The Great Portland Street dealer did not know who the tall dark man in gray was, nor had he observed him with sufficient attention to describe him minutely. He did not even know which way this person had gone after leaving the shop. For a time Mr. Wace remained in the shop, trying the dealer's patience with hopeless questions, venting his own exasperation. And at last, realizing abruptly that the whole thing had passed out of his hands, had vanished like a vision of the night, he returned to his own rooms, a little astonished to find the notes he had made still tangible and visible upon his untidy table.

His annoyance and disappointment were naturally very great. He made a second call (equally ineffectual) upon the Great Portland Street dealer, and he resorted to advertisements in such periodicals as were likely to come into the hands of a bric-a-brac collector. He also wrote letters to *The Daily Chronicle* and *Nature,* but both those periodicals, suspecting a hoax, asked him to reconsider his action before they printed, and he was advised that such a strange story, unfortunately so bare of supporting evidence, might imperil his reputation as an investigator. Moreover, the calls of his proper work were urgent. So that after a month or so, save for an occasional reminder to certain dealers, he had reluctantly to abandon the quest for the crystal egg, and from that day to this it remains undiscovered. Occasionally however, he tells me, and I can quite believe him, he has bursts of zeal in which he abandons his more urgent occupation and resumes the search.

Whether or not it will remain lost forever, with the material and origin of it, are things equally speculative at the present time. If the present purchaser is a collector, one would have expected the enquiries of Mr. Wace to have reached him through the dealers. He has been able to discover Mr. Cave's clergyman and ''Oriental''—no other than the Rev. James Parker and the young Prince of Bosso-Kuni in Java. I am obliged to them for certain particulars. The object of the Prince was simply curiosity—and extravagance. He was so eager to buy, because Cave was so oddly reluctant to sell. It is just as possible that the buyer in the second instance was simply a casual purchaser and not a collector at all, and the crystal egg, for all I know, may at the present moment be within a mile of me, decorating a drawing-room or serving as a paper-weight—its remarkable functions all unknown. Indeed, it is partly with the idea of such a possibility that I have thrown this narrative into a form that will give it a chance of being read by the ordinary consumer of fiction.

My own ideas in the matter are practically identical with those of Mr. Wace. I believe the crystal on the mast in Mars and the crystal egg of Mr. Cave's to be in some physical, but at present quite inexplicable, way *en rapport,* and we both believe further that the terrestrial crystal must have been—possibly at some remote date—sent hither from that planet, in order to give the Martians a near view of our affairs. Possibly the fellows to the crystals in the other masts are also on our globe. No theory of hallucination suffices for the facts.

THE STAR

IT WAS ON the first day of the new year that the announcement was made, almost simultaneously from three observatories, that the motion of the planet Neptune, the outermost of all the planets that wheel about the sun, had become very erratic. Ogilvy had already called attention to a suspected retardation in its velocity in December. Such a piece of news was scarcely calculated to interest a world the greater portion of whose inhabitants were unaware of the existence of the planet Neptune, nor outside the astronomical profession did the subsequent discovery of a faint remote speck of light in the region of the perturbed planet cause any very great excitement. Scientific people, however, found the intelligence remarkable enough, even before it became known that the new body was rapidly growing larger and brighter, that its motion was quite different from the orderly progress of the planets, and that the deflection of Neptune and its satellite was becoming now of an unprecedented kind.

Few people without a training in science can realize the huge isolation of the solar system. The sun with its specks of planets, its dust of planetoids, and its impalpable comets, swims in a vacant immensity that almost defeats the imagination. Beyond the orbit of Neptune there is space, vacant so far as human observation has penetrated, without warmth or light or sound, blank emptiness, for twenty million times a million miles. That is the smallest estimate of the distance to be traversed before the very nearest of the stars is attained. And, saving a few comets more unsubstantial than the thinnest flame, no matter had ever to human knowledge crossed this gulf of space, until early in the twentieth century this strange wanderer appeared. A vast mass of matter it was, bulky, heavy, rushing without warning out of the black mystery of the sky into the radiance of the sun. By the second day it was clearly visible to any decent instrument, as a speck with a barely sensible diameter, in the constellation Leo near Regulus. In a little while an opera glass could attain it.

On the third day of the new year the newspaper readers of two hemispheres were made aware for the first time of the real importance of this unusual apparition in the heavens. "A Planetary Collision," one London paper headed the news, and proclaimed Duchaine's opinion that this strange new planet would probably collide with Neptune. The leader writers enlarged upon the topic. So that in most of the capitals of the world, on January 3rd, there was an expectation, however vague, of some imminent phenomenon in the sky; and as the night followed the sunset round the globe, thousands of men turned their eyes skyward to see—the old familiar stars just as they had always been.

Until it was dawn in London and Pollux setting and the stars overhead grown pale. The winter's dawn it was, a sickly filtering accumulation of daylight, and the light of gas and candles shone yellow in the windows to show where people were astir. But the yawning policeman saw the thing, the busy crowds in the markets stopped agape, workmen going to their work betimes, milkmen, the drivers of news-carts, dissipation going home jaded and pale, homeless wanderers, sentinels on their beats, and in the country, laborers trudging afield, poachers slinking home, all over the dusky quickening country it could be seen—and out at sea by seamen watching for the day—a great white star, come suddenly into the westward sky!

Brighter it was than any star in our skies; brighter than the evening star at its brightest. It still glowed out white and large, no mere twinkling spot of light, but a small round clear shining disc, an hour after the day had come. And where science has not reached, men stared and feared, telling one another of the wars and pestilences that are foreshadowed by these fiery signs in the Heavens. Sturdy Boers, dusky Hottentots, Gold Coast Negroes, Frenchmen, Spaniards, Portuguese, stood in the warmth of the sunrise watching the setting of this strange new star.

And in a hundred observatories there had been suppressed excitement, rising almost to shouting pitch, as the two remote bodies had rushed together, and a hurrying to and fro to gather photographic apparatus and spectroscope, and this appliance and that, to record this novel astonishing sight, the destruction of a world. For it was a world, a sister planet of our earth, far greater than our earth indeed, that had so suddenly flashed into flaming death. Neptune it was, had been struck, fairly and squarely, by the strange planet from outer space and the heat of the concussion had incontinently turned two solid globes into one vast mass of incandescence. Round the world that day, two hours before the dawn, went the pallid great white star, fading only as it sank westward and the sun mounted above it. Everywhere men marveled at it, but of all those who saw it none could have marveled more than those sailors, habitual watchers of the stars, who far away at sea had heard nothing of its advent and saw it now rise like a pigmy moon and climb zenithward and hang overhead and sink westward with the passing of the night.

And when next it rose over Europe everywhere were crowds of watchers on hilly slopes, on house-roofs, in open spaces, staring eastward for the rising of the great new star. It rose with a white glow in front of it, like the glare of a white fire, and those who had seen it come into existence the night before cried out at the sight of it. "It is larger," they cried. "It is brighter!" And, indeed the moon a quarter full and sinking in the west was in its apparent size beyond comparison, but scarcely in all its breadth had it as much brightness now as the little circle of the strange new star.

"It is brighter!" cried the people clustering in the streets. But in the dim observatories the watchers held their breath and peered at one another. *"It is nearer,"* they said. *"Nearer!"*

And voice after voice repeated, "It is nearer," and the clicking telegraph took that up, and it trembled along telephone wires, and in a thousand cities grimy compositors fingered the type. "It is nearer." Men writing in offices, struck with a strange realization, flung down their pens; men talking in a thousand places suddenly came upon a grotesque possibility in those words, "It is nearer." It hurried along awakening streets, it was shouted down the frost-stilled ways of quiet villages, men who had read these things from the throbbing tape stood in yellow-lit doorways shouting the news to the passers-by. "It is nearer." Pretty women, flushed and glittering, heard the news told jestingly between the dances, and feigned an intelligent interest they did not feel. "Nearer! Indeed. How curious! How very, very clever people must be to find out things like that!"

Lonely tramps faring through the wintry night murmured those words to comfort themselves—looking skyward. "It has need to be nearer, for the night's as cold as charity. Don't seem much warmth from it if it *is* nearer, all the same."

"What is a new star to me?" cried the weeping woman kneeling beside her dead.

The schoolboy, rising early for his examination work, puzzled it out for himself—with the great white star, shining broad and bright through the frost flowers of his window. "Centrifugal, centripetal," he said, with his chin on his fist. "Stop a planet in its flight, rob it of its centrifugal force, what then? Centripetal has it, and down it falls into the sun! And this—!"

"Do *we* come in the way? I wonder—"

The light of that day went the way of its brethren, and with the later watches of the frosty darkness rose the strange star again. And it was now so bright that the waxing moon seemed but a pale yellow ghost of itself, hanging huge in the sunset. In a South African city a great man had married, and the streets were alight to welcome his return with his bride. "Even the skies have illuminated," said the flatterer. Under Capricorn, two Negro lovers, daring the wild beasts and evil spirits, for love of one another, crouched together in a cane brake where the fireflies hovered. "That is our star," they whispered, and felt strangely comforted by the sweet brilliance of its light.

The master mathematician sat in his private room and pushed the papers from him. His calculations were already finished. In a small white phial there still remained a little of the drug that had kept him awake and active for four long nights. Each day, serene, explicit, patient as ever, he had given his lecture to his students, and then had come back at once to this momentous calculation. His face was grave, a little drawn and hectic from his drugged activity. For some time he seemed lost in thought. Then he went to the window, and the blind went up with a click. Half way up the sky, over the clustering roofs, chimneys and steeples of the city, hung the star.

He looked at it as one might look into the eyes of a brave enemy. "You may kill me," he said after a silence. "But I can hold you—and all the universe for that matter—in the grip of this little brain. I would not change. Even now."

He looked at the little phial. "There will be no need of sleep again," he said. The next day at noon, punctual to the minute, he entered his lecture theater, put his hat on the end of the tables as his habit was, and carefully selected a large piece of chalk. It was a joke among his students that he could not lecture without that piece of chalk to fumble in his fingers, and once he had been stricken to impotence by their hiding his supply. He came and looked under his gray eyebrows at the rising tiers of young fresh faces, and spoke with his accustomed studied commonness of phrasing. "Circumstances have arisen—circumstances beyond my control," he said and paused, "which will debar me from completing the course I had designed. It would seem, gentlemen, if I may put the thing clearly and briefly, that—Man has lived in vain."

The students glanced at one another. Had they heard aright? Mad? Raised eyebrows and grinning lips there were, but one or two faces remained intent upon his calm gray-fringed face. "It will be interesting," he was saying, "to devote this morning to an exposition, so far as I can make it clear to you, of the calculations that have led me to this conclusion. Let us assume—"

He turned towards the blackboard, meditating a diagram in the way that was usual to him. "What was that about 'lived in vain'?" whispered one student to another. "Listen," said the other, nodding towards the lecturer.

And presently they began to understand.

That night the star rose later, for its proper eastward motion had carried it some way across Leo towards Virgo, and its brightness was so great that the sky became a luminous blue as it rose, and every star was hidden in its turn, save only Jupiter near the zenith, Capella, Aldebaran, Sirius and the pointers of the Bear. It was very white and beautiful. In many parts of the world that night a pallid halo encircled it about. It was perceptibly larger; in the clear refractive sky of the tropics it seemed as if it were nearly a quarter the size of the moon. The frost was still on the ground in England, but the world was as brightly lit as if it were midsummer moonlight. One could see to read quite ordinary print by that cold clear light, and in the cities the lamps burnt yellow and wan.

And everywhere the world was awake that night, and throughout Christendom a somber murmur hung in the keen air over the countryside like the belling of bees in the heather, and this murmurous tumult grew to a clangor in the cities. It was the tolling of the bells in a million belfry towers and steeples, summoning the people to sleep no more, to sin no more, but to gather in their churches and pray. And overhead, growing larger and brighter as the earth rolled on its way and the night passed, rose the dazzling star.

And the streets and houses were alight in all the cities, the shipyards glared, and whatever roads led to high country were lit and crowded all night long. And in all the seas about the civilized lands, ships with throbbing engines, and ships with bellying sails, crowded with men and living creatures, were standing out to ocean and the north. For already the warning of the master mathematician had been telegraphed all over the world, and translated into a hundred tongues. The new planet and Neptune, locked in a fiery embrace, were whirling headlong, ever faster and faster towards the sun. Already every second this blazing mass flew a hundred miles, and every second its terrific velocity increased. As it flew now, indeed, it must pass a hundred million of miles wide of the earth and scarcely affect it. But near its destined path, as yet only slightly perturbed, spun the mighty planet Jupiter and his moons sweeping splendid round the sun. Every moment now the attraction between the fiery star and the greatest of the planets grew stronger. And the result of that attraction? Inevitably Jupiter would be deflected from his orbit into an elliptical path, and the burning star, swung by his attraction wide of its sunward rush, would "describe a curved path" and perhaps collide with, and certainly pass very close to, our earth. "Earthquakes, volcanic outbreaks, cyclones, sea waves, floods, and a steady rise in temperature to I know not what limit"—so prophesied the master mathematician.

And overhead, to carry out his words, lonely and cold and livid, blazed the star of the coming doom.

To many who stared at it that night until their eyes ached, it seemed that it was visibly approaching. And that night, too, the weather changed, and the frost that had gripped all Central Europe and France and England softened towards a thaw.

But you must not imagine because I have spoken of people praying through the night and people going aboard ships and people fleeing towards mountainous country that the whole world was already in a terror because of the star. As a matter of fact, use and wont still ruled the world, and save for the talk of idle moments and the splendor of the night, nine human beings out of ten were still busy at their common occupations. In all the cities, the shops, save one here and there, opened and closed at their proper hours, the doctor and the undertaker plied their trades, the workers gathered in the factories, soldiers drilled, scholars studied, lovers sought one another, thieves lurked and fled, politicians planned their schemes. The presses of the newspapers roared through the nights, and many a priest of this church and that would not open his holy building to further what he considered a foolish panic. The newspapers insisted on the lesson of the year 1000—for then, too, people had anticipated the end. The star was no star—mere gas—a comet; and were it a star it could not possibly strike the earth. There was no precedent for such a thing. Common sense was sturdy everywhere, scornful, jesting, a little inclined to persecute the obdurate fearful. That night, at seven-fifteen by Greenwich time, the star would be at its nearest to Jupiter. Then the world would see the turn things would take. The master mathematician's grim warnings were treated by many as so much mere elaborate self-advertisement. Common sense at last, a little heated by argument, signified its unalterable convictions by going to bed. So, too, barbarism and savagery, already tired of the novelty, went about their mighty business, and save for a howling dog here and there, the beast world left the star unheeded.

And yet, when at last the watchers in the European States saw the star rise, an hour later it is true, but no larger than it had been the night before, there were still plenty awake to laugh at the master mathematician—to take the danger as if it had passed.

But hereafter the laughter ceased. The star grew—it grew with a terrible steadiness hour after hour, a little larger each hour, a little nearer the midnight zenith, and brighter and brighter, until it had turned night into a second day. Had it come straight to the earth instead of in a curved path, had it lost no velocity to Jupiter, it must have leapt the intervening gulf in a day, but as it was it took five days altogether to come by our planet. The next night it had become a third the size of the moon before it set to English eyes, and the thaw was assured. It rose over America near the size of the moon, but blinding white to look at, and *hot*; and a breath of hot wind blew now with its rising and gathering strength, and in Virginia, and Brazil, and down the St. Lawrence valley, it shone intermittently through a driving reek of thunderclouds, flickering violet lightning, and hail unprecedented. In Manitoba was a thaw and devastating floods. And upon all the mountains of the earth the snow and ice began to melt that night, and all the rivers coming out of high country flowed thick and turbid, and soon— in their upper reaches—with swirling trees and the bodies of beasts and men. They rose steadily, steadily in the ghostly brilliance, and came trickling over their banks at last, behind the flying population of their valleys.

And along the coast of Argentina and up the South Atlantic the tides were higher than had ever been in the memory of man, and the storms drove the waters in many cases scores of miles inland, drowning whole cities. And so great grew the heat during the night that the rising of the sun was like the coming of a shadow. The earthquakes began and grew until all down America from the Arctic Circle to Cape Horn, hillsides were sliding, fissures were opening, and houses and walls crumbling to destruction. The whole side of Cotopaxi slipped out in one vast convulsion, and a tumult of lava poured out so high and broad and swift and liquid that in one day it reached the sea.

So the star, with the wan moon in its wake, marched across the Pacific, trailed the thunderstorms like the hem of a robe, and the growing tidal wave that toiled behind it, frothing and eager, poured over island and island and swept them clear of men. Until that wave came at last—in a blinding light and with the breath of a furnace, swift and terrible it came—a wall of water, fifty feet high, roaring hungrily, upon the long coasts of Asia, and swept inland across the plains of China. For a space the star, hotter now and larger and brighter than the sun in its strength, showed with pitiless billiance the wide and populous country; towns and villages with their pagodas and trees, roads, wide cultivated fields, millions of sleepless people staring in helpless terror at the incandescent sky; and then, low and growing, came the murmur of the flood. And thus it was with millions of men that night—a flight no-whither, with limbs heavy with heat and breath fierce and scant, and the flood like a wall swift and white behind. And then death.

China was lit glowing white, but over Japan and Java and all the islands of Eastern Asia the great star was a ball of dull red fire because of the steam and smoke and ashes the volcanoes were spouting forth to salute its coming. Above was the lava, hot gases and ash, and below the seething floods, and the whole earth swayed and rumbled with the earthquake shocks. Soon the immemorial snows of Thibet and the Himalaya were melting and pouring down by ten million deepening converging channels upon the plains of Burmah and Hindostan. The tangled summits of the Indian jungles were aflame in a thousand places, and below the hurrying waters around the stems were dark objects that still struggled feebly and reflected the blood-red tongues of fire. And in a rudderless confusion a multitude of men and women fled down the broad river-ways to that one last hope of men—the open sea.

Larger grew the star, and larger, hotter, and brighter with a terrible swiftness now. The tropical ocean had lost its phosphorescence, and the whirling stream rose in ghostly wreaths from the black waves that plunged incessantly, speckled with storm-tossed ships.

And then came a wonder. It seemed to those who in Europe watched for the rising of the star that the world must have ceased its rotation. In a thousand open spaces of down and upland the people who had fled thither from the floods and the falling houses and sliding slopes of hill watched for that rising in vain. Hour followed hour through a terrible suspense, and the star rose not. Once again men set their eyes upon the old constellations they had counted lost to them forever. In England it was hot and clear overhead, though the ground quivered perpetually, but in the tropics, Sirius and Capella and Aldebaran showed through a veil of steam. And when at last the great star rose near ten hours late, the sun rose close upon it, and in the center of its white heart was a disc of black.

Over Asia it was the star had begun to fall behind the movement of the sky, and then suddenly, as it hung over India, its light had been veiled. All the plain of India from the mouth of the Indus to the mouths of the Ganges was a shallow waste of shining water that night, out of which rose temples and palaces, mounds and hills, black with people. Every minaret was a clustering mass of people, who fell one by one into the turbid waters, as heat and terror overcame them. The whole land seemed a-wailing, and suddenly there swept a shadow across that furnace of despair, and a breath of cold wind, and a gathering of clouds, out of the cooling air. Men looking up, near blinded, at the star, saw that a black disc was creeping across the light. It was the moon, coming between the star and the earth. And even as men cried to God at this respite, out of the East with a strange inexplicable swiftness sprang the sun. And then star, sun and moon rushed together across the heavens.

So it was that presently, to the European watchers, star and sun rose close upon each other, drove headlong for a space and then slower, and at last came to rest, star and sun merged into one glare of flame at the zenith of the sky. The moon no longer eclipsed the star but was lost to sight in the brilliance of the sky. And though those who were still alive regarded it for the most part with that dull stupidity that hunger, fatigue, heat and despair engender, there were still men who could perceive the meaning of these signs. Star and earth had been at their nearest, had swung about one another, and the star had passed. Already it was receding, swifter and swifter, in the last stage of its headlong journey downward into the sun.

And then the clouds gathered, blotting out the vision of the sky, the thunder and lightning wove a garment round the world; all over the earth was such a downpour of rain as men had never before seen, and where the volcanoes flared red against the cloud canopy there descended torrents of mud. Everywhere the waters were pouring off the land, leaving mud-silted ruins, and the earth littered like a storm-worn beach with all that had floated, and the dead bodies of the men and brutes, its children. For days the water streamed off the land, sweeping away soil and trees and houses in the way, and piling huge dykes and scooping out Titanic gullies over the countryside. Those were the days of darkness that followed the star and the heat. All through them, and for many weeks and months, the earthquakes continued.

But the star had passed, and men, hunger-driven and gathering courage only slowly, might creep back to their ruined cities, buried granaries, and sodden fields. Such few ships as had escaped the storms of that time came stunned and shattered and sounding their way cautiously through the new marks and shoals of once familiar ports. And as the storms subsided men perceived that everywhere the days were hotter than of yore, and the sun larger, and the moon, shrunk to a third of its former size, took now fourscore days between its new and new.

But of the new brotherhood that grew presently among men, of the saving of laws and books and machines, of the strange change that had come over Iceland and Greenland and the shores of Baffin's Bay, so that the sailors coming there presently found them green and gracious, and could scarce believe their eyes, this story does not tell. Nor of the movement of mankind now that the earth was hotter, northward and southward towards the poles of the earth. It concerns itself only with the coming and the passing of the Star.

The Martian astronomers—for there are astronomers on Mars, although they are very different beings from men—were naturally profoundly interested by these things. They saw them from their own standpoint of course. "Considering the mass and temperature of the missile that was flung through our solar system into the sun," one wrote, "it is astonishing what a little damage the earth, which it missed so narrowly, has sustained. All the familiar continental markings and the masses of the seas remain intact, and indeed the only difference seems to be a shrinkage of the white discoloration (supposed to be frozen water) round either pole." Which only shows how small the vastest of human catastrophes may seem, at a distance of a few million miles.

IN THE ABYSS

THE LIEUTENANT STOOD in front of the steel sphere and gnawed a piece of pine splinter. "What do you think of it, Steevens?" he asked.

"It's an idea," said Steevens, in the tone of one who keeps an open mind.

"I believe it will smash—flat," said the lieutenant.

"He seems to have calculated it all out pretty well," said Steevens, still impartial.

"But think of the pressure," said the lieutenant, "At the surface of the water it's fourteen pounds to the inch, thirty feet down it's double that; sixty, treble; ninety, four times; nine hundred, forty times; five thousand three hundred—that's a mile—it's two hundred and forty times fourteen pounds; that's—let's see—thirty hundred-weight—a ton and a half, Steevens; *a ton and a half* to the square inch. And the ocean where he's going is five miles deep. That's seven and a half—"

"Sounds a lot," said Steevens, "but it's jolly thick steel."

The lieutenant made no answer, but resumed his pine splinter. The object of their conversation was a huge globe of steel, having an exterior diameter of perhaps eight feet. It looked like the shot for some Titanic piece of artillery. It was elaborately nested in a monstrous scaffolding built into the framework of the vessel, and the gigantic spars that were presently to sling it overboard gave the stern of the ship an appearance that had raised the curiosity of every decent sailor who had sighted it, from the pool of London to the Tropic of Capricorn. In two places, one above the other, the steel gave place to a couple of circular windows of enormously thick glass, and one of these, set in a steel frame of great solidity, was now partially unscrewed. Both the men had seen the interior of this globe for the first time that morning. It was elaborately padded with air cushions, with little studs sunk between bulging pillows to work the simple mechanism of the affair. Everything was elaborately padded, even the Myer's apparatus which was to absorb carbonic acid and replace the oxygen inspired by its tenant, when he had crept in by the glass manhole, and had been screwed in. It was so elaborately padded that a man might have been fired from a gun in it with perfect safety. And it had need to be, for presently a man was to crawl in through that glass manhole, to be screwed up tightly, and to be flung overboard, and to sink down—down—down, for five miles, even as the lieutenant said. It had taken the strongest hold of his imagination; it made him a bore at mess; and he found Steevens, the new arrival aboard, a godsend to talk to about it, over and over again.

"It's my opinion," said the lieutenant, "that that glass will simply bend in and bulge and smash, under a pressure of that sort. Daubrée has made rocks run like water under big pressures—and, you mark my words—"

"If the glass did break in," said Steevens, "what then?"

"The water would shoot in like a jet of iron. Have you ever felt a straight jet of high pressure water? It would hit as hard as a bullet. It would simply smash him and flatten him. It would tear down his throat, and into his lungs; it would blow in his ears—"

"What a detailed imagination you have," protested Steevens, who saw things vividly.

"It's a simple statement of the inevitable," said the lieutenant.

"And the globe?"

"Would just give out a few little bubbles, and it would settle down comfortably against the day of judgment, among the oozes and the bottom clay—with poor Elstead spread over his own smashed cushions like butter over bread."

He repeated this sentence as though he liked it very much. "Like butter over bread," he said.

"Having a look at the jigger?" said a voice behind them, and Elstead stood behind them, spick and span in white, with a cigarette between his teeth, and his eyes smiling out of the shadow of his ample hat-brim. "What's that about bread and butter, Weybridge? Grumbling as usual about the insufficient pay of naval officers? It won't be more than a day now before I start. We are to get the slings ready today. This clean sky and gentle swell is just the kind of thing for swinging off twenty tons of lead and iron; isn't it?"

"It won't affect you much," said Weybridge.

"No. Seventy or eighty feet down, and I shall be there in a dozen seconds, there's not a particle moving, though the wind shriek itself hoarse up above, and the water lifts halfway to the clouds. No. Down there—" He moved to the side of the ship and the other two followed him. All three leant forward on their elbows and stared down into the yellow-green water.

"*Peace*," said Elstead, finishing his thought aloud.

"Are you dead certain that clockwork will act?" asked Weybridge, presently.

"It has worked thirty-five times," said Elstead. "It's bound to work."

"But if it doesn't?"

"Why shouldn't it?"

"I wouldn't go down in that confounded thing," said Weybridge, "for twenty thousand pounds."

"Cheerful chap you are," said Elstead, and spat sociably at a bubble below.

"I don't understand yet how you mean to work the thing," said Steevens.

"In the first place I'm screwed into the sphere," said Elstead, "and when I've turned the electric light off and on three times to show I'm cheerful, I'm swung out over the stern by that crane, with all those big lead sinkers slung below me. The top lead weight has a roller carrying a hundred fathoms of strong cord rolled up, and that's all that joins the sinkers to the sphere, except the slings that will be cut when the affair is dropped. We use cord rather than wire rope because it's easier to cut and more buoyant—necessary points as you will see.

"Through each of these lead weights you notice there is a hole, and an iron rod will be run through that and will project six feet on the lower side. If that rod is rammed up from below it knocks up a lever and sets the clockwork in motion at the side of the cylinder on which the cord winds.

"Very well. The whole affair is lowered gently into the water, and the slings are cut. The sphere floats—with the air in it, it's lighter than water; but the lead weights go down straight and the cord runs out. When the cord is all paid out, the sphere will go down too, pulled down by the cord."

"But why the cord?" asked Steevens. "Why not fasten the weights directly to the sphere?"

"Because of the smash down below. The whole affair will go rushing down, mile after mile, at a headlong pace at last. It would be knocked to pieces on the bottom if it wasn't for that cord. But the weights will hit the bottom, and directly they do the buoyancy of the sphere will come into play. It will go on sinking slower and slower; come to a stop at last and then begin to float upward again.

"That's where the clockwork comes in. Directly the weights smash against the sea bottom, the rod will be knocked through and will kick up the clockwork, and the cord will be rewound on the reel. I shall be lugged down to the sea bottom. There I shall stay for half an hour, with the electric light on, looking about me. Then the clockwork will release a spring knife, the cord will be cut, and up I shall rush again, like a soda-water bubble. The cord itself will help the flotation."

"And if you should chance to hit a ship?" said Weybridge.

"I should come up at such a pace, I should go clean through it," said Elstead, "like a cannon ball. You needn't worry about that."

"And suppose some nimble crustacean should wriggle into your clock-work—"

"It would be a pressing sort of invitation for me to stop," said Elstead, turning his back on the water and staring at the sphere.

They had swung Elstead overboard by eleven o'clock. The day was serenely bright and calm, with the horizon lost in haze. The electric glare in the little upper compartment beamed cheerfully three times. Then they let him down slowly to the surface of the water, and a sailor in the stern chains hung ready to cut the tackle that held the lead weights and the sphere together. The globe, which had looked so large on deck, looked the smallest thing conceivable under the stern of the ship. It rolled a little, and its two dark windows, which floated uppermost, seemed like eyes turned up in round wonderment at the people who crowded the rail. A voice wondered how Elstead liked the rolling. "Are you ready?" sang out the Commander. "Aye, aye, sir!" "Then let her go!"

The rope of the tackle tightened against the blade and was cut, and an eddy rolled over the globe in a grotesquely helpless fashion. Someone waved a hand-kerchief, someone else tried an ineffectual cheer, a middy was counting slowly: "Eight, nine, ten!" Another roll, then with a jerk and a splash the thing righted itself.

It seemed to be stationary for a moment, to grow rapidly smaller, and then the water closed over it, and it became visible, enlarged by refraction and dimmer, below the surface. Before one could count three it had disappeared. There was a flicker of white light far down in the water, that diminished to a speck and vanished. Then there was nothing but a depth of water going down into blackness, through which a shark was swimming.

Then suddenly the screw of the cruiser began to rotate, the water was crickled, the shark disappeared in a wrinkled confusion, and a torrent of foam rushed across the crystalline clearness that had swallowed up Elstead. "What's the idee?" said one A. B. to another.

"We 're going to lay off about a couple of miles, 'fear he should hit us when he comes up," said his mate.

The ship steamed slowly to her new position. Aboard her almost every one who was unoccupied remained watching the breathing swell into which the sphere had sunk. For the next half hour it is doubtful if a word was spoken that did not bear directly or indirectly on Elstead. The December sun was now high in the sky, and the heat very considerable.

"He'll be cold enough down there," said Weybridge. "They say that below a certain depth sea-water's always just about freezing."

"Where'll he come up?" asked Steevens. "I've lost my bearings."

"That's the spot," said the Commander, who prided himself on his omniscience. He extended a precise finger southeastward. "And this, I reckon, is pretty nearly the moment," he said. "He's been thirty-five minutes."

"How long does it take to reach the bottom of the ocean?" asked Steevens.

"For a depth of five miles, and reckoning—as we did—an acceleration to two foot per second, both ways, is just about three-quarters of a minute."

"Then he's overdue," said Weybridge.

"Pretty nearly," said the Commander. "I suppose it takes a few minutes for that cord of his to wind in."

"I forgot that," said Weybridge, evidently relieved.

And then began the suspense. A minute slowly dragged itself out, and no sphere shot out of the water. Another followed, and nothing broke the low oily swell. The sailors explained to one another that little point about the winding-in of the cord. The rigging was dotted with expectant faces. "Come up, Elstead!" called one hairy-chested salt, impatiently, and the others caught it up, and shouted as though they were waiting for the curtain of a theatre to rise.

The Commander glanced irritably at them.

"Of course, if the acceleration's less than two," he said, "he'll be all the longer. We aren't absolutely certain that was the proper figure. I'm no slavish believer in calculations."

Steevens agreed concisely. No one on the quarter-deck spoke for a couple of minutes. Then Steevens's watch-case clicked.

When, twenty-one minutes after, the sun reached the zenith, they were still waiting for the globe to reappear, and not a man aboard had dared to whisper that hope was dead. It was Weybridge who first gave expression to that realization. He spoke while the sound of eight bells still hung in the air. "I always distrusted that window," he said quite suddenly to Steevens.

"Good God!" said Steevens, "you don't think—"

"Well!" said Weybridge, and left the rest to his imagination.

"I'm no great believer in calculations myself," said the Commander, dubiously, "so that I'm not altogether hopeless yet." And at midnight the gunboat was steaming slowly in a spiral round the spot where the globe had sunk, and the white beam of the electric light fled and halted and swept discontentedly onward again over the waste of phosphorescent waters under the little stars.

"If his window hasn't burst and smashed him," said Weybridge, "then it's a cursed sight worse, for his clockwork has gone wrong and he's alive now, five miles under our feet, down there in the cold and dark, anchored in that little bubble of his, where never a ray of light has shone or a human being lived, since the waters were gathered together. He's there without food, feeling hungry and thirsty and scared, wondering whether he'll starve or stifle. Which will it be? The Myer's apparatus is running out, I suppose. How long do they last?

"Good Heavens!" he exclaimed, "what little things we are! What daring little devils! Down there miles and miles of water—all water, and all this empty water about us and this sky. Gulfs!'' He threw his hands out, and as he did so a little white streak swept noiselessly up the sky, traveling more slowly, stopped, became a motionless dot as though a new star had fallen up into the sky. Then it went sliding back again and lost itself amidst the reflections of the stars, and the white haze of the sea's phosphorescence.

At the sight he stopped, arm extended and mouth open. He shut his mouth, opened it again and waved his arms with an impatient gesture. Then he turned, shouted, ''El-stead ahoy,'' to the first watch, and went at a run to Lindley and the searchlight. ''I saw him,'' he said. ''Starboard there! His light's on and he's just shot out of the water. Bring the light round. We ought to see him drifting, when he lifts on the swell.''

But they never picked up the explorer until dawn. Then they almost ran him down. The crane was swung out and a boat's crew hooked the chain to the sphere. When they had shipped the sphere they unscrewed the manhole and peered into the darkness of the interior (for the electric light chamber was intended to illuminate the water about the sphere, and was shut off entirely from its general cavity).

The air was very hot within the cavity, and the india-rubber at the lip of the manhole was soft. There was no answer to their eager questions and no sound of movement within. Elstead seemed to be lying motionless, crumpled up in the bottom of the globe. The ship's doctor crawled in and lifted him out to the men outside. For a moment or so they did not know whether Elstead was alive or dead. His face, in the yellow glow of the ship's lamps, glistened with perspiration. They carried him down to his own cabin.

He was not dead they found, but in a state of absolute nervous collapse, and besides cruelly bruised. For some days he had to lie perfectly still. It was a week before he could tell his experiences.

Almost his first words were that he was going down again. The sphere would have to be altered, he said, in order to allow him to throw off the cord if need be, and that was all. He had had the most marvellous experience. ''You thought I should find nothing but ooze,'' he said. ''You laughed at my explorations, and I've discovered a new world!'' He told his story in disconnected fragments, and chiefly from the wrong end, so that it is impossible to retell it in his words. But what follows is the narrative of his experience.

It began atrociously, he said. Before the cord ran out the thing kept rolling over. He felt like a frog in a football. He could see nothing but the crane and the sky overhead, with an occasional glimpse of the people on the ship's rail. He couldn't tell a bit which way the thing would roll next. Suddenly he would find his feet going up and try to step, and over he went rolling, head over heels and just anyhow on the padding. Any other shape would have been more comfortable, but no other shape was to be relied upon under the huge pressure of the nethermost abyss.

Suddenly the swaying ceased; the globe righted, and when he had picked himself up, he saw the water all about him greeny-blue with an attenuated light filtering down from above, and a shoal of little floating things went rushing up past him, as it seemed to him, towards the light. And even as he looked it grew darker and darker, until the water above was as dark as the midnight sky, albeit of a greener shade, and the water below black. And little transparent things in the water developed a faint glint of luminosity, and shot past him in faint greenish streaks.

And the feeling of falling! It was just like the start of a lift, he said, only it kept on. One has to imagine what that means, that keeping on. It was then of all times that Elstead repented of his adventure. He saw the chances against him in an altogether new light. He thought of the big cuttle-fish people knew to exist in the middle waters, the kind of things they find half-digested in whales at times, or floating dead and rotten and half eaten by fish. Suppose one caught hold and wouldn't leave go. And had the clockwork really been sufficiently tested? But whether he wanted to go on or go back mattered not the slightest now.

In fifty seconds everything was as black as night outside, except where the beam from his light struck through the waters, and picked out every now and then some fish or scrap of sinking matter. They flashed by too fast for him to see what they were. Once he thought he passed a shark. And then the sphere began to get hot by friction against the water. They had underestimated this, it seems.

The first thing he noticed was that he was perspiring, and then he heard a hissing, growing louder, under his feet, and saw a lot of little bubbles—very little bubbles they were—rushing upward like a fan through the water outside. Steam! He felt the window and it was hot. He turned on the minute glow lamp that lit his own cavity, looked at the padded watch by the studs, and saw he had been traveling now for two minutes. It came into his head that the window would crack through the conflict of temperatures, for he knew the bottom water was very near freezing.

Then suddenly the floor of the sphere seemed to press against his feet, the rush of bubbles outside grew slower and slower and the hissing diminished. The sphere rolled a little. The window had not cracked, nothing had given, and he knew that the dangers of sinking, at any rate, were over.

In another minute or so, he would be on the floor of the abyss. He thought, he said, of Steevens and Weybridge and the rest of them five miles overhead, higher to him than the very highest clouds that ever floated over land are to us, steaming slowly and staring down and wondering what had happened to him.

He peered out of the window. There were no more bubbles now, and the hissing had stopped. Outside there was a heavy blackness—as black as black velvet—except where the electric light pierced the empty water and showed the color of it—a yellow green. Then three things like shapes of fire swam into sight following each other through the water. Whether they were little and near, or big and far off he could not tell.

Each was outlined in a bluish light almost as bright as the lights of a fishing-smack, a light which seemed to be smoking greatly, and all along the sides of them were specks of this, like the lighted portholes of a ship. Their phosphorescence seemed to go out as they came into the radiance of his lamp, and he saw then that they were indeed fish of some strange sort, with huge heads, vast eyes, and dwindling bodies and tails. Their eyes were turned towards him, and he judged they were following him down. He supposed they were attracted by his glare.

Presently others of the same sort joined them. As he went on down he noticed that the water became of a pallid color, and that little specks twinkled in his ray like motes in sunbeam. This was probably due to the clouds of ooze and mud that the impact of his leaden sinkers had disturbed.

By the time he was drawn down to the lead weights he was in a dense fog of white that his electric light failed altogether to pierce for more than a few yards, and many minutes elapsed before the hanging sheets of sediment subsided to any extent. Then, lit by his light and by the transient phosphorescence of a distant shoal of fishes, he was able to see under the huge blackness of the superincumbent water an undulating expanse of greyish-white ooze, broken here and there by tangled thickets of a growth of sea lilies, waving hungry tentacles in the air.

Farther away were the graceful translucent outlines of a group of gigantic sponges. About this floor there were scattered a number of bristling flattish tufts of rich purple and black, which he decided must be some sort of sea-urchin, and small, large-eyed or blind things, having a curious resemblance, some to woodlice, and others to lobsters crawled sluggishly across the track of the light and vanished into the obscurity again, leaving furrowed trails behind them.

Then suddenly the hovering swarm of little fishes veered about and came towards him as a flight of starlings might do. They passed over him like a phosphorescent snow, and then he saw behind them some larger creature advancing towards the sphere.

At first he could see it only dimly, a faintly moving figure remotely suggestive of a walking man, and then it came into the spray of light that the lamp shot out. As the glare struck it, it shut its eyes, dazzled. He stared in rigid astonishment.

It was a strange, vertebrated animal. Its dark purple head was dimly suggestive of a chameleon, but it had such a high forehead and such a braincase as no reptile ever displayed before; the vertical pitch of its face gave it a most extraordinary resemblance to a human being.

Two large and protruding eyes projected from sockets in chameleon fashion, and it had a broad reptilian mouth with horny lips beneath its little nostrils. In the position of the ears were two huge gill covers, and out of these floated a branching tree of coralline filaments, almost like the tree-like gills that very young rays and sharks possess.

But the humanity of the face was not the most extraordinary thing about the creature. It was a biped, its almost globular body was poised on a tripod of two frog-like legs and a long thick tail, and its fore limbs, which grotesquely caricatured the human hand much as a frog's do, carried a long shaft of bone, tipped with copper. The color of the creature was variegated: its head, hands, and legs were purple; but its skin, which hung loosely upon it, even as clothes might do, was a phosphorescent grey. And it stood there, blinded by the light.

At last this unknown creature of the abyss blinked its eyes open, and, shading them with its disengaged hand, opened its mouth and gave vent to a shouting noise, articulate almost as speech might be, that penetrated even the steel case and padded jacket of the sphere. How a shouting may be accomplished without lungs Elstead does not profess to explain. It then moved sideways out of the glare into the mystery of shadow that bordered it on either side, and Elstead felt rather than saw that it was coming towards him. Fancying the light had attracted it, he turned the switch that cut off the current. In another moment something soft dabbed upon the steel, and the globe swayed.

Then the shouting was repeated, and it seemed to him that a distant echo answered it. The dabbing recurred, and the globe swayed and ground against the spindle over which the wire was rolled. He stood in the blackness, and peered out into the everlasting night of the abyss. And presently he saw, very faint and remote, other phosphorescent quasi-human forms hurrying towards him.

Hardly knowing what he did, he felt about in his swaying prison for the stud of the exterior electric light, and came by accident against his own small glow lamp in its padded recess. The sphere twisted, and then threw him down; he heard shouts like shouts of surprise, and when he rose to his feet he saw two pairs of stalked eyes peering into the lower window and reflecting his light.

In another moment hands were dabbing vigorously at his steel casing, and there was a sound, horrible enough in his position, of the metal protection of the clockwork being vigorously hammered. That, indeed, sent his heart into his mouth, for if these strange creatures succeeded in stopping that his release would never occur. Scarcely had he thought as much when he felt the sphere sway violently, and the floor of it press hard against his feet. He turned off the small glow lamp that lit the interior, and sent the ray of the large light in the separate compartment out into the water. The sea floor and the man-like creatures had disappeared, and a couple of fish chasing each other dropped suddenly by the window.

He thought at once that these strange denizens of the deep sea had broken the wire rope, and that he had escaped. He drove up faster and faster, and then stopped with a jerk that sent him flying against the padded roof of his prison. For half a minute perhaps he was too astonished to think.

Then he felt that the sphere was spinning slowly, and rocking, and it seemed to him that it was also being drawn through the water. By crouching close to the window he managed to make his weight effective and roll that part of the sphere downward, but he could see nothing save the pale ray of his light striking down ineffectively into the darkness. It occurred to him that he would see more if he turned the lamp off and allowed his eyes to grow accustomed to the profound obscurity.

In this he was wise. After some minutes the velvety blackness became a translucent blackness, and then far away, and as faint as the zodiacal light of an English summer evening, he saw shapes moving below. He judged these creatures had detached his cable and were towing him along the sea bottom.

And then he saw something faint and remote across the undulations of the submarine plain, a broad horizon of pale luminosity that extended this way and that way as far as the range of his little window permitted him to see. To this he was being towed, as a balloon might be towed by men out of the open country into a town. He approached it very slowly, and very slowly the dim irradiation was gathered together into more definite shapes.

It was nearly five o'clock before he came over this luminous area, and by that time he could make out an arrangement suggestive of streets and houses grouped about a vast roofless erection that was grotesquely suggestive of a ruined abbey. It was spread out like a map below him. The houses were all roofless inclosures of walls, and their substance being, as he afterwards saw, of phosphorescent bones, gave the place an appearance as if it were built of drowned moonshine.

Among the inner caves of the place waving trees of crinoid stretched their tentacles, and tall, slender, glassy sponges shot like shining minarets and lilies of filmy light out of the general glow of the city. In the open spaces of the place he could see a stirring movement as of crowds of people, but he was too many fathoms above them to distinguish the individuals in those crowds.

Then slowly they pulled him down, and as they did so the details of the place crept slowly upon his apprehension. He saw that the courses of the cloudy buildings were marked out with beaded lines of round objects, and then he perceived that at several points below him in broad open spaces were forms like the encrusted shapes of ships.

Slowly and surely he was drawn down, and the forms below him became brighter, clearer, were more distinct. He was being pulled down, he perceived, towards the large building in the center of the town, and he could catch a glimpse ever and again of the multitudinous forms that were lugging at his cord. He was astonished to see that the rigging of one of the ships, which formed such a prominent feature of the place, was crowded with a host of gesticulating figures regarding him, and then the walls of the great building rose about him silently, and hid the city from his eyes.

And such walls they were, of water-logged wood, and twisted wire rope and iron spars, and copper, and the bones and skulls of dead men.

The skulls ran in curious zigzag lines and spirals and fantastic curves over the building; and in and out of their eye-sockets, and over the whole surface of the place, lurked and played a multitude of silvery little fishes.

And now he was at such a level that he could see these strange people of the abyss plainly once more. To his astonishment, he perceived that they were prostrating themselves before him, all save one, dressed as it seemed in a robe of placoid scales, and crowned with a luminous diadem, who stood with his reptilian mouth opening and shutting as though he led the chanting of the worshippers.

They continued worshipping him, without rest or intermission, for the space of three hours.

Most circumstantial was Elstead's account of this astounding city and its people, these people of perpetual night, who have never seen sun or moon or stars, green vegetation, nor any living air-breathing creatures, who know nothing of fire, nor any light but the phosphorescent light of living things.

Startling as is his story, it is yet more startling to find that scientific men, of such eminence as Adams and Jenkins, find nothing incredible in it. They tell me they see no reason why intelligent, water-breathing, vertebrated creatures inured to a low temperature and enormous pressure, and of such a heavy structure, that neither alive nor dead would they float, might not live upon the bottom of the deep sea, and quite unsuspected by us, descendants like ourselves of the great Theriomorpha of the New Red Sandstone age.

We should be known to them, however, as strange meteoric creatures wont to fall catastrophically dead out of the mysterious blackness of their watery sky. And not only we ourselves, but our ships, our metals, our appliances, would come raining down out of the night. Sometimes sinking things would smite down and crush them, as if it were the judgment of some unseen power above, and sometimes would come things of the utmost rarity or utility or shapes of inspiring suggestion. One can understand, perhaps, something of their behavior at the descent of a living man, if one thinks what a barbaric people might do, to whom an enhaloed shining creature came suddenly out of the sky.

At one time or another Elstead probably told the officers of the *Ptarmigan* every detail of his strange twelve hours in the abyss. That he also intended to write them down is certain, but he never did, and so unhappily we have to piece together the discrepant fragments of his story from the reminiscences of Commander Simmons, Weybridge, Steevens, Lindley, and the others.

We see the thing darkly in fragmentary glimpses—the huge ghostly building, the bowing, chanting people, with their dark, chameleon-like heads and faintly luminous forms, and Elstead, with his light turned on again, vainly trying to convey to their minds that the cord by which the sphere was held was to be severed. Minute after minute slipped away, and Elstead, looking at his watch, was horrified to find that he had oxygen only for four hours more. But the chant in his honor kept on as remorselessly as if it was the marching song of his approaching death.

The manner of his release he does not understand, but to judge by the end of cord that hung from the sphere, it had been cut through by rubbing against the edge of the altar. Abruptly the sphere rolled over, and he swept up, out of their world, as an ethereal creature clothed in a vacuum would sweep through our own atmosphere back to its native ether again. He must have torn out of their sight as a hydrogen bubble hastens upwards from our air. A strange ascension it must have seemed to them.

The sphere rushed up with even greater velocity than, when weighed with the lead sinkers, it had rushed down. It became exceedingly hot. It drove up with the windows uppermost, and he remembers the torrent of bubbles frothing against the glass. Every moment he expected this to fly. Then suddenly something like a huge wheel seemed to be released in his head, the padded compartment began spinning about him, and he fainted. His next recollection was of his cabin, and of the doctor's voice.

But that is the substance of the extraordinary story that Elstead related in fragments to the officers of the *Ptarmigan*. He promised to write it all down at a later date. His mind was chiefly occupied with the improvement of his apparatus, which was effected at Rio.

It remains only to tell that on February 2, 1896, he made his second descent into the ocean abyss, with the improvements his first experience suggested. What happened we shall probably never know. He never returned. The *Ptarmigan* beat about over the point of his submersion, seeking him in vain for thirteen days. Then she returned to Rio, and the news was telegraphed to his friends. So the matter remains for the present. But it is hardly probable that any further attempt will be made to verify his strange story of these hitherto unsuspected cities of the deep sea.

A DREAM OF ARMAGEDDON

THE MAN WITH the white face entered the carriage at Rugby. He moved slowly in spite of the urgency of his porter, and even while he was still on the platform I noted how ill he seemed. He dropped into the corner over against me with a sigh, made an incomplete attempt to arrange his traveling shawl, and became motionless, with his eyes staring vacantly. Presently he was moved by a sense of my observation, looked up at me, and put out a spiritless hand for his newspaper. Then he glanced again in my direction.

I feigned to read. I feared I had unwittingly embarrassed him, and in a moment I was surprised to find him speaking.

"I beg your pardon?" said I.

"That book," he repeated, pointing a lean finger, "is about dreams."

"Obviously," I answered, for it was Fortnum-Roscoe's *Dream States,* and the title was on the cover.

He hung silent for a space as if he sought words. "Yes," he said at last, "but they tell you nothing."

I did not catch his meaning for a second.

"They don't know," he added.

I looked a little more attentively at his face.

"There are dreams," he said, "and dreams."

That sort of proposition I never dispute.

"I suppose—" he hesitated. "Do you ever dream? I mean vividly."

"I dream very little," I answered. "I doubt if I have three vivid dreams a year."

"Ah!" he said, and seemed for a moment to collect his thoughts.

"Your dreams don't mix with your memories?" he asked abruptly. "You don't find yourself in doubt; did this happen or did it not?"

"Hardly ever. Except just for a momentary hesitation now and then. I suppose few people do."

"Does *he* say—" he indicated the book.

"Says it happens at times and gives the usual explanation about intensity of impression and the like to account for its not happening as a rule. I suppose you know something of these theories—"

"Very little—except that they are wrong."

His emaciated hand played with the strap of the window for a time. I prepared to resume reading, and that seemed to precipitate his next remark. He leant forward almost as though he would touch me.

"Isn't there something called consecutive dreaming—that goes on night after night?"

"I believe there is. There are cases given in most books on mental trouble."

"Mental trouble! Yes. I dare say there are. It's the right place for them. But what I mean—" He looked at his bony knuckles. "Is that sort of thing always dreaming? *Is* it dreaming? Or is it something else? Mightn't it be something else?"

I should have snubbed his persistent conversation but for the drawn anxiety of his face. I remember now the look of his faded eyes and the lids red stained—perhaps you know that look.

"I'm not just arguing about a matter of opinion," he said. "The thing's killing me."

"Dreams?"

"If you call them dreams. Night after night. Vivid!—so vivid . . . this—" (he indicated the landscape that went streaming by the window) "seems unreal in comparison! I can scarcely remember who I am, what business I am on. . . ."

He paused. "Even now—"

"The dream is always the same—do you mean?" I asked.

"It's over."

"You mean?"

"I died."

"Died?"

"Smashed and killed, and now, so much of me as that dream was, is dead. Dead forever. I dreamt I was another man, you know, living in a different part of the world and in a different time. I dreamt that night after night. Night after night I woke into that other life. Fresh scenes and fresh happenings—until I came upon the last—"

"When you died?"

"When I died."

"And since then—"

"No," he said. "Thank God! That was the end of the dream. . . ."

It was clear I was in for this dream. And after all, I had an hour before me, the light was fading fast, and Fortnum-Roscoe has a dreary way with him. "Living in a different time," I said: "do you mean in some different age?"

"Yes."

"Past?"

"No—to come—to come."

"The year three thousand, for example?"

"I don't know what year it was. I did when I was asleep, when I was dreaming, that is, but not now—not now that I am awake. There's a lot of things I have forgotten since I woke out of these dreams, though I knew them at the time when I was—I suppose it was dreaming. They called the year differently from our way of calling the year. . . . What *did* they call it?'' He put his hand to his forehead. "No," said he, "I forget."

He sat smiling weakly. For a moment I feared he did not mean to tell me his dream. As a rule I hate people who tell their dreams, but this struck me differently. I proffered assistance even. "It began—'' I suggested.

"It was vivid from the first. I seemed to wake up in it suddenly. And it's curious that in these dreams I am speaking of I never remembered this life I am living now. It seemed as if the dream life was enough while it lasted. Perhaps— But I will tell you how I find myself when I do my best to recall it all. I don't remember anything clearly until I found myself sitting in a sort of loggia looking out over the sea. I had been dozing, and suddenly I woke up—fresh and vivid— not a bit dreamlike—because the girl had stopped fanning me.''

"The girl?''

"Yes, the girl. You must not interrupt or you will put me out.''

He stopped abruptly. "You won't think I'm mad?'' he said.

"No,'' I answered; "you've been dreaming. Tell me your dream.''

"I woke up, I say, because the girl had stopped fanning me. I was not surprised to find myself there or anything of that sort you understand. I did not feel I had fallen into it suddenly. I simply took it up at that point. Whatever memory I had of *this* life, this nineteenth-century life, faded as I woke, vanished like a dream. I knew all about myself, knew that my name was no longer Cooper but Hedon, and all about my position in the world. I've forgotten a lot since I woke— there's a want of connection—but it was all quite clear and matter of fact then.''

He hesitated again, gripping the window strap, putting his face forward and looking up to me appealingly.

"This seems bosh to you?''

"No, no!'' I cried. "Go on. Tell me what this loggia was like.''

"It was not really a loggia—I don't know what to call it. It faced south. It was small. It was all in shadow except the semicircle above the balcony that showed the sky and sea and the corner where the girl stood. I was on a couch— it was a metal couch with light striped cushions—and the girl was leaning over the balcony with her back to me. The light of the sunrise fell on her ear and cheek. Her pretty white neck and the little curls that nestled there, and her white shoulder were in the sun, and all the grace of her body was in the cool blue shadow. She was dressed—how can I describe it? It was easy and flowing. And altogether there she stood, so that it came to me how beautiful and desirable she was, as though I had never seen her before. And when at last I sighed and raised myself upon my arm she turned her face to me—''

He stopped.

"I have lived three-and-fifty years in this world. I have had mother, sisters, friends, wife and daughters—all their faces, the play of their faces, I know. But the face of this girl—it is much more real to me. I can bring it back into memory so that I see it again—I could draw it or paint it. And after all—''

He stopped—but I said nothing.

"The face of a dream—the face of a dream. She was beautiful. Not that beauty which is terrible, cold, and worshipful, like the beauty of a saint; nor that beauty that stirs fierce passions; but a sort of radiation, sweet lips that softened into smiles, and grave grey eyes. And she moved gracefully, she seemed to have part with all pleasant and gracious things—''

He stopped, and his face was downcast and hidden. Then he looked up at me and went on, making no further attempt to disguise his absolute belief in the reality of his story.

"You see, I had thrown up my plans and ambitions, thrown up all I had ever worked for or desired for her sake. I had been a master man away there in the north, with influence and property and a great reputation, but none of it had seemed worth having beside her. I had come to the place, this city of sunny pleasures, with her, and left all those things to wreck and ruin just to save a remnant at least of my life. While I had been in love with her before I knew that she had any care for me, before I had imagined that she would dare—that we should dare, all my life had seemed vain and hollow, dust and ashes. It *was* dust and ashes. Night after night and through the long days I had longed and desired—my soul had beaten against the thing forbidden!

"But it is impossible for one man to tell another just these things. It's emotion, it's a tint, a light that comes and goes. Only while it's there, everything changes, everything. The thing is I came away and left them in their Crisis to do what they could."

"Left whom?" I asked, puzzled.

"The people up in the north there. You see—in this dream, anyhow—I had been a big man, the sort of man men come to trust in, to group themselves about. Millions of men who had never seen me were ready to do things and risk things because of their confidence in me. I had been playing that game for years, that big laborious game, that vague, monstrous political game amidst intrigues and betrayals, speech and agitation. It was a vast weltering world, and at last I had a sort of leadership against the Gang—you know it was called the Gang—a sort of compromise of scoundrelly projects and base ambitions and vast public emotional stupidities and catchwords—the Gang that kept the world noisy and blind year by year, and all the while that it was drifting, drifting towards infinite disaster. But I can't expect you to understand the shades and complications of the year—the year something or other ahead. I had it all—down to the smallest details—in my dream. I suppose I had been dreaming of it before I awoke, and the fading outline of some queer new development I had imagined still hung about me as I rubbed my eyes. It was some grubby affair that made me thank God for the sunlight. I sat up on the couch and remained looking at the woman and rejoicing—rejoicing that I had come away out of all that tumult and folly and violence before it was too late. After all, I thought, this is life—love and beauty, desire and delight, are they not worth all those dismal struggles for vague, gigantic ends. And I blamed myself for having ever sought to be a leader when I might have given my days to love. But then, thought I, if I had not spent my early days sternly and austerely, I might have wasted myself upon vain and worthless women, and at the thought all my being went out in love and tenderness to my dear mistress, my dear lady, who had come at last and compelled me—compelled me by her invincible charm for me—to lay that life aside.

" 'You are worth it,' I said, speaking without intending her to hear; 'you are worth it, my dearest one; worth pride and praise and all things. Love! to have *you* is worth them all together.' And at the murmur of my voice she turned about.

" 'Come and see,' she cried—I can hear her now—'come and see the sunrise upon Monte Solaro.'

"I remember how I sprang to my feet and joined her at the balcony. She put a white hand upon my shoulder and pointed towards great masses of limestone, flushing, as it were, into life. I looked. But first I noted the sunlight on her face caressing the lines of her cheeks and neck. How can I describe to you the scene we had before us? We were at Capri—''

''I have been there,'' I said. ''I have clambered up Monte Solaro and drunk *vero Capri*—muddy stuff like cider—at the summit.''

''Ah!'' said the man with the white face; ''then perhaps you can tell me—you will know if this was indeed Capri. For in this life I have never been there. Let me describe it. We were in a little room, one of a vast multitude of little rooms, very cool and sunny, hollowed out of the limestone of a sort of cape, very high above the sea. The whole island, you know, was one enormous hotel, complex beyond explaining, and on the other side there were miles of floating hotels, and huge floating stages to which the flying machines came. They called it a pleasure city. Of course, there was none of that in your time—rather, I should say, *is* none of that *now*. Of course. Now!—yes.

''Well, this room of ours was at the extremity of the cape, so that one could see east and west. Eastward was a great cliff—a thousand feet high perhaps—coldly grey except for one bright edge of gold, and beyond it the Isle of the Sirens, and a failing coast that faded and passed into the hot sunrise. And when one turned to the west, distinct and near was a little bay, a scimitar of beach still in shadow. And out of that shadow rose Solaro straight and tall, flushed and golden crested, like a beauty throned, and the white moon was floating behind her in the sky. And before us from east to west stretched the many-tinted sea all dotted with sailing boats.

''To the eastward, of course, these little boats were grey and very minute and clear, but to the westward they were little boats of gold—shining gold—almost like little flames. And just below us was a rock with an arch worn through it. The blue sea-water broke to green and foam all round the rock, and a galley came gliding out of the arch.''

''I know that rock,'' I said. ''I was nearly drowned there. It is called the Faraglioni.''

''*I Faraglioni?* Yes, *she* called it that,'' answered the man with the white face. ''There was some story—but that—''

He put his hand to his forehead again. ''No,'' he said, ''I forget that story.

''Well, that is the first thing I remember, the first dream I had, that shaded room and the beautiful air and sky and that dear lady of mine, with her shining arms and her graceful robe, and how we sat and talked in half whispers to one another. We talked in whispers not because there was anyone to hear, but because there was still such a freshness of mind between us that our thoughts were a little frightened, I think, to find themselves at last in words. And so they went softly.

''Presently we were hungry and we went from our apartment, going by a strange passage with a moving floor, until we came to the great breakfast room—there was a fountain and music. A pleasant joyful place it was, with its sunlight and splashing, and the murmur of plucked strings. And we sat and ate and smiled at one another, and I would not heed a man who was watching me from a table near by.

''And afterwards we went on to the dancing-hall. But I cannot describe that hall. The place was enormous—larger than any building you have ever seen—and in one place there was the old gate of Capri, caught into the wall of a gallery high overhead. Light girders, stems and threads of gold, burst from the pillars like fountains, streamed like an Aurora across the roof and interlaced, like—like conjuring tricks. All about the great circle for the dancers there were beautiful figures, strange dragons, and intricate and wonderful grotesques bearing lights.

The place was inundated with artificial light that shamed the newborn day. And as we went through the throng the people turned about and looked at us, for all through the world my name and face were known, and how I had suddenly thrown up pride and struggle to come to this place. And they looked also at the lady beside me, though half the story of how at last she had come to me was unknown or mistold. And few of the men who were there, I know, but judged me a happy man, in spite of all the shame and dishonor that had come upon my name.

"The air was full of music, full of harmonious scents, full of the rhythm of beautiful motions. Thousands of beautiful people swarmed about the hall, crowded the galleries, sat in myriad recesses; they were dressed in splendid colors and crowned with flowers; thousands danced about the great circle beneath the white images of the ancient gods, and glorious processions of youths and maidens came and went. We two danced, not the dreary monotonies of your days—of this time, I mean—but dances that were beautiful, intoxicating. And even now I can see my lady dancing—dancing joyously. She danced, you know, with a serious face; she danced with a serious dignity and yet she was smiling at me and caressing me—smiling and caressing with her eyes.

"The music was different," he murmured. "It went—I cannot describe it; but it was infinitely richer and more varied than any music that has ever come to me awake.

"And then—it was when we had done dancing—a man came to speak to me. He was a lean, resolute man, very soberly clad for that place, and already I had marked his face watching me in the breakfasting hall, and afterwards as we went along the passage I had avoided his eye. But now, as we sat in an alcove, smiling at the pleasure of all the people who went to and fro across the shining floor, he came and touched me, and spoke to me so that I was forced to listen. And he asked that he might speak to me for a while apart.

" 'No,' I said. 'I have no secrets from this lady. What do you want to tell me?'

"He said it was a trivial matter, or at least a dry matter, for a lady to hear.

" 'Perhaps for me to hear,' said I.

"He glanced at her, as though almost he would appeal to her. Then he asked me suddenly if I had heard of a great and avenging declaration that Evesham had made. Now, Evesham had always before been the man next to myself in the leadership of that great party in the north. He was a forcible, hard, and tactless man, and only I had been able to control and soften him. It was on his account even more than my own, I think, that the others had been so dismayed at my retreat. So this question about what he had done reawakened my old interest in the life I had put aside just for a moment.

" 'I have taken no heed of any news for many days,' I said. 'What has Evesham been saying?'

"And with that the man began, nothing loth, and I must confess even I was struck by Evesham's reckless folly in the wild and threatening words he had used. And this messenger they had sent to me not only told me of Evesham's speech, but went on to ask counsel and to point out what need they had of me. While he talked, my lady sat a little forward and watched his face and mine.

"My old habits of scheming and organizing re-asserted themselves. I could even see myself suddenly returning to the north, and all the dramatic effect of it. All that this man said witnessed to the disorder of the party indeed, but not to its damage. I should go back stronger than I had come. And then I thought of my lady. You see—how can I tell you? There were certain peculiarities of our relationship—as things are I need not tell you about that—which would render her presence with me impossible. I should have had to leave her; indeed, I should have had to renounce her clearly and openly, if I was to do all that I could do in the north. And the man knew *that*, even as he talked to her and me, knew it as well as she did, that my steps to duty were—first, separation, then abandonment. At the touch of that thought my dream of a return was shattered. I turned on the man suddenly, as he was imagining his eloquence was gaining ground with me.

" 'What have I to do with these things now?' I said. 'I have done with them. Do you think I am coquetting with your people in coming here?'

" 'No,' he said; 'but—'

" 'Why cannot you leave me alone. I have done with these things. I have ceased to be anything but a private man.'

" 'Yes,' he answered. 'But have you thought?—this talk of war, these reckless challenges, these wild aggressions—'

"I stood up.

" 'No,' I cried. 'I won't hear you. I took count of all those things, I weighed them—and I have come away.'

"He seemed to consider the possibility of persistence. He looked from me to where the lady sat regarding us.

" 'War,' he said, as if he were speaking to himself, and then turned slowly from me and walked away.

"I stood, caught in the whirl of thoughts his appeal had set going.

"I heard my lady's voice.

" 'Dear,' she said; 'but if they have need of you—'

"She did not finish her sentence, she let it rest there. I turned to her sweet face, and the balance of my mood swayed and reeled.

" 'They want me only to do the thing they dare not do themselves,' I said. 'If they distrust Evesham they must settle with him themselves.'

"She looked at me doubtfully.

" 'But war—' she said.

"I saw a doubt on her face that I had seen before, a doubt of herself and me, the first shadow of the discovery that, seen strongly and completely, must drive us apart forever.

"Now I was an older mind than hers, and I could sway her to this belief or that.

" 'My dear one,' I said, 'you must not trouble over these things. There will be no war. Certainly there will be no war. The age of wars is past. Trust me to know the justice of this case. They have no right upon me, dearest, and no one has a right upon me. I have been free to choose my life, and I have chosen this.'

" 'But *war*—,' she said.

"I sat down beside her. I put an arm behind her and took her hand in mine. I set myself to drive that doubt away—I set myself to fill her mind with pleasant things again. I lied to her, and in lying to her I lied also to myself. And she was only too ready to believe me, only too ready to forget.

"Very soon the shadow had gone again, and we were hastening to our bathing-place in the Grotta del Bove Marino, where it was our custom to bathe every day. We swam and splashed one another, and in that buoyant water I seemed to become something lighter and stronger than a man. And at last we came out dripping and rejoicing and raced among the rocks. And then I put on a dry bathing-dress, and we sat to bask in the sun, and presently I nodded, resting my head against her knee, and she put her hand upon my hair and stroked it softly and I dozed. And behold! as it were with the snapping of the string of a violin, I was awakening, and I was in my own bed in Liverpool, in the life of today.

"Only for a time I could not believe that all these vivid moments had been no more than the substance of a dream.

"In truth, I could not believe it a dream for all the sobering reality of things about me. I bathed and dressed as it were by habit, and as I shaved I argued why I of all men should leave the woman I loved to go back to fantastic politics in the hard and strenuous north. Even if Evesham did force the world back to war, what was that to me? I was a man with the heart of a man, and why should I feel the responsibility of a deity for the way the world might go?

"You know that is not quite the way I think about affairs, about my real affairs. I am a solicitor, you know, with a point of view.

"The vision was so real, you must understand, so utterly unlike a dream that I kept perpetually recalling trivial irrelevant details; even the ornament of a bookcover that lay on my wife's sewing-machine in the breakfast-room recalled with the utmost vividness the gilt line that ran about the seat in the alcove where I had talked with the messenger from my deserted party. Have you ever heard of a dream that had a quality like that?"

"Like—?"

"So that afterwards you remembered details you had forgotten."

I thought. I had never noticed the point before, but he was right.

"Never," I said. "That is what you never seem to do with dreams."

"No," he answered. "But that is just what I did. I am a solicitor, you must understand, in Liverpool, and I could not help wondering what the clients and business people I found myself talking to in my office would think if I told them suddenly I was in love with a girl who would be born a couple of hundred years or so hence, and worried about the politics of my great-great-great-grandchildren. I was chiefly busy that day negotiating a ninety-nine-year building lease. It was a private builder in a hurry, and we wanted to tie him in every possible way. I had an interview with him, and he showed a certain want of temper that sent me to bed still irritated. That night I had no dream. Nor did I dream the next night, at least, to remember.

"Something of that intense reality of conviction vanished. I began to feel sure it *was* a dream. And then it came again.

"When the dream came again, nearly four days later, it was very different. I think it certain that four days had also elapsed in the dream. Many things had happened in the north, and the shadow of them was back again between us, and this time it was not so easily dispelled. I began I know with moody musings. Why, in spite of all, should I go back, go back for all the rest of my days to toil and stress, insults and perpetual dissatisfaction, simply to save hundreds of millions of common people, whom I did not love, whom too often I could do no other than despise, from the stress and anguish of war and infinite misrule? And after all I might fail. *They* all sought their own narrow ends, and why should not I—why should not I also live as a man? And out of such thoughts her voice summoned me, and I lifted my eyes.

"I found myself awake and walking. We had come out above the Pleasure City, we were near the summit of Monte Solaro and looking towards the bay. It was the late afternoon and very clear. Far away to the left Ischia hung in a golden haze between sea and sky, and Naples was coldly white against the hills, and before us was Vesuvius with a tall and slender streamer feathering at last towards the south, and the ruins of Torre Annunziata and Castellamare glittering and near."

I interrupted suddenly: "You have been to Capri, of course?"

"Only in this dream," he said, "only in this dream. All across the bay beyond Sorrento were the floating palaces of the Pleasure City moored and chained. And northward were the broad floating stages that received the aeroplanes. Aeroplanes fell out of the sky every afternoon, each bringing its thousands of pleasure-seekers from the uttermost parts of the earth to Capri and its delights. All these things, I say, stretched below.

"But we noticed them only incidentally because of an unusual sight that evening had to show. Five war aeroplanes that had long slumbered useless in the distant arsenals of the Rhinemouth were manœuvring now in the eastward sky. Evesham had astonished the world by producing them and others, and sending them to circle here and there. It was the threat material in the great game of bluff he was playing, and it had taken even me by surprise. He was one of those incredibly stupid energetic people who seem sent by heaven to create disasters. His energy to the first glance seemed so wonderfully like capacity! But he had no imagination, no invention, only a stupid, vast, driving force of will, and a mad faith in his stupid idiot 'luck' to pull him through. I remember how we stood out upon the headland watching the squadron circling far away, and how I weighed the full meaning of the sight, seeing clearly the way things must go. And then even it was not too late. I might have gone back, I think, and saved the world. The people of the north would follow me, I knew, granted only that in one thing I respected their moral standards. The east and south would trust me as they would trust no other northern man. And I knew I had only to put it to her and she would have let me go. . . . Not because she did not love me!

"Only I did not want to go; my will was all the other way about. I had so newly thrown off the incubus of responsibility: I was still so fresh a renegade from duty that the daylight clearness of what I *ought* to do had no power at all to touch my will. My will was to live, to gather pleasures and make my dear lady happy. But though this sense of vast neglected duties had no power to draw me, it could make me silent and preoccupied, it robbed the days I had spent of half their brightness and roused me into dark meditations in the silence of the night. And as I stood and watched Evesham's airplanes sweep to and fro—those birds of infinite ill omen—she stood beside me watching me, perceiving the trouble indeed, but not perceiving it clearly—her eyes questioning my face, her expression shaded with perplexity. Her face was grey because the sunset was fading out of the sky. It was no fault of hers that she held me. She had asked me to go from her, and again in the night time and with tears she had asked me to go.

"At last it was the sense of her that roused me from my mood. I turned upon her suddenly and challenged her to race down the mountain slopes. 'No,' she said, as if I jarred her with gravity; but I was resolved to end that gravity, and made her run—no one can be very grey and sad who is out of breath—and when she stumbled I ran with my hand beneath her arm. We ran down past a couple of men, who turned back staring in astonishment at my behavior—they must have recognized my face. And half-way down the slope came a tumult in the air, clang-clank, clang-clank, and we stopped, and presently over the hill-crest those war things came flying one behind the other."

The man seemed hesitating on the verge of a description.

"What were they like?" I asked.

"They had never fought," he said. "They were just like our ironclads are nowadays; they had never fought. No one knew what they might do, with excited men inside them; few even cared to speculate. They were great driving things shaped like spear-heads without a shaft, with a propeller in the place of the shaft.''

''Steel?''

''Not steel.''

''Aluminum?''

''No, no, nothing of that sort. An alloy that was very common—as common as brass, for example. It was called—let me see—'' He squeezed his forehead with the fingers of one hand. ''I am forgetting everything,'' he said.

''And they carried guns?''

''Little guns, firing high explosive shells. They fired the guns backwards, out of the base of the leaf, so to speak, and rammed with the beak. That was the theory, you know, but they had never been fought. No one could tell exactly what was going to happen. And meanwhile I suppose it was very fine to go whirling through the air like a flight of young swallows, swift and easy. I guess the captains tried not to think too clearly what the real thing would be like. And these flying war machines, you know, were only one sort of the endless war contrivances that had been invented and had fallen into abeyance during the long peace. There were all sorts of these things that people were routing out and furbishing up; infernal things, silly things; things that had never been tried; big engines, terrible explosives, great guns. You know the silly way of the ingenious sort of men who make these things; they turn 'em out as beavers build dams, and with no more sense of the rivers they're going to divert and the lands they're going to flood!

''As we went down the winding stepway to our hotel again, in the twilight, I foresaw it all: I saw how clearly and inevitably things were driving for war in Evesham's silly, violent hands, and I had some inkling of what war was bound to be under these new conditions. And even then, though I knew it was drawing near the limit of my opportunity, I could find no will to go back.''

He sighed.

''That was my last chance.

''We didn't go into the city until the sky was full of stars, so we walked out upon the high terrace, to and fro and—she counselled me to go back.

'' 'My dearest,' she said, and her sweet face looked up to me, 'this is Death. This life you lead is Death. Go back to them, go back to your duty—'

''She began to weep, saying, between her sobs, and clinging to my arm as she said it, 'Go back—Go back.'

''Then suddenly she fell mute, and, glancing down at her face, I read in an instant the thing she had thought to do. It was one of those moments when one *sees*.

'' 'No!' I said.

'' 'No?' she asked, in surprise, and I think a little fearful at the answer to her thought.

'' 'Nothing,' I said, 'shall send me back. Nothing! I have chosen. Love, I have chosen, and the world must go. Whatever happens I will live this life—I will live for *you!* It—nothing shall turn me aside; nothing, my dear one. Even if you died—even if you died—'

'' 'Yes?' she murmured, softly.

'' 'Then—I also would die.'

''And before she could speak again I began to talk, talking eloquently—as I *could* do in that life—talking to exalt love, to make the life we were living seem heroic and glorious; and the thing I was deserting something hard and enormously ignoble that it was a fine thing to set aside. I bent all my mind to throw that glamour upon it, seeking not only to convert her but myself to that. We talked, and she clung to me, torn too between all that she deemed noble and all that she knew was sweet. And at last I did make it heroic, made all the thickening disaster of the world only a sort of glorious setting to our unparalleled love, and we two poor foolish souls strutted there at last, clad in that splendid delusion, drunken rather with that glorious delusion, under the still stars.

"And so my moment passed.

"It was my last chance. Even as we went to and fro there, the leaders of the south and east were gathering their resolve, and the hot answer that shattered Evesham's bluffing forever, took shape and waited. And all over Asia, and the ocean, and the South, the air and the wires were throbbing with their warnings to prepare—prepare.

"No one living, you know, knew what war was; no one could imagine, with all these new inventions, what horror war might bring. I believe most people still believed it would be a matter of bright uniforms and shouting charges and triumphs and flags and bands—in a time when half the world drew its food supply from regions ten thousand miles away—"

The man with the white face paused. I glanced at him, and his face was intent on the floor of the carriage. A little railway station, a string of loaded trucks, a signal-box, and the back of a cottage, shot by the carriage window, and a bridge passed with a clap of noise, echoing the tumult of the train.

"After that," he said, "I dreamt often. For three weeks of nights that dream was my life. And the worst of it was there were nights when I could not dream, when I lay tossing on a bed in *this* accursed life; and *there*—somewhere lost to me—things were happening—momentous, terrible things. . . . I lived at nights—my days, my waking days, this life I am living now, became a faded, far-away dream, a drab setting, the cover of the book."

He thought.

"I could tell you all, tell you every little thing in the dream, but as to what I did in the daytime—no. I could not tell—I do not remember. My memory—my memory has gone. The business of life slips from me—"

He leant forward, and pressed his hands upon his eyes. For a long time he said nothing.

"And then?" said I.

"The war burst like a hurricane."

He stared before him at unspeakable things.

"And then?" I urged again.

"One touch of unreality," he said, in the low tone of a man who speaks to himself, "and they would have been nightmares. But they were not nightmares—they were not nightmares. *No!*"

He was silent for so long that it dawned upon me that there was a danger of losing the rest of the story. But he went on talking again in the same tone of questioning self-communion.

"What was there to do but flight? I had no thought the war would touch Capri—I had seemed to see Capri as being out of it all, as the contrast to it all; but two nights after the whole place was shouting and bawling, every woman almost and every other man wore a badge—Evesham's badge—and there was no music but a jangling war-song over and over again, and everywhere men enlisting, and in the dancing halls they were drilling. The whole island was awhirl with rumours; it was said, again and again, that fighting had begun. I had not expected this. I had seen so little of the life of pleasure that I had failed to reckon with this violence of the amateurs. And as for me, I was out of it. I was like a man who might have prevented the firing of a magazine. The time had gone. I was no one; the vainest stripling with a badge counted for more than I. The crowd jostled us and bawled in our ears; that accursed song deafened us; a woman shrieked at my lady because no badge was on her, and we two went back to our own place again, ruffled and insulted—my lady white and silent, and I aquiver with rage. So furious was I, I could have quarrelled with her if I could have found one shade of accusation in her eyes.

"All my magnificence had gone from me. I walked up and down our rock cell, and outside was the darkling sea and a light to the southward that flared and passed and came again.

" 'We must get out of this place,' I said over and over. 'I have made my choice, and I will have no hand in these troubles. I will have nothing of this war. We have taken our lives out of all these things. This is no refuge for us. Let us go.'

"And the next day we were already in flight from the war that covered the world.

"And all the rest was Flight—all the rest was Flight."

He mused darkly.

"How much was there of it?"

He made no answer.

"How many days?"

His face was white and drawn and his hands were clenched. He took no heed of my curiosity.

I tried to draw him back to his story with questions.

"Where did you go?" I said.

"When?"

"When you left Capri."

"South-west," he said and glanced at me for a second. "We went in a boat."

"But I should have thought an aeroplane?"

"They had been seized."

I questioned him no more. Presently I thought he was beginning again. He broke out in an argumentative monotone:

"But why should it be? If, indeed, this battle, this slaughter and stress *is* life, why have we this craving for pleasure and beauty? If there *is* no refuge, if there is no place of peace, and if all our dreams of quiet places are a folly and a snare, why have we such dreams? Surely it was no ignoble cravings, no base intentions, had brought us to this; it was Love had isolated us. Love had come to me with her eyes and robed in her beauty, more glorious than all else in life, in the very shape and colour of life, and summoned me away. I had silenced all the voices, I had answered all the questions—I had come to her. And suddenly there was nothing but War and Death!"

I had an inspiration. "After all," I said, "it could have been only a dream."

"A dream!" he cried, flaming upon me, "a dream—when, even now—"

For the first time he became animated. A faint flush crept into his cheek. He raised his open hand and clenched it, and dropped it to his knee. He spoke, looking away from me, and for all the rest of the time he looked away. "We are but phantoms," he said, "and the phantoms of phantoms, desires like cloud shadows and wills of straw that eddy in the wind; the days pass, use and wont carry us through as a train carries the shadow of its lights—so be it! But one thing is real and certain, one thing is no dreamstuff, but eternal and enduring.

It is the centre of my life, and all other things about it are subordinate or altogether vain. I loved her, that woman of a dream. And she and I are dead together!

"A dream! How can it be a dream, when it has drenched a living life with unappeasable sorrow, when it makes all that I have lived for and cared for, worthless and unmeaning?

"Until that very moment when she was killed I believed we had still a chance of getting away," he said. "All through the night and morning that we sailed across the sea from Capri to Salerno, we talked of escape. We were full of hope, and it clung about us to the end, hope for the life together we should lead, out of it all, out of the battle and struggle, the wild and empty passions, the empty arbitrary 'thou shalt' and 'thou shalt not' of the world. We were uplifted, as though our quest was a holy thing, as though love for one another was a mission. . . .

"Even when from our boat we saw the fair face of that great rock Capri—already scarred and gashed by—the gun emplacements and hiding-places that were to make it a fastness—we reckoned nothing of the imminent slaughter, though the fury of preparation hung about in puffs and clouds of dust at a hundred points amidst the grey; but, indeed, I made a text of that and talked. There, you know, was the rock, still beautiful for all its scars, with its countless windows and arches and ways, tier upon tier, for a thousand feet, a vast carving of grey, broken by vine-clad terraces and lemon and orange groves and masses of agave and prickly pear, and puffs of almond blossom. And out under the archway that is built over the Marina Piccola other boats were coming; and as we came round the cape and within sight of the mainland, another string of boats came into view, driving before the wind towards the south-west. In a little while a multitude had come out, the remoter just specks of ultramarine in the shadow of the eastward cliff.

" 'It is love and reason,' I said, 'fleeing from all this madness of war.'

"And though we presently saw a squadron of aeroplanes flying across the southern sky we did not heed it. There it was—a line of dots in the sky—and then more, dotting the south-eastern horizon, and then still more, until all that quarter of the sky was stippled with blue specks. Now they were all thin little strokes of blue, and now one and now a multitude would heel and catch the sun and become short flashes of light. They came, rising and falling and growing larger like some huge flight of gulls or rooks or such-like birds, moving with a marvellous uniformity, and ever as they drew nearer they spread over a greater width of sky. The southward wing flung itself in an arrow-headed cloud athwart the sun. And then suddenly they swept round to the eastward and streamed eastward, growing smaller and smaller and clearer and clearer again until they vanished from the sky. And after that we noted to the northward and very high Evesham's fighting machines hanging high over Naples like an evening swarm of gnats.

"It seemed to have no more to do with us than a flight of birds.

"Even the mutter of guns far away in the south-east seemed to us to signify nothing. . . .

"Each day, each dream after that, we were still exalted, still seeking that refuge where we might live and love. Fatigue had come upon us, pain and many distresses. For though we were dusty and stained by our toilsome tramping, and half starved and with the horror of the dead men we had seen and the flight of the peasants—for very soon a gust of fighting swept up the peninsula—with these things haunting our minds it still resulted only in a deepening resolution to escape. Oh, but she was brave and patient! She who had never faced hardship and exposure had courage for herself—and me. We went to and fro seeking an outlet, over a country all commandeered and ransacked by the gathering hosts of war. Always we went on foot. At first there were other fugitives, but we did not mingle with them. Some escaped northward, some were caught in the torrent of peasantry that swept along the main roads, many gave themselves into the hands of the soldiery and were sent northward. Many of the men were impressed. But we kept away from these things; we had brought no money to bribe a passage north, and I feared for my lady at the hands of these conscript crowds. We had landed at Salerno, and we had been turned back from Cava, and we had tried to cross towards Taranto by a pass over Monte Alburno, but we had been driven back for want of food, and so we had come down among the marshes by Pæstum, where those great temples stand alone. I had some vague idea that by Pæstum it might be possible to find a boat or something, and take once more to sea. And there it was the battle overtook us.

"A sort of soul-blindness had me. Plainly I could see that we were being hemmed in; that the great net of that giant Warfare had us in its toils. Many times we had seen the levies that had come down from the north going to and fro, and had come upon them in the distance amidst the mountains making ways for the ammunition and preparing the mounting of the guns. Once we fancied they had fired at us, taking us for spies—at any rate a shot had gone shuddering over us. Several times we had hidden in woods from hovering aeroplanes.

"But all these things do not matter now, these nights of flight and pain. . . . We were in an open place near those great temples at Pæstum at last, on a blank stony place dotted with spiky bushes, empty and desolate and so flat that a grove of eucalyptus far away showed to the feet of its stems. How I can see it! My lady was sitting down under a bush resting a little, for she was very weak and weary, and I was standing up watching to see if I could tell the distance of the firing that came and went. They were still, you know, fighting far from each other, with those terrible new weapons that had never before been used: guns that would carry beyond sight, and aeroplanes that would do—What *they* would do no man could foretell.

"I knew that we were between the two armies, and that they drew together. I knew we were in danger, and that we could not stop there and rest!

"Though all these things were in my mind, they were in the background. They seemed to be affairs beyond our concern. Chiefly, I was thinking of my lady. An aching distress filled me. For the first time she had owned herself beaten and had fallen a-weeping. Behind me I could hear her sobbing, but I would not turn round to her because I knew she had need of weeping, and had held herself so far and so long for me. It was well, I thought, that she would weep and rest and then we would toil on again, for I had no inkling of the thing that hung so near. Even now I can see her as she sat there, her lovely hair upon her shoulder, can mark again the deepening hollow of her cheek.

" 'If we had parted,' she said, 'if I had let you go.'

" 'No,' said I. 'Even now, I do not repent. I will not repent; I made my choice, and I will hold on to the end.'

"And then—

"Overhead in the sky flashed something and burst, and all about us I heard the bullets making a noise like a handful of peas suddenly thrown. They chipped the stones about us, and whirled fragments from the bricks and passed. . . .' "

He put his hand to his mouth, and then moistened his lips.

"At the flash I had turned about. . . .

"You know—she stood up—

"She stood up, you know, and moved a step towards me—

"As though she wanted to reach me—

"And she had been shot through the heart."

He stopped and stared at me. I felt all that foolish incapacity an Englishman feels on such occasions. I met his eyes for a moment, and then stared out of the window. For a long space we kept silence. When at last I looked at him he was sitting back in his corner, his arms folded, and his teeth gnawing at his knuckles.

He bit his nail suddenly, and stared at it.

"I carried her," he said, "towards the temples, in my arms—as though it mattered. I don't know why. They seemed a sort of sanctuary, you know; they had lasted so long, I suppose.

"She must have died almost instantly. Only—I talked to her—all the way." Silence again.

"I have seen those temples," I said abruptly, and indeed he had brought those still, sunlit arcades of worn sandstone very vividly before me.

"It was the brown one, the big brown one. I sat down on a fallen pillar and held her in my arms. . . . Silent after the first babble was over. And after a little while the lizards came out and ran about again, as though nothing unusual was going on, as though nothing had changed. . . . It was tremendously still there, the sun high and the shadows still; even the shadows of the weeds upon the entablature were still—in spite of the thudding and banging that went all about the sky.

"I seem to remember that the aeroplanes came up out of the south, and that the battle went away to the west. One aeroplane was struck, and overset and fell. I remember that—though it didn't interest me in the least. It didn't seem to signify. It was like a wounded gull, you know—flapping for a time in the water. I could see it down the aisle of the temple—a black thing in the bright blue water.

"Three or four times shells burst about the beach, and then that ceased. Each time that happened all the lizards scuttled in and hid for a space. That was all the mischief done, except that once a stray bullet gashed the stone hard by—made just a fresh bright surface.

"As the shadows grew longer, the stillness seemed greater.

"The curious thing," he remarked, with the manner of a man who makes a trivial conversation, "is that I didn't *think*—I didn't think at all. I sat with her in my arms amidst the stones—in a sort of lethargy—stagnant.

"And I don't remember waking up. I don't remember dressing that day. I know I found myself in my office, with my letters all slit open in front of me, and how I was struck by the absurdity of being there, seeing that in reality I was sitting, stunned, in that Pæstum Temple with a dead woman in my arms. I read my letters like a machine. I have forgotten what they were about."

He stopped, and there was a long silence.

Suddenly I perceived that we were running down the incline from Chalk Farm to Euston. I started at this passing of time. I turned on him with a brutal question, in the tone of "Now or never."

"And did you dream again?"

"Yes."

He seemed to force himself to finish. His voice was very low.

"Once more, and as it were only for a few instants. I seemed to have suddenly awakened out of a great apathy, to have risen into a sitting position, and the body lay there on the stones beside me. A gaunt body. Not her, you know. So soon—it was not her. . . .

"I may have heard voices. I do not know. Only I knew clearly that men were coming into the solitude and that that was a last outrage.

"I stood up and walked through the temple, and then there came into sight—first one man with a yellow face, dressed in a uniform of dirty white, trimmed with blue, and then several, climbing to the crest of the old wall of the vanished city, and crouching there. They were little bright figures in the sunlight, and there they hung, weapon in hand, peering cautiously before them.

"And further away I saw others and then more at another point in the wall. It was a long lax line of men in open order.

"Presently the man I had first seen stood up and shouted a command, and his men came tumbling down the wall and into the high weeds towards the temple. He scrambled down with them and led them. He came facing towards me, and when he saw me he stopped.

"At first I had watched these men with a mere curiosity, but when I had seen they meant to come to the temple I was moved to forbid them. I shouted to the officer.

" 'You must not come here,' I cried, '*I* am here. I am here with my dead.'

"He stared, and then shouted a question back to me in some unknown tongue.

"I repeated what I had said.

"He shouted again, and I folded my arms and stood still. Presently he spoke to his men and came forward. He carried a drawn sword.

"I signed to him to keep away, but he continued to advance. I told him again very patiently and clearly: 'You must not come here. These are old temples and I am here with my dead.'

"Presently he was so close I could see his face clearly. It was a narrow face, with dull grey eyes, and a black moustache. He had a scar on his upper lip, and he was dirty and unshaven. He kept shouting unintelligible things, questions, perhaps, at me.

"I know now that he was afraid of me, but at the time that did not occur to me. As I tried to explain to him, he interrupted me in imperious tones, bidding me, I suppose, stand aside.

"He made to go past me, and I caught hold of him.

"I saw his face change at my grip.

" 'You fool,' I cried. 'Don't you know? She is dead!'

"He started back. He looked at me with cruel eyes. I saw a sort of exultant resolve leap into them—delight. Then suddenly with a scowl, he swept his sword back—*so*—and thrust."

He stopped abruptly.

I became aware of a change in the rhythm of the train. The brakes lifted their voices and the carriage jarred and jerked. This present world insisted upon itself, became clamorous. I saw through the steamy window huge electric lights glaring down from tall masts upon a fog, saw rows of stationary empty carriages passing by; and then a signal-box, hoisting its constellation of green and red into the murky London twilight, marched after them. I looked again at his drawn features.

"He ran me through the heart. It was with a sort of astonishment—no fear, no pain—but just amazement, that I felt it pierce me, felt the sword drive home into my body. It didn't hurt, you know. It didn't hurt at all."

The yellow platform lights came into the field of view, passing first rapidly, then slowly, and at last stopping with a jerk. Dim shapes of men passed to and fro without.

"Euston!" cried a voice.

"Do you mean—?"

"There was no pain, no sting or smart. Amazement and then darkness sweeping over everything. The hot, brutal face before me, the face of the man who had killed me, seemed to recede. It swept out of existence—"

"Euston!" clamored the voices outside; "Euston!"

The carriage door opened admitting a flood of sound, and a porter stood regarding us. The sounds of doors slamming, and the hoof-clatter of cab-horses, and behind these things the featureless remote roar of the London cobble-stones, came to my ears. A truckload of lighted lamps blazed along the platform.

"A darkness, a flood of darkness that opened and spread and blotted out all things."

"Any luggage, sir?" said the porter.

"And that was the end?" I asked.

He seemed to hesitate. Then, almost inaudibly, he answered, *"No."*

"You mean?"

"I couldn't get to her. She was there on the other side of the temple— And then—"

"Yes," I insisted. "Yes?"

"Nightmares," he cried; "nightmares indeed! My God! Great birds that fought and tore."

THE MAN WHO COULD WORK MIRACLES

A PANTOUM IN PROSE

IT IS DOUBTFUL whether the gift was innate. For my own part, I think it came to him suddenly. Indeed, until he was thirty he was a skeptic, and did not believe in miraculous powers. And here, since it is the most convenient place, I must mention that he was a little man, and had eyes of a hot brown, very erect red hair, a moustache with ends that he twisted up, and freckles. His name was George McWhirter Fotheringay—not the sort of name by any means to lead to any expectation of miracles—and he was clerk at Gomshott's. He was greatly addicted to assertive argument. It was while he was asserting the impossibility of miracles that he had his first intimation of his extraordinary powers. This particular argument was being held in the bar of the Long Dragon, and Toddy Beamish was conducting the opposition by a monotonous but effective "So *you* say," that drove Mr. Fotheringay to the very limit of his patience.

There were present, besides these two, a very dusty cyclist, landlord Cox, and Miss Maybridge, the perfectly respectable and rather portly barmaid of the Dragon. Miss Maybridge was standing with her back to Mr. Fotheringay, washing glasses; the others were watching him, more or less amused by the present ineffectiveness of the assertive method. Goaded by the Torres Vedras tactics of Mr. Beamish, Mr. Fotheringay determined to make an unusual rhetorical effort. "Looky here, Mr. Beamish," said Mr. Fotheringay. "Let us clearly understand what a miracle is. It's something contrariwise to the course of nature done by power of Will, something what couldn't happen without being specially willed."

"So *you* say," said Mr. Beamish, repulsing him.

Mr. Fotheringay appealed to the cyclist, who had hitherto been a silent auditor, and received his assent—given with a hesitating cough and a glance at Mr. Beamish. The landlord would express no opinion, and Mr. Fotheringay, returning to Mr. Beamish, received the unexpected concession of a qualified assent to his definition of a miracle.

"For instance," said Mr. Fotheringay, greatly encouraged. "Here would be a miracle. That lamp, in the natural course of nature, couldn't burn like that upsy-down, could it, Beamish?"

"*You* say it couldn't," said Beamish.

"And you?" said Fotheringay. "You don't mean to say—eh?"

"No," said Beamish reluctantly. "No, it couldn't."

"Very well," said Mr. Fotheringay. "Then here comes someone, as it might be me, along here, and stands as it might be here, and says to that lamp, as I might do, collecting all my will—'Turn upsy-down without breaking, and go on burning steady,' and—Hullo!"

It was enough to make anyone say "Hullo!" The impossible, the incredible, was visible to them all. The lamp hung inverted in the air, burning quietly with its flame pointing down. It was as solid, as indisputable as ever a lamp was, the prosaic common lamp of the Long Dragon bar.

Mr. Fotheringay stood with an extended forefinger and the knitted brows of one anticipating a catastrophic smash. The cyclist, who was sitting next the lamp, ducked and jumped across the bar. Everybody jumped, more or less. Miss Maybridge turned and screamed. For nearly three seconds the lamp remained still. A faint cry of mental distress came from Mr. Fotheringay. "I can't keep it up," he said, "any longer." He staggered back, and the inverted lamp suddenly flared, fell against the corner of the bar, bounced aside, smashed upon the floor, and went out.

It was lucky it had a metal receiver, or the whole place would have been in a blaze. Mr. Cox was the first to speak, and his remark, shorn of needless excrescences, was to the effect that Fotheringay was a fool. Fotheringay was beyond disputing even so fundamental a proposition as that! He was astonished beyond measure at the thing that had occurred. The subsequent conversation threw absolutely no light on the matter so far as Fotheringay was concerned; the general opinion not only followed Mr. Cox very closely but very vehemently. Everyone accused Fotheringay of a silly trick, and presented him to himself as a foolish destroyer of comfort and security. His mind was in a tornado of perplexity, he was himself inclined to agree with them, and he made a remarkably ineffectual opposition to the proposal of his departure.

He went home flushed and heated, coat-collar crumpled, eyes smarting and ears red. He watched each of the ten street lamps nervously as he passed it. It was only when he found himself alone in his little bedroom in Church Row that he was able to grapple seriously with his memories of the occurrence, and ask, "What on earth happened?"

He had removed his coat and boots, and was sitting on the bed with his hands in his pockets repeating the text of his defense for the seventeenth time, "*I* didn't want the confounded thing to upset," when it occurred to him that at the precise moment he had said the commanding words he had inadvertently willed the thing he said, and that when he had seen the lamp in the air he had felt that it depended on him to maintain it there without being clear how this was to be done. He had not a particularly complex mind, or he might have stuck for a time at that "inadvertently willed," embracing, as it does, the abstrusest problems of voluntary action; but as it was, the idea came to him with a quite acceptable haziness. And from that, following, as I must admit, no clear logical path, he came to the test of experiment.

He pointed resolutely to his candle and collected his mind, though he felt he did a foolish thing. "Be raised up," he said. But in a second that feeling vanished. The candle was raised, hung in the air one giddy moment, and as Mr. Fotheringay gasped, fell with a smash on his toilet-table, leaving him in darkness save for the expiring glow of its wick.

For a time Mr. Fotheringay sat in the darkness, perfectly still. "It did happen, after all," he said. "And 'ow I'm to explain it I *don't* know." He sighed heavily, and began feeling in his pockets for a match. He could find none, and he rose and groped about the toilet-table. "I wish I had a match," he said. He resorted to his coat, and there were none there, and then it dawned upon him that miracles were possible even with matches. He extended a hand and scowled at it in the dark. "Let there be a match in that hand," he said. He felt some light object fall across his palm, and his fingers closed upon a match.

After several ineffectual attempts to light this, he discovered it was a safety-match. He threw it down, and then it occurred to him that he might have willed it lit. He did, and perceived it burning in the midst of his toilet-table mat. He caught it up hastily, and it went out. His perception of possibilities enlarged, and he felt for and replaced the candle in its candlestick. "Here! *you* be lit," said Mr. Fotheringay, and forthwith the candle was flaring, and he saw a little black hole in the toilet-cover, with a wisp of smoke rising from it. For a time he stared from this to the little flame and back, and then looked up and met his own gaze in the looking glass. By this help he communed with himself in silence for a time.

"How about miracles now?" said Mr. Fotheringay at last, addressing his reflection.

The subsequent meditations of Mr. Fotheringay were of a severe but confused description. So far as he could see, it was a case of pure willing with him. The nature of his first experiences disinclined him for any further experiments except of the most cautious type. But he lifted a sheet of paper, and turned a glass of water pink and then green, and he created a snail, which he miraculously annihilated, and got himself a miraculous new toothbrush. Sometime in the small hours he had reached the fact that his will-power must be of a particularly rare and pungent quality, a fact of which he had certainly had inklings before, but no certain assurance. The scare and perplexity of his first discovery was now qualified by pride in this evidence of singularity and by vague intimations of advantage. He became aware that the church clock was striking one, and as it did not occur to him that his daily duties at Gomshott's might be miraculously dispensed with, he resumed undressing, in order to get to bed without further delay. As he struggled to get his shirt over his head, he was struck with a brilliant idea. "Let me be in bed," he said, and found himself so. "Undressed," he stipulated; and, finding the sheets cold, added hastily, "and in my nightshirt—no, in a nice soft woollen nightshirt. Ah!" he said with immense enjoyment. "And now let me be comfortably asleep. . . ."

He awoke at his usual hour and was pensive all through breakfast-time, wondering whether his overnight experience might not be a particularly vivid dream. At length his mind turned again to cautious experiments. For instance, he had three eggs for breakfast; two his landlady had supplied, good, but shoppy, and one was a delicious fresh goose-egg, laid, cooked, and served by his extraordinary will. He hurried off to Gomshott's in a state of profound but carefully concealed excitement, and only remembered the shell of the third egg when his landlady spoke of it that night. All day he could do no work because of this astonishingly new self-knowledge, but this caused him no inconvenience, because he made up for it miraculously in his last ten minutes.

As the day wore on his state of mind passed from wonder to elation, albeit the circumstances of his dismissal from the Long Dragon were still disagreeable to recall, and a garbled account of the matter that had reached his colleagues led to some badinage. It was evident he must be careful how he lifted frangible articles, but in other ways his gift promised more and more as he turned it over in his mind. He intended among other things to increase his personal property by unostentatious acts of creation. He called into existence a pair of very splendid diamond studs, and hastily annihilated them again as young Gomshott came across the counting-house to his desk. He was afraid young Gomshott might wonder how he had come by them. He saw quite clearly the gift required caution and watchfulness in its exercise; but so far as he could judge the difficulties attending its mastery would be no greater than those he had already faced in the study of cycling. It was that analogy, perhaps, quite as much as the feeling that he would be unwelcome in the Long Dragon, that drove him out after supper into the lane beyond the gas-works, to rehearse a few miracles in private.

There was possibly a certain want of originality in his attempts, for apart from his will-power Mr. Fotheringay was not a very exceptional man. The miracle of Moses' rod came to his mind, but the night was dark and unfavorable to the proper control of large miraculous snakes. Then he recollected the story of "Tannhäuser" that he had read on the back of the Philharmonic program. That seemed to him singularly attractive and harmless. He stuck his walking-stick— a very nice Poona-Penang lawyer—into the turf that edged the footpath, and commanded the dry wood to blossom. The air was immediately full of the scent of roses, and by means of a match he saw for himself that this beautiful miracle was indeed accomplished. His satisfaction was ended by advancing footsteps. Afraid of a premature discovery of his powers, he addressed the blossoming stick hastily: "Go back." What he meant was "Change back;" but of course he was confused. The stick receded at a considerable velocity, and incontinently came a cry of anger and a bad word from the approaching person. "Who are you throwing brambles at, you fool?" cried a voice. "That got me on the shin."

"I'm sorry, old chap," said Mr. Fotheringay, and then realizing the awkward nature of the explanation, caught nervously at his moustache. He saw Winch, one of the three Immering constables, advancing.

"What d'yer mean by it?" asked the constable. "Hullo! It's you, is it? The gent that broke the lamp at the Long Dragon!"

"I don't mean anything by it," said Mr. Fotheringay. "Nothing at all."

"What d'yer do it for then?"

"Oh, bother!" said Mr. Fotheringay.

"Bother indeed! D'yer know that stick hurt? What d'yer do it for, eh?"

For the moment Mr. Fotheringay could not think what he had done it for. His silence seemed to imitate Mr. Winch. "You've been assaulting the police, young man, this time. That's what *you* done."

"Look here, Mr. Winch," said Mr. Fotheringay, annoyed and confused, "I'm very sorry. The fact is—"

"Well?"

He could think of no way but the truth. "I was working a miracle." He tried to speak in an off-hand way, but try as he would he couldn't.

"Working a—! 'Ere, don't you talk rot. Working a miracle, indeed! Miracle! Well, that's downright funny! Why, you's the chap that don't believe in miracles. . . . Fact is, this is another of your silly conjuring tricks—that's what this is. Now, I tell you—"

But Mr. Fotheringay never heard what Mr. Winch was going to tell him. He realized he had given himself away, flung his valuable secret to all the winds of heaven. A violent gust of irritation swept him to action. He turned on the constable swiftly and fiercely. "Here," he said, "I've had enough of this, I have! I'll show you a silly conjuring trick, I will! Go to Hades! Go, now!"

He was alone!

Mr. Fotheringay performed no more miracles that night, nor did he trouble to see what had become of his flowering stick. He returned to the town, scared and very quiet, and went to his bedroom. "Lord!" he said, "it's a powerful gift—an extremely powerful gift. I didn't hardly mean as much as that. Not really. . . . I wonder what Hades is like!"

He sat on the bed taking off his boots. Struck by a happy thought he transferred the constable to San Francisco, and without any more interference with normal causation went soberly to bed. In the night he dreamt of the anger of Winch.

The next day Mr. Fotheringay heard two interesting items of news. Someone had planted a most beautiful climbing rose against the elder Mr. Gomshott's private house in the Lullaborough Road, and the river as far as Rawling's Mill was to be dragged for Constable Winch.

Mr. Fotheringay was abstracted and thoughtful all that day, and performed no miracles except certain provisions for Winch, and the miracle of completing his day's work with punctual perfection in spite of all the bee-swarm of thoughts that hummed through his mind. And the extraordinary abstraction and meekness of his manner was remarked by several people, and made a matter for jesting. For the most part he was thinking of Winch.

On Sunday evening he went to chapel, and oddly enough, Mr. Maydig, who took a certain interest in occult matters, preached about "things that are not lawful." Mr. Fotheringay was not a regular chapel goer, but the system of assertive skepticism, to which I have already alluded, was now very much shaken. The tenor of the sermon threw an entirely new light on these novel gifts, and he suddenly decided to consult Mr. Maydig immediately after the service. So soon as that was determined, he found himself wondering why he had not done so before.

Mr. Maydig, a lean, excitable man with quite remarkably long wrists and neck, was gratified at a request for a private conversation from a young man whose carelessness in religious matters was a subject for general remark in the town. After a few necessary delays, he conducted him to the study of the Manse, which was contiguous to the chapel, seated him comfortably, and, standing in front of a cheerful fire—his legs threw a Rhodian arch of shadow on the opposite wall—requested Mr. Fotheringay to state his business.

At first Mr. Fotheringay was a little abashed, and found some difficulty in opening the matter. "You will scarcely believe me, Mr. Maydig, I am afraid"— and so forth for some time. He tried a question at last, and asked Mr. Maydig his opinion of miracles.

Mr. Maydig was still saying "Well" in an extremely judicial tone, when Mr. Fotheringay interrupted again: "You don't believe, I suppose, that some common sort of person—like myself, for instance—as it might be sitting here now, might have some sort of twist inside him that made him able to do things by his will."

"It's possible," said Mr. Maydig. "Something of the sort, perhaps, is possible."

"If I might make free with something here, I think I might show you by a sort of experiment," said Mr. Fotheringay. "Now, take that tobacco-jar on the table, for instance. What I want to know is whether what I am going to do with it is a miracle or not. Just half a minute, Mr. Maydig, please."

He knitted his brows, pointed to the tobacco-jar and said: "Be a bowl of vi'lets."

The tobacco-jar did as it was ordered.

Mr. Maydig started violently at the change, and stood looking from the thaumaturgist to the bowl of flowers. He said nothing. Presently he ventured to lean over the table and smell the violets; they were fresh-picked and very fine ones. Then he stared at Mr. Fotheringay again.

"How did you do that?" he asked.

Mr. Fotheringay pulled his moustache. "Just told it—and there you are. Is that a miracle, or is it black art, or what is it? And what do you think's the matter with me? That's what I want to ask."

"It's a most extraordinary occurrence."

"And this day last week I knew no more that I could do things like that than you did. It came quite sudden. It's something odd about my will, I suppose, and that's as far as I can see."

"Is *that*—the only thing. Could you do other things besides that?"

"Lord, yes!" said Mr. Fotheringay. "Just anything." He thought, and suddenly recalled a conjuring entertainment he had seen. "Here!" He pointed. "Change into a bowl of fish—no, not that—change into a glass bowl full of water with goldfish swimming in it. That's better! You see that, Mr. Maydig?"

"It's astonishing. It's incredible. You are either a most extraordinary . . . But no—"

"I could change it into anything," said Mr. Fotheringay. "Just anything. Here! be a pigeon, will you?"

In another moment a blue pigeon was fluttering round the room, and making Mr. Maydig duck every time it came near him. "Stop there, will you," said Mr. Fotheringay; and the pigeon hung motionless in the air. "I could change it back to a bowl of flowers," he said, and after replacing the pigeon on the table worked that miracle. "I expect you will want your pipe in a bit," he said, and restored the tobacco-jar.

Mr. Maydig had followed all these later changes in a sort of ejaculatory silence. He stared at Mr. Fotheringay and, in a very gingerly manner, picked up the tobacco-jar, examined it, replaced it on the table. *"Well!"* was the only expression of his feelings.

"Now, after that it's easier to explain what I came about," said Mr. Fotheringay; and proceeded to a lengthy and involved narrative of his strange experiences, beginning with the affair of the lamp in the Long Dragon and complicated by persistent allusions to Winch. As he went on, the transient pride Mr. Maydig's consternation had caused passed away; he became the very ordinary Mr. Fotheringay of everyday intercourse again. Mr. Maydig listened intently, the tobacco-jar in his hand, and his bearing changed also with the course of the narrative. Presently, while Mr. Fotheringay was dealing with the miracle of the third egg, the minister interrupted with a fluttering extended hand—

"It is possible," he said. "It is credible. It is amazing, of course, but it reconciles a number of difficulties. The power to work miracles is a gift—a peculiar quality like genius or second sight—hitherto it has come very rarely and to exceptional people. But in this case . . . I have always wondered at the miracles of Mahomet, and at Yogi's miracles, and the miracles of Madame Blavatsky. But, of course! Yes, it is simply a gift! It carries out so beautifully the arguments of that great thinker"—Mr. Maydig's voice sank—"his Grace the Duke of Argyll. Here we plumb some profounder law—deeper than the ordinary laws of nature. Yes—yes. Go on. Go on!"

Mr. Fotheringay proceeded to tell of his misadventure with Winch, and Mr. Maydig, no longer overawed or scared, began to jerk his limbs about and interject astonishment. "It's this what troubled me most," proceeded Mr. Fotheringay;

"it's this I'm most mijitly in want of advice for; of course he's at San Francisco—wherever San Francisco may be—but of course it's awkward for both of us, as you'll see, Mr. Maydig. I don't see how he can understand what has happened, and I dare say he's scared and exasperated something tremendous, and trying to get at me. I dare say he keeps on starting off to come here. I send him back, by a miracle, every few hours, when I think of it. And of course, that's a thing he won't be able to understand, and it's bound to annoy him; and, of course, if he takes a ticket every time it will cost him a lot of money. I done the best I could for him, but of course it's difficult for him to put himself in my place. I thought afterwards that his clothes might have got scorched, you know—if Hades is all it's supposed to be—before I shifted him. In that case I suppose they'd have locked him up in San Francisco. Of course I willed him a new suit of clothes on him directly I thought of it. But, you see, I'm already in a deuce of a tangle—''

Mr. Maydig looked serious. "I see you are in a tangle. Yes, it's a difficult position. How you are to end it . . ." He became diffuse and inconclusive.

"However, we'll leave Winch for a little and discuss the larger question. I don't think this is a case of the black art or anything of the sort. I don't think there is any taint of criminality about it at all, Mr. Fotheringay—none whatever unless you are suppressing material facts. No, it's miracles—pure miracles—miracles, if I may say so, of the very highest class."

He began to pace the hearthrug and gesticulate, while Mr. Fotheringay sat with his arm on the table and his head on his arm, looking worried. "I don't see how I'm to manage about Winch," he said.

"A gift of working miracles—apparently a very powerful gift," said Mr. Maydig, "will find a way about Winch—never fear. My dear Sir, you are a most important man—a man of the most astonishing possibilities. As evidence, for example! And in other ways, the things you may do . . ."

"Yes, I've thought of a thing or two," said Mr. Fotheringay. "But—some of the things came a bit twisty. You saw that fish at first? Wrong sort of bowl and wrong sort of fish. And I thought I'd ask someone."

"A proper course," said Mr. Maydig, "a very proper course—altogether the proper course." He stopped and looked at Mr. Fotheringay. "It's practically an unlimited gift. Let us test your powers, for instance. If they really are . . . If they really are all they seem to be."

And so, incredible as it may seem, in the study of the little house behind the Congregational Chapel, on the evening of Sunday, Nov. 10, 1896, Mr. Fotheringay, egged on and inspired by Mr. Maydig, began to work miracles. The reader's attention is specially and definitely called to the date. He will object, probably has already objected, that certain points in this story are improbable, that if any things of the sort already described had indeed occurred, they would have been in all the papers a year ago. The details immediately following he will find particularly hard to accept, because among other things they involve the conclusion that he or she, the reader in question, must have been killed in a violent and unprecedented manner more than a year ago. Now a miracle is nothing if not improbable, and as a matter of fact the reader *was* killed in a violent and unprecedented manner a year ago. In the subsequent course of this story that will become perfectly clear and credible, as every right-minded and reasonable reader will admit. But this is not the place for the end of the story, being but little beyond the hither side of the middle. And at first the miracles worked by Mr. Fotheringay were timid little miracles—little things with the cups and parlor fitments, as feeble as the miracles of Theosophists, and, feeble as they were, they were received with awe by his collaborator. He would have preferred to settle the Winch business out of hand, but Mr. Maydig would not let him. But after they had worked a dozen of these domestic trivialities, their sense of power grew, their imagination began to show signs of stimulation, and their ambition enlarged. Their first larger enterprise was due to hunger and the negligence of Mrs. Minchin, Mr. Maydig's housekeeper. The meal to which the minister conducted Mr. Fotheringay was certainly ill-laid and uninviting as refreshment for two industrious miracle-workers; but they were seated, and Mr. Maydig was descanting in sorrow rather than in anger upon his housekeeper's shortcomings, before it occurred to Mr. Fotheringay that an opportunity lay before him. "Don't you think, Mr. Maydig," he said, "if it isn't a liberty, I—"

"My dear Mr. Fotheringay! Of course! No—I didn't think."

Mr. Fotheringay waved his hand. "What shall we have?" he said, in a large, inclusive spirit, and, at Mr. Maydig's order, revised the supper very thoroughly. "As for me," he said, eyeing Mr. Maydig's selection, "I am always particularly fond of a tankard of stout and a nice Welsh rarebit, and I'll order that. I ain't much given to Burgundy," and forthwith stout and Welsh rarebit promptly appeared at his command. They sat long at their supper, talking like equals, as Mr. Fotheringay presently perceived with a glow of surprise and gratification, of all the miracles they would presently do. "And, by the bye, Mr. Maydig," said Mr. Fotheringay, "I might perhaps be able to help you—in a domestic way."

"Don't quite follow," said Mr. Maydig, pouring out a glass of miraculous old Burgundy.

Mr. Fotheringay helped himself to a second Welsh rarebit out of vacancy, and took a mouthful. "I was thinking," he said, "I might be able *(chum, chum)* to work *(chum, chum)* a miracle with Mrs. Minchin *(chum, chum)*—make her a better woman."

Mr. Maydig put down the glass and looked doubtful. "She's— She strongly objects to interference, you know, Mr. Fotheringay. And—as a matter of fact— it's well past eleven and she's probably in bed and asleep. Do you think, on the whole—"

Mr. Fotheringay considered these objections. "I don't see that it shouldn't be done in her sleep."

For a time Mr. Maydig opposed the idea, and then he yielded. Mr. Fotheringay issued his orders, and a little less at their ease, perhaps, the two gentlemen proceeded with their repast. Mr. Maydig was enlarging on the changes he might expect in his housekeeper next day, with an optimism that seemed even to Mr. Fotheringay's supper senses a little forced and hectic, when a series of confused noises from upstairs began. Their eyes exchanged interrogations, and Mr. Maydig left the room hastily. Mr. Fotheringay heard him calling up to his housekeeper and then his footsteps going softly up to her.

In a minute or so the minister returned, his step light, his face radiant. "Wonderful!" he said, "and touching! Most touching!"

He began pacing the hearthrug. "A repentance—a most touching repentance— through the crack of the door. Poor woman! A most wonderful change! She had got up. She must have got up at once. She had got up out of her sleep to smash a private bottle of brandy in her box. And to confess it too! . . . But this gives us—it opens—a most amazing vista of possibilities. If we can work this miraculous change in *her* . . ."

"The thing's unlimited seemingly," said Mr. Fotheringay. "And about Mr. Winch—"

"Altogether uniimited." And from the hearthrug Mr. Maydig, waving the Winch difficulty aside, unfolded a series of wonderful proposals—proposals he invented as he went along.

Now what those proposals were does not concern the essentials of this story. Suffice it that they were designed in a spirit of infinite benevolence, the sort of benevolence that used to be called post-prandial. Suffice it, too, that the problem of Winch remained unsolved. Nor is it necessary to describe how far that series got to its fulfilment. There were astonishing changes. The small hours found Mr. Maydig and Mr. Fotheringay careering across the chilly market-square under the still moon, in a sort of ecstasy of thaumaturgy, Mr. Maydig all flap and gesture, Mr. Fotheringay short and bristling, and no longer abashed at his greatness. They had reformed every drunkard in the Parliamentary division, changed all the beer and alcohol to water (Mr. Maydig had overruled Mr. Fotheringay on this point), they had, further, greatly improved the railway communication of the place, drained Flinder's swamp, improved the soil of One Tree Hill, and cured the Vicar's wart. And they were going to see what could be done with the injured pier at South Bridge. "The place," gasped Mr. Maydig, "won't be the same place tomorrow. How surprised and thankful everyone will be!" And just at that moment the church clock struck three.

"I say," said Mr. Fotheringay, "that's three o'clock! I must be getting back. I've got to be at business by eight. And besides, Mrs. Wimms—"

"We're only beginning," said Mr. Maydig, full of the sweetness of unlimited power. "We're only beginning. Think of all the good we're doing. When people wake—"

"But—," said Mr. Fotheringay.

Mr. Maydig gripped his arm suddenly. His eyes were bright and wild. "My dear chap," he said, "there's no hurry. Look"—he pointed to the moon at the zenith—"Joshua!"

"Joshua?" said Mr. Fotheringay.

"Joshua," said Mr. Maydig. "Why not? Stop it."

Mr. Fotheringay looked at the moon.

"That's a bit tall," he said after a pause.

"Why not?" said Mr. Maydig. "Of course it doesn't stop. You stop the rotation of the earth, you know. Time stops. It isn't as if we were doing harm."

"H'm!" said Mr. Fotheringay. "Well." He sighed. "I'll try. Here—"

He buttoned up his jacket and addressed himself to the habitable globe, with as good an assumption of confidence as lay in his power. "Jest stop rotating, will you," said Mr. Fotheringay.

Incontinently he was flying head over heels through the air at the rate of dozens of miles a minute. In spite of the innumerable circles he was describing per second, he thought; for thought is wonderful—sometimes as sluggish as flowing pitch, sometimes as instantaneous as light. He thought in a second and willed. "Let me come down safe and sound. Whatever else happens, let me down safe and sound."

He willed it only just in time, for his clothes, heated by his rapid flight through the air, were already beginning to singe. He came down with a forcible, but by no means injurious bump in what appeared to be a mound of fresh-turned earth. A large mass of metal and masonry, extraordinarily like the clock-tower in the middle of the market-square, hit the earth near him, ricochetted over him, and flew into stonework, bricks, and masonry, like a bursting bomb. A hurtling cow hit one of the larger blocks and smashed like an egg. There was a crash that made all the most violent crashes of his past life seem like the sound of falling dust, and this was followed by a descending series of lesser crashes. A vast wind roared throughout earth and heaven, so that he could scarcely lift his head to look. For a while he was too breathless and astonished even to see where he was or what had happened. And his first movement was to feel his head and reassure himself that his streaming hair was still his own.

"Lord!" gasped Mr. Fotheringay, scarce able to speak for the gale. "I've had a squeak! What's gone wrong? Storms and thunder. And only a minute ago a fine night. It's Madig set me on to this sort of thing. *What* a wind! If I go on fooling in this way I'm bound to have a thundering accident! . . .

"Where's Madig?

"What a confounded mess everything's in!"

He looked about him so far as his flapping jacket would permit. The appearance of things was really extremely strange. "The sky's all right anyhow," said Mr. Fotheringay. "And that's about all that is all right. And even there it looks like a terrific gale coming up. But there's the moon overhead. Just as it was just now. Bright as midday. But as for the rest— Where's the village? Where's— where's anything? And what on earth set this wind a-blowing? *I* didn't order no wind."

Mr. Fotheringay struggled to get to his feet in vain, and after one failure, remained on all fours, holding on. He surveyed the moonlit world to leeward, with the tails of his jacket streaming over his head. "There's something seriously wrong," said Mr. Fotheringay. "And what it is—goodness knows."

Far and wide nothing was visible in the white glare through the haze of dust that drove before a screaming gale but tumbled masses of earth and heaps of inchoate ruins, no trees, no houses, no familiar shapes, only a wilderness of disorder vanishing at last into the darkness beneath the whirling columns and streamers, the lightnings and thunderings of a swiftly rising storm. Near him in the livid glare was something that might once have been an elm-tree, a smashed mass of splinters, shivered from boughs to base, and further a twisted mass of iron girders—only too evidently the viaduct—rose out of the piled confusion.

You see, when Mr. Fotheringay had arrested the rotation of the solid globe, he had made no stipulation concerning the trifling movables upon its surface. And the earth spins so fast that the surface at its equator is traveling at rather more than a thousand miles an hour, and in the latitudes at more than half that pace. So that the village, and Mr. Maydig, and Mr. Fotheringay, and everybody and everything had been jerked violently forward at about nine miles per second— that is to say, much more violently than if they had been fired out of a cannon. And every human being, every living creature, every house, and every tree— all the world as we know it—had been so jerked and smashed and utterly destroyed. That was all.

These things Mr. Fotheringay did not, of course, fully appreciate. But he perceived that his miracle had miscarried, and with that a great disgust of miracles came upon him. He was in darkness now, for the clouds had swept together and blotted out his momentary glimpse of the moon, and the air was full of fitful struggling tortured wraiths of hail. A great roaring of wind and waters filled earth and sky, and, peering under his hand through the dust and sleet to windward, he saw by the play of the lightnings a vast wall of water pouring towards him.

"Maydig!" screamed Mr. Fotheringay's feeble voice, amid the elemental uproar. "Here!—Maydig!"

"Stop!" cried Mr. Fotheringay to the advancing water. "Oh, for goodness' sake, stop."

"Just a moment," said Mr. Fotheringay to the lightnings and thunder. "Stop jest a moment while I collect my thoughts. . . . And now what shall I do?'' he said. "What *shall* I do? Lord! I wish Maydig was about."

"I know," said Mr. Fotheringay. "And for goodness' sake let's have it right *this* time."

He remained on all fours, leaning against the wind, very intent to have everything right.

"Ah!" he said. "Let nothing what I'm going to order happen until I say 'Off!' . . . Lord! I wish I'd thought of that before."

He shifted his little voice against the whirlwind, shouting louder and louder in the vain desire to hear himself speak. "Now then!—here goes! Mind about that what I said just now. In the first place, when all I've got to say is done, let me lose my miraculous power, let my will become just like anybody else's will, and all these dangerous miracles be stopped. I don't like them. I'd rather I didn't work 'em. Ever so much. That's the first thing. And the second is—let me be back just before the miracles begin; let everything be just as it was before that blessed lamp turned up. It's a big job, but it's the last. Have you got it? No more miracles; everything as it was—me back in the Long Dragon just before I drank my half-pint. That's it! Yes."

He dug his fingers into the mold, closed his eyes, and said "Off!"

Everything became perfectly still. He perceived that he was standing erect.

"So *you* say," said a voice.

He opened his eyes. He was in the bar of the Long Dragon, arguing about miracles with Toddy Beamish. He had a vague sense of some great thing forgotten that instantaneously passed. You see, except for the loss of his miraculous powers, everything was back as it had been; his mind and memory therefore were now just as they had been at the time when this story began. So that he knew absolutely nothing of all that is told here, knows nothing of all that is told here to this day. And among other things, of course, he still did not believe in miracles.

"I tell you that miracles, properly speaking, can't possibly happen," he said, "whatever you like to hold. And I'm prepared to prove it up to the hilt."

"That's what *you* think," said Toddy Beamish, and "Prove it if you can."

"Looky here, Mr. Beamish," said Mr. Fotheringay. "Let us clearly understand what a miracle is. It's something contrariwise to the course of nature done by power of Will. . . ."

THE STORY OF THE LATE MR. ELVESHAM

I SET THIS story down, not expecting it will be believed, but, if possible, to prepare a way of escape for the next victim. He perhaps may profit by my misfortune. My own case, I know, is hopeless, and I am now in some measure prepared to meet my fate.

My name is Edward George Eden. I was born at Trentham, in Staffordshire, my father being employed in the gardens there. I lost my mother when I was three years old and my father when I was five, my uncle, George Eden, then adopting me as his own son. He was a single man, self-educated, and well-known in Birmingham as an enterprising journalist; he educated me generously, fired my ambition to succeed in the world, and at his death, which happened four years ago, left me his entire fortune, a matter of about five hundred pounds after all out-going charges were paid. I was then eighteen. He advised me in his will to expend the money in completing my education. I had already chosen the profession of medicine, and through his posthumous generosity, and my good fortune in a scholarship competition, I became a medical student at University College, London. At the time of the beginning of my story I lodged at 11A University Street, in a little upper room, very shabbily furnished, and drafty, overlooking the back of Shoolbred's premises. I used this little room both to live in and sleep in, because I was anxious to eke out my means to the very last shillingsworth.

I was taking a pair of shoes to be mended at a shop in the Tottenham Court Road when I first encountered the little old man with the yellow face, with whom my life has now become so inextricably entangled. He was standing on the curb, and staring at the number on the door in a doubtful way, as I opened it. His eyes—they were dull grey eyes, and reddish under the rims—fell to my face, and his countenance immediately assumed an expression of corrugated amiability.

"You come," he said, "apt to the moment. I had forgotten the number of your house. How do you do, Mr. Eden?"

I was a little astonished at his familiar address, for I had never set eyes on the man before. I was annoyed, too, at his catching me with my boots under my arm. He noticed my lack of cordiality.

"Wonder who the deuce I am, eh? A friend, let me assure you. I have seen you before, though you haven't seen me. Is there anywhere where I can talk to you?"

I hesitated. The shabbiness of my room upstairs was not a matter for every stranger. "Perhaps," said I, "We might walk down the street. I'm unfortunately prevented—" My gesture explained the sentence before I had spoken it.

"The very thing," he said, and faced this way and then that. "The street? Which way shall we go?" I slipped my boots down in the passage. "Look here!" he said abruptly; "this business of mine is a rigmarole. Come and lunch with me, Mr. Eden. I'm an old man, a very old man, and not good at explanations, and what with my piping voice and the clatter of the traffic—"

He laid a persuasive skinny hand that trembled a little upon my arm.

I was not so old that an old man might not treat me to a lunch. Yet at the same time I was not altogether pleased by this abrupt invitation. "I had rather—" I began. "But *I* had rather," he said, catching me up, "and a certain civility is surely due to my grey hairs." And so I consented, and went away with him.

He took me to Blavitski's; I had to walk slowly to accommodate myself to his paces; and over such a lunch as I had never tasted before, he fended off my leading questions, and I took a better note of his appearance. His clean-shaven face was lean and wrinkled, his shriveled lips fell over a set of false teeth, and his white hair was thin and rather long; he seemed small to me—though, indeed, most people seemed small to me—and his shoulders were rounded and bent. And, watching him, I could not help but observe that he too was taking note of me, running his eyes, with a curious touch of greed in them, over me from my broad shoulders to my sun-tanned hands and up to my freckled face again. "And now " said he, as we lit our cigarettes, "I must tell you of the business in hand.

"I must tell you, then, that I am an old man, a very old man." He paused momentarily. "And it happens that I have money that I must presently be leaving, and never a child have I to leave it to." I thought of the confidence trick, and resolved I would be on the alert for the vestiges of my five hundred pounds. He proceeded to enlarge on his loneliness, and the trouble he had to find a proper disposition of his money. "I have weighed this plan and that plan, charities, institutions, and scholarships, and libraries, and I have come to this conclusion at last,''—he fixed his eyes on my face,—''that I will find some young fellow, ambitious, pure-minded, and poor, healthy in body and healthy in mind, and, in short, make him my heir, give him all that I have.'' He repeated, ''Give him all that I have. So that he will suddenly be lifted out of all the trouble and struggle in which his sympathies have been educated, to freedom and influence.''

I tried to seem disinterested. With a transparent hypocrisy, I said, ''And you want my help, my professional services maybe, to find that person.''

He smiled and looked at me over his cigarette, and I laughed at his quiet exposure of my modest pretense.

''What a career such a man might have!'' he said. ''It fills me with envy to think how I have accumulated that another man may spend—

''But there are conditions, of course, burdens to be imposed. He must, for instance, take my name. You cannot expect everything without some return. And I must go into all the circumstances of his life before I can accept him. He *must* be sound. I must know his heredity, how his parents and grandparents died, have the strictest inquiries made into his private morals—''

This modified my secret congratulations a little. ''And do I understand,'' said I, ''that I—?''

''Yes,'' he said, almost fiercely. ''You. *You*.''

I answered never a word. My imagination was dancing wildly, my innate skepticism was useless to modify its transports. There was not a particle of gratitude in my mind—I did not know what to say nor how to say it. ''But why me in particular?'' I said at last.

He had chanced to hear of me from Professor Haslar, he said, as a typically sound and sane young man, and he wished, as far as possible, to leave his money where health and integrity were assured.

That was my first meeting with the little old man. He was mysterious about himself; he would not give his name yet, he said, and after I had answered some questions of his, he left me at the Blavitski portal. I noticed that he drew a handful of gold coins from his pocket when it came to paying for the lunch. His insistence upon bodily health was curious. In accordance with an arrangement we had made I applied that day for a life policy in the Loyal Insurance Company for a large sum, and I was exhaustively overhauled by the medical advisers of that company in the subsequent week. Even that did not satisfy him, and he insisted I must be re-examined by the great Doctor Henderson. It was Friday in Whitsun week before he came to a decision. He called me down quite late in the evening,—nearly nine it was,—from cramming chemical equations for my Preliminary Scientific examination. He was standing in the passage under the feeble gas-lamp, and his face was a grotesque interplay of shadows. He seemed more bowed than when I had first seen him, and his cheeks had sunk in a little.

His voice shook with emotion. ''Everything is satisfactory, Mr. Eden,'' he said. ''Everything is quite, quite satisfactory. And this night of all nights, you must dine with me and celebrate your—accession.'' He was interrupted by a cough. ''You won't have long to wait, either,'' he said, wiping his handkerchief across his lips, and gripping my hand with his long bony claw that was disengaged. ''Certainly not very long to wait.''

We went into the street and called a cab. I remember every incident of that drive vividly, the swift, easy motion, the contrast of gas and oil and electric light, the crowds of people in the streets, the place in Regent Street to which we went, and the sumptuous dinner we were served with there. I was disconcerted at first by the well-dressed waiter's glances at my rough clothes, bothered by the stones of the olives, but as the champagne warmed my blood, my confidence revived. At first the old man talked of himself. He had already told me his name in the cab; he was Egbert Elvesham, the great philosopher, whose name I had known since I was a lad at school. It seemed incredible to me that this man, whose intelligence had so early dominated mine, this great abstraction, should suddenly realize itself as this decrepit, familiar figure. I dare say every young fellow who has suddenly fallen among celebrities has felt something of my disappointment. He told me now of the future that the feeble streams of his life would presently leave dry for me, houses, copyrights, investments; I had never suspected that philosophers were so rich. He watched me drink and eat with a touch of envy. "What a capacity for living you have!" he said; and then, with a sigh, a sigh of relief I could have thought it, "It will not be long."

"Ay," said I, my head swimming now with champagne; "I have a future perhaps—of a fairly agreeable sort, thanks to you. I shall now have the honor of your name. But you have a past. Such a past as is worth all my future."

He shook his head and smiled, as I thought with half-sad appreciation of my flattering admiration. "That future," he said; "would you in truth change it?" The waiter came with liqueurs. "You will not perhaps mind taking my name, taking my position, but would you indeed—willingly—take my years?"

"With your achievements," said I, gallantly.

He smiled again. "Kümmel—both," he said to the waiter, and turned his attention to a little paper packet he had taken from his pocket. "This hour," said he, "this after-dinner hour is the hour of small things. Here is a scrap of my unpublished wisdom." He opened the packet with his shaking yellow fingers, and showed a little pinkish powder on the paper. "This," said he—"well, you must guess what it is. But Kümmel—put but a dash of this powder in it—is Himmel." His large greyish eyes watched mine with an inscrutable expression.

It was a bit of a shock to me to find this great teacher gave his mind to the flavor of liqueurs. However, I feigned a great interest in his weakness, for I was drunk enough for such small sycophancy.

He parted the powder between the little glasses, and rising suddenly with a strange unexpected dignity, held out his hand towards me. I imitated his action, and the glasses rang. "To a quick succession," said he, and raised his glass towards his lips.

"Not that," I said hastily. "Not that."

He paused, with the liqueur at the level of his chin, and his eyes blazing into mine.

"To a long life," said I.

He hesitated. "To a long life," said he, with a sudden bark of laughter, and with eyes fixed on one another we tilted the little glasses. His eyes looked straight into mine, and as I drained the stuff off, I felt a curiously intense sensation. The first touch of it set my brain in a furious tumult; I seemed to feel an actual physical stirring in my skull, and a seething humming filled my ears. I did not notice the flavor in my mouth, the aroma that filled my throat; I saw only the grey intensity of his gaze that burnt into mine. The draft, the mental confusion, the noise and stirring in my head, seemed to last an interminable time. Curious vague impressions of half-forgotten things danced and vanished on the edge of my consciousness. At last he broke the spell. With a sudden explosive sigh he put down his glass.

"Well?" he said.

"It's glorious," said I, though I had not tasted the stuff.

My head was spinning. I sat down. My brain was chaos. Then my perception grew clear and minute as though I saw things in a concave mirror. His manner seemed to have changed into something nervous and hasty. He pulled out his watch and grimaced at it. "Eleven-seven! And tonight I must—Seven—twenty-five. Waterloo! I must go at once." He called for the bill, and struggled with his coat. Officious waiters came to our assistance. In another moment I was wishing him good-bye, over the apron of a cab, and still with an absurd feeling of minute distinctness, as though—how can I express it?—I not only saw but *felt* through an inverted opera-glass.

"That stuff," he said. He put his hand to his forehead. "I ought not to have given it to you. It will make your head split tomorrow. Wait a minute. Here." He handed me out a little flat thing like a seidlitz-powder. "Take that in water as you are going to bed. The other thing was a drug. Not till you're ready to go to bed, mind. It will clear your head. That's all. One more shake—Futurus!"

I gripped his shriveled claw. "Good-bye," he said, and by the droop of his eyelids I judged he too was a little under the influence of that brain-twisting cordial.

He recollected something else with a start, felt in his breast-pocket, and produced another packet, this time a cylinder the size and shape of a shaving-stick. "Here," said he. "I'd almost forgotten. Don't open this until I come tomorrow—but take it now."

It was so heavy that I well-nigh dropped it. "All ri'!" said I, and he grinned at me through the cab window as the cabman flicked his horse into wakefulness. It was a white packet he had given me, with red seals at either end and along its edge. "If this isn't money," said I, "it's platinum or lead."

I stuck it with elaborate care into my pocket, and with a whirling brain walked home through the Regent Street loiterers and the dark back streets beyond Portland Road. I remember the sensations of that walk very vividly, strange as they were. I was still so far myself that I could notice my strange mental state, and wonder whether this stuff I had had was opium—a drug beyond my experience. It is hard now to describe the peculiarity of my mental strangeness—mental doubling vaguely expresses it. As I was walking up Regent Street I found in my mind a queer persuasion that it was Waterloo station, and had an odd impulse to get into the Polytechnic as a man might get into a train. I put a knuckle in my eye, and it was Regent Street. How can I express it? You see a skillful actor looking quietly at you, he pulls a grimace, and lo!—another person. Is it too extravagant if I tell you that it seemed to me as if Regent Street had, for the moment, done that? Then, being persuaded it was Regent Street again, I was oddly muddled about some fantastic reminiscences that cropped up. "Thirty years ago," thought I, "it was here that I quarrelled with my brother." Then I burst out laughing, to the astonishment and encouragement of a group of night prowlers. Thirty years ago I did not exist, and never in my life had I boasted a brother. The stuff was surely liquid folly, for the poignant regret for that lost brother still clung to me. Along Portland Road the madness took another turn. I began to recall vanished shops, and to compare the street with what it used to be. Confused, troubled thinking was comprehensible enough after the drink I had taken, but what puzzled me were these curiously vivid phantasmal memories that had crept into my mind; and not only the memories that had crept in, but also the memories that had slipped out. I stopped opposite Stevens', the natural history dealer's, and cudgeled my brains to think what he had to do with me. A 'bus went by, and sounded exactly like the rumbling of a train. I seemed to be dipped into some dark, remote pit for the recollection. "Of course," said I, at last, "he has promised me three frogs tomorrow. Odd I should have forgotten."

Do they still show children dissolving views? In those I remember one view would begin like a faint ghost, and grow and oust another. In just that way it seemed to me that a ghostly set of new sensations was struggling with those of my ordinary self.

I went on through Euston Road to Tottenham Court Road, puzzled, and a little frightened, and scarcely noticed the unusual way I was taking, for commonly I used to cut through the intervening network of back streets. I turned into University Street, to discover that I had forgotten my number. Only by a strong effort did I recall 11A, and even then it seemed to me that it was a thing some forgotten person had told me. I tried to steady my mind by recalling the incidents of the dinner, and for the life of me I could conjure up no picture of my host's face; I saw him only as a shadowy outline, as one might see oneself reflected in a window through which one was looking. In his place, however, I had a curious exterior vision of myself sitting at a table, flushed, bright-eyed, and talkative.

"I must take this other powder," said I. "This is getting impossible."

I tried the wrong side of the hall for my candle and the matches, and had a doubt of which landing my room might be on. "I'm drunk," I said, "that's certain," and blundered needlessly on the staircase to sustain the proposition.

At the first glance my room seemed unfamiliar. "What rot!" I said, and stared about me. I seemed to bring myself back by the effort and the odd phantasmal quality passed into the concrete familiar. There was the old looking-glass, with my notes on the albumens stuck in the corner of the frame, my old everyday suit of clothes pitched about the floor. And yet it was not so real after all. I felt an idiotic persuasion trying to creep into my mind, as it were, that I was in a railway carriage in a train just stopping, that I was peering out of the window at some unknown station. I gripped the bed-rail firmly to reassure myself. "It's clairvoyance, perhaps," I said. "I must write to the Psychical Research Society."

I put the rouleau on my dressing-table, sat on my bed and began to take off my boots. It was as if the picture of my present sensations was painted over some other picture that was trying to show through. "Curse it!" said I, "my wits are going, or am I in two places at once?" Half-undressed, I tossed the powder into a glass and drank it off. It effervesced, and became a fluorescent amber color. Before I was in bed my mind was already tranquilized. I felt the pillow at my cheek, and thereupon I must have fallen asleep.

I awoke abruptly out of a dream of strange beasts, and found myself lying on my back. Probably everyone knows that dismal emotional dream from which one escapes, awake indeed but strangely cowed. There was a curious taste in my mouth, a tired feeling in my limbs, a sense of cutaneous discomfort. I lay with my head motionless on my pillow, expecting that my feeling of strangeness and terror would probably pass away, and that I should then doze off again to sleep. But instead of that, my uncanny sensations increased. At first I could perceive nothing wrong about me. There was a faint light in the room, so faint that it was the very next thing to darkness, and the furniture stood out in it as vague blots of absolute darkness. I stared with my eyes just over the bedclothes.

It came into my mind that someone had entered the room to rob me of my rouleau of money, but after lying for some moments, breathing regularly to simulate sleep, I realized this was mere fancy. Nevertheless, the uneasy assurance of something wrong kept fast hold of me. With an effort I raised my head from the pillow, and peered about me at the dark. What it was I could not conceive. I looked at the dim shapes around me, the greater and lesser darknesses that indicated curtains, table, fireplace, bookshelves, and so forth. Then I began to perceive something unfamiliar in the forms of the darkness. Had the bed turned round? Yonder should be the bookshelves, and something shrouded and pallid rose there, something that would not answer to the bookshelves, however I looked at it. It was far too big to be my shirt thrown on a chair.

Overcoming a childish terror, I threw back the bedclothes and thrust my leg out of bed. Instead of coming out of my truckle-bed upon the floor, I found my foot scarcely reached the edge of the mattress. I made another step, as it were, and sat up on the edge of the bed. By the side of my bed should be the candle, and the matches upon the broken chair. I put out my hand and touched—nothing. I waved my hand in the darkness, and it came against some heavy hanging, soft and thick in texture, which gave a rustling noise at my touch. I grasped this and pulled it; it appeared to be a curtain suspended over the head of my bed.

I was now thoroughly awake, and beginning to realize that I was in a strange room. I was puzzled. I tried to recall the overnight circumstances, and I found them now, curiously enough, vivid in my memory: the supper, my reception of the little packages, my wonder whether I was intoxicated, my slow undressing, the coolness to my flushed face of my pillow. I felt a sudden distrust. Was that last night, or the night before? At any rate, this room was strange to me, and I could not imagine how I had got into it. The dim, pallid outline was growing paler, and I perceived it was a window, with the dark shape of an oval toilet-glass against the weak intimation of the dawn that filtered through the blind. I stood up, and was surprised by a curious feeling of weakness and unsteadiness. With trembling hands outstretched, I walked slowly towards the window, getting, nevertheless, a bruise on the knee from a chair by the way. I fumbled round the glass, which was large, with handsome brass sconces, to find the blind-cord. I could not find any. By chance I took hold of the tassel, and with the click of a spring the blind ran up.

I found myself looking out upon a scene that was altogether strange to me. The night was overcast, and through the flocculent grey of the heaped clouds there filtered a faint half-light of dawn. Just at the edge of the sky, the cloud canopy had a blood-red rim. Below, everything was dark and indistinct, dim hills in the distance, a vague mass of buildings, running up into pinnacles, trees like spilt ink, and below the window a tracery of black bushes and pale grey paths. It was so unfamiliar that for the moment I thought myself still dreaming. I felt the toilet-table; it appeared to be made of some polished wood, and was rather elaborately furnished—there were little cut-glass bottles and a brush upon it. There was also a queer little object, horse-shoe-shaped it felt, with smooth, hard projections, lying in a saucer. I could find no matches nor candle-stick.

I turned my eyes to the room again. Now the blind was up, faint specters of its furnishing came out of the darkness. There was a huge curtained bed, and the fireplace at its foot had a large white mantel with something of the shimmer of marble.

I leant against the toilet-table, shut my eyes and opened them again, and tried to think. The whole thing was far too real for dreaming. I was inclined to imagine there was still some hiatus in my memory as a consequence of my draft of that strange liqueur; that I had come into my inheritance perhaps, and suddenly lost my recollection of everything since my good fortune had been announced. Perhaps if I waited a little, things would be clearer to me again. Yet my dinner with old Elvesham was now singularly vivid and recent. The champagne, the observant waiters, the powder, and the liqueurs—I could have staked my soul it all happened a few hours ago.

And then occurred a thing so trivial and yet so terrible to me that I shiver now to think of that moment. I spoke aloud. I said, "How the devil did I get here?" . . . *And the voice was not my own.*

It was not my own, it was thin, the articulation was slurred, the resonance of my facial bones was different. Then to reassure myself I ran one hand over the other, and left loose folds of skin, the bony laxity of age. "Surely," I said in that horrible voice that had somehow established itself in my throat, "surely this thing is a dream!" Almost as quickly as if I did it involuntarily, I thrust my fingers into my mouth. My teeth had gone. My finger-tips ran on the flaccid surface of an even row of shriveled gums. I was sick with dismay and disgust.

I felt then a passionate desire to see myself, to realize at once in its full horror the ghastly change that had come upon me. I tottered to the mantel, and felt along it for matches. As I did so, a barking cough sprang up in my throat and I clutched the thick flannel nightdress I found about me. There were no matches there, and I suddenly realized that my extremities were cold. Sniffing and coughing, whimpering a little perhaps, I fumbled back to bed. "It is surely a dream," I whimpered to myself as I clambered back, "surely a dream." It was a senile repetition. I pulled the bedclothes over my shoulders, over my ears, I thrust my withered hand under the pillow, and determined to compose myself to sleep. Of course it was a dream. In the morning the dream would be over, and I should wake up strong and vigorous again to my youth and studies. I shut my eyes, breathed regularly, and, finding myself wakeful, began to count slowly through the powers of three.

But the thing I desired would not come. I could not get to sleep. And the persuasion of the inexorable reality of the change that had happened to me grew steadily. Presently I found myself with my eyes wide open, the powers of three forgotten, and my skinny fingers upon my shriveled gums. I was indeed, suddenly and abruptly, an old man. I had in some unaccountable manner fallen through my life and come to old age, in some way I had been cheated of all the best of my life, of love, of struggle, of strength and hope. I groveled into the pillow and tried to persuade myself that such hallucination was possible. Imperceptibly, steadily, the dawn grew clearer.

At last, despairing of further sleep, I sat up in bed and looked about me. A chill twilight rendered the whole chamber visible. It was spacious and well-furnished, better furnished than any room I had ever slept in before. A candle and matches became dimiy visible upon a little pedestal in a recess. I threw back the bedclothes, and shivering with the rawness of the early morning, albeit it was summer-time, I got out and lit the candle. Then, trembling horribly so that the extinguisher rattled on its spike, I tottered to the glass and saw—*Elvesham's face!* It was none the less horrible because I had already dimly feared as much. He had already seemed physically weak and pitiful to me, but seen now, dressed only in a coarse flannel nightdress that fell apart and showed the stringy neck, seen now as my own body, I cannot describe its desolate decrepitude. The hollow cheeks, the straggling tail of dirty grey hair, the rheumy bleared eyes, the quivering, shriveled lips, the lower displaying a gleam of the pink interior lining, and those horrible dark gums showing. You who are mind and body together at your natural years, cannot imagine what this fiendish imprisonment meant to me. To be young and full of the desire and energy of youth, and to be caught, and presently to be crushed in this tottering ruin of a body. . . .

But I wander from the course of my story. For some time I must have been stunned at this change that had come upon me. It was daylight when I did so far gather myself together as to think. In some inexplicable way I had been changed, though how, short of magic, the thing had been done, I could not say.

And as I thought, the diabolical ingenuity of Elvesham came home to me. It seemed plain to me that as I found myself in his, so he must be in possession of *my* body, of my strength that is, and my future. But how to prove it? Then as I thought, the thing became so incredible even to me, that my mind reeled, and I had to pinch myself, to feel my toothless gums, to see myself in the glass, and touch the things about me before I could steady myself to face the facts again. Was all life hallucination? Was I indeed Elvesham, and he me? Had I been dreaming of Eden overnight? Was there any Eden? But if I was Elvesham, I should remember where I was on the previous morning, the name of the town in which I lived, what happened before the dream began. I struggled with my thoughts. I recalled the queer doubleness of my memories overnight. But now my mind was clear. Not the ghost of any memories but those proper to Eden could I raise.

"This way lies insanity!" I cried in my piping voice. I staggered to my feet, dragged my feeble, heavy limbs to the washhand-stand, and plunged my grey head into a basin of cold water. Then, toweling myself, I tried again. It was no good. I felt beyond all question that I was indeed Eden, not Elvesham. But Eden in Elvesham's body!

Had I been a man of any other age, I might have given myself up to my fate as one enchanted. But in these skeptical days miracles do not pass current. Here was some trick of psychology. What a drug and a steady stare could do, a drug and a steady stare, or some similar treatment, could surely undo. Men have lost their memories before. But to exchange memories as one does umbrellas! I laughed. Alas! not a healthy laugh, but a wheezing, senile titter. I could have fancied old Elvesham laughing at my plight, and a gust of petulant anger, unusual to me, swept across my feelings. I began dressing eagerly in the clothes I found lying about on the floor, and only realized when I was dressed that it was an evening suit I had assumed. I opened the wardrobe and found some ordinary clothes, a pair of plaid trousers, and an old-fashioned dressing-gown. I put a venerable smoking-cap on my venerable head, and, coughing a little from my exertions, tottered out upon the landing.

It was then perhaps a quarter to six, and the blinds were closely drawn and the house quite silent. The landing was a spacious one, a broad, richly carpeted staircase went down into the darkness of the hall below, and before me a door ajar showed me a writing-desk, a revolving bookcase, the back of a study chair, and a fine array of bound books, shelf upon shelf.

"My study," I mumbled, and walked across the landing. Then, at the sound of my voice a thought struck me, and I went back to the bedroom and put in the set of false teeth. They slipped in with the ease of old habit. "That's better," said I, gnashing them, and so returned to the study.

The drawers of the writing-desk were locked. Its revolving top was also locked. I could see no indications of the keys, and there were none in the pockets of my trousers. I shuffled back at once to the bedroom, and went through the dress suit, and afterwards the pockets of all the garments I could find. I was very eager; and one might have imagined that burglars had been at work, to see my room when I had done. Not only were there no keys to be found, but not a coin, nor a scrap of paper—save only the receipted bill of the overnight dinner.

A curious weariness asserted itself. I sat down and stared at the garments flung here and there, their pockets turned inside out. My first frenzy had already flickered out. Every moment I was beginning to realize the immense intelligence of the plans of my enemy, to see more and more clearly the hopelessness of my position. With an effort I rose and hurried into the study again. On the staircase was a housemaid pulling up the blinds. She stared, I think, at the expression of my face. I shut the door of the study behind me, and seizing a poker, began an attack upon the desk. That is how they found me. The cover of the desk was split, the lock smashed, the letters torn out of the pigeon-holes and tossed about the room. In my senile rage I had flung about the pens and other such light stationery, and overturned the ink. Moreover, a large vase upon the mantel had got broken—I do not know how. I could find no checkbook, no money, no indications of the slightest use for the recovery of my body. I was battering madly at the drawers, when the butler, backed by two women-servants, intruded upon me.

That simply is the story of my change. No one will believe my frantic assertions. I am treated as one demented, and even at this moment I am under restraint. But I am sane, absolutely sane, and to prove it I have sat down to write this story minutely as the thing happened to me. I appeal to the reader, whether there is any trace of insanity in the style or method of the story he has been reading. I am a young man locked away in an old man's body. But the clear fact is incredible to everyone. Naturally I appear demented to those who will not believe this, naturally I do not know the names of my secretaries, of the doctors who come to see me, of my servants and neighbors, of this town (wherever it is) where I find myself. Naturally I lose myself in my own house, and suffer inconveniences of every sort. Naturally I ask the oddest questions. Naturally I weep and cry out, and have paroxysms of despair. I have no money and no checkbook. The bank will not recognize my signature, for I suppose that, allowing for the feeble muscles I now have, my handwriting is still Eden's. These people about me will not let me go to the bank personally. It seems, indeed, that there is no bank in this town, and that I have taken an account in some part of London. It seems that Elvesham kept the name of his solicitor secret from all his household— I can ascertain nothing. Elvesham was, of course, a profound student of mental science, and all my declarations of the facts of the case merely confirm the theory that my insanity is the outcome of overmuch brooding upon psychology. Dreams of the personal identity indeed! Two days ago I was a healthy youngster, with all life before me; now I am a furious old man, unkempt and desperate and miserable, prowling about a great luxurious strange house, watched, feared, and avoided as a lunatic by everyone about me. And in London is Elvesham beginning life again in a vigorous body, and with all the accumulated knowledge and wisdom of threescore and ten. He has stolen my life.

What has happened I do not clearly know. In the study are volumes of manuscript notes referring chiefly to the psychology of memory, and parts of what may be either calculations or ciphers in symbols absolutely strange to me. In some passages there are indications that he was also occupied with the philosophy of mathematics. I take it he has transferred the whole of his memories, the accumulation that make up his personality, from this old withered brain of his to mine, and, similarly, that he has transferred mine to his discarded tenement. Practically, that is, he has changed bodies. But how such a change may be possible is without the range of my philosophy. I have been a materialist for all my thinking life, but here, suddenly, is a clear case of man's detachability from matter.

One desperate experiment I am about to try. I sit writing here before putting the matter to issue. This morning, with the help of a table-knife that I had secreted at breakfast, I succeeded in breaking open a fairly obvious secret drawer in this wrecked writing-desk. I discovered nothing save a little green glass phial containing a white powder. Round the neck of the phial was a label, and thereon

was written this one word, *"Release."* This may be—is most probably, poison.
I can understand Elvesham placing poison in my way, and I should be sure that
it was his intention so to get rid of the only living witness against him, were it
not for this careful concealment. The man has practically solved the problem of
immortality. Save for the spite of chance, he will live in my body, until it has
aged, and then, again, throwing that aside, he will assume some other victim's
youth and strength. When one remembers his heartlessness, it is terrible to think
of the ever-growing experience, that . . . How long has he been leaping from
body to body? . . . But I tire of writing. The powder appears to be soluble in
water. The taste is not unpleasant.

There the narrative found upon Mr. Elvesham's desk ends. His dead body lay
between the desk and the chair. The latter had been pushed back, probably by
his last convulsions. The story was written in pencil, and in a crazy hand quite
unlike his usual minute characters. There remain only two curious facts to record.
Indisputably there was some connection between Eden and Elvesham, since the
whole of Elvesham's property was bequeathed to the young man. But he never
inherited. When Elvesham committed suicide, Eden was, strangely enough,
already dead. Twenty-four hours before, he had been knocked down by a cab
and killed instantly, at the crowded crossing at the intersection of Gower Street
and Euston Road. So that the only human being who could have thrown light
upon this fantastic narrative is beyond the reach of questions.

POLLOCK AND THE PORROH MAN

IT WAS IN a swampy village on the lagoon river behind the Turner Peninsula
that Pollock's first encounter with the Porroh man occurred. The women of that
country are famous for their good looks—they are Gallinas with a dash of
European blood that dates from the days of Vasco da Gama and the English
slave-traders, and the Porroh man, too, was possibly inspired by a faint Caucasian
taint in his composition. (It's a curious thing to think that some of us may have
distant cousins eating men on Sherboro Island or raiding with the Sofas.) At any
rate, the Porroh man stabbed the woman to the heart as though he had been a
mere low-class Italian, and very narrowly missed Pollock. But Pollock, using
his revolver to parry the lightning stab which was aimed at his deltoid muscle,
sent the iron dagger flying, and, firing, hit the man in the hand.

He fired again and missed, knocking a sudden window out of the wall of the
hut. The Porroh man stooped in the doorway, glancing under his arm at Pollock.
Pollock caught a glimpse of his inverted face in the sunlight, and then the
Englishman was alone, sick and trembling with the excitement of the affair, in
the twilight of the place. It had all happened in less time than it takes to read
about it.

The woman was quite dead, and having ascertained this, Pollock went to the
entrance of the hut and looked out. Things outside were dazzling bright. Half a
dozen of the porters of the expedition were standing up in a group near the green
huts they occupied, and staring towards him, wondering what the shots might
signify. Behind the little group of men was the broad stretch of black fetid mud
by the river, a green carpet of rafts of papryus and water-grass, and then the
leaden water. The mangroves beyond the stream loomed indistinctly through the
blue haze. There were no signs of excitement in the squat village, whose fence
was just visible above the canegrass.

Pollock came out of the hut cautiously and walked towards the river, looking over his shoulder at intervals. But the Porroh man had vanished. Pollock clutched his revolver nervously in his hand.

One of his men came to meet him, and as he came, pointed to the bushes behind the hut in which the Porroh man had disappeared. Pollock had an irritating persuasion of having made an absolute fool of himself; he felt bitter, savage, at the turn things had taken. At the same time, he would have to tell Waterhouse—the moral, exemplary, cautious Waterhouse—who would inevitably take the matter seriously. Pollock cursed bitterly at his luck, at Waterhouse, and especially at the West Coast of Africa. He felt consummately sick of the expedition. And in the back of his mind all the time was a speculative doubt where precisely within the visible horizon the Porroh man might be.

It is perhaps rather shocking, but he was not at all upset by the murder that had just happened. He had seen so much brutality during the last three months, so many dead women, burnt huts, drying skeletons, up the Kittam River in the wake of the Sofa cavalry, that his senses were blunted. What disturbed him was the persuasion that this business was only beginning.

He swore savagely at the black, who ventured to ask a question, and went on into the tent under the orange-trees where Waterhouse was lying, feeling exasperatingly like a boy going into the headmaster's study.

Waterhouse was still sleeping off the effects of his last dose of chlorodyne, and Pollock sat down on a packing-case beside him, and, lighting his pipe, waited for him to awake. About him were scattered the pots and weapons Waterhouse had collected from the Mendi people, and which he had been repacking for the canoe voyage to Sulyma.

Presently Waterhouse woke up, and after judicial stretching, decided he was all right again. Pollock got him some tea. Over the tea the incidents of the afternoon were described by Pollock, after some preliminary beating about the bush. Waterhouse took the matter even more seriously than Pollock had anticipated. He did not simply disapprove, he scolded, he insulted.

"You're one of those infernal fools who think a black man isn't a human being," he said. "I can't be ill a day without you must get into some dirty scrape or other. This is the third time in a month that you have come crossways-on with a native, and this time you're in for it with a vengeance. Porroh, too! They're down upon you enough as it is, about that idol you wrote your silly name on. And they're the most vindictive devils on earth! You make a man ashamed of civilization. To think you come of a decent family! If ever I cumber myself up with a vicious, stupid young lout like you again—"

"Steady on, now," snarled Pollock, in the tone that always exasperated Waterhouse; "steady on."

At that Waterhouse became speechless. He jumped to his feet.

"Look here, Pollock," he said, after a struggle to control his breath. "You must go home. I won't have you any longer. I'm ill enough as it is through you—"

"Keep your hair on," said Pollock, staring in front of him. "I'm ready enough to go."

Waterhouse became calmer again. He sat down on the camp-stool. "Very well," he said. "I don't want a row, Pollock, you know; but it's confoundedly annoying to have one's plans put out by this kind of thing. I'll come to Sulyma with you, and see you safe aboard—"

"You needn't," said Pollock. "I can go alone. From here."

"Not far," said Waterhouse. "You don't understand this Porroh business."

"How should *I* know she belonged to a Porrohman?" said Pollock, bitterly.

"Well, she did," said Waterhouse; "and you can't undo the thing. Go alone, indeed! I wonder what they'd do to you. You don't seem to understand that this Porroh hokey-pokey rules this country, is its law, religion, constitution, medicine, magic— They appoint the chiefs. The Inquisition, at its best, couldn't hold a candle to these chaps. He will probably set Awajale, the chief here, on to us. It's lucky our porters are Mendis. We shall have to shift this little settlement of ours— Confound you, Pollock! And, of course, you must go and miss him."

He thought, and his thoughts seemed disagreeable. Presently he stood up and took his rifle. "I'd keep close for a bit, if I were you," he said, over his shoulder, as he went out. "I'm going out to see what I can find out about it."

Pollock remained sitting in the tent, meditating. "I was meant for a civilized life," he said to himself, regretfully, as he filled his pipe. "The sooner I get back to London or Paris the better for me."

His eye fell on the sealed case in which Waterhouse had put the featherless poisoned arrows they had bought in the Mendi country. "I wish I had hit the beggar somewhere vital," said Pollock, viciously.

Waterhouse came back after a long interval. He was not communicative, though Pollock asked him questions enough. The Porroh man, it seems, was a prominent member of that mystical society. The village was interested, but not threatening. No doubt the witch-doctor had gone into the bush. He was a great witch-doctor. "Of course, he's up to something," said Waterhouse, and became silent.

"But what can he do?" asked Pollock, unheeded.

"I must get you out of this. There's something brewing, or things would not be so quiet," said Waterhouse, after a gap of silence. Pollock wanted to know what the brew might be. "Dancing in a circle of skulls," said Waterhouse; "brewing a stink in a copper pot." Pollock wanted particulars. Waterhouse was vague, Pollock pressing. At last Waterhouse lost his temper. "How the devil should *I* know?" he said to Pollock's twentieth inquiry what the Porroh man would do. "He tried to kill you off-hand in the hut. *Now,* I fancy he will try something more elaborate. But you'll see fast enough. I don't want to help unnerve you. It's probably all nonsense."

That night, as they were sitting at their fire, Pollock again tried to draw Waterhouse out on the subject of Porroh methods. "Better get to sleep," said Waterhouse, when Pollock's bent became apparent; "we start early tomorrow. You may want all your nerve about you."

"But what line will he take?"

"Can't say. They're versatile people. They know a lot of rum dodges. You'd better get that copper-devil, Shakespear, to talk."

There was a flash and a heavy bang out of the darkness behind the huts, and a clay bullet came whistling close to Pollock's head. This, at least, was crude enough. The blacks and half-breeds sitting and yarning round their own fire jumped up, and someone fired into the dark.

"Better go into one of the huts," said Waterhouse, quietly, still sitting unmoved.

Pollock stood up by the fire and drew his revolver. Fighting, at least, he was not afraid of. But a man in the dark is in the best of armor. Realizing the wisdom of Waterhouse's advice, Pollock went into the tent and lay down there.

What little sleep he had was disturbed by dreams, variegated dreams, but chiefly of the Porroh man's face, upside down, as he went out of the hut, and looked up under his arm. It was odd that this transitory impression should have stuck so firmly in Pollock's memory. Moreover, he was troubled by queer pains in his limbs.

In the white haze of the early morning, as they were loading the canoes, a barbed arrow suddenly appeared quivering in the ground close to Pollock's foot. The boys made a perfunctory effort to clear out the thicket, but it led to no capture.

After these two occurrences, there was a disposition on the part of the expedition to leave Pollock to himself, and Pollock became, for the first time in his life, anxious to mingle with blacks. Waterhouse took one canoe, and Pollock, in spite of a friendly desire to chat with Waterhouse, had to take the other. He was left all alone in the front part of the canoe, and he had the greatest trouble to make the men—who did not love him—keep to the middle of the river, a clear hundred yards or more from either shore. However, he made Shakespear, the Freetown half-breed, come up to his own end of the canoe and tell him about Porroh, which Shakespear, failing in his attempts to leave Pollock alone, presently did with considerable freedom and gusto.

The day passed. The canoe glided swiftly along the ribbon of lagoon water, between the drift of water-figs, fallen trees, papyrus, and palm-wine palms, and with the dark mangrove swamp to the left, through which one could hear now and then the roar of the Atlantic surf. Shakespear told, in his soft blurred English, of how the Porroh could cast spells; how men withered up under their malice; how they could send dreams and devils; how they tormented and killed the sons of Ijibu; how they kidnapped a white trader from Sulyma who had maltreated one of the sect, and how his body looked when it was found. And Pollock after each narrative cursed under his breath at the want of missionary enterprise that allowed such things to be, and at the inert British Government that ruled over this dark heathendom of Sierra Leone. In the evening they came to the Kasi Lake, and sent a score of crocodiles lumbering off the island on which the expedition camped for the night.

The next day they reached Sulyma, and smelt the sea breeze; but Pollock had to put up there for five days before he could get on to Freetown. Waterhouse, considering him to be comparatively safe here, and within the pale of Freetown influence, left him and went back with the expedition to Gbemma, and Pollock became very friendly with Perera, the only resident white trader at Sulyma—so friendly, indeed, that he went about with him everywhere. Perera was a little Portuguese Jew, who had lived in England, and he appreciated the Englishman's friendliness as a great compliment.

For two days nothing happened out of the ordinary; for the most part Pollock and Perera played Nap—the only game they had in common—and Pollock got into debt. Then, on the second evening, Pollock had a disageeable intimation of the arrival of the Porroh man in Sulyma by getting a flesh-wound in the shoulder from a lump of filed iron. It was a long shot, and the missile had nearly spent its force when it hit him. Still it conveyed its message plainly enough. Pollock sat up in his hammock, revolver in hand, all that night, and next morning confided, to some extent, in the Anglo-Portuguese.

Perera took the matter seriously. He knew the local customs pretty thoroughly. "It is a personal question, you must know. It is revenge. And of course he is hurried by your leaving de country. None of de natives or half-breeds will interfere wid him very much—unless you make it wort deir while. If you come upon him suddenly, you might shoot him. But den he might shoot you.

"Den dere's dis—infernal magic," said Perera. "Of course, I don't believe in it—superstition; but still it's not nice to tink dat wherever you are, dere is a black man, who spends a moonlight night now and den a-dancing about a fire to send you bad dreams— Had any bad dreams?''

"Rather," said Pollock. "I keep on seeing the beggar's head upside down grinning at me and showing all his teeth as he did in the hut, and coming close up to me, and then going ever so far off, and coming back. It's nothing to be afraid of, but somehow it simply paralyses me with terror in my sleep. Queer things—dreams. I know it's a dream all the time, and I can't wake up from it."

"It's probably only fancy," said Perera. "Den my niggers say Porroh men can send snakes. Seen any snakes lately?"

"Only one. I killed him this morning, on the floor near my hammock. Almost trod on him as I got up.''

"Ah!" said Perera, and then, reassuringly, "Of course it is a—coincidence. Still I would keep my eyes open. Den dere's pains in de bones.''

"I thought they were due to miasma," said Pollock.

"Probably dey are. When did dey begin?''

Then Pollock remembered that he first noticed them the night after the fight in the hut. "It's my opinion he don't want to kill you," said Perera—"at least not yet. I've heard deir idea is to scare and worry a man wid deir spells, and narrow misses, and rheumatic pains, and bad dreams, and all dat, until he's sick of life. Of course, it's all talk, you know. You mustn't worry about it—But I wonder what he'll be up to next.''

"*I* shall have to be up to something first," said Pollock, staring gloomily at the greasy cards that Perera was putting on the table. "It don't suit my dignity to be followed about, and shot at, and blighted in this way. I wonder if Porroh hokey-pokey upsets your luck at cards.''

He looked at Perera suspiciously.

"Very likely it does," said Perera, warmly, shuffling. "Dey are wonderful people.''

That afternoon Pollock killed two snakes in his hammock, and there was also an extraordinary increase in the number of red ants that swarmed over the place; and these annoyances put him in a fit temper to talk over business with a certain Mendi rough he had interviewed before. The Mendi rough showed Pollock a little iron dagger, and demonstrated where one struck in the neck, in a way that made Pollock shiver; and in return for certain considerations Pollock promised him a double-barrelled gun with an ornamental lock.

In the evening, as Pollock and Perera were playing cards, the Mendi rough came in through the doorway, carrying something in a blood-soaked piece of native cloth.

"Not here!" said Pollock, very hurriedly. "Not here!"

But he was not quick enough to prevent the man, who was anxious to get to Pollock's side of the bargain, from opening the cloth and throwing the head of the Porroh man upon the table. It bounded from there on to the floor, leaving a red trail on the cards, and rolled into a corner, where it came to rest upside down, but glaring hard at Pollock.

Perera jumped up as the thing fell among the cards, and began in his excitement to gabble in Portuguese. The Mendi was bowing, with the red cloth in his hand. "De gun!" he said. Pollock stared back at the head in the corner. It bore exactly the expression it had in his dreams. Something seemed to snap in his own brain as he looked at it.

Then Perera found his English again.

"You got him killed?" he said. "You did not kill him yourself?"

"Why should I?" said Pollock.

"But he will not be able to take it off now!"

"Take *what* off?" said Pollock.

"And all dese cards are spoiled!"

"*What* do you mean by taking off?" said Pollock.

"You must send me a new pack from Freetown. You can buy dem dere."

"But—'take it off'?"

"It is only superstition. I forgot. De niggers say dat if de witches—he was a witch—But it is rubbish—You must make de Porroh man take it off or kill him yourself—It is very silly."

Pollock swore under his breath, still staring hard at the head in the corner.

"I can't stand that glare," he said. Then suddenly he rushed at the thing and kicked it. It rolled some yards or so, and came to rest in the same position as before, upside down, and looking at him.

"He is ugly," said the Anglo-Portuguese. "Very ugly. Dey do it on deir faces with little knives."

Pollock would have kicked the head again, but the Mendi man touched him on the arm. "De gun?" he said, looking nervously at the head.

"Two—if you will take that beastly thing away," said Pollock.

The Mendi shook his head, and intimated that he only wanted one gun now due to him, and for which he would be obliged. Pollock found neither cajolery nor bullying any good with him. Perera had a gun to sell (at a profit of three hundred percent,), and with that the man presently departed. Then Pollock's eyes, against his will, were recalled to the thing on the floor.

"It is funny dat his head keeps upside down," said Perera, with an uneasy laugh. "His brains must be heavy, like de weight in de little images one sees dat keep always upright wid lead in dem. You will take him wiv you when you go presently. You might take him now. De cards are all spoilt. Dere is a man sell dem in Freetown. De room is in a filty mess as it is. You should have killed him yourself."

Pollock pulled himself together, and went and picked up the head. He would hang it up by the lamp-hook in the middle of the ceiling of his room, and dig a grave for it at once. He was under the impression that he hung it up by the hair, but that must have been wrong, for when he returned for it, it was hanging by the neck upside down.

He buried it before sunset on the north side of the shed he occupied, so that he should not have to pass the grave after dark when he was returning from Perera's. He killed two snakes before he went to sleep. In the darkest part of the night he awoke with a start, and heard a pattering sound and something scraping on the floor. He sat up noiselessly, and felt under his pillow for his revolver. A mumbling growl followed, and Pollock fired at the sound. There was a yelp, and something dark passed for a moment across the hazy blue of the doorway. "A dog!" said Pollock, lying down again.

In the early dawn he awoke again with a peculiar sense of unrest. The vague pain in his bones had returned. For some time he lay watching the red ants that were swarming over the ceiling, and then, as the light grew brighter, he looked over the edge of his hammock and saw something dark on the floor. He gave such a violent start that the hammock overset and flung him out.

He found himself lying, perhaps, a yard away from the head of the Porroh man. It had been disinterred by the dog, and the nose was grievously battered. Ants and flies swarmed over it. By an odd coincidence, it was still upside down, and with the same diabolical expression in the inverted eyes.

Pollock sat paralyzed, and stared at the horror for some time. Then he got up and walked round it,—giving it a wide berth—and out of the shed. The clear light of the sunrise, the living stir of vegetation before the breath of the dying land-breeze, and the empty grave with the marks of the dog's paws, lightened the weight upon his mind a little.

He told Perera of the business as though it was a jest,—a jest to be told with white lips. "You should not have frighten de dog," said Perera, with poorly simulated hilarity.

The next two days, until the steamer came, were spent by Pollock in making a more effectual disposition of his possession. Overcoming his aversion to handling the thing, he went down to the river mouth and threw it into the sea-water, but by some miracle it escaped the crocodiles, and was cast up by the tide on the mud a little way up the river, to be found by an intelligent Arab half-breed, and offered for sale to Pollock and Perera as a curiosity, just on the edge of night. The native hung about in the brief twilight, making lower and lower offers, and at last, getting scared in some way by the evident dread these wise white men had for the thing, went off, and, passing Pollock's shed, threw his burden in there for Pollock to discover in the morning.

At this Pollock got into a kind of frenzy. He would burn the thing. He went out straightway into the dawn, and had constructed a big pyre of brushwood before the heat of the day. He was interrupted by the hooter of the little paddle steamer from Monrovia to Bathurst, which was coming through the gap in the bar. "Thank Heaven!" said Pollock, with infinite piety, when the meaning of the sound dawned upon him. With trembling hands he lit his pile of wood hastily, threw the head upon it, and went away to pack his portmanteau and make his adieux to Perera.

That afternoon, with a sense of infinite relief, Pollock watched the flat swampy foreshore of Sulyma grow small in the distance. The gap in the long line of white surge became narrower and narrower. It seemed to be closing in and cutting him off from his trouble. The feeling of dread and worry began to slip from him bit by bit. At Sulyma belief in Porroh malignity and Porroh magic had been in the air, his sense of Porroh had been vast, pervading, threatening, dreadful. Now manifestly the domain of Porroh was only a little place, a little black band between the sea and the blue cloudy Mendi uplands.

"Good-bye, Porroh!" said Pollock. "Good-bye—certainly not *au revoir*."

The captain of the steamer came and leant over the rail beside him, and wished him good evening, and spat at the froth of the wake in token of friendly ease.

"I picked up a rummy curio on the beach this go," said the captain. "It's a thing I never saw done this side of Indy before."

"What might that be?" said Pollock.

"Pickled 'ed," said the captain.

"*What?*" said Pollock.

" 'Ed—smoked. 'Ed of one of these Porroh chaps, all ornamented with knife-cuts. Why! What's up? Nothing? I shouldn't have took you for a nervous chap. Green in the face. By gosh! you're a bad sailor. All right, eh? Lord, how funny you went! Well, this 'ed I was telling you of is a bit rum in a way. I've got it, along with some snakes, in a jar of spirit in my cabin what I keeps for such curios, and I'm hanged if it don't float upsy down. Hullo!"

Pollock had given an incoherent cry, and had his hands in his hair. He ran towards the paddle-boxes with a half-formed idea of jumping into the sea, and then he realized his position and turned back towards the captain.

"Here!" said the captain. "Jack Philips, just keep him off me! Stand off! No nearer, mister! What's the matter with you? Are you mad?"

Pollock put his hand to his head. It was no good explaining. "I believe I am pretty nearly mad at times," he said. "It's a pain I have here. Comes suddenly. You'll excuse me, I hope."

He was white and in a perspiration. He saw suddenly very clearly all the danger he ran of having his sanity doubted. He forced himself to restore the captain's confidence, by answering his sympathetic inquiries, noting his suggestions, even trying a spoonful of neat brandy in his cheek, and, that matter settled, asking a number of questions about the captain's private trade in curiosities. The captain described the head in detail. All the while Pollock was struggling to keep under a preposterous persuasion that the ship was as transparent as glass, and that he could distinctly see the inverted face looking at him from the cabin beneath his feet.

Pollock had a worse time almost on the steamer than he had at Sulyma. All day he had to control himself in spite of his intense perception of the imminent presence of that horrible head that was overshadowing his mind. At night his old nightmare returned, until, with a violent effort, he would force himself awake, rigid with the horror of it, and with the ghost of a hoarse scream in his throat.

He left the actual head behind at Bathurst, where he changed ship for Teneriffe, but not his dreams nor the dull ache in his bones. At Teneriffe Pollock transferred to a Cape liner, but the head followed him. He gambled, he tried chess, he even read books; but he knew the danger of drink. Yet whenever a round black shadow, a round black object came into his range, there he looked for the head, and—saw it. He knew clearly enough that his imagination was growing traitor to him, and yet at times it seemed the ship he sailed in, his fellow-passengers, the sailors, the wide sea, was all part of a filmy phantasmagoria that hung, scarcely veiling it, between him and a horrible real world. Then the Porroh man, thrusting his diabolical face through that curtain, was the one real and undeniable thing. At that he would get up and touch things, taste something, gnaw something, burn his hand with a match, or run a needle into himself.

So, struggling grimly and silently with his excited imagination, Pollock reached England. He landed at Southampton, and went on straight from Waterloo to his banker's in Cornhill in a cab. There he transacted some business with the manager in a private room; and all the while the head hung like an ornament under the black marble mantel and dripped upon the fender. He could hear the drops fall, and see the red on the fender.

"A pretty fern," said the manager, following his eyes. "But it makes the fender rusty."

"Very," said Pollock; "a *very* pretty fern. And that reminds me. Can you recommend me a physician for mind troubles? I've got a little—what is it?—hallucination."

The head laughed savagely, wildly. Pollock was surprised the manager did not notice it. But the manager only stared at his face.

With the address of a doctor, Pollock presently emerged in Cornhill. There was no cab in sight, and so he went on down to the western end of the street, and essayed the crossing opposite the Mansion House. The crossing is hardly easy even for the expert Londoner; cabs, vans, carriages, mail-carts, omnibuses go by in one incessant stream; to any one fresh from the malarious solitudes of Sierra Leone it is a boiling, maddening confusion. But when an inverted head suddenly comes bouncing, like an india-rubber ball, between your legs, leaving distinct smears of blood every time it touches the ground, you can scarcely hope to avoid an accident. Pollock lifted his feet convulsively to avoid it, and then kicked at the thing furiously. Then something hit him violently in the back, and a hot pain ran up his arm.

He had been hit by the pole of an omnibus, and three of the fingers of his left hand smashed by the hoof of one of the horses,—the very fingers, as it happened, that he shot from the Porroh man. They pulled him out from between the horses' legs, and found the address of the physician in his crushed hand.

For a couple of days Pollock's sensations were full of the sweet, pungent smell of chloroform, of painful operations that caused him no pain, of lying still and being given food and drink. Then he had a slight fever, and was very thirsty, and his old nightmare came back. It was only when it returned that he noticed it had left him for a day.

"If my skull had been smashed instead of my fingers, it might have gone altogether," said Pollock, staring thoughtfully at the dark cushion that had taken on for the time the shape of the head.

Pollock at the first opportunity told the physician of his mind trouble. He knew clearly that he must go mad unless something should intervene to save him. He explained that he had witnessed a decapitation in Dahomey, and was haunted by one of the heads. Naturally, he did not care to state the actual facts. The physician looked grave.

Presently he spoke hesitatingly. "As a child, did you get very much religious training?"

"Very little," said Pollock.

A shade passed over the physician's face. "I don't know if you have heard of the miraculous cures—it may be, of course, they are not miraculous—at Lourdes."

"Faith-healing will hardly suit me, I am afraid," said Pollock, with his eye on the dark cushion.

The head distorted its scarred features in an abominable grimace. The physician went upon a new track. "It's all imagination," he said, speaking with sudden briskness. "A fair case for faith-healing, anyhow. Your nervous system has run down, you're in that twilight state of health when the bogles come easiest. The strong impression was too much for you. I must make you up a little mixture that will strengthen your nervous system—especially your brain. And you must take exercise."

"I'm no good for faith-healing," said Pollock.

"And therefore we must restore tone. Go in search of stimulating air—Scotland, Norway, the Alps—"

"Jericho, if you like," said Pollock, "where Naaman went."

However, so soon as his fingers would let him, Pollock made a gallant attempt to follow out the doctor's suggestion. It was now November. He tried football; but to Pollock the game consisted in kicking a furious inverted head about a field. He was no good at the game. He kicked blindly, with a kind of horror, and when they put him back into goal, and the ball came swooping down upon him, he suddenly yelled and got out of its way. The discreditable stories that had driven him from England to wander in the tropics shut him off from any but men's society, and now his increasingly strange behavior made even his man friends avoid him. The thing was no longer a thing of the eye merely; it gibbered at him, spoke to him. A horrible fear came upon him that presently, when he took hold of the apparition, it would no longer become some mere article of furniture, but would *feel* like a real dissevered head. Alone, he would curse at the thing, defy it, entreat it; once or twice, in spite of his grim self-control, he addressed it in the presence of others. He felt the growing suspicion in the eyes of the people that watched him,—his landlady, the servant, his man.

One day early in December his cousin Arnold—his next of kin—came to see him and draw him out, and watch his sunken, yellow face with narrow, eager eyes. And it seemed to Pollock that the hat his cousin carried in his hand was no hat at all, but a Gorgon head that glared at him upside down, and fought with its eyes against his reason. However, he was still resolute to see the matter out. He got a bicycle, and, riding over the frosty road from Wandsworth to Kingston, found the thing rolling along at his side, and leaving a dark trail behind it. He set his teeth and rode faster. Then suddenly, as he came down the hill towards Richmond Park, the apparition rolled in front of him and under his wheel, so quickly that he had no time for thought, and, turning quickly to avoid it, was flung violently against a heap of stones and broke his left wrist.

The end came on Christmas morning. All night he had been in a fever, the bandages encircling his wrist like a band of fire, his dreams more vivid and terrible than ever. In the cold, colorless, uncertain light that came before the sunrise, he sat up in his bed, and saw the head upon the bracket in the place of the bronze jar that had stood there overnight.

"I know that is a bronze jar," he said, with a chill doubt at his heart. Presently the doubt was irresistible. He got out of bed slowly, shivering, and advanced to the jar with his hand raised. Surely he would see now his imagination had deceived him, recognize the distinctive sheen of bronze. At last, after an age of hesitation, his fingers came down on the patterned cheek of the head. He withdrew them spasmodically. The last stage was reached. His sense of touch had betrayed him.

Trembling, stumbling against the bed, kicking against his shoes with his bare feet, a dark confusion eddying round him, he groped his way to the dressing-table, took his razor from the drawer, and sat down on the bed with this in his hand. In the looking-glass he saw his own face, colorless, haggard, full of the ultimate bitterness of despair.

He beheld in swift succession the incidents in the brief tale of his experience. His wretched home, his still more wretched schooldays, the years of vicious life he had led since then, one act of selfish dishonor leading to another; it was all clear and pitiless now, all its squalid folly, in the cold light of the dawn. He came to the hut, to the fight with the Porroh man, to the retreat down the river to Sulyma, to the Mendi assassin and his red parcel, to his frantic endeavors to destroy the head, to the growth of his hallucination. It was a hallucination! He *knew* it was. A hallucination merely. For a moment he snatched at hope. He looked away from the glass, and on the bracket, the inverted head grinned and grimaced at him—With the stiff fingers of his bandaged hand he felt at his neck for the throb of his arteries. The morning was very cold, the steel blade felt like ice.

THE MOTH

(GENUS UNKNOWN)

PROBABLY YOU HAVE heard of Hapley—not W. T. Hapley, the son, but the celebrated Hapley, the Hapley of *Periplaneta Hapliia,* Hapley the entomologist. If so, you know at least of the great feud between Hapley and Professor Pawkins, though certain of its consequences may be new to you. For those who have not, a word or two of explanation is necessary, which the idle reader may go over with a glancing eye, if his indolence so incline him.

It is amazing how very widely diffused is the ignorance of such really important matters as this Hapley-Pawkins feud. Those epoch-making controversies, again, that have convulsed the Geological Society, are, I verily believe, almost entirely unknown outside the fellowship of that body. I have heard men of fair general education even refer to the great scenes at these meetings as vestry-meeting squabbles. Yet the great Hate of the English and Scotch geologists has lasted now half a century, and has "left deep and abundant marks upon the body of the science." And this Hapley-Pawkins business, though perhaps a more personal affair, stirred passions as profound, if not profounder. Your common man has no conception of the zeal that animates a scientific investigator, the fury of contradiction you can arouse in him. It is the *odium theologicum* in a new form. There are men, for instance, who would gladly burn Professor Ray Lankester at Smithfield for his treatment of the Mollusca in the Encyclopædia. That fantastic extension of the Cephalopods to cover the Pterpodos— But I wander from Hapley and Pawkins.

It began years and years ago, with a revision of the Microlepidoptera (whatever these may be) by Pawkins, in which he extinguished a new species created by Hapley. Hapley, who was always quarrelsome, replied by a stinging impeachment of the entire classification of Pawkins.[1] Pawkins, in his "Rejoinder,"[2] suggested that Hapley's microscope was as defective as his powers of observation, and called him an "irresponsible meddler"—Hapley was not a professor at that time. Hapley, in his retort,[3] spoke of "blundering collectors," and described, as if inadvertently, Pawkins's revision as a "miracle of ineptitude." It was war to the knife. However, it would scarcely interest the reader to detail how these two great men quarreled, and how the split between them widened until from the Microlepidoptera, they were at war upon every open question in entomology. There were memorable occasions. At times the Royal Entomological Society meetings resembled nothing so much as the Chamber of Deputies. On the whole, I fancy Pawkins was nearer the truth than Hapley. But Hapley was skillful with his rhetoric, had a turn for ridicule rare in a scientific man, was endowed with vast energy, and had a fine sense of injury in the matter of the extinguished species; while Pawkins was a man of dull presence, prosy of speech, in shape not unlike a water-barrel, over-conscientious with testimonials, and suspected of jobbing museum appointments. So the young men gathered round Hapley and applauded him. It was a long struggle, vicious from the beginning, and growing at last to pitiless antagonism. The successive turns of fortune, now an advantage to one side and now to another—now Hapley tormented by some success of Pawkins, and now Pawkins outshone by Hapley—belong rather to the history of entomology than to this story.

But in 1891 Pawkins, whose health had been bad for some time, published some work upon the "mesoblast" of the Death's Head Moth. What the mesoblast of the Death's Head Moth may be, does not matter a rap in this story. But the work was far below his usual standard, and gave Hapley an opening he had coveted for years. He must have worked night and day to make the most of his advantage.

[1] "Remarks on a Recent Revision of Microleptdoptera." *Quart. Journ. Entomological Soc.* 1863.

[2] "Rejoinder to certatn Remarks," &c. *Ibid.* 1864.

[3] "Further Remarks," &c. *Ibed.*

In an elaborate critique he rent Pawkins to tatters,—one can fancy the man's disordered black hair, and his queer dark eyes flashing as he went for his antagonist,—and Pawkins made a reply, halting, ineffectual, with painful gaps of silence, and yet malignant. There was no mistaking his will to wound Hapley, nor his incapacity to do it. But few of those who heard him—I was absent from that meeting—realized how ill the man was.

Hapley had got his opponent down, and meant to finish him. He followed with a simply brutal attack upon Pawkins, in the form of a paper upon the development of moths in general, a paper showing evidence of a most extraordinary amount of mental labor, and yet couched in a violently controversial tone. Violent as it was, an editorial note witnesses that it was modified. It must have covered Pawkins with shame and confusion of face. It left no loophole; it was murderous in argument, and utterly contemptuous in tone; an awful thing for the declining years of a man's career.

The world of entomologists waited breathlessly for the rejoinder from Pawkins. He would try one, for Pawkins had always been game. But when it came it surprised them. For the rejoinder of Pawkins was to catch the influenza, to proceed to pneumonia, and to die.

It was perhaps as effectual a reply as he could make under the circumstances, and largely turned the current of feeling against Hapley. The very people who had most gleefully cheered on those gladiators became serious at the consequence. There could be no reasonable doubt the fret of the defeat had contributed to the death of Pawkins. There was a limit even to scientific controversy, said serious people. Another crushing attack was already in the press and appeared on the day before the funeral. I don't think Hapley exerted himself to stop it. People remembered how Hapley had hounded down his rival, and forgot that rival's defects. Scathing satire reads ill over fresh mould. The thing provoked comment in the daily papers. This it was that made me think that you had probably heard of Hapley and this controversy. But, as I have already remarked, scientific workers live very much in a world of their own; half the people, I dare say, who go along Piccadilly to the Academy every year, could not tell you where the learned societies abide. Many even think that Research is a kind of happy-family cage in which all kinds of men lie down together in peace.

In his private thoughts Hapley could not forgive Pawkins for dying. In the first place, it was a mean dodge to escape the absolute pulverization Hapley had in hand for him, and in the second, it left Hapley's mind with a queer gap in it. For twenty years he had worked hard, sometimes far into the night, and seven days a week with microscope, scalpel, collecting-net, and pen, and almost entirely with reference to Pawkins. The European reputation he had won had come as an incident in that great antipathy. He had gradually worked up to a climax in this last controversy. It had killed Pawkins, but it had also thrown Hapley out of gear, so to speak, and his doctor advised him to give up work for a time, and rest. So Hapley went down into a quiet village in Kent, and thought day and night of Pawkins, and good things it was now impossible to say about him.

At last Hapley began to realize in what direction the preoccupation tended. He determined to make a fight for it, and started by trying to read novels. But he could not get his mind off Pawkins, white in the face, and making his last speech—every sentence a beautiful opening for Hapley. He turned to fiction—and found it had no grip on him. He read the "Island Nights' Entertainments" until his "sense of causation" was shocked beyond endurance by the Bottle Imp. Then he went to Kipling, and found he "proved nothing," besides being irreverent and vulgar. These scientific people have their limitations. Then, unhappily, he tried Besant's "Inner House," and the opening chapter set his mind upon learned societies and Pawkins at once.

So Hapley turned to chess, and found it a little more soothing. He soon mastered the moves and the chief gambits and commoner closing positions, and began to beat the Vicar. But then the cylindrical contours of the opposite king began to resemble Pawkins standing up and gasping inefectually against checkmate, and Hapley decided to give up chess.

Perhaps the study of some new branch of science would after all be better diversion. The best rest is change of occupation. Hapley determined to plunge at diatoms, and had one of his smaller microscopes and Halibut's monograph sent down from London. He thought that perhaps if he could get up a vigorous quarrel with Halibut, he might be able to begin life afresh and forget Pawkins. And very soon he was hard at work, in his habitual strenuous fashion, at these microscopic denizens of the way-side pool.

It was on the third day of the diatoms that Hapley became aware of a novel addition to the local fauna. He was working late at the microscope, and the only light in the room was the brilliant little lamp with the special form of green shade. Like all experienced microscopists, he kept both eyes open. It is the only way to avoid excessive fatigue. One eye was over the instrument, and bright and distinct before that was the circular field of the microscope, across which a brown diatom was slowly moving. With the other eye Hapley saw, as it were, without seeing.[4] He was only dimly conscious of the brass side of the instrument, the illuminated part of the tablecloth, a sheet of notepaper, the foot of the lamp, and the darkened room beyond.

Suddenly his attention drifted from one eye to the other. The tablecloth was of the material called tapestry by shopmen, and rather brightly colored. The pattern was in gold, with a small amount of crimson and pale-blue upon a grayish ground. At one point the pattern seemed displaced, and there was a vibrating movement of the colors at this point.

Hapley suddenly moved his head back and looked with both eyes. His mouth fell open with astonishment.

It was a large moth or butterfly; its wings spread in butterfly fashion!

It was strange it should be in the room at all, for the windows were closed. Strange that it should not have attracted his attention when fluttering to its present position. Strange that it should match the tablecloth. Stranger far to him, Hapley, the great entomologist, it was altogether unknown. There was no delusion. It was crawling slowly towards the foot of the lamp.

"*Genus unknown,* by heavens! And in England!" said Hapley, staring.

Then he suddenly thought of Pawkins. Nothing would have maddened Pawkins more—And Pawkins was dead!

Something about the head and body of the insect became singularly suggestive of Pawkins, just as the chess king had been.

"Confound Pawkins!" said Hapley. "But I must catch this." And, looking round him for some means of capturing the moth, he rose slowly out of his chair. Suddenly the insect rose, struck the edge of the lampshade—Hapley heard the "ping"—and vanished into the shadow.

In a moment Hapley had whipped off the shade, so that the whole room was illuminated. The thing had disappeared, but soon his practiced eye detected it upon the wall-paper near the door. He went towards it, poising the lampshade

[4] The reader unaccustomed to microscopes may easily understand this by rolling a newspaper in the form of a tube and looking through it at a book, keeping the other eye open.

for capture. Before he was within striking distance, however, it had risen and was fluttering round the room. After the fashion of its kind, it flew with sudden starts and turns, seeming to vanish here and reappear there. Once Hapley struck, and missed; then again.

The third time he hit his microscope. The instrument swayed, struck and overturned the lamp, and fell noisily upon the floor. The lamp turned over on the table and, very luckily, went out. Hapley was left in the dark. With a start he felt the strange moth blunder into his face.

It was maddening. He had no lights. If he opened the door of the room the thing would get away. In the darkness he saw Pawkins quite distinctly laughing at him. Pawkins had ever an oily laugh. He swore furiously and stamped his foot on the floor.

There was a timid rapping at the door.

Then it opened, perhaps a foot, and very slowly. The alarmed face of the landlady appeared behind a pink candle flame; she wore a nightcap over her gray hair and had some purple garment over her shoulders. "What *was* that fearful smash?" she said. "Has anything—" The strange moth appeared fluttering about the chink of the door. "Shut that door!" said Hapley, and suddenly rushed at her.

The door slammed hastily. Hapley was left alone in the dark. Then in the pause he heard his landlady scuttle upstairs, lock her door and drag something heavy across the room and put against it.

It became evident to Hapley that his conduct and appearance had been strange and alarming. Confound the moth! and Pawkins! However, it was a pity to lose the moth now. He felt his way into the hall and found the matches, after sending his hat down upon the floor with a noise like a drum. With the lighted candle he returned to the sitting-room. No moth was to be seen. Yet once for a moment it seemed that the thing was fluttering round his head. Hapley very suddenly decided to give up the moth and go to bed. But he was excited. All night long his sleep was broken by dreams of the moth, Pawkins, and his landlady. Twice in the night he turned out and soused his head in cold water.

One thing was very clear to him. His landlady could not possibly understand about the strange moth, especially as he had failed to catch it. No one but an entomologist would understand quite how he felt. She was probably frightened at his behavior, and yet he failed to see how he could explain it. He decided to say nothing further about the events of last night. After breakfast he saw her in her garden, and decided to go out to talk to her to reassure her. He talked to her about beans and potatoes, bees, caterpillars, and the price of fruit. She replied in her usual manner, but she looked at him a little suspiciously, and kept walking as he walked, so that there was always a bed of flowers, or a row of beans, or something of the sort, between them. After a while he began to feel singularly irritated at this, and to conceal his vexation went indoors and presently went out for a walk.

The moth—or butterfly, trailing an odd flavor of Pawkins with it, kept coming into that walk, though he did his best to keep his mind off it. Once he saw it quite distinctly, with its wings flattened out, upon the old stone wall that runs along the west edge of the park, but going up to it he found it was only two lumps of gray and yellow lichen. "This," said Hapley, "is the reverse of mimicry. Instead of a butterfly looking like a stone, here is a stone looking like a butterfly!" Once something hovered and fluttered round his head, but by an effort of will he drove that impression out of his mind again.

In the afternoon Hapley called upon the Vicar, and argued with him upon theological questions. They sat in the little arbor covered with briar, and smoked as they wrangled. "Look at that moth!" said Hapley, suddenly, pointing to the edge of the wooden table.

"Where?" said the Vicar.

"You don't see a moth on the edge of the table there?" said Hapley.

"Certainly not," said the Vicar.

Hapley was thunderstruck. He gasped. The Vicar was staring at him. Clearly the man saw nothing. "The eye of faith is no better than the eye of science," said Hapley, awkwardly.

"I don't see your point," said the Vicar, thinking it was part of the argument.

That night Hapley found the moth crawling over his counterpane. He sat on the edge of the bed in his shirt-sleeves and reasoned with himself. Was it pure hallucination? He knew he was slipping, and he battled for his sanity with the same silent energy he had formerly displayed against Pawkins. So persistent is mental habit, that he felt as if it were still a struggle with Pawkins. He was well versed in psychology. He knew that such visual illusions do come as a result of mental strain. But the point was, he did not only *see* the moth, he had heard it when it touched the edge of the lampshade, and afterwards when it hit against the wall, and he had felt it strike his face in the dark.

He looked at it. It was not at all dreamlike, but perfectly clear and solid-looking in the candlelight. He saw the hairy body, and the short, feathery antennæ, the jointed legs, even a place where the down was rubbed from the wing. He suddenly felt angry with himself for being afraid of a little insect.

His landlady had got the servant to sleep with her that night, because she was afraid to be alone. In addition she had locked the door, and put the chest of drawers against it. They listened and talked in whispers after they had gone to bed, but nothing occurred to alarm them. About eleven they had ventured to put the candle out, and had both dozed off to sleep. They woke up with a start, and sat up in bed, listening in the darkness.

Then they heard slippered feet going to and fro in Hapley's room. A chair was overturned, and there was a violent dab at the wall. Then a china mantel ornament smashed upon the fender. Suddenly the door of the room opened, and they heard him upon the landing. They clung to one another, listening. He seemed to be dancing upon the staircase. Now he would go down three or four steps quickly, then up again, then hurry down into the hall. They heard the umbrella-stand go over, and the fanlight break. Then the bolt shot and the chain rattled. He was opening the door.

They hurried to the window. It was a dim gray night; an almost unbroken sheet of watery cloud was sweeping across the moon, and the hedge and trees in front of the house were black against the pale roadway. They saw Hapley, looking like a ghost in his shirt and white trousers, running to and fro in the road, and beating the air. Now he would stop, now he would dart very rapidly at something invisible, now he would move upon it with stealthy strides. At last he went out of sight up the road towards the down. Then, while they argued who should go down and lock the door, he returned. He was walking very fast, and he came straight into the house, closed the door carefully, and went quietly up to his bedroom. Then everything was silent.

"Mrs. Colville," said Hapley, calling down the staircase next morning. "I hope I did not alarm you last night."

"You may well ask that!" said Mrs. Colville.

"The fact is, I am a sleep-walker, and the last two nights I have been without my sleeping mixture. There is nothing to be alarmed about, really. I am sorry

I made such an ass of myself. I will go over the down to Shoreham, and get some stuff to make me sleep soundly. I ought to have done that yesterday.''

But half-way over the down, by the chalk-pits, the moth came upon Hapley again. He went on, trying to keep his mind upon chess problems, but it was no good. The thing fluttered into his face, and he struck at it with his hat in self-defence. Then rage, the old rage—the rage he had so ften felt against Pawkins—returned once more. He went on, leaping and striking at the eddying insect. Suddenly he trod on nothing, and fell headlong.

There was a gap in his sensations, and Hapley found himself sitting on the heap of flints in front of the opening of the chalk-pits, with a leg twisted back under him. The strange moth was still fluttering round his head. He struck at it with his hand, and turning his head saw two men approaching him. One was the village doctor. It occurred to Hapley that this was lucky. Then it came into his mind, with extraordinary vividness, that no one would ever be able to see the strange moth except himself, and that it behoved him to keep silent about it.

Late that night, however, after his broken leg was set, he was feverish and forgot his self-restraint. He was lying flat on his bed, and he began to run his eyes round the room to see if the moth was still about. He tried not to do this, but it was no good. He soon caught sight of the thing resting close to his hand, by the night-light, on the green tablecloth. The wings quivered. With a sudden wave of anger he smote at it with his fist, and the nurse woke up with a shriek. He had missed it.

"That moth!" he said; and then, "It was fancy. Nothing!"

All the time he could see quite clearly the insect going round the cornice and darting across the room, and he could also see that the nurse saw nothing of it and looked at him strangely. He must keep himself in hand. He knew he was a lost man if he did not keep himself in hand. But as the night waned the fever grew upon him, and the very dread he had of seeing the moth made him see it. About five, just as the dawn was gray, he tried to get out of bed and catch it, though his leg was afire with pain. The nurse had to struggle with him.

On account of this, they tied him down to the bed. At this the moth grew bolder, and once he felt it settle in his hair. Then, because he struck out violently with his arms, they tied these also. At this the moth came and crawled over his face, and Hapley wept, swore, screamed, prayed for them to take it off him, unavailingly.

The doctor was a blockhead, a half-qualified general practitioner, and quite ignorant of mental science. He simply said there was no moth. Had he possessed the wit, he might still, perhaps, have saved Hapley from his fate by entering into his delusion and covering his face with gauze, as he prayed might be done. But, as I say, the doctor was a blockhead, and until the leg was healed Hapley was kept tied to his bed, and with the imaginary moth crawling over him. It never left him while he was awake and it grew to a monster in his dreams. While he was awake he longed for sleep, and from sleep he awoke screaming.

So now Hapley is spending the remainder of his days in a padded room, worried by a moth that no one else can see. The asylum doctor calls it hallucination; but Hapley, when he is in his easier mood, and can talk, says it is the ghost of Pawkins, and consequently a unique specimen and well worth the trouble of catching.

A SLIP UNDER THE MICROSCOPE

OUTSIDE THE LABORATORY windows was a watery gray fog, and within a close warmth and the yellow light of the green-shaded gas lamps that stood two to each table down its narrow length. On each table stood a couple of glass jars containing the mangled vestiges of the crayfish, mussels, frogs, and guinea-pigs, upon which the students had been working, and down the side of the room, facing the windows, were shelves bearing bleached dissections in spirit, surmounted by a row of beautifully executed anatomical drawings in white wood frames and overhanging a row of cubical lockers. All the doors of the laboratory were panelled with blackboard, and on these were the half-erased diagrams of the previous day's work. The laboratory was empty, save for the demonstrator, who sat near the preparation-room door, and silent, save for a low, continuous murmur, and the clicking of the rocker microtome at which he was working. But scattered about the room were traces of numerous students: hand-bags, polished boxes of instruments, in one place a large drawing covered by newspaper, and in another a prettily bound copy of ''News from Nowhere,'' a book oddly at variance with its surroundings. These things had been put down hastily as the students had arrived and hurried at once to secure their seats in the adjacent lecture-theater. Deadened by the closed door, the measured accents of the professor sounded as a featureless muttering.

Presently, faint through the closed windows came the sound of the Oratory clock striking the hour of eleven. The clicking of the microtome ceased, and the demonstrator looked at his watch, rose, thrust his hands into his pockets, and walked slowly down the laboratory towards the lecture-theater door. He stood listening for a moment, and then his eye fell on the little volume by William Morris. He picked it up, glanced at the title, smiled, opened it, looked at the name on the fly-leaf, ran the leaves through with his hand, and put it down. Almost immediately the even murmur of the lecturer ceased, there was a sudden burst of pencils rattling on the desks in the lecture-theater, a stirring, a scraping of feet, and a number of voices speaking together. Then a firm foot-fall approached the door, which began to open, and stood ajar, as some indistinctly heard question arrested the newcomer.

The demonstrator turned, walked slowly back past the microtome and left the laboratory by the preparation-room door. As he did so, first one, and then several students carrying notebooks, entered the laboratory from the lecture-theater, and distributed themselves among the little tables, or stood in a group about the doorway. They were an exceptionally heterogeneous assembly,—for while Oxford and Cambridge still recoil from the blushing prospect of mixed classes, the College of Science anticipated America in the matter years ago,—mixed socially, too, for the prestige of the College is high, and its scholarships, free of any age limit, dredge deeper even than do those of the Scotch universities. The class numbered one and twenty, but some remained in the theatre questioning the professor, copying the blackboard diagrams before they were washed off, or examining the special specimens he had produced to illustrate the day's teaching. Of the nine who had come into the laboratory, three were girls, one of whom, a little fair woman wearing spectacles and dressed in grayish green, was peering out of the window at the fog, while the other two, both wholesome-looking, plain-faced school-girls, unrolled and put on the brown holland aprons they wore while dissecting. Of the men, two went down the laboratory and sat down in their places, one a pallid, dark-bearded man who had once been a tailor, the other a pleasant-featured, ruddy young man of twenty, dressed in a well-fitting brown suit, young Wedderburn, the son of Wedderburn the eye specialist. The others formed a little knot near the theatre door. One of these, a dwarfed, spectacled figure with a hunch back, sat on a bent wood stool, two others, one a short, dark youngster, and the other a flaxen-haired, reddish-complexioned young man, stood leaning side by side against the slate sink, while the fourth stood facing them and maintained the larger share of the conversation.

This last person was named Hill. He was a sturdily built young fellow of the same age as Wedderburn, he had a white face, dark gray eyes, hair of an indeterminate color, and prominent, irregular features. He talked rather louder than was needful, and thrust his hands deeply into his pockets. His collar was frayed and blue with the starch of a careless laundress, his clothes were evidently ready-made, and there was a patch on the side of his boot near the toe. And as he talked or listened to the others, he glanced now and again towards the lecture-theatre door. They were discussing the depressing peroration of the lecture they had just heard, the last lecture it was in the introductory course in Zoölogy. "From ovum to ovum is the goal of the higher vertebrata," the lecturer had said in his melancholy tones, and so had neatly rounded off the sketch of comparative anatomy he had been developing. The spectacled hunchback had repeated it, with noisy appreciation, had tossed it towards the fair-haired student with an evident provocation, and had started one of those vague, rambling discussions on generalities so unaccountably dear to the student mind all the world over.

"That is our goal, perhaps,—I admit it,—as far as science goes," said the fair-haired student, rising to the challenge. "But there are things above science."

"Science," said Hill, confidently, "is systematic knowledge. Ideas that don't come into the system must anyhow—be loose ideas." He was not quite sure whether that was a clever saying or a fatuity, until his hearers took it seriously.

"The thing I cannot understand," said the hunchback, at large, "is whether Hill is a materialist or not."

"There is one thing above matter," said Hill, promptly, feeling he had a better thing this time, aware too of someone in the doorway behind him, and raising his voice a trifle for her benefit, "and that is—the delusion that there is something above matter."

"So we have your gospel at last," said the fair-haired student. "It's all a delusion, is it? All our aspirations to lead something more than dogs' lives, all our work for anything beyond ourselves. But see how inconsistent you are! Your socialism, for instance. Why do you trouble about the interests of the race? Why do you concern yourself about the beggar in the gutter? Why are you bothering yourself to lend that book"—he indicated William Morris by a movement of the head—"to every one in the lab?"

"Girl," said the hunchback, indistinctly, and glanced guiltily over his shoulder.

The girl in brown, with the brown eyes, had come into the laboratory, and stood on the other side of the table behind him with her rolled-up apron in one hand, looking over her shoulder, listening to the discussion. She did not notice the hunchback, because she was glancing from Hill to his interlocutor. Hill's consciousness of her presence betrayed itself to her only in his studious ignorance of the fact; but she understood that and it pleased her. "I see no reason," said he, "why a man should live like a brute because he knows of nothing beyond matter, and does not expect to exist a hundred years hence."

"Why shouldn't he?" said the fair-haired student.

"Why *should* he?" said Hill.

"What inducement has he?"

"That's the way with all you religious people. It's all a business of inducements. Cannot a man seek after righteousness for righteousness' sake?"

There was a pause. The fair man answered with a kind of vocal padding, "But—you see—inducement—when I said inducement—" to gain time. And then the hunchback came to his rescue and inserted a question. He was a terrible person in the debating society with his questions, and they invariably took one form,—a demand for a definition. "What's your definition of righteousness?" said the hunchback, at this stage.

Hill experienced a sudden loss of complacency at this question, but even as it was asked, relief came in the person of Brooks, the laboratory attendant, who entered by the preparation-room door, carrying a number of freshly-killed guinea-pigs by their hind-legs. "This is the last batch of material this session," said the youngster who had not previously spoken. Brooks advanced up the laboratory, smacking down a couple of guinea-pigs at each table, and the discussion perished abruptly as the students who were not already in their places hurried to them to secure the choice of a specimen. There was a noise of keys rattling on split rings as lockers were opened, and dissecting instruments taken out. Hill was already standing by his table, and his box of scalpels was sticking out of his pocket. The girl in brown came a step towards him, and leaning over his table, said softly, "Did you see that I returned your book, Mr. Hill?"

During the whole scene, she and the book had been vividly present in his consciousness, but he made a clumsy pretense of looking at the book and seeing it for the first time. "Oh, yes," he said, taking it up. "I see. Did you like it?"

"I want to ask you some questions about it—sometime."

"Certainly," said Hill. "I shall be glad." He stopped awkwardly. "You liked it?" he said.

"It's a wonderful book. Only some things I don't understand."

Then suddenly the laboratory was hushed by a curious braying noise. It was the demonstrator. He was at the blackboard ready to begin the day's instruction, and it was his custom to demand silence by a sound midway between the "Er" of common intercourse, and the blast of a trumpet. The girl in brown slipped back to her place, it was immediately in front of Hill's, and Hill, forgetting her forthwith, took a notebook out of the drawer of his table, turned over its leaves hastily, drew a stumpy pencil from his pocket, and prepared to make a copious note of the coming demonstration. For demonstrations and lectures are the sacred text of the College students. Books, saving only the professor's own, you may—it is even expedient to—ignore.

Hill was the son of a Landport cobbler, and had been hooked by a chance blue paper the authorities had thrown out to the Landport Technical College. He kept himself in London on his allowance of a guinea a week, and found that with proper care this also covered his clothing allowance, an occasional waterproof collar, that is, and ink and needles and cotton and suchlike necessaries for a man about town. This was his first year and his first session, but the brown old man in Landport had already got himself detested in many public-houses by boasting of his son "the professor." Hill was a vigorous youngster, with a serene contempt for the clergy of all denominations, and a fine ambition to reconstruct the world. He regarded his scholarship as a brilliant opportunity. He had begun to read at seven, and had read steadily whatever came in his way, good or bad, since then. His worldly experience had been limited to the Island of Portsea, and acquired chiefly in the wholesale boot factory in which he had worked by day, after passing the seventh standard of the Board School. He had a considerable gift of speech, as the College Debating Society, which met amidst the crushing machines and mine models in the Metallurgical Theatre downstairs, already recognized, recognized by a violent battering of desks whenever he rose. And he was just at that fine emotional age when life opens at the end of a narrow pass, like a broad valley at one's feet, full of the promise of wonderful discoveries and tremendous achievements. And his own limitations, save that he knew that he knew neither Latin or French, were all unknown to him.

At first his interest had been divided pretty equally between his biological work at the College and social and theological theorizing, an employment which he took in deadly earnest. Of a night, when the big museum library was not open, he would sit on the bed of his room in Chelsea with his coat and a muffler on, and write out the lecture notes and revise his dissection memoranda until Thorpe called him out by a whistle,—the landlady objected to open the door to attic visitors,—and then the two would go prowling about the shadowy, shiny, gas-lit streets, talking, very much in the fashion of the sample just given, of the God Idea and Righteousness and Carlyle and the Reorganization of Society. And in the midst of it all, Hill, arguing not only for Thorpe but for the casual passer-by, would lose the thread of his argument, glancing at some pretty, painted face that looked meaningly at him as he passed. Science and Righteousness! But once or twice lately there had been signs that a third interest was creeping into his life, and he had found his attention wandering from the fate of the mesoblastic somites or the probable meaning of the blastopore, to the thought of the girl with the brown eyes who sat at the table before him.

She was a paying student; she descended inconceivable social altitudes to speak to him. At the thought of the education she must have had and the accomplishments she must possess, the soul of Hill became abject within him. She had spoken to him first over a difficulty about the alisphenoid of a rabbit's skull, and he had found that, in biology at least, he had no reason for self-abasement. And from that, after the manner of young people starting from any starting-point, they got to generalities, and while Hill attacked her upon the question of socialism,—some instinct told him to spare her a direct assault upon her religion,—she was gathering resolution to undertake what she told herself was his aesthetic education. She was a year or two older than he, though the thought never occurred to him. The loan of "News from Nowhere" was the beginning of a series of cross loans. Upon some absurd first principle of his, Hill had never "wasted time" upon poetry, and it seemed an appalling deficiency to her. One day in the lunch hour, when she chanced upon him alone in the little museum where the skeletons were arranged, shamefully eating the bun that constituted his midday meal, she retreated and returned, to lend him, with a slightly furtive air, a volume of Browning. He stood sideways towards her and took the book rather clumsily, because he was holding the bun in the other hand. And in the retrospect his voice lacked the cheerful clearness he could have wished.

That occurred after the examination in comparative anatomy, on the day before the College turned out its students and was carefully locked up by the officials, for the Christmas holidays. The excitement of cramming for the first trial of strength had for a little while dominated Hill to the exclusion of his other interests. In the forecasts of the result in which every one indulged, he was surprised to find that no one regarded him as a possible competitor for the Harvey Commemoration Medal, of which this and the two subsequent examinations disposed. It was about this time that Wedderburn, who so far had lived inconspicuously on the uttermost margin of Hill's perceptions, began to take on the appearance of an obstacle. By a mutual agreement the nocturnal prowlings with Thorpe ceased for the three weeks before the examination, and his landlady pointed out that she really could not supply so much lamp-oil at the price. He walked to and fro from the College with little slips of mnemonics in his hand, lists of crayfish appendages, rabbits' skull-bones, and vertebrate nerves, for example, and became a positive nuisance to foot-passengers in the opposite direction.

But by a natural reaction Poetry and the girl with the brown eyes ruled the Christmas holiday. The pending results of the examination became such a secondary consideration that Hill marveled at his father's excitement. Even had he wished it, there was no comparative anatomy to read in Landport, and he was too poor to buy books, but the stock of poets in the library was extensive and Hill's attack was magnificently sustained. He saturated himself with the fluent numbers of Longfellow and Tennyson, and fortified himself with Shakespeare, found a kindred soul in Pope and a master in Shelley, and heard and fled the siren voices of Eliza Cook and Mrs. Hemans. But he read no more Browning, because he hoped for the loan of other volumes from Miss Haysman when he returned to London.

He walked from his lodgings to the College with that volume of Browning in his shiny black bag, and his mind teeming with the finest general propositions about poetry. Indeed he framed first this little speech and then that with which to grace the return. The morning was an exceptionally pleasant one for London, there was a clear, hard frost and undeniable blue in the sky, a thin haze softened every outline, and warm shafts of sunlight struck between the houseblocks and turned the sunny side of the street to amber and gold. In the hall of the College he pulled off his glove and signed his name with fingers so stiff with cold that the characteristic dash under the signature he cultivated became a quivering line. He imagined Miss Haysman about him everywhere. He turned at the staircase, and there, below, he saw a crowd struggling at the foot of the notice board. This, possibly, was the biology list. He forgot Browning and Miss Haysman for the moment, and joined the scrimmage. And at last with his cheek flattened against the sleeve of the man on the step above him, he read the list:

"*Class I.*
H. J. Somers Wedderburn.
William Hill."

And thereafter followed a second class that is outside our present sympathies. It was characteristic that he did not trouble to look for Thorpe on the Physics list, but backed out of the struggle at once, and in a curious emotional state between pride over common second-class humanity and acute disappointment at Wedderburn's success, went on his way upstairs. At the top, as he was hanging up his coat in the passage, the zoölogical demonstrator, a young man from Oxford, who secretly regarded him as a blatant "mugger" of the very worst type, offered his heartiest congratulations.

At the laboratory door Hill stopped for a second to get his breath, and then entered. He looked straight up the laboratory and saw all five girl students grouped in their places, and Wedderburn, the once retiring Wedderburn, leaning rather gracefully against the window, playing with the blind tassel and talking, apparently, to the five of them. Now Hill could talk bravely enough and even overbearingly to one girl, and he could have made a speech to a roomful of girls, but this business of standing at ease and appreciating, fencing, and returning quick remarks round a group, was, he knew, altogether beyond him. Coming up the staircase his feelings for Wedderburn had been generous, a certain admiration perhaps, a willingness to shake his hand conspicuously and heartily as one who had fought but the first round. But before Christmas Wedderburn had never gone up to that end of the room to talk. In a flash Hill's mist of vague excitement condensed abruptly to a vivid dislike of Wedderburn. Possibly his expression changed. As he came up to his place Wedderburn nodded carelessly to him, and the others glanced round. Miss Haysman looked at him and away again, the faintest touch of her eyes. "I can't agree with you, Mr. Wedderburn," she said.

"I must congratulate you on your first class, Mr. Hill," said the spectacled girl in green, turning round and beaming at him.

"It's nothing," said Hill, staring at Wedderburn and Miss Haysman talking together, and eager to hear what they talked about.

"We poor folks in the second class don't think so," said the girl in spectacles.

What was it Wedderburn was saying? Something about William Morris! Hill did not answer the girl in spectacles, and the smile died out of his face. He could not hear and failed to see how he could "cut in." Confound Wedderburn! He sat down, opened his bag, hesitated whether to return the volume of Browning forthwith, in the sight of all, and instead drew out his new notebooks for the short course in elementary botany that was now beginning, and which would terminate in February. As he did so a fat heavy man with a white face and pale grey eyes, Bindon, the professor of Botany who came up from Kew for January and February, came in by the lecture-theatre door and passed, rubbing his hands together and smiling in silent affability, down the laboratory.

In the subsequent six weeks Hill experienced some very rapid and curiously complex emotional developments. For the most part he had Wedderburn in focus—a fact that Miss Haysman never suspected. She told Hill (for in the comparative privacy of the museum she talked a good deal to him of socialism and Browning and general propositions) that she had met Wedderburn at the house of some people she knew, and "He's inherited his cleverness; for his father, you know, is the great eye specialist."

"*My* father is a cobbler," said Hill, quite irrelevantly, and perceived the want of dignity even as he said it. But the gleam of jealousy did not offend her. She conceived herself the fundamental source of it. He suffered bitterly from a sense of Wedderburn's unfairness and a realization of his own handicap. Here was this Wedderburn had picked up a prominent man for a father, and instead of his losing so many marks on the score of that advantage, it was counted to him for righteousness! And while Hill had to introduce himself and talk to Miss Haysman clumsily over mangled guinea-pigs in the laboratory, this Wedderburn, in some backstairs way, had access to her social altitudes, and could converse in a polished argot that Hill understood perhaps, but felt incapable of speaking. Not of course that he wanted to. Then it seemed to Hill that for Wedderburn to come there day after day with cuffs unfrayed, neatly tailored, precisely barbered, quietly perfect, was in itself an ill-bred, sneering sort of proceeding. Moreover, it was a stealthy thing for Wedderburn to behave insignificantly for a space, to mock modesty, to lead Hill to fancy that he himself was beyond dispute the man of the year, and then suddenly to dart in front of him, and incontinently to swell up in this fashion. In addition to these things Wedderburn displayed an increasing disposition to join in any conversational gouping that included Miss Haysman, and would venture, and indeed seek occasion to pass opinions derogatory to Socialism and Atheism. He goaded Hill to incivilities by neat, shallow, and exceedingly effective personalities about the socialist leaders, until Hill hated Bernard Shaw's graceful egotisms, William Morris's limited editions and luxurious wallpapers, and Walter Crane's charmingly absurd ideal workingmen, about as much as he hated Wedderburn. The dissertations in the laboratory that had been his glory in the previous term, became a danger, degenerated into inglorious tussles with Wedderburn, and Hill kept to them only out of an obscure perception that his honor was involved. In the Debating Society Hill knew quite clearly that, to a thunderous accompaniment of banged desks, he could have pulverized Wedderburn. Only Wedderburn never attended the Debating Society to be pulverized, because—nauseous affectation!—he "dined late."

You must not imagine that these things presented themselves in quite such a crude form to Hill's perception. Hill was a born generalizer. Wedderburn to him was not so much an individual obstacle as a type, the salient angle of a class. The economic theories that, after infinite ferment, had shaped themselves in Hill's mind, became abruptly concrete at the contact. The world became full of easy-mannered, graceful, gracefully dressed, conversationally dexterous, finally shallow Wedderburns, Bishops Wedderburn, Wedderburns, M.P., Professors Wedderburn, Wedderburn landlords, all with finger-bowl shibboleths and epigrammatic cities of refuge from a sturdy debater. And every one ill clothed or ill dressed, from the cobbler to the cab runner, was a man and a brother, a fellow-sufferer, to Hill's imagination. So that he became, as it were, a champion of the fallen and oppressed, albeit to outward seeming only a self-assertive, ill-mannered young man, and an unsuccessful champion at that. Again and again, a skirmish over the afternoon tea that the girl-students had inaugurated, left Hill with flushed cheeks and a tattered temper, and the Debating Society noticed a new quality of sarcastic bitterness in his speeches.

You will understand now how it was necessary, if only in the interests of humanity, that Hill should demolish Wedderburn in the forthcoming examination and outshine him in the eyes of Miss Haysman, and you will perceive, too, how Miss Haysman fell into some common feminine misconceptions. The Hill-Wedderburn quarrel, for in his unostentatious way Wedderburn reciprocated Hill's ill-veiled rivalry, became a tribute to her indefinable charm. She was the Queen of Beauty in a tournament of scalpels and stumpy pencils. To her confidential friend's secret annoyance, it even troubled her conscience, for she was a good girl, and painfully aware, from Ruskin and contemporary fiction, how entirely men's activities are determined by women's attitudes. And if Hill never by any chance mentioned the topic of love to her, she only credited him with the finer modesty for that omission.

So the time came on for the second examination, and Hill's increasing pallor confirmed the general rumor that he was working hard. In the Aërated Bread Shop near South Kensington Station you would see him, breaking his bun and sipping his milk, with his eyes intent upon a paper of closely written notes. In his bedroom there were propositions about buds and stems round his looking-glass, a diagram to catch his eye, if soap should chance to spare it, above his washing-basin. He missed several meetings of the Debating Society, but he found the chance encounters with Miss Haysman in the spacious ways of the adjacent Art Museum, or in the little Museum at the top of the College, or in the College corridors, more frequent and very restful. In particular they used to meet in a little gallery full of wrought-iron chests and gates, near the Art Library, and there Hill used to talk, under the gentle stimulus of her flattering attention, of Browning and his personal ambitions. A characteristic she found remarkable in him was his freedom from avarice. He contemplated quite calmly the prospect of living all his life on an income below a hundred pounds a year. But he was determined to be famous, to make, recognizably in his own proper person, the world a better place to live in. He took Bradlaugh and John Burns for his leaders and models, poor, even impecunious, Great Men. But Miss Haysman thought that such lives were deficient on the aesthetic side, by which, though she did not know it, she meant good wallpaper and upholstery, pretty books, tasteful clothes, concerts, and meals nicely cooked and respectfully served.

At last came the day of the second examination, and the professor of botany, a fussy conscientious man, rearranged all the tables in the long narrow laboratory to prevent copying, and put his demonstrator on a chair on a table (where he felt, he said, like a Hindoo god) to see all the cheating, and stuck a notice outside the door, "Door Closed," for no earthly reason that any human being could discover. And all the morning from ten to one the quill of Wedderburn shrieked defiance at Hill's, and the quills of the others chased their leaders in a tireless pack. So also it was in the afternoon. Wedderburn was a little quieter than usual, and Hill's face was hot all day, and his overcoat bulged with textbooks and notebooks against the last moment's revision. And the next day, in the morning and in the afternoon, was the practical examination, when sections had to be cut and slides identified. In the morning Hill was depressed because he knew he had cut a thick section, and in the afternoon came the Mysterious Slip.

It was just the kind of thing that the botanical professor was always doing. Like the income tax, it offered a premium to the cheat. It was a preparation under the microscope, a little glass slip, held in its place on the stage of the instrument by light steel clips, and the inscription set forth that the slip was not to be moved. Each student was to go in turn to it, sketch it, write in his book of answers what he considered it to be, and return to his place. Now to move such a slip is a thing one can do by a chance movement of the finger, and in a fraction of a second. The professor's reason for decreeing that the slip should not be moved depended on the fact that the object he wanted identified was characteristic of a certain tree stem. In the position in which it was placed it was a difficult thing to recognize, but once the slip was moved so as to bring other parts of the preparation into view, its nature was obvious enough.

Hill came to this, flushed from a contest with staining reagents, sat down on the little stool before the microscope, turned the mirror to get the best light, and then out of sheer habit shifted the slip. At once he remembered the prohibition, and with an almost continuous motion of his hands, moved it back, and sat paralyzed with astonishment at his action.

Then slowly he turned his head. The professor was out of the room, the demonstrator sat aloft on his impromptu rostrum, reading the "Q. Jour. Mi. Sci.," the rest of the examinees were busy and with their backs to him. Should he own up to the accident now? He knew quite clearly what the thing was. It was a lenticel, a characteristic preparation from the elder-tree. His eye roved over his intent fellow-students and Wedderburn suddenly glanced over his shoulder at him with a queer expression in his eyes. The mental excitement that had kept Hill at an abnormal pitch of vigor these two days gave way to a curious nervous tension. His book of answers was beside him. He did not write down what the thing was, but with one eye at the microscope he began making a hasty sketch of it. His mind was full of this grotesque puzzle in ethics that had suddenly been sprung upon him. Should he identify it? Or should he leave this question unanswered? In that case Wedderburn would probably come out first in the botanical list. How could he tell now whether he might not have identified the thing without shifting it? It was possible that Wedderburn had failed to recognize it, of course. Suppose Wedderburn, too, had shifted the slide? He looked up at the clock. There were fifteen minutes in which to make up his mind. He gathered up his book of answers and the colored pencils he used in illustrating his replies, and walked back to his seat.

He read through his manuscript and then sat thinking and gnawing his knuckle. It would look queer now if he owned up. He *must* beat Wedderburn. He forgot the examples of those starry gentlemen, John Burns and Bradlaugh. Besides, he reflected, the glimpse of the rest of the slip he had had, was after all quite accidental, forced upon him by chance, a kind of providential revelation rather than an unfair advantage. It was not nearly so dishonest to avail himself of that as it was of Broome, who believed in the efficacy of prayer, to pray daily for a First-Class. "Five minutes more," said the demonstrator, folding up his paper and becoming observant. Hill watched the clock hands until two minutes remained, then he opened the book of answers, and with hot ears and an affectation of ease, gave his drawing of the lenticel its name.

When the second pass list appeared, the previous positions of Wedderburn and Hill were reversed, and the spectacled girl in green who knew the demonstrator in private life (where he was practically human) said that in the result of the two examinations taken together, Hill had the advantage of a mark, 167 to 166, out of a possible 200. Every one admired Hill in a way, though the suspicion of "mugging" clung to him. But Hill was to find congratulations and Miss Haysman's enhanced opinion of him, and even the decided decline in the crest of Wedderburn tainted by an unhappy memory. He felt a remarkable access of energy at first, and the note of a Democracy marching to Triumph returned to his Debating Society speeches; he worked at his comparative anatomy with tremendous zeal and effect, and he went on with his aesthetic education. But through it all, a vivid little picture was continually coming before his mind's eye, of a sneakish person manipulating a slide. . . .

No human being had witnessed the act, and he was cocksure that no Higher Power existed to see it, but for all that it worried him. Memories are not dead things, but alive; they dwindle in disuse, but they harden and develop in all sorts of queer ways if they are being continually fretted. Curiously enough, though at the time he perceived clearly that the shifting was accidental, as the days wore on his memory became confused about it, until at last he was not sure, although he assured himself that he *was* sure, whether the movement had been absolutely involuntary. Then it is possible that Hill's dietary was conducive to morbid conscientiousness,—a breakfast frequently eaten in a hurry, a midday bun, and, at such hours after five as chanced to be convenient, such meat as his means determined, usually in a chophouse in a back street off the Brompton Road. Occasionally he treated himself to threepenny and ninepenny classics, and they usually represented a suppression of potatoes or chops. It is indisputable that outbreaks of self-abasement and emotional revival have a distinct relation to periods of scarcity. But apart from this influence on the feelings, there was in Hill a distinct aversion to falsity, that the blasphemous Landport cobbler had inculcated by strap and tongue from his earliest years. Of one fact about professed Atheists I am convinced: they may be, they usually are, fools, void of subtlety, revilers of holy institutions, brutal speakers, and mischievous knaves; but they lie with difficulty. If it were not so, if they had the faintest grasp of the idea of compromise, they would simply be liberal Churchmen. And, moreover, this memory poisoned his regard for Miss Haysman. For she now preferred him to Wedderburn so evidently that he felt sure he cared for her, and began reciprocating her attentions by timid marks of personal regard,—at one time he even bought a bunch of violets, carried it about in his pocket, and produced it with a stumbling explanation, withered and dead, in the gallery of old iron. It poisoned, too, the denunciation of capitalist dishonesty that had been one of his life's pleasures. And, lastly, it poisoned his triumph over Wedderburn. Previously he had been Wedderburn's superior in his own eyes, and had raged simply at a want of recognition. Now he began to fret at the darker suspicion of a positive inferiority. He fancied he found justification for his position in Browning; but they vanished on analysis. At last, moved curiously enough by exactly the same motive forces that had resulted in his dishonesty, he went to Professor Bindon and made a clean breast of the whole affair. As Hill was a paid student, Professor Bindon did not ask him to sit down, and he stood before the Professor's desk as he made his confession.

"It's a curious story," said Professor Bindon, slowly realizing how the thing reflected on himself, and then letting his anger rise. "A most remarkable story. I can't understand your doing it, and I can't understand this avowal. You're a type of student—Cambridge men would never dream—I suppose I ought to have thought— Why *did* you cheat?"

"I didn't—cheat," said Hill.

"But you have just been telling me you did."

"I thought I explained—"

"Either you cheated or you did not cheat."

"I said my motion was involuntary—"

"I am not a metaphysician, I am a servant of science—of fact. You were told not to move the slip. You did move the slip. If that is not cheating—"

"If I was a cheat," said Hill, with the note of hysterics in his voice, "should I come here and tell you?"

"Your repentance, of course, does you credit," said Professor Bindon; "but it does not alter the original facts."

"No, sir," said Hill, giving in, in utter self-abasement.

"Even now you cause an enormous amount of trouble. The examination list will have to be revised."

"I suppose so, sir."

"Suppose so! Of course it must be revised. And I don't see how I can conscientiously pass you."

"Not pass me!" said Hill. "Fail me!"

"It's the rule in all examinations. Or where should we be? What else did you expect? You don't want to shirk the consequences of your own acts?"

"I thought perhaps," said Hill. And then, "Fail me! I thought, as I told you, you would simply deduct the marks given for that slip—"

"Impossible!" said Bindon. "Besides, it would still leave you above Wedderburn. Deduct only the marks! Preposterous! The Departmental Regulations distinctly say—"

"But it's my own admission, sir."

"The Regulations say nothing whatever of the manner in which the matter comes to light. They simply provide—"

"It will ruin me. If I fail this examination, they won't renew my scholarship."

"You should have thought of that before."

"But, sir, consider all my circumstances—"

"I cannot consider anything. Professors in this College are machines. The Regulations will not even let us recommend our students for appointments. I am a machine, and you have worked me. I have to do—"

"It's very hard, sir."

"Possibly it is."

"If I am to be failed this examination I might as well go home at once."

"That is as you think proper." Bindon's voice softened a little, he perceived he had been unjust, and, provided he did not contradict himself, he was disposed to amelioration. "As a private person," he said, "I think this confession of yours goes far to mitigate your offence. But you have set the machinery in motion, you know, and now it must take its course. I—I am really sorry you gave way."

A wave of emotion prevented Hill from answering. Suddenly very vividly he saw the heavily-lined face of the old Landport cobbler, his father. "Good God!— What a fool I have been!" he said hotly and abruptly.

"I hope," said Bindon, "that it will be a lesson to you."

But curiously enough they were not thinking of quite the same indiscretion. There was a pause.

"I would like a day to think, sir, and then I will let you know—about going home, I mean," said Hill, moving towards the door.

The next day Hill's place was vacant. The spectacled girl in green was, as usual, first with the news. Wedderburn and Miss Haysman were talking of the Meistersingers, when she came up to them.

"Have you heard?" she said.

"Heard what?"

"There was cheating in the examination."

"Cheating!" said Wedderburn, with his face suddenly hot. "How?"

"That slide—"

"Moved? Never!"

"It was. That slide that we weren't to move—"

"Nonsense!" said Wedderburn. "Why! How could they find out? Who do they say—"

"It was Mr. Hill."

"*Hill!*"

"Mr. Hill!"

"Not—surely not the immaculate Hill?" said Wedderburn, recovering.

"I don't believe it," said Miss Haysman. "How do you know?"

"I *didn't*," said the girl in spectacles. "But I know it now for a fact. Mr. Hill went and confessed to Professor Bindon himself."

"By Jove!" said Wedderburn. "Hill of all people— But I am always inclined to distrust these philanthropists-on-principle—"

"Are you quite sure?" said Miss Haysman, with a catch in her breath.

"Quite. It's dreadful, isn't it? But you know, what can you expect? His father is a cobbler—"

Then Miss Haysman astonished the girl in spectacles.

"I don't care. I will not believe it," she said, flushing darkly under her warm-tinted skin. "I will not believe it until he has told me so himself—face to face. I would scarcely believe it then," and abruptly she turned her back on the girl in spectacles, and walked to her own place.

"It's true, all the same," said the girl in spectacles, peering and smiling at Wedderburn.

But Wedderburn did not answer her. She was, indeed, one of those people who are destined to make unanswered remarks.

THE REMARKABLE CASE OF DAVIDSON'S EYES

I

THE TRANSITORY MENTAL aberration of Sidney Davidson, remarkable enough in itself, is still more remarkable if Wade's explanation is to be credited. It sets one dreaming of the oddest possibilities of intercommunication in the future, of spending an intercalary five minutes on the other side of the world, or being watched in our most secret operations by unsuspected eyes. It happened that I was the immediate witness of Davidson's seizure, and so it falls naturally to me to put the story upon paper.

When I say that I was the immediate witness of his seizure, I mean that I was the first on the scene. The thing happened at the Harlow Technical College just beyond the Highgate Archway. He was alone in the larger laboratory when the thing happened. I was in the smaller room, where the balances are, writing up some notes. The thunderstorm had completely upset my work, of course. It was just after one of the louder peals that I thought I heard some glass smash in the other room. I stopped writing, and turned round to listen. For a moment I heard nothing; the hail was playing the devil's tattoo on the corrugated zinc of the roof. Then came another sound, a smash—no doubt of it this time. Something heavy had been knocked off the bench. I jumped up at once and went and opened the door leading into the big laboratory.

I was surprised to hear a queer sort of laugh, and saw Davidson standing unsteadily in the middle of the room, with a dazzled look on his face. My first impression was that he was drunk. He did not notice me. He was clawing out at something invisible a yard in front of his face. He put out his hand, slowly, rather hesitatingly, and then clutched nothing. "What's come to it?" he said. He held up his hands to his face, fingers spread out. "Great Scott!" he said. The thing happened three or four years ago, when everyone swore by that personage. Then he began raising his feet clumsily, as though he had expected to find them glued to the floor.

"Davidson!" cried I. "What's the matter with you?" He turned round in my direction and looked about for me. He looked over me and at me and on either side of me, without the slightest sign of seeing me. "Waves," he said; "and a remarkably neat schooner. I'd swear that was Bellows's voice. *Hullo!*" He shouted suddenly at the top of his voice.

I thought he was up to some foolery. Then I saw littered about his feet the shattered remains of the best of our electrometers. "What's up, man?" said I. "You've smashed the electrometer!"

"Bellows again!" said he. "Friends left, if my hands are gone. Something about electrometers. Which way *are* you, Bellows?" He suddenly came staggering towards me. "The damned stuff cuts like butter," he said. He walked straight into the bench and recoiled. "None so buttery, that!" he said, and stood swaying.

I felt scared. "Davidson," said I, "what on earth's come over you?"

He looked round him in every direction. "I could swear that was Bellows. Why don't you show yourself like a man, Bellows?"

It occurred to me that he must be suddenly struck blind. I walked round the table and laid my hand upon his arm. I never saw a man more startled in my life. He jumped away from me, and came round into an attitude of self-defense, his face fairly distorted with terror. "Good God!" he cried. "What was that?"

"It's I—Bellows. Confound it, Davidson!"

He jumped when I answered him and stared—how can I express it?—right through me. He began talking, not to me, but to himself. "Here in broad daylight on a clear beach. Not a place to hide in." He looked about him wildly. "Here! I'm *off*." He suddenly turned and ran headlong into the big electro-magnet— so violently that, as we found afterwards, he bruised his shoulder and jawbone cruelly. At that he stepped back a pace, and cried out with almost a whimper, "What, in Heaven's name, has come over me?" He stood, blanched with terror and trembling violently, with his right arm clutching his left, where that had collided with the magnet.

By that time I was excited, and fairly excited. "Davidson," said I, "don't be afraid."

He was startled at my voice, but not so excessively as before. I repeated my words in as clear and firm a tone as I could assume. "Bellows," he said, "is that you?"

"Can't you see it's me?"

He laughed. "I can't even see it's myself. Where the devil are we?"

"Here," said I, "in the laboratory."

"The laboratory!" he answered, in a puzzled tone, and put his hand to his forehead. "I *was* in the laboratory—till that flash came, but I'm hanged if I'm there now. What ship is that?"

"There's no ship," said I. "Do be sensible, old chap."

"No ship!" he repeated, and seemed to forget my denial forthwith. "I suppose," said he, slowly, "we're both dead. But the rummy part is I feel just as though I still had a body. Don't get used to it all at once, I suppose. The old shop was struck by lightning, I suppose. Jolly quick thing, Bellows—eigh?"

"Don't talk nonsense. You're very much alive. You are in the laboratory, blundering about. You've just smashed a new electrometer. I don't envy you when Boyce arrives."

He stared away from me towards the diagrams of cryohydrates. "I must be deaf," said he. "They've fired a gun, for there goes the puff of smoke, and I never heard a sound."

I put my hand on his arm again, and this time he was less alarmed. "We seem to have a sort of invisible bodies," said he. "By Jove! there's a boat coming round the headland! It's very much like the old life after all—in a different climate."

I shook his arm. "Davidson," I cried, "wake up!"

II

It was just then that Boyce came in. So soon as he spoke Davidson exclaimed: "Old Boyce! Dead too! What a lark!" I hastened to explain that Davidson was in a kind of somnambulistic trance. Boyce was interested at once. We both did all we could to rouse the fellow out of his extraordinary state. He answered our questions, and asked us some of his own, but his attention seemed distracted by his hallucination about a beach and a ship. He kept interpolating observations concerning some boat and the davits and sails filling with the wind. It made one feel queer, in the dusky laboratory, to hear him saying such things.

He was blind and helpless. We had to walk him down the passage, one at each elbow, to Boyce's private room, and while Boyce talked to him there, and humored him about this ship idea, I went along the corridor and asked old Wade to come and look at him. The voice of our Dean sobered him a little, but not very much. He asked where his hands were, and why he had to walk about up to his waist in the ground. Wade thought over him a long time—you know how he knits his brows—and then made him feel the couch, guiding his hands to it. "That's a couch," said Wade. "The couch in the private room of Professor Boyce. Horsehair stuffing."

Davidson felt about, and puzzled over it, and answered presently that he could feel it all right, but he couldn't see it.

"What *do* you see?" asked Wade. Davidson said he could see nothing but a lot of sand and broken-up shells. Wade gave him some other things to feel, telling him what they were, and watching him keenly.

"The ship is almost hull down," said Davidson, presently, *apropos* of nothing.

"Never mind the ship," said Wade. "Listen to me, Davidson. Do you know what hallucination means?"

"Rather," said Davidson.

"Well, everything you see is hallucinatory."

"Bishop Berkeley," said Davidson.

"Don't mistake me," said Wade. "You are alive, and in this room of Boyce's. But something has happened to your eyes. You cannot see; you can feel and hear, but not see. Do you follow me?"

"It seems to me that I see too much." Davidson rubbed his knuckles into his eyes. "Well?" he said.

"That's all. Don't let it perplex you. Bellows, here, and I will take you home in a cab."

"Wait a bit." Davidson thought. "Help me to sit down," said he, presently; "and now—I'm sorry to trouble you—but will you tell me all that over again?"

Wade repeated it very patiently. Davidson shut his eyes, and pressed his hands upon his forehead. "Yes," said he. "It's quite right. Now my eyes are shut I know you're right. That's you, Bellows, sitting by me on the couch. I'm in England again. And we're in the dark."

Then he opened his eyes. "And there," said he, "is the sun just rising, and the yards of the ship, and a tumbled sea, and a couple of birds flying. I never saw anything so real. And I'm sitting up to my neck in a bank of sand."

He bent forward and covered his face with his hands. Then he opened his eyes again. "Dark sea and sunrise! And yet I'm sitting on a sofa in old Boyce's room!—God help me!"

III

That was the beginning. For three weeks this strange affection of Davidson's eyes continued unabated. It was far worse than being blind. He was absolutely helpless, and had to be fed like a newly-hatched bird, and led about and undressed. If he attempted to move he fell over things or struck himself against walls or doors. After a day or so he got used to hearing our voices without seeing us, and willingly admitted he was at home, and that Wade was right in what he told him. My sister, to whom he was engaged, insisted on coming to see him, and would sit for hours every day while he talked about this beach of his. Holding her hand seemed to comfort him immensely. He explained that when we left the College and drove home,—he lived in Hampstead Village,—it appeared to him as if we drove right through a sandhill—it was perfectly black until he emerged again—and through rocks and trees and solid obstacles, and when he was taken to his own room it made him giddy and almost frantic with the fear of falling, because going upstairs seemed to lift him thirty or forty feet above the rocks of his imaginary island. He kept saying he should smash all the eggs. The end was that he had to be taken down into his father's consulting room and laid upon a couch that stood there.

He described the island as being a bleak kind of place on the whole, with very little vegetation, except some peaty stuff, and a lot of bare rock. There were multitudes of penguins, and they made the rocks white and disagreeable to see. The sea was often rough, and once there was a thunderstorm, and he lay and shouted at the silent flashes. Once or twice seals pulled up on the beach, but only on the first two or three days. He said it was very funny the way in which the penguins used to waddle right through him, and how he seemed to lie among them without disturbing them.

I remember one odd thing, and that was when he wanted very badly to smoke. We put a pipe in his hands—he almost poked his eye out with it—and lit it. But he couldn't taste anything. I've since found it's the same with me—I don't know if it's the usual case—that I cannot enjoy tobacco at all unless I can see the smoke.

But the queerest part of his vision came when Wade sent him out in a bath-chair to get fresh air. The Davidsons hired a chair, and got that deaf and obstinate dependent of theirs, Widgery, to attend to it. Widgery's ideas of healthy expeditions were peculiar. My sister, who had been to the Dog's Home, met them in Camden Town, towards King's Cross. Widgery trotting along complacently, and Davidson evidently most distressed, trying in his feeble, blind way to attract Widgery's attention.

He positively wept when my sister spoke to him. "Oh, get me out of this horrible darkness!" he said, feeling for her hand. "I must get out of it, or I shall die." He was quite incapable of explaining what was the matter, but my sister decided he must go home, and presently, as they went up the hill towards Hampstead, the horror seemed to drop from him. He said it was good to see the stars again, though it was then about noon and a blazing day.

"It seemed," he told me afterwards, "as if I was being carried irresistibly towards the water. I was not very much alarmed at first. Of course it was night there—a lovely night."

"Of course?" I asked, for that struck me as odd.

"Of course," said he. "It's always night there when it is day here— Well, we went right into the water, which was calm and shining under the moonlight— just a broad swell that seemed to grow broader and flatter as I came down into it. The surface glistened just like a skin—it might have been empty space underneath for all I could tell to the contrary. Very slowly, for I rode slanting into it, the water crept up to my eyes. Then I went under, and the skin seemed to break and heal again about my eyes. The moon gave a jump up in the sky and grew green and dim, and fish, faintly glowing, came darting round me—and things that seemed made of luminous glass, and I passed through a tangle of seaweeds that shone with an oily luster. And so I drove down into the sea, and the stars went out one by one, and the moon grew greener and darker, and the seaweed became a luminous purple-red. It was all very faint and mysterious, and everything seemed to quiver. And all the while I could hear the wheels of the bath-chair creaking, and the footsteps of people going by, and a man with a bell crying coals.

"I kept sinking down deeper and deeper into the water. It became inky black about me, not a ray from above came down into that darkness, and the phosphorescent things grew brighter and brighter. The snaky branches of the deeper weeds flickered like the flames of spirit lamps; but, after a time, there were no more weeds. The fishes came staring and gaping towards me, and into me and through me. I never imagined such fishes before. They had lines of fire along the sides of them as though they had been outlined with a luminous pencil. And there was a ghastly thing swimming backwards with a lot of twining arms. And then I saw, coming very slowly towards me through the gloom, a hazy mass of light that resolved itself as it drew nearer into multitudes of fishes, struggling and darting round something that drifted. I drove on straight towards it, and presently I saw in the midst of the tumult, and by the light of the fish, a bit of splintered spar looming over me, and a dark hull tilting over, and some glowing phosphorescent forms that were shaken and writhed as the fish bit at them. Then it was I began to try to attract Widgery's attention. A horror came upon me. Ugh! I should have driven right into those half-eaten—things. If your sister had not come! They had great holes in them, Bellows, and—Never mind. But it was ghastly!''

IV

For three weeks Davidson remained in this singular state, seeing what at the time we imagined was an altogether phantasmal world, and stone blind to the world around him. Then, one Tuesday, when I called, I met old Davidson in the passage. ''He can see his thumb!'' the old gentleman said, in a perfect transport. He was struggling into his overcoat. ''He can see his thumb, Bellows!'' he said, with the tears in his eyes. ''The lad will be all right yet.''

I rushed in to Davidson. He was holding up a little book before his face, and looking at it and laughing in a weak kind of way.

''It's amazing,'' said he. ''There's a kind of patch come there.'' He pointed with his finger. ''I'm on the rocks as usual, and the penguins are staggering and flapping about as usual, and there's been a whale showing every now and then, but it's got too dark now to make him out. But put something *there,* and I see it—I do see it. It's very dim and broken in places, but I see it all the same, like a faint specter of itself. I found it out this morning while they were dressing me. It's like a hole in this infernal phantom world. Just put your hand by mine. No—not there. Ah! Yes! I see it. The base of your thumb and a bit of cuff! It looks like the ghost of a bit of your hand sticking out of the darkening sky. Just by it there's a group of stars like a cross coming out.''

From that time Davidson began to mend. His account of the change, like his account of the vision, was oddly convincing. Over patches of his field of vision the phantom world grew fainter, grew transparent, as it were, and through these translucent gaps he began to see dimly the real world about him. The patches grew in size and number, ran together and spread until only here and there were blind spots left upon his eyes. He was able to get up and steer himself about, feed himself once more, read, smoke, and behave like an ordinary citizen again. At first it was very confusing to him to have these two pictures overlapping each other like the changing views of a lantern, but in a little while he began to distinguish the real from the illusory.

At first he was unfeignedly glad, and seemed only too anxious to complete his cure by taking exercise and tonics. But as that odd island of his began to fade away from him, he became queerly interested in it. He wanted particularly to go down into the deep sea again, and would spend half his time wandering about the low-lying parts of London, trying to find the water-logged wreck he had seen drifting. The glare of real daylight very soon impressed him so vividly as to blot out everything of his shadowy world, but of a nighttime, in a darkened room, he could still see the white-splashed rocks of the island, and the clumsy penguins staggering to and fro. But even these grew fainter and fainter, and, at last, soon after he married my sister, he saw them for the last time.

V

And now to tell of the queerest thing of all. About two years after his cure, I dined with the Davidsons, and after dinner a man named Atkins called in. He is a lieutenant in the Royal Navy, and a pleasant, talkative man. He was on friendly terms with my brother-in-law, and was soon on friendly terms with me. It came out that he was engaged to Davidson's cousin, and incidentally he took out a kind of pocket photograph case to show us a new rendering of his *fiancée*. "And, by-the-by," said he, "here's the old *Fulmar*."

Davidson looked at it casually. Then suddenly his face lit up. "Good heavens!" said he. "I could almost swear—"

"What?" said Atkins.

"That I had seen that ship before."

"Don't see how you can have. She hasn't been out of the South Seas for six years, and before then—"

"But," began Davidson, and then, "Yes—that's the ship I dreamt of. I'm sure that's the ship I dreamt of. She was standing off an island that swarmed with penguins, and she fired a gun."

"Good Lord!" said Atkins, who had never heard the particulars of the seizure. "How the deuce could you dream that?"

And then, bit by bit, it came out that on the very day Davidson was seized, H.M.S. *Fulmar* had actually been off a little rock to the south of Antipodes Island. A boat had landed overnight to get penguins' eggs, had been delayed, and a thunderstorm drifting up, the boat's crew had waited until the morning before rejoining the ship. Atkins had been one of them, and he corroborated, word for word, the descriptions Davidson had given of the island and the boat. There is not the slightest doubt in any of our minds that Davidson has really seen the place. In some unaccountable way, while he moved hither and thither in London, his sight moved hither and thither in a manner that corresponded, about this distant island. *How* is absolutely a mystery.

That completes the remarkable story of Davidson's eyes. It is perhaps the best authenticated case in existence of a real vision at a distance. Explanation there is none forthcoming, except what Professor Wade has thrown out. But his explanation invokes the Fourth Dimension, and a dissertation on theoretical kinds of space. To talk of there being "a kink in space" seems mere nonsense to me; it may be because I am no mathematician. When I said that nothing would alter the fact that the place is eight thousand miles away, he answered that two points might be a yard away on a sheet of paper and yet be brought together by bending the paper round. The reader may grasp his argument, but I certainly do not. His idea seems to be that Davidson, stooping between the poles of the big electro-magnet, had some extraordinary twist given to his retinal elements through the sudden change in the field of force due to the lightning.

He thinks, as a consequence of this, that it may be possible to live visually in one part of the world, while one lives bodily in another. He has even made some experiments in support of his views; but, so far, he has simply succeeded in blinding a few dogs. I believe that is the net result of his work, though I have not seen him for some weeks. Latterly, I have been so busy with my work in connection with the Saint Pancras installation that I have have had little opportunity of calling to see him. But the whole of his theory seems fantastic to me. The facts concerning Davidson stand on an altogether different footing, and I can testify personally to the accuracy of every detail I have given.

THE CONE

THE NIGHT WAS hot and overcast, the sky red-rimmed with the lingering sunset of midsummer. They sat at the open window trying to fancy the air was fresher there. The trees and shrubs of the garden stood stiff and dark; beyond in the roadway a gas lamp burnt, bright orange against the hazy blue of the evening. Further were the three lights of the railway signal against the lowering sky. The man and woman spoke to one another in low tones.

"He does not suspect?" said the man, a little nervously.

"Not he," she said peevishly, as though that too irritated her. "He thinks of nothing but the works and the prices of fuel. He has no imagination, no poetry—"

"None of these men of iron have," he said sententiously. "They have no hearts."

"*He* has not," she said. She turned her discontented face towards the window. The distant sound of a roaring and rushing drew nearer and grew in volume; the house quivered; one heard the metallic rattle of the tender. As the train passed there was a glare of light above the cutting and a driving tumult of smoke; one, two, three, four, five, six, seven, eight black oblongs—eight trucks—passed across the dim grey of the embankment, and were suddenly extinguished one by one in the throat of the tunnel, which, with the last, seemed to swallow down train, smoke, and sound in one abrupt gulp.

"This country was all fresh and beautiful once," he said; "and now—it is Gehenna. Down that way—nothing but pot-banks and chimneys belching fire and dust into the face of heaven— But what does it matter? An end comes, an end to all this cruelty—*tomorrow*." He spoke the last word in a whisper.

"*Tomorrow*," she said, speaking in a whisper too, and still staring out of the window.

"Dear!" he said, putting his hand on hers.

She turned with a start, and their eyes searched one another's. Hers softened to his gaze. "My dear one," she said, and then: "It seems so strange—that you should have come into my life like this—to open—" She paused.

"To open?" he said.

"All this wonderful world—" she hesitated and spoke still more softly— "this world of *love* to me."

Then suddenly the door clicked and closed. They turned their heads, and he started violently back. In the shadow of the room stood a great shadowy figure— silent. They saw the face dimly in the half-light, with unexpressive dark patches under the pent-house brows. Every muscle in Raut's body suddenly became tense. When could the door have opened? What had he heard? Had he heard all? What had he seen? A tumult of questions.

The new-comer's voice came at last, after a pause that seemed interminable. "Well?" he said.

"I was afraid I had missed you, Horrocks," said the man at the window, gripping the window-ledge with his hand. His voice was unsteady.

The clumsy figure of Horrocks came forward out of the shadow. He made no answer to Raut's remark. For a moment he stood above them.

The woman's heart was cold within her. "I told Mr. Raut it was just possible you might come back," she said, in a voice that never quivered.

Horrocks, still silent, sat down abruptly in the chair by her little work-table. His big hands were clenched; one saw now the fire of his eyes under the shadow of his brows. He was trying to get his breath. His eyes went from the woman he had trusted to the friend he had trusted, and then back to the woman.

By this time and for the moment all three half understood one another. Yet none dared say a word to ease the pent-up things that choked them.

It was the husband's voice that broke the silence at last.

"You wanted to see me?" he said to Raut.

Raut started as he spoke. "I came to see you," he said, resolved to lie to the last.

"Yes?" said Horrocks.

"You promised," said Raut, "to show me some fine effects of moonlight and smoke."

"I promised to show you some fine effects of moonlight and smoke," repeated Horrocks, in a colorless voice.

"And I thought I might catch you tonight before you went down to the works," proceeded Raut, "and come with you."

There was another pause. Did the man mean to take the thing coolly? Did he after all know? How long had he been in the room? Yet ven at the moment when they heard the door, their attitudes—Horrocks glanced at the profile of the woman, shadowy pallid in the half-light. Then he glanced at Raut, and seemed to recover himself suddenly. "Of course," he said, "I promised to show you the works under their proper dramatic conditions. It's odd how I could have forgotten."

"If I'm troubling you—" began Raut.

Horrocks started again. A new light had suddenly come into the sultry gloom of his eyes. "Not in the least," he said.

"Have you been telling Mr. Raut of all these contrasts of flame and shadow you think so splendid?" said the woman, turning now to her husband for the first time, her confidence creeping back again, her voice just one half-note too high. "That dreadful theory of yours that machinery is beautiful and everything else in the world ugly. I thought he would not spare you, Mr. Raut. It's his great Theory, his one discovery in Art—"

"I am slow to make discoveries," said Horrocks, grimly, damping her suddenly. "But what I discover—" He stopped.

"Well?" she said.

"Nothing," and suddenly he rose to his feet.

"I promised to show you the works," he said to Raut, and put his big, clumsy hand on his friend's shoulder. "And you are ready to go?"

"Quite," said Raut, and stood up also.

There was another pause. Each of them peered through the indistinctness of the dusk at the other two. Horrocks's hand still rested on Raut's shoulder. Raut half fancied still that the incident was trivial after all. But Mrs. Horrocks knew her husband better, knew that grim quiet in his voice, and the confusion in her mind took a vague shape of physical evil. "Very well," said Horrocks, and, dropping his hand, turned towards the door.

"My hat?" Raut looked round in the half-light.

"That's my work-basket," said Mrs. Horrocks, with a gust of hysterical laughter. The hands came together on the back of the chair. "Here it is!" he said. She had an impulse to warn him in an undertone, but she could not frame a word. "Don't go!" and "Beware of him!" struggled in her mind, and the swift moment passed.

"Got it?" said Horrocks, standing with door half open.

Raut stepped towards him. "Better say good-bye to Mrs. Horrocks," said the ironmaster, even more grimly quiet in his tone than before.

Raut started and turned. "Good-evening, Mrs. Horrocks," he said, and their hands touched.

Horrocks held the door open with a ceremonial politeness unusual in him towards men. Raut went out and then, after a wordless look at her, her husband followed. She stood motionless while Raut's light footfall and her husband's heavy tread, like bass and treble, passed down the passage together. The front door slammed heavily. She went to the window, moving slowly, and stood watching—leaning forward. The two men appeared for a moment at the gateway in the road, passed under the street lamp, and were hidden by the black masses of the shrubbery. The lamplight fell for a moment on their faces, showing only unmeaning pale patches, telling nothing of what she still feared, and doubted, and craved vainly to know. Then she sank down into a crouching attitude in the big arm-chair, her eyes wide open and staring out at the red lights from the furnaces that flickered in the sky. An hour after she was still there, her attitude scarcely changed.

The oppressive stillness of the evening weighed heavily upon Raut. They went side by side down the road in silence, and in silence turned into the cinder-made by-way that presently opened out the prospect of the valley.

A blue haze, half dust, half mist, touched the long valley with mystery. Beyond were Hanley and Etruria, grey and dark masses, outlined thinly by the rare golden dots of the street lamps, and here and there a gaslit window, or the yellow glare of some late-working factory or crowded public-house. Out of the masses, clear and slender against the evening sky, rose a multitude of tall chimneys, many of them reeking, a few smokeless during a season of "play." Here and there a pallid patch and ghostly stunted beehive shapes showed the position of a pot-bank, or a wheel, black and sharp against the hot lower sky, marked some colliery where they raise the iridescent coal of the place. Nearer at hand was the broad stretch of railway, and half invisible trains shunted—a steady puffing and rumbling, with every run a ringing concussion and a rhythmic series of impacts, and a passage of intermittent puffs of white steam across the further view. And to the left, between the railway and the dark mass of the low hill beyond, dominating the whole view, colossal, inky black, and crowned with smoke and fitful flames, stood the great cylinders of the Jeddah Company Blast Furnaces, the central edifices of the big ironworks of which Horrocks was the manager. They stood heavy and threatening, full of an incessant turmoil of flames and seething molten iron, and about the feet of them rattled the rolling mills, and the steam hammer beat heavily and splashed the white iron sparks hither and thither. Even as they looked a truckful of fuel was shot into one of the giants, and the red flames gleamed out, and a confusion of smoke and black dust came boiling upwards towards the sky.

"Certainly you get some fine effects of color with your furnaces," said Raut, breaking a silence that had become apprehensive.

Horrocks grunted. He stood with his hands in his pockets, frowning down at the dim steaming railway and the busy ironworks beyond, frowning as if he were thinking out some knotty problem.

Raut glanced at him and away again. "At present your moonlight effect is hardly ripe," he continued, looking upward; "the moon is still smothered by the vestiges of daylight."

Horrocks stared at him with the expression of a man who has suddenly awakened. "Vestiges of daylight! Of course, of course." He too looked up at the moon, pale still in the midsummer sky. "Come along," he said suddenly, and, gripping Raut's arm in his hand, made a move towards the path that dropped from them towards the railway.

Raut hung back. Their eyes met and saw a thousand things in a moment that their lips came near to say. Horrocks's hand tightened and then relaxed. He let go, and before Raut was aware, they were arm in arm, and walking, one unwillingly enough, down the path.

"You see the fine effect of the railway signals towards Burslem," said Horrocks, suddenly breaking into loquacity, striding fast and tightening the grip of his elbow the while. "Little green lights and red and white lights, all against the haze. You have an eye for effect, Raut. It's a fine effect. And look at those furnaces of mine, how they rise upon us as we come down the hill. That to the right is my pet—seventy feet of him. I packed him myself, and he's boiled away cheerfully with iron in his guts for five long years. I've a particular fancy for *him*. That line of red there,—a lovely bit of warm orange you'd call it, Raut,— that's the puddler's furnaces, and there, in the hot light, three black figures— did you see the white splash of the steam hammer then?—that's the rolling mills. Come along! Clang, clatter, how it goes rattling across the floor! Sheet tin, Raut,—amazing stuff. Glass mirrors are not in it when that stuff comes from the mill. And, squelch!—there goes the hammer again. Come along!"

He had to stop talking to catch at his breath. His arm twisted into Raut's with benumbing tightness. He had come striding down the black path towards the railway as though he was possessed. Raut had not spoken a word, had simply hung back against Horrocks's pull with all his strength.

"I say," he said now, laughing nervously, but with an undernote of snarl in his voice, "why on earth are you nipping my arm off, Horrocks, and dragging me along like this?"

At length Horrocks released him. His manner changed again. "Nipping your arm off!" he said. "Sorry. But it's you taught me the trick of walking in that friendly way."

"You haven't learnt the refinements of it yet then," said Raut, laughing artificially again. "By Jove! I'm black and blue." Horrocks offered no apology. They stood now near the bottom of the hill, close to the fence that bordered the railway. The ironworks had grown larger and spread out with their approach. They looked up to the blast furnaces now instead of down; the further view of Etruria and Hanley had dropped out of sight with their descent. Before them, by the stile, rose a notice board, bearing, still dimly visible, the words "BEWARE OF THE TRAINS," half hidden by splashes of coaly mud.

"Fine effects," said Horrocks, waving his arm. "Here comes a train. The puffs of smoke, the orange glare, the round eye of light in front of it, the melodious rattle. Fine effects! But these furnaces of mine used to be finer, before we shoved cones in their throats and saved the gas."

"How?" said Raut. "Cones?"

"Cones, my man, cones. I'll show you one nearer. The flames used to flare out of the open throats, great—what is it?—pillars of cloud by day, red and black smoke, and pillars of fire by night. Now we run it off in pipes and burn it to heat the blast, and the top is shut by a cone. You'll be interested in that cone."

"But every now and then," said Raut, "you get a burst of fire and smoke up there."

"The cone's not fixed, it's hung by a chain from a lever and balanced by an equipoise. You shall see it nearer. Else, of course, there'd be no way of getting fuel into the thing. Every now and then the cone dips and out comes the flare."

"I see," said Raut. He looked over his shoulder. "The moon gets brighter," he said.

"Come along," said Horrocks, abruptly, gripping his shoulder again, and moving him suddenly towards the railway crossing. And then came one of those swift incidents, vivid, but so rapid that they leave one doubtful and reeling. Half way across, Horrocks's hand suddenly clenched upon him like a vice, and swung him backward and through a half turn, so that he looked up the line. And there a chain of lamp-lit carriage-windows telescoped swiftly as it came towards them, and the red and yellow lights of an engine grew larger and larger rushing down upon them. As he grasped what this meant, he turned his face to Horrocks and pushed with all his strength against the arm that held him back between the rails. The struggle did not last a moment. Just as certain as it was that Horrocks held him there, so certain was it that he had been violently lugged out of danger.

"Out of the way!" said Horrocks, with a gasp, as the train came rattling by, and they stood panting by the gate into the ironworks.

"I did not see it coming," said Raut, still, even in spite of his own apprehensions, trying to keep up an appearance of ordinary intercourse.

Horrocks answered with a grunt. "The cone," he said, and then as one who recovers himself—"I thought you did not hear."

"I didn't," said Raut.

"I wouldn't have had you run over then for the world," said Horrocks.

"For a moment I lost my nerve," said Raut.

Horrocks stood for half a minute, then turned abruptly towards the ironworks again. "See how fine these great mounds of mine, these clinker heaps, look in the night! That truck yonder, up above there! Up it goes, and out-tilts the slag. See the palpitating red stuff go sliding down the slope. As we get nearer, the heap rises up and cuts the blast furnaces. See the quiver up above the big one. Not that way! This way, between the block heaps. That goes to the puddling furnaces, but I want to show you the canal first." He came and took Raut by the elbow, and so they went along side by side. Raut answered Horrocks vaguely. What, he asked himself, had really happened on the line? Was he deluding himself with his own fancies, or had Horrocks actually held him back in the way of the train? Had he just been within an ace of being murdered?

Suppose this slouching, scowling monster *did* know anything? For a minute or two then Raut was really afraid for his life, but the mood passed as he reasoned with himself. After all, Horrocks might have heard nothing. At any rate, he had pulled him out of the way in time. His odd manner might be due to the mere vague jealousy he had shown once before. He was talking now of the ash-heaps and the canal. "Eigh?" said Horrocks.

"What?" said Raut. "Rather! The haze in the moonlight. Fine!"

"Our canal," said Horrocks, stopping suddenly. "Our canal by moonlight and firelight is an immense effect. You've never seen it? Fancy that! You've spent too many of your evenings philandering up in Newcastle there. I tell you, for real florid effects— But you shall see. Boiling water—"

As they came out of the labyrinth of clinker heaps and mounds of coal and ore, the noises of the rolling mill sprang upon them suddenly, loud, near, and distinct. Three shadowy workmen went by and touched their caps to Horrocks. Their faces were vague in the darkness. Raut felt a futile impulse to address them, and before he could frame his words they passed into the shadows. Horrocks pointed to the canal close before them now: a weird-looking place it seemed, in the blood-red reflections of the furnaces. The hot water that cooled the tuyeres came into it, some fifty yards up—a tumultuous, almost boiling affluent, and the steam rose up from the water in silent white wisps and streaks, wrapping damply about them, an incessant succession of ghosts coming up from the black and red eddies, a white uprising that made the head swim. The shining black tower of the larger blast-furnace rose overhead out of the mist, and its tumultuous riot filled their ears. Raut kept away from the edge of the water and watched Horrocks.

"Here it is red," said Horrocks, "blood-red vapor as red and hot as sin; but yonder there, where the moonlight falls on it and it drives across the clinker heaps, it is as white as death."

Raut turned his head for a moment, and then came back hastily to his watch on Horrocks. "Come along to the rolling mills," said Horrocks. The threatening hold was not so evident that time, and Raut felt a little reassured. But all the same, what on earth did Horrocks mean about "white as death" and "red as sin"? Coincidence, perhaps?

They went and stood behind the puddlers for a little while, and then through the rolling mills, where amidst an incessant din the deliberate steam hammer beat the juice out of the succulent iron, and black, half-naked Titans rushed the plastic bars, like hot sealing-wax, between the wheels. "Come on," said Horrocks in Raut's ear, and they went and peeped through the little glass hole behind the tuyeres, and saw the tumbled fire writhing in the pit of the blast-furnace. It left one eye blinded for a while. Then with green and blue patches dancing across the dark they went to the lift by which the trucks of ore and fuel and lime were raised to the top of the big cylinder.

And out upon the narrow rail that overhung the furnace Raut's doubts came upon him again. Was it wise to be here? If Horrocks did know—everything! Do what he would, he could not resist a violent trembling. Right underfoot was a sheer depth of seventy feet. It was a dangerous place. They pushed by a truck of fuel to get to the railing that crowned the place. The reek of the furnace, a sulfurous vapor streaked with pungent bitterness, seemed to make the distant hillside of Hanley quiver. The moon was riding out now from among a drift of clouds, half way up the sky above the undulating wooded outlines of Newcastle. The steaming canal ran away from below them under an indistinct bridge, and vanished into the dim haze of the flat fields towards Burslem.

"That's the cone I've been telling you of," shouted Horrocks, "and, below that, sixty feet of fire and molten metal, with the air of the blast frothing through it like gas in soda-water."

Raut gripped the handrail tightly, and stared down at the cone. The heat was intense. The boiling of the iron and the tumult of the blast made a thunderous accompaniment to Horrocks's voice. But the thing had to be gone through now. Perhaps, after all—

"In the middle," bawled Horrocks, "temperature near a thousand degrees. If *you* were dropped into it—flash into flame like a pinch of gunpowder in a candle. Put your hand out and feel the heat of his breath. Why even up here I've seen the rain-water boiling off the trucks. And that cone there. It's a damned sight too hot for roasting cakes. The top side of it's three hundred degrees."

"Three hundred degrees!" said Raut.

"Three hundred centigrade, mind!" said Horrocks. "It will boil the blood out of you in no time."

"Eigh?" said Raut, and turned.

"Boil the blood out of you in—No you don't!"

"Let me go!" screamed Raut. "Let go my arm."

With one hand he clutched at the handrail, then with both. For a moment the two men stood swaying. Then suddenly, with a violent jerk, Horrocks had twisted him from his hold. He clutched at Horrocks and missed, his foot went back into empty air; in mid-air he twisted himself, and then cheek and shoulder and knee struck the hot cone together.

He clutched the chain by which the cone hung, and the thing sank an infinitesimal amount as he struck it. A circle of glowing red appeared about him, and a tongue of flame, released from the chaos within, flickered up towards him. An intense pain assailed him at the knees, and he could smell the singeing of his hands. He raised himself to his feet and tried to climb up the chain, and then something struck his head. Black and shining with the moonlight the throat of the furnace rose about him.

Horrocks he saw stood above him by one of the trucks of fuel on the rail. The gesticulating figure was bright and white in the moonlight, and shouting, "Fizzle, you fool! Fizzle, you hunter of women! You hot-blooded hound! Boil! boil! boil!"

Suddenly he caught up a handful of coal out of the truck and flung it deliberately, lump after lump, at Raut.

"Horrocks!" cried Raut, "Horrocks!"

He clung crying to the chain, pulling himself up from the burning of the cone. Each missile Horrocks flung hit him. His clothes charred and glowed, and as he struggled the cone dropped and a rush of hot suffocating gas whooped out and burned round him in a swift breath of flame.

His human likeness departed from him. When the momentary red had passed Horrocks saw a charred, blackened figure, its head streaked with blood, still clutching and fumbling with the chain and writhing in agony—a cindery animal, an inhuman, monstrous creature that began a sobbing, intermittent shriek.

Abruptly at the sight the ironmaster's anger passed. A deadly sickness came upon him. The heavy odor of burning flesh came drifting up to his nostrils. His sanity returned to him.

"God have mercy upon me!" he cried. "Oh, God! what have I done?"

He knew the thing below him, save that it still moved and felt, was already a dead man—that the blood of the poor wretch must be boiling in his veins. An intense realization of that agony came to his mind and overcame every other feeling. For a moment he stood irresolute, and then, turning to the truck, he hastily tilted its contents upon the struggling thing that had once been a man. The mass fell with a thud and went radiating over the cone. With the thud the shriek ended, and a boiling confusion of smoke, dust, and flame came rushing up towards him. As it passed he saw the cone clear again.

Then he staggered back and stood trembling, clinging to the rail with both hands. His lips moved, but no words came to them.

Down below was the sound of voices and running steps. The clangor of rolling in the shed ceased abruptly.

THE LOST INHERITANCE

"MY UNCLE," SAID the man with the glass eye, "was what you might call a hemi-semi-demi millionaire. He was worth about a hundred and twenty thousand. Quite. And he left me all his money."

I glanced at the shiny sleeve of his coat, and my eye traveled up to the frayed collar.

"Every penny," said the man with the glass eye, and I caught the active pupil looking at me with a touch of offense.

"I've never had any windfalls like that," I said, trying to speak enviously and propitiate him.

"Even a legacy isn't always a blessing," he remarked with a sigh, and with an air of philosophical resignation he put the red nose and the wiry moustache into his tankard for a space.

"Perhaps not," I said.

"He was an author, you see, and he wrote a lot of books."

"Indeed!"

"That was the trouble of it all." He stared at me with the available eye, to see if I grasped his statement, then averted his face a little and produced a toothpick.

"You see," he said, smacking his lips after a pause, "it was like this. He was my uncle—my maternal uncle. And he had—what shall I call it?—a weakness for writing edifying literature. Weakness is hardly the word—downright mania is nearer the mark. He'd been librarian in a Polytechnic, and as soon as the money came to him he began to indulge his ambition. It's a simply extraordinary and incomprehensible thing to me. Here was a man of thirty-seven suddenly dropped into a perfect pile of gold, and he didn't go—not a day's bust on it. One would think a chap would go and get himself dressed a bit decent—say a couple of dozen pairs of trousers at a West End tailor's; but he never did. You'd hardly believe it, but when he died he hadn't even a gold watch. It seems wrong for people like that to have money. All he did was just to take a house, and order in pretty nearly five tons of books and ink and paper, and set to writing edifying literature as hard as ever he could write. I *can't* understand it! But he did. The money came to him, curiously enough, through a maternal uncle of *his*, unexpected like, when he was seven-and-thirty. My mother, it happened, was his only relation in the wide, wide world, except some second cousins of his. And I was her only son. You follow all that? The second cousins had one only son, too; but they brought him to see the old man too soon. He was rather a spoilt youngster, was this son of theirs, and directly he set eyes on my uncle, he began bawling out as hard as he could. 'Take 'im away—er,' he says, 'take 'im away,' and so did for himself entirely. It was pretty straight sailing, you'd think, for me, eh? And my mother, being a sensible, careful woman, settled the business in her own mind long before he did.

"He was a curious little chap, was my uncle, as I remember him. I don't wonder at the kid being scared. Hair, just like these Japanese dolls they sell, black and straight and stiff all round the brim and none in the middle, and below, a whitish kind of face and rather large dark grey eyes moving about behind his spectacles. He used to attach a great deal of importance to dress, and always wore a flapping overcoat and a big-rimmed felt of a most extraordinary size. He looked a rummy little beggar, I can tell you. Indoors it was, as a rule, a dirty red flannel dressing-gown and a black skull-cap he had. That black skull-cap made him look like the portraits of all kinds of celebrated people. He was always moving about from house to house, was my uncle, with his chair which had belonged to Savage Landor, and his two writing-tables, one of Carlyle's and the other of Shelley's, so the dealer told him, and the completest portable reference library in England, he said he had,—and he lugged the whole caravan, now to a house at Down, near Darwin's old place, then to Reigate, near Meredith, then off to Haslemere, then back to Chelsea for a bit, and then up to Hampstead. He knew there was something wrong with his stuff, but he never knew there was anything wrong with his brains. It was always the air, or the water, or the altitude, or some tommy-rot like that. 'So much depends on environment,' he used to say, and stare at you hard, as if he half-suspected you were hiding a grin at him somewhere under your face. 'So much depends on environment to a sensitive mind like mine.'

"What was his name? You wouldn't know it if I told you. He wrote nothing that anyone has ever read—nothing. No one *could* read it. He wanted to be a great teacher, he said, and he didn't know what he wanted to teach any more than a child. So he just blethered at large about Truth and Righteousness, and the Spirit of History, and all that. Book after book he wrote and published at his own expense. He wasn't quite right in his head, you know, really; and to hear him go on at the critics—not because they slated him, mind you—he liked that—but because they didn't take any notice of him at all. 'What do the nations want?' he would ask, holding out his brown old claw. 'Why, teaching—guidance! They are scattered upon the hills like sheep without a shepherd. There is War, and Rumours of War, the unlaid Spirit of Discord abroad in the land, Nihilism, Vivisection, Vaccination, Drunkenness, Penury, Want, Socialistic Error, Selfish Capital! Do you see the clouds, Ted?'—my name, you know—'Do you see the clouds lowering over the land? and behind it all—the Mongol waits!' He was always very great on Mongols, and the Spectre of Socialism, and such-like things.

"Then out would come his finger at me, and, with his eyes all afire and his skull-cap askew, he would whisper: 'And here am I. What do I want? Nations to teach. Nations! I say it with all modesty, Ted, I *could*. I would guide them; nay! but I *will* guide them to a safe haven, to the land of Righteousness, flowing with milk and honey.'

"That's how he used to go on. Ramble, rave about the nations, and righteousness, and that kind of thing. Kind of mincemeat of Bible and blethers. From fourteen up to three-and-twenty, when I might have been improving my mind, my mother used to wash me and brush my hair (at least in the earlier years of it), with a nice parting down the middle, and take me, once or twice a week, to hear this old lunatic jabber about things he had read of in the morning papers, trying to do it as much like Carlyle as he could; and I used to sit according to instructions, and look intelligent and nice, and pretend to be taking it all in. Afterwards, I used to go of my own free will, out of a regard for the legacy. I was the only person that used to go and see him. He wrote, I believe, to every man who made the slightest stir in the world, sending him a copy or so of his books, and inviting him to come and talk about the nations to him; but half of them didn't answer, and none ever came. And when the girl let you in—she was an artful bit of goods, that girl—there were heaps of letters on the hall-seat waiting to go off addressed to Prince Bismarck, the President of the United States, and such-like people. And one went up the staircase and along the cobwebby passage,— the housekeeper drank like fury, and his passages were always cobwebby,—and found him at last, with books turned down all over the room, and heaps of torn paper on the floor, and telegrams and newspapers littered about, and empty coffee-cups and half-eaten bits of toast on the desk and the mantel. You'd see his back humped up, and his hair would be sticking out quite straight between the collar of that dressing-gown thing and the edge of the skull-cap.

" 'A moment!' he would say. 'A moment!' over his shoulder. 'The *mot juste,* you know, Ted, *le mot juste.* Righteous thought righteously expressed—Aah!— concatenation. And now, Ted,' he'd say, spinning round in his study chair, 'how's Young England?' That was his silly name for me.

"Well, that was my uncle, and that was how he talked—to me, at any rate. With others about he seemed a bit shy. And he not only talked to me, but he gave me his books, books of six hundred pages or so, with cock-eyed headings, 'The Shrieking Sisterhood,' 'The Behemoth of Bigotry,' 'Crucibles and Cullenders,' and so on. All very strong, and none of them original. The very last time but one that I saw him he gave me a book. He was feeling ill even then, and his hand shook and he was despondent. I noticed it because I was naturally on the look-out for those little symptoms. 'My last book, Ted,' he said. 'My last book, my boy; my last word to the deaf and hardened nations'; and I'm hanged if a tear didn't go rolling down his yellow old cheek. He was regular crying because it was so nearly over, and he hadn't only written about fifty-three books of rubbish. 'I've sometimes thought, Ted—' he said, and stopped.

" 'Perhaps I've been a bit hasty and angry with this stiff-necked generation. A little more sweetness, perhaps, and a little less blinding light. I've sometimes thought—I might have swayed them. But I've done my best, Ted.'

"And then, with a burst, for the first and last time in his life he owned himself a failure. It showed he was really ill. He seemed to think for a minute, and then he spoke quietly and low, as sane and sober as I am now. 'I've been a fool, Ted,' he said. 'I've been flapping nonsense all my life. Only He who readeth the heart knows whether this is anything more than vanity. Ted, I don't. But He knows, He knows, and if I have done foolishly and vainly, in my heart— in my heart—'

"Just like that he spoke, repeating himself, and he stopped quite short and handed the book to me, trembling. Then the old shine came back into his eye. I remember it all fairly well, because I repeated it and acted it to my old mother when I got home, to cheer her up a bit. 'Take this book and read it,' he said. 'It's my last word, my very last word. I've left all my property to you, Ted, and may you use it better than I have done.' And then he fell a-coughing.

"I remember that quite well even now, and how I went home cock-a-hoop, and how he was in bed the next time I called. The housekeeper was downstairs drunk, and I fooled about—as a young man will—with the girl in the passage before I went to him. He was sinking fast. But even then his vanity clung to him.

" 'Have you read it?' he whispered.

" 'Sat up all night reading it,' I said in his ear to cheer him. 'It's the last,' said I, and then, with a memory of some poetry or other in my head, 'but it's the bravest and best.'

"He smiled a little and tried to squeeze my hand as a woman might do, and left off squeezing in the middle, and lay still. 'The bravest and the best,' said I again, seeing it pleased him. But he didn't answer. I heard the girl giggle outside the door, for occasionally we'd had just a bit of innocent laughter, you know, at his ways. I looked at his face and his eyes were closed, and it was just as if somebody had punched in his nose on either side. But he was still smiling. It's queer to think of—he lay dead, lay dead there, an utter failure, with the smile of success on his face.

"That was the end of my uncle. You can imagine me and my mother saw that he had a decent funeral. Then, of course, came the hunt for the will. We began decent and respectful at first, and before the day was out we were ripping chairs, and smashing bureau panels, and sounding walls. Every hour we expected those others to come in. We asked the housekeeper, and found she'd actually witnessed a will—on an ordinary half-sheet of notepaper it was written, and very short, she said—not a month ago. The other witness was the gardener, and he bore her out word for word. But I'm hanged if there was that or any other will to be found. The way my mother talked must have made him turn in his grave. At last a lawyer at Reigate sprang one on us that had been made years ago during some temporary quarrel with my mother. I'm blest if that wasn't the only will to be discovered anywhere, and it left every penny he possessed to that 'Take 'im away' youngster of his second cousin's—a chap who'd never had to stand his talking not for one afternoon of his life."

The man with the glass eye stopped.

"I thought you said—" I began.

"Half a minute," said the man with the glass eye. "*I* had to wait for the end of the story till this very morning, and I was a blessed sight more interested than you are. You just wait a bit, too. They executed the will, and the other chap inherited, and directly he was one-and-twenty he began to blew it. How he did blew it, to be sure! He bet, he drank, he got in the papers for this and that. I tell you, it makes me wriggle to think of the times he had. He blewed every ha'penny of it before he was thirty, and the last I heard of him was—Holloway! Three years ago.

"Well, I naturally fell on hard times, because, as you see, the only trade I knew was legacy-cadging. All my plans were waiting over to begin, so to speak, when the old chap died. I've had my ups and downs since then. Just now it's a period of depression. I tell you frankly, I'm on the look-out for help. I was hunting round my room to find something to raise a bit on for immediate necessities, and the sight of all those presentation volumes—no one will buy them, not to wrap butter in, even—well, they annoyed me. I'd promised him not to part with them, and I never kept a promise easier. I let out at them with my boot, and sent them shooting across the room. One lifted at the kick, and spun through the air. And out of it flapped— You guess?

"It was the will. He'd given it me himself in that very last volume of all."

He folded his arms on the table, and looked sadly with the active eye at his empty tankard. He shook his head slowly, and said softly, "I'd never *opened* the book, much more cut a page!" Then he looked up, with a bitter laugh, for my sympathy. "Fancy hiding it there! Eigh? Of all places."

He began to fish absently for a dead fly with his finger. "It just shows you the vanity of authors," he said, looking up at me. "It wasn't no trick of his. He'd meant perfectly fair. He'd really thought I was really going home to read that blessed book of his through. But it shows you, don't it?"—his eye went down to the tankard again,—"it shows you, too, how we poor human beings fail to understand one another."

But there was no misunderstanding the eloquent thirst of his eye. He accepted with ill-feigned surprise. He said, in the usual subtle formula, that he didn't mind if he did.

THE FLOWERING OF
THE STRANGE ORCHID

THE BUYING OF orchids always has in it a certain speculative flavor. You have before you the brown shriveled lump of tissue, and for the rest you must trust your judgment, or the auctioneer, or your good-luck, as your taste may incline. The plant may be moribund or dead, or it may be just a respectable purchase, fair value for your money, or perhaps—for the thing has happened again and again—there slowly unfolds before the delighted eyes of the happy purchaser, day after day, some new variety, some novel richness, a strange twist of the labellum, or some subtler coloration or unexpected mimicry. Pride, beauty, and profit blossom together on one delicate green spike, and, it may be, even immortality. For the new miracle of Nature may stand in need of a new specific name, and what so convenient as that of its discoverer? "Johnsmithia"! There have been worse names.

It was perhaps the hope of some such happy discovery that made Winter-Wedderburn such a frequent attendant at these sales—that hope, and also, maybe, the fact that he had nothing else of the slightest interest to do in the world. He was a shy, lonely, rather ineffectual man, provided with just enough income to keep off the spur of necessity, and not enough nervous energy to make him seek any exacting employments. He might have collected stamps or coins, or translated Horace, or bound books, or invented new species of diatoms. But, as it happened, he grew orchids, and had one ambitious little hothouse.

"I have a fancy," he said over his coffee, "that something is going to happen to me today." He spoke—as he moved and thought—slowly.

"Oh, don't say *that!*" said his housekeeper—who was also his remote cousin. For "something happening" was a euphemism that meant only one thing to her.

"You misunderstand me. I mean nothing unpleasant—though what I do mean I scarcely know.

"Today," he continued after a pause, "Peters are going to sell a batch of plants from the Andamans and the Indies. I shall go up and see what they have. It may be I shall buy something good, unawares. That may be it."

He passed his cup for his second cupful of coffee.

"Are these the things collected by that poor young fellow you told me of the other day?" asked his cousin as she filled his cup.

"Yes," he said, and became meditative over a piece of toast.

"Nothing ever does happen to me," he remarked presently, beginning to think aloud. "I wonder why? Things enough happen to other people. There is Harvey. Only the other week, on Monday he picked up sixpence, on Wednesday his chicks all had the staggers, on Friday his cousin came home from Australia, and on Saturday he broke his ankle. What a whirl of excitement!—compared to me."

"I think I would rather be without so much excitement," said his housekeeper. "It can't be good for you."

"I suppose it's troublesome. Still—you see, nothing ever happens to me. When I was a little boy I never had accidents. I never fell in love as I grew up. Never married—I wonder how it feels to have something happen to you, something really remarkable.

"That orchid-collector was only thirty-six—twenty years younger than myself—when he died. And he had been married twice and divorced once; he had had malarial fever four times, and once he broke his thigh. He killed a Malay once, and once he was wounded by a poisoned dart. And in the end he was killed by jungle-leeches. It must have all been very troublesome, but then it must have been very interesting, you know—except, perhaps, the leeches.''

"I am sure it was not good for him," said the lady, with conviction.

"Perhaps not." And then Wedderburn looked at his watch. "Twenty-three minutes past eight. I am going up by the quarter to twelve train, so that there is plenty of time. I think I shall wear my alpaca jacket—it is quite warm enough— and my grey felt hat and brown shoes. I suppose—"

He glanced out of the window at the serene sky and sunlit garden, and then nervously at his cousin's face.

"I think you had better take an umbrella if you are going to London," she said in a voice that admitted of no denial. "There's all between here and the station coming back."

When he returned he was in a state of mild excitement. He had made a purchase. It was rare that he could make up his mind quickly enough to buy, but this time he had done so.

"There are Vandas," he said, "and a Dendrobe and some Palæonophis." He surveyed his purchases lovingly as he consumed his soup. They were laid out on the spotless tablecloth before him, and he was telling his cousin all about them as he slowly meandered through his dinner. It was his custom to live all his visits to London over again in the evening for her and his own entertainment.

"I knew something would happen today. And I have bought all these. Some of them—some of them—I feel sure, do you know, that some of them will be remarkable. I don't know how it is, but I feel just as sure as if someone had told me that some of these will turn out remarkable.

"That one"—he pointed to a shriveled rhizome—"was not identified. It may be a Palæonophis—or it may not. It may be a new species, or even a new genus. And it was the last that poor Batten ever collected."

"I don't like the look of it," said his housekeeper. "It's such an ugly shape."

"To me it scarcely seems to have a shape."

"I don't like those things that stick out," said his housekeeper.

"It shall be put away in a pot tomorrow."

"It looks," said the housekeeper, "like a spider shamming dead."

Wedderburn smiled and surveyed the root with his head on one side. "It is certainly not a pretty lump of stuff. But you can never judge of these things from their dry appearance. It may turn out to be a very beautiful orchid indeed. How busy I shall be tomorrow! I must see tonight just exactly what to do with these things, and tomorrow I shall set to work.

"They found poor Batten lying dead, or dying, in a mangrove swamp—I forget which," he began again presently, "with one of these very orchids crushed up under his body. He had been unwell for some days with some kind of native fever, and I suppose he fainted. These mangrove swamps are very unwholesome. Every drop of blood, they say, was taken out of him by the jungle-leeches. It may be that very plant that cost him his life to obtain."

"I think none the better of it for that."

"Men must work though women may weep," said Wedderburn, with profound gravity.

"Fancy dying away from every comfort in a nasty swamp! Fancy being ill of fever with nothing to take but chlorodyne and quinine—if men were left to themselves they would live on chlorodyne and quinine—and no one round you but horrible natives! They say the Andaman islanders are most disgusting wretches—

and, anyhow, they can scarcely make good nurses, not having the necessary training. And just for people in England to have orchids!''

"I don't suppose it was comfortable, but some men seem to enjoy that kind of thing," said Wedderburn. "Anyhow, the natives of his party were sufficiently civilised to take care of all his collection until his colleague, who was an ornithologist, came back again from the interior; though they could not tell the species of the orchid, and had let it wither. And it makes these things more interesting."

"It makes them disgusting. I should be afraid of some of the malaria clinging to them. And just think, there has been a dead body lying across that ugly thing! I never thought of that before. There! I declare I cannot eat another mouthful of dinner."

"I will take them off the table if you like, and put them in the window-seat. I can see them just as well there."

The next few days he was indeed singularly busy in his steamy little hothouse, fussing about with charcoal, lumps of teak, moss, and all the other mysteries of the orchid cultivator. He considered he was having a wonderfully eventful time. In the evening he would talk about these new orchids to his friends, and over and over again he reverted to his expectation of something strange.

Several of the Vandas and the Dendrobium died under his care, but presently the strange orchid began to show signs of life. He was delighted, and took his housekeeper right away from jam-making to see it at once, directly he made the discovery.

"That is a bud," he said, "and presently there will be a lot of leaves there, and those little things coming out here are aërial rootlets."

"They look to me like little white fingers poking out of the brown. I don't like them," said his housekeeper.

"Why not?"

"I don't know. They look like fingers trying to get at you. I can't help my likes and dislikes."

"I don't know for certain, but I don't *think* there are any orchids I know that have aërial rootlets quite like that. It may be my fancy, of course. You see they are a little flattened at the ends."

"I don't like 'em," said his housekeeper, suddenly shivering and turning away. "I know it's very silly of me—and I'm very sorry, particularly as you like the thing so much. But I can't help thinking of that corpse."

"But it may not be that particular plant. That was merely a guess of mine."

His housekeeper shrugged her shoulders.

"Anyhow I don't like it," she said.

Wedderburn felt a little hurt at her dislike to the plant. But that did not prevent his talking to her about orchids generally, and this orchid in particular, whenever he felt inclined.

"There are such queer things about orchids," he said one day; "such possibilities of surprises. You know, Darwin studied their fertilisation, and showed that the whole structure of an ordinary orchid-flower was contrived in order that moths might carry the pollen from plant to plant. Well, it seems that there are lots of orchids known the flower of which cannot possibly be used for fertilisation in that way. Some of the Cypripediums, for instance; there are no insects known that can possibly fertilise them, and some of them have never been found with seed."

"But how do they form new plants?"

"By runners and tubers, and that kind of outgrowth. That is easily explained. The puzzle is, what are the flowers for?

"Very likely," he added, "*my* orchid may be something extraordinary in that way. If so, I shall study it. I have often thought of making researches as Darwin did. But hitherto I have not found the time, or something else has happened to prevent it. The leaves are beginning to unfold now. I do wish you would come and see them!"

But she said that the orchid-house was so hot it gave her the headache. She had seen the plant once again, and the aerial rootlets, which were now some of them more than a foot long, had unfortunately reminded her of tentacles reaching out after something; and they got into her dreams, growing after her with incredible rapidity. So that she had settled to her entire satisfaction that she would not see that plant again, and Wedderburn had to admire its leaves alone. They were of the ordinary broad form, and a deep glossy green, with splashes and dots of deep red towards the base. He knew of no other leaves quite like them. The plant was placed on a low bench near the thermometer, and close by was a simple arrangement by which a tap dripped on the hot-water pipes and kept the air steamy. And he spent his afternoons now with some regularity meditating on the approaching flowering of this strange plant.

And at last the great thing happened. Directly he entered the little glass house he knew that the spike had burst out, although his great *Palæonophis Lowii* hid the corner where his new darling stood. There was a new odor in the air, a rich, intensely sweet scent, that overpowered every other in that crowded, steaming little greenhouse.

Directly he noticed this he hurried down to the strange orchid. And, behold! the trailing green spikes bore now three great splashes of blossom, from which this overpowering sweetness proceeded. He stopped before them in an ecstasy of admiration.

The flowers were white, with streaks of golden orange upon the petals; the heavy labellum was coiled into an intricate projection, and a wonderful bluish purple mingled there with the gold. He could see at once that the genus was altogether a new one. And the insufferable scent! How hot the place was! The blossoms swam before his eyes.

He would see if the temperature was right. He made a step towards the thermometer. Suddenly everything appeared unsteady. The bricks on the floor were dancing up and down. Then the white blossoms, the green leaves behind them, the whole greenhouse, seemed to sweep sideways, and then in a curve upward.

At half-past four his cousin made the tea, according to their invariable custom. But Wedderburn did not come in for his tea.

"He is worshipping that horrid orchid," she told herself, and waited ten minutes. "His watch must have stopped. I will go and call him."

She went straight to the hothouse, and, opening the door, called his name. There was no reply. She noticed that the air was very close, and loaded with an intense perfume. Then she saw something lying on the bricks between the hot-water pipes.

For a minute, perhaps, she stood motionless.

He was lying, face upward, at the foot of the strange orchid. The tentacle-like aerial rootlets no longer swayed freely in the air, but were crowded together, a tangle of gray ropes, and stretched tight with their ends closely applied to his chin and neck and hands.

She did not understand. Then she saw from under one of the exultant tentacles upon his cheek there trickled a little thread of blood.

With an inarticulate cry she ran towards him, and tried to pull him away from the leech-like suckers. She snapped two of these tentacles, and their sap dripped red.

Then the overpowering scent of the blossom began to make her head reel. How they clung to him! She tore at the tough ropes, and he and the white inflorescence swam about her. She felt she was fainting, knew she must not. She left him and hastily opened the nearest door, and, after she had panted for a moment in the fresh air, she had a brilliant inspiration. She caught up a flower-pot and smashed in the windows at the end of the greenhouse. Then she re-entered. She tugged now with renewed strength at Wedderburn's motionless body, and brought the strange orchid crashing to the floor. It still clung with the grimmest tenacity to its victim. In a frenzy, she lugged it and him into the open air.

Then she thought of tearing through the sucker rootlets one by one, and in another minute she had released him and was dragging him away from the horror.

He was white and bleeding from a dozen circular patches.

The odd-job man was coming up the garden, amazed at the smashing of glass, and saw her emerge, hauling the inanimate body with red-stained hands. For a moment he thought impossible things.

"Bring some water!" she cried, and her voice dispelled his fancies. When, with unnatural alacrity, he returned with the water, he found her weeping with excitement, and with Wedderburn's head upon her knee, wiping the blood from his face.

"What's the matter?" said Wedderburn, opening his eyes feebly, and closing them again at once.

"Go and tell Annie to come out here to me, and then go for Dr. Haddon at once," she said to the odd-job man so soon as he brought the water; and added, seeing he hesitated, "I will tell you all about it when you come back."

Presently Wedderburn opened his eyes again, and, seeing that he was troubled by the puzzle of his position, she explained to him, "You fainted in the hothouse."

"And the orchid?"

"I will see to that," she said.

Wedderburn had lost a good deal of blood, but beyond that he had suffered no very great injury. They gave him brandy mixed with some pink extract of meat, and carried him upstairs to bed. His housekeeper told her incredible story in fragments to Dr. Haddon. "Come to the orchid-house and see," she said.

The cold outer air was blowing in through the open door, and the sickly perfume was almost dispelled. Most of the torn aerial rootlets lay already withered amidst a number of dark stains upon the bricks. The stem of the inflorescence was broken by the fall of the plant, and the flowers were growing limp and brown at the edges of the petals. The doctor stooped towards it, then saw that one of the aerial rootlets still stirred feebly, and hesitated.

The next morning the strange orchid still lay there, black now and putrescent. The door banged intermittently in the morning breeze, and all the array of Wedderburn's orchids was shriveled and prostrate. But Wedderburn himself was bright and garrulous upstairs in the story of his strange adventure.